BAD IDEA: THE COMPLETE COLLECTION

NICOLE FRENCH

BAD IDEA

BOOK ONE OF THE BAD IDEA SERIES

I

SPECIAL DELIVERY

CHAPTER ONE

Layla

BOOM!

The 6 train stops with a thunderous jolt and a screech of breaks. A minute later, I jog up the stairs of the subway stop on Park Avenue and Twenty-Third, following the herd of people exiting the station.

Straight up Park is the elegant architecture of Grand Central Station; the other way, the looming buildings of the Flatiron District. It's one-thirty on a Monday, and people scurry on and off their lunch breaks. I hear Spanish, some kind of Creole, English speakers with myriad accents, all jumbled together with the horns and throttle of the cars making their way through the impermeable Manhattan traffic. A few of the nearby corners boast coffee carts and nut vendors, the smells from which waft through the frigid January air. This is New York, chaotic and colorful, a city I have come to adore since moving here to start college.

I glance around for a coffee shop. That's the one thing I miss about Seattle: decent coffee on every corner. The cheap stuff from the carts here makes my stomach hurt if I have too much. Since I already had two cups before my eight o'clock class this morning, I'm at my limit for what Quinn, my roommate, dubs "Borough Battery Acid."

"Excuse me, miss."

A deep baritone voice interrupts my thoughts, and I twist around to get out of the owner's way. The stereotype about people in New York is that they're mean, but that's wrong. It's just that there are certain social codes everyone here knows—codes like "don't stand like an idiot in the middle of a busy sidewalk," "don't stand in front of the subway car doors during rush hour if you're not getting off at the next stop," and "never, ever drive through a crosswalk when pedestrians are present." "I'm walking here!" is a real saying; I've used it myself. In a city of almost eight million people stuffed into a few small boroughs, no one has the patience for those who don't know the rules.

Yeah. It's a lot different than Washington.

"Sorry," I say quickly as I step to the side.

The speaker is obscured by a tower of boxes stacked on a creaky dolly, which he's trying to maneuver through the crowds.

"No problem, sweetie."

He pushes by, providing an excellent view of a set of wide shoulders and a prize-worthy ass in tight blue cargo pants. Seriously, the way some men's butts look in uniforms should be illegal. Sometimes I wish that catcalling were normal for women to do, not just men. It would level the playing field a bit. Plus it would be really satisfying to whistle after someone who looks like this guy.

Curious to see if his face is as good-looking as the rest of him, I watch to see if the hot delivery guy will turn around. But he just continues doggedly about his business like everyone else.

I shrug and check my watch again. Time to go. A small deli on the corner catches my eye. It's not exactly espresso, but it will do the trick. My stomach will just have to deal.

———

"Fox, Lager, and Associates, how may I help you?"

The receptionist's voice rings out loud and clear while I wait in the small conference room behind the donut-shaped desk. The office is cool and modern, with blonde wood floors and furnishings capped with brushed metal fixtures. The name partners, Steven Fox and Gerald Lager, pose with boy bands and pop singers in dozens of photos lining the walls along with gold records from said artists.

I was hired take the place of the regular night receptionist while she's on maternity leave. It's the kind of job I hope will look good on law school applications in a few more years. I'm the perfect candidate: nineteen, in my second year at NYU. Major...yeah. That's a different story. I'm supposed to be an attorney one day—my promise to become pre-law was the entire reason they agreed to send me to NYU.

I sit alone at the long oval table, peering at the pictures and trying to distract myself from first-day nerves. The perfect, white-toothed celebrities only make me that much more self-conscious. This is an entertainment firm, where everyone works for perfect-looking people and looks like they could be one of them. April, the current receptionist, could be doing spreads at *Vogue*. I, on the other hand, with my petite, curvy stature and thick wavy hair, don't look much like a fashion model. Anything but, really.

"Layla?"

Karen, the office manager and my new boss, stands in the doorway. Even at first glance, you know Karen is the kind of woman you don't want to mess with. A thirty-something woman with a business degree and a penchant for very high-heeled shoes, Karen was born and raised in the Bronx and is the third child out of five from a family of Puerto Ricans who operate a lot of the hot dog carts in Central Park. She was the first of her family to go to college, and she didn't mess around, graduating summa cum laude from NYU's school of business. These are all such critical elements of her personality that she divulged them to me during my interview. It was a scare tactic, I guess—she thinks I'm just a rich kid from the suburbs, and she wanted me to be afraid of my boss.

Well, she got what she wished for. Karen scares the hell out of me. Still, maybe we're more alike than she realizes. Like my dad, a native of Brazil, Karen takes major pains to erase any implications of her less than affluent upbringing. She wears shoes that no office manager in Manhattan has any business buying, and the waterfall of straight, caramel-colored hair is most likely the product of a very sleek and expensive way of taming hair that probably looks naturally a lot like mine—wavy and unruly.

She obviously works really hard to fit in here. It reminds me of my dad's insistence on trading in his BMW every year whether we need to or not, or the way he refuses to let anyone call me anything other than American. I'm not Latina, I'm American. I'm not Brazilian, I'm American. He's terrified of anyone thinking of me or us as something different.

I pull at the hem of my H&M skirt as I stand. I don't look terrible, but my skirt is slightly wrinkled after I sat in class all morning, and my gray sweater is pilling everywhere. My parents might have money, but they don't share it with me. My dad, for all his pretentions, is also a big fan of the "bootstraps" mentality. He pays for my tuition, but beyond that, I'm on my own.

"Are you ready?" Karen asks.

The only thing Karen can't mask is her speech. A thick Bronx accent curves over every word. But accents don't bother me. I've been deciphering my dad's Portuguese-laced English my entire life.

I nod, holding up a pad of paper and pen. "Absolutely."

Karen leads me through the halls while lecturing me on my duties. The office is constructed like a horse shoe, with Karen's and the partners' offices lining the exterior arc. Inside the shoe, junior associates, assistant, and one intern all sit around small wooden desks, which are blocked off from the front lobby and reception area by the conference room in the middle of everything.

I listen, take notes, and look curiously around at the groups of assistants with headsets and the few attorneys whose doors are open. Every so often, Karen stops and squints her eyeliner-laden lids as if examining me for character defects or an inability to understand the basic tasks of answering phones and keeping things stocked. I just nod, jot a few more details on my legal pad, and we continue with the training.

We circle back to the lobby, where April is answering phones.

"April will continue training you through your first shift," Karen informs me, tapping her long, manicured nails on the lacquered wood bar rimming the reception desk. "After that, you're on your own. Think you can handle it?"

Her condescension grates, but I'm not about to tell her that. She seems like the type who, when it really comes down to it, wouldn't mind breaking a few of those pretty nails on someone's face if they cross her the wrong way.

I blink and smile. "Got it."

———

THE JOB IS CAKE. If I have nothing to do in between phone calls, I'm allowed to study or read. No problem here; what college student doesn't want to get paid to study?

Sometime around six o'clock, April's giving me the low-down on office gossip when the elevator doors open. Although during my shift several clients and couriers have already arrived, some of them even recognizably famous, this is the only person who causes April to tense. Her pale, porcelain face flushes a girlish pink.

Immediately, at least three instant message windows appear on her computer from some of the assistants in the back:

Jenny: Is he here?

Marie: It's six—who just arrived?

Paula: Damn, I'm on a call!

I look at April. "What's going on?"

She shakes her head and swallows audibly, like something is caught in her throat. Before I can ask again, April pushes her blonde hair behind her ears and somehow finds a way to speak to the person walking into the lobby.

"Oh, ah, hi, Nico," she stammers almost a little too loudly.

I suppress a chuckle and shuffle my training notes instead of greeting this Nico person, whoever he is. Give me a break. I've met at least four genuinely famous people today—one of them a Top-Forty pop star—and I didn't flinch. What's this guy got that he makes a bunch of hotshot lawyers act like clucking hens?

But when I do look up, it's like the air evaporated from my lungs, like I've been hit hard by a sack of bricks. As if someone has slapped me hard across the face. Or submerged my body in a bucket of numbing ice water. My vision actually blurs, and I can't feel my legs.

It's a really, really good thing I'm sitting down.

He is so unbelievably beautiful. I say that instead of sexy or handsome or good-looking because these words don't cover it. They're too external, too superficial for the charisma that radiates from the man in front of me. His appeal could obviously make a nun toss out her habit, and I'm no nun. Neither, from the way she's squirming uncomfortably in her seat, is April.

On paper, he would probably come across as average. Obviously no big success career-wise—just a twenty-something FedEx courier, dressed in the same dark blue and purple uniform as the rest of them. He's not terribly tall either, maybe five-ten or eleven in boots. I estimate that in heels I'd be eye-to-eye with him, maybe an inch or two shorter.

But his lack of height is tempered by a pair of broad, toss-a-girl-over-them shoulders and biceps that ripple clearly, even under the thick fabric of his uniform. His FedEx shirtsleeves are rolled up over a set of muscular forearms, and his skin is tanned and smooth, the color of the coffee and rich cream. A fringe of short black hair just sticks out from the edges of his FedEx cap, the bill of which is curled over a pair of black eyes that twinkle mischievously beneath thick lashes.

Then he smiles. I'm seriously not sure why the building didn't blow a fuse—that grin adds about ten thousand watts to this room alone. It's the most thoroughly panty-dropping smile I have ever seen. And Holy Mary, Mother of God, it's not even pointed at me yet.

Like I said: a sack of bricks.

"How you doin', April?"

If his smile causes all the blood to drain out of my head, his voice makes it all flood back in again. I've heard that voice before, and now that I think about it, I recognize the shape of those big shoulders too. It's the guy from the street, Mr. Ass of the Year. And his front side *definitely* matches the promise of the back.

His voice holds traces of the same accent that Karen has, but his is softer somehow, muted in his velvety baritone. It's a gorgeous, deep voice, the kind you want whispering in your ear in some dark alley while he's got you pressed against a brick wall, hands up your skirt, hot mouth against your ear while he—

Whoa. Steady, girl. You're at work.

I know I'm staring, but it takes me a few seconds to shut my mouth and make sure I can actually move my legs. April has obviously learned to recover faster. Even though she's barely said anything, she's already standing up. My feet are still numb.

"Not bad, Nico." April giggles at him. "Today's my last day on the night shift. Will you miss me when I'm gone?"

"Of course I will, hon, of course I will," Nico croons. "Is this the new girl?"

His jet-black gaze briefly sweeps over me from my head down to my waist, which is likely all that's visible from where he stands. He gives me an inquisitive half-smile. I open my mouth to reply, but nothing comes out.

"Yeah," April's saying, but I can barely hear her. "This is Layla."

CHAPTER TWO

Nico

HOLY SHIT. AND I MEAN, WOW. HOLY. SHIT. SITTING IN FRONT OF ME IS ONE OF THE hottest girls I have ever seen. Wait, no. Hot is the wrong word. She's not hot like a video girl—she's covered up, for one thing, and for another, she doesn't look like she's been injected full of silicone.

Beautiful? I don't know. Beautiful doesn't seem to cover it either. For once I'm glad of my bad habit of chewing on my lower lip, because if I didn't, I swear to God, my jaw would have dropped to the fuckin' floor when I saw her.

The girl looks a little out of place in this office full of skinny, rich, white people and the models and actors they represent. Don't get me wrong—the fancy law firm, or whatever the fuck this place is, is one of my favorite spots on my route. The secretaries like to flirt, and Karen, the office manager, parades around in her too-tight pants. I get free coffee, sometimes a celebrity sighting. By the time six o'clock rolls around, I am in serious need of some relief from the monotony of delivering packages all day long, and the staff at Fox and Lager are usually willing to provide it.

But this girl is different. For one, you can tell she's not wrapped up in the dumb fantasy of the city yet. I don't mean that starry-eyed look new people have when they're first here. No, she's got that in spades. I mean that assumption that New York City is the only place in the world worth living. People live here long enough, and they can't be happy anywhere else.

She's young. Too young for me, I can already tell. She almost looks like she could be from my neighborhood. She's got a head full of hair that's begging to be grabbed, full lips that make an O-shape that's sending some nasty thoughts straight to my dick, and soft, fair skin that's just a shade darker than April's. But then she blinks, and I get a look at those baby-blues, eyes that skewer straight through my gut. Holy shit.

I'm about to dive into those sapphire beauties when Karen steps out and starts clattering across the hardwood floor. I swear to God, I have never seen this chick in anything less than five-inch heels. The woman sways her hips like a burlesque dancer on ecstasy and makes RuPaul look like Martha Stewart.

April stops talking as Karen approaches. Both she and the new girl are scared of their boss. I get it. Karen's got that hard edge like so many of the girls I grew up with, and I don't blame her. New York's a harsh place to grow up, especially for a girl. Too many boys thinking they're men. Too many men thinking women are their play-things, or even worse, their punching bags. With two sisters and a single-mom at home, I've had a front-row seat to some of the shitheads this city has to offer.

I look up. Karen's frowning. She just caught me staring at the new girl. Shit, what was her name, again? I was so lost in that heart-shaped mouth I don't remember a thing. Karen narrows her eyes at the girl. *Damn, New Girl. Sorry about that.*

"Layla's our new receptionist from NYU. We're hoping she'll do all right."

Layla. That's right.

Karen turns up her accent. Yeah, I know what she's doing. The way you speak tells people your tribe. A Hassidic Jew from Brooklyn is going to talk differently than Haitians in Jamaica Queens or a Dominican cat from the Heights. Karen and I are both Puerto Rican—at least, I'm half, anyway—and right now she's telling the two white girls that she and I belong in a way they don't. I stifle a smile. They wouldn't be so intimidated if they'd seen Karen dancing on the bar two weeks ago. Get a few drinks into her, and she turns into *Coyote Ugly.*

"Same ol', Karen, you know," I answer after she asks how I'm doing.

Now I can't take it anymore. Blue Eyes is still staring at me, her mouth still just a little bit open. I want to stick my finger in between those soft lips. I want to tell her to suck it and see just how hard she can.

Shit.

I reach out my hand, although in a much nicer way than what I'm imagining. "I'm Nico. Your friendly neighborhood FedEx delivery man."

What. The. Fuck. Your friendly neighborhood FedEx delivery man? I sound like Mister Rogers with this shit. This girl is gonna think I'm an idiot.

For a few more seconds, she keeps staring, and I'm struck with this strange feeling that those big eyes see right through my shit. Like she can see any secret I've ever kept locked behind the swagger and smile. And the weird thing is, I want her to see it. Does she want to know about when K.C. and I used to shoplift candy and beer from the corner bodega when we were kids? Or about my first fight, the one with David Caldero, after he told everyone at school that my little sister was a slut? Because I'd tell her everything and more. Suddenly, I'm an open book.

Slowly, slowly, she reaches up, like she's about to touch a hot iron, and takes my calloused fingers. Then she smiles, and I swear to God, if I wasn't already holding onto the top of the desk, I probably would have fallen over it anyway.

Lightning. There's no other way to describe what's shooting through every bone, every vessel, every nerve of my body right now.

"Nice to meet you," she says in a voice that's low and just a little bit husky. "I'm Layla." For no reason that I can tell, she blushes, a head-to-toe rosy hue that makes her look like one of the Renaissance paintings at the Met. "I guess I'll be seeing you every day at six."

My big dumb grin is still pasted on my face like a fuckin' weirdo, but I can't move. An electric current is buzzing up my arm between her hand and mine, and the longer

I hold on, the longer I'm going to need it. Two seconds in, and I already feel like I have to be around this girl to survive.

Wait, *what*?

The shock of that thought yanks me out of my daze. I pull my hand back, even though I still can't stop smiling. "I guess you will, NYU."

For a moment more, we just gaze at each other, me clutching the desktop, her clenching the arms of her chair. She presses her thighs together, and *fuck* if that isn't like another lightning bolt straight to my cock. Well, what do you know? This girl wants me too. As in, wants me bad.

"Ahem."

Karen clears her throat. April snorts, and I catch Layla give her a dirty look before they both resume a couple of bland expressions like puppets. I clear *my* throat and pull a little at my collar. Suddenly, the thing is feeling very tight.

"So, ah, yeah," I say. "I got a few for you today, ladies."

God, I sound like a douchebag. Like the beginning of a porn video where some asshat in a too-tight UPS uniform starts boning the secretary with a line like "Do you wanna see my package?" I set my clipboard onto the desk and turn to unload several large boxes from the dolly, conscious the whole time that there are three pairs of female eyes staring straight at me. April flits around to check the names on the labels in order to alert the assistants in the back. I can't help but wish it was Layla. I'm dying to see what *she* looks like from the back. If that ass is as sweet as her lips.

Shit. I'm going to get myself in trouble thinking things like that. *Say something, asshole.*

I clear my throat. Again. "So, you gonna do the honors, NYU?"

I hand Layla the clipboard, which she stares at until Karen snatches it.

"I'll take care of that," she purrs, signing with vigor. She shoots Layla another dirty look after she returns the board to me. "But Layla, this will be your job most evenings, got it? Sorry, Nico. You know we gotta teach these young kids everything these days. You workin' the door at AJ's this weekend?"

"Every Saturday," I confirm. "You know I gotta pay the bills."

"You know I do," Karen cheers with a flirty smile.

Damn, I hope Karen doesn't come by this weekend. She's nice enough here, but every time she and her posse show up at AJ's, the Chelsea club where I work Saturday nights, things get rowdy, and I'm always the one who gets called in to settle them down. It's fuckin' embarrassing, if you want to know the truth. Karen's a grown woman. She needs to learn to hold her shit.

"See you tomorrow, Nico."

Karen taps her fingernails on the desktop cheerfully before clacking back to her office in her noisy damn shoes. I like heels as much as the next man, but Karen really does look like one of the drag queens at Chang's. April disappears with some of the smaller packages, leaving me alone with Blue Eyes while I wait for the elevator. I wonder what kind of shoes she's wearing.

I swallow. *Say something, Nico. Don't be a fuckin' chump.*

"Your first day going all right, NYU?"

She jerks a little at the sound of my voice. She's a daydreamer; that much is obvious. I have never wanted to know what someone was thinking so badly. I punch the elevator button and pray it's stuck at the top of the building with a stop on every floor. I want as much time as I can get here, even though at the same time, I don't know what the fuck to say.

"Um, yes," she says. That flush rises up her neck again. Damn, now I *really* want to know what she was thinking about.

"Where you from, NYU? Kansas?" Her blush is so cute, I can't help but tease her.

And then she snorts. She actually snorts, like a damn baby horse. It's the cutest sound I have ever heard in my life.

"Are you serious? Kansas? Why would you say that?"

I grin. She's mad. Her cheeks are a red, and her eyebrows are scrunched together. It's fucking adorable.

"Just 'cause you got that Dorothy look all about you, NYU," I egg her on a little more. "Bright lights, big city, and all that. So, Kansas? Am I right? Or is it Iowa?"

The look of complete and utter disgust on her face is priceless. I could tease her all day long.

"Um, *neither*," she pronounces. "Definitely not. Washington, actually." And then, after a moment, she adds, "Just outside of Seattle."

"Ah, okay then."

I'm such a stereotypical New Yorker. Name any place outside of the tristate area. If it's not Los Angeles, all I see are cornfields. Seattle? It rains there a lot, right? And their sports teams suck.

Right now, I'm at a loss. I want to keep talking, want to keep making her mad or sad or happy or whatever other emotions are possible on that beautiful face. But all I can do is look at my clipboard like I have something super important to check. No more deliveries today. Yes, it is Friday. Uh-huh, my name is definitely still Nico—says so right here. Nicolás Soltero: FedEx courier, sometimes-doorman, and lame-ass loser who just lost his game.

The elevator bell signals the opening doors, and I sigh with relief as I back the dolly into the car. I need to get my shit together and figure out how to talk to this girl without acting like an idiot.

"See you tomorrow, NYU." I raise a hand in mock salute. Jesus. Now I'm a motherfuckin' ship captain.

"It's Layla!" she calls out, but not before I shoot her a wink and smile one last time.

I'm thrilled when the doors close and she can't see me collapse against the wall. I can't breathe, like one of the guys at the gym just landed a punch to my gut.

Holy shit.

Holy. Shit.

I am in serious fuckin' trouble.

The doors open on the bottom floor, and Flaco, my route partner, is standing impatiently in the lobby. His skinny arms are crossed, and he's actually tapping his foot like a damn girl.

"Yo," he says when he sees me rolling out the empty dolly. "What the fuck took you so long? Happy hour's done in forty-five, and I cannot *wait* to get my drink on."

But I must look a little shaky still because Flaco leans down, lurching over me with his big, lanky body. He grabs my cheeks, checking my eyes like I'm in a coma. For a second, I think he's going to kiss me.

"*Pendejo!* What the fuck are you doin', man?"

I bat his hands away, and he jumps back like a hopping spider.

"Just checkin'," he says with a horsey laugh. "You looked kind of crazy there. Everything okay?"

I nod. I'm not going to tell him about this girl—no *way*. Flaco gave me this building a long time ago so he could take the modeling agency next door. He never has any luck with anyone, but that doesn't stop him from trying. I keep telling him you can't hit on clients—that's an easy way to get fired. But that never stops him. He hears about the cute new receptionist at the law firm, he's gonna be stealing the dolly tomorrow. Guaranteed.

———

WE DROP off the truck and file the paperwork to finish the day's route right. Within an hour, we're out of these monkey suits and on our way to Traveler for some hard-earned beers.

"Yo, Frankie!" I call out, banging my hands on the bar top.

Fridays are my nights out, since I usually have to work Saturdays, and Sundays I'm either fixing shit around my mother's place or watching my baby niece, Alejandra, while my sister, Maggie, studies for her night classes. Fridays are my days to let loose.

"Hey, Nico. What's happening, man?"

Frankie, the bartender, has known me since I first started at FedEx. When I first got the job, I was crazy excited. Good wages, benefits to share with everyone, even a pension if I stay long enough. It meant no more getting school supplies from the YMCA. No more choosing between the phone bill and the electricity. It meant I could move the fuck out of my mother's tiny one-bedroom apartment and the store room at the back of my gym. I could get my own place. That was *definitely* the best part.

But five years later, after driving the same goddamn routes and hefting the same goddamn boxes day in and day out, I'm getting tired. This job is starting to feel like the rest of this city has for all twenty-six, almost twenty-seven years of my life. Tired. Dirty. Same fuckin' attitudes, same fuckin' shit.

This year is the last year that any of me and my three siblings live with our mom. Selena left for Vermont with her boyfriend, Maggie finally moved in with Jimmy, her kid's father, and come June, Gabe graduates high school and is off to college. I'm so fuckin' proud of my little brother—full scholarship to CUNY, that smart kid. Makes everything worth it. Ma will finally have the place to herself, which she deserves more than any of us.

And now, finally, I can get the fuck out of New York.

"What're you drinking tonight, man?" Frankie slides a coaster my way.

I twist my lips, looking around the bar. Flaco is already hitting on a pack of Happy Hour chicks. They're cozied up at the pool table, where he's bent over one girl, trying to sneak a feel under her dress while he "teaches" her how to shoot. I snort. The guy is corny as fuck, but I can't deny he's got some game.

One of the other girls, a friend, gives me a smile and a wave. She's blonde and cute. There are a lot of cute girls in New York. But I know her type. Probably works as somebody's assistant somewhere, or maybe she's an intern. She'll be looking for a fun night here and there, maybe even looking for a ring one day, but not from a guy like me. I'd be something to remember when she's older, that time she went slumming with the dude from uptown.

Some nights I'm willing to play the part. A few well-placed Spanglish phrases, maybe boss her around a little, and I'll get an invitation back to the apartment in the Village she probably shares with three other girls. We'll hook up a few more times, but after a while she'll get bored. She'll meet an investment banker, some guy who's worth trapping. An asshole who'll make her a millionaire even while he's cheating on her every chance he gets.

Sometimes I'm okay playing that part. But tonight, I'm just not in the mood.

"Just a PBR," I tell Frankie when I swing back around. "Looks like Flaco's taken care of."

I push the brim of my hat up so I can watch the Knicks game on TV, ignoring the sound of the bar behind me. But I can't focus.

Fuck me, that girl. It doesn't take much to conjure that face again. That long black hair. That pale olive skin. Those bright blue eyes that basically shot an arrow through my chest. How old is she? I get a lot of practice looking at IDs—she's not more than twenty, twenty-one at most. Too young. But damn if I can't just see those full, heart-shaped lips pouting at me, ready to be kissed. Fuck if I can't imagine them wrapped around my—

The bar suddenly explodes at some play that just happened. But I have no fuckin' clue what it was. Shit. This is bad.

"Hey, fuckface! You gonna join us or what?"

I turn around and find Flaco with his arms slung around two girls, both giggling up a storm. He's grinning like an idiot, and behind him, I see Goldilocks giving me the eye. The way she's looking at me, I know I'll get lucky tonight if I want, maybe even in the cab on the way to her place.

I finish my beer and get up, thinking I might as well take advantage of the distraction. But I have a feeling I'm going to be thinking about someone else with long black hair and blue eyes the entire time.

CHAPTER THREE

Layla

THE SUBWAY RIDE BACK TO MY DORM IS SWEATY, GRAY, AND MOSTLY UNEVENTFUL. AT seven-thirty, the 6 train to Canal Street is still packed enough that there is condensation on the windows. The lights flicker when the car twists a little or swings on the track.

I barely notice any of it, with Nico's smile flashing through my head. It's ridiculous, really. We spoke—if you can call my minor paralysis speaking—for all of five minutes, maybe. He's a tattooed delivery guy, pretty much the exact opposite of anyone my family would want for me. I shake my head, catching a few curious looks from other people on the train. *Whatever.* Like there aren't thousands of crazy people in this city.

On a single train car, you can easily hear four or five different languages being spoken. It's a far cry from the Seattle suburb where I grew up, always an outcast among the skinny blonde women and their cloned daughters.

It didn't help that physically, I take after my father. I inherited his dark hair, his wide, full lips, and the shadows under his eyes. The only features I get from my mother, a blonde, picture-perfect Stepford wife, are her fair skin, her long, straight nose, and her blue eyes that glow in the right light. It wasn't until we visited Brazil, when I was fifteen, that I realized where I got my hips from. My father's side of the family endowed me with an ass that gets some attention in New York, but that used to make me cry when I didn't fit into the size-zero jeans the rest of my friends wore in high school.

So I wasn't like the rest of my friends, but I'm not like my father's family either. I don't look exactly like all of them either. Nor do I speak Portuguese. My dad staunchly refused to teach me, and my mother never learned it either.

Maybe that's why I became obsessed with New York when I visited in high school with my parents. It's a city full of in-betweens. Of people like me.

I spill off the train with the rest of the crowd after the black and white sign for Canal Street blurs in front of my window. I hurry the five-block walk, watching for black ice around gutters and curbs while dodging the Chinatown crowds. Canal Street is a rainbow of activity, even at eight o'clock at night in the middle of winter. The tchotchke shops are still open, their wares toppling onto the sidewalks, red lanterns, kites, t-shirts, shop after shop of cheap produce, fish, and meat. I pass the bakery where I sometimes buy pork buns for twenty cents each—change I could scrounge up on the street if I needed to. Not tonight. They're good, but they don't fill you up.

Lafayette is *the* social spot at NYU. Like many of the dorms for upperclassmen, it's a repurposed apartment building with full kitchens so students don't have to eat at the dining halls. The rooms also have high ceilings and large balcony spaces no one is supposed to use (though everyone does). The top floor is a penthouse usually inhabited by seniors who throw monthly parties on the roof. In short, Lafayette is a party house, and my roommates and I have embraced the chaos of living here.

I share apartment 5E, a two-bedroom place, with my three best girlfriends I met last year as freshmen: Shama, Jamie, and Quinn. Shama and Jamie are both from inland New Jersey, both journalism majors, both hilarious. They share the first bedroom.

Quinn, my roommate, is a no-nonsense girl from Boston, extremely motivated, and the most serious of the four of us. She's a little uptight—the only one of us still a virgin because of her "standards." We tease her about it sometimes, but honestly, I envy her. Quinn knows exactly what she's going to do for the next twenty years. She knows who she's going to marry (although she hasn't met him yet), what kind of medicine she's going to practice, where she's going to do her residency, how many kids she wants, and what sort of nanny she'll hire to take care of them.

Despite my father's insistence that I am going to law school after I graduate, I haven't even been able to pick a major yet.

I unlock the door to find Shama and Jamie lounging on the couch, watching reruns of—you guessed it—*Sex and the City* with Vinny, a friend who lives down the hall. Vinny and I have been friends since discovering a mutual love of soccer. His real name is Mervin, but his freshman roommates declared that utterly too nerdy, christening him Vinny from that day forth. Those guys were assholes, but apparently Vinny never liked Mervin anyway, and his middle name, Eustace, isn't much better. Like so many kids who come to college to reinvent themselves, Vinny took the moniker and ran with it.

"Hey!" Vinny stands up from the couch to give me a high five. "There she is! Dude, I need some guy time. These chicks are too much for me."

Jamie and Shama throw chips at him from either side, keeping their eyes glued to the TV. They are both *Sex and the City* fanatics and couldn't care less what a cliché that makes them. Thankfully, they agreed to watch only a few episodes per week when Quinn and I are in the apartment, considering how we quickly tire of Carrie Bradshaw's constant "wondering." Honestly, that chick never stops to answer any of her damn questions.

"That show is *nothing* like New York," I snark. How could a show claiming to represent this place be all about rich white people? Even from my sheltered, NYU-centric perspective, I know that's incorrect.

"Dude," Vinny says. "Preaching to the choir. But I had no idea there was so much sex. Those chicks are doing it, like, all the time! Do you think women in New York come that fast too?"

He pushes a gangly hand through his close-cut brown hair, clearly daydreaming about screwing his next date in a swing like the woman is currently doing on the screen. She moans in ecstasy.

"I doubt it on both counts." I hang my shoulder bag on the hook by the door, then put my parka over it.

Vinny pouts. "That's too bad, I could really use some lovin'. Those chicks are old, but they would be all right."

"They are not old!" Shama hurls another chip at Vinny's face. "You just like girls who look like preteens. Tell him, Lay, so I don't have to."

She sighs when Carrie kisses Mr. Big. Vinny picks the chip off the front of his shirt and pops it in his mouth.

"These bitches be *crazy*," he jokes.

"Shut *up*, Vinny!" Several more chips catapult toward his head.

From anyone else, calling my friends bitches would be enough to earn a lot more than a chip thrown at his head, but because Vinny is such a dork, not quite having grown out of his teenage-looking body and cracked voice, it just sounds funny. Shama's right, though. He does tend to date really thin women, but I suspect it's mostly because he's nervous about his own less than muscular physique.

Not like FedEx guy, I think to myself. And...*damn*. There's that smile again, flashing like it did the entire ride home. And my knees start to feel weak. And my mouth starts to drop.

I dodge the hailing finger foods and head into the kitchen to rustle up some food. It's been a long time since that cheap coffee.

"Come on, dude," I say to Vinny. "Let's have a drink and I'll tell you all about my new job."

I grab a soda from the fridge. It's a weekday so I'm not having any of the cheap beer we have stacked on one side. None of us drink during the week. I still have reading to do for my eight a.m. class, and I can't study if I'm sloshed.

Vinny, however, doesn't have the apartment's discipline. He doesn't have the grades either. He pops open his beer with gusto and takes a long drink while I find some carrots and hummus in the fridge and sit down at the breakfast bar in the kitchen.

"Thanks, man," he says. "I've already had a couple. I'll bring you guys a six pack tomorrow. Is that all you're eating for dinner?"

"You better, you lush!" Shama yells, allowing me to sidestep the question about my dietary habits.

The truth is, it's hard to eat well in such an expensive city. And unlike most of the kids I live with, I don't get allowance checks from my parents every month. Sometimes it's a choice between my social life and dinner. Okay, so it's not the smartest thing in the world, but I can eat when I'm old. I'm only going to be young and in the center of the universe once. The upside of coming home ten pounds lighter at my first Christmas break was that my mother was thrilled. Her greatest fear was that her daughter would gain the dreaded Freshman Fifteen, and instead I managed to lose the baby fat she was always haranguing me about.

"Cheers to your first day as a lackey, kid." Vinny clinks his can to mine. "Did you meet Katie Derek?"

"Not on the first day. But she did call a few times."

I take a long drink of my Diet Coke. I've got a decent night of studying ahead of me, so I need whatever help caffeine can give me. It's not going to be easy going to school full time and working an additional twenty-five hours per week, but I need the money more than I need the spare time. I'll just have to make it work.

Vinny nods. "That's really too bad. Anything else happen?"

I hide behind my can. Vinny's not exactly perceptive, but I doubt I can mask the heat rocketing up my neck.

"Um, not really," I lie. Hey, losing my power of speech because of a delivery guy's smile isn't really news, right? "They just taught me how to answer phones and stuff. My boss is kind of a bitch. She'd eat you alive, Vin."

Unfortunately, it doesn't take more than another brief memory of Mr. FedEx Man's gorgeous smile to make my face color all over again. Nico. The memory of his name makes me shiver.

"You met a guy."

I find Quinn standing in the open doorway in her sweaty gym clothes, water bottle in hand. She stares at me with a cocked eyebrow that immediately makes me feel like I have done something dirty, and she *knows* it. And she would, too. That's how tight Quinn and I are.

"Hi, Quinny Winny," I say in the baby voice I know she hates, but also can't help but love. I raise my can in her direction. "My *quin*tessential, quinniest Quinn. How was your day, darling?"

"Hi, babe." She gives me a quick air kiss before dropping her bottle in the sink. "You don't want to touch me—I'm stank right now."

"You work too hard," I counter.

It's a familiar, unspoken routine we go through almost daily. Quinn kills herself at the gym; I tell her she's overworking. At this point she usually makes some derogatory comparison of herself to me or another roommate, which is my cue to offer lavish praise.

Quinn arrived in New York about fifty pounds heavier than she is now and with an even bigger chip on her shoulder because of it. She was determined, like me, like all of us, to carve out a different spot for herself in this world than the one she grew up in. The first time we all tried out our fake IDs, she took one look at the scantily clad women in the club, said "Oh, *hell* no," and went straight to the twenty-four-hour Student Athletic Center. There would be no more being "the chubby one" for Quinn Bishop. Since then she's dropped that weight (sometimes more when she's being obsessive) and enjoyed herself thoroughly at the clubs and bars we frequent, but there's still a significant part of Quinn that will probably never be content with her body image.

"Not all of us were blessed with an ass you can bounce quarters on, unlike someone else I know, Barros."

Right on cue.

I glance down at said body part and shrug. "Eh, I'm pretty sure yours wins in a bikini contest these days, my love. I've seen you changing in the morning, and honey, let me tell you, meeeooowww."

I imitate an obnoxious purring noise, and she finally cracks a smile. I may not be able to catcall the hot FedEx guys I see, but I can do it to my roommates whenever I want.

"So who's the guy?" She opens a Diet Coke of her own and leans on the bar across from Vinny and me.

Her Shirley Temple curls escape around her forehead, but the rest are still swept back in a knot. I catch Vinny sneaking a peek down her tight work-out shirt and shoo him a way before answering.

"Get out of there, perv." I bat my eyes at Quinn, who's glaring at Vinny. "Only I get to check out the goods in this house. Oh, he's no one."

"Bullshit." Quinn takes a sip. "I saw that blush before I even opened the damn door. Out with it, Barros."

Vinny turns curiously, and Jamie and Shama's heads pop over the back of the sofa like puppets. I blush again.

"Okay, fine, you bitch. You win." I take a deep breath and sigh, amazed at how quickly I turn into your average, flustered romance character. I might even start biting my lip. Ugh. "Guys, I think I'm in love."

"In love?"

Jamie's voice squeals as she and Shama join us at the table. The TV is off, and all eyes are on me. Now that I have an audience—am I sure about this?

I close my eyes. There is that hundred-watt smile, those black, twinkling eyes, that deep, melodic voice. He's like some big, sexy panther I want to hunt me. It's not even about his body, which is pretty gorgeous as far as I can tell. It was something else, something that made every cell in my body seize up and shift toward his magnetic center. Oh yes, this is definitely love, or at least lust of the highest degree—how could anything else hit me this hard?

"I met the most beautiful man today," I proclaim and proceed to tell them all about Nico. It doesn't take long. But I give as much detail as I can, sighing like an idiot in between sentences.

"You are *so* going to marry him!" Jamie pronounces at the end of my story.

Shama grins while Vinny does his best to appear embarrassed, even though he's just as charmed as everyone else. It's not every day that someone walks in and starts talking about love at first sight.

I'm not an idiot. I know I'm young and that what I'm feeling could be nothing in the grand scheme of things. But I've never felt anything like that. There's a reason people compare it to a lightning bolt. You're hit all at once by that flash.

"I'm happy for you, babe. I really am." Quinn's tone tells me she's going to say something I don't want to hear.

I sigh, preparing myself for the inevitable. "But?"

"Layla, really. A FedEx guy? And how old do you think he is?"

I shrug, trying to play off her concerns like they don't matter, even though I know they probably do. I have no idea how old Nico is. He has one of those faces that hides his age, and his hat blocked any potential bald spots. He could be twenty, or he could be forty. God, I can just imagine my parents' faces—especially my dad's—if I brought home a thirty-something FedEx man. The thought alone makes me turn bright red.

"Don't know, don't care," I insist a little too loudly.

Okay, so, the idea of dating a thirty-five-year-old does make my skin crawl a little bit. After all, I'm only nineteen. Someone that age would literally be old enough to be my father. But there's no way Nico is that old. No one that gorgeous could be closer to my parents' age than mine.

"He's probably just a few years older than us," I say to Quinn. "And no, Miss

Snob-and-a-half, I don't care he's a FedEx courier. You don't know him any more than I do. He's probably a starving artist or something, just doing it to pay his bills. We'll all probably be there in two more years in this economy, you know."

"Ugh, don't remind me." Vinny gets up and stretches. "I have my first internship interview next week with Goldman Sachs. Do you know only one out of thirty interviewees gets this position? I told my mom she should be proud I even made it past the five hundred applications." He shakes his head. "You guys have it so easy in journalism. You can apply to marketing, newspapers, whatever. It's, like, the world's most universal degree."

Jamie and Shama clink water glasses.

"Don't we know it!" Shama cheers.

Quinn just gives me the side eye while I sip my Coke. The deadline for choosing a major by the end of the semester has been ticking away like a bomb. My friends are all moving down their paths in life, sorting out real internships, not just receptionist jobs, and I'm still...in between. Like always.

"Maybe he'll be your valentine this year." Jamie steers us back to Nico. "It's only two weeks away."

Jamie's our house romantic, even more than Shama. While it's grating at times to have every major relationship in any of our lives compared to Carrie and Mr. Big, I'll be honest—sometimes her brand of optimism is just what I'm feeling. It's certainly what I'm feeling right now.

Quinn snorts. "I doubt the FedEx workers are Valentine's Day fanatics. I bet they get sick of it because of all the extra packages."

"God, Quinn, why do you have to be such a downer?" Shama looks at me and grins. "You should just ask him out if you like him that much."

"No *way*."

Vinny slams his beer on the counter behind us. The action causes the beer to overflow, and he cries out, jumping up and slurping noisily at his can. Quinn snatches a dishtowel from the counter and starts mopping up the liquid. She really hates a messy kitchen, even though it's kind of a hopeless battle with four of us sharing it.

"Thanks." Vinny flops his gangly hands on the counter while Quinn cleans.

"Goddamn klutz," she mutters, chucking the towel at his head before settling back at the bar. "Finish it up, will you?"

"What I was trying to say was, you want to play it cool, kid," Vinny says as he wipes up his mess. "Dudes love a good chase. Tease him a bit, make him want you, but don't dish it out on a silver platter, you know?"

"I agree," Shama chimes in. "Vinny's actually right."

"Playa knows."

The rest of us to burst into laughter. Vinny is the absolute last thing from a player.

"Considering the source, it's not a bad idea," I admit.

"All right, how about this?" Shama continues. "Get him to ask *you* out."

"Hmmm," I say. "You think?"

Shama nods. "Do it."

I tap my finger on my lips, contemplating. "Quinn," I say just as my friend opens her mouth to object, "I promise. If he's over thirty-five—"

"Twenty-five," she counters with a look that means business.

"Thirty." I don't wait for her approval because I already know I wouldn't write him off because of age. "If he's older than thirty, no-go."

Now I actually do bite my lip. I *really* hope he's not thirty.

"It's on," Jamie says. "Guys aren't that hard to figure out. Drop a few hints, wear a low-cut shirt, and he'll make you his valentine all on his own. You'll see."

And with that, Operation FedEx Guy is officially in effect. But underneath the cheers and laughter of my roommates, the real question is, how in the hell am I going to get the best-looking man I've ever seen to ask me out when I can barely move around him in the first place?

CHAPTER FOUR

Layla

I SLIDE INTO A ROUTINE PRETTY QUICKLY. EVERY DAY AFTER MY MORNING CLASSES, I GO TO the gym, get changed into whatever sexy-yet-office-appropriate outfit I manage to scrounge up, and then take the train up to Fox and Lager. It's harder than I thought getting a moment alone with Nico—it seems like the entire office is waiting for him to arrive. Karen tends to stay until just after six so she can flirt with him, and a lot of the assistants decide they need to "get coffee" right at that time.

Give me a break. By six o'clock, the coffee is stale and ready to be thrown out. And as soon as Nico's gone, the whole office practically empties.

Luckily, even the preternaturally thirsty assistants don't want to hang around late on a Friday, and even Karen leaves early to meet up with friends for Happy Hour. By five-thirty, I'm mostly alone, twiddling my thumbs at the desk. It's casual Friday, so today I'm wearing my favorite dark blue jeans that pull attention to my ass, a clingy black sweater, and I actually took the time to dry my hair so that it lays in loose, thick waves over my shoulders. I'm no Gisele Bündchen, but I think I look pretty good.

I'm also getting impatient. Valentine's Day is in a week, and I've made absolutely no inroads with my cute FedEx guy. If anything, my inability to speak is getting worse. He comes in, full of swagger that no delivery guy has any right to have. Winks at me, and my knees go weak. Chats it up with Karen or one of the other assistants, but overall hasn't made any direct conversation with me other than a brief "Hey, NYU" or "How's it going?"

Not exactly the stuff of romance novels.

"Well, hello there. You must be the new girl."

I turn from sending a fax to find a man I haven't yet met leaning over my desk. His lavender striped tie hangs over the rounded wood edge, perilously close to my open cup of coffee.

The man smiles, the kind of cocky smile that tells me he's used to being adored.

"Now that's a nice face to see when you walk in the door," he says with a wink.

I give him a stiff smile back. "Better watch your tie."

The man stands up to shake my hand as I introduce myself.

"I'm Layla, sir."

"Oh, don't sir me, Layla, please. We're too friendly around here for that. You can call me Alex."

April told me about Alexander Farrell, Esquire, last week. He isn't a part of the firm, just a tenant who rents out office space with two other lawyers. Clean-shaven in a tailored, pinstriped suit, Alex is probably somewhere in his mid-to-late forties, but still looks good for his age, I have to admit. He has a full head of boyishly floppy hair, salt-and-peppered brown and casually mussed. He's also clearly fit, with muscles that stretch against the fabric of his shirt.

"Lovely to meet you, Layla."

He smiles again, revealing an impeccable set of white teeth that have to be capped. They look like my mom's. His skin is also a little too tan for someone who works in an office for twelve hours a day. My literature professor would call him a dandy.

His brown eyes twinkle as he leans on the desktop, as if gearing up for a good gab. "So, what's your story? Why are you here? Who is Layla? Tell me everything, now."

This time I can't help but smile back. He's kind of ridiculous, but this Alex guy has that kind of affable demeanor that draws people in. I bet it wins him a lot of clients.

"Well," I say slowly. "I'm a student at NYU. I moved here from Washington last year."

"Washington? No kidding. Where are your parents from? That skin and that hair —I'm guessing...Persian? Italian? Except the blue eyes...Irish?"

When I shake my head, Alex purses his lips like he's deep in thought.

"I give up." He grins. "Come on, what are you? Tell old Alex."

There's that question again. And what do I say? Half-Brazilian? It's not a part of me I've ever been taught to know. White? English? Washingtonian?

I just offer another polite smile. "My mother is originally from California, and my dad is from Brazil."

"Brazil! That's it!" Alex slaps the top of the desk in triumph. "I knew there was...something...about you. Something special." But before I can even have time to feel awkward about the infatuation with my ethnicity, he's on to the next question. "What about school? What are you studying there?"

So much for avoiding the awkward.

I clear my throat. "I'm planning to go to law school eventually, I guess." My dad's stern face pops into my head. Oh yeah, it's definitely going to be law school. "I thought this would be a good place to start learning about it."

"Do you like it so far?"

"This is only my first week, but everyone seems nice."

"Well, I sure hope so, my darling." Alex stands up and straightens his tie and shirt cuffs. "They treat you bad, just tell 'em to see old Alex. We're lucky to have such a beautiful addition to the office, so they'd better be grateful."

He winks again when the phone starts ringing. I'm not completely sure of what to make of his flirty comments. It didn't feel like anything was wrong, and he's such a nice guy; I don't want to jump to any conclusions. But the phone provides a welcome escape. So does the elevator as it chimes open.

Nico

Six o'clock is quickly becoming my favorite time of day. I know what she's doing. Last week she was wearing shapeless office clothes, the kind she probably borrowed from a friend until she got a new paycheck. This week she's been dolled up, hair down around her shoulders, something that should be illegal on her lips, and pants and skirts that basically force me to stand behind the stack of packages every day to keep from embarrassing myself.

Because it just doesn't care. My cock doesn't care that this girl is obviously too young for me. It doesn't care that she has the entire world there for the taking, and I'd only hold her back. All it cares about is the way her ass looks every time she bends over the desk to grab something, or the way her eyes gleam when they seek me out across the room me.

Fuckin' traitor.

We haven't been able to talk, so all I can do is smile like some kind of clown. She seems to like it, but I feel like an idiot. But what can I say? The girl makes me grin. On Wednesday, I managed to make her laugh out loud when she was on the phone, and I practically combusted. Now it's a daily goal, even when Karen is looking in on us or decides she needs to come out to join the fun. All of a sudden, I'm putting on a comedy act for the entire fucking floor. Because seriously, I could listen to that laugh for the rest of my life.

See? Dangerous.

Today, the office is practically deserted when I arrive late. I'm tired. It's been a long week, and an even longer fuckin' day. I had to help Flaco with some of his packages after staying up with Alejandra all night while my sister pulled an all-nighter. Maggie really has to get some better study habits.

But it's not just that. It's Allie's jackass dad being a shithead again, which means that Maggie is crashing with me right now. It's Gabe spending all the food stamp money on cereal when Ma sent him shopping, so I had to chip in an extra hundred to their grocery bill on top of paying my own rent. It's the truck getting a flat tire on Forty-First today and half the FDNY yelling at me and Flaco for getting in their way. Nothing like being screamed at in the middle of Park Avenue by New York's Bravest.

Fuck.

So I'm not feeling like such a comedian today. And I sure as fuck want to kick that asshat attorney in the face when I see him hanging over Layla's desk. I know that dude. I've watched him hit on April and every other chick in this building countless times. The guy doesn't wear a ring, but I happen to know he's married. You know how? Because his *wife* has shit delivered to his office almost every day.

"Remember what I told you," says Dickhead when I roll into the lobby. "You tell them to see me."

See you about *what*, asshole?

He stands up, actually points his fingers at Layla like guns, and makes clicking sounds at her. She gives him a little smile, and I want to punch him in his stupid fake teeth. The guy has to be at least forty, if not more. He's old enough to be her dad, and he's looking at her like she's something to eat.

Fuck. This is not what I want to be doing right now. All I want is to finish this delivery and run up my tab at Traveler. Pretend this day never happened. And I definitely don't want to watch the girl who's been in my head for the past week smiling at the biggest douchebag in Manhattan.

"I'll let you know how it goes," Layla says to Captain Asshat before he walks past me like I'm a piece of furniture. Yeah, fuck you too, buddy.

Still, when Layla turns to me, her blue eyes glow like stars in the middle of this bland, boring office. She grins. It's not the tight, polite smile she was just giving that clown. It's huge and lights up her whole face. And the fuck if I don't grin right back.

It's then I realize that for the first time, we're alone. No Karen. No assistants. No Fuckface von Douchebag, Esquire. Just us.

"Hey there, NYU," I say as I pull everything up to her desk.

She takes a drink of something from a paper cup and spills a little when I speak. I have to look away when a drop of water hangs on her bottom lip. Whoa. Would it be weird if I just kissed her? Yeah, it would be weird. But all of a sudden, that's all I can think about doing after this shitty, shitty day. I get the feeling that kissing Layla would make everything else disappear because I wouldn't be able to think of anything else but her. Hell, that's basically where I'm at just being in the same room as her.

She gives me a little scowl as she wipes water off her chin, but I can tell she's glad I'm here. She knows it, and I know it. The excitement is written all over both our faces.

"Look what you made me do." Her tone is more teasing than mad. "A menace, that's what you are."

"Aw, I'm sorry, sweetie. You need some help?"

I don't even wait for her to say yes. I just want to be near her, that's all. Nothing inappropriate. Nothing "improper." Today, I just need to be next to this girl who lights up whenever she sees me.

So I drop the dolly and walk around the desk to squat next to her. I grab another napkin off the desktop, and she stares, mouth slightly open, as I dab at the water drops on her collarbone.

What a total sham. Nothing improper? This is the definition of improper. But I can't stop dabbing, can't stop pressing the napkin over her dewy skin, wishing to God that it was my fingers or my mouth instead.

The donut-shaped desk encircles us, forces us close together, and now that I'm near enough to smell her, I realize this was a really bad idea. She smells like coconuts and flowers, a mix that goes straight to my head and other parts lower down.

I'm not much for fancy shit. I shower at night after I've been out all day, and I slap on whatever deodorant I bought on sale last time I was at the Duane Reade. All of a sudden, I'm very, very conscious of the way Layla's nipples have hardened through her thin black sweater, conscious of the way my pants are suddenly *very* tight. She inhales sharply. I consider the fact that I have been heaving boxes around this city for the last eight hours.

Fuck. She must think I absolutely *reek*.

Quickly, I shuffle to the other side of the desk to start unloading and scanning packages. This day. This god*damn* day. If I just ruined my chances with this girl, I'm going to kick my own ass.

And that's when I realize I actually want a chance with NYU. Layla. I want to go on a date with her. I want to take her out to dinner and hold her hand while we walk around the city. I want to know what kinds of sounds she makes when I kiss her, or maybe even when I do other things to her too. And I kind of want those things more than anything else I can think of.

Fuck. The timing could not be worse. No. I can't do this right now.

"How old are you, NYU?" I blurt out before I can stop myself. It's harsh, and a little sudden, but we might as well put it out there.

"Twenty-one," she answers automatically, a little too quickly.

I just cock my eyebrow. I've been a doorman for too long not to know when people are lying about their age. "What's your real age?"

She sags a little in her chair, and her cheeks turn red. Fuck. It makes me want to lick them.

"Nineteen."

Shit. I knew that's what she would say, but for some reason, hearing it out loud makes the reality of our seven-year age gap hit home. Maybe even eight depending on her birthday. I'll be twenty-seven in a few months. What am I going to do, bring a teenager home to meet my mother?

For real: the thought of bringing anyone home to meet my mom scares the shit out of me.

"What about you?" Layla asks. It's the most she's ever said to me out loud. She sits up a little straighter.

I sigh. "Twenty-six."

I hate the way my age hits her too. The way she frowns, like she knows it's not good. She was probably hoping I'd say twenty-two, twenty-three. Too bad, baby. Even if I wanted to move forward with this thing, it's clear now that I'd never be anything more to her than a good time. Another dude to slum with before she goes back to her rich parents, wherever they live. Washington, did she say?

"So, Nico." Layla pulls me out of my hurricane of doubt. She stands, rebounded from the revelations. "Got big plans this weekend?"

Can she see the fear I'm feeling? She's hopeful, all big blue eyes as she leans over the desk. I exhale. No, I really can't do this with her. So even though I'm dying to make her laugh again, I just shrug and set one of the packages down with a thump.

"Not really," I say. "Working at AJ's, you know. Take it easy on Sunday, maybe go see some art or something."

"You like art? Really?"

I look up, no longer needing to pretend I'm annoyed with her. These rich girls—all the fucking same. They see the uniform, the scuffed shoes, the brown skin. They think the only thing I'm good for is watching sports and drinking beer. Don't get me wrong, I like sports, and I like beer. But can't I have other interests too?

"I could like art." I scan another package. "Why does that surprise you? You think the FedEx means Philistine?"

Her rosebud mouth drops open, and I can't quite hide my smirk. That's right, baby. I can use big words too.

"No," she insists, a little too emphatically. "I—no. No, no, no, that's not what I meant. I'm so sorry, it's just that my roommates and I were talking, and—oh my God, that made me sound like such an asshole, didn't it? *Shit!*"

Before I can help it, I'm chuckling. She's flustered and red-faced and grabbing at her hair, and it's so fucking cute I can't help but laugh while she babbles on—something about how she wondered to her roommates if I was an artist or some shit like that.

I lean over the desk and touch her shoulder. "Hey."

There it is again—that lightning buzz. She stops talking immediately and blinks her big blue eyes.

"It's okay. You're not an asshole."

She swallows. "What kind of art do you like?"

She's biting her lip. *Biting* her fucking *lip*. I mean, I know I do the same thing when I'm nervous, but I'm pretty sure if I looked like that when I did it, I wouldn't be able to walk down the street without being molested. I turn and unload more boxes just so I don't haul her over the desk and bite that lip for her.

Walk away, man. Just walk away.

"Pretty much all art." I lift set another box onto the stack. "I draw a little in my spare time, but mostly I just like to see it. There's a new exhibit at the Met opening up this weekend, so I might go to that. Y'know, if they'll let in some uncouth spic like me to mix with the college girls like you."

She flushes again, and I'd feel bad if it wasn't so damn cute.

"I really didn't mean it like that." She looks down at her hands. "I'm not..."

She's ashamed. I was just giving her shit—anyone who looks at her can see that rich or not, she's not just some uptight white girl, but now I'm starting to see that Layla's not really sure about that herself. And here I am throwing around racial slurs just to make her uncomfortable because I'm in a shitty mood. *I'm* the asshole.

"Hey, it's cool, sweetie," I say. "I'm just giving you a hard time. I can see you're good people."

Her smile is instantaneous. It makes my chest swell about five times its size, not to mention makes all the other shit from today seem to disappear. Fuck. How am I supposed to say no to that?

Suddenly, the answer is simple: don't.

Don't say no to the pretty girl.

Don't say no to what every part of my body is telling me to do.

Don't say no at all.

"Listen." I hand her the clipboard to sign for the packages and shift between the balls of my feet. Fuck, I'm nervous. Why am I so nervous? "Music should be good this weekend, if you and your friends want to stop by AJ's. I'll put you on the list."

She cocks her head to the side with a sly grin—a grin I'm starting to recognize. It's the look she gets when she's trying to get me to flirt with her. She thinks she's being coy, but what she doesn't know is that her plain attraction is getting harder and harder to ignore. So I'm not going to anymore.

"Even if I'm only nineteen?" she jokes.

"Wait a second." I shake my head in fake-confusion. "You said you're twenty-one. I can't let any minors into the club."

I'm rewarded with a giggle. A fuckin' giggle. And I fuckin' love it.

"Right, right. Yeah, I'm twenty-one."

"That's what I thought."

I watch happily as she bites her lip again. Yeah, she likes my smile. Well, that's good, since I can't stop doing it around her.

"Great." She focuses really hard on rearranging a set of pens in their small plastic cup. "I don't know what we have going on this weekend, but I'll see if my roommates are interested. Maybe we'll see you there."

She's playing casual, but I bet she'll be there. Fuck, I hope she'll be there. Time to go while I'm ahead.

"Yeah, yeah, no worries." I tug the now-empty dolly backward. The elevator opens immediately after I tap the call button. "See you later, NYU."

I don't look at her. I don't want to see if she's smiling or biting her lip again. I'm not sure I can take either in this mood.

"Hey, Nico," she calls just as I'm rolling backward into the elevator. "Out of curiosity, do you even remember my name?"

I look up. Because how could I not, with a question like that? And her eyes glow, and she's looking at me, half-uncertain, half-flirtatious. All the way gorgeous.

"How could I forget?" I say simply. "Layla's a beautiful name."

CHAPTER FIVE

Layla

SATURDAY NIGHT ROLLS AROUND AT AN EXCRUCIATINGLY SLOW PACE. JAMIE, SHAMA, AND Quinn convince me that showing up at AJ's right at ten, when the band actually starts, would come across as desperate. It's...hard, but I have to admit they're probably right.

That look on his face when he found out I was nineteen just about killed me. And, yeah, I'm not going to pretend I'm not a little disappointed by it. But twenty-six isn't *that* old, you know? Seven years. I'll be twenty in July. The more I think about it, the more it seems like nothing.

But I don't want him to look at me like that again. Like I'm a child. Some kind of forbidden fruit. And to do that, I need to not look like a kid waiting for Santa Claus every time I see him. I need to play it cool.

So on Saturday, after pre-gaming with shots of the 99 Bananas Jamie managed to buy off one of the upperclassmen (oh my *God*, that stuff is rank), the girls and I decide to start the night at Fat Black's, an NYU dive bar off Washington Square Park. Shama's boyfriend is a DJ there, so she wants to stop by for a little action. The plan is to saunter over to AJ's sometime after midnight as if we just "happened" to find the time.

"He asked me for fifteen minutes in the DJ booth," Shama says with a sly grin while we're getting ready in the tiny bathroom. "What was I supposed to say?"

"Because *that's* not desperate." I elbow her in the ribs.

I can't blame her. It's rough when we're all hooking up on the single scene, and her guy can't come too. Poor Shams ends up being the odd one out too much of the time.

The small tiled sink is cluttered with tubes of mascara and other cosmetics. We all have our signature looks that play up our best features. Jamie usually focuses on her lips with a slash of red lipstick, while Shama almost always teases her long black hair into waves. Quinn tames her curly hair and highlights her bone structure and lips in shades of pink. I, on the other hand, do my best to pull focus to my eyes, lining them with a lot of black that makes the blue pop, even at night. Tonight I make sure to look my absolute best, taking the time to straighten my thick hair so that it hangs almost to my waist.

Shama ribs me right back while she wraps another piece of hair around her curling iron. "Hell, no. Helps keep things fresh! Maybe you need to invite FedEx behind the desk again, huh?"

I already told her about yesterday's interlude, when Nico was literally touching the skin two inches above my breasts. They were heaving. My breasts were actually heaving, like I was some idiotic character in a bad book about pirates and fair maidens. Heaving bosoms. Christ.

"You should have pulled his hand lower."

Shama winks at me in the mirror, and I can't help but crack up. She has a bit of an exhibitionist streak, and I wouldn't put a quickie in the DJ booth past her.

We make a damn fine posse. Shama wears a white mini-dress that makes her skin and hair glow. Jamie and Quinn are both dressed in tight jeans and shimmery tank tops beneath their jackets. I'm wearing a short LBD that hugs my body, and a pair of thigh-high black boots that show off my legs. Shama lends me some of the gold bangles she brought back from her trip to India last summer, and I wear a pair of gold hoops to match. I feel sexy and sophisticated—much different from "office" Layla.

When we stride into the bar like we own the place, I know my efforts haven't been in vain. At least three groups of guys all turn our direction, and at least two of them start preening like peacocks to catch my eye.

I pay them no attention while the girls and I find a table. Shama slips away to say hi to her man and returns within a few minutes with a round of beers, which we all accept eagerly.

"Truth or dare?" Quinn points the neck of her beer bottle in my direction.

Okay, so it's juvenile, but we use it as a way to break the ice with random strangers. Plus it's hilarious. Maybe not the best way to come off as "sophisticated," but right now I'm thinking we should just get the goofy out of our systems before we go to AJ's.

After Jamie requires Quinn to do the chicken dance in the middle of a slow song for a solid minute, Quinn earns her right to choose the next victim. She points at me, and I can tell it's going to be something good.

"Dare," I say obediently. There is really no point in choosing truth; we tell each other everything anyway.

"All right, Barros," she says, tossing her brown ringlets over her shoulder. "You're so hot for FedEx Guy that the pheromones are practically oozing out of your pores. I think you need to expel some of that excess energy before we embark on Mission 'Court the Courier.' Your dare, should you choose to accept it, is to make out with one of the men in this room for at least a minute. I'm talking solid tongue twister here, babe."

I blanch as Jamie and Shama whoop their support for the plan. There's only one guy I'm interested in making out with tonight (although I'm not planning on it happening for a while longer), and he isn't present. But maybe Quinn has a point. It might do me some good to release this pent-up energy.

"Fine," I relent to the girls' cheers.

I stand up, smooth my skirt, and straighten my boots as I survey the room. Who's half-decent looking and would be game for some fun without getting too handsy? Peering around, I light my eyes on Mike, a guy I hooked up with once at a party freshman year. We made out on a couch for a while before the cops shut everything down. Thirty minutes without going past first base. I smile. He'd be game.

"Target acquired," I inform my friends, then weave my way to where Mike stands at the bar.

I can feel the girls' eyes on me as I approach him, and the competitor in me relishes the attention. I do well under pressure. But it's more than that. Am I this girl, deep down, who goes around kissing strangers, especially when I already know there's only one person I want to be kissing? Not really. But sometimes it feels good to be something different from what I think I am. From Layla, the straight-A student. Layla, Daddy's good little Catholic girl. Layla, future lawyer.

Sometimes it feels good to be a little bad.

"Hey, Mike." I tap him on the shoulder.

He looks like every other guy in this bar in a striped button-down shirt, tailored jeans, and a carefully manicured chin-strap. His hair is gelled so that it looks like he just rolled out of bed, but sleek, like it's been covered in oil. I actually hate this style— these kinds of dress shirts look like pajamas, and I can't stand to touch hair with more product in it than mine. Every douchey investment banker and business student in Manhattan likes this look; it's about as generic as you can get.

Mike turns with a puzzled look that evolves into mild recognition.

"Layla," I prompt. "Remember, we met at that party last year in Brittany Hall..."

His recognition clearly grows, and his brown eyes widen with appreciation as he looks me up and down. If I didn't already know I look good tonight, Mike's expression would tell me.

"Yeah," he says. "I remember. How're you doing? Been a while."

He's close enough that I can smell the beer on his breath. His eyes are a little glazed, and the tip of his nose is red. Good, he'll be more likely to play along.

"I'm good, really good. So listen," I rush on before he can ask me another inane question. I'm not interested in flirting, just getting my dare over with so we can go. It's almost eleven, and Quinn wants to go to another bar before AJ's.

"What's up? Can I get you a drink, by the way?"

"No, thanks. I have one at my table. But I do have a favor to ask."

Mike cocks an eyebrow. "Sure, what's the problem?"

"Well, I kind of made a stupid bet with my friends. See, I told them you and I kind of hooked up at that party, and they don't believe me because they thought you were cute. I sort of bet them twenty bucks that you maybe wouldn't mind doing it again right here." I lower my eyelids in that come-hither look that works so well with guys like him. "Right now."

Mike gulps visibly, and I'm satisfied to see a familiar hunger as he stares at my lips.

"Could you help a girl out?" I step closer and float a hand up his arm.

He looks at it, and then looks back at me. "Uh, sure," he says after taking another big gulp of his beer. He wraps a slightly awkward hand around my waist and tugs me close. "I think I could do that. If you give me your number this time."

I don't say anything, just give him a sly smile. He leans in for the kill, setting his lips on mine and pressing his tongue into my mouth. It's pleasant—I remember it from last time. Enough to stir some tingles in my toes and make my breath come up short. But if I can still count the seconds in my head to a minute without hesitation, the guy isn't that good of a kisser. That's the thing about a great kiss: when it happens, you shouldn't be able to think at all.

And fifty-nine, and sixty! I pull away.

"Thanks again," I say, leaving him slightly confused and catching his breath. "Why don't you write down your number and I'll call you some time?"

"You're going so soon?"

He's obviously disappointed; I step beyond his reach before I start to feel the evidence of his excitement against my leg. Yeah, no thanks.

"Girls' night." I raise my hands as if to say, "What can you do?"

He nods as if he understands entirely, then scribbles down his number on a bar napkin. "Call me. We can hang out again. For more than just a minute."

"Sounds like a plan." I tuck the napkin into my small black purse and give him a quick salute before weaving back through the crowd to where the girls are all cackling like crazy into their drinks. Their triumphant expressions make it easier to ignore the sinking feeling in my stomach, like I've just done something wrong.

"Happy? That poor guy thinks I'm actually into him now." I pull out the napkin and push it on the table to Quinn. "Maybe you could use this instead."

Her face is bright red from laughing so hard, and she fights to catch her breath before she answers. "Oh, God. That was so worth doing the chicken dance. So. Worth. It."

I just take a large gulp of my drink. I've made out with my fair share of guys—I'm in college, for crying out loud—but for some reason I feel kind of dirty. It was just a kiss, fairly innocent, but still. I never believed in soulmates before—you wouldn't either if you'd grown up with my parents, two diehard Catholics who would rather throw themselves off a cliff than get a divorce. But right now, I have this distinct feeling that there is someone out there really meant for me, and for once, I don't want to share my kisses with anyone else.

A pair of twinkling black eyes under a curved brim flashes through my mind. I want to get out of this bar right now.

"All right, babe, your turn," Quinn interrupts my brooding. "You earned it, that's for sure."

I drain the rest of my beer. "I think I'm going to reserve my call for next time. Shama saw her man. Can we go?"

CHAPTER SIX

Nico

IT'S ALWAYS THIS TIME OF YEAR THAT I REGRET THIS JOB. I STARTED WORKING THE DOOR four years ago, after I'd been boxing enough that my shoulders got big. K.C., my best friend and a badass DJ, hooked me up with a job at his first regular gig, and it snowballed from there. I'm not huge or anything, but apparently, I have a knack for scaring off assholes and, according to K.C., attracting enough hot girls to get the party started.

Whatever. It's an extra two hundred dollars in my pocket every week. And usually I don't complain about a job that's this easy until it's the middle of January and I'm sitting on my ass in twenty-degree weather. That two hundred dollars can go fuck itself. I'll stay poor in my nice, warm apartment.

Two people leave the bar, and I let in another two—this time a man and woman, clearly on a date. She's got curly black hair that reminds me a little of Layla's on the first day I saw her. I hope she does her hair like that again. I liked it.

I shake my head, realizing I am already so pussy-whipped that I am thinking about a girl's *hair*. Maybe it's better she and her friends didn't show tonight after all.

A blast of freezing wind whips off the river, just a few blocks away. It hasn't snowed in several weeks, but gray-colored sludge leftover from the last storm is still piled at the ends of the sidewalks, leaving icy sinkholes that are easy to mistake for concrete. Everyone in the line is moaning and groaning because of the wind. Whatever. They should try sitting in it for six straight hours.

"Jesus!" A sharp voice echoes down the street. "I don't care how cute this guy is, he is *not* worth losing body parts. I am not about to get fucking frostbite so you can get laid, babe."

I smirk as a group of girls join the line snaking down the block. They're all dressed in tiny skirts and skin-tight shirts. We'll see how long they last.

"Ugh," another one complains. "Okay. I'll walk up there and see if I can do anything."

I snort. The club is *packed* tonight, and there is a line of people waiting. *Good luck, ladies. I don't care how short your skirts are, you're not getting in.*

"Hey, man. Can we, um, offer you a little extra to get us out of the cold?"

The next two people in line are a couple of douchey-looking bros who probably work on Wall Street. One of them is holding out a too-obvious twenty in his sleazy little palm. I look down at the cash, and then back at his smarmy face.

"Sorry," I reply shortly. "We're at capacity. I can't let you in."

"I could make it worth your while, dude. I'm sure guys like you could use a little extra cash."

The other guy holds out a hundred folded up into a square. He gives a little nod, like he's trying some kind of Jedi-mind trick on me. I hate that a part of me wants to take it, because the fact is, I could use the money, especially this week. But if the fire marshal comes, I lose my job, and that's a lot more money. Not to mention, I don't appreciate these kinds of bullshit assumptions. They don't know me. They don't know what I need or not. Fuck these guys. For real.

"No can do," I bark again. "Back behind the line."

The two guys grumble, but do what I say. I check the time. Fuck. It's just after midnight, but with the crowd like this, I have at least three more hours of this shit to deal with.

"Um, Nico?"

I look up again, full of irritation. "*What?*"

Bright blue eyes, beacons in the dark. Long black hair that's even straighter than usual. And a coat that's hanging open to reveal a dress that is *way* too short and that she makes look *way* too good.

Layla.

"Hey!" I jump off my stool. "NYU!"

Before I can stop myself, I pull her into a quick embrace and kiss her cheek. Big mistake. There's that coconut scent again, plus something that's just...her. Flowers? Soap? Something warm and sweet that I can't put my finger on. One whiff triggers an express line to my cock, even in this fucking cold.

"You made it," I say as I step back.

She looks stunned, but looks me up and down anyway. Not much to see. I'm in my big black parka and a black knit hat that covers my ears—about as basic as it gets.

"Not too far from campus for you?" Shit, was the kiss too much? Is she going to say anything?

She shakes her head, like she's exiting a trance. "Nah," she says with a smile. "We were in the area anyway, so I thought we should stop by. My roommates and me, that is. But it's all full, isn't it?"

At that moment, the thick steel door opens, and two couples leave the club, arms wrapped tightly around each other's waists, laughing as they grope for each other's mouths. I feel a momentary twist of jealousy at the sight of them.

I turn back to find Layla watching me.

I grin. "Not full anymore. How many you got?"

"J-just four," she stutters as another gust of wind blows down the street. Those boots are sexy, but she's got to be freezing.

"All girls?"

She rubs her arms and nods.

"As cute as you?"

She flushes and gives me a shy smile. Even in this cold, it makes me melt.

"Perrrfect," I say. "Bring 'em up, sweetie."

She waves to the girls at the back of the line, and they scuttle up to us.

"Nico, these are my roommates: Jamie, Shama, and Quinn," Layla says, pointing to each as they pull out their IDs.

I take a cursory glance at each one. They're all fakes, but good fakes. Fakes that won't fuck over the bar owner if by chance an undercover cop shows up. It doesn't happen a lot, but definitely more than it used to. One of the many changes after 9/11.

"Hey, man, what the fuck!" protests one of the investment-banker douches who tried to bribe me.

I turn and glare.

"You got a problem with these ladies, my friend?" I ask in a don't-fuck-with-me voice that you only learn if you grew up in certain neighborhoods in this city.

Too bad this dude doesn't get the message. He's been too busy nursing his entitled ass out in Connecticut or someplace like that to learn basic commonsense in New York: Don't piss off the doorman.

"We've been waiting for over an hour in this fucking weather, man." This idiot just doesn't know when to stop. "It's not cool to let in a bunch of skanks just because you want some easy pussy."

"Ex*cuse* me? What the—"

One of Layla's friends—I think the one named Quinn—starts to snap back at the guy, but I'm already done. It's motherfuckers like this that make me want to leave this city and never look back. I have the guy shoved against the icy brick wall of the building before anyone can say another word. Grant, the other bouncer, stays by the door. He knows I can handle myself.

"Listen, you pencil-dick, Gordon-Gecko-wannabe *fuck*," I pronounce as evenly as I can. I have an audience with the girls, not to mention the line of people that have become really, really quiet. But I don't care. "You will apologize to my friends here, and you will do it nicely. And then you will get the *fuck* out of here before I have to beat some manners into that slimy little mouth of yours. You got that?"

The banker murmurs a quick apology before skulking away with his friend. Most of the people look awkwardly in other directions, obviously not wanting to be the next person tossed out of the club line. Layla and her friends just stare with open mouths. Shit. So much for a good impression.

"Sorry about that," I say uneasily as I sit back on my stool. "Those kind of entitled assholes think they can say whatever they want. I, uh, hope it didn't ruin your night."

All four nod, like they're too stunned to respond. Fuck. I don't usually lose my temper like that anymore, but something about that guy, and the way he was talking about Layla and her friends...I don't know. It just got to me.

"Uh, how much do we owe you for the cover?" Layla squeaks.

Immediately, I soften. "Nothin', sweetie. It's on me. You girls go on and enjoy yourselves, okay?"

The girls murmur their thanks, clearly shaken up by what they just saw, and file through the door now held open by Grant. But I can't help it. I don't want Layla to go in thinking I'm some kind of thug, so I grab her hand and pull her back. Her eyes are still big, and the shock in them makes me feel very small. She looks down at my clutch on her fingers.

"You look really nice tonight, Layla," I say quietly. I use her name, not "sweetie" or "NYU." I want her to know that I see *her*.

She opens and closes her mouth a few times. I really fucked up. So much for the chance I was hoping for.

"Thanks," she whispers.

"Come out and say hi again if you have a second."

Then I let her go. Because the way this night has gone, I doubt she'll have a second for me again.

––––––

Layla

The dancehall group lives up to the hype. For the next hour and a half, I actually forget that I'm here to flirt with the doorman, throwing myself into the music with my room-mates and having the time of my life. I love dancing for the same reason I love playing sports. It forces you to live in the moment, controlling every movement of your body as you lose yourself in your surroundings. You can't think about anyone or anything else.

It's a nice way to ignore what just happened out there. You see things like that in movies, but it's not the same when, in real life, the man you're lusting over defends your honor. I don't even care that he just threatened to beat the crap out of some stranger. I don't care that I should probably have turned around and left. What really scares me is how turned on I was when he did it. That's what I'm trying to forget.

After ninety straight minutes of dancing, I'm sweaty, tired, and ready for a break. The band is done, and now there's a DJ who will play until last call, sometime around four. Shama split a while ago to meet up with Jason, and both Quinn and Jamie have cozied up to dance partners of their own, so I won't be missed. I get a cup of water at the bar, retrieve my coat from where it's stashed behind a speaker, and head outside to fulfill my promise to Nico.

At this point, the line to get into the club is gone. Nico sits alone on his stool, hands shoved into his pockets while he stares at the concrete, deep in thought. Plumes of white escape his lips and nose as he breathes.

"Cold?" I ask.

He looks up, clearly surprised to see me. And then that grin appears again. I'm really never going to get used to that.

"Nah," he says. "I could walk across Antarctica in this coat and still be hot. You okay, though? That outfit can't be too warm."

I look down to where my open coat reveals my dress. "I'm good. It's really hot in there right now."

The chilly wind actually feels refreshing. I shift back and forth on my feet, unsure of what else to say. Usually I'm pretty good at flirting, but with him, it's like eighty percent of my vocabulary goes on vacation. How am I supposed to charm him if I can't find words—any words at all?

I look back up to find him watching me intently, and before I know it, I blurt out, "You have a terrific smile, you know."

That, of course, earns me another ear-splitting grin, which just about makes me lose my footing. Christ, what is happening to me? I look back down and tap the pointed toes of my shoes together. One, two, three. Anything to avoid staring at him like an idiot.

A gloved finger reaches out and tips my chin up so I'm looking into a pair of impossibly dark eyes. This close, I can see that they're brown, not black. An insanely, chocolatey, dive-into-them dark brown.

Nico's expression softens. "Thanks, sweetie," he says gently and drops his hand, almost as if the contact makes him nervous too. "I'm sorry about what happened before. With those guys. I was already pissed off, and when he called you a—"

"It's okay," I cut in even while I'm trying not to flush. "Forget about it, really."

Nico pauses, like he's not sure whether to believe me. Then he sighs. "Did you like the music?"

I nod. "I did, yeah. Dancehall is really fun. Kind of reminds of samba, a little."

"You dance samba?"

"Yeah. A little, since my dad is Brazilian. We've gone for Carnaval a couple of times. I picked up a few moves."

Nico scans me up and down, appraising. "Yeah, I can see that. You got a little of the look of some Brazilians I've met. You speak Portuguese?"

I flush again. "A little. We, um, didn't speak it much in the house. My mom doesn't speak it at all."

Nico nods again, as if that confirms something untold about me. What, I don't know.

"Well, let's see it."

"See what?"

Nico raises one black brow. "Come on, NYU. You were just telling me how good you can samba. Was that all just talk?"

I giggle. "This isn't samba music," I say lamely, earning another raised brow.

"Come on…" he cajoles with another grin. "I'm not going to believe you otherwise."

"Okay, okay," I relent. "But only if you do it with me."

To my surprise, he hops off his stool and holds out his gloved hands. Even through the thick leather, I can feel that electric spark.

"Show me," he says.

So I do. We move awkwardly through the basic steps, which he keeps trying to dance like they're salsa. Eventually, though, he gets the rhythm, and I speed up so we roughly match the grinding pace of the dancehall vibrating from inside the club. In Brazilian samba, the feet move so quickly you can hardly discern one step from another—it's all in the hips. Soon mine are shaking all over the place, and I let go of his hands so I can move forward and back and turn to the music the way my cousins taught me a few years ago, the way I would practice in my bedroom when my parents weren't home. Nico tries to follow, going faster and faster until finally we trip over each other's feet, and I topple into his arms.

"Careful!" he exclaims, but we're both laughing like crazy.

I inhale his scent and am barely able to stand upright when I pull away. Nico resumes his seat and looks me over, like he's checking to see if everything is in order. I pull nervously at my skirt.

"Okay, NYU," he says as he chuckles. "I guess you really are Brazilian. You move like one, anyway."

Inside, I feel a twinge. Is that what I am? I never felt like it until I moved here and everyone insisted on it.

"What about you?" I ask, diverting the attention from me. "What kind of name is Nico?"

"It's short for Nicolás Soltero," he pronounces. "I'm a mutt too, like you. My mom's, um, Puerto Rican, and the other half is Italian, Puerto Rican, and some other stuff too. I grew up with my moms, though, so her side's the only one that really matters."

"You never saw your dad?" I blurt out, aware too late of how rude my question is. Nico's dark eyes grow even darker, but he gives me a rueful smile.

"No, sweetie, I didn't," he says kindly. "He ran with some bad dudes, got locked up before I was born. I don't know where he is now. But...whatever. It's in the past."

An awkward silence grows as we stare at each other. Anything that comes to mind to say seems completely inadequate and ignorant. In my suburban existence, I've never really known anyone who lived a truly hard life as a kid. Even in Brazil, my only real exposure to poverty came from the inevitable drives through the slums that surround all the major cities. We didn't actually spend time there.

"Are you close to your mom?" I ask.

Nico gives me that rueful smile again and nods, suddenly absorbed with picking lint off his jeans. "Yeah, she still lives in Hell's Kitchen, in the same apartment I grew up in. My sisters and I go over there on weekends."

"How many sisters do you have?"

"Just two."

"Younger or older?"

"Younger. Everyone's younger than me. And they are total bitches too, let me tell you."

I have to laugh at the matter-of-fact way he says it, but honestly, I'm jealous. I'm an only child, and it was a bit lonely growing up without much family in Washington.

"It's great you are all close, though," I say. "I bet your mom likes it, too."

He nods, but doesn't say anything. We stand together for a moment more until I shiver and zip up my coat. The post-dancing heat has definitely worn off, and the chill from the river penetrates my clothes more with every gust.

"You should go back in, sweetie," Nico says. "You look like your lips are gonna turn blue."

I smile, but nod because he's right. "Yeah, I should check on my roommates. We'll probably get going home soon."

He reaches out and touches my elbow for a second. "Thanks for keeping me company, Layla. And for showing me your dance moves."

A shiver that is completely unrelated to the cold shimmies down my back.

"Anytime," I manage, and walk back inside.

A half an hour later, the DJ is starting to slow down. The bar will probably stay open for another hour or more, but the majority of the crowd leaves with us. I look for Nico, but his stool has been moved inside.

"Jeez, he didn't even say goodbye," sniffs Quinn as we walk to the subway station.

I shrug. He likely had better things to do than search out a bunch of college kids. That we shared a moment together is sufficient for me. Wherever Nico is now on this cold, late night, I hope he's warm and safe.

CHAPTER SEVEN

Layla

I SPEND MOST OF SUNDAY TRYING TO GET AHEAD OF MY READING AND ASSIGNMENTS FOR the week. I've only had this part-time job for a few weeks, but the suck on my time is starting to get the best of me. I need to be more disciplined.

Sometime around four o'clock, my cell phone buzzes on my desk.

With an annoyed expression, Quinn looks up from her bed, where she's surrounded by books. "*Senhora* Barros?"

I nod. Like clockwork, my mom calls every Sunday while my dad lies down for a nap after lunch. I duck out of the room and into the hall, where I won't disturb anyone. Most students are probably doing the same thing we are, so the normally bustling thoroughfare is empty.

"Hi, Mom," I answer once my door is shut behind me.

"Hi, honey. How are you this week? How is the paper going?"

When we'd spoken last week, I mentioned a paper that would be due this Monday. I'm not surprised she's asking about it. She knows sometimes I procrastinate, and one of the conditions of even being in New York is that I maintain straight As. Otherwise, it's back home and to a state school for me.

"It's fine," I say. "Mostly drafted. I have a bit of editing to do tonight, but it shouldn't take me long."

I don't include the fact that I've got another hundred pages of reading to get through before I can actually start on it. But I'll deal.

"Good, good. How are your grades looking this semester?"

She asks me that question every week—I know it's because my dad makes her. He can't be bothered to call me directly. Too tied up with work.

I sigh. "It's still early, Mom, like I told you last week. I won't really know until I get my papers back and we take our midterms."

"There's no reason to be curt, Layla."

I stifle a groan. Sometimes my mom is the most sensitive person on the planet. According to her, everything out of my mouth should be the equivalent of roses and sunshine. Polite. Demure. But it's no use arguing either—I learned that a long time ago.

"Sorry," I mutter. "But there's really nothing to report. I will let you know when there is."

Mom sighs prettily. I can just imagine her on the other side of the phone. She's a timid West Coast princess, raised in Pasadena before meeting my dad while he was studying medicine at UCLA. Dad was the big rebellion of her life, and only because he was a Brazilian medical student instead of an American one. Still a doctor. Still wealthy, conservative, and everything else her family expected of her. He just had an accent, is all.

The story of how they fell in love isn't well known—not to me, not to anyone—and I suspect it's because it was a forbidden affair. I don't know her family well; they never seemed to approve of my dad or me. It doesn't matter that my dad comes from money too or that his skin is as light as theirs. She was only eighteen when they met; my dad was almost twenty-eight. We see her parents every few years or so, usually when they come to marvel at the big house my dad's career as a plastic surgeon has bought their daughter. But Dad doesn't waste time placating his in-laws anymore. He usually has better things to do.

For a minute, I consider telling Mom about Nico. Maybe she'll get it instead of insisting I get on the first plane back to Seattle. There are some similarities: the age difference, Nico's ethnic background. The fact that I'm almost as young as she was when she fell in love.

But my parents aren't happy with each other these days. Once they were in love— their wedding pictures, the shots at the Rio cathedral of my mom drenched in lace and my dad, dashing in his black tuxedo, are a testament to that. But these days they are more indifferent than anything else. I haven't seen them kiss each other in years, and Mom is usually more concerned with the state of her antiques collection than with her husband. It's been like that for as long as I can remember.

The only clue to anything beyond their pleasant détente was a comment my mom made when we attended her cousin's wedding a few years ago. They were another young couple, marrying right out of college. The ceremony was short and sweet, but it wasn't until the bride tossed her bouquet into a crowd of thrashing bridesmaids that I heard my mother speak to herself.

"No one should get married that young," she murmured.

Before I could reply, she had located her glass of white wine and found her old friends, her slim, blonde form disappearing through the crowd.

So, I keep my mouth shut while Mom conveys the news from the week: that she has been appointed treasurer of the local Rotary club, that Maura Smith's son has been accepted to UW with early admission, that Dad is leaving for some kind of conference tomorrow, so he can't talk just now. I sigh and lean back against the wall. She doesn't explicitly come out and say it, but my mom is worried about something.

Another Sunday, another absence. Lately it seems like every time I talk to them he's on his way out of town or working late. In Brazil, it's common for wealthy men of a certain age and wealth to have mistresses. I remember when one of my cousins mentioned something about their grandfather's girlfriend and just shrugged when I started to ask about what Mamãe, our grandmother, must have thought. Considering how badly my dad always wanted to be considered American, I hoped he would forego that family tradition.

"Anything else to report, honey? How's the new job? Any young men you're interested in?"

I could tell her about Nico now. Part of me wants to. There's a side of my mom that likes to indulge me. When I had my first boyfriend in high school, she kept the secret for over a month before I told my dad.

Sometimes I tell her about the dates I've been on or the guys I meet. Sometimes. But not this one. I'm not ready to be told he's too old, too poor, too whatever. I'm not ready for the low, shameful sighs that will feel just as harsh as any winter wind.

Besides, there's nothing to tell.

"Nothing new," I say. "How's church?"

She takes my cue like I didn't just brush her off and starts talking about the Mass this morning. I push ungrateful thoughts of my dad aside and do my best to listen. It's hard, though, when there are so many things between us that we'd both like to say but can't.

———

Nico and I don't get much of a chance to talk the week after seeing each other at AJ's. Karen is almost always there to sign for the packages and flirt with him. He catches me glaring at her once and winks when she turns her back. I flush. He just smiles wider. And honestly, I don't even care that he caught me looking jealous. This bitch is derailing all of my carefully laid plans, and I'm running out of time.

By the time I close the office on Thursday, I'm starting to stress. Valentine's Day is tomorrow. I know it doesn't really matter if he asks me out for exactly that day, but I'm my father's daughter: a goal setter and extremely competitive, even with myself. There is nothing I hate more than losing.

It's seven forty-five in the morning on Friday, and Jamie and I were up late studying for our tests. Vinny and I are stopping for coffee at Reggie's, the local café across the street from the College of Arts and Sciences building. Huddled in our parkas in the February wind, we stand in the long line of students snaking out onto the sidewalk. Washington Square Park, the unofficial "quad" of the NYU campus, is a freaking wind tunnel during the winter.

"Relax, kid," Vinny says. "If it's meant to be, it's meant to be. There's plenty of time to let the guy into your pants."

I bang my palm into my forehead. "Jesus, Vin, it is way too early in the day to be talking about my pants or anyone sneaking into them."

Vinny snorts. "You make it sound like I'm talking about little trolls who come out at night."

"Pants trolls?"

"Yeah. They climb in when you're asleep. Have a party. Brush their hair. Yell at goats. They're a bunch of little perverts."

The students in front of us snicker, but we ignore them as the line inches forward. I nudge Vinny, but I'm still laughing.

"You're such a weirdo," I say.

I'm practically drooling at the smell of fresh coffee. Coffee is my lifeline, and I haven't had any yet this morning. Four hours of class per day, working twenty-five hours per week, plus finding enough time to study, work out, and maintain an active social life is exhausting. I need my caffeine.

"Jesus," I say, catching a glimpse of myself in the mirror. I touch the hollows in my cheeks lightly in my mild horror. "Well, he's not going to be asking me out with these freakin' suitcases under my eyes. I look like my grandmother."

"Whatever," Vinny scoffs. "It's still early, and you look fine. Just rub Vaseline under them like my Bubbe does."

"How do you even know she does that?" The line moves forward again, and at last I'm able to order. "Large Americano, no room," I say, wincing a bit as I hand over the four dollars to the waifish guy behind the counter. Four dollars is way too much for a cup of coffee, but I just can't take the battery acid this morning. I need something stronger.

"I don't know how you drink that without eating anything," Vinny remarks after putting his own order for white chocolate mocha with caramel on top and a blueberry scone.

I have to laugh; it's always guys who order the girliest drinks. I empty one sugar packet into my coffee and stir it for a moment before taking a long, satisfying sip.

"No money," I say as we walk past the other students still waiting for their turn to order. "I've told you this before. My parents are paying for tuition and dorm fees, but I have to pay for everything else. That's food, insurance, transportation, books, spending money..." I tick off each item with my gloved fingers. "And I spent too much already last weekend. So, the choice is food or coffee. If I eat, I fall asleep in class. Coffee, and I'm hungry, but alert. Let me tell you, my folks won't give a shit that I'm eating well if my grades suck. And my mom always wants me to lose weight anyway."

Vinny just shrugs before we cross the street to an NYU building now jammed with students. A massive purple banner bearing the university logo flaps in the harsh breeze, just above the brass rotating doors.

"All right, Lay, I'll see ya," Vinny says as he leaves me standing in line for the elevators. His class is on the first floor, lucky bastard. "And don't worry!" he calls from down the hall, attracting the tired glances of a few other students. "It'll all work out in the end. You'll get laid before you know it! Trolls or no trolls!"

I turn red and try to look as if I'm not the one whose sex life has just been broadcast all over campus. As I step forward in line, I pass a jumble of cardboard hearts decorating the student center window next to the stairs and sigh. Today is Valentine's Day, but I am singularly without a Valentine. One can only hope.

———

As it happens, Karen calls in sick to work today, so I'm left alone at the desk without her imperious glare and with a little extra spring in my step. I know there's a better than decent chance that Nico has a date for tonight—with my luck, he probably has a girlfriend. But I can't *not* try to make something happen. It doesn't matter that he's seven years older than me, and it doesn't matter that he's just a FedEx guy (though my parents and Quinn would certainly disagree on both counts). Whether it's lust or actually some weird form of love at first sight, I can't deny this feeling. And I'm petrified of regret—always have been. It's just not in me to be passive.

As if solely to boost my confidence before six, Alex keeps stopping by my desk all afternoon to chat. He asks how my weekend was, demands to know what I'm study-ing, compliments my outfit. It's flattering, if slightly annoying and verging on inap-propriate.

"So," he says on his fourth "coffee break." "Here's a new topic of conversation for you. Is there a Mr. Barros, Ms. Barros?" He waggles his eyebrows in a way that makes them look like lively caterpillars.

I can't help but giggle. "Ah, no, not at the moment."

"And how is it that a gorgeous girl like you is single? I just flat out don't believe it."

I giggle again, even though I'm pretty sure this counts as sexual harassment. The consistent eye rolls in his direction from other female employees tell me I'm not the only one who gets this kind of attention. In a weird way, his charm offensive reminds me of my dad. He's also tall and handsome and has that same charisma. I try not to wonder if my dad talks to the receptionists in his office like Alex is talking to me.

"What can I say?" I ask, tossing my hands up. "I'm a particular woman who knows what she particularly wants."

At that moment, the elevator doors open, and he whom I particularly want *very* badly wheels in his dolly with a large smile that fades immediately at the sight of the attractive attorney leaning over my desk.

Nico

"You'll have to tell me more about that some time."

Asshat is back. Son of a *bitch*. This time he's leaning so far over Layla's desk she practically has to recline her seat.

A glance at Karen's shut door tells me she's gone. If this guy weren't here, I'd be able to do what I've been planning all week: ask Layla out on a date.

This guy. All his packages come from fashion designers and modeling agencies—he represents some of the biggest names in the business. But right now, the only name he's into is the girl whose face has been imprinted on my brain for the last two weeks, the girl I *still* haven't managed to get a moment alone with. The way he's sneaking looks down her shirt makes me want to toss him down the stairs and teach him the real meaning of "New York state of mind."

"Maybe over lunch?" he's saying. "I'm a member at the Princeton Club, you know."

I roll the dolly into the lobby, and just like last time, while Layla glances at me with a friendly smile, this shithead doesn't even look my way. Go figure. To people like him, people like me are invisible. Yeah, forget that.

Layla smiles, but it's not the kind of smile she gives me when I tease her about her hair or her dance moves. It's the kind of smile that's uncomfortable, the kind of smile that says she wants this asshole out of her personal space, but doesn't feel like she can tell him that.

"That's so nice of you," she says, "but I doubt I could make time. My class schedule is pretty tight. I'm downtown all morning before I come here, and I have to study for midterms."

Behind them, I snort as I start to unload packages. There's only a few for them today, but I'm taking my sweet time. Dickwad doesn't even notice, but I see Layla bite her lip at my response. There's my girl.

My girl. Fuck me, I haven't even taken her out yet, and I'm already thinking things like that. What the fuck is wrong with me?

"Well, the offer's open anytime." Twatwaffle winks as he pushes off the desk.

I'm still staring daggers at the guy when Layla reaches up to tap my hand. I practically jump, and she scoots back a little. It's then I realize I'm still glaring—at her.

"H-hi there," she says just before she bites her lip again. Fuck me, she *really* has to stop doing that.

She offers a shy smile, and it pretty much melts away the jealous rage. I smile back, and she relaxes.

"Hey, NYU, you fixing a date with the geriatric ward?" I toss my head in the direction he went. It's none of my business, but I can't help but ask.

Layla just snorts, and like always, it's pretty much the cutest thing I've ever seen. "Absolutely not. Alex is a flirt, but he's married. I don't think he really means anything by it."

"Oh, he means something all right," I say, leaning onto the desk. "Pretty girl like you, of course he does, sweetie. But he's kind of old for you, don't you think?"

God, I'm an asshole. It's none of my business if she wants to flirt with her co-workers, which she wasn't even doing in the first place. I'm fishing. I want her to say she doesn't like him, that she likes me instead.

"Well, *I* don't mean anything by it," she says.

Immediately, I feel better. Too much better. To cover it up, I make a big deal out of scanning all of the packages I've lined up on the desktop. Be cool, Nico. Jesus, I am better than this.

"So, what are you doing tonight for Valentine's Day?" Layla asks, standing up and leaning over to watch me at work. "Got big plans with a sweetheart?"

I look up and see her staring at me, a waterfall of her wavy hair dropping down one shoulder. She's so damn beautiful, and I can barely register what she's saying. Wait...Valentine's Day...is tonight. I think about that fucker asking her out for a drink after work, which I know he will, and suddenly the only thing I want Layla to say is that she's got plans. With me. The invisible FedEx guy.

"Not much," I say, trying to be playful as I mimic the sing-song quality of her original question. We're both trying to play it cool. I'm failing miserably. "I'll probably go out for a drink when I'm off. Isn't that what you're supposed to do on Valentine's Day if you're single? Drink yourself stupid?"

Layla chuckles. "Sounds about right. I'll probably do the same, I guess."

She nods nonchalantly as if in agreement, but my heart is soaring at the word when she agrees with the word 'single.' I didn't think she had a boyfriend, but somehow, I'm really damn glad she confirmed it.

"You're going out drinking, too, NYU? No boyfriend to give you hearts and flowers?" God, I really can't help myself. "I'm sure Legal Beagle back there would take you to the Princeton Club."

She snorts again, holding in her laughter as she glances nervously back toward the hallway. "I don't think he looks anything like a beagle."

I just shake my head, enjoying this little game we're playing.

"Please," I say as I restack the packages neatly on top of the desk. I've probably reordered them five times at this point, and now I'm going to do it again. Anything to stay here and make her blush. I lean onto the wood surface. "Dude was looking at you like a bloodhound."

This time she full-on giggles, and the sound makes me feel like I'm walking on air. How can someone's laugh do that?

"Maybe," she says. "Anyway, yeah, I'm planning to spend some quality time at the bar tonight, just like you. No boyfriends in sight."

"Well, then we should probably do it together. Be a shame to drink alone, don't you think?"

I'm an asshole. I should just tell her I want to take her out. That I want to go on a proper date, not just sit together at a shitty bar or run into each other at all my different jobs, where I have to act like I don't really care so much if she smiles or looks hot in a dress. I want to get her alone so I can show her just what those tight pants she wears do to me. I want to kiss her until we both can't think straight anymore.

"You think?" she parrots me.

Her eyes are suddenly a pool of light I want to dive into. I don't say anything, suddenly paralyzed that I royally fucked this up by not asking for a date like a gentleman. This isn't the kind of girl you have a drunken hookup with at a bar. She's the kind of girl you take home to meet your mother.

My mother? What the fuck is wrong with me?

"Yeah, that could be cool," she continues.

That's it. I'm done. I can't stop the giant monkey-grin on my face when I realize she's just agreed to a date. Suddenly, we're exchanging numbers on Post-It notes, and I'm tucking that thing into my breast pocket like it's made of solid gold. I don't even care that today is the most overrated, overhyped, loved up day of the year. The only thing I care about is that the girl of my dreams just agreed to spend it with me, not some rich asshole with a club membership. Me. Nico.

"I get off between seven and eight most nights, and I can come straight from work," I tell her as I hand her my number. "Text me when you're home and ready to go? Want to meet up around nine for dinner? And drinks, of course."

She stares at the number for a second, as if it says something more complex than just ten simple digits. Then she tucks the small blue slip into her purse and pats it, as if to assure me she'll keep it safe. She nods, and her blue eyes sparkle when they turn to me. Now this is definitely a legitimate date.

"Yeah," she says softly. "That sounds good."

"All right, sweetie." I tip my head to one side, mimicking the same action she's doing. "I guess this means you're my Valentine, huh?"

She gulps and grabs the edge of the desk, but doesn't say anything. It's probably for the best. I'm barely keeping it together myself.

I collect the clipboard and the dolly and wheel back to the elevators, careful to avoid her gaze in case she can see just how damn excited I am. I wink again—corny shit is becoming a habit with this girl—but when the elevator doors close, I collapse against the wall and exhale heavily. Holy. Shit.

CHAPTER EIGHT

Layla

At exactly seven-thirty, I sprint into the apartment, tearing off my clothes because I have less than an hour and a half to get ready for what feels like the most important night of my life. He called me at seven and said he would pick me up at Lafayette at nine, maybe a bit later depending on the train. I gave him the address, biting back all the other things I wanted to say. Things like, by the way, the sound of your voice makes my panties basically disintegrate or, oh hey, I'm in love with you and want to have your babies.

I have about a million questions I want to ask him. I want to get to know the man behind that gorgeous face, the person who exudes that magnetic charisma. What are his siblings like? How did he come to love art? Why wasn't he scared that guy would beat him up outside the club? Is he content working as a FedEx guy? Has he ever lived outside of New York? Where does he see himself in ten years?

I don't even care about looking desperate anymore. I'm just giddy about the prospect of having him all to myself for an entire evening.

While I'm tearing literally every single piece of clothing I own out of the tiny closet Quinn and I share, all my roommates crowd into my bedroom and alternately coach and tease me. Jamie, predictably, is almost as giddy as I am. Shama is more practical, trying to help me find an outfit. Quinn just sits on her bed with her books open and acts the part of the cynical peanut gallery.

"I mean, it's one thing if it's just a little fling," she says to Jamie, who's looking through my jewelry. "But let's be honest. It's not like she can have a real relationship with a twenty-six-year-old FedEx thug from Hell's Kitchen."

Shama and I both turn from the closet and glare at her.

"Seriously?" I say. "You don't even know him. Why are you being so negative about this?"

"I'm being realistic," Quinn counters. She turns to Jamie. "Lay's just mad because she knows she's slumming and doesn't want to face up to the truth."

"*What* the fuck..." Shama trails off behind me.

I hurl a sweater onto the floor and march into the center of the room, where I face Quinn with my hands on my hips.

"What the hell, Quinn?" I say directly.

She just stares at me calmly and sets her book aside. "Lay, calm down."

I rub my forehead. "I'm calm. I'm not the one being racist."

"Oooh, here we go," Shama says.

Jamie shakes her head. "Guys, we don't really need to do this, do we?"

Quinn's forehead wrinkles as she stares at me. "Are you serious? What did I say that was racist? Is he not from a shitty part of town? Is he not a FedEx guy? Is he not twenty-six?"

"Just because his family doesn't have money doesn't make him a thug," I retort. "And Hell's Kitchen is not that bad anymore, either. Would you be saying this about him if he were white? Would you be saying that about him if he wasn't Puerto Rican?"

"No, I wouldn't be saying it if I hadn't seen him shove and physically threaten a couple of guys just for saying something he didn't like," Quinn says. "He's dangerous, Layla, and you know it."

"Those guys were being assholes to all of us, and *you* know it!" I argue back. "He was defending *your* honor. And if it had been a nice investment banker from Stamford, you'd have been all over it. I can't believe you right now!" I look to Jamie and Shama, who are studiously avoiding my gaze. "You guys. Come on. Back me up here."

Jamie just swallows and goes back to looking through jewelry. Shama sighs.

"I think you're both right," she says diplomatically. I roll my eyes. I expected more from her. "Quinn, you can't make massive generalizations about someone based on one interaction and a few things you know about him," Shama continues. "Coming from someone of your background—no, girl, really—it does come off sounding racist. So you need to be aware of that." She turns to me. "Still, Lay, you can't deny that what he did was kind of scary. Hot, yeah. But Quinn's got a point. I do think you need to be careful with him."

I sigh and pick my sweater up off the floor.

"I'm not 'slumming'," I mutter as I turn back to my closet. "I think I just want to get ready on my own."

Behind me, Quinn sighs. "Stop. I'll go." I stare at my clothes while listening to her gather up her books. On her way out, she pauses behind me. "I hope you have fun tonight, babe. Be safe."

She goes to the other room while Jamie and Shama stay, and we fumble around in awkward silence for the next twenty minutes while they help me pick out what I'm going to wear. It's starting to snow outside, so my outfit needs to be warm, but I don't want to look like the Michelin Man either.

"Hair curly or straight?" Jamie asks as she goes back to perusing my jewelry box.

I have a bit of decent jewelry courtesy of our trips to Brazil. My dad's family lives in the center of Minas Gerais, the gold and gemstone mining state, so I picked up a few quality pieces when we visited.

"Curly, definitely curly," I say. "If it gets snow on it, it'll just get wavy anyway, plus I don't really have time to straighten it. He's going to be here in less than an hour now."

Shama critically flips through a few more outfits.

"I think you should just wear jeans and some sexy shirt," she says. "You don't want to look like you're trying too hard, and this is a last-minute thing. He didn't make reservations anywhere, did he?"

I shake my head and wonder if that should bother me as I continue towel drying my hair. I know we're just supposed to be drinking, but should I expect anything more because it's Valentine's Day? Nico mentioned dinner, but no reservations.

"No, I think we're just going to play it by ear. Grab food somewhere easy and then find a bar or something like that." I walk back into the bathroom to grab the leave-in conditioner that will keep my curls in check throughout the night.

"K, these are the jeans," Shama announces when I return.

She's laid a pair of moto-style gray jeans on the bed that usually fit me like a second skin, flattering my ass and making my legs look a little longer than usual. They have a few tears in the knees, so they look nowhere near formal. The opposite of try-hard.

Shama yanks several different tops for me to choose from—all of them, I notice, are cropped. I can't argue with that; my abs are one of my best assets. I pick one of the ones I brought home from Brazil last summer: a magenta shirt with long sleeves and two long panels of extra fabric extending from my ribs that I wrap around the remainder of my torso to fit as I like. When I'm done, only small patches of my stomach and waist peek through the twisted fabric. I tie it just above my belt, leaving a sliver of skin exposed around the top of my pants. My abs are on display in the tight material, but not so much I look open for business. Mom would be proud.

Jamie does my makeup, keeping it natural with only a bit of liner and mascara to make my blue eyes pop, and just a dab of lip gloss. My hair, now mostly dried, falls over my shoulders in thick, wavy ribbons. With my brown leather boots, I feel completely and perfectly ready for my super incredibly casual Valentine's Day date.

"Wait!" Jamie cries out as I start to leave the room. It's almost nine, and I figure I should make peace with Quinn before I go. Jamie shuffles over, carrying a couple of gold necklaces and a pair of hoops to match.

"You said he's Puerto Rican, right?"

I nod. "Part, anyway. He's half Italian too."

"Well, you should play up your Brazilian half. So he doesn't think you're just a dumb white girl, you know?"

I roll my eyes, and Shama snickers beside me.

I bite my lip. "You think a couple of chains are going to change the fact that I'm not *not* a dumb white girl?"

Jamie just gives me a long look. "No, that's Quinn."

"Hey!" Quinn shouts from the sofa.

I sigh. I don't really want to have the "what am I?" conversation with my room-mates right now, and I'm not interested in starting another fight with Quinn. I am what I've always been: Layla. If Nico is the kind of guy who's going to call me a coconut—a brown person who acts white—he's not going to be worth my time anyway. I'm not going to try to act like someone I'm not.

I also can't help but wonder if perhaps that's why I sometimes feel like a little kid when Nico looks at me. I wonder if maybe it's not because I'm so much younger than him. I haven't even considered that an issue—not since chatting him up outside the club. But maybe he sees me as some rich white girl, or at least as a Latina who is trying to be white. He wouldn't be the first.

So I let Jamie clasp the three gold chains around my neck the way all the Puerto Rican and Dominican girls do while I put gold hoops through my ears. I do look a little less like the Stepford side of my family and more *brasilera*—it reminds me of the time I went clubbing with my cousins in Vitoria, and they dressed me up like a doll. I run my hands up my top. I'm not pretending to be anything I'm not. Really.

I walk out to the common area, and Quinn looks up from the couch, where she's paging through one of her textbooks. She looks me over and nods appreciatively.

"You look great," she says simply. "And I'm sorry."

I don't waste time walking over to her and wrapping her in a big hug, which she returns. "I'm sorry too. You're not racist. You're my best friend, and I love you."

"I love you too, you idiot."

Then my cell phone rings.

"He's he-ere!" Jamie shrills from my room, earning shrieks and laughs from Shama behind her.

"Shh, shut up!" I answer the phone once they quiet into hushed giggles together on the couch with Quinn, openly eavesdropping on my conversation. It's one of those sisterly moments that, despite the annoyance, I actually really love them for. "Hey, Nico?"

"Hey, sweetie."

His voice sounds even deeper on the phone, and I swear it vibrates down my arm and through my chest. Shama fake-swoons at the sound that carries through the room. I shoot a quick grin to my roommates and turn my back on them to listen.

"You here?"

"Downstairs. I'm outside."

"Sounds good," I say. "I'll be right there."

I hang up the phone and pull on my gray wool jacket, fluffing my curls a little in the mirror next to the door. "Okay, girls, last-minute check. Anything out of sorts?" I twirl in front of them.

"You look hot, mama," Quinn pronounces. "If he doesn't try his damnedest to nail you tonight, then something is seriously wrong with him."

"You guys going out tonight?"

They all nod. Shama wants to meet up with Jason again at Fat Black's, so they are all planning to stay there for the evening.

"We'll be back late, babe," Quinn informs me. "So if you need to get your hooch on in our room, you have until two a.m. or so."

She grins when I throw the nearest piece of mail at her, but only because she knows she was right to tell me.

"Only if I'm lucky. Don't wait up, girls," I say and promptly leave before another round of teasing can commence.

———

WHEN I EXIT THE BUILDING, I immediately spot Nico leaning against a lamppost, casually dressed in a pair of dark blue jeans, a black thermal shirt that hugs his trim torso in all the right places, and a leather jacket. He's wearing the same black beanie from last weekend, and I have to remind myself not to tear it off. I'm dying to know what his hair looks like under all those hats. God, I hope he's not bald on top.

The sly grin he breaks into has me stumbling down the stairs from my building, prompting him to push off the post and meet me at the bottom just as I'm catching my footing.

"You all right, sweetie?" he asks.

His question is innocent, but his knowing smile says different. He knows exactly the effect he has on me.

"Fine, fine," I say. "These sidewalks are slippery in the snow."

I brush off the flakes that are starting to fall on my shoulders, as if to demonstrate their threat. Nico nods and sucks on his full bottom lip, which, if we had been walking, would have made me stumble again.

"What's up, NYU?" he says gently, taking my hands gently into his and tugging me close to kiss me lightly on the cheek.

Electricity sparks all over my skin despite the cold. God, he smells good. I don't reply, but only because, well, I can't.

Nico, as I had anticipated, definitely does not have anything planned for the evening, so we decide to walk through Nolita and Little Italy to see if there are any restaurants that aren't too crazy. It is, after all, the number one date night of the year. He holds my hand securely despite the bulk of our gloves. I find myself wishing that it wasn't cold so that I could feel the warmth of his fingers.

"What about this place?" I ask.

We stop in front of a small bistro in an old brick building on Elizabeth Street that is only about half full of people. The menu posted on the window shows a number of French-style foods and a wine list. It's nothing too elaborate, but the food they're serving looks edible and not terribly expensive. I'm just eager to get out of the snow that is still falling in small flakes.

"Sounds good to me," Nico says, and holds the door open as we walk inside.

CHAPTER NINE

Nico

ONCE AGAIN, I FEEL LIKE A COMPLETE ASSHOLE. I'M OUT ON VALENTINE'S DAY IN NEW York City, and I completely forgot the most basic thing: reservations. Everywhere decent is filled up because, you know, it's the busiest night of the year. And I'm stuck wandering around with Layla like a bum. She's going to think I don't give a shit about tonight. About her.

It's not like I don't know how to do this. I'm just a little rusty. It's been a long time since my last girlfriend—three years, to be exact. And twenty-three-year-olds aren't exactly known for being masters of romance. But still. I should have known better.

The hostess seats us at a small table in the window where we can people watch, mostly other couples out on similar kinds of dates. I offer to take Layla's coat because I'm not a complete Neanderthal. But it turns out that was a mistake, because what I see just about knocks me the fuck out. Suddenly, I can't quite breathe the right way. Between the skin-tight jeans she's wearing and a shirt-thing that I'm really not sure how the fuck stays on, she looks like a package I want to unwrap. Like, right the fuck *now*.

"Damn," I breathe, and she looks over her shoulder to find me practically drooling. Fuck *me*, her ass looks good in those pants.

When I realize she's caught me staring, my mouth snaps shut, and I try to smile, although I have a feeling I look more like a serial killer. Layla sits down smugly. Yeah, she knew exactly what she was doing wearing that outfit.

Luckily, I didn't mess around either. A leather jacket might not be the best choice when there's a blizzard threatening outside, but the only stuff she's seen me in are the baggy FedEx uniforms and the puffy coat I wear at the club. Between my job and the gym, I actually work out pretty hard most days, and I'm wearing a black t-shirt that shows it off. From the way Layla's looking at me right now, the shirt is doing its job.

Unfortunately, she's not the only one who notices. The hostess, a cute little thing with long brown hair, bats her eyelashes as she hands me a menu. She's pretty, sure, and if Layla weren't around, I might be a little interested. But it's the same look I get all the time. They see the tattoos, they see the dark skin, and they see a bad boy and nothing else. Right now, I can't see anything but the girl across the table, the girl who seems to see *me*. And I want this chick to stop flirting with me in front of my date.

"Should we get a bottle?" I ask Layla when the hostess asks for drink orders.

Her eyes bulge slightly as she nods. She's only nineteen—I wonder if this is the first time anyone has ordered a bottle of wine at dinner who wasn't her dad. Shit, I'm not sure *I've* ever ordered a bottle of wine at dinner.

"Um...that one," I say, pointing to a random name on the list. I have no fuckin' clue what I'm doing. Usually I drink PBR or whatever cheap beer is handy.

The hostess walks away with another wink my way, but I ignore her, especially since I see that Layla has noticed the flirting too and is not happy about it. Okay, time to distract. I'm not going to let this date be ruined in the first five minutes.

I tug off my beanie and set it on the table. When I look up, Layla is staring at me, mouth slightly open, as I push a hand through my short, curly hair. Really? All I had to do was take off my hat to get her to look at me that way?

I clear my throat.

"You clean up good, NYU," I say, trying for some levity. "But I already knew that. A lot different than your usual look in the office."

Immediately, she smiles. She does look different. With the gold chains and the tight clothes, she sort of looks like some of the girls from my neighborhood. I can't decide if I like it or not.

"Oh. Yeah, thanks," she says as she opens her menu.

I watch her for a second. She's fidgeting, tapping a finger on the side of her menu, avoiding my gaze. Does she really not know the effect she has on me?

"Well, I think you'd look good in a paper bag," I tell her, provoking another shy smile.

A silence falls, and we both become really interested in looking through our menus. Layla seems surprised when I order the steak. I want to ask her why, but I don't want to hear her say what I'm pretty sure she was thinking: that she thought I was too poor to order the most expensive thing on the menu.

No. I'm not going there tonight. Not when I've been thinking about this date for the last two weeks and definitely not when she hasn't said anything. I'm not going to let the chip on my shoulder fuck things up.

"I'll have the side salad," she says, handing her menu back to the waiter.

Now I'm the one who's surprised. "You're only going to eat a side salad?"

Layla just looks uncomfortable, but smiles at the waiter and nods. "I had a big lunch," she says to me.

I don't believe her. "Whatever you say, sweetie," I say.

I have two sisters—I know how chicks are. Layla's nineteen and obviously does *something* to keep her ass looking like that. Guaranteed she can put it down. Which means she's not ordering for one of two reasons: she doesn't want me to think she's fat (yeah, not possible), or she can't afford it.

It's then I consider that maybe Layla isn't exactly the same as the rich kids she goes to school with. Her jewelry and her nice clothes tell me she comes from some-thing, but she's also working twenty-five hours a week on top of going to school. It's not full-time work like my sister, but she's no slouch. Rich kids don't have to work as receptionists.

I hope she'll tell me what's up, but she doesn't say a word. Okay, then. Time to move on.

We continue sipping our wine way too quickly, making awkward conversation about the weather and the recent subway repairs on Forty-Ninth Street until our food arrives. It's…weird. And really fuckin' awkward.

I don't get it. The energy I feel with this girl in every other place is like the way the air feels right before a thunderstorm. Sparks everywhere. All she has to do is smile, and I'm on fuckin' fire. But now, on an actual date, sitting across from one another, we can't get up a conversation any better than one I'd have with my Great Aunt Cecelia. And she speaks this really weird Creole dialect that I barely understand.

I watch as Layla drains her second glass of wine and reaches for the bottle, and it's then I realize the problem. We're both nervous.

———

Layla

To hell with playing nice, I decide just as our food arrives. Nico and I have been staring awkwardly at each other for the last fifteen minutes while we drank an entire bottle of wine. My lips are feeling loose. I have questions. He has stories. With a little liquid courage, I'm ready to dive in.

"So, Nico," I say, spearing a piece of lettuce with my fork. "What's with working at FedEx?"

He frowns at me mid-bite of his steak, then swallows heavily. "What do you mean?"

"Do you like it there? How long have you worked there? Is that all you want to do for a living?"

This strategy can go either way, I know. Some guys would take these kinds of questions to mean I think he's a loser, like I'm giving him the third degree in order to make him feel like shit about himself, make him think he should change. More often than not, I've found those guys are just insecure in general. There's a reason they always think they're under attack.

I hope he's not like that. I don't want Nico to feel persecuted here, but our date so far has been about as exciting as dry toast. If this is how "nice" girls behave all the time—non-confrontational and demure—I can't for the life of me understand how any of them ever have fun.

Nico peers at me with a raised eyebrow, as if he's trying to figure out where I'm going with my questions, and then shrugs. "It's not a dream job or anything, but it pays good. I've been there for almost seven years now."

I almost choke on my lettuce. That would have made him, well, my age when he started working for them. I can't imagine having the same job for that long. If I had to answer phones at Fox and Lager for seven years, I'd strangle myself. With the telephone cord.

But before I can respond, he continues.

"I was actually in school before then, but I had to drop out when my mom got hurt. I was the only one old enough to help out when she couldn't work. My buddy got me the job at FedEx, and I've been there ever since."

He takes another large bite of his steak, but keeps his intense black gaze trained squarely on me, watching my reaction carefully.

I swallow. "Your mom. Is she okay now?"

His expression softens, almost as if he's relieved that I'm not trying to tear apart what he does. He nods.

"Yeah, she's fine, but she can't really work much anymore. Her back's all messed up. The doctor says she has a couple of ruptured discs."

"Jesus, that's terrible." I'm shooting for kind here, even though I'm wondering what kind of ruptured disc problem keeps you housebound for seven years. "She's lucky she has you to help."

"Well, it's not just me anymore," he says gruffly. "But when I started, my sisters were both in high school, and my brother was just a kid. We didn't have health insurance, so when I was old enough to get a job with benefits, I was able to claim them as dependents and get everyone medical."

I try to maintain a neutral expression and tone that echoes the one he's kept firmly in place, but it's hard. I can't imagine having to support three younger siblings at my age. I also want to ask why his mother didn't have health insurance, but something in his darkened expression tells me he doesn't want to talk about this anymore.

"So what about now?" I ask. "Do you ever think of going back? To school, I mean?"

He considers the thought again, chewing carefully. "I've thought about it. But honestly, I actually want to be…well…it's kind of dumb."

I lean forward over my plate, curiosity getting the better of me. He is so much more interesting than the watery cucumbers in my garden salad. "What? What is it?"

He grins, and I almost knock over my wine.

"Well," he says. "The engineering degree was really more because I thought it would be a good idea than something I was really interested in. But since I was a kid, I actually wanted to become a firefighter. Like, for the FDNY. Those guys are tough, and they live a kick-ass life. You get to be active, save people's lives, and once you're hired, you pretty much have a job for life unless you do something to really screw it up. And then, after 9/11…well, you were here. You know what happened."

We both grow quiet at the mention of 9/11. I was only a freshman when it happened, had only been in the city for three weeks, and the memory of it was seared into my heart. Like most people who were actually in the city for it, neither of us elaborate. It was only a year and a half ago that the city shut down, filled with the ghostly debris of death and asbestos in the wake of one of the biggest tragedies in American history. Most of us still don't have the words for it. I think the shock that everyone in the country felt was the only reason my dad didn't yank me out of New York immediately.

Nico continues. "I just kept coming back to the firefighters. I always wanted to be one before, but those guys were really heroes. Some of them gave their lives to help the people who were trapped in those buildings. I just…I remember thinking after that, I want to do that. I want to be someone people think about as a hero." He bites his lip and gives a sheepish grin. "I sound like a little kid, don't I?"

"Not at all," I say, completely charmed. "Why don't you do it?" I take another bite of salad and wait pointedly for his answer.

"I've tried," he confesses. "It's not that easy. I applied twice to the FDNY and was turned down both times. Once because I wasn't qualified, and the other because they were full up. I'm out of time. They don't hire anyone over twenty-nine."

"Aren't you only twenty-six?" I ask.

He shrugs. "I'll be twenty-seven in September. But first I have to get the invite to take the exam. Then I have to go through academy...if they even reopen their hiring to begin with. I'd be twenty-seven, almost twenty-eight by the time I could even start. Time's pretty much up."

Nico signals to the waiter for another bottle of wine, stopping any more questions I have. Well, I did sign up to drink, didn't I?

"You know," he says. "I've thought about becoming a cop, because I hear sometimes that can help you get into the academy, too, but I don't know. I don't really like cops."

I snort. "Who does?"

He grins. "You get pulled over a lot, NYU?"

I say nothing, just purse my lips. He's got me there. He's nice enough, though, to let that line of conversation die.

"So, my turn for twenty questions. What're you studying in college? What do you want to be when you grow up? Tell me all about Layla."

Something about the way he rolls the syllables of my name over his tongue sends ripples all over my skin, the kind that make me want to throw myself across the table to see what else that tongue can do. I cringe a bit at the backhanded reference to my age, but maybe he's just kidding. I hope.

"Well," I say as I stab another piece of lettuce. "I'm kind of figuring that out. I'm supposed to go to law school."

"Supposed to?"

I shrug. "It's the only way I could convince my dad to let me come to NYU instead of staying home and going to UW."

"So, what are you, pre-law?"

I shake my head. "NYU doesn't have a pre-law program, so I can pretty much choose anything. I'm still figuring out my major."

Nico cocks his head to the side. "Don't you have to do that soon? Before your junior year or something like that?" When he catches my surprised look, one black brow arches. "Hey, I put in a couple of years. I remember a little bit about it."

I finish chewing my lettuce and sigh. "It's a sore subject."

"Well, what classes have you enjoyed the most?"

"That's the problem," I say after a big gulp of wine. "I sort of like everything. I'm taking a literature class right now, and that's great. Biology was fascinating. This religious studies seminar I took last semester blew my mind." I look up. "Did you know that in one version of the Gospel, the direct translation of Christ's death actually says he was hanged, not crucified?"

Nico blinks. "I did not know that."

I shrug and go back to forking my limp lettuce. "Anyway. Yeah. I guess I'm having a hard time deciding exactly what I want to study. But I have to declare soon. This is my last semester of prerequisites. I have to start my major classes next year."

Nico watches sympathetically. "I get it. It's hard having that kind of decision forced on you, especially when there are so many amazing things in the world to see, and too much shit to figure out about yourself, right?"

I blink away the sudden tears that are welling up. Somehow, this conversation ended up touching on a bunch of nerves. I've known this guy for all of a couple of weeks. How does he know the questions that are brewing inside me—questions I haven't even been able to put into words yet?

"Hey."

Nico puts his fork down and reaches over to touch my hand. There it is again—that strange tingle that happens when we touch. I shiver, despite the fact that inside the restaurant, it's actually pretty warm.

"Layla?"

I look up, blinking away the wet sheen clouding my vision. When it clears, I just see Nico. Instantly, I feel better.

"You'll be all right," he says as he squeezes my hand. "You're smart, sweet, and you obviously did something right to end up where you are. You'll figure it out in the end."

The confident, kind look in his eyes just about breaks me. "Thanks," I say as I take back my hand and swipe under my eyes before I actually do cry and trash my eye makeup. "Sorry. I didn't mean for things to get so heavy."

Nico takes another bite of steak and grins. "I'll take heavy over bullshit any day of the week, baby. I like real."

I finish my salad and set the plate aside, picking up my wine and taking a long drink to chase away the emotions clouding my head. Nico refills my glass with the last of the first bottle while the waiter opens our second. But what really surprises me is when he cuts off a portion of his steak and plops it on my plate along with a handful of fries.

"What's this?" I ask.

He just shrugs adorably. "You need to eat, baby. Nobody can drink a bottle of wine on iceberg lettuce. So, your family's from Brazil, right? You go there a lot?"

Still marveling at the way he just pivoted from the steak, I start to cut up my food. I can't deny that I'm still starving. I'm also starting to feel the pleasant wooziness of alcohol rising in my head and dissipating the last of my nerves.

"Just a few times," I say. "The last time was when I was in high school, for Carnaval."

"Carnaval," he repeats with a clipped "r", the way Spanish speakers, not Brazilians, would say it. "That must have been crazy. I'm so fuckin' jealous."

I take another, smaller bite of my steak and nod. "Yeah, it's pretty nuts."

"Do you go to the parades, like in Rio?"

I shake my head. "No, those are mostly for tourists, although a lot of people watch them on TV. My dad's family goes up to Salvador, in Bahia, where they rent a condo on the beach. The city has these giant trucks, they're called *trios electricos*, and the samba bands play on top of them, blasting their music to the crowds. Everyone parties in the streets for six days straight. When you're tired, you go sleep in the house; when you're thirsty, you drink the cheap beer all the vendors have; when you're hot, you go run in the ocean. It's amazing." I sigh. "I wish I was there now. It starts next week, you know."

I sit back in my chair and smile, a little lost in the fond memories.

"Did you ever go to a soccer game?" Nico asks, interrupting me from my samba daydream. He's just finished his steak and has assumed the same comfortable, slightly glazed-eye position that I'm in. Apparently, the wine has loosened up us both.

I smile. "Hell yeah, I did. Played too." I take another bite, satisfied with the shocked look on Nico's face.

He leans forward. "Seriously? You, playing? I thought chicks didn't really get into sports there; at least, that's what the Brazilians I've met say."

I nod, swirling my wine glass meditatively. "It's kind of true, actually. Most of the girls just go to the gym. But I played soccer through high school, and so I played on the beach with my cousins, too. It's where I get all my moves." I gyrate my neck a bit, demonstrating one of said moves, and earn a laugh in return. "You like soccer?"

Nico nods, eyes blazing. "A little, yeah. I play in the park sometimes too, but I suck. What position did you play?"

"Striker," I say with a wink and a grin. "I know how to score."

And that's all it takes to jumpstart the connection I knew was there all along. We talk about everything and nothing, finishing the second bottle of wine and ordering a slice of mediocre chocolate cake to share just so we won't have to leave. I tell him about the lonely house where I grew up, what my parents are like, and how my biggest dream right now is to stop living off my parents when I graduate. He tells me about how he likes to draw in his spare time, how he lives in Dominican City, sometimes with his sister and her kid when she's on the outs with her boyfriend, and how his favorite sibling is his baby brother, Gabriel, who's just a couple of years younger than me. He's proud of Gabe, who is getting ready to go to school at CUNY next year. Nico has about half his tuition money saved so far.

The job at FedEx makes more and more sense. Nico carries the burdens of a lot of people on his big shoulders, burdens that require a full-time job that, after so many years, pays well and comes with excellent benefits.

"Gabe's crazy smart. Just like you, baby," he says. The second bottle of wine has also made him a lot more familiar, and I like it. "You'd like him."

"You sound like you want to set me up with him," I joke. "Maybe I'm out with the wrong brother."

That earns me a dark glare almost immediately, and I start to giggle almost uncontrollably. Nico leans over the small table, now cleared of all dishes besides our wine glasses and the empty bottle. He covers my hand with his. I try to pull it back, playing the coquette, but he presses it tightly to the tablecloth.

"Oh, no," he growls, causing my heart to skip a few beats. "You definitely got the right brother, NYU."

I stop laughing, caught in the intensity of his gaze, now just a few inches from my own.

"Did I?" I ask.

He grunts and signals for the check. "I think," he says as he drains the last of the wine in his glass, "that it's time we get out of here. Don't you?"

I couldn't agree more.

CHAPTER TEN

Layla

WE ARE BOTH FAIRLY DRUNK WHEN WE STUMBLE OUT OF THE RESTAURANT. WE GRAB desperately at each other's arms to steady ourselves on the slippery sidewalk, each unable to stifle our elation. Nico's deep laugh reverberates down the snow-brightened street, echoing off the brick apartment buildings and fire escapes. We might be drunken fools, but we're fools together, and the night couldn't be going any better.

"So, where to, NYU?" Nico says, tucking an arm around my waist as we start in the general direction of Lafayette.

The snow is falling harder now, covering downtown Manhattan in a magical layer of quiet and white. Even the rumble of the subway beneath us is muted. Despite the fact that there are still people on the street, it suddenly feels like we are the only two people in a city of millions.

"That depends," I say as I lean more into the crook of his big shoulder. I've been dying for this kind of contact all night. Actually, for two weeks. "On what you're interested in doing."

I'm not intending to be suggestive, and so I blush when he winks at my comment.

"Oh jeez, men are such perverts," I say, elbowing him softly in the side. "All I meant was what you wanted to drink. We *are* out drinking, aren't we?"

"Sure, sure, sweetie. Whatever you say, NYU."

"Why don't you ever call me by my name?" I ask suddenly, breaking away to look at him. We're standing under a lamppost on a corner, and I watch as the snowflakes create a bright halo behind his head, falling on his broad shoulders and atop his beanie. "It's always 'NYU' or 'sweetie' or something with you. Never my name. Are you afraid of it or something?"

He raises one mischievous eyebrow and pulls me a little closer so I can see his full expression. He has dimples; I can't believe I didn't notice them before.

"But you are sweet, Layla. It fits."

"I'm not so sweet."

I lay a hand on his chest as if to push him away. He glances down at it and back up to me, his gaze resting on my lips before returning to my eyes.

"Oh, I bet you are," he says.

He sticks his hand in between his teeth to pull off one glove, then the other, which he shoves in his pocket. A lightly calloused fingertip traces my cheekbone, dropping down my nose and over my lips. Suddenly, I can't breathe.

"Do you want me to kiss you, Layla?"

Nico's deep voice reverberates through the quiet of the snow, and my own voice deserts me completely, leaving me only to nod, dumbfounded. He drifts his thumb over my lips.

"You sure you want a man like me?"

His voice dares me to say yes while he frames my chin and cheeks with both hands.

I should probably say no. He's too old for me. Too poor. Too uneducated. Too dangerous. But right now, none of that means a thing. It doesn't matter that this is a bad idea.

"I'm sure," I whisper. I don't know if he heard me, but it's all I was able to get out. *I'm sure.*

"You have a snowflake here," he says, and leans down to kiss my upper lip. He hums. "You see? I was right. So very sweet."

He dips his head again while cupping the back of mine, then slowly teases my mouth open. And *Christ*, does he taste better than I ever thought he could.

I angle my face, allowing him to run his tongue lightly over my bottom lip before he slips it inside my mouth. A pang of desire shoots down my spine when he sucks my lip between his teeth. I welcome his invitation to come even closer when he wraps his arms around my waist and pulls me firmly against his body. Gently, the hands at my chin tip my face to the side so he can deepen the kiss even more.

The snow-flurried lights around me spin, and not just in that too-much-wine kind of way. This is what I have been waiting for. Not just for the last two weeks. I have been waiting for this kiss my entire fucking life. Every kiss I've experienced before now was child's play, the tentative, floundering advances of teenage boys and not-yet men. There should be another word for this kind of kiss. Something that conveys the way the Earth tilts a little when his lips are on mine, the way the sky changes color a little when our tongues coil together. Nothing comes close to this man's mouth. Nothing.

A small moan escapes when I come up for air, and I'm pleased to find Nico's breathing is on the rough side too.

"My roommates are out for the night," I mumble into his lips, barely managing to get out the words before he devours me all over again. At this rate, I won't be able to make it home by myself anyway. His lips are soft, his tongue is firm, and his insistence with both of them makes it hard to think at all.

"Oh yeah?" he purrs, gently pulling my hair back to nip over my neck and behind my ear. The wet imprints of his lips chill in the wind, causing goosebumps to rise all over my skin and make me forget completely that we are standing in the middle of a relatively crowded street, probably attracting a number of curious looks from passersby. "They won't be back at all?"

"No, not until late," I slur, leaning back to make my neck more available to his advances. "They won't mind if you're there, either. But we'll have some privacy. Mmm, that feels good."

He returns to my mouth, and his hands reach gingerly under the confines of my unbuttoned jacket, sliding cautiously over my ass. He squeezes lightly—he wants more, and so do I.

"I'd be all right with that," he murmurs against my lips.

It takes another thirty seconds of him sucking on my lower lip before I can answer. When I do, my voice is hoarse, but urgent.

"Let's go."

―――

Nico

We practically sprint back to her dorm, stopping here and there when I can't fuckin' take it anymore and have to kiss her against a dark wall or on an empty street corner. I can't explain it. Something happened. All that electricity that's been building for the last two weeks finally sparked, and now it's full-fledged fire. It's like now I can't stand more than six inches between us at all times, and if I don't get another taste every few seconds, I'll stop breathing. In the space of a few minutes, Layla went from sweet to essential.

I really am completely fucked.

Somehow, when I don't have my tongue down her throat or my hands on her ass, we get back to her building. Layla sobers a little and touches her hair, but lets me keep her other hand firmly in mine. If she thinks I'm letting her go now, she's crazy.

I glance around curiously as we stop at the security desk. It's been a while since I've been in a college dorm. During the year and a half I spent at CUNY, I lived at home, although I did visit a few friends at NYU and Fordham. I forgot how busy they are. Even at eleven o'clock at night, the lobby is bumping with the chatter of students, most of them looking readier to go out than stay in.

I smirk as I hand my ID to the security guard, and he copies the information with a bored look. All the better if everyone is out for the night. If I have my way, Layla's going to be making a lot of noise.

Once we're let through, I recapture Layla's hand while she leads me to the elevator banks. A few of the students wave at her, and I notice more than one frat-looking dude looking her up and down, and then at me with a little annoyance. I scowl. I know these guys. They'll grow up to become the next generation of Wall Street assholes, like the ones at the club last weekend. Scumbags who will trade people's lives away for some extra coin. They see Layla as a commodity, not the special, luminous person she is.

I grip her hand harder, and she leans on my shoulder.

"Don't worry," she murmurs into my ear. "We're almost there."

She trembles when I grin at her. It's a good thing she seems to like my smile, because I seriously can't stop around her.

"Hey, Layla."

A gawky kid who looks about six inches too tall for his shirt gives Layla a wave and looks me up and down curiously as we all enter the elevator. I glare. Christ, this girl really turns me into an animal. I'm almost afraid of what I'm going to be like once we're finally alone together.

"Oh, hey, Vin," Layla says. She tugs on my arm, urging me to look at the kid. "Nico, this is my friend, Vinny. We've known each other since we first started at NYU."

I give the kid another look, but now I can tell by the way he's glancing between me and Layla that he's not interested in her—just looking out. I relax. Preppy shitheads with too much entitlement? They can fuck the hell off, and I'm happy to help them do it. Scrawny guy down the hall watching her back? Him I can deal with.

"Hey, man, nice to meet you," I say, holding out my hand.

Vinny accepts, still looking at me like he's afraid I'm going to kill him. Is it fucked up I kind of like it? Is it fucked up that I kind of want this kid to put the word out about Layla's new thug boyfriend, just so those other pricks will lay off?

Whoa. *Boyfriend*?

"Good to meet you too," Vinny says, interrupting me from my sudden panic.

The doors open, and we follow him into a hall that's lined with doors, a lot of them decorated with pictures, magazine cutouts, whiteboards scribbled with notes. The exact opposite of my building's sober halls.

"Have a good night, you two," Vinny says with a wink at Layla, although not until I'm well out of swinging arm's distance.

His lanky form bounds away, and I have to smile a little. He kind of reminds me of Gabe, all arms and legs, not quite grown into his body. I hope he's a good friend to Layla.

"This is me," Layla says as she stops in front of one of the doors.

She unlocks it, then turns around and pauses, biting her lip a little. Those big blue eyes flicker up at me, and suddenly her awkward friend is the last thing on my mind. She bites her lip. I rock a little closer.

"It's, um, small," she says as I close the gap between us.

I prop my hand on the door, right beside her head. Slowly, I run my nose down her cheek, enjoying the way her inhale sharpens and her fingernails claw at the door.

"Did you change your mind?" I ask, even though suddenly I'm terrified she has. I'll stop if she wants. I have the sneaking feeling I'd do anything this girl wanted. But I really, really don't want to.

And thank fuck, she shakes her head.

"N-no," she breathes as her hands grasp at my belt buckle. "I just—"

Before she can speak again, I crash my lips against hers, effectively shutting off any worries she might have about whether or not I want to be here. She's surprised at first, but after a second returns the kiss whole-heartedly—and I mean *really* gives as good as she gets. Suddenly, her arms are wrapped around my neck, and she's got a leg slung up on my hip so she's grinding against me in a way that shoots pretty much every conscious thought I have straight to my cock. My hands find her ass and lift her up against the door, and before I know it, I'm about two seconds from yanking down her jeans and taking her right here in the hallway.

A door slams. Layla freezes, then squirms until her feet are back on the carpet.

"I-um-I—"

Christ, she's cute when she's flustered. Her nose is pink, and her eyes are brighter than normal. I just grin and try to adjust my pants as subtly as I can. It's not easy. She's got me hard as a rock.

"Layla?" I say, stopping her stuttering.

She blinks. "What?"

"Open the door. Right the fuck now." I cock my head. "Please."

CHAPTER ELEVEN

Layla

THE GIRLS, THANK GOD, HAVE CLEANED UP THEIR STUFF IN THE COMMON AREA. WE'RE not terrible about keeping things neat, but there is always the chance I might find someone's books piled on the coffee table or a box of tampons that haven't been put away. True to their words, the place is empty.

As the door shuts behind us, I suddenly feel inexplicably nervous to be alone with Nico. My buzz is mostly gone, and we're a long way from the romance of streetlights and falling snowflakes. One kiss, and I almost just let him fuck me in the middle of my hallway. Seriously, what that man can do with his mouth should be illegal.

But now that we're inside the homely apartment I share with three other people, will I look as good? Or will he take a look at the posters of Jennifer Lopez and Carrie Bradshaw that Shama and Jamie have plastered all over the common area and think he's walked into a den of teenage ridiculousness?

I didn't need to worry. When I turn to hang my coat in the closet next to the door, I almost immediately feel a pair of strong arms wrap around my waist from behind. Nico presses his face into my hair and inhales deeply. I turn to face him and welcome another long, thorough kiss that leaves me breathless.

"Hi," he says against my nose, flashing that smile that shoots another pang of desire straight between my legs. Yeah, I have nothing to worry about.

"Hi," I answer, and fit my lips again to that mouth, that incredible mouth that's going to be my undoing.

I walk backward with him into my bedroom, yanking off his jacket and tossing it over my desk chair. Like magnets, his hands come right back to my body, tracing the uneven lines of the fabric wrapped around my waist. He shudders slightly when his fingers catch on the edges and come across itinerant patches of bare skin.

"I like this shirt," he grumbles before he slips his tongue around mine.

As his hands slide below the waistband of my jeans, his fingers hook the straps of my underwear, a thong. He groans audibly. Oh, he wants me, but not nearly as much as I want him.

I push him over to my bed, and he sits down obediently, placing his hands on my hips while I lean over to kiss him again. My hair falls around us, forming a dark cocoon of desire. He slides his palms up to tug off my shirt, only to find that the straps won't budge.

"Uh-oh," he says with a cheeky grin as he jerks playfully at the knot next to my belt buckle. "I think we've got a problem here."

I smile and untie the knotted fabric at my waist so he is holding the ends. "It's kind of like a bandage."

Nico pulls one of the newly freed ends, and I start to spin in his arms until the strips of fabric are completely unraveled down to the floor. He easily tugs the rest of the top over my head and lets it fall while he reaches eagerly for my newly bared skin. His fingertips are feather-light over my torso, thumbs pressing gently up the soft skin of my stomach and around my rib cage until he reaches the clasp of my bra and unhooks it. I let the straps fall down my arms along with the rest of it, and suddenly I'm standing before him half naked, my skin and nipples perked in the cool night air.

He stares at me wordlessly, his hungry gaze roving over my body. Nervously I move to cross my arms over my chest, but he grabs them and holds them down to my sides.

"Don't," he orders softly.

"Is...is everything okay?"

My voice sounds so weak, so unsure. What is it about this man that makes me lose my usual bravado?

But Nico looks up and smiles kindly, shaking his head. Then he leans in and places a soft kiss directly between my breasts, taking time to inhale slowly and exhale there. His lips float over the curve of one breast, then the other before both of his hands cup them gently.

"So...beautiful," he murmurs, his low voice rumbling against my skin as he pulls one nipple into his mouth, rolling the taut edge between his teeth until I shudder.

"Aah!" I yelp as I tug on his hair, sinking my fingers into the tight black curls that literally had me speechless when he removed his hat in the restaurant. All I wanted to do was grab them.

I press him closer as he performs the same ritual on the other side, teasing the nipple with that sinfully talented mouth until I'm tingling absolutely *everywhere*. He moves back and forth between each side until I can't take it anymore. Roughly, I push him back.

He knows what I'm after. Eager to feel his skin against mine, I claw impatiently at his shirt as his hands search for the zipper of my jeans. His shirt falls to the floor next on the growing piles of clothes, and I take a second to look at what I've got.

Even half-hidden in the shadows of the unlit room, he's perfect enough that I can't quite breathe properly. Though it's dark, I can still see the contours of his abs and the lines of his chest, which is smooth, with only a thin smattering of hair in the center. It's just the right amount. This guy is naturally just that gorgeous.

He watches with hooded eyes as I reach forward and run my fingers over the lines of his tattoos, a half-sleeve of various black designs that arches over his shoulder on one side and down just to his elbow. I had noticed the edges of that one at dinner, when it stuck out of the sleeve of his t-shirt, but was too entranced with our flirting to think about it.

Over his heart is a large black compass, bigger than the span of my hand. I want to ask him what that's for—Nico doesn't really seem like the nautical type. But right now, I'm caught up in the smooth contours of his pectoral muscles, the sinewy slopes of his shoulders and biceps. The taut lines of his stomach ripple and shift under my fingertips. Lifting boxes all day definitely does this body good.

"Like what you see?" he asks playfully.

He leans back on his elbows now, unabashedly giving me a full view of his shirt-less chest while he runs his eyes over me. We're both staring now, equally caught up in seeing each other's bodies for the first time.

I stare back, brazen, and lick my lips. "Yes."

There's no getting around it, no reason to play games anymore. I'm getting exactly what I wanted—or at least I hope I am.

"Your turn."

His voice is gravelly, suddenly overcome with want. He stands up, close enough that the tips of my breasts graze the front of his chest, causing both of us to suck in desperate inhalations. With a deviant grin, he unbuttons my jeans in a hurry, then slips his hands under the waistband so he can grab my ass, pull me firmly against him, and squeeze as he kisses me again.

Suddenly all the urgency from the restaurant, the street, the hallway is back, multiplied by ten. My hands fly around his neck. I grind into the hard length I feel against my hip as one of his hands slips lower down the cleft of my ass, dragging my pants with it until a finger lightly brushes the dampness through the thin silken fabric. I moan into his lips, and the pressure of his fingertip increases slightly as his breathing grows more ragged.

"Christ, baby," he groans against my mouth in between kisses. "You're so fucking wet, Layla."

I whimper again, wordlessly imploring him to tear my jeans off already so he can move that hand farther, down to touch that spot that would make me lose the last remnants of control I still possess. Every cell in my body is screaming for me to fuck this man, to let him slide into me again and again, to put him into my mouth and do the dirtiest things I can think of just to undo him the same way he's undoing me now.

But somehow, just as he pulls his hands out and starts to peel my jeans over my hips, the realization that I'm about to sleep with someone I hardly know pops into my head, a miniature version of my mother chiding me. Her conservative instincts combined with my father's strict Catholicism echo through every word. "No one likes a slut, Layla." She has never actually said such a thing to me, but I can hear her. And the thing is, I'm only nineteen. That voice, imagined or not, still has serious clout.

"Wait," I say breathlessly as Nico sucks on the edge of my ear.

He doesn't seem to hear me, concentrated as he is on removing the barriers between us. His own jeans have somehow come undone as well, revealing a solid bulge encased in gray boxer briefs that don't leave much to the imagination. It wouldn't take much to get them out of the way and see what's really underneath that fabric. I groan. Damn my mother, and damn my imagination. Just…damn.

I summon every particle of will left in my treacherous body.

"Nico, *wait.*"

———

Nico

Shit. I was really hoping I had imagined it the first time, but then it's clear. Despite the fact that I'm hard as a rock and she's basically a water fountain, she's asking me to stop.

Shit.

She pulls her hands back from around my neck and pushes me away a little, forcing me to release her earlobe from between my teeth. She shudders at the friction of my teeth, and I'm full of regret already. The only thing I want to do is strip her naked and show her what a fucking real man can do to a body like this. Make her lose control like I already know she's going to make me do.

But then I look down and catch her gaze. And my hands still on her hips.

She's watching me with a funny mixture of free and frustrated, her blue eyes still dark and dilated with desire. She covers her breasts with her arms, and giggles a little when I frown playfully at the movement. No, don't do that! She's too beautiful to cover up.

"Nico...I—I just want you to know...I'm not going to sleep with you tonight. I sort of have this rule, you see. I don't sleep with men on the first date."

For a minute, I'm stunned. It's not that I've never heard that line before—plenty of girls have similar dumb rules. But for real. As if I give a fuck whether or not she gives it up on date one or date one hundred. Can't she feel this energy between us? If there is one thing I have ever been sure of in this short, fucked-up life of mine, it's that our bodies were made for each other. Mine is fuckin' *craving* hers at this point, and considering the way her nipples are staring at me like headlamps, she's dying for me too.

But again, it's the look on her face that stops me from flipping her over and showing her just how badly we both want it. As turned on as she obviously is, she's scared too. Those big blue eyes are as wide as the sky, and she's got her lip in a death clench between her teeth as she watches my reaction.

It's then that it finally occurs to me that maybe she's feeling the same thing I'm feeling. Something that goes deeper than just bodies. That maybe she doesn't just see a pretty face and nice abs—that maybe she wasn't just after fucking the FedEx guy like everyone else in that stupid office.

Maybe when we touch, she feels the same spark. Maybe this spark is more than just fire.

I glance over her body again—it's right there, and I can't help but look—but I settle my hands on her hips and gently stroke her hipbones. She closes her eyes, almost like she's in pain. Oh...baby. I'm right here with you.

"Are you going to kick me out?" I ask softly. "Or...can I at least stay the night?"

I run my hands around her bare back and gently pull her closer, so that our bodies just barely touch. She keeps her arms in front of her chest, but relaxes a little into me. Her arms are surprisingly cool, and she leans into my warmth.

"You want to stay?" she wonders. "With me? In this tiny bed?"

I almost laugh, but I'm surprised by her obvious shock. She thinks I was only coming up here for one thing. Don't get me wrong. I was *definitely* coming up here for that. But we haven't even fucked yet, and already Layla means so much more than sex to me. I hate that she can't see it.

So I lean down and land a tender kiss on her lips, one that I hope tells her the things I can't quite say yet. I run my hands up and down her spine, hoping to tell her with my touch. Tell her not to worry. Tell her she's safe with me.

"Of course I want to stay with you, sweetie. What kind of guy do you think I am?"

She cracks a smile, and my heart cracks in half. "I don't know. I guess the kind who smashes himself onto a twin mattress with a girl even if she doesn't put out?"

I laugh this time, then gather her close and kiss her again because I can't not. She relaxes more, and her arms drop while she buries her face in my chest. It feels so good I laugh some more.

"Well," I say with a few more kisses on top of her head. I worry her earlobe again between my teeth and enjoy her hum in response. "As long as the girl's hot and won't mind if I try some stuff on her later."

"You better be careful," she purrs, arching her neck to the side to give me better access. "She'll probably try some stuff on you too."

"God, I fuckin' hope so," I growl against her neck.

She giggles. The sound is fucking music to my ears. I could die a happy man if the last thing I ever heard was Layla's laugh. Then she pushes away reluctantly and grabs my shirt from the floor to hold against her breasts.

"Awww," I fake moan, flopping my hands out as I collapse back onto the bed. "Don't do that. Booooo."

I'm being a clown, but it only makes her laugh more. She turns back to face me, unable to conceal her grin. That smile. It fuckin' slays me.

"I'm just going to slip into some pajamas, if that's all right with you," she says shyly, even as her eyes run down the length of my body again. "Jeans are kind of uncomfortable."

I can't even hide the sly smile that arises at the thought of her taking off her pants.

"You mind if I make myself comfortable too, baby?" I ask, gesturing down at my jeans, which are still partially open and not hiding a damn thing about how turned on I still am.

She blushes visibly in the dark light, but shakes her head with another grin. "Not at all."

She grabs some clothes from her dresser and leaves the room. I'm a little disappointed that she won't let me watch her change, but I get it. I'm not *that* much of a creep. While she's gone, I pull off my jeans, shoes, and socks, and stack my clothes on her desk chair. Then I get into her bed to escape the chill, taking a look at the room she lives in.

In some ways, the way she lives reminds me of my mom's cramped apartment. I never slept in a room by myself until I moved out of there. The mishmash of posters and pictures taped all over the walls reminds me a little of how Ma used to let my sisters, brother, and me decorate her place. Almost as if to make up for the fact that we didn't have our own space, she gave us hers.

This is a small room, split between the two sets of clunky wood furniture that each clearly belong to Layla and her roommate. Layla's bed is crammed against the right side of the room, with a desk on the other side of the bed, and a dresser beyond that. I look around curiously at little ways she's made the space her own: a really beautiful painting of something that looks like tribal art is tacked over her dresser, and a bulletin board crammed with photos is next to that. Her desk is cluttered with an open jewelry box, a bunch of books and scattered papers, cosmetics, and a computer.

I'm tempted to ask her if I can get online. I don't have a computer, so I don't check my email that often.

But then again, who's going to email me?

A few minutes later, Layla comes back looking cute as fuck in a pair of minuscule cotton shorts and a cotton tank top that makes it more than obvious she's not wearing a bra. Her hair is pulled back in a long ponytail, one I could easily see myself pulling while I do extremely dirty things to her.

But not tonight, I remind myself. Fuck. This is going to be torture. But I wouldn't want to be anywhere else.

I watch curiously as she reaches to the side of the bed and pulls a blue curtain around the wire that I hadn't noticed suspended from the ceiling. It's sort of like a hanging shower curtain that surrounds the bed and wraps the two of us with a little bit of privacy. Once we're immersed in a sheath of darkness, she leans over me, surrounding me with that sweet coconut smell of hers, and switches on her bedside light. It casts a low, ambient glow through the dark blue material.

I grin. "Nice cave."

Layla sits on the bed next to me. "Quinn and I had to rig something in here, if just to preserve our friendship."

"I could have used one of these when I was growing up."

"Tight quarters?"

"You could say that. Get under here."

She slides in eagerly as I yank back the covers to make room for us both on the narrow mattress. I catch her glancing down my body, pausing briefly on the bulge in my briefs. With a soft hum, she tucks securely into the crook of my arm like she's meant to be there, laying her head on my chest. She sighs. I sigh. And then, because I just fuckin' have to, I tip her chin up and kiss her again, another deep, long kiss with just enough tongue to let her know I still want her more than anything, but mostly that I'm just happy to be with her.

"You're so beautiful," I tell her again, unable to keep it back.

My filter is shot to hell with this girl. Her face sees through my damned soul. I have a feeling I couldn't hide anything from her if I tried.

She shivers, but I don't think she's cold. We lie here, listening to each other breathe in the quiet of the room. The combination of the wine and her warm body next to me soon causes my eyelids to droop.

"Nico?" she asks in a voice low and sleepy.

"Yeah, baby?"

"Thanks for staying. I...I had a good time."

I hug her tighter, enjoying the feel of her legs entwined with mine, the curve of her lower back under my hand. It doesn't matter how we do it. Together, we just fit. Absently, I brush a kiss over the top of her head. She inhales, then exhales, long and content.

"Anytime, baby," I say. And I mean it.

We both close our eyes. Our heartbeats find a similar rhythm as we drift off to sleep.

CHAPTER TWELVE

Layla

I AWAKE THE NEXT MORNING TO THE SOUND OF THE CURTAIN SLIDING BACK ON THE clothesline, and Nico is pulling his pants on. God, he looks even better in the light than he did at night—I don't think I've ever had beer goggles work in reverse before. Now the chiseled muscles of his stomach and chest are in full relief in the morning light, and the black of his tattoos are even more visible. I sigh as the rest of the night comes back to me.

Most of our "sleep" consisted of more groping and making out under the thick comforter, even after my roommates clambered in sometime after three. It was simply impossible to sleep soundly while pressed against his body. For some reason, the knowledge that Quinn was snoring on the other side of the thin curtain made the gorgeous man feeling me up that much hotter, and I couldn't find a way to say no to his urgent kisses and roving hands. By the morning, I was no longer in possession of my pajama shorts, although I did manage to keep on my underwear and camisole. It took every iota of willpower I had not to tear off his boxer briefs and mount him like a damn pony at about four a.m.

But hey, he never promised to be a gentleman. And I never promised to be a lady.

"Hey," I say drowsily, knowing I must look like a complete wreck.

Curly hair rarely ever looks cute first thing in the morning, and in my half-drunken haze, I didn't take the time to clean the makeup off my face last night either. I glance across the room at the full-length mirror on the closet door, which reveals several curls sticking out from behind my ears like antennas. With a clap, I grope around my desk for another hair band (since my last one was apparently lost in all the activity) and hastily pile my hair into a messy bun. On the bright side, at least none of my makeup is too badly smudged. I'm pretty sure Nico kissed most of it off.

Nico watches me with an amused smile as he gingerly pulls back the curtain the rest of the way, breaking the sanctuary I built for us last night.

"Hey, baby," he whispers.

Quinn emits a whale-sized snore across the room, earning an amused glance and a chuckle from Nico.

"Where you going so early?" I ask as I sit up fully.

Much to my disappointment, he pulls his shirt on over his shoulders and sits down to put on his shoes. "I figured I should leave before your roommates wake up."

I glance at the clock on my desk. It's just past seven. "Nico, there is no way they're going to wake up before ten. Besides, they won't care if you're here. Jamie or Shama, or both, probably have guys in their room too. Come on, it is way too early on a Saturday for you to be rushing out."

He smiles again and lies down beside me, and I let him pull my head into his chest for a quick embrace as he kisses my forehead. It's a sweet gesture, the kind that makes me want to think maybe this means more to him than a casual hookup. God, I hope so.

"You're even gorgeous in the morning," he murmurs. "It's insane. Who are you? Where did you come from?"

I push myself to sit up fully and smile over him. "You're not so bad yourself, Mr. Soltero. Take your shoes off. Shirt too. I can make it worth your while."

But he shakes his head ruefully and sits back up, then stretches his beanie back over his head. I know it's cold outside, but it makes me sad. His hair is thick and glossy. I could run my fingers through it all day.

"I'm really not ditching you, sweetie, I promise. I just have some errands I need to run today, and I'm up, so I figured I'd get them out of the way. Listen..." He traces the cream piping on my eggplant-colored comforter. "Shit...do you want to meet up later this afternoon? I have to work at AJ's again tonight, but I'd like to see you...if you're okay with that."

It's the game he's struggling with; I know because I'm struggling too. It's not cool to want to see someone so soon—especially not the same *day* after you've hooked up. If you're the guy, you're supposed to play it cool, wait a few days until you send the girl a casual text to meet up somewhere. If you're a girl, well, you're just supposed to wait, and under no circumstances do you call the guy before he calls you. It sucks. Hard. Hardly anyone actually dates anymore, and if they do, they do their best to downplay it.

So when he comes right out and tells me that he wants to see me again, I'm over the fucking moon. Calling me the same night he got my number. Taking me out for the first time on Valentine's Day. Staying the night with me—without even having sex. And now asking for another date in just a few hours? I guess we're breaking all the rules.

I try to stifle a wide grin, but it's a complete failure. My friends always tease me for having such a transparent face. Normally it doesn't bother me; it's something that keeps me honest. But in this case, I wouldn't mind shielding my hand a bit more.

"Sure," I reply, trying my best to sound nonchalant. "I don't have much going on today. I guess that sounds good."

Nico raises one black eyebrow. He sees right through me, which only makes me grin harder. "You guess, huh? Well, good, NYU. I'll call you after I get my stuff taken care of. Say, around four?"

I nod. He leans in for a brief but thorough kiss, unable to completely subdue a grunt of pleasure before he breaks away.

"Take care, beautiful," he says as he draws the curtain back around the bed.

I fall into my pillow, listening to the sound of his feet tiptoeing through the apartment. The front door only squeaks a little when it opens, but I don't close my eyes again until it shuts.

———

Nico

After spending the morning fixing the busted pipe under my mom's sink and listening to her nag at me for wearing jeans to Mass, I finally manage to get out of Hell's Kitchen to get a haircut and meet up with K.C. for lunch.

K.C., whose real name is Kevin Carlos, is my best friend. Really, he's another brother, my twin, since our moms are both from the same part of Puerto Rico. We grew up together in the Kitchen, went to the same elementary school together, high school, ran with the same kids. K.C. and I are ride or die. There is nothing I wouldn't do for him, and him for me.

"Whazzup, *maricón*!" he hollers when I enter our favorite Dominican restaurant up on One-Forty-First and Broadway.

It's no different than every other mom and pops' place in West Harlem, but this one has a cute waitress K.C. likes to flirt with. He's not allowed to fuck her because we like the chicken here too much.

"Hey, *mano*," I greet him with a slap and a hug. "How's LA? You missin' New York yet, motherfucker?"

K.C. left a year ago for a job out in LA, but he comes back all the time to visit, usually when he's booked a gig at one of the clubs. I'm proud of my friend. He started out hoofing around boxes of records for some of the early beat boys in our neighborhood, and now he's really starting to make a name for himself as a DJ. A big radio station just hired him to do their hip-hop programming while he spins at clubs on both coasts.

"Miss this shitty weather?" K.C. gestures outside, where the snow is piled up on the sidewalks. "*Fuck* no. Gimme palm trees and beaches. Girls in bikinis, if you please!"

I pull off my jacket and my hat, eager to get warm. Last night the snow was pretty, but today it's gray sludge and just causes a bunch of delays. Took me an extra hour just to get up here on the 1 train.

Lula, the waitress K.C. likes, comes over holding her notepad and rattles off a bunch of insults at him in Spanish. Her dialect is a little different from ours—she moved here from Panama, and I know she gets lost sometimes in the slang that gets thrown around by all the different groups in New York. K.C. always liked to mess with her that way, so now she messes with him.

"Nico, *que quiere*?" she asks me after she's done trading barbs with K.C.

I order my favorite chicken plate, and she leaves us with a pitcher of Coors Light that K.C. ordered. I roll my eyes.

"*Coño*, it's fuckin' twelve-thirty," I say as he pours us both pints. "You don't think it's a little early?"

"Shut the fuck up," K.C. says. "This is basically water. Stop bein' a pussy and drink."

I just look at the beer skeptically. I still want to get in a workout at the gym before I catch up with Layla. The last time I sparred on a stomach full of beer, I was in the bathroom for an hour puking my guts out. *No bueno.*

"Come on, *cabrón*," K.C. jeers. "We're celebrating. Fuck your boxing shit. You ain't gonna need that when you come to LA with me."

"Come again?" I ask, sitting back as Lula brings a water for me. "*Gracias, linda.* K.C., what are you talking about?"

K.C. leans over the table, his round white face practically glowing with excitement. It's funny. He's never the best-looking dude in the room. Always a little pudgy with skinny arms and a gut, he's so light-skinned that he looks like he was shipped straight from Spain, which is only more obvious by the fact that he started shaving his head a couple of years ago. Dude looks like the Man in the Moon.

But K.C.'s energy is contagious. Wherever he goes, he's the life of the party, because he has this ability to attract everyone's energy. We've been friends our whole lives, getting into trouble together our whole lives. He was always the instigator; I just played along, even if sometimes I paid a higher price.

"Nico, I did it, man," he says in a low voice, like he's telling me a secret. "I got the job."

"You got the...oh!"

A light bulb goes off. It's the club gig at Venom, the hottest new spot in LA that basically pretends to be New York in the middle of California. I don't know what that means, exactly, but choosing K.C. to be their DJ every Friday night is a good idea. He couldn't be more New York if he tried. It also makes him a genuine name in the business.

"Yo, man, congratulations!" I shoot him a fist bump. "That's amazing, *mano*! When do you start?"

"Next month."

Lula brings over our chicken, and K.C. whistles at her as she goes. She looks back with a raised eyebrow. She's dressed like a million other girls on the block with the gold chain around her neck, her hair pulled into a tight brown bun, and her nails done long with crazy designs on a few of them. If there's one thing that girls in this neighborhood do, it's their hair and nails.

I think about Layla. She was trying to look a little like a girl from the block last night, and it was working for her, no doubt, but I think she looks cuter when she's a little more low-key, the way she dresses at the office. Even more when she's wearing barely anything at all.

"Hey! Earth to Nico. Where the fuck you at, man?"

I blink. My food is sitting in front of me, untouched. "Sorry. Just lost for a second, I guess."

"I know that look," K.C. says as he shoves a forkful of beans and rice into his mouth. "You got some last night, didn't you?"

I don't say anything, just take a bite of my food. Unfortunately, K.C. can read me like a book.

"Oh, shit! Was it that NYU girl from the law firm? You finally hit that, bro?"

Yeah, I told him. K.C. and I don't have secrets, although right now, I'm kind of wishing we did.

I just shake my head. "No, no. It's not like that. We just hung out last night. We had a good time."

"Valentine's Day, man? I can't believe you fell for that. NYU must have some serious game."

I think back to Layla's interactions this week—the way she tried to flirt with me in the office, but usually got just as tongue-tied as I did. The way her big blue eyes watched my every move. The way her body shook when I touched her.

No, it might have started a little like a game, just like it always does when you first meet someone. But by the time we were sitting across a table from one another, neither one of us were playing anymore. We were just trying to keep up with what was happening.

"Oh, shit," K.C. says, interrupting my reminiscing. He gives me a knowing look as he drains his beer. "It's like that, huh?"

I frown and shake my head. "Nah, man. It's cool. She's just cool, that's all."

"Uh-huh."

I ignore him and focus on my food. The melt-in-your-mouth chicken doesn't really taste like anything right now. But I can't hide from K.C. He knows exactly what I'm thinking and why.

"Yo, did you tell her about—"

"No," I say quickly. "It hasn't come up."

There's another long look from my friend.

"Nico, if you changed your mind, I kinda need to know," K.C. says. "They can find somebody else, but you can't blow them off last minute."

I stab at my chicken. I really don't want to talk about this right now. I managed to stop thinking about it all night last night, and I really don't want to worry about it today when I see Layla again. It occurs to me that maybe I should just call it off. That maybe I should tell her I thought about it, and the timing's no good. That I can't get into a relationship right now.

But then I remember the fact that when we kissed, it was like a lightning bolt ran through both of us. That when she touches me, my heart and my cock feel like they're going to explode. I already know she isn't someone I'm going to be able to ignore for the next three months. Not when I'll be seeing her beautiful face every damn day.

Maybe there's a way around it. Layla's a girl who seems down for a good time. Shit, she and her friends built curtains around their beds. Don't tell me that's just because they like to sleep with privacy. I know the truth, even if the thought of Layla bringing another guy back to her room makes me want to cut someone.

But it also makes me remember the score. For a girl like her, I'm just a good time, nothing else. I need to remember that.

"You don't have to worry," I assure K.C. "Nothing's changed."

CHAPTER THIRTEEN

Layla

"I DON'T KNOW HOW YOU TALKED ME INTO THIS TODAY," I GRUMBLE AS I LEAVE THE cycling studio at the Student Athletic Center. "You guys were out later than me. I was counting on you just wanting to sleep all day and ply your hangovers with coconut water."

"A workout a day keeps the goddamn cellulite away, babe," Quinn quips far too cheerily for my taste as she takes a large drink of said coconut water.

Her mom, the pearl-wearing wife of a state senator in Massachusetts, is so hyped about Quinn's relatively new workout obsession that she sends her daughter a crate of the stuff every month to keep her hydrated on the treadmill. I don't know. Regular water always worked for me.

We are both covered in sweat after hauling through a grueling spinning class at the Student Center. Despite her snoring, Quinn bounced out of bed just after eight and yanked me out the door with her to class so that Jamie could have some time alone with the guy who had escorted her home the night before. Shama, it turned out, had just gone home with Jason.

"You could also say it's payback for not letting me get a glimpse of Mr. Perfect," Quinn says with a smirk. "I had to listen to you getting busy with FedEx Guy all fucking night, and I don't even get a glimpse of his ass come morning? So not fair, babe."

I smile, happy that Quinn's nasty reservations about Nico seem to have disappeared since last night.

"Well, whatever your intentions, the end result is also that I am allowed to have a scone this morning at Reggie's," I say as we walk into the locker room to shower and change out of our sweaty clothes. I pull out my wallet and count the cash I still have left for my spending money for the week. I have two wrinkled dollars. Shit. "Maybe not. On second thought, tea and oatmeal at home will be just fine."

"Isn't that, like, all you've been eating for the past week?" Quinn asks as she wraps herself in a towel.

We walk into the showers in our flip-flops. I rush into one of the stalls so she can't examine my face while I ignore her question.

"I get paid next week," I call to her over the roar of the showers and the curtained barrier between us. "I'll be able to go shopping then." I don't like to talk about money with the girls—especially not with Quinn—in part because that would mean disclosing the fact that I am not particularly good with it.

The truth is, I unfortunately haven't managed to budget particularly well over the past few years—to be honest, it's really more a problem of spending the cash set aside for essentials on things like bar covers. Every weekend I tell myself that this time I'll stay in, study, and save my money. And every weekend there is some great new place to see, new music to hear, people to meet. How many nineteen-years-olds in New York City can resist that? So I figure this is the time in my life where I can actually handle the tradeoff—meager living for the sake of a rocking social life—because when it really comes down to it, the contents of my cupboard are not going to give me memories I'll cherish for the rest of my life.

"You've been losing more weight, babe," Quinn calls over the roar of the showers with a hint of reproach that I suspect has more to do with envy than actual concern. Her obsession over her own weight has been deflected onto us more than once. "You need to take better care of yourself. You're gonna make yourself sick."

I mimic her words ungraciously to myself under the steam of my shower. It's easy for her to say. Unlike my roommates, I don't have parents who send me spending money. It was a point of pride in the beginning, when I'd see my roommates gleefully open checks each month that would cover any and all extraneous expenses. I told myself I was the one with character; I wasn't just the average rich kid whose parents did everything for her.

Eighteen months later, those checks are still coming for all of my friends, who have the time to commit to unpaid internships because they don't have to work for real money in the most expensive city in the country. It's a hard pill to swallow when I'm expected to work twenty-five hours a week on top of my course load just to pay for food, books, school supplies, transportation, my cell phone, and student health insurance. Nor do they have to, as I will probably have to do this week, walk the forty blocks between school and the dorms in the freezing cold just to save the last two dollars in their wallets. I wouldn't mind being spoiled just a little.

I really hope it doesn't snow again this week.

But there's always a bright side, right? If my parents weren't so hell-bent on teaching me "good American values" (in my dad's thick Brazilian-accented English), I wouldn't have gotten that job, and I wouldn't be meeting up with a certain gorgeous FedEx courier in a few hours. Just the thought of his thousand-watt smile brings one to my own lips. I'll make the best of my accidental diet and wear my super skinny jeans—the ones I bought on a whim, that I can only fit into when I've had the stomach flu.

"I'm fine," I say loudly so Quinn will be sure to hear. I finish rinsing the conditioner out of my hair and turn off the water. I wrap myself back up in the towel before stepping out of the shower. "Healthy as a horse."

Quinn soon joins me, and we walk back to our lockers to get dressed.

"I'm serious, Lay," she says. "You hear about it all the time. Don't you remember how many kids in our dorm last year got the flu? Knocked half the floor out because everyone was too busy partying to take care of themselves." She grimaces. "I do *not* miss the shit they fed us in the dining hall, that's for sure."

I have to agree with her on that count. Tea and oatmeal is infinitely preferable to the slop they fed us last year. I lost ten pounds within a few months of entering college just because I hated the dorm food so much. But honestly, what girl isn't okay with losing a little extra here and there? The battle of the bulge is real, my friend.

Quinn and I sit in the back of the subway car so we have a little privacy to talk. I love that I have the kind of girlfriends who aren't shy about details. She wants to know everything, from the size and shape of his dick (I can't tell her exactly, but I have a pretty good idea) to the expression on his face when he came (also not something I could say yet, although we both came close a few times). Like the best friend that she is, she sighs appropriately where she's supposed to, demonstrates obvious shock when I tell her that all we did was tease each other all night like horny high school students, and reacts with surprise and frustration when I mention that he left early this morning.

"Wait, *what*? He stayed the entire night and then just bounced at the crack of dawn?"

We emerge from the train station on Canal Street, diving immediately into the usual droves of tourists in Chinatown. The street is typically busy for a Saturday morning, and we maneuver in between other pedestrians until turning off onto our street.

"He said he had errands to do. I think he was kind of embarrassed," I say as I side-step a small pile of snow that's littered with cigarette butts and empty beer cans.

Quinn scrunches her lips together, running a hand thoughtfully through her dark Shirley Temple curls. "You don't think that's kind of weird that he just up and left? Like he was trying to ditch you or something?"

"I really don't think so," I insist. "We didn't actually have sex or anything, so it's not a 'fuck and run' situation."

Quinn chuckles. "Oh, what would we do without the knowledge of Liz Phair? But seriously, Lay, you don't think he's trying to play you, just up and going the way he did? I'm only asking because I don't want you to get hurt. FedEx guys can be dangerous too."

Annnnd she's back. I should have known that Quinn wouldn't be able to hear about last night without casting her pessimistic spin on the situation.

We push through the glass doors into our building and flash our IDs to the security guard sitting at the stairs.

"Hey, Bill," we both greet him. He looks sleepily at us through his glasses as we pass, but doesn't answer.

"It's really not like that. We're meeting up this afternoon again," I inform Quinn once we are in the elevator. "Honestly, I think it's more that he was weirded out by being in a dorm. I mean, imagine you're twenty-six, you live on your own, and then you go home with a chick who has to pull a curtain around her bed when you're getting busy."

"Dudes don't care about shit like that," Quinn retorts. "They care about the getting-busy part, not the privacy. Any one of them would get down in the middle of the street with the right girl. Some of them do."

The elevator doors open to reveal a girl stepping out of one of the doors on our floor. She bears the tell-tale signs of a walk of shame: short, tight skirt carrying the wrinkles of a night spent on the floor, hair mussed and tied back awkwardly, smudged black makeup under her eyes, and high stiletto heels hanging from her fingers. She gives her date, a junior named Mike standing in his boxers and a wrinkled t-shirt, a quick kiss before darting past us on her "walk of shame." Mike watches her leave with a very satisfied grin before nodding a hello at us as we pass.

"What's up, ladies?" he asks, looking Quinn and me up and down while licking his lips. "Have a good night? I know I did."

I scowl at him. "Dude, gross."

"Keep it in your pants, Mikey. Nobody wants whatever venereal disease you're spreading this week," Quinn shoots back at him.

Mike shuts his door, but not before muttering "bitch" just loud enough that we both can hear it.

Quinn looks back to me with a knowing look. "Like I said, babe. Dudes don't care."

———

AFTER SHOWERING and doing a load of laundry with Quinn in the basement, I find myself sitting at my desk later that morning, split between figuring out my finances for the month and doing my reading for my British Literature survey. We are reading Spenser's *The Faerie Queene*, which is long, written in Renaissance English, and not particularly motivating me to focus. I sigh and pick up the stack of bills that arrived in the mail this week.

Ten minutes later, Quinn walks in to find me banging my head on my desk and groaning into the oak surface.

"What's up, buttercup?" she asks as she sets her laundry basket on the floor and begins putting away her folded clothes.

I shuffle the bills underneath the rest of the papers on my desk and look up. "Nothing. You know, the same old poor college student bit."

"You need to borrow money?"

It's the same charade we go through every few months. It's hard keeping up with these girls, but I don't like having to sacrifice my social life just so I can have a few extra dollars in my savings account. No, it's not the "grown-up" thing to do, but I'm just a college student—what do I really have to save for? I also don't like playing the "get free drinks" game with men in bars like Jamie does; it makes me feel cheap. But I'm in college in New York City—I'm supposed to have fun, right?

"No, thanks, I'll manage," I mumble into my papers, just as I always do. Quinn always offers, and I always decline. It's become an awkward routine over the last year and a half.

"You really need to start managing your money, honey," Quinn says, coming up to rub me on the shoulder supportively. "Take a couple of free drinks here and there. Hell, my dad sent a little extra this month—why don't you just take it? Use it to pay off some of these bills." She lifts up one of the credit card statements shoved under my books. "Jesus, Layla, does that say what I think it does?"

I snatch the bill away and shove it back into the pile with the rest, suddenly as protective over them as a guard dog.

"It's *fine*," I snarl. "I don't need your help, Quinn. Don't worry about it. It's no big deal."

"Layla, thousands of dollars of debt is a big deal, and you're behind two payments. If you keep letting that go, it's going to ruin your credit. Seriously, just let me help you out—"

"I said it's *fine*, Quinn! Seriously, it's none of your business."

I slam my book shut and thrust it into the messenger bag that hangs off the side of my desk chair before locking the stack of bills into the front drawer of my desk. I stand up in a huff and sling the bag over my shoulder, only to be met by Quinn blocking the exit.

"Layla."

"Quinn."

She doesn't leave room for movement, and we stare at each other with our arms crossed. Quinn and I can both be stubborn asses at times, and this appears to be one of them. I place my hands on my hips and glare at her, but she doesn't budge. Yep, that's us: stubborn as freaking mules.

"You need to talk to your parents about this," she states clearly. "I know your folks want you to learn to stand on your own and all, but I really don't think they understand just how expensive this city—"

Ignoring just how childish it makes me, I blow a raspberry, and Quinn finally steps back to avoid my spit, giving me the space to flounce around her and grab my down coat from the closet.

"Layla," she calls out as I stomp out of our room. "What are you, five?"

Shama and Jamie are in their room studying too, but I can see a flutter of movement from their desks as they notice the scuffle. It's not uncommon for Quinn and me to butt heads from time to time, so they know the signs.

"Layla, your parents would help if you just asked them," Quinn continues as she follows me out. "It's not like they're hurting for cash. Your dad is the best plastic surgeon in Seattle, for crying out loud."

I stop just as I grab the doorknob, suddenly seething and wanting something to take out my frustration. It's one of those times where I miss the combative outlet of soccer, where it's acceptable to kick the shit out of a ball and run over anyone who gets in my way. Everything that was good about this day—about this weekend—has just evaporated, and Quinn only wants to push me further into the abyss. She doesn't get it. None of them do.

My dad is the definition of the macho Brazilian father. Sure, he'd love to help his little girl, just like he'd love any reason to cart his kid back from the big bad city and force her to live at home until she's married. It doesn't help that my mom thinks the same way. Neither of them understood in the first place why I had to leave home for college, let alone move to New York. There is nothing they'd like better than to cut off my tuition checks and force me to transfer to the University of Washington. Credit card debt and a too-old boyfriend would be the perfect excuses.

I turn once again to glare at Quinn, who has suddenly become my scapegoat. I've told her about my dad—she knows I'd rather pull out my fingernails one by one than ask him for money.

"Well, my folks don't own half of fucking New England like yours," I spit out. "My dad might make some money, but *I* wasn't raised with a silver spoon."

"Layla," she starts again, earning one more glower from me even as her voice starts to rise.

"Don't," I order her, and shut the door behind me.

CHAPTER FOURTEEN

Layla

It takes me a good hour and a half of walking around the snow-lined streets of Lower Manhattan before I'm ready to apologize to Quinn. She'll forgive me—she always does, just like I forgive her for spouting off at me. I know in another week or two I'll bear the brunt of one of her shitty moods to make up for it.

As much as I hate to admit it, I know Quinn is right. I need to get that shit paid off, and soon—otherwise it will eat at my credit score. Law school isn't cheap, and federal loans don't cover all of the tuition. God, if I've heard that from my father, I've heard it a million times.

But by the time I return to my dorm, the girls have all left—most likely to the library. Instead of being responsible and doing the same, I spend the last ninety minutes walking around Soho, window-shopping for things I can't possibly afford, and trying to figure out exactly how I am going to pay off the debt I somehow racked up in the last year and a half. So far, the only solutions I've come up with are selling my body on the street or giving up my social life for a while.

I continue to brood through another bowl of oatmeal and prep for my date with Nico. I decide to go totally casual this time, the better to help me play nonchalant when I certainly can't depend on my face to do it. My curls have air-dried again around my shoulders with appropriate devil-may-care waywardness, and I'm just wearing my favorite gray Rolling Stones t-shirt with jeans and brown boots. I dress up the outfit with a little bit of jewelry, but it's still very "I was just hanging out when you happened to show up." It also feels a lot more like me than the decked out look I was rocking last night.

Nico calls up to the room promptly at two.

"I'll be right down," I tell him as I jot a quick apology note and leave it on top of a candy bar I picked up for Quinn. That bitch better appreciate it—it was purchased with my last dollar from the bottom of my purse. I pull my coat back on and skip the elevator, running two at a time down the stairwell to meet Nico outside.

He's taken a shower and changed his clothes since departing from my room this morning and is dressed as casually as I am in a pair of fitted jeans and a white t-shirt, over which he wears his black parka and a Yankees hat on backward. New York is still mostly white, courtesy of the snowfall the night before, and his big black boots will make walking through the snow much easier. I'm dressed similarly for the cold, in my big down coat and a cream-colored wool cap pulled over my curls.

"Hiya, sweetie," he says with a light peck on my lips, and I thrill at the rumbling of his low voice against my skin. "You wanna go to the Cloisters?"

I frown, adjusting my hat against the cold. It's not snowing anymore, but the winds have definitely picked up, and the "Cloisters," whatever they are, sound suspiciously outdoors and possibly expensive. "What's that?"

"Art, remember?" He gives me a crooked smile, recalling the conversation we had at the office. "You'll like it, I promise. You up for an adventure?"

I squint at him, feigning suspicion, then shrug. I still have a little bit left on one of my credit cards. "Sure, why not?"

———

THE CLOISTERS, I soon find out, are castle-style buildings that house a large collection of medieval art. It's an extension of the Metropolitan Museum of Art, located at the very northern tip of Manhattan.

Nico and I catch the A train uptown, enjoying the hour-long ride tucked into each other's sides while we chat amiably about our mornings. He tells me about Mass with his family and makes me giggle when he describes the way his brother managed to spill wine down his shirt when he was taking the Eucharist. I recount the boring details of the gym and skate briefly over my disagreement with Quinn without giving him all the gory details about my finances.

"Sounds like she's just looking out for you," Nico says at one point. "Your girl sees you stressing over a stack of bills; she just wants to help you figure it out."

"I know," I admit. "I was kind of a bitch to her, so I left her a little apology gift before I came down for you. But...well...it's really none of her business unless I want it to be, right?"

Nico's quiet, like he knows I'm second-guessing that statement myself. Then he shrugs and shifts his gaze around the subway car, checking out the other people. We sit a bit awkwardly until finally he breaks the silence, although still not looking directly at me.

"Look, Layla, I don't know what's going on between your friends and your family...it's not really my business either—"

"That's not what I meant," I start to protest, but his dark, piercing eyes silence me as he continues.

"It isn't my business," he repeats. "You don't know me. But since you brought it up, it sounds like you're behind on things enough that your friend feels like she has to step in. So I'll say this, and then I'll shut the fuck up about it so I don't sound like your dad or something. Don't fuck with your money. I've been there, owing money and not being able to eat, and it fuckin' sucks. If you need help, ask someone—your dad, your friends, whoever's willing. Don't be so proud you just screw yourself later, all right?"

He holds my gaze for a beat as a rush of blood rises in my face. Finally, I tear myself away and sit forward so that his arm falls from around my shoulder. I take a few deep breaths, trying to push away the hot tears and shame of knowing he's right —they're all right—down where I can ignore them again. I feel like an idiot. How immature must he think I am, that he has to give me life advice? I wanted him to look at me like an adult...but I literally stuck my tongue out at Quinn like a little kid. How grown up am I?

"It's nothing to worry about," I insist once I'm able to look at him again. I force a smile. "Really. Quinn's kind of a drama queen, and sometimes I am too. Please don't worry about me. What else did you do this morning?"

Nico cocks his head to the side, measuring my response before he decides to let it go. I'm already figuring out that Nico is not the kind of person who will press you to talk if you don't want to. He has patience that my friends and I don't have.

The train emerges from the underground tunnel, elevated as we pass a cluster of tall brick tenement buildings. I've never been inside buildings like them, even though there are plenty in plain view everywhere you go here, lining the periphery of the island and most of the outer boroughs too. But anyone who has ever watched music videos knows they look like a prison on the inside, with shitty florescent lighting, thin walls, small windows.

"Projects," Nico says knowingly, catching me staring at the buildings.

I turn. "I know." I pause for a moment, and then a question bubbles up before I can stop it. "Do you live in the projects?"

He snorts, and I immediately feel foolish all over again.

"No, sweetie, I don't," he says kindly.

I want to explain that I didn't necessarily ask because he's not white—didn't I?— but because he said he knows what it's like to be poor. It never occurred to me before now that maybe he still is. These buildings line the edges of the island almost all the way around. Why wouldn't he live in one?

Nico's hand slips up my back and squeezes my shoulder. Great, now he feels sorry for me. But my curiosity, that stubborn bitch, gets the best of me.

"Did you ever live in one of them?"

I don't know what made me ask. Something about the way he talks about his family, sharing bedrooms, or the way his mother doesn't seem to be able to do much for herself anymore. Or maybe it's just the look on his face when he saw the buildings. A shadow lurks under that bright smile. I want so badly to know this man sitting next to me on the train, but I don't know how to do it besides ask the questions, dumb or not.

As if on cue, Nico's expression darkens as he looks back at the buildings receding into the distance.

"No," he says carefully. "But...I might as well have."

"What does that mean?"

He chews on his lower lip for a moment, considering. "Tell me something, NYU. How many bedrooms did you have in your house growing up?"

I frown. There's that moniker again, and this time it feels like a designation, a reminder of the difference in our social...I don't know what to call it. Stations? Upbringings? I want a word that won't sound so permanent.

I don't want to do this—we'll get nowhere comparing that sort of thing, and it will make me look like a spoiled brat. Which, compared to him, maybe I am.

"What does that have to do with anything?" I ask.

"Just tell me, baby," he cajoles. "I won't judge. But it matters."

I look back at the tenement buildings, now almost out of sight, and then back at him.

"I know what poverty looks like, if that's what you're getting at," I say carefully. "I've seen the *favelas*—the slums—in Brazil. I've driven through places where people live in houses literally built out of crumbling bricks and metal scraps they steal off railroad cars. Whatever's inside those buildings, I promise it's about ten times better than those people live."

"You think those *favelas*—" he pronounces the word carefully, testing out the unfamiliar accent, "—are worse than the projects?"

"Yeah, I do," I contend mulishly. "I've seen kids there running around the streets with open sores all over their legs. Half the women are forced into prostitution because they can't make enough money as maids to eat. People 'disappear' all the time, and the cops won't go there because the gangs are stronger than they are. You know, when my dad was a kid, most of the *favelas* weren't even included as part of the city, so they didn't even get basic services like water, electricity, and sanitation. So yeah, I think it's worse."

"People die in the projects here," Nico counters. "There are some places here that a pretty rich girl like you should never, ever go by yourself because you might disappear too."

He leans in, close enough so that his nose is almost touching mine, and his sooty eyes burn with a kind of intensity that holds me still even though I want to turn away. I shake my head, trying my best to break the connection. It doesn't work.

"I get it. There's poverty everywhere. But it's real life, not a rap song. I'm sorry, but you can't tell me that a building with plumbing and lighting and walls that are all of the same material is worse than the worst living conditions in a developing country."

Nico shakes his head and rubs his face. "Layla, that's not what I'm saying," he says, clearly a little frustrated. "My mother was born in a place like that. She grew up in a ghetto outside of San Juan. Trust me, I know it's better here."

I frown. "Then what's your point?"

He presses his full lips together. "Just that it's not really fair to make those comparisons in the first place. Just because those buildings have basic utilities doesn't mean they're safe. And just because someone calls one of them 'projects' doesn't mean they're hell on Earth. Have you ever actually been inside one of those buildings, NYU?" he asks, his voice dropping into a decibel that's almost menacing.

The man who shoved the testy investment banker against a wall like he was as light as a scarecrow is back, and I don't want to be on his bad side. I gulp, and I swear I can feel Nico relishing my discomfort.

"No," I admit.

"So answer the question, NYU. How many bedrooms did you have in your house growing up?"

"Five," I admit, my voice small as I focus on folding my scarf in my lap.

Nico sits back in his seat and waits until I finally look to see his face, half satisfied, but half...resentful? Regretful? I can't tell.

"We had one," he says as the train dips back down into the tunnel system below the city. We turn away from the window and face the inside of the car, which is old and covered in graffiti, and mostly emptied of people now that we've passed through Harlem.

I gape, but not at the vandalism. "You had *one* bedroom? Weren't there, like, four of you in that place?"

"Five," he corrects me. "Sometimes six if my mom had a boyfriend. My sisters slept on the Murphy bed. Gabe slept in the bedroom with our mom or on the floor until he was seven; then he got my spot on the couch when I left."

I'm the only child in my family. My parents have three extra bedrooms that sit empty in our big suburban house, kept sparkling for relatives who never come to visit. Nico's family had one to share. Jesus.

"How old were you when you left?" I ask, unable to conceal the awe in my voice, along with the guilt.

"Fifteen," Nico says in a heavy voice.

"That's young," I remark, and he blinks and straightens slightly.

"Um, yeah. I was in a program for a few years that...brought inner city kids to the country to see what that's like. But eventually I came back to Hell's Kitchen and got my shit together enough to go to school for a little while. You know the rest."

It's clear by his tone that he doesn't want to linger on this story, but I can't help myself. "And your mom still lives in that apartment?"

He rubs hands together impatiently. "Yes. Layla, I don't really want to talk about my past anymore though, all right? My point was just that things can be bad here too. My family didn't even have it as bad as some, but a lot of people who live in those buildings over there, they still had it better than us. 'Projects' is just a word, baby. It doesn't tell you everything."

I nod, now wanting more than ever to know more of his story, how he grew up. I want to know how a family of five could get along living together like that for years. I wonder if it's even legal. But somehow, I know that pressing the issue will probably only make Nico withdraw further, and that's the last thing I want.

Instead, we let the rumble of the train and the hum of other conversations fill the new silence that grows between us. As we sit back on the hard subway seats, I can't help but wonder just how much of his life in New York Nico has spent in train cars just like these. I also wonder if he has ever wanted to leave.

————

The Cloisters is about a ten-minute walk up a hill from the second to last stop on the route. As we trudge up the snowy drive, a large tower comes into view. It doesn't actually look so much like a castle as like the Roman-style basilicas in Europe and, as it happens, Brazil. A large tower rises above a square-shaped building, in the center of which is an outdoor garden space guests can roam during the spring and summer months.

We walk around the gated building and locate the entrance on one side. Once we're inside, Nico pulls out a season pass to show the ticket-booth attendant and hands over the "suggested" student fee before I'm able to take out my wallet.

"You didn't have to do that," I say while I attach the small "M" clip to my sweater. I tuck my hat and mittens into my satchel and sling my overcoat through the straps.

"Please," he says. "You're my date, and you're just a poor college student."

In light of our earlier conversation, I can't help but feel guilty that he's paying despite my obvious privilege compared to his family, but I shake it off as he grabs my hand and tows me into the museum like he owns the place.

He knows it as if he owns it too. I have my very own tour guide, because Nico has memorized just about every piece of art in the museum and all the trivia to go with it.

"So, get this," he rambles as we walk around the stone interior. "The museum is constructed from parts of five different medieval buildings from Europe. The rich guys who funded the place—Rockefeller, I think, and some other cats—actually purchased parts of churches and abbeys in Southern France and had them shipped over here, brick by brick, to reconstruct. On the tip of fuckin' *Manhattan*. Is that crazy, baby, or what?"

I have to agree that it is, and look on in awe as we walk in and out of the various buildings—the cloisters for which the place is named—peering at the medieval art and sculptures that adorn every room. We are mostly alone; few people want to make the trip up here in the snow, I suppose. Nico eventually steers me into a large room where the walls aren't lined with paintings, but with tapestries.

"These are my favorites," he informs me, guiding me toward the first in a large series of woven works.

"Oh!" I cry in delight and surprise. "Hey, I know these! These are the Unicorn Tapestries. We read about these in my art history class last year."

Nico stands behind me and rests his hands on my hips as we examine the first tapestry in the series, *The Start of the Hunt*. Like the others in the room, the tapestry is massive, some twelve by fourteen feet, according to the placard next to it.

"Amazing, isn't it, sweetie?" His deep voice rumbles with pleasure, and I have to fight myself not to turn around to look at him instead of the art. "Look at all the detail. Can you imagine how long it took to do this by hand?"

It's as detailed and intricate as any painting. The tapestry portrays eleven men and their hunting paraphernalia, all with a somewhat confused intent to kill the mythical creature that's spearing one of the dogs in the side with its horn. The creature doesn't want to be trapped or chased—that's obvious, and the irritation on its face is just as clear as the befuddlement on those of its captors, maybe from the fact that they had even located a mythical creature to begin with. The desire to kill it—the most rare and valuable animal in the world—for nothing but sport is obviously the paradox of the story.

Nico keeps hold of my hand as he escorts me to the next few tapestries in the series, which cover the progress of the hunt, the unicorn becoming more and more trapped as the hunters got their act together. The fifth tapestry, of which only a few torn fragments are present, consists of a woman who appears to be taming the unicorn to the point where it's oblivious to a dog biting its flank, thus allowing for its capture and death, portrayed in the sixth, bloodiest tapestry. We study them as Nico pulls me in front of him and wraps his arms around my waist. We're quiet, almost as if paying respect to the fallen beast.

"The myth is that a unicorn can only be tamed by a virginal maiden," Nico says as he leans his chin on my shoulder. "What do you think, sweetie? Could you tame a unicorn?"

"Well, first I'd have to be a virgin, wouldn't I?" I respond somewhat wryly. "Unfortunately, that ship has sailed."

"You're still a lovely, virtuous maiden," Nico says as he sets a soft kiss on my neck. "You could probably tame a wild beast if you met him."

Again, I have to resist the urge to twist around in his arms. I really wish I could see the look on his face as he says that, but I'm scared what he might see on mine.

"Is that a challenge, Mr. Soltero?" I'm joking, but inwardly I'm begging for it to be true.

He growls in return, a deep, pleasant vibration against my neck. "You're welcome to try. Come on, milady. Let me show you the garden before they close."

On our way out, I glance at the seventh and final tapestry: *The Unicorn in Captivity*. The unicorn, apparently back from the dead, sits happily tethered to a tree, completely encircled by a fence. It looks happy to be there, as if all it had wanted all along was to belong to someone. Still, the pitiful size of the fence makes its happiness pathetic, and I wonder briefly if that was what Nico thought of when he joked about being tamed by a virtuous maiden. I hope not.

CHAPTER FIFTEEN

Nico

I REALLY NEED TO TELL HER. BUT WHEN SHE LOOKS AT ME LIKE THAT, LIKE SHE REALLY *wants* to tame the beast within, the beast she doesn't really even know yet, I don't want to say that this whole thing needs to stay casual, that I can't get into anything serious right now. I want to throw myself onto my knees and tell her she's basically already tamed me. That I'm hers. If she wants me.

Fuck me. What am I supposed to do when she looks at me like that?

We walk out into the deserted courtyard that looks out onto the Hudson River. The temperature is dropping, and I have an arm around her waist as we stride around the grounds. It's not easy since we're both wearing these giant parkas, but I make it work.

"Usually this is a really nice garden," I tell her. "They do all this landscaping to make it true to the way things looked back in the medieval times. Same flowers, same patterns."

I don't know why I feel like I have to be a tour guide. Maybe it's because I don't have anything else to give her but my city. I know everything about New York, but I don't have the money to show her all the fancy things about it. All I can offer is what I know. The deals, like attending the Met on donation only or the cheap Pakistani food you can get in the garage off Houston. The secret spots in Central Park that the tourists never find. This city is the only thing I can give her, but this city is all I want to escape.

"Do you like to garden?" she asks. "Since you spent all that time in the country?"

The country. Shit. I'm already regretting telling her that white lie. Yeah, I was out in the country for a few years as a teenager, but it wasn't on some homestay holiday. I shake my head, wanting to put *that* piece of bullshit behind me. She doesn't need to know.

So instead I play it off like a joke. "In New York? Oh, yeah, I got a farm on my fire escape. They call me Old MacDonald, NYU. E-I-E-I-O!"

She giggles with me while I sing out, loud and clear, about cows and horses and whatever other barnyard animals I can think of. God, I could listen to her do that forever. It makes me forget about the obvious differences between us, about the nasty fact that we come from completely different worlds.

"You know, I have an idea for you," she says once I'm done.

Our breaths come out like ghosts while we walk. The temperature is starting to drop again, and the sun is falling down to the bluffs across the river. It's still pretty early, but the sight of it puts me in a bad mood. It means I'm going to have to say goodbye to her soon and go back to my real life. Another night checking IDs and collecting money. You get an extra shift, you take it. Work, work, work.

"What's that, baby?" I ask, not wanting to spoil the moment.

"Well," she says slowly. "I was thinking about what you said last night. About wanting to be a firefighter and all that."

"Yeah?" I'm a little suspicious, but curious too. I've been burned too many times by the FDNY. All I ever wanted was to be one of those dudes on the trucks, but for whatever reason, I've never been good enough for them.

"Well, have you ever actually asked the people who choose the new entries why they make the choices they do? Like, have you ever asked them what they're looking for in an applicant?"

I don't really know what to say. "No, not really," I admit. "They have the application, so I put my information on it and sent it in. They keep saying no. What else can I do?"

Layla steps lightly, like she's trying to see if she can walk without leaving footprints on the hard-packed snow. I grip her tighter around the waist and watch her progress. She fails every time, but she doesn't stop trying.

"Well," she starts again, "when I first applied last year for jobs in the city, I didn't get a single call back on my resume. My dad is really good at getting the jobs he wants in a country that doesn't really like accents." She pauses, measuring her words. "He told me that if you want to break into a new industry, you have to figure out what they want that's not in the application. He suggested I call some places I thought I might like to work for and ask for information only. Ask them what they like in an applicant and tell them I'm thinking about applying, but I want to build my skill set before I apply."

She takes a deep breath and peeks at me, like she's worried about what I'll think. She seems thoughtful, if somewhat placid, before continuing.

"So I did. And I found out that even though the internship positions said no experience was needed, they were still interested in people who knew things like how to proofread a paper or how to use data entry software. They liked someone who had proven interest in the job, even if they didn't have working experience. So last summer I volunteered for the legal department at my dad's practice. It was ridiculously boring, but I learned a lot of that kind of stuff. When I was interviewed for the position at Fox and Lager, they actually said it was that experience—the fact that I had done it of my own volition—that got me the position over older, more experienced candidates."

"Well, that, and you're super hot," I joke.

She tries to smack my shoulder, but I catch her arm and pull her close so I can press my nose in her neck. She smells even better than I remember. And suddenly I really want to stop talking about this. Jobs. Family. Our pasts. This day got really heavy, really fast.

We stop by one of the pillars that holds up the giant stones of the building, and I turn her to me. She rests her cheek on my chest.

"Maybe you should try again," she says softly, toying with the zipper of my jacket. "You could find out what they want and do that first. It couldn't hurt to ask."

I want to ask why she cares so much. Why does it matter if I'm a FedEx guy or a doorman or a firefighter? They're all blue-collar jobs, the kind of jobs that no one who ends up with this girl will ever have. Her father's a doctor, for fuck's sake. She's going to end up married to someone like him, someone who can buy her more of that gold jewelry she likes to wear, someone who can take care of her. Someone who's nothing like me. I'm just a pit stop on the way to her future. She knows it, and I know it.

Except, fuck. What if she doesn't?

I can't help but smile a little.

Because I can't not kiss her right now, I tip her head up and press my mouth to hers. Her lips are soft and warm, even in the winter air. But just when she's opening for something deeper, I stop, tuck a misbehaving curl behind her ear, and trace the rest of her cheek with my finger.

Things are getting a little too real with her today. But I think I always knew it would be like that with Layla.

"You're a smart girl," I say as I loosen my grasp around her waist.

"Um, thanks?"

She looks uncertain. I get it. Our kisses are electric—she's probably wondering, just like I am, why exactly I pulled away. But it's nothing I want to talk about right now.

So instead, I make a big production of stepping away to check my watch. Yeah, it's time to go anyway.

"Time's up, sweetie. I gotta be downtown at AJ's by ten. You wanna stop by tonight with your friends again? You could stay until closing and we could continue our date…"

I shouldn't ask her, but still, I can't help it. The more time I spend with Layla, the more time I *want* to spend with her. *Tonight,* I tell myself. Tonight I can tell her the truth. I'll explain why this can't go on past May, why it's best maybe to nip it in the bud.

But she just smiles sadly and shakes her head.

"I want to, but I really have to get some studying done tonight and tomorrow. I'm kind of behind in my school work right now, and I can't afford to be hungover tomorrow. I'm sorry."

I ignore the way my heart sinks in my chest when she says no. I don't want to wait until Monday to see her again. But this is probably for the best. Maybe I need some space too to figure out what the fuck I'm doing here.

"Nah, baby, don't apologize. School comes first, always." My phone buzzes in my pocket, and for once, I'm glad for the interruption. "Hold on." I step away to take the call. "Hey, Lionel. What's up?"

Lionel is the manager at AJ's and a good friend of K.C.'s.

"Hey man. Just want to let you know the show tonight is cancelled. The band is stuck in Boston because of the blizzard up there. Grant can probably handle the door if you want a night off."

Is it sad that I'm excited? I shouldn't be. I can always use the extra money this job brings in each week. But right now, all I can think is that maybe I can talk Layla into studying with me tonight instead of with her friends. Except my sister has taken over the apartment with her kid, and there is no way I'm bringing Layla around Maggie, the viper. She'd call Selena, and then whatever this is will be over before it's even started. My sisters eat the girls I date for breakfast.

But K.C. is leaving for LA tonight. He's got an apartment just sitting there across the river, a place I sometimes crash when the city gets a little too much. It's quieter than Manhattan. A good place to tell Layla exactly what's going on in my life.

I hang up and face her with a new bounce in my step.

"So, NYU," I say, unable to keep the grin off my face. She doesn't like it when I call her that, which for some reason makes me want to do it even more. She's cute when she's annoyed. "Looks like the show is cancelled tonight—'inclement weather' in Boston."

"You don't have to work tonight after all?"

I shake my head. "I was wondering…"

I reach out to twirl a piece of her hair around one finger. She watches the action like it's the most interesting thing she's ever seen.

"Would you be interested in studying with me tonight? I'll leave you alone, I promise. Except, you know, when you don't want me to."

I wink. It makes me look like an idiot, but she doesn't seem to mind my goofy side. In fact, I'd say she likes it.

"Just a quiet night in?" she asks shyly. "That won't be boring for you?"

I shake my head. She really has no idea. I never get quiet nights in. If I'm not working at FedEx until close to nine, I'm at the gym or working odd jobs at clubs around town. Suddenly, I'm ready to beg her to do it. An entire night alone with this girl sounds like a dream come true.

"It'll be perfect," I say honestly. "Especially with you there."

She tips her head to one side, considering the idea for a moment even though I can already see on her face she's going to say yes. She wants more time just as bad as I do

"Yeah, okay," she says finally, and I can't even try to hide my grin. "But *only* if you give me some time to study, okay?"

"Sure, sure, baby, I'll just watch TV or something." I hook an arm through hers and start walking us back to the train station. The sky is turning a purplish-gray as twilight falls, and I'm suddenly aware that I'll be spending the night with this girl for the second night in a row. I can't even remember the last time I spent one night with someone, let alone two. Not since Jessie.

I shake that memory out of my head. No, I can't think about that. Right now, I just hope I can keep some kind of self-control if that's what Layla needs.

"So listen, sweetie," I say as we walk down the drive. "I was wondering if you'd be willing to go to New Jersey…"

CHAPTER SIXTEEN

Layla

I$_{T}$ DOESN'T TAKE ME LONG TO PACK UP MY BOOKS AND A FEW THINGS INTO AN OVERNIGHT bag once we return to the dorm. Shama and Jamie are out, but I find Quinn sitting on her bed reading when I walk into our room with Nico at my heels, his hands eagerly on my hips. She glances at him curiously, then back at me, and smiles like a cat that just ate the canary.

"Well, hello, there," she croons, standing up and fluffing her curly ponytail. "You must be FedEx man. I'm Quinn. Roommate. Best friend. You know the drill."

I can tell Nico wants to laugh by the way his eyes twinkle, but he doesn't, just extends a big hand out to shake Quinn's.

"Nico," he says. "Nice to meet you. How you doin', Quinn?"

"Not as good as you, I'm guessing," she says as she sits in her desk chair. "Where are you two kids coming from?"

I tell her about our afternoon at the Cloisters, which has her looking at Nico with obvious approval. Museums are classy places to take someone on a date, and Quinn's a total snob. She won't date a guy who wears sneakers to a bar, and she'll never accept a movie offer (or something equally standard) until her third date. She says she likes to make sure they're willing to work for it. There is a reason she doesn't get a lot of dates. I secretly think these kinds of mind games are the reason she's still a virgin at almost twenty—she can't find anyone willing to jump through these damn hoops for her.

"So where to now?" she asks, drumming her fingernails on her desktop.

Nico sits down on my mattress while I rifle through my drawers, searching as unobtrusively as possible for underwear that's appropriately sexy but won't be uncomfortable the next morning. Hmmm, maybe I should just bring two sets.

"New Jersey," I say, bracing myself for what I know will be her obvious scowl.

Quinn is from Boston, and the only thing Bostonians look down on more than

New Yorkers (specifically Yankees fans) is New Jersey. It's a constant source of genial conflict in our apartment, considering both Jamie and Shama grew up there. To Quinn, New Jersey is the land of shitty Springsteen cover bands and big-haired bridge-and-tunnel girls. Jamie and Shama just start shouting about Boston and Marky Mark whenever the topic comes up, but Quinn's opinion never changes. New Jersey isn't the kind of place you go if you can avoid it.

"Why? What's over there?" Her face is thankfully blank when I turn around, and I breathe a sigh of relief. Nico doesn't need to know just how entitled my roommates can be. At least not yet, anyway.

"My friend has an apartment in Hoboken," he says, repeating the same thing he told me on the train. "I'm housesitting for him for a while. It's a good place to relax and...uh...study."

He shoots a devious grin in my direction, and I flush, knowing that Quinn certainly saw that look too. To her credit, she nods approvingly, although the quick flash in her eyes tells me there's no way she thinks I'm going to do any studying there. Whatever. From out of Nico's range of sight, I stick my tongue out at her, and she blinks before training her gaze back on Nico.

"I'm going to use the bathroom before we go, sweetie." With a peck on my cheek, he leaves me alone with Quinn's imperious attitude.

"Will you stop it?" I hiss, shoving a few other pieces of clothes in my bag before starting on my books. "I love you, but I have a dad of my own if I want someone to give my dates the third-degree."

"Third-degree, please. It was a couple of questions. I'm just doing my best friend job, babe," she retorts. She comes next to me so we can speak in low tones Nico won't be able to hear through the thin walls.

"You never did this before. Not even with Teddy, and you fucking *hated* him," I say in a loud whisper.

Teddy was my disaster of a boyfriend from freshman year to whom I lost my virginity. He cheated on me a few weeks later, leaving me furious and heartbroken, though surprisingly not as torn up as I might have expected, all things considered. Just goes to show that I wasn't really as in love as I'd thought.

"That's because you were obviously not in love with Teddy," Quinn echoes my thoughts. "But you are definitely falling for this one, Lay. He's hot—I'll give you that. I just want you to be careful."

"I'm *being* careful," I insist, zipping up my bag and grabbing a few cosmetics from the small caboodle on my desk. "Yes, I like him. And I think he likes me too. But we're just starting this, for Christ's sake."

"You're taking off at a sprint, babe. Your first date was yesterday, and you're already going home with him for a weekend." Quinn cocks her head knowingly before she shrugs and goes to flop back down on her neatly made bedspread. "For what it's worth, he seems nice, even if he does have a temper," she informs me, ever so nonchalant as she picks up her marketing book and flips through it. "But you don't really know him yet, and you're heading off to New Jersey with the guy after, like, five minutes. I worry because I love."

I soften at her words. I get that she cares. I'm lucky to have three friends like that who watch my back and who are willing to protect me against the shitheads roaming New York. But Nico's not one of them.

"Thanks, Quinny," I say as I zip up my bag. "You *are* the best. I'll text you later, okay? Just to let you know I'm safe."

She sighs, then leans over so she can reach into the desk drawer next to her bed.

"Here," she says. She turns back and flings an unopened box of condoms at me.

I catch them in my chest and look up, grinning. "Really, Quinn? Didn't know you even had any in stock. I'm impressed."

"Shut up, you whore," she orders me, sinking back down in her pillow with a red face. "Like I said, be safe."

———

THE PATH TRAIN to Hoboken doesn't arrive as often as the subway, so Nico and I have about a fifteen-minute wait. Once we're on, the trip under the Hudson is fast. Our stop is the second one across the water, and after we arrive, Nico immediately walks me down the street in search of food. Both of our stomachs are grumbling, so we find a cheap Chinese place and order some boxes to go before getting a cab to his friend's apartment.

"So, who's the friend that owns this place?" I ask once we're on our way to an address on the outer edge of Hoboken that directly faces Manhattan across the river. My stomach growls—the lo mein smells amazing.

"My boy, K.C.," Nico says fondly. "My best friend. We've known each other since we were kids in the Kitchen. His mom knew my mom, and we lived in the same building, so I was always over at their house." He leans over conspiratorially to whisper: "Don't tell my mom, but K.C.'s mom is a better cook."

I laugh as the cab pulls up outside a building on a darkened road. It doesn't look dangerous per se—just deserted. The street, which needs to be repaved, is lined with tall, somewhat dilapidated brownstones, remnants of a time when the area had a bit more money. I know enough about Hoboken to know that it's already in the midst of a revitalization, considering its proximity to New York and the availability of space to young professionals. But I wouldn't want to walk alone at night here.

Nico pays the cabbie and we step out, the frozen snow crunching loudly under our feet and the tires as the car pulls away. Nico leads me up the steps of the building and pulls out a key to unlock the door. He guides me into the foyer of the building and up a few flights of stairs that lead to the third floor.

"He owns the top floor," Nico informs me as he unlocks the door. It swings open, and we step inside one of the nicest places I've seen since moving to New York.

The space alone tells me why people even bother moving to Hoboken—the living room we step into is easily bigger than the entire apartment I share with three other girls. It's huge, with high ceilings and massive windows at one end that open out to the street and offer a faint view of the Midtown skyscrapers that twinkle across the darkened river. The place has obviously been fixed up, with gleaming hardwood floors, walls that have all been painted a soft sage green, a large sectional sofa that faces a flat-screen TV mounted on one wall. A baby grand piano sits in the other corner of the room. I twirl around for a moment in it, my arms stretched out on all sides as Nico watches with amusement.

"Ahhh," I sigh, coming to a stop. "I haven't been able to do that inside since coming to the city. This place is gorgeous! What does your friend do?"

Nico smirks. "He's a DJ. He mixes at a bunch of clubs, but he also does the programming for one of the radio stations in LA He's mad talented."

I gaze around, taking in the posh surroundings. "He must be."

"Wait 'til you see the rest."

I'm quickly taken on a tour of the rest of the floor, which includes a dining room and big kitchen to the left of the living room, a hallway lined with a bathroom and framed black and white photos (several of which include Nico), and two huge bedrooms, one of which holds a set of turn tables and several instruments. The walls are padded with leather. This isn't the shared apartment of a college kid, like me, or a poor twenty-something, like Nico. This is a grown-up's apartment, through and through.

"Is this room...soundproofed?" I ask, reaching out to touch the leather. It's soft against my fingers, and my voice is a bit muted in here.

Nico nods. "Yeah. K.C. records on his own sometimes. Pretty sweet, isn't it? It's my room when I stay here, too." He gestures toward a small futon in the corner of the studio. It's folded up as a couch right now. "I'd probably just sleep in the bedroom this week," he says as if reading my mind. "Would you—do you want to see it?"

Something in his voice makes me feel shy as he takes my hand and leads me down the hallway to the master bedroom. He takes my bag, drops it to the floor beside the door, and pulls me inside.

My first thought upon walking into this room is that it so absolutely screams sex that I'm almost literally thrown off balance. It's not sleazy—not like a porn set or anything like that—but unlike the demure polish of the rest of the apartment, this is clearly the room of a bachelor who is looking to get laid, and as frequently as possible. The entire room is bright white, right down to the walls, the painted wood floors, the soft cotton curtains fluttering over the large window, and the modern-style canopy bed dressed with white linens and a twisting drape of translucent muslin hung lazily around the frame.

On the opposite wall, facing the window, there is a huge painting—the only color in the room—done in a Jackson Pollock-esque style using rainbow splatters of paint. It appears to be a close up of a woman's erect nipple and a man's mouth, teeth bared, about to close down on it. My own breasts tingle at the sight, instantly bringing to mind the attention Nico paid to them just last night. I glance back at him, and he is watching my reaction with a knowing smirk on his face, gently rubbing his fingers over my knuckles.

"Jesus," I breathe. "You really can't be in this room and not think about sex, can you?"

Nico tips his head back and laughs.

"No doubt, baby, no doubt," he agrees. "I call it K.C.'s fuck pad. It really is, isn't it?"

"He, um, must get around. How do you sleep in here alone?"

The bed is perfectly made, like it's waiting for someone to throw back the covers. As I think about how many women have been lured to this exact spot I'm standing in, made to feel the exact things I'm feeling...a shudder of revulsion slides down my spine. The room is so obvious—too obvious, really. It *is* a fuck pad, but I can't under-stand how any woman could enter the place and not know she was one of a long succession of other conquests that preceded her.

My arms wrap around my middle as I shrink into myself. I don't want him to think I'm intimidated by this place, but I can't help it. He says he housesits the place when K.C. is gone, which seems to be a lot. But Nico's young, gorgeous, and has the charm of an R&B song. How many other girls has he brought back here?

Suddenly, I feel a little dirty. And not in the way I want to feel around Nico.

"I...Nico, don't take this the wrong way, but..." I trail off, struggling to vocalize my thoughts. "Has anyone slept in the fu—this room recently...with you?"

He blinks at me for a moment, and then bursts into a peal of laughter that bounces around the airy high ceilings and light furnishings. "Oh God, Layla," he gasps. "You are awesome."

"That doesn't really answer my question," I point out, squeezing my stomach. Does that mean he has? The thought makes my stomach twist into knots, even though I know I have no right to be jealous.

"Ah," he gasps through a few more chuckles. "Sorry. That was just funny. No, baby, the answer is *no*. I haven't brought anyone but you back to the fuck pad. That would be K.C.'s M.O., not mine."

Privately I wonder why not. Nico's got the looks and the charisma to take home just about any girl he wants. Hell, half my office would come running if he crooked his fingers. They already do the second the elevator doors open.

But Nico's expression is kind as he strokes my shoulder lightly. Hope springs warm in my belly—maybe he really is the good guy I want so badly for him to be. One thing is for sure. I don't want to be another conquest of this room, no matter who's the conqueror.

"Do you think we could sleep on the futon?" I ask. "Or maybe the couch?"

Nico sobers, considering the room again before reaching down to grab my bag.

"Abso-fuckin'-lutely," he declares, and we march back down the hallway to the recording studio and its conveniently soundproofed walls.

CHAPTER SEVENTEEN

Nico

I KNEW IT WAS GOING TO BE A GAMBLE TAKING HER INTO THAT ROOM. K.C. IS AN ANIMAL, and for all his goofy looks, the guy gets more play than anyone I know. Helps when you have extra cash and a place like this to take the girls.

But I'm actually thrilled that Layla wasn't feeling it. That the tension running through her body wasn't the good kind. She's been nervous around me before, but not in the way that makes her shrivel up like a raisin. She looked worried. She looked scared.

Now I'm even starting to wonder if I should have just taken her to my place. The more time I spend with this girl, the more I want her to see all sides of me. Maybe she wouldn't care that I live in a crappy railroad apartment in Harlem. Maybe she would actually be all right with just plain Nico.

The longer we're away from K.C.'s porn-set bedroom, the more relaxed Layla becomes. We go back to the kitchen and eat dinner, sitting across from each other on the counters and grinning over the takeout boxes she suggests we use instead of K.C.'s fancy dishes. Then she sets up her books at the dining table and studies while I park myself on the sofa and watch TV. It's weird. We're not doing anything but just being together, but it's nice. I feel calmer, lighter just knowing she's there, doing her thing in the next room. I feel happy just being around her.

It's fully dark outside when I wake up about two hours later with the TV still blaring with some sports trivia. I'm laid out on K.C.'s massive sofa, and Layla is bent over me, looking cute and uncertain as she taps my shoulder.

I blink lazily, then my eyes widen as I become aware of the situation going on underneath my jeans. Morning wood is a real thing, but I'm telling you, it doesn't just happen in the morning. Especially not around a girl like this.

Layla doesn't seem to notice as she sits next to me on the couch. Naturally, I slide my arm around her waist and nuzzle my head in her lap. Her hands thread into my hair, and we both sigh, content. Her coconut scent surrounds me, and it doesn't take me long to move from content to something else. She seems to feel the same, as I feel her fingers drift down my neck and start playing with the collar of my shirt.

I turn in her lap to look up at her.

"Hey beautiful." My voice is still scratchy from sleep. Her hand falls on my chest, and I take it, eager for her touch. "You all done?"

She nods, her eyes wide, like she's mute. I smile. She shivers.

Ah. So it's like that, huh?

"Come here."

I pull her down until she collapses along the length of the couch, spooned comfortably toward the television with her back fitted to my front.

I grab the remote control from the coffee table and flip around, trying to find something that's not a total mood killer. Eventually, I land on a channel that's broadcasting a live concert by Sade. Fuck, yes. I could not have asked for anything better. The velvety texture of her voice fills the room, and I'm humming along with her as I skim my hand up and down the length of Layla's thigh. She wiggles her heart-shaped ass in reaction and hums lightly. It's torture, but I love it just the same.

"Mmmm."

She makes that sound when she likes what I'm doing. She did it a lot last night too. So, I keep doing the same thing, running my hand up and down her curves, light and flirtatious, just enough to drive her as crazy as she's driving me.

Then she turns in my arms and burrows further into my warm chest as she slips her hand under my shirt. The effect is instantaneous—I'm hard as a rock in seconds. But I don't hurry anything. It feels really good just to touch her like this, to have her touch me too.

"This okay, baby?" I ask, pulling up the edge of her shirt so I can mirror her actions and brush the delicate skin over her ribs. Her skin is butter-soft.

"Mmmm, yes. Yes, it's...ah...just fine."

I lean into her neck, feather a few kisses down the side, where whatever scent she wears is the strongest. She arches against me, rubbing her hips against the serious *hard*ship in my pants. This is a dangerous game we're playing, one I'm not sure I'll win. But I don't kiss her—not yet. I know the second I do that, it's over. There will be no more gentle flirtation, no more teasing. Just pure, all-consuming lust.

Slowly, I graze my fingers over her oblique muscles, testing to see just how far she's going to let me go. Layla works out. Not crazily like some of the girls I see at the gym, but just enough that her body is taut and soft at the same time. My fingertips tease farther and farther up her shirt while I nip at her ear. Then I finally brush my knuckles under the curves of her breasts and caress the incredibly soft skin between them. She squirms, her breath hot against my ear. So I do it again and again, trailing my hand back down her ribs and stomach and then up again.

I want to leave no part of her untouched. I want her to feel it tingle from head to toe, long after I'm gone.

I continue worshipping her like that for what seems like hours, occasionally pressing kisses on her collarbone, her neck, her ear, her cheek. But aside from the fact that I could do this forever and be a happy man, I'm not going to make a move here beyond a little petting on the couch. I need her to give me the green light. I can give her at least that much.

Then, just as I skim back down again to play with her navel, Layla seizes up.

"Stop," she breathes into my neck. "Stop!"

I pull my hand away, confused. She obviously likes what I'm doing. Her nipples are visibly hardened through her shirt, and her breath is harsh and staggered. If she doesn't want to do more, I'll be disappointed, but it will be okay. I just like touching her. Maybe she doesn't realize that no matter what, it's okay. I just want to be with her.

I open my mouth to say just that, but I can't. So instead, I just ask, "What's wrong, baby?"

Layla bites her lip and shakes her head. Okay, now I'm worried. Is it just me, or is she about to cry?

"N-nothing," she says, even as she twists away from me and swings her feet to the floor.

I stand up with her and take her hands.

"Hey," I say. "You okay?"

Her gaze is hungry as she stares at me, the bottom of her t-shirt caught up a little on her hip, the top button of her jeans already undone. The thought of what's below it makes my cock stand to attention. Seriously, does she have any idea? Does she have any fucking clue what she does to me?

———

Layla

"T-take—take off your shirt," I blurt out before my nerves get the best of me.

The concern on Nico's face is adorable. He's not sure if I like what's happening, or maybe he's not sure if I'm going to stop him again. Truth be told, I probably like it too much. If I'm being honest with myself, there is a chance that Quinn is right, and I'm right on the precipice of falling in love with this man, even after such a short time. It's scary, and I doubt he feels the same way, but I can't say no to him either.

My mother would toy with her big diamond solitaire and tell me to wait—even until marriage—to let a boy do the things I want Nico to do to me. *Especially* because I might be falling for him. *Nobody respects easy women, Layla*, she'd intone every time I'd want a skirt that was too short for her tastes or wear a little too much eyeliner. If she could have had it tattooed above my vagina, I think she would have.

But in this moment, it's easy to push her warnings aside in the face of my visceral, all-consuming desire for this man. I can't remember ever wanting something as badly as I do in this moment. Not the soccer state championship. Not visiting my dad's country and meeting my family. Not my admittance to NYU. Nothing even comes close to how badly I want Nico. Right here. Right now.

And it must be all over my face, because the confusion disappears from his features, and a sly, panty-melting smile spreads across instead. Suddenly, I feel like prey, and he's the predator that just sighted me. But instead of running, I want nothing more than to be hunted. Consumed.

"Your wish is my command."

Nico sits up and yanks the t-shirt over his head, revealing that broad, muscular chest I spent the last night cuddled into. I take a moment to ogle him openly, studying the way his tattoos emphasize the taut lines of his deltoids and biceps, the way his skin stretches over his pecs and the ridges of his abs. In contrast to the thick black hair on his head and the five o'clock shadow he's currently sporting, his chest is bare, impossibly smooth, almost glossy, like petrified wood. Seriously, no one has any right to look that good.

"Your turn, baby. Fair's fair."

I remove my t-shirt and toss it to the floor, then reach down and tug off my jeans too, even though he's still in his. I'm vulnerable, standing before him like this in nothing but a black lace bra and matching panties, one of the few nice sets of lingerie I own. This isn't my darkened bedroom at midnight or the dim light of the morning. The lights are on, and I'm on display. Will he like what he sees?

Nico's eyes are hungry. I can feel the heat of them as they pass over the shape of my shoulders, breasts, stomach, legs, lingering for a moment at the lace-covered shadow between my thighs. I'm thankful I had everything groomed just a few days ago. He's incredibly good-looking, but I'm no slouch, either. I need to remind myself that sometimes.

Without breaking his searing gaze, Nico unbuckles his belt and lets his jeans drop to the floor, where he kicks them away. Oh, and he looks good too, even though it was only this morning that I saw him just like this. The hard muscles of his thighs and V-shaped abs disappear under the tight silhouette of his boxer briefs, which don't leave much to the imagination. I haven't yet seen what's under there, but it's obvious he's got more than enough to satisfy any woman. I bite my lip. He wants me. I don't need to doubt that.

"Jesus, Layla," Nico whispers, breaking my trance, though he still seems to be lost in one too.

He reaches out a tentative hand and strokes my arm, then catches my hand and pulls me against his solid body. I can feel him ready against my thigh, hard as steel. It only makes me want him more.

"You are so goddamn beautiful, it hurts," he mutters against my lips.

Then he tilts my chin, just like he did last night, and kisses me—*finally*—for the first time all evening.

That's it. I'm done for.

"Shut up," I mumble and open my lips to welcome his tongue, so eager to twist and tangle deliciously with mine.

I moan when his hands slide down to knead rhythmically at my ass, something that quickly makes him fall short of breath. Hmmm. Six flights of stairs? Next to nothing. A couple handfuls of my backside, and Nico can't exhale properly. It's hard not to feel smug.

"You're thinking too much," he says as he bends a little and lifts me easily so I wind my legs around his waist.

Obediently, I wrap my arms around his neck and bring his mouth back to mine. Between that and the fact that he's got a death grip on my ass, he barely manages to stumble down the hall to the recording studio, where the futon now lays open. Sometime while I was studying, he must have come back here to make the bed, since now it's dressed with some very soft-looking sheets and a fluffy blue comforter.

With a groan of frustration as he breaks the kiss, Nico kneels down and sets me gently on the mattress. Then he crawls up the length of my body, covering me completely with his broad, solid warmth while I lie back. Balanced with his forearms on either side of my head, he shelters me as our eyes meet.

He plants a gentle kiss on my lips. "You don't…I mean…" He chews on his lower lip as he figures out what to say. It's a habit we share.

I do my best to wait patiently.

"I guess what I'm trying to say is, we can stop whenever you want." He kisses me again, then chews for a moment on his lower lip. "I don't want you to feel like just because I brought you all the way here, I'm expecting something."

I have to quirk an eyebrow at that one. "Not even a little?"

A pair of dimples emerges in full force with a sheepish smile. If he wasn't so tan, I'd probably be able to see him blushing. As it is, his expression is completely endearing.

"Well, I'm not going to say I don't *want* anything more to happen," he admits. "But want's not the same thing as expect."

"So if I told you to get *this*—" I gyrate against the long length currently nestled between my legs, blocked only by two thin pieces of fabric—"off of me, you'd be just fine with it?"

I roll my hips again, earning a long, low growl from the bottom of his significantly deep voice.

"I might be a little disappointed." He leans down to nip lightly at the soft skin under my jaw. Then he pushes himself back up slightly to look at me, his features turning serious again. "Is that what you want, Layla? You just have to say the word. I don't want you to feel like I'm trying to pressure you. You deserve…well, you deserve the best any guy can give you. A fuck lot better than me."

We stare at each other, all remnants of the joking mood gone. My heart is beating so loud and fast, I wonder if he can feel it against his chest. It's getting harder and harder to keep my feelings at bay here, getting harder to convince myself I'm just another girl to him, that he couldn't possibly feel what I have been feeling. The way he's looking at me, the way he's tried so hard to respect me and impress me, the fact that *he*'s initiated this entire day's worth of second and third date material…could it be possible that he feels the same kind of connection I do? Could he be…falling…too?

"Layla," he whispers hoarsely. "Give a guy a break here."

I blink, then take a deep breath as I trace a finger across the strong line of his cheekbone, down the square jaw that's dusted with stubble. And then I kiss him, gently. He stays perfectly still as I nibble my way around the contours of his lips and beg entry with my tongue, slipping it in for a second to touch his. Just a touch, just a touch. When I lay my head back on the pillow, he's a statue, his eyes closed, but mouth still half open.

"Don't stop," I whisper.

Nico's eyes pop open, dazed, as if he's not sure I said what I said.

"Please," I add for good measure.

"Thank fucking God," he exhales deeply.

And then he collapses forward with another kiss as deep and penetrating as mine was light and tentative. Keeping his mouth firmly fused to mine, he rolls to his side in order to have better access to the rest of my body. My hands tug at his hair, leaving the rest of me open for his exploring fingers. And explore they do. His free hand travels down the front of my body, tracing its former path between my breasts and ribs, dipping into my belly button and then finally slipping under the fabric of my panties.

"I like these," he says, low and fierce as his lips feather down my neck.

I just whimper as his fingers continue their quest, my breathing turned haggard with need. He's gentle, mapping the terrain by touch, investigating the soft skin and hair in order to locate the most sensitive spot on my body. When I quiver, he lingers; when I shake, he looks elsewhere. His finger toys with my damp entrance as he hums low with anticipation.

"What do you feel like here?" he wonders, his voice vibrating against my earlobe.

I can't answer, but it doesn't matter. He bites the edge of my ear as his finger slides in, a delicate intrusion that has me gasping almost immediately.

"You like that, baby?" he rumbles before seizing my ear and biting a little harder this time.

The slight pain sends a direct bolt of pleasure to where his finger slips in and out of me a few more times. He adds a second finger and pushes them both in deeper. Inside me, they curl upward, finding contact with a cluster of nerves I didn't even know existed. As he moves them again, finding a more consistent rhythm, I moan, loud and long.

"Yesssss," I hiss as my hips start to move in time with his hand, thrusting down to create even more of that delicious friction. It feels so good, almost more than I can take. If this is what he can do with just his hand, I'm almost scared to see what he can do with the rest of his body.

His kisses flutter to my neck, over the tops of my breasts before he buries his face between them. The light scrape of his rough cheeks against the sensitive skin is almost enough to send me over alone—almost anything could push me over the edge with the way he's fucking me with his hand. My moans have disappeared now, replaced by pants and squeaks as I grind harder. It's coming, that familiar precipice I'm hurtling toward faster than ever before.

Then, mimicking the painting in the bedroom next door, Nico's teeth close over one lace-covered nipple. His thumb presses down on my clit while his fingers continue their onslaught. And I come with a long, loud shout. My entire body clenches and shakes around his fingers while they continue to thrust to some silent beat. He sucks at my breast, hard and unforgiving, helping me ride out my orgasm until it finishes its flight from my head to my toes.

Just as the shaking starts to abate (but not completely), Nico pulls his hand out quickly, leaving me panting as he sits up and pulls off my panties with renewed urgency. His hand trails a thin, damp line down my thigh as he does; the sensation only turns me on again, even in my post-orgasmic haze. That's me. That's what he makes me do.

"Now I want to feel you do that," Nico growls, reaching into the small side table next to the futon where apparently he (or K.C.?) keeps a small stash of condoms. The foil rips, and I watch, practically salivating as he tugs down his briefs and rolls the condom over himself. He's perfect, just like I knew he would be—not too big, not too small, the perfect extension of his already gorgeous body.

Before I know it, he's back on top of me, covering me again with that body, his cock teasing just where his hand was before. He sits up and pulls my legs around his hips. Then he grabs my ass with a satisfied grunt and angles me to receive him better.

"Do you want this too?" he asks, teasing me a little more, forcing me to open to him like the petals of a flower.

We both look down, transfixed by the sight of him rubbing up and down the sensitive juncture. I rock my hips, trying to sneak him inside, but he keeps teasing me. I whimper.

"Tell me." His deep voice is rough with want, and our bodies are slick where they meet. It's cold outside, but very hot in this room. "Tell me what you want, Layla."

Again, my hips rock toward him, and again he evades my attempt to coerce him inside.

"Tell me," he orders again.

"I-I want you," I say in words that stutter, completely undone with frustration and desire. I still can't think straight; anything my body is doing is out of instinct. "P-p-*please*."

"Yesssssss," Nico groans, and then slams into me so hard I yelp at the impact, grasping desperately at the sheets over my head for anything to help me bear it.

He starts to move, slowly at first but eventually gaining a steady rhythm that reignites that familiar rising heat at my core. I raise my hips and start meeting him pound for pound. He's starting to lose it too. The concentration on his face gradually gives way to raw, animal instinct as he closes his eyes and leans back, embracing the feeling of me, the feeling of us.

"That's it, baby," he groans as he thrusts deeper, his hold on the backs of my thighs so tight it will probably leave bruises. I couldn't care less. "Squeeze me tight. God, you feel so *fucking* good!"

One of his hands finds my clit again, pinching it lightly between his thumb and forefinger as he continues with his merciless pace. My body starts to spasm all over again, and I pray he's not going to stop this time before I'm completely done.

"Please, Nico," I whimper, totally helpless as I climb higher and higher.

"That's right, baby," he growls. "Go ahead. Let me feel it!"

Tremors shoot up and down every limb, every bone, every nerve in my body. Nico stills as I clench around him, crying out my second orgasm of the night in moans that must penetrate the soundproofed walls around us. How could they not? Everything he's doing has me in pieces. Then he moves again, and I open my eyes just in time to see him shut his eyes tightly as he falls apart, collapsing over me as his control shatters, right along with mine.

———

WE LIE HERE for some uncountable time after, crumpled atop the mangled sheets as we catch our breath and find our senses again. Eventually, Nico staggers away to dispose of the condom in the bathroom, returning with a damp washcloth that he presses gently between my legs. In some ways, it's a more intimate gesture than being inside me; I stay perfectly still until he's finished. It never would have occurred to Teddy, despite his wealthy Connecticut upbringing and pretensions, to take care of me this way. It's yet another barrier that Nico dismantles with every kind, thoughtful gesture.

I sigh as he slides us both under the covers and gathers me against him.

"Thank you for that," he whispers against my ear. "You really are incredible, you know that?"

Another kind of heat glows in my chest, but this one has nothing to do with sex. I sigh again, blissfully content. His breath is warm against my neck, and his body is strong and solid wrapped around mine. I feel precious and protected. Like nothing bad could ever happen to me here with him.

"Did you want me too?" I wonder sleepily, the post-sex haze hitting me hard as my eyelids involuntarily flutter closed.

Nico hugs me closer, draping one heavy leg over mine and slipping a lean, muscled arm around my waist so he is curved completely around the back of my body. He fits there. We fit, like two crooked pieces of the crazy jigsaw puzzle of this city, with its eight million other parts.

He yawns and drops butterfly kisses over the edge of my ear and the spot on my neck just behind it.

"Layla, I wanted you the second I saw you sitting behind that desk." He burrows his head into my neck. "I knew you'd taste sweet, baby, and I was right."

I sigh one last time with utter and complete satiety as the room falls dark, and we both succumb to sleep.

CHAPTER EIGHTEEN

Layla

SOMETIME THE NEXT MORNING I WAKE UP WITH A STALE TASTE IN MY MOUTH, FEELING LIKE my head is being squeezed tightly in a vise. K.C.'s recording studio has no windows, so the only light filtering into the room comes from the tiny crack at the bottom of the door. I reach a lazy arm to my side, where Nico spent the night curled around my body like a clamshell, but I only find rumpled sheets. He is nowhere to be found.

Cautiously, I slide out from under the twisted mess of sheets and comforter and attempt to stand up. I crouch awkwardly and feel around the floor for my clothes—or at least something to drape around my naked body. The movements make me wince slightly and remind me of what happened on this futon.

My night passed blissfully, if not quite restfully, considering I was woken up two more times by prowling fingers and inquisitive lips looking to explore just about every surface of my body. Nico's got stamina far beyond mine—I feel like a wrung-out sponge. But even in my half-asleep state, I couldn't say no to him, which is why I'm now sore all over. Wincing again, I reach around the padded walls for the light switch, taking care to avoid the places where I think the drums and guitars are set up near the door.

"Ow! Shit!" I yelp as I step on the sharp edge of a soundboard. I hop in the direction of the door, find the switch, and rescue myself from the dark.

After I pull on the leggings and tank top I brought with me, I pad down the hall to the bathroom. I splash water over my face and brush my teeth, eager to cleanse the residue of sleep. I didn't drink anything last night, but my face feels hot and cloudy, like I'm hungover. I throw another splash of cold water over it, then tie my hair up in a messy knot on top of my head. There: comfortable, yet effortlessly sexy. At least, that's what I'm going for, even if I'm not quite feeling that way. Fake it 'til you make it, right?

I'm drawn to the kitchen by the smell of coffee and find Nico setting donuts on a plate, wearing nothing but his jeans. They hang slightly loose on his hips, revealing the mouth-watering contours of the muscles that dip below his waistband, under which he's obviously got nothing else on. A small bouquet of tulips is arranged in a vase on the kitchen table—purple, my favorite color. I wonder if he figured that out from the color of my bedspread at the dorms. My body starts humming again at the sight of his smooth, broad back. He turns around and smiles. The hum intensifies.

"Hey, good morning, Sleeping Beauty." He places a final donut on the plate and comes over to smack a kiss on my lips. "How you feeling?"

I smile up at him. "Pretty good. Ah, a bit worn out."

That earns me a devilish grin—he knows exactly why I'm worn out. "What can I say, baby? You're irresistible. Plus, I don't remember a whole lot of complaining."

I duck my head into his bare chest as a tell-tale blush rises up my neck. No, I definitely didn't complain at all. In fact, contrary to what my sore parts are telling me, I want more. So much more.

But instead of saying so, I focus on the plate of pastries and the smell of coffee, hopping up onto the counter next to him. Nico steps easily between my knees and delivers another sweet kiss, tasting a little of fresh donuts and cinnamon.

"Mmm," he vibrates against my lips. "That's what I want for breakfast."

I giggle into his kiss. "Maybe. But those donuts look good too. Where did you get them?"

He picks up an apple fritter and splits it in half, holding one out to me and taking a bite of the other. "I ran out while you were sleeping and picked them up from the shop a few blocks away."

"Like that?" I nod at his bare chest as I accept the donut and take a bite.

He looks down at his shirtless form and back up to me somewhat sheepishly. "Well, I did wear a coat and shoes. But I couldn't find my shirt anywhere, and I didn't want to wake you up. You looked so cute with your head buried under the pillows."

I stifle my laugh with another bite of fritter. I wonder if his coat was open or closed. The fine folks at the donut shop must have gotten quite an eyeful.

"Do you work out?" I ask suddenly.

Some people are lucky enough to look like models without doing much, but I doubt he has a six-pack just from pushing boxes all day long.

Nico laughs. "Other than my job, you mean? Um, yeah, I do. I mean, I try."

"What do you do?"

He smirks. "There's a boxing gym around the corner from my mom's place. Sometimes I'll go and mess around. Been doing it since I was in—um, since I was a teenager."

I lean back a little, looking him over. Another component of Nico's personality emerges. His physique starts to make sense—he's definitely built like a boxer.

"Did you ever compete?" I ask.

He tips his head back and laughs. "Fuck, no. I wanted to keep my teeth and my brain cells. But I like the training. Sometimes it feels good just to take your frustrations out on a heavy bag. Living in this city…"

He trails off, suddenly struck by some unknown specter from his past. His face darkens. I desperately want to know what he's thinking about, but I don't want to pry.

So I'm a little disappointed when he slips away to grab two coffee cups from one of the cabinets. "You like cream and sugar in your coffee, baby?"

"Yes, please," I say, and tell him when to stop as he doctors up my cup. I inhale and take a long sip. "God, that's good."

It's utter ambrosia to my woozy head, and my stomach growls in response, eager for sustenance after a long night of activity. I scarf down the rest of my fritter and reach to the plate beside me for one of the chocolate donuts.

"Yum," Nico concurs as he picks up his second donut as well. "God, I'm going to miss this in LA."

"You're going to LA?" I break off a piece of donut and toss it in my mouth. "That sounds fun. When?"

His head snaps up, and I find him staring at me like he's just ran over my new puppy and is afraid to tell me. The light of the morning seeps out of the room, and the hunger in my stomach turns to a giant ball of dread. Bad news.

———

Nico

I can't believe I did that. I mean, I can't *fucking* believe I just did that. I had a plan for how to tell her. I woke up this morning, tossed and turned about the fact that I'd let things get as far as they did without telling her the truth. I stole out this morning, not even bothering to find my shirt, even though it's fuckin' twenty-eight degrees outside. Left her in the bed, sleeping like a damn angel, and crept out like the thief I am when it was still practically dark to get donuts and coffee. I practiced what I was going to say the entire way there and the entire way back.

And all for what? So she can think I'm an asshole just using her for sex? Waiting until I fucked her until I mentioned offhand that I'm out of here?

I am a fuckin' asshole. She's going to hate me. Fuck, *I* hate me right now.

"I, uh, shit, baby." I stumble over my words like I've got a sudden speech impediment. Shit. Shit, shit, motherfucking *shit*.

Suddenly the donuts are all in the wrong places on the plate, and I have to rearrange them. Layla watches until I'm done and crosses her arms while I brush my hands off on my jeans. I don't know where the fuck to put them—I hook my thumbs in my belt loops, but that just makes me feel like Fonzi. So I fold my arms over my chest, even though that probably makes me look even more like a bouncer.

No, I think. You look like an asshole.

"I meant to tell you…I didn't want to spoil things…but, Layla…"

She's watching me, her big blue eyes already full of mixed emotions: regret, fear, frustration, and that hint of desire that never seems to go away. I know, baby. I feel it too. Fuck, looking at her in a thin white tank that's clinging to *everything*, I'm feeling it coming like a freight train.

Just say it, you mother. Fucking. Pussy.

"I'm moving to LA in May." The words burn, just like I knew they would. "K.C. knows some people out there; he hooked me up with a job doing security for one of the clubs where he just got a job. It's been in the works for a while…but he just found out that it's a done deal. So…yeah. I'm going."

She drops the donut she's holding on the counter, and the dread in my belly turns much darker. Shit. Fuck, fuck, *shit*. I was right. This meant something more to her, maybe as much as it has to me. All sorts of emotions filter across her beautiful face: frustration, sadness, which eventually morphs into anger.

I should have just stayed the fuck away.

"You knew this," she says, horrified. The tension in her voice is already tightening, like a rubber band ready to snap. "You knew you were leaving in a couple of months, and you—"

She mashes her lips together, and I know what she's thinking. We didn't make love last night, but we weren't exactly fucking. Not the first time, and not the second or third either. But whatever it was, it was a fuck lot more than just a good time.

"—did that to me anyway," she continues. "Tell me all this stuff about how much you wanted me, you touch me and kiss me like you want us to be lovers, bring me fucking breakfast in the morning!"

The rubber band snaps. Suddenly, she's gesturing wildly to the set up in the kitchen with the food and the flowers, her hands flailing around and threatening to knock the coffee mugs off the counter. She hops off the counter and starts pacing angrily around the kitchen. I stay perfectly still. If she's anything like my sisters, one wrong move, and the whole place will get smashed.

"Layla."

I'm a statue. I keep my voice low, calm, and begging for her to look at me, even though my insides are completely twisted up.

Layla whirls around and glares.

"So that's it?" she demands, trying and failing to keep the shake out of her voice. The sound makes my heart jump. "Was this all some ploy to nail some college chick? Was this your plan all along, to tell me how special I am, fuck me, make me fall in— fall into bed with you, all the while you're secretly planning to run off to fucking *California*?!"

She stops at the far end of the kitchen, where a cloudy window faces the back of another brick townhouse. This would have been the part where my sisters would start throwing kitchen utensils and breaking dishes, but Layla just grips the countertop and bows her head. I know without asking that she's trying not to cry. She's trying not to look weak, like she cares as much as she does.

I only know because I'm trying to do the same thing. I've known this girl less than two weeks; been with her for maybe forty-eight hours. But as I see her there, so clearly in pain—pain that *I* caused—the truth is so fuckin' clear. It's a fact that hits me with so much force that I actually have to grab the edge of the stove to keep from falling down.

Fuck me. What am I going to do?

Finally, after several minutes of trying to get myself together, I find my voice again.

"Layla," I say again, this time more softly.

I push off the stove and shuffle toward her. She doesn't move, just keeps standing at the window. I can feel the warmth of her body from inches away, and it's causing me physical pain not to touch her, even a little.

So I do. Because I really am an asshole.

I slide my hands tentatively up her arms to rest on her shoulders. Then I lean down and rub my nose down her neck. Because really, this might be the last time I get to do it.

"Please," I say into her warm, soft skin. "I didn't mean to tell you like this. I didn't mean for all this to happen."

She sighs, and for a second I think she might forgive me. But then she ducks out of my reach to the other side of the kitchen. It's for the best. I can't be close to her and keep my hands to myself. I don't think she can either.

"Why are you even going there?" she asks me, her voice suddenly sharp. "You're a New Yorker if I've ever met one. This city is in your blood. Is this just a spontaneous move? Something that just came up?"

I shake my head, shifting awkwardly in my sneakers. "Ah, no, not exactly. I've been trying to figure it out for a while now. I was in LA for a few weeks last year and met some of the people K.C. set me up with. It's been in the works since then, and stuff just came through for me."

I don't mention the people who are waiting there for me. People I haven't been talking to much for the past few weeks because I'm too wrapped up with Layla. People like Paul, the owner of the club where I'm supposed to be working. People like Jessie, the girl I spent a good chunk of that time with.

Layla's mouth opens and closes a few times. "But…you don't really *have* to leave, do you?" she pleads, and it just about breaks my heart. "I mean, it's not like you've signed a contract, right?"

From anyone else, it might sound pathetic. But from her, I get it. If it were me on the other side, I'd already be on my knees, begging her to stay. But there are other things to think about here. Things like, I'm nowhere near good enough for Layla, that she deserves better than a fuckin' delivery man or a part-time doorman. Things like, sometimes I feel like I have to get out of this fuckin' cesspool of a city or else I'll die. Or I'll never figure out what or who I am without the chains of this place holding me down.

"No, I do have to go, baby," I say quietly, and watch her face fall. "And not just because I already made the commitment. I've spent almost twenty-seven years in this city. Never lived anywhere else, never had any other job. My sisters are old enough now to help out with our mom, and my brother's eighteen, almost done with school. I need to try to do something different with my life, but everything I try here goes nowhere. It's time."

I sigh and take a deep breath as I voice all the things I'm not sure I've ever said out loud, but have been thinking for years.

"I don't want to work at FedEx forever, baby—you gotta understand that. I feel like this is my shot at something new, and I have to take it. Just like what you're doing here, away from your family and where you grew up."

"You've lived somewhere else," she argues stubbornly, unwilling to let it go. "Those years in the country, when you were in high school, right?"

"That was in juvie, Layla," I admit quietly, dropping the other bomb I hadn't ever planned on telling her. That she didn't just sleep with a guy with no future, but one with a fucked-up past too. A criminal. "Juvenile detention. It doesn't exactly count as a positive experience outside the city, you know what I mean?"

She's stunned. I'd be willing to bet I'm the first person she knows with a record. I was a minor, it's true, but a record is still a record. It's something I have to explain to any employer for the rest of my life.

"What did you do?" she asks, unable to hold back her curiosity. There's a gleam in her eyes I've seen before. This turns her on.

I *hate* that it turns her on.

"Hung out with the wrong crowd. Got caught with some kids holding up bodegas. The third time they kicked my ass out to the center for almost two years. I got out just in time to finish high school." I raise an eyebrow. "Do you hate me now?"

I can see plainly she doesn't. But more than that, I can see that she's not scared of me. The gleam is gone, and she's not looking at me any differently than before. I'm still just Nico to her.

I'm shocked by how relieved I am.

"Please," she says. "If I was going to be judged for every stupid thing I did in high school, I wouldn't have any friends left in the world. Have you held up any bodegas since then?"

We both know I haven't. There is no way I'd have the job at FedEx if I had an adult record. I barely got it as is, and that's only because Flaco was friends with the hiring manager.

The conversation lulls, and I feel like the space between us is huge, like these two bombs having created a chasm between us. Was I really so stupid to have fooled myself into believing she wouldn't care? Of course she cares.

"Layla, please believe me when I say this," I start to say.

She looks up, and my throat tightens at the pain shining bright in her eyes. Fuck. *Fuck.*

"I didn't expect to meet you when I did," I ramble on. "Didn't expect to feel what I do this intense, this fast. You're so...fuck, you're so everything. Beautiful, smart, sexy as hell, fun to be around, easy to talk to...the whole package, really. I...I swear to God, I didn't expect to like you this much, baby."

My voice cracks like a teenager's when I finish. I'm so weak. I should just be the asshole she thinks I am. I should just let her fucking go.

"I could go with you," she blurts out, pulling me out of my thoughts. The next words follow in a rush. "I could transfer to USC or UCLA or some other school in LA. I could fly out with you when I finish the school year in May. It wouldn't be that hard..."

Even as she trails off, we both know how nuts it sounds. She's thinking about jumping ship for a guy she literally met two weeks ago. It's crazy. And yet, I can see in her eyes she's serious.

So now I have to break her heart again. Because even though I have to leave this city, I can't take her with me.

"Shit. Baby, that's so sweet, and I'm honored that you would even offer to do that for me." I walk slowly to her, like I'm approaching a wild animal. I take her hands, playing with the edges of her fingertips. "God, you're so beautiful..." I whisper.

She blinks hopefully. My heart drops another story.

"We both know you need to stay here, finish what you started. You have your friends, your degree...law school eventually, right? Coming out to LA will only put you behind, and baby, you can't do that for someone you've only known a few days. I can't let you do that for me."

I take a deep breath, lean in to kiss her lightly on the lips. She doesn't respond as my words sink in. I'm numb and falling apart at the same time. Maybe this is the real difference between our ages. She's still young enough to be optimistic, to throw caution to the wind for her heart, but I know the realities of everyday life. The complications of mine are only going to hold her back. And I won't do that.

"Let's just enjoy the time we have left together," I say, because I'm still too weak to let her go completely. How can I live in this city for three more months, knowing that this beautiful, amazing creature is in it?

But then she says the one thing I knew she would. The smart thing to say. And I know I'm wrong. Our age difference doesn't mean shit.

"No." Layla pushes off the counter and out of my grasp. She shakes her head and shuffles backward out of the kitchen. "No, no. I-I can't."

I watch dazedly as she disappears down the hallway toward the bedrooms and returns with her overnight bag. I watch as she stuffs the books on the dining table back into her messenger bag, as she pulls on her boots and coat. I watch because I'm stuck in place, like a statue.

"I have to go," she says, as if it isn't obvious. "I can't do this with you. It's…it's going to hurt too much. It already does."

Her voice cracks across the last words, and she swipes viciously at the tears falling down her cheeks. Fucking *fuck*. All I want to do is go to her, wrap her in my arms, tell her I'll stay, tell her I'll do whatever she wants if she'll just stop crying.

But instead, I keep watching as she heaves her bags over her shoulder.

"Layla." I finally find my voice just as she opens the heavy front door. "I'm sorry."

She turns around and stares at me, her deep blue eyes shooting a bullet right through my fuckin' heart. I chew on my lower lip, unsure of what else to say. I want to grab her, tell her this has been a sick joke, show her that I'm willing to make it work no matter what, that this feeling between us is too special, too rare to just throw aside for things like jobs and school.

That's what she does to me. She makes me hope in ways I never thought I could.

But then Layla turns away again, her eyes cast downward

"I know," she says finally. "I'm sorry, too."

And then she pulls the door shut behind her, and I, like the lonely, downtrodden, fucking asshole I am, let her find her own way back to Manhattan, back to where she belongs.

II

STAY

CHAPTER NINETEEN

Layla

BETWEEN HIKING THROUGH THE UNPLOWED STREETS OF HALF OF HOBOKEN AND WAITING for the slow Sunday trains to carry me back across the Hudson and up to Canal Street, it takes me almost two solid hours to get back to the dorms. It's past noon when I arrive irate, tired, and feeling like I've been run over by a truck. All of it makes me a little woozy when I stumble into the apartment. The girls, who are scattered about the place studying, look up at my entrance, their curious expressions immediately melting into concern as they get a good look at me.

"Layla!"

Quinn leaps out of the small dorm armchair and runs to my side. She dumps my bags next to the closet and guides me to the couch where Jamie is sitting. Shama comes out of her room, takes one look at me, and heads to the kitchen to make some tea.

"Dang," Jamie says as she scoots over to make room for my dazed form. "You don't look so good, Lay. Are you all right?"

I shake my head, the memories of last night and this morning replaying yet again. It's all been on terrible repeat for the past two hours. I nearly went back to Hoboken twice, but stopped the second time when I realized I probably wouldn't be able to find my way there on my own. With my friends surrounding me, it all comes crashing down one last time, and the dam inside me finally breaks. The tears start coming. And they just. Don't. Stop.

"Holy shit, babe, what is it?" Quinn asks, rubbing my back. "What did that bastard do to you?"

I choke out a few more sobs and breathe heavily, trying to rein in my emotions enough to tell them what happened. "He's...he's great. We slept together. It was... (sob)...amazing. And then he told me...he's...(sob)...leaving!"

Another flood of tears pour down my cheeks after that last word, and I can feel, rather than see, my roommates trading triplet looks of worry as they pat my back and murmur that everything is going to be all right. I know what they're thinking. This isn't like me. I don't break down crying after one night with a guy. I barely cried after breaking up with Teddy, and he took my V-card and cheated on me. This is just different. I'm not even sure I can explain why or how. But I feel like my heart was made of porcelain and was hurled against a wall.

Eventually, I calm down and stop shaking enough to accept a cup of chamomile tea from Shama. She folds herself down onto the rug and hugs my knees while Quinn and Jamie wrap around me from either side. I'm so thankful that I live with these girls —who else has roommates who will literally stop whatever they are doing just to help you cry over a guy?

"I'm sorry," I say, wiping the tears off my face with the back of my sleeve. "I'm better now. Really."

"Bastard," Quinn remarks as we sit back. "Fuck and run. Just like we said, right? Seriously. Guys are shit."

"He's not shit, Quinn," I insist, maybe a little too vehemently. "He's lost. There's a difference. He didn't have the opportunities we have, you know?" I stop, swallowing back the pain I feel. "He grew up with practically nothing, in a freaking one-bedroom apartment shared with five people. He's barely ever left New York! Now that his siblings are all grown, he finally gets the chance to make a better life for himself. I'm heartbroken, but I can't begrudge him that."

It's not until I say the words that I realize they're true. I look out the window, which faces east. It only looks out to another brick apartment building, but beyond that, I can imagine the river, and beyond that, the brownstone. I wonder if Nico is still there.

"Well, he didn't have to screw you on his way out," Quinn says harshly.

Jamie nods on my other side, as does Shama from her spot on the floor, although I can see she's a little less sure. Jamie tends to side with Quinn on just about everything, but since she started dating her DJ, Shama has been a lot more circumspect about the dramas of our love lives. Jason's another local boy from Queens, and Quinn had *plenty* to say about him when he first came around, until Shama told her where she could stick her opinions. I do wonder, though, sometimes if he's really as nice to her as she makes him out to be. I've heard her crying in the shower sometimes when she thinks no one can hear.

I take a sip of tea with a brief smile at Shama before replying. She squeezes my knee.

"It's not like that," I say quietly, even though I know Quinn won't believe me. "What I feel…I'm pretty sure he feels it too. I think he's sad to leave me. I think…" I take another sip of tea to give myself time to sniff back the tears that are yet again on the edge of falling. "I think his heart is breaking just like mine."

"Whatever." Quinn's pronouncement isn't quite as tough as she'd like. "You're done with him anyway. You can't let him just crush your heart like this, so it's better to let him go now than to get even more attached, right?"

"Right," I say glumly, even though I don't really feel it.

It *is* why I left like I did. I just don't know how I'm going to deal with seeing him every day. The assistants are going to think it's weird that I have to go to the bathroom every day at exactly six p.m. Shit, should I look for another job?

I shiver suddenly, pulling my jacket tighter around me and rocking into it as I sip my tea.

"Are you feeling okay, Layla?"

Shama looks at me from her spot on the floor, and I can see in her eyes that it's not just my emotional state that has her concerned. She's looking over my entire body like there is something wrong with me.

"Actually, no," I admit, realizing that my head is suddenly pounding and my hands feel really clammy. "I started feeling kind of funny on my way home. I thought it was just because I was so upset."

Quinn immediately slaps her hand over my forehead while Shama twists her lips to the side, considering.

"Oh my God," Jamie says next to me, even as she scoots a bit away. "You know the juniors at the end of the hall? Like, four apartments are all down with mono. I bet you have that."

Quinn's eyes roll so far into the back of her head I think they might stay there.

"Well, since Layla hasn't been sticking her tongue down any of their mouths or using their toothbrushes, I doubt she has mono, J." She looks back at me. "Wait, you haven't hooked up with any of them, have you?"

I swipe her hand off my forehead and give her a pointed look. "Do you really think I wouldn't have told you if I had been hooking up with our neighbors? Or used their toothbrushes?"

Jamie giggles, earning a sharp look from Quinn, who immediately puts her hand up to my forehead again. I roll my eyes. Shama smirks.

"Okay, so you don't have mono. But you do feel warm, Lay," Quinn announces after she removes her hand. "I think you might be getting sick."

I nod. "Well, something is definitely wrong. I thought I just had a stuffy head from crying so much, but I'm starting to get chills."

I let them shuffle me into my room and tuck me into bed with tea. The sound of them squabbling about the best way to get me better while trying not to infect themselves with whatever I've got is actually kind of comforting. Quinn, of course, suggests that the three of them disinfect the apartment while I'm sleeping, but that's quickly vetoed by Shama and Jamie, who are both studying for a marketing exam tomorrow. Jamie suggests getting some wonton soup and having Quinn sleep in her and Shama's room, all suggestions that are given serious consideration while they fluff my pillow and tuck me in.

"That's too many blankets, J," Quinn scolds Jamie, urging her to take one off.

"Dude, she says she has chills," Jamie says, but she folds the extra blanket down by my feet anyway. If there is a pecking order in this apartment, Quinn is definitely at the top.

I smile. It's not quite my mom's chicken soup and the down comforter in my old bedroom, but it feels good to be babied by my roommates. I promise each of them I'll take care of them the next time they get sick too. They hush me with more tea and extra pillows before leaving me to sleep off my cold.

Just as my eyes are starting to close, my phone buzzes on the desktop. I pick it up —it's a text from Nico. He doesn't usually text much—neither of us do, since it's an extra cost on top of our cell phone bills.

Nico: just wanted to make sure u got home ok

I should just leave it alone, but I can't help it. Quickly I text him back:

Me: Im home thx.

A few minutes later, the phone buzzes again. My eyelids are really heavy by this point, but like an addict, I pick it up again.

Nico: Im sorry Layla please.

Please what? Please forgive him? Please take him back? Please believe that he's sorry? I don't know what he's trying to say, and my brain feels too thick to figure it out. Without sending a reply, I set the phone to silent and place it back on the desk, letting the fog roll over my senses until I fall asleep.

———

IN THE MORNING, the fog is still there, and everything feels about ten times worse. My throat is sore, and my fever remains along with a pounding headache. After more than fourteen hours of sleep, I still feel completely exhausted; even the trip from my bed to the bathroom is tiresome.

The girls are all asleep still, so I shuffle into the kitchen to make another cup of tea, moving as quietly as I can. A knock at the door tells me it's seven-fifteen—the time I normally catch the shuttle up to campus with Vinny for our eight o'clock classes. Shit. There is no way in hell I'm going to class feeling like this.

I trudge to open up the door, and sure enough, Vinny is standing there, looking particularly lanky in a pair of skinny jeans under his puffy jacket.

"Whoa," he says, looking at me still in my t-shirt and yoga pants.

My hair is still in a messy bun, flyaways probably rioting around my face like a lion's mane the way they do when I've been rolling around in my sleep. At this rate, I'm going to have dreadlocks by the end of the week. It's a far cry from my normal school attire, which is usually office-appropriate for the afternoon.

"I take it you're not ready for class," he says with a smirk. "Rough night?"

"You could say that," I say, turning my back to retrieve the boiling kettle from the stovetop. "And yeah, I'm not going."

When Vinny makes to enter the apartment, I hold a hand out to stop him. "You don't want to come in here, dude. I'm sick."

Vinny's a total hypochondriac, so that halts him in his tracks, and even sends him a few steps back from the doorway. He immediately starts searching through the pockets of his messenger bag for hand sanitizer.

"Bummer," he says as he digs through the bag. "Sorry, man. You want me to talk to your professors or anything?"

It's a nice offer, but I shake my head as I pour my tea. "No, I'll just email them. They probably won't believe me anyway without a doctor's note, so I'm not going to stress about it. I'll be better by tomorrow, I hope."

"Okay. Ah, yes! I knew I had this in here!"

Triumphantly, Vinny pulls out a bottle of sanitizing gel and squeezes a much larger amount than necessary onto his hands. The smell of alcohol stings my nostrils all the way inside the apartment.

"Dude," I say as I watch him. "Going a little overboard, aren't you?"

"Don't nobody want your germs, L-Boogie," he says as he finishes rubbing his hands together.

He sticks the sanitizer back in the front pocket of his bag, then takes a few more steps back into the hallway. I can see the desire to cover his mouth and nose with his jacket sleeve flickering across his features.

"I guess I'll see you later. Feel better."

"Thanks," I say as I walk up to the doorframe.

Vinny dances a few more steps down the hall, clearly focused on keeping a perimeter. I roll my eyes and shut the door. I don't have time to be sick, so I really hope I'll be better tomorrow.

―――――

UNFORTUNATELY, I'm not better at all. In fact, I'm much worse, tired to the bone and feverish. I can hardly talk because my throat hurts so badly, and for the second day in a row, I have to skip classes and call in sick to work, much to Karen's obvious irritation. I don't even have to fake the sick voice on the phone—my sore throat gives me an inimitable scratchiness that I couldn't have created better if I'd tried.

At six-thirty the night before, right after he would have dropped off the packages at Fox and Lager, Nico texted me again.

Nico: everything ok? where have u been?

I didn't respond. I don't have the energy to deal with how he makes me feel. All day I've been falling in and out of feverish sleep and trying my hardest to gulp down glasses of water and zinc-vitamin C supplements. My stomach is starting to act up too, so I'm not always able to keep everything down. In short, I'm in hell.

Sometime around nine o'clock the next night, there's a light tap on my bedroom door, and I stir out of another restless nap as it opens and Quinn pops her head in.

"Hey sickie," she says. "You look like the prettiest picture of death I've ever seen."

"Thanks," I croak and yank my covers over my head.

"No hiding, Sleeping Beauty. There's someone here to see you. You up for some company?"

"Tell Vinny that hand sanitizer isn't going to solve this problem," I grumble. Oh, the dark feels good on my eyes.

"Vinny? That skinny kid down the hall?"

The sound of the deep voice has me batting the comforter from my head with energy I didn't know I possessed. Quinn enters the room gingerly, having avoided it for the last two days while sleeping on the couch. She's followed by Nico, who's still dressed in his FedEx gear. The sleeves of his navy uniform are rolled up to his elbows, exposing his powerful forearms. I sigh, amazed that I can even notice details like that in this state.

And then I remember that he's leaving and pretty much taking my heart with him.

Lacking any shame about being a third wheel, Quinn flops down on her bed, clearly unwilling to leave me alone with the "shit-eating bastard," as she's called him since Sunday. Nico glances at her, then pulls his cap off his head and comes to sit in the desk chair next to my bed.

"Hey," I squeak out, sitting up on my elbows. I know I probably look like a gargoyle, but I'm honestly too tired and too shocked to care. "What are you doing here?"

"I heard you were sick," Nico replies softly. "Karen was all bent out of shape because her assistant had to man the front desk." He reaches out a big hand to touch my forehead briefly with his knuckles. "I wanted to see how you were doing."

I squirm uncomfortably under my sheets, suddenly feeling even hotter under his gaze. God, how could I have forgotten how gorgeous this man is in two days? Oh, right, a hundred-and-three-degree fever might have had something to do with it. I reach up to smooth back my hair, which is still tied in a bedraggled knot, frizzy tendrils sticking out from my temples and around my neck.

"Stop," Nico says, pressing my hand back down. "You're beautiful."

Behind him, Quinn's expression softens at his words before she re-hardens her sharp features. She is really determined to dislike Nico. But it's difficult to hate a guy who's taking the time to visit a girl on her sickbed.

"How did you get up here?" I ask. Visitors have to be signed in by residents of the building; otherwise they aren't even allowed in the front doors of the building.

"He called *me*," Quinn says behind him, clearly disapproving. "About thirty times until I finally agreed to go down there. How did you get my number anyway, you wily bastard? Drug the security guard?"

Nico smirks over his shoulder at her. "I asked around until I found someone who knew you. You poor college kids'll do anything for twenty bucks. Some blonde girl was very helpful."

"I'll bet it was Darla," Quinn says as she lies back on her pillow to ruminate. "That bitch has been trying to stick it to me since first semester last year, when her boyfriend hit on me at a party."

I have to smile at the idea of Nico stalking the kids entering and leaving Lafayette until he met someone in the building—which probably houses about two thousand students—who knew me and my roommates and who would give one of our numbers to a complete stranger. No doubt his charm helped tremendously.

He looks back at me and flashes that smile I just can't resist, and it's then I recall why I left Hoboken to begin with. He's leaving. There's nothing I can do about it. And there's no way I can avoid getting hurt if I keep seeing him until it happens. Underneath the fever, the sore throat, the headache, my heart breaks all over again.

"Well, as you can see, I'm sick but on the mend," I say a little too curtly. "I'm tough. I'll be better soon."

I lie back down on my pillow and turn my head away from him as if I want to go back to sleep. Behind him, Quinn looks on with concern.

"Listen, Layla," Nico says. "I don't want to keep you from getting better. I just wanted to say hi, and—" He cuts himself off, suddenly aware of Quinn's imperious stare behind him. He turns around to face her. "Uh, Quinn? Do you think I could have a second alone with your roommate?"

Quinn doesn't answer, just looks at me for a reply.

I nod. "It's okay. I'll be fine."

She stares back at Nico purposefully and stands up, brushing imaginary creases out of her jeans. "Okay, Casanova, you get your way. But I'm warning you—you make her cry again, and I'll cut your balls off and serve them to the pigeons for breakfast."

She strides out of the room without waiting for a response, leaving Nico and me watching the door close with our mouths hanging open. I'm the first one to laugh, and Nico looks back at me with a sheepish smile.

"You know, I think she'd really do it."

We share a laugh that almost immediately gives way to awkward silence. Things aren't easy between us anymore. They're weird, I'm weak, and I want him to go.

"Soooo…" I say. "I'm kind of tired, you know."

"I know, I'm sorry," he says. "I just…I didn't have the time to tell you this before you left K.C.'s, but listen. I might stay. It's a long shot, but I sent in another application to the fire department. So, you know, maybe three's a charm, right?"

He looks so hopeful as he says it, his eyes shining, obviously willing me to smile and be hopeful with him. And I can't lie—some small flicker of hope does alight inside me. But he knows and I know that that same application has already been turned down twice already, and he's already committed to the job in LA My head still feels cloudy, and I don't know what to think.

I snuggle farther into my sheets. Is he expecting me to invite him into my bed with open arms for this? Hope. What does that even mean?

My head hurts so much.

"I can't really think about all of this right now," I tell him, effecting a yawn and closing my eyes a few times. It's not an act—I'm incredibly tired.

Disappointment plays over Nico's dark features, but he just gives me a smile and a nod.

"Sure, baby," he says, standing up. "I'll see you at work, okay? Feel better, beautiful."

"Mmm," I answer, barely cognizant of the fact that he is leaving as I fall headlong back into another feverish dream.

I was so tired I forgot to tell him not to call me "baby" anymore.

CHAPTER TWENTY

Nico

The blare of my alarm clock wakes me at nine a.m. on Wednesday, and my head is fucking *pounding* with it. It took everything I had to walk away from Layla when she was lying there, weak and sick. She looked like a ghost. The most beautiful ghost I ever saw in my life, but a ghost of her usual vivacious self.

Normally I'd be running. I have too many things on my plate, too many people who depend on me. I can't afford to get sick. But every bone in my body was telling me to stay and take care of her. Take her back to Hoboken where she can have a real bed to lay on, fuck pad or not. Take the next day or the week off and just help her get better.

But she didn't want me there—that much was obvious. And despite the fact that she's a five-foot-two white girl, Quinn kind of scares me.

So I left. Since I couldn't really handle going back to my place with Maggie and her kid, and the idea of sitting around K.C.'s place smelling Layla on my sheets made me feel fuckin' miserable, I called Flaco and met up with him at the Traveler for one or eight beers.

And now I am fuckin' paying for it.

God, I hope she's better.

My phone buzzes on the nightstand next to my futon. I clap my hand on it and open it up without checking who it's from.

"Yeah?"

"*Papito* Nico?"

I sit up straight at the sound of my mother's voice. She's not usually one to call. She doesn't even have a cell phone, and the phone in her apartment is in the kitchen, rather than a decent place to sit and chat.

"*Sí, Mamá, que pasa?*" I answer, and she continues to rattle on in Spanish.

"Did you forget?" she asks me, her voice insistent. "Did you forget about the Mass this morning?"

"Did I forget about..." I rub my forehead viciously, wondering what the fuck she's talking about. I usually take my mother to Mass on Sundays, not Wednesdays.

"It's Ash Wednesday, Nico. You were supposed to be here thirty minutes ago to take me to the church. Now Gabe is missing his classes this morning to go."

Ah, *shit*. That's right. I was supposed to bring Ma to Mass this morning and have a bunch of dirt smeared on my head so she can believe I'm a good Catholic. I'm not. The only time I go to church is with my mother, and I fight the entire time not to fall asleep. I'm not even sure if I believe in God anymore, not when I look around and see the shit deal he gives people who don't deserve it.

But if it helps my mother to think I'm a believer, I don't mind kneeling with her once a week to keep her happy. And she won't go anywhere these days without one of us with her.

"So?" she's saying. "You will go?"

"Huh? What?" I rub my head again. Fuck, I do *not* like being this hungover during the week.

"Wake up, Nico! I said church. I want to see that you got your ashes today, okay?"

I grumble to myself. It's too late to get to a morning Mass, and standing in line with thousands of other New Yorkers is not really how I want to spend my lunch break. But my mother is waiting, and she will seriously wait all day until I stop by her apartment to show her my dirty forehead.

I sigh. "Yeah, Ma, I'll go. And then I'll come by after work, okay?"

I can pretty much hear her smiling over the phone.

"*Bueno*," she replies. "Okay."

———

FOUR HOURS, a couple of Advil, and some cold Chinese food later, I'm taking an early lunch just off Park while Flaco gets ahead on our route. My head isn't feeling as awful anymore, and I keep looking around for Layla as I approach St. Andrew's, which is just a few blocks from her office. I hope she's feeling better. I hope she's good enough to get back to work, where, even if I can't talk to her around her boss, at least I can flirt with her a little behind Karen's back.

I can respect that she doesn't want to see me anymore. But I don't want her to hate me. I don't think I could handle a world where Layla Barros hates me.

The good thing about being Catholic in New York: there's a church a few blocks from everywhere. I read somewhere that the Catholic Church is the largest landowner in New York City, and I don't doubt it.

It's not a process I like. I'm not a good Catholic—I ask too many damn questions. Every time the priest declares some kind of truth supposedly rooted in scripture, I always want to raise my hand and ask how he *really* knows about heaven and hell, about mortal sins, and on and on. How can anyone really know? And what's wrong with a little ignorance anyway? Maybe the world would be a better place if sometimes people just said "I don't fuckin' know" instead of insisting that they do all the time.

Or maybe it's just guilt that keeps me away from the Church. I haven't always been a good man. I try to do the right thing now, but there was a long time, especially when I was younger, when I did wrong without thinking twice. Too much stealing, too much fighting. When it feels like the whole world has more than you do for no real reason, it's easy to justify a lot to yourself: I'll do what it takes to survive. For fifteen-year-old me, that meant too many nicked bags of chips at the bodegas, too many dime bags sold at the school yard, too many fights at the basketball courts or down by the river.

This priest isn't much of a public speaker, so I spend most of the short Mass thinking about Layla and the conversation I had with K.C. last night after I got back from the bar. One thought keeps coming back to me. It's better she knows now. Not just about my move to California to get away from this life, but about my past too. Because no matter how hard I try to rise above it, in New York, I'll always be just another bad egg from the barrio. I'll always be a bad idea.

Except to her, this little thought keeps saying in the back of my mind. And, apparently, K.C.

"Why didn't you just tell her the truth?" K.C. asked me last night when I got back from the bar. "Tell her what you're thinking, or just move the fuck on."

Apparently, Flaco texted him while we were out, told him I wouldn't shut up about Layla. I don't even remember. I had too many beers trying to forget her helpless face. They didn't work.

So K.C. called me, half-drunk himself where he was out at another hot party in LA Another party, another room full of actresses and models. But he still calls me—that's friendship.

"Otherwise just switch buildings with Flaco. Then you don't have to see her no more, bada bing, you're done."

I had to roll my eyes. K.C. only ever talks like a character from *Goodfellas* when he's trying to impress some girl with his New York charm. On cue, I heard a giggle through the phone.

"Besides," K.C. continued. "There's plenty of fish in the sea, *mano*. And one particularly hot fish been asking about you a lot lately."

I begged off when I heard more laughter on the phone, but the conversation stayed with me all through today too.

He's talking about Jessie, of course, the waitress/actress I hooked up with when I visited K.C. in December. She's tall and blonde and basically any guy's wet dream. And up until two weeks ago, we were still talking. A few flirty phone calls, a few hot texts. She even sent me a couple of dirty pictures in the mail. But it's been over two weeks since we last talked. Not since I walked out of an elevator and tripped over two eyes the color of the sky.

Two blue eyes that looked at me yesterday like I made her ill.

Luckily, it's a short and sweet Mass to accommodate the loads of other guilty New York Catholics also here to get their marks, just like me. I'm relieved when we are told to move forward to receive our blessing. I just want to get out of here.

Then I see her. At first I do a double-take, not sure if I'm imagining her thick black hair and slim form, or if it's really her. But then she turns, and I take in her profile, the small, straight nose, the rose-petal lips. The cheekbones that are a little more defined than normal. The body that would make any man forsake Jesus himself just to get a look.

Layla.

She looks tired still, and it looks like she's lost some weight. Her cheeks are a little hollowed out, and the circles that are always kind of under her eyes are just a little darker. Even dressed for comfort in black pants and a shapeless gray sweater, with her hair down in messy waves, she's still the most beautiful woman I've ever seen.

Christ. I really am a lost man.

"Psst!"

I cut in line so we're walking next to each other. Before I can stop myself, I reach out and tap her on the shoulder. She starts, then sees me and relaxes. I can't even pretend I'm not thrilled to see her. I smile like an idiot, even if she's staring at me with shock and confusion.

"Hey, NYU," I whisper, catching a few glares from other churchgoers. I couldn't give a shit. "Fancy seeing you here. You feeling better, sweetie?"

She glances around, like she's scared we're going to get caught by the priest. It's cute. I've been kicked out of Mass too many times to count, but I could see Layla as one of the little kids in the front pew, dressed in white with her hands tucked in her lap. I'll bet she never even got detention.

"A bit," she whispers back. "Do you...do you come to Mass often?"

It's a polite way of asking if I'm actually religious. We haven't talked about it at all—I didn't know she was Catholic, and I definitely didn't say anything to her about it. Suddenly, I'm filled with the fear that she regrets the entire weekend. Some of the sluttiest girls I've ever met were Catholic, but the nice ones don't sleep with boys they just met within twenty-four hours of their first date. For some reason, the idea of Layla as a nice Catholic girl is really disappointing.

I turn, and she's eying me curiously as if she's thinking the same thing.

I smirk. "Nah. I go with my mom sometimes on Sundays, but usually I'm in bed. Today I'm in the doghouse because I forgot to take her to church for her blessing this morning. So if I don't go today, she'll be on my ass for weeks about not having ashes on my forehead. She checks, you know. Ash Wednesday, and she's like a motherfu— um, a drill sergeant."

"My dad does the same thing," Layla whispers back with a hushed giggle. "He's scared I'm going to get corrupted in the city. Do you know he called me at four-thirty in the morning—well, his time, anyway—to remind me to go? And I have to send a picture to prove I was here."

She rolls her eyes, which just makes me grin again like an idiot. I don't know. Maybe I feel some relief, knowing she doesn't totally hate me. That she's not here to confess everything we did. Because a world where I'm not allowed to worship Layla's body is not a world I want to live in.

"Parents," I say. "Can't live with 'em, but they force you to anyway, right?"

Fuck, this girl turns me into a corny bastard. What kind of line is that? I sound like a Will Smith song.

But Layla giggles aloud this time, earning more glares from the people in front of us. My chest feels like it's about to explode.

"Couldn't we just steal some dirt or something off the ground outside?" she asks. "I'll swipe your forehead if you swipe mine."

I feign outrage. "That is totally sacrilegious, NYU. And nasty, girl. Do you know what kinds of things people do in this city? I don't want none of that near my forehead."

She giggles yet again—fuck, I just want to hear that sound on repeat—but sobers up as we move forward to the priests in front of the lines, each holding a cup of ashes.

Paired together, I suddenly feel like we're about to receive a blessing before taking our vows. And I can't lie—the idea of doing just that makes a whole bunch of other things flash through my mind. Layla in a white dress. Layla carried over across the doorway of a house. Layla pregnant, and then holding our child.

Jesus *fucking* Christ. I have got to get it the fuck together.

We obediently bow our heads as each priest quietly intones the words of Genesis 3:19: "Remember that thou are dust, and to dust thou shalt return." Two quick swipes cross my forehead, and I'm officially marked as a child of Christ.

Layla bobs and crosses herself before filing off to the side to leave the church. I do the same and follow her outside as we both tug on our coats.

In the bright light of the afternoon, I watch curiously as she takes out a few pieces of bread and tears off a piece. She chews it slowly, like it might make her sick, then swallows it with a swig from her water bottle. To my surprise, she offers me the bag.

"I'm good," I say, surprised by the food. "Wow, sweetie, you really do the whole thing, don't you? I, uh, had no idea you were so devout."

She's fasting. After being sick for three days, she's fasting.

Layla just shrugs. "Meh, not really. My parents are hardcore Catholics, so it's kind of habit now."

"Yeah?" I ask. "My mom does it too. She says it's fine to have milk if you need it to get through the day, though." I'm trying to stay light-hearted, but Layla really doesn't look that good. She shouldn't be fasting when she's sick. "You a good Catholic girl, NYU? Should I be worried about corrupting you, or has that ship already sailed?"

She laughs out loud at that one, and doesn't bother to hide it since we're not in the church anymore.

"Maybe it's because I haven't been to Mass since Christmas with my parents, and I'm feeling a little guilty," she admits with a smirk.

I can't help myself. "You been naughty, huh?"

Almost immediately, a blush appears in her cheeks, and she can't meet my gaze. I know exactly what she's thinking about—the feel of me, my hands, my lips, my cock, all doing things to her that no nice Catholic girl should let me do, things the priest inside would no doubt condemn. And now I'm thinking of them too, with a sudden need to adjust my pants *outside a fucking church.*

"Excuse me!"

Other people exiting St. Andrew's push past us with some nasty glares, even pushing Layla a few steps closer to me. I should let her be, but all I can see is the way she's staring at my lips right now like she wants to suck them off my face. And fuck if I wouldn't let her, church or no church. In the mood I'm in, I'd take her right on the altar.

So I lean close to her ear so that my lips brush the soft skin by her earring. Her scent is everywhere, it shoots straight to my dick. Fuck, I want her. The weekend didn't do anything to get rid of that need. Three days later, and I still want her more than I've wanted anything in my life.

"Don't worry," I say in a low voice I can't quite control. "I liked you naughty, NYU."

That's me, Nico Soltero. Asshole and glutton for punishment.

Just as I start to drift my lips around the edge of her earlobe, she steps back. Her cheeks are even redder now, and she's licking her lips, even shaking a little. But instead of saying anything, she reaches into her messenger bag and pulls out a disposable camera. She snaps a photo of me, and then of herself.

"For my dad," she says in a voice that quavers. "I need to be good."

Good. Fuck. She hasn't mentioned her family much, but I can see they put a lot of pressure on her. And I am one hundred percent sure that the conservative Catholic father who will receive that photograph won't want a bastard street urchin like me hanging around his daughter.

I'm an idiot. It's better that things are ending now, before they get too out of hand. I'm capable of ruining Layla's life, and that's the last thing I want to do. Already she means too much for me to do that.

"Understood," I say, leaning in to kiss her one last time on the cheek before she can step away. Hey, I said it's better things are ending. I didn't say it would be easy. "I'll see you at six, all right?"

"Sure," she mumbles with another confused look.

I take a few steps back, even though every nerve in my body is screaming to stay close. I turn away, already thinking that I should take K.C.'s advice and switch buildings with Flaco. The less I see of those big blue eyes, the better.

Still, I can't quite do it. But Layla can. When I turn around to tell her one last thing—I don't even know what to say, just *something* to keep her talking to me, smiling, laughing, anything—she's gone, disappeared through the crowds on her way to work.

I stand there like an idiot for a good minute, hoping to see her shiny black hair, before I'm able to shake off the dread that's settled in my bones.

"Get a fuckin' grip, Soltero," I mumble to myself, startling an old woman coming out of the church.

Nodding at her politely, I clap on my FedEx hat and check my watch. It's one forty-five. Time to get back to work.

———

Layla

"Eyes up, Layla."

I snap my head up to find Karen staring down at me over the wood desktop. There's less than an hour and a half left in my shift—and I'm having a hard time staying awake.

"What's going on with you?" she asks sharply. "Are you *still* sick?" She snarls it, as if she thinks I was lying about the last two days.

I glance around the lobby. No one is here; it's been a slow day, and I suspect people are doing less business because of the snow outside, which has been coming down hard since about three o'clock. It's going to be a bitch to get home.

To top things off, I've also been feeling progressively worse as the afternoon has passed. Having eaten nothing but a slice of bread for breakfast and the baguette for lunch, I'm feeling seriously low-energy and want nothing more than a quick dinner and my bed. My sore throat seems to have returned, and I'm starting to feel a bit nauseous too, probably from low blood sugar.

Being sick also makes me crabby, and for a split-second I consider asking Karen what the hell she thinks is going on with me, considering I've been out with the flu for two days and probably still look like death. But instead I smile demurely and say, "I'm sorry, Karen. I'm just tired. I'll perk up, I promise."

"You weren't sleeping at your desk, were you?"

I shake my head. I wanted to, but it was only a momentary resting of my eyes, right? "No, I was just thinking about something. I have midterms in a few weeks, so I'm trying to get ahead on some stuff. There's this one concept for my English class that's got me stumped—"

"Okay, okay, fine." She's irritable, and keeps checking her watch as she teeters back into her office. According to one of the assistants, Karen has a new boyfriend, so she's always waiting for him to call. When he doesn't, she gets bitchy. Clearly, he doesn't call much.

I glance at the clock. It's five minutes to six, which means a certain FedEx courier is due any minute. I sigh. I feel like shit and not at all like summoning enough bravado to deal with his suggestive banter and not profess my undying love in the process. It was hard enough not jumping him outside a church. Christ, if my dad knew the kinds of thoughts that were going through my head about him, I'd be on the first plane back to Seattle.

I pick up the phone and dial one of the legal interns.

"Hey Ann, I need a bathroom break. Could you man the desk for a few minutes?"

A few minutes later, I'm hiding out in the utility closet across from the bathrooms when the elevator bell rings, and I hear Nico's big voice echoing through the lobby. Ann returns his greeting with an irritatingly obvious giggle, which makes me want to run out there and kick her out. They continue to make polite, if flirtatious conversation, and I'm surprised that Karen doesn't come out to join them. I grip the edge of the utility door, gritting my teeth while Ann tells Nico all about the classes she's currently taking at Cardozo, where she's in law school. He makes a joke I can't quite understand, causing her to laugh like a freaking hyena.

"Oh, for fuck's sake, he's not *that* funny!" I mutter, knowing full well I've definitely exhibited equally hyena-like laughter. That's just the effect Nico has on women.

"You okay out there, Layla?" Nate, another intern, enters the utility room to make copies. I jump and pretend that I haven't been crouched at the door like a crazy stalker, eavesdropping on the FedEx guy. In the background, Ann says goodbye to Nico just before the elevator doors close.

"Fine and dandy," I tell him. I grab at a couple of pens in a plastic bin near my head. "Just getting some supplies for the front desk." I smile and dart out of the closet before he can question me further.

Ann stands up with a smile when I arrive and take back my seat.

"You can have me trade places with you any time," she says with a dreamy smile. "That dude is smoking hot!"

I shrug as if I don't know what she's talking about. "I guess. I never really noticed."

"Right," she says, clearly disbelieving. She leans in so she can speak quietly. "Don't worry, I won't tell anyone." Before I can deny her tacit accusation, she reaches up and grabs the large paper bag perched on top of the desk. "He brought you this."

She gives me a conspiratorial wink and walks to the back hallway before I can reply, leaving me sitting with the paper bag on my lap.

I pull it open and find a carton of matzo ball soup, a potato knish, and a carton of milk, along with various utensils to eat everything, all purchased from the Jewish deli around the corner. The soup is still hot and smells amazing, but I know there's no way Karen would be okay with me eating something like this at my desk. Ignoring the way my stomach is growling, I put the food back in the paper bag for later, but leave the milk out when I see the small note taped to the side.

Thought you should make your one meal of the day a good one. I hear soup is good when you're sick, and you looked hungry. Don't make me worry about you, beautiful.

—Nico

I blink at the stark scrawl on the lined yellow paper, suddenly unable to keep the tears from clouding my vision. It's a small gift, but it's so thoughtful. How am I supposed to ignore him when he's like this? How am I supposed to let him go when he tries to take care of me?

Reluctantly, I crumple the note up, although I shove it into my purse instead of the trash. For a few moments, I stare at the milk, debating about whether or not to drink it as if the actual nutrients running through my bloodstream might cause me to fall even more for this man than I already have, which I definitely don't want. Then my stomach growls again. It's been a long time since that bread.

"Fuck it," I whisper, and tear into the carton, downing the whole thing in just a few seconds. It's just milk, right?

But as I count the minutes passing by until I can leave at seven, the rest of the paper bag full of sustenance catches my eye. And I know it will never be just milk with him.

CHAPTER TWENTY-ONE

Layla

THE SOUP HELPS MORE THAN I WANT TO ADMIT, AND BY THE END OF MY SHIFT, I'M READY to do more than just go back to the dorms. One of the benefits of sitting in bed for two days is that I've actually managed to get ahead on my homework. For once, I have nothing to do before class tomorrow. So even though I should probably go home and rest, I decide to take advantage of the fact that the snow has stopped and walk all the way home.

Walking is probably my favorite part about living in this city. I feel safer in many parts of Manhattan at any time at night than I do on the quieter streets of Seattle, or even the suburb where my parents live. I can walk down Fifth Avenue at one a.m. and not feel scared. There are always people around, always lights on, always cars passing and trains running. One day maybe I'll get sick of the craziness of it all, but right now, the cacophony is just what I need to drown out the warring arguments in my head.

I hadn't expected to see Nico today and definitely hadn't expected him to make me practically combust on the steps of a church less than five minutes after I'd been blessed to start a season of attrition. If God is actually real, He has a messed-up sense of humor. And that moment, when Nico's lips just barely touched my ear...gah. I wanted nothing more than to grab his ears and pull him in for another soul-searing kiss, the kind that makes me forget all the reasons we probably won't work out, that makes me forget my own name.

But I made the right decision walking away. He wants to fool around for three more months. It would be fun, but if I feel this strongly now, I can't imagine what kind of pain I'll feel when he leaves. By then I'd be one hundred percent in love with him, if I'm not already.

Wait. Hold the phone. *Love*?

I hug my arms around myself, trying to collect my emotions back into a place where I can manage them. No. You're not in love with him. It's not possible. You're too young for this, and he's too old for you.

I repeat the words silently, willing my body and my heart to believe them. It doesn't work.

I think back on the two nights we've spent together, the easy hours in each other's company, where the conversation had come more naturally with him than with anyone else. The way he touched me...like he knew my body better than I did...and now the returning shock that I'm the only one who felt that connection.

I think back to that moment in the kitchen, when Nico came clean about his plans and neatly brushed away any possibility of making things work in other ways. His face drawn in obvious sorrow, with tiny lines I hadn't noticed before crinkling around his dark eyes. His mouth, chewing ferociously on his lower lip every time he shook his head "no" to one of my suggestions.

He was genuinely sad; none of it smacked of a play to get rid of me. But what do I know? I'm just a naïve nineteen-year-old who's fallen for a man seven years her senior. A man who's explained why he has to leave her. Truthfully, I don't know what I am to him, and that's only going to lead to heartbreak. It already has.

And yet his words keep floating back. *I like you naughty, NYU.* I shiver, and not because of the cold. Yeah, I like me naughty too. With him. Naked. Mmmm.

Damn it, Layla, get a hold of yourself. I have to keep repeating the mantra as I turn onto my street and step through the leftover snow drifts. He's leaving. I just need to keep telling myself that anytime I start getting pulled back into the Nico vortex. He's leaving. He's leaving.

He's...right in front of me?

As I approach my dorm, I find Nico leaning against the side of the brick building, about fifty feet from the entrance, intently watching the students as they come and go. His back is to me, but I would know those shoulders, that cap-covered head, that denim-clad ass anywhere.

He's hunched over in his leather jacket and a pair of cuffed dark jeans and has replaced his FedEx cap with his favorite, beat-up Yankees hat. His shoulders sag with fatigue, and his head rests lightly against the side of the building. I can tell from the way he keeps rubbing his hands together and shoving them back into his pockets that he's been standing there a while. Even without seeing his face, I can feel the magnetic attraction between us. He's here waiting for me, and my body, the traitor, wants to run right to him.

"Hey, Layla."

One of the kids from my dorm greets me as he passes by with a few friends, completely blowing my cover. Nico turns around in surprise, nodding at the kid before resting his dark, searching eyes on me. We stare at each other for a minute, not saying anything.

"Hey," he finally says. "I was just—"

"Stalking me?" I finish for him.

I walk a few steps closer so that we don't have to yell over the din of the street. It's not a busy location, set well off Canal, but this is still New York. There's no such thing as a quiet street.

He gives me a sheepish half-smile, baring one dimple that I immediately want to nuzzle. Shit. He's leaving, Layla. He's going to break your heart.

"I wanted to make sure you were okay," he says. "Quinn said you weren't home, and she wouldn't let me up."

He reaches a hand out to touch my mitten, but I step back. If I let him touch me, I'm as good as gone. I might as well just throw myself into the abyss right now.

He shifts back and forth from foot to foot, like he's nervous about something. "Listen, Layla. I just wanted to say...ah, I'm not good at this...I, uh..."

Suddenly it's not hard to keep him at bay. Watching him hem and haw like this is worse than being made into self-imposed star-crossed lovers. At least Romeo actually *wanted* to be with Juliet. At least he fucking *tried* to make something happen. Nico wants to have his cake and eat it too. He wants to fuck me, make me fall in love with him, and leave me after. Well, fuck that. I'm not just going to lay my heart on the pavement for him to run over.

"You know what, don't worry about it," I say, stepping widely around him to make my way down the street to the dorm.

I hear his heavy footsteps on the sidewalk as he follows, so I walk faster, hoping he'll get the hint.

"Come on, baby, please don't do this."

"I am *not* your baby!"

I whirl around, suddenly furious. He has no right to play games with me like this; to fuck me senseless on Saturday, drop me for a job in California on Sunday, then give me a "maybe I will, maybe I won't" spiel on Tuesday. I know why he has to go; I get it. But I don't appreciate being treated like a placeholder for what he really wants. A way to kill time until he leaves. It doesn't matter if he knows the best delis in the city or he's the kind of guy who will make romantic gestures like waiting for you for possibly hours in the freezing cold.

"You're *leaving*," I seethe. Yes, I can do this. Just as long as he doesn't touch me. "Sure, it'll be great for the next three months. I know this is great. You think I don't know that? I do. But you're leaving, Nico, so what's the fucking point?"

"The point is us, Layla!"

He steps back, unable to keep still as he swings his arms out wide, as if trying to expel excess energy and demonstrate just how big "us" really is. When he finally stops and faces me, his expression is determined and his eyes flash under the streetlamp.

"It's us, baby! You know, just like I do, that I'm not going to be able to stay away from you any more than you're going to be able to stay away from me. We'll have to see each other every day until May, and it's not like this is ever going to fade away. One fuckin' touch, and you melt in my hands. And you know what? It's the same for me. All you have to do is pout those beautiful goddamn lips of yours, and I'm ready to hop your desk and do you in front of your whole office!"

"So, you want to fuck me, and I want to fuck you?" I paraphrase cruelly. "Big *fucking* surprise."

"Don't say that," he orders curtly. "And don't play dumb. You and I both know it's more than that."

"We've been on one—no, two, I guess—dates," I snap. "We've known each other for about five fucking minutes. It's just sex."

I hate the words as they roll out of my mouth. I hate them because I know them for the lie they are.

"Fuck that. You know it's way more than sex."

Nico tears his cap off his head and smacks it irritably against the wall before clapping it back on backward. It makes his dark eyes and brows stand out now that the bill doesn't cast a shadow over his face. His eyelashes are a thick fringe that only intensifies the frustration painted on his strong features.

"Fine!" I burst out. "So there's a connection!" My voice falters. I inhale deeply to control myself before continuing. "So what? You're still *leaving*."

"Yeah, I'm leaving!" He shouts it out like he can't quite believe it himself. Maybe he can't. "I have to do this, Layla! I have to get the *fuck* out of this garbage can of a city, at least try, or else I know I'll never leave, and I'll be stuck with this same shitty life forever. I'm not going to get into the FDNY, just like every other fuckin' time I've tried. So, I have to...*fuck*! I have to do something!"

He looks at me, those deep-set brown eyes ripped with fury and pain. I want to look away—I don't want to feel sorry for him. Sorry means I care, and caring is one more step closer to that L-word I've been trying to avoid. But I'm already crying. I'm already here with him, stuck in this abyss. I fell in the second he stepped off that elevator.

"You got your chance, NYU," Nico says, invoking that nickname that speaks of everything I have, everything he's trying for. "You're living it right now. And I wouldn't take that from you by even letting you consider coming with me. But I gotta take mine, Layla. Don't you get that?"

The way his voice cracks on that last word practically breaks my heart. He holds my gaze, not letting me look away, forcing me to feel the earnestness, the pain he feels. We stand together for a moment, our breaths heaving, uncertain of anything but the obvious chemistry crackling between us. This is infuriating, wanting him so badly but at the same time knowing I shouldn't do anything about it.

"Of course I get it," I say, trying and failing not to let my voice, which is still slightly hoarse, split over the words. "I'm not a monster. But I...I don't want my heart to be broken in the process. And Nico, you will—you *will* break my heart."

There. I've finally said it out loud. Now he knows how I feel and how I'm afraid to feel. Maybe now he'll walk away, because I am steadily losing the strength to do it again.

"I don't want to say goodbye to you yet, Layla."

"Just..."

I falter on the words when his eyes glimmer. The way he's looking at me, I want nothing more than to throw myself into his big arms and tell him we'll just live in the now, that LA can go to hell, and we'll deal with his departure when it actually comes.

But I know I won't be able to do that.

"Just go, Nico," I finally say, my tone defeated.

I can't look at him, knowing that with one smile, one flash of his eyes, I'll be jumping into his arms. I study the texture of the bricks behind him. The way the color of the stone changes when it's wet with melted snow. I take a deep breath.

"I'll deal with seeing you at the office. But I can't do more than that."

I hate that fate is so unkind as to hand me the most intense connection of my life, and two days later steals it back again. I hate that I can't even take a last glance at him as I walk away.

"Layla, please."

I continue to walk slowly toward the dorm, to where I can be protected by the flurry of students loitering around the entrance. My footsteps drag—whether because

I'm still a little sick or because underneath it all, I don't really want to leave him, I don't know. But it's got to be what's best. It's just got to be.

"Layla, please!"

Just before I reach the street, Nico's hand catches mine and pulls me back to face him.

"Please," he says one last time, his voice catching again.

It's then I make the mistake of looking into his eyes, burning bright with a combination of desire, pain, and obvious…love, maybe? Whatever it is, it's strong, and he searches my face for something of the same, his eyes drawing hungrily over my face, my lips as he cups my cheeks between his leather-encased palms.

"You're like a magnet. I can't just stay away," he says and bends down to kiss me.

"Stop," I whisper just before he touches me. "You're leaving."

"I don't fuckin' care," he growls and kisses me, opening my mouth with his tongue and plundering until every inch of my body practically melts into him.

I succumb, wrapping my arms around his head and pulling him closer, sucking on his bottom lip so hard I wonder if I've drawn blood. His hands reach inside my coat, clasping my ass so he can grind his hips into me. Even as I moan into his mouth, I hear a couple of whistles from students passing us, even a "Get a room," but it's hard to do much more than register anything when his lips are on mine.

Which they won't be…for long. Eventually my brain catches up with my body, realizing a clear, important truth: nothing about this situation has changed with that kiss. I still want him, and he is still going to leave me cold.

I am stronger than I thought.

"Stop!"

I shove him back, and we gape at each other, our lips swollen and hungry. The air swirls with the heavy mists of our breath and a few errant snowflakes, and I ignore the curious students who walk around us.

"What?" Nico gasps. "What is it?"

He reaches for me again, but I step out of his grasp, backing farther down the sidewalk.

"I *do* fucking care," I huff at him, still trying to catch my breath. "And that doesn't change the fact that you're still going to break my heart."

And with that, before he can whisper another word that will make me stay or surprise me with another kiss that's sure to paralyze me for good, I turn on the heel of my boot and run the last few steps into the dorm. This time he doesn't follow, and I force myself not to look back to see if he's still there.

CHAPTER TWENTY-TWO

Nico

THE NEXT DAY, I SWITCH BUILDINGS WITH FLACO. I MUST LOOK LIKE AN EVEN BIGGER IDIOT than I thought, because he doesn't even put up a fight about missing out on the modeling agency. It should feel like the jackpot. I get to be the hot delivery guy to a floor full of eight-foot-tall Amazons who'd *all* like to go slumming in between TV executives and the CEOs they're escorting in between modeling gigs. But even after I get two numbers slipped to me on the first day alone, I couldn't care less.

All I see are big blue eyes with a sweep of black lashes. A heart-shaped mouth that's a puzzle-piece match to mine. Layla.

The rest of the week and the next drag on, and every day I try something, anything, to make me stop thinking the way I do. I go out to Jersey, but all I can see is her there. I come back to Manhattan, but I only wish she were with me. I spend the entire weekend helping my mom weed through her magazine collection. I take extra shifts at AJ's and even volunteer to work the door Sunday night at another club uptown.

I even volunteer to watch my sister's kid, Alejandra, at night and in the morning, because I'm not sleeping anyway. It's a good idea at first—Allie's a great distraction. But then it gives Maggie a minute to patch things up with her boyfriend, and by the next week, they move back to his apartment. So now I'm alone at my place again, with nothing but my thoughts and my sketchbook. And there's only one thing I've been interested in drawing.

By Friday the next week, I am breaking the fuck down. I take my lunch break in the truck, watching the entrance of the Fox and Lager building like a fucking stalker. It's been over a week since I last saw her, and like a junkie, I need my fix. I tell myself that it's because I just want to make sure she's okay. She didn't look like she had totally recovered from the flu. I want to make sure she's taking care of herself.

Flaco, like the friend he is, keeps me company, eating his sandwich like a horse and shaking his head at how pathetic I am.

"I told you," he says through a mouthful of chicken cutlet. "She looks fine. She was out sick a few more days, but she's been there all week, and she looks fine, *mano*."

I set my sandwich on the dashboard of the truck. The pastrami tastes like cardboard anyway.

"Nico," Flaco says. "Why don't you just tell her?"

"Tell her what?" I'm absent, keeping my stare glued to the glass double-doors of the building. If I look away, I might miss her when she arrives.

Flaco smacks me on the shoulder. "What do you think? That you're fuckin' in love with her."

My head snaps at him like it was on a slingshot. "*What?*"

Flaco rolls his bug-eyes. He's a tall, skinny dude with big eyes and lips like a frog. Flaco, another word for skinny in Spanish, isn't his real name (which is actually Juan). But he's been a skinny fuck since grade school and never grew out of it.

"Don't play," he says simply. "I been watchin' you fall all over yourself for NYU princess. You in love with her, bro. Don't deny it."

I frown. "That's crazy. I barely know her."

"Psssh, whatever," he says, tossing his gangly hands up in the air. "That don't mean shit. My parents got married four days after they met. They seen each other across the club, and blammo! That was it. Next stop, Atlantic City."

I haven't met Flaco's parents, but he's told the story a lot. We talk a lot of shit about girls, but you don't grow up listening to mambo kings and bachata ballads without becoming romantics at heart. His parents are actually still together after they met at an early Hector LaVoe show up in the Bronx. Love at first sight, the way Flaco tells it. It's easy to imagine—salsa is sexy as fuck. I bet a lot of babies got started at those concerts back in the day.

"Still," I say, even though I'm back to staring at the building. "It's not the same thing."

And it isn't. I met Layla in the middle of my delivery route, not a sexy concert. Flaco's parents are cut from the same cloth—both Puerto Rican, both new immigrants, both living in the same neighborhood. Layla and me, we're from totally different worlds.

"Whatever," Flaco says as he turns back to his sandwich. "You a fool in love, bro. No doubt."

Layla arrives at one-fifty, ten minutes before her shift starts. I see her walking down the street from the subway entrance. She looks...good. Skinny, but good. Better than I want her to look now that we're split. I really am a selfish bastard.

She glances nervously toward the FedEx truck, and I'm glad we have tinted windows so she can't see me watching her like some *Fatal Attraction* psycho. Fuck, I'm freaking myself out here.

Still, I take her in, follow her every step. She's so serious, her big eyes scanning around, already with the watchfulness New Yorkers have so they don't get taken for a ride. Everyone in this city is suspicious, and Layla, even though she doesn't have that jaded edge to her yet, has already learned to be cautious around strangers.

She doesn't smile. Even from across the street, I can see that the twinkle in her eyes is dulled. I want to tell myself it's just because she was sick, even though I know better. A couple of construction workers catcall her—the kind who will catcall anything with a skirt—and she ducks her head as she passes, but doesn't show the fear I know she must have. I clench my fists, fighting the urge to jump out and shield her from their whistles, maybe even teach some of these assholes some respect. I have sisters. I know how scary these streets can be to women, especially young pretty ones like Layla.

My eyes skim over the determined set of her shoulders, the sway of her hips, the way she glances from side to side as she walks. I'm not watching in a sexual way, although I feel that too. Fuck, how could I not, especially now that I know the way our bodies fit together? But now it's more like I'm making sure she's all right, just making sure she's healthy and happy, like I want her to be. I'm a man obsessed. A man...fuck me. A man in love.

Shit.

Flaco's licking his chops, looking more like a frog than ever as he watches realization dawn on my face. He gives me a pat on the back, the way you might comfort a kid who just lost his favorite stuffed animal.

"There you go, *papi*," he says with a rueful shake of his head. "Now you just gotta tell her."

I bang my head on the steering wheel. Flaco's right. This changes everything.

CHAPTER TWENTY-THREE

Layla

A fter a week and a half of not seeing Nico, I'm feeling completely normal and also completely terrible. I still miss him. How crazy is that? It's been almost as long as the time I actually knew him, and I still feel like my heart has been torn out of my chest.

It doesn't help that every time the new FedEx guy comes in, he stares at me like I'm a kid who just lost her favorite stuffy. Flaco—he says that's his name, even though it makes Karen laugh—has big, expressive eyes, not unlike a frog's. When he's done flirting with Karen in Spanish (apparently, they're from the same neighborhood), he nods at me every night and clicks his tongue, like even he thinks this situation between me and Nico is ridiculous.

He's probably right. Every time the doors open at six, I find myself praying it's Nico who'll roll in today's packages, not Flaco.

But it never is.

By Saturday, I'm fed up with my shitty mood, and so are the rest of my roommates. We've got a few more weeks until midterms, so this is our last chance to get out and party for a while, and I'm determined to make the best of it.

"Bitches," I announce on Saturday afternoon after I get back from the gym. "Where are we going tonight? Because I am *done* feeling sorry for myself over a freaking FedEx guy."

"Jesus. Fucking *finally*," Quinn says from the couch, setting her pencil down on her book with satisfaction. "I was wondering when you were going to snap out of it."

I toss my ponytail over my shoulder and put my hand on my hip. "Someone tell me where the party is tonight, because I am bringing it. End of story."

———

SINCE BEING sick caused me to drop a few pounds, I'm feeling confident enough to slip on a short, body-con, sea-blue dress that normally I don't have the guts to wear. Jamie flatirons my hair so it hangs in a long, dark waterfall down my back, and I use extra liner around my eyes to make them pop with the color of the dress. With my thigh-high leather boots, I feel ready to kick some serious ass, or at least play some serious game. Anything, really, to get over Nico.

The girls are more than ready to have me back, considering I was so AWOL the weekend before.

"It always feels like one of us is a third wheel when you're not around, Lay," Shama privately tells me as we're walking behind Jamie and Quinn down the hall to the elevators.

I grin. I know what she means. For some reason a group of four just works better. Everyone always has someone to talk to.

We decide to go to a lounge in Chelsea called The Grotto, where Jason, Shama's boyfriend, is DJing for the night. I try to ignore the fact that the bar is three blocks from a certain music venue where a certain FedEx courier works on the weekends. I try to ignore the temptation to just walk by AJ's "on my way" to the other venue. But I've decided tonight is a perfect night to get the hell over him, and so I decide to do my best to distract myself.

The Grotto is a typical midtown lounge: small and low-lit, with the exposed brick walls and square ottomans surrounding small tables. It's the kind of sexy place where people sit a little lower to the floor than they would normally, making you feel like you're almost already in bed with them. Since Jason usually plays electronic remixes of popular songs, an impromptu dance floor has sprung up in the back near the raised booth where he's mixing tracks, one hand clasping a set of large headphones to his left ear.

Jason looks up when we arrive and winks when he sees Shama, who practically blooms right there on the dance floor. Whatever I might think of the guy, I like that he makes her happy. The rest of us wave to him and find our way to a small table where we can share a couple of ottomans.

"Damn, girl, you lost your ass," Jamie tells me as we squeeze onto one of the square-shaped cushions together.

"I did not!" I exclaim, looking behind me at where my backside meets the cushion.

My dress definitely doesn't fit quite as second-skin as it used to, but my booty didn't disappear in a week and a half. Jamie elbows me, and I look to the right, where she's gazing.

A small group of three guys sits around the table next to ours, clearly scoping us out. They've got that advertising/finance look about them that you see all over New York—manicured stubble, stylishly worn jeans, gelled hair that's carefully mussed. One guy with glasses and dark facial hair that's been shaped into a chinstrap around the edge of his jawline is watching me with obvious interest. He's a bit thinner than the types I normally go for, lacking the big, toss-me-over-them shoulders like Nico's—shit, I wasn't going to think about him tonight!—but he's not bad-looking. Full lips and pretty eyes. Plus, I have a bit of a thing for men who wear glasses.

When I smile at him, he elbows his friend in the side and mouths "Hi" to me.

"He's cute, Lay," Jamie says.

Quinn is watching the group too, and I can already tell she likes what she sees.

Quinn goes for men who are more polished, like these—guys who look like they could finance more than a few drinks.

"See the blond one in the gray pants?" she whispers across the table. "That shirt was in the Armani spread in GQ last month. That's a three-hundred-dollar shirt."

Well, I guess we know which one she likes. The guys stand up, and we pretend not to watch as they make their way awkwardly around the scattered ottomans to where we sit.

"Hey," says Mr. Armani.

He's tall and lanky, with combed, dark blond hair and eyes so blue they've got to be tinted with contacts. So not my type, but Quinn's all smiles as she responds with a carefully nonchalant "Hey" in kind. The other one with him, a shorter guy with a big nose who's wearing a muscle t-shirt, is already making eyes at Jamie. And they say that people of my generation don't know how to speak to each other.

"Mind if we join you ladies?" says Glasses, looking directly at me. I give him my best flirty, come-hither smile and nod.

"You'll have to get your own seats," I say. "We're already squeezed onto ours."

"Can we get you some drinks first?" he asks.

Shama volunteers to go with the guys to help them bring back drinks—honestly, it's more to make sure nothing extra gets put into them than to actually help carry them to the table. None of us have had the pleasure of being roofied, but we've all known someone who's experienced it at some point.

The boys return with our orders, and I happily accept my whiskey and soda from Glasses, who pulls up another ottoman to sit next to me.

"I'm Blake," he says over the din of the bar where Jason has started to pump up the dance music.

He reaches out to shake my hand, and I resist yanking my hand from his weak grip. There's nothing worse than when a guy's handshake feels like a dead fish; it doesn't bode well for the strength of his other body parts.

"I'm Layla," I tell him, and take a long sip of my drink.

It's a little bitter, just the house generic, but I can't afford the good stuff. Mixed drinks just go down way too fast.

"That's quite a drink you've got there, Layla," he says.

I raise my eyebrows with a mild frown and look at his drink, which is a mostly-juice cranberry vodka. Gross. Honestly, that's sorority girls' bread and butter, one step from a cosmopolitan. This guy might as well announce he's got a vagina with that drink.

Me, I can't with super sweet girly drinks, with the exception of the occasional margarita or caipirinha. It's my dad who gave me the taste for whiskey. In Brazil, we attended formal functions with his family, when one of my cousins graduated from secondary school or college. It was customary to place a bottle of scotch at every table in addition to the open bar. That never failed to lead to some crazy party and some of the best nights of my life. To me, whiskey always tastes like a really good time.

"I don't think I've ever seen a girl order straight liquor before," Blake continues.

He winks at me knowingly, as if my drink is some huge joke. What the hell? Is he serious? I know I'm not the only woman in New York who enjoys hard alcohol without a fruity accompaniment.

"It's not straight whiskey," I correct him. "It's mixed with soda. You know, the bubbly water?"

This guy is already getting on my nerves. Deep down I know the reason I'm being kind of a bitch isn't really because my drink choice doesn't fit Blake's gender stereotypes. He's just like any other guy—grasping at straws to make conversation with a girl in a bar. He's nervous, just like they all are.

No, I'm being a bitch because Blake just isn't what I want. His hair is floppy and too long, not short and clean cut. The line of scruff around his jaw bristles, and his eyes, even behind those glasses, just don't flash the way Nico's—

Damn it, Barros! Without thinking, I slam the rest of my drink and set the glass down on the table with a clink of ice cubes.

"Whoa, there," Blake says. "You're a live one. You need another, honey?"

"Sure."

I stand up. Blake's eyes rake over the contours of my body. I never should have worn this dress. Even in the shadows of the lounge, the clingy blue silk basically puts everything on display. I follow him to the bar and stand behind him as he flags the bartender's attention.

"Hey, you want to take a shot with me?" he calls over the clamor.

I nod. Why the hell not? It's going to take some serious beer (or whiskey) goggles to make this guy—or any guy, I'm starting to realize—look good tonight, and I really need someone to take my mind off you-know-who.

The bartender pours us a couple of kamikazes and we toss them back after clinking the shot glasses together. Inwardly I cringe at the sickeningly sweet mixture as it goes down, but free drinks are free drinks. Beggars can't be choosers and all that.

Blake hands me my second whiskey and soda, which I shoot down almost as quickly. Blake's only taken a few sips of his second cranberry vodka when I grab his hand, ignoring the clammy, limp-fish texture more easily this time. I can feel the alcohol thrumming through me, and I need some body-on-body contact to get rid of this yearning I have for a certain other, very hard, tattooed body. Someone whose hands have probably never been clammy in his life.

"Let's dance!" I yell.

The bar is filling up really fast, and people are feeling Jason's current mix.

Blake's eyes widen. I can tell he's not much of a dancer by the way he nervously glances back and forth between the crowd and me. I shake my hips provocatively. He slurps back the rest of his drink and follows me to the dance floor, where everyone is busy grinding to the seductive hip-hop beats Jason is currently spinning.

I was right. Blake is a terrible dancer. He rests his hands on my hips like dead weights and starts rubbing back and forth against my ass like he's were a pendulum on a clock, except with absolutely no rhythm. I pull away slightly so I can groove on my own to the music, but allow him to keeping touching me while I twist from side to side in slow, sinewy motions.

"Damn, you are so fucking hot," he breathes, turning me around and pulling my body close to his again. "You're like some gorgeous, exotic princess or something. Where are you from? Italy? Morocco? I dated a Persian girl once; she looked kind of like you. So hot."

Ugh, I hate it when these kinds of guys do this, start to play that stupid geography game just because I have dark hair and a bigger butt than your average Connecticut trust-funder. Like they all jerked off watching *Aladdin* too many times as kids, and now they want to sleep with Princess Jasmine. *What are you, what are you, what are you?* Never who. They want a label, not a person.

I cringe when he rubs his lips on the sensitive hollow above my collarbone. He wraps his hands around the small of my back and drifts his fingers lower to graze my backside. I shut my eyes and ignore him while we dance, but it's hard. He's hot and sweaty and hardly moving while plastered against my body. The song blends into another I don't like so much, so I take the opportunity to pull away, fanning myself. Blake doesn't seem put off, just grazes my body up and down with his eyes.

"Hey," he says as he grips my waist again.

His chapped lips linger too close to my ear, and I fight the urge to jerk away.

"Yeah?"

"So, my friends and I were planning to go to this other place a few blocks away to hear some music. You girls want to come?"

"Let's find out."

I turn on my heel, eager to get away from his clingy hands. Like a puppy, he follows close behind.

"Blake wants to go to another bar," I announce to everyone as we return to where our little group is sitting, with the exception of Shama, who has joined Jason in the DJ booth.

Quinn is currently deep in drunken conversation with her lanky investment banker, who seems to be more interested in her breasts than what she's saying, and Jamie has her tongue halfway down the throat of Blake's other friend. Jesus, we're a mess. These guys are gross, and we are being gross with them. The girls look up, their eyes glazed with alcohol.

"Where?" Quinn asks. Her eyes sharpen—she's always been good at handling her liquor. I can tell her brain is fighting her body. She's looking for a reason to stop.

"This place called AJ's," Blake volunteers. "It's just three blocks up Tenth. They usually do live music. The band tonight is this sick hip-hop group."

Quinn immediately narrows her eyes at me, but I just purse my lips and stare at the ceiling, like Blake didn't just name the exact club where the man I'm trying to forget works.

"I just want to hear some 'sick hip-hop,' Quinny," I whine.

Her lips twitch, and I can tell she's trying not to laugh. Jamie, unfortunately, doesn't have as good of a poker face.

"What's so funny?" Blake asks as both of my roommates start giggling like crazy.

"Nothing," I say, pulling on his arm. He wraps it around my waist like a dead snake. "They're just silly drunks. Before we go, maybe a couple more shots?"

———

"I just wanna see him," I tell Quinn as we're finishing the icy three-block walk to AJ's. "You said yourself, I look hot tonight. I want him to know just what he's leaving in New York."

My self-control has predictably collapsed after two more kamikazes, and it looks like Quinn's has too. Under normal circumstances, I might have expected her to play sister's keeper to my drunken idiot and hold me back from making stupid decisions when I'm intoxicated. The only problem is, we're all three sheets to the wind, and irresponsible behavior seems to be in the air. Shama stayed behind to make the moves on Jason in the DJ booth, leaving Jamie, Quinn, and me to meander happily to the bar that we all know I shouldn't be anywhere near. Even Jamie is letting her investment banker of the night manhandle her on the street in between texting her ex-boyfriend, the dickhead lawyer she dated all last year. We need a straight-minded intervention, but there's none to be had.

"You sure you're going to be okay?" asks Quinn as we turn the corner onto the street where AJ's is.

I can hear the bass reverberating down the block, and just ahead of us, Blake and his friends are raising their hands with excitement, doing some mock breakdancing moves. Christ, these guys are idiots. It's not even the right kind of music for that.

"When we've got guys with moves like that? How can I *not* be okay?"

We giggle helplessly as we watch our impromptu dates strutting up to the bar entrance, blocking the chair where the doorman sits. Which doorman is actually sitting there is still unclear. But it *is* Saturday night.

"Okay, babe." Quinn squeezes my arm. "Just be smart, okay? Remember he's a manipulative ass who just wants to fuck you and leave."

I nod as the boys turn to gesture toward us, handing the doorman thirty extra dollars for our cover. Quinn and Jamie's dates pull them into the bar and there, of course, is Nico. His deep eyes drill into me, then flash back to Blake, who has his clammy fish hand extended my way.

"You coming, sexy?" Blake asks with a leer. "I took care of your cover."

I glance down and realize that my coat is open and my revealing dress is on display. No wonder the walk was so cold. I've gone sans bra (the dress won't allow it), so the headlights are on full blast too.

I clap my coat closed instead of taking his hand. Blake winks at me in that irritating way that men do when they buy you something with the full expectation of reaping the benefits later. Damn, I really shouldn't have let him pay for all those drinks, and definitely not for the cover.

Nico seems to be of the same mind. He whips the ten-dollar bills back at Blake, who takes it, obviously confused.

"It's cool, man, she's a friend," Nico clarifies, now staring at me again. "How you doin', NYU?"

And now it's back to "NYU." I smart. He only seems to call me that when he thinks I'm acting...I don't know, really young. Privileged. Immature. Definitely nothing good.

"You know this guy, honey?" Blake says.

Nico's face blackens at the word "honey." I fight my own glare. I'm not sure this guy actually knows my name. But I nod, and Blake grins.

"Too bad, we could have all gotten in for free."

"Yeah," I mumble. "You go on in. I'm just going to say hi for a second."

"You sure, Lay?" Quinn is standing beside me, now staring drunk daggers in Nico's direction.

"Yeah, I'm sure."

I still haven't been able to stop looking at him, and his black eyes have been glued to mine since I spoke. Jamie whistles and follows her date inside with Blake. Quinn and her blond investment banker follow close behind, with Quinn singing "Fuck and Run" just loudly enough that Nico is sure to hear it.

"Balls to the pigeons, motherfucker," she hisses at him.

He jerks his head at her, but before he can reply, the door closes behind all of them, leaving the two of us alone in the cold.

"She's a real piece of work," Nico remarks.

I have to fight not to lick my lips. Even covered by his thick parka and beanie, he looks so damn good. Just like always.

There's no one else in line for the club; just the two of us on the street. His eyes soften as they fall back on me.

"Hey, beautiful."

Nico's voice is muffled slightly against the snow-covered ground, and even with the music pounding from the club, it feels like we are encompassed in silence.

"Hey," I murmur.

"You look gorgeous tonight, baby. I like your hair straight like that. And that dress...goddamn, baby. For real."

I glance down at my boots and dress, conscious again of the effort I put into everything tonight. I hadn't planned to come here. At least, not consciously.

"Thanks." I look back up again. "How's it going?"

He glances back as the doors to the club open, but relaxes when it's only a few patrons coming out for a smoke break.

He sighs. "Slow as fuck, actually. No one's out because of the snow, and my boss won't let me go until the band is gone. Grant—the bouncer on tonight—said he'd take over two hours ago, but the asshole said no. So, I'm stuck here freezing my dick off until last call." He rubs his hands together and blows out a long, steamy breath over his fingertips between leering up at me. "I don't suppose you want to keep me warm, do you, NYU?"

I start at that mega-watt smile, open and close my mouth a few times before I'm finally able to stutter, "Uh, n-no thanks."

"Too bad. So, you and Clark Kent, huh?"

I glance at the door and chuckle. Blake does kind of look like a skinny Clark Kent. If Clark Kent had facial hair that made you want to punch him.

"Um, yeah, I guess he's my date."

"I see. You move fast, baby."

I want to look away from Nico's sad expression, but somehow, I can't. And then the anger builds at his comment. Fuck this. He's the one leaving me. I'm just doing what I have to do here.

I flip my hair back over my shoulder. "Yeah. I do. I gotta get back to my date now."

I turn on my heel without waiting for his answer and flounce into the bar, leaving Nico and his puppy dog eyes to ponder *that* while he's outside in the cold.

––––

The next few hours seem like a fight as the effects of more alcohol seem to darken my mood even more as the night progresses. A fight to keep Blake's clammy hands off my ass, a fight to make sure Jamie and Quinn don't do anything inordinately stupid with their dates, a fight not to run back outside and throw myself at Nico. They're all fights I'm losing, and I'm at the point where I don't feel like I'm in control anymore. The band isn't terrible, but the club is a lot less crowded than it was the first time I was here. I feel on display every time Blake shoves his obvious erection against my leg in rhythm-less time to the music.

"Dude!" I say for the fifth time. "Some space, please!"

I haven't let him buy me any more drinks since we've arrived. I even bought a couple for him with money I don't really have in hopes of erasing the "you owe me" look in his eyes. So far, it hasn't been working.

"Come on, honey," he slobbers in my ear, tightening his grip on my ass. "You're so hot. I just want to dance with you."

He smells like vodka and sweat, and suddenly I want to get as far away from this dude as possible. I try to push him off me, but with little success as he only pulls me closer and goes in for a rubbery kiss.

"Dude, I said to fucking stop!" I shout, trying to be heard above the blare of the music.

Suddenly, Blake flies backward toward the bar, and a cool rush of air flows against my body as I'm left alone on the dance floor. Nico is standing over the prostrate form of my "date", fists clenched and eyes flashing murder. The bouncer—Grant, I presume—lugs up Blake and starts steering him toward the club entrance while Nico follows.

"What the fuck, man!" Blake protests, holding the back of his head while he stumbles along with Grant. "I wasn't doing anything wrong!"

"Get the fuck out of here."

The deep tenor of Nico's voice is menacing enough that it still carries through the club without yelling. He's not the biggest guy in the club—next to Grant's hulking form, he almost looks small—but between the tension radiating through his chest and the black expression that threatens violence to anyone who would cross him, he's definitely the scariest.

He turns to me, his eyes still flashing. "You." He stalks over to where I stand on the dance floor and takes my arm. "Get your coat. We're leaving."

"Get your own fucking coat," I spit, trying unsuccessfully to pull away. "I'm not going anywhere with you. You're not my man. You don't give a shit about me. Just 'fuck and run,' right? Well, I have friends here—"

"Your 'friends' left an hour ago with that douchebag's posse!" Nico thunders, his New York accent getting thicker with every word.

A few people stop dancing to watch the commotion.

"You're making a scene!" I hiss through clenched teeth.

"I don't give a shit." He scowls at our onlookers, and they immediately turn away. "My shift is up, and I'm not leaving you here by yourself. Get your fuckin' coat, Layla, because otherwise we're leaving without it, and you're just gonna have to freeze."

I stare at him for a solid ten seconds, but he doesn't blink, just keeps his stony grip on my arm until finally I relent.

"Fine!" I grit through my teeth. "Let's go."

CHAPTER TWENTY-FOUR

Nico

SHE'S LUCKY GRANT WAS THERE, IS ALL I CAN SAY. I'M STILL SHAKING AS I DRAG HER OVER to Tenth Avenue to catch a cab. I don't have any patience for the train tonight, and I sure as fuck can't deal with anymore slimy motherfuckers eye-fucking Layla in that underwear she calls a dress.

Fuck, this girl makes me feel out of control. *Fuck.*

Once we're safely in the cab, it doesn't take long for the stop and go rhythm of the engine to lull her to sleep against the car window. The driver gives me a knowing look, and I have to bite back the urge to tell him to mind his own fuckin' business. I haven't said a word since we left the club, and I'm still too pissed off to be nice.

But the anger wears off a little as we shoot up the Westside Highway. Asleep, Layla's lost that angry pout—the pout I put there. Her words ring in my mind. *Just fuck and run. You don't give a shit about me.*

No, I think. She's drunk. She doesn't really think that.

I'm so lost in my thoughts that I barely notice when the cab stops in front of my building. Layla is still asleep, so I pay the cabbie and walk around the other side to help her out.

"Come on, baby," I mutter, wrapping an arm around her waist and lifting her out of the car.

She wakes up and starts walking, but leans on me in her daze.

"Hey." She looks around drowsily. "This isn't my dorm."

"It's my apartment." I tug gently on her arm. "I didn't know if your friends took those other assholes home, and I don't want you there with them."

She looks equal parts tired and curious, but the anger is still gone. She lets me guide her into the building, and suddenly I'm self-conscious, seeing the old place with new eyes, the way she must see it. It's one of the prewar stone buildings that are all up and down the West Side, but far enough uptown that it's not in the greatest shape. I wonder what she thinks of the cracked black and white tiles of the lobby floor, the streaks of mold and cracks running up the walls, the splotchy graffiti tags on the elevator door. It isn't the worst-looking apartment building I've ever seen—not by a long shot—but it isn't exactly her posh dorm with the security guard.

I lead her into the tiny, fluorescent-lit elevator that barely fits the two of us, and she lets me tuck her hand in mine as I press the number four and close the accordion-style gate.

She wrinkles her nose. "It smells like pee in here, Nico."

I swallow back a sharp retort and just sigh. She's not wrong, but she sounds like a spoiled fuckin' princess. It's just another reminder of the miles of difference between us. At least this building even has a working elevator. We could be taking the stairs.

The elevator stops. I walk her onto my floor, which is only lit by the ghostly moonlight coming in through the windows. My landlord barely pays for the elevator maintenance. The cheap bastard would never shell out for hallway lights.

Layla follows me down the hallway over more cracked tiles until we reach the apartment marked 406.

"This is me," I say as I dig my keys out and unlock the door.

It's nothing to be proud of, although because of rent control and a shady landlord, my place is a lot bigger than you'd usually get for this price. Keeping Layla's hand in mine, I lead her down the very long, dark hallway that connects the two bedrooms, living room, and kitchen. It's kind of like what realtors call a "railroad" apartment, where all the rooms are lined up one on top of the other, one after another, except this one has the hallway down one side, and the rooms jut off.

I knock on lights as we go, gesturing silently at the kitchen, with its sink half full of dishes, the living room where I keep a faded plaid couch I picked up for free and my TV, and a third common room that I never use because it's full of Maggie's crap and a cot Gabe sometimes uses when he needs a break from our mom.

Layla follows me into the kitchen, where I open the fridge and pull out a beer for me and a bottle of water for her. She twists it open and takes several long, grateful pulls of the cold water. It's hypnotic, watching her lips on the bottle, sucking on it like that. It reminds me of something else she's sucked on before.

Goddammit, Nico. That is *not* where your mind should be.

She looks up and catches me staring. I swallow, then take the bottle from her and toss it into the bin by the sink before handing her another.

"Feel better?" I ask after she's done with the second.

Looking a lot more alert and a lot less drunk, she throws the second bottle in the recycling bin and straightens up.

"Yes," she says. "Thank you."

"So," I say.

"So."

I cross my arms. "What the fuck, Layla?"

She jerks her head up, blue eyes blazing. Ah, there's that anger again. "What's *that* supposed to mean?"

"It means what it means." I yank off my hat and shove it into my coat pocket, then run a hand through my hair, not caring if it stands up. "Let's see. I bring you food, and you ignore it like I don't fucking exist. You kiss me, then run off. So I leave you alone, just like you want. But knowing how I feel about you, you still decide to show up at my fucking place of work, blitzed out of your mind, and proceed to let some dude molest you on the dance floor right *fuckin'* in front of me!"

The memory is too much, and a torrent of Spanish escapes my mouth, causing Layla's eyes to widen and her mouth to drop, even though I doubt she knows what I'm saying. Sometimes English cuss words aren't enough.

Finally, I stop, out of breath, and glare at her. "I think that about covers it."

She shuts her mouth, then glares right back. "So?"

I gape, about to lose it all over again. "So? So, I don't deserve to see you being dry-humped right in front of me by some Opie-lookin' motherfucker who doesn't know when to stop! You shouldn't be doing that kind of shit with other guys, Layla!"

"You have *no* right to say that!" she retorts, finally starting to yell just as loudly as I am. "I don't know if you're dense or something, because you obviously haven't noticed the most obvious fucking thing! I don't give a shit about other guys, whether it's on the street or at a party or at a fucking bar. The only person I am currently interested in fucking or loving or doing anything else with right now, is you! And *you don't want me like that!*"

We stare at each other across the kitchen, chests heaving, both of us out of breath. Suddenly, I can't take it anymore. It's too hard. All of this with her is too fuckin' hard. Without thinking twice, I hurl my half-empty beer bottle into the sink, where it breaks with a nasty crash.

"Fuck!" I shout. "Do you ever fuckin' listen? Don't want you, Layla? I want you more than anything in the fuckin' world!"

I take two big steps across the kitchen so I'm all up in her space, nose to nose, surrounded by her scent of coconut and liquor while I back her against the counter.

"Don't want you?" I repeat through gritted teeth. Fuck, she smells good. I'm angry and hard all at once. How can I want someone who makes me this crazy? I take a long inhale. "One breath, and it's like I've never had oxygen. One look at your blue eyes, and water never existed. Fuck, Layla, I don't just want you. I *need* you."

We stand like this for a moment, nose to nose, just staring at each other, breathing the same air and each other's intoxicating scents. She gulps, frozen in place, even while her eyes start to water. What is she thinking? Was it too much? Should I have kept it to myself?

Too late. I'm all in now, for better or for worse. Because the second I saw this girl, I knew on some level she was it. Finally, I raise my hand slowly and run it through her hair, caressing the silky strands meditatively. She closes her eyes as if in pain and leans into my touch.

Stay. The word echoes through my head. That's all I have to do to fix this.

"You want me to stay, Layla?" I ask softly.

Her eyes blink open at my words, like she's unsure if I actually said them.

"I wouldn't do it for anyone else," I continue, my voice shaking with the effort of reining in my emotions. Something in my stomach drops, even while my heart thumps in my chest harder than it ever does at the gym. "You're killing me here, baby. Tell me what to do. You tell me to stay…I'll stay."

"Nico…" She stares at me like she's hypnotized.

And then I can't take it anymore. I can't stand being this close to her and not touch her everywhere. If she can't understand what I'm trying to say with my words, then I'll have to show her, any other way I know how.

"Come with me," I breathe, taking her hand in mine. It's strange. My hands are so much bigger than hers, but they still seem to fit. "Right now."

She lets me lead her out of the kitchen and down the hall, and I walk us into my bedroom at the end. I kick the door shut behind us, closing us in darkness lit only by the snow and the moonlight shining through my fire-escaped window. I yank her to me without another word.

Her lips find mine in the dark, and she devours my mouth, like I'm also the air she needs to live. I don't fight it. I can't anymore. I've got my hands around her waist, our bodies flush together, opening my mouth as wide as I can, urging her as deep as she can go. I also can't seem to get anywhere near as close as I need to be.

With a few quick yanks, I get her dress unzipped and over her head, leaving her standing in just her underwear and her boots, those boots that should be illegal. I want to take a moment to enjoy the beauty in front of me, this girl who looks like a piece of art to me. But I need her more than that, and so I pull her back against me, grinding anxiously while my tongue licks and twists, my teeth occasionally biting her lower lip, sucking on it like candy. I should leave her alone, I know. But she tastes better than anything in the world, and I'm a starving man.

"Don't think I want you?" I breathe in between kisses that are so sweet, yet still almost painful.

She's already wrenched off my coat and is pawing at my t-shirt. My hands grab at her ass, and I rub my cock into her through my jeans.

"Can you feel how I want you, baby? Can you feel that?"

She groans into my mouth, and the feel of it travels straight to my dick. I can't wait anymore. I need her, yesterday. And by the way she's ripping off my belt buckle and my jeans, she can't wait either.

I toss her roughly onto the bed so I can unzip her boots and drop them on the floor with the rest of her clothes. I tear off my clothes too, enjoying the way her gaze follows the lines of my muscles, the tattoos on my arms and chest. *Yeah, you like that, baby*. I smirk before I tackle her back onto the bed.

"I don't want to be nice anymore," I say against her throat. "You want me to fuck you, baby?"

A soft moan erupts from her throat as I move down her body, burying my nose in between her breasts, and inhale in their soft fullness. Does she ache like I ache? I want her so bad it hurts.

"Tell me," I demand, dragging my teeth over one nipple and then the other. I pull one into my mouth deeply, using my teeth enough that she arches with another excited moan. "You like that?" I ask before performing the same savage suck on the other side.

But she's lost her words, like she can't answer in anything but whimpers as I continue to torture each hardened nipple, using my free hand to massage one breast as I suckle the other. I'm torturing myself too. Because I know once I'm inside her, I'm not going to last more than a minute—that's how turned on I am right now.

"Tell me what you want." I sit up. I need to slow down, otherwise I'm going to lose it all over her.

I trace my palms down the sides of her body to finger the edges of her panties. I tug the sides part-way down her legs before pulling them back into place. One finger draws over the fabric down the center of her pussy, just over her clit before toying through the damp fabric with the place I *really* want to be. She wriggles against my touch. Fuck me, I'm still about to explode.

"You're wet again, baby," I whisper, entranced by what I'm doing as her hips writhe up to meet my finger, trying to pull it inside her, panties be damned. "Always so wet for me. Do you want me to touch you here?"

I brush again over that sensitive spot, and she moans again, louder this time.

"Yessss," she whimpers. "Please, Nico, I want you."

"I need to taste you first," I decide as I pull my hand away.

So I get rid of her underwear completely, leaving her naked. I graze my lips up her legs, twirling my tongue over the soft skin of her inner thighs before covering that hot, dark space between them. She shudders as my tongue touches her entrance, the tip of it flicking against the edges before dipping inside.

Jesus Christ Almighty. If heaven has a taste, this is it.

"Oh Jesus!" she cries out, reaching down to clasp my head. Her fingernails dig into my scalp. My tongue dives deeper.

Her insistence only turns me on more. I don't just want to make her come; I want to make her fucking shatter the same way she shatters me, inside and out. With a free hand, I pinch her clit softly and massage the sensitive nub, causing her to writhe even more as I continue to lap at her like I can't get enough. She's a flavor I've never had and craved all my life. I'll never get enough of her. Never.

I continue to tease her, rubbing her clit and fucking her with my tongue until all at once, her entire body convulses, her thighs clenching around my head as the waves of one orgasm and then another match the rhythm of my fingers.

"Nico," she whimpers as the waves have passed. I sit up and wipe my mouth with my arm, but she pulls me back down to her.

"Fuck me, please!" she begs. "Fuck me hard, now!"

I kiss her roughly, and she moans again in my mouth. I can still taste her on my lip —can she taste herself? The fuck if it doesn't turn me on even more.

"I need you," she whimpers as her teeth nip at my tongue and she sucks roughly on my lips.

Without speaking, I scramble out of my underwear. I grab a condom from the bedside table and rip it open with a fever while Layla watches, blue eyes blazing in the striped light of the moon through the blinds.

"That's right, baby," I mutter as I slide on the latex. "Beg for it. You want it bad, don't you?"

She stares up at me, completely enthralled as I cover her with my body. She's soaking wet and ready for me.

"You want it, Layla?" I ask again before pulling her lower lip in between mine. I bite down just a bit. I can tell it hurts a little, but I can also tell she likes it.

"Yes," she mumbles when I finally release her lip.

I slide in just an inch or so, then pull back out. Looks like I'm feeling masochistic tonight. This is as much torture for me as it is for her.

But I can't stop. She wanted to toy with me. Now I want to toy with her.

"What was that, baby? I couldn't quite hear you."

In again, just a little, and right back out.

"I want it," she says louder, trying in vain to lift her hips to pull me inside. But I don't let her, I just keep making enough friction to get her even wetter, even more ready for me. Because when I take her, I know I won't be gentle. When I take her, it's going to rock both of us to the core.

"What was that?" I ask again. "Tell me, Layla! I need to hear it!"

"Fine, fine, *fine*! I want you, okay! I lo—I want you so fucking bad!"

"FUCK!" I shout.

With both hands, I flip her onto her stomach and haul her hips up so I can slam into her with everything I have. With one harsh thrust, I enter with enough force that she barks at the intrusion. She's tight. I'm hard. Together we're dynamite.

"God, Nico," she groans as I pound into her, picking up the pace to generate that incredible friction we make together.

Fuuuuck me, it's too much, it's just too fucking much. I can feel her tightening around me as the tension inside her rises again. Twice in a row is not something that happens a lot, at least not to most of the girls I've known. But I know I'm rubbing the right spot, particularly as she angles her hips down to receive me deeper, feel me more intensely.

"You wanna come again, baby?" I ask, dipping my head down to nip at the edge of her ear.

She likes it—she likes my animal side, the side that bites and nips at her like the dog I am. I'm following my instincts now, and as I sit up, taking a handful of her full, luscious ass, watching my cock moving between her legs, my hand reaches back and then lands with a crack on her cheek.

"Ah!"

She jumps while I take handfuls of her flesh as I pound away. I want her to feel me everywhere. I want her to know without a doubt that no one else will ever do this to her like this. That nothing else compares to what we are together. And fuck if I don't want to punish her—and myself—for trying to forget it.

"Goddamn, baby," I grunt. I'm starting to lose control.

I spank her again—I can't help it—just hard enough to make her cry out for more. But I'm not going to last much longer. This is too much, even for me.

So I slide my hand under her stomach to play with her clit again, to push her over the edge so I can fall right with her. Every part of my body feels like it's expanding as she grips the edges of the mattress, taking every slap of our bodies, every twitch of my fingers, all driving us closer, closer.

"Shit, Nico, I think I'm going to come," she cries over her shoulder. Her words are barely understandable. She's so close; I just need to hold on...come on, hold on, Nico.

"Wait for me, baby," I order, my breath and voice obviously ragged, like I'm running a marathon. "Just. A. Little. Bit. More!"

I crash into her two, three, four more times before I can feel her seize around me. On the fifth thrust, she starts to shake, unable to keep herself together any longer. She cries out a long stream of insensible words. And then we both fall completely apart, careening loudly into a void where neither of us knows our names. We only know each other.

CHAPTER TWENTY-FIVE

Layla

Sᴀʀᴘ ʀᴀʏꜱ ᴏꜰ ʟɪɢʜᴛ ꜱʜɪɴᴇ ᴅɪʀᴇᴄᴛʟʏ ɪɴ ᴍʏ ᴇʏᴇꜱ ᴛʜʀᴏᴜɢʜ ᴄʜᴇᴀᴘ ʙʟɪɴᴅꜱ ᴏᴠᴇʀ ᴛʜᴇ single window in the bedroom. It takes me a second to remember where I am. To take in the unfamiliar sights, unfamiliar smells. But I have no problem remembering this very familiar touch.

Nico himself is wrapped completely around me, one big arm draped across my waist and one muscled leg thrown over both of mine. He holds me tightly as he sleeps, head burrowed into the crook between my shoulder and neck. I'm his own personal teddy bear. A quick glance at the alarm clock on the nightstand tells me it's just after six-thirty in the morning.

I'm in his apartment. Not his friend's fancy digs, but where he actually lives. Sleep and hangover fade away as curiosity takes over. Without moving, I look around the room, absorbing the place that Nico calls home.

It's a small, simple room painted white. It smells like dust and, well, sex, obviously from last night. A beat-up wood wardrobe stands next to the door, with a small green armchair in the corner next to it. The futon bed we're lying on is shoved in the opposite corner. It occurs to me that Nico has spent most of his life on futons or couches. I wonder if he's ever owned a real mattress.

The single window looks out to the side of a neighboring building with a peek-aboo view of the Hudson, and under it is a small desk on which are scattered a few bills, a pamphlet for the California State Driver's Test, and a large black sketchbook that has seen better days. The walls are bare except for a couple of tribal masks hanging above the bed and a framed picture on the window sill of what looks like Nico and his family members.

There are a few pieces of laundry strewn around the floor—a pair of shoes kicked off under the desk, a t-shirt or pair of shorts crumpled in the corner—but for the most part, Nico seems to keep his things in order, primarily by not having much to order in the first place. It's an austere existence, and I find myself wondering if he's been living in this place long. I'm also somewhat comforted by the fact that there appear to be absolutely no remnants of female visitors in the room—not a spare hairband on the desk, no random bobby pins in the corners. It's the room of a man who spends his time here alone.

It's then that the memories of the night before come flooding back, enhanced by a distinct soreness between my legs and on my ass. He's insatiable, and he brings it out in me too. There's a faint throb as I recall just how Nico's mouth felt down there, how hard he claimed me as his own.

So much for getting over him. So much for a clean break. Now I'm right back to where I was a week ago, and my heart sinks down to the lobby at the realization. No. I'm not going to let this happen again. I'm not going to pretend to myself that everything is going to be all right when I know that he'll just break my heart.

Very, very slowly, I unwind his arm and leg. He snorts and rolls to the other side of the bed, freeing me to look for my underwear, which was tossed somewhere at some point during the night. I find them slung over the small lamp sitting on the nightstand beside the bed.

My fingers brush the edge of the sketchbook. I'm tempted to look inside. But I don't want to snoop, and I'm sure whatever he's drawn in there is intensely personal. Not to mention, it would only make me that much more invested when I'm trying to detach all over again.

There are five text messages from my roommates and four missed calls from Quinn alone. Apparently, I set my cell phone on silent when I was sick and forgot to take it off. I scroll through the text messages to see what terror I've caused.

Quinn (1:31 AM): We r going home. U ok?

Jamie (1:53 AM): Home now. U all right? Pls call quinn shes worried.

Quinn (2:44 AM): Layla where r u?? alan said blake left w o u!!

Quinn (3:05 AM): trying 2 call pls pick up girl!!

Shama: (3:30 AM): Srsly u need 2 call Quinn she is going insane. What happened last night?

Quinn (3:45 AM): OMG LAYLA IF I DON'T HEAR FROM U BY 2MORROW MORNING IM GOING 2 CALL THE COPS!

I glance back at Nico, who is now snoring audibly, and gingerly stand up from the bed. A stack of folded t-shirts sits on the armchair, so I grab one, slip it on, and tiptoe out of the room and into the kitchen, hoping to God his sister is an early riser.

Once I'm safe in the living room, I dial Quinn's number. It goes to her voicemail, and I leave a hushed message letting her know where I am and that I'm safe.

"Don't worry!" I whisper before hanging up.

When I creep back into the bedroom, Nico is lying on his back, blinking up at the ceiling. He glances at me and smiles gently. *There it is*, I think as my knees tremble. That smile. My fucking kryptonite.

"Hey." Nico sits up. The blankets fall down, revealing the expanse of his defined chest and a few tiers of mouth-watering abs that point to exactly nothing underneath the thin fabric. "I thought maybe you'd left."

I shake my head. "No. But I should get going."

I sit on the edge of the bed and tug off his t-shirt so I'll be able to pull on my dress, which I struggle to turn the right-side back out after I find it on the floor. Behind me, the sheets rustle. Nico's legs slide to either side of me as he wraps his arms around my naked torso, pulling me close. The feel of his smooth, warm skin against my back is enough to make me arch my neck, welcoming the feel of his body around me. How, *how* am I going to walk away from this again?

"I meant what I said," he murmurs against my shoulder.

I freeze in his arms, and then crane my head around to look back at him. "Yeah?"

Honestly, I'm not sure what he means. We both said a lot of things last night. And did a lot of things.

He meets my gaze, unblinking and without a trace of guile. "Yeah. I need you, Layla."

Slowly the fear and anxiety over losing him seeps out of my body, replaced with relief and elation. I should have known I couldn't fight this. I couldn't really ever say no to him. And apparently, by some miracle…he can't say no to me either.

I twist around to straddle him.

"Yeah?" I ask again, stamping a kiss on his mouth. "Yeah?"

I give another, and then another, and giggle as he flips me onto my back and pummels my neck and shoulders with kisses every time I ask "Yeah?"

Finally, Nico stops, hovering over my face so we are nose to nose.

"You sure you want to be with a big fuckin' loser like me, Layla?" he asks softly.

The doubt on his handsome face just about breaks my heart. I want to tell him he's not a loser, that he's determined and honest and honorable and dedicated. I want to tell him he's one of the best people I've ever met. I want to tell him that all he has to do is touch me and my entire being, mind, body, spirit, all come alight. But instead I just lift my head to kiss him lightly.

"Yeah," I say as I fall back on the pillow. "I do."

"Then I'll stay," he says. He touches his forehead to mine. "I'll stay for you."

Before I can take a second to comprehend what he just said, Nico gives me another drowsy kiss, this one long and thorough. Then he rolls onto his back and pulls me securely into the crook of his shoulder with my head resting on his chest. Together we sigh, long and content. This is where I belong.

"What is this?" I ask as I play over the tattooed symbols over his heart. "Is it a clock or something?"

Nico doesn't move his head, but his other hand falls over mine, stilling it on his chest.

"It's a compass."

"A compass?" I blink. It's…confusing. "Are you secretly a sailor? Do you take to the Hudson at night, like a weird nautical superhero?"

Nico snorts. "Yeah, *no*. But I bet you'd like to see me in tights, wouldn't you, NYU?"

I punch him lightly in the side. "Seriously. What is it?"

He sighs. "Um…well…you know I was incarcerated for a while…"

"You were in juvenile detention," I correct him. "That's not the same thing."

He unravels his arms and lies on his side so we're facing each other. His eyes are dark and solemn.

"Baby, jail's jail. They just call it something different when you're under eighteen." He weaves his fingers with mine and continues his story.

"I was sent to Tryon when I was fifteen, like I told you. It's about two hours from here, outside of Albany, middle of fuckin' nowhere. You hear gunshots during the day instead of at night because of all the deer hunters. It's a big property with bunkhouses, a main hall, classrooms, all of it surrounded by a nice razor-wire fence."

Nico watches as he rubs his thumb over my knuckles, but I know right now he doesn't see the way our hands fit. He's lost in another place.

"They dictated everything to us. Uniforms. How many books we could have in our rooms. Where to keep our fuckin' underwear." He scowls. "We couldn't go anywhere without being watched by the guards. Up at seven, brush our teeth, wash our face, take a piss. All with some dude watching.

"Everyone was angry. Everyone there was fucked up, drugged up. A lot of fights. A lot of lockdowns. There was a kid in my bunkhouse who once swallowed screws that he tore out of the furniture with his fingernails. That's how bad he wanted out of there."

I don't say anything now, just listen in shock. I don't know what I'd been expecting, but it wasn't this. Nico just plows on.

"I was there for over a year and a half," he says softly. "I didn't see my mom or my brother or sisters—they couldn't—well, they couldn't visit. K.C. came a couple of times, but that was it."

Still I stay quiet. There's something I'm missing here, but I don't want to pry. Not when he's already opening up. But what would keep a mother from visiting her child for almost two years?

"Anyway," Nico says, "before I left, I had this teacher, Ms. Alvarez. She knew what I'd done—everyone knew, because everyone did it. I wasn't the first one to knock over a bodega too many times. I wasn't the first one whose family couldn't get food stamps because their moms were undocumented."

He looks straight at me for a second, checking for my reaction at that revelation about his mother. I do whatever I can not to move a muscle.

"Gabe was just six, you know. Six-year-olds eat a lot."

"I bet they do," I say softly.

Suddenly, things make sense. Why he and his family would be crowded into a one-bedroom apartment. Why at just nineteen, he had to support his siblings. Why his mother wouldn't be able to visit her son at a detention center, a place that would almost certainly require identification.

"Wait," I interrupt my own thoughts. "When you were released, who did the state give custody to? You were a minor, right?"

Nico swallows and nods. "Remember how I told you that K.C.'s mom and mine are tight?"

I nod.

He shrugs. "They grew up together. *Tía* was our legal guardian until I could take over. And I wasn't allowed to do that until I got the FedEx job." Under my cheek, I can feel his body tighten. "Fucked up, huh?"

I frown. Something wasn't adding up. "I thought you said your mom was from Puerto Rico. That would make her a U.S. citizen, wouldn't it?"

Nico sighs and runs a hand over his head. "She is from Puerto Rico. But she was born in Cuba. Her parents fled when Castro came into power and she ended up in San Juan. I—honestly, Layla, I don't know the whole story. I don't even know how she got here, only that she followed Alba, K.C.'s mom. My mother's had a hard life, running from place to place, trying to find some place that's better. She doesn't really like to talk about the details."

It doesn't take much for me to piece the rest together. A woman who's lived her life on the run, taking shelter where she was able. How much she must have been taken advantage of because of her status. Four kids from three different fathers. A part of me wonders what the story is there. How many of those men promised to help her with citizenship only to leave her when it got hard.

"She could get amnesty," I pipe up. "There's got to be some kind of asylum she can claim because of the Castro regime. You and your siblings could sponsor her. There's no *way* they'd make her leave her entire family." I sit up, suddenly full of energy.

But Nico just chews on his lip. "I—Layla, you think I haven't looked into that before?" He shakes his head. "Lawyers cost money, baby. Money we don't have. And Ma...she's too scared. You don't know, baby. What do you think happens every time one of the buildings in our neighborhood gets torn down so fat cats can build a new high-rise? ICE, baby. Immigrations fuckers are *everywhere*, and a lot of times, they look just like me."

He pulls me back down on his chest before I can say something else. I open my mouth, full of arguments, but then realize I don't know nearly enough about this issue to make any of them. This isn't a fear my family has ever had. My father has been a naturalized citizen since I was a little kid. He's only ever been in this country legally.

"Anyway," Nico pivots away from his mother. "Ms. Alvarez came to see me before I left for Tryon. She was my English teacher, but she always used to catch me doodling on the scrap paper she gave the class—for notes, since a lot of us couldn't afford notebooks and school supplies. So, she brought me a sketchbook to take with me. She said people get lost in places like Tryon, and I would need to keep track of myself in there to find my true north. Especially so that when I came back to my ma, I'd still be her Nico." He chuckles slightly and squeezes my fingers. "Corny, huh?"

I don't laugh at all.

"No," I say as I study the compass on his chest more closely. Up close, I can see that the edges are done with a design that looks something like a barbed wire. "I don't think that's corny at all."

Nico shrugs, the action causing the tattoos to ripple.

"Well, corny or not, she was right," he says. "I went in there one way and came out another. But when the other kids were fighting or goading the guards, getting doped up by aides or locked up in solitary, I just drew. I wasn't good at it or anything, but it kept me focused. I drew my family and my friends. Things that reminded me of home and where I came from. I drew the places I wanted to go in my life, the things I wanted to see or do. And I drew this and had it put over my heart after I finally got out."

"True north," I murmur, sliding my fingers over the big compass as wide as my hand that's inked over his chest. "Did you find it?"

Nico gives me a small, sweet smile as he pushes some hair out of my face.

"Not yet, Layla," he says in a voice so low I can barely hear its vibration. "But I have faith."

We stare at each other, caught for a minute in a trance. Then Nico sighs and pulls me close again.

"Come on, baby, let's go back to sleep. It's too damn early to be up on our day off."

"What if I'm not tired?" I ask playfully, jabbing him in the side with my fingers.

That gets me flopped on my back again, with Nico peering at me from above. Gone is the melancholy man, and back is that mischievous boy who has stolen my heart. Nico's still a thief, just of a different sort.

"Oh, I could probably find ways to tire you out again, NYU," he says with a sly grin, and proceeds to show me just how.

CHAPTER TWENTY-SIX

Nico

"So where is your sister?" Layla asks sometime around one in the afternoon.

It's been hours of sleeping, fucking, sleeping, fucking. No, that's wrong. I feel like a pussy saying "making love," but this hasn't been just sex. If I'm being honest, it's never just sex with Layla. I'm going to have to get used to that.

So, we're only a little bit closer to making it out of the bedroom for the day than we were at seven this morning. I ran into the kitchen a couple of times to grab us whatever food I had left in the house. Leftover rice and beans probably isn't the most nutritious thing I could have given Layla, but it tastes damn good after the workout we've had. Now, though, we've both had our fills of salty leftovers, so we've decided to grab some sandwiches at the diner on the corner before I have to put Layla on a train back to Chinatown. She needs to study, and I am not going to get in the way of my baby's future. No fuckin' way.

I shrug on a black hoodie over a t-shirt and jeans while Layla pulls on her dress from last night. Fucking hell. Her coat only goes to her hips, and with those boots, she's going to earn a whistle from every motherfucker on the block. Suddenly, the idea of making her ride the train alone sounds absolutely terrible.

I whistle at her anyway.

She blushes, then scowls. "Shut up."

She throws a pillow at me. I parry it away and pull her flush against me. All of a sudden, I'm starving all over again, and not for food.

"That dress should be burned," I say as I nibble on her ear. "You have no idea how your ass looks in that thing. It makes me want to do very, very dirty things to you, Ms. Barros."

"You have a thing for asses, don't you?" she asks as I nuzzle deeper into her neck.

In response, my hands drift down to grab that exact part of her body, and she squeaks loudly.

"Maybe a little," I say with a chuckle. "But yours takes the motherfuckin' cake, baby."

I squeeze her again before letting go, shaking my head. I'm a little scared to walk outside with her, you wanna know the truth. She has no idea as she ties up her hair into a knot on top of her head and checks herself in the mirror next to my door. She could stop traffic without batting an eyelash. In this neighborhood, a girl like Layla is every guy's wet dream.

"Seriously, though," she says. "Did we wake anyone up last night? Or today, for that matter?"

I shake my head again before putting on my Yankees cap backward. "No, sweetie, there's no one here but us. My sister's back with her boyfriend, so her room is empty right now."

"How often does she come?"

I pick up my clothes off the floor and toss them into the basket next to the armchair. Sitting down on the bed, I start putting on my black Adidas sneakers. "Maggie and Jimmy—that's Allie's dad—are kind of...well, they have a hard time with self-control, let's just put it that way. They try to make it work for Allie's sake, but sometimes she needs a break. So I keep the room empty for them."

I don't tell her that it's because I'm pretty sure one day Jimmy is going to get locked up himself again. I don't have proof of it, but I've seen my sister applying thick makeup to her cheek or eyebrows one too many times. I've talked to her enough times to be told to fuck off, but we grew up with too many of our mom's shitty boyfriends not to know the signs of an abusive relationship. One day I hope she and Allie will just come to stay. I wouldn't mind. Jimmy wants to question that, he can talk to me. Or my fist.

Layla watches me like she's trying to figure something out, then just goes back to putting on her coat.

"How old is your niece?" she asks.

I look up. "Allie's three."

"What's Allie short for?"

"Alejandra, actually," I clarify with the correct Spanish pronunciation. "But that's way too serious a name for a baby, you know? So we call her Allie."

Layla smiles. "That's cute. I hope I can meet her one day."

I smile back, and then I shake my head. Whoa. The idea of Layla holding a little black-haired baby sounds *way* too good to me. You are twenty-six, Nico. She is nineteen. You are both way too young to be thinking about kids.

"How can you afford this apartment by yourself?" Layla interrupts me. "It's huge."

I look around, trying to see what she sees. My place isn't that nice, but it is pretty big as far as New York apartments go, which is why I've never moved. I forget that until I go into the rat traps that pass as studios these days. Even though I'm not in one of the ritzier areas of the island, this is still Manhattan, which is crazy expensive. So when K.C.'s cousin left the city and offered his lease to me, I jumped. Getting a rent-controlled apartment in Manhattan is like winning the lottery.

I finish tying my shoes, stand up, and grab my leather jacket off the back of my desk chair. Then I grin. "Rent control, baby." I grab Layla's hand. "Come on, let's get you something to eat."

―――

Layla

We walk a few blocks over to Broadway, and it's then I realize just how far uptown we are. The street sign on the corner reads "W 138th Street: Dominican City." Looking around, I see immediately that this is a completely different world than the streets of lower Manhattan. The buildings, most of them brick apartments and brownstones like the rest of the island, are clearly not as well maintained as in the more affluent and predominantly white neighborhoods below 95th Street. Sprawling stains and graffiti mark up several buildings and their ragged awnings; laundry hangs out to dry from more than one window, even in this cold.

A few blocks from City College, this section of Broadway bustles with a completely different energy, particularly since ninety percent of the voices I hear speak Spanish. About half of the signs on the local businesses, which at first glance include a couple of bodegas, tchotchke shops, a laundromat, and a bunch of restaurants, are written in Spanish as well, and most of the people passing us on the street look like they are either completely or part Hispanic.

We pass a group of girls chatting loudly in a mix of Spanish and English. They are loud and jovial, expansive with slicked bangs, long acrylic nails, gold monogram necklaces. One catches my eyes for a split second before she yells "*Coño!*" and launches into a tirade in Spanish that I can't understand. So very different from the contained mannerisms of my father's wealthy family in Brazil and my mom's in Washington.

We pass another small group of men lounging on the steps of a building next to a Dominican restaurant. One wears a bandana tied around his forehead, and another fiddles with the ends of a set of cornrows. They can't be older than me—as evidenced by their hairless faces that make them look more innocent than they probably want. Bandana catches me looking at him and nods with a smile.

"Hey ma," he jeers, flashing a set of bright white teeth.

It's hardly the first catcall I've received in New York. But for some reason I'm more put off than normal by it. Maybe it's because I already feel like I stick out in this neighborhood, but I don't like the way the man's eyes peruse me like a piece of meat he's thinking about buying.

Nico shoots Bandana a dirty look and grabs my hand, which effectively shuts the guy up. It's like an unspoken code: don't check out another dude's woman when he's standing right there—not unless you want trouble.

At that thought, a small thrill runs up my spine. Apparently, now I'm Nico's woman. I like the idea. A lot.

Nico tows me to a diner near the subway entrance on the corner of 137th and holds the door open as we enter. It's a long, thin space, with a counter on one side where singles eat, and several small tables against the opposite wall all the way to the back. The white, linoleum-tiled floors are as grimy as the large man flipping burgers behind the counter, and the smell of frying potatoes and sizzling meat is dense in the air.

I follow Nico to a small table in the back, and we are followed by a waitress clearly from the neighborhood, if the length of her fingernails and curly black hair are any indication.

She rattles off a few questions in Spanish to Nico, either because she recognizes him or just assumes he speaks Spanish. Nico doesn't even look at the menu, just grins at the waitress and rattles off a ridiculously fast answer in response, causing the girl to giggle. Mid-order, he interrupts himself in English, looking at me.

"Oh, baby, you like steak, right?"

I raise an eyebrow. "Dude. I'm Brazilian. We practically live on barbecue."

That earns me another heart-stopping grin before he turns back to the waitress and finishes our orders. She picks up our menus and struts away in her high tops, but not before she gives me a sharp, suspicious glare.

"What, I don't even get to pick out my own food now?" I joke.

Nico reaches across the table and picks up my hand, swirling his thumb across the lines of my palm. It's amazing how such a simple touch makes me want to drag him out of the restaurant and back to his bedroom. If my lady parts didn't need a serious rest, I probably would.

"Sorry," he admits with another sly smile. "But there's really only one thing to order here. They make the best cheese steak outside of Philly."

I'm really going to have to hit the gym hard tonight. First gobs of heavy beans and rice for breakfast, and now a greasy sandwich for lunch. I haven't worked out all week, and I'm already hitting my calorie limit before my day is halfway over.

"So...I didn't realize you speak Spanish so well," I venture. I don't want to say it directly, but it's kind of intimidating. He mentioned it before, and I've definitely heard him curse in it, but he speaks it like it's his native language.

"What? *Sí, sí, lo hablo*," he confirms with another cheeky smile. "Of course I do. My mom doesn't speak much English, baby. Spanish is my first language."

That surprises me. Of course she speaks Spanish—I should have already realized that. But she must have lived in the states for, well, close to thirty years if she had Nico here. How could you live in a place for that long and not learn the language?

"Wait," I say. "I have a question. If you're mom is from Cuba, doesn't that make you Cuban, not Puerto Rican?"

Nico glances around and then gives me a funny look. "Ah, I don't know, you want to know the truth. I mean...she grew up in Puerto Rico, lived there since she was two. Ethnically, there's not that much of a difference. Culturally, that's all she knows. It's how she talks, in the food she likes, in everything about her. She calls herself *boricua*, even though there are plenty who would say she's not." He shrugs. "My dad's part Puerto Rican too. I think that qualifies me." He taps his fingers on the table. "Are you any less American because your dad's from Brazil?"

I frown. It's not quite the same thing, but I see what he's saying. I don't really feel as American as a lot of the white kids whose families have been here for centuries. But Nico's words remind me more of Brazil, which, much like the United States, is a country full of immigrants, stemming back hundreds of years, all mixed with indigenous groups too (some more than others). Most of my dad's family only came to Brazil following World War II, over from Italy like a lot of other wealthy families. But they wouldn't call themselves Italian. Not anymore.

"What about you?" Nico interrupts my train of thought. "Don't you understand any Spanish? It's pretty close to Portuguese, right?"

I shake my head. "My parents didn't speak Portuguese at home, remember? I picked up a few words when we visited Brazil, but I don't speak it that well. And my dad wanted me to take French instead of Spanish in school. He thought it was more civiliz—"

The word's halfway out before I can censor myself completely. I clap my hands across my mouth, but Nico looks at me knowingly.

"More civilized than Spanish?" he asks, suddenly preoccupied with stirring the straw around in his water. When he looks up, his eyes are dark and searching.

My face flushes. "*I* don't think that," I say. "My dad...shit. I'm sorry. My dad can be kind of an asshole."

But Nico just shakes his head. "Don't worry about it, baby. I get it. He's just looking out for you."

I frown. "What do you mean?"

Nico raises one brow, like he's surprised I don't understand. "Layla, a lot of immigrants don't want their kids to learn English like a second language. And if their kids can pass as white, even better. They think it makes their lives are just easier." He shrugs, like it makes perfect sense.

I think about my dad, about how he's always cursing his accent, which he can never quite get rid of. How he would always refuse to teach me Portuguese when I was little, no matter how many times I asked. The way he won't let anyone call him or me Latino, unless it's on a college application.

You're not like them, he'll so often say when we pass people with darker skin, who look like they might be Mexican or South American. *Why would you even want to be?*

I look at Nico. He's so beautiful, it makes my chest hurt. Like me, like so many people in this city, he comes from a mix of ethnicities—Cuban, Puerto Rican, Italian, maybe more. But his skin is too dark for anyone to confuse him with a white man. I can't deny that it's probably put him at a disadvantage that I've never felt because of the way I look.

But at the same time...I envy him. Even with the complex cultural background he claims, he knows who and what he is. That's a knowledge that feels like it's been kept from me my whole life.

"Would you do it?" I ask. "Keep your kids from learning Spanish?"

He looks up in surprise. "Of course not. I love my culture. I wouldn't want them to lose out on knowing that side of themselves."

He watches me for a moment, but I look away first, out the window.

"I wouldn't want that either," I murmur softly.

On the street, more groups of kids walk past, chattering loudly in a patois of Spanish, English, and what sounds like bits of Creole thrown in there. They look so comfortable with each other, speaking languages that wouldn't be considered legitimate by anyone else but the people who live in this small corner of New York. And yet...they are languages, nonetheless.

"There's a good Brazilian barbecue place in midtown," Nico jerks me out of my thoughts once again. "We should go there sometime."

He's looking at me with a kind expression. I wonder for a moment if he can read my thoughts.

"Are you talking about Marcio's?"

"Yeah, you been there?"

I nod. "Yeah, my dad and I went when I started school. It was okay. They didn't really have very good side dishes, and that's the best part. No *farofa* or beans or anything. It was just meat and a salad bar."

Nico furrows his brow, and I'm taken by how adorable his face becomes when he's confused. He usually looks so sure of himself, his dark features lightened by the constant smile and laughter he's never afraid to display. He twists his full lips around as he ponders my remark.

"What's fa-dow-fa?" he asks in a poor imitation of my accent.

I almost laugh, he's so damn cute trying to pronounce a Brazilian word.

"*Farofa* is a side dish made of ground yucca. It's usually cooked with things like pork rinds and egg and beans. Salty and so good. But most Brazilian places in the US don't ever have it. Actually, the best barbecue I've had in the US is in Boston—they have a pretty big Brazilian community up there. We went there to look at schools when I was applying, and my dad and I went out for *churrasco*. Not as good as in Brazil, but not bad."

All this talk of barbecue makes my stomach growl, and it's right then that the waitress returns with our food—two massive steak sandwiches in toasted hoagies, piled with thinly sliced French fries on the side. She also sets down two sodas with a lightning-fast comment to Nico, who replies in kind with what must be a big, booming joke. His bright smile and deep voice has her in giggles, and as she shuffles off, I catch her glancing back at him in a way that doesn't hide her attraction. I sigh; I think I'm going to have to get used to that. I also think I'm going to have to learn Spanish.

I look back at my food and take a sip of the soda. At the taste, I raise an eyebrow.

"Ginger ale?"

"Hangover," he says through a mouthful of sandwich. "Thought you could use it."

"I don't have a—" I start to say, but stop when I realize he actually called that one correctly.

As giddy as I am about being with my new man today—not to mention the fact that he is going to stay my man until further notice—my head is undeniably foggy in the aftereffects of too much to drink last night and not enough sleep. I look down at my sandwich and realize the best thing I can do is eat, if only to soak up the remnants of the alcohol still in my system.

"Wait, baby, hold on." He brushes my hands off the sandwich and takes off the top of the hoagie so he can press a handful of French fries on top before replacing the bread. "You gotta eat it like that. That's how everybody eats 'em here. It's the best. Trust me, NYU."

Gingerly, I hold the now stuffed sandwich up and take a small bite, and then a bigger one.

"Well?" Nico's expressive features are wide, eager to see what I think.

I grin. "Dude. That is *really* good."

"Ha, HA!" He laughs, slapping the tabletop. "Didn't I tell you, baby?"

I feel somehow like my ability to enjoy this sandwich is a test of some sort, which I just passed with flying colors. I am triumphant.

We drink our ginger ales and polish off the rest of our sandwiches, with Nico eating the last third of mine. I can eat a lot, but it was way too much, even for me. He drops some cash on the table to pay for the meal, waving away my efforts to split the tab with him.

Nico walks me to the subway station and waits with me just outside the turnstiles for the train. People pass us on their way downtown. People who look like him, and people who look like me too. Sort of.

"Well, NYU, what do you think?"

He hooks his thumbs in the pockets of my coat and pulls me close, so we are almost forehead to forehead, allowing me to look into those gorgeous chocolate eyes of his. This close, I can see that they have small flecks of gold that glisten under the lights of the station. Nico smiles, but I see a hint of trepidation. He's waiting for something, but I don't know what.

"What do I think about what?"

Unnerved myself now, I lick my lips, which are still salty from the sandwich. Nico's gaze follows the motion, then snaps back up.

"Here. My neighborhood. My place. You think you wouldn't mind visiting me up here in the ghetto?"

Oh. He's worried I might feel his neighborhood isn't good enough. Guilt floods through me. Sure, I feel a little out of place here, but that has nothing to do with the economic class of the neighborhood. To begin with, Dominican City is hardly a slum; it's just middle-class New York. It's a million miles from Seattle suburbs, but that's exactly why I like it here.

"Please," I say with a snort and a light slap on his chest. "You and I both know this is the last thing from a ghetto. Plus, that sandwich alone is enough reason for me to come back."

That earns me a quick laugh, and he gives me a thorough, relieved kiss, slipping a little tongue in there for good measure and a mischievous squeeze of his favorite part of my anatomy.

We hear the train approaching with a groan down the track, so Nico gives me one more quick kiss before turning to go. I don't want to leave, but I'm dying to change out of this dress, and I really need to get some homework done. And maybe take a quick nap.

"I'll see you tomorrow, beautiful. Go study," he rumbles in my ear, and I swear the vibration I feel is from more than just the train.

I pass through the turnstile and into the waiting car. Through the scratched window, I smile as Nico blows me a kiss. Then he turns back up the stairs to the neighborhood that he navigates with such ease and comfort. And I go back to my neighborhood, where I may or may not belong.

CHAPTER TWENTY-SEVEN

Layla

On Monday afternoon, after I'm done with classes, Nico insists that we meet for lunch instead of waiting until six to see each other. I agree, knowing there's no guarantee we'll get a chance to talk, and even if we do, it would only be for ten minutes or so. Even though it's only been a short time since the cheesesteak, I'm about ready to tackle him across the bistro table. I never knew watching a man eat a club sandwich could be such a turn-on.

We chat amiably while I dip my spoon into a cup of tomato-basil soup and Nico wolfs down his sandwich before my shift starts at two.

"I'm just glad to be out of that room," I say, leaning back in the chair. "I had some serious cabin fever after studying for the past two days."

"You look better than you have in a while," Nico says after he polishes off the last of his sandwich. "Too skinny, but definitely better."

I look down. I have probably lost close to ten pounds in the last two weeks, which has made my clothes start hanging off my hips in a way I don't like, but I still wouldn't necessarily call myself skinny. True, I'm currently borrowing a bunch of Jamie's clothes because I no longer have the curves to fill out mine, but I'm no Victoria's Secret model.

"You're crazy," I tell him as I dip my spoon into my soup for another bite. "Don't like what you see anymore?"

His eyes darken at the suggestion, and he gives me a look of such pure and unadulterated lust that I actually drop my spoon onto the table with a loud clatter of metal on metal.

"What do you think?" he asks evenly. His tongue runs over the contours of his lower lip on the pretext of licking off some stray mustard. I follow it, transfixed. All right, Mr. Soltero. Two can play that game.

Not one to be outmatched, I retrieve my soup spoon and dip it into my soup again. I slowly take a bite, taking some extra time to lick every drop of soup off the utensil and suck it for a moment before letting it pop out of my mouth.

He watches my progress like a big panther stalking its prey. Then he blinks, and that predatory expression vanishes as his gaze drops to my soup. "Is that all you're having for lunch?"

A taxicab blasts its horn right in front of the shop, as if to emphasize the ridiculousness of that possibility. So much for maintaining the mood.

I roll my eyes and take another bite. "You sound like Quinn. She's always haranguing me about what I eat."

Nico nods. "Yeah, well, she's a smart girl. Speaking of...what did she say about us? She still want to chop up my balls?"

I almost spit out my soup. But then I swallow and grimace. "Maybe a little. Quinn kind of likes to hold a grudge."

The third-degree I had to take when I got home on Sunday was worse than my dad. Quinn didn't let up for at least an hour, peppering me with questions about where Nico lived, what he did, whether I was safe, was he really going to stay or was he just blowing more hot air just to get laid. It took me smacking her in the face with my pillow to get her to shut up—well, that and assuring her at least ten times that Nico wasn't actually going anywhere. I found I still needed that assurance myself. I could hardly believe it was true.

"She can hold a grudge if she wants," Nico says. "She looks out for you. I can get behind that." He looks me over again. "Seriously, baby, we need to fatten you up. You want me to go back in and get you a cookie or something?"

I blanch and shake my head at the idea. I'm still trying to pay off my bills, and this soup was expensive enough. "I'm good, really. I had a big breakfast." It's a lie. I had my regular fifty-cent bagel and cheap coffee. But he doesn't need to know that.

Like he knows I'm lying, Nico just frowns. But before he can respond, my phone blares out the bossa nova riff that's my dad's ringtone. Knowing my dad, he won't be satisfied with voicemail.

As I answer, I make a face at Nico, who just sits back with a curious expression, his arms crossed over his broad chest. The motion makes his forearms bulge slightly through his rolled-up sleeves. Yum.

"Hi, Dad," I say, slightly annoyed.

"Layla. What are you doing?"

My father's voice booms over the tiny speakers of my phone, so loud I swear Nico can probably hear him over the din of the cafe. I try not to roll my eyes. It's never just hello with him. It's always making sure I'm doing the right thing.

"I'm good, Dad," I say wearily. "Just at lunch."

I stand up with my tray as I talk and carry my now-empty container of soup inside to throw it out. Nico follows, taking my tray from me to dispose of our trash while I stand at the long line of counter seating that runs along the deli window. I lean onto the counter and watch the people passing on their lunch break.

"Did you go to your doctor's appointment this morning? Did he do another spleen exam?"

I nod, even though my father can't see me. "Yes, Dad. I was appropriately poked and prodded, I promise."

My dad had apparently thought that Jamie wasn't wrong about the mono. Although the nurse practitioners at the student health center hadn't seen any reason to give me a blood test, Dad told me I needed to have them check for strep throat and my spleen health. I've never said "spleen" so many times in my life.

"Layla, don't be smart to me. I'm a doctor. You should be grateful you have one in the family."

Now I do roll my eyes at Nico, who has come up behind me and rests his chin on my shoulder. He wraps his big arms around my waist and pulls me against his solid frame while my dad continues to lecture. I suck in a breath at the feel of him and angle my neck willingly as he buries his face into it. It doesn't matter to either of us that we're standing in the middle of a crowded deli. In the afternoon. While I'm on the phone with my father.

Clearly I'm not the only one who's hard up after just a few days.

"Layla, are you all right?" my dad asks as I squeak loudly when Nico nips at the edge of my ear. "What was that?"

"I'm fine, Dad, just out to lunch with...a friend. Ah!" I cry out when Nico's fingers, which have been toying with the bottom of my blouse, give me a quick pinch at the waist.

"Layla?"

"Dad, sorry, I'm in the middle of a restaurant." I try as hard as I can to keep an even tone while Nico continues his stealthy exploration of my midsection.

"Just a friend, huh?" he rumbles against my neck.

I try to elbow him in the gut, but he dodges it, yet somehow manages to hold me tighter as he nibbles my earlobe. Now I can definitely feel something hard pressing into my backside through the material of my pants. It's getting hard to talk.

"Your mother wants to book your flight home for the summer," my dad is saying. "So you need to call her and give her your finals schedule."

"I need...oh...I'll need time to clean out my dorm room too, um..."

I haven't told my dad yet that I don't want to come home this summer—that I have the idea of continuing at Fox and Lager, maybe picking up an extra job to pay my way. But this isn't the time to have that conversation.

Nico's hands rub small circles into the bare skin of my belly, teasing the skin just above my waistband. His tongue flickers softly at the delicate skin under my jaw, causing me to grip the countertop more firmly to keep my balance.

"Dad?" I say, interrupting my father's diatribe about proper cleaning methods.

"Layla, I am talking to you. Are you listening?"

"Dad, I need to go," I squeal as Nico sinks his teeth into the side of my neck. "I'm going to be late for work!"

"Layla, make sure you call your mother later, and—"

"Gotitdadloveyoubye!"

I spit the words out as fast as I can so I can twist quickly around to smack Nico in the shoulder. He catches my hand and pulls it up around his neck, crushing his lips to mine and sliding his tongue into my mouth before I can get any more words out. My indignation is gone as I sink into the kiss and twist my hands into the curls sticking out at the bottom of his cap.

"You need a haircut," I mutter a little too forcefully against his lips.

"Just a friend?" he mumbles. His hands reach down to pinch my side again, causing me to jerk in his arms.

"Ah! Don't!" I cry, giggling helplessly as he continues his onslaught of kisses and tickling. A few of the other patrons are blinking at us from their spots in line, but I don't care. "I'm sorry! Uncle! Uncle! Ah, what do you wish I'd said?"

He stops, leaning down to settle his forehead on mine. "Are you ashamed to tell your dad about me, sweetie?"

Immediately, I lean back. "Oh my God, Nico, *no*! Not at all!"

It's the last thing I want him to think. He doesn't have to say it, but I know he thinks about the difference in our backgrounds. It's in the way he looks around my dorm, at the computer on my desk and the loads of groceries my roommates buy each week. He knows I don't come from exactly the same kind of money they do, but my family clearly has a lot more than his does. I wouldn't be here if they didn't.

"I'd love to tell my dad about you, but what should I say? We haven't even talked about what we are. Do I tell him I'm with the guy I'm sleeping with?" I ask softly, reaching up to hold his face between my hands. "Trust me. My dad needs to be eased into things. I'd prefer if you stayed alive."

Nico just stares at me for a long moment, his big eyes clouded with sadness. My heart sinks. Shit. But the questions still remain... *Is* he my boyfriend? Am I his girlfriend? He's staying in New York for me, says he needs me. But we haven't used formalized language to each other. Nothing's "official."

I'm two more seconds from yelling "I love you!" at the top of my lungs just to wipe that puppy dog look off his face when Nico steps out of my grasp and then takes one of my hands in his.

"Just tell them you're with Nico," he announces with a grin. Then he pulls me out the door, effectively ending our standoff.

———

THE AFTERNOON GOES SLOWLY, thankfully, so I have a lot of time to work on my homework. No matter what, I have to keep up with my studying. That's what I'm here for, after all, and there is no way I'll convince my dad to let me stay in New York for the summer if my grades aren't top-shelf.

By the time six o'clock rolls around, the office is practically dead. Karen is in the back working on the firm's tax documents with their accountant, but most of the attorneys have cleared out for the night, along with their assistants. Except for one.

I'm in the middle of taking notes on *The Tempest* when a loud voice with way too much swagger interrupts me.

"Well, well, well, if it isn't Emily Dickinson."

When I look up, I can't help but smile when I find Alex leaning over the top of the desk, right at my shoulder.

"I take that to be a reference to the fact I've had to stay at home a bit recently?" I ask sweetly.

"That and the fact that you're an English major. I could call you Emily Brontë if you like her better. I think she died of tuberculosis. Whatcha readin' there, kid?"

He speaks in that sort of faux-folksy cadence, the way rich people do when they want to sound familiar to not-so-rich people. I've heard Alex do this with his clients, usually the young female ones, who are often starving artists or models he's trying to "discover." It only vaguely registers that he has me grouped in with them. It's odd.

When I don't answer right away, he crooks his head to read the title at the top of the page.

"Ah, The Bard!" Alex stands back up and grins. "*The Tempest* is one of my favorites. 'We are the stuff as dreams are made on, and our little life is rounded with a sleep.' *I* actually played Ferdinand in college."

He waggles his eyebrows at me in a way that makes me laugh. He's so cheesy, but he's the kind of guy who could probably charm the pants off a snake. It explains why he's so successful.

"Oh?"

I set the book down. Alex is kind of foppish, so I could imagine him, twenty or more years ago, as the romantic lead in a Shakespearean comedy. He leans back on the desk, taking my comment as an invitation to chat. Behind him, the elevator bell rings, and I don't have to look around him to know that the sound of squeaky wheels on the tiled floor means the arrival of the real romantic lead in my life. Jeez, I guess Alex isn't the only one who's cheesy.

Alex ducks back, but turns immediately back to me when he sees that it's only the FedEx man. Unlike the other people at the firm, he doesn't greet Nico. He doesn't even acknowledge his presence. I, on the other hand, have to fight not to follow the man around the room. And I'd like nothing more than for Alex to disappear.

"Hi, Nico," I say as neutrally as I can, so as not to make Alex suspect anything untoward.

Nico nods at me with a brief, bright smile that quickly shutters as he looks at Alex, who has continued talking as if no one is there.

"Yeah, I did a stint with the Princeton Shakespeare Company," he says as he doodles on a pink Post-It. "*And* I designed the logo for the show. See?"

He flips the pad around to show me a small, unremarkable insignia. I "ooh" and "ah" politely, but have to stifle a grin when Nico rolls his eyes and mouths the sounds to me from behind Alex's shoulder. Ever oblivious, Alex turns the pad back around to admire his drawing.

"You would have made a great Miranda to my Ferdinand," he says with a leer. "Young. Impressionable. Gorgeous. A perfect fit."

A loud thump of a package landing on the floor briefly interrupts Alex's flirting, but he pays it no mind.

"So, what's your secret?" Alex says as he frankly looks me up and down. "Juice cleanse? One of my clients did some lemonade diet and lost fifteen pounds in two weeks. Best thing she's done yet for her career."

Another package slams on top of the first.

I glance uncomfortably at my thinner form, then back up at the older man. "Um, no secret. Just being sick."

Alex pushes off the desk and snaps me with a finger gun, completely oblivious to the harsh glares of the dark-eyed courier behind him. "Well, you look hot, kid. Keep it up, and I might be helping you sign a modeling contract." Alex flashes me a grin and cocks his head. "Maybe we should have a lunch meeting to talk about your future, huh? What do you say, next Tuesday around noon?"

"I need you to sign this, Layla."

The clipboard is thrust almost violently between Alex and me, and it's all I can do not to gasp at the thin-lipped, barely contained anger practically pulsing out of Nico's handsome face. Turns out a jealous Nico is a hot Nico.

"Thanks," I say with what I hope is a reassuring smile as I take the papers to sign.

Surely he knows he has nothing to worry about. To Alex, I also smile, but for a different reason. "I can't, unfortunately. I come here straight from classes."

"Another time, then." Alex walks backward toward his office. "Later, cutie," he says before he disappears down the hall.

When I give Nico back his clipboard, I'm confronted by five feet, eleven inches of very *un*amused FedEx courier. I tip my head to the side and swallow back a laugh.

"Is he like that every day with you?" he asks between clenched teeth as he takes back the clipboard and sets it on top of his other packages.

I glance in the direction of Alex's office, then back to my jealous deliveryman. "No. Just every now and then when he feels his midlife crisis setting in."

The joke relaxes some of the tension in Nico's jaw, but only just. I stand up and lean over the desk so I can touch his shoulder.

"Hey," I say softly.

He looks down at my hand and then up at me. There is more in his expression than just jealousy. Fear, maybe. And some of the sadness I glimpsed after the conversation with my dad.

Before I can say anything more, he grasps my face between his big palms and lays a deep, fierce kiss that takes all the oxygen out of my lungs. Just as quickly, he breaks the kiss, still nose to nose.

"Next time you tell that motherfucker you got a man," he says.

He gently bites my lips one more time before releasing me. I stumble backward into my chair, thankful it's there since I've temporarily lost my ability to stand up.

Nico flashes me a quick grin before the elevator doors open behind him like magic. One of the interns comes in and races around the desk for the new packages, oblivious to the sexual tension in the room. Nico waits until he leaves, then steps backward into the elevator.

"I'm coming down tonight after work," he says. "I need some quality time with my *girlfriend*."

His still-dark expression doesn't leave any room for argument. Wordlessly, I nod, but I thrill at the sound of the word "girlfriend." He didn't exactly give me a choice in the matter. But as the doors close over his broad smile, I also know I couldn't care less.

III

VIVIR SIN AIRE

CHAPTER TWENTY-EIGHT

Layla

Two weeks later, I've just finished my last round of midterms, and Nico has set aside Saturday afternoon before his shift at AJ's for us to celebrate. We haven't been able to see each other much with the exception of a few stolen kisses at the office and an innocent lunch date here and there (once which turned into a very not-innocent rendezvous in the back of his delivery truck).

On Friday, I decide to make the most of my class-free morning and pick out something new to wear. I'm almost finished paying off my credit card bills, but I want to use a little something of this week's paycheck to find something that fits. I still haven't gained back the weight I lost after getting the flu. It's weird, but I've just chalked it up to the stress of midterms and subsisting on bagels and cheap coffee. Really, you wouldn't want to eat most of the time if that's all you could afford either.

"Damn, Layla!" Vinny yelps as we walk up Third Avenue.

We're going to one of the places that sells crop tops and tight pants on five-dollar racks. That's all I can afford right now, and Vinny's looking to spruce up his own look before going out with a new girl from his accounting class this weekend. I've told him I'll help him look less like a scrawny nineteen-year-old and more like a proper player. Whatever that means.

"What?" I ask.

"Dude, you have, like, no ass anymore. What happened?"

"Um, you *know* what happened," I say. "That's what two weeks of barely eating will do for you."

"I know, but *jeez*. That was over a month ago, and you look even skinnier. I never thought I'd see the day where you lost 'dat ass'."

Vinny knows he's the only guy I'd ever let talk about my ass like that without an elbow to the ribs, but I wince anyway as I glance at my reflection in a shop window.

He's right—my butt and legs look more like an actual model's these days: scrawny and too-long. Maybe I should take Alex up on his offer.

"You should love it," I joke. "I look just like the girls you date."

Vinny looks at me critically, like he's checking me out for the first time. "Maaaaybe," he says. "Maybe I'd make a play if I thought you'd stay this way."

"You're disgusting."

He grins. "I can't help I like girls who look like models!"

"You like girls who look like they're twelve," I retort.

Vinny shrugs, as if to admit his guilt freely. Then he slings a skinny arm over my shoulder and squeezes. "It doesn't matter anyway," he says. "You wouldn't be you without your booty. Doesn't your man miss it?"

I sigh. Nico has commented a few more times about needing to fatten me up. It's always a joke, but I know he misses my curves. I've had to borrow a pair of Jamie's jeans since most of mine slide off my hips at the moment. Even though we're now the same size, they still don't look right since Jamie is about three inches taller than I am.

"Besides," Vinny adds, "I'm pretty sure your boyfriend would kick my ass if I made a play for his girl anyway."

I grin. I'm still getting used to thinking of myself as "Nico's girl." And Vinny's not totally wrong. I stick my tongue out at my reflection and urge Vinny to keep moving. "Well, that's why we're going shopping, right? So I don't look like such a paperclip in my clothes. Come on, let's help me get my ass back."

————

IN THE STORE, I almost immediately find the kind of dress I'm looking for. It's a bright blue, floral tea dress covered with polka dots that will hopefully flatter what's left of my hourglass shape down to my knees, covering up the expanse of pasty skin that only comes from being inside too much. Tea skirts aren't usually my thing—that's usually more my mother's look—but in this case the swishy bell-shaped skirt might give me the illusion of a shapelier figure.

Unfortunately, things don't go as planned. In the dressing room, I'm faced again with the shock of just how much weight I've actually lost.

"Shit," I mutter after I put on the dress. The look…is not good. The bodice hangs like an empty sack from my torso, and the skirt falls limply over my nonexistent hips. I look like a deflated party balloon.

A brief knock signals the salesgirl, whose name I think is Mandy. I open it. The look on her face tells me she knows exactly why I'm not happy.

"Oh, honey," she says. "That is not the dress for you."

"You don't say," I reply dryly. I pick up the fabric that pooches out around my hips. "Got any suggestions? I've…lost some weight recently, so I'm not sure of my size anymore."

"Well, that sure ain't it," she says as she checks the tag scratching at my back. "Size six? Ha. I'd say you're at least a two, lucky girl. You'll make a killing at the sample sales."

"Yeah, I'm thrilled," I say dryly.

She laughs and shakes her head. "All right, then, what are we looking for?"

"Something that makes me look like I'm not a stick figure," I say, making her laugh again. "Something that will make my boyfriend think I'm sex on heels. He…

likes a woman with some curves. Which I used to have, but can't quite seem to gain back."

A woman with a lot of curves of her own, Mandy nods appreciatively. She twists a lock of her curly hair thoughtfully, perusing my form up and down while she thinks. She's nice, like a grown-up version of Shirley Temple.

After a moment, her eyes light up and she grins devilishly. "Got just the thing, hon. Be right back."

I wait irritably in my polka-dotted trash bag. Even though a part of me—the part that was constantly berated by my mother not to eat too much—*is* slightly triumphant at being this thin, I'm almost as frustrated with that feeling as I am at the fact that none of my clothes fit. Having grown up in a town that was mostly full of anorexic blonde girls, it took a lot of work (with the help of our yearly visits to Brazil) to learn to accept my body—muscular and curvy as opposed to lithe and underweight—as pretty. This feels like just another loss. I liked my curves. I liked my ass. I want them back!

Mandy's brisk knock sounds again, and I open it to find her holding a dress out to me with a satisfied smirk on her face. It's a light, undeniably sexy affair: bright crimson fabric sprinkled with a small flower print, sewn in a bias cut to cling to my breasts and my hips, with the tiniest of tiny spaghetti straps. She knows she's done well—the dress is really cute and sexy as hell.

"That's going to be way too small," I say, noting the size at the back of the hanger. "I've never been that small in my life. Maybe when I was ten or something."

"Just *try* it," Mandy insists, thrusting the dress at me. "It's meant to stretch, and if it's a little tight, you know your man won't mind. Now put it on and let's see."

I shrug, but allow her to shut the door since she's obviously not going anywhere until I've tried it on. I slip out of the baggy, polka-dotted embarrassment and pull the little red dress over my head. After I've tugged everything into place, I take a breath, turn around, and look at myself in the mirror.

"Holy shit," I breathe.

"Good?" Mandy's voice cuts through my shock.

The dress doesn't look good. It looks fucking amazing. Way better than anything at a five-dollars-or-less place should look. Stopping just before being indecently tight, it clings to every inch of me and gives the illusion of curves in exactly the right places. I turn around and want to jump with glee. Suddenly, I have an ass again—albeit a much smaller one than before, but it's still there. I turn back; my boobs also look awesome. Bonus.

"Oh yeah," I finally answer. "You did really good."

"Let's see, girl."

I slip into the espadrilles I brought to try on with dresses and open the door. I sashay down the hall of dressing rooms to examine myself in the mirror at the end. Mandy lets out an encouraging whistle as I walk, causing me to smile back at her just as I walk past where Vinny is waiting in an armchair for me. He drops his magazine.

"Hey!" he crows. "Look, you found your ass again!"

I turn back at him from where I'm standing on the pedestal in front of the three-paned mirror.

"Shut up," I say, but it's with a grin. I don't remember the last time I felt this good, and he and I both know it.

———

"Vinny!" I call from my chair in the waiting area of Zara. Vinny swears by their jeans, although I'm not convinced they look any better than Levi's. He's been trying on different cuts for the last hour, and I only have twenty minutes to grab lunch before I catch the subway up to work.

I decided not to wear the dress, which is tucked safely into a shopping bag at my feet, opting instead to wear the clingy black skirt and red blouse Mandy hooked me up with. She found me two more skirts and three shirts that kept me within my fifty-dollar budget. They're all totally cheap knockoffs that will fall apart within a month, but everything makes me look halfway normal again until I can eat enough ice cream to get my figure back.

Vinny pops his head out of the dressing room and turns around to show me his butt. "What do you think?"

I slide back into my chair. "They look exactly the same as the last four pairs you modeled for me. Your ass is bony no matter what."

Vinny turns to me and frowns. "Why are you so grumpy? I thought girls loved shopping."

I sit back up and roll my eyes. "You have got to learn to stop stereotyping, my friend."

I do actually like shopping. Just not shopping for men's jeans with the nineteen-year-old equivalent of Simon Doonan, apparently. For two hours straight.

Vinny shrugs. "I only have three more pairs, and then we can go, I promise. We can stop for falafel for lunch. On me."

I perk up. Falafel sounds really good. With extra hummus. "All right, let me see them."

Vinny disappears back into his dressing room while my phone rings in my purse. I take it out and answer it tentatively. It's my parents' house line, which means it's my mom. She doesn't usually call me during the week, preferring to keep her communication to her standard Sunday time.

"Mom? Everything okay?"

"Y-yes. Everything's fine. I just…well, I thought I would call to say hello."

I frown. This is weird. "Uh, okay. Hi."

"How are you doing today?"

Vinny pops out in a pair of jeans that are almost as tight as mine. I shake my head furiously and mouth "NO" as overtly as possible. He droops and disappears again.

"I'm fine, Mom," I say. "Just out with a friend shopping right now. What are you up to?"

"Oh, well…I just finished coffee with Catherine Kramer. You remember her, Lindsey's mother?"

I nod, even though she can't see me. "Yeah, I remember Lindsey. How is she?"

"Still at the University of Washington. Catherine says she likes it there."

I roll my eyes. Here we go again. "Dad must be jealous."

There's a long pause, and I think I can hear the sound of Mom's nails tapping on something—a counter, the top of her steering wheel, maybe the side of the telephone.

"Mom?" I finally ask after she still says nothing.

"Catherine and Mel are splitting up."

She says it quickly, like she's taking some terrible medicine. It's hard for Cheryl Bagley Barros to admit difficult truths, even when they're not necessarily about her.

Even so, the news isn't unexpected. I have at least four friends whose parents split after they left for college.

"I'm sorry for them. Poor Catherine. Poor Lindsey," I say. Vinny pops out of the dressing room again, sees the look on my face, and turns right back around, clearly sensing that the fashion show is over.

"Well, I don't think you should transfer to UW unless you really want to," Mom says, increasingly blustery, as if the words will cut her tongue if she says them too slowly. "NYU was your dream. You shouldn't give it up, no matter what your father says."

I frown. She's all over the place. But more importantly, she's breaking with my dad's line again, which is even stranger.

"Layla, do you have enough money?"

If I wasn't already sitting, that question would have bowled me over. My mother, one half of the "earn what you get" Barros pair, is asking me about my financial situation? Is the world on fire or something?

I don't literally know how to answer. "Ah…"

"I'm going to send you some money," Mom hurries on. "I know how expensive that city is. You should be focusing on your grades, not working yourself to death."

"But, what about…Dad says…" I'm stumbling. What is going on here?

"This is what family is for," Mom says. "I'll send you a check in the mail tomorrow. It should be there next week. Deposit it right away, understand?"

I push my hand back into my hair. I cannot believe what I am hearing. "Um, yeah. Okay. No problem."

I want to ask how much. Is she talking twenty bucks here? A few hundred? A few thousand? I don't want to get my hopes up, and I'm afraid if I ask, she'll back out of the whole thing. Because the truth is, I could really, *really* use the extra cash. A little bit more, and I won't have any more debt to pay off. And then I could start saving for the summer.

I'm just about to suggest as much when my mom interrupts me.

"Layla?" There's a little more strength in her voice, like now that she's gotten out something she'd been holding onto for a while, she can speak with her normal, even cadence.

"Yeah?"

A deep breath. Okay, maybe not quite so much confidence as I'd originally thought.

"Don't tell your father," she says quickly, and then with a hurried "I love you," she hangs up.

"Dude, did someone die?"

I look up to find Vinny standing in front of me, two pairs of jeans draped over his forearm. He looks a little worried, which means the expression on my face must look way worse.

"You know," I say as I stand up. "I'm not quite sure."

CHAPTER TWENTY-NINE

Nico

It's close to noon when I roll up to Layla's dorm on Saturday. I've been looking forward to this for the last two weeks. Layla's the brightest spot in my life right now, and I need more of that brightness. After telling K.C. that I wasn't going to be coming out to LA after all, I had to listen to him badger me for close to an hour, and almost every day since.

"I can't believe you," he kept saying. "You're finally free. Gabe's almost out of school. No more kids to watch over, no more field trips to sign. What are you doing?"

He threatened to tell Jessie and all of our other friends on me, and after that, started listing all the reasons why I had wanted to leave New York in the first place.

Shitty job.

Shitty family.

Shitty apartment.

Shitty everything.

Except her. In the middle of the slog, there's Layla, sitting at her desk every day waiting for me. But I need more than a kiss or two behind the desk and the occasional lunch break. I need to know that I'm making the right decision staying here for her.

I wait outside her dorm, ignoring the curious looks from her classmates as they check me out. I know what I look like: older dude creeping outside the dorm. In my faded t-shirt and old Yankees cap, my tattoos sticking out of the sleeves and the St. Christopher medallion hanging on a chain, I don't exactly look like the nice Connecticut kids who go to this school. A few of the girls scan me up and down—there's that familiar look, half scared, half curious. Nothing like the kind, open way Layla looks at me. The way I hope she'll never stop looking at me.

"Hey," she says when I call up to her dorm. "You downstairs?"

Just the sound of her voice makes my chest tight. One day I'm going to get up the guts to tell her how I really feel. Maybe today.

"Yeah," I say. "Do you want to sign me in, or are you ready?"

Part of me hopes she'll say no, even though I know if I get her alone right now, we won't leave her room for the rest of the day. And that's not what I have planned.

"No, I'm ready. Be down in a few."

I see her before she sees me, and for a second, I can't breathe. She's wearing this red thing that's hugging her body like a second skin. I'd march her upstairs to change if I could say anything at all—that's how hot she looks. It doesn't look like she's wearing much makeup or anything. Instead, she's simple, with her hair in a braid over her shoulder, pulled back so her blue eyes shine, a little too big in her face these days. My heart practically stops. That's the thing about Layla. She has no fucking clue how beautiful she really is.

She finds me, and her wide-eyed features move to a smirk. She can see my reaction—I'm doing nothing to hide it. I suck on my bottom lip, shift my weight onto one leg, and actually stumble backward, almost missing the lamppost before finally I manage to find my way to her. Then she laughs, the sound of it filling the street and my whole body, and bounds down the last few steps from the building and into my waiting arms.

"Damn," I mutter as I push up the brim of my hat so I can see her better.

I slip a hand around her tiny waist and pull her close while still taking her in. God, *how* does she always smell this good? "That is some dress, baby. You look smokin'."

She grins, and my heart swells.

"Thanks."

"What's the occasion? I thought we were just going to the park." I gesture toward the backpack I have over my shoulder. "I brought a lunch."

"You packed a picnic?" she practically squeals. Damn, she's cute when she's excited. "No one has ever packed me a picnic before!"

"It's nothing big," I mumble. "Just some bagels and stuff. I thought you might be hungry."

And right then, I blush. I doubt she can see it, but I can feel my face get hot just the same. Who knew packing some food could make her so freaking happy? I grin again. I can't help it. She's so damn adorable, and when she smiles at me like that, all the other shit in my life melts away.

Layla tips up onto her toes to kiss my cheek, but I turn at the last second and capture her lips, pulling her even closer. I savor her, enjoying her mouth, the way it makes the rest of the world disappear. Unfortunately, the taste of her also shoots straight to my cock, and I'm already regretting not asking her just to sign me in. It's obvious I'm not the only one feeling hard up. My hand slips down and lightly squeezes her ass before I groan and force myself to stop. She doesn't need me mauling her in the middle of the street.

"Aah," I moan lightly against her lips. "Maybe we just need to go back up to your room instead. Fuck the park. I need you more than bagels."

But Layla just groans back with humor and frustration and pushes her head into my chest.

"My roommates," she mumbles against my collarbone. "They're all there right now. No go."

I close my eyes. "Damn. Of course they are." Because that's just the kind of luck I have.

Checking to make sure curious students aren't watching us anymore, I adjusted the front of my pants. The Mets. My counselor at Tryon. My mother's plumbing problems. Okay, that about did the trick.

"All right, beautiful," I say. "The park it is. And then *mi casa* for sure."

———

TWO HOURS LATER, we're lying in the middle of Sheep Meadow on the threadbare blanket I brought, our bellies full of bagels. We're surrounded by at least a few hundred other New Yorkers taking advantage of the warmer-than-average April weather. This goddamn city. If you're not living in some tiny box, you can't get away from fucking people. All I want is to be alone with Layla, and other than my shitty apartment, there's literally nowhere else for us to go.

Layla's shucked her sweater and lies with her head on my thigh, clearly enjoying the sunshine. She's nearly asleep, but I'm just entranced, watching my girl all blissed out. The sun bounces off her soft skin, and her lips are curved into a small, sweet smile. I've started drawing her from time to time, usually like this, when she's asleep or almost there. She doesn't know it. The drawings are just for me, reminders of why I'm staying.

I toy with the thin straps of her dress, pulling them over her shoulders, then putting them back, running the backs of my fingernails over the delicate bones of her clavicle, up the long line of her neck. It's meditative, even though I can tell by the way her nipples perk through her dress that she's turned on. I am too...but now I'm not in as much of a hurry to get her alone. I don't get a lot of moments like this. Moments where everything is perfect.

Layla opens her eyes, lazy, contented, the same bluebird color as the sky. Then she registers the touch of my fingers grazing across her sternum, and a spark reappears.

I quirk a black brow. "You keep lookin' at me like that, NYU, and you're asking for some trouble."

Her lips curve into a smirk. "Promise?"

So it's like that, huh? I know from past conversations that Layla can be kind of competitive. I'm not normally so much, but she's fun to play with. This is how we ended up doing it like rabbits on the balcony of her dorm—I bet her she wouldn't have the guts.

Glancing around to make sure no one is looking at us, I slip my fingers, the ones toying with her dress, down a little farther to tickle the swell of her breast through the fabric. My thumb brushes over her nipple, once, twice. Her mouth falls open in surprise.

I raise one eyebrow. "Too much for you, NYU?"

Her surprise flattens, and she rises to the challenge, just like I knew she would.

"Bring it," she mouths.

Before I know it, I flip her onto her back, one arm braced behind her head. I don't know what it is about Layla, but she turns me into a predator in the space of a second. My shoulders block the sunlight over her, but she doesn't care as she stares up at me with naked desire. Then she closes her eyes, clearly ready to be kissed.

And I can't...move. It's like every nerve in me is stalled, unable to move. I'm...paralyzed. Layla brings out so much in me—awe, lust, fear, adoration. Love. The word echoes through my head, just like it did when Flaco said it. And suddenly I feel like I can't breathe.

So instead of kissing her, which is all I really want to do, I sit up and pull my hat down over my face.

Layla opens her eyes. "Hey. What just happened?"

"Nothing."

I squint into the sunlight. Layla props up onto her elbows, not bothering to hide her disappointment.

"What are you talking about? What happened to bringing it?"

Fuck. I swipe my hat off my head, then put it right back on. "Well, you seemed short of breath. We've been out a while. I don't want to overwhelm you, you know. You have been sick."

It's a stupid excuse. Layla is plenty healthy, and I'm being a chicken shit. I'm a scared little kid, scared to tell her how I really feel. About this city. About my life. About her.

She pushes herself up completely.

"Stop that," she says.

I turn the bill of my hat around so she can see my face. "What? Stop what?"

"Talking."

Before I can respond, she grabs a handful of my shirt and crushes her lips to mine. A groan escapes, buried deep in my throat. Every doubt I've had is suddenly gone, swallowed by the taste of her. Of Layla.

It takes me a second, but then I'm meeting her kiss for urgent kiss, snaking an arm around her waist and lifting her into my lap to bring our bodies closer, as close as we can. Somehow the hem of her dress pushes past her knees with the movement, and as she begs my lips to open with sweet, urgent flicks of her tongue, I palm her thigh, only inches from her ass, that part of her I can't ever get enough of. She fits. We fit. Better than I ever thought possible.

She winds her arms around my neck, welcoming me closer, without a care in the world about the fact that we have an audience of literally hundreds surrounding our very public display of affection. But one of us has to be smart about this. I don't give a fuck about what people think about me, but I'm pretty sure that neither Layla nor her uptight parents would appreciate videos of their daughter showing up on the internet.

I pull away and find another couple sitting a few feet from us watching over the tops of their sunglasses with disapproving looks. "Get a room," one of them mutters before they both turn back to their newspapers. Layla buries her face into my neck in embarrassment, oblivious to the way the feel of her lips only make the, ah, problem in my pants get that much...harder.

"We should probably take their advice." I gently bite her earlobe in that way that always makes her whimper. Fuck, I'd take her right here if it wouldn't get us both arrested.

I'd take her for the rest of my life.

Fuck, Nico. What are you doing?

She shivers. "Let's go," she murmurs. "Now."

We pack up the picnic in record time and practically sprint across the field onto one of the paths that lines the surrounding area. Both of us are laughing almost uncontrollably. I pull her onto one path, then another, until we're running under green wood arches of the Central Park Dairy, which is by some miracle empty. We twist around, arms about each other's waists, sneaking kisses until finally we slam against one of the doors, and I bury my face in the soft skin of Layla's neck all over again.

The backpack hits the floor. Her mouth meets mine in a frenzy, nipping and sucking, twisting and diving with my tongue until we are both completely out of breath.

"How…ah…how well do you know…this park?" she gasps in between hurried kisses.

I chew on my lower lip before kissing her again. "Better than most. Why?"

You know why, you bastard. It's all over her innocent face. Well, maybe not-so-innocent.

I press my forehead against the door over her shoulder, then glance from side to side, nervous of the onlookers I know will eventually come upon us here. It's a visitor's center, after all.

Then I look back at her, tensing when her hands reach around to my ass and grab, hard. Fuuuuuuck.

"I…I don't think I can wait," she whispers in a throaty voice. "To get to your apartment, I mean."

Sex is painted clearly across her sweet face. Her lips fall open into a shape that would fit perfectly around my—

My hands tighten even more around her thighs. "Are you serious? Because I ain't fuckin' around, Layla. You have no idea what I'm feeling right now, baby."

"Oh, I think I do." Heavy-lidded, she rolls her hips against the fucking pipe I have in my jeans, which grows even harder when she moans a little.

Jesus *Christ*. This girl is seriously going to be the death of me.

Layla sucks on my lower lip like a lollipop, slips her tongue into my mouth, and welcomes me into hers. My arms hold her up, hold her close. I feel her light that I increasingly depend on to keep me steady in this dreary life. I'm a drowning man, and she's my anchor.

I lift her off the ground and stumble us into a hidden alcove off the main arched corridor of the old wood building. I'm not sure how I even know it's there—it's like I have some weird sixth sense for where we need to go to be together. With the sky quickly covering with clouds and the new green of the trees offering a bit of cover from all the eyes around us, this is the best sanctuary we can get, the closest thing to a corner all our own. With Layla in my arms, open and eager, the rest of the city fades away.

Her body is warm. Her hands are everywhere, finding their way under the hem of my shirt, yanking at the buttons of my jeans, even as I'm shoving her skirt up and pulling her underwear to the side. The humidity is rising—it's like we want to melt into each other, and everything else is just in the way.

"Hold on," I mutter as she tries to steer me inside her. It's hard to find the condom in the back of my jeans with her lips fused to mine, but I manage to get it and put it on.

I can't hear, see, sense anything but her. It doesn't matter that we're in the middle of the day. It doesn't matter that we're in the middle of this fuckin' zoo we call a park. All I can think about is her, how badly I need to be inside her right fuckin' now.

And then our bodies find each other, and I can't think at all. I move automatically, and she arches violently as I spear her against the rough wall. She's as desperate as I am, wriggling against me, eager to find that friction I know she needs to get off.

"Fuck!" My voice is hoarse; I'm struggling to be quiet. There are voices down the path, but for now we're still hidden by the trees.

I bury my face in her neck as I pound away. Her nails bite into my shoulders as she whimpers in my ear. I'm so close, but I can feel by the way she's tightening around me that she's right there with me. Come on, Nico. You gotta last a little longer. Football. Dirty socks. Cockroaches.

"Please," I whisper.

"Nico!" she cries, almost too loud.

But she's coming—finally. I can feel it in the way her entire body tightens around me, the way her fingers tear at my skin, how her thighs turn to rocks around my waist. I cover her mouth with mine as I let go myself, shoving into her with one last painful, beautiful thrust. Our muscles throb. Our bones shake together, in waves that match the ebbs and flows of the wind blowing through the leaves above us.

Slowly, slowly, her feet fall to the ground. I feel the slick of her as I slide out and her skirt falls back into place. Layla takes in a deep breath. I try to remember how to breathe at all. But my hands don't leave her waist. I'm stuck in place, my forehead pressed against hers for a few more blissful moments before I finally reach down to get rid of the condom.

"Fuck," I whisper.

Our breaths mingle. I shudder.

"You said it," Layla whispers back.

We both close our eyes and listen to each other's breaths as we catch our breath and our hearts begin to slow.

"You." My voice is haggard. I shake my head from side to side. "You wreck me, Layla. You really do."

I don't know if that's a good thing or a bad thing, but I decide not to think too much of it. Instead, I focus on the look on her face as she traces the line of my jaw, on her soothing touch instead of the terrifying sense of feeling completely undone. I don't move or break eye contact until her finger touches my lips, swiping meditatively back and forth over the bottom one. She seems as entranced as I am. Small mercies.

I exhale through my nose, and then, because I can't not do it, cup her face with one hand and kiss her again, savoring every dip and valley of her lips, tasting deeply, slowly, exquisitely. It's not a kiss that says I need to fuck you. It's a kiss that says I love you. *Te amo.* However you say it in Portuguese. It doesn't matter; it's all the same thing.

My eyes shut. It's almost too much to bear.

I'm just about to tell her what I'm feeling when the sound of a few Japanese tourists crushing through the park ruins the moment. We break the kiss. Suddenly the air is heavy—sweat beads around my collarbone. I swipe off my hat and wipe the sweat before replacing it with the bill to the front. Layla stares at me hard, her chest rises and falls with each breath. The moment might be over, but the tension between us still crackles.

The chatter of the tourists dies away as they finish taking pictures of the quaint little building, unaware of where we stand in the shadows. Then a few of them scream when a loud clap of thunder sounds from the sky. A spring storm, right on time.

I glance through the trees, now bristling in a bit of heavy wind.

"It's going to rain," Layla says.

She's right. The dark alcove of what used to be an old dairy might be enough to shelter us, but if the wind blows anything sideways, we'll get soaked.

Another clap of thunder. I look up to the sky, and hold her tighter. "We need to find a cab."

Layla

Fat drops of warm rain splatter on my bare shoulder by the time we exit the park somewhere by Lincoln Center. The wind has picked up some more—now the sky is covered more with low-lying gray clouds that are nearly black. It's a typical spring storm in New York—the kind that sweeps in on a warm day and leaves just as quickly. Another clap of thunder sounds, and as if some god turns a key, the clouds open and it starts to absolutely pour.

"Come on!" Nico yells.

The light turns on Amsterdam, and he tugs me across the street. Out of nowhere, a wave of sudden nausea hits me, and I stumble on a crack in the sidewalk.

"Whoa, you okay?" Nico calls through the roar of the weather.

I nod my head as we keep walking, even though I feel like crap. What the hell is happening to me?

Soon the combination of the jog and the withering humidity is too much, and it doesn't take longer than a block before I have to stop again. I grab the railing of a set of brownstone stairs. Nico whips around as I collapse on the bottom stair, holding my stomach while the rain hammers down in fat sheets. I will not puke in the middle of the Upper West Side. I will not puke, I will not puke. Will. Not.

"Baby, what's wrong?"

Nico's at my side in a moment, sliding an arm around my rib cage while I bend over. I breathe deeply as the nausea subsides. Damn. Quinn isn't going to let me hear the end of this. And neither will my father.

"I'm fine," I say. "This weather is just kind of kicking my ass. Give me a second."

Nico looks at me up and down, and before I can say anything more, he slips another arm under my legs and lifts me up like I weigh nothing. With a wicked grin and brief peck on the cheek, he carries me briskly down the block.

We stop in front of a boutique, one of those places that would have said no to Julia Roberts in *Pretty Woman*. With me in his arms, Nico busts through the glass doors, startling the waifish salesgirls lounging behind a display of beige skirts.

"She's not feeling too well," he tells them with his trademark smile as he sets me neatly on the bench by the entrance. "Can she hang out here while I find a cab?"

With his rain-soaked shirt hugging his muscles transparently, he's putting on the best wet t-shirt contest in the world. Even through the nausea, I can't help but appreciate the view.

The salesgirls clearly like what they see too. One of them stumbles as she takes in the soaking wet god in front of her. She barely glances at me, despite the fact that I am dressed in red in a store devoid of color.

"S-sure," she says. "Take as long as you need."

Nico gives me a gentle kiss. "Stay here, baby. I'll get us a cab."

———

IT TAKES close to thirty minutes for Nico to get a cab, leaving me thirty minutes to wilt on the bench, pressing my temple against the cold glass wall of the store and willing the waves of nausea that just won't quite die to go away, away, away. I have had one offer of help from the salesgirls, the bitches, and it isn't until Nico lifts me up again that I realize just how shitty I do feel. I want to lie down right here on the cold white marble and go to sleep. I want to be anywhere else than a New York City cab.

And I want to know what the hell is going on.

The cab is even worse than normal. The interior stinks of cheap air freshener and hot dogs, and the driver, a taciturn guy named Karim, is blasting some kind of South Asian music featuring an ear-piercing female singer. Karim drives even more erratically than most New York cabbies, whipping and winding around the corners, jerking at the stoplights hard enough to throw me against the thick plastic barrier between the front and back seats.

Ten blocks down Broadway, and it's too much.

"Stop," I say weakly. "Stop, I need to get out. I'm going to be sick."

There's nothing a New York cab driver fears more than people throwing up in his cab. I spoke softly, but almost immediately, the cab pulls over.

"Out," Karim orders.

"Hold on, man, just give her a second," Nico's arguing. "She doesn't feel good, but she'll be all right."

"I need out," I manage to say. "*Now.*" That final lurch did it for me.

"Out!" yells Karim, and he slams his hand on his horn, prompting Nico to shuffle quickly out of the cab and come around to help me out. He stands me up on the curb and tosses a few bills at the cabbie, who zooms away.

The sky thunders. My stomach rolls. I sprint to a trashcan on the corner, where the stench of urine and rotten garbage lingers. Everything I've eaten today comes up.

"Shit!"

Nico's voice is frantic behind me while his hand is at my back, holding back my hair as I lose my cookies on a busy street corner in the middle of New York City.

"Nasty!" I hear someone sneer as they pass by.

My thoughts exactly. If I didn't feel so awful, I'd be incredibly embarrassed.

When I stand up, all the blood rushes from my head. There's another clap of thunder, and I barely register a flash of lightning against the dark gray of the sky and tall buildings.

"Nico," I mutter, just before I fall forward into his arms.

CHAPTER THIRTY

Layla

THERE'S A RINGING SOUND IN MY HEAD. IT COMES AND GOES, LIKE A TIMER GOING OFF, BUT just a bit slower. It's steady, but annoying. And it's making my head hurt more than it already did.

I groan. I just want it to stop. Ugh.

"Layla?"

The voice is warm, kind, and male, but not one I recognize. He repeats my name, and something rustles around my body. I'm in bed, but it's not *my* bed. My hands grasp at the sheets, and my eyes open.

"There she is. I thought you were coming around."

I stare through a foggy haze until my vision focuses on a round, tanned face framed by a mane of tawny blond hair. He looks like the human version of Simba from The Lion King.

Dressed in purple scrubs, Simba smiles sweetly. "Hey there. Welcome back."

I frown. My vision is a little hazy, but it's clearing up quickly. Looking around, I see that I'm in a small corner of a hospital, partitioned off from the rest of a busy ER by two hanging curtains that encircle my hospital bed. They are light blue, speckled with small pink teddy bears. My wrist aches a little. I look down to find an IV drip line inserted into my vein, just below the oversized sleeves of a hospital gown. It makes me feel faint again, so I lie back against my pillow and close my eyes again.

"You okay, there, honey?" Simba—the nurse, it appears—does a quick check of my vitals, taking my temperature and blood pressure in record time before making quick notes on my chart at the end of the bed. "I'm Tad, the nurse on call here tonight. You had quite a spell at the park."

I clear my throat, coughing a bit. I blink, trying to remember the name he just told me, but still, all I can come up with is Simba. "What...what happened?"

"You fainted, dear." His expression is kind and honest. "Right in the middle of

Lincoln Center, if you can believe that. You're lucky your boyfriend was there to catch you, otherwise you'd probably have a nice little gash and a concussion too. It's nothing major—just dehydration. Your doctor ordered an IV drip to help."

He taps the bag hanging from the rod next to my left elbow. I just nod as he continues checking me out. Where is Nico? Where are my clothes, my things? A pounding headache rips through the side of my head, but disappears quickly. God, I feel like shit. This is worse than any hangover I have ever had.

"Baby?"

A familiar deep voice rumbles, and a brown hand gingerly pulls the curtain aside. Nico's head pops in, his Yankees cap crooked and propped so far up that the bill points almost to the ceiling, the way it looks when he's been taking it on and off in quick succession. His worry transforms into relief when he sees I'm awake, and he wastes no time moving to sit on the edge of my bed.

"Hey," he murmurs sweetly as he takes my hand and brushes a thumb over my knuckles.

I squeeze gently, and he leans in to nuzzle my nose with his.

"You might want to give her some space," says Simba.

Nico sits up, obviously annoyed. The thunder in his expression is enough to cause the nurse's mouth to close mid-sentence.

"I'll let the on-call doctor know you're awake," Simba says as he ducks away.

Nico turns back to me. "You need space, baby?" he asks with a sneaky grin. "Is *Lion King* right?"

I giggle. "You see it too?"

"How could I not? He looks like he just ran in from the Serengeti. Was off chasing wildebeests and shit."

I giggle again. Nico lifts a hand up to cup my face, then runs it down my neck to rest on my shoulder. He exhales, long and slow between full, pursed lips.

"You scared me, sweetie." His voice is almost too low to hear. He studies the edge of my hospital gown, fingering the coarse fabric.

"I'm sorry." My own voice is coarse, unused, though it hasn't really been that long that I was out.

"Layla, you got nothing to be sorry about." Nico's deep eyes fill with kindness.

"I know. I just...I'm pissed I ruined our date."

At that, Nico tips his head back and laughs loudly, big from his belly. "Our date? You were worried about ruining our *date*?"

"Well, it was important!" I protest, suddenly irritated that he finds this so funny. I want to shove him aside, but I've got a freaking needle stuck in my arm. "You went through all that trouble with the picnic. And it was our first big date since...you know. Since you decided to..."

"Stay?"

Nico just laughs harder, his whole body shaking. I cross my arms and fume, which only makes him laugh even more. I stare at the stupid teddy bears until finally he calms down long enough to catch his breath.

"Only you...shit...ah, my stomach hurts," he stutters, still chuckling every few words. "Only you would faint in the middle of the fuckin' street, baby, and then worry that you ruined our date. God, you are so fuckin' cute!"

I stick my lower lip out and frown, but I can't keep the sour expression for long. Nico's big hands capture my face as he gives me a gentle kiss, ending with a nip of my bottom lip and the promise of more once I feel better. He leans his forehead onto mine again and sighs.

"Don't ever fuckin' do that to me again, all right?"

It's then I realize that he was genuinely scared, that most of his laughter is rooted in fear. I whimper and accept another kiss with a closed mouth, conscious that I haven't brushed my teeth since losing my lunch. Then I scoot over on the bed and pull him beside me so I can rest on his broad chest.

"How long was I out?" I ask, winding an arm around his middle while one of his wraps around my shoulder.

Nico kisses the top of my head and rests his chin there for a second. "About an hour and a half. You just…shit, baby. I thought you were dying or something. You just collapsed. Your eyes rolled back in your head, and you just looked…gone."

I exhale sharply. I obviously can't remember what it felt like to pass out, but I can imagine how scary it would be to see Nico do something like that. Instinctively, I burrow a little closer.

"I'm sorry. I didn't mean to scare you."

He just hugs me tighter. "And I told you. Nothing to be sorry for. We just…*I* just need to take better care of my girl."

I sigh, but don't reply. I love that he wants to take care of me, but I don't want to be another burden in his life. He already takes care of so many people.

But he speaks before I can say as much.

"Layla," he says, and I'm struck by the way his voice, normally so deep and strong, quivers slightly around my name. "Layla, baby, I—"

But before he can finish his sentence, we're interrupted by a tall woman in a white coat and a stethoscope.

"Ms. Barros?" she asks as she pulls the curtain aside. It's not really a question, since she's reading my name from the chart.

Nico stands up, and the doctor looks him over.

"I hear this guy is your hero."

Nico suddenly looks bashful, and I smile back at the doctor. "I guess he is."

"Lucky you." She moves to the other side of the bed to sit next to me on a rolling stool. "I'm Dr. Andrews. I just wanted to check in, make sure you're feeling better now that you've woken up. Tad said your vitals are good."

I nod. "Okay."

She looks at the IV bag. "Well, you took almost two full bags—you were pretty dehydrated. You don't have a concussion thanks to this guy, but you should continue to hydrate at home and try to take it easy. It's so easy to relapse when you've had mono this badly."

I blink. "Wait…what?" Did she say mono? "No, no. I had the flu a few weeks ago. It's just a relapse from that."

Dr. Andrews pages through the chart again. "Um, no dear. We did a blood test just to check for some things, and you came up positive for mono. Mr. Soltero told us that you had been sick recently. It wasn't hard to put two and two together." She flips the papers back down. "Sometimes mono is hard to diagnose. It can look like the flu in the beginning. Let me guess: you've been a little more tired than usual and lost a bit of weight recently."

"More like a lot," Nico pipes up.

I swallow. My chest feels like it's made of ice. I know it's not cancer or anything, but this is the last thing I need. It's the middle of the semester. I have finals coming in a few more weeks. I can't be this sick right now.

"You'll need to take it easy over the next few weeks," Dr. Andrews is saying. "I'm going to prescribe some anti-nausea medication to make sure you can keep food down, but more importantly, you need to be getting enough sleep. I'm guessing you've been feeling tired a bit?"

I nod. I have, but I figured that was just because, you know, I hadn't exactly been sleeping a ton. Like every other college student.

"Well, then," Dr. Andrews says. "No hot baths. Minimize your caffeine intake. No alcohol, or even tea, which is a diuretic."

Nico takes my hand as my mouth falls open. No caffeine? How am I supposed to make it through eight-a.m. classes without caffeine?

The doctor continues to rattle off a bunch more suggestions for a speedy recovery. I'm left feeling like an invalid. I basically have to be treated like I'm on hospice for a week or two. This is seriously the last thing I need right now. I glance up at Nico, who is listening intently to every word she says. Shit. Like a twenty-six-year-old wants to play nursemaid to his new girlfriend. How fucking romantic.

"Ms. Barros?" Dr. Andrews pulls my attention. "Do you have any questions?"

I blink. "No. No, I think I got it."

Dr. Andrews replaces the chart at the end of my bed. "All right, I'm going to get your paperwork started to go home. As soon as it's finished, you're free to go."

"Sounds good. Thank you."

She ducks out with a polite nod, and Nico immediately resumes our previous position with my head back on his chest. He hums a little as he strokes my hair. I close my eyes. Nowhere feels as good as right here.

"Mono," he murmurs. "Damn."

"I'm okay." I say, gripping him closer.

His warmth emanates through the thin cotton of his t-shirt, soft and worn under my cheek. He smells so good—an antidote for any ailment. But then the realization hits me of just what I've been diagnosed with. Mono is a kissing disease. Which means if I have it, Nico probably does too. Or will, unless I stop kissing him now.

Double damn.

"God, Layla," he breathes. He kisses my forehead. "I just...I feel...Layla, I really lo—"

My heart is starting to beat a little quicker at the cadence of his words when a familiar voice cuts through the beeps and hustle of the hospital.

"No, no, Mr. Barros, I'm here now."

I flop back into my pillow while Nico chuckles and shakes his head beside me. Apparently, hospital beds are the absolute worst places for emotional confessions.

Quinn blusters through the curtain, batting it out of her way as if it's no more than a spider web. Her other hand clasps her phone to her ear; she's obviously talking with my father.

"She's awake," she tells him. "Okay. Here she is." Quinn shakes her head as she holds the phone to me, her palm covering the speaker at the bottom. "You," she says before tsking. "What are we going to do with you? It's your dad. And he is *pissed*, Lay."

I scowl at the phone. "Do I have to?"

Before Quinn can give me a sharp retort—which I'm certain she's been saving up since my dad is no picnic to deal with—Nico plucks the phone away and holds it to his ear.

"Mr. Barros?" he says while Quinn and I just stare in shock.

Quinn glances at me in one of those secret, telepathic messages only best friends can perform. Her confused expression clearly asks, "Has he ever talked to your dad before?"

I just shrug and shake my head. I'm equal parts curious and terrified by this turn of events.

"This is Nico Soltero, sir. Layla's—ah—friend." Nico glances at me and raises his big shoulders. He clearly isn't sure what he's supposed to say here. "She's just sleeping, sir. Yes. Yes, I was with her. No, sir, I didn't do anything to her."

At that, I reach out, beckoning for the phone. Nico shakes his head and waves my hand away.

"No, sir, I'm not a student. I, uh, I'm a friend of hers from work. We were at the park. A picnic, sir. No, sir, I wasn't planning to assault your daughter in any way. I mean, unless she asked me to, sir. That was a joke, sir."

Nico turns back to me with wide eyes, but I can tell by the appearance of his dimples that he's pretty tickled by the conversation. I struggle to sit up and try for the phone again, but he dodges my reach as he hops off the bed.

"Nico," I hiss. "Give it to me. Now!"

"Oh, look, sir, she's awake. She wants to talk to you. Yes, Mr. Barros, nice talking to you, too."

He hands me the phone with a shit-eating grin. I want to hurl it at him and kiss him at the same time. No one ever gives my dad a bad time. But I know I'm going to have to pay for it in just a second.

"Hi, Dad," I say reluctantly.

"Layla, who was that?" My dad's voice is sharp and insistent. He's clearly not amused with the conversation.

I sigh. "Just like he said, Dad. Nico is a friend from work."

"Why were you with him alone in a park? He said his name is Nico? What kind of name is that? It sounds Greek. You were with a strange Greek man at the park?"

I roll my eyes. Only my dad can make a spring day in the park sound like a lecherous activity. Of course, it was pretty damn lecherous at one point, but he doesn't need to know that.

"It's a nice day," I say. "No strange Greek men involved. Nico and I both had some free time, so we met up for lunch. Is that a crime?"

"What did he do that made you pass out? He says his name is Soltero? Where is he from?"

My heart picks up a beat, and I glance at Quinn, who is now watching me sympathetically. She's no stranger to my dad's third-degree.

"I just walked too far, Dad," I mumble, ignoring the second question about Nico's name. "The weather is super humid here, and we got caught in a rainstorm. It changed quickly, and we had to run across the park to get out of the rain. I over-exerted. That's what the doctors say."

"Yes, I know. Dr. Andrews also said you have mononucleosis. This is a serious thing, Layla."

Great, so he's been on the phone with the hospital too. Now I'm wishing I hadn't given them permission to disclose my records to him, doctor or not. But that's the condition of being on his health insurance.

"Layla, your mother and I think you should come home."

It's the sentence I've been waiting for all semester—the last three, to be exact—and frankly, I'm surprised it hasn't come sooner. I sit up farther, bracing myself for an argument, and Nico, who is now beside me with a comfortable hand on my leg, frowns in confusion.

"Dad," I say. "It's too late in the semester for that. Classes are done in less than two months. I'm fine, really."

"You are not fine!" he roars into my ear so loudly before continuing in a quick, almost unintelligible onslaught of Portuguese, full of idioms I can't follow. I have to hold Quinn's phone away until he calms down. Both Quinn and Nico watch with wide eyes, and I bite my lip. My dad only speaks Portuguese to his family or when he's really, really angry. He doesn't do well when he loses control of the situation.

"Dad?" I say once he's finally done.

There's a long pause on the other side of the line. Then, finally: "What, Layla?"

I exhale. If he's back to my name, I'm on the way into the clear. "I'll be back in May. I promise."

I can't look at Nico's face when I say it. He just promised to stay, and here I am, promising my father I'll leave New York, if only for the summer. But there is no way in hell I'll be able to convince my folks to let me stay here for the summer, and the money my mom sent already went to paying off the rest of my bills. Without being able to work, I won't be able to save up enough to stay.

"I can manage, okay?" I continue. "No more walks in the rainstorms, I promise. I'll be careful."

My dad grumbles something unintelligible before answering. "May," he barks and hangs up.

I hold the phone away, somewhat dazed, before Quinn takes it. She and Nico both watch with obvious concern as I slide back against my pillows. Suddenly, I'm exhausted again.

"He's...worried," I say as I curl into Nico's chest when he pulls me close again.

"He cares," Quinn says. She takes a seat in the small chair next to the bed. "We all do."

"Yeah," Nico murmurs as he lightly strokes my hair. "We do."

CHAPTER THIRTY-ONE

Layla

I WAKE UP THE NEXT MORNING IN A PILE OF BLANKETS, MY SKIN CLAMMY UNDER THE weight of a rumpled twist of sheets and an extra comforter. It's been a restless night, one made worse by the return of nausea whenever the pills wore off. *Mono*, said the doctor. Fuck.

Nico and Quinn brought me home together after the hospital, arguing in the cab most of the way. Quinn was more in line with my father, convinced that Nico was at least partially responsible for my condition, while Nico insisted the entire time that he had no idea I wasn't feeling well.

Stuck between them, I was too tired to defend Nico, and I collapsed into my bed almost immediately when we got back to Lafayette. I woke several times during the night, usually to shove a blanket off my sweaty body, and then again to pull it back on when I was chilled to the bone. Some of my memories were tinted with the proximity of a warm, comforting body and a kind hand on my forehead. The sounds of a baritone hum and the occasional "Shh."

It's not until I finally climb out of bed sometime past nine in the morning that, when I nearly step smack onto a pile of curled-up man, I realize how many of the fevered dreams were real. Nico is asleep in a nest of extra blankets and cushions pulled off the couch. His jacket, cap, and shoes are folded neatly on my desk chair, but otherwise he still wears the jeans and wrinkled shirt from the day before. He's snoring slightly and some spit has dried on the pillowcase under his mouth. He's adorable.

Careful not to disturb him, I tiptoe out to the kitchen, closing the bedroom door gently behind me. Quinn is sitting at the bar, calmly paging through a textbook while she sips a cup of coffee. A glance at the couch tells me she spent the night there. Again. My stomach plummets with guilt.

"Hey there, sickie!" she greets me with a smile. "How're you feeling, babe?"

I take a seat, wrapping my bathrobe tightly around my waist. "Okay. Better than last night." I look at the couch again. "I'm so sorry you're sleeping out here again."

"Bah, it's fine," she says. "Seriously, if I was the one with mono, you'd be kicked to the curb." She looks past me toward the closed door of our bedroom. "I take it Special Delivery is still asleep?"

I nod. "Yeah. I can't believe he stayed."

Even in my achy condition, my heart swells a little at the thought. I stare at the big oak door separating his sleeping form from the common room.

"He's sweet, Lay."

Quinn's voice is softer, more forgiving than usual. It's the first time she's really acknowledged anything good about Nico. For most of the time he and I have been seeing each other, she's been a consistent Devil's Advocate, and it's caused some tension between us over the past several weeks.

"He is," I agree. "Very."

I sigh again and run a hand through my bedraggled hair. I no doubt look horrendous after spending a day at the hospital and a night twisting around.

"I'm going to take a shower." I get up, holding the edge of the bar to keep myself steady. I'm still so weak; already I'm feeling tired all over again.

Quinn nods and turns back to her textbook.

"I'm glad he's here," she says. "He'll take care of you."

———

It's NOT until I'm in the shower that Quinn's last words really sink in, and I start to think about what this situation means for me and Nico. That there is no way I'm going to be able to convince my parents to let me stay in New York this summer. In six more weeks, I'm going to have to go back to Washington for the summer, leaving when Nico and I have barely had time to start. It's not that long to solidify a new relationship, and now I might have to spend half that time staying away from him if I don't want to get him sick too.

My heart suddenly feels like it's been smashed with a hammer. Tears spring to my eyes, and a sob chokes in my throat. I know I'm being melodramatic, but as I stand under the running water, thinking about my misfortunes—the bills that keep piling up as I skip more days off work, the fact that just after Nico promised he would stay, I have to leave for the entire summer, and now that I'm sick, our time together will be shortened even more—I can't see the bright spot in any of it. Except Nico.

I love him. That's really all it boils down to. The words come easily in my mind. I love him with every fiber of my being, and every new thing I discover about him makes me fall harder. I love him like crazy, and when it really comes down to it, no one says no to that.

Except this goddamn body.

I slap an angry hand on my thigh, hard enough to leave a red mark that fades beneath the water. A rush of nausea rises. I dart out of the shower just in time to make it to the toilet, heaving up what little I've been able to eat in the last twenty-four hours in a mess of choked sobs as water runs off my body and onto the warped boards of the bathroom floor.

Once I finish my shower, I hobble back to my room, catching a concerned glance from Quinn as I pass. Nico is still passed out on the floor—considering how worried he was, he was probably up more than I was. I manage to put on one of the t-shirts he's left behind on some other, much happier day and creep back into my bed without waking him. All of the drama running through my brain is suddenly replaced by complete and total fatigue as I drift off to sleep, to a place where none of this can harm either of us.

———

Nico

After spending an hour or so in the morning making sure Layla's going to be okay, I finally have to leave in time to meet my mom and brother for noon Mass. I didn't want to leave. It went against every instinct I had letting her stay by herself. But she has three other girls to check on her, and Quinn actually promised to send me updates if there were any changes. Rest and water. That's all the doctor said she needs. Having me hover isn't going to help.

Gabe meets me outside the church, holding one of his button-up shirts for me to shrug on before we run into the church.

"I don't know why you bother," he says as he watches me struggle to roll up the sleeves. "She's still gonna be mad you're wearing jeans."

Gabe's taller than me, but skinnier, and sleeves that button around his chicken arms won't even come close around mine. Forget about the collar.

"Whatever," I say as I finish with the sleeves. I smooth down the shirt and glance at my worn Converse. "I'm here, aren't I? I'd rather be sleeping."

"With your girl?" Gabe says. "I don't blame you. She's fine as hell, Nico. You lucky I didn't see her first."

I snort. From anyone else, the idea of some other guy looking at Layla like that would be enough for some serious words, but from my goofy-ass brother, it's just funny.

"Last time I wore a t-shirt, she wouldn't stop with it for like a week," I say before shaking my face a little, like I'm preparing for a fight. "Let's go in before Ma interrupts the priest to come get us."

We shuffle toward our customary pew in the middle of the old church as quietly as possible while a lector is intoning one of the liturgies in Spanish. Shit. I knew I was late, but not that late.

My mother guilts as many of her kids as she can into coming to church on Sundays, and this week she managed to snag all of us. She's on the end of the worn wood pew, followed by the short, round silhouettes of my sisters, and my niece Allie. I nod at everyone as Gabe and I slide into the pew behind them. Allie twists around with her tiny-toothed grin. I grin back, and she giggles.

"*Tío!*" she half-squeals, half-whispers.

"Hey, *linda!*" I whisper with a wink. "Turn around, *mamita*, okay? Otherwise you're gonna get the *chancleta* from *Abuela*."

Allie's eyes pop open in fear. All kids in this neighborhood grow up worried about getting the *chancleta*, the house slipper that doubles as a weapon when kids misbehave. She turns back around, but I've caught the attention of her mother instead. Great. The priest announces the Gospel, and the entire church stands with echoes of hundreds of feet on the stone floors.

"Where you been? Allie and I came to the apartment last night, but you never came home." Maggie stares pointedly at me over her shoulder, even as her hands are clasped in front of her like she's caught up in the prayer. I know better. My sister is the least penitent person on the planet.

I just nod my head toward the talking priest, as if to tell her to pay attention. She just screws her round face into an even deeper scowl. Honestly, I'm not sure I've seen my sister smile in about five years.

"You been downtown again? With that young girl?" She says it with a snarl, like spending time with Layla is the equivalent of doing coke or running around with a bunch of hoods.

"Gabe said that's *all* he's been doing," says Selena, my other sister, in a loud whisper behind our mother's back. "Nico's too good for the Kitchen these days. Spends all his time downtown now." She whistles lightly and chants "*chavos, chavos*" under her breath.

I roll my eyes. Selena gives me a sly smile before she re-clasps her hands in her lap and bows her head like she's listening really hard. The action makes her giant earrings jangle a little.

"You're just jealous you ain't got a man," I retort, but a little too loudly, since my mom's head pops up.

Selena's mouth pops open like she wants to shout back at me. It was a cheap shot —she only just broke up with her boyfriend and moved back home.

The priest ends the Gospel reading, and all at once, the entire church says "*Gloria a ti, Señor Jesus.*"

"*Mira!*" hisses my mother as we all sit back down. We obediently look up, but instead of saying anything, she fixes us with The Look, the one I've seen all my life, especially in church. It's a look that, if we were little, would tell us we better shut up. It's a look that tells us she's got something for us when we get home, something we're not going to like. It doesn't matter that we're grown adults. The Look never changes, and it always hits your bones.

All four of us quiet immediately.

I glance at Gabe, who's suddenly looking everywhere but at me, like the little snitch he is. He's the only one who knew about Layla, and the little shit's been blabbing to the two biggest busybodies in Manhattan. Now I don't just have to spend the rest of my day fixing shit, but I have to listen to my sisters nag at me while I do it. Fuckin' great.

BY THREE-THIRTY, the novelty of interrogating my love life has worn off, and Selena and Maggie have finally left our mom's apartment. She's having me check the electrical work on the stove, which has been acting funny. The landlord needs to replace it, but Ma's too scared to ask for anything like that. It doesn't matter that Robbie's name is on the lease now and that we have legal rights to decent living conditions. She's lived for too long in this place doing whatever this fucking slumlord wanted because she was terrified he'd evict her, or worse. Half of this building lives in fear of ICE (U.S. Immigration and Customs Enforcement). So I still to do what I can to help.

"Okay," I say in Spanish as I shove the stove back against the wall. "That should hold the wires together for now until I can find someone to replace the whole system.

But you need to be careful until then—just run one thing at a time in the kitchen. Otherwise it's gonna blow a circuit, and then you won't be able to watch your telenovelas."

Her mouth twists into a smirk at the little joke. She doesn't even like telenovelas, even though they are the only things she watches anymore. I speak in Spanish, not because she can't understand English, but because my mother still doesn't speak it back. I used to wonder how my mother could live in this country for thirty years but never learn English, but as I got older, the answers became clearer. Even though she came from Puerto Rico and lived there since she was a little girl, my mom wasn't a citizen because she was born in Cuba. She's lived her entire life in shadows, terrified of deportation. And for a long time, we hid with her. Now we're more like her shields.

Back in the day, our building sounded more like San Juan than the mainland, but that's changed a lot as the neighborhood started to gentrify. Still, most of the people here are still like Ma. People who came here scared, many of them maybe legal, maybe not. People who never quite shook off that fear and the hardness that comes from it. I know that at some point we're going to have to figure out a different situation for her. One day this place will be sold out from under her to some high-rise developer, just like all the other buildings in Midtown, and she'll have nowhere to go. I only pray I'll know what to do when it happens.

But things are a little better now. For one, she doesn't have to worry about raising kids anymore now that we're all grown. There's no more asking K.C.'s mom to sign parental consent forms as our guardian, or latching onto less-than-nice dudes to make ends meet when she was in between odd jobs. The first thing I did when I started at FedEx was to transfer her lease under my name and start paying the rent. But she still won't open the door to people she doesn't know. Which means when things break, it's still up to me to fix them.

"*Ven, papi*," she beckons me to a spot on the couch, the same faded, flowered sleeper we've had since I was a kid. For a long time, this couch was my bed.

I sit down. "*Que pa'o, Mami?*"

"This girl?" she asks. "The *blanquita* Gabe was talking about? Who is she?"

I frown. *Blanquita* isn't exactly the nicest word for what Layla is: a rich girl, probably a white girl. Someone who thinks she's better than everyone else. Stuck-up.

"Did Gabe call her that?"

Ma shrugs, but shakes her head. Which means it was probably one of my sisters. Maggie, I'm guessing.

I chew on my lip, a habit I get from my mother, but I can't will away the tight feeling in my chest when I think about Layla. We've texted a few more times today, and honestly, I'm dying to get back down there, even if it's just to kiss her goodnight. I'm not sure how much longer I'll be able to go without telling her just how I feel.

"I see..." my mother says as she watches my face.

I sigh. My mom's always been able to read me like a book. So I shrug. There's no use hiding it.

"She's nice," I say. "She's smart."

Ma doesn't reply. Not all Puerto Rican women are loud and obnoxious. My sisters have no problem fulfilling that stereotype, but my mother is the quiet type. Her silences speak just as loudly, and right now, this one is screaming doubt.

She hums a little under her breath and nods. She pushes back her hair, which is coarse, threaded with gray through the black, and tied into a little knot at the back of her head. It sticks out around her face a little, just like always. She could never afford to have it done when we were kids, and she refuses the money I give her for it now. *Stupid*, she says. *Waste of money.*

"Gabe said that she goes to college," Ma states. "She's white?"

I swallow roughly. "No. She's Brazilian. Her dad's from Rio, I think."

I don't answer the question about her family's money. I know my mother. She's had a hard life. Her whole life, she was the kind of person who cleaned other people's houses instead of having hers cleaned. Layla hasn't said much about her dad's family, but she said she drove through the slums in Rio. She didn't get out and stay.

Ma just wrinkles her nose. "They don't speak Spanish." It's not a question.

I roll my eyes. "No, they don't. But she doesn't really speak Portuguese either, so..."

My mother's big eyes flash dangerously. Fuck, that was the wrong thing to say. To someone like my mother, that right there is a sign that Layla really is a *blanquita*, no matter where her dad was born. And from what Layla has told me, her dad is exactly the kind of man my mother despises. The kind of man who turns his back on his own.

I sit silently. There's no use arguing about it with her. My mother is stubborn, completely immovable. I know she'll love Layla when she meets her—one day, maybe, in the very distant future. But for now, maybe it's easier to just pretend things don't matter.

"It's no big deal," I mutter in English, sitting forward and examining my hands.

"'No big deal'," Mom repeats in her thick accent before reverting back to Spanish. "What does this mean? Is this '*no big deal*' the reason you are not going to Los Angeles?"

I look up sharply. When I broke the news earlier today that I was staying, Ma was so happy she cried and made *arepas*. No one else knows yet, but it's different with her. She's my mother.

"She—I—"

The words won't come out the way they're supposed to. I want to say no, say I decided I was better off staying here. I want to say Layla had nothing to do with it, even though she had everything to do with it.

My mother puckers her lips and makes a sort of squeaky sound between them while she raises her almost non-existent eyebrows. It's a look I know well. It means I'm full of shit.

I hang my head.

After a few moments, I feel a hand on my back, urging me to sit up. Ma cups my face with her hand and runs her coarse thumb over my cheekbone.

"My beautiful boy," she says. "If you reach too high for the stars, you're going to fall."

My throat feels thick. This is not what I was expecting her to say, but I shouldn't be surprised. "But—"

"*Mira*," she commands. "I didn't want you to go to move away, but I knew it would make you happy. This girl, I don't know her, but I don't think she will. Too different. You need to be your own man now. You don't need her to hold you back and hurt you later when she becomes tired with you." She clasps my hand. "Believe me, *papito*. I know. That's what they always do."

A hundred things fly through my head. That Layla would never do that. That she's not like the assholes that used my mother and left her worse off than she was before. That when I'm with her, I don't feel like some loser from the *barrio*, or some brown-skinned guy she wants to get off with, but just me, just Nico.

But Ma has always had the ability to puncture fantasies. If I'm being honest, it's probably one of the reasons I've been trying to leave for so long. As much as I love my family, I wouldn't mind taking a break from people who have a tendency to shoot each other down, even if it is out of a sense of survival.

"Okay, Ma," is all I have to say in the end. "I gotta go. I have to be at work in a few hours."

I lean down and deliver kisses on both my mother's cheeks. She clasps my face tightly before letting me go. We don't say I love you before I leave. Those are not words my mother uses lightly, if at all.

Long after I leave, her words echo through my head. Somehow, someway, they hit their mark. And when I get on the train, I go uptown to my empty apartment instead of downtown, where Layla sleeps, thinking I'll be back.

CHAPTER THIRTY-TWO

Layla

"Oh, shame take all her friends then! But howe'er
Thou and the baser world censure my life,
I'll send 'em word by thee, and write so much
Upon thy breast, 'cause thou shalt bear 't in mind:
Tell them 'twere base to yield where I have conquer'd.
I scorn to prostitute myself to a man,
I that can prostitute a man to me:
And so I greet thee."

Quinn intones another quote from the massive English study packet. My British Literature exam is next week, and it won't be easy. I'm terrible at memorizing texts verbatim, and it's ten times worse when it's for a class that, up to now, has focused almost solely on medieval epic poetry and Renaissance literature. I thought that Nico would be upset that I had to forgo our usual Friday night date, but he immediately switched nights with the other doorman at AJ's so we could go out tonight instead. Seriously, he's almost as bad as Quinn about making sure I do my schoolwork.

The last few weeks haven't been as bad as I thought. I spent a little over a week recovering and forcing Nico to stay at his place instead of mine, and since then, I've taken an extra week off on the doctor's orders to avoid a relapse. No late nights. No long days walking around the city. Class, studying, and only on the weekends is Nico willing to hang out for more than an hour, usually bringing me up to his place to hole up for a movie night. It's been nice. And then it got boring. Fast.

Seriously. I didn't move to New York to watch reruns of *You've Got Mail*. And there is no way that Nico's not bored either. I'm pretty much done with him treating me with kid gloves, and I think it's been affecting our normal rapport. I can't really tell you why, but something's different. Little things. I'll catch Nico looking out the window, gazing off into space in the middle of a conversation. Or maybe his mom or one of his siblings call, and he looks like he's in pain. Nothing big. But I can't help but feel like I've only added to his burdens.

Well, no more of that.

"Ooh, an easy one," I say. "That's *The Roaring Girl*, by Middleton and Dekker. Published in 1611. It's about a crossdressing chick named Moll, and that's the scene where she basically tells the guy to fuck off, that she can be the seducer, and then they sword-fight. I love that play." I chuckle. "Some days I'd love to toss these stupid binding things we have to wear, and be all, fuck you, I can be a man too! I could even get a sword and take up dueling."

"I wouldn't mind seeing you wielding a rapier," Quinn remarks as she marks the passage, indicating I know it. "You probably shouldn't say 'fuck' in your exam, but otherwise you got it. That's the last one. You're getting better at this, babe."

"And it only took me two whole days!"

I'm finally starting to feel caught up with the classes I missed while I was sick. Quinn and I have been quizzing each other on and off for the last forty-eight hours, and we've earned a much-needed night out. I'm rallying with an extra Diet Coke while I wait for Nico to pick me up. My doctor gave me the okay to drink caffeinated beverages again (thank *God*), but I'm supposed to keep it to two a day for a while. I've been saving this one.

Nico and I haven't really been able to *go out* go out since I was in the hospital, so tonight he's taking me to one of those huge midtown clubs where celebrities are always in the VIP rooms, and where I never go simply because I can't afford a thirty-dollar cover. He used to work there, so we can get in for free. I'm excited to see what this kind of place is like, considering I've generally stuck to the small bars and cabarets that proliferate downtown Manhattan. But mostly I'm excited because K.C., *the* K.C., is spinning there tonight, and I finally get to meet Nico's very best friend.

That is, if Nico actually shows up.

I glance at the clock on my desk, which reads 10:09. Nico's very late, over two hours, in fact. According to a rushed call at eight, he had dinner with his family and lost track of the time. He had to take the train back up to his apartment, and then he was coming back downtown to pick me up. There have been no phone calls since.

One by one my roommates have left, not wanting to spend our one night out this week sitting around waiting for my boyfriend to show up. Shama took off at about nine to hang at Fat Black's with Jason, and Jamie followed about twenty minutes later after hearing that Jason had brought friends.

"I think that's enough," I tell Quinn.

She sets the study packet down. I can tell she's feeling antsy too. Out of the four of us, she's easily the best student, and has been saying "no" more often than not to going out in order to get an A in her Organic Chemistry class. Tonight is also her much-needed break too, and I know she doesn't want to miss it.

I lumber off my bed to check my appearance again in the full-length mirror we keep by the door. This is the fifth time in an hour I've done this.

"Babe, you still look gorgeous," Quinn says from her bed.

Quinn's got her second-best dark jeans, a gorgeous green shirt that brings out her eyes, and her new designer heels that she bought with some of the money her dad sends her each month. I try not to stare enviously at them; my own shoes, which I bought in Brazil two years ago, were beautiful when I bought them, but the heels have definitely seen better days.

I've still stepped it up a notch, since I'm supposed to be going to such a high-profile club. I borrowed a gold, sequined-covered mini-dress from Shama that she bought at a sample sale last year, which I've paired with my black strappy stilettos and a vintage black clutch. Jamie helped me teased my curls out Beyoncé-style. I look approvingly at myself in the mirror. While I was on bed rest, Nico and the girls have been stuffing me silly, and I've finally gained a bit of the weight back that I lost. I fill out this dress the way I'm supposed to, and I look appropriately diva-esque for a nightclub. Too bad there's no one here to take me.

"You sure you don't want to go to the club too?" I ask. "It would be better than Fat Black's again..."

"I...yeah. Probably not," Quinn says as I turn around. "I won't leave you here by yourself, babe, but I don't really want to be the third wheel either. Unless you wanna just say 'fuck him' and come with me?"

I purse my lips, considering. It's a tempting thought. I'm trying not to be too pissed about Nico's disappearance, but the truth is, I'm starting to feel stood up. He should have been here a long time ago. Shades of Teddy, my asshole of an ex who used to skip out on our dates all the time, are also messing with my mind.

"No," I finally say with a shake of my head. Nico's not the type to play me like that. "Something has probably happened. But, Quinn, don't waste your night. You should go ahead."

I sit back down on the bed and gather up my study materials, trying my hardest not to glance at the phone that has been sitting silent on my desk.

"Are you sure?" Quinn's asking to be nice, but she's already standing up.

I smile. "Of course. I have this to keep me company." I hold up the study packet, and Quinn makes a face. "You go have fun. I'll be fine."

She evaluates me for a second, then grabs her coat and purse off her bed.

"Give him hell," Quinn says as she passes by, her heels clicking on the wood floor. The clock now says it's closer to ten-thirty. Yeah, I think to myself, I probably will.

———

It's almost eleven by the time my phone finally buzzes next to my feet on the coffee table. I almost fall over in my frenzy to grab it: a text message from Nico, asking me to meet him on the street. I sigh.

For the last half hour, I've been alternating between pacing around the apartment and watching crappy television, finding it difficult to evict the nasty suspicions that have gotten stuck in my head and won't leave. New York's an easy place to lead a double life—most people who live here rarely venture outside of where they work and live, so getting lost in the eight million people who live here is as simple as taking your date to a different neighborhood. People get conned every day. Jamie once went on a blind date with someone who faked losing his wallet at the restaurant, then talked his way up into our dorm so he could make out with her and leave, but not before stealing her cell phone and Discman. Two weeks later, Shama spotted him at a local Starbucks, giving other NYU students a totally different name.

By the time Nico pulls up in a cab, I'm standing in the lobby of my building literally tapping the sole of my sandal on the hard linoleum. The weather has warmed up a bit during the days, but it's still cold at night. My head, however, has been getting hotter and hotter with every minute. Once I knew Nico wasn't maimed or disfigured, my imagination spiraled out of control. There's a surprising amount of pessimism I can develop in just twenty minutes.

I get into the cab without touching Nico or looking at him, trying not to be affected by the scent of his body wash or the fact that he looks really freaking good dressed up in a pair of slim black pants and a fitted gray shirt. No hat to cover up his thick black hair that he's actually styled a little for the occasion.

I stare at my lap. He might look like a million bucks, but that doesn't make him any less late.

"Fifty-Seventh and Eighth," he calls to the cabbie before turning to me with that hundred-watt smile that seems to glow, even in the dark cab interior. "Hey, baby," he says. "Damn, you clean up nice. This dress is crazy sexy. I haven't seen you like this in a while."

I feel the wall of irritation and suspicion start to crack as he scoots closer to give me a kiss on the cheek and rests one warm hand on my knee, causing unsolicited tingles to ripple up my thigh. I almost return the kiss—I know the addictive softness of those lips, and I haven't been able to feel them since Monday. I miss him.

Then I remember that he's almost three hours late. And that he's been acting kind of weird in general. One phone call. That's all I got.

"Where were you?" I ask before he manages to brush a kiss across my lips.

Nico pulls back, his dark features twisted with confusion. "What do you mean? I called to let you know I was going to be late."

I look down at where my hands grip my black velvet clutch and rub my thumb over the vintage ball clasp, avoiding his gaze.

"That was two and a half hours ago, Nico. You couldn't have called again? When I wasn't imagining you dead, I thought you were standing me up, and so did my roommates."

I can't bring myself to tell him I have also been imagining him with another woman for a lot of that time.

Nico sighs impatiently and rubs the back of his neck. "Baby, I was on the train. It took me forty minutes to get to my place once I left Hell's Kitchen. I got home, showered, changed—believe me, you do not want me to take you to a club in my Yankees hat and a t-shirt with bathroom caulk smeared all over it. By the time I left my place, it was almost ten. Took me an hour to get here because the train was late, and then I had to catch a cab."

I look up and find him watching me with raised brows and his head cocked to one side knowingly, as if he's waiting for me to smile and forgive him immediately. I'm close, but not quite there. Instead, I frown.

"I just think it's weird," I say. "Almost three hours to get up to your place and back? If you went somewhere or—or saw someone else, you should just tell me."

I know I'm starting to sound paranoid, but I can't help it. The green-eyed monster arrived the moment Quinn walked out that door and I was left by myself.

Nico sighs and runs a hand back over his head again. I notice he got a haircut today—his thick black curls are cut closer than normal. The curved shape of his head is that much clearer, and I want to run my hands over it. I look down and scowl.

"Please don't tell me you're one of those crazy jealous chicks, Layla," he says finally. "I don't have the patience for that kind of shit, and I really didn't peg you for that."

"So you just happened to be super late and went to this mysterious family dinner, and didn't think to tell me about it? I don't even get a quick text to let me know when you're on your way? Something doesn't add up. What's really going on?"

I'm met with a hard look I've never seen in Nico's eyes, which are usually so buoyant and full of life. Actually, that's not true. I've seen it before—when those Wall Street idiots tried to bribe him outside of AJ's and started making cracks about me. It's the kind of look he gives when he thinks people are being stupid *and* insulting. I have to fight not to cower back into my seat; I feel like it turns me to stone.

The cab stops and Nico flips a couple of bills at the driver before jerking the car door open. He pulls me out behind him roughly, but slows down when the heel of my stiletto hooks on a crack in the pavement. Then he tows me past the very long line of people waiting to get into the club, and I try to ignore their dirty looks as we pass.

"Nico, we're not done talking," I say, trying to slow him down, but he just keeps walking, his hand a vise around my wrist.

"Hey, Cameron!" he booms, his deep voice catching the notice of a small man with a blond goatee. Standing just outside the club in a suit and a long black overcoat, and carrying a clipboard, the man smiles when he sees us approach and holds out his hand to pull Nico in for a one-armed hug. Nico returns the embrace tightly, but doesn't let go of my wrist.

"Nico, my *man*, what the fuck're you doin' here?" Cameron has a Queens accent so thick it sounds like he's talking through the skinny end of a Coke bottle. He looks me up and down, appreciatively lingering on my bare legs. "And who is this gorgeous girl you got with you? What are you doin' these days, datin' models now?"

Beside me, Nico stiffens. I blush, even though I know it's just flattery. I'm cute, but I'm no model.

"This is Layla," Nico introduces me with a quick grin. I'm so confused—I thought he was mad, and now he looks thrilled to have me with him. "Baby, this dickhead is Cameron. We used to work the door here together a few years back."

"Yeah, except they had to fire his ass because I could do it better alone," Cameron jokes, earning a slug on the shoulder and a playful "shut the fuck up!" from Nico.

"Don't listen to him," Nico says. "He's a dirty fuckin' liar. They'd take me back any time."

"Yeah, yeah, yeah. So, Layla." Cameron turns to me. "What is it you do when you're not making this asshole the luckiest man in New York?"

"I'm a student at NYU."

"She's Brazilian, Cam," Nico puts in. "Baby, Cameron lived in Sao Paolo for a couple of years. You had a girl down there, right, Cam?"

Cameron turns back to me with a grin and nods. "*Você fala português?*" he asks in surprisingly good Portuguese.

I smile uneasily. It's a question I get a lot when people find out about my dad's side of the family, and one that's always embarrassing to answer, especially in New York, where everyone loves to put their ethnic heritage on display. But just when I'm about to tell Cameron that my Portuguese isn't particularly good, I catch Nico's look of obvious pride.

So I nod and respond in kind, albeit a bit stunted. "*Sim, eu falo um pocinho.*"

Cameron and I chat for a few more moments in stunted Portuguese, and I'm lucky that the questions he asks are relatively simple. With every answer I give, Nico smiles a little bit wider, almost like he's proud of me for speaking my family's language. I get it. It's the same, slight proud, slightly turned on feeling I get when he speaks Spanish with obvious confidence and comfort. I'm still confused about what's going on between us, but his pleased expression makes the rest of my irritation melt away.

"All right," Cameron says with a laugh when I tell him about running half naked through the streets at *Carnaval* two years ago. "Your lady's got some guts, Nico, that's for sure."

"She's the best," Nico agrees with a look that's more than a little heated. He pulls out a fifty and slips it into Cameron's hand, but his friend puts it right back in Nico's jacket pocket.

"No need, brother, no need," he tells him with a wink back at me. "On the house for you and *a brasileira*. Anytime, man. *Tchau, beleza.*"

CHAPTER THIRTY-THREE

Nico

SHE'S PISSED. SHE'S TRYING HARD NOT TO BE, BUT IT'S OBVIOUS SHE'S STILL MAD WHEN WE walk into the club. And she's right—I should have called. I have a cell phone. I could have texted. But I didn't.

I can't exactly say why. After the day I had...it just felt like one more thing, you know? One more thing after I had to sit and listen to Maggie bitch for hours about Jimmy—again. One more thing after I was on my knees caulking my mom's toilet and fixing the rusty hinges on the murphy bed.

One more thing after Gabe busted in around noon and started messing shit up and then got into a shouting match with Selena and Ma that I had to break up before my sister broke more than one vase. One more thing after I had to sit on the phone for two hours paying Ma's bills because Maggie's too fuckin' flaky to do it and Ma still doesn't speak enough English to do it herself.

So if I'm being honest, the last fuckin' thing I want to do tonight is hang out at a club full of the same assholes who treat me and my family like shit ninety percent of the time. I know Layla and I have barely been able to do anything for weeks. And yeah, I know she's got cabin fever, and I promised her a big night out. But all I want to do is cart her up to my apartment, have sex until we can't think straight anymore, and then pass out in front of the TV.

Instead I'm here, dressed up in a monkey suit, trying to ignore the way every other dude in the club is staring at my girl like they want to eat her.

To be fair, Layla does look delicious. I don't know where she got that gold dress, but the thing is short enough that it should be illegal, stopping right below her ass with a back that is basically nonexistent. When I take her coat to check, my heart just about stops.

It's also when I feel really fuckin' bad for blowing off half the night. The Roxy is just another club to me, but I knew tonight was special to Layla. She really took the time to dress up, and now I'm feeling proud (okay, maybe a little nervous) to show her off.

To me, this place is the same as every other club in New York: big, loud, crammed with people, and clouded with cigarette smoke. I'm hoping the cigarette ban passes, even though people complain that it's one more way New York is being sanitized. Well, you know what? This city could use some fuckin' sanitizing. Speaking as someone who comes home every weekend stinking of other people's ashes, I'd throw a party if the ban passes. Drinks on me, motherfuckers.

A DJ stands in a booth elevated in the middle of a mirrored dance floor, surrounded by people writhing around to his techno-soul mix. But Layla's looking around with big eyes, and it occurs to me that she hasn't been to a big club like this in New York. She's a poor student, and even though her fake ID is a pretty good one, it still wouldn't have passed Cameron without me. They get raided too often to let in a bunch of underage kids, especially after security everywhere went up 9/11. Besides, NYU kids usually stick to the bars around the Village or go to Webster Hall.

"Come on," I call into her ear over the music, getting a brief whiff of her coconut scent. It's a breath of fresh air in this nicotine factory. "Once we find my friend Nina, we won't have to pay for drinks."

Layla nods at me, although she hasn't spoken since her weird exchange with Cameron outside. Sometimes she seems almost ashamed of the fact that she's part-Brazilian, like she really believes some of the shit her dad tells her. Like she would rather just focus on the white side of her family. Maybe it's because her Portuguese isn't that good—she stumbled over a bunch of words and couldn't quite understand everything Cameron said. But I was proud of her for trying.

We grab a couple of seats at the crowded bar and wait, letting the loud noise fill the awkward space between us until I spot Nina, one of the bartenders. But as soon as Nina turns around, I already know this was a bad idea. Female bartenders tend to show off the goods for better tips. It's been a while, and I'm no expert, but Nina looks like she's had some serious, um, enhancements in that neighborhood. It doesn't help either that she's looking at me like she wants me to check them out hands on.

Okay, yeah, we used to hook up sometimes. But it wasn't anything big, and Nina's seen me with other girls. Then again, none of them looked like Layla either.

"Hey, handsome," Nina says as she leans over the bar to kiss my cheek, far enough that her new additions are basically served on a platter. I don't miss the way Layla's eyes follow Nina's hand down my arm, where it squeezes my bicep for a second before letting go.

"I see someone's still hitting the gym," Nina says appreciatively before finally standing up straight. "Who's this?"

She looks at Layla, who looks like she wants to cut someone. Shit. I really should have just told the cab to go to my apartment. I could have enjoyed the damn dress up there.

"This is my girlfriend, Layla." I place an arm around Layla's shoulders. She stiffens, but doesn't move my hand. "Baby, this is Nina. We go way back working here together."

But Nina smiles and winks at Layla. I relax. Nina's cool. She knows the score. Hopefully, Layla can see that too.

"Nice to meet you, hon," Nina says. She glances around the bar, where people are waving at her, trying to catch her attention. "We're pretty busy tonight. What'll you guys have?"

I smack a twenty on the counter, which Layla watches with big eyes. I forget sometimes that even though she's the one who comes from a nice family, between the two of us, I'm the one who actually makes a little cash. For now, anyway.

"What the fuck are you doing?" Nina asks. "You know you're not paying for shit."

I smirk. This is a game we're required to play. "Tips, girl. Just take it. I'll have a Tito's and tonic, and..." I turn to Layla. "What do you want, baby?"

Layla softens at the nickname and lets me pull her a little closer. She's a little overwhelmed by this place, by Nina. Shit, what's she going to do when I introduce her to K.C.? I kiss her a little on the cheek, and she thaws a little more. Okay, okay. Good sign. Maybe the night's not a total wash.

"Whiskey soda," she murmurs, and leans her head on my shoulder while I pass her order to Nina.

Nina gives us another wink, then grabs our drinks and disappears down the bar to flirt with more customers and collect the massive tips those tits will get her. Layla just sips her drink.

"You still mad?" I ask her. My voice is already starting to hurt from shouting over this shitty house music. The bass is so loud I can feel it thumping through the bar top. K.C. hasn't started his set yet—he's known for doing a good mix of Latin and electronica, which will be better than this Eurotrash garbage.

Layla shrugs, just sucks on her drink and avoids my eyes. I sigh and look around the room. I spot K.C. and wave him over from where he's flirting up not just one, but three women at the same time. The guy's got serious game, I'll give him that. He catches sight of me, and starts pushing through the dance floor.

"You don't believe me?" I call to Layla, who turns back around to face me. "Ask K.C. He was with me most of the day."

She turns around to see who I'm waving at and spots K.C. waving back. We watch as he weaves through the masses of people, wearing his backward red Yankees cap and a goofy smile even while he gives at least five girls on the way a smile or a wink. He sticks out. No one else but him would have been allowed into a club like this with a hat, hoodie, or sneakers, but he's wearing all three.

It's not until he's almost here that I realize he's got my brother Gabe with him too. Suddenly, I'm nervous. I didn't want to make a big thing of it, but Layla hasn't met any of my friends or family. Other than Ma and K.C., no one even knows yet that I'm staying. They don't know that she's the reason why.

"Hey, *mano*, what's up?" K.C. greets me with a quick slap to the back and a fist bump. Gabe reaches around him to slap my hand.

"What the fuck are you doing here?" I ask, looking at my kid brother up and down. It's not like I've never snuck him into a bar. But I came out to get away from my family. I love them, but for fuck's sake, I needed a break tonight.

"K.C. hired me to help him lug his records," Gabe says, clearly excited to be in a place like this.

I glance at K.C., who just shrugs. I know what he's thinking. That Gabe's eighteen, a man now, can make his own damn decisions. But he knows I don't like my kid brother in a place like this. It's one thing to tag along with me to AJ's, which is a small enough club that I can keep an eye on him. It's a total other to be in the Roxy, where if you stumble around the wrong corner, you're as likely to find people selling blow as anything else.

"Well, you better be doing a good job, kid," I tell him. I pull Layla in front of me, but keep an arm around her waist. "Guys, this is my girl, Layla."

She softens again when I say that, and I smirk, even though for some reason, saying that to K.C. and Gabe like this makes my chest feel tight. It's one thing to tell the doorman or the bartender, people I used to know but barely see anymore, about me and Layla. It's another to introduce her to the most important people in my life.

Layla openly looks over K.C. and Gabe, who are doing the same thing to her. Gabe's dressed up a little, wearing his Sunday shirt from H&M and the pair of black pants I bought him for his graduation. With his black hair combed back, he's made a lot of effort to look more grown up than he is in church clothes and a pair of shoes that look a couple sizes too big for him.

We don't look much alike. I'm a little on the shorter, bulkier side, while Gabe tops six feet and is skinny as a telephone pole. Gabe's also fair like his dad, a light-skinned Cuban guy who still comes around every so often. I take more after my mom, with her darker skin. But Gabe and I both have the same eyes and lips. People still look at us and know we're brothers.

"Hello." He holds out his hand to Layla. "I'm Gabe, Nico's brother. You must be Layla. He was talking about you tremendously today."

I have to hide a smile. Gabe's trying really hard to speak what he calls "proper English." He's nervous about going to college this fall, and when I told him that Layla goes to NYU, he was curious about her right away.

"Hey, *manito*," I cut in in Spanish so I don't embarrass him. "You sound like an ass."

Layla blinks between us, unaware of what I've said, while K.C. starts cackling, although he's more interested in sizing up Layla than moderating my exchange with my brother.

Layla smiles shyly and shakes both of their hands and accepts kisses on both cheeks from K.C. "It's nice to meet you guys. I've heard a lot."

"Good things, I hope. I can't trust this fuck to be honest," K.C. jokes.

"Hey, hey, easy."

I swat his hand away good-naturedly. K.C. mimes a punch at my shoulder, and finally Layla smiles—really smiles—as she watches our exchange.

"Gabe was with me all day today too, baby," I tell her. "He can tell you what a fucking mess the trains were."

She looks at Gabe curiously. "You went up to Nico's apartment with him? Why?"

"He has booze up there," Gabe says with a sly wink. "I'm only eighteen, so I can't buy." He holds up a wrist that's bare in contrast to the green paper bands wrapped around Nico's and mine. "I needed to pregame."

"You don't have a fake ID?" she asks.

It's cute how shocked she is. I know the first thing all the college kids do is buy a fake, but no one local does it. No one needs to if you have the right connections.

"Nah, what do I need that for when my brother knows everyone at the hottest clubs? Besides, most of the weekends I'm supposed to be studying anyway."

We launch into a discussion of Gabe's last semester of high school and his acceptance to CUNY. I'm so fuckin' proud of my kid brother. He's insanely good at math and didn't fuck up the way I did in high school. I made sure of that. His counselor at school even helped him get a full scholarship, so he's going to have nothing else to do but study next year. He's going to finish college if it's the last thing I make him do.

"I'm mostly excited to move uptown," Gabe's saying. "Nico's place is right by the college. No commuting from Hell's Kitchen. I don't care what Ma says. She drives me nuts."

"Well, she must be happy that you'll be living with your brother," Layla says cautiously.

I smile at her. She's trying to be nice without encouraging him to say anything bad about our mom. I want to tell her not to worry. We love her, but she drives all her kids crazy.

"What?" Gabe stares at me with obvious confusion. "Bro, what is she talking about? I thought you were moving to LA."

K.C.'s eyes go wide. "Oh *shit*," he mutters into his cup. "Dude, you didn't tell him?"

Layla glances between us with confusion. Suddenly, my chest feels tight again.

"Uh, yeah," I say. "I realized I'd be crazy to leave the greatest city in the world for fuckin' LA. So yeah, bro, I'm stayin'. You'll still get my room, though."

For some reason, I can't quite meet my brother's eyes, so instead I fix my gaze on the chick grinding on some dude behind him. She's hot, and the guy is pretty into it, inching up her skirt. Normally it might turn me on, make me want to do the same thing with Layla, but instead I just hug her closer to me so she can't see my face. Her coconut scent is there again, and my chest relaxes.

Gabe's skinny face flickers back and forth between Layla and me for a moment before settling into a neutral smile.

"Well, hey, that's great, I guess," he says. "Great, bro. Mom must be happy."

"Um, yeah," I say. "Yeah, she's happy."

"Too bad I won't get my own place, though."

He lifts his water cup toward me in silent salute while he steals one last glance at Layla. I give a tight smile and squeeze Layla around the waist. For some reason, in this moment, she feels like a lifeline. Like if I let her go, I'd drift away into this sea of nothingness that surrounds us.

K.C. has been weirdly quiet this whole time, watching the exchange over the rim of his cup. He looks at me carefully, and I just focus on finishing the strong-ass vodka tonic Nina made me. Girl was trying to fuck me up, that's for sure.

"Come on, dude," K.C. says suddenly, hitting Gabe on the shoulder. "We need to set up."

Gabe nods. "All right. See you guys."

Suddenly, I don't want to sit here anymore. Layla's not stupid. She's going to turn around with her blue eyes full of questions that will gut me. I can hear them already. *Why didn't you tell your brother you were staying? What did your mother really say when you told her? Why was K.C. staring at me like that?* And I can already feel the liquor loosening up my inhibitions.

She doesn't need to know what I'm feeling right now. That even though I made my choice, that I can't imagine leaving this girl, this woman who makes my heart feel like it's beating for the first time, being in this place, in this city, still makes me feel like I'm drowning.

"Come on, baby," I say, full of sudden decision. I tip back the rest of my drink, and then take Layla's empty plastic cup and toss both of them into a nearby trashcan. "Let's dance."

I pull her into the middle of the crowd, letting the deep bass and drum filter through the floor into our bodies. Layla closes her eyes and sways her hips to the music. Even in the dim atmosphere of cigarette smoke cut through every so often with strobe lights, she looks like the sun. I'm reminded of the fact that much like this city, I can't seem to escape her orbit. The only difference is that with her, I don't want to.

A salsa beat starts to mix into the deep bass. K.C. is starting his set, and the crowd cheers in response. I pull Layla closer, wrapping her arms around my shoulders and nuzzling her cheek. She melts into me, moving in time to the rhythm I set with my hips. I'm not a professional, but I'm a decent dancer. You don't grow up in New York without hearing a lot of music. Filtering out of the shops. Blasting out of boom boxes or people's headphones on the subway. It's everywhere here.

"I'm sorry I didn't believe you," Layla shouts in my ear.

She's got her fingers in my hair, and the way she's moving her hips against mine has me standing at half-mast. There is nothing more I'd rather do than just take her home right now and forget the way this city makes me feel—like I'm stuck in a marriage I can't get out of.

Instead, I shrug and kiss her on the forehead, letting my lips linger a touch too long. "Think about it, sweetie. I'm staying in New York for you. If I wasn't interested anymore, I would just leave, wouldn't I? Go to LA like I originally planned."

I try to ignore the way that statement makes me feel. The way it makes my chest constrict all over again, the way it makes me feel like I can't breathe. I press my forehead into her neck and inhale. She's my lifeline. She has no idea, but that's what she is these days.

I need to treat her better for it, instead of like I resent her.

Now we're swaying to our own beat, separate from whatever it is that K.C.'s playing. I grip her waist, holding her as tight to me as I can. What would she do if she knew how much I need her right now? Does that make me pathetic? I really don't know.

"I was dumb," she says. "Do you forgive me?"

I stand up straight, tip her chin up with a finger so I can look directly at her. Her eyes glow, two glittering blue lights that shine brighter than any strobe. Gently, I kiss her, my lips opening wider than I intended, as if by instinct. But her tongue welcomes mine, twists around, slowly, meticulously until we're both out of breath. When I break away, her face is flushed. My chest hurts, but in a totally different way. There's so much I want to say to her, but it's too soon. Isn't it?

"Already done, baby," I say instead. "And I'm sorry I was so late and didn't call. Now we need to make up."

I touch my forehead to hers, and my hands slip down to cover her ass in the crowded club. I have no shame with her. There's no way she misses the way she makes me feel against her leg. Instead, she grinds against it. I kiss her again.

"I think it's time to go," she says when I let her go, still a little breathless.

But now I'm not quite so eager to leave. We just got here, after all. The feel of her body, the thump of the music. All of it's invaded me, hypnotized me, just the way New York always seems to do. Now my instincts aren't to get out, but interested more in the torture of delayed gratification.

I squeeze her ass a little tighter and start to move in time to the music again.

"Not yet," I say with a grin. "We should probably stay more than five minutes. I need to dance with my baby."

CHAPTER THIRTY-FOUR

Nico

"WHAT DO YOU THINK OF THIS ONE?"

After spending the rest of last night and a solid chunk of Sunday morning making up, Layla and I decide to visit the Met before she has to go back downtown to do her homework. I still haven't been able to shake that tightening I feel in my chest, and the Met is one of the few places in New York that doesn't make me crazy. So I take her back downtown to change her clothes, and then we run back uptown to check out a special exhibit.

The Met is doing a special on the works of William Blake, a favorite of Layla's. She'll actually get some extra credit for going to the exhibit, so it's a double-win. I just like the drawings. All around these massive poems, which I'm honestly not that big on, this Blake guy made these intricate watercolors and etched designs. I have to laugh at the title of the exhibit: "The Marriage of Heaven and Hell." It could not fit my life better.

Layla's pointing to a larger watercolor next to the fourth plate of the poem. "The Good and Evils Angels" presents two angels, one brown, the other white, both naked, arguing over the child held in the arms of the white, supposedly "good" angel. The "evil" angel seems to be flying out of a collection of flames, but is shackled to them by one foot. The child looks like it wants to escape from the arms of the "good" angel.

I cock my head as I study the drawings. "I like the way he draws the body. Very detailed, anatomically. I mean, he's no Michelangelo, but everything is very clear."

It's something I try to do when I draw too. Since I've still been too chicken shit to tell Layla how I really feel—about her, about LA, about everything—this morning, I decided the next best thing was to let her look through my sketchbook. No one sees that. That shit is private.

She paged through it for about an hour, and at one point, when she found the cache of pencil drawings at the end that are mostly of her, I escaped to the shower. I just couldn't deal with the possibility that she didn't like them.

I didn't need to worry. When I came back in, she showed me just how much she liked them, and then we both needed another shower.

"He was more a poet than an artist," Layla says. "Do you think the bad angel isn't 'bad' because he wants to be, but because he's forced there?"

I frown, staring at the shackle. "I don't know. Could be. I don't think anyone really wants to be bad, really, but sometimes you have to do those things every now and then, and then it's easier to get sucked further into it. Everything in life is that way, you know?" I look at her and smile, trying to shake off the echoes of my own life. "But he looks pretty possessed, NYU. I don't think I'd give my kid to that dude."

She laughs as she moves to look at the next plate, but my thoughts still linger with the evil angels. It's too close to home.

I look at the picture for a few more minutes, and just when I'm about to follow Layla, my cell phone buzzes in my pocket. Maggie. Fuck. My sister doesn't exactly call just to chat.

"Yo, what's up, Mag?" I say in a quiet voice, so as not to disturb the other people looking at the exhibit. It's not that big of a deal, though—the Met is fairly loud, as museums go. Layla watches curiously as I chat with my sister in Spanish. I don't need this room full of rich white people knowing my family's business.

"Nico, hey...I just wanted to know if, um, Allie and I could come stay for a bit. Just until we find a place for ourselves, really."

I swear silently to myself. The last time this happened, my sister had a nasty bruise on her face. "What happened? Did Jimmy..."

"No, no, nothing like that, I swear it. It's just that things aren't really so hot with him. He's...I don't know. He's so hot and cold."

"Forget him, Maggie. Tell him to fuck off. You don't need that shit."

A few of the other people looking at the pictures jump a little at my words and put a few extra feet between us. I roll my eyes. Forget them too.

The weight of my sister's sighs seems to push physically through the phone. "It's complicated, Nico. He's Allie's father. He just needs a little space sometimes, that's all."

I pace around in a small circle, trying to keep my temper in check. It's the same old excuses for Jimmy, same old shit about how Maggie and he can't seem to get along, how he needs a break from his own kid, how they always need everyone else— meaning me—to pick up the slack. It's bullshit. This isn't what grown-ups do. They don't get to take timeouts from their own fuckin' lives. They deal with their shit.

I close my eyes and rub my face. I want to tell my sister to deal with her own shit. Get her own place instead of leeching off me. Tell Jimmy where to shove it and stop putting her kid through this garbage. But then I think of Allie, and I don't want to consider what might happen if I forced her mother to grow the fuck up.

"Sure," I bite out. "The room's open. I'll see you tonight, okay?"

"Thanks, Nico. You're the best."

"Yeah," I say with a grimace I'm glad my sister can't see. "Later."

I shove my phone in my pocket and walk over to Layla, who's given me a bit of space while I talked to my sister. Suddenly, I need to hold her.

"Who was that?" she asks as I wrap my arms around her waist from behind and press my nose into her hair.

"Oh, that was Maggie," I mumble, and then force myself to look at the artwork, the title page from "The First Book of Urizen."

On the front is a painting of a very old, Gandalf-looking dude. I don't want to look at this shit right now. I just want to look at Layla. I nuzzle her neck, nipping just above her collarbone on that spot that I know she loves. This girl and her magic skin. It's anywhere, anytime with her, and I know she'd be game if I could find a decent spot. Even in the middle of the MET.

"What—what did she want?" Layla asks, her voice all breathy and light.

I'm having a hard time focusing. I really just want to lose myself in her again, but there are people around. Right now, I'm trying to think of any secret spots in this part of the city where we could be alone. Maybe the park again, if we could deal with the rain today...

"Mmm...She and Jimmy broke up again. She wanted to make sure her room would be there for her and Allie. And that I could pay for them, of course."

The tightening in my chest grows. There goes my hard-on. I rest my chin on Layla's shoulder and let out a long sigh.

"You don't sound too happy about that."

To my frustration, Layla steps away and turns to face me. I shove my hands in my back pockets.

"It's fine, I guess," I say, and suddenly I can't keep all of this in. "I'm used to it. But Maggie's just such a fuckin' freeloader, though, you know? I want to tell her no, she's gotta grow up, get a real damn job, and stop fuckin' around with Jimmy, who acts like he doesn't have a kid to take care of. But I can't say no to Allie."

Layla stands quietly, obviously unsure of what to say. She doesn't have family like this, I'm sure. Brothers and sisters from three different dads. A mother who came here illegally and can't speak English. Siblings who can't keep their shit together, who have babies out of wedlock with men who can't grow up. Usually I'm not embarrassed by my family because everyone I know has a family just like them. It's only one more reason why Layla and I really do come from completely different worlds.

"What about Gabe?" she asks. "Will he be able to move in with you still this summer?"

I sigh. "Yeah, I'm not going to make him sleep on the couch while he's going to school. I tried that, and it doesn't work. I'll probably give him my room so he can have some privacy, and I'll take the living room."

It's the last thing I want to do, but Gabe will need a place to study. One of us kids is going to finish college—Maggie and Selena didn't even start. The heaviness in my chest grows. There goes my privacy, not to mention the one space where Layla and I can be alone. But what else can I do?

"That's life, right?" I say.

And then I can't take this anymore. I can't take the pity that's practically painted all over her beautiful face. I can't take her looking at me like she's sorry for me, like I'm a stray dog she wants to rescue. This is my life, not an afterschool special. I plaster a grin on my face, the one that always makes her smile back. Then I grab her hand. "Come on, baby, let's go see the mummies."

———

Layla

Although the original plan was for him to drop me off at a subway stop before heading across town to his apartment, Nico ends up accompanying me back down to my place. It's weird, but I get the feeling he doesn't want to say goodbye, maybe doesn't want to go back uptown. We grab some Chinese pastries to snack on while I do laundry, but we both know the main reason he came all the way down here was to get me naked. My roommates are out. Walking around the Met without being able to do anything more than hold hands or kiss and hug was basically two straight hours of foreplay.

So literally the moment I arrive from putting my clothes into one of the washers in the basement, the door slams shut behind me, and I'm shoved against one of the walls of the common area, my lips thoroughly crushed by Nico's. There's that need again—that same intense desire that drove him last night and once more this morning. The second the door closes, he's voracious.

His hands slide eagerly down my waist to grab my ass and pull me into the erection that's straining against his jeans.

"I've been staring at this gorgeous ass all day," he mumbles against my lips. He sucks on the edge of my tongue, eliciting a moan from deep in my chest.

"Fuck," I breathe when he releases me. He bends his legs and pulls both of mine around his waist so that he can carry me into my bedroom, but we only make it as far as the common area couch before we topple over the back, landing on the cushions in a pile of giggles.

"Stop that," he chides. "I'm supposed to be seducing you."

He's trying to sound harsh, but I can feel his chest vibrate with suppressed laughter. He repositions us so I'm sitting up on the couch and commences to tear off my shirt and unbutton my jeans as quickly as he can move his fingers.

"Getting greedy, are we?" I ask, although I'm happy to assist with his shirt too. I've been dying to get my hands on that smooth skin all day.

"I need you naked," he growls, and gives me another breath-shattering kiss before I can respond.

He sits up onto his knees and pulls my jeans off, tossing them onto the floor before he yanks off his own pants. He angles himself over my body and nips along the edge of my neck, making me arch my back farther toward him. I want more, but he's focused on tonguing the soft skin in the hollow of my collarbone, alternately licking and biting in a way that I know is going to leave some marks tomorrow morning.

His lips reach my chest, and he slides the straps of my bra over my shoulders and pulls down the soft cotton cups so that my breasts bob over them, trussed and available for his pleasure. It's a favorite technique of his; I think he likes the way I look all bound up.

"Beautiful," he breathes, cupping them with both hands as he sinks to his knees between my straddled legs. Delicately he takes one nipple in between his teeth, rolling the sensitive nub between them and tonguing it in a way that causes me to cry out as I grab his head to pull him closer.

"Don't," he orders gruffly as he releases my breast from his grip to take my arms and hold them firmly to my sides. "Don't move. You just have to take it, baby. Understand?"

The dark, hungry look in his eyes brooks no other response than the small nod I manage to give him. He needs control—it's like he's been starving for it for the last twenty-four hours. I'm not arguing—he is insanely hot when he's ordering me around.

"Good," he clips, and leans back to suck my other nipple deep into his mouth.

His hands glide down my abdomen, gripping my thighs for a moment before he slips both of his thumbs under the thin layer of cotton that covers the sensitive heat between my legs. I moan again, resisting the urge to push against his thumbs for a deeper connection as they brush up and down the juncture of soft skin, hair, and nerves.

"Does that feel good, baby?" he asks softly, his eyes clouded with obvious desire. "Do you like it when I touch your pussy?"

"Yes," I whisper, unable to move my eyes from the dark hold of his.

He hooks his fingers under the elastic band of my panties and draws them down my legs so that I'm fully exposed. He draws one finger down, toying slightly with my entrance that's becoming wetter by the second.

"It's starting to grow out," he says, entranced by the path of his hand.

If my face weren't already red from wanting him, I would have blushed. "It, uh, needs to be waxed. I have an appointment next week."

Nico shakes his head with a hungry smile, the kind you might see on a cartoon wolf. "No, baby, let it grow a little. It's sexy."

He slips his finger inside me, then another, curving the ends to massage the bundle of nerves inside my darkest place. My hips jerk and grind involuntarily. He leans over my body, taking my earlobe into his mouth so that I can feel the heat of his body hovering over me while he fucks me with his hand.

"God, Layla," he growls into my ear. "You are so fucking hot, you know that? So wet and willing."

"Ah!" I cry out, no longer able to form coherent words in response to the building tension. He's coiling me up like a spring, and I'm about ready to burst.

"You want to come, baby?" he asks, slipping a third finger in to join the other two's internal massage.

"Ummmm," I moan, pressing my chest upward so that the sensitive ends of my nipples rub against the smooth lines of his chest. He increases his fingers' tempo, and I feel my muscles start to tighten.

"Bear down, baby," he orders me. "Do it. Now."

So I do, almost as if I'm trying to pee, and almost immediately my entire body is wracked with the unbelievable spasms of my release as I come hard onto his hand. "AaaaaaAAAAH, NICO!"

"That's it, Layla," he growls, rubbing out the rest of my release as I claw the couch cushions under my head. "Just let it go."

Finally, he withdraws and shucks his underwear.

"Come here," he orders, pulling my legs forward and flipping me over so I'm on my knees, my chest resting on the couch with him behind me.

He loves this position, where he can see his favorite part of my body and take me with the kind of ferocity he almost never lets loose anywhere else. I can't argue—the angle he finds, combined with his touch on my clit, makes me come again and again and again. It's hard to argue with that.

I'm so wet that he doesn't even have to push when he slides into me. His hands find my ass and knead it hard. I tighten around him, relishing the sumptuous friction of our bodies, pushing and pulling together. From this angle, I feel the whole of him as he seeks my limits, over and over again.

"Fuck, baby," Nico groans over my shoulder. He starts to move faster, no longer concerned with the evenness of his rhythm, but obviously overcome himself. I slip my hand under my legs, reaching below to where I can cup his balls in my fingers, squeezing them just enough to push him over the edge.

"Shit! Layla!" he cries, and emits a long, deep groan as he comes, jerking in my hand and then collapsing over my body as he pumps out the last of his release. I don't come with him, which is unusual. It's also unnecessary, considering the body-melting orgasm I experienced just moments before. I honestly don't think I could have handled another one anyway.

We lie together, him piled on top of me, for a moment as we catch our breaths. Nico presses a soft kiss between my shoulder blades, and I sigh, sated.

"You're incredible," he whispers into my back.

"So are you, Mr. Soltero," I murmur back. I awkwardly readjust my bra so it's back on normally. He likes the trussed-turkey look, but once my euphoria dies down, I don't love the way the underwire digs into my skin.

Nico gently pulls out and pads to the bathroom to dispose of the condom I didn't even realize we used. Huh. It's not good that I get so lost with this man, I can't even keep track of our protection.

He returns with a damp cloth, which I accept to clean myself off while he gathers up our clothes. He's completely unabashed by his nakedness, moving easily around the room, checking to make sure we haven't left any telltale items of clothing for my roommates to find and tease us about. Two weeks ago, Jamie found his underwear shoved under a couch cushion (we looked and looked, but couldn't find it). Nico had to suffer the girls' merciless taunting about the bright orange color for at least a week every time he called.

He catches me watching and rewards me with a grin that erases the slight sadness on his face.

"Like what you see, baby?" he asks as he stands up. The spring light shines through the windows, casting deep shadows over his muscles.

I bite my lip, trying unsuccessfully to kill my blush. I nod. "I might."

I stand up and help him straighten up the room so that we can move to my bed. It's not that my roommates would necessarily be put off by the fact that we just had sex on the living room couch. But it's still better not to confront them with two naked people lying in the middle of the common area where we sit on a regular basis.

Nico follows me into my bedroom, where we toss our clothes onto my desk chair and crawl into my tiny bed together, my makeshift curtain closing us in a blue cocoon. I snuggle up against his warm chest and he folds me close, using one hand to cradle my head and run his fingers through my loose curls. It's a gesture he does a lot, one that makes me feel so loved and cherished. One that makes my heart open to the love I feel too.

My eyes blink open when the thought hits me, just like it does every time. I don't just like this man. I am completely in love with this man. I love every single thing about him—his dark, expressive eyes, his gorgeous smile, his casual, "I just want to have fun" demeanor, and the obvious compassion it masks. I love him. So much. Sometimes so much it hurts.

I had an inkling of it before, but once I knew that things were free to progress naturally, I've been content to leave that possibility aside as our relationship grew naturally. But now it doesn't feel like something I can ignore anymore. Right here in his arms, this is where I definitely belong.

"Music?" he mumbles through the silence that's descended.

I push myself off his chest. "What do you feel like listening to?"

He shrugs. "What do you have?"

I twist around and pull my case of CDs from underneath my bed, and then toss it at him with a thumb. He sits up and starts paging through my collection, which isn't bad for a nineteen-year-old. Most of my extra money in high school went to record stores.

"You have very eclectic tastes," Nico remarks as he thumbs through. "Who's Aimee Mann?"

"Portland singer," I say. "Sort of like Joni Mitchell."

Nico makes a face. "Pass." He keeps looking. "You're such a Seattleite. Look at all this grunge."

"Hey, it's my hometown," I joke. "If I didn't own any Nirvana and Pearl Jam records, they wouldn't let me on the plane home."

He pauses. "Who's Timbalada?"

I glance. "Oh, that's a samba band. Loud. Carnaval-kind of stuff."

Nico looks over the album cover curiously. "I'll have to check them out. But not right now." He flips again and pulls out another CD. "Maná? I wouldn't have expected you to know them."

I nudge him in the shoulder. "Come on. They're internationally known."

"It's a Mexican rock band, NYU. And you're—"

"A sheltered white girl?"

Nico doesn't answer, but I know he's thinking it. And, well, he's not wrong, at least partly.

I shrug. "I had a Spanish *au pair* when I was a kid. She really liked Maná."

"Put it on."

I turn around and slip the disc into the small stereo on the edge of my desk. Almost immediately, the room fills with the sounds of a live audience clapping, followed by the soft guitar tones of the unplugged album. I don't understand Spanish, and I don't really care for most of this band's other stuff I've heard, but this album is one of my favorites. Fher Olvera, the singer, has a soft, melodic voice that's soothing, especially when he's backed up with only acoustic guitars and light percussion.

We lie back in the pillows for a bit, letting the gentle sounds wash over us. Beside me, Nico murmurs the lyrics, obviously familiar with the music.

I turn over to lie on his chest, and his arm wraps around my waist.

"Tell me what it means?" I ask.

He gives me a sad smile, then looks past me with a sort of far-away expression. "Okay."

Another song starts up. It's my favorite on the album—melancholy and sweet. Nico starts to translate over Olvera's rueful voice.

"So, he's saying how he wishes he could live without water. How nice it would be to live without air. How I wish I could love you a little less. How I wish I could live without you."

The percussion picks up a little, and the sad strums of the guitar fill the air.

"That's so sad," I murmur against Nico's warm chest.

"It is," he agrees. "But it's beautiful. It's like...he's really just saying the truth. That when you love someone, really love them and need them, to live without them *is* to live without water or air. Because to need someone that much...hurts a little, you know? The fear that you'll lose them is always there. And so maybe there's a part of you that wishes you didn't need them so badly."

He drifts off, and his arms tighten around me. My hand presses just a little harder into his chest. A finger reaches under my chin and tips my head up to look at him.

Nico's eyes, so dark they're almost black, are fathomless. I could fall into them, and I want to. But though they glisten a little with such clear adoration that tugs at my heart—that bittersweet pain the song talks about—there's still that edge, that worry, that pain that never quite leaves them. That expression that shows just how much of the world Nico has to carry on his broad shoulders.

He kisses me and tastes like chocolate—the bitter kind that's not quite sweet. Our tongues tangle, but it's not a kiss built in a frenzy of desire. It's adrift in something much more potent. Something sweet. Something painful. Love.

Nico's phone buzzes on the desk on the other side of the curtain, and he groans as he stretches up to grab it.

"Shit, it's my mom," he mutters, and swings his legs off the bed to get up while he answers the call. "She wanted me to go to Mass with her tonight since I skipped this morning. Hold on, baby."

Watching him babble in quick-tongued Spanish, I'm struck again by just how dedicated he is to his family, and how much they appear to take advantage of that. I've only barely met Gabe, but even he seemed to take for granted his brother's continued generosity. Paying his sister's rent and his brother's tuition, doing his mother's errands and taking her to church. Why does Nico have to shoulder all of these burdens? When does he get to follow his own dreams?

I suddenly feel guilty for coming down so hard on him last night; it's clear they all take up more of his time than they should.

That's when my second epiphany of the day hits me. I love this man. And because I love him, I know that he deserves more than just me.

Nico says goodbye to his mother and sets his phone down on my desk. He turns around to find me watching him. Damn. Damn, oh damn me and my mother's giant eyes that show everything I'm thinking.

"What's with the glum face, sweetie?" Nico asks.

He tugs the curtain back in place and slides back under the comforter to cover me with his body. He's still warm, and oh, his skin feels so good on mine. For a second I'm tempted to slip my hands farther down his body and start an encore round of what we just did on the couch. From the look in his eyes, I'd guess he's thinking the same thing.

"Let's turn that frown upside down," he rumbles, and starts nibbling on my earlobe in that way he knows drives me crazy. So when I don't respond, he pulls his head up, his eyes wide and perplexed. "Hey. What's wrong, sweetie?"

His lips are so close, and all I want is to pull them back down to me, to make him kiss me everywhere, devour me in that way only he can do that makes us both stop thinking. Damn, this is going to be hard.

"You...you should go to LA," I say, my voice small and uncertain. As soon as it's out, I hate it, but I know it's the right thing.

Nico's eyebrows furrow, and he purses his lips. This is definitely not what he was expecting. "What?"

"You—" I stop to clear my throat, which has suddenly become inexplicably clogged. "You should go to LA," I repeat.

He rolls off to one side so his back is against the wall, keeping one arm draped over my stomach. With his fingers, he toys with my navel and traces the lines of my hipbones. We lie here for a moment in silence, digesting the words I've just thrown out there.

"Why?"

I take a deep breath. I have to get through this without crying. I know I can do it. Because I love him.

"Because. I see what you mean now, about how your family depends on you, too much, really. You deserve a chance to try on your own, just like I have. You deserve a chance to start fresh and figure out what you really want in life."

"Yeah, but I already told you, Layla. I want you."

It's an offering, not so much a defense, an argument he seems to be making as much to himself as he is to me. As if I'm supposed to feel better about it, or maybe he's looking for me to insist on him staying again. Moving across the country alone is definitely daunting—I know, having done it. But I just give him a weak smile and trace a finger down his nose.

"I know you do," I say quietly. "But we've only been dating, what, a few months? I hate to say it, but it's not enough to keep you here. I l—"

I cut myself off before those three dangerous words slip out of my mouth, words certain to put my heart out there to be trampled. Words that, more importantly, might make him feel like he has to stay. Think, Layla!

"I just know you need to do this," I say instead. "I can see it."

"And…what about us, though?"

A crease forms in between his eyebrows, and I feel his grip on my waist tighten a little. I shake my head and push a hand into my hair meditatively. We both know the answer to that.

I started school with a "boyfriend" back home with whom I actually tried to make something work from thousands of miles away. It was a naïve fairy tale, one that only fifteen-year-olds believe in. I went into it thinking it might work out—after all, we promised to email every day, call, all of that. But after a month or so, it petered out— we lost interest, or someone "accidentally" hooked up with someone new. I honestly don't remember. There was a little heartache, but nothing to what I'd feel if I ever found out Nico did something like that.

No, if there is one thing I'm absolutely sure of, it's that long distance relationships never work.

"We'll just enjoy the next few weeks together," I say much more optimistically than I feel. I have to, since I'm sure my despair is completely obvious. "Do you think you can wait until I go home for the summer too? Then, you know, it will feel like we're both leaving, and not just you."

Nico worries his bottom lip with his teeth for a second. "Are you sure about this, Layla? Because I meant it. I'll stay if you want me to."

I take a deep breath, fighting the urge to say, "Never mind." But what do they say? If you love something, set it free? In my heart, I know this is right, even if it means I'm going to lose him in a few more weeks. I love him, and I can't be the reason he holds himself back.

"I'm sure." My voice creaks. "I'm sure."

Nico presses his forehead against mine, pulling me close to him so that our bodies line up together. I can feel him twitching against my thigh, already gearing up for round two. But his eyes are solemn.

"You really are amazing."

I close my eyes because I know if they're open, he'll see the way his words just completely broke my heart. He wants to go; deep down, he's wanted it this entire time.

I pull him in for a kiss so he can't see the pain that I know writes itself clearly across my face. His kiss can erase everything, and I feel the unspoken love there as my mouth opens to his. I welcome him as he rolls me over onto my back, pushing my legs open to him. He'll be ready again soon, but for now I'm content to bask in the sweet attention of his lips, keeping him close so he can't see the few errant tears slip down my cheeks. I want him to make slow love to me until I can't feel anything else but his touch, so that I can forget, if just for a few minutes, that I've just told the man whom I am increasingly learning to need like air and water that he should leave me. I'll take every single moment with him I can get, because soon, I'm going to lose him for good.

CHAPTER THIRTY-FIVE

Nico

"I LIKE THIS ONE. IT LOOKS LIKE SOMETHING BATMAN WOULD DRIVE."

Gabe stands next to a shiny sports car, a Mitsubishi Eclipse. I scowl.

"Maybe if Batman were a fourteen-year-old girl," I say. "I just need something that's going to get me around. Small. Easy to park. Cheap and won't break."

"You sound like a soccer mom, Nico," my little brother says as he wistfully draws a hand over the top of the black sports car.

It's such a weird thing to be doing, shopping for a car. I'm a New Yorker, born and bred. I only got my license when I decided to apply to FedEx. I'm the only one in my family who even has one. There's no point to it in a city like this.

But now, things are different. Three weeks ago, Layla told me to go to LA, and even though I could tell it killed her to say it, at the same time, that metal band that had been slowly tightening around my chest disappeared. It's not like I won't carry the same burdens. I'll still pay for the apartment for Maggie and Allie, still keep up with Ma's rent. I'll still be calling back to make sure Gabe is helping Ma around the house. But for the first time in my life, I'm going to be something else than what this city and everyone in it expects of me. I'll be free.

And it's a great feeling, so long as I don't think too hard about the one person I wish I could take with me. Layla hasn't said a word about it since that night. We've gone on like we always do. Dates on Fridays, maybe sneaking dinner or lunch during the week, seeing each other at work for a few minutes everyday until yesterday, when we both served our last days on the job—Layla only while she takes the summer off, but me for good. Her semester's done, and I turned in my uniform to FedEx last night. Layla's flying home tonight. I've got one last shift at AJ's, and then I'll be driving out to California tomorrow.

But first I need a car.

"This one has low mileage," I say as I look over a maroon Toyota Camry. "It's not flashy, but I don't want to spend my entire paycheck on fuckin' gas money."

Gabe looks the car over with a frown that practically falls off his face. "You're gonna look like a soccer mom too. You planning to make some babies out there? Should we go stroller shopping?" He nudges me in the ribs. "Jessie know about your plans, man?"

I rub the back of my neck. Jessie isn't someone I want to think about right now. After I told K.C. that I was coming out to LA for sure, he started talking. Which also means everyone else in LA knows I'm coming too. Which means Jessie knows.

Two days after that, I got the new hire paperwork in the mail from the club where I'll be working. A week ago, I signed the year-long contract and sent it back to LA. Everything I own is either boxed up or shoved into duffel bags. This is really happening.

"Come on," Gabe says as he elbows me. "You telling me that a car like this is going to impress a fuckin' model?"

He makes it sound like Jessie is some big deal, but the truth is, she's only done a little catalog work and mostly just waits tables and does promotional appearances for a living. We met last year when I was visiting K.C. She was one of the go-go dancers at a club where he was spinning. But to a kid like Gabe, the only woman hotter than Jessie is J. Lo. She's blonde, tan, has legs for days. And yeah, okay, we hooked up while I was out there for a few weeks. And again when I went back in December.

But I still haven't taken her calls in months—not since Valentine's Day, to be exact. I can't even remember what she looks like anymore. It's hard to get excited about this move when I'm walking away from a pair of bright blue eyes that can see into my soul. A body that was made for my touch. A heart that feels like it's my other half.

I shake my head. No, I can't be thinking like this again. Layla told me to go. This is what she wants to do. A part of me has known from the beginning that this wasn't ever going to work out. As much as I care about her, we come from two different worlds. She knows it too. I can see it in the way she hedges about me when her dad calls and asks about the guy in the hospital. The way she checks out the crumbled bricks of my building and the stains on the lobby floor. I don't know what she'd do if I ever brought her back to the apartment where I grew up. Brazilian last name or not, my mother and my sisters have already labeled her *la blanquita,* and that won't change anytime soon.

"Did you ever think of just asking her to go with you?"

I look up from the Camry. "Who?"

Gabe rolls his eyes. It's one of the things we both do exactly the same. "Who do you think, man? Maggie? Ma?"

I mirror his expression, and then cross my arms. I don't want to admit how many times I've thought about it. How many times the words almost fell out of my mouth. "I...yeah. No." I shake my head and rub my face. I need to shave. "Why do you ask?"

"Well, if I had a supermodel waiting for me to make a real woman out of her on the beach..." Gabe mimics like he's giving it to a girl doggy-style.

"*Coño,* stop! You look like an idiot."

I smack him in the shoulder, more because he looks stupid than because I'm embarrassed. Gabe brags a lot about girls, but I'm pretty sure my little brother is still a virgin. First of all, his hands are in completely the wrong place when he does that.

Gabe laughs. "All I'm saying is, I'd be a little more excited to meet her on the beach, Nico."

Then he looks at me sadly, with a face that says more than he wants to admit. I know why he's here. He won't say anything, but Gabe wants me to stay too. Now he's going to be the only man in the family, the youngest, surrounded by the crazy women in our family. And I feel guilty too for leaving him. To tell the truth, I'm not sure how he's going to handle college and living with Maggie and Allie. I have a feeling I'm going to be making a lot of phone calls to get him to do his homework.

"Yeah, well..." I say, suddenly really interested in the trunk of the Camry. "Jessie's fine, but she's not—"

"NYU?" Gabe says it right after I cut myself off.

I sigh and shut the trunk. "Yeah. Well."

Gabe leans on the top of the car and stares me down. We may not look a lot alike, but we both have our mom's eyes, the ones that can stare a hole through you.

"Fuck, man, *stop!*" I finally say. "I'm not going to ask her to do that, all right?"

"Why the fuck not? You obviously want to. I saw you two. She's crazy about you, and you're obviously into her. What's the worst that could happen?"

"Gabe, she moved to New York because she wanted to be *here*," I say flatly. "Layla's smart. What am I going to do, ask her to trade NYU for community college while I try out a different life? Let her sit at home while I'm gone every weekend at K.C.'s gigs?" I shake my head. "I don't even know what's going to happen to me out there. She's too good for that life. She's too good for *me*."

There they are. The words I haven't ever said out loud, the words I've always known. But they're true. Her parents may not give her much to spend, but Layla comes from money. She comes from a nice house, a nice family, a safe neighborhood, not a shitty one-bedroom apartment full of kids with different daddies on a block where gunshots were just part of the background noise.

Until now, these differences didn't seem so bad. Layla still thinks they don't mean anything. But I see where she's going. In two more years, she'll be done with school, moving on to law school or a career that will surround her with more people just like her. People with means. People with direction.

Gabe just looks at me with big, sad eyes, like he sees the thoughts going through my head. And because he can't dispute them—he knows what we are just as well as I do—he says nothing. Not for the first time, I think I might be doing the wrong thing. Gabe has a chance to break this shitty cycle, better than the rest of us. I've been riding his ass for years to get the grades he has. I hope he'll be able to do as well without me around.

"Do you want to test drive anything?"

A salesman has approached us in the lot. I tip the bill of my hat up and rub my forehead. Gabe scowls at the Camry. I swallow. This move feels shitty enough without doing it in a soccer mom's car. I look around the lot, and nothing seems inspiring. Until I see the exact car I want, sitting in a corner with the exact amount I have in my budget.

"Yeah," I say with a smile. "That one. I'll test drive the Wrangler."

Gabe looks to where I'm pointing at the soft-top Jeep, and with a whoop, follows me and the salesman to the car. It's a terrible car for New York. But for LA, with the constant sunshine, with music blasting out the open roof, this car is perfect. And if I'm going to do this, I might as well do it right.

———

THREE HOURS LATER, I've just dropped Gabe off at my apartment—well, *his* apartment now—and I'm driving back downtown to pick up Layla. I've never driven a car in New York, only the FedEx truck. The weather is nice today, so I took off the canopy. With wind blowing and my stereo blasting while I cruise down the Westside highway, I'm feeling good.

The station changes, and the piano riffs shift over to the newest single from Alicia Keys. At first I go to change the station—it's not really the kind of music I usually like. But I leave it on, because there's some nostalgic value in it today. Alicia and I didn't run in the same circles—she's a few years younger than me—but I remember seeing her around the neighborhood when we were growing up. My younger sister, Selena, knew her a little back when she was still Alicia Cook.

The music is a reminder that things can change. Already Hell's Kitchen is becoming a place where investment bankers move instead of new immigrants. Alicia's music proves that some people from this place can become something different than just another kid from the block.

Suddenly, the world feels a little lighter. The wind blowing around me is warm. The trees lining the highway are full of bright green leaves.

Maybe anything is possible after all.

———

Layla

The loud scratch of packing tape fills the room as Quinn closes the last box of her things. Mine are stacked in a corner, ready to be taken to the storage facility we're all sharing. Jamie and Shama already left for New Jersey yesterday morning, and Quinn and I have been eating out of takeout containers while we wait for her train this afternoon. I'll see our boxes are picked up by the storage center before I'm the last to go on a red-eye flight tonight. Nico wanted to take me to the airport, but he was offered double to do security for a big event at AJ's—his last before he leaves for LA tomorrow anyway.

I told him not to worry about it. I know he could use the money for his trip across the country. And that's true, but the real reason is that I'm not sure I can take a teary goodbye at the airport. I'm not sure I can even handle it on a crowded sidewalk this afternoon.

"Well, that's it." Quinn comes to sit next to me on my mattress. The cheap vinyl squeaks under our weight. She wraps a thin arm around me and pulls my head onto her shoulder. "You okay?"

I know what she's talking about. I'm going to miss her this summer—I'll miss all of my roommates. But I'll see them again in a few months when we move into a new dorm on Union Square. We'll pick up right where we left off, just like this year. So this isn't really goodbye. Not for us, anyway.

I sit up and wipe the mascara under my eyes. They've been watering all day. "I'll be fine."

Quinn looks like she doesn't believe me. "It's okay to be sad, Lay."

I shrug. I've spent so much of the past three weeks vacillating between moping around and trying to pretend like everything will be fine. The effort is giving me whiplash.

"What does Romeo have planned for today?"

I blink. "We're going up to the Cloisters again. He said he wanted to e-end where we s-started." The tears start to well up before I can stop them, and I swipe angrily while Quinn looks on. "God, this is ridiculous! We barely know each other!"

Quinn pulls my hand away and squeezes it for a second before letting go. "I don't think it's ridiculous. And it's been long enough."

I give her a look. "Come on. You've been against this relationship from the start."

"I had my reservations, sure," Quinn admits. "But he won me over. Even if..."

I look up curiously. "Even if what?"

She twists her lips around. "Well...even if it was never going to work out. Come on, Layla, just listen," she says when I open my mouth to speak. "He's nice. And overall, he's been really good to you. I know you love him—you don't have to say it; it just shows. He probably loves you too. But you guys come from two completely different worlds. And eventually, those worlds are going to grow further and further apart."

"That's ridiculous—" I start to protest, but Quinn just shakes her head.

"It's reality, babe," she breaks in. "Think about where you'll be in ten years, and where he'll be. You'll be, what, a lawyer? Doing real, important things with your life? And where is he going to be? Still working doors at nightclubs? Delivering packages? He has no future, Lay."

The words sound harsh, but Quinn's voice is actually kind. Her expression is full of pity, like she's sorry to have to break the news to me. I close my eyes. This isn't what I want to hear. Because when I see Nico, I don't see any of the things other people see. I don't see the bad neighborhood, the dead-end jobs, the messy home life, and so on. I just see Nico, someone with whom I feel more right, more myself than with any person I've ever known.

How could that be wrong?

But it doesn't matter now. He's leaving. This is over. Done.

I stand up and run my fingers under my eyes. Quinn stands up with me and checks her watch.

"It's that time," she says. "My train leaves at 2:30. I need to get going to the station."

On my now-empty desk, my phone buzzes with a message.

"I'll walk you down," I say. "He's here."

———

Quinn and I exit onto the sidewalk. I look to the lamppost where Nico usually waits for me, but he's not there. Quinn nudges me in the shoulder.

"Over there," she says, and points across the street.

He's standing against the door of a shiny black Jeep, waiting like the entire city belongs to him. It's a warm spring day, and he's wearing his dark jeans and a worn t-shirt that hugs the contours of his shoulders. The dark lines of his tattoo snake out of one sleeve around his right bicep. I can see the tip of the compass tattoo on his chest peeking out of the collar, and a thin silver chain glints around his neck. With his

Yankees hat pulled low over his face, he looks like the definition of the bad boy everyone thinks he is.

But I know better.

He spots me and raises a big paw.

"Have fun," Quinn says. "Love you."

I give her a tight hug. "Love you too. Call me when you're in Boston."

"Call *me* when you're in Seattle." She releases me, then checks me over. "Take care of yourself, Lay. Have fun today. And have some fun at home. Try not to spend your *whole* summer arguing with your dad, okay?"

I nod. "Love you."

"Love you too. See ya, babe," Quinn says, and with a terse wave at Nico, walks to Canal Street to catch a cab for Grand Central.

I turn back to the man waiting for me and quickly cross the street.

"Hey, sweetie," he says as he takes my hands and pulls me to him for a quick kiss.

I ignore the throbbing in my chest. Shit. Everything is going to hurt today, isn't it?

Nico looks me up and down with a sly smile. "Beautiful as ever. Goddamn, I'm going to miss you."

I swallow and look away, blinking back the tears that are already threatening to fall. Shit, I'm really going to be a mess by the end of this day. I gulp them back and finally manage to look back.

"Let's not...let's not do that until the very end, okay?" I suggest.

Nico looks at me for a second, then nods. "Deal. You wanna check out my new ride? Not bad for a delivery boy, huh? Gabe talked me into it."

I look over the Jeep. It's not exactly my dad's BMW, but it's definitely sexy. I'm sure Nico's going to look really good driving the thing in LA. Around all the pretty blonde girls in bikinis. I cringe.

"It's nice," I say.

Nico tips his head back and laughs loudly. "You sound thrilled. I know, I know, it's kind of a piece of junk. But it'll be good for sunny days like this." He pulls open the passenger side door for me and ushers me in. "Come on, baby. Let's go."

———

Nico

She's incredibly quiet as I steer the Jeep back uptown, swerving around cars to the top of the island. It's hard to enjoy the drive when Layla is so miserable.

She's as beautiful as ever in a light blue sundress that matches her eyes. I keep staring at her like an idiot. I don't want to make things weird, but this day was never going to be light and fun. It's the end. So, my brain is already watching her hard, taking mental pictures so I won't forget. Her sky-blue eyes turn to me. Those eyes that have been watering since I saw her.

Click. Committed to memory.

"Hey," I say, just to break the awkward silence. "I got something for you."

I reach to the backseat and grab a package that I wrapped in newsprint. Layla takes it like it's made of gold. This is one of the things I'm going to miss about her the most. She'll never be the type to look at the way something's wrapped on the outside and judge. Layla is the kind of person who cares about what's inside.

"For me?"

I nod. "Open it."

She unwraps the newspaper, then pulls out the picture within a frame. It's a charcoal sketch I did of her one night while she was sleeping. She's on her back, arms folded over her head, the sheet just barely covering her naked body. I remember the night I drew it. I had just come back in from the bathroom in the middle of the night and saw her asleep, her hair spread on the pillow under her while the moonlight shone through my bedroom window, lighting up her skin in the night. She was the most beautiful thing I'd ever seen. Fuck. She still is.

"Oh my God," she murmurs as she floats her hand over the drawing, careful not to touch the paper, which isn't covered by glass. "Oh my God, Nico. This is amazing."

I could tell her she won't ruin it—it's been treated with my sister's hairspray to make sure the charcoal won't fade. That shit is basically shellac. But I like the awe in the way Layla hovers her fingers. There aren't a lot of people who look at anything I do like that.

Click.

But then she turns, and she looks like she's about to cry again. It's not doing good things to the cracks already running through my chest. And for the first time, I'm actually sad I'm *not* on the subway or in the back of a cab, because if I'm driving, it means I can't pull her close and hug her until she stops crying.

"Oh, baby...hey...fuck..." I trail off. I can't cuss her tears away. My hand falls off the gearshift, and I grapple for hers. "I'm sorry. I thought you'd like it."

She sniffs and wipes at her eyes. "I—I do like it. I love it. So much."

I glance at the picture in her lap, with its carved wood frame I found at a flea market in Chelsea. It's not much, but I thought it would look good with the rough charcoal. I'm no real artist, but it seems to have hit its mark. In the last three weeks, things have been good between us, but she's pulled back a bit. I get it. I probably have too. Sometimes she'd look at me, and I'd see a glimmer of that heat, that emotion that I suspect is always going to be between us. She'd look like she wanted to say something. Those three words, the three words I've been keeping back since...well, since I met her, I guess.

But it would only last a moment, because then she'd turn away, and we'd be back to casual and carefree.

Inwardly, I'm shaking my head. I've been crazy about this girl from the moment I saw her. This is some Romeo and Juliet shit going on. But I know this is right, even if it hurts. I can't stay here anymore. And she can't come with me.

Layla finally touches the drawing, and I smile a little. I needed to tell her how I felt, somehow. I think maybe now she can see it.

CHAPTER THIRTY-SIX

Layla

We wander around the museum for a few hours, taking our time with the paintings and the tapestries and all of the other medieval art that's there. It's three o'clock on a Tuesday, so we're basically the only ones at The Cloisters. Nico's never more than a few inches away from me, his hands always touching somewhere: my hand, my waist, the back of my neck. We say little, just enjoying each other's company. Every time we stop in front of another piece, he slips his arms around my waist and knots his fists there so he can rest his chin on my shoulder. I have no idea what the last five pieces are that we've looked at, because every time he does it, I just close my eyes, relishing the feel of his cheek, warm and slightly scratchy against mine, or his unique scent, soap and some sort of musk that's only Nico.

I try not to think about the fact that this is the last day I'll ever do this. I try not to count down the times I'll get to feel his warmth around me.

I fail miserably.

We wander past the unicorn tapestries, and I find that I can't even look at them. In some way, I had known even on our first day that I wasn't going to be able to keep this beautiful man. The caged animal reminds me of the fact that Nico is going to be free. It makes me feel a little better. Only a little.

"You hungry?" he murmurs as one hand drifts down my arm and grasps my fingers.

I nod. "A little."

My stomach is actually in knots. I doubt I could eat anything today, but Nico doesn't like it when I don't take care of myself. Since I ended up in the hospital, he started bringing me snacks and water every time he saw me. Karen actually got mad at how much food I had stashed behind the receptionist desk.

"There's a cafe downstairs."

Nico leads me to the basement level of the museum. He buys us a bottle of water to share and a chocolate chip cookie, and we carry them outside into the small cloister garden, where we sit on the wide stone wall overlooking the Westside Highway, the Hudson River, and New Jersey beyond that. West. Where we're both going. Just not together.

"Here."

Nico pulls the cookie out of the bag and breaks it in half. I nibble on my piece, but it tastes like sawdust. I hate that we're here. I hate that this day is here.

"Come on, baby," Nico cajoles. "You gotta be hungry since you skipped lunch."

I just look out toward the river. It's a much different scene from the last time we were here. It's spring now, and the park that the museum looks over is covered by trees in full bloom. All shades of green line the river bank on either side, muffling the sounds of cars. A warm breeze sweeps through the courtyard every so often. It's a beautiful spring day, but the sound of the wind rustling the leaves sounds like crying. It sounds like how I feel.

The wind causes my hair to fly around and into my face; I'm glad, because it hides the tears that are threatening to fall again. *Don't go.* The words sit on my tongue, waiting to be said. It's selfish, but a part of me wishes he had brushed off my order. A part of my heart is breaking because I'm not enough for him to stay.

Nico brushes the hair out of my face, but the wind just tosses it back into my eyes. He pulls off his cap and sets it backwards on my head with a smirk. But his lopsided smile disappears when he catches my unguarded face. The regret I see there, the concern, the—dare I say it?—love, breaks my heart all over again. And finally, my tears begin to fall.

"Aw, baby," he murmurs as his thumb wipes one tear away, then another.

The sweet gesture doesn't do anything but make them come even more. I don't move, don't even try to make them stop. Just like the first time we met, I'm frozen— by his touch, by the depth in his eyes, by everything about him.

Nothing else in my life seems as real as this man. Washington feels a million miles away. Am I really going back there tonight? California—what's that? School, my friends, all of the vibrant things I've seen and done since living in this city...everything pales next to him.

What am I going to do without you?

Nico leans in, his hand still cupping my cheek, and presses an impossibly soft kiss on my lips. He starts to move away, but I pull him back, and the kiss slowly morphs into something so much deeper. We savor each other, tongues twisting, lips drinking, hands grasping, but slowly, slowly. This is a kiss that's saying everything our voices can't. I feel it, and I think Nico does too.

When I pull away, his eyes are wet and shining, and his breath is haggard. I lean in and kiss him once more, echoing the soft touch of his first one. Full circle, over and over again.

"I think," he starts when I pull back. His voice is choked. "I think we should go. Layla...Jesus. I need you so fucking bad right now."

My chest expands. I nod.

"Let's go," I whisper.

———

WE SAY little as Nico drives us back to Lafayette, even less as I sign him into the nearly-empty building and escort him up to my room. The apartment is bare. Nothing in the kitchen, no sheets on the plastic-covered mattresses. All my things are boxed up, ready to be taken into storage or in the duffel bags I'm bringing home with me.

As soon as the door closes, Nico pulls me into him, wrapping me into a kiss so painfully deep that I can't think of anything else. Our hands are everywhere, pulling off each other's clothes like butterflies shedding their chrysalises. Nico walks me backward to the couch and gently pushes me down. But then he stops when I lie back, naked. His gaze drifts over me, like he's trying to memorize the curves of my body. Then his dark eyes blacken as he kneels in front of me and lays his head on my stomach.

My hands drift over the smooth skin of his shoulders, tracing the tattoos that cover one side.

"Don't forget about me, okay?" he says in a voice so low I almost can't hear it. But that baritone rumbles against my skin.

Before I can answer, he presses kisses over my navel, drifting down over my hip bones, over the soft skin of my inner thighs. The light stubble scratches the sensitive skin, and my hips jerk a little at the feel of it. His tongue and lips drift to my center, finding that sensitive bundle of nerves that makes my thoughts stop completely.

My fingers weave into his thick hair while he licks softly. His eyes are closed, and I watch him work in a trance, as if he's committing this most intimate taste to memory too.

My body starts to shake, and I can't keep my gaze straight anymore. I fall back into the couch cushions as Nico picks up his pace, humming a little as he goes, like someone tasting exotic chocolate or their favorite foods.

"Please," I whimper, although for what, I'm not sure. Please let me come? Please stay? Please...

"Let go," Nico says, his breath warm and his voice low. "Let me feel you let go, Layla."

The sound of my name, when usually I'm "sweetie," "baby," or "NYU," is my undoing. My body seizes, and suddenly I'm no longer preparing to lose the first person I've ever really loved in my short life. Right now, I'm flying.

"Nico!" I cry, my hands grasping at the pillows, at his hair, at anything to keep me anchored as one orgasm flies through me, and then, almost as suddenly, another in quick, body-wrenching spasms.

And it's only when the last gut-wrenching tremor has rippled through every cell in my body that Nico presses his nose into that most intimate part of me, inhales deeply, and then lifts himself up to kiss me gently. I can taste myself on his lips, on his tongue. The knowledge of it makes me shiver.

"I..." I say in between long, languid kisses. "I..."

But the words won't come. Not the ones I want to say. The ones my heart is too scared to admit anymore.

"I know," Nico says softly in between kisses. "I know, baby."

Then he reaches down and grabs a condom from his pants. I shouldn't do this—I know I shouldn't—but I pull the condom away and toss it to the floor.

"It's okay," I say softly. "I'm on the pill."

Nico's brow furrows adorably. "I—you don't have to—"

"I'm safe," I tell him. "I was tested last month at the hospital."

Nico gulps. "I was, too, just after we met."

I pull him into me. I close my eyes as he nudges at my entrance. It's stupid, but just once, I'd like to know there's nothing between us.

"You sure?" he asks, even as he pushes in slightly. There's pain in his voice. He wants this as badly as I do.

I raise my eyes, and neither of us can look away.

"I'm sure," I whisper.

Slowly, he fills me, one solid inch at a time. The muscles in his arms—the cut lines of his biceps, forearms, triceps, even in his chest—tremble with the effort to go slow.

"Jesus," he whispers as he seats himself completely. "You feel so fucking good, Layla."

I slide my arms up his shoulders and clasp them around his neck.

"Kiss me," I ask. "Please."

So he does, with the same long, languorous licks that just tore me apart only minutes before, the pace of his hips matching every delicious movement he makes with his tongue. This isn't sex. It's making love, the culmination of the entire, bitter-sweet afternoon. I can't imagine a better way to say goodbye to him, even though at the same time, it's going to make it that much harder when I actually have to do it. It's for the best that we waited until now to do it like this. If sex had been like this for the entire three months, there's no way I could have said goodbye. There's no way I could have ever let him go.

"Layla," he says after he sucks on my bottom lip hard enough to bite a little. He's starting to lose that careful control. "Baby—I—I'll—"

I cup his face between my hands and kiss him again, shuttering the words that are failing. He thrusts again, then again, but his forehead wrinkles. He's stuck on something—something that's keeping him from letting go.

"I—" he starts again, but stumbles once more.

I trace my thumbs over his sharp cheekbones, trying to memorize every dip and valley in this beautiful face.

"What is it?" I ask. "What do you need?"

"I—" He jerks again as he thrusts even deeper. "God, Layla. I just..." His eyes scrunch closed, then pop open, black and fathomless. "I need to hear you...say it..."

My mouth drops open. "Say what?"

He pushes even further, making my body writhe like a wave.

"Say..." Beads of sweat gather over his forehead with the effort of his control. "Say that you'll never forget me," Nico whispers as his eyes shut tightly. "That you'll never forget us."

The memories of the past few months hit me like an avalanche. The lightning connection of our first touch. The kiss in the snow. Every afternoon. Every lazy morning. Every look, every touch, every tear, every kiss. Every single moment is imprinted into the threads of my being. If my life is a tapestry, this man has forever altered its weave.

"I promise," I tell him. "I'll never forget us. Never."

And it's then, with a pained howl that cuts through the air, that Nico finally lets go. We both let go, together.

CHAPTER THIRTY-SEVEN

Nico

WE LIE THERE FOR WHAT SEEMS LIKE AN HOUR, WRAPPED UP TOGETHER ON THE COUCH, not wanting to let each other go. We sleep a little, tangled and uncomfortable, but neither of us wants to get up or admit that the shadows falling across the wall are growing longer and longer. Because then it will be time to say goodbye. And I'm still not sure I'm going to be able to do it.

My watch alarm beeps at six-thirty, telling me it's time to go back to my apartment and get ready for my last shift at AJ's. I'd take any excuse to call in sick, but I can't lie. Between the Jeep and the three-month's rent I just paid for Gabe and Maggie, I pretty much wiped out my savings. The extra few hundred dollars will help pay my way across the country. Away from my girl.

Layla sits up, her mussed hair a black waterfall over her shoulders. She wipes her fingers under her eyes, and I take in the simple form of her naked body: her small, perfect breasts, the curves of her hips and waist, the graceful lines of her legs. All before she covers up with her dress.

"I guess..." she trails off, suddenly intent on finding the rest of her clothes.

"Yeah."

I sit up and grab my jeans and shirt off the floor. We're both silent, overly focused on adjusting and readjusting fabric. Anything to delay the inevitable.

Eventually, there's nothing left to do. I clap on my cap, and Layla buckles her sandals.

"I guess I should—"

"I'll walk you down," she says, and my heart sinks with relief. No goodbyes yet. I still have a few more minutes.

We ride down to the lobby together in silence, ignoring the bored security guard as Layla signs me out. Then she walks me out to where the Jeep is parked out front, clean and gleaming in the sun.

I unlock the door and toss my hat inside. I want to see her clearly when I have to do this. I turn around, feeling like my chest is about to split open.

"Well, sweetie," I say. "This is it."

Layla looks up, her blue eyes matching the color of the sky shining through the buildings behind her. I can admit it—it's hard to beat New York in the spring. It's hard to leave the city when it's like this. When there's someone like her in it.

"I just want to say..." I start saying some lame piece-of-shit goodbye, because what else can you say when you have to do something like this?

But Layla stops me by jumping forward and wrapping her arms around my neck. It takes me a second to register that like a faucet, she started sobbing—not just crying the little streams of tears that have been threatening all day, but big, body-shaking sobs. She lets out all the emotion I know she's been trying to keep back all day. Maybe for the last three weeks, if she's anything like me.

I hold her close, trying to absorb the pain I feel emanating from her in waves, a pain that echoes through my bones. It's weird, but I don't know if I've ever seen a girl cry like this before. Little kids, sure. Allie cries like crazy when she's mad. But Maggie and Selena learned quick that tears won't get you much. Soltero kids don't cry, because otherwise, they get their ears swatted.

But Layla didn't grow up like that, and in its own way, it's a beautiful thing to see. She lets me gather her into my shoulder while she falls apart. It's amazing. I've never known anyone so pure, so open to feel what she feels.

Layla has no remorse for her feelings. She lets them pass through her, like everyone should do, but that so many, including myself, don't. It's contagious, and before I know it, there are actually a few tears sneaking out of my eyes while I absorb the sobs that wrack through her small body.

"Shhhh," I croon, rocking us back and forth on the sidewalk.

We catch a few curious looks as people walk by, wondering what I've done to upset this girl. I shoot them glares and press kiss after kiss onto Layla's head. She can cry as long as she wants. No one has ever cried for me like this before, and I'll be damned if I'm going to tell her it's wrong. She deserves better than me—and one day, she'll find it. But for now, I can be here for her, even though I'm the asshole breaking her heart.

Eventually, her sobs subside. Layla pushes away from my chest, hiccupping a little and pushing stray tears from under her eyes. Her makeup disappeared a long time ago, and her big blue eyes are still watery, but she's still the most beautiful girl I've ever seen. No. The most beautiful *woman*.

Come on. Say it, you pussy. Tell her you love her. At least give her that.

Layla takes a few long, deep breaths. "I guess...I guess it's time."

I nod, still holding her hand. I don't want to let go, but I have to. I have to go to work, and she's got a plane to catch.

"I..." I shift from foot to foot, kicking a tiny rock onto the street. Then I look up. "I'll never forget you, Layla. Ever. You should know...that I...I lo—"

"I know," she interrupts me before the words can leave my mouth.

She gives me a small, sad smile. She doesn't want to hear it. I try to ignore the way the words sit in my chest like rocks. So it's like that.

I nod. "Okay." I open my mouth, then close it, then open it again to say the only thing I can think of. "I guess I'll go, then."

I lean over and press one last kiss on her forehead. Layla closes her eyes, and I inhale that coconut-flowered scent I can't ever get enough of.

"Be good, baby," I murmur.

I sound like a fucking preschool teacher, but I don't care. I mean it, especially since I can't say the words I really want to say. I just want the best for her. I want her to have everything good this shitty life has to offer.

She steps away and swipes beneath her eyes again. "Okay. You better go." She folds her arms around her waist in a hug.

Fighting the urge to fold her back into my arms, I nod. "Okay."

I get into my car, and with a quick press of my hand to the window, I turn on the ignition and pull away.

It takes me about a half of a block before I'm already regretting it. It takes less than another before I'm banging on the steering wheel and shouting at myself inside my head. *You should have asked her to come! You should have told her you love her! You should have asked her to come, asked her to wait, asked her to stay in the city until you can come back.*

Fuck it. This isn't how I should end things. Not with Layla.

I'm three blocks from her dorm and already pulling my cell phone out of my pocket when a loud bang on my window makes me jump. When I look, there she is, standing in the middle of Canal Street traffic, her hand pressed against the glass, more tears streaming down her face while she struggles to catch her breath.

The cars are moving ahead of me, but I don't care. In less than a minute, I've double-parked the car and jumped out into the street, ignoring the honking horns and New Yorkers cursing me from the cabs and trucks trying to get down the thoroughfare. All I see is Layla.

"What is it?" I say as I kiss her lips over and over again.

She hiccups back a sob, returns the kisses, returns them all.

"I just…" she hiccups again. "I needed to say…"

"What baby?" I ask. "Tell me."

"I love you."

The words are so quick, I'm almost not sure she said them. But when I pull back to look at her face, I can see them shining through her big, sad eyes. My heart expands and breaks all at once. This is why people say not to fall in love. Because it makes you feel like flying and jumping off a cliff at the same time.

But it's still love. And I don't regret a thing.

I press my forehead into hers. "I love you too." My eyes are closed. God, this hurts. "Layla, I—"

"Get the fuck out of the road!"

The shouts of angry New Yorkers interrupt our moment, and Layla steps away. I fight the urge to pull her back. I already miss her so fucking badly.

"I'll see you," she says with a limp wave. "Drive safely."

I smile, but as the honking behind us picks up, all I can do is nod and get back into the Jeep.

"Be good!" I shout again as I start the engine.

Layla nods, but she's already jogging back down the street, wiping her eyes and hugging herself around her waist. Instead of jumping out of the car and chasing her down like I should, I just watch in the rearview mirror while she disappears around the corner. And then, like the fuckin' coward I am, I step on the gas and drive on, ignoring the earthquake going on in my chest.

Because the truth is, love was never going to be enough. We had a good run, but she's better off. A real future between us was never going to happen. She might be the best thing that ever happened to me, but I was always a bad idea.

EPILOGUE

MAY 2004: ONE YEAR LATER

Nico

THE SHADOWS OF THE PALM TREES ARE LONG AND THIN, STRETCHING DOWN SUNSET Boulevard like spider legs. The engine of the Jeep kicks. I'm still regretting buying this hunk of junk. Sure, it looks great when I go to the beach—it's one of the few cars in LA that still gets points for charm. But the thing guzzles gas and breaks down every other month. For real, I never thought I'd miss the subway until I had to pay for car repairs.

But now I'm done with it. I'm dropping this thing off with some starving artist in West Hollywood before I go to K.C.'s going away party. He says it's for us both, but there aren't that many people who will want to say goodbye to some random security guy. I didn't think it was possible, but people in LA are even more shallow than New Yorkers. If you don't know anyone important, you're no one. I controlled the names on the list, but after they got through the door of whatever club we were at, I might as well have been a shadow.

But now it's over. This crazy fuckin' year is over, and I could not be more ready. In two days, K.C. and I will start the long-ass drive back to New York in his Yukon, which never breaks down and has air conditioning. He's taken a job at a radio station in the city, one that won't require him to play clubs up and down the Eastern seaboard (unless he wants to) and will pay a lot more money. I'm proud of my friend, who's really hitting the good life these days. But more than that, I'm actually excited about my own life for the first time.

I've finally got a reason to go back that doesn't involve obligations. No back-rents to pay, no bathrooms to caulk, no boyfriends to beat up. I didn't think I'd miss the city this much, but I really have. I think the real reason I left was because it always felt like New York didn't want me, instead of the other way around. I kept giving that city everything I had, and it kept shitting all over me. My family's shit. My friends' shit.

But now New York is finally giving me a break. I'm looking at a future I want there, a job I want, and I'm going to go back and be somebody.

My phone buzzes in my pocket. It's probably K.C., wondering where the fuck I am. He wants to make an entrance together, the two of us. It's nice the way he always wants to include me, but it's unnecessary. I've never needed to be the center of attention like he does.

"Yo, man, I told you, I'm just dropping off the car, and then I'm on my way." I practically yell so he can hear me over the roar of traffic. Sunset Boulevard at the tail end of rush hour is a bitch. And you know what no one ever tells you about convertibles? They're fuckin' loud. And you get a lot of bugs flying into your mouth.

"N-Nico?"

It's a voice that's uncertain and small. A voice that's shaking and barely audible over the combination of wind, car horns, and rolling tires. It's a voice that blows through my head like a grenade. And not just because I haven't heard it since she told me two months ago, in no uncertain terms, to fuck the hell off. Her voice creaks and shakes over my name. She stammers, which is not something she ever does unless she's really scared or really nervous. The girl I know is usually calm and well-spoken. She's never, ever sounded like this.

"Layla?" I call out. "Is that you?"

"I-I want you to k-kill him," she stutters words that are cracked and raw. "I want you to come with your-your boys, your friends. Flaco. K.C. Who—I don't know— who-whoever you would bring to help you. And I-I want you to beat the sh-shit out of him, j-just like you would have, w-way back w-when...you know...w-when you were y-younger..."

All the hair on the back of my neck, the tops of my arms stands up, even under the warm California sun. It's eighty-five degrees in the shade today, and I'm sweating in my tank top, but I've got goosebumps all over. Layla has asked me for a lot of things over the course of this crazy fuckin' year, but she's never asked for anything like this. The whole time I've known her, she's barely even mentioned the past that always seemed to follow me around like a black cloud. Unlike everyone else who's ever known about the kind of person I used to be, she never treated me like a thug. Even when she was pissed as hell at me, when her friends told her I was no good, when everyone, including me, told her I was just a bad idea, I was always a person to Layla. I was only ever Nico.

Cutting off a white Mercedes and earning a loud "Fuck you!" from its driver, I pull the car over to the side of the road and shut off the engine.

"Where are you?" I demand.

"I'm-I'm at a payphone," she stutters. "T-two blocks from h-his place. H-he...I c-can't..."

She trails off as a siren sounds behind her. I can hear the noise of whatever busy street she's on. Her boyfriend lives somewhere close to my old place—I know that from our last incredibly painful conversation—but otherwise I can't picture her. Two blocks from his place could mean anywhere. It could mean some nasty alley closer to the River, or it could be just a block from CUNY. I check my watch. It's ten at night in New York right now. Even though the city lights never allow the sky to completely dim there, there are plenty of streets that are dark enough on their own.

All I know is that something happened. Layla's scared, angry, and alone somewhere up in West Harlem, and I'm stuck here in the land of eternal sunshine. I close my eyes. I can't go there. If I start imagining some of the places I *know* Layla shouldn't be, combined with the fact that I'm three-thousand miles away from her, I'll go motherfuckin' crazy, right here in Beverly Hills.

"Layla, what the fuck is going on?" I snatch off my sunglasses and throw them on the seat next to me. "What did that motherfucker do to you?!"

But all I get is a patchy response, since I'm far enough into the Hills that my reception cuts off. Fuck! I can only hear every other frantic word she's saying.

"He...to...me...I don't...help...he's coming...need...go!"

Then the line goes dead.

"*Coño!*" I roar, startling an elder lady out walking her dog. I try to call back the payphone number, but there's no answer. When I try Layla's cell phone, an operator tells me it's no longer in service. I let out a torrent of Spanish that would have caused my mother to rinse my mouth out with soap, no matter if I'm twenty-seven years old or not, and hammer my fists on the steering wheel for a solid ten seconds. The old lady stares at me with her mouth open, and when I look up, practically runs away from the car.

I don't know what to do. I don't know what to think. The girl I've been in love with since the second I saw her just called me, freaking out after her shithead boyfriend did *something* to her. Layla's not a drama queen. And she wouldn't hurt a fly. She wouldn't have made that request if something seriously fucked up hadn't happened.

I slam the steering wheel again, this time making the horn honk at another couple of pedestrians. They glare at me; I stare a hole through the window. I should be careful, I know. In a neighborhood like this, being a brown dude throwing a tantrum in his shitty car is enough to get me arrested, and I cannot afford to have a record that's anything but squeaky clean. It would throw *everything* I have lined up in jeopardy.

But instead of acting calmly, I spring into action. The Jeep screams away from the curb, and there's only one path on my mind: drop this hunk of junk off with the buyer—I don't even care how much they want for it. At this point, I'd pay them to take the thing off my hands. Fuck this car. Fuck the party. Fuck California and all three-thousand and some miles in between me and the girl I'd tear through steel doors to get to. I just want it all gone so I can get my ass to the airport and onto whatever red-eye flights they have available.

K.C.'s going to have to make the drive by himself. I gotta get back to New York.

LOST ONES

BOOK TWO OF THE BAD IDEA SERIES

I

SAUDADE

CHAPTER ONE

AUGUST 2003

Layla

Fifty-eight...fifty-nine...

I turn from the register in the empty juniors' department at Nordstrom. It's exactly three thirty, and I'm officially off the clock for good.

"Sarah, I'm out of here," I tell my twenty-something manager, who's busy digging through boxes in the stockroom.

Sarah pushes her picture-perfect, light-brown hair out of her face. It always takes her a moment to remember the temporary employees like me. I'm not sure that in three months she's even managed to learn my name.

"Oh...right," she says. "When are you here tomorrow?"

I smile tightly. "Today's my last day. I'm headed back to school."

Realization dawns on her vapid face. Sarah's nice, but her world doesn't extend very far beyond the sales floor. "Oh! Well, thanks for the great work this summer. Let me know if you need a reference."

"Layla." I nod. "Will do. Good luck with...everything."

There's not much else to say. I'm practically skipping out of the door after I go through employee security for the last time, grab my purse, and sprint to my car. This giant brick building in the middle of downtown Bellevue has felt like a prison for the last three months, and now I'm free. Two weeks of vacation with my parents, and after that, I can go back to New York, back to the city that's been calling my name since May.

It's true what they say: you can never go home again. Fewer of my high school friends came home this year, so I feel like a stranger in the town where I grew up. On top of that, my dad seems to be working even more than normal, often spending his nights at his office while my mom disappears to the country club with her chardonnay-drinking friends.

The bright side is that their negligence has only given me more time to save money. Between working overtime at the mall and answering phones at my dad's office, I've managed to save enough that I won't have to work during the school year. The problem with boring jobs, though, is that they leave too much time for daydreaming, and I have an active imagination. I had two goals this summer: make money and forget about a certain handsome ex-New Yorker who broke my heart last spring.

Well...I succeeded at one.

The long afternoon shifts don't keep me from imagining him striding around every corner. They don't stave off dreams of how he spots me, picks me up, and swirls me around like the guys in cheesy romance movies. They don't calm my heart every time I see a FedEx truck. Do you know how hard that is? Those things are everywhere.

Broad shoulders and strong hands, the kind that lifted me up like I weighed next to nothing. Tattoos that decorated an excruciatingly defined body, under which lay a heart of gold. A smile that made me lose my footing regularly, and which could probably power all of Manhattan during an outage.

But in the end, the fantasies hurt. I remember that I'm stuck here, and he's in California after he left New York to seek a real future for himself elsewhere and wouldn't let me come with him. And I remember that after exchanging a few phone calls once he got there, and then even fewer text messages, he changed his number and hasn't called me back since.

That's when the real pain starts. So I try to think about how I'm going back to New York in two weeks with a savings account full of money. Which means I won't have to work at the entertainment law firm anymore—a relief, since the place would no doubt remind me of the man I met there. Instead, I can focus on my classes and getting the kinds of internships that will help me get into law school.

If, of course, that's still what I'm going to do. The idea has been sounding worse and worse to me lately, although I haven't mentioned it to my parents. Since they've shown absolutely no interest in me, I've chosen not to bring it up, and they haven't either. Works for me.

Surprisingly, both of their cars are in the driveway when I pull up to our house in Redmond. Despite the fact that I grew up here, it's never totally felt like home. For one thing, it's huge, far too big for just three people. With six bedrooms sitting on three acres of lush forest, it's more like a museum than a home. My mother has stocked it with priceless antiques, and the immaculate white carpet has never seen a shoe, much less a dropped backpack or spilled snacks. Everything has its place, but none of those places ever seemed to fit me. Let's just put it this way: when I saw *Beauty and the Beast*...I felt for the Beast, not Belle. I understood why he was such a dick locked up in the big castle. The guy was *lonely*.

"Layla?"

My dad's deep voice echoes through the long hallway when I enter the house. I remove my shoes and carefully place them in the hallway closet, then pad into the kitchen, where I find him and my mother sitting together at the marble-topped island, both of them holding their favorite drinks: scotch on the rocks for my dad, dry white wine for my mom.

It wouldn't be such a strange sight if it weren't four in the afternoon. My parents like their cocktails, but they aren't exactly lushes. They'll usually wait until at least five to break out the alcohol.

"Sit down, Layla," my dad orders, his thick Brazilian accent more pronounced than usual.

I slide onto a stool across from them at the island. At first glance, they don't look any different than normal. I suspect that Mom has occasionally taken advantage of the fact that her husband owns a successful cosmetic surgery practice—her glossy exterior never seems to change, while the rest of my friends' parents have all gotten older. She's still the same bottle-blonde, white-toothed, blue-eyed ingénue she's always been, despite having celebrated her forty-second birthday last month. Same tasteful blue sundress, same mid-height pumps, same pearl necklace and solitaire ring.

Dad's slightly more olive-toned skin shows his age a bit more, and his thick black hair is shot through with silver on the sides. He wears one of his many starched, button-down shirts and shiny leather loafers. On his wrist is one of the tastefully expensive watches he gets for Christmas from his wife. But unlike my mother's blasé sweetness, my father is always stern. Sergio Barros never, ever smiles. That, more than the fact that he has over ten years on her, is why he has more wrinkles than his wife. His forehead is always puckered when he frowns.

Today they both look a little more their ages than usual. Dad really does look fifty-eight, and Mom really does look forty-two, mostly because their faces are shot through with something different. Sadness, maybe? Dread?

I grip the edge of the counter, already bracing myself for something. "What's up?"

Mom takes a long drink of wine. Her tennis bracelet clinks against the glass.

"We waited as long as we could," Dad says. "Your mother and I, we wanted to give you one last summer here before...well, it's time."

My gaze ping-pongs between them. "Time for what?"

"Your mother and I have decided we will no longer live together."

Silence drops on the table like an anvil while his words echo around the big house. In here, everything has its place. Nothing feels shattered...yet. I'm not even sure if I heard him correctly.

My parents have never been happy together—that much was always clear. They're an odd couple—a Pasadena princess with a magnanimous foreigner many years her senior. My dad is loud and authoritative while my mom is diminutive and quiet. They've never been affectionate, never even socialized together beyond work events. Once, when my mother had too many glasses of wine and my dad was working late, I asked her if she loved him. She laid her head in my lap and cried. I was twelve.

They've always treated each other with indifference, the way one might treat a piece of outdated furniture. It's fine until it starts to get beat up. It's fine until it gets in your way. When things get in my mother's way, she turns around and ignores them. When things get in my father's way, he attacks.

Living.

Apart.

"Wha-*what*?" I finally stutter. "You're getting a...*divorce*?" The word is not even in my parents' vocabulary. "But...you're the most Catholic people on the planet." I'm shooting back and forth between them. "You wouldn't even let me go to a Protestant youth group in high school, for Christ's sake! You don't believe in divorce!"

"Layla!" chastises my father. "There's no need for that kind of language. And we're not getting a divorce. We are separating. There is a difference."

Beside him, my mother snorts. It's the first noise she's made, and if I hadn't been looking at her when she did it, I might have missed it. She hides her face in her glass like she didn't say anything, but Dad shoots her a dirty look nonetheless. I wait for the sharp retort that should knock her down a peg—the kind I just received. But none comes.

"Is the difference that you're planning to get back together?" I ask, trying and failing to keep the sharpness out of my voice, which is already starting to quiver.

My dad tightens his jaw. "It's not so simple."

"Yes, it is, Serge," my mother interrupts.

Dad and I both stare at her, dumbfounded. My mother never, ever interrupts my father. But she isn't looking at him when she says his name. She's looking at me.

"We're not getting divorced because the church doesn't allow it, even if the state does," Mom tells me. "And...well, that's just the way it's going to be."

She casts another long look at my father, who doesn't have the decency to meet her gaze. It's clear which one of them refuses to do this. And fighting my father is usually not worth the battle.

"But effectively," she continues, "we *will* be divorced."

This causes my glance to flicker back to Dad. We're Catholic, yes, but it's mainly a choice fueled by my father's occasional guilt. Mom converted to marry him, so this isn't her hang-up. But my dad...yeah. I could see him refusing to sign divorce papers on account of the church. He doesn't wear that St. Christopher medallion around his neck because he's confident about getting into heaven. There's a reason why he calls me on Sundays to see if I go, why he made me send pictures last year after I received my blessing on Ash Wednesday. He's the guiltiest person I know.

"So, what, you're going to move to an apartment downtown or something for a while?" I venture back at my dad. "Leave Mom in this giant house by herself? What kind of life is that?"

"Not one I want," Dad puts in. "The house was sold in the spring, before you came home. We've been renting it since then."

That explained why both my parents had been even more anal-retentive than normal about keeping the place clean. The house wasn't even ours anymore.

"So...where are the two of you going?"

My mother takes another long slug of wine, but she lets my father talk.

"I've sold my practice," Dad replies as he swirls the ice around in his drink. "And bought a share in another. In Vitória."

Vitória. Brazil? I shove a hand through my hair. This makes no sense. Absolutely no sense at all.

"B-but...you hate Brazil," I sputter. "You've spent most of your life trying to act like you're not even from there!"

"Layla, Brazil is my country. Of course I do not hate it," Dad replies wearily after taking a long drink of his scotch. "I've made a good life here, it's true, but it was hard. Very hard. Now your mother and I have little in common anymore. I've made my fortune. My daughter is grown. I am tired of fighting so hard for what I have. It is time for me to go home."

"I-I still don't understand." I'm reeling. What is happening right now? "You won't even let me tell people I'm Brazilian."

"That's because you're *not*!" my father returns sharply. "You're American. Look at you. You have blue eyes, your skin is white like snow, and you speak only English. You were born here, and thank God for that." He leans in, the angles of his face softening slightly. "It will never be as hard here for you as it was for me, Layla. Besides, is this not what you want? To leave this place? How much did we have to fight for you to come home this summer at all?"

This close, I can see the way the dark circles, the ones I get too when I'm stressed, make his eyes look like they've been etched with black. My father is tired. He never wants to tell me about the problems he's had, only gestures to them obliquely like this. Sometimes I try to imagine. Racial slurs thrown at him when he first arrived here in the seventies, maybe? Assumptions that he was the groundskeeper at Stanford, not a medical student? He and my mother must have caught some kind of wrath when they started dating. Harassment? Attacks?

I'll never know. But obviously it was bad enough that he feels he needs to shield me from it. Bad enough that he learned to hate himself and now wants to run away.

I look up. "Where's Mom going?"

"Pasadena."

My mom has a quiet voice, one that comes from years of learning how to play second fiddle to Sergio Barros, preeminent surgeon and life of the party. She fiddles with the stem of her wine glass before she meets my gaze.

"I'll be staying with your grandparents," she tells me, "while I look for a new house down there."

I blink. "You're moving in with your parents?"

My mother is forty-two. She's a grown woman, and not just that, a *rich* grown woman. Even if she wants to house hunt for a while, there's no reason she has to stay with her parents while she does it. She could rent an apartment or even a house somewhere in the LA area.

I glance between the two of them as my chest starts to feel like it's icing over, a thin crust of frozen water, delicate enough that it might shatter. This is where I grew up. While it's never been the warmest place in the world, it's always been familiar. *They* have been familiar.

Slowly, I push back from the counter as tears cloud my vision. The chair leg drags on the marble floor, and the screech echoes through the high-ceilinged rooms.

"Where are you going?" my dad barks as I walk away.

I turn up the stairs that lead to the six empty bedrooms. The house echoes with every one of my steps—it's never had enough to fill it, but it's the only home I've known.

"I need a few moments," I say, barely hearing my own voice.

"Not too long," Dad calls, always controlling, always assuming he's in the right, even when he's the one delivering the bomb that blows everything up. Until he drops the other one: "We have a lot to do. I leave in three days, and you'll be going to Pasadena with your mother."

CHAPTER TWO

Nico

THE JEEP RUMBLES TO A STOP, AND I PULL THE PARKING BREAK AND SIT FOR A MINUTE. THE soft top is off, and early evening California sun beats down on me and the pavement. Across the street, the disc-shaped Capitol Records building practically shimmers in the heat. It's almost six o'clock, but it's still hot as fuck. Not humid like August usually is in New York, but nastier. In New York, the grime is gray and sticky, but every so often a rain shower or a snowstorm washes everything away. The heat in LA feels dirtier somehow. It flickers with a layer of smog that bakes in the sun all year round. It doesn't matter that the sky is always blue and the palm trees sway in the breeze that sometimes comes up from the ocean. LA heat is tinted yellow, and it cuts you through like a rusty blade.

The door to Venom, the nightclub across the street and my place of work, opens, and a few of the staff exit the building. One of them says hi, but they know my routine. I usually take a few minutes in my car, just to be alone, before I go in. The Wednesday-night DJ is already setting things up at the booth and doing his sound check. It's drum and bass night, which means I'm going to need about ten Advil tomorrow morning to get rid of my headache. The sun will go down in another couple of hours, and the club will open to a mix of tourists, wannabe actors, and the people they want to impress. All of them have to pass by me. I'll be dressed in my black monkey suit, my hair slicked back like a gangster while I check names and IDs, just like I do every other night.

It's a job I didn't mind so much in New York, but that was only because I did it for extra cash. It was never a career. It was never the defining part of my life. Now I'm working security six nights a week at Venom, where K.C., my best friend from back home, DJs every Saturday. It's one of the biggest clubs in LA, but Venom is the cheesiest place on the planet. Go-go dancers and caged girls, strobe lights and disco balls.

And the people who come here...forget about it. I haven't seen normal-colored teeth or real tits in three months. I feel bad for the bouncers. About half their job consists of kicking people out who are fucking or doing blow in the bathrooms. I can't even imagine wanting to fuck the kinds of people who go to places like this. I'd be getting STD tests every week for the rest of my life.

I work from seven thirty to four. Go home and sleep until noon. Get up. Go to the gym. Get dressed in the black tie and collared shirt I have to wear every damn night. Repeat.

It's getting harder not to admit that coming here was a mistake, even if it's only been a few months. At least the money's good. I make enough to pay my little brother, Gabe's, tuition at CUNY and my mother's rent, plus help out my sisters, Maggie and Selena, so they can focus on work and Maggie's kid, Allie. My family is taken care of, and since I'm three thousand miles away, they can't come running to me for every little thing. It's nice to have a break from them. I think.

My phone rings in my pocket. I pull it out. "Hey, Jess."

"Hey. Everything okay? You seemed kind of mad when you left."

I sigh. Jessie's my roommate, but obviously wants to be more. And yeah, there have been a few times in the past couple of months where I've been a little weak and given in. What would you do if you were living with an actual model who handed out blowjobs like candy? When I come home from the club, I'm so tired that I don't usually stop to wonder why she's there waiting for me instead of going home with her own dates. And yeah, so maybe sometimes I close my eyes and pretend she's someone else. Someone with black hair and blue eyes. Someone I still see almost every night when I fall asleep anyway.

Layla.

I didn't think it would be this hard to forget her. I got here, and all I wanted was to hear her voice. Make her laugh. It was so hard that I almost quit my job the first week to drive up to Seattle to see her. I had to "lose" my phone in the Pacific Ocean to stop myself from calling and texting her, and I changed my number to a fuckin' 323 area code so she couldn't call me either. Do you know how hard it was to give up my 212 number? That's OG New York right there. I'll never get that back.

We only knew each other for a couple of months. And yeah, we both fell pretty hard. But Layla is young—only nineteen, or maybe twenty by now. I think she had a birthday over the summer. She was going to move on from a futureless loser like me anyway at some point, so it might as well have been last May. I just didn't think I wouldn't be able to let her go.

"I'm fine, Jess," I say, forcing myself back to the present. When I start daydreaming about Layla, it's a rabbit hole I can't always escape. "Just don't want to go to work, that's all."

"Want me to come down and keep you company? You know Craig doesn't mind when I hang out."

It's true. Craig, the club manager, loves it when Jessie stands outside with me. She's gorgeous and blonde, and in California, that draws people in like flies. The only problem is, Jessie starts taking things like that to mean we're more than we are. She starts putting her hands all over me, calling me baby, her big brown bear. It makes me cringe. I'm not a fuckin' stuffed animal, and I'm certainly not hers. Any other guy would give his left nut to get with a girl like Jessie, but anything more than scratching the occasional itch just feels wrong. I can't tell you the reason.

Yes, you can, you cowardly fuck. One big reason. One achingly beautiful, blue-eyed reason with a heart-shaped mouth and an ass that won't quit. A heart that speaks to mine in a secret language that has no words.

I guess I'm a fuckin' poet tonight. Just call me Mother fuckin' Goose.

"No, it's fine," I say. "It's going to be busy tonight. I'll probably be in and out anyway."

It's a lie. Wednesdays are the slowest nights of the week. But I'm just not in the mood to deal with Jessie's clinginess right now. If I hadn't signed a lease on the apartment, I would have already moved out.

"Okay," she says. "I guess I'll just have to cheer you up when you get home."

She doesn't say anything wrong. But the way she talks, she makes it sound like it's our place. Like we share everything about it together, instead of the living room and kitchen. Like we don't have separate bedrooms, separate lives.

Who am I kidding? Maybe we don't.

"I'll probably just stay at K.C.'s tonight, hang out with him," I tell her.

K.C. is in Vegas this week doing a party. But I have the key to his very nice West Hollywood apartment, and our arrangement here is the same as it was in New York: when he's out of town, I get to use his place to get a little quiet.

And yeah, more often than not, I end up using it just to mope around and think about the girl I wish was there with me.

"Okay," Jessie's saying, a little sadly.

I sigh, trying not to be bothered by it. I came out here *not* to take on other people's clingy shit.

"See you," I say and hang up the phone before she can reply.

I lean back in my seat and pull the bill of my Yankees cap down low over my face, taking a few more minutes before I have to go into the club. Just like always, those two blue eyes pop up. Shadowed by a fringe of long black lashes. Wide and open. Bluer than the sky above me, bluer than the ocean just fifteen minutes down the road. I let them wash over me and pretend Layla's right there, seeing into my soul the way she always could, penetrating but not painful.

My chest hurts. I rub my face. Usually when I give myself a few seconds to do this, I can push her memory away and get back to my real life. Like a true addict, I just need a quick hit. But today, it's just making me want more, and it hurts like hell that I can't have it.

My thumb slides over the buttons on my phone, automatically tapping out her number. Who was I kidding? I'd never forget it. It might as well be tattooed onto my chest, right over the compass that's already there.

Before I know it, the phone is ringing. Three times, four times. I start to panic. What the fuck am I doing? She doesn't want to hear from me. I haven't called her in two months, like some fuckin' asshole who sleeps with a girl and pretends she's a stranger after she puts out. What the fuck am I going to say?

I'm just about to hang up when she answers.

"Hello?"

Her voice is shaking a little, and my heart shakes right along with it. Fuck. Does she know it's me? What am I going to do? I'm paralyzed. But I can't hang up now that I hear the voice that's been haunting my dreams for the last three months. Like a true addict, I can't let go.

"Hello?" she asks again. "Who is this?"

She's been crying. Her voice is thick, like it's speaking through molasses. I can imagine her, red-rimmed eyes, rose-petal mouth that's pink and swollen. Sad, but beautiful. Always so damn beautiful.

"Hello?" she asks again, now a little bit irritated too.

"Hey, beautiful," I say softly. "It's me."

Layla is silent. I can hear her shuffling around a little bit. I try to imagine where she is right now. Home, I think. She was going home for the summer—home to finish recuperating from a nasty bout of mono in the spring. Is she in her bedroom? A living room? I don't even know exactly where her family lives, just that it's somewhere near Seattle. Is it a big house? Her dad's a big-time plastic surgeon, so I doubt it's small. Do they live in a city, or a small town? Does she have pets?

Suddenly it's killing me not to know these details. I should know these things. I *want* to know these things.

"Hey," she says finally. "Hi."

"Hi," I say back. I sound like a fuckin' parrot. But I don't know what else to say. I just wanted to hear her voice, and now that I have, I want her to talk so I can keep listening.

"Um...yeah. It's...been a while."

I chew on my lip. "I lost my phone," I blurt out. "In the ocean. I had to get a new one and lost all my contacts."

"You lost your phone in the ocean?"

I can hear the smile in her voice, and I grin too, even though she can't see me. "Okay, I threw it in the ocean. By accident. When I got mad one night."

She giggles. Fuck me, that sound kills me, and suddenly I'm laughing right with her, hard enough that my eyes start watering. But then she quiets down, just as quickly.

"Did you lose your number too?"

Shit. She's got me there. I ghosted her, and we both know it. It was an asshole move. No question about it.

"I...uh..." I trail off, searching for an excuse. But I got nothing. I could never lie to her.

"It's okay," she says quietly. "I get it. It was...hard."

I swallow. "Yeah. I...shit. I'm sorry, baby."

The word snakes out of my mouth before I realize it. But somehow, I don't mind it. I realize that no matter where we are or who we're with or how long it's been, on some level, Layla is always going to be my baby. That's just how it will be. The thought is weirdly comforting.

"I know," she says after a moment. "So, um, why are you calling?"

I sigh, drumming my fingers on my thigh. "Honestly...I'm not really sure. I guess I just wanted to hear your voice."

I shouldn't say these things. If it was hard before, it's going to kill me when I have to hang up. If she's feeling what I'm feeling, she's been having just as hard a time being apart. I hope that's not the case. Or maybe I do.

"Tell me about your life," I say quickly, trying to make things light, but sounding more like a shitty game show host. Heartbreaking dickhead for five hundred, Alex. "I mean, how you been, NYU? How was your summer?"

"I've been...good," she says low, in a voice that sounds about the farthest from good I can think of.

She goes quiet, and it's only after another minute that I realize she's crying again, long slow tears that are almost silent. Almost, but not quite.

"Layla, what is it?" I ask, sitting straight up and grabbing the steering wheel.

I'm an idiot. What the fuck are you going to do, Andretti? Drive to Seattle just to give her a hug? She doesn't want to see you.

"Baby, talk to me," I demand, because that's all I can do.

Did I do this? Is she crying because of me? Fuck, I should have just left her alone.

"I...my parents," she hiccups. "My parents are getting divorced. They...they just told me a few minutes ago. My dad is going back to Brazil. He's leaving in three days."

"Holy shit," I breathe. "Oh fuck, sweetie. I'm so sorry. Layla, really, I am."

She sniffs back a few more tears. "I know you are," she says in a thickened voice. "I know it's not like he's dying or anything. And I barely even live here anymore. They're not...well, they've never really been happy."

My heart just about breaks listening to her try to diminish her own pain. Make it sound small. Like it doesn't matter. I mean, sure, Layla grew up with a bit of a silver spoon. She was lucky enough to have an intact family, not the kind I grew up with, four kids from three shitty dads and a single mom. But I know what it's like to have your father leave. Mine split when I was a baby, and I watched Maggie and Selena's abandon them later on. It feels like shit no matter how old you are, no matter how much money you have. Abandonment is abandonment, plain and simple.

Just like you did to her, you selfish asshole. Fuck. What am I doing here?

"So your mom, though," I say, trying to change the subject. "She's going to stay in Seattle? At least you'll still be able to go home, right?"

Another shuddering breath. "No. She's...she's moving to be close to her family too. In Pasadena." Another sniff. "I have to go with her this weekend before school starts."

See, the fucked-up thing is that I have no idea what that last sentence was or anything else Layla says as she tells me about her parents' split. I barely hear how her dad got mad at her for calling herself Brazilian, or how her mom said maybe five words while she guzzled red wine—or was it white? Everything jumbles together after Layla says "Pasadena."

Pasadena is fifteen, maybe twenty minutes from where I'm parked right now. Pasadena means I don't just have to dream about those big blue eyes anymore. Pasadena means I might actually get to see them.

"Let me see you," I blurt out without thinking, interrupting her discussion of the sale of her house. "Please. I know the phone thing was fucked up. But I won't ghost you like that again, I promise. I *promise*, Layla."

She's silent for what feels like an hour. I get it. If she'd done that to me, I'd be thinking twice about whether or not to let her back in. But already I'm glad I called. The truth is, Layla and I are supposed to be in each other's lives. Maybe not as lovers, but at least as friends.

"I'll pick you up," I rush on. "Show you around town. We can even go to one of those cheesy movies you love. Seriously. I'm your friend, Layla. No matter what, I'll always be that."

I sound pathetic, I know. But now the only thing I can think about is seeing her again, touching her. Not in a sexual way, although the sex with her was always fuckin' mind-blowing. Like out-of-this-world, forget-my-own-name, lose-myself-completely kind of sex. But right now, I just miss the feel of her. The way her head fit exactly into the crook of my shoulder. The way her fingers always curled around one of my wrists when I held her cheek. The way my fingertips molded exactly to the grooves up and down her spine.

Right now I'd do anything to get her to agree. Get down on my knees. Run naked down the I-10. Wear bright pink ties to the club for a month. Anything.

"Okay," she says softly and immediately, shocking the hell out of me.

I blink. "What?"

She giggles again, and I practically float out of my seat. *Fuck*, this girl absolutely wrecks me. She always did.

"Really?" I ask. I need to make sure this isn't a joke.

She giggles again. "Yeah. I'll call you on Saturday."

I close my eyes, letting the sound of her sweet laughter seep in. Already, I'm feeling more energized to go into the club. Because now I have something to look forward to.

And I can tell you what: Craig could offer me an entire week's extra salary. I don't care if I make half of my weekly tips; there is no fuckin' way I'm working Saturday night.

CHAPTER THREE

Nico

THE WEEK FLIES BY AND AT THE SAME TIME MOVES INCREDIBLY FUCKIN' SLOWLY. BUT eventually it's Friday, and I'm helping K.C. schlep his bins of records back to his Yukon after my shift and his extra set. Layla's plane gets in tomorrow, and since Wednesday I've been doing nothing but count down the hours until I get to see her. Maybe it makes me a pussy, but I don't fuckin' care. In less than twenty-four hours, I get to see my girl.

My girl. It's a little crazy how fast I slide into thinking that way again, but I can't help it. I have a feeling that no matter how long it's been, whether we're twenty or eighty, Layla's always going to be my girl.

"Yo, Earth to Nico. Where the fuck you at, man?"

I look up from the box I've been balancing on the tailgate for the last few minutes. Daydreaming. Again.

I shake my head. "Sorry. Layla gets in tomorrow. I can't really focus."

K.C. whistles long and low. "That's right, that's right, NYU's comin' to town. You gonna tell old girl?"

I frown and recoil. "Dude. Don't call Jessie that. That's all she needs, man, is for people to be thinking that we're something we're not."

"Aren't you livin' with her?" K.C. looks down his nose like he's an old man. "What would *you* call it?"

I scowl and shove the box of records farther into the car. "I'd call it 'roommates.'"

"Yeah, roommates with benefits. Pssh." K.C. waves the thought away. "Bro, you ain't foolin' *no*body. No. One. Roommates, my ass," he chuckles to himself as he goes back into the club for more records.

"Whatever," I mutter as I follow.

But he's got a point. I haven't told Jessie that my plans this weekend consist of staying at K.C.'s empty apartment with another girl. I don't want her anywhere near Layla.

I grab another bin of records and shake away the thought. It's time for Jessie and me to have a real talk about where we stand, but that can wait another week. The only thing I want to think about right now is Layla.

———

Layla

The Town Car pulls up in front of my grandparents' big white house at about two in the afternoon. Ostentatious with palatial white columns and a half-acre yard, it's about the same size as our house in Redmond—or what *used* to be our house, before the moving company arrived yesterday to pack up everything we owned and ship it to a storage facility.

Stepping out of the car, I rub my face while the driver goes around to the back for our suitcases. Mom has several trunks of clothing being shipped here next week, but everything important to me is in these three bags, which will be going to New York with me. When my parents broke their news, I figured I would leave this weekend, be there on Monday when they open the dorms for students. But that phone call changed everything.

Nico. The timing of his call was one of the weirdest things I've ever experienced. Does that guy have Spidey sense or something? I've been fine—well, as fine as I could have been with a broken heart—all summer. And the second my parents drop this huge bomb, he calls.

I know this isn't going anywhere. One week, that's the most we have together before I have to get back to school. We've called and texted back and forth every day since Wednesday. I might be wrong, but I'm pretty sure he's excited to see me too. I don't know what else he's thinking, but I know that much.

"Layla, are you coming?"

I turn around to where Mom is halfway up the walkway. Our suitcases are stacked on the front stoop, while I'm standing here like an idiot on the sidewalk.

I blink. "Sorry," I say and follow my mother into the house.

It's empty except for a small woman with black hair and dark skin who pops into the hallway carrying a dust cloth.

"Hello," Mom greets her slowly, speaking in very loud, slow words. "You must be the new housekeeper. I'm Cheryl, Jerry and Cece's daughter. This is my daughter, Layla."

"Martina," the woman says cautiously, although she offers a kind smile.

Martina leaves the cloth on the entry table and accepts my handshake, although Mom doesn't offer one. The woman looks at me curiously and a little bit knowingly. I wonder if she's heard about my dad.

"Hello," she says in thickly accented English.

"Nice to meet you. Where are you from?" I ask. Mom looks at me sharply, but doesn't say anything.

This time Martina's smile is more genuine. "Panama City," she says. "*Habla español?*"

"No, she does not," Mom cuts in. "Her father is Brazilian, not *Hispanic*."

I frown at her, the way she says "Hispanic" like it's a dirty word. Like it's something bad.

"Actually," I tell Martina, "*estoy..ap-apren...diendo. Es correcto*?" When Martina nods at my poor phrasing, I smile. "I'm learning," I say again in English. "Maybe you can help me practice."

Martina smiles brightly, but when she catches my mother's sharp look, she picks up her cloth and murmurs, "*sí, sí*" before darting into another room.

"What do you mean, you're learning Spanish?"

I turn around to my mother with a hand on my hip. "I have to take a foreign language before I graduate. Spanish is way more practical than French. I started at the community college this summer, remember?"

My mother quirks an eyebrow and taps a long finger on her lips. "I don't remember that."

"That's because you were swimming in your wine glass," I mutter, too low for her to hear.

"What's that?"

I look up. "Nothing. It was just something I did on the side."

"Does your father know?"

I shrug. "He knew I was getting ahead with my degree. But Dad's not here anymore, is he?"

It's the first time either of us has talked about the fact that this morning, my father took one plane while we took another. Permanently. Mom hasn't mentioned it once, and it's gotten to the point where I wonder if she's actually aware this is happening. Or, I consider, maybe she's happy. She wasn't any more affectionate toward my dad than he was to her. My father has a tendency to micromanage every aspect of my life, and it drives me absolutely crazy. I wonder the extent to which he did that to Mom too.

"Well," Mom says. "It's your life. I suppose you'll be able to help us communicate better with the help, at any rate."

I roll my eyes. "Only if you stop saying things like 'the help.'"

"Layla, please. You're in Pasadena now. Everyone says 'the help.'"

I wander into the foyer of the big house. I've been here a few times in my life, but we were pretty isolated in Washington. My mom's family didn't get along very well with my dad. They barely came to visit, and he didn't usually come the few times we visited them. I'm as much a stranger in this house as I would be in any other.

"Where are Grandma and Grandpa?" I wonder.

Behind me, Mom's nails tap the glass entry table. She checks her watch. "Well, right now is Mother's weekly hair appointment, and Daddy's probably at the golf course. They'll be home in time for cocktails, I'm sure. They *never* miss that."

"Well, I'll probably miss them, then," I say as I grab one of my bags and start toward the stairs. "Do you know which room I'm in?"

My mother's hand closes around my wrist. "What do you mean, you'll miss them?"

I look down at her hand, then back up at her face. Not for the first time today, tension crackles between us.

"I'm going out with a friend," I inform her. "I'll probably be back kind of late. Do you know if there are any spare keys?"

Mom just stares at me, then releases my wrist. "Layla, this is a strange city. We just got here. I really think it would be best if you stayed here tonight and we relaxed with Grandma and Grandpa. I'm sure they're excited to see you—"

"Thrilled, clearly," I say sarcastically. "That's why they're here waiting for us, right? The grand welcoming committee? Oh, wait, except they're *not*."

Mom bites her perfectly painted lip and frowns. "That's really uncalled for. But aside from that, you're my daughter, and I'm saying you need to stay. You can't just go out whenever you want."

I cross my arms, prepared to stare my mother down. I've been looking forward to this all week—the one bright spot in the tornado that just hit my family.

"And *I'm* saying I'm twenty years old and can make those decisions for myself." I tip my head, daring her to contradict me.

Mom starts, and as I catch a glance at myself in the giant mirror over the doorway, I'm struck by what she must see. My dad does the same thing when he gives an order. Stands the same. Looks the same.

Immediately, I drop my arms. "I'm going out," I repeat. "You don't like it, I can leave too."

The "too" echoes around this cavernous house like I shouted it into a quarry. Mom's blue eyes squint, and for a second, I feel bad. It's not fair for me to make those kinds of threats when her husband left her. But she doesn't get to tell me what to do any more than he does. Not anymore.

"All right, then," she says at last. "I'll get you a key before you leave."

———

A FEW HOURS LATER, I'm sitting on the front stoop while my mom is inside taking a bubble bath. Nico is supposed to be here in ten minutes, but I didn't feel like being in that mausoleum anymore. Despite the fact that they are well into their seventies and could potentially break a hip or something, my grandparents lived in a house that's full of sharp corners and glass fixtures. After I changed into a pair of shorts and a tank top that befit the hot weather, I was tiptoeing everywhere, terrified I'd accidentally knock over a vase or maybe a tasteful figurine. My grandmother has a thing for Chinese statues.

Outside, the sunshine feels nice, but a little heavy. It's not like the sun in Seattle, which always seems to be tempered by the trees. The sun in LA has nothing to mitigate it—no clouds, nothing. But right now the warmth of the sidewalk is a nice balance with the cold house behind me.

It makes me wonder what New York is like right now. I thought about taking some of my earnings and going back this summer for a visit, but no one would have been there. My friends were all home or working full-time internships. I'd have stayed in a hotel, felt like a stranger in a city that's closer to home than anywhere right now.

Instead, I put my energy into getting ready for the school year, working and starting a major that I only regret when it makes me think of Nico. The combination of a few Latin American studies electives I took my freshman year start a nice foundation for a Latin American studies major, something I decided to pursue in May. It's not something I've told anyone. But after I had said goodbye to this man, felt that gaping hole in my life without him, I realized Nico had still left me with something else: a desire to know more about the side of myself that my father had never been willing to show me. It's not my fault that my dad hated his foreignness so much he refused to teach his only daughter about her cultural roots. I realized I could learn about them, at least some of them, on my own.

I never told my dad that I had decided on this major instead of a more typical prelaw major like economics or English. I never told him I was taking Spanish at the community college instead of French with the check he gave me. I never told him that I'd switched my fall schedule, and I marveled at my luck that for once, he wasn't micromanaging my classes.

And now that he's gone, I know why he didn't pry. He was already out the door.

I kick at a rock on the front drive. Right now, the idea of taking intermediate Portuguese and Afro-Brazilian musicology sounds terrible. My dad and his "country" can fuck off. Maybe I can find some classes on Caribbean culture instead. I try not to think about why I might want to do that. Why another man's ethnic background might sound better than my own. A man who also left me.

A man who's pulling up right now.

Nico's black Jeep rumbles up the hill with a roar. Every muscle in my body tenses, and just when the Jeep backfires, it's like a spring is released inside me. I'm scrambling off the step, suddenly freed from this smoky haze I've been living in for the past few days, hell, for the past three months. Like it always did when he was around, my body *moves* without thinking.

So before Nico's even pulled to a stop, I'm sprinting down the lawn, reaching him just as he steps out of the car. I barely register the open, eager look on his face before I tackle him against the door, barely hear the boisterous "Hey!" from his deep voice as I grab him. But he reacts quickly. I'm swept off the ground as his big arms encircle my waist, and my arms wrap a death grip around his neck.

Suddenly I'm crying. My chest shakes with the tears that have been trapped since Wednesday. I am surrounded by Nico. This body, this touch—everything from last spring is here. The wanting, the magnetic attraction, the *rightness* I always felt with him. How could I have forgotten his clean, masculine scent? The way his skin seems to radiate at least a degree or two above my body temperature? The way his shoulders fit exactly against the hollow of my cheek, underneath my arms?

The answer is that I haven't. Not really. These facts have been living like shadows in the back of my thoughts all summer, jumping out in my daydreams. But now he's here, in the flesh, and it's awakening all sorts of things that had gone dormant out of self-preservation.

I sob. Hard, painful sobs that make my chest rattle. Even though he left me too, I know I'm safe here with him now. I know he'd never hurt me that way. He'd never make me feel as cold, as lonely, as my father did this morning when he boarded his plane with a wave, not a hug.

One of Nico's hands cradles my head against his shoulder, but he doesn't let me touch the ground for one, ten, thirty seconds? It could have been ten minutes. A low hum vibrates through his chest while he sways me back and forth, and we squeeze the life out of each other while my tears flow.

"It's okay," he murmurs into my hair. "It's going to be okay. I got you, baby."

I let out my frustrations, my hurts, both from Nico's absence and the loss of my family. I let out everything onto his big warm shoulder until finally my tears abate. Then he sets me down in the still-open driver's seat.

"Hey," he says softly, pushing my hands from my face so he can run his thumbs under my eyes and brush away the last of my tears.

"Shit," I mutter, making him laugh.

And for the first time, I finally see him. The familiar square jaw. The wide, friendly smile that seems brighter than the sun. The chocolate-brown eyes that twinkle under thick lashes.

"I haven't seen you in three months, and your first word is 'shit'?" Nico asks with a grin.

I laugh and roll my eyes. "No. I'm just mad because I probably have mascara all over my face. And you look...well, you look like you."

Meaning he looks perfect. Because he really does. I didn't think Nico could look better than he did in New York, but I have to admit: California looks good on him. His skin has gotten a little darker from the sun and has a new glow that sets off his bright smile and dark eyes against the white of his t-shirt and backward Yankees cap. His plain t-shirt strains against the curves of his biceps and pectorals. He worked out in New York, but he looks like he's really been going at it this summer. His muscles practically cut through the cotton.

"You're beautiful," he says simply as he wipes away the remnants of my smeared makeup.

He pulls down the visor over the dashboard so I can look in the mirror. It looks like he got whatever was there. I look sad and blotchy, but at least the reddened skin makes my blue eyes pop.

I turn back to him, suddenly nervous. "What, um, I—" It's so strange. I have no idea what to say.

Nico looks at me, and his gaze drops to my mouth. Unconsciously, his tongue slips out and licks at his full bottom lip.

"You're beautiful," he says again, this time more softly. "I forgot—I mean, I didn't forget—but I...shit. I always thought I knew what you looked like until I saw you again. You knock me out every time."

He steps in between my legs and takes my hands in his. Tentatively, he fingers my knuckles, then looks at my lips again. He bends down.

But just as he's about to kiss me, I catch movement in the window behind him. My mother, standing in the frame with a glass of wine, watching the whole thing. And the look on her porcelain face is not good. She looks scared. And more than that, she looks impossibly sad.

It's then I realize what I'm doing. Throwing myself at a man who left me and cut me off all summer. In front of my grandparents' neighbors. In front of my mother, who's got to be dealing with her own pain, even if she doesn't show it.

What the hell am I doing?

Nico, sensing my change in mood, stands up straight and drops my hands. He steps away, rubbing the back of his neck.

"Ah...yeah," he says, suddenly looking around the neighborhood uneasily. "You want to scoot over? Then we can get out of here."

"Where are we going?" I ask as I follow his request.

Nico gets into the driver's seat. "I want to show you LA, baby," he says and starts up the Jeep.

CHAPTER FOUR

Nico

I ACTUALLY HADN'T CONSIDERED WHERE I WOULD TAKE LAYLA, DESPITE THE FACT THAT I had days to figure it out. I had a few ideas in mind, but they all flew out of my head when I saw her sitting on that step, looking more beautiful than I'd ever imagined for the past few months. Her hair seemed darker, shinier. Her lips seemed fuller, her legs longer. And by the time I'd parked and she tackled me against the car door, I couldn't think at all, couldn't fuckin' breathe because she felt so good.

The trees looked brighter. The unnaturally green grass rich people water to death looked like it was in fuckin' technicolor. With Layla in my arms, I felt like I'd been seeing black and white for the last three months only to have the whole world turn into one of those new 3-D movies.

Then she started to cry, and it was over. All my ideas that this was going to be some kind of beautiful reunion, that we were going to pick right up where we left off, vanished. The only thing I could see or hear or feel or sense was her. The only thing I wanted to do was take away her pain.

But how the fuck do I do that?

Luckily, she solves my problem as I start driving: "Let's go to the beach."

I nod. "You got it, baby."

She's quiet for most of the thirty-minute drive. This is a Layla I don't know very well. She was never a loudmouth, but she was always full of questions, things she wanted to know about me. Since the roar of the road doesn't make for good conversation, she just tugs on her long hair and gazes at the palm trees, the concrete buildings, the traffic as we take the back roads through downtown LA.

I peek at her when we idle at stoplights, trying to spot any differences. They're small, but they're there. Her hair is a little bit longer, dropping past her shoulder blades in a loose braid I want to wrap around my fist. She's gained back the weight she lost last spring—yeah, I noticed *that* as soon as she stood up. With the tight shirt and tiny shorts that show off most of her legs, with her curvy body pressed up against me, I *really* noticed that.

You horny asshole. Get it together. She is *not* here so you can get your rocks off.

But the biggest difference is in the way she holds herself. The smile that was all over her face when I arrived is gone. Whether it's the shit that's going down in her family or something else, there's a sadness that wasn't there before. Her eyes look more tired than a twenty-year-old's should. Every now and then they close, her long black lashes hovering over her cheeks like fans for one, two seconds before they lift again. I know that look. It's a look that says, "I'm just trying to fuckin' deal."

It's not until I've exited the freeway onto Sepulveda and have just turned onto Ardmore that I realize I've been so absorbed by her, I've driven on autopilot straight to my neighborhood. Shit. Thirty minutes with Layla, and I'm already losing my head. This is the last place I should be taking her.

I could drive north to Malibu, maybe, or south to Newport or Laguna Beach. Maybe we could hike Griffith Park and make out behind the Hollywood sign. Anywhere but here. But instead, I find myself parking around the block from my building knowing that even if I can't take her there, I can at least show her the places that have become *my* places here in LA, even if they aren't quite home. Just as much as I ever did, I want Layla to know me, to see me for what I am.

I didn't realize how much I missed that feeling until I pulled up to her grandparents' fancy house.

"Where are we?" she asks as she gets out of the car.

I close the door and take her hand. She glances at our entwined fingers, but doesn't pull away. It's natural. I don't think I could be next to her and not touch her.

"Manhattan Beach," I say as we start toward the main strip.

She gives me a look. "Out of all the places to live in LA, you ended up in Manhattan Beach? Don't you think that says something?"

I give her a sly grin. "You can take the boy out of New York, right?"

She chuckles, but she looks a little sad.

"This place actually makes a decent sandwich," I say as we pass Becker's, one of the only basic delis for miles. "Over there they make açai bowls and smoothies, but they don't really fill you up. That's my new gym—it's not my old spot back in Hell's Kitchen, but they have a good trainer."

Layla holds my hand tight, like she's afraid she might lose me, but takes in the neighborhood. I see her gaze float over the sushi restaurants and yoga studios, the way all the buildings are nicely painted with matching colors.

"This is a really nice area," she remarks after I point out a few more places.

Her words aren't meant to hurt, but they do a little. Threaded through them is surprise—surprise that someone like me would be living in a place like this. She probably thought I'd be somewhere like East LA or Maywood—not because of the way I look, but because of where she knows I've lived before. A one-bedroom apartment shared between my mother and her four kids. A railroad up in Harlem with about as much charm as a sardine can. Compared to those places, Manhattan Beach is the Ritz.

Lennox, one of the neighborhoods in LA that actually reminds me a little of home, isn't actually that far from here, and sometimes I'll stop there for dinner when I miss hearing Spanish. But even there, I'm still an outsider. In a room full of Mexicans, Guatemalans, Colombians, Salvadorans...I sound different. I speak a different kind of

Spanish, a different kind of Spanglish. It's close, and there are a lot of similarities. But it's not like home.

"The club must pay well," Layla says after we cross Hermosa and turn onto The Strand, the big pedestrian promenade that runs alongside the beach. A few roller bladers whiz by us, and Layla jumps a little closer.

"Whoa," she laughs as I tuck her into my side.

"You okay?" I ask.

She's jumpy, like she's not sure what's about to happen next. I don't think it's just me.

After we pass the volleyball nets, we step onto the beach, past the sunbathers, where we can walk mostly alone. It's one of the things I actually like about California —unlike New York, where everyone is crammed together, here you can always find a spot by yourself, even in the middle of LA.

Layla takes off her sandals and holds them in one hand as we walk.

"So," I say, reaching for small talk. "What, um, classes are you taking this year?"

She takes a deep breath and tugs on her braid again. "Oh...well. Yeah, they're...you know, I don't really want to talk about it." Another big sigh.

"What?" I ask. "Don't want to take them anymore?"

"I...you're not going to believe this." She rubs her face, and her forehead wrinkles adorably. "I decided to be a Latin American studies major. So I could, um, get to know my culture better." She makes a face. "Now it seems really dumb."

I frown. "That doesn't seem dumb. That seems awesome, baby. Shit, I wish *I* could be a 'Latin American studies major.'"

She laughs, then blows a long stream of air from her lips. "I don't know how I'm going to focus. I'm taking Spanish, Portuguese, and a few other classes this fall. And all I'm going to think about is, well, *you*"—she gives me a sheepish shrug—"and my asshole dad who just fucking abandoned me and my mom. Sounds like a *great* way to spend the next two years."

I wait for her to say more. I don't know the whole story. I do know that her dad went from being an uptight, controlling-as-fuck Latino father to announcing he was straight-up leaving her and her mother. And yeah, I can see how that probably hurts. A lot.

"Plus..." she trails off, looking out to the water. "I don't...I don't want to be like him. I thought I wanted to learn about my culture, learn about that part of me that he always tried to hide. But if Brazilian culture is what made him...I don't know that I want any of it." She sighs. "Maybe I should just be the nice white girl he always wants everyone to think I am."

I frown. She's talked about this before. Her dad, like a lot of immigrants who've experienced prejudice and hate for not being "American" enough, went through a lot to keep his daughter from being different. But in the process, he alienated her from a whole part of her identity.

"Even if you hate your dad right now..." I venture, "you shouldn't let that make you hate what you are. He's not Brazil, baby. He's just one man. And that shouldn't stop you from learning about who you are."

We walk a little more, letting the sound of the gulls flying down the beach fill the air. I try not to notice the way the sun gleams off Layla's skin, or the way her legs, long and tan from the summer, are in the shortest shorts I've ever seen. Okay, they're not really that short, especially by LA standards. It's just that some animal in me wakes up around Layla, one that wants to cover her up and show her off at the same time. Because my girl is that beautiful.

You asshole. She's not your girl anymore.

The idea hurts. A lot.

"So, your dad," I say, just to interrupt my own thoughts. "When he bounced. Did he say why?"

Layla sniffs. "Are we really going to spend this time talking about that?"

I shrug. "What do you want to talk about? The weather? It's the same thing every day here. Sunny and boring as fuck."

She smirks. "You don't sound as if you like it here very much."

I shrug. "It's okay. Different. But don't think you get to change the subject that easily, beautiful."

For that, I get another small smile.

"You still think I'm beautiful?" she asks.

I stop walking and turn so I can push her hair out of her eyes. "I'll always think you're beautiful, Layla."

She stares at me for a moment with her wide blue eyes the color of the ocean, then swallows and starts walking again.

"He just left," she says. She lets me keep her hand in mine, but stares down at the sand while she talks. "We all went to the airport together. He barely said a word to my mom, kissed me on the cheek, and got on his plane while we waited for ours. Did you know he sold his practice? All of it. Apparently they'd been planning it since last year. I just—" She breaks off, stopping for a moment to look out at the ocean. "I just feel really stupid," she says quietly.

I squeeze her hand. "You're not stupid, sweetie. Not even close."

She pushes her hair out of her face defiantly. "Yes, I am. All of those years, he was such a control freak. He told me what to do, told my mom what to do. I thought it was because he cared so much, but obviously not. Because if you care about someone, you don't just up and leave them!"

"No," I agree with her. "You don't."

She gives me a piercing blue look, and I know what she's thinking: that I left her too. Although if she said so, I'd say I left New York, not her. More and more, I'm wondering why. I look away.

She walks a little closer to the water, then, without warning, plops down in the sand. I fall down next to her, and we sit together, looking out at the ocean. Down the way, a few surfers flounder around in the whitewash, and a couple of others are riding the waves farther out. We watch the way they move up and down on the waves like second nature, fall, paddle back out. It's one of those things that makes me feel like an alien in California. I can barely even swim.

"It's not the same," I venture after a few minutes.

Layla turns sharply. "What's not the same?"

"Your dad," I say, but then I surprise her. "Versus someone like mine."

Her expression softens. She knows this is hard for me, that I don't normally like to talk about my father, if I can even call him that.

"Your dad stuck around your whole life," I say. "Mine split before I was even crawling. He didn't ever want to know me at all."

"So you're saying it's okay what mine did?" she asks defensively.

"No, baby, I'm not. But I'm saying...I doubt he did it because he wanted to get away from you. It sounds like maybe he waited until he knew you were going to be okay. He put up with a lot of unhappiness, living in a place where people only heard his accent, only ever looked at him like a *foreigner*." I say it like a dirty word. "Maybe he saw his chance to go home, and he took it."

It's a familiar story—the same one I had to tell her last spring. Under normal circumstances, I'd want to break the nose of anyone who made Layla feel like this. But a part of me understands her dad too, and I never thought I'd be saying that. I understand how it feels to sacrifice everything you want so that everyone you care about will be okay. I understand the need to escape that kind of pressure. It's what I'm doing out here.

"He'll come back," I tell her with more assurance than I feel. "Maybe not permanently, but he'll be back for you."

Layla's quiet for a moment, running her tongue over her bottom lip while she thinks things over. I really wish she wouldn't do that; it makes it hard to focus.

"You think?" she asks.

I take her hand and pull it across my knees so I can toy with her fingers.

"I know," I say. "You're...there's no way he doesn't love you, baby. Anyone who knows you would love you."

She stills for a second, then lays her head on my shoulder. My chest tightens. It's crazy how easily we fit. How could I have convinced myself she was just another girl? How could I have convinced myself we were anything but right together?

I close my eyes. I don't give a shit about the sunset that's starting in front of us. I just want to focus on this feeling. The solid weight of her nestled up against me. The smooth skin of her palm under my calloused thumbs. The scent of her. It's not coconut anymore—she stopped using whatever it was that made her smell like a piña colada. But a hint of something sweet is still there, subtle and intermingled with whatever intoxicating thing makes her smell like her.

I kiss her lightly on top of her head. She sighs.

"You okay, baby?" I whisper.

She exhales. "I'm fine," she says. "I'll be fine." Then, so quietly I wonder if she even wanted me to hear it: "I miss you."

But I did hear it. And it fuckin' guts me. I miss her too. More than I've ever admitted to myself before now. But I can't say it back, because then I'd have to admit that this whole fuckin' thing was a mistake, that I never should have left New York, never should have left her.

And I'm just not ready to do that yet.

I shift, and she sits up and looks at me. I lean in and press my forehead to hers, my eyes closed. Without me thinking about it, my hand cups her cheek. I can feel, rather than see, her shudder, can feel the skin of her forehead frown against mine with the pain. I get it, baby, I want to say. Neither of us can pull away.

Fuck it.

"I...it's not enough," I admit.

"What's that?"

"Saying 'I miss you.' It's weak. Like something you'd say when you're away from home for a weekend. Not...not like this."

My hand slides down her shoulder, and Layla takes it between both of hers.

"Brazilians have a word for that, you know," she says as she sits back and plays with my fingers. "*Saudade*. It's...it's hard to explain because there isn't a translation.

But the way I had it explained to me, it's like when you yearn for something or some-one. Like your heart speaks to their heart, and when they're gone, it's that emptiness that remains. It's a longing, maybe for something that never even happened."

Slowly, I nod. "Sow-dodgy?" I repeat, trying out the unfamiliar syllables. They say Portuguese and Spanish are twin languages, but they sure as fuck don't sound like it to me.

Layla smiles and nods. "That's pretty much it." She repeats the word, but smooths out the syllables, so it sounds less choppy and more like a waterfall.

Damn. That's one hell of a word. And it fits perfectly. Because it doesn't make sense why we should miss each other like this after having, what, a few months in New York? We've been apart longer than we were ever together. But it only took one second of seeing Layla again for me to see a future I could never have with her, and for that hole in my chest to open up all over again. *Saudade*? Yeah, I get it.

"So how do I say it?" I wonder. "I *saudade* you, baby?"

She chuckles and shakes her head. "It's not a verb. It's something you have. Like, I have *saudade*." She looks at me, and her eyes match the color of the sky behind her, and my heart pounds in my chest.

"*Eu tenho saudade*," she whispers in Portuguese

Her eyes lock with mine. They shimmer like the ocean next to us, deep and open. I could get lost in those eyes. I'd look at them the rest of my life if she'd let me.

"*Para ti*," I whisper back in Spanish, so low my voice is almost carried away on the wind. But not quite. For you. Only for you.

"*Sim*," she says.

"*Sí*," I say.

Yes. Both words mean the same. They sound the same. Spelled out, there's one letter of difference, but when you say them, it doesn't matter. The differences don't really matter.

We lean into each other like magnets while the sound of the waves crashing on the beach overwhelms the air. *Eu tenho/Yo tengo saudade* indeed. I'll long for this girl for the rest of my life, whether I'm with her or not. I know now this longing will never go away. I had it before I even met her.

She leans into the pain, rubs her nose against mine, searching for something until her mouth finds mine. Her lips are soft, open, pliant, and *fuck*, it's like they've never been gone. It's a kiss that's full of sorrow and longing, a kiss where Layla pours out her grief, and I take it. I cup her beautiful face with both hands and guide her again and again. I can't go with her where she's going next week. I can't help her bear the weight of what's happening to her family. But right now, I can help absorb some of that pain. I'd take it all if I could.

CHAPTER FIVE

Layla

WE KISS. AND THEN WE KISS SOME MORE. WE KISS UNTIL THE ANGER AND SADNESS AND desolation I've been carrying around with me for the past three days actually melts a little. That's what this man does to me, what he's always done to me. And the longer we sit together, enveloped in each other's touch and taste, the more I'm ready to get off this stupid beach and go somewhere we can be alone.

"I, um," I try to speak as Nico cups the back of my head to pull me into yet another kiss that sweeps every painful, conscious thought away.

"What?" he grumbles before slipping his tongue in to dance with mine. "What is it, baby?"

My hands grip his t-shirt, and I'm having a hard time finding words. There's only one thing I want right now. It doesn't matter that we'll have to say goodbye again in a week. I just want him closer, in the closest way two people can get.

"Go," I manage to get out. "Alone. You. Me." Finally, I manage to evade his next kiss so I can look him in the eye. "*Please.*"

His lips tug to one side with a smirk that reveals a dimple. Then he opens his mouth to answer, but his cell phone rings. When he pulls it out, a name is flashing brightly, even under the glare of the sun.

"Who's Jessie?" I ask

Nico presses the silence button and shoves his phone in his pocket.

"Um, yeah. Jessie's my roommate. I wish..." he trails off before placing a light kiss on the top of my head. "I wish you didn't have to be so far away."

"Me too—" I start to say before I realize that I don't have to. New York is calling my name, it's true, like a ghost I can't quite shake. My family's house in Washington is gone, and I'm certainly not at home here in my grandparents' museum of a house. I might only have a dorm room to go to, but it will be filled with my best friends, and one small corner will be mine. I can't wait.

But. My mother does live here now. It would be a simple thing to get state residency, and I could transfer schools. I *could* come to LA, I *could* stay, and maybe this ache that's been in the pit of my stomach since May would finally go away. New York, I love. But maybe I love someone else more. Maybe he's sitting next to me right now.

I'm just about to say so when a name echoes from down the beach.

"Nico!"

It's a woman's voice, and she calls his name again as she jogs toward us.

"Fuck," Nico mutters under his breath as the woman approaches. His arm falls from around my shoulders, and I try not to be hurt when he scoots slightly away.

We both watch the woman as she comes closer. The first thing I notice is that she's stunning—tall, thin, blonde, and tan, and showing it all off in a pair of skin-tight leggings and a sports bra that bares an incredibly toned stomach. Her sun-streaked hair is pulled into a high ponytail on top of her head. From the way her skin glistens slightly in the sun, it's clear she's been out for a run.

"Oh my God," she says as she comes to stand in front of us. She reaches an arm over her head and stretches, making her belly even flatter than before. "Do you *ever* check your phone, hon? I've been trying to call you for the last hour."

Hon? I tense further, and her sharp brown eyes zero in on the movement.

"Hi," she says as she extends a hand. "I'm Jessie."

My voice freezes in my throat as I hear the name. Jessie. Nico's roommate. Who looks like she should be on the cover of a fashion magazine and who also happens to call him "hon." *This* is Jessie?

Beside me, Nico is rubbing the back of his neck and assiduously avoiding either of our gazes.

I look back at the Amazon standing in front of me. "I-I'm Layla," I say, accepting her handshake. "I'm...a friend. From New York."

"She's just in town for a bit," Nico finally breaks in. "We thought we'd catch up. We, uh, go way back."

Jessie quirks an eyebrow between us. "Huh. Must be *way* back. You never mentioned Laura before."

Nothing. Nico says nothing.

"Layla," I say with a sharp look at him. "It's Layla, not Laura."

She blinks at me like an owl, and then flips her ponytail back and smiles brightly. "Lara. Got it. Well, I have to finish my run and get going. I have that photo shoot tomorrow morning, so I need to get to sleep early."

She looks at me as she says photo shoot, as if I'm supposed to be impressed. Well, mission accomplished. In all her blonde, statuesque glory, Jessie makes me feel like a freaking hobbit.

"Anyway, babe, I was just asking you to pick up some toilet paper, okay? Also, I think we're out of condoms," she says to Nico, whose head immediately snaps up at the word.

Something inside me also springs into action. Whoever this Jessie person is, she's clearly more than just a roommate. Roommates don't call each other babe or hon. They don't buy each other condoms. Not unless they're *my* roommate, Quinn, and considering we are both heterosexual females in only a slightly codependent, but completely platonic friendship, I'd say she's fairly harmless. *Jessie* is anything but.

"You know what?" I say as I get up. "I have to get going too."

I try to brush off all the sand that is sticking to my legs, and, of course, it won't go anywhere. I'm a sandy mess while I'm standing beside the next Cindy Crawford. Fucking great.

Jessie watches me with barely masked amusement while Nico scrambles up beside her.

"Hold on," he says to me. "I'll drive you back to Pasadena."

"No, really, it's okay." I hoist my purse over my shoulder, where, of course, it keeps falling down. "I have some things I wanted to grab in Santa Monica anyway. I was going to take a bus over there to meet my mom for dinner."

"Oh, you don't have a car?" Jessie says it like it's the worst thing in the world. Like I'm some pitiful child because I have to take public transportation.

"Like he said, I'm just visiting," I say through my teeth.

It's a lie. Mom is probably swimming in a vat of white wine with Grandma right about now. The first thing I'm going to do when I get off the beach is figure out how the hell to take a bus back to Pasadena, maybe even get a cab if I really have to, because there is no way in hell I'm going to ride in the car with Nico. I'll break, I know it, and I just can't deal with that right now.

That ache is back, only this time, it scissors through me like a blade. I catch Jessie looking at Nico like he's a piece of meat—no, like something she knows *intimately*. Her mouth twists knowingly. The blade twists too.

"I'll see you," I mutter as I turn away. "Nice to meet you, Jessie."

"You too, hon," she calls. "Have a nice trip back to New York!"

But I'm already too far down the beach to answer. And all I can think as the wind whips my hair in front of my face, as the sand builds up around my stumbling feet, is that I need to get the hell out of this city and away from this man as fast as I can.

————

Nico

After Layla practically sprints off the beach, I turn back to Jessie, who is still watching Layla with a *really* satisfied expression. She looks at me, and the satisfaction turns to fear.

"What the fuck was that?" I demand.

Jessie bites her lip. "What? We *are* out of toilet paper."

"Condoms? Really? That was some manipulative bitch shit there, Jess."

Jessie bites her lip and tosses her long ponytail over her shoulder. "It's not like we've never used them."

I scoff. "What, three, four times this whole summer? You made it sound like we're a serious couple."

"What about you? I thought you were going to K.C.'s for the weekend. You think it felt good for me to run into you making out with some rando on the beach? People here *know* me, Nico. They're going to think you're cheating on me!"

My mouth falls open. "And why the fuck would they think that when we're not together, Jessie?"

Jessie gives me an equally disbelieving look that makes me want to tear my hair out. I mean, I'm not stupid. I notice how she cozies up to me. Makes me dinner or hangs off me at the club, like I belong to her or something. That's usually when I take off for the weekend. Give her a little space. Remind her that I need mine.

She crosses her arms and nudges me in the shoulder. "I know we're not together, together," she says finally. "But...come on. You've never thought about it? We have a good connection, and we already live together."

I bury my face in my hands and groan. "Are you really asking me this right now? Right after you just chased another girl off the beach?"

"Please. Like that easy piece would ever be able to satisfy someone like you. Her shorts were about two inches long. Cheap."

"*Don't* talk about her like that," I growl.

"Whatever. How old is she, twelve? You need a woman, Nico, not a little girl."

I brush the sand off my shorts roughly. Jessie leans away to avoid getting it in her eyes. I couldn't care less.

"I'ma say this *once*," I state as evenly as I can. It's hard, because I'm that pissed off. "You wanna stay on my good side, Jess? Then you better respect my friends and family, and that goes *double* for Layla. Otherwise, you can fuck off. If it's between you and that girl, I choose her every time. You got that? *Every. Time.*"

Jessie's eyes widen. She's only ever known me as good-time Nico. Nico at the club. Nico at the beach. She might be my roommate, but she doesn't know shit about the real me. Not like Layla.

"Fuck!" I shout, startling a bunch of seagulls a few feet away floating in the whitewash.

Jessie leans away, but doesn't move when I glare at her. I pull out my phone and dial Layla's number. If I'm lucky, she's still in the neighborhood, although at the pace she was running she's probably already up to Hermosa by now.

It goes to voicemail. Then again. And again. With another grunt, I shove my phone in my pocket and start jogging in the direction of my car.

"Where are you going?" calls Jessie.

"To clean up this fuckin' mess you made!" I yell, not even bothering to turn around.

———

Two hours and about ten voicemails later, I'm done driving around Santa Monica hunting for Layla, and I'm pulling up in front of her grandparents' big house in Pasadena. I'll wait here all night if I have to, but she's going to see me.

Before I get out of the car, I send one last text.

Me: You're mad, I get it. Please, Layla. Im begging here.

I sit there for a few minutes, waiting for her to respond. It gives me a few seconds to take in the neighborhood, really take it in. Even in the dark, it's clear the grass is way too green for late summer in Southern California. The columns and sparkling white paint makes the Spanish-style houses pristine, and the crack-free sidewalks and the tag-free garage doors continue that perfection. Manhattan Beach is nice, but this neighborhood is where the really rich live. Most of them would probably assume I was here to work on their yards.

Well, fuck 'em. I'm only here for one thing, and she's pissed as hell at me.

I'm just about to get out of the car when she actually texts me back.

Layla: I'm at the airport.

The airport? What the fuck?

Me: Why? You were supposed to stay another week.

This time, the response is immediate.

Layla: Got an earlier flight.

I wait a moment, but no other texts come. She's gone.

I sigh and clap the phone shut. Fuck. I don't want her to leave like this. I'm just not sure I can live in a world where Layla Barros hates my guts. I start the Jeep, suddenly full of decision. I may not be able to follow Layla back to New York, but the fuck if I'm going to let her leave thinking I'm some two-timing asshole. If I really step on it, maybe I can catch her.

Thirty minutes later, I'm jogging into the airport and scanning the ticketing area for a head of black hair and a pair of blue eyes. United? Delta? I shake my head, trying to remember which airline she took coming down here. It doesn't mean she's on the same one back to New York, but I'll take that chance. Rich people like her family can afford to prefer one airline over another.

I have to find her before she goes through security. Fuckin' 9/11. Never thought I'd miss the days when people could run all the way to the gates, but I'm about two seconds from buying a ticket myself just to get through security.

Security. That's a thought. I follow the people funneling out of the ticketing area toward the clogged security checkpoint. It's not too crowded here tonight, which makes it a little easier for me to spot her, just as she's handing her ID and ticket to the security agent. Her brown-black hair, wavy around her shoulders, gleams under the fluorescent lights.

"Layla!" I shout over the crowds. Several heads turn as I weave around to get to her. "Layla!" I call, over and over again.

Finally, she hears me. It's useful sometimes having a voice that's deep, that carries. I can boom like a cannon when I want. Her blue eyes are wide with surprise as she pulls her ticket and ID out of reach of the agent.

"Stop," I say, half out of breath as I reach her. I'm blocked by the thin barrier strap.

She just stares. "What are you doing here?"

"Ma'am?" says the ticket agent, and taps her hand impatiently on the desk. "There's a line."

Layla shakes her head. "Oh, right. Sorry."

She follows me over to a bank of chairs, towing her suitcase like she's in a trance.

We sit down, and she stares at me suspiciously. She also looks tired again. Did I do that, or was she like that before?

"What are you doing here?" she asks again.

"I...shit...hold on..." I'm still trying to catch my breath. I've been sprinting around since I parked the car. I'm in good shape, but the combination of running and the adrenaline rush takes its toll.

Layla glances back at the line of people. "My flight leaves in forty-five minutes. I need to get through security."

"Just...wait a second...fuck..." I take a deep breath as I whip off my hat and turn it backwards. I don't want anything to keep me from seeing her face. Then I take both of her hands, holding them firmly with mine. I'm not letting her leave until I say whatever I'm going to say.

"Why are you leaving now?" I ask.

Okay, it's not what I practiced in the car for the, but I need to know. I was planning on having a week with her, not just one fucked-up afternoon.

Layla bites her lip, which is trembling. "It's...it's just too hard. This place. I don't belong here. Not with my mom's ridiculous, stuck-up family. And not with you. You're...you're taken, Nico."

"I am not *taken*," I snap. "Jessie is full of shit. She was just trying to make you jealous."

"And why is that?" Layla asks sharply. Her blue eyes glint with a bit of steel.

That's my girl, I think to myself, in sort of a proud, distant way. She's sweet, but she's learning not to take shit from people. Not even me.

I take another breath. "Okay. I'm not going to pretend there's nothing between her and me. But it's always been casual, Layla. Usually it's..." I sigh. "Usually it's just when I'm missing you."

"You fuck another woman because you miss me?" Layla's voice cuts through the noise of the airport. "That's gross. You're using her. Should I go fuck other guys just to get over you?"

"*Fuck* no," I start to growl, but manage to hold myself back.

The truth is, I have no say over who Layla gets with. I don't want to know about it. I don't want to *think* about it. I imagine if I had been in her spot, if I had watched some dude walk up to her, call her pet names, tell her they were out of contraceptives. Fuuuuuuck. *Mine*, I'm thinking, from some primal place that doesn't have a conscience.

But I don't have a right to feel this way. Not anymore.

"You can do whatever you want," I say hollowly. "And so can I. You're right about Jessie, I don't need to be using her, and I don't. We're friends with benefits. She knows the score."

"Does she?"

"*Yes*," I insist.

Layla and I stare at each other. I'm still holding her hands, only now they're in a death grip. She pulls them away and shakes out the spots where her skin turned white. Then she stands up and puts her backpack on.

"I can't do this right now," she says. "I have enough drama in my life. I just...I just need to get back to New York."

"Layla." I stand up and take her shoulders, forcing her to look at me. "I'm sorry. I didn't...I didn't mean for this to happen."

"I know," she says, but continues to avoid my gaze. "You never do."

Those beautiful blue eyes are welling up with tears again, and it just about kills me that I put them there. I want to do anything but let her leave. I want to take her home with me and hole up in my room and pretend that nothing out there can hurt her, can hurt us. Not school. Not her family. Not Jessie. When it's just us, everything is fine.

I slide a finger under her chin and tip it up so she can't look anywhere else but at me.

"Please," I say. "Stay the week."

I'm working hard to be gentle, even though there's a big part of me that wants to toss her over my shoulder and carry her out whether she wants to come or not. But Layla is fragile right now. More than anything, she needs to know I care.

And then, because I can't do anything else, I kiss her, right here in the middle of the airport. I can't avoid the electricity that seems to shoot through us when we touch, that turns to a thunderclap whenever we kiss. What starts as gentle turns hungry in about two seconds, and suddenly, airport or not, Layla is devouring me just like I'm devouring her. The three months we've been apart come roaring back—three months of longing, three months of loneliness, three months of reaching to the other side of my bed only to find it empty. I barely register the thud of her bag as it drops to the floor, followed by my hat as her hands weave into my hair. My hands drift down and get solid handfuls of her ass—fuck, this ass that dreams are made of—and suddenly we're practically tearing at each other in front of hundreds of strangers.

"Mmph," she groans unintelligibly into my mouth, a half-pained sound that sends a lightning bolt straight to my dick.

"Fuck your flight," I grumble in her ear as I kiss along the line of her jaw. "I'll buy you a new ticket. Goddammit, Layla, just let me take you home."

She stiffens in my arms. "What home?"

Shit. How does a kiss that lasts maybe ten seconds make me completely forget about the rest of my life? I'm not this kind of person, the guy who plays two women, who tries to fuck one and mess around with the other. *Fuck* me.

"*Your* home?" she demands. Where you live with...her?"

Layla presses a hand on my chest and shoves me away. There are new tracks of tears on her cheeks, which she swipes at angrily and then stoops down to pick up her backpack. Taking hold of her carry-on, she faces me again.

She's so angry. My baby's fierce, even when she's mad at me. Maybe *especially* when she's mad at me. Her blue eyes glitter like the Pacific at night, just when the moon is rising over it. I wanted to show her that moon tonight.

"You're an asshole," she pronounces in an even voice that still manages to shake me to the core. "Go back to your *home*. Go back to Jessie."

Then she turns and starts walking down the long hallway, passing this security checkpoint, I'm guessing to find another so she can get the fuck away from me.

I want to chase her down all over again. I want to show her that yeah, maybe I'm an asshole, but I'm *her* asshole, that I'd never do anything to hurt her if I could help it.

But instead I just watch her go, watch the defiant sway of her hips in those shorts that really should be illegal. Watch the way she occasionally paws at her face, wiping away tears I put there. As much as a part of me wants to beg her to stay another day, a week, a month, a lifetime, I know it's best if I don't. Letting her walk away gets harder every time I do it. I'm not sure how many more times I can.

CHAPTER SIX

Layla

I'T'S TWELVE O'CLOCK WHEN I TUMBLE INTO SHATZI'S, THE JEWISH DELI AROUND THE corner from campus, and set my giant bag of books on the floor with a loud thump. My roommates, Shama, Jamie, and Quinn, all look at the stack with big eyes.

"Damn, babe," Quinn remarks. "Did you bring the entire library to lunch with you?"

I roll my eyes as I take a seat. "This is what I get for starting a major so late in the game. I have to catch up. Portuguese *and* Spanish, through level three. And my other two classes are seriously reading-intensive." I let my face fall into my hands. "What the fuck was I thinking?"

"*The Wretched of the Earth*?" Shama picks up one of my books curiously.

Quinn frowns. "The sounds like a ball of laughs."

"It's interesting," I say, taking the book back from Shama and paging through it. "It's this account of the psychological effects of colonialism. Frantz Fanon wrote it about his experiences during the French-Algerian war."

"Why are you reading about Algeria as a Latin American studies major?" Quinn shakes her head, as if she still can't believe my choice. I still can't believe it myself. And although my dad's sudden departure at first put the same sour look on my face about it, once I realized that my major is exactly the opposite of anything he wanted me to study in college, I came back to it with a renewed sense of purpose. It means I'll probably have to take classes through next summer to graduate on time, but the good thing is that a few of my general education classes from freshman and sophomore years will count.

I got lucky too. After spending most of my summer taking intensive Spanish at the local community college when my parents weren't looking, I was able to place into an intermediate Spanish class this semester. It's going to be hard, and I already know I'll be imagining Nico the entire time. But he's right. I can't let what's happening with my family dissuade me from my original goals—to learn about myself. My dad already took that from me once. He's not taking it again.

I shake my head. In the last two weeks, I've been doing everything I can not to think about Nico. Ignoring his calls, which have finally dropped off. Pretending the punching bag I take my frustrations out on at the gym is his stupid, gorgeous face.

The first few days back were the hardest, when I was here alone. But as my room-mates, Quinn, Jamie, and Shama, all arrived and we started to settle into our new dorm on Union Square, it's become a little easier. Classes start on Monday. Nothing like a bunch of food for my brain to distract me from my heart.

"It's for my African Diaspora class," I say, taking back the book. When Quinn's confused frown deepens, I shake my head. "Quinn. There are black people in Latin America. Lots of them. Afro-Latino history is a major part of the regional history."

Quinn looks at Jamie and Shama for support, but neither of them meets her eye. Quinn turns back to me.

"But you're not black. Was this the only class that was open?"

I sigh, irritated. "Do you have a problem with me taking a Black studies course, Quinn?"

There's an awkward silence. Shama watches the tension between Quinn and me while Jamie picks at something invisible in her pastrami sandwich.

"I just think it's weird," Quinn says finally. "You decide all of a sudden that you're going to learn about your culture. But this isn't your culture. You're paler than I am, and that's saying something."

I scowl, and Shama shakes her head. "Oh my God," she murmurs to herself.

"What?" Quinn asks. "It's not like Shama just stood up today and said, I'm going to major in Chinese because India's in Asia too. It's a huge continent."

Shama buries her face in her hands. I just glare.

"Half of my family comes from a Latin American country, Quinn," I say. "And even if they hadn't, it doesn't mean I can't learn about this stuff if I want to. Maybe *you* should take the class with me."

"And have a bunch of liberal guilt shoved down my throat? No, thank you. Besides, this isn't you learning about yourself. Or anything practical, for that matter. It's you learning about *him*."

"What the hell is that supposed to mean?" I demand.

"You know exactly what it means," Quinn counters. "I just hope you're not doing this for Special Delivery, Lay. FedEx guy doesn't care if you know about his mixed racial background."

"Quinn!" Jamie finally pipes up. "I think we should talk about something else."

I stand up. My chair squeaks loudly, even over the din of the diner. Quinn stares at me. Then, finally, she exhales heavily.

"Okay," she says. "Okay, I'm sorry. It's none of my business anyway."

"No," I say, slowly sitting down. "It's not."

"I know," Shama says as she pounds a hand unnecessarily hard on the bottom of a ketchup bottle. "Let's talk about where we're going to go tonight. It's our first night out together now that everyone is back. What'll we do?"

Both Quinn and Jamie hum with agreement. I sigh. I'm still annoyed, but Jamie's right. We should just let it go. The semester starts on Monday, and we're supposed to be celebrating. I don't want to ruin it by fighting with Quinn.

"Okay," I say. "But it better be someplace good."

OLD HABITS DIE HARD. Despite best-laid plans to do something out of the ordinary, we end up at our favorite bar near campus, Fat Black's, where the bouncer takes a look at our fake IDs and waves us in without a second glance. I don't actually mind. It's just so nice to be back in New York, like coming home after a long trip away. The heartbreak of summer starts to fade away with the familiar smell of stale alcohol and the sexual energy crackling around the bar.

The girls and I don't skimp, either. Working at Nordstrom had its perks, including a discount that helped me beef up my wardrobe. I should have known my dad was leaving just by the way he gave me money for the school year. By the way my mom suddenly put extra money into my savings every now and then. Unlike the last two years at NYU, I'm actually starting the school year ahead of the game financially.

I'm guessing by the effort we've all put into tonight that my roommates haven't had many chances to go out this summer either. Shama and Jamie visited each other a few times, since they only live a few towns from each other in Jersey, but Quinn spent most of the summer taking an MCAT prep course in Boston. Everyone has on their finest "come fuck me" gear—short skirts, high heels, and we spent the last hour and a half doing and redoing each other's makeup.

Shama's boyfriend, Jason, is DJing, although for the first time, she doesn't immediately say hi to him. Normally she'd want to take advantage of the fact that the elevated DJ booth blocks on the dance floor from seeing anything below the waist. Instead, she takes a seat on the barstool next to me and sends covert glances his way.

"What gives?" I ask nodding to where Jason is watching her from the booth.

She glares at him, then turns to me. "Oh. *That*." She shakes her head. "I found an email from an old girlfriend on his computer last night. Asking him to hook up."

I suck in a breath. "You don't think they..."

Shama gives a small shrug that just about breaks my heart. "I don't know. We barely got to see each other this summer. I came into the city a few times, but he was working so much he couldn't even get out to Jersey."

I frown at Jason, who is now bent over his turntables. This isn't good. Our yearly schedules are one of the things that sometimes gets in the way of dating people who aren't also students. I get that Jason works a lot, like most people trying to make a living in this expensive city, but not visiting his girlfriend once in three months? That's messed up.

"I don't want to talk about it," Shama says as we turn around to the bar. "I just want to drink. Have a couple of guys buy me drinks. Make him jealous so I can yell at him or have makeup sex or whatever ends up happening later."

The four of us order a round of cheap shots, then another, and it doesn't take long for the room to start spinning. And while the alcohol quiets the ache that seems to throb inside me no matter what, it also makes me really, really...horny. Um, yeah. I said it.

It's been more than three freaking months since I've had sex. And the side effect of making out with Nico on the beach is that it awakened a beast inside me. A beast that really, *really* needs to be fed.

"That one," I whisper to Shama, who, after nearly two hours of intermittent dancing and drinking, is the only one of our foursome left sitting with me at the bar.

Quinn has cozied up with a business grad student in the corner, and Jamie has disappeared to find her new boyfriend, Dev.

Shama follows my gaze across the bar. "Who?"

Before I can say anything, Quinn and Jamie reappear with their companions. Quinn pops up on the stool next to me while the business student waves over a bartender.

"Who's that guy?" Quinn asks, her voice slightly slurred.

"Who?" Jamie giggles as Dev suddenly becomes very interested in touching her neck.

Quinn nods over my shoulder. "The guy across the room. The one who looks like Antonio Banderas with glasses. He's staring at you, babe. Do you know him?"

I look where Quinn gestured. It's the same guy I just pointed out to Shama, and he is indeed watching me intently through a pair of glasses while he holds his beer bottle in a death grip. He's tall and lanky, with a face that's shadowed in the dim club light, but I can just make out the thin line of facial hair around his jaw, a mop of wavy black hair, and glasses that sort of look like Malcolm X's. I don't know who he is, but he's hot. Dark. Exactly what I'm looking for tonight.

"And...she's gone," Shama says behind me while I'm locked in a stare with Mystery Man.

I pay her no mind as I slide off my chair.

My skin feels prickly. Uncomfortable. Like all the hairs on it are standing up, but not from fear. More like I'm a cat that's been pet the wrong way, and now I need someone to smooth everything back into place. Who am I kidding? Someone? One person.

Except he's three thousand miles away, and I'm standing in this bar with a blood alcohol level that should probably be illegal. The hell if I'm going to waste my temporary loss of inhibitions. *Don't be easy*, my mom would say. Well, I'm about ready to say fuck it. Fuck her stupid conservative advice. What did it get her? A divorce? A husband who left her? Who the fuck cares if I'm easy?

"Lay, where are you going?" Quinn asks. Shama and Jamie trade glances, as if to say "of course" to Quinn's controlling behavior.

"I'm just going to say hi," I say, still watching the stranger. But before I can leave, Quinn grabs my arm and pulls me back to face her.

"Hey," she says. "Not for nothing, but something seems off to me about that guy. He's a little intense, don't you think?"

I look back to Glasses, who, very subtly, tips his chin at me like a short summons. Quinn's right. He *does* look intense. But that also might just be what I need right now.

"I'll be fine," I say, shaking her hand off irritably. "It's just a conversation."

Glasses watches me intently as I weave through the crowd. He takes a long drink without breaking eye contact, then sets his empty bottle on a table when I approach. He stands there, still looking, but not saying anything for a solid ten seconds. I stand awkwardly. Didn't he ask me to come here?

"Um, hi," I say, giving a light wave. I cock my head, waiting for a response. An introduction. Any of the normal niceties that would make this a little more comfortable.

Glasses nods. "I saw you dancing before."

His voice is low, but not quite as low as I would have expected from someone with such an imposing presence. It has a lilt I don't recognize. Like so many people in this city, he was born somewhere else. Italian, maybe. It's hard to tell from just a few words.

Glasses doesn't say anything else, so I nod and focus on my drink. He watches while I polish off the rest of it quickly. The alcohol goes straight to my head. Damn. I don't normally pound whiskey—I usually get it because it's better for sipping. But this guy makes me nervous. I have this urge, this immediate desire. I really want him to like me.

"Let's go," he says, and before I can reply, he walks around me.

I turn, and like he's Moses and the Red Sea, the crowd parts on either side of him, opening a space in the middle of the dance floor. He turns around and jerks his head at me, like he's surprised I didn't automatically follow. I set my drink on the table. And then, for some reason I can't really fathom, I do as I'm wordlessly told.

I understand now why birds in the wild do mating dances. I've danced with plenty of guys in clubs. I've let them touch my body, kiss my lips, even cop a feel here and there. It's not always what I want to do, but it's better than the alternative of telling them to fuck off and starting some drama. But this...this is different. This guy doesn't touch me; in fact, he stays a solid foot away from me while we dance. He circles around me with every step, forcing the crowd to back up around him while he moves, his gaze slowly raking up and down my body. I never knew it was possible to be turned on and terrified at the same time, but here I am.

He circles again, and at the end of the song, he closes a big hand around my wrist and pulls me close. His touch feels like a brand. Then he leans down so his lips are next to my ear, and his scent surrounds me—something salty, warm, overlaid with a sharp cologne.

"Your name?" he asks. His breath smells of some kind of sweet liquor. Rum, maybe. It's a bit like cachaça, the sweet Brazilian liquor my dad likes in the summertime.

"L-Layla," I stutter. "Yours?"

"Mmmmm," Glasses hums, but doesn't answer my question. His grip around my wrist tightens, and he tugs me closer. "Let's dance, Layla."

So we do. While my roommates watch with wide, speculative eyes, I let the handsome stranger wrap a long arm around my waist and pull me close. I let him guide me around the dance floor with hip movements that seem almost sinful. I let him dust his lips over my ears and shoulders, but he never goes farther than that. His hands drift to my waist, but never lower, never farther up. He's a tease, and it only makes that wanting, that painful desire, throb all the more.

And at the end of the dance, we do it again. And again. And at the end of those, when I've had three more drinks and can barely remember my own name, much less to ask him his, I say yes. I say yes to the tall, handsome stranger when he asks me to leave with him. I say yes, because he makes me feel like I can forget.

CHAPTER SEVEN

Nico

"ID, PLEASE."

The two girls hand me the cards, which thankfully, are real. It's harder to get a decent fake out here. California IDs are hard to forge, and it seems like underage people here just don't really go out to clubs. They'd rather party on the beach or at someone's house, smoke weed or drink shitty beer. I don't mind. Makes my job easier.

The girls, a couple of twenty-two-year-olds who seem to giggle more than talk, give me a couple of twittery grins. With their bleached blonde hair, they might as well be canaries. A pair of slutty Tweety Birds.

"So, handsome. You, um, want to come inside and buy us some drinks when you get a break?" one of them asks as she runs her finger down my lapel.

I smile grimly, remove her hand, and give them back their cards. "I'm good, thanks. It's twenty each for the cover."

"You sure?" her friend asks. "We, um, come as a set."

Canaries who are about as subtle as a steamroller. *Coño.* And the thing is, ninety-nine percent of dudes in my situation would be tripping all over themselves at a proposition like that. A threesome, offered on a platter, with two hot girls? I couldn't be less interested.

I still can't get those two blue eyes out of my mind. I might as well just accept it. I'm done. When she got on that plane, she basically took my heart and my dick with her. I should just make my mother happy and become a priest.

"What do you think, *papi*?" asks the taller of the blondes. "What time are you off? We could use a Spanish lesson."

I wasn't interested before, but now I'm pissed. These chicks are no different than the others who hit on me every week. They see the suit, the brown skin, maybe even the tattoo on my chest if my shirt is open. They want to get off with a brown guy. They want to go slumming.

Fuck. That.

"I'm good, ladies," I say as evenly as I can manage. "I gotta keep up my standards."

The short one's mouth drops open, revealing some stained molars. Great, so they're probably into meth too. Fuckin' winners we got out here tonight.

"Did you hear what he just said?" she says to her friend.

But I turn to the street, like I can't hear them as they walk by me into the club. I rub my hand over my face. It's one of those things that I actually miss about New York: the way people just say what they think, and no one cares. Sure, sometimes people could be fuckin' assholes, but at least they're assholes up front. Douchebags at AJ's, the club where I used to work, didn't pretend to be anything but that. Vapid women who only wanted one thing didn't couch their come-ons with racist fuckin' innuendo. It was black and white, and it's the hardest thing about living here, how people seem to talk all the time and say fuckin' nothing.

My phone rings in my pocket, pulling me out of my irritation. Gabe, my little brother.

"Yo, *mano*, what's up?" I answer, maybe a little too eagerly.

It's good to hear from him. We talk a lot, every few days usually, about what's going on with Ma or our sisters. Gabe is the man of the house now, so to speak. He's in my old room up by CUNY, about to start school. It's his job now to make sure that little things around our mother's apartment stay fixed, that the rent gets paid on time, that her utilities stay on. It's his job because our mother's immigration status is not exactly legal, and she's terrified of getting caught.

"It's good, it's good," Gabe says. "School starts on Wednesday. I'm pretty excited."

"You should be, you smart fuck. You're gonna do great, I know it."

Gabe's smart, but I know he's nervous about starting college. I understand why. I did a year and a half at City before I had to drop out to work. It wasn't easy. There was a big damn gap between what I learned to do in high school and what they expected me to know in college. I'm worried about my baby brother, but I know he can do it. He's a way better student than I was at his age.

"So," I say. "Did you find out the number for the writing center on campus? And all those free tutors I told you about?"

"Yes, for the fuckin' millionth time, yes, I have all the tutoring shit squared away, okay?"

I chuckle. "Good. I'm just checkin', just checkin'. So what's up?" He doesn't normally call me. Like a lot of kids his age, Gabe already texts more than he talks.

Gabe pauses. "I, uh, I was just wondering if you got my letter."

I almost laugh. "You sent me a *letter*? What are you, my fuckin' pen pal now? We gonna start trading drawings and locks of hair?"

"Shut the fuck up," Gabe says. "And you're the artist, *maricon*, not me. I just sent you something, okay? I was wondering if you got it."

I shake my head, even though he can't see me. "Nah, man, no letter. I'll check my mailbox when I get home, all right?"

"Sure. I just didn't want you to miss it."

"Everything okay?" Suddenly, I'm worried. Gabe's not exactly the kind of kid who would sit down at the kitchen table to compose a novel to send to someone. I'm honestly kind of surprised he even knew how to buy a stamp and address the envelope properly.

"Yeah, sure. Everything's fine."

But there's a beat before he says it, and I'm not buying it. I know my family. "Gabe. What's wrong?"

He sighs. "Nothing. Yet. It's just that...yeah. Mr. Ramirez is gone. Sounds like Immigration was making the rounds last week. And there's another rumor that Mr. Pineo wants to sell the building."

Shit. This is not good. Mr. Pineo is the old-as-fuck Italian who owns my mother's building. To be real, the dude's a slumlord and was probably mixed up with the mob back in the day. Now he's just a grouchy old man who takes wads of cash each week from his tenants in exchange for cheap apartments that wouldn't have a chance in hell at meeting New York City housing standards.

But the neighborhood is changing. Hell's Kitchen isn't crime central the way it was when I was a kid. More and more of the buildings are being bought by developers interested in building skyscrapers for the Wall Street hacks to live in. One of these days, Mr. Pineo will decide he can make more money without collecting cheap rents, and my mother, along with the rest of his tenants who may or may not be there legally, will be shit out of luck.

Immigration pokes around the building every now and then because it's full of people who speak English with an accent, but they rarely get anyone because most of the building is from Puerto Rico, which means they are all citizens. But my mom, even though she's from San Juan too, is a different case. Smuggled to Puerto Rico as a baby from Cuba, she looks like a Puerto Rican and talks like a Puerto Rican. It's the only culture she's ever known, but to the U.S. government, she's as Cuban as they come and here without permission.

Mr. Ramirez was a newer neighbor, one from Ecuador. I don't know if he knows about my mom, but I don't want to wait to find out.

"Have Ma stay uptown for a while," I say. "You or Maggie can stay in the Kitchen. Just until you know ICE isn't poking their nose around anymore, and you find out more about Pineo's plans. Maggie would probably appreciate the extra space."

Gabe exhales loudly. "Fuck that. I'm taking the apartment for myself. Ma can come help with Allie. That kid never stops crying, and I'm going to need to study!"

I chuckle. "You just gotta find her Dora the Explorer. She has that, she never cries."

"Dora the Explorer," Gabe says, like he's writing it down. "Got it."

"Anything else? You need money? For food, utilities, school supplies, whatever?"

"We're good, man," Gabe says. "Your last check came two days ago, and I just got a job on campus so you won't have to pay for everything, okay? We're fine."

"Everyone else good? You hear from Flaco—"

"Nico, we're *fine*," Gabe says. Then he pauses. "Just check your mailbox." Then, with a quick goodbye, he hangs up.

The rest of the night is slow. Labor Day weekend, said the manager. Most people are out of town for the long weekend, partying it up in Vegas or getting out of the city. I wouldn't mind camping on the beach or something like that. Not that I ever have before, but something tells me I'd like it. Especially if I was with the right person.

Her face pops up again, like clockwork. Whenever I start daydreaming, there she is.

This time, I don't even fight it. I pull out my phone and text her again. I haven't stopped in the last week. She won't take my calls, but sometimes she'll respond to my texts. K.C. thinks I'm crazy for caring so muc. Why should it matter if a girl three

---

Me: hows the night? its nine oclock and im already bored as fuck. LA ppl suck.

It doesn't take long to get a response. I nod to myself. A good sign. Sometimes she
doesn't answer at all.

Layla: Im out w the girls. yeah, LA ppl do suck.

It's not an overt insult, but I'm pretty sure that's for me. Or maybe Jessie. Or
maybe us both. Well, she's allowed a pot shot or two after what happened. I just want
to keep her talking.

Me: Hot night? Send me a pic.

It's a long shot, I know, not to mention torture. I know what kinds of Band-Aids
Layla tries to pass as clothing when she and her friends go out. She's probably
looking at the message right now thinking, what the fuck is this guy's problem?

I hope she asks. I hope I can tell her that my problem is her. That she needs to get
her ass on a plane so we can finish what we started.

My phone buzzes, and I flip it open with surprise. It's a picture, probably taken by
one of her friends, grainy the way most cell phone pictures are. My phone barely gets
them at all, and I'll have to delete it immediately to save memory, but *damn*, I'm glad I
asked. Layla's tiny black dress might as well be underwear. It's small and tight, even
for her. Her hair is wavy around her shoulders. Even with the lack of focus, I can still
see the tilt of her hips, the defiant posture, the eyes that stare a hole through me.

My baby is mad. And she wants to show me what I'm missing. Well, message
fuckin' received. She wants to play games, I'm up for that. It's better than the silent
treatment.

Me: u wanna take that off and show me what else im missing?

Not my finest, I know. But the green-eyed monster showed its face for a moment,
and suddenly I'm not feeling like such a "nice guy" anymore.

It backfires, though, because she doesn't text back. Two hours later, my phone
buzzes in my pocket again. I open it up to find another picture from Layla. I check my
watch—it's close to 3:00 a.m. New York time. I don't know why she'd be texting me
now unless it was to—

I can't even finish my thought. The picture is grainy and kind of out of focus, but I'd know those shoulders, that hair, that *ass* anywhere. There's Layla, wrapped like a vine around some dude in the middle of what looks like a crowded dance floor. His hands are hovering just over that part of her body I'd secretly love to have tattooed with: "Property of Nico fuckin' Soltero, so step the fuck off." Her hands are shoved into this creep's hair, and he's staring at her neck like she's a piece of meat he's going to bite into. It takes me a solid ten minutes to realize there's a caption. A fuckin' nasty one too.

Layla: This is what you're missing. So you can fuck off.

I swear. In Spanish. In the dirtiest phrases I can think of, ones I couldn't translate if I tried. Because when I see this picture, I am barely literate. It takes everything I have not to hurl my phone on the ground and kick the shit out of it.

And it takes hours—many of them—for it to occur to me that the text wasn't written in the usual shorthand that Layla uses when she texts. That maybe she wasn't the one who sent it. All I can see is some bloodsucking motherfucker about to kiss my girl. And my girl is going to kiss him back.

———

IT'S ALMOST four when I unlock the door to my apartment. It's not until I've taken off my shoes and tossed my jacket over the back of the couch that I realize my bedroom light is on.

I push open the door. My room looks the same as always: simple, with a twin bed in one corner and my clothes hanging from a rack, since it doesn't actually have a closet, a ratty armchair in one corner, and a small desk pushed under a window. The only difference is Jessie.

Things have been weird between us. I still haven't forgiven her for fucking up things between Layla and me, and she's done a pretty good job of staying out of my way. Which is why it's strange to find her sitting cross-legged on my bed like a fairy, paging through my sketchbook.

"What the fuck are you doing?"

Jessie starts and looks up. She's dressed like she was just out, in a skin-tight dress that's basically a shirt because of the way she's sitting. I can see her red underwear. It has white hearts on it. Her makeup is smudged a little under her eyes, and her blonde hair, which is usually all done up, is stringy and messy over her shoulders.

"This is that girl," she says with a slight slur.

I frown and walk in, pulling off my tie in the process. "What are you doing in my room?"

"This is that girl from the beach," Jessie replies as she gets up from the bed. Damn, she's really drunk. She doesn't even bother to pull down her skirt.

I turn around after I toss the tie on my armchair and start undoing the button of my shirt. Jessie stands in front of me and doesn't even try to hide the way her eyes raze up and down my body.

I take the open sketchbook out of her hands, close it, and put it on top of my dresser. "You're toasted, Jess. Go to bed."

"I'm not drunk," Jessie says. "I was. But I'm not anymore."

"Don't you have an audition tomorrow?" I take off my shirt and toss it on the chair too. I'm grabbing a t-shirt out of my dresser when I feel a set of cold hands sliding around my waist from behind.

"Mmmm," Jessie hums as she presses her face into my back. "I swear, you just get hotter every day, babe. It's not fair."

I take her hands, which are knotted around my stomach, and push them away. "Jess. What are you doing?"

She pulls back with a pout, and I put on my shirt. I'm not in the mood to be ogled like a piece of fuckin' meat.

"What do you think I'm doing?" she says snottily when I turn around. "I'm doing the same fucking thing we've been doing for months. You *never* say no to me. Then Baby Spice shows up on the beach all of a sudden, and now you're a Boy Scout. What gives?"

I'm about to open my mouth to tell her she better keep Layla's name out of hers when I catch a look at my bed behind her. In my shock at finding Jessie paging through my sketchbook, which is fuckin' *private*, I hadn't noticed the ten or so envelopes scattered all over my bedspread.

"What the fuck is this?" I ask as I stride around Jessie and start picking everything up. "You went through my mail?" I look up, shaking the letters. "What the fuck is wrong with you?"

"I should say the same thing," Jessie returns, coming back to the corner of the bed. "What the fuck is wrong with *you*, Nico?"

I glare at her. This is insane. I don't want to have a fight with my roommate/fuck-buddy about her boundary issues. I just want to get some fuckin' sleep.

Jessie wiggles her nose like a rabbit. "I was just bringing it in to put on your desk," she says. "I promise. But then I saw your sketchbook open on the bed. I didn't know you could draw like that."

I just grip the stack of mail harder. I haven't actually drawn much in the last few months, but when I have, it's only been one thing. Or one person, actually.

"There are a lot of pictures of...her," Jessie ventures again. She pops her lower lip out in a pout I've seen in some of her photos. It's a look she wants to make her "signature," whatever the fuck that means. All I know is that she spends a lot of fuckin' time practicing it in the bathroom.

I frown. "Yeah. There are."

"I didn't see any of me."

I just sift through the mail. Bill, bill, another bill. Nothing interesting. I want her to get the fuck out of my room. I want to sleep. Jerk off. Dream the dreams that are going to drive me crazy, since I know I'll be thinking about that fucking almost-kiss all night long.

"I also saw this."

Jessie flips a letter to me, one she must have been sitting on, or maybe one she's been holding the whole time. When I see the scrawl over the front, I smirk.

"Who's it from?" Jessie asks as she watches me open it.

"My little brother."

I tear open the envelope. I'm still curious about why the fuck Gabe would send me something.

The reason becomes clear as I take out a wrinkled piece of paper. It's rough, torn out of a newspaper. No note or anything—Gabe's not the type. But the message is clear.

"The FDNY?" Jessie scoffs next to me. "Are you kidding?"

I give her a look. "What's so funny?"

"Haven't you applied to take the exam about five times?"

I frown. "Twice. They weren't hiring then."

I look back at the clipping, which states clearly that the FDNY is holding another exam in less than two months. An open application. Anyone who's qualified can take it.

"Holy shit," I mumble, flipping the page over and then back again. I know from previous attempts that this only happens maybe once every five years.

"This is ridiculous," Jessie says as she snatches the page away.

"Hey!" I bark. "What the fuck!"

But Jessie's already crumpled up the page and tossed it in the waste bin under the desk. She turns around with a hand on her hip. She looks every inch the party girl—a little worn down from the night, but still glamorous, tan, everything most women in California try to be. You'd never know she grew up in a trailer in Nowhere, Oregon.

"*That* is a waste of your time," she says as she walks back to where I stand. "You're here now. Not in New York. Why do you keep looking back to a place that clearly doesn't want you? A girl who doesn't want you. A job that doesn't want you. Last year, you couldn't *wait* to leave New York."

I open my mouth to argue with her, but the thing is, she's right. New York only ever treated me like shit. I was born into a situation where people looked at me like I was nothing because of my family, my neighborhood, my skin color, the way I talked. Every time I tried to do better for myself, it just pushed me back down again. The FDNY was always a pipe dream.

"People like you and me," Jessie begins as she reaches a slow hand to stroke my shoulder. She traces the lines of the tattoo that snake out from underneath my right sleeve. "We have to leave the places we come from. You can't be something in a place where you've only ever been nothing."

It's the one thing Jessie and I do have in common—the fact that both of us came from so little. Raised in a trailer by a deadbeat father, she knows exactly what it means to need to get away from a past that pigeonholes you. She's been running from hers her whole life.

She draws a line down the center of my chest, scraping her fingernail up my abs, pulling the shirt with it, then back down. Her hand tugs suggestively on my belt buckle.

"I bet I could bring you back to the here and now," she says, stepping a little closer while her hands pull slowly at the leather.

She gives me a little nudge, then another, until I hit my mattress and sit down on it. Without waiting for me, Jessie finishes unbuckling my pants and sinks down to the floor. And I'm not going to lie. She's a beautiful girl, and the look of her there, on her knees for someone like me...it turns me the fuck on.

Looks like I didn't lose my dick after all.

"You want this?" Jessie asks as she unzips my pants and pulls down my briefs. It's pretty fuckin' clear I do.

I close my eyes as she takes me in her mouth. Like magic, a pair of sad blue eyes flash in my mind. She's always there, lurking behind my thoughts. But then I think of that dude's hands, grainy, but obvious, all over Layla's ass. His tongue slipping out like a snake while he touches her body.

I growl. Jessie, not realizing why, releases me and smiles.

"I guess that's a yes," she says haughtily.

I glare at her and wrap her ponytail around my fist so she has to look at me.

"It's just sex," I state clearly. "That's all. And when you're done, it's back to your own room."

Jessie gulps, but her brown eyes gleam. She nods.

"It's just sex," she repeats. "Fine."

She bends back to her work, taking me further while I rock my hips forward. Maybe it makes me an asshole, but I need this. I need the control. I need the release. I need to feel like I'm not being played from three thousand miles away.

But every time I close my eyes, the hair wound around my hand is black, not blonde. And the eyes that look up at me from that vulnerable position are a bright, all-seeing blue. Eyes that know the truth that echoes through my soul.

I slam my hand on the wall above Jessie's head with a force that makes her jerk. *You're mine*, those eyes say. And the fuck if it's not true.

———

I DON'T SLEEP. Usually I sleep like the dead, especially after a long night at the club and definitely after sex. Jessie was true to her word. She shuttled back to her room, leaving me to lie in mine, staring at the popcorn ceiling while I wait for sleep to come.

It doesn't. And I know why.

With a sigh, I roll off the bed and pad to my desk, where I sit down and reach underneath for the wastebasket. I pull out the crumpled piece of paper, open it, and smooth it out on the desktop. There's a corny-looking dude on the front, smiling while he carries an ax. But in serious block letters, the announcement is clear: there's an open test date for the exam.

I pick up my phone and open my messages from Layla. Before the anger in my chest takes over, I delete the shitty picture of her in the club. She obviously didn't take it—maybe she didn't send it either. And I don't want to think of her like this, angry and out of control.

Without thinking about the fact that it's almost 8:00 a.m. New York time, my thumbs slide over the buttons, punching out a message. It's all I've thought about all night. Sometimes it feels like all I can ever think about.

Me: I miss u.

I say it because I mean it. Because even though I'm angry, I know she has the right to kiss whoever the fuck she wants. Because I'm the one who left, I'm the one who shacked up with another woman. Because a part of me knows I have nothing more to lose by saying it, and if there's any way I can keep some piece of her in my life, I'll do whatever it takes. She's always looked at me like she believes I can be anything. And the thing is, when she looks at me like that, I start to believe it too.

When I'm done, I punch in the number on the flyer. I won't be telling anyone else about this—not for a while yet. But I have to try. I'll regret it if I don't.

CHAPTER EIGHT

Layla

The tiny, inconsequential ding of my phone is a small sound, but it might as well be a knife by the way it's stabbing through my brain.

I am not exaggerating, I swear. My eyes open like creaky windows. Everything is foggy and out of focus. How much did I have to drink last night?

The first, second, and third round of shots, I remember. The weird, peacock-style dancing in the middle of the club. Another three drinks. Getting way nastier than I ever intended with Intense Dude on the dance floor. Leaving the club with—

My heart gives a couple of chest-shaking thumps as the rest of the night comes back to me. A cab ride that felt more like war than foreplay. Some fairly intense petting that led to...

I squeeze my thighs together. Yeah, they're naked all right, and the ache between them brings the rest of the night back to me. My eyes are open wide as I absorb the geography of a bedroom that is definitely not mine: the faded gray carpet, the bay window with flaking paint and bars over it. The clothes that are slung over the open doors of a closet. The stack of books on a very messy desk, and the pair of wayfarer glasses perched on top of them.

Giancarlo. That was his name. He finally told me through a thick South American accent, but only after we'd made out for an hour and I refused to leave with him without having a name to give my girlfriends. Giancarlo from Argentina, from a suburb of Buenos Aires, the name of which I couldn't possibly remember right now. A twenty-three-year-old exchange student at CUNY, here to study business or something like that. A bunch of other stuff that reappears in my memory like the teacher's voice in Charlie Brown. Wa-wa-wa. Thanks, alcohol.

Slowly, I peek to my left, where I'm greeted by the long, sleeping form of the man himself, draped casually in his peach-colored sheets. Up close, he's even bigger than I remember—well over six feet. He's on his stomach, his hands clutching a pillow to his chest. In his sleep, his frown is only slightly lessened, but the rounded edges of his face soften a bit. Dark, curly brown hair that flops a little on top. Uneven stubble. Shadows under his eyes that look like mine, like my family's in Brazil. His full lips and chin pout slightly. He's still handsome, but almost boyish, despite his size.

That prickly feeling is back. I can't tell if I like it or not. It's unfamiliar, exciting. Everything about this moment, this guy, is different. I don't go home with men I don't know. I don't get blackout drunk in bars. I don't wake up with parts of my memory too blurry to see clearly.

I turn onto my side. There's a small envelope icon on my phone—a string of text messages I don't remember getting or sending, the last of which arrived at about eight o'clock this morning—all of them back and forth with that stupid 323 number I both hate and love. I miss the New York number, the one I still remember by heart. Well, I miss a lot more than that. Careful not to wake the sleeping giant next to me, I scroll through them.

The messages turn from playful to irate to sad, culminating with a photo that apparently I sent sometime around midnight. It's a terrible picture of me and Giancarlo, wrapped up with each other on the dance floor. Giancarlo looks like he's about to eat me alive. I look like I'm just trying to hold on for dear life.

And this went to Nico.

Fuck. It had to have been Quinn. There's no one else who would have snapped this and then sent it to him with that kind of message. I scroll back through his responses, all of them coming in within the past couple of hours. He must have seen these when he got home from the club. To her. To Jessie.

Nico: wtf layla

Nico: i dont get it. why send that at all?

Nico: Fuck. FUCK.

Nico: i hope u were safe

Nico: u know what? its fine. i want u to be happy.

Nico: I miss u.

They're just words. Three little words that feel like hammers on this fragile wall I've contrived around my heart. You miss me? You *miss me*?! I want to shout, hurl my phone across the room. Let it drown in the Hudson, right into the water just like he did with his. But at the same time, I feel like crying. He says he wants me to be happy, and as angry as I still am, I want him to be happy too. I'm also mad at myself for leaving the way I did. Maybe he shouldn't have kissed me like that, but in the end, it's not like we were going to get back together or anything. He can do whatever he wants, and so can I.

So why does the thought of that still make me feel so freaking terrible?

Tears spring, and I work to blink them away, grasping at the sheets in this unfamiliar room until my vision clears. Beside me, Giancarlo snorts, and it snaps me out of my anger. I remember that I'm not in my room at all, but in a stranger's. Someone who might not take it so kindly if I startle him out of his sleep.

Suddenly the only thing I can think about is getting out of this place. I want to get back to my other strange bed, the one that belongs only to me, at least for the next nine months. I want to bury myself under my familiar purple comforter, wrap the curtains around my bed, and stay asleep until Monday.

Very, very carefully, I slip out of bed, wincing at the creak of floorboards under my feet. After I manage to track down my clothes, Giancarlo emits a loud snore. I can't help wondering how I ever thought this guy even approximated Nico. Because that's what I was doing, right? This guy's hair is black, but it's longer, the curls almost too shiny at his temples. His jaw is more rounded, his cheekbones less pronounced. His skin is more golden than brown, and his shoulders lack the lean, corded muscle Nico's have. He's handsome, sure, but a terrible substitute for the man who, as of yet, has no replacement.

This was supposed to help me forget. But now I only feel that much worse.

Clasping my heels in one hand, I tiptoe toward his bedroom door, but just when I'm about to make my escape, the hinge creaks loudly. I freeze. Giancarlo rolls over and sits up a little, blinking in the sunlight because he puts on his glasses. His gaze focuses on me with growing recognition.

With his glasses, he looks a little older. His eyes harden with that same look I remember, even through my drunken memory. It's sharp. Possessive. Hungry.

"Hello," he says sleepily in that same, thickly accented voice. "You are leaving."

I nod, keeping the doorknob in my hand. It wasn't really a question, but I'm answering it anyway. "I need to get going."

Giancarlo pushes off the covers and gets up, giving me a full view of, well, everything. He's even bigger than I thought, probably close to six-four, maybe even taller. His shoulders slope, and although he's not cut the same way that Nico is, the guy is clearly no slouch. He stretches, and his cock, half-erect, points at me. I look away.

"I will walk you to the subway," he says even as I turn away.

"Um, no, that's okay."

I already have one foot out of his room, but now I feel like I should close the door or something, give him some modesty that he doesn't already have. He's still brutally naked, scratching his head without a care that his penis is just hanging out there, waving in the wind. I shouldn't feel that weird about it, considering we had sex last night, but I do. I don't know this person. I don't want to see all of this. Somehow, his nakedness feels weirdly dominant.

"I really have to get back. I'm supposed to meet my friends for breakfast." Lie. All lies. Good God, I just want to get out of this room, dive into a vat of coffee, and crawl into my own bed.

Giancarlo looks up from his dresser, where he pulls out a pair of briefs. He tugs them on, finally covering up that...thing. Even half-erect, he's pretty damn big. Shit, *how* did that fit in me? No wonder I'm sore.

"Are you sure?" he's asking. "I will only take a second."

"No, I'm fine," I say. "Um...thanks. For..."

He smiles. His teeth are a little crooked, but only slightly. He has a nice smile. I feel kind of bad for blowing him off.

"Before you leave, I can give you my number?" he asks.

Damn it. I knew that question was coming. "Do you have a card?"

It's a tactic I actually picked up from Quinn. She does it in situations where she wants guys to feel important while also giving herself an out. This guy won't. He's a student, like me. There is absolutely no reason for him to have a business card, which will, in turn, make him feel ashamed. And hopefully he won't call me again.

Giancarlo scratches his head and shoves a big hand into his curly hair. I think it's working. I owe Quinn a drink. Or, I think as a bout of nausea rises and falls, maybe just a coffee.

But when Giancarlo smiles, it changes him completely. He goes from being stern and slightly scary to magnanimous and almost sweet. "It's okay," he says. "No card."

He reaches a hand out and waits patiently. He shrugs, and the movement is so charming, I can't help but smile back and hand him my phone. I watch as he punches his number into it and calls himself. His phone buzzes on the bedside table, and he smiles as he hangs up mine and gives it back to me.

"There," he says. "Easy."

"Uh, okay," I say. "I guess...I'll see you around?"

Giancarlo nods. "Yes."

It's abrupt. I can't quite tell if that's a dismissal or not. But in the end, I give a muffled "okay" and scoot my way out of the apartment.

Outside, it takes me a second to find my bearings. We took a cab last night, and I have no idea where I am other than roughly suspecting I'm still in Manhattan. Maybe? At least, I don't remember crossing any bridges. I walk up a short hill, keeping my skirt pulled down with both hands while my tiny purse keeps sliding down my arm. Ugh. I am a total cliché, dressed like a streetwalker while I complete a "walk of shame." Emphasis on shame.

Once I reach the end of the block, I realize with both relief and dread that I know exactly where I am: West 144th and Broadway. Just a few blocks from another apartment where I used to spend a *lot* of time. I turn down the street, and despite the fact that it's a cloudy, nondescript day, despite the fact that the air is full of emotionless car honks and subway rumbles, despite the fact that the catcalls I receive make my skin crawl as I walk as fast as I can down Broadway, just about every conflicting emotion I've been feeling for the past week and a half comes bubbling up to the surface.

Because everything about this neighborhood is him. Correction: everything about this neighborhood is *us*. Every bodega is a place where we bought drinks, gum, condoms, snacks together before racing up to his apartment to have our way with each other. There's the Dominican restaurant that makes his favorite chicken; there's the cheesesteak place where he flirted shamelessly with me over ginger ale. His laundromat. His grocery store.

His...brother?

My eyes are so full of threatening tears that when I turn into the subway entrance, I run smack into a familiar lanky form.

"*Oye*, watch it!" Two hands land on my shoulders to steady me as I almost teeter down the steps. Then: "NYU?"

I blink furiously, willing the tears to recede. They finally do, and then I look up. "Gabe! Hey."

Nico's younger brother, Gabriel, looks me over like he's checking that I'm actually here. As if realizing he's touching his brother's girl, he yanks his hands away like I'm made of fire, and it's then he gets a look at what I'm wearing. His eyes almost fall out of his head.

I immediately blush. Yep, what I'm doing is *that* obvious. I didn't even wear a jacket last night since the late summer nights are still warm enough to go without. This dress is basically lingerie, and I'm wearing five-inch heels at eight in the morning.

"Ah, how you doin'?" Gabe asks, clearly working very hard *not* to move his gaze from my eyes. He's staring so hard I might end up with a hole through my head.

I shrug. "I'm okay. You? How's school? You started at CUNY last week, right?"

Gabe nods, like he's not sure what I just said. "Um, yeah. It's good, I guess. A lot harder than high school. So, you, um..."

He trails off, and I can tell he's struggling to find a way to ask me what I'm doing in this neighborhood dressed like this without coming right out and saying it. I bite my lip. This is the last thing I want. After those stupid photos—fucking *Quinn* sent them, I'm sure of it now—Nico is going to think I'm stalking his family now just to niggle him. I might be mad at him, but I don't want to hurt him. I'd never want that.

"I just crashed at a friend's place," I offer.

He must know it's a lie, but Gabe's shoulders relax visibly. "Okay, okay," he says. "Fun night?"

Shyly, I nod. "Yeah. Maybe too much fun. I need to get going, though. Lots to do before my classes start this week."

Gabe looks me over a little more frankly. It's not a look like some of the ones I got walking down the street. It's a look that's more critical. And I can only guess who's going to hear about what he sees.

"Yeah, me too," he says as he meets my eyes again. "It was good seeing you, NYU." He leans in, like an afterthought, and gives me a quick kiss on the cheek. A familiar greeting I've only experienced in Brazil. It's a move that's both awkward and sweet. When he finishes, I smile.

"You too," I say. "Later."

I watch for a moment as he walks up the street toward the apartment I used to know so well. I wonder what it looks like now. I wonder if it's changed.

And before I wonder more, my cell phone buzzes again in my purse. Speak of the devil.

Nico: Im sorry.

I deflate right there on the subway steps. All the anger I felt is gone. I don't like being mad at him. And if this little walk through memory lane has shown me anything, it's that I don't want to have a life where I don't know him anymore.

I press the call button. His deep, scratchy voice answers almost immediately.

"Layla?"

I sigh. I'm still standing in the middle of the subway stairs, but there's nowhere for me to go. "Hey."

"Hey, baby."

The familiar moniker guts me. How can something that feels so good hurt so much? Tears rise again.

"I just..." I trail off. "I saw all your texts. Nico, I'm so sorry about that photo. I didn't take it or send it, I swear."

"But that's you, right?" His voice isn't mad—just sad. Dejected.

I gulp. "Yeah."

He sighs. "Well, I'm not gonna pretend I liked it. But...hey. I don't exactly have a right to be angry over here." He pauses. "Are you happy?"

No. "Sure."

There's another long sigh. "Where are you?"

I glance around like he can see me. "Um, just on the street. Getting some breakfast."

I know that Gabe is going to call him and spill the beans, but I don't want to rub it in his face. Nico's smart. He'll put two and two together, and if he wants to ask me about it, he can.

"I just wanted to say...I'm sorry," I rush on. "And that I'm not...well, I'm not mad at you anymore, okay? I shouldn't have run off like that. I was just in a really messed-up state of mind, with my dad and everything."

"Of course, of course, sweetie." Nico's voice is warm, and it makes my heart lift a little. Gah...I miss him so freaking much.

He pauses, and we sit there silently on the phone together. It's quiet on his end; he can no doubt hear the sounds of cars and the rumble of the trains on mine.

"We friends again?" he asks finally. "I just want to be your friend, Layla. Tell me I can at least be that."

I let out a breath I didn't know I was holding. "Of course. Nico, I'll always be your friend."

"Even when you tell me to fuck off?"

I can't help but smile. "Even then."

He chuckles. "Okay, then. Maybe don't send me any more photos like that, okay? I might be your friend, but I'm not *that* kind of friend."

"Okay," I agree. "That's fair. I don't really want to hear about...you know...either."

An awkward silence falls, like there's something Nico wants to say. But doesn't.

"Of course," he says finally. "It's a deal." There's another brief pause, and then I hear a rustling in the background. "I actually need to get some sleep," he says. "I got home not that long ago."

"I need to go too."

"Okay, baby. Be good."

A few minutes later, I step onto a crowded train, ignoring the knowing looks of a few passengers: the *what a slut* expression of the woman sitting with her kid, the curious leers of the two boys on the bench across from me. I shrink into myself, trying to avoid the touch of other people's bodies. It's hard; the train is jammed with morning commuters, even though it's Saturday. But unlike last night, when I was craving the feel of skin on skin, now the thought of a random person's touch feels repulsive. And yet, my skin still has that sensation of displacement. It covers my body, making me feel like a stranger in my own skin. That prickly feeling is still there. If anything, it's gotten worse.

II

"I GOT YOU."

CHAPTER NINE

NOVEMBER 2003

Nico

The worst thing about studying is the sound. Last week I invested in a new pair of headphones and a couple of CDs because I can't stand the scratch of pencil on paper or the way my breathing picks up when I concentrate. But when I move to a public place, I get too distracted. I like to people-watch too much. I notice too many things to focus on a piece of paper with a bunch of dry questions. It's ironic: the qualities that I think would make me a great firefighter are what might make me fail this stupid test.

It takes me a while to get into the groove, so when I do, I don't get out for a while. It's not until Jessie's cold fingers slide over my shoulders and slip under the collar of my t-shirt that I even realize anyone is in my room with me.

"Jesus!" I start and yank off my headphones, then turn around in my seat. "You scared me."

Jesse looks curiously around me at the papers scattered over my small desk. "What are you doing, sketching?"

I fiddle with my pencil, tapping the eraser on the desk. "Not exactly."

Jessie leans over me, a long waterfall of blonde hair draping over my neck. She's been at a photo shoot and had some extensions put in. She looks like she's been dipped in makeup, and her hair is about a foot longer than it was this morning. The ends are itchy on my skin, and her bright red nails dig into my shoulder. Why girls think they look better when they add all this fake shit to their bodies makes no fuckin' sense. I want to be able to pull hair without worrying it's going to come off, if you know what I mean. I want to be able to kiss a woman's skin without getting a mouthful of makeup.

Well, one woman's skin. But she's not here right now. We've been talking every now and then over the past two months, but it's hard. Layla and I...we can't not be in each other's lives, but at the same time, it's painful. I know she's doing a lot of things I don't want to know about. Going out with her friends. Meeting other men—she's beautiful, how could she not? And there is plenty about my life I can't tell her either.

Details about Jessie, who, if I'm being honest, acts more and more like my girlfriend these days and less like a roommate. And if I'm being *really* honest, I don't do much to stop her. I get tired of sleeping alone, even if the body next to me isn't totally the one I want.

"What's this?" Jessie asks, squinting down at the stack of practice tests and the legal pad full of notes.

I repress the urge to shut the book and turn over my messy chicken scratch. It's been a while since I took notes on anything, and I wasn't exactly a great student before. No one but Gabe even knows I'm taking this test. Not K.C. Not my mother. Not Layla. No one. I'm not sure why I haven't told anybody. Maybe it's because I don't want to hear the obvious: that I'm not exactly a brain, and only the top five percent of test-takers even have a chance at a call back. I looked it up. The last time they held this test, they had thirty thousand applicants. That means maybe fifteen hundred of them got a real interview. The odds aren't great.

But that hasn't stopped me from trying my best over the last two months. I'm twenty-seven now, having celebrated my birthday checking IDs last week. The FDNY doesn't hire anyone over thirty, and they won't do this again for another four or five years. This is my last chance.

"Seriously, what the hell is this?" Jessie asks again as she pushes me to the side and starts leafing through my notes. She picks up one of the practice exams that I've taken at least three times. It's highlighted in four different colors. "The FDNY? Seriously?" She flips through some of the other tests. "How long have you been doing this?"

I trade my pencil back and forth between my hands. Jessie's looking at me like I've betrayed her, but honestly, this isn't any of her business. She and I don't really talk much, considering we're on completely different schedules, and when we overlap, it's usually for sex, and that's about it. Sometimes we do nice things for each other, like make an extra cup of coffee in the morning, or order the takeout the other likes. But those are roommate things, right?

Sure, asshole. Keep telling yourself that.

"A while," is all I say.

Jessie stands up with a pout. "You could have told me."

I shrug. "We'll see what happens."

She tips her head like she's trying to figure something out. Then that look appears —one I know pretty well at this point. One side of her painted pink lips lifts as she leans over, giving me a nice view down her shirt. She's a typical California girl, tan and golden in a pair of short shorts and a loose white tank top. She's pretty; some might say gorgeous. But as she sinks to her knees and runs her hands suggestively up my thighs, I'm not feeling it. At all.

"I can't," I say as I lift her hands off me. "Look, I'm sorry. But I'm taking the test next week when I go home for Thanksgiving, and I'm still not doing very well on the last section."

Jessie frowns and stands back up. "You know, I'm getting kind of sick of this shit from you."

"And what shit would that be?"

"This hot and cold bullshit," she snaps. "You were kind of off when you first got here, but I figured that was just getting used to each other again. You mostly got back to normal though, and that Nico wouldn't say no to some cookie if it was two a.m.

and he had the flu." She squints her eyes a little. "Is it that girl? The one from the beach that day?"

Now it's my turn to frown. "I told you not to talk about her."

"You told me not to say anything disrespectful. I'm not."

I stare at her for a moment. Then I shrug. "Yeah. Well. That was almost three months ago, Jess."

"And you've been kind of different for three months. I know you still talk to her."

"So what? We're friends. She gives me study tips." It's a lie, sort of. Even though Layla has no idea I'm doing this, picking her brain about her classes tells me a lot about what a good student looks like. My girl is smart. Really smart.

Jessie, on the other hand, isn't exactly big on education. She moved to LA when she was seventeen, as soon as she graduated high school. As far as she's concerned, there's nothing else but LA, nothing but modeling and auditions and nightlife.

She grimaces. "Why? What's the fucking point?"

I scowl at the mess of papers, feeling my face get hot. This is exactly why I didn't want to tell anyone. "You know why."

Her frown deepens. "Why would you want to be a firefighter anyway? You're a promoter. You could make more money doing that than you ever would at the FDNY. And you won't die of lung cancer or whatever before you're fifty."

I roll my eyes and slump back in my chair. "I'm a doorman, not a promoter. And maybe I want to do more with my life than check IDs, Jess."

"Like be a big, strong fireman? What are you, three, watching Sesame Street? Should I get you a play ax too?"

I just stare her down. That's fucked up, and she knows it. Jessie knows how many times I've applied to the FDNY. She knows it's all I've ever really wanted to do—I told her that last year, when we first met.

"Maybe," is all I say finally. "Can't hurt to try again."

Jessie steps closer, forcibly takes my hands in hers, and pulls me off my chair. We're basically eye to eye. I'm not a huge guy—I've got big shoulders, but I'm not quite five-eleven—and Jessie tops five-ten in bare feet.

"I don't want to be mean here," she starts.

I cross my arms. "Then don't."

"Nico." She tugs my chin so I'm looking at her. "They. Don't. Want. You. I'm sorry, but it's the truth. Hon, you need to come back down to reality and join the rest of us."

"Should I say that to you every time you get turned down for a job?" I ask. "You think being a supermodel is any less of a pipe dream?"

Jessie rolls her eyes. "It's not the same thing. And second of all, I'm getting work regularly these days. You...you're not going to be a firefighter, Nico. Maybe it's your record; I don't know. But it's time for you to just give it up. Come back to earth, baby." Her hand slips across my chest and up my neck, and her thumb brushes over my lower lip. "I could probably convince you to stay if you let me."

We stare at each other. And I almost let her pull me closer. I almost follow her into her bedroom, have my way with her, just like she wants, just like sometimes I do. But then she quirks a slim blond brow, like she already knows what I'm going to do. And it's that knowing that makes me sit my ass back down and pick up my pencil.

"I can't," I say again. "I have to study. I don't have time to fuck around."

She flinches a little. I feel bad. No one likes being told they're a waste of time. I know better. I rub the back of my neck.

"Look," I say, softening as I take her hand and play with her knuckles. "I'm sorry. We can hang out when I get back on Friday, okay? You can come by the club if you want."

Jessie presses her lips together and tosses her hair over her shoulder. "Friday. Yeah, okay." She looks at me like she's hoping I'll pull her into my lap and assure her with...something.

But I don't. Because that's not what we do. As much as I yearn for it sometimes— the feel of a body next to mine, the touch of someone who doesn't just want to fuck me, but actually wants *me*, the person, *Nico*—it isn't with Jessie, and it's not fair to make her think otherwise. I might be a weak motherfucker for letting my dick take over from time to time, but I can at least give her that.

———

JESSIE'S COMMENTS are still ringing in my head hours later, to the point where I have to stop studying and go to the gym. But they don't go away. And when I get back, I'm dying to call the one person I know who never has anything but good things to say about what I can do with my life. The one person who's ever believed in me unconditionally.

But I won't. I only let myself call Layla once a week—twice if she texts me first. It's better for us both if we keep a little distance.

So I'm surprised when my phone buzzes on my desk around six, just when I'm getting ready for work. We just talked last night for over an hour. Sometimes it feels like Layla has a sixth sense for when I need her most.

I pick up the phone. Fuck distance. I need to hear her voice.

"Hey, baby," I answer with a grin. "Twice in two days. Lucky me."

I can practically hear her smiling through the phone, and fuck, it feels good. I shouldn't call her baby. I know that. But she'll always be that to me, and I think she knows it too, because she doesn't tell me to stop anymore.

"Hey," she says. "What are you doing?"

"Getting ready for work."

"What are you going to wear?"

It's a familiar game we play. I usually ask her what she's wearing whenever I call, partly because I'm hoping she'll say nothing, and partly because I just want to imagine her.

I look at myself in the mirror. "Same black monkey suit as always. Black shirt, black tie tonight. I'm feeling dangerous."

"Oh?"

I smile into the mirror. We might be three thousand miles apart, but I can still read my girl like a book. She's imagining me right now, and she likes what she sees, so I make a mental note to take this shirt and tie with me to New York later this week. I kind of look like Zorro in this shit, but it's not a bad look.

"What about you?" I ask. "It's Saturday night. What are you wearing?"

"Um..." she drifts off. "Black pants, a blue shirt, and my black boots. The girls and I are about to go out to meet Jamie's boyfriend and his friends. They're business students."

I shove the growl that rises automatically back down my throat. Meeting up with a bunch of dudes sounds like a great recipe for meeting a new boyfriend. I can just see these fuckers now with their shiny leather shoes and their striped shirts and gelled hair, buying Layla and her friends drinks and expecting more afterward. I want to fly across the country tonight and punch every one of them in their entitled fuckin' faces.

Whoa, there. Calm the fuck down, hot shot.

"Good, good," I lie. "I hope you have fun."

"Are you okay? You sound kind of sad."

I snort. This girl can read me like a book too—she always could.

"I—I'm just nervous," I admit as I sit down on the bed. "I...yeah. I've got this test thing coming up."

"What test?"

I'm not going to tell her what it's for. As much as I'd love Layla in my corner, cheering me on, it would be unfair to her. I know her. She'd get her hopes up like crazy, imagining I'm going to be moving back to the city next year.

But it can't hurt to tell her a little right? I could seriously use her optimism. So I tell a white lie.

"Uh, it's for a first responder thing." It's not a total lie. Firefighters are a type of first responders.

"What, like an EMT?"

"Yeah," I say, deciding to go with it. "Like an EMT. I decided...well, yeah. I'm sick of this club shit. And I want to do something different with my life. But first I have to take the entrance exam for the program, so I'm studying for that."

"What?!" Her enthusiasm blasts through my phone's tinny speakers. "Nico, that's *amazing!*"

My face practically splits in half when I hear the excitement in her voice. *This* is what I needed. Not the doubt dripping off Jessie or the worry that my brother projects even though he sent me the test announcement to begin with. Everyone needs someone in their life who really believes in them, and for me, Layla is that person. I never want to lose that.

"God, I wish I could see you right now," she says. "I just want to tackle you. I want to give you the biggest hug to wish you good luck. You can do this, Nico. You're so smart. If you're putting your mind to it, I *know* you'll kick that exam's ass!"

Fuck. It's so easy to forget what this feels like when you've never really had it before. How many people have had this kind of faith in me? I could count them on one hand. Layla gives it so freely, and it feels so crazy good. I close my eyes as she keeps going, not really listening to all of the praise she gives, but just absorbing her enthusiasm, letting her belief in me sink in. Hoping I can take that with me after we hang up.

"I want to see you," I blurt out, interrupting her from her onslaught. "I'm—shit, I should have told you before. But I'm going to be in town for Thanksgiving next week. Do you—are you—you're not going to be around, are you?"

Shit. Of course she's not, you idiot. And fuck me, if I'd really thought about this before, I would have arranged my trip so I was in LA when she got here. Because in all likelihood, this is where Layla is going to be spending her breaks. Her mom lives here now. And I just fucked up my next chance to see her.

"Actually, yeah, I will."

The words are a fresh breeze. My eyes pop open. "Seriously?"

"Yeah. My mom is going to Cabo or something with my grandparents. She wanted me to come too, but I just...I didn't want to."

She trails off, and I can hear the sadness in her voice. I know the last few months have been hard for her. She doesn't hear from her dad much these days, and her mom sends money but never calls. I don't get the feeling that Layla's family was ever that affectionate. Her dad is a typical, domineering Latino father, but it doesn't sound like either of her parents balanced that sternness with warmth. Which is crazy, because when I'm around their daughter, all I want to do is hug her. Okay, and other things too. But it's impossible not to love her.

Despite the sadness in her voice, I can barely hide the excitement in mine. "So, that means I get to see you this week?" Okay, I can't actually hide it at all. And I don't give a fuck.

There's a swift intake of breath, and I can practically see Layla squirming on her bed. Is it the same kind as last year, with the makeshift curtains she hangs around a twin mattress? The one where we used to get it on like rabbits, not giving a shit that her roommate was snoring maybe ten feet away?

The thought of it, snores and all, actually gets me more excited.

"Yes," she breathes, and I'm practically bowled over by another wave of anticipation. Suddenly, I don't give a fuck that I'm really going to New York to take that test. I'm just excited I get to see my girl.

"Layla?"

"Yeah?"

"I know we promised not to talk about it...but are you seeing someone right now, baby?"

She hesitates, and my heart stops in my chest. No. Please, no. I'll take whatever I can get from her. But god*damn* I really need her to be single right now.

"Not really," she says slowly. "Nothing...nothing serious."

I exhale, long and loud. "Good."

"Good?"

"*Good*," I repeat. "Because when I see you, I want to kiss you, baby. And I really fuckin' hope you'll let me."

She doesn't answer at first. Then, a few seconds later, there's a giggle. It's not a yes, but it's on the right track.

CHAPTER TEN

Layla

I'M SITTING ON THE COUCH, TRYING TO FIND SOMETHING, ANYTHING TO DO WITH MYSELF. I hate waiting like this more than anything else—waiting for the stupid phone to ring, waiting for the seconds to tick by, waiting for the moment—whatever is going to happen in it—to occur.

It's been like this for days, ever since that phone call on Saturday night. Quinn's been yelling at me all week to calm the fuck down because I'm so jumpy. But I can't help it. I'm pretty much beside myself with anticipation over seeing him. Seeing Nico.

My phone buzzes on the coffee table, and I leap for it, practically falling over my feet to get it. Behind me, there's a snort: Quinn, studying in the kitchen. But I'm too annoyed to respond, because the number on the front is *not* the one I've been waiting for.

"Not him?" she asks dryly.

I shake my head. "No."

It's Giancarlo, the Argentinian student I met at Fat Black's. He calls a lot, at least two or three times a week. Sometimes I like it, sometimes I don't. Most of the time I send him to voicemail—the guy is a little intense, and I'm not really in the headspace for dealing with a new relationship. But the guy is nothing if not persistent.

I'd never say this to my roommates, but it kind of feels good to be pursued like this. Sometimes, usually when I just can't deal anymore with listening to Jamie and Dev cuddling on the couch, or Quinn's bitching gets to be too much for me, I pick up the phone.

Giancarlo and I have met up maybe three times since that first night, and it's usually led to something similar; a lot of drinking and me waking up in his apartment uptown. But every morning I feel weird as I do the walk of shame back to the subway, avoiding the catcallers and practically sprinting past Nico's old block, where his brother now lives.

I silence the call. Giancarlo is the least of my concerns right now. I go back to freaking out about what's going to happen when Nico shows up.

Will he be happy to see me?

Will he act like it's no big deal?

Will he act like the last six months haven't happened?

Do I want him to?

Quinn looks up from her books. "Can you find something to do over there, babe? You're making *me* nervous."

I look down at the foot that is currently shaking and tuck it under my skirt. "Sorry."

Quinn tugs off her glasses and sets them on the counter. She shuts her book, gets up, then hands me a piece of mail over the back of the couch. It's a familiar envelope, one that makes me relieved and sad at the same time.

"Check from your mom?" she asks.

I rip open the envelope and nod. "Yep."

It's the same check I've started getting every month. Mom doesn't pick up the phone either when I call. She's usually busy at the country club, perfectly happy living at her parents' house. And after September, the checks started to arrive like clockwork every few weeks just as her phone calls became less and less frequent. This time there's not even a note—just cold, hard cash represented by Mom's soft script, all of it a way to mitigate her own pain and guilt.

Still, it's better than my dad, who hasn't called in months. I never thought I'd wish for the day my dad went back to being grossly overbearing, but his silence hurts worse than his sharp words ever did. If it's a choice between them, I'd rather be scolded and yelled at. I'd rather fight than be abandoned.

"When's he supposed to be here?" Quinn interrupts as she puts on her coat.

I glance at the clock that's next to the kitchen. "Any minute."

A phone buzzes, and I practically jump three feet in the air to check if it's mine. It's not.

"Sorry. That's my cue, jumpy," Quinn says as she checks her phone. "That was Shams and Jamie. We're going out so you crazy kids can have some privacy."

"Quinn, you don't have to leave." My reply is weak, and we both know it. There is nothing I'd like more than an empty apartment, even though a part of me knows it would probably be smarter to have a chaperone.

She smirks and pats me on the head like a baby. "You're so cute, Lay. Like a little kid waiting to get up on Christmas morning."

"Yeah, except this package might break my heart again," I grumble.

Quinn looks on sympathetically. "He was an ass," she states simply. "He left you and immediately shacked up with another chick. Don't let him forget it, and you'll be fine."

We're both remembering the day the girls arrived back from summer and found me curled up in my bed. They took me to the nearest diner and plied me with hot chocolate and home fries while I cried my eyes out. It was so much worse than when he'd left.

But it's different now. I know things aren't ever going to be serious between us. They can't, not when he lives so far away. But it feels good to have him in my life again, so much better than when he wasn't. I'd rather have him as a friend than as nothing at all.

With another warning look, Quinn grabs her purse and coat and heads out.

"Don't forget," she calls. "Total. Ass."

The door slams behind her, and I'm left in the worst possible position: alone with my thoughts. Trepidation. Fear. Excitement. Happiness that I will get to see the man I fell so hard for. The man I still love, if I'm being completely honest. Anger. Betrayal. Sadness. Mourning. All of it.

My phone buzzes again. There's that stupid 323 number. Suddenly paralyzed, I watch it light up, then finally pick it up on the fourth ring.

"Hello?"

"Hey, baby! I'm outside your building."

His deep voice erases the cacophony in my head, leaving only one feeling. The excitement bubbles up in my chest before I can stop it. Despite my desire to stay cool, I'm already grinning.

"I'll be right down," I say and hang up before he can answer, suddenly unable to move fast enough. I put on the first shoes I can find—a pair of bright blue stilettos I wore over the weekend. They don't exactly go with my outfit, a black skirt and graphic t-shirt, but I don't care. I just need to get downstairs.

I fly down the two flights of stairs instead of taking the elevator. The sandals pinch my toes, but I can't feel a thing. His energy is magnetic, pulling me close though I can't see him.

I burst outside, where it's sprinkling with a chilly November rain, a layer of clouds low over the city. Broadway is jammed even more than normal at this time of the day, full of honking cars trying to make their way around the square. It takes me two seconds of scanning the traffic before I spot him across the street, exiting from the Union Square subway station. He's all in black: black jeans, black sneakers, his familiar black leather jacket, and a tight black beanie that covers his short black curls. Nico locates me, and his face lights up with that hundred-watt smile I dream about almost every night.

"Layla!" he calls, weaving through the traffic toward me as quickly as he can. But I'm faster.

I skip across the pavement, out to where he stands in between the cars, and tackle him. It's pure impulse; my body couldn't have done anything different as I squeeze him with everything I have, legs wrapped tightly around his waist, arms clasped around his neck. He holds me just as tightly, so tight I can barely breathe.

Our noses touch, and before I can even start to think about standing on my own again, he's kissing me, fast and hard, and I'm kissing him back, with all the urgency and wanting and loneliness that I've been carrying around in the pit of my heart since we said goodbye. Our tongues meet, our hands grapple, and it's not until a chorus of horns blasts that we finally break away with hoarse breaths.

Nico walks us back to the sidewalk and deposits me on the ground, though his arms don't leave my waist. He kisses me again and again, but can't stop grinning that silly grin that I know is mirrored on my face. I can't help it. I don't care about anything else that's happened between us. I'm just so fucking glad to see him.

"*Fuck*, it's good to see you," he says in between joyful kisses.

He grins again, and it lights up the otherwise cloudy day. He laughs, and I laugh along with him. He pulls me into another tight embrace and swings me around the sidewalk, almost causing my feet to smack passersby. I couldn't care less, lost in my laughter and joy.

"Thanks," he says after he sets me down.

"For what?"

Another crooked smile spears me. "For letting me kiss you."

"Oh." A blush rises up my neck. Who was I kidding? I wasn't ever going to say no. "Come on," I say as I take his hand. "No one's home."

With a different light in his eyes, Nico follows me into the building. While we sneak excited looks at each other, I sign him in with the security desk, then lead him up the stairs to my floor.

We practically jog the whole way up. Nico's grasping at my waist from behind, like he can't stand not to touch me. I know the feeling. Every few feet I turn around and grin at him, just to make sure he's really here. I don't know why he's so freaking happy right now—it can't just be because of me or because of Thanksgiving. But I don't care. Right now, we get to be together.

Once we make it inside the apartment, I turn to give him the requisite "this is my new place" speech, but I'm not even able to get a word out before Nico snakes a hand around my waist and pulls me in for another kiss, the kind that would get us both arrested if we did it on the street. The apartment disappears as his hands are suddenly everywhere—my waist, my back, my ass with a grip that will probably leave bruises.

Nico groans into my mouth as his hands find their target. "Bed," he mutters before diving into my mouth again. "Now."

I can't answer, just manage to walk us toward the bedroom I share with Quinn. A different color flashes in my mind with every step I take as we fumble at each other's clothing, too fast to even remove anything properly. There's no time for words; our mouths are everywhere. My knees buckle when I hit the edge of my bed, and I fall into the pillows with Nico on top of me. My wandering hands have managed to remove his beanie at least, and my fingers thread into his thick hair, which has grown long enough in the last three months that I can really grab it.

Nico grunts against my lips, reaching down to shove the hem of my skirt to my hips, rip off my underwear, and undo his pants. I'm slick, ready; I was ready hours ago. Days. In less than a second, he's ripped open a condom and is inside me with a shock that stretches me and makes me shout as he buries himself deep and moans into my neck. My hands find the taut curves of his ass and squeeze.

"Nico!" His name erupts from my throat. This wasn't what I was expecting, and yet, it's like nothing else was ever going to happen.

He huffs my name back, thrusting furiously into me, hurtling both of us toward that edge. It doesn't take long for both of us to come. The friction between our bodies, even fully clothed but for where our bodies join, is too much.

"Fuck, Layla!" Nico moans as he moves even more erratically. He pushes up slightly on his forearms, angles me to take him deeper as he finds the last few, frenzied strokes that make me fall apart completely.

"Nico! GOD!" I shout.

Nico's body shakes right along with me, and he tips his head back to howl at the ceiling. My name, over and over again, like a wolf to the moon. Then our bodies puddle together, his hands on my ass, mine around his waist as we struggle to regain our breaths. Our chests move in tandem. Nico inhales deeply into my hair and sighs with utter content.

"God, I've missed this," he breathes. "I fucking miss *you*."

My breath hitches again. I forgot just how good that deep bass feels, vibrating against my skin. I sigh, my voice suddenly small.

"I missed you too," I whisper and breathe deeply. And in. And out. I seem to have lost all ability to function correctly, so lost am I in him. Talk about zero to sixty in no time flat.

"Damn," he breathes. "God, I...that wasn't really what I was planning to do when I saw you, you know."

Slowly, my heart rate calms, and my senses return. As I consider what's just happened, my bare legs, still wrapped around his waist, shiver in the cold.

"Off," I mumble, shoving ineffectually at his leather-covered shoulders. Jesus, we couldn't even manage to take off his jacket.

Nico frowns, but obligingly pushes up and discreetly refastens his pants before turning back around. I've scrambled fully onto the bed. My underwear has disappeared, but I've managed to yank the thick knit of my skirt back over my legs, now wanting nothing more than to dive under my covers in shame. This isn't how it's supposed to be with us. I'm not supposed to be some cheap, easy piece that he can use whenever he comes to town.

I look at everything but him.

"Hey." The word is gentle, floats like a breeze while I bury my nose into my arms. My feet are cold; I shove them under my pillow at the edge of the bed.

"Hey," Nico says again.

The bed shifts under his weight. It's a crappy mattress, and I roll into him. The contact is the last straw, and I suck in a sob just as it's starting to escape.

Nico slips a few fingers under my chin and forces me to look at him. His eyes are wide, still sparkling with the leftovers of lust, and his dark brows are slightly furrowed with concern. He looks different in ways I hadn't realized, hadn't had time to notice because of how overcome I'd been with desire. His skin is even darker than the last time I saw him, more coffee than cream now, whereas before it had been the color of a rich café au lait. The fine hairs around his forehead have been bleached by the California sun, and if I'm not wrong, he has a few tiny wrinkles around his eyes. He looks like he's been outside a lot, playing at the beach. Having a great time. Without me. With someone else.

Jessie, tall and blonde, rises in the back of my mind. I hiccup another sob as tears spill down my cheeks.

"Aw, baby, please don't cry."

Nico cups my face and kisses me, oh-so-softly, over and over with his full lips. The kisses aren't about sex, but about love and compassion, and they just make me cry harder.

"Please," he whispers as he pulls me against him, tucking my face into the coarse leather. "Fuck, baby, I can't take it when you...what can I do? Tell me what to do."

I grasp at his coat, ignoring the bite of the cold zipper under my palm. The only thing I can feel is my heart splitting in two all over again. Who am I kidding? It was never really back together in the first place.

So he rocks me, then lays us back on the throw pillows shoved against my wall and strokes my back while I cry on his chest. Even through his jacket, I can feel the warmth of his body, the solid blocks of his muscle, the thump of his heart against my hand. I had no idea what was going to happen when we came together again, but I certainly never expected this. I never expected sky-high ecstasy follow by gut-twisting pain.

Nico croons softly until my sobs slowly subside. Eventually I wipe the last tears away, confident no more will come. I sit up, but still avoid looking at him, choosing instead to dash to the bathroom to wash away the mascara I'm sure is all over my face. I don't even look in the mirror until I'm done scrubbing. The cold water is a welcome distraction. Everything is different under the harsh fluorescent lights. We're not reuniting lovers anymore. I'm that sad girl who gets left by everyone. He's the boy that still doesn't want me in the end.

When I come out, Nico is sitting against the pillows, his feet crossed on the floor in front of him, beanie on his lap like a guilty schoolboy. He looks up, dark eyes wide, like he's expecting some kind of punishment.

"I'm...I'm sorry about that," I say.

"Sorry about what? Crying?" He smiles ruefully. "You don't have to worry, beautiful. You can cry on my shoulder any time."

"Of course I can't," I say a little too sharply. "That's just the point. You don't live here. And I just fucked another woman's boyfriend."

My voice cracks a little at the end, and the tears rise again. I walk past him to my desk and flop down in the chair. It's too much—his warmth, his scent, his gorgeous face. I can't sit next to him like this and not kiss him or cry, and I don't want to do either.

Nico scoots over on the bed so only the small frame separates us. He leans over and takes my hand gently in his, brushing over my knuckles like he always does. Or did.

"Don't..." he starts, then trails off. He bites his lip, clearly trying to figure out the right thing to say. "Please don't feel bad, baby. Layla, this wasn't wrong."

"It *was* wrong," I snap bitterly. I jerk my hand away and scoot out of his reach. "I helped you cheat on your girlfriend." I practically spit the word out, hating how my voice quavers around it. Girlfriend. I was that for all of a minute.

"Jessie is *not* my girlfriend." When I don't answer, Nico swears. "Layla, I'm serious. I don't want you thinking that about yourself. Besides, don't you have a boyfriend? That dude from the picture?"

I scowl. "I told you there was nothing serious."

Nico looks at me like he doesn't quite believe me, even if *he*'s the one living with a girl he's sleeping with. If that's not a girlfriend, I don't know what is.

After a moment, he gets off the bed and kneels in front of me, cupping my face between his hands so I have to look at him. He tries for a kiss, but I lean back. So he stops, though his hands stay where they are.

"Listen to me," he says, low and soothing. "This wasn't wrong."

"How can you possibly say that?" I whimper, unable to keep the quavering at bay.

A tear falls down my cheek, and Nico sighs as he gently brushes it away with his thumb. He kisses the spot where it fell, and this time I don't pull away, even though a few more tears fall behind the first.

"Because you're Layla," he replies. "Because it's us. It's always been that way with us. Layla, I couldn't be around you and not need to fucking touch you, baby. And because...shit, because you can't help it any more than me, can you?"

I sniff back a few more tears. "Would Jessie be okay with those reasons?" It's a shitty question to ask, but I can't help myself. He's not wrong about us, but that doesn't make this okay.

Nico drops his hands and looks down at the floor guiltily.

"Probably not," he admits. "But that's my fault, not yours. And maybe it makes me an asshole, but I'm not sorry. Jessie knows the score. I never made her any promises I couldn't keep. And I...fuck. Layla, I could never be sorry about anything we do together. That's the truth."

"But you'll still leave me for another woman."

My words are tart. I can't help it. I know I'm the one who convinced him to go, but it still hurts that he has someone else waiting in the wings.

"That's not fair." Nico stands up and shoves his hands into his coat pockets. "I don't know what you want me to say here. I just wanted to see you. To tell you I'm sorry about how things worked out. I'm sorry I didn't answer your calls and everything—I just...shit, Layla, I just didn't see the point, you know? I missed you, you missed me, but we can't be together. The timing is just shitty. And you know what I'm trying to do out there."

"Is it working?" I ask, although my tone still isn't exactly generous. "Are you happy with everything? With her?"

"Are you happy with him?"

I bite my lip. I have no idea how to answer that question. So I ask another one. "Are you thinking of coming back?"

He can't quite meet my eyes. Of course he's not coming back. He's only been there for six months. It wouldn't be much of a go of it if he turned around and came right back.

"I see," I say. "So you just came here to fuck me and leave me all over again. I get it."

Nico's expression darkens. "That is *not* why I'm here, and you know it." He looks like he wants to say something cutting, just like me, but just as quickly, his expression softens. He sits next to me on the couch and takes my hand. "Five days. I have five days in New York, and I wanted to spend as much of them as I can with you, Layla. For the next five days, I'm yours. Unless you don't want me."

I bury my face in my arms. I can't say that. I could never say that. So instead, I collapse on his shoulder and let him rock me again until the guilt goes away.

"You think we should go to confession?" Nico jokes.

I snort. In a weird way, it would be fitting. I haven't been to confession since my dad left, and since then, I've been sinning left and right. But I don't think I could ever repent for anything I do with this man. Everything about him feels right. Even when it hurts.

So I sit up and wipe the tears away. Again.

"I want you," I admit. "I'll probably always want you."

One side of Nico's full mouth quirks with a half-smile. "Yeah?"

I sigh. "Yeah. But I want to do something different than mope about the fact that you're leaving again. If we only have five days, then I want to do them right."

CHAPTER ELEVEN

Nico

"Okay," I say once Layla stops crying. I'm glad—not because I don't want her to feel what she feels, but because I fuckin' hate it when my girl is sad. And I hate it even more that I'm the one who made her cry. "What should we do, then? Hang out here? Go get some food? When do you take off for Thanksgiving with your friends?"

"Um, never?" She swipes under her eyelids again. "I'm not going anywhere for Thanksgiving."

I know I shouldn't like it, but after she cries, her eyes turn this crazy shade of aquamarine. Right now they shine, and I can't look away.

I frown. "You're not going home with Quinn or one of them?"

She shakes her head. "My roommates are all going somewhere with their families. I'll probably just stay here and get ahead on schoolwork."

Huh. This is not what I expected at all. Despite the fact that Layla comes from so much more than I do, I actually have more of a home to go back to than she does. The shitty one-bedroom where my mother still lives might not be much, but it's the place where I grew up. And when all of my siblings and I get together there, we might drive each other crazy, but it's the most natural thing in the world.

Layla doesn't have that anymore. My chest physically hurts as I realize the pain she'll be going through over the holidays.

"Fuck that."

I shake my head. The idea of Layla sitting alone in this dorm room eating takeout while I'm gorging myself on turkey and sweet potatoes goes against everything I know is right.

"You're coming home with me."

Her eyebrows shoot up. "Seriously?"

I nod. The idea is scary. Between my sisters and my mother, I'm basically feeding her to the wolves. But it also sounds right. I'm home for the holidays. Celebrating with my family, and Layla should be there. It will maybe make up a little for this colossal fuckup that just happened. You don't take someone you don't care about home to meet your mother. And, I realize with an ache in my chest, there's no one I care about more.

I kiss her—because her lips just beg for it, and because the way they open in surprise is too fuckin' adorable not to. I kiss her again, and again, until the room is full of her laughter, chasing away her tears.

"One rule," I confirm. "No holding back, baby. My mother puts something on the table, you gotta eat it."

Layla just giggles. Mother*fucker*. I forgot how beautiful that sound is. My grin is so big I feel like my face is going to split into pieces.

"Okay," she says. "Stuff myself silly. Got it. What can I bring?"

Layla

We meander around Union Square a while, hand in hand, talking about everything and nothing. In a way, it's like he never left. I tell him about my classes—despite Quinn's reservations at the beginning of the quarter, my African Diaspora class has ended up being one of my favorites. Where I went to school in Washington, black history was one-sided, had one month where when you learned anything about it. The teachers usually recycled the same few faces: Martin Luther King, Malcolm X. Sometimes they brought up Oprah.

But in this class I've been learning that because of slavery, Africans came to this part of the world almost concurrently with Europeans. I'm learning about how deeply entrenched racism is in just about every country in the Americas; how deeply entwined that history is with my history, my family's history. And more evidently, Nico's family's too.

"Do you consider yourself black?" I ask him after I mention a book we just finished, Piri Thomas's *Down These Mean Streets*. It's a book that made me think a lot about Nico and his mother when I read it—a memoir of a Puerto Rican man from Spanish Harlem figuring out his identity as both black and Latino. Even though it was written in 1967, a lot of it seemed relevant to Nico's life. At least, so far as I could tell.

Nico blinks, clearly surprised by the question. Whatever he was expecting me to say right then, it wasn't that.

"No," he says finally. "Do you?"

I can't tell for sure, but his expression isn't one I've seen before. Guarded, sharp. Maybe a little scared.

I shrug. "No. But I'm not. My dad is a light-skinned Brazilian, and my mom's about as Aryan as it gets with her blue eyes and blonde hair. It's not really up for discussion."

"And it is with me?"

I glance at him nervously. "You act like I'd think it was terrible if you said yes."

Nico shakes his head. "It's not that. I just...no. No, I don't consider myself black. To start, it's not something most people say to me. I mean, sure, there's some African in there somewhere. My mom's darker than me, from Cuba, right? It's in the blood over there. At the same time, I grew up *boricua*, or Puerto Rican, even if plenty of people would say that I'm not actually from the island. But I grew up speaking Spanish, you know?"

I frown. "I don't get it. If you know you're part black, doesn't that make you black?"

"I think there's a difference," he says carefully, "between having somebody's DNA running through your veins and having it come out on your skin, versus being a part of a culture, you know? Maybe that's what that cat in the book was talking about, what he was struggling with. Like, I could see how it would be hard for him in *El Barrio*, especially in the sixties. That racism you're talking about, it's everywhere. Puerto Rican, Cuban, Dominican, whatever—a lot of people don't want to be seen as black because they think it makes them less Latino. Less...I don't know...pure, I guess."

I twist my mouth around. I wouldn't necessarily look at Nico and say he's black, but you can tell he's a mix of a bunch of things, and that black is probably one of them. He makes it sound like it's a choice he has. It's confusing.

"Shit," he continues. "You wanna talk DNA, most of the people in this country are technically people of color. You know, if you want to go by the one-drop rule. But one drop, ten drops, none of it matters if you don't look the way that people see you." He looks at me knowingly. "I think you know that. Technically you and I are probably the same percentage Latino, whatever that really means. But which one of us looks it, huh?"

I look down at our joined hands. My much lighter skin contrasts with the deep tan of his.

Nico shrugs. "In New York, you know, sometimes it's just about how you show it. I look mixed, so I guess if I wanted people to think I was black, I could be. Other people don't have that choice, like my sisters."

"What do you mean?"

We take a seat on a bench that faces Gramercy Park. We've been walking a while now, having circled the park a couple of times. I like this part of the city. It's quieter, full of classic old brownstones that feel like an Edith Wharton novel. Like someone wearing petticoats and carrying a parasol should walk around the corner.

Nico doesn't say anything for a while, so I wait. His answers have my mind working a mile a minute.

"My dad was half Italian, half Puerto Rican," he says finally. "I think. I ran into him a few times when I was a kid. He was a little dark, but not too dark. I get my hair from him, and also my nose. Selena and Maggie on the other hand, their dad was from Cuba, and dude was like, *black* black. Like, you-wouldn't-be-asking-this-question black. They both have darker skin, much darker than mine." He pauses, and taps his finger to his lips. "Then there's Gabe's dad, David. That asshole's family is from the Dominican Republic, but the way he tells it, he descended from Christopher fuckin' Columbus. He's fair—really fair, like you. And Gabe looks like that, doesn't he? Like, until he opens his mouth and starts talking, it's not really obvious what he is, huh?" Nico pauses again, mulling. "I guess...for some people, maybe the lucky ones, race is a decision more than something they just are. For others, the ones who can't hide it, it's just a fact. To me, that's where you really see racism. That lack of choice. That's why, you know, racism isn't just about how others hate you for your skin color. It's about a system that also makes you hate yourself."

I frown. I've read *Invisible Man*. I've read Kate Chopin. Most of my life I've barely considered myself Latina because other than a few oblique references to my "exotic" black hair or curvy physique, I mostly "present" or "pass," as my professor would call it, like I'm white. I checked the Latino/Hispanic boxes on my college applications mostly to be considered for scholarships and affirmative action, not because I really thought of myself a part of that category.

Until now. Still, I'm not sure that I agree with Nico about everything. Identity isn't just skin-deep, and it's not something I could choose like a mask either because I have light skin. It's hard to claim a trauma I've never personally experienced. Not in the ways that Nico, his sisters, or even my father surely have. But I'm not just written through with my mother's privilege either, totally oblivious to these issues because I don't experience them at all.

I really don't know. But the whole question does make me understand more why my father works so hard to distance himself from people of color. I just wish he had shared those hardships with me instead of pushing me away. Maybe we could have borne them together.

I shake my head. "Tell me about your test," I pivot. "I'm so excited for you."

Nico brightens, clearly happy to change the subject. I don't blame him. It's complicated—maybe too complicated for an afternoon still. If he was paler, I'd be able to see him blush, but Nico just shoves his hands in his pockets and pushes a nonexistent rock aside with his toe.

"Um, yeah," he said. "It's no big deal. It just sounded like..." he sighs, like he's trying to decide whether to tell me something. "I just don't want to do the same old shit for the rest of my life. You know what I figured out this summer? That I fuckin' hate nightclubs. I hate everyone there except K.C. I hate the people. I hate the music. I just want to do something I actually like. And saving lives sounds pretty damn good." He shakes his head and runs a hand over his beanie. "I don't know. I'm not much of a student. I'm not smart like you, baby."

I don't say anything for a long time. Finally, he looks at me, his eyes big and nervous.

"What?" he asks. "You think it's a bad idea?"

His face is full of doubt, and I hate it. I want him to see himself like I see him. I want him to see how smart he is, how kind, how full of joy, full of so much to offer the world. This is why we need each other in our lives. Nico buoys me, makes me think in ways no one else does. Maybe I can do the same for him.

"I am *so* fucking proud of you," I tell him solemnly. "You are super smart—way smarter than me. And I think it is *awesome* you are doing this. You'll kick ass if you give it your best. I know you will."

Slowly, as my words sink in, warmth flows into the endless black of his eyes. I press a gentle kiss to his full lips, but his arms snake around my back, and he holds me close as he turns the kiss into something much more intoxicating. When he lets me go, his face is a curious mix of desire and gratitude. He blows out a long breath.

"Thanks, baby," he says. "I needed that."

We get up and continue walking, circling back down through the Flatiron District and back to the Village. It's a good place to walk. The affluent neighborhood is full of quiet, brownstone-lined streets with trees that still have the last of their fall foliage. Eventually the conversation rolls around to our personal lives. Nico keeps looking around as we pass other men, and he stiffens a little whenever someone with glasses walks by.

"So, your new man," he says, like it's totally normal that he's bringing this up after we just had sex and spent a good part of the afternoon together. "What's he like?"

I give him a funny look. "Well, like I said, he's not my man. We hang out sometimes. Second of all, do you really want to hear about this?"

Nico's face darkens. "No," he admits. "But I probably better. Just in case."

"Just in case what?"

"Just...in case," he says cryptically. He presses a kiss to the back of my hand and gives me a smile that's tinged with pain. "Look. I'm not going to pretend I like it. But...it is what it is. And I need you in my life, Layla, which means I need to hear about what's going on in yours. You're so beautiful..." He hooks my chin with a finger. "Of course you're gonna have a boyfriend. I'm honestly surprised this joker hasn't tried to lock that down yet."

I sigh. Nico shrugs.

"So, who's the bum?" he jokes.

I roll my eyes. "He's Argentinian. A student at City College."

Nico perks up. "Yeah? I wonder if Gabe knows him. What's his name?"

I narrow my eyes. "Giancarlo. Why would Gabe know him?"

Did Gabe tell him about seeing me uptown that one time? Nico hasn't said anything about it, but you never know...

Nico gives me the biggest, fakest, widest-eyed look I've ever seen. "Maybe they have a class together or something. Maybe they can be friends. We could invite him to Thanksgiving too. You, me, my crazy family, and your new boyfriend."

"Only if we invite Jessie."

We're both laughing, and it feels good to joke about this, even if the idea of each other being with someone else makes both of us kind of sick.

"Okay, okay," Nico says after a bit. "Maybe not. I'm not sure I could sit across from Jack in the Box—"

"Gian*carlo*," I correct him.

"What'd you say? Evita?"

"Stop." I nudge him in the shoulder, but I can't help but laugh a little.

"Whatever. El Tango Shithead." Nico grins. "You know I'm never gonna like anyone you go out with, baby. Nobody's good enough for my NYU."

My smile falls, but before I can say anything, Nico slings a heavy arm around my shoulder and lays a thick kiss on my temple.

"What next?" he asks.

I shrug. "I need to study some more this evening. Boring, I know."

He immediately turns us back in the direction of the dorms. But I'm surprised to find another silly grin on his face.

"What?" I ask as he steers us back down Broadway.

"You need to study?" he repeats. "Me too."

I never realized how much fun that sentence could be before now.

CHAPTER TWELVE

Layla

ON THURSDAY AFTERNOON, I'M STANDING NERVOUSLY ON A CORNER IN HELL'S KITCHEN. For the rest of the week, Nico and I haven't been able to see each other as much as we wanted. He was busy with family stuff on Tuesday and Wednesday while I finished a few midterm papers on top of my normal coursework. We were able to grab dinner together (okay, and a bit more than that in my room), but that's about it.

My roommates all left for their various holiday destinations last night, and Nico is staying with me tonight before he goes back to LA in the morning. After dropping his stuff off at my dorm, we left for Thanksgiving dinner. At his mother's place.

Even in the cold, his palm is a little sweaty as he holds my hand tightly. He's nervous too.

"Have you ever brought a girl home with you before?" I wonder as we walk down Forty-Ninth Street. Nico stops in front of an ordinary brick apartment building.

I've heard about this place a few times. You wouldn't know by looking at it that it's breaking down from the ground up because the landlord doesn't bother to do any maintenance, forcing the residents to fix their own broken pipes or electrical problems...or not. Nico doesn't talk much about his childhood, but I know it was hard. I know that his mother moved here when she was young and raised her kids, four of them from three different fathers, in a tiny apartment in an expensive city. I can imagine how hard it was for a single working mother to keep track of her kids in a city like this. There's a reason why Nico got into enough trouble as a teenager to land himself in a detention center.

He squeezes my hand again.

"You're the first," he admits as he looks at the building.

"Good thing we're just friends, then."

For that, I get a strange look, something crossed between confusion and irritation.

"Yeah," he says finally. "Good thing."

I haven't been around this part of the city much. Times Square is only a few blocks east, but once you cross Eighth Avenue, it's a completely different world. Hell's Kitchen is a neighborhood that's changing fast. The street we're on is an even mix of fancy new restaurants and mom-and-pop shops that you know have been there forever. A tapas bar next to a barbershop. A cigar store next to a boutique. Across the street from Nico's building looms the red-brick walls of the local church, along with a fenced parish school.

"Did you go there?" I ask, nodding at the playground equipment locked on a blacktop behind a chain-link fence.

Nico follows my gaze and shakes his head. "Private school? Oh no, we couldn't afford that, NYU. My school was about six blocks from here."

Oh. Of course. I want to smack myself for even asking.

"We'd go to church there, though," he says, nodding at a sign for a Spanish Mass posted next to the church doors. "Every damn Sunday." He winks at me. "You better be careful. If my mother likes you enough, she'll start dragging you with her."

I smile. Is it weird that doesn't sound so terrible? I'm no fan of Mass, but I spent enough time kneeling with my parents at St. Anne's at home that the familiarity sounds...nice. Maybe even nicer if Nico were with me.

"Don't forget," Nico says as he leads me up the steps of his building. "Every bite on your plate."

"Got it. You'll have to roll me out of here." I bare my teeth in a silly grin.

That finally earns me a smile. Nico smacks a loud kiss on my cheek and nuzzles me. "Come on, baby. Let's go eat."

———

THE APARTMENT IS at the top of a third flight of narrow stairs, and the building has no elevator. It's not nice by any stretch of the imagination, but it's not as bad as I thought, considering the way he's referred to it. The white walls are dingy, sure, littered with scrapes and stains, and the bottom floor bears more than a few graffiti tags, but it's not like the walls are literally coming down around us or anything.

Even though it's not as loud as the street, the building is far from quiet. Music vibrates from several doors we pass, and beyond one comes the sound of shouting voices. The halls are narrow, and privately I wonder if Nico's mother, whom he said has had some back problems, has trouble walking up and down these stairs every day. Managing them with four squirrelly kids...eesh.

We stop at an unassuming door, and with another shy smile, Nico unlocks it.

Despite only having six or seven people in it, the apartment feels packed. The front door opens directly into a room that's maybe four hundred square feet. In one corner, an open door peeks into what I assume is the bedroom; through another clamors the sounds of pots and pans.

This is it: the place where Nico became Nico. The furniture has been pushed to the walls to make room for two card tables that take up most of the center, covered in a white lace tablecloth and surrounded by folding chairs. There's barely enough space to fit the setup in front of a faded orange couch, which is covered with plastic. The walls, which look like they haven't been painted in a long time, are littered with posters and paraphernalia: postcards of saints and other Catholic iconography, a few framed, yellowing photos of what looks like Nico and his siblings when they were kids, an ornate, bronze-framed mirror above the sofa. An open closet to my right reveals a stowed Murphy bed and some shelves covered by thin curtains.

Even my dorm room, which I share with Quinn, is clearly split between the two of us. She has her half, which she decorates the way she wants, and I do the same with mine. Things are separate. Neat. This room is completely different. I don't know this family, but I can tell that all of them are scattered throughout the small space. I doubt that anyone but Gabe is a J. Lo fan, just like I'm pretty sure that a poster of an unfamiliar male singer on the opposite wall probably belongs to one of his sisters. I'm guessing that the signed Yankees baseball in the tiny curio shelf by the door belongs to Nico. This apartment isn't just his mother's—it belongs to everyone who was raised here.

"*Tío!*" A loud shriek erupts through the chatter, and a tiny, black-haired girl shoots out from under the table, smack into Nico's legs, which she proceeds to climb like a tree.

Laughing, Nico helps her into his arms and peppers her face with kisses until she falls apart laughing.

"Stop!" she cries, giggling helplessly. "Keep going! Stop! Keep going!"

With one last smack on her cheek, Nico turns the little girl toward me. They look alike. She has his same latte-colored skin and sparkling black eyes. He gazes at her with obvious adoration.

"*Mamita,*" he addresses her, "this is my friend, Layla. Layla, this is Allie, my niece. She's my sister Maggie's daughter." Looking up, he scans the room for Maggie, who raises her hand from the couch. Her face is hard, but it softens a little as she looks at her daughter.

I wave back shyly, then turn to Allie. "*Encantada,*" I say to her.

Her entire tiny face grins, and she addresses her uncle. "*Ella habla español?*"

I can barely understand her, but Nico turns to me with a half-grin that brings out one of his dimples. "You speak Spanish now, baby?"

I flush. "Um, a little. I'm trying to learn."

The half-grin turns to a full one, both dimples puckering his cheeks, and I blush. Across the room, Maggie's eyebrows pop up. Gabe stands up from his seat at the table and sidles around to us.

"Hey, NYU," he greets me with the same nickname his brother sometimes uses. He looks at me knowingly. I wonder again if he's said anything about our awkward meeting.

He kisses me lightly on both cheeks, and I relax into the familiar gesture. My mom's family never does this—they barely touch anyone—but my dad's family does. When I visited them a few years ago, I thought I'd never get all the lipstick off my cheeks. Then again, I wasn't sure I wanted to.

I think of my dad then, and wonder where he is right now. What he's doing. If he's happy now that he's home.

Nico jokes a little more with Allie before he puts her down and pulls out a chair for me at one of the tables.

"You want a drink, baby?" he asks, holding up the paper bag of beverages he brought.

I shake my head. "I want to give your mother the appetizers I picked up. Also, I need to use the restroom."

Nico gives me a funny look and points at the kitchen. "Just through there."

I walk into the kitchen, where two women who could be sisters are arguing in Spanish as they lean over a sauce pan full of rice and a cooked half-turkey. They both are short and slight, barely clearing five feet tall, and with identically pulled-back hair that flies out around their temples. The younger, whom I'm guessing is Selena, Nico's youngest sister, speaks in rapid, irritable Spanish with the other, waving around her long, painted fingernails and making the costume earrings that hang almost to her neck swing wildly. The older woman, obviously Nico's mother, listens stolidly, occasionally clicking her tongue and shaking her head at her daughter's opinions.

They silence immediately when I walk in.

"Hello-*hola*," I venture, holding out a hand. "Um, *yo soy Layla. Un amigo de Nico.*"

"It's *una amiga*. You're a girl," Selena says as she shakes my hand. "And I speak English."

I flush. "Oh, um, I know. Nico just told me that your mom doesn't." This is weird. I don't like talking about the woman as if she's not right there.

Selena smirks. "She can speak a little. And she understands everything, so you don't have to worry."

I flush. "Oh. Right. Okay."

I turn to Nico's mother and hold out my hand. She looks at it for a moment, then shakes it lightly, her hand barely moving.

"Carmen," she says, continuing quietly in heavily accented English. "Nice to meet you."

I nod shyly and hold out the food I brought. I am Cheryl Barros's daughter; I know better than to visit someone's house empty-handed.

Carmen accepts the bag and pulls out the selection of French cheese and baguettes that cost me about half of my budget for the week. I didn't know what to bring, so I just bought the kinds of things my mother would. Carmen takes out a Saran-wrapped lump of *bleu*, then looks at Selena and says something in Spanish that I can't understand.

Selena examines it. "It's cheese, *Mami*. The good kind." She looks at me, and there's a little kindness in her brown eyes.

"Oh. Thank you," Carmen says to me. She holds up the cheese, and then hands it and the bag to her daughter, who moves around the tiny kitchen looking for a plate.

"Of course," I say. "Thanks for having me."

We stand awkwardly until I remember the other reason I came in.

"Um, could you tell me where the bathroom is?" I ask quietly as I look around and see nothing like it. "*El baño?*"

Both women look at me strangely, echoing that same expression I just got from Nico. Okay, I know my Spanish is bad, but is it really *that* bad?

"Over there," Selena says, pointing to the corner.

I follow her gesture and immediately realize why I missed it. The door to the "bathroom" looks like a cabinet, a flimsy stall made of painted plywood that surrounds a toilet installed in the middle of the kitchen. No sink, unless you count the one in the kitchen. A door that would only provide privacy if you're sitting down. That's it.

I swallow and meet both Carmen and Selena's faces straight on. I know then what they're expecting—what they've all been expecting since I walked in. I'm the rich white girl, someone who should think she's too good for this place, for them.

But it's just a bathroom. It's just an apartment. And ultimately, the only things that matter are the people inside it.

So I meet both of their gazes and smile. "*Gracias*," I say and push the door open.

———

IN THE END, it's a pretty normal Thanksgiving. The only difference is that I only understand about ten percent of what's said. All of the Solteros fall in and out of torrents of Spanish that are very different from the stiff, formal version I'm learning. I'm quiet for most of the meal, trying to understand what I can, listening intently whenever Nico leans over to translate.

But besides that, it's the same, just dished out on a mixed set of dishes instead of my mother's china. The half-turkey is just as moist, and they put marshmallows on the pan of sweet potatoes too. There are a few dishes that are unfamiliar, Puerto Rican-style foods that are clearly favorites of Nico's and his siblings'. I make sure to take a second serving of the *arroz con gandules*, the yellow rice dish with peas and peppers. It's not hard—it's freaking delicious.

After a while, the family lapses comfortably into raucous conversation with each other, appearing to forget that I'm even there. Nico and his sisters throw insults at each other over the pumpkin pie, Gabe gets in trouble for talking with his mouth full, and Allie breaks every awkward silence with some adorable phrase. I try to smile when, every so often, I catch Carmen openly examining me, but for the most part, I eat my food and feel thankful that I've been included.

At the end, after Nico and Gabe have finished clearing the dishes away, Carmen looks around the table with a contented expression, in that same way any parent looks when all their kids have come home together.

"*Listos?*" asks Carmen.

Her kids stop talking, and like a wave, everyone stands up.

"Where are we going?" I ask.

It's very abrupt. One minute, we're sitting around, laughing, but also talking kind of awkwardly, and the next, everyone is getting ready to go. Most Thanksgivings I've been to usually end when people migrate to a living room to watch football and loosen their pants while they sink into a food coma. Except, I realize, the television in the corner is maybe big enough for one or two people to watch. And there aren't enough comfortable seats for everyone to relax.

Nico winks as he hands me my coat. "We're going to *Tía* Alba's place," he says. "K.C.'s mom. It's where we always go after the meal at Thanksgiving and Christmas. She puts on a party for all the family."

I cover up, trying and failing to swallow the newly formed lump in my throat. Party? Family?

"Come on, baby," Nico says, taking my hand in his as we follow his family out the door. "Let's go."

CHAPTER THIRTEEN

Nico

It's dark as we follow my family out into the cold night air and start down the street to the high-rise where Alba, K.C.'s mother, lives.

The dinner went well, I think. My sisters were a lot nicer than I thought they would be, being relatively careful only to talk about Layla when she was legitimately out of earshot. Gabe was his usual eager-ass self, working hard to entertain my guest while he threw around big words, trying to sound smart while Allie threw pieces of *pasteles* at his face. Ma was Ma, quiet and watchful as always. I can't tell yet what she thinks of Layla. She's never been the type to trust outsiders, and even if Layla has a last name like Barros, she's still an outsider.

Jesus Christ, I'll never forget the look on her face when she followed my mother out of the kitchen carrying the plate of that smelly fuckin' cheese. I had no idea what she'd brought for dinner. I could have told her that my family wasn't going to eat food that smelled like it had been lost under the couch for two weeks. I'm more adventurous than the others, but even I didn't want to eat that stuff. It smelled like feet.

But her face. Her poor, beautiful, embarrassed face. You could tell she knew the mistake she'd made as soon as she set the platter of that crap on the table. We all stared at it. No one wanted to touch it. And then she turned to me.

"I brought cheese," she said and bit her lip.

Yeah. I was already a goner before she did that, but I can't say no to that face. Not when she looks at me like that, dying for *someone* to like her. So I leaned over, loaded a piece of bread with the slimy blue shit, and took a giant bite while my sisters laughed behind their hands and my brother watched with eyes about the size of our dinner plates.

"Ewwww!" Allie cried from across the table. "He just ate the mold!"

"Hush!" snapped Maggie.

"It's delicious," I said with my mouth full.

Beside me, Layla looked like sun was beaming straight out of her face. I'm not going to lie; that shit tasted like feet too. But I'd eat a whole closet of shoes to make her happy. And after catching her watching us with a gleam in her eye, I think my mother knows it too.

Layla looks up at the high-rise with surprise when everyone starts through the revolving glass door. "K.C.'s mom lives here?"

She was expecting another apartment like my mom's. Maybe something a little bigger that could accommodate all the family, but roughly the same. That used to be the case—Alba, my mother's best friend, used to live just downstairs from us in a bigger two-bedroom place. But the first thing K.C. did when he started to make some money was upgrade his mom's apartment.

It's hard not to be jealous. I'd love to do something like this for my mom one day, but who knows if that will ever happen. Nice apartments usually require all the tenants' names to be on the lease, and that's not something my mom is willing to do.

"K.C.," is all I say, and Layla nods. She's been to his apartment in Hoboken. That place is crazy nice.

We take the elevator up to the fifteenth floor, and as soon as the doors open, salsa music floats down the hall. Layla looks at me nervously.

"I thought this was just a family thing," she says.

I squeeze her hand. "It is, sweetie. But this family is...big. It's a generous term. You'll see."

Inside is a familiar scene to me, but Layla holds my hand like she's about to drown. Alba has a big space, even bigger with her furniture pushed to the walls for the party. Her big table is filled with a potluck of foods, mostly leftovers people brought from their own Thanksgivings. The place is full of people I grew up with. People I call family, but who are really just a part of the extended network that helped raise my mother and, by default, her kids. Countless *tías* and *tíos*, their kids, and their kids' kids scurry around the apartment. Layla watches curiously as I greet most of them with a quick *"bendición,"* accepting kisses to my cheeks from the aunties and a few uncles too, letting the older ones murmur *"Dios te bendiga."* It's close to fifteen minutes before we're able to make our way to the far side of the room, where I can toss our jackets on a pile by the balcony and get us some drinks.

Layla's a champ. She clutches my hand with a death grip, but nods politely at everyone she meets and accepts kisses where they're offered. They look curiously at her, but she's not the only stranger at the party. A few other people have brought their girlfriends or boyfriends to meet the family too. It's hard. I can't come out and say that's what she is, because she's not. Every time I have to say she's just my "friend," there's this stabbing in my chest, so eventually I just tell them she's Layla and let them make whatever assumptions they want.

Most of the people here are Puerto Rican, which means the older ones mostly speak Spanish, but the younger ones, like me, speak English peppered with Spanish or a mix of both. There's a playlist blasting a mix of Latin music from Alba's stereo, and already the group is getting boisterous. Even the line of men standing against the picture windows like a line of pigeons are starting to move a little with the music.

Beside me, Layla polishes off her cup of *coquito*. "Wow," she says. "That is *really* good."

I smirk, then take her cup for a refill. Alba really went all out this year. *Coquito*, the coconut and rum drink, is usually something we have at Christmas. I wonder if my mom asked for it since I won't be around this year. K.C. was moaning all last week about missing it since he was hired for a big party in Vancouver over the weekend.

Layla starts to loosen up. She still looks a little like a scared deer, but her hips are starting to undulate to the music, some random bachata song.

I nurse a beer, but my eyes stay on her. She catches me watching and immediately turns red. It's fuckin' adorable.

I snake a hand around her waist. "You want to dance, baby?"

"What?" Maggie's loud fuckin' voice blasts from at least three people over. "*You want to dance? Since when do *you* dance?*"

I roll my eyes. My sister had a few drinks already back at the apartment, and the people she's standing with shake their heads and laugh. There is nothing Maggie likes more than giving me shit. I give her a rude hand gesture behind Layla's back, which Maggie ignores. Behind her, Selena covers a laugh, and across the room, Ma watches us with interest.

"I can dance," I insist. I look back at Layla. "I *can* dance."

"I didn't say you *can't*," Maggie says as she moves over to us. "I said you don't. You hate bachata. You don't even like salsa."

Layla watches our exchange curiously, but stays silent. I feel myself turning a little red.

"Maybe I like it better now," I say, starting to move my shoulders and hips a little with the music. I don't know what it is, but something about being here with Layla makes me want to show off. "Maybe I just needed to stop hearing it every damn day like I did living with you. I can only take so much Marc Anthony, Mags."

Maggie pouts, but she can't totally hide her smile as I start moving a little more. I'm not a great dancer or anything, but I have a few moves. I'm not doing it for her, though; I'm doing it for Layla. I'm doing it because of the way her mouth falls open as she watches my hips. Just then, the music shifts. The bright guitar of the bachata fades away, and a sultrier beat replaces it, accompanied by the telltale horn section of salsa and the crooning voice of Marc Anthony, the man himself. I recognize the tune—it's hard to live in New York and not hear this voice. Especially living with Maggie, the man's superfan.

"Well?" Maggie asks Layla. "You gonna dance with my brother or what?"

Layla flushes, but I'm already halfway to the dance floor, hand at my stomach as I step backward with the beat. God, this girl turns me into such a fuckin' cornball. But I don't care. She's laughing, and I'm feeling on top of the world tonight. If all I ever did for the rest of my life was make her laugh, I'd die a happy man. So I hold out a hand.

"Come on, baby. I'll teach you how to move."

Layla lets me lead her to the center of the party crowd, and she watches carefully as I take both of her hands and instruct her on the steps, just like Ma taught me when I was a kid.

"Move your right foot back, two, three, left foot forward, two, three. Yeah, like that, sweetie. On your toes, not your heels. Yeah, you got it."

She follows my feet, and after a bit, she starts to move naturally. It's a basic step, much more basic than some of the moves other people are doing. The real experts are the older ones who moved here from one of the islands or who grew up when salsa really got going. Layla's doing pretty good, actually. She might look like a white girl, but she doesn't move like one.

Back and forth we move, until I get bored. I pulled her close. Her flowery scent surrounds me and makes it hard to think. It's been three days of this. Three days of hugs in public places, of holding hands across a dinner table or a coffee shop, of one quickie in her room on Tuesday before her roommates returned from their classes. I'm ready to do a lot more than that. I want to take my time with her, again and again. I want her to know how much she means to me, get as close as we can for as long as we can until I have to go. Tonight is ours, and I want to make the best of it.

"Get ready, baby," I say.

Before she can ask for what, I slip a hand around her back and twist her around the combos my mom taught me long ago. Ma loves to dance, so she made Gabe and me both learn with her. I bitched about it a lot when I was a teenager, but I'm sure as fuck glad she taught me now.

I turn Layla through one, two, three separate maneuvers that include ducking her under one of my arms and pulling her backwards against my chest. With the last one, she yelps a laugh, catching the attention of a few other people on the floor. Plenty of people have been watching us—Layla really doesn't know how beautiful she is. But now Ma stops her conversation with Alba and zeroes in on us as I continue to turn Layla around the floor. She's not sure about Layla yet; my mother is a hard nut to crack. But when Layla laughs, I think I can see Ma soften.

"You're doing pretty good, baby," I say as I turn her around some more. "You got the hips down, that's for sure."

I spin her out and do a little shimmy of my own. Watching me, Layla trips over her own feet. It's hard not to feel smug as I catch her and pull her flush against my body. I know that look in my girl's eyes. It's that look she gets when I've done something that gets under her skin. She's thinking about one thing, and now it's all I can think about too.

I hold her waist in the middle of the crowd. We're both breathing hard now; there's a thin sheen of sweat on Layla's brow, and her rose-petal lips are open slightly. Our eyes meet. In the middle of this loud, crazy room, we're both silent.

If this were a club, with dimmed lights and people we didn't know, we'd already be all over each other. I probably would have dragged her to a dark corner somewhere to cop a feel, drive her crazy with my fingers, watch her lose herself in the dark. Or maybe we'd have already left, gotten lost on some street corner or in the back of a cab, racing against time to reach the moment when we have to come together, public place or not. Central Park. The bathroom at AJ's. An alley by her dorm. How many times did we forget where we were, who we were, out of the blind need for each other's bodies?

I'm wearing the same black shirt and pants I told her about last week, the ones that made her growl and kept me up half the night fantasizing. I've unbuttoned my shirt a few buttons and rolled up my sleeves to combat the heat, and by the way her gaze drifts down every so often, it's clear she likes the way my tattoos poke out on my chest and over my elbow.

She's wearing a little black dress, one that's a far cry from her club wear, but which does fuckin' nothing to hide her curves. Caught slightly with sweat, the dress clings. Fuck me. If we were even close to alone, I'd have already torn it off.

But we're in a room full of my relatives, many of them watching the show we've put on, watching how the new girl, the *blanquita* (a term I've heard a couple of times when they thought I wasn't listening), is going to fare at the family party. As Layla catches her breath, she looks around, blue eyes wide. The joy disappears from her face.

"You okay?" I step closer.

Layla presses her lips together and waves a hand at her face. "Yeah. I'm just going to get some air, okay? It's hot. There's a balcony, right?"

I nod and point toward an open door that's covered by retractable shades. "Over there. I'll get you another drink."

Layla escapes to the balcony while I go to the kitchen for another beer and a bottle of water for Layla. When I come back out, Gabe is waiting for me in the hallway.

"Hey, *papi*," I greet him, tossing him the water. I reach back into the kitchen and grab another.

"You were tearing it up out there with NYU," Gabe remarks as I shotgun my beer. Shit, that's good.

I nod. "Yeah, she was doing pretty good for a first-timer."

We stand there for a second, gulping down our drinks. Then it gets awkward.

"So?" he asks.

It's the first time we've had a second without the fuckin' sonar ears of the women in our family. Allie skids by on the floor, having lost her shoes a while ago so she can slip and slide around the hardwood floors in her tights.

I polish off the rest of my drink "So what?"

"The test, dickhead. How did it go yesterday?"

I glance around, making sure no one is listening, and most of all that Layla can't hear us.

"I don't know," I say with a shrug. "It didn't seem that hard to me. But it's still a pretty fuckin' long shot."

Gabe nods, but to my surprise, he claps me on the shoulder.

"If anyone can do it, it's you, bro," he says. "For real."

I study him like he's joking. Gabe's softer than the rest of us, being the youngest and all, but no one in my family gives out compliments too often. We love each other, but Carmen Soltero's kids are realists.

"Thanks, man," I say. "That means a lot."

Gabe shrugs like it means nothing, but doesn't meet my eye. Besides my mother, he's the one I worry about most. He's never said it, but I know he didn't want me to move away. It's hard enough being a dude in this family without being the only one.

I toss my can into a trash bin and carry the water out to the party. A glance around the room tells me Layla is still on the balcony. I cross the room and push open the blinds, ready to pull my girl back into another round of dancing/foreplay. But what I see stops me in my tracks.

Layla stands at the balcony, looking out at the city, her arms wrapped around her waist. She's not doing it because it's cold outside, even though it is hovering just above forty. It's a posture I know and hate—she only does it when she's upset. Scared, maybe.

"Hey," I say, immediately dropping the water on a lounge chair and crossing to her.

She turns, clearly trying desperately not to cry.

"Whoa." I pull her close, sweaty shirt be damned. "Hey, what is it, sweetie? What's wrong?"

My words don't help for shit. She just starts crying into my shirt, her hands curling tightly at my collar. I keep one hand at her waist and slide the other up her back to the nape of her neck, cradling her against me. I don't know exactly what's wrong, but I can guess. She hides it well, but my girl's been carrying a lot.

"Do you know," she says once her tears finally stop. "Neither of my parents called me today? I know they're out of the country, but it's not like they can't afford a phone call." She sniffs against my shoulder. "I'm sorry. I—"

"It's okay, baby," I tell her as I stroke up and down her back. "You got nothing to be sorry about. I know it's hard not being with your family around the holidays."

"No," Layla says. "No, that's not it." She lifts her head and looks at me even while she wipes her tears from under her eyes with her fingers. "It's...I never had this, you know? In my family, Thanksgiving is a formality. Mom usually hired a caterer, or maybe we'd go eat with one of my dad's partners. At Christmas, we'd exchange gifts in the morning, and then spend the rest of the day at church. I..." She breaks away for a second to wipe her eyes. "And I miss it. Isn't that crazy? I actually miss those weird, cold holidays. Because it's what I knew."

I rub her shoulders. "Of course you do, baby. It was home."

She sniffs and looks back toward the party. "But then I'm here. There's so much love in there, Nico. It's amazing. And it...well...it just made me feel really alone for a second. Like, I'm missing what I never had at all." She rubs her forehead. "I'm sorry. I didn't want to ruin your night. Really, I'm so grateful you brought me here tonight."

She looks out to the city twinkling below. Alba's apartment looks east toward Times Square, and from here the lights of the Broadway theaters and billboards glow between the buildings. Layla's face is lit by the glow too, a sort of blue hue that fits her mood. My girl is incredibly beautiful, but she's also so sad. I hate it.

"They're a pain in the ass." I jerk my head toward the party. "Always bitching at each other, getting into trouble. One wrong thing, and you get a house slipper thrown at you—I'm not kidding. They're like fuckin' heat-seeking missiles."

Layla chuckles.

"No family's perfect, Layla," I tell her as I press my forehead to hers.

"True," she agrees. She closes her eyes and sighs. "I do miss mine."

Fuck. There's not much I can say to that, and I'm not going to blow it off like it's not important. Her parents aren't together anymore, and she has no siblings. No matter how distant or cold they might have been, the family she had is gone. I have the same one as ever, full of drama, judgment, insecurity, and, yeah, love. I never thought I'd be the luckier of the two of us, but here we are.

So, I hold her tight and let her feel what she feels. We look out to the city. Layla shivers.

"Come on, sweetie," I say. "Let's go back inside."

We walk back to where the party is in full swing. Even more "relatives" have arrived, and the music has been turned up some more. Even Ma is on the dance floor, swishing her skirt around her knees with the first smile I've seen in a while. I have to grin. My mother doesn't smile that much, so when she does, I know it's because she's truly happy.

"You want to dance some more?" I ask Layla, still holding her hand.

She shakes her head. "Not yet. I just want to watch for a bit. You should if you want, though."

I don't. I don't want to be anywhere but with this work of art next to me. That's what she is to me, and I wish I could tell her without making us both miserable tomorrow morning. Instead, I lean against one of the walls and move her so she's sandwiched between my legs and leaned against my torso while we watch the party. I wrap an arm across her sternum, and the other around her waist, like two solid locks around her broken heart, and if I'm being honest, mine. It's already getting late, and my flight leaves early so I can be back in time for work. Tomorrow I'll feel like shit, having to leave this girl who makes me feel like I can do anything, who trusts me with her soul, and who I want to trust with mine.

But I don't want to think about that right now. I nuzzle into Layla's neck, a low hum escaping from my chest after I inhale her floral scent. We are both full of words we can't say, promises we can't keep. But what we feel—neither of us can hide that.

"I'm glad you're here," I say as I set my chin on her shoulder.

Layla sighs. "Thank you for bringing me," she whispers, turning her face to mine.

I know I shouldn't. I'll catch a torrent of shit about this for a month, from my mother, my sisters, every Puerto Rican in a twenty-block radius wanting to know who this is, this first girl I've ever brought home. The first girl I've danced with. The first girl I've ever kissed in front of all these people.

But I don't care.

Tenderly, I press my lips to Layla's. It's a church kiss, the kind you'd do in a chapel full of people. It's not our most passionate kiss, the kind that makes me want to rip both our clothes off. Totally chaste, especially by our standards. But it's a kiss full of those words that neither of us will say out loud. It's a kiss I'll never forget.

CHAPTER FOURTEEN

Layla

It's past two when we finally make it back to my dorm. The building is empty; almost everyone has gone home for the break, so our footsteps sing on the stairs, echoing up the concrete stairwell until we get to my floor. There's a nip in the air, almost like it might snow for the first time this winter. Snow will always make me think of Nico—our first kiss was shadowed by soft flakes.

When my door closes behind us, in the apartment that's still dark, we face each other, consumed by the sudden silence.

Nico was quiet the rest of the night—careful with me, always holding me, touching me. We danced a bit more, mostly to slower songs, but for the rest of the night, even if we were chatting with some distant relative or one of the impossible number of aunties at the party, he always had at least one arm around me, one hand touching me somewhere. His blatant affection in front of his family was unexpected, but also its own weird kind of foreplay. Because as soon as we're inside, that feeling, that desire to be close, blooms bright within me.

He follows me into my room, and practically runs into me when I stop suddenly and start to undress for bed. Nico watches, transfixed as I remove my shoes, tights, the thin sweater I had over my dress.

"Help me out here, will you?" I just want to get into bed with him. Curl up with his arms around me. Get closer than we've been all night. Than we've ever been.

"Jesus," he breathes as he pulls the zipper down my back. The thin straps hang a bit off my shoulders, and then the silky fabric falls to the floor.

"You are so goddamn beautiful, Layla." Nico draws a line down my vertebrae.

I shiver and smile shyly over my shoulder. "You always say that."

His black eyes are full of promise. "It's always true."

Up until now, his touch has been tender, but strong. All night long. We danced a few more times, but no more fancy moves. It was all holding me, guarding me from the scary things in the world, even though he knew what hurt was on the inside.

Now his touch is just as strong, but as he places his hands on my bare skin, his strength and tenderness is threaded with a different kind of electricity too. He presses his hands all over me, drawing his fingers, palms over my skin as if to memorize the contours of my body, but also to imprint his touch there so it won't ever leave. Almost a massage, but I'm anything but relaxed. My skin buzzes with each powerful handprint.

I turn around to face him, and his brow furrows with concentration as he continues the pressure: over my chest, between my breasts, down my stomach, where they fan out over my waist. His eyes follow his hands, brows crinkled as he memorizes my body. As his palms slide behind, over my ass, and then he's crouching, following that same forceful yet tender touch down the outside of my thighs.

He presses his nose into my thigh and inhales deeply. I want to grab his hair and pull his face more to the center, but he has his own agenda.

"I can't," he murmurs into my leg before he stands back up. "It's too...God, it's too fuckin' much."

There's no one here. No roommates to worry about. No students on the other side of the thin walls. We can be as loud as we want, wherever we want.

But we're quiet, the only sounds between us our breaths, both suddenly hoarse as we stare at each other. Nico's chest is suddenly heaving, and his breath is ragged. Harsh. My chest feels like it's being squeezed, and a wave of longing suddenly erupts all over my bare skin. He's right in front of me, staring at me while a muscle ticks in his jaw. We're both paralyzed by how much we want each other, unable to move.

"Nico," I say, barely able to get out the word.

His eyes open wide, and my voice, small and timid, cuts through the silence. My eyes are watering, not from tears, but from desire. I want him so badly I can't see straight. I wonder if it will always be like this.

"Please," I say. I swallow hard, barely able to do it because my throat is so tight. "Please."

Nico frowns, almost like he's in pain. His mouth—that full mouth, with the lower lip that's soft, plump, begging for me to suck on it—falls open.

Then he's full of action. His hands find my thighs, and with a quick, graceful movement, I'm lifted up and set on the desk behind me. He snakes a hand behind my neck while the other clasps my back, and with a determined, forceful look, he sets his mouth to mine.

It's the kiss we've both wanted all night. While we sat next to each other at his mother's apartment, our knees continually touching, feet brushing under the table. While we walked hand in hand to Alba's party, body to body in the packed elevator. While we twirled and turned around the crowded dance floor. Even while we stood against the wall together, when he wrapped me in his strong arms and made me feel safer than I'd felt in months.

All that time, I still wanted this kiss. I was starved for this closeness.

It's the kiss we wanted and couldn't have until now, when his fingers and mouth possess me with a kind of certainty I lack. My hands move on their own, up his chest, then down his arms, clutching the bulges of his biceps, that raw, animal strength that he controls so elegantly. His touch is delicate yet firm as we move in a dance reminiscent of the one we did earlier. All of it says the same thing he murmured to me all night.

I got you, baby.

He doesn't say it now, but the words release knots in my shoulders and back I didn't know were there, a ripple that flutters through me. Nico senses the change. The hands at my neck and waist relax, and his mouth breaks away as he rubs his nose against mine. He kisses me again. Once. Twice. Worries my lower lip between his teeth a little until I squeak. It's only then I can feel his smile against my mouth.

"Do you ever feel this way?" he wonders as his mouth travels across my face, down to my neck where he sucks, hard, at that soft spot just below my ear.

Goose bumps immediately erupt all over my skin. "What way?"

His hands slide up my thighs, then grab my ass and squeeze. "Like we can't get close enough?"

My arms wrap around his neck so I can press my body against his. I want to feel every edge of him, hard and soft. I want there to be nothing between us. Not even a sliver of light.

"Layla," Nico says in between kisses that seem to grow deeper and deeper, like he wants to swallow me whole and also dive into me himself. "Layla."

It's then I realize that he's waiting for me to take the next step. He'll do this all night—just feel our bodies together, the way our skin produces a new kind of warmth. He'll keep rubbing his hands over my skin with a pressure that's demanding, but never out of control. Kiss after hungry kiss. Touch after starving touch.

He's waiting for me to tell him he can let go. Even now, when I can feel the shape of his desire throbbing between us, the length of him that begs to come inside, he protects me.

"I know one way we can," I finally say.

Nico watches as I press him back just an inch or two, and proceed to undress him. Like he did with me, I take my time about it, unbutton each button of his black shirt, push the tailored material over his broad shoulders, and watch it fall to the ground. I slide my hands over his chest, pausing slightly as I trace the delicate work of the tattoo over his chest. Half-compass, half-clock. A reminder that he has only one life, one direction to find. A direction he's searching for now in California.

The thought makes my chest squeeze, and I push it away. As if sensing my shift, Nico catches my hand and kisses it.

"Do you know what I'm thinking right now, baby?" he asks, the deep bass of his voice pulling me out of my brooding.

I blink at him. It's written all over his face, just like I'm sure it's written across mine. But we've done this before. And just like I don't want to think about the fact that he's going back to California tomorrow, I don't want to think about what happened the last time we said the word love.

They tell you how good it feels when you find love for the first time. But no one ever tells you how much love hurts when you have to let it go. And the way I'm feeling tonight, I'm not sure I can take it if I hear him say it again just to walk away. I'm not sure my heart can take it.

"I know," I finally say. "I know."

Nico nods, that same delicate pain I feel is etched over his strong face. His gaze drops to my lips as he reaches into his pocket.

"Please," he says as he presses a condom into my hand. "Please let me come closer."

I take the condom, and he kisses me, slow and steady, absorbing the waves of emotion, pain, love, tenderness that wash over us again and again. Still controlled. Still waiting for me to take this at my own pace.

We're both silent as I unbuckle his pants and push them and his briefs down. I hold him in my hand for a moment, and he shudders. It would be so easy to take him again, with nothing between us. So easy. So natural.

But I don't want to regret anything I do with Nico. Not ever again. So I roll the condom on while he groans slightly, then guide him toward me. He looks down, watches for a moment as he finds his way inside, finding that place where his body fits perfectly, deeply within mine. Then he finds my face again, his black eyes fathomless.

"Come here," I say as I slip my hands around his neck.

So he does. But this time his kiss isn't measured, isn't quite as thorough. It's hungrier, belying the control he's losing. The rest of him is still, though his hands take hold of my thighs so tightly it almost hurts. It turns me on even more.

"I don't want to move," he says in between kisses that are losing their control. "I don't want to ruin it."

I tilt my hips, taking him even further. He groans.

"You won't," I say as I bite his lip. "I need it just as bad as you do."

Slowly, slowly he obeys. His lips float over mine, his breath uneven as he starts to move.

I fall back, only barely registering that he catches me with a strong arm. His lips catch one of my nipples as he picks up his pace, his cock moving in time with his lips.

"Nico," I whisper, my voice hardly more than a whimper.

My legs wrap automatically around his waist as he thrusts even deeper. A moan erupts from deep within my chest. My words are no longer any language I know.

"I got you," he keeps saying against my neck, my chest, my ear, his breath now coming in torn waves. "Let go, Layla."

It's not just the friction of him as he moves steadily, finding that spot only he seems to find. Nor is it the way his lips feel, feather-light as they drift staccato touches over my neck and collarbone, or the way his hands knead the fullest parts of my body with aplomb. It's all of it—his complete and utter *want* of me that undoes me in the end.

The world explodes behind my closed eyelids as it hits me, a detonation of color and light that's brighter than the center of Times Square itself. My body tightens; every muscle seizes, and I squeeze him tightly, wanting him deeper still as I fall apart around him.

"Layla," he shudders, his hips continue to move. "Baby. I. *Fuck*."

His words dip into unintelligibility right along with mine. He calls my name out just as I call his. We fall into each other, completely laid out as the world envelopes us together.

"Layla." My name echoes across his lips. "Layla."

———

"I CAN TELL ABOUT YOUR MOM," I say much later, when Nico and I are curled up in my twin bed. I lie on his chest, tracing the outlines of the compass tattoo. It splays over his heart, about a hand's width. He has one arm draped over my shoulders, the other tucked behind his head.

"What's that?"

"That she's not here legally."

Beneath me, he tenses. It's not a secret—he told me a long time ago that Carmen doesn't have papers—but it's not something he likes to discuss. A few seconds pass before he replies.

"How's that?" he asks finally.

"Little things. You can see the difference." I massage his tricep, which has suddenly gone stiff. "Between her and K.C.'s mom. Alba is so open, and it seems like she's done all right for herself."

Nico relaxes a bit. "Well, K.C. paid for that apartment a few years ago. But yeah, *Tía*'s done pretty good. She got a job housekeeping at one of the big hotels and then started her own business."

"She just seems comfortable. Your mom seems...I don't know. Closed off, somehow."

My fingers trace a path down his sternum, in the hollow between his chest muscles. He's smooth there, only a few stray hairs. The black ink on his chest and encircling most of his right arm shines in the moonlight.

"Plus, you know, her apartment gives it away too," I add. "The bathroom doesn't exactly meet housing code. I'm guessing people don't live in that kind of place legally."

Nico snorts. "You'd be surprised, NYU. Plenty of people live in even worse places just for cheap rent." He sighs. "So it was that bad, huh?"

Shit. I'm such a jerk. Here I am, with the clueless audacity to explain to Nico about his family's own semi-poverty. And now he's clearly thinking that somehow I'm put off by it all, when that's the last thing I'm thinking.

I sit up so I can lean over him. My hair falls over my shoulder, and he immediately starts to play with it, studiously avoiding my gaze.

"Hey."

I wait until he looks up, his black eyes big and vulnerable.

"It's not the Ritz," I say, "but it doesn't have to be. It was warm and full of people who love each other. I don't give a shit about the bathroom or any of that. It felt like a home."

Finally, the tension in his body releases. Both of his hands slide up my back and pull me down. His kiss is soft.

"You feel like home to me," he says very, very softly. "You always do."

I close my eyes as he kisses me again. My mouth opens to him reflexively, wanting to take him deeper. But as he rolls me onto my back, ready to start round two of what never seems to fade no matter how many times we do it, one thought keeps screaming through my head.

"I could come with you," I blurt out when his mouth moves to my neck.

He stops, pushes up on his hands so he's looking down at me with a frown. "What?"

"To California," I rush on. "I could move there. Finish the semester at NYU and leave. Apply to transfer in the spring. It's not too late, I—"

"Layla," Nico says, and the resignation in his voice makes my chest ache.

"Please." My voice shakes around the word, and with it, another round of tears threatens. God, I just can't stop them tonight.

But he needs to know. I want to know about his family not because I think they're strange, but because tonight I felt like they were people I could maybe be a part of one day. It's a feeling I didn't even know I wanted until I met this man. Here with him, in this safe cocoon of love and sex and warmth, one thing is certain: that when we're together, things are better. I'd give up everything I had if it meant we could stay this way for good.

But Nico doesn't smile. He doesn't laugh and kiss me again with relief, tell me he's been dying for me to suggest it again, that he regrets ever leaving. He just stares at me, his mouth hanging open slightly.

"The answer is no, isn't it?" I ask, utterly crestfallen.

Nico exhales, long and heavy. His head hangs. "Yeah, baby. The answer's no."

I roll out from under him and curl into myself, willing the pain lancing through my chest to abate. It does not. Not even close.

"Layla..."

"Why? Why don't you want me?"

"Baby, come on. It's not that. You know it's not that. Layla, will you look at me, please?"

I turn back over so we are both on our sides facing each other. I'm naked, but it's my emotions that are making me feel this vulnerable. Like I'm about to break.

"Why did you come to New York?" Nico asks as he takes one of my hands between us and strokes a finger over my knuckles.

My throat is too choked to answer.

"Do you know who you are?" he continues, gazing at our joined hands. "Like, one hundred percent? Who Layla is, what you want, what you need, in ways that you know aren't going to change?"

Yes, I want to say. I want you. I need you. But instead I gulp the words down. Because he and I both know the real answer.

"No."

Nico's black eyes drill through me, like he knows who and what I am in a way I still don't. I could say I have everything figured out, but the truth is, the only thing I feel like I know is him. That I love him.

"I'm not letting you give this up," he says. "You came to New York to figure that out. You need to be here. I'm not letting you get lost in my life when I don't even know what the fuck my life is supposed to be yet. I don't even know where I'm going to be in the next few months."

I frown, confused. "What does that mean? Where would you be if not LA?"

He blinks sharply, but then turns his gaze to our hands. "I'll probably be there. But I...I just don't know, Layla. I have shit to figure out about myself, about what I'm doing with my life. And you do too."

They're good reasons, all of them. What he's saying makes sense. But all I hear is the same truth I hear from my mother every time she pushes off my next trip to visit, or every time my dad doesn't answer his phone. *I don't want you.*

"I think you should go," I whisper, curling away from him. Oh, my chest hurts. My heart feels swollen, like it's about to explode. My lungs feel like they've turned to stone. I can't breathe. Why doesn't he want me? Doesn't he feel what I feel?

"Layla," Nico says, placing a hand on my shoulder and trying to turn me toward him. I don't move. "Baby, please. I just want what's best for you. I...I love you. You know that, don't you?"

That's when the tears finally let go. Those words should feel good, but they cut so deeply, just like I knew they would. Does he love me? I know he means it, but I'm not convinced he understands it. Those words—those three simple words that I'm always yearning to hear from him—don't make me feel better; they only make the pain worse. I may be young, but I know that's not what love should do. It shouldn't make you feel abandoned. Like you're nothing.

"Please," he murmurs behind me. "Let me stay. Just for tonight. Please."

I sigh, keeping my face toward the wall so he won't see the goddamn rivers sliding down my cheeks. "Okay." It hurts, but I also know I can't say no to him. I could never ask him to leave and truly mean it.

"Will I..." he asks tentatively as he gently strokes my back. His fingers fit into the groove of my spine, sliding down and scooping back up. "Will I get to see you at Christmas in LA?"

I can't speak for a moment. This hurts so much. And the idea of sitting in that big stupid house, having vapid conversations with my grandparents, pretending everything is fine. Seeing Nico during the day only to know he's going home to another woman at night.

It's too much to take.

"No," I say quietly, keeping my eyes trained on the wall in front of me.

His heartbeat behind me quickens for a moment, then calms.

"Okay," he says. The single word is full of so much understanding. "Okay."

III

THE TANGO

CHAPTER FIFTEEN

DECEMBER 2003

Layla

I TAP MY PENCIL ON THE TOP OF MY DESK. TAP-tap-tap-tap-tap. IT'S A MACHINE GUN. IT'S a woodpecker. It's a...

"Layla!"

I turn around. "What?"

Quinn tosses her book on the bed and crosses her arms. "What do you think?"

Our bedroom door opens, and Shama pops her head inside, quickly followed by Jamie.

"Everything all right in here?" Shama asks.

I frown at Quinn. "It's fine."

"Oh, that's rich." Quinn stands up and makes a big show at brushing off her yoga pants. She recently started wearing them everywhere after someone at the gym told her she had a nice ass. If I have to hear about her squat routine one more time, I swear to God, I'm going to scream.

Instead I glare at her. "What's that supposed to mean?"

"It means it's the same damn answer you've been giving us for weeks, Sylvia Plath. Everything's 'fine.' Your soup is 'fine.' Your classes are 'fine.' You haven't even wanted to go out since Thanksgiving. I know you're still pining over Special Delivery—"

"Oh my God, *don't* call him that, Quinn."

"It's getting ridiculous!" she explodes, falling back onto her mattress. "He's gone. He doesn't live here anymore, and he didn't want you to be with him. I know it's sad, Lay, and I know you were into him, but you have *got* to move on, babe!"

I stare at the ground, trying unsuccessfully to let her words roll off me. Does she think I haven't told myself this a thousand times? We've had this conversation. And to be honest, it hurts a little to have her minimize a relationship when she knows that "into him" doesn't even begin to cover how I felt about Nico. How I still feel. How painful it still is.

"I want my friend back," she continues. "I want fun, snarky Layla who liked to joke in bars and was up for late-night study sessions. Do you know what time you went to sleep last night? Nine thirty. My great-grandmother doesn't go to bed that early."

Shama and Jamie edge their way into the room and sit down on my bed. Quinn and I haven't been getting along as well as we used to, and our roommates have taken to trying to distract us when we bicker. It was never unusual for Quinn and me to butt heads from time to time, but it's been getting worse. She wants me to be something I'm not—her sidekick, someone to go out and be her "wingman." Play stupid games in bars and judge the men who try to buy us drinks. But I'm just not in the mood these days. I'll snap out of it at some point, I'm sure, but for now, I'm just not interested in listening to her wax melodic about her future as an orthopedic surgeon or evaluate men's footwear.

I yank on the end of my ponytail. "Whatever." Original, I know. But I'm not really interested in coming up with pithy comebacks either.

Quinn's eyes practically roll up to the ceiling. "You've been moping around this apartment for the last four months like friggin' Charlie Brown. Did you even pass your classes this semester, Lay?"

"I did just fine in my classes, thanks."

And it's true. I did. I couldn't sleepwalk through those like I have everything else the last three weeks. Learning about Latin American politics hasn't been easy, considering everything about it reminds me of the two men in my life who tore it apart in quick succession, one, two, three. But in its own way, it was kind of cathartic. At least it makes me *feel* something.

"Lay, you have been a little..." Shama starts uneasily.

"A little what?"

"Glum?" Jamie suggests while toying with the bedspread.

"I was going to say suicidal," Quinn remarks.

I turn back to her. "That's not even funny."

"Please. You're about five minutes from slitting your wrists."

"Quinn!"

Quinn looks sheepishly at Shama, whose older brother actually *did* attempt suicide a few years ago. He wasn't successful, but it's not even close to a funny joke, especially in this circumstance.

"Sorry, Shams," she says.

"Super heartfelt," I mumble as I turn back to my desk to finish writing the letter for my dad for Christmas. I can feel, rather than see, my roommates glancing at each other.

"Right," Quinn spits. "Because you're one to give practice lessons on empathy. Do you even know what's been going on in Shama's life recently? Did you know that Jason cheated on her?"

"Hey!" Shama pipes up again. "We do *not* know that Jason's been cheating! I just told you that he's been a little weird lately."

"Whatever." Quinn waves away her complaints. "He's a dick, and you're finally seeing it. He blew you off *again* the other night. The writing's on the wall, babe."

"God, do you *always* have to be so fucking insensitive?" I shove my papers to the side and get up, grabbing my coat off the back of my chair and shoving my arms into it violently. "You're always like this, you know? Always thinking the worst about anyone the rest of us date. You just have to call Nico 'Special Delivery,' insult him just because he's trying to figure out his life. And just because Jason had a bad night, you think he must be cheating on Shama. How about Jamie's boyfriend? Is Dev secretly gay or something?"

"I'm just looking out for you," Quinn counters.

"No, you're nagging us." I tie my scarf around my throat so tightly it almost chokes. "If I wanted the third fucking degree, I'd fly to Brazil to have my father give me one the right way."

"That's hilarious. If you were like this all summer, I'm not surprised your dad barely wants to speak to you these days. Isn't that why you're staying here over Christmas?"

"Quinn," Jamie chides quietly. "You didn't have to go there."

I stand still, though my body shakes with anger. Only a week ago, I finally heard from my dad—a terse, scratchy call that informed me he wouldn't be traveling to the States for Christmas. My mom seemed happy enough when I told her I'd be staying here. She had wanted to go to a retreat with friends in Arizona anyway. Even though I hadn't wanted to spend Christmas at my grandparents' cold house in Pasadena, the fact that neither of my parents wanted to spend the holidays with me at all hurts. And Quinn knows it.

But she doesn't apologize, just folds her arms stubbornly. Without another word, I walk out, ignoring the weak pleas from Jamie and Shama to stay.

"There she goes," calls Quinn.

The front door slams behind me before I can even think about answering.

I walk around Union Square for a while, aimlessly window-shopping on Broadway while I try to stay warm. My gloves and hat are still at the dorm, sitting on my desk, on top of papers full of comments like "Intelligent, but needs passion" or "Adequate; you can do more." I wasn't lying. My grades are fine. I'll probably finish the semester with an A- average, just a slight dip from the near-4.0 I carried over the last two years. The change would have been enough to earn my father's ire a year ago —he would have been calling me at 4:00 a.m. every morning after midterms to make sure I was studying extra. But considering how interested he's been in my life these days, I doubt he'll notice anything at all.

Still, Quinn's right about one thing, as much as I hate to admit it. I've been going through the motions for most of the semester, and definitely for the last three weeks. She's right about my mood. She's right that I've been in a funk. And if I'm being honest, she's probably right about Jason and Shama too. I just really, really don't want her to be. And most of all, I just want her to leave me alone.

I want everyone to leave me the hell alone.

But they don't. Not in real life, and not in my mind either. Nico, of course, is everywhere I go, his memory embedded into the concrete slabs and lampposts of the city. I don't need Quinn to tell me that I'm still pining for him. I miss him like crazy. I tried to let go, but we still text back and forth here and there, even send each other a few pictures. There's one photo that someone took of him on the beach. I actually had it printed out, and I keep it in my desk drawer for when I just can't take it anymore and have to see his face. The edges are already worn and creased.

Eventually I find myself walking steadily west, zigzagging past the closed stores on Seventh, stopping for tea in Chelsea, and eventually ending up in the same neighborhood where I was only three weeks before. Standing awkwardly on the corner of Ninth Avenue and Forty-Ninth Street, I look up and down the brick walkups, up toward the high-rise buildings that crowd the horizon. At almost five o'clock, the sky is starting to dim, but not enough to see the halo cast by the city against the darkness. I haven't seen stars in months. You can't when you're inside New York's odd corona.

I try to imagine what this neighborhood was like when Nico was growing up. A glance down Forty-Ninth tells me that the closer you get to the river, the darker and quieter the streets get. Down at the end of the block, a few buildings have boarded-up windows and some tags sprayed over the brick sides. Past Tenth, it's practically black. Not a place that, even now, I'd probably want to walk alone.

Nico grew up in New York during the eighties. I've seen pictures. My father used to travel here sometimes; once we even came on vacation as a family in the nineties. I was only thirteen, but I remember even then the way my dad skirted around certain blocks like the plague. How he wouldn't take the subway for fear of being mugged. And yeah, he might have been overprotective. I've certainly never felt unsafe here. But looking down Ninth Avenue, I can easily imagine how that shadow might have taken over a lot of the city at certain points in time. How maybe it's not really ever vanquished, just being held at bay.

Maybe that's all Nico will ever be for me too. A shadow I just have to keep at bay.

My heart aches. Most days I don't regret anything that happened between us. But there are times, like right now, when I wish to God I could just get rid of all of it so I could stop feeling this way.

"Layla?"

I turn around at the familiar voice. "Giancarlo?"

The tall, lanky form of the Argentinian lopes down Forty-Ninth. It's been well over a month since I saw him last—a few weeks before Nico arrived Thanksgiving, when I was too excited to think of being with anyone else but him. And for the last three, not being able to keep my mind off him.

"Hello," Giancarlo says almost formally, unafraid to let his accent out. He uses it like a point of pride.

I notice then that he's dressed up in a tie, a collared shirt, and slacks underneath his long black coat. He wears the same square-toed loafers so popular with the European crowds here. I see them at the clubs a lot. His thick black hair is combed back from his face, and his smile, if a bit brusque, screams confidence.

"It has been a while," he pronounces, even as he slides a familiar hand around my back and kisses both of my cheeks. "You are good?"

"I...yeah. I'm good," I agree, still slightly stunned to see him. "What are you doing in this part of town?"

Giancarlo frowns, his deep-set eyes growing a little dark. "Why? Is there a reason you wouldn't want me to see you here?"

Suddenly flushed, I shake my head and shove my hands deeper into my pockets. "Um, no. No, I don't think so," I say, only just realizing the second "no" makes me sound guilty.

Giancarlo examines me, and I have to force myself not to look away. I haven't seen him for a while. I had forgotten just how intense his dark eyes are. Intimidating, and...a little arousing. I shift back and forth on my feet.

"St. Andrews is the closest Spanish Mass for me," he says abruptly, finally breaking the awkward silence.

The well-lit doors of the red-brick building just down the block are open, welcoming Spanish speakers around Hell's Kitchen for evening Mass, the same church where Nico and his family went while he was growing up. Where Carmen and her kids still go. A priest stands outside, accepting the handshakes and occasional kisses of the parishioners. It's a Friday night. Not a busy night for church, but a steady trickle of people enter the double doors.

"Would you like to come with me?"

I look back at Giancarlo, who still hasn't turned his gaze from me. "What?"

He shrugs. "You are Catholic, no? Your family is Brazilian."

I haven't been to Mass in months, not since my father left. This time last year, they would have asked if I had started celebrating the Advent. Had been giving confession before Christmas.

I finger the new gold watch on my wrist, the early Christmas gift from my dad. On the back of the face is an engraving: *a minha filha*, which means "to my daughter." Apparently now that he's living in Brazil again, he's actually comfortable using Portuguese with me in a way he never would have before.

"Sure," I say finally. "Why not?"

I follow Giancarlo into the church, nodding politely when the priest greets us both in Spanish. I know enough now to answer politely in kind.

It's an older building, probably built sometime in the early nineteen hundreds. Sturdy and tall, the inside opens into high, arched ceilings that tower above the T-shape of a traditional basilica. It's a familiar shape, one that reminds me of St. Anne's, the big cathedral in Seattle my parents and I attended every Sunday, but which also recalls the smaller churches in Brazil. The ones my dad might be visiting with his family these days.

I glance around, weirdly hopeful and nervous. But no, I don't see Nico. There's no sign of the shoulders I'd know anywhere. And of course not. He wasn't coming back for Christmas because of all the time he took off at Thanksgiving.

"You are practicing your Spanish," Giancarlo observes as we walk down the aisle. With a hand at my back, he steers me into a pew near the middle, a few rows away from the families sitting closer to the altar.

I nod as I sit down. "My class is immersion-based, five days a week. We've been learning really fast. My instructor says I have a pretty good ear."

Giancarlo examines me a moment, then proceeds to reel off a succession of quick Spanish, out of which I catch maybe four or five words.

I blush. "Okay, maybe not that good."

He smirks and pushed his glasses up his long nose. "It takes a long time to learn another language unless you are really talented at them. You shouldn't be hard on yourself. I learned English in a few months once I moved here, but not everyone can do that."

I look down at my hands, unsure of how to take his comments. They don't criticize me directly. Obviously, he must know the difference between learning a language in class instead of by living in a native-speaking country.

"Shhh," he says.

I frown. Did I say something?

But he points a finger toward the front of the church. "It's starting. I will help you translate."

CHAPTER SIXTEEN

Layla

Even spoken in a different language, the ceremony is comforting and familiar. The whiff of incense in the dimly lit space puts me into a sort of trance while the priest intones the opening lines of Mass. I've only ever associated Catholicism with my parents and my upbringing. To be honest, I'm not even sure I believe in most of it anymore. But the familiarity is balm to my tired heart. The rhythm of the homily is the same in Spanish as in English, and Giancarlo translates the readings and the sermon to me, his voice low and soothing in my ear. By the time I've taken the Eucharist, swallowed my bit of dry bread and the overly sweet wine that every church on the planet blesses, I feel a little more at peace.

We file out silently ahead of most of the other attendees as the pipe organ plays behind us. It wasn't a full Mass, only thirty minutes, but it was long enough to cultivate that heavy sense of peace and foreboding I always feel leaving a church. My soul is somehow lighter and heavier, all at the same time.

"What's up, NYU?"

Almost to the exit, I swing around to find Gabriel, Nico's brother, striding up the aisle, followed by the short, slight figure I recognize as Carmen, his mother.

Oh. Shit.

"Hey," I greet Gabe as he gives me a quick kiss on the cheek. "How are you?"

"Good, good," he says. We step to the side of the door to let the other parishioners leave. "Just taking *Mami* to Mass. One of us takes her most days."

As if on cue, Carmen joins us, and with a careful, guarded nod, accepts my brief embrace.

"*Hola*, Carmen," I say.

She nods again, but remains silent, looking suspiciously at Giancarlo, who sort of looms next to us. Gabe is pretty tall, but Giancarlo still has a few inches on him. The two of them make Carmen and me look like dwarves.

"Oh," I start. "Sorry. Um, *perdón*. *Eso es mi amigo, Giancarlo. El está de Argentina*." I stumble through the rudimentary phrases I manage to piece together for Carmen, even though I know she understands English perfectly well. It just seems rude to speak in a language she can't return. "Giancarlo, *esa es* Carmen Soltero *y su niño*, Gabriel."

Gabe snorts at the awkward introduction, and I shoot him a dirty look. He just laughs harder.

"*Encantado*," Carmen murmurs to Giancarlo, who shakes her hand limply.

Gabe, suddenly serious, also shakes Giancarlo's hand. "It is a pleasure to meet you."

I frown. From what I know of Gabe, he only speaks that formally when he's trying to impress. He puffs his chest out a little at Giancarlo, and beside me, the taller man stiffens.

The three of them trade pleasantries in Spanish for a bit while I try to follow along as best I can (mostly unsuccessfully). Giancarlo remains stiff. Everyone does, actually. Carmen keeps squinting at him, like she's trying to figure something out about him.

"Okay," she pronounces awkwardly in English once there's a lull in the conversation. Then to me: "Nice to see you, Layla."

I nod and lean in to give her another kiss on the cheek, which she accepts awkwardly. "*Adiós, señora*."

Gabe snickers at the formal address of his mother, for which he receives a quick smack in the belly from her purse. I roll my eyes, and he laughs. Carmen proceeds to drag her son out of the church.

"See ya, NYU!" Gabe crows loudly, earning another smack on the way out. "I'll tell *Nico* you said hi!"

I'm smiling when I turn back to Giancarlo, relieved that the interaction wasn't as awkward as it could have been. But his murderous face flattens my cheer.

"This boy. He is a lover of yours?" he demands.

I balk, glancing wildly around the church in case someone heard us. "What? *No!*"

Giancarlo grabs my hand and tows me outside. Across the street, Gabe and Carmen enter their building without another look at us. Giancarlo scoffs, then continues steering me toward Ninth Avenue.

"*Mamarrachos pobres*," he mutters.

"Poor what?" I ask. I know enough Spanish to figure out the second word, but not the first.

Giancarlo looks at me with surprise, and if I'm not mistaken, a little embarrassment. It seems to make him angry. "It's...an expression. In Argentina, we say it to...it refers to people who have no...it is for people who are from the country."

I frown. "What does that have to do with Carmen and Gabriel? They're from New York."

"It's...you can hear from the way they talk," he says. "No class. They are Puerto Rican, no? None of them speak Spanish the right way."

"What does that mean, the 'right way'?" I ask, getting defensive on the Solteros' behalves. "My teacher says that Spanish has hundreds of different variations and dialects. It's a huge, diverse language group, just like English."

"Yes, but Puerto Ricans, they don't speak Spanish," Giancarlo retorts, clearly annoyed. "They speak a mix. Sometimes Spanish, sometimes English. Like they can't choose. Even words that sound like Spanish are actually from English." He wrinkles his long nose, like he's smelling something bad. "It is, how do you say...*sucio*."

"Dirty?" I translate out loud. "What?"

"You want to speak a language, speak the language," Giancarlo says. "Choose. Don't mix them, like dishwater."

He turns abruptly and guides me into a tapas bar on the corner.

"*Una mesa por dos*," he rattles to the hostess, and then gets annoyed when the poor girl doesn't speak Spanish.

"Just the two of us, please," I tell her.

She seats us at a small table near the back of the dimly lit restaurant, and I sit back into the plush bench seat while Giancarlo folds his long legs under the table.

"Are you...are you always so abrupt with people?" I ask him after he's settled in.

He blinks at me through his glasses. "How do you mean?"

I shrug, trying not to look away from his piercing gaze. "I mean...it's not her fault that she doesn't speak Spanish. You were kind of rude."

"She works at a tapas restaurant. You don't think she should learn the language?"

"She's selling appetizers, not Spanish courses," I joke.

As if he notices that he's compromising his own character, Giancarlo flashes a sudden smile. It's a little shocking how much it changes his face. He goes from stern into a handsome rogue in two seconds flat, and I can't help but smile back.

"Maybe you're right," he says, covering my hand with his big one. "This is why I need you around. You make me a nicer person." Before I can ask exactly what he means by that, he removes his hand and picks up his menu. "I will order, okay?"

"Okay," I say, sensing it would probably be better to let him have his way at this point than to argue anymore. Giancarlo's stubbornness seems a lot like my dad's—not worth the fight. In a weird way, it's sort of soothing.

A waitress arrives and stutters through the night's specials before Giancarlo orders in quick succession. It's too much for just the two of us, but I don't argue. I am hungry. He also orders a bottle of wine, and we clink glasses when it arrives.

"*Salud*," he says and nods with approval when I say it back. "Good. Your accent is not so terrible."

I smile. "Um, thanks."

We sip together while Giancarlo continues to study me. He never stops watching.

"I miss you," he says abruptly just before taking a long drink of his wine.

I glance around, unsure if I just heard him correctly. "What?"

He shrugs, like he's just informed me that it's raining outside. "I miss you these last months. I'm not afraid to say it, like some of these men. I know you are busy. But I wonder why you don't call."

"You didn't call me either." And immediately, I wonder why suddenly I care, even though moments ago I didn't.

Giancarlo shrugs again, like it doesn't make a difference. After that display outside the church, I'm certainly not about to tell him that the reason I haven't called is because I've been heartbroken. That even though I refused to go to LA for Christmas, Nico and I still talk sometimes. That we haven't been able to stop sending each other the occasional text or even a blurry picture here and there. That I don't want to cut him out of my life, even though having him in it hurts.

"Are you, how do you say, seeing someone else?"

I squint. "Didn't you already ask me that?"

"No," Giancarlo says. He leans back when the food arrives, but continues speaking, like the server isn't even there. He has a habit, I've noticed, of treating certain people like furniture. It's chilly. "I asked if *that* boy was your lover. You say no. So...is there another?"

I take a piece of fried zucchini and dip it into a cup of aioli. "Um, no." I hate the way my heart squeezes when I say that. I hate that it's the truth.

"So you are free for me."

I balk. Is this guy for real? We barely know each other—a few random hookups do not a relationship make. I'm not sure we've even had an entire conversation. Most of our interactions have consisted of late-night booty calls the few times my roommates were paired off with significant others, and I was left alone at the apartment and couldn't take it anymore.

I think of the things I know about him, things gathered from early morning musings after sex, just when we were falling asleep. He's from Buenos Aires, I know that. The son of a shipping manufacturer there, sent here to get his degree before he goes home to run the family business. I know he's an only child, like me. And, as I recall the way he moved through the Mass with practiced ease, that he's staunchly Catholic.

"I—what—" I sputter.

"No," Giancarlo says, cutting me off. "We won't start this tonight. You are different. I can tell."

I frown. Different from what? I have no idea what he's talking about.

"My woman has to have her head right," he continues. "You will, I know you will." He leans over the table. "Look at this face. This is the face of someone who is going places. And I want to take you with me. You are beautiful. Smart. I know you will be perfect for me."

I stare, holding my zucchini, half-eaten. This has got to be one of the strangest conversations I've ever had.

"When you return home from Christmas, you will decide," he says. He plucks the zucchini from my hand and pops it into his mouth.

"I, um, well, I'm not going anywhere for Christmas," I tell him as I watch, transfixed, while he finishes my food. "I'm just staying here."

I haven't even told my roommates that. They'll all invite me home with them, and I'm just not in the mood to play nice with other people's families again. I just want to be alone.

Giancarlo swallows, then gives me a slow, sweet smile. "We'll have Christmas together, then," he says. "Go to Mass. And I can help you practice your Spanish."

I open my mouth to argue, insist that I was looking forward to having my apartment to myself for the holiday, that I wanted the alone time. But the truth is, I'm not. I know exactly what I'll be doing—just what Quinn says, moping around New York like I did tonight. I'll probably find my way to the MET, to the Cloisters, even around Central Park in the freezing rain, just because they are places where Nico and I spent time together. I've been as sad and lonely with people as I'll be by myself. I don't want to feel this way anymore.

"Okay," I agree. "It's a date."

Giancarlo nods with approval. "*Sí,*" he replies. "*Good.*"

CHAPTER SEVENTEEN

LAYLA

A few nights later, after Quinn and Jamie have already left for break, I'm in my room trying trying to watch a movie. Quinn was in a giant huff after I refused to apologize. I don't know what I have to apologize for. Being sad? She was the one who attacked me.

Shama knocks on my bedroom door, roller bag in hand. She sees me lounging on my bed, watching *Crybaby* on the little TV that Quinn and I share.

"Oooh," she says as she abandons her bag and comes to sit next to me. "I love this one."

"Yeah," I say as I sit up. "Quinn might be a bitch sometimes, but she's got a great DVD selection."

We watch while Johnny Depp teaches the blonde girl how to French kiss. It's hot for a second, but before long, we're both giggling uncontrollably when the characters start wiggling their tongues at each other like snakes. It's the corniest damn movie, but I remember falling in love with Johnny Depp back when it first came out.

Looks like I had a thing for bad boys even then.

Shama sniffs and wipes at her eyes. I turn curiously. I doubt it's the snake-tongues that are making her cry.

"You okay, Shams?" I ask her.

Shama shrugs. "Yeah. It's just...Quinn's probably right. About Jason. He forgot to call me last night. Said he had a last-minute gig at Fat Black's. But I called to see if he was there, and they had someone else booked." She grimaces. "I sound pathetic, don't I? Checking up on my boyfriend."

I don't say anything. I don't want to be like Quinn, so judgmental, telling Shama what to think about her own life. It doesn't sound good, it's true. So maybe Quinn is right. But she might be wrong too.

"I think you need to just ask him," I say. "And then trust your gut, not mine or Jamie's or Quinn's. You know what's best for you."

Shama sighs. "Do I? Sometimes I just want to fast-forward through this part of our lives. Get to the part where we know better already." She stands up and grabs her rolling bag's handle and gives me a one-armed hug. "Have a good break. Unless you want to change your mind and come home with me...you'll get a lot of really delicious Indian food and only thirty-four questions about your major and career plans."

I snicker. A little parental badgering doesn't sound that awful. Actually, it sounds kind of nice.

But instead, I say, "I'm good," and walk her to the door for another real hug. "Have a good break, Shams."

———

AN HOUR LATER, I'm awakened by the buzz of my phone on my desk. I turn off the *Crybaby* credits and look at the number. Giancarlo.

"Hello?"

"What are you doing?" His voice, as always, is abrupt and direct.

"I...I just woke up," I say, sitting up and pushing a tired hand through my hair. A glance at the clock tells me it's almost four thirty.

"Meet me at Rockefeller Center."

He doesn't make requests, I'm starting to notice.

"I just woke up," I repeat. "What time?"

"I'm here now. Have you ever seen the tree?"

"No."

"Then meet me here."

I stare at myself in the mirror across the way. I look pale, with dark circles under my eyes. Even though I've been sleeping more than usual, I always feel tired.

I think of Giancarlo's intense energy—the way he seems like he knows exactly what he wants. From me. From his life. His direction is invigorating. I wasn't quite sure what to make of it all last night, but I can't shake off the fact that being around him made me feel something other than half-asleep for the first time in weeks. Maybe he's what I need to wake up.

I push off the bed and walk toward the closet. "Okay," I agree. "I'll be there in about an hour."

———

FIFTY-FIVE MINUTES LATER, I step out of the Forty-Seventh Street stop dressed practically in jeans, boots, and my parka, looking around for Giancarlo, who said he would meet me at the stop. Feeling self-conscious, like I'm being watched, I see nothing. I don't really want to wait by myself here forever. Rockefeller Center is always busy, especially this time of year. But for some reason I feel like a sitting duck just standing here beside a subway stop.

"Did you think I wouldn't be here?"

Giancarlo steps out of the shadows of a building next to the stop, one hand shoved into the pocket of the same long black wool coat he wore yesterday. He dresses a little more formally than most guys his age—like he's forty-three, not twenty-three. He carries a large brown paper bag in his other hand.

I shake my head. "I wasn't worried. What's that?"

"You'll see." He places an authoritative arm around my shoulder and pulls me close. "Don't worry. *I* would never forget about you."

We walk down Forty-Eighth and across the street. Giancarlo guides me around the iconic buildings until we reach the familiar skating rink. It's one of those surreal places in New York where you don't really feel like you're in a real city, but on a movie set—a place you've seen so many times in so many different films that when you see it, you can't escape the déjà vu.

"You know, you're lucky to meet me," he says as he guides me around the rink. "A lot of boys might want you to look perfect all the time, but I don't mind the 'natural look.'"

He looks pointedly at my hair, which is arranged on my shoulder in its air-dried waves. I tried to tame it, but it wasn't cooperating, so I just shoved a hat on top and left.

"Um, thanks," I say, trying to ignore the way his compliment doesn't really feel like one.

We stop and watch the skaters below. The rink is pretty full, with a long line of people waiting. Giancarlo looks bored.

"Do you want to skate?" I ask playfully.

He rolls his eyes. "I would never do that. They look ridiculous. Only a few of them can skate at all, and the others look like clowns." He shakes his head. "I don't waste my time on things that don't matter." He looks down and gives me a sly half-smile. "Not like you, of course. Don't worry."

He keeps saying that. *Don't worry.* I want to say that I don't, but I'm not sure it's true.

I turn toward the rink. "I don't know. It looks kind of fun. Don't you like to try new things?"

"Only when I know I'll be good at them," Giancarlo answers. "Otherwise, there's no point." He pushes off the railing and takes my hand. "Come."

He leads me to the other side of the rink, where crowds of people are all posing in front of the famous Rockefeller Christmas tree. I've never actually seen it in person even though I've lived here for the better part of three years. It's another phantom from movies, a glittering giant of golden light.

"Too much," Giancarlo mutters as he surveys the tree.

I blink. "You think?"

"Look at it. A hundred feet tall, covered in gold, sparkly fake presents. It has, how do you say, no class. Like what Americans think rich looks like."

"Why did you take me here, then?"

Giancarlo shrugs, reaches down for my hand, but before he can take it, I put it in my pocket. "You wanted Christmas," he says with a slight frown at the movement. "This—big tree, lots of presents—is Christmas in America, no?"

I turn back to the tree. Even though I never came to see it last year, there is actually something comforting about it. How many movies have I seen it in? And how many trees have I decorated with my mother, albeit on a much smaller scale.

"I suppose it is a little," I admit. "But I'm not just an American."

Giancarlo snorts. "Yes, you are. Your father went to Brazil by himself, didn't he?"

I open my mouth with a quick retort, but find I have none. Maybe he doesn't mean it to, but the comments sting. Granted, Giancarlo knows only a little about my family's situation—little bits and pieces I've told him. Maybe not enough to use it as the weapon it sounds like.

We stare up at the lights for a few more minutes. I want to enjoy the beauty of it, but I can feel Giancarlo's disdain, even though he doesn't say anything else. I've never been to Argentina, even though it borders Brazil. But I know that economically, it shares a lot of the same problems as my father's country. A lot of concentrated wealth, and a lot more poverty than here.

But Giancarlo's family isn't poor. His tastes, styles, even his casual entitlement belies an upbringing that's pretty far from the slums. I glance at the sturdy gold ring on his index finger, his shiny black shoes, then look back at the tree, trying to see what he sees.

"Are you finished?" he asks a few seconds later.

I sigh. If it were just me, I might have stayed longer. Found a seat on a bench with a coffee, spent some time watching the crowds. Tried to have a conversation. It's the kind of thing Nico and I would have done together, content just to be in each other's presence, no matter where we were.

But this wasn't even my idea in the first place, Giancarlo doesn't seem like the kind of guy who likes to people-watch. I'm also not sure I want to see what he's like when his own plans are disrupted.

———

TO MY SURPRISE, instead of leading me to the street for a cab or even to say goodbye at the subway, Giancarlo guides me up Fifth with a firm hand at my elbow. He stops in a deli for a couple of hot teas, which we carry up the street as we walk. I'm still thinking about his reaction to the tree, and finally, I can't keep back my questions anymore.

"Your family in Argentina," I start slowly. "What do they do?"

Giancarlo frowns. He does that a lot, and it makes his thick black brows furrow over his glasses, like a scholar deep in thought. It's attractive...but intimidating. Which is basically him in a nutshell.

"Why do you want to know?" he asks.

Now it's my turn to frown. "Curiosity. I just want to know more about you, I guess."

He presses his lips together, like he's trying to decipher if I'm telling the truth. Then his shoulders seem to relax. "My father, he owns a shipping company in Buenos Aires. It controls almost ten full percent of Argentinian exports."

"Oh...so it's...a good business?" I don't know how to ask if his family makes money without sounding like a gold digger or something equally awful. I have no idea if ten percent of Argentinian exports is a lot, but I assume it is.

Giancarlo smirks. "It's excellent. My father is one of the most successful men in Buenos Aires. They have asked him to run for mayor. There has even been talk of him becoming president, but he said no. His work is *too* important. And one day, *I* will take over."

"Oh," I say. "Well, that must be...nice." I'm not sure how to respond to that. "Then why do you live in that apartment?"

The question jumps out before I can stop it, before I realize how terrible and rude it is. But I'm still curious. If Giancarlo's family is wealthy enough to send him as an international student to study in the U.S., he obviously isn't poor. It's a little strange that he lives in such a brittle little place. Close to his school, yes. But there are nicer places in that part of the city too. Places where a shipping magnate would seem more likely to house his son.

He shrugs. "He pays for my tuition," he says. "But my father insists that I earn the rest of my money. I don't have a golden fork like some people."

I twist my lips. "What?"

"You know. The golden fork. That rich children have. It's a saying, no?"

"The golden..." I trail off, thinking it through. "Ohh! You mean a silver spoon!" I erupt with laughter. "It's 'silver spoon,' not 'golden fork,' silly."

Now he scowls, confused. "Why would it be silver? Gold is the more valuable metal."

I shrug, still giggling. "It just is. The saying is, 'born with a silver spoon.'" I nudge his shoulder, although my shoulder only comes just above his elbow. He really is tall. "It's okay. I figured it out in the end."

Giancarlo grunts. "It's not polite, you know, to tease a person still learning the language. I am trying my best."

At first I think he's joking, but his black look tells me he's not. Instantly, I feel awful for teasing him.

"Hey, I'm sorry," I say, tugging on his sleeve. "Really, I am. You're right, that was mean."

Giancarlo examines me skeptically over the rim of his cup, and for a half-second, I think he's going to tell me to fuck off (albeit in a much more refined way). My parents would like him. He's strong and solid, just like my dad. He's cultured, on his way to being educated, and comes from money. Motivated. Everything my mom wanted to marry, and my father wants to be. Or wanted.

Suddenly, I feel really scared about what would happen if he told me to fuck off. Suddenly, I really don't want him to.

"I'm sorry," I say again, more softly.

At last, Giancarlo smiles, a broad smile that completely transforms his otherwise stern face into something much more charismatic. "What, you think I can't take a joke?"

I'm awash with relief—more than I should be, considering I don't really know this guy very well. I shouldn't care so much what he thinks.

We keep walking, sidestepping around a few homeless people piled under an awning. I glance back at them, considering whether to give the extra dollar or two in my purse, but Giancarlo tugs me onward. Across the street, several closed designer boutiques are still lit up with ostentatious Christmas displays in the windows: sleek mannequins in the front posed in thousands of dollars' worth of merchandise. It's the haves and have-nots in this city in high relief.

Giancarlo ignores the sleeping people, but glares at the boutiques. "You see, in my country, it's not like here."

"No?"

Giancarlo shakes his head, and the movement causes a lock of thick black hair to fall over his brow. He tries to give me another smile, this time less genuine. It's obviously not a natural expression for him, since it looks more like a grimace. Then he pushes his glasses up his nose, looking halfway between a librarian and a rake.

"Not so many gifts," he continues. "We have presents, of course, but most people make them instead of buy them. And maybe only a few. The rest of the time, we do other things. It's not so much a holiday about presents, all of these flashy things"—he gestures in the direction of the stores—"but more about family. God. The soul." He looks directly at me, and his eyes practically flash under a streetlight. "The things in life that really matter, don't you think?"

It's hard to look away when he stares at me like that. Searching, like he wants to know the depths of my soul; the soul he's talking about.

But eventually, I nod. "Yes."

Giancarlo turns, like I just passed some sort of test. We keep walking steadily north, up toward the park. The Plaza Hotel looms in front of us, with its gold-lit green roof and gold-leaf trim. Another famous symbol of wealth and status in New York.

"My parents are like yours too," I tell Giancarlo after I toss my empty cup into the trash. "They have money, but they really wanted me to make my own. I ended up sick last year trying to make enough to live in this city. It's so expensive."

Giancarlo grunts in agreement. "And now?"

"Now...I'm getting help from my mother. They aren't as...strict as they were before."

I don't mention that my parents are also too busy wallowing in their own misery to pay attention to mine. I try to focus on the silver lining. No one is breathing down my neck anymore. I can live my own life.

My roommates never understood why I had to work as much as I did, and even Nico sometimes treated me like a spoiled princess just for struggling through it. But Giancarlo clearly knows. He knows how hard it is to have had something once and to have to go without it. To figure out that life on your own, all at once.

"What about you?" I ask. "You said your father insisted that you work, right? Where's that?"

"Yes, I work," Giancarlo replies slowly, almost like it's a secret he shouldn't share with me. "But it's complicated." He pronounces the word slowly, one syllable at a time in his thick Argentine accent: "com-plee-cay-ted." "My visa doesn't allow me to work outside of the campus. And those jobs don't pay very much money."

I frown. "So...what do you do?"

"I work for a club promoter downtown. Help bring in people. Go out and get college girls, young people to come to his events." He looks at me meaningfully. "So, if sometimes I don't answer the phone late at night, that's why. Sometimes I am at work. It's cash, so I have to do what they say."

His words are foreboding somehow, even though nothing specific about them is a threat. Like he's warning me against something, but I don't know what.

I continue to brood about this a few more blocks, until I realize that we've crossed the street, right under the lit awnings of the plaza, and are standing at the corner of Fifty-Ninth Street: at the entrance of Central Park. I look around the corner, bewildered, then at Giancarlo, who stops a few steps ahead of me, like he was about to pass into the trees and only just realized that I hadn't followed.

"What?" he asks impatiently. "What's the problem?"

I peer into the trees, toward the blackness beyond them. "Um, it's the park."

Giancarlo looks at me like I'm missing some brain cells. "Yes..."

I frown. "It's after dark. In New York City. And you want to go into Central Park?"

He says nothing, just crosses his arms over his lapels and waits. I glance down the path, which is unlit and opaque. I feel like a storybook character trying to decide whether to go down the friendly, well-lit 6 train entrance across the street, or the fore-boding, wolf-ridden path of Central Park at night.

Giancarlo sighs, then takes a few long steps back to me. He picks up my hands and holds them to his chest. "Do you really think I would ever let anything happen to you, *mi joya*?"

I bite my lip and try to pull my hands away, but he doesn't let me. "*Joya*? What does that mean?"

"It means you are a jewel. A precious gem. I would protect you always."

He squeezes my hands, then waits for me to respond. When I don't immediately, he just sighs and kisses me lightly on the forehead before releasing me. It's the first gesture that's actually been sweet with him, not tinged with a little too much intensity, or something else I can't quite name. It melts me a little. Enough to do something I know I shouldn't.

But really. Who's even here to care?

I follow Giancarlo into the park, which eventually doesn't seem quite so dark as my eyes get used to walking without the glare of the city streets. As we progress, the sounds of the city dim. I actually hear a couple of squirrels scamper here and there, even a few birds getting ready for bed. It makes me wonder why people always tell you not to go into the park at night. It doesn't seem scary at all. The quiet is actually really nice.

Giancarlo keeps a brisk pace, then takes a quick left, and then another until we are suddenly out in the open again, facing another iconic site: the enormous boulder that towers over the Pond, a crescent-shaped pool at the southeast corner of the park. He gives me a wolfish grin, then scrambles up the rock, slipping a little in his loafers on his way to the top. He turns around. The scramble causes his glasses to fall slightly down his face, and he pushes them up with another half-smile.

"Come on," he calls.

Mindful of the slippery soles of my leather boots, I manage to get to the top, and am once again completely awestruck by the view of the Plaza and midtown over the tops of the Central Park trees and the mirror-like surface of the Pond.

Giancarlo drops his paper bag on the rock and bends down to pull a few things out of it. Bemused, I watch curiously as he folds and bends a few pieces of paper around some wire frames until they have formed two rounded paper lanterns. He takes a couple of candles from the bag and sets them inside the lanterns.

"One thing about this city," he says as he works, "you can find anything from anywhere. I found these in Chinatown last week."

"What are they?" I ask curiously.

"*Globos*." He twists a few things together, then sets the candles in place and pulls out a lighter. "Well, almost. They aren't quite the same thing, but they will work."

He hands me one of the lanterns, and I hold it up while he lights it from underneath. Before I know it, the lantern is flying out of my hands into the darkness.

"Oh!" I cry with surprise. "It floats!"

"Now light mine."

On my tiptoes, I obey, lighting Giancarlo's lantern so he can release it into the night sky, hovering just below the first.

"Instead of staring at a big fake tree," he says as we watch them float, "in my country, this is what we do. And at the New Year, everyone lights *globos* all together, and we set them into the sky, like stars."

He stares at the lanterns flying above us for a moment, but in that moment, I'm transfixed by him. It's the first softness I've seen in his usually stern face. Watching the lights with something close to wonder, he almost looks childlike.

"You miss home," I observe.

Giancarlo gives me a shrug, another almost-smile. "I miss some things, yes." He looks back at the lanterns. "It's a little different when you do this with so many people around you." He shrugs again. "I didn't think it would be so lonely to light only two."

I try to imagine what a sky would look like, filled with football-sized golden cylinders, illuminating the park from above. Magical, I'm sure. Beautiful.

"Still," Giancarlo says as we watch the glowing lights float farther and farther into the sky, "it's nice to share it with someone, even now."

"Yes," I agree. "It is."

Beside me, his hand takes mine. This time, I don't pull away as we continue to watch the two lonely lanterns, tiny golden orbs against the black night sky. They float together through the dark, up and up, only drifting away when we can barely see them anymore, and then, with a brief flash of fire, burn quickly until they disappear into ashes and wisps of smoke.

Giancarlo turns, his face no longer lit by the warmth of a candle, but by the cold moonlight rising over the city. He kisses me, and I let him, taken in by the feel of his lips, the tightness of his clutch. He knows I will come with him after this, up to his apartment, or bring him back to mine, where I'll let him have his way with me like he has before. Mostly in ways where he is concerned with his own pleasure, his own tastes, and mine are afterthoughts. But right now he wants me, and that feels good. Better than good. Right now, it's something I crave.

Still. Even as I stand on this rock, in this beautiful park, kissing another man, I can't help thinking of another one far away from his family near Christmas. I can't help wondering what he's doing now. And if he's thinking of me too.

CHAPTER EIGHTEEN

DECEMBER 2003

Nico

"Get the fuck outta here."

I help Ben, one of the other bouncers, toss a couple of drunks out of the club, pushing them beyond the fake velvet ropes of Venom to the street, where a line of cabs waits on the corner.

"Man, fuck you, you fuckin' wetback!" one of them calls at me drunkenly. "You're lucky I don't call the cops on you! Have your brown ass arrested in a *second* for assault!"

I roll my eyes and cross my arms in front of my chest. "So I guess you don't care if they find the blow in your pocket, huh? You guys must really like living on the edge."

"Monkey!" the guy shouts, even as his friends start dragging him away from the club. I take a step forward, like I'm ready to come at him, but they jog away before I can do anything else.

"You okay, man?" Ben asks.

I shrug. It's nothing I haven't heard before. That doesn't make it get under my skin any less, but these two aren't worth the fight. "I'm fine. They're just high."

For the first time since coming out to LA, I'm genuinely tired of it here. As in, ready to fuckin' pack my shit and leave. But I'm realizing that it's not the city itself I'm tired of, even though, yeah, there are some things I would change. And I'm thinking that maybe it wasn't New York I was tired of before. After all, I would kill for a Gray's Papaya right about now. And don't even get me started on my mother's cooking.

No, it was my life that I was sick of, a life that followed me across the country. I've been doing the same things for a decade. I've been sitting on stools like this, checking IDs at clubs like these, for almost ten years. I came out to LA thinking the beaches and the palm trees would give me something different, show me a different side of the country, a different way of being. But all I ended up with was a job just like all the others. Tagging on someone else's coattails, just like I always did. Fighting against the stupid fuckin' stereotypes that everyone seems to see when they look at me. The only difference is that things are hotter here.

I'm tired of staring at people's grumpy faces for hours at a time.

I'm tired of picking drunk people up off the cement while they scream racist slurs.

I'm tired of arguing with entitled fuckheads who think a twenty is going to buy my favor.

I'm fucking tired of all of it. A lot more tired than a twenty-seven-year-old guy has any right to be.

"Seriously, man," Ben say as he lumbers back onto the stool left for us outside. "You been a little down lately. Everything all right?"

I shrug. I don't know what to say. Yeah, this last month hasn't been my best. I've been going through the motions—here, at the gym, at home. I feel like I'm stuck in the mud, waiting.

Last week, I got a call from Gabe telling me that one of his friends from high school got a letter from the FDNY containing his test results and his list number, the number he ranked among applicants. The lower, the better—the lowest are called up first to interview and take the medical exams. His friend scored somewhere around two thousandth out of everyone who applied. Which means I probably did even worse if I haven't gotten anything.

I'm starting to think that Jessie was right. That all that studying, all that time and hope that I might actually be able to do the thing I've wanted to do since I was a little kid was just a waste. And here I am, in a different city, but with the same issues I've always had. Just fuckin' stuck.

Ben goes back inside, and out of habit, I pull out my phone and scroll through the string of text messages I still have from Layla—messages I never erase, even though they take up too much room on this piece of shit flip phone.

I don't have any right to call her like I do—after Thanksgiving, she stopped calling me completely, only responding here and there to texts. I fucked up, I know. Made her feel like I wasn't as interested as her. But I couldn't tell her the truth because I know my girl. She gets more excited about my future than anyone. She dreams quicker, more eagerly than anyone I've ever known. Layla lives on a different level, one where her own dreams haven't ever really been crushed. She doesn't know yet what it feels like to fall. Really fall. I hope she never does.

I scan the messages we send from time to time. Maybe we shouldn't be in contact at all. I'm not going to lie—it didn't take long before I started letting Jessie crawl back into my bed again. But fuck, I'm lonely. It's not fair to her when half the time I have my eyes closed, pretending she's someone else. Covering her mouth with my palm so her voice doesn't interrupt my fantasies. Jessie doesn't realize that when she's asleep and I'm sketching, it's not her face that floods the pages of my book.

Those eyes are blue, not brown.

That hair is black, not blonde.

God, I miss her. And I regret so fuckin' much not begging her to come here for Christmas. I should have just told her everything about the test. *Coño*, you fuckin' idiot. What the fuck were you thinking?

"Hey."

I turn around to find the club manager walking out with an envelope—tonight's tips.

"We're at last call," he says, handing me the money. "You can go home now."

The envelope is thin. It's been slow as fuck tonight, just like I knew it would be on Christmas Eve. I use it to salute him, though he's already carrying my stool back inside.

"Thanks," I say, but he's already too far away to notice.

———

THE APARTMENT IS empty when I get back. Jessie left yesterday to spend Christmas with her family after asking me about fifteen times to come with her. Christmas in Oregon. It was tempting. Another change of pace. She all but guaranteed a white Christmas, nestled in the big evergreen trees we don't have in New York. Something else besides sunshine and palm trees, concrete and asshats.

But the idea of sitting at a kitchen table in a room full of white people staring at me like I kidnapped their daughter doesn't sound so great. Especially not when it's with a girl I'm trying to get away from, even though every time I try, we just seem to get closer. Maybe it's because Jessie and I are both equally stuck. Maybe it's because we are both equally lonely. Whatever it is, something brings her into my room in the middle of the night. And something keeps me from kicking her out when we're done.

I unlock the door to the apartment and take a moment to enjoy the solitude. It's not often I get to be alone like this. I still like it. A lot. I dump the mail on the table, then grab a water from the fridge before I start shuffling through the envelopes. Cable bill. Shit, a doctor's bill for Allie—poor kid had chicken pox, looks like. Notice for next term's tuition for Gabe. Bills, bills, bills, most of them other people's.

Then a letter pops up that makes me feel like the floor just dropped out from under me. The return address is in big blocked letters, with my name printed clearly across the front.

The FDNY.

I sink into a chair in the kitchen and stare at the envelope. This is late. Maybe too late. Everyone else has heard already. I'm probably at the end of the list. The pity letter they only send because they have to.

With hands that tremble, I tear open the envelope and pull out the flimsy piece of paper like I'm ripping off a Band-Aid. At the top, in big, broad letters, reads "Notice of Results." And right under that, my name and a number.

Nico Soltero: 23

At first I'm not sure I see it. Maybe I'm imagining that I just got a number that puts me within the top twenty-five scores of a test that seven thousand people took with me on that day alone. I'm not sure there isn't a zero at the end, or maybe two. I flip the letter over. Look over the next page, which contains another application for the fitness exam, and a note that says a packet for my background check is on its way. No, this isn't a prank. This is real.

Twenty-three. Twenty-fuckin'-three. Me, Nico Soltero, the fuckup kid who at one point wasn't even sure he was going to graduate high school. The guy who thought he was going to end up delivering packages or pouring drinks for the rest of his life because they were the only jobs anyone was willing to give my criminal ass. I just got an A on a fuckin' test. Not just any test. The most important test of my life.

And there's only one person I want to tell.

It's late, too late, but I'm dialing anyway while I rush around the apartment, my fingers slipping over the keys. Maybe it's just early enough here that she'll be up soon. The phone rings four times, and I'm just about to hang up when I hear her voice, faint and groggy.

"Nico?"

I sit down on the bed, tugging off my tie. "Hey, baby."

"Hey...what's...up?"

Goddamn. I can just see her. Face a little puffy, bleary from sleep. Her brown-black hair curled from the way she sweats just a tiny bit around her neck when she's really out. I can see her rubbing her lips, trying to wake up. They'll be swollen a little, the color of rose petals in the Central Park gardens.

Fuck. Just the thought of them gets me hard. I wish to God I was there with her, wish I could help her wake up the right way. Down, boy. That's not why you're calling.

"I just...how are you?"

I don't know why I can't get it out. I stare at the paper, looking at the numbers. Twenty-three. Out of thousands. It's a good number. No, a fuckin' great number. It means I'm pretty much guaranteed for the series of interviews. And maybe, just maybe, the academy as a cadet.

But then my heart sinks as I realize the hurtles I'm actually facing. This test wasn't ever going to be the hardest thing I had to face in trying to get this job. I might have been just a minor when I robbed that bodega with some other kids in high school, but the guilty verdict for assault—an assault I didn't even commit—is permanent. The fact that I lived in a juvenile detention facility is not something I'll ever be able to erase. And no one is going to think that someone who used to be a criminal could be a new hero for New York City. No one.

I open my mouth, trying to figure out how to answer her question. But then I hear another voice. A deep voice that calls her name.

"Layla?"

I stiffen. "Who was that?"

Layla's silent for a second. I hear her palm cover the phone speaker while she talks to someone, her voice muffled through her hand. Then she gets back on.

"Sorry," she said. "I'm back. What was it you were trying to say?"

I open my mouth to tell her the news. But that voice±that very male voice—echoes through my head, and I can't see straight. My fist closes, and the paper in it crumples.

"Nothing," I say in some feat of magic, since I manage to keep my voice level. "I just wanted to wish you a Merry Christmas, sweetie."

"Oh."

She pauses. Her thoughts are so loud, I can practically hear them through the phone. I just wish I knew what they were. I wish I knew who that guy was. I wish I was there to kick his fuckin' ass out of her apartment. *Mine*, I want to shout, with every bone in my body.

But I stay quiet.

"Merry Christmas, Nico," she says, her voice small and very far away.

And then we hang up. Because there isn't anything else to say.

CHAPTER NINETEEN

JANUARY 2004

Layla

"Giancarlo, please. We need to go. My friends are waiting for us."

"Your friends, your friends. That's all I hear about—your friends."

I lean against the doorframe of Giancarlo's bedroom, waiting impatiently for him to finish putting on his shoes. He's been dragging all evening, clearly unhappy about coming downtown to meet Shama, Jamie, and Quinn. My roommates all got back from break last night, but I was holed up at Giancarlo's apartment uptown until tonight. We ended up spending most of the last few weeks together, cocooned at his place or mine. Somehow I woke up, and it was almost the end of January.

Maybe it's too soon to spend so much time together, but I couldn't help but like having him with me when I opened the impersonal checks from my mother and father. I think he liked having me there too when he opened the small package from his family containing some treats from home. We even went to Mass on Sundays. It was...nice. Better than being lonely, even if he is kind of intense.

Like right now.

He sighs. The head-to-toe black he's wearing doesn't help his sullen expression. It's his preferred color, but his skin is too pale for it, though I'd never tell him that. It would just be asking for a fight. And Giancarlo, I've learned, doesn't give up on a fight.

"Do I really have to go?" he demands. "They're your friends. What do they care about me? I don't need friends."

I wilt. This is not how the evening was supposed to go. It's going to look really bad if I show up at the bar having promised new boyfriend without said boyfriend in tow. And then there's the other side of the equation: that things between Giancarlo and me don't seem quite official until someone outside of the two of us actually acknowledges our existence. Sees us. Interacts with us. Approves of us. Giancarlo doesn't even have a roommate, and since my roommates have been gone...well, let's just say you can't live in a cocoon forever.

His cantankerous attitude remains through the subway ride downtown, all the way to the tiny bar, where I scan for my friends from the entrance.

"I don't know why we are here," he grumbles as he stands behind me. "I could have worked tonight. Do you have any idea how many jobs I have given up this month to be with you?"

I push him in the side light-heartedly, hoping I can get him to smile. It's not something he does a lot, but I know I can get him there, my friends might actually like Giancarlo.

"Dude," I say. "Lighten up, will you? Don't be a grouch around my friends."

Giancarlo just glares at me. "You think this is a joke? You think it's cheap to take you out, buy you things? Pay for the privacy of my apartment? Do you have any idea how much this night will cost me?"

My cheeky smile falls as I turn to him. "Hey, I'm sorry. I wasn't making light of you. I was just trying to get you to lighten up so you can enjoy yourself. And like I keep telling you, you do not have to pay for me at all."

He just pushes his glasses up his nose, but his glare doesn't waver. I take a deep breath. There's a tightness in my stomach when he does that, and I don't know why. A knot of tension that never quite dissipates, bad as I want it to.

"Layla, are you my woman, or not?" he asks, pulling me close to him.

I bite my lip. Shit. There's that question again. I place my hands on his arms and rub up and down, hoping to calm him. I had hoped things would be better tonight.

"I didn't mean it," I murmur into his ear. "You're not a grouch. And I am really grateful that you're here."

Giancarlo remains stiff for a few more seconds, but slowly I feel him relax a bit under my touch. "Good," he breathes at last. "You have no idea how scared I get sometimes. You say things like that to me, and I worry I'm going to lose you. I don't know what I would do alone, here in this city, without you by my side. I need you, Layla."

It's something he started saying a lot, and I only recently learned the price of not returning the sentiment.

———

SAY IT," he said. "Why can't you just say it?"

I frowned as I dropped a handful of sliced peppers into the pan, letting the sizzle pop and crackle through the air. The question wasn't out of nowhere, although usually it would come up either after we'd just had sex or when he would appear after a night at his job and had had a few drinks. I didn't know if it was because school was starting again or that my friends were returning, but there in the kitchen was the first time he'd ever asked me like it was an average, everyday request.

"It's only been a month..." I started slowly. "Not even. And you want me to say I'm yours? Aren't we moving fast enough already? We went from a first date to practically living together in the space of three weeks."

It was hard to admit, but I had been there before, hadn't I? I had fallen for a man within a day of meeting him—head over heels within twenty-four hours of our first date. A man who, in the end, didn't want me the way I wanted him.

"I need you," Giancarlo said again, pacing up and down the small, tight space. He stopped behind me and wrapped his arms around my waist, nuzzling into my neck, his breath warm and heavy. "I need you, Layla. I don't know why. I don't know how. But I do. I need to know you're mine, amor. Say it."

I took a deep breath. My body didn't melt into his embrace. Instead, I stood stock-straight as I felt his growing erection against me. Intensity turned him on, I knew. But I didn't like the way he conflated that intensity with love. The lines between them became very blurry.

"I..."

Giancarlo pulled away and then leaned against the counter so he faced me. "It's just us now, don't you know that? No families. Nobody. We only have each other. If I lose you, I'll...I just need to know, amor. I need to know you belong to me."

But I couldn't say it. I couldn't tell him I was his, couldn't say I belonged to someone else. I'm honestly not sure I could ever say that to another person.

Except one.

The thought entered my head before I could stop it, and I pushed it away and turned back to the vegetables, hissing in the pan. The sound echoed through the air, taking up the space where my words should have been. Why couldn't I just say it? He so clearly needed me to. And it did feel so, so good to have someone want me the way he did.

But my mouth wouldn't move. I stared at the vegetables, feeling Giancarlo's temper building beside me, a powder keg ready to burst. It was strangely familiar. My father, of course, was the same way, with a temper that would turn to shouting if you pressed the wrong button. I winced, bracing myself for an onslaught.

Suddenly, the spatula was swatted out of my hand, and before I could say anything, the pan was slammed off the stove and into the wall in the corner. Flecks of hot oil bit into my skin, and I jumped back against the sink.

"Ow! Okay, okay, okay!" I shouted. "I-I need you too, I guess. Is that what you need to hear? Jesus!"

Giancarlo stood next to the still-red burner on the stove, its coil as red and angry as his face. He hurled the spatula at the pan, and I stared at them both, bewildered by the oily vegetables now staining the walls and the linoleum.

"Don't placate me," he bit out, then stomped out of the apartment, slamming the heavy door behind him.

It took me five full minutes to stop shaking, to get down on my knees and clean up the stir fry, to go without eating because that was all the food in his apartment, and I was too scared to see what he would do if he came back to find me gone. And he did come back, several hours later, smelling a little of Malbec and something else I couldn't place. He scooped me against his big body, full of apologies and sex. And in my daze, I accepted both.

———

"THERE SHE IS! LAYLA!"

I snap out of the memory and scan the bar, a little place on the Lower East Side where Shama wanted to go tonight. She and Jason broke up over the break, so Fat Black's is off-limits for a while, at least for her. I'm glad they're done even though my friend is heartbroken. Getting a text in the middle of the night from your naked boyfriend wouldn't be so bad, but it's fucked up when the text was clearly sent by the woman naked with him.

It was Quinn's voice I heard. A second later I spot all of my roommates waving furiously from a booth.

"Come on," I say and pull Giancarlo with me.

They've met before, of course, but it's been a long time since that night in September. Jamie's snuggled into Dev's side, and Quinn and Shama stand up to give me tight hugs.

"We missed you!" they both yelp as we all sit down. I relax a little. It's good to know that Quinn and I don't have to be weird now.

"Guys," I say, tugging on Giancarlo's hand to pull him into the booth with me. Reluctantly, he follows. "This is Giancarlo. Giancarlo, this is Quinn, Jamie, and Shama. And that's Dev, Jamie's boyfriend."

Dev gives a tip of his head, but turns quickly back to Jamie to resume their reunion as well. Quinn and Shama turn to us, openly assessing Giancarlo, who remains tense.

"So, Harry Potter," Quinn says, "Layla says you're in school. What's your major?"

"Who is Harry Potter?" Giancarlo turns to me, ignoring the question.

"You don't know who Harry Potter is?" I ask. "Those books are huge right now."

"He's a wizard!" Shama pipes up. She cocks her head, looking at Giancarlo. "Yeah, I sort of see it. I mean, he's not exactly the little schoolboy type, but the glasses and the scarf...good call, Quinn."

Quinn smirks. Giancarlo scowls.

"Maybe he'd like Voldemort better," Quinn remarks dryly as she stirs her drink. Shama and Jamie start to laugh.

"Quinn!" I hiss.

She shrugs. "Anyway. Major, V-man?"

Giancarlo clears his throat. "Business."

"Oh? What kind? Finance? Econ?"

Again with the throat clearing. "Um, finance, I think. After I finish, I will go back to Buenos Aires and learn my family's business." He turns to me with a sober look. "Layla will come with me too."

He gives me that long, slow smile that makes my insides melt a little, and it almost distracts me from the fact that he thinks I'm going to move to a completely different hemisphere with him. Almost.

"What's that?" I ask as lightly as I can. "This is news to me." I grin at my friends, trying to play it off as a joke, but no one looks amused.

"Whoa," Jamie says as she breaks from a kiss with Dev. "Did I hear you're moving to Argentina? That's *awesome*! And your dad will be so happy since you'll be closer to Brazil, right?"

"Is this true?" Quinn's voice is a lot more sober than Jamie's, but I do find the courage to look at her.

Feeling the tension radiating around the table, but especially from the tall glass of intensity sitting next to me, I chew on my upper lip for a minute before answering.

"No," I say. "It's just an idea I guess."

I don't even have to look at Giancarlo to know that he's glaring at me. His message tone rings, a loud blare that can still be heard inside the club. He checks it, then shoves it back in his pocket.

"I have to go," he says as he stands up. "Come. We need to talk."

And with a curt nod at my friends, Giancarlo tugs me back out of the booth and through the club without even giving me a second to grab my coat from the hanger. It's not until we're back outside on the sidewalk that he whirls around, the tails of his long black coat flying behind him like a cape.

"What the fuck was that?" he demands, nose tinged red with anger. A couple entering the lounge sidesteps away from him, even though he's not even shouting.

Arms crossed, I hold myself tightly, shivering in the icy wind. I'm wearing a thin sweater and jeans, and it's thirty degrees outside. "What are you talking about?"

"You think I *like* being made a fool? Is that why you brought me here?"

"N-no!" I proclaim. "Come on, please. Giancarlo, we were only joking around. That's what we do."

"And you? Joking around?" he comes closer, grabbing my arms and pulling me to him. "*I* wasn't joking when I said I wanted you with me. I *always* want you with me, Layla. Don't you feel the same for me?" His hands drift up my neck, clasping me there and turning my face toward his. "No," he says, before I can reply. "You don't take this serious. I can see it in your face."

He releases me with enough gusto that I fall back a step or two. I'm so cold that my teeth are chattering, but my mouth falls open anyway in shock. Is he serious right now? I've been with him literally every day for the last month. How could he possibly think that I'm not serious?

"I should walk away while I can," Giancarlo snarls. "You're only going to ruin me, I can see it. Nothing but fun and games to you, like a child."

"No!" I finally burst out.

The tension that's been stewing in my stomach finally flowers into something more explosive. I couldn't say why, but the idea of him walking away, of leaving me, just like everyone else always seems to do, is suddenly too much to bear. It's enough that it shutters the anger at his unfair accusations, at the feeling like I'm being rail-roaded into this conflict whether I want it or not.

"I'm serious," I say reaching out for his sleeves. "I'm serious. You just took me off-guard with the Argentina comment, okay? But you know I'm serious about you, Giancarlo. You must know that."

He lets me pull him close, but remains a statue as I press slow, tentative kisses around his jaw. There is no response, and his skin there, the skin he keeps meticulously shaved, is chilled in the wind. At last he takes a step back and draws his knuckles slowly across my cheek. I lean into the touch, not daring to break eye contact as he levels his cold stare at me.

"I don't believe you," he says, as he pushes my face roughly to the side. "I have to go. Maybe that will give you some time to consider what you really think of me. Maybe then you'll appreciate what we have."

And with another scowl, he turns and walks swiftly down the street, coattails flying. I stand there, shivering in the wind hurling down Houston until he disappears around the corner.

"You okay, sweetie?"

A deep voice startles me with its familiarity. Its low timbre. Its faint New York accent. I turn around, but of course, it's not him. The doorman is dressed in the universal uniform of black, but he's not Nico.

"You want me to kick his ass for you?" he offers kindly.

I almost say yes. I'm mad and scared and I just want this feeling to go away. But then I catch the way the guy's eyes drift down to the cleavage apparent in my flimsy black shirt.

I shiver again and shake my head. "No. No, thanks."

"Anytime," he says just before I duck back inside the bar.

———

As if my roommates all made an agreement not to press me about Giancarlo for a certain period of time, no one brings up his sudden disappearance. We share a few rounds, and slowly the ball of stress in my stomach unravels—a little—while I listen to them tell stories about their breaks. We let Quinn brag about her family's trip to Miami Beach, ooh and ahh as Jamie and Dev recount visiting Jamie's mom, and boo accordingly as Shama debriefs us on her and Jason's breakup. A few hours later, I'm not checking my phone for messages every few minutes anymore. Jamie and Dev have graduated to the dance floor, and Shama's found herself a rebound.

"I don't get it."

I turn back to the table, where Quinn is finishing her fourth vodka soda. The music in here is really loud, but her disapproval echoes across the table.

"What don't you get?" I ask.

Quinn looks toward the door, like she's expecting Giancarlo to walk back in.

"What you see in Severus Snape."

"Annnnd here it is," I mutter.

"What?"

"I knew you wouldn't be able to help it," I snap. "You just couldn't let an entire evening pass without judging my life, could you?"

"Calm down," Quinn says. "He was a dick, and you know it."

"He was a dick because *you* were a dick!" I counter. "You couldn't have just been nice? Welcoming to my new boyfriend for once? Christ, you didn't even like Nico until you physically saw him nursing me back to health last spring."

"And I was still right about him, wasn't I? I said he was the 'fuck and run' type, and he was! And I'm right about this one too. Gian*carlo's* a selfish prick, Lay. I can see it all over his Potter-looking face."

"Will you make up your mind which character he's going to be?" I snap as I cross my arms over my chest. "Your snide insults aren't as effective when you jump around."

"He takes off for his so-called 'job' at the mysterious club. Does he not see that we are college kids out for the night? Jesus, even that shit-eating bastard Jason used to hook us up at Fat Black's, and he was cheating on Shams the whole time!"

I roll my eyes. "I get it now. You're just pissed that he didn't invite you for free drinks. After you were busy insulting, no less." I cross my arms. "Your entitlement is incredible, you know that? I had really hoped that a month away would have cooled your desire to criticize every part of my life, but it's like it got worse." I take a drink, polishing off the rest of my whiskey diet. "When you left, you were mad because you wanted me to move on from Nico. Well, I did, and now you can't handle it. I'm happy now. Can't you just be okay with that?"

"This is you happy? You're a shell. You spent the entire ten-minute conversation brokering his interactions. Not to mention the mommy act you had to pull when you got in."

"That's it!" I toss a few bills on the table to pay for my drinks, grab my coat, and scoot out of the booth.

"Layla, come on. Don't be so dramatic."

I whirl around, not caring in the slightest how dramatic that makes me look. "You did *not* just say that to me."

Quinn shrugs. "If the shoe fits..."

I shake my head, biting back the words I *really* want to say. "I'm going home. I need to cool off."

"Is that the room we share, or Argentina?"

"Try not to wake me when you get back," I call out as I exit the bar.

When I get outside, I ignore the leering smile of the doorman, deciding to waste a few extra dollars on cab fare instead of walking the several frigid blocks to the nearest subway stop. Sitting in the back of the cab by myself, while the city races by, I'm struck by how alone I feel. New York is an incredibly dense place, where everyone is literally stacked on top of one another. And yet, sitting in this cab, I feel so incredibly alone.

My phone buzzes in my pocket. I pull it out and open the message there.

Giancarlo: I'm sorry. I will see you tomorrow? You have no idea how important you are to me. x

---

I pause, reading the brief sentences over and over again. Giancarlo has a way of loading his words with more than they say on the outside, but it's hard to tell with a text message. I'm never quite sure what he really means by these things, and if I get it wrong, I might pay for it with yet another argument.

But the bench beside me is empty. I rub my forearm, remembering another cab ride. One where I sat in someone's lap, was utterly wrapped up in his lips, his mouth, his arms, his hands. Where I felt like I was the center of his universe in those moments, like for him, the sun rose and set with me.

All before it was ripped away. Time and time again.

I touch my lips, then look down at my phone.

Me: You are important to me too. x

The phone buzzes quickly after that, more x's and o's, more messages with all the ways he's going to make the night up to me. I respond to them briefly, then tell him I'm home well before I am. For the rest of the drive, I lean my head against the window and close my eyes, willing that ball in my stomach to loosen completely, and the voice in my heart that aches for another to quiet into the night.

CHAPTER TWENTY

FEBRUARY 2004

NICO

I pull hard on the underside of the bleachers. One more. Two more. Last one. You can do it.

"Ahhhh!" I growl as I pull up the last time, holding my body for an extra second before dropping to the ground. I'm so covered in sweat from the end of my workout, I'm not sure I could have held on anymore if I tried.

Still, I jog in place for a second, shaking out the pain coursing up and down my arms. It's a good pain—a burn that tells me I'm making progress.

On the other side of the bleachers, a group of high school girls giggle at me from the middle of the field as I jog back to the track for my cool-down. I probably should have kept my shirt on, but it's too damn hot for that. Way hotter than normal even for LA in February. If you want to know the truth, I'm getting tired of the damn sunshine. Right now New York is covered in slush, and they're supposed to have a snowstorm next week. I'd be happy to be there if just for the change of pace.

I finish the last loop of the mile, ignoring the way the girls are eyeing me. Kids. I sprint the last hundred meters on the track, huffing out short, sharp breaths in time with my feet. I want this. I want this job more than just about anything. I had one of the top scores of the test, and now I want one of the top physical assessments too. I know that it doesn't really matter as long as I pass. It's the background checks that are really important to getting one of the coveted FDNY spots. But I can't afford to have an application that's anything less than stellar. They already know about my pas, and the two big blemishes against met: two years in detention for aggravated assault. I was only fifteen, but still prosecuted as an offender instead of a delinquent, putting a permanent mark on my record.

But they could have just tossed my application right then and there, and then didn't. So I have to try. If FedEx can see past my mistakes, maybe the FDNY will too, and I'm determined to make the rest of my application shine.

I know you can do it.

Layla's voice sings through my brain as I jog back to my apartment, keeping a quicker pace than normal. I wish I could tell her what she does for me, how her faith keeps me going. I've left her alone since Christmas, when I heard that male voice on the other end of the line. I'm not going to lie. That knowledge cuts me too. I hate knowing that she's moving on, even though she has every right. I hate thinking about the fact that another dude is touching her, loving her. Doing things to her that only *I* should do.

So I don't. Instead, I think about the good stuff. When we do share a few text messages back and forth, she asks about my EMT test, and like an idiot, I tell her it's going well. I tell her I have an interview—which is true—and let her praise and faith and optimism wash all over me.

I'm so proud of you. You're going to be great. You're so freaking smart. Words I'd never heard in my life—words I never thought I needed to hear—until I met her.

The problem with thinking about her as much as I do is that it usually leads to thinking about other stuff too. The glow in her eyes when she sees me naked. The texture of her lips when I suck on them. The swell of her ass when I take a nice handful...

I grunt, forcing myself to run a little faster. Fuck. I'm going to need a really cold shower now. It's been more than two months since I saw her last, but it. Never. Ends. Normally I wouldn't let myself get so caught up in those fantasies, but I need her words right now. My test is next week.

I have just enough time to get home, shower, and pack up my stuff before my shift tonight. I have an early flight to New York in the morning, with the weekend to spend with my family before my interview on Monday. And yeah. Okay. I'm hoping to see her too. I just want to make sure she's okay.

Yeah, you keep telling yourself that, mano. K.C. isn't even here, but I can hear him, loud and clear. Whatever, man, I think back at him. You've never been in love. You don't know how it is.

First, though, I have to tell her I'm coming.

I get back to the apartment, where most of my stuff has been packed into boxes. Jessie's supposed to find a new roommate by the time I get back, which will give me the last few weeks of February to move my things into storage and K.C.'s place in WeHo.

Jessie is sitting at the table, looking sullenly through her email.

"Hey," I say as I toss my keys into the bowl. "How's the search?"

Her answer is the same as it's always been: a scowl. She wasn't happy when, after she got back from the holidays, I broke the news: I was moving out. And when I say not happy, I mean she hurled a vase at my head, then tried to get me into bed, then a salad bowl joined the vase. So yeah, I think getting out is the right decision, aside from just being the right thing to do. And you know what? It feels good to do the right thing.

I promised I'd stay until she found a roommate, but slowly, I've been bringing my stuff over to K.C.'s and have been spending more and more nights over there. It doesn't make sense for me to find another apartment if I'm not sure what I'm doing here, and my boy is nice enough to let me sleep on his couch. Sometimes I think I should just get on the plane now. Go back to my old apartment and wait out the results of my next test in New York. Try to convince Layla to dump that fuckwad she's with and come back to me, where she belongs.

But what if I fail? Even worse, what if I get all the way to the end only to have my past pull the rug out from under me? Then I'd be right back where I started. Same old life. Same old shit.

I can't do that. Because as much as I don't want to admit it, Jessie's right. I can't go back to a city that doesn't want me. I need to make something of myself first. At least in LA I'm head of security instead of just a minor employee. There's room for growth in that. Or maybe I can actually take that EMT exam. Maybe I'll even go back to school.

Jessie huffs at her computer. "Not anyone worth having here. People are psychos; you know that."

I get a glass of water, gulp it down, and immediately refill it. "Jess, you have to give some of them a chance. At least meet a few."

"Why?" she asks sullenly.

I sigh. "We really gonna do this again? You and I should not be living together, Jessie."

She rolls her eyes, but she knows it's the truth. It's not good, this situation. A year ago, we had some fun together, but that was before things got...complicated...in my life. It was before I gave my heart to someone else. Jessie deserves more than that. She doesn't deserve to be used like a Band-Aid when I'm missing someone else.

I walk over to where she sits and look over her shoulder at a response to her Craigslist ad. I shrug, standing back up. "She looks nice."

"*She*," Jessie spits out. "I don't want to live with a girl. They're too catty." She shuts her laptop and spins around to me, slipping her hands up my bare skin naturally. "Come on. Stay. This is getting ridiculous, don't you think?"

I step out of her grasp. It would be easy, like it's been so many other times, to let her do what she wants to do—use me for some kind of self-esteem boost, let me use her to distract myself. And fuck, I am feeling pretty fuckin' hard up these days. But she always feels like shit when we're done, and so do I. If we were good together, good for each other, it wouldn't be like that. And I'd be thinking of her when I close my eyes, not someone else.

"I gotta pack, Jess," I say as I walk to my room. "Keep looking. You'll find someone."

———

THAT FEELING DOESN'T GO AWAY, EVEN after I jump into a freezing cold shower. I'm still a bit hard; it's all anticipation.

"Fuck this," I mutter and turn the water on warm again while I wash up. I might as well take care of this while I'm in here. I work in an industry with a lot of scantily dressed women. I can't be checking IDs with half a boner.

Layla. I'll call eventually, but right now, I imagine what she would do if I showed up and surprised her. Outside her dorm, maybe, where I used to wait against the lamppost. Wait, no. She doesn't live there now.

Her office, then, where we first met. Doesn't matter that she doesn't work there anymore either; this fantasy is working for me. Yeah...I thought about bending her over that desk lots of times.

Now I'm fully hard, and without a second thought, I start rubbing one out, focusing more on one particular idea that I've imagined so many times that I've even sketched it once or twice.

She's sending a fax or filing papers or whatever shit she did behind that donut-shaped desk. If I remember right, it's about three and a half feet high, tall enough that when she stood, it came well above her waist. I see her there, standing in one of those tight skirts she preferred, the high-heeled shoes that made her legs look crazy long.

How many times did I imagine coming up behind her and caging her to the desk with both hands while I nosed her hair off her neck and kissed her bare skin? How many times did I imagine slipping a hand between her legs and slowly, slowly, tugging her skirt over her hips? Sliding a finger inside her with my thumb on her clit, just the way I know she likes until she's practically dripping down my arm.

And then, just when I'd know she was ready, I'd unzip my pants and pull out my dick. I'd be a fuckin' rock, so fucking hard for her, and she'd arch as I'd gently push inside, little by little. No condom, no nothing. Just me. Just her.

"Quiet, baby," I'd have to tell her. "They'll hear you."

But she can't be quiet. My girl never could. And because I'd just have to fucking have her, right then and there, I'd keep thrusting, take hold of her ass with one hand, flick her clit with the other, and keep going until she'd be writhing all over that desktop like a snake, begging me to give it to her, harder, faster, deeper.

"Baby..." she'd moan, all breathy and light like she does when she's just about to lose it. "Nico...*please.*"

I press one hand into the shower tile as the other takes over, stroking furiously as I let my imagination go. Turning her around. Riding her all over that fucking desk. Sometimes I imagine that some of the stuck-up lawyers at that place walk in, the ones who always flirted with her in front of me, treated me like a piece of furniture. Like I wasn't there. I imagine they'd see me giving it to her, see her face contorted with desire, see her grasping at the edges as I ram into her again and again.

"Hey!" they'd shout. "You can't do that! Get off her!"

"Get the fuck out," I'd snarl just as she'd fall apart, twisting and moaning as she'd come hard all over me. "She's mine."

"Fuuuuuuuuuccccccckkkk," I moan, clapping my hand against the shower tile again and again as I come. It seems like it lasts forever as I let it pour over me and through, massaging out the last of it until everything is spent.

For a moment after, I rest my forehead against the tile, letting the water rinse off the rest of my body, which is filled with the peace that only comes from that sort of release. I know in a few minutes, it's going to be even worse. With my head filled with images of her, I'll want to topple into bed and hold her for the rest of the night.

But she's not here. And that bed is empty. And I've got to get to work before—hopefully—I can see her again for real.

———

A FEW HOURS LATER, I'm standing outside, my bag in hand. K.C. is going to drive me to the airport after his gig and my shift are up.

I finger my cell phone. Maybe I shouldn't call. Maybe I shouldn't even tell her that I'm coming. She's trying to move on, and I should let her. But...I can't. I just have to know she's okay. I haven't seen her in almost three months. Dinner can't hurt.

The phone rings three, four times. Of course. It's almost eleven o'clock on a Friday night in New York. She's at a bar with her friends, maybe out with her...man. She's not going to be able to talk to me.

But then she picks up.

"Hello?"

I listen hard for any sounds behind her. A deep voice. The clink of glasses or blare of music. But it's silent.

"Hey, baby," I say as I relax into my seat. "It's...yeah, it's me."

There's a sigh, low and content. Fuck, I forgot how good that sound makes me feel. It's the sound she used to make whenever we hugged, whenever she relaxed into my arms. She made it when she was happy. I lived for that sound. I would do anything to hear it again.

"I know who it is, silly," she says. "How are you? It's been a while."

I exhale. "I'm good, baby, I'm good. How about you? Still with Evita?"

She giggles. It makes my chest hurt, but in a good way.

"That's not very nice," she says. "But yeah, we're still together."

"Getting serious, huh?" Please say no. Say you're barely dating. Say you dress like a nun whenever you're around him and that he's never touched anything except to hold your hand. Say he hasn't even done that.

"I guess," she says. "A little. We've been dating for over two months, now."

"So he's probably got big plans for you on Saturday, huh?"

"Saturday..." she says, and I wait while she figures it out. "Oh, you mean Valentine's Day."

I frown. She doesn't sound like someone whose boyfriend is getting ready to woo her, or whatever the fuck you'd call it. It's a statement, not a question.

"Everything okay with you?" I ask. "What's wrong?"

"Nothing, nothing. I-he-um, he has to work on Valentine's Day. He works at a club like you do. He's a promoter."

Immediately, I tense. Promoters are assholes. Two-bit fuckin' salesmen who sell sex and drinks to get as many hot girls as they can into the club. Their job is to flirt, and I've literally never met one I liked. I don't know this guy, and I wasn't ever going to like him, but now I know for a fact he's not good enough for Layla.

"He didn't take the night off to spend it with you?" I ask.

"He's just a poor student, remember?" she says hurriedly, which makes me think I'm not the first person who's said this too her. "Give him some slack. I thought you of all people would respect someone with a good work ethic."

I pause. Layla's not usually defensive like this. Maybe I'm going about this the wrong way.

"That's cool, that's cool, baby. Sounds like your man has a good head on his shoulders."

It just about kills me to say it. If you have a woman like Layla, you don't work on the one fuckin' night of the year you're supposed to show her you love her. You buy her every fuckin' rose in Manhattan. You take her out for a night on the town. You never stop kissing her because her mouth tastes better than water. It feels better than air.

Fuck. Three thousand miles away, and I'm still a fuckin' pussy. I can't just say how I feel.

"So, listen," I push on. "I'm coming to town to check up on my family, see friends, all that. Since your man has to work, maybe we could grab dinner. A drink or what-ever. Just as friends, I promise."

There's a silence. I have to smile. I can easily imagine an arched black brow over a suspicious blue eye.

"Seriously?" she says. "You think you and I can have dinner 'just as friends'?"

I chuckle with her. Obviously Layla and I will never be "just friends," but I don't fuckin' care. That horse's ass left the most beautiful fuckin' girl in New York by herself on Valentine's Day. This is his fault, plain and simple.

"Just as friends," I lie without a single regret. And then, taking a chance: "What Evita doesn't know won't hurt him, you know."

But she doesn't laugh. Not like she would have a few months ago, when she knew I was just joking. Instead there's another sigh, this one long and sort of sad.

"Hey." Suddenly I'm not in the mood to joke. I just want to finish my shift and catch my flight. I want to look into her face and find out what the *fuck* this asshole is doing to make her sound like that. "You okay?" I ask again.

"Saturday it is," she says finally, and her tone is a little lighter as she scoffs. "Just as friends, you got that, Soltero?"

I grin, big and bright, feeling like a fighter who just got a K.O. "You got it, baby. Just as friends."

CHAPTER TWENTY-ONE

Nico

I DRUM MY FINGERS ON THE BAR AT THE TRAVELER, MY FAVORITE OLD PLACE FROM WHEN I worked at FedEx. I got here early enough to have a drink with Flaco after he finished his shift. I'm hoping it helps me get rid of some of this nervous energy.

"That's great, man, that's great," he says after I tell him about the interview coming up. "You'll fuckin' kill it, I know it. Just one more step 'til we get you back, right?"

They offered me a spot to take the physical on Wednesday, right after the psych interview. From what I hear, most guys have to wait months, sometimes over a year to do that. It's a good sign. Right after they sent me my list number, I received a fat packet in the mail and spent most of the holidays writing down every piece of information about myself. An investigator has been calling, asking me all sorts of questions, and I put it out there, told her everything I could think of, including all about my record and the stint at the facility upstate. The FDNY now knows me better than I know myself. They probably know what color my underwear is on any given day.

I shrug. I don't want to count my chickens, as they say, but at the same time, I know I wouldn't have gotten this far if I didn't have at least a decent shot of making it to the academy. I'm close—real close.

"How's the, uh, apartment?" I change the subject.

Flaco gives me a dry look down his long nose. "She's fine, man."

I hold my hands up innocently. "Who's fine? I didn't ask about—"

"She's fine. NYU is the same as always, just like she was last week, and the week before that when you asked about whether the maintenance people fixed the locks. Stop playin'. Nobody is that interested in brass fittings."

I snort and take a drink of my beer. Layla's dorm is on Flaco's FedEx route, and sometimes he drops off packages there. Care packages from students' families, things like that. He's seen her a few times, usually when she's on her way out.

"Fine," I say. "Fine. I'm just checkin.'"

Flaco pats my shoulder sympathetically. "I got you, *papi*, I got you. It's not easy when your woman is with another dude."

My head snaps up. "How did you know that?"

Flaco strokes his chin for a second, looking uneasy. "Shit. You didn't know?"

"No, I knew. I just didn't realize everyone else did too."

He grimaces, spreads his wide lips in a way that makes him look more like a frog than usual. "Yeah, well. Maybe I should have told you. Homeboy lives in my building."

I stare at him. "Are you serious?"

Flaco nods. "Yeah. I see them around the neighborhood sometimes. He likes that Chinese joint on 140th. She—yo, man, you sure you want to know this?"

I look down to where I've just torn a couple of the bar coasters to shreds. I drop the last few pieces and push the mess to the side. "No, I'm fine. It's all good."

"I'm not going to lie, Nico, the dude gives me the creeps. He's tall, and every time I see him, he's dressed all in black. Lookin' like the grim fuckin' reaper, chattin' up those cats that hang outside the Dominican restaurant on 138th."

I sit up a little straighter. I know those dudes. The faces change over the years, but their essence stays the same: wannabe thugs who dabble in drugs, selling dime bags to the kids at City College.

"You want me to keep tabs on him?" Flaco asks.

I scowl. I don't want to know this shit. I don't want to know anything about this dude or the stupid shit he's into. What do I care if he smokes pot every now and then? I've certainly done worse myself.

"It's fine," I grit out between my teeth. "It'll be fine."

"Well, if you want to know more, you can probably just ask her yourself."

I swing around on my barstool to where Flaco is looking. There's Layla, standing in the door of the bar, shaking snow off her parka.

Flaco slides off his stool and drops a twenty on the bar. "See you, *mano*. And hey...be smart, eh?"

With a clap on my shoulder, Flaco leaves, giving Layla a greeting and kiss on the cheek before he points her in my direction. When she sees me, her face lights up in a bright smile, and it feels for a moment like the bar freezes. Or maybe my heart stops. I don't know, but it's always like this when we haven't seen each other for a while. Like the electricity that's always there—shit, that was there even before we met—just continues to build when we're apart instead of lessening. And when it doesn't have a way to escape as often as it should...*boom*.

Layla chews on her lower lip for a minute while she finishes removing her coat, giving me a second to run my gaze over her, checking for little things. She cut her hair again and straightened it so it flows down her back. She's dressed conservatively in a modest gray sweater and black pants, but they don't do anything to hide my girl's beauty. You couldn't hide it with a garbage bag.

My girl. I really need to stop calling her that. Problem is, I'm not sure if I can.

She hangs her coat on the rack by the door and starts toward me slowly, but soon picks up the pace so that by the time she reaches the bar she's practically running. I'm grinning like an idiot, already off my stool, arms spread when she launches at me. Her arms lock around my neck as I pick her up in a tight embrace, swaying side to side. My heart squeezes as I bury my nose in her hair. There's no other way to say it. I'm not really home until I have Layla in my arms.

We hug way longer than anyone who is "just friends" should, but slowly, eventually, Layla steps away, looking sheepish.

I push the brim of my Yankees hat up and smile. "Hey, baby. God*damn,* it's good to see you."

I'm rewarded with another grin, and for a second, we just stand there, grinning like idiots in the middle of the bar.

"Can I get you guys something?" Frankie, the bartender, asks.

Layla nods. "Um, sure. I'll have a—"

"Whiskey diet," I interrupt her. "And another beer for me. Thanks, Frankie."

I toss a couple of bills on the bar, a pile of payments that Frankie will tally at the end of the night, just like he always did. Some things never change. It's actually kind of a comfort.

Layla gives me another shy smile. "You remembered my drink."

I tip my head. "Of course I do. I remember everything about you, sweetie. So tell me, how you doin'?"

She's shy at first, but soon I get her to tell me about school, her classes, her job. She dances around the subject of her boyfriend, but that's okay. I'm going to need another few drinks anyway before I can hear about that.

"That's crazy," I say when she tells me about some of the things she's learning in her South American history class. "You mean they used to measure their heads and everything? Just to prove that black people weren't as human as the Europeans?"

She nods solemnly. "I know, it's horrific. We are learning about stuff like that every day. The teacher is kind of militant, but it's really eye-opening. It's part of the whole history of colonialism. You start to see how these things became so entrenched in our cultures."

I have to smile. A year ago, even a few months ago, Layla wouldn't have been using the term "our" like that. She'd mention her "dad's culture" or "his country," like the fact that he's Brazilian was totally separate from her.

Layla sighs. "I think maybe that's why my dad is the way he is. Maybe it's why he never wanted me to learn about Brazilian culture. He's always telling me how lucky I am that I look white."

I stroke a finger down the smooth, pale skin of her arm. I can't help it. She's so lost in thought that she barely notices.

I've never met her dad, but I already knew this about him. I know so many like him, people who want to pretend like the native or the black parts of their heritage don't exist. They talk up the fact that their ancestors came straight from Madrid or wherever, like they come from the blood of kings. Sometimes it's little things too, like how K.C.'s grandma always calls Ma and my sisters "*negra*" as a term of endearment, but never her own kids. She means it kindly, but it was always a way to point out that they were different from her light-skinned family.

Layla taps her mouth, thinking. It's distracting—she licks a drop of Coke off her top lip, and I spend a good minute and a half staring at the bar and thinking about *Abuela* before I can sit comfortably again.

She catches me looking and blushes. Fuck, she's beautiful.

"You have to stop looking at me like that," she says, turning back to the bar.

I want to hook a finger under her chin and turn her back to me, kiss that blush off her face, or maybe make it darker. I don't want her to look away from me, ever. Still, she's right. I shouldn't touch her like that, or look at her like this.

My mouth, though, has other ideas.

"Did you know it's an anniversary today?" I ask abruptly. "Ours, I mean. You and me."

She looks up with wide, blue eyes. "I didn't know you remembered."

I scoff. "It's easy to remember our first date since it was on Valentine's Day, baby. But even if it wasn't, I'd never forget that night." I take another drink of my beer, lost for a second in the memories. "It was snowing, just like tonight, you remember?"

The blush on her face deepens. "I remember."

I peek at her sideways. If I look at her straight on, she'll see every dirty thought I have. "You remember how I kissed you in the snow? You had a snowflake on your lip."

That same lip falls in response, like it's waiting for me to kiss her again. This is so strange. I've never been next to Layla and not been able to kiss her. And yeah, that only makes me want to that much more.

She swallows and turns to her drink. I open my mouth to tease her a little more, but something on her face stops me. Her bright eyes are sad—a new kind of sad, but a sad I recognize. I've seen it in my mother and my sisters. I can't quite put my finger on it, but it puts me on edge.

"Your man," I say softly, though my voice deepens. "Is he good to you?"

"Yes."

Her voice is low and quick. She continues to study the bar. Call me crazy, but it's not the most reassuring response in the world.

She looks up, and I freeze. Her eyes, always wide, always as blue as a summer sky, are glossy and bright. They flicker from side to side, like she's watching for something. She reminds me of those tiny animals in Disney movies who are being chased by the big bad wolf. She looks...timid. Scared.

Immediately, I'm off my stool and reaching for her, but she leans away, like she's scared of my touch. Like she's scared of me.

"Hey," I say. "What is it?"

"Nothing," she murmurs down to the bar. "It's just...I probably shouldn't be here."

"Why?"

She looks up, her face impatient and annoyed. "You know why."

I chew on my lip for a second. Fuck it. If we're already in forbidden territory, I might as well just lay it out there. It's a kamikaze mission, but I never seemed to care about myself when it came to Layla. Why start now?

"I meant what I said, you know," I say.

"What's that?"

She's trying so desperately to keep it cool and casual, but she's also failing miserably. Her eyes keep drifting to my lips, and every now and then she sneaks a look at the tattoo that snakes down my arm. My muscles flex in response, as if they crave her touch.

"When I said I love you," I rush on. "I know it was a long time ago, but I meant it."

"W-why are you saying this to me?"

Why indeed. I don't even know.

Yes, the fuck you do, you asshole.

"Because," I say. "You should know if someone loves you, no matter what you want to do about it. And if that motherfucker you're with doesn't treat you like the princess you are, he ain't worth your time, baby. He doesn't deserve you."

She stares at me, blinking for a minute. Her eyelids twitch—that's how hard she's thinking. I'd kill to be inside that beautiful mind of hers, to know where her thoughts are at right now. But before I can ask, decision sweeps over her.

"This was a mistake," she says, pushing off her stool. "I have to go."

"Layla," I say, but she's already winding her way out.

"I have to go," she calls. She grabs her coat off the rack by the door, and in the space of five seconds, she's gone.

———

Layla

"Fuck," I breathe as soon as I'm outside. "Oh, *fuck*."

The snow is falling even harder than before, and in the hour and a half that I was inside the bar, Park Avenue has been covered with an inch of white. The snow quiets the city, and I breathe heavily into the silence, lost in the muted sounds of the street.

What was he doing? What the *hell* was he doing in there?

The same thing he always does. Makes me fall in love with him. Reminds me of how well we fit. Causes that awful tug-of-war in my heart between what I want and what I know is right. But just when he makes me give in, he'll leave me all over again.

It didn't escape me that we had an entire conversation without bickering or getting angry. No hypersensitive accusations or vindictive, cutting remarks. Between Quinn and Giancarlo, it's been months since I've had a conversation that didn't devolve into some kind of fight. We fight and then we make up, like Giancarlo says. He always says makeup sex is the best kind of sex, but it's not until I was sitting there with Nico that I realized how badly I wanted the other kind. All the other kinds. And not with Giancarlo, but with him.

Fuck. I'm a terrible person.

I lean against the brick building, still working to catch my breath. I wanted him so badly I could barely speak in there. I had to get out before I did something stupid. Giancarlo would kill me if he knew I was here. I don't even want to think about what he'd do if he knew the thoughts that were going through my head.

The door to the bar swings open, and Nico steps out into the cold, looking frantically up and down Twentieth. He's putting on his gloves, but stops and shoves them into his pocket when he spots me holding myself against the wall.

"Why did you do that?" he asks sharply as he bounds down the steps. "Why did you run away from me?"

"I shouldn't be here," I say, pushing off the brick. I start walking toward Park.

"Layla," he calls as his boots pad through the snow. "Goddammit, will you stop?"

He snags my arm and tugs me to a halt.

"What?" I cry. "What do you want from me?"

"I don't want anything," he says, but his voice shakes. "Just to see you. To make sure you're okay. Call me crazy, but I just had this feeling I needed to check on you."

There goes his gaze again, drifting down my body and up again, resting on my lips. But it's not a lecherous look, not one that's purely physical. It bears a hunger I recognize because I feel it too. And it's only made worse because it's like I'm standing in front of a buffet I can't touch. I'm starving, but I'm not allowed a bite.

"Do you not understand how much this hurts?" I say. "How painful it is to see you and know it can't work? To—"

Before I can continue, he pulls me into him and wraps me up in a kiss. It's the kind of kiss I didn't realize I had been missing, that I'd blocked out of my mind, papering it over as best I could with another man's lips, another man's touch. Nico's lips are full and soft, his tongue is wet and firm, and his arms, wrapped securely around my shoulders and my waist, hold me steady, like he knows that without them I'd be lost in the euphoria that only he causes.

A few second later—or maybe minutes, I really can't tell with him—he breaks away, leaving only a small space between our mouths, where our breaths, white and warm in the chilly night, still mingle together.

"I'm sorry," he whispers as he presses his forehead to mine. His eyes close, in a pain that matches the cyclone whipping around my chest.

Finally, what I've done hits me. He's with someone. I'm with someone. And here we are, making out like nothing's changed. But everything's changed. And it hurts. So. Bad.

I push him away, putting at least three feet between us.

"I have to go," I choke out, taking one step back, and then another. "I have to go."

This time, he doesn't follow.

CHAPTER TWENTY-TWO

Layla

I WALK LONGER THAN MY LEATHER BOOTS CAN REALLY TAKE IN THE NEWLY FALLEN SNOW, and eventually I end up on the subway, heading uptown. But that feeling in my stomach, that knot of tension that always seems to be there these days, has just doubled, and I don't seem to want to go anywhere.

Quinn and Shama will both be at the apartment, avoiding the hordes on Valentine's Day, and I'm tired of fighting with Quinn about my bad decisions. She'll take one look at my face and know immediately I've been doing something I shouldn't. And then she'll open her mouth, and Shama will crowd in, and just the thought of it makes me feel claustrophobic.

He kissed me. After he said he wouldn't. He said he loved me, and then he kissed me, and what's worse, I kissed him back.

And it felt. So. Good. I hadn't kissed him since Thanksgiving, since he broke my heart for the third time. I had imagined it plenty in moments of weakness, but oh, *God*, my imagination really can't do justice to his mouth, the exact right pressure of it, the way he commands my body with every flick of his tongue. Even through his parka, I could feel his rigid stacks of muscle. It was everything I could do to keep from grabbing his bicep right there in the bar. It strained against the cotton sleeve, the black, tattooed lines just visible under the thin white fabric.

Right there on the train, I gasp at the memory, causing the man reading the *New York Post* across the aisle to look up, alarmed. Quickly, I switch my gaze to an ad for HPV testing. It features a couple smiling and embracing each other—a black man and a white woman. They look happy, his arms wrapped around her waist. My heart twists. I miss him still. I miss him, and I don't want to anymore.

The train pulls to a stop at 137th and Broadway, and I get off without thinking, purely on autopilot. I'm staring at the mosaic sign, built into the tiled walls, and it occurs to me that I'm at City College. Well, of course I am. Giancarlo lives here. Still, I find myself walking up the west side of the street instead of the east, and I realize it wasn't to Giancarlo's apartment that my body intended to go.

I pause at the corner of 139th. I come up here all the time now, day or night. Giancarlo lives only a few blocks north, where the shops turn from selling *quinceañera* cakes and Dominican food to stereos and discounted ENYCE threads. Quinn still makes a face whenever I say I'm heading uptown—she thinks of Harlem as untouchable and dangerous, something out of a Spike Lee movie (so what if he mostly films in Brooklyn). She, like so many people I know at my school—like me only a year ago—didn't really understand that wealth in New York exists on a spectrum, just like anywhere else. And that just because you don't have it doesn't mean you don't have worth.

I look down the street where I *used* to spend so much time. Like most of the streets up here that jut off Broadway, 139th is poorly lit, with streamers of laundry flapping across the fire escapes like bats, even in the snow. I can just make out the familiar concrete blocks that arch over the entrance, welcoming me there. In my mind, I see the tiny elevator, the black and white tiled floors, the tagged walls of the lobby. I see the narrow gray apartment and the small white room where I spent some of the most contented hours of my life.

He might be there now. He might be sleeping on the couch or something, or in his old room if his sister or brother isn't staying there right now. He might be there if I rang the buzzer, might forgive me for running away from him, might take me in his arms and continue what we started in the snow...and the hell if my entire body isn't aching to do just that.

"Hey, ma! What you doin' tonight, baby?"

A car blasting merengue drives by, and I cower toward a bodega entrance as a couple of guys hanging out the windows whistle. It's certainly not the first time that's happened, but there's something alarming about the catcalls tonight. I feel like prey more than I ever have in this city.

"Move," I tell myself. "You have to move." I'm a sitting duck, just standing on the street like this, whether it's in the middle of the West Village or up here. That's the number one rule of New York City: movement.

"NYU?"

I turn around, and there's Gabe, exiting the bodega, a six-pack of Coke under one arm.

I smile and give a weak wave. "Gabe, hi."

"Hey," he says, all friendly as he gives me a quick kiss on the cheek. "You okay? You look lost."

I shake my head. "No, not lost, just...anyway. I know my way around up here."

Gabe nods knowingly. "Yeah, I've seen you around. Plus, Nico..."

I blush, even though I know I have no reason not to. It's not just because I was making out with his brother maybe an hour ago, right?

"My, um, boyfriend lives a few blocks from here," I say, shoving my hands into my pockets and nodding up Broadway. "I was just on my way there to wait for him until he gets off. He works at a club in midtown, I think."

"Oh, I'll walk you."

"No, that's ok—"

"Yeah, no," Gabe interrupts as he hooks his free arm through mine and starts walking, fairly dragging me along with him. "My brother would kill me if I let you walk around by yourself at night."

We walk in silence, letting the noises of the neighborhood replace conversation. West Harlem doesn't get quiet until really late. It's only about eleven now. Some of the curio shops are still open, with cheap suitcases piled on the sidewalk, although the owners are starting to bring them in. The big Dominican restaurant on 141st is still mostly full, and music echoes every so often from an opening door.

"So you know Nico's in town, right?"

"I—" I open my mouth to say that I saw him, but then realize that Gabe would want to know where he ended up. "Yes, I know. He's here to visit family, right? You guys must be happy to have him back for a little bit."

"Here to visit...is that what he told you?" Gabe gives me a funny look.

I blink. "Yes, why? Is that not right?"

Gabe frowns, and it's the first time he's ever really looked much like his brother. Their eyes are the same—sooty and black with a twinkle—but the guileless expression on Gabe's face most of the time is a lot different than the mischief and passion I know on Nico's.

"No, that's right," he says, in the end, and lapses back into silence. "Just visiting family," he murmurs, like he's telling himself the fact.

"Is everything all right?" I ask. "Like...with your mom?"

It's not until I say it that I realize I'm probably overstepping. Gabe gives me a sharp look, pauses for a second, then relaxes.

"He told you about her, huh?"

"I didn't mean to impose. Sorry, I shouldn't have said anything."

Gabe wrinkles his long nose. "Nah, it's okay. She's still in her apartment. For now. The whole thing is really stressing us out, and it's worse for Nico since he's so far away right now."

I stay quiet, since Gabe is apparently feeling chatty. Nico never liked to talk that much about his mother's residency issues. He always treated them like a lost cause.

"We're probably going to move her up here," Gabe's saying, "since her new land-lord's got eyes for developing."

"What do you mean?"

Gabe shrugs. "Little things. A bunch of other places in the neighborhood have been bought over the last few years. Some of the other tenants have been pushed out. A couple even by having Immigration mysteriously knock on their doors. The land-lord refuses to do repairs, cuts off the heat. We're all kind of spooked. It's their M.O. when they want to vacate rent-controlled apartments."

"That's awful!" I reply, totally aghast. "How can they do that?"

Gabe sighs, causing his lips to flare. "They can do a lot of things. Housing in New York is pretty fucked up if you don't have a lot of money." His fingers twitch at my elbow, like he's itching to rub them together. "That's why I want to be a doctor one day. Nico shouldn't be the only one to take care of this kind of thing."

I nod, considering yet again how little I understand about Nico's responsibilities to his family and the burdens that made him leave. My anger thaws. He left because he needed to find out who he was without all of this. How could he make promises without that knowledge?

I get it. I really do. But it doesn't make missing him any better.

We cross Broadway at 144th Street, and Gabe looks on curiously as I stop in front of Giancarlo's building. I doubt he's actually there, since he had to work tonight, but since I'm here, I might as well try.

I press the apartment buzzer.

"Hello?"

"Hey," I say in surprise when I hear the familiarly accented voice. "You're here."

There's a few beats, and I wonder if Giancarlo heard me. Then the same voice answers from above.

"I am here."

I look up. There's Giancarlo, looking down at us from two stories above with a face like thunder.

"Hey, man," Gabe calls warily, waving a big hand.

Giancarlo glares at him, then at me. "I will let you in."

He disappears, and Gabe looks at me. "He seems...nice."

I sigh. "He can be intense, but he means well."

"Yeah..." Gabe looks back at the window, but it's clear he doesn't believe me. "You sure you don't want to come home with me? I bet Nico would love to see you."

I shiver, more at the thought of telling Giancarlo I'm leaving than at the idea of going with Gabe. "No, that's okay. I'll be fine."

Again, Gabe looks skeptical. But when the buzzer to the door sounds, and I pull it open, his lanky shoulders fall.

"Okay. But, um, hey."

I turn back, waiting, still holding the door open.

Gabe glances up toward the window once again, then back at me. "I, uh...listen, you're welcome at my place anytime. If you need somewhere to crash or whatever. Just...come ring the bell. Okay?"

I take a deep breath and try to give him the friendliest smile I can. "Thanks, Gabe. I will."

The response seems to appease him, and he relaxes. "Okay. See you, NYU."

I watch him leave, then enter the building and start up the big stairs, only to be shocked when I find Giancarlo waiting for me on the second landing.

"Jesus!" I cry out, holding a hand to my heart. "You scared me! What are you doing lurking on the stairwell?"

"Who the *fuck* was that?"

I freeze in front of him. Giancarlo looks me over, his eyes grazing over my body slowly, taking in the tight black pants, the jewelry, the makeup—all the little signs that I wasn't just sitting at home for the evening, pining away for him.

"Come upstairs," he says, and starts toward his place without waiting.

The door slams heavily beside us, and he whirls around like a cyclone.

"Where the fuck were you? Out with him, this little boy?"

I swallow guiltily. "No, I wasn't. Gabe saw me get off the subway and offered to walk me home. You met him once before, remember?" A thought occurs to me. "Why aren't you at work? It's only eleven o'clock."

"I finished early." He takes a step closer so that we're nose to nose. I can see myself in his smudged glasses. "I went to your apartment to surprise you. You were not there."

I gulp. "Um, no. I wasn't."

Giancarlo's dark eyes narrow. He worries his jaw back and forth for a minute, and a muscle on one side starts to tick. "Who is he?"

I frown. "Who?"

"The man you are fucking behind my back. Making me a fool? Being a fucking whore?"

"Hey, I wasn't doing anything! I just met a friend for a drink because *you* had to work on Valentine's Day. I wouldn't have been out at all if you had just told me you got the night off."

Giancarlo takes a step toward me, and I step backward.

"I knew it," he gritted out. "I knew you were always going to cheat on me like this. I knew better than to trust someone like you."

I suddenly feel like I'm drowning. Where is this coming from? Sure, Nico kissed me, but I put a stop to it and left. I did the right thing, whether Giancarlo knows it or not. He has no reason to say any of this.

Or does he? Does the fact that I'm still in love with someone else show all over my face?

"You never loved me from the beginning," Giancarlo continues, spitting the words out like poison. "Admit it. Admit that you were only using me. Using me like the *puta* you are."

"Using you for what?" I pipe up, finally finding my voice. "This shitty apartment? The crappy takeout food we eat?" I can practically feel my roommates sitting on my shoulders, cheering me on. *That's it, Lay. Don't let Snape get away with that shit.* "What exactly am I using you for?"

Giancarlo's face darkens further. "I suppose that's better than the two rooms you share with four girls? You always want me to fuck you in the middle of the room, like we're animals. You're a spoiled brat who doesn't appreciate the privacy here, no? The privacy *I* pay for!"

"I think you mean the privacy your daddy pays for, don't you?" I cut back. "And it's not like this is a palace or anything. You live in a shitty one-bedroom in the worst building in the neighborhood."

A hand, fast as lightning, snakes out immediately and grabs my wrist. Giancarlo jerks me close, but even when I stumble next to him, my wrist stays steady, held fast near his chest while my body weight tugs on it. His hand is immovable—I'm caught.

"Did you sleep with him?"

"Who?"

"Whoever the fuck you were with?" Giancarlo looks closer. "I'm not stupid. I know you were with someone."

"No," I say as evenly as I can, even though my heart is thumping wildly. "I didn't sleep with anyone."

"Did you kiss him?"

Giancarlo's eyes drop to my lips, like he's studying them for imprints of Nico's mouth. As searing as the kiss was, I half wonder if he can see remnants. And it's then I know that my guilt is surely written through my thoughts and on my face. It spreads, just like the realization spreads over Giancarlo.

"H-he kissed me," I whisper. "I stopped him. And ran off. Straight here. I—I didn't want to. He just did it, and I left. I'm so—"

"Ahhh!"

Giancarlo shoves me away from him, finally releasing the iron grip on my wrist and causing me to fall back several steps from the force while he paces the living room like a caged animal. I rub my wrist—it's red from his grip—and cower slightly into the corner. I've never seen him like this, not even when I angered him in the kitchen. Not even the other week when he couldn't keep an erection and blamed me for it. My heart falls. Nothing I say here will make it better; nothing is going to alleviate my guilt. Because I did kiss another man, and in doing that, I hurt this one badly.

Then someone else's face flashes through my mind, someone I haven't thought about or spoken to more than a few times in the last several months. Someone too busy wallowing in her own misery to care about her daughter's life.

My mother. I remember her all those years, dealing with my father's late nights at the office. Realizing that in Brazil, where more than one of my uncles have not-so-secret extra-marital affairs, her husband is probably already involved with another woman if he wasn't before. I wonder if he was unfaithful all those years where they clearly didn't love each other. I wonder if she knew I was going to be like him.

The realization guts me, and I start to cry.

"Giancarlo," I creak, unable to wait for him to speak. I'm full of remorse and self-hatred, and it pours from me like a river. "Giancarlo, please. It was an accident. I didn't think anything would happen, but I should never have gone. I should have just stayed at home and waited for you, I know that now. Please, please forgive me. He's no—"

I'm about to saying "nothing," but that's not true either. My heart squeezes as I admit to myself that Nico will always be someone to me. And that all I can do is try my best to be present with the person I'm with instead of the person who never wanted me like I wanted him anyway.

Giancarlo has stopped pacing, and is now standing in the doorway of the kitchen, arms folded across his chest. He's breathing normally now, like somehow my outpouring of emotion tempers his. Maybe, I think, he just needed to see I cared.

Slowly, he approaches me and raises his hand. I flinch, and he arches a thick eyebrow in response.

"You are afraid of me?" he asks in a low purr.

My jaw trembles, and I swipe at the tears falling down my cheeks. "N-no."

Again, the eyebrow rises. "Maybe you should be." He glances at my reddened wrist. "Now you'll learn."

The words land between us, and I'm not sure if they are a threat or a warning. I freeze, feeling again like prey, except this time the predator is someone I know intimately, not strangers in a car. Giancarlo maintains his penetrating stare, and it feels like some sort of test. But in the end, his shoulders relax.

"You are sorry?" he asks.

Miserably, I nod.

"You want to...how do you say...make it up for me?"

A bit less certain, I nod again.

His gaze flickers over me, like he's measuring me up. He huffs. "Okay. Tomorrow."

I blink. "What?"

"Tomorrow," he repeats more firmly. "I have some money that needs to be taken to a store in the Bronx, but I can't go because of work. It's a payment for something my boss bought for the club."

I frown. "What did your boss buy—"

"What does it matter?" he spits out curtly. "Televisions. For the walls. It's none of your business, only a way for you to show me I can trust you. Can I trust you, *amor*?"

I look up. There's that word. Love. For all his anger, Giancarlo uses it so freely. From the beginning, he's been dedicated to whatever we are, jumping ahead and waiting patiently for me to join him. Maybe his anger is related to the fact that I've been holding back. That in my heart, maybe I've been waiting for someone else.

"Okay," I relent. "Sure. I can take it."

He relaxes visibly, then takes my hand and pulls me into him, turns me around so my back is to his front and he can press his face into my neck.

"Oh, my love," he whispers, before he launches into Spanish colloquialisms I can't quite understand. "You make me crazy, do you know that?"

I soften into him, desperate for the touch. My eyes close, and I sink into the feel of a body sheltering mine.

His hand slides up my back and into the hair at the base of my neck. But just as I relax a little more, he grabs my hair and winds it around his wrist, pulling it taut so my neck is cranked back, exposed to him.

"Go," he says before he draws his teeth across my bared skin. He yanks at my hair, jerking my neck up, and points me down the hall. "Into the bedroom. Take off your clothes. We will finish this in there."

In the end, I follow his orders. I walk into the bedroom, remove my clothes, and curl up on his faded, peach-colored sheets, feeling as naked inside as I am out. My skin pebbles in a room that's never quite warm enough, and I wait for what seems like forever until Giancarlo finally follows me in. Outside the windows, a siren sounds.

Giancarlo looks me over and nods with approval, then strips off his own clothes. I can't help it—I compare him to Nico. His body isn't as cut; Giancarlo is long and lean, but he's no athlete. His pale torso is softer, lacking the definition and raw strength of Nico's even though he's several inches taller. He removes his glasses and sets them next to the bed, then kneels in front of me on the mattress and takes a handful of my hair, pulling my head back. Pain prickles through my scalp.

"You want me to kiss you?" he asks in a voice that's low, still laced with threat.

I gulp. Then I nod, although I'm not so sure. But I need something to replace the imprint of lips still throbbing on mine.

Giancarlo inspects me, his dark gaze traveling over my body. "Maybe later," he says. "If you're good." He continues his examination. It strikes me how little we've really been like this together. Most of the times we've had sex have been in the dark, shrouded by alcohol and other ways of blurring the moment.

"You're beautiful," he says, like he's surprised.

I look down my body. I haven't been exercising as much as I usually do, since the time away usually earns Giancarlo's ire, but I think I look okay. "Thanks."

He reaches between my legs, slipping his fingers inside suddenly. I arch against the intrusion, ignoring the way I want them to feel like someone else's. I ignore how clinical it feels, how his fingers actually pinch a little inside me, having not taken any time at all to ready me. My body squeezes in response, and not in a good way. It curls inward, trying to protect itself.

"Does that feel good?" Giancarlo asks as he presses a thumb on my clit. He watches the movement distantly, like he's observing a lab rat or something, though his cock stands upright, pointing directly at me. "Do you like that?"

I nod, closing my eyes against the feeling. I frown, ignoring the way the tip of his cock brushes against my leg. His fingers are pressing too hard, pushing too far.

"Hold on," I say, reaching down to take his hand.

I pull it back a little bit, urging a lighter touch, and Giancarlo stops completely.

I open my eyes and look down. "What?"

"Nothing." He looks away. His erection softens, and I already see the anger building on his face.

"I need to go," he says suddenly, standing up. "You are not in the right mind for this tonight. Maybe I need to give you time to get your head right."

For some reason, the words stir something deep inside me. A jab to my heart. I couldn't tell you why. I couldn't have even explained it to myself. But the only thing going through my head was *not again*. I spring forward and grab his hand before he's off the bed completely.

Giancarlo turns around. "What?"

"Don't go," I say. "I'm sorry. It was my fault. Sometimes I act before I think. I didn't mean to make you feel bad."

His eyebrow quirks. "I don't like that."

Don't like what? Being challenged? Being corrected?

I don't say anything—just swallow my words and nod. "I understand. Please. Let's start over. Let's make up."

He sits back on the bed and beckons for me to sit on top of him. When I pause, he frowns. Immediately, I scurry forward and obey when he moves my legs so that I straddle him. But when I lean forward to kiss him, a hand closes around my neck.

"I didn't say you could do that," he says. "Not yet. You don't deserve it yet."

I wilt, and the guilt still lodged in my stomach blooms.

"Are you going to listen to me?" he says as his hand slides up my throat and takes hold of my chin so I can't look away.

I blink slowly. Then I nod. "Oh-okay."

His eyes are actually brown, but right now they look black. They always look black, deep and foreboding. "Good," he says. "Now, take me in your hand. Get me hard."

When I don't move, his eyes flash dangerously. The hand at my chin slides down my neck, and his long finger wrap around it and squeeze slightly.

"Giancarlo," I say, my voice cut off a little from the pressure. "I can't—I can't breathe."

"Do what I say," he prods.

My heart pounding in my chest, I reach between us. Giancarlo intercepts my hand and squeezes some lubricant on it, then nods for me to continue. I rub my fingers together, then take his soft penis in my hand. It's squishy, like holding an overripe banana. Giancarlo's hand around my neck loosens its grasp, and I can breathe normally again. His fingers drift over my skin. In the mirror over the bed, I can see the slight red marks left there, quickly fading away.

In my hand, he turns harder.

"This is what a woman does for her man." He looks down, entranced by the movement of my fingers. "I want you to come," he orders as he places his thumb on my clit and starts to rub it meditatively while keeping his other hand around my neck. It's an odd position, sort of being held like a puppet in reverse.

We continue touching each other, his eyes boring into me, expectant and fierce. I already know there's no way I'm going to orgasm like this.

Giancarlo swears in Spanish, a phrase I don't recognize. He's fully hard now, watching. His thumb on me presses harder, just a little too hard to feel good as his finger slides inside me again.

"Are you close?" he asks as the fingers around my throat tighten just a little, though not enough to cut off my breathing. I shake my head, but the hand remains.

"Are you close?" he asks again, this time with more of an edge.

I'm scared to say no. I'm scared to tell him the truth, tell him that I'm miles away from where he wants me to be. But I've hurt him enough tonight already, and it seems like this means a lot to him, this control. He's looking for something I can't produce, and what he's doing with his hand isn't going to get me there. I can't just come on demand.

But I can fake it.

"Yeah," I whisper, purposefully breathy, sounding almost as though he's squeezing my windpipe all over again, even though he's not.

Giancarlo sighs, his chest shuddering as he grows even harder.

"Do it," he says. "I want you to come. Right now."

Um, what? What the fuck kind of fool thinks that women can just come on command? I know it happens in shitty romance novels, but this is real life.

I know it's a bad precedent to set. I know if I do this, he'll expect that his commands will undo me every time, when just like anyone, I need so much more than that.

But all I want is for him to stop looking at me like I'm a terrible person. Or maybe I just want to stop feeling like a terrible person. I want him to look at me like I'm precious and important. And Giancarlo, despite his flaws, has always needed me. He's always done that.

"Oh, GOD," I shout, manufacturing desire with the best imitation I can. It's hard. When I come, I'm not usually conscious of what I actually sound like. I'm just...in the moment.

But instead, I will my body to shake—not actually that difficult with all the tension coursing through me. I toss my head back and moan toward the ceiling, ride his hand as if it's undoing me for real.

"I'm coming!" I shout again and again. "Oh, God! I'm *COMING*!"

And then, slowly, I let myself come down from the manufactured high and fall forward onto his shoulder. Honestly, forcing myself to mimic the relaxation of post-coital haze is harder than pretending an orgasm. Especially when I'm still so tense. So worried. So needy.

But Giancarlo doesn't seem to notice. Instead, he pushes me back upright, then fixed his hand back around my throat and urges my hand to keep working his cock.

"Slap me," he orders.

My hand stills. "What?"

"Hit me. I want you to." Giancarlo sticks out his chin, like he's daring me to punch him, then turns his face to the side. "Do it. Now. And don't stop with your other hand."

Slowly, I keep rubbing his cock, which is now basically stone. Is he serious? He really wants me to hit him? I can't imagine doing that to anyone I care about, ever.

"Layla." Giancarlo growls. His eyes bore into me, two black rubies that glint under the fluorescent lighting "Now. Hard."

So I do. Slowly, I draw back my free hand, watching as anticipation grows on Giancarlo's angular features. He nods slightly, and like a spring being let loose, I whip it forward and land it straight across the side of his face.

"Fuck!" he shouts. In my hand, his cock spasms, jetting a sudden, sticky release on his stomach and my thighs. The hand around my neck flops down, then he grabs my hand and continues sliding our fists together up and down his cock until he's finished completely.

"Fuck," he murmurs, looking down. "Look at this mess." His gaze returns to me, dazed, but still hardened. "Clean it up."

Again, I look up, unsure if he's serious. Jesus, he's not asking me to lick it up or anything like that, is he?

"What are you waiting for? Take care of your man. Go to the bathroom and get me a towel."

Without saying anything, I slide off him, then tiptoe out of the bedroom. When I return, dampened washcloth in hand, Giancarlo has already mopped off the mess with his t-shirt, and is waiting expectantly for me, rubbing himself and already partially hard again.

"What-why did you have me get this?" I ask, holding up the towel.

"For later," he says. "Put it on the nightstand and come here."

I follow his orders, and when I reach his side, he puts an arm around my back. He looks at me, up and down, the blackness in his eyes softened slightly from before.

And it's then, finally, that he kisses me. His lips are soft, though not as soft as the ones that kissed me before. His tongue is firm, though it doesn't quite move in that way that makes me melt. But his hands stroke up and down my back gently, with a softness I've been craving.

My body softens toward him.

"I need you," he says, over and over again. "Don't you need me too?"

And in that moment, those three words are the only things I want to hear.

"Good," he says as he grazes his teeth up my neck. It doesn't matter that I never responded. "Now turn over."

And I do. Feeling like a shadow of myself, I let Giancarlo take out what he needs on my body, alternately soft and harsh as his mood evolves. At one point, he turns me over, claps his hands on top of mine and barely lets me move against his mattress. Shouts his dominance while he takes me from behind, while I bury my silence into the pillow, waiting for it to be over. It isn't an act of pleasure; it's an act of penance. Like a priest, Giancarlo has determined my punishment for my sins. And now I have to take it.

CHAPTER TWENTY-THREE

Nico

I DUMP THE BOX OF OLD MAGAZINES INTO THE DUMPSTER AND THEN JOG THE REST OF THE way up the stairs. Gabe, Selena, and I are all helping Ma clean out her apartment. The lease—the lease in *my* name—is up at the end of the month, and for the first time in almost ten years, the landlord asked me for verification that I actually live here and wanted all residents' names and ID numbers on the new lease. I checked, and he's been asking everyone in the building for the same thing.

Bastard. He knew exactly what would happen. He knew there was no way in hell my mother was going to put her name on any kind of legal document. He knew she would move out, leave her home—tiny, run-down home that it is, but still a home nonetheless—before she made herself vulnerable that way.

I have a couple of days between my interview and my physical, and even though I've worked out a few times, a little extra labor is the best way to get rid of the jitters I feel. Well, there's one other distraction I can think of, but she won't have anything to do with me.

I tried to call Layla this morning, when I thought that maybe she'd have cooled off enough to accept my apology for last night. If I'm being honest, I'm not really sorry. I don't care if she's with someone else, I'll never be sorry for anything we are together.

The only thing I'm sorry for was the look on her face when she said that loving me hurt. That pain makes me feel like my guts are being torn out.

Which is why, in the end, I didn't call her again. I don't want to hurt her, even if it's physically painful to leave her alone. Knowing she's probably staying a few blocks from where I am made for a night of really shitty sleep, I can tell you that.

"I still think you should just tell her your plans," Gabe says when he confronts me after I tell him what happened. "They're going to hire you. Peter didn't even get an interview yet," he says, referring to his friend who also applied. "In six months, you'll be a fuckin' firefighter for real. FDNY, man. That's the shit." He nudges me in the shoulder. "*You're* the shit."

I smile at the ground and rub the back of my neck. "We don't know what's going to happen."

And that's the truth. I hoist another big box of linens down the stairs so my brother doesn't have to see how scared I am that I'm going to get to this final stage and not make it. It's the same reason I haven't told Layla. I don't think I could take getting her hopes up that I'm coming back to New York only to rip them away again.

I want this so bad. I'm scared to admit to myself how badly I want it—more than anything I've ever imagined for myself. I want this more than I wanted to get out of juvie, back when I was seventeen and locked in a jail for kids. I want this more than I wanted the job at FedEx, which was the first time I was ever given a legit job. I want it more than I wanted to leave New York...and I never thought I'd want anything more than that.

For the first time, I feel like I'm on the precipice of doing something great. Not just a change. Not just something to help me or my family get by. But something truly worth doing in my life.

I never had that kind of opportunity. And now that it's here, I don't know how I'll handle it if—no, *when* it does get ripped away.

"Yeah, well," Gabe interrupts my thoughts as he arrives at the rented truck with me. "I guess she got Lurch anyway."

I look up from the back of the cab, frowning, and turn my cap on backward so I can look at him. "Who the fuck is 'Lurch'?"

Gabe blinks uneasily. "Um, Layla's boyfriend. At least, that's what I think he looks like—that guy from *The Addams Family*. He lives up by CUNY. Maybe five, six blocks from our place."

"And how the fuck do you know this?" My voice is sharper than I intend it to be.

Now it's Gabe's turn to rub the back of his neck. "I might have walked her there last night. She was standing on our corner looking like a lost kitten. It was, I don't know, like ten, eleven? Something like that? I just figured you'd want me to walk her to wherever she was going."

"You thought right," I say. "Thanks. So you met her...the guy?"

Gabe nods and makes a face. "Yeah. Dude was wack. Tall, pale, skeleton-looking asshole with glasses. He talked to her like he was her dad, all pissed that she missed curfew." I must have a pretty awful expression, because when Gabe looks up, he actually takes a step back. "Sorry. You want me to stop?"

I shake my head. "No, it's okay."

"He's actually in one of my classes."

I stop. "Serious?"

Gabe nods. "Yeah, my algebra class. But he's always missing or leaving early, or else he's on his phone, texting someone while the instructor talks. She fuckin' *hates* him because he doesn't listen for shit."

I snort, even though I probably shouldn't take so much pleasure in that. But if I'm being honest, the guy is a little intimidating. He's everything I'm not—smart, college kid, from a good family, probably rich. Way closer to what Layla's family would want for her than I am.

So yeah, it's nice to hear he's not perfect.

"You think he's into something?" I ask, thinking of Flaco's comments about the guys on the block.

Gabe shrugs. "I don't know. But it's weird how he's always up and leaving. His phone buzzes and 'boom,' he's gone. She said yesterday that he works at a club, but I don't know, man. What kind of club business takes you out of class at nine thirty in the morning?"

I frown. I don't know where this guy works, but I've worked in nightclubs for a long time. It's not impossible that Evita has errands for a manager first thing in the morning, but most people who work in the nightlife industry keep hours like bats. And I don't know a single promoter who starts their job before noon.

"Hey." Gabe stops walking toward the buildings when he notices I haven't followed. "You want me to keep an eye on him?"

It's tempting. But I don't need my little brother getting involved with this guy, especially if he's into anything bad. Gabe needs to focus on school. That's it.

"Nah, man, it's okay. Thanks, though."

We jog back up the stairs to where Ma and Selena are finishing up. Alba is coming over tomorrow morning to help everyone clean the place. There's no deposit to get back, but we don't need to get slammed with an exit fee.

Ma walks out of the kitchen carrying a box of dishes. The apartment is looking really bare. We got rid of the last of the furniture a few days ago, and they've been moving her things gradually uptown so as not to attract the suspicion of the landlord up there. The move is almost done; all that's left is to take a few more boxes uptown and haul the rest to the Salvation Army. Then we clean and get the hell out.

"*Ay, bendito*," Ma remarks for the tenth time as she looks over the empty living room. It seems bigger now that it's not crammed with furniture and the clutter of four kids. She's been sighing like that for the last few days.

"It's hard to say goodbye," she says in Spanish.

My mother moved here when she was ten, so I'm pretty sure she could speak English if she wanted to. But for most of her life, living in the shadows the way she has, she's kept to the community of people from Puerto Rico and other Hispanic countries that originally populated this part of Hell's Kitchen, until one by one, most of them left, scattered across New Jersey and the Bronx as it became harder and harder to pay the rent in this part of the city. We've been seeing it our whole lives, especially after the police cleaned up the neighborhood. It was only a matter of time for us too.

I walk over and put my arm around her shoulder, and Ma lays her head against me for a moment. She says nothing more, but I know what she's feeling. She and Alba moved into the building when they both had K.C. and me in tow, and until I was eighteen, the apartment was under Alba's name, just like anything else my mom needed legal identification for. But Alba moved out years ago, and eventually so did most of the other people. Things are changing. It's time for her to change too.

And she deserves more than this. More than living in a place that doesn't meet housing codes and has a bathroom in the middle of the kitchen. More than moving from building to building like a fugitive. Always living in fear of being discovered. Constantly worried that one day, her habit of staying out of the way is going to catch up to her. I want more for my mother. More for all of us.

Still, I get it. This was our home, for better or for worse. The scent of beans and rice, always cooking on the little stove, still lingers in the air. If I listen hard enough, I can hear the shouts of laughter when my siblings and I would chase each other around the room until one of us got a house slipper thrown at us.

But I can hear other sounds too—the shouts and screams when my mother fought with David, Gabe's dad, or one of the other shitheads who preyed on her vulnerability until I was old enough and big enough to tell them all to fuck off. It took threatening to take away Gabe and Selena and Maggie to get her to stop with those types, but she's stayed good to her word, even now, when all of us are finally grown. Things are better; our family finally has a peace we rarely had when I was growing up. But all of us still bear the scars of those times, inside and out.

I squeeze her shoulders and then take the last box from her. No matter what happens with my job, I decide then and there that after it's all over, the next thing on my agenda will be to get my mother on the path to legal residency. And my brother and sisters—they have to help too. Plenty must have changed since she was told in the seventies she had no chance. It's been over twenty years. She deserves more.

———

BY THE TIME Gabe and I load the rest of the boxes into the truck, it's close to dinner. Ma wants to stay one last night in the apartment by herself on the mattress that's getting tossed in the morning, probably to say goodbye to the first place that was only hers. She didn't have much time to herself—just a few months after I left and Gabe moved out. I can't actually tell if she was happier alone.

I still want to work out or do something to burn off some steam before my interview tomorrow, which will probably mean running up and down the Hudson until I get too cold to do it anymore, then picking up some food uptown before I get a good night's sleep.

"We'll see you up there?" Gabe asks as he shuts the cab. Selena is waiting in the front seat, messing around on her phone.

I nod and hand him the keys. "Yeah. See you there."

They drive off, and I take a final look around the neighborhood. I don't know how much I'll come back here anymore. Probably every now and then to see Alba, who's really like my second mother. But beyond that...this is a goodbye for me too. Really, it's a goodbye for all of us.

My phone buzzes in my pocket, and I answer it without looking, still stuck in my memories.

"Hello?"

"N-Nico?"

The voice, small and tentative, cuts through the rumble of car horns and people.

"Layla? What is it? What's wrong?" I swear to God, if that motherfucker hurt her, I'll kill him myself.

"I'm fine," she says, and relief floods me. "I just...I need your help."

"Where are you?" I demand, already jogging toward Tenth Avenue to hail a cab.

There's a long pause, and I wonder for a second if she's messing with me. But then she answers, and I'm not sure if I heard her correctly.

"Hunt's Point?" I ask. "Is what you just said? That your boyfriend sent you to Hunt's fuckin' *Point*?"

"Y-yes," she says, and then rattles off an address. For a second I feel like I'm about to faint. Because Layla just told me she's alone in one of the most dangerous neighborhoods in New York, and I'm standing here like an idiot, miles away.

"Don't move," I order as a cab pulls over. "I'll be there in twenty minutes."

CHAPTER TWENTY-FOUR

Nico

Hunt's Point is a weird neighborhood, with some buildings taller than my old seven-story building in Harlem, and others that are supposed to be single-family homes. The cab zips past a few clusters of people on the darker corners—dealers, some of them, a few gang members, and some lone women I'd guess are prostitutes.

This part of the city is much more spacious than the narrow streets I grew up on, but the sly crime and deviance that hangs in the air reminds me of Hell's Kitchen when I was a kid. It's nicer now, but when I was little, the Kitchen was so populated with junkies and criminals that my mother felt safer walking us down the center of the street than the sidewalks. More than one kid I went to school with is already dead, having met an early end in a life of crime or drugs. Hunt's Point has that same air of hopelessness and abandonment. It's a feeling that's getting harder and harder to find in the city these days, but still exists in a few pockets.

The cab stops in front of the address Layla gave me—a pawnshop, where the neon "OPEN" sign flickers, orange and tinged with dirt in the twilight.

"Thanks, man," I say as I hand over the fare. "Can you wait a few minutes?"

The cabbie, an older Russian guy who seems like he's been doing this for a long time, looks at me like I'm crazy. "No."

I sigh. "Fine. Thanks again."

I push open the door to the pawnshop to find Layla cowering next to one of the glass cases while the owner, a short, fat dude with a trimmed gray mustache, stares at her like he's not sure if he should smack her or feed her dinner.

Layla looks up, and her big blue eyes flood with relief.

"Hi," she says in almost a whisper as I join her.

"Hey," I say, a little too sharply as I approach.

I can't help it. I sat in the back of that cab for twenty-eight minutes, twenty-eight minutes of texting her constantly to make sure she was okay, twenty-eight minutes for my worry to turn into about a million other emotions until it finally landed on anger, pure and simple. So now I'm fuckin' pissed. I'm pissed she's here. I'm pissed that she thought it would be a good idea for her to come to this neighborhood by herself. And I'm *really* fuckin' pissed at the motherfucker who sent her.

Everything about Layla sticks out in a place like this. Her privilege shouts itself in her big blue eyes that look at the world without any hardness, in the quiet polish of her clothes, her genuine leather shoes, and the gold jewelry that won't rub off to brass or nickel in a few weeks.

What the *fuck* was this guy thinking?

Then it hits me: he knew *exactly* what he was doing. Motherfucker sent his naive, rich girlfriend here precisely because the pawnbroker would see her and say what he says next.

"She's short."

He speaks Spanish directly to me, in a Dominican accent that Layla can't understand yet because of the way he removes letters and even whole words. Don't get me wrong. I'm impressed by the progress she's made in less than a year. She's smart and definitely has a knack for language. But as cute as it is to hear her ask "Where is my backpack?" in textbook Spanish, she can't understand the rapid-fire dialects you hear in New York.

"You know Giancarlo?" the broker continues, still in Spanish.

I shake my head. "No. But he's gonna get to know me pretty soon."

"The cocksucker sent his girl here a thousand short. Don't tell me it wasn't on purpose."

I don't argue with the man. He's not the kind who will take no for an answer. He's the kind of guy who probably has a Glock handy by the register, who'll shout for a couple of dudes to hold you down while he rips your watch and anything else of value off your body. Jack-Me-Off knows this, which is why he sent his Bambi-looking girlfriend instead. And on some level, Layla knows this too; it's why she called me to come get her.

"What did he say?" she whispers, her blue eyes large and afraid. I hate that look. That look makes me want to break the neck of the fucker who put it there.

I blink between the broker and Layla. She doesn't notice the way my fists ball up, but he does.

"Her watch," he says to me. "I told her I wanted the watch, and everything will be okay. But she doesn't understand."

"Did you try in English? She doesn't speak Spanish."

"I told her." The broker shrugs, which tells me his English probably wasn't good enough to explain what he wants, and the conversation probably consisted mostly of pointing and yelling at Layla.

I turn to where she's watching the exchange, her arms folded around her waist. She's scared, shrunken into herself. The sight makes me that much angrier, but I swallow it back with difficulty.

"Baby, he needs your watch."

Her face screws up with confusion. "What? Why? I gave him the money."

I sigh, and the broker starts tapping his fat fingers on the glass.

"El reloj!" he shouts, pointing at her wrist.

"Oye, calma!" I snap, then turn back to Layla, who is clasping her wrist. "Baby, your man,"

I trip over the phrase; it sounds *so fuckin' wrong* out of my mouth. This dude's not a man, not by any stretch of the imagination. And even if he was, the only way that fucking sentence works is *with me*. As in, your man is me. Nico. I, Nico, am your man. No one the fuck else, and especially not that piece of shit motherfucker.

I clear my throat. "He didn't give you enough money. He still owes a thousand dollars. The broker here says he'll take your watch instead."

"What? No! There must be some mistake. Giancarlo said this would cover everything he paid for the TVs. They were for the club he works for, he said."

I have to force myself not to roll my eyes. I'd bet my foot Gian*carlo*—the name makes me want to vomit—owes money for something a lot bigger than some used televisions. This shit has gambling or drug money written all over it.

I just shake my head. "No, sweetie. There's no mistake. Layla, I think you should just give him the watch."

Layla's mouth opens and closes a few times as she processes what's happening. Yeah, I know, baby. Your boyfriend's a dick. He shorted you on purpose so you'd get stuck with the bill, because he was betting no one would take advantage of your pretty, innocent face. He's a cowardly fuck, and he was doing it to save his own ass.

I hate that I can't just pay the debt for her. But the shitty Casio on my wrist is worth maybe fifteen dollars, and I only have twenty more in my pocket. Nothing else on me is worth a dime.

The broker lets out a growl and another machine-gun fire of Spanish, cursing Giancarlo. I don't argue with any of it. But this guy is getting impatient, and soon he's not going to care that Layla's a sweet, innocent girl. He'll get that watch, whether she wants to give it up or not.

"Layla," I say again, trying for a calmer tone. "It's just a watch."

"But m-my dad gave me this watch," she says. "It was m-my Christmas gift this year."

Shit. I can see her now, carrying this flashy piece of jewelry around with her, the one thing her father has done in six months to show her he cares about her at all. That's another guy I wouldn't mind punching one day because of the way he makes her look.

I sigh and take her hand. "Layla."

I don't have to say anything else. She can see it on my face. With eyes that water and a chin that quivers, she nods, then pulls off the watch and sets it on the glass in front of the broker.

"G-good?" she asks him. "*B-bueno?*"

He examines the watch, a delicate little thing that's clearly well made. Then he looks at her, a little bit of kindness written across his hard features.

"*Sí,*" he tells her. Then to me: "Tell *la blanquita* she needs a new boyfriend. The one she's got is bad news. And if you see that motherfucker, tell him he's not welcome in my shop no more. Any bitch who has to send his woman to pay his debts for him wants a beating."

My fists curl tightly. I don't want to think about beating this dude's face. It's too tempting, and Layla doesn't need to see me like that.

With a curt nod, I turn to Layla. "You're good, baby. Let's go."

———

Layla

After Nico practically jogs us to the other side of the highway so that we are firmly out of Hunt's Point, he calls a cab from the shelter of a gas station, and we ride in silence while the tinny voice of some kind of Middle Eastern music fills the air.

Nico's mad. He's *really* mad. I'm still trying to figure out how I feel as I curl my fingers around my bare wrist. I still don't completely understand what happened back there. I don't know why the broker thought Giancarlo owed more money than he did. I'm sure there was some kind of misunderstanding, but when Nico told me to give him the watch, there was something in his eyes that told me not to argue. Nico was scared too. And that scared me more than anything.

One day, my father is going to ask me what happened to my watch. Well, he'll ask if he ever comes back to see me. A pang shoots through my heart at that thought, but I push it away. It's another issue I'm so very tired of thinking about.

It's not until the cab comes to a stop much quicker than I expected that I realize Nico hasn't told the driver my address, but his.

"I can walk," I say after we get out. "Giancarlo's apartment is only a few blocks from here. I can wait there for him if he's not already home, find out what happened."

Nico looks at me like I'm crazy. "Abso-*fuckin'*-lutely *not*," he pronounces. "If you think I'm going to let you walk around by yourself right now, you are even crazier than I thought."

"What the fuck is *that* supposed to mean?" I demand.

"It means you should have known better than to go running up to the worst part of the *South fuckin' Bronx* by yourself!" Nico explodes, right there on the sidewalk, startling a group of teenage girls passing by.

"Ohhh," one of them titters to the other.

Nico gives them a black look, and they scurry up the hill. He turns back to me.

"Look," he says. "It's getting late. I'm tired, I need dinner, and I have a...thing tomorrow that I can't fuck up. I don't have time to take you back downtown right now, and honestly, I don't have any more cash for a cab. Can you please just stay with me tonight?"

I look dubiously at the familiar gray building, then back at him. "You want me to stay here. With you. Are you forgetting what happened the last time we were together? Nico, I have a boyfriend."

"Yeah, where's your boyfriend now?"

"At work!" I protest.

"I'll believe that when I fuckin' see it."

"You want to go to the club?" I ask, though part of me doesn't want to go. Part of me wonders if maybe Nico is right.

His jaw ticks when he grinds his teeth together. Nico sighs audibly. "Look, I'll be good, I promise. But if Evita's just a club promoter, baby, I'm the fuckin' Easter Bunny."

"What is that supposed to mean?"

He sighs. "Nothing. It means nothing."

I cross my arms. There's a tension in the pit of my stomach, a warring between wanting to stay with him because, if I'm being honest, Nico makes me feel safe, and always will. But the other side of me feels guilty. Giancarlo wouldn't like it. He wouldn't like me staying at some stranger's place. And after what happened last night, I'm genuinely scared of what he would do if he found out.

Nico's gaze loses its hardness. His big black eyes turn tender, and I see then how very afraid he was for me tonight—more afraid, maybe, than even I was. I'm not sure I want to know why.

"Please." He swallows heavily. "Layla. I just need to know you're safe, okay? My head's going to be all types of fucked up tonight if I don't know where you are."

I take a deep breath and look up at the gray stone arch. With its tagged exterior, the crumbling mortar, it's nothing special to look at. But weirdly, it does feel a little like home. Everything I ever experienced here only ever felt like home. The good and the bad.

I called Shama about this mess, but she was at work and didn't answer. I'll have an apartment full of judgmental roommates waiting for me when I get back, ready to shit all over Giancarlo, tell me all the mistakes I'm making, judge, judge, judge. And if I go to Giancarlo, he'll be asking me questions all night. And when he finds out whom I was with...the thought makes me shudder.

Maybe this is better. Maybe I don't have to tell anyone where I am at all.

CHAPTER TWENTY-FIVE

Layla

HOME.

The word echoes through my mind when I wake up the next morning. Slowly, in the dim light, the room comes into focus. It's familiar, but not the one I'm used to seeing here. That one, the plain white bedroom on the other side of the far wall, is now occupied by Nico's brother, Gabe. Poor Gabe. He had a taste of freedom for just over six months before he was right back to living with his mom.

Nico and I are on the pull-out couch in the living room, a space that's cordoned off by a couple of screens that block the open doorways leading from one side into the hallway, and through the other into the small TV room and the kitchen. It used to serve as a storage space for Nico and his family, giving his mother a little extra room in her tiny apartment in Hell's Kitchen. There is even more stuff now, he explained sheepishly last night, because they've been slowly moving her up here.

Several cardboard boxes are stacked against the plastered walls, and another side of the room contains a jumble of other household goods: a couple of old brass lamps, a stack of faded sheets, a box of cords, an old TV, and two or three laundry baskets with what look like children's clothes that Allie has grown out of. Faint scents of rice and beans filter through the air, and even this early, the bright guitar of a bachata song fades in every now and then from the street below. It's not a nice apartment by any stretch of the imagination, but I don't feel awkward here. I never did.

Despite the chill of the room, I'm warm. It's because, I soon realize, I'm in an equally familiar position: wrapped in five feet, elevenish inches of Nico. He's curled around me like a shrimp, one big arm draped across my middle, the other wormed under my neck to hold me securely against his broad, warm body. Apparently, it didn't matter how vehemently we both insisted we would stay away from each other through the night. Our bodies were determined to do differently.

I can't say I'm surprised. And even though I know it's wrong, I don't move away.

Nico's nose is buried in the back of my neck, and his warm breath feels so good. His fingers tighten reflexively now and then, and every few breaths, a low hum escapes his lips as he dreams. His biceps flex, a sturdy armor. Even in his dreams, he protects me.

My phone blinks on top of the suitcase beside the couch: filled with messages, no doubt, from my roommates and Giancarlo. I texted all of them last night, but everything I said was lies. The twist in my stomach reminds me: I am not a good person. My roommates think I'm staying with my boyfriend; Giancarlo thinks I went to stay with them. None will be happy about where I am now.

I sigh. The world outside this room feels heavy. But the person in it is not someone I should be with. And he's also not someone I have ever been able to say no to.

Nico stirs again, inhaling deeply. The hand at my waist tightens, and his hips flex into me from behind. Well...*something* is definitely awake. Instinctively, he grinds into me again, and a light groan erupts from his lips as he burrows his face further into my neck and shoulder, lips and mouth seeking.

"Mmmm, Layla," he murmurs as his fingers locate the hem of my t-shirt. I gasp as they slide underneath, skin on skin as his lips meet the soft spot under my ear.

"Ah!" I gasp as his teeth find my earlobe.

"Mmmmm." Nico's deep voice is a motor as the hand at my stomach drifts farther south and starts to slide under the waistband of my jeans.

"Nico," I whisper.

"Just five minutes, baby."

His voice slurs a little; he's not completely awake. But as much as I want to stay here, want to let his fingers continue their path, I know I have to stop this. I have to stop before we make this mistake all over again, and I'm eaten alive with guilt more than I already am.

"Nico," I say, wriggling against him.

Shit, that really doesn't help. The rock-hard length of him pressed against my ass just gets even harder, and he groans as he thrusts lightly. Shit.

"Nico, you have to stop!"

"Hm? What?" The hand at my stomach starts. His whole body tenses. "Oh," he says. "Damn." But he doesn't move away immediately. "Damn," he murmurs again, and then, finally, withdraws his arms and rolls away.

His absence is sudden and acute. And now I am freezing.

I roll over to find him lying on his back, hands clasped over his broad chest while he stares up at the ceiling with a pained expression. Perhaps feeling my gaze, he turns to me.

"Hey," I say softly.

He presses his full lips together. "Hey. Um, sorry about that. I...I was asleep, I guess. Hard to control myself when I'm not conscious."

I give a lopsided smile. Is it fucked up that I like that I have this effect on him? This is definitely not someone who ever needs help getting things started.

"It's okay," I say. "Old habits die hard, right?"

His smile isn't the big, bright one I usually get. He doesn't even bare his teeth.

"I—this is hard," he admits, turning back to the ceiling. He pushes his hands into his hair, which is a little longer than usual. "I don't know how to do this." His eyes sharpen. "I don't want you to see that guy anymore, Layla."

All the warmth of this moment disappears. "You have no right to say that."

"I have a right as your friend."

"Do friends dry hump each other in their sleep?"

Nico groans, loud and long, into his elbow. The movement makes the tattoos over his right bicep ripple. I try not to drool.

"Fuck," he whispers loudly. I know he's struggling to keep it down because his family is still asleep. Then he looks at me with a dagger-like expression. "*You* called *me*, you know."

I scowl back. "Do you wish I hadn't?"

"No. Yes. No. Fuck!"

Nico sits up, and the covers fall down. His white t-shirt isn't leaving much to the imagination, and neither are his boxer briefs. Jesus, he has *really* been working out in LA.

"I'm glad you called," he says. "But you shouldn't have been up there in the first place. Layla, I don't know what kind of shit your *boyfriend*"—he spits out the word, like it gives him a bad taste in his mouth—"is into, but he should know better than to send his innocent girlfriend in his place to deal with a fuckin' gangster!"

"I see. So you think I'm too ignorant and stupid to understand what was going on?" I ignore the fact that I *didn't* actually know what was going on. Gangster?

"Fuck—*me cago*—no, I didn't mean it like that."

But I'm already swinging my legs out of the bed and searching for my shoes. I slept in my clothes last night, too wary of what might happen if there were only a few pieces of underwear between Nico and me. Nico's feet hit the floor with a thump, and then he's coming around the mattress to stand in front of me.

"Layla."

I look up, and despite the anger I feel—at him, at Giancarlo, at myself for even being in this situation—I still want to do what comes most naturally. Nico's dense, close-cut hair is sticking up a little around the crown of his head, and there's a solid day and a half's worth of black stubble on his cheeks and chin. He rubs his eyes, which have shadows underneath them. But his lips look so soft and full, and all I want to do is throw my arms around those broad shoulders and kiss him until neither of us is mad anymore.

Okay, I want to do a lot more than that.

Nico puts his hands on my shoulders and stills me. I look up, expecting to see disdain. Condescension. Someone who thinks I'm stupid, because in my heart, I know I'm being horrible to someone who helped me last night. But all I see is concern and maybe a little frustration warring across his face. His eyes drift to my mouth again, and without thinking, I lick my lips. His eyes dilate.

"Fuck," he murmurs as he closes them. He exhales forcefully, then looks straight at me. "Don't go back there."

My mouth drops. That was not what I was expecting him to say. "What?"

"I—" He rubs the back of his neck uneasily. "You don't—I mean—look, I wasn't going to say anything, but there's a chance I'm moving back to New York. I don't know when. But possibly within a few months. You don't need someone like him, Layla. Not when you and I..."

"What do you mean, there's a chance you're moving back?"

The words seem to crackle in the air. I'm honestly not sure if I really heard him say that.

Now Nico's the one who looks guilty.

"Ah, yeah. I wanted to tell you, but I didn't want to get your hopes up."

I don't say anything. Just wait for him to say whatever this is.

"It's...you remember that EMT test I told you about?" he ventures.

I still say nothing. He blinks, his expression black and uneasy. Suddenly I feel like I'm made of glass, about to shatter.

Nico takes a deep breath. "It was, um, actually the FDNY entrance exam. I took it last November. And then...well, I did pretty well. Actually, I did great."

"Of-of course you did," I murmur, more to myself than to him. "Of *course* you did."

"Well, um, yeah. So I was called up this week to, um...keep interviewing." He keeps going, now in a sudden rush. "I had the physical on Tuesday. The psych interview is today. You should have seen me the last few months, baby, I've been working out like a beast. It's basically all I do, other than work. Anyway, they seemed to think I did well on that, and now the psych interview is this morning. I still don't know...I don't know. I have a record, and they may decide in the end that someone with a history of assault isn't worthy of the FDNY. But I had to try, you know? It's...it's what I've always wanted..."

For a long time I sit there, taking in his words. Nico's quiet now, watching to see what I'll do. He chews on his lips and cracks his knuckles—he's never been good with silence.

"I just...I just..." I shake my head, back and forth, trying to register what he's telling me.

He's coming back. He's coming back to New York. And he knew all this time that he was trying to do that. Every time I asked to be together, he knew.

He knew. And he always said no.

Suddenly, it's hard to breathe. I suck in the air, hiccuping around each breath.

"Layla?" Nico sits next to me, worried. "Are you all right?"

"I...can't..." I take another deep breath. "I can't *believe* that you are doing this to me...again!"

Nico's brow screws up in confusion. "What?"

"Did you know?" I demand, my voice already choking up. "Did you know that you might be coming back? Have you known this whole time?"

"What? I, well—" He's stumbling, unable to put together a complete sentence.

"Of course you did," I continue without waiting. "You applied. You took a test. You knew even then that you had made the final cut, and *you didn't tell me*?"

"I just...Layla, do you have any idea how many times I've applied for the FDNY over the years? This was a long shot. I still can't even believe I got this far!"

"Who the fuck *cares*?" I snarl. "You don't get it, do you?" My voice cracks, and I can feel my chest cracking right along with it. "All I've wanted is you. All year. Ever since you left. And every time I'm starting to think about moving on again you pop back into my life, every time, sweep me right back in, make me love you, all just to leave me. I can't take it, anymore, Nico!"

He sinks down onto the bed with a dazed expression, like he can hardly believe what he's hearing. I can hardly believe it myself. I look around frantically for my shoes. I just want to go. I want to leave and bury myself under a mountain of blankets. I want to find a place in this world, this life, where this ache in my chest can finally go away.

"Layla." He says my name slowly, deliberately.

"I have a boyfriend," I say, though the words are weak.

"Who, that asshat from Argentina? The guy who robs his girlfriend blind and lies the fuck about it?"

"Shut up."

"No." He kicks at his shoes lying on the floor; they flop over.

I spy my boots behind a box and make a grab, hopping wildly around the room while I put them on. "Come back to New York," I say. "Don't come back to New York. But whatever you do, don't do it for me."

The words bite; they don't sound nearly as indifferent as I intend them. I'm crying too hard to look apathetic anyway.

"Layla, please. I'll—listen, I'll be back in a few months. In May. I don't live with Jessie anymore, baby. I've been staying with K.C. for a while now. I just...tell me it's not too late. It's you and me, Layla. *You* and *me*. You can't tell me that you and fuckin' Evita have anything on that!" He squats down, cups my face between his hands. "You don't need him. You have me."

I lean into the touch—that warm, familiar touch. Nico has always been a furnace when I'm with him—he radiates heat all the time. I close my eyes, enjoying the roughness of his calluses against my skin, the gentleness of the thumb lightly brushing my cheekbone. When I open them, he's giving me that look—that Nico look, black and fathomless, but open and full of love. Love he's never given completely, but that I wanted so badly.

"I don't want to be alone," I admit, for the first time that I can remember.

And I don't. Because being alone hurts. It reminds me that the person I want to be with doesn't want me back. It reminds me that even if he loves me, he still chose a life without me. Without us. And every single time I think of it, it's like he drives a knife further and further into my heart.

"Baby..."

"I don't want to be in love with you anymore," I whimper and fall into his chest.

He starts for a second in surprise, but quickly folds his arms around me, holding my shaking form as the tears fall before I can stop them. I start to shake violently, as much for the pain of loving him as for the pain of admitting I don't want to anymore. Giancarlo might say mean things. He might yell or shout or throw the occasional dish. But nothing hurts more than this man's love. Or, I should say, nothing hurts more than loving him.

I jerk away, pawing at my face. I'm so tired of crying for this man, for the pain of being without him.

"And if you aren't hired?" I ask. I can see the suggestion hurts him, just like it hurts me to say it. Nico would be a brilliant firefighter—he's a natural hero. Any fool could see that.

But I still need to know the answer to that question. I need to know what he wants from us.

"Are you—are you coming back to New York? Are you coming back here?"

Nico opens and closes his mouth, like he wants to say yes, but then his chest deflates. "I—no. No, I'm not."

And there it is. The answer that's been breaking me from the start. The reason I need to convince me that he really doesn't feel the same way about me as I feel about him.

We stare at each other for a long time, and it's almost like time acts as a magnet.

The longer we stare, the closer we get, until our lips are almost touching. Suddenly all I can think about is that those lips showed me what love felt like. That maybe I never knew what that really felt like until I met him.

That maybe I never will again.

And then our lips are touching. I'm not sure if I start the kiss or if he does, but quickly, it takes over both of us. And just as organically, his hands are back on my skin, sliding up and down my legs, up and down my body like he's trying to commit every imprint to memory.

He's warm. So warm. When the world is literally freezing, and the people in it offer the shelter of an igloo, this man heats my soul like fire. He pulls me flush against him so we're chest to chest, legs against legs, so my soft parts meet his hard ones, and he throbs against my core.

"Layla," he utters before taking another kiss, and then another one as he turns me toward the bed. His hands slip down, take a firm hold of my ass, that body part he seems to love so much.

"Nico," I whisper against his lips, soft and sensuous, that pillow over my face. "Please," I murmur against him, arching up to rub myself against his cock. I want him. My body craves kindness. It craves love. It craves a man who won't hurt me, even when he's angry. A man who won't leave me when I'm at my most vulnerable.

Which, I realize, is exactly what he's going to do. If we do this, it will feel good, so *so* good in the moment. I'll lose myself in him in the way only Nico can make me do. But afterward, we'll be right back where we are: he's getting on a plane back to LA, and I'll be here with guilt eating a hole through my stomach, feeling more lost, more alone, more hopeless than ever.

"No," I say against his mouth. And then I pull away. Tears stream down my face in hot tracks. The glass is shattering. "I'm sorry. I just...I can't anymore." I suck in a desperate sob. "Please. I need to go."

Nico covers my hands with his, holding them against his chest for a moment. His thumbs brush over the tops of my palms, and we stare at each other, caught again in each other's thralls. When it's just us together, things seem so simple. Him. Me. Everything else just fades away.

"Five minutes," he relents as he steps away to grab some clothes. "And then we'll leave together."

———

We ride the 1 train downtown together, and Nico holds my hand the entire time. I don't argue. I'm too weak to say no. It's platonic, I tell myself, even though I know it's a lie. I insist it doesn't matter that I spent the night in this man's bed. We didn't do anything.

Nico plays his thumb over the ridges of my knuckles, and we sway a little on our seats as the train starts and stops, then dips below the street.

"What are you going to tell him?" he asks quietly after we've passed a few more stops.

I consider the question. "I...I guess I'll tell him the truth. That I sold my watch to pay his debt, and I'll ask him to pay me back. He will. Giancarlo doesn't like to be indebted to anyone."

I don't want to think about what that might mean about last night. Nico thinks

Giancarlo sent me there because he's a coward who couldn't pay his own debt. But a small part of me, one I'm not quite ready to listen to, says it's something different. That I was sent to that pawnshop to make a point. To be taught a lesson about control.

Which means that he can't ever know who helped me out of there. And when I see him again—today, tomorrow, or later this week—I'm going to have to pretend like everything went fine. Like, as he would say, I'm *his*.

"Just promise me this," Nico says after the train leaves Seventy-Second Street.

I gulp. "What's that?"

He pulls a little on the brim of his favorite old Yankees hat, then pulls it around so it's backwards. It's something he does when he wants to see me clearly. Or maybe when he wants me to see him.

"The second that guy does anything to you—"

"Who says he's going to do something to me?" I interrupt a little too vehemently.

Nico sighs. "Okay. If. *If* he does anything to you..." Any softness in his eyes evaporates. They are black and stony. "You call me. No matter what time it is. No matter what coast I'm on. You call me."

It's a look that gives me shivers, but I don't look away. I can't.

"We'll see," I say in a voice that's weak. Even saying the words makes me feel out of breath.

"Oh. Okay. But...you deserve the best, sweetie," Nico says, and when he swallows, a muscle in his jaw ticks. "Don't let anyone make you believe otherwise."

Slowly, I nod. He squeezes my hand. I don't ever want him to stop.

"Fifty-Ninth Street Columbus Circle." The conductor announces the stop over the scratchy intercom. It's intelligible only to people who live here and have already memorized most of the stops on the map.

Nico looks up as the train slows in front of the station. The doors open, and he looks at me helplessly.

Then, without warning, he darts in and stamps a kiss on my lips.

"Be good," he says like always, before I can say anything more, and then skips off the train before the doors close.

The train starts to move again. I twist in my seat, my fingers over my mouth. Nico stands on the platform, his duffel bag slung over his shoulder. He raises a big hand at me while the train moves away. I set my palm to the window and watch him fade into darkness.

IV

HOMEWARD

CHAPTER TWENTY-SIX

MAY 2004

Layla

The phone buzzes violently on my desk, waking me up from a peaceful sleep, sprawled across the desktop. It's almost 6:00 p.m. on a Friday, and I've fallen asleep on my books. Again.

It's not a surprise. I haven't been sleeping well, not since February. Everything these days seems to make me feel uneasy. Every cab that passes seems like it's about to hit me. Every sidewalk grate feels like it's about to open up. I often wake in the middle of the night with my heart pounding, but I never know why.

This is the first time I've been home all week, since Giancarlo always wants me to stay with him. He refuses to sleep in my twin bed with me, and I don't blame him. It's a tiny mattress for such a tall guy. After the incident with the pawnshop, guilt has eaten me alive. And it's like Giancarlo knows it, sometimes pushing my boundaries, pushing my limits until we're yelling at each other or I'm kowtowed in front of him, a pathetic mess.

And every time I think I'm ready to leave him for good, he falls to the old gray carpet, blocking my exit.

"*Amor*," Giancarlo moans as he wrapped his arms around my knees. I close my eyes at the pain of the word, hearing the echoes of someone else's voice around it. "My love, I need you. Forgive me. You make me so crazy. Love makes me crazy."

He tips his face up and lays his head on my thigh. Reflexively, my hands will slip into his hair, and he'll close his eyes, content now that the storm is over.

Maybe I shouldn't stay. The hand prints on my wrist still sting, even if I can't see the red marks anymore. His other words rankle through my head: *whore, bitch,* puta, not quite tempered yet by time. But he inhales my skin like I'm life itself. Like I'm a drug he can't quit. And that feeling is a drug to me too.

I need you. His words float through the air, and so do someone else's. *October.* I think about it all the time—the month when Nico received the newspaper clipping.

He knew he might come back, yet never chose to tell me. So my heart falls every time the realization hits that I never factored into Nico's decision, though I offered time and time again to adjust my life around his. My heart falls, right into Giancarlo's waiting hands.

Sometimes I still want to call Nico. And at first, after he left in February, he would call a lot. Every day. Every other day. He'd ask if I'd told Giancarlo what had happened. Asked if I had confronted him about the pawnshop.

I didn't tell him I'd been too afraid to do it. That I didn't want to see what Giancarlo would do if he knew I'd called Nico. If, by some trick, he discovered I'd spent the night with another man. Had let him kiss me. Had kissed him back. Had very nearly done so much more.

So instead, I told him that Giancarlo was clean and it was all a big misunderstanding. I told him that I had gotten my watch back, though it's probably on some other girl's wrist in the Bronx somewhere.

I don't think Nico believed me, because he asked me again to cut Giancarlo loose. Told me in a frenzy he wanted me no matter what. And this time, he promised that even if the FDNY didn't hire him in the end, that he wanted me to come out there, just like I'd offered last year.

And that, really, was what did it.

———

"Is THAT WHAT YOU THINK?" I demanded, anger simmering inside me, turning me into a keg of gunpowder that had just been lit. "After all this time, you think you can just snap your fucking fingers and I'll jump to your side! Nico, you had your chance! Again and fucking again! What can't you understand about that?"

The words burst out of me like fireworks, and when I finished, I slumped against the wall while Quinn watched from her bed knowingly. I knew better than to expect her sympathy by that point. We were basically strangers most of the time.

"Layla," Nico started again, his voice full of mourning. "Please, baby —"

"I am not your baby!" I shouted directly into the phone. "Stop tormenting me! I am with someone else! Just..." My voice trailed off, losing its fire the more I spoke. Before long, I choked back a great sob. "Just leave me alone," I whimpered, and then hung up the phone.

He called again. And again. But by the end of the week, the phone calls stopped. And by the end of the month, the texts did too.

———

THAT WAS IN MARCH. Two months later, my chest feels hollower than ever.

I rub my face and pick up my phone, then sit up straight as I see the number. It's not one I recognize, but the area code is familiar—Brazil.

"Dad?" I perk up as I answer.

It's maybe the third time all year I've heard from my father. Once after he arrived in Brazil, a brief conversation at New Year's, and now this. He says it's because of the cost of international phone charges, but I doubt that's the reason. He's been busy. Busy joining a new practice in Vitória, his hometown. Busy setting up a house with his new girlfriend. Too busy for me.

But last month, my mother informed me that I was going to Brazil for the summer instead of to Pasadena. Considering at that point I had no job lined up for the summer, it was ideal timing. All the anger and pain I'd been harboring toward my dad all year melted away as I realized that he was ready to see me again. That he still wanted me in his life. I'm leaving in a week once the semester is over, with plans to meet Giancarlo in Buenos Aires about halfway through. I can't wait.

"Layla, what is this?"

My dad is always like this—he starts conversations like we're already in the middle of them, continuing a thought process that started well before we began speaking. No hello, no "how are you doing?" Usually I can keep up with him, but right now I'm silent because I'm trying to figure out what the hell he's talking about.

"Layla?" he repeats.

"What?" I ask. "What's what?"

"This grade I see on your transcript. Three point seven last term. Layla, this is not acceptable."

"Dad, that's from last semester," I protest weakly. I'm honestly shocked it took this long for him to say anything about it, but since I've barely heard from him all year, I thought it might fly. "It was one B minus. I know it's not my best, but it was just one B!"

"And this term? What will your grades be? Cs? Ds?"

"I don't know," I reply lamely. "I really don't. Finals are next week."

It's a lie. My grades have been falling. I'm not flunking or anything, but I've been pulling late night after late night doing whatever extra credit I can to pull up some of my absences. My language classes are good, but the others, my South American history class and Latin American literature, are lagging. I'll be lucky if I pull a B in either one.

"Layla, I'm not paying a fortune for you to go to that school so you can screw up. We had a deal. You go to school in this dangerous city, now do this ridiculous major instead of business like we talked about, you have to keep your grades."

Maybe it's the lack of sleep. Maybe it's the fact that I haven't slept in my bed in five days, using my dorm like a locker room. But suddenly, I've had it. I'm sick of being talked down to, like everyone in my life seems to do. He left. He doesn't want to finance my education anymore, fine, but this is bullshit.

"We also had a deal that you'd stick around and be my father instead of calling once every six months," I retort.

My father's silence echoes through the receiver. He's thousands of miles away, but his disappointment is palpable. The hairs on my arms rise.

"Is that correct?" he says finally, in that low voice I recognize all too well. My father is calmest when he's beyond angry. He sounds like that when he's about to pull the trigger on something truly nasty.

"Y-yes," I venture, forcing myself to hold my ground. I'm in the right here. I am. I am a grown fucking woman, and I don't deserve to be spoken to like a little kid. "That's correct."

I study the smudged notes on the desk. Damn, I probably have pencil smears on my cheek. While I wait, I doodle a flower in one corner, then a clock that looks strangely like a compass. Once I realize what I've drawn, I scowl and cross it out.

"Well," he says. "Since you know so much...you can forget about coming to Brazil this summer."

My heads snaps up, and my hand flops to the desk. "What?"

This is the one thing I've been looking forward to—knowing that at the end of this tortuous year, I'll be studying for the LSATs at the beach, getting to know the side of the family I mostly know through history books. The side of me I want so badly to understand. Portuguese and Spanish are the only classes I'm still getting As in. I was excited to show my father what I've learned.

"Dad." I try to stop him, all pretense of dignity gone. "Daddy. I haven't seen you since September. It's been almost a year! Please, don't do this!"

"You should have thought of that before you threw your education away," he barks.

I sink back into my chair, feeling like a balloon that's just been popped. "It's been almost a year," I repeat softly.

It's hard to believe. So much has happened this year. I didn't realize until this moment how much I needed to see my dad. How much I need his rough grounding. But this, this indifference, like he doesn't actually care whether or not I'm there...it hurts more than the yelling. It stabs even harder than any punishment he could conjure.

There's a voice in the background—female. Her.

"*Momento, amor,*" Dad says to her.

Again, that stabbing feeling. It's a pet name I've never heard him use for me or my mother because of his strict adherence to English. The only time I've ever heard him use Portuguese at all is when we visited his family. Never to us. We were always separate from that life.

"I have to go," Dad says, now to me. The anger is gone from his voice, but it's still firm. Immovable. "You will study in Pasadena, at your grandparents' house. Find an LSAT class, and tell your mother to send me the bill. *My* daughter will not fail, Layla. This is your future."

The word echoes across miles. There's no arguing with him, not unless I'd like a worse punishment, like withholding tuition for next year. Poke the bear, and I'm finishing college at whatever Cal State school I can get into. I shut my eyes and murmur my assent. But even after he hangs up with barely a kind word of goodbye, I can't help but wonder: how can a man claim to know my future when he barely knows me anymore?

———

A FEW HOURS LATER, after I've finished an extra-credit paper for my literature class, I hear the arrival of my roommates as they return from the gym. Quinn's busy jabbering about the summer classes she's taking so she can double-major in biology and chemistry. All of my roommates are actually staying here through the summer— Quinn to take classes while Jamie and Shama start their summer internships. Two hours ago, I had a plan for the summer. Now I'm just wallowing.

"Hey," Quinn says, visibly cool as she tosses her gym bag on her bed. Shama follows her in and flops onto mine.

"Did you get your paper done?" Shama asks.

Out of my three roommates, she's the only one still reliably friendly these days. Quinn hasn't forgiven me for staying with Giancarlo after the pawnshop incident, and Jamie pretty much goes along with however Quinn feels.

"Yeah," I say. "I'm just working on some other stuff now."

Quinn grabs her towel off a hook and looks over my shoulder on her way to the shower. "Since when are you taking economics?"

I scowl and shove the papers aside. "I'm not. Giancarlo is struggling in it, so I told him I'd help him a little."

At the mention of his name, Quinn's face grows dark. "I see. So now you're doing his homework for him too?"

"*No*," I say. "He has a hard time because of the language differences. I'm just helping."

Quinn peers at the notes sitting in front of me, an outline for a response paper. I turn them over.

"Let it go, Quinn," Shama says. "It's her choice if she wants to help him."

Quinn just wrinkles her button nose and shakes her head. "Pathetic," she mutters as she leaves the room.

"It's...nice of you to help," Shama offers, even though she's having a hard time masking her skepticism too.

I sigh and push my hands over my face. I feel tired. Really tired. "It's what you do, right? When you lo—care about someone?"

Almost five months I've been dating this guy, and still I can't bring myself to say that L-word. He says it all the time. Calls me his "love." His "*amor*." Usually after a fight, but still. At least he says it.

I just...can't. I take it, like the drug that it is. But I just can't give it back.

I really am a terrible person.

"So, are you ready for Brazil yet? Puh-*lease* tell me I get to come too."

It's a joke, of course. Shama is trying to be nice, trying to elevate the mood after Quinn's and my icy exchange. But I just sit there, staring at the mess of papers on my desk.

"Lay?" she asks. She gets up from the bed and comes to sit on the edge of the desk. "What's wrong?"

I huff. "It doesn't matter. It's nothing." I look up at her. "My dad, um, canceled the trip."

Shama covers her mouth in surprise. "What? Oh no!"

I nod, then get up and go to the bed. Shama follows, and I curl into a corner, hugging a pillow into my chest.

"He's mad about my grades. He thinks I need to stay in Pasadena and take an LSAT class there instead of studying on the beach."

Saying the words deflates me even further. I badly need a change of pace this summer. LA just spells out pain, and I have absolutely no desire to spend my summer being picked at by my mother and grandmother over white wine. The energy of New York, which used to be so invigorating and addictive, just feels oppressive.

"He's right."

Quinn enters the room, dressed in yoga pants and a t-shirt, a towel wrapped around her wet hair.

I look up. "Right about what?"

"You need to get out of here. Get your head right."

I roll my eyes. Here we go again.

"Quinn, I don't really think she needs to hear this right now..." Shama starts as she pats my shoulder.

"You haven't even been here for most of this conversation," I cut in. "And here's the truth: if I want your advice, I'll ask for it."

Quinn rolls her eyes as she pulls off her towel and hangs it on the closet door rack. "Surprise, surprise. Little Miss Angst is pushing everyone away. How're those grades, kid? Still failing your history class?"

"It's a B minus, not an F, for Christ's sake. Why is everyone freaking out about this?"

"Because we know you're better than this." Quinn pauses, one hand still in her hair, then marches over to where I'm sitting.

"I don't need a fucking lecture, right now, Quinn." I turn into my pillow.

"I beg to differ." She opens her mouth, like she's about to go on yet another tirade about my life choices. But then she rubs a hand across her face. "I can't believe I'm about to say this, but I honestly think you need to go home to your mommy. You need a break, Lay. And I really think that if you just put some space between you and South American Snape, you'll figure out that he's no good for you."

Beside me, Shama groans to herself.

"Honestly," I say, a lot more evenly than I feel, "what the fuck do you know about it?"

Quinn frowns slightly, clearly taken aback by my directness. "What-what do you mean?"

"I *mean*...what the fuck would you know about being in a relationship? You talk to me like I'm a little kid, but who's the twenty-one-year-old virgin in this apartment, huh? Who's the one who, in three years of college, has been on maybe two or three dates max with anyone?"

"Lay..." Shama tries to calm me, but I fling her hand aside.

"Oh, *I* see," Quinn says, stomping back to her desk. She picks up a hairbrush and starts yanking it through her wet hair. "Because I care more about my grades than screwing abusive randos all over Manhattan, I'm an idiot. I make smart choices, so I'm the bad guy. Sure, that makes total sense."

"If you call living like a nun a smart choice, sure," I retort. "At least my life isn't fucking G-rated. At least I'm trying to have real fucking experiences in New York instead of living my life wearing a virtual chastity belt."

The hairbrush sails across the room and smacks the wall above my head, landing innocuously on the bed between Shama and me.

"Whoa," Shama mutters.

I glare at Quinn. "What the *fuck*?"

"What the fuck yourself!" Quinn's face is red, and her voice is shaking with anger. "That was a low blow, even for you!"

I open my mouth with another retort ready, but Quinn just keeps going.

"I don't care what you're doing with your sorry fucking summer!" she shouts. "Knowing you, you're just going to be miserable and pathetic anyway. I'm actually glad you'll be gone. All year, all we've listened to is you moaning and groaning about your parents, about Nico!"

"Quinn, that's unfair," Shama puts in. "Layla barely talks about any of that stuff."

"Well, she's been moping around since September—same fucking thing!" Quinn crosses her arms and glares at me. "I'm sick of it. I didn't come to college to be your therapist. You're pissed because I refuse to enable your shitty life choices; well, tough. Maybe we don't need to be friends, then."

My mouth drops. I'm not sure I just heard that correctly. This is Quinn. We fight, we make up. There's always been a certain degree of push and pull in our friendship, but it's mostly been productive. We challenge each other, I thought. Like all good relationships do...right? We've just been in a rough patch...

Beside me, Shama's shaking her head, but she says nothing more. Quinn doesn't say anything either, just pops her hip out and waits for my response.

She means it. She really means that we shouldn't be friends. I didn't know people even did that, actually cut others off cold turkey. Slowly, I uncurl myself from my pillow and shuffle off the bed.

"All right," I say more to myself than anyone else. "Fine. You want me gone, I'm gone."

Like a zombie, I get up and start packing the things I need for class next week. My roommates are in for the night, studying through the weekend for finals. But Quinn is basically telling me to leave. She hasn't spoken the words, but everything in her posture, her words, says just that.

When I'm done shoving everything into my messenger bag, I find my coat and shoes, all under Quinn's nasty gaze. I have enough clothes at Giancarlo's to last me through the week. Toothbrush, hairbrush, and I can get out of here.

Jamie pops in with her phone to her ear. "Hey, I'm thinking of ordering pizza. You guys wanna split—oh. Hey, what's going on?"

I finish tying my shoes and stand up with my bag. "I'm leaving." I give Jamie a weak smile, but I can't even look at the other two. I have never in my life felt more like a pariah.

"Later," Jamie says as I pass, and on my way out the door, I can hear her asking, "What was that about?"

"Drama," Quinn answers as the door shuts behind me. "Her usual fucking drama."

I take the stairs all the way down to the main floor and walk out into the late spring sunshine. It's May in New York, which is usually my favorite time of year. A bunch of vendors are setting up booths for a craft bazaar in Union Square, where they'll have local artists showing off their work before Memorial Day. It's the kind of thing I usually love about New York, but right now I hate it. The sunniness of all of it makes me want to kick down all the stands.

I pull out my phone and call the only person I can think of. The only person who ever seems to care about me these days.

He answers on the first ring. "Layla?"

"Giancarlo. I—" I can't even get the words out before I start to cry. Of course, it's here on the street where I start to blubber. Not in the privacy of the apartment upstairs. Not even in the vacant stairwell where no one would see me. It's here, on one of the busiest streets in the city, with my classmates and other strangers looking at me, the strange girl breaking down on the sidewalk.

I wipe my eyes and turn toward the windows. Inside, the security guard looks up, but does nothing.

"It's Quinn, she..." I hiccup back my tears, and my throat hurts with the effort.

"Come here," Giancarlo orders. "Come now."

I wait a few seconds, for what, I don't know. A few words of kindness? Some comfort? I know that's what he's offering, but I don't feel it.

"You don't need them. They're bitches, all of them. You don't need to be around girls who treat you like this. I told you this for weeks, months. Why don't you listen to me?"

The ground under my feet rumbles with a train's passing through the massive Union Square station below. It's a slow vibration that seeps into my bones, and for a second, I think of another voice that makes my insides shake in the same way. I close my eyes and will the feeling away. He's not going to help me now.

"*Amor?*"

Love. He only says it after he's snapped at me. But he still says it.

"You don't need them," he says again. "Only we matter. Just you and me."

I exhale. "I'm coming. See you soon."

CHAPTER TWENTY-SEVEN

Nico

I START AWAKE ON K.C.'S COUCH, MY CHEEK STICKY AGAINST THE BLACK LEATHER. Everyone thinks that leather couches are nice because they're expensive, but they kind of suck to sleep on, especially when it's hot. K.C. has a really great apartment in West Hollywood, but it's still just a one-bedroom. And the walls are fuckin' thin.

There's a loud thump on the drywall just above my head. And another. And another. Followed by the low moan of a woman's voice.

Oh, so *that's* what woke me up.

"Ummmmmmeeeeeeeeee!"

The moan sounds again, followed by a high squeal. I pull a pillow over my face, and try to block out the sound of my best friend fucking whatever random girl he picked up at Venom tonight, but no such luck. Jesus Christ, this girl sounds like a character from the movie *Babe*. K.C. is basically fucking a CGI pig.

I have got to find my own place.

I sit up and flip on the TV, knowing there's no way I'm going to be able to sleep while they're going at it. But, of course, late-night television isn't much better. It's either infomercials or reruns of the shit they can't play during primetime. *Showgirls* is just going to make this situation that much more awkward.

I yank a pair of jogging pants out of the duffel bag that's spilling clothes all over K.C.'s living room floor and get dressed, trying my best to block out the noises still shouting from the bedroom. The sky out of K.C.'s windows is turning lighter. I pull on my sneakers and lace them tight. I might as well use the time now that I'm up. It'll be better than working out mid-afternoon anyway, before I have to be at work.

A jog around the neighborhood turns into a full-on run. A little over an hour later, I'm flopping on the sand at the Santa Monica Pier, breathing hard after pounding the pavement for nine miles. It's longer than my usual run, but I'm in good enough shape to take it.

I strip off my t-shirt, which is damp with sweat anyway, and use it to mop off my face and neck. Fuck. That felt good. I've been pushing myself harder than I probably should lately, like I have all this pent-up tension to release. New York feels like a magnet, pulling me back with everything there, but keeping me at arm's length too.

My family. Ma is driving Gabe and Maggie crazy, and he said a few weeks ago that the landlord started asking who she is. It's not the worst thing in the world, of course. He can't legally require her to provide proof of residency, but if he asks for ID from all his tenants, he could ask for hers too. ID that she doesn't have.

Something has to be done there, but I don't know what. I really don't know what the fuck we could do to help her. All I know is that I could do it better if I were there.

And then there's the job. It's been almost three months since I had my interview at the FDNY headquarters. Finished the background check, took the physical, kicked its ass, then sat through a psych interview that I was told would take fifteen minutes but ended up taking an hour. Since then, they picked at my record a little, but there's been no official news since March. No email. No phone call. No, hey, sorry, we went with a dude who isn't a criminal, you fuckin' asshole. Anything would be better than this limbo. I've been literally homeless for months, waiting around to see if I should sign a lease on a new place out here or keep saving my money for the move back to New York.

And the anxiety, of course, only makes me want to call one person—the only person whose blind faith calms me down and makes me fly all at once. I wouldn't have been able to go through the whole application in the first place if she hadn't said, over and over again, how much she believed in me. How much she knew I could do it, even if she didn't know what "it" really was. Who knew that having my own personal cheerleader, even from three thousand miles away, could be so effective?

But we haven't talked since March, since I begged her to leave that guy and be with me, and she told me to fuck off. I've sent texts. No answer. Tried to call a few times. No answer. I can't stand the not knowing. Is she still with that motherfucker? Did she break it off and make things right with her friends? Most of all, it's driving me crazy that I don't know if she's safe.

But she told me to stop calling. She told me we were done. I hurt her—I know I did—for not believing in us the way she did. For not taking that leap with her, and letting her fall on her own.

Fuck. I'll never regret anything more than that. Never.

I stare at the ocean, watching the slow glimmer of the sun rising across the white-blue waves. This early in the morning, it's still clean and smooth, without the winds that chop it up later in the day. A row of surfers rides a wave breaking off the pier.

I watch them for a few minutes. I thought about surfing when I first came out here —Jessie goes sometimes—but I'm a terrible swimmer. It's one of those things I missed out on growing up. We visited public pools a lot, especially since New York is a fuckin' sweatbox in the summer, but the only swim lessons my mom could afford were the ones Alba's boyfriend gave me and K.C. when we were kids, which mostly consisted of tossing us in the pool to find out if we would sink or swim. I know it's one of those things Ma feels guilty about. After all, her own father died drowning. But it can't be helped now. I'll do my best to make sure Allie learns to swim, that's for sure.

The surfers make it look so easy, their boards cutting across the sleek surface. But I've messed around in the whitewash just enough to know it's probably really hard.

When I first moved out here, K.C. and I actually rented boards. Too scared to paddle out for real, we spent most of the time pulling kelp out of our mouths and freezing our asses off because we didn't get wetsuits. The Pacific Ocean is really fuckin' cold, even in California, and the currents underneath those glassy waves are a fuck lot stronger than you'd think.

It makes me consider what other things might be harder than I thought. As a kid, I grew up in a city full of contrast. I shared that tiny apartment in a building full of people living the same way. People who worked hard for every scrap of food they had, who banded together to survive in a neighborhood where you were just as likely to get mugged as looked at. Everything felt so damn hard. My mother's job. Paying the rent or the electricity or the phone bill. Sharing food between the five of us. It was like there was a ceiling, low and hard, ready to smack you down if you tried too hard to stand up too fast. The world was small and harsh and cold.

But three blocks away was Times Square. You'd cross Eighth Avenue, and suddenly you were in the theater district, blinded by lights, ladies in fur coats, men flipping tips around like it was nothing. I remember walking by one of those theaters with K.C., thinking about how easy everything seemed for them. I had just found out that I was hired at FedEx, and K.C. and Flaco and I were going down-town to celebrate. I was on my way to get my first tattoo—the compass on my chest.

The world was bigger that day. I was just a kid, having dropped out of community college to help my mom. But I had a job, a real job that would take me out of the crappy back room where I was living at my boxing gym, a job that would keep food on the table for my brother and sisters, make it so we could afford things like regular dentist appointments and school supplies.

I remember walking by those rich people and feeling like nothing could touch me. I felt larger than life, even when a tall man in a black suit stared me down after I acci-dentally bumped into his daughter.

I start, suddenly remembering those big blue eyes.

Holy shit. Holy *fucking* shit. It was her. The girl I bumped into that day. The girl with eyes the color of the summer sky. *How the fuck* could I have forgotten that?

The memory comes flying at me like a one-two combo to the gut—Layla, an awkward girl with a mouthful of braces and way too much black hair. Me, a cocky nineteen-year-old bouncing down the sidewalk with my boys. She must have been there on vacation—they were seeing a Broadway play, like so many tourists do. *Phantom* or *Cats* or one of those overpriced shows. For a second, even then, the world stopped right there, on one of the busiest streets in New York. All I could see were her eyes before her dad called her away.

Oh God. What am I doing? What am I *fucking* waiting around for?

I can't breathe. The best moments of my life have always been with her. Right from the start. They were *always* meant to be with her.

I pull out my phone, ready to tell her as much. That no matter what news comes from the FDNY, I need to get back to where I belong. I need to be with her, whether she wants to come here or wants me there. Layla and I are meant for each other—I've never been surer of anything in my life. We can make it work. I'm not going to pussy out anymore.

I punch in her number and hit send. The phone rings. Three, four times, then goes to voicemail like it always does. Her voice, bright and warm, echoing through my ear, but I cut it off and dial again. I'll dial the rest of the day if I have to. I need to tell her how I feel.

Except.

Her words come back. *It hurts too much.*

Yeah, baby. It does.

I love her. I do. I love her enough that I put my phone back in my pocket. I've been selfish, and I fucked things up. I have no one to blame but myself for the failure of this relationship. For the fact that she moved on with someone else. If he makes her happy—it's a big if, but I'm not there, so what do I know?—*if* he does, I have to be okay with that. Because I love her enough to do the same thing she did for me.

I love her enough to let her go.

"Hey."

I look up. I've been so lost in my thoughts that I didn't even notice the person approaching until she plops down on the sand next to me.

"Jess. Hey. What are you doing over here? So early, too."

Jessie looks down over her sports bra and shorts and then back at me. "Same thing you are, looks like. I have a shoot this afternoon, so this was the only time I could work out."

Fitness was one of the few things Jessie and I always had in common—it was actually one of the things we would do together every now and then. Since she's an aspiring model, she has to look good. Exercise is part of her job.

"How've you been?" she asks. "Did you find out about your job yet?"

I examine her, a little taken aback by her casual attitude. She wasn't exactly nice the last time we talked, when I turned over my key to her apartment at the end of April.

"Um, no. I'm still at K.C.'s place until I hear. It's been a while. I'm guessing I didn't get in."

She frowns. "Really? I thought it all went so well."

I hunch my shoulders. The sun is getting hot. "Yeah, well. You never know, I guess."

"I guess." She traces a finger around the sand. "Well, if you want to stop by our—I mean, my—place, I still have some of your mail there."

I frown. "Really? You want me to come by? When I left, you threw a lamp at me and told me to burn in hell before I came back."

Jessie cringes. "Yeah, so maybe that wasn't my best moment."

She gives me a shy smile, the one that's been getting her a bunch of jobs lately. Last week I saw her face on the side of a billboard.

"I just...I liked you, you know?"

The smile is still there, but it's sad now. I watch her for a second, then realize that she's telling the truth. Jessie could be pretty damn manipulative, but this isn't one of those times. And it's got to be hard for her to admit this. Like most people, she's not great at saying how she feels.

I sling an arm around her shoulder and give her a quick hug. "It's okay. I get it."

She nods. "I thought you would. That girl..."

"Yeah," I say. But I don't continue the conversation.

We sit there for a moment together, then Jessie stands up and dusts off her legs. "Come on," she says. "I drove here today because I wanted to run north. I'll give you a ride back to the apartment, and then I can drop you downtown on my way to work. I have a shoot in Culver City."

I watch her for a second, looking for an ulterior motive. But there doesn't seem to be any.

"Okay," I say and follow her off the beach.

———

BACK AT THE APARTMENT, I noticed immediately that my old bedroom door is closed and there are boxes everywhere.

"New roommate?" I ask, looking around.

Jessie follows my gaze. "Oh, um, no. I'm moving out. I can't afford the place by myself, and I don't want another roommate. The lease is up this month. Time to move." She pauses biting her lower lip for a second. "I think I could use some time by myself, you know?"

I nod. "Yeah, I know."

"Anyway, the mail is in my room."

I follow her into her bedroom, also lined with boxes, and wait awkwardly while she fishes a paper bag of mail out of her closet.

"Here," she says, handing it to me and then proceeding to watch me. "Come on. I know there's an FDNY letter in there for you."

My head snaps up. "You couldn't have fuckin' led with that one?"

She giggles. "I had to play with you a little, you know."

I roll my eyes, but immediately dig into the bag. It doesn't take long. Soon I find the thin envelope with the thick FDNY letters printed on the front. I turn it back and forth in my hand. Jessie walks up and clasps my face between her hands.

"Hey," she says. "Good luck."

Then she kisses me. Her lips are soft, and her hands feel good when they slip down my neck and over my bare chest. It's nice enough that the tension in my stomach lets up a little. The noises I've been hearing from K.C.'s bedroom sing through my mind. I wouldn't mind getting laid right now. It actually might help.

But something's not right. It's never been right. And I'm not going to do this to her again.

I pull away. "Jess..."

She steps back with a sigh, but for once, she's not angry. I'm reminded that for all of her cynicism, Jessie's not a bad girl. She's lost, trying to figure out how to be more than the place she came from. Trying to play catch-up with everyone else, just like me.

She looks me over, her big brown eyes suddenly sympathetic.

"You really love her, huh?"

I pull at the backwards brim of my hat, then twist it around to the front. "Yeah. I do."

The admission cuts deep, an arrow into my heart. There's a reason, I realize, why Cupid carries an arrow. Love is a weapon. It spears.

"I think you shouldn't give up on her."

I frown, surprised. "What?"

Jessie sits down on her bed, folds her long legs up underneath her chin, but doesn't look at me, just keeps her eyes focused on her flowered bedspread. "I was mad about it for a while—okay, I was more than mad. I was really, really jealous. But that's just because I..." She shrugs. "Look, I've never felt that way about anyone, the way you feel about her. I think if I did...I probably wouldn't give it up without a fight."

"Yeah, well." I sink into the chair across from her and turn the letter over and over in my hands.

"People like us," Jessie says, "we're always so scared. You ever notice that? Scared to try. Scared to do more. Scared to succeed, maybe."

"That's because we know what it's like to fail," I joke. "We were born into failure, not victory, like them."

"You really believe that?"

I think about Layla. The way, even with everything going on around her, she's never been afraid to try. With jobs. With school. With us. I thought it was her age, her naiveté that made her so ready to give everything up, to move out here with me. To give it her all. But now that Jessie's talking, I realize that maybe it was also my fear that held us back.

All my life they've called me a fighter. I've used my fists more than once, in ways I haven't always been proud of, but mostly I was just trying to find something better for my family and me than the lot we were dealt. I didn't grow up with anywhere near the resources someone like Layla has had access to. School always felt like a struggle, because who was going to help me with my homework? No one was watching where I went or what I did because my mother was too busy working and trying to take care of her three younger kids.

But I wasn't born into failure either. It's not as simple as that. We had Alba and her family looking out for us. I got into some trouble that will follow me for the rest of my life, but I've still worked my ass off to avoid selling dope or stealing shit for a living. So I know what it's like to try. Maybe it's time to accept that I can also succeed, just like anyone else.

I turn the letter over, fearful, but also excited about what might be inside.

"Open it," Jessie says. "Come on. They're offering you the job, I know it."

I slide my thumb underneath the edge of the paper. Suddenly, I feel like I'm about to throw up. I've never wanted anything this badly before. Never tried so hard to get it. Hours of time, forcing my brain through those books, forcing my body through the workouts. If I don't get it...fuck. The idea is paralyzing.

"Nico," Jessie says, but I can barely hear her.

"Okay," I say.

Before I hesitate again, I rip my finger through the paper, then pull out the letter inside.

Dear Mr. Soltero...

"Well?" Jessie asks. "*Well?* What did they say, you asshole? Don't keep me in suspense!"

I read it once. Then I read it again. And again. Then, finally, I look up. For the first time in my life, my shoulders feel light. The future seems wide open.

CHAPTER TWENTY-EIGHT

Layla

I finish typing the last few sentences of Giancarlo's economics paper, then email it to him and shut my computer. It's not a great paper, written in the last twenty-four hours. I had to skip one of my classes today to finish it, but it's the best I could do with such short notice.

I blink, trying to kick out Quinn's disapproving looks, Shama and Jamie's pitiful faces last Friday. I've barely seen any of them since I walked out, sneaking in during hours I knew they wouldn't be there to grab some stuff to bring up here. But the commute back to campus from here isn't easy every day of the week. And staying with Giancarlo all the time isn't easy either. Sometimes he's sweet, other times unbearably terse. I never know which version of him I'm going to get.

"Please," he begged as he curled up on the bed last night and pressed his face into my shoulder. "*Amor*, I need your help."

It wasn't until he told me he would lose his student visa if he failed his class that I finally gave in. What was I supposed to say to that? Tell him he had to leave the country because I wasn't willing to type a five-page paper?

I yawn, repressing the urge to collapse across the desk. I need some coffee, but Giancarlo's out, and my bank account is down to its last few pennies. I need to call my mother and figure out this summer. Try to convince her to let me stay here, although every mention of that makes Giancarlo get that crazy look in his eye. He wants me to come with him to Buenos Aires. That's a discussion for when we're both getting a decent night's sleep, I guess.

I look out the window, where the sun peeks between the buildings, gleaming through the fire escape. From here, the iron bars look a lot like a jail. I try not to think about how this place is starting to feel like one too.

When he said "you and me," I didn't realize it would mean demanding to know where I was every second of every day. I didn't realize it would mean sporadically checking my cell phone messages to make sure I wasn't cheating on him or talking to anyone else. But every time I start arguing with what he says or does, he reminds me of one fact, one truth that digs so deeply. *Only me,* he says over and over again. *I'm the only one here for you.*

It hurts. It all hurts. And even though sometimes he hurts too, Giancarlo is the only one who's here. The only one who stays.

With a sigh, I flip open my history textbook, finally ready to finish my last paper. I haven't done very well in this class, so I need to do well on this to pull my grade out of the B-minus range. There's a lot to do.

The front door opens and shuts with a slam, and a few minutes later Giancarlo walks in, chattering on the phone.

"Hello," he says curtly after he hangs up, but he stops and waits until I look up from the desk.

I try to give a bright smile. *"Bueno. Estoy tratando de escribir mi papel."*

Giancarlo frowns at my clunky Spanish while he takes off his glasses and polishes them. Even though he knows I'm taking accelerated Spanish classes, he doesn't like to speak it with me. My poor accent, which sounds more Brazilian than any kind of Hispanic, is frustrating, apparently. "Like talking to a toddler," he said just last week. "Waste of my time."

He flops down on the unmade bed, an old mattress balanced on a squeaky metal frame, and it's then I notice that his eyes look a little glassy. Sometimes they look that way when he gets back from his job, doing whatever it is the club has him doing at all hours of the night and day. He's a promoter, or so he told me once. Apparently that means he does everything, including buying televisions and selling his girlfriend's watch to do it, though I'd never say anything about it now.

He flips on the television to a rerun of some crime show, which is all he ever likes to watch. It's the kind my dad likes, but which bores me to death.

I look up irritably. "Do you have to do that? I have a final exam tomorrow and a paper due."

Giancarlo frowns. "I had to work all day today. I need some time to relax. This is my apartment."

I blink between him and the screen, trying to figure out if he's for real. "Um, okay. Well, I guess I can go downtown to work at the library. They're open all night."

I stand up and start gathering my things together, but in a minute, I'm surrounded by Giancarlo's arms, pulled tight against his tall form.

"I'm sorry," he murmurs into my ear. "Forgive me. Stay. This is your home too."

Home? I'm not sure how I feel about that.

He keeps me trapped against his body, and I can feel something starting to grow against the small of my back. He's most attracted when I'm trapped.

"Giancarlo," I say, gently unwrapping his arms from around me. "I need to study. Please?"

He pumps his growing erection lightly against my hip, then releases me with a reluctant groan. "Fine," he says, like a child, and then flops back on the bed, but turns off the TV. "You are so lucky to have me, you know that? How many men would be this patient with their woman?"

Wise enough not to answer that question, I turn back to the desk and try to keep writing, even though it's that much harder to focus with a restless, long-limbed Argentinian flopping around on the bed behind me.

Eventually, I'm able to focus more, and I write and study for a few more hours, taking notes and doing the best I can to learn the history of Spanish migration patterns that I should have learned a month ago. As I scratch out some notes about the recent timeline of travel patterns from Cuba through Venezuela, something catches my eye.

"Holy shit," I breathe.

"What?" Giancarlo asks irritably from the bed, where he's lying. "What are you gasping about?"

I read over the words, unsure if I understand them correctly.

In 1999, the Clinton Administration passed a series of laws opening up travel to Cuba for educational purposes. Through the Bush Administration restricted these measures in 2003, family visitations were actually expanded beyond humanitarian relief. Currently, any close relative of a Cuban national can visit the country. Critics of this law have said it was too lax because visitors are not required to bring any documentation of their family's presence in Cuba to visit.

2003. I flip the page back and forth, looking for more information, but there's nothing. Barely a mention of the new laws, but immediately, I jump to the computer and start searching for more information, although I soon realize I don't have the expertise to parse the legal jargon online. I need to talk to a lawyer.

Correction: Nico's *family* needs to talk to a lawyer.

But one thing is clear. *Not required to bring any documentation.* Maybe I'm reading this wrong, but it looks like under the auspices of tightening regulations, the travel laws to Cuba for family have actually been relaxed in some ways. All Nico or one of his siblings has to do is say they are visiting a relative there, and they could potentially get a license to go. Get Carmen's birth certificate. Set her on the path toward citizenship.

I skim the article again while my heart picks up a few beats. The whole story isn't here—it doesn't say what to do, or whom to talk to about getting the license needed to travel. But this small paragraph is everything. This could change Carmen's life. It could change her whole family's life.

I stand up suddenly, clapping the book under one arm.

Giancarlo looks up from the TV and glares at me. "What are you doing?"

I glance around for my jacket, barely noticing him in my flurry of thoughts. "I need to go out for a bit."

"What? Where?"

My skin prickles. Finally I locate my jacket under a pile of Giancarlo's laundry and shove my arms through it. I look like crap in leggings and an old t-shirt, my hair tossed up into a bun after I pulled an all-nighter last night writing papers for two. Carmen and her kids are going to think I look crazy. But it doesn't matter. They need to know this right freaking now.

"Um, some friends down the street. I just found some information that will help them." For some reason, I don't want to tell Giancarlo what's going on. I mean, he might understand. After all, he's here on a visa too. But the way he's looking at me tells me he's in one of those moods where he won't even want to let me out of the room, much less on a five-block walk.

Suddenly I'm in a hurry. Like if I wait around this apartment, I'll be talked out of it. Convinced this is nothing, that I have nothing to tell them, nothing to offer anyone else but him, in this strange, dingy little cocoon he's constructed here.

"Do you remember Gabe?" I say, hoping the memory will soothe him a little. "My friend from down the street? His mother, she, um, well, anyway, I just read something in here that could help them. It has to do with her status, you know? I just really want to show them."

Giancarlo pushes up from the bed and walks over in his socked feet. His normally glossy hair looks dull, flattened on one side from lying down for so long, and his five-o'clock shadow is patchy. He still hasn't lost that glazed look in his eyes.

"I can tell him tomorrow in our class. You don't need to leave."

He reaches a hand out for the book and waits. I stare at it. Suddenly I feel like the book symbolizes something I'll never get back if I give it up.

"Um, no thanks," I say. I hug the book to my chest and step toward the bedroom door. "I don't want it to get lost in translation." I open it before he can reply, slipping on my sneakers as I hop out. "It's fine. They only live a few blocks away. I'll be back in an hour, maybe less."

"Layla!"

I skip to the front door and let it slam over my name, and without thinking, I'm scurrying down the stairs to the lobby, like a mouse escaping a bloodthirsty cat.

This is silly. What am I running from? This is Giancarlo, my boyfriend, not some terrible monster. We are practically living together now—he always wants me with him, and even though sometimes his attention chafes, I know it's just because he cares. Because he wants me.

He wouldn't hurt me. He wouldn't.

Wouldn't he? A voice echoes, one that isn't Quinn or Nico or my other friends and family, but maybe a little bit of all of them. Maybe a little myself too. My wrist throbs. So when I hear a door open and footsteps sound in the building, I rush out the front door into the night.

It doesn't take long to walk-run the five or so blocks to Nico's old apartment, skipping around the groups of people arriving home from work and leaving classes at this time of night. It's twilight, and the last glow of the sun has set over the river, which glimmers down the hill through the tall buildings, alight with a purple hue, the color of a fresh bruise.

I stop in front of the arched entrance to the familiar gray stone building, smiling politely at an older couple who walk by.

"*Buenas noches,*" I say, aware that I probably sound like a textbook, not someone familiar with the local lingo, but they smile like they would to a child and nod politely.

Then I turn back to the building. My fingers hover over the call buttons to buzz the apartment. For a second I'm not sure if I should press them. Gabe might not even be there, although I'd bet my foot that Carmen is. I could just call Nico, weird as it might be after not taking any of his calls or texts for months. But maybe he should tell his mother, not me. They could do with the information what they liked. Maybe this isn't my business.

No, I decide. This doesn't need a translator, and it doesn't have to be yet another thing on Nico's shoulders. And Carmen deserves to see the words herself, hear it straight from the source that someone in her family can go and get her the documents she needs to be here legally.

But just as I'm about to press the button, a hand closes over my wrist, and I'm yanked around with a force that nearly pulls my arm out of its socket.

"Come!" Giancarlo shouts as he fairly drags me back toward Broadway.

"Hey!" I wrench my arm out of his grasp, then clasp my wrist to my chest. "What are you doing?"

"What am *I* doing?" he demands. "I'm coming after my woman, who just leaves in the middle of the night for no reason! What the fuck do you *think* I should be doing?"

He makes another grab at my wrist, and to avoid the curious looks of another woman walking down the street, I let him tow me back to his apartment, trotting next to him the entire way. Inside, Giancarlo drags me down the hall, practically flings me into his bedroom, and slams the door.

"Where. The fuck. Did you go?"

I take a step back. His eyes are less glassy, but still dilated. Yeah, he definitely took something when he was out. But it's the look of complete blackness on his face right now that really terrifies me. It's a look devoid of any love or compassion or tenderness. Only contempt. Rage.

"What-what do you mean?" I stutter. "I told you where I was going."

I take a step backward again, and my heel hits the bottom of the bed frame. Giancarlo approaches, forcing me to look up. He's so much taller than me; I have to crane my neck to look him in the eye.

He snags my wrist again to hold me in place. "You were going to *him*, weren't you?"

I frown. "Who?"

"Whoever you're *fucking* behind my back. That boy, maybe. The one that walked you here."

Shit. Not this again. I swallow. "P-please. Listen to yourself. You sound crazy right now. I don't know what you did at work or if maybe you took something. I...I won't judge you, I promise. But I really don't think you're yourself right now—"

"I'm *fine*." Giancarlo bites out the words, and I shake slightly. "You are *mine*," he spits. "We talked about this."

"No, *you* talked about this," I say, struggling unsuccessfully to get back my wrist. "I've never said anything like that, ever!"

"So now you lie to me too, eh?" he asks, his accent suddenly a thick syrup over his words. "You lie to me about where you go, you lie about why—you lie about all of it, don't you? *Don't you?*"

His words shake, and his voice rises slightly with a mild hysteria. I take a deep breath, willing my racing heart to calm down. Every cell in my body is screaming to *get out*. I'm overreacting. He wouldn't do anything to hurt me. He...wouldn't.

"Were you going to play his little whore? Suck his cock, do all the dirty things you never want to do for me? Eh? Is that where you were running to? Hmm?"

My entire face screws up. "Are you fucking serious right now? I t-told you where I was going! You're acting nuts!"

His hands land on my shoulders like dead weights, and he starts pushing me down to the carpet. "You say you're my woman? Prove it. On your knees."

I struggle against his force. "What? *No*? I'm not doing anything like that to you right now!"

"Yes, you are!" he roars, pushing me down hard enough that my knees land on the floor with a crack. Suddenly I'm shoved against the back of the bed, pinned there by his legs while he struggles to unbutton his pants.

"Stop!" I cry out, pushing against his iron thighs. "What are you doing?!"

But my struggles only get me yanked under my arms and tossed onto the bed. Giancarlo straddles me, his half-erect penis hanging out of his pants while he pins my arms above my head. Pain lances through the shoulder he wrenched on the street.

I shriek: "Get off me!"

"Stay DOWN!" Giancarlo shouts. "You're *my* woman! *Mine!*"

"I am NOT!" I scream, and in a reflex that's purely rooted in fight-or-flight mode, my hands fly out with curled fingers, flailing wildly to beat off his much larger form. "LET ME FUCKING GO!"

And suddenly I'm off the bed like a doll and tossed backward with a loud thud as my head whips against the plaster over the bed. Then Giancarlo's on top of me again, and his hands close around my neck, holding me against the pillow while he straddles my body all over again. I fight to suck in air, but none comes as his hands tighten around my windpipe.

"Giancarlo!" I wheeze, but the word barely makes it through his grip. I try to pound my chest, let him know I can't breathe, but his steel-like grip remains.

"Are you going to calm down?" he says, over and over again. "Are you? Are you going to calm the *fuck* down?"

The world starts to feel brighter, but also fades a little—out of fear or lack of oxygen, I can't say. Either way, I've never been more terrified, and my body freezes. I couldn't have moved if I wanted to. All I want is to run. But instinct takes over—before I can run, he has to let me go.

"Are you going to calm down?" he asks for the last time. He stares at me, his black eyes shining through smudged glasses.

Somehow, with my last remnants of oxygen, I nod, a tiny shake of my head that quivers under his grip. *Please*, is all I can think, a prayer to someone out there. God. Jesus. A saint. The universe. *Please don't let him kill me. I don't want to die.*

His eyes clear suddenly, like a fog has lifted. As if he realizes where we are, what he's doing, Giancarlo's hands let go, and he lifts off me suddenly. I remain frozen for a half-second while I inhale a massive breath. And then, as the oxygen goes to my brain, my heart, my soul, my body erupts into sudden action.

Giancarlo watches dumbfounded with a big hand thrust into his thick black hair, as I jump off the bed, grab my purse off a chair. I don't even think about what I'm doing as I grab a few books, my computer, shove them into a bag.

"Wait," Giancarlo says as he finds his voice. He stumbles toward me, reaching out. "*Amor*, please, stop. I didn't mean to—"

His hand finds my elbow, and I spring out of reach, a textbook under one arm. My jacket is on the other side of the room, but that can stay. I'm a whirlwind, I just need to get out.

"No!" I shout, as I sprint toward the door.

"Layla!" Giancarlo shouts, still stumbling, tripping in his faze over the thick carpet and falling to the floor.

It gives me the extra few seconds I need to make my escape. This time, I don't scurry. I fucking run.

I sprint down the stairs, two at a time, run out the building and ignore the shouts of my name echoing down the block from two stories up. I dash down two blocks on Broadway, ignoring the concerned looks on people's faces as I wipe away tears and struggle for breath after breath. I still feel like I can't breathe. I need...I need something.

I feel around in my pocket, but realize too late that I've left my phone there in my hurry to leave. I need to call someone. Let them know I'm coming. Figure out what the fuck I'm going to do next.

If I had been thinking clearly at the time, I probably wouldn't have stopped on my way to the subway that night. I wouldn't have spied a pay phone across the street, dodged oncoming traffic flying down Broadway in order to get to it. I wouldn't have fished the dollar out of my purse I needed to make long distance phone calls. I would have just kept going.

But at that moment, I needed to hear his voice more than I needed to be safe. To me, they were the same thing.

"Hello?"

The deep, melodic tone is instant balm to my soul, but also opens up wounds even further. The chaos of the last twenty minutes breaks over me like a waterfall, and the tears immediately turn to choked sobs.

"N-Nico?"

It's loud. There's static on the other end of the line, like he's outside, maybe driving somewhere. And for a second, I'm not sure if he can hear me. Or if he even wants to at all.

"Layla?" His voice is scratchy. Worried. "Is that you?"

"I-I want you to k-kill him," I stutter automatically into the phone, my words caught on the sobs. I barely even know what I'm saying as all the pain and frustration of the last few weeks, months, shit, the entire year, pours out of me. "I want you to come with your-your boys. Flaco. K.C. Who—I don't know—who-whoever you would bring to help you. And I-I want you to beat the sh-shit out of him, j-just like you would have, w-way back w-when...you know...w-when you were younger."

I don't really know what he was like back then. He's told me a little about it, and I've seen for myself that he's no one to mess with. I've seen him wrangle unruly men at bars like they were nothing, seen his fists curl with the urge to fight. I know at the very least that when he told me to call him, threatening to take care of anyone who hurt me, he meant it.

My fear has suddenly been replaced with anger, an anger I've never known before. It's a rage that burns white, like a glowing iron that's so hot the red has all but disappeared. More than anything else, I'm angry that I don't have the power to fight back the way I want to. That I'd never be able to.

But maybe Nico could. Maybe he would. For me.

The buzz behind the phone dies down, but his voice still crackles, like he's getting out of range.

"Nico?" I ask again. "Are you there?"

At first there's no answer. Then he's back: "Where are you?"

"I'm-I'm at a pay phone," I manage. "T-two blocks from h-his place. H-he...I c-can't..." The words choke in my mouth. How can I tell him this? I don't even know how to explain it to myself.

The line breaks up again, but occasionally there's some swearing. "Motherfucker" breaks through a few times, but I can't tell anything else.

This was a mistake. I shouldn't have called. And as I look through the window of the phone booth to see Giancarlo jogging erratically down the other side of the street, I realize just how stupid my mistake really was.

"I have to go," I say quickly. "I'm sorry. He's coming toward me, and I don't know what he's going to do. I need to get help, okay? I need to go!"

I don't wait to hear Nico's response, just drop the phone as Giancarlo spots me and start sprinting down the street.

"Layla!" he shouts.

My feet trip on the pavement, but I manage to keep my footing. Several cars honk as I run into oncoming traffic, but the gamble means I reach the subway entrance a full block earlier than Giancarlo. I jog down the stairs, praying for a train, not considering what I'll do if he corners me in the station while I wait.

The attendant in the booth watches curiously as I hurriedly swipe my MetroCard. I exhale with relief as a train pulls up almost immediately.

"Layla!" Giancarlo shouts from the other side of the turnstiles, blocked by a flush of people exiting the platform. "Come back *now*!"

But I just stare, deadened, crying, terrified, as the scratched glass subway doors close between us, cutting off his voice. His black stare pins me to the hard, plastic seats as the train leaves, and we dive underground into blackness.

I ride it all the way down to the last stop, and then back up to Union Square. And then I wait a solid ten minutes behind a statue, waiting for Giancarlo to appear on my street. When he doesn't, I dodge across the street like a shadow and into my building. And it's only with a nod at the security guard that at last I feel safe.

CHAPTER TWENTY-NINE

Nico

The phone rings. And rings. And rings. And again, goes to voicemail. Fuck. *Fuck*. I've been trying to call her for the last hour, and nothing. I thought at first she was stuck in the subway, but it's ringing too many times for that. Layla either doesn't have her phone—which would, I guess, explain why she was calling from a pay phone—or she's ignoring me again.

I feel like I'm going crazy. Today was supposed to be a good day. A day to say goodbye to LA in style before K.C. and I drive back to New York together. As fate would have it, I wasn't the only one fed up with California.

"Too much fuckin' sunshine," he said as we sat on the balcony of his apartment a few weeks ago with a couple of beers.

He's been out here almost three years. He's had enough. So when a radio station in New York offered him a job, K.C. took it. It'll allow him the freedom to play only the shows he really wants to play while at the same time making a decent steady income.

Our plan was to sell as much of my stuff as we could, then drive back to New York in his Yukon, which doesn't break down every month like my crappy Jeep and also has the benefits of air-conditioning. I was on my way to sell the stupid thing, then go to the goodbye party for us (okay, mostly K.C.) at some lounge in WeHo. I barely managed to get through the sale, but a solid chunk of that money just went to a last-minute plane ticket.

My cab stops, and I jump out after tossing a few bills toward the driver. I jog into the party, which is in full swing now. It's mostly full of people from Venom, here before the club opens, and a bunch of other industry types who are just strangers to me. These people are here to say goodbye to K.C. and mingle with each other. Everyone in LA is out to get something. If you're like me, with nothing to offer except a best friend who's starting to make a real name for himself, you're not worth much except as a point of contact.

But it's a good feeling not to be riding on my friend's coattails anymore. A feeling I was enjoying an hour ago while I drove up Sunset, thinking about the next steps I'll take in another week or so when I arrive for my first day at the FDNY Academy. I was feeling great before I got that phone call.

"Yo!" K.C.'s voice echoes through the crowd when I storm into the lounge, even though it's immediately swallowed by the conversations around us. "There he is: Mr. FDNY!"

A few people cheer and clap toward me, but I ignore them as I walk toward my friend. As soon as he catches the thunder on my face, K.C. immediately pushes a girl off his lap and stands up.

"Hey!" she crows, but he waves her away.

"What's up?" he asks. "What's going on?"

"I need a favor," I say. "I gotta leave for New York tonight. Now. It's Layla—her boyfriend—"

"Who, Mrs. Perón? She spill something on her dress?"

If I wasn't so pissed off, I'd laugh. K.C. took the Evita nickname and ran with it, probably because he knows just how hard it is for me that Layla has a boyfriend. But I'm not in a laughing mood, and the jokes stop immediately.

"Yo," K.C. demands. "What'd that motherfucker do?"

I shake my head. "I don't know, man. I don't know. She called, freaking out on the street somewhere, asking me to fuck him up."

"Is she okay? Where the fuck is she?"

I gotta give it to my friend. He's only met Layla a few times, but like any best friend would, he knows how important she is. Dude's already bouncing on his heels like he's ready to jump clear across the country to have my back.

"I don't know," I say, over and over again while I pace around in a circle. I really do feel like I'm about to go crazy. "I don't fuckin' know. I was on my way to sell the Jeep, and the phone cut out. She's not answering hers. I don't know what the fuck is going on, and I'm fuckin' freaking out." I clasp his shoulder. "You gotta drive yourself, man. I need to be on the next flight out of here."

K.C. nods. "Yeah, yeah, of course. Go get your girl, man. Tell her we're gonna fuck that motherfucker *up* when we get back. Tell her I'ma cut off that *pendejo*'s balls myself."

I give a slight smile, but it's just talk right now. K.C. would probably help me take that fucker down if I really wanted—he had my back plenty of times when we were younger. But right now, he doesn't know what he's saying. He doesn't know how capable I feel of outright murder.

Still, one thing is more important than that. I need to get to Layla. I need to find my girl.

"Thanks, *mano*," I say. We slap hands, and K.C. pulls me in for a quick hug.

"Anytime, man, anytime. Your stuff is all packed?"

I nod. "I'm going back to the apartment to grab as much as I can. Everything else is in the corner."

"I got it, I got it. See you in a few days."

I turn to leave, start weaving my way around the people who are mostly there just to see K.C. A few from Venom reach out to say hi, but I ignore them, only one thing on my mind.

"Nico!"

I turn back to K.C.

"Don't do anything stupid," he calls out. Then, with a funny half-salute: "Wait 'til I get there."

———

IT'S NOT until I'm waiting for my crazy fuckin' expensive red-eye flight to New York to board, that I finally get some answers. My Yankees hat is wrinkled, the bill crunched, since I've taken it on and off so many times in the last four hours. I just dropped half the money I got for the Jeep on this ticket, but I don't even care. I'd sell a kidney right now if it would get me to New York faster.

I've called everyone I can think of trying to get some answers. Gabe's been walking up and down Broadway all damn day, but he hasn't seen anything. I even called Quinn, Layla's so-called best friend, blowing up her damn phone for hours, but nothing. No texts. Nothing.

But it's Quinn's number on my phone right now. Finally, some answers.

"Hello?" I answer in a rush. "Quinn? What the fuck is happening back there? Have you heard from her?"

I'm loud and frantic, and the businesswoman sitting next to me in the crowded waiting area gives me a dirty look. I glare at her and stand up, pacing toward the big windows of the gate.

"It's all right," Quinn says. "She's here, okay? Sorry I didn't see your calls until now. I left my phone at the gym."

Relief floods me—and when I say floods me, I mean practically knocks me down. I brace a hand on a pillar to hold myself up.

"Fuck," I exhale. "Thank God. Can I—can I talk to her? Is she there?"

"Yeah, she's here. She's still a little shaken up, but I think she'll want to say hi."

There's a rustle on the other end of the line, and a few moments later, sweetest fuckin' thing I've ever heard in my life sounds through the phone.

"Nico?"

My body sags against the pillar. "Baby?"

There's a sniffle, like she's trying not to cry again, and suddenly, I feel like doing the same.

"Hey," she says. "Are you—are you okay?"

"Am *I* okay? Jesus Christ, Layla." I rub my face with my hand. Goddammit. This flight is too slow. This world is too slow. I need to be with her *now*. "What's going on?"

"Give me that." Quinn's voice sounds in the background, and there's another shuffle before she comes back on the line. "Hey."

"Hey your fuckin' self," I snap. "I want to talk to Layla." I have no patience with this chick's bullshit. Not now.

"She needs a moment," Quinn says. "It's been a shitty fucking night, Special Delivery, and I don't think she should have to talk about it *again*."

"What do you mean, *again*?" I ask, ignoring the stupid nickname that doesn't even work anymore, considering I'm no longer a FedEx guy.

"I mean the cops have been here all goddamn night, and she's been grilled over and over again while they took her statement. Fucking vultures. You'd think *she* was the one being accused of sexual assault, not the fucker who actually did it."

At the words "sexual assault," I have to close my eyes as I pressed my forehead hard against the pillar. It doesn't help. I can still only see red.

"What happened?" I grit out.

"You want me to say?" Quinn asks, clearly speaking to someone away from the phone. Layla. Goddammit, I just want to talk to *her*, not pushy Massachusetts princess.

"Quinn—" I bite out.

"He tried to rape her," she states bluntly. "Tried to force her to suck him off. When she didn't want to do that, the asshole threw her on the bed, tried to fucking *strangle* her, and then started, you know, the next step. He was pissed because she had gone somewhere without telling him or some bullshit like that. We're pretty sure he was on something. Not like that fucking matters."

"*Fuck!*" I slap my palm against the pillar hard enough that the pain of it vibrates up my arm. If I felt like murder before, now I feel like I could take out this entire fucking building.

The attendants at the desk look at me, alarmed, as do several other people waiting to board the plane. I glance at them, but turn around. I need to keep my cool. Hardest thing I've ever had to do, but I can't get kicked off this flight.

For a second, I wonder if Quinn is embellishing, making the story more than it really is. But I remember Layla's voice—the terror I heard when she called. No matter what happened, that wasn't fake. That was real. And I want to *kill* the motherfucker who made her sound like that.

"Let me talk to her," I say once I'm able to think clearly again. Well, as clearly as I can.

"Don't upset her, Romeo," Quinn says. "She's been through enough today already, you hear me? She's been through enough this entire fucking year. It's really late over here, and we all need to get some sleep after this fiasco."

"Quinn. *Please.*"

"All right, all right."

There's some more shuffling as the phone is handed back to Layla.

"Hey," she says. "I—sorry. I just...yeah. I can't really talk about it anymore."

"You don't need to be sorry for anything," I tell her. "And you don't need to talk. I just needed to know you're okay, baby. I've been going crazy over here."

She sniffs again. Fuck, I didn't want to make her cry.

"I'm okay," she says. "You don't have to worry, okay? My friends are here. We're getting everything figured out. I'm sorry to take you away from whatever you're doing. I shouldn't—I shouldn't have called you like that."

"Baby, didn't I tell you to call me if he ever did anything to you? *Didn't I?*"

There's silence for a second. Then a very small: "Yes."

"So you just did what I asked. I'm glad you did. And I'm so fuckin' glad you're all right."

"I am," she says. But she still sounds sad. "So, um, yeah. You can go back to whatever it is you're doing today. Hanging out with your friends or Jessie or whatever..."

I hate the way her voice quivers. She sounds so weak, so tired. Then I realize that she doesn't know. We haven't talked in weeks, months. She doesn't know the results of my interview. She doesn't know that I'm on my way to New York.

"Layla," I say, trying and failing to keep my voice from shaking. "I—I'm at the airport."

"Oh? Where are you going?"

"I'm coming to you, sweetie."

Around me, the airport buzzes, but I can only hear this girl. She's the center of this moment, her gravity, her power over my mind, my heart, makes everything else silent, obsolete. Why the fuck did I ever try to fight it?

"What?" she asks finally. "What do you mean?"

"I got in," I tell her softly, turning my face back toward the pillar and pulling my cap low. "To the FDNY. I start the academy in two weeks."

I wish to God I were there, watching her face while I tell her. I'd be down on my knees right now. Begging her to forgive me for waiting this long to tell her the truth: I belong to her.

"That's...oh, Nico. That's amazing. I knew you could do it..."

I can feel her grappling with her answer, unsure of exactly what to say. It's not the overjoyed response I was hoping for, but of course, she's not exactly herself. I close my eyes in pain, imagining her curled up on her bed or the couch. Holding her stomach the way she does when she's hurting. Curled into herself.

I want to wrap myself around her. Tell her it's going to be all right. Tell her that I'm there, that I'll make sure she's safe, that I'll never leave her again.

"Now boarding all seats for Flight 117 to New York/La Guardia Airport."

The call for general boarding rings out, pulling me back to this moment. Seven hours. Seven more hours, and I'll be there. I can tell all of this to her in person and more.

"Layla?" I ask as I turn toward the gate.

"Yeah?"

"I'm coming back," I tell her again, willing her to understand. "So don't—don't do anything, okay? Don't go anywhere, because I'm coming straight to you. And, baby? I love you. I love you so fuckin' much. Do you hear me, Layla? *I love you.*"

There's another long pause, and I wonder for a minute if I've lost her. If she missed all of it. But I'd tell her again. I'll tell her over and over until she believes that what I say is true.

"I hear you," she says, small and quiet. "I'll be here."

CHAPTER THIRTY

Layla

THE NEXT MORNING, I WAKE UP FEELING LIKE I'VE BEEN RUN OVER BY A TRAIN. Everything is stiff. Worn out. But a quick glance at the mirror across the room reveals I don't look as bad as I feel—the red marks are starting to bruise now, but it's nothing a little concealer and a scarf won't hide. It's the emotions of the last twenty-four hours that have gotten to me.

I press a hand to my head as the events of yesterday return. Sitting in our living room for two hours with the police officers that came to take my statement after Quinn insisted that we call them. But there was really little they could do other than that. There wasn't enough evidence of assault for them to press charges, nor could they do anything to help me get my things from Giancarlo's apartment.

"Tomorrow," they said. "If you have bruising or something like that."

I never thought I'd be one of those girls. The ones who have to answer questions like the cops asked me. The one who has to defend my own attack.

"What were you wearing?" the police officer wanted to know. "Did you do anything to provoke him?"

And I honestly couldn't answer no—that was the worst part. Because I did scratch him, didn't I? I did yell. I did push him away. Didn't I assault him too? Sort of?

Shama and Quinn sat there with me, angry and defiant while I recounted the events, but I couldn't tell with whom. Giancarlo? Or me, for bringing it all down on myself?

After the very *long* interview with the cops, I tumbled into my bed, and it was only when I was nearly asleep that I heard Nico's voice again, frantic and worried.

One more thing to feel guilty about.

I'm coming back, he said.

Don't go anywhere.

I love you.

They were all the words I'd been dying to hear for months, almost a year now. Words that should have made everything feel better. And while they did soothe the pain some, a new feeling sprang in my heart, one I hadn't felt before with him: fear.

Because I saw the looks on all my roommates' faces when I arrived at the apartment last night, blotchy and red-eyed, my hair a mess and my clothes stretched out of shape. I saw their faces after they listened to me tell my story three times: once to them, once to the R.A. down the hall, and once more to the policemen. They looked tired. Fatigued. I could see the effects my choices had on the people in my life. Their bitter disappointment in me.

I'm not sure I can deal with that look on Nico's face when he arrives.

"I still think you need to call your mom," Quinn says as she finishes primping her hair in the mirror over her desk.

I curl back into my bed. The girl has been up and chipper for over an hour.

Quinn turns around. "Did you hear me? Lay, you could probably just take incompletes with the rest of your classes and finish your final projects this summer. Take your last final tomorrow and go. Write your paper from home. Get yourself together."

She means Pasadena, of course, but Quinn doesn't really understand how much I *don't* want to go back there. If my roommates have been judgmental this semester, I don't even want to think about what my mother and grandparents will say. Probably truck me off to some kind of therapist or rehab center, although for what, I don't know. But it will come with a lot of long looks, breathy sighs, and several phone calls to my father. Brazil will be put off for years. My grandparents will resume their lives at the country club while my mom keeps running down to Cabo or the spa or wherever she goes in her spare time. And I'll be left in that big, empty house, in that big, empty room. Alone.

I shake my head stubbornly. "I need to finish here. And then..."

I can't finish the sentence. I don't know what's going to happen. Nico's on a plane right now, due to arrive sometime past 9:00 or 10:00 a.m. I don't know what his plans are. I don't even know what *we* are.

All I know is that I don't want him to look at me the way Quinn is right now. I don't want him to come back here and find me in pieces. *I* called *him*, raving like a crazy woman on the street. Made him jump on a plane to rescue me. The least I can do is put things back together, at least a little. Have some kind of plan for what to do next.

I shake my head again. "I can't even take today off. I've missed too many classes this term already. I should go for the final review."

I get out of bed and trudge toward the closet, ready to pick through the remainder of my clothes that aren't up at Giancarlo's.

Quinn watches me dubiously. "Um...okay. Do you want me to wait for you?"

I give a small smile through the closet mirror. "No. You go ahead. I'll see you later tonight."

She stands up. "Okay. Well, I'm going to go grab some breakfast on campus, then. See you tonight."

———

TEN MINUTES LATER, I'm feeling a little better, dressed in gym clothes. I decide this is what I need best. A workout, which I haven't gotten in weeks, since Giancarlo never wanted me to leave his place. It will clear my mind before classes. Everything feels better with an endorphin boost.

I run around Union Square, over to Palladium, the NYU dorm with the gym in the basement, and spend the next hour running out my troubles on the treadmill, trying to decide a plan of action. Going to class is about as far as I get, but it's a better plan than nothing.

I'm rounding the corner, almost back to my dorm, when I spot a familiar tall figure lounging by the entrance of the building. Immediately, my heart starts beating wildly with an eerie sense of déjà vu.

Giancarlo recognizes me and starts toward me at a run. I bolt the other direction, dodging people as I fight to cross Fourteenth Street onto the flat concrete expanse of Union Square.

"Layla!" Giancarlo calls behind me, loud enough that I know he's close.

My legs, worn out after running for so long at the gym, won't move fast enough. I run toward the nearest subway entrance, but just as I arrive, an influx of people pours from the station. I jerk around the entrance, but I'm not fast enough. A big hand snags my elbow, pulling me into a sturdy male wall.

"Hello, *amor*." Giancarlo's lips are warm and sinister against my throat as he locks one arm around my chest, the other pressing something sharp—I'm guessing a knife —discreetly against my stomach.

"Let me go," I say, although not loud enough to stop anyone as he turns me away from the crowd. To anyone else, we are locked in a lover's embrace. And with the knife at my side, I'm too petrified to move.

"Now, why would I do that, hmm?" Giancarlo nuzzles into my neck familiarly, which was once something I liked, but now makes me ill. "I came here to see you." When he leans back, his dark eyes are ice-cold. "We have some unfinished business." He hails a cab, which immediately pulls to the curb next to us. "Get in."

"No," I whisper, though the knife stays at my side.

Giancarlo raises a black brow and squeezes my arm hard. "Get in," he says, "before I make you. And I think that is not what you want."

Before I can answer, he turns me roughly toward the open door, twisting my ankle hard against the concrete and forcing me to fall onto the vinyl seats. Unable to run, I'm shoved inside the cab, which smells of body odor and stale pizza, the prick of the knife at my waist the entire time.

"Broadway and West 144th," he barks at the driver, who immediately takes off down the street.

The taxi takes a sharp right on Broadway and stops for a moment in traffic just in front of Carlyle, where another cab has stopped by the curb. I look out of the window just in time to see a familiar pair of broad shoulders emerge from the back seat, with a familiar worn Yankees cap turned backwards so that I can see the black and white emblem.

"Nico!" I shout with a voice that's hoarse from yesterday. I bang on the glass window, but the mix of cars and horns and glass muffles my sounds, which is immediately silenced when Giancarlo yanks me back toward his body.

"Stop," I whimper. "Please, just let me go."

But the car speeds on with the traffic, and Nico's strong frame gets smaller and smaller.

"Nico," I murmur, even while I'm pressed against another man. But it's no use. He can't hear me. He doesn't even know I'm gone.

———

Nico

I've been pacing outside Layla's dorm on Union Square for twenty minutes when her roommate, Quinn, finally calls me back.

"Jesus!" she says. "I was in class, you know. My professor had to ask me to leave because my fucking bag wouldn't stop buzzing."

"Where's Layla?" I demand. "I've been standing outside your building for the last half hour. She's not picking up the landline."

"How should I know where she is?" Quinn asks. "The psycho wanted to go to class today. It wouldn't be the first time she just took off without telling anyone."

"Did she? Go to class?"

There's a pause. "Hold on. Her lit class actually meets across the hall from mine."

I haven't hopped around this much since I was eighteen, training as a boxer because I had too much angry energy and nowhere decent to put it. I could use a heavy bag right now, actually, except a part of me would be perfectly happy delivering this rage to the man who deserves it. Eight-foot-tall, tango-dancing fuckboy who doesn't know how to keep his fuckin' hands to himself.

Just the thought makes me see red again.

"She's not there." Quinn's voice sounds far away through the receiver, but I can still hear the fear there. "Nico, she's not there."

"Meet me here," I say. "Now."

Another twenty minutes later, Quinn, Shama, and Jamie, all of Layla's roommates and so-called best friends, let me into their suite. I bust through the door, dump my bags in their living room, and then jog around the bedrooms. It's exactly as I thought: no Layla.

I return to the living room, where all of the girls are just *sitting* there, lounging on the couch and at their kitchen table, watching me with strange expressions while I bounce around their apartment like a fuckin' pinball.

"What the hell is wrong with you?" I demand from Quinn when I finally stop looking around. "Why are you just sitting there? Aren't you supposed to be her best friend?"

"Isn't she supposed to be *mine*?" Quinn retorts as she stands up from the couch, her face red and angry. "You haven't been around this year. It's been one fucking thing after another with that girl. She keeps falling apart and expecting us to pick up the pieces. I'm sorry, but I didn't come here to be her fucking social worker! I have my own shit to take care of!"

I swear in Spanish and yank off my hat. "And you?" I ask the others. "You think it's okay to just sit here? Where do you think she is, huh?"

I know I'm acting crazy. She could be anywhere. She could be at the gym, a bookstore. Maybe she went out for coffee. But something in my gut tells me otherwise. I know Layla. She knew I was coming. She wouldn't just disappear like this for hours. Something is very, very wrong.

I scoop my jacket off the sofa. "If she's been falling apart, maybe it's because she knew she didn't have a real support system to help her deal with all this shit. Maybe it's because in the end, she knew her friends didn't really have her back."

I'm just about to go when Shama speaks up. "Where are you going?"

I turn around. "Look, if there's any chance at all that motherfucker knows you called the police, my best bet is that she's with him. If they didn't file charges, he could get her to recant her statement. Or, you know, get rid of the evidence altogether. You follow me?"

As the realization of what I'm talking about dawns on their faces, Shama and then Jamie both stand up and grab their coats off the back of the chairs.

"Are you coming?" Shama asks Quinn.

But Quinn just looks away. "I can't do this anymore with her," she says. "I'm sorry. But I'm done."

They stare at her for a second, like they're not sure they actually heard her correctly. Shama gives Quinn a dirty look as she crosses the room to join me.

"That's messed up, Quinn," she says as she grabs her keys off the table. "Seriously. That's messed. Up."

Jamie follows, looking more uncertain. But then they turn to me.

"Let's go get her," Shama says. And without another look at their roommate, we leave.

CHAPTER THIRTY-ONE

Layla

"GET INSIDE."

"No."

"Layla!" Giancarlo hustles me out of the cab, keeping his steel grip around my arm while he pays the cab driver and then tows me toward his building. I look up and down the street, hoping that someone—*anyone*—will recognize me, but for once there aren't even any people around at this time of day. Go figure. The one time I need the eight million people in this city to show up, and no one's around.

"Please," I say as Giancarlo unlocks the door. Like a scared rabbit, I don't dare run. He'd catch up to me in a second, and on my twisted ankle, I wouldn't get far anyway. "What do you want? My friends will know I'm gone soon."

He gives me a black, contemptuous look. The door opens, and he drags me through the lobby and up the stairs to his apartment. Every step hurts.

"You really think they'll come here for you?" he snarls. "After everything that happened?"

I open my mouth to answer, but he's right. He's been there every time I was upset, every time Quinn or someone else turned away. I haven't been the easiest person to be around this past year. I know that. And somehow, in the last six months, Giancarlo positioned himself as the only person I could turn to when things were hard. When everything seemed to hurt, he was there, even if sometimes he seemed to make it hurt a little more.

"I still don't understand," I mutter after the heavy door of the apartment bangs shut.

Giancarlo whirls around, his black shirt flapping with the motion.

"You think you can just walk out on me like that?" he demands. "You think you can call the fucking police, and I won't find out about it?"

Before I can respond, he grabs my hand again and starts dragging me toward his bedroom. I pull away, but his grip is too strong, and my ankle gives. I hop behind him, my bad foot dragging on the dusty wood floors, until he swings me into his room and slams the door behind us.

"H-how did you know?" I ask as I shuffle backward until the bed hits my knees, forcing me to sit.

Giancarlo paces the room like a panther, a trapped cat. He pushes his broad hands through his thick black hair over and over again, though pieces of it still fall forward.

"How did I know?" he asks, as if to himself. "How did I *know*?"

He stops mid-pace and turns to me. "They knocked on my door late last night. Asked me questions for two hours. Why am I here? Where are my papers? Do I know *you*?"

He takes steps toward me, and I scramble onto the bed, ignoring the pain lancing through my ankle.

"Do you know what they do if I have a record?" Giancarlo demands, eyes widened and crazed, his normally near-perfect grammar disappearing into his accent. "I lose my visa! I go back to Buenos Aires! Back to my father, my family, all in shame!"

My chin trembles as I try to remain calm.

"You have to call them," he continues. "You need to go to the police. Tell them it was a lie. They won't do anything to you—you're a citizen. Me, they might kick out of the country! Tell them it was a mistake, a lover's quarrel went wrong, that you shouldn't have called them."

"B-but it wasn't a lover's quarrel," I whisper. "You tried to choke me."

Giancarlo's eyes darken.

"You really want me to be angry, don't you?" he asks, his voice tripping over itself, rippling with anger. "You are trying to make me lose control, eh?"

"I-I'm not trying to do anything," I say. "And I'm—I was never going to press charges, okay? My roommates called the cops, Giancarlo. I just wanted to leave. That's all."

"You want to leave?" he asks, quirking his head, like the concept just occurred to him. "You want to leave *me*?"

I stare at him, dumbfounded. I don't know if he's on something again, or if this is just part of his personality, a part that might have been lurking there the whole time. He was always possessive, and at times I thought I liked it. But right now...he's just acting unhinged. And it scares me even more.

"P-please," I say, cowering against the wall at the back of the bed. "Just let me go, okay? You can keep whatever's here. You can—I won't bother you again. No police."

"She wants to go," Giancarlo mutters, more to himself than to me. He takes a step backward, then another until he's halfway out the door. "She wants to go."

When he's out of sight, I slump against the wall, but my heart speeds up. His footsteps scramble erratically down the hall, and I listen with dread as a drawer opens and closes in the kitchen, and his footsteps track closer.

"Do you see?!" he cries as he rushes back in the room, knife in hand, maybe the same knife he used to corner me in the Square.

I stare at it, bug-eyed as I scrambled back on the bed. "W-what are you doing? Giancarlo, what are you doing with that?"

Arm trembling, he points the knife straight at me, then turns it back and cuts into the skin of his other wrist. A thick line of blood wells immediately, and when he pulls the knife away, it drips onto the carpet.

"This is what you do to me!" he shouts, arm shaking as blood seeps down his forearm. "You kill me! You rip me to shreds, just like this knife!"

"What—oh my God, *stop*!" I yelp, as he moves to pierce his skin again. "What are you doing?"

"We are for each other—you don't run from me! If you try to leave, this is your fault. I will do it, I *will*! Because you are *mine*!"

"No, I'm NOT!" I'm crammed against the wall, ignoring the pain throbbing through my leg, terrified out of my wits, but the words escape regardless.

Giancarlo stares at me, like he can't believe what he just heard. For a second I wonder if this is just a bad dream, if maybe I'm still back at my room, asleep in my bed, waiting for Nico to arrive. But then his long arm snakes across the mattress, grabs hold of my bad ankle, and yanks.

"Get *OFF*!" I shriek, writhing like an animal even as pain sears.

"Quiet!" he roars, as he tackles me back down.

Blood drips onto my clothes from his open wound, smears against the white of my t-shirt as I fight him off. But even with his arm cut open, he's still much stronger than me as he wrenches my legs open and covers me with his body. I'm all too conscious of the knife pressing into the mattress by my head even while I twist under his weight.

His hands fumble over my body, looking for something to hold on to—skin, clothes, thighs, breasts. I don't know what he wants; I'm not even sure he knows what he wants.

"Please!" I beg, my voice throttled by the sobs twisting my throat. I've never felt so many emotions at the same time—terror, rage, confusion. "Don't do this, Giancarlo. Please don't."

"Why, so you can run to the cops again? Tell them I'm nothing but a dirty criminal, just like all the other *putos* around here?! Do you know what they'll do to me? I'll be finished, deported like a dirty criminal!"

His glasses slide down his long nose as he spits out the last words. I continue to struggle against him, pushing with all my might even as he reaches around my neck with his bloodied hand and wraps my hair around his fist. He yanks my head still, forcing me to look at him.

"Kiss me," he orders. "Do it."

"*STOP!*" I shriek as loudly as I can.

His palm hits my cheek with a loud crack, and the pain burns down my face.

"Shut up!" he roars.

But I don't stay quiet. I can't. I should be terrified into submission; my flight reflex would normally kick in by now. But something in me comes apart, like a spring door busted open. My anger flies like a spray of water from a broken hose—angry, loud, but ultimately useless.

"*Stop!*" I shout, again and again. But my cries only earn me harder and heavier blows. I don't stop either. I just keep shouting, keep crying. It's the only thing I can do.

———

Nico

"That one, right?" Shama says as the cab pulls down West 144th.

I nod. Yeah, this is the right building, the same place where Flaco's lived for the last ten years. Jamie looks around with big eyes in a way that tells me the girl probably hasn't ever ventured above Eighty-Fifth Street.

"Jesus," she whispers. "She lives here?"

"No," I snap as I hand some money to the cabbie. Jesus, between the cab from La Guardia and the one up here, I just dropped close to a hundred dollars today, but it's honestly the last thing on my mind. "She lives with you, right?"

Jamie and Shama shrug, which tells me just how absent Layla has been from their lives lately. They're hurt, and I get it. But it also tells me how abusive this asshole has really been. Isolation is one of the first things shitheads like this do. I've seen it with Maggie over and over again.

We pile onto the curb and find Gabe standing there, skinny arms crossed over his chest.

"Hey," he says.

He gives Jamie a clear look up and down. She blushes. I roll my eyes. Looks like my little brother's been learning some moves in college, but they're not exactly subtle.

"*Yo!*" I snap my fingers in front of his face. "Not why we're here, Casanova. Put it back in your pants."

Gabe swallows. "Sorry, sorry. Yeah. Um. A guy coming out said he was in Apartment 3F. Says everyone knows where the Clark Kent-lookin' motherfucker lives with Nico Soltero's old girl."

It's not his fault, but the way he says that so matter-of-factly pisses me off even more. It must show all over my face, because Shama and Jamie both take a step back.

"Anyway..." Gabe says with a wide-eyed look as I swallow my anger. "Apparently the place used to get raided all the time because the old tenant dealt, but rumor has it the apartment is still on the same lease. It's a front for something."

I exhale roughly through my nose. I knew this dude was bad news. Ten to one the sketchy fuckin' run to Hunt's Point had something to do with the old tenant and whoever actually has their name on the lease. This is no place for Layla, as naive as she can be.

"Ev-everything okay?" Jamie asks.

I gulp down my anger. Save it for Evita.

"Fine," I say as I walk up to the buzzer and press Flaco's button. The buzzer goes off, and the door clicks open. I turn to everyone else. "Let's go."

We're quiet as we trudge up the two flights of stairs, even when we run into Flaco on the first floor, rubbing his hands together as I approach.

"You look way too excited," I tell him.

"Man, you ain't even know," he says eagerly. "I been waiting *months* to kick this motherfucker's ass."

"You really think she's here?" Gabe asks as he jogs behind us.

I shrug. I hope to God she is. I haven't thought yet about what I'll do if I don't find her here. But I don't have to answer, because as soon as we get to the third floor, I hear a scream through one of the doors. It's muffled, but I'd know it anywhere.

"Layla," I breathe and run the rest of the way to the apartment.

The door is actually unlocked. The stupid motherfucker must still be high, because he brought Layla here against her will and didn't even think to lock the goddamn door.

Calling this place a shithole would be nice. The ugly stained carpet, the faded leather couch that looks like it's seen its fair share of parties. The dinge that lines the crown molding, the popcorn texture of the walls, the rim of dust settled over the furniture. I barely have time to notice any of it, because I'm only one step in when Layla screams again.

"Get *off* me!"

I sprint down the short hallway to a closed bedroom door, which I hit with the full force of my shoulder, using my body like a battering ram. It flies open, and inside is Layla on her back on the bed, legs kicking wildly under the force of tall man who's doing his fucking best to hold her down. The grayish, peach-colored sheets are tinged with blood—it's everywhere, including all over my girl. Fear locks my muscles until I realize that the blood isn't hers. It's his, gushing from a nasty cut on his arm.

"What the fuck..." Gabe's voice trails off behind me, and Flaco clicks his tongue, but I barely hear them. Layla screams again, and instinct takes over.

"GET THE FUCK OFF HER!" I roar, taking exactly three steps to where I can grab the man off Layla and spin him around.

It takes me two more steps to shove him against the window hard enough to crack the glass. A half-second more to get a good grip of his shirt and look at his snarling face. Then my hand pulls back, like it's caught on a spring, and I let it all go.

My fist hits his face with a sickening, yet satisfying crunch as bone meets bone. It's been a while since I've done this, but my hands haven't forgotten the feel. His face contorts, and blood gushes from his nose almost immediately. Good, I broke it. That knife-edge nose is going to have a nice crooked line from now on, and he'll know it came from me.

I land another hard punch to his gut, and just as he's keeling over, the breath knocked fully out of him, another uppercut to the bottom of his jaw. He slumps against the wall, but I don't stop. The rage—that rage that almost ruined me when I was a kid, that tossed me in a youth jail for two years and probably would have landed me in a real one if it hadn't been for some luck—is taking over.

But if it's her frenzied shriek that awakens the monster inside, it's her terrified whisper that calms me down.

"Nico?"

My fist hangs in mid-air, ready to take the next punch. To his kidney. His stomach. Maybe his face again, although I can't afford to break my hand a week before I start the academy. But her voice—small, afraid, but still unbearably fucking sweet—holds me still. Maybe it saves me too.

Evita—because the *fuck* if he gets the dignity of a real name now—is only half-conscious as blood still pours out his nose and the rest of him wilts against the peeling paint. Most of the blood on Layla was, in fact, his. That cut on his arm is still seeping down his wrist and dripping on the carpet, adding to the mess from his nose. I release my hold on his collar, and he sinks down to the floor, gasping for breath. When I turn around, Layla is standing in the doorway, held up by Shama and Jamie, who is also staring at me with her mouth hanging open. Layla's hurt. She limps on one foot, and I exhale, resisting the urge to finish the job. He hurt her. He hurt my—he hurt Layla.

"Nico," she says again, pulling out of the wave that's threatening to break all over again. She reaches a hand toward me. "Please. Please, I just want to go."

"Nico," Gabe says as he approaches. "We gotta get her out of here."

Flaco sits down on the bed. "Don't worry, *mano*. I'll take care of this. Fuckface here ain't goin' nowhere 'til you get back."

I nod, slowly back away from Evita's slumped form. My entire body is vibrating. "Okay. Okay."

"Hold on. They can't leave like that."

Shama leaves Layla and rummages around Jack Rabbit's closet. He might be lying on the floor, but I'm still not going to call this motherfucker by his name.

She tosses me a t-shirt and throws another at Layla. It's only then that I realize I'm pretty much covered in blood, and so I strip off my shirt and change into his. It's too tight. He might be taller than me, but he's thinner, and the cotton pulls across my chest. My nose wrinkles. It smells like him, like shitty cologne and cheap red wine and stale cigarettes. Fuck, I hate this guy so much.

"Let's go, man," Gabe says. "Let's go."

I stride to where Layla stands, and without asking, I sweep her up into my arms and tuck her into my shoulder.

"I got you, baby," I tell her as I walk out of the apartment. "I got you."

"Wait," she murmurs, then calls back to Shama: "The book on the desk."

She doesn't say anything else as I carry her down to the street, where Jamie is waiting with a cab. She doesn't argue as I keep her securely on my lap, hold her tight against me, unwilling to let go even a little. She doesn't budge, doesn't move, just shakes silently in my arms. And because she doesn't fight what's got to be a suffocating hold, that's how I know my girl is really broken. And it breaks me too.

CHAPTER THIRTY-TWO

Nico

SOMEHOW, WE MAKE IT BACK TO MY OLD APARTMENT ON 139TH. IT'S ONLY FIVE BLOCKS away, but it feels like five miles. I could have stayed in the back of that cab for hours, holding her, stroking her back, kissing her hair until those goddamn shakes disappear.

But they didn't. If I hadn't been holding her so close, I wouldn't have known it, but because she's burrowed into my chest, I can feel the faint vibrations persist after the cab stops outside the building, after I carry her out and hold her while Gabe unlocks the door, and all during the cramped elevator ride to the fourth floor.

Once we're inside, Gabe walks Shama and Jamie to the train to make sure they get home safe. I keep reminding myself that Flaco is still at the apartment, making sure that motherfucker doesn't leave before I can deal with him properly. I don't know. Just the thought of him makes my head feel like it's about to explode all over again. I can smell his fucking blood on Layla—blood from that cut on his arm. I hope she's the one who gave it to him. I hope my baby fought like hell.

When I walk in, Layla still cradled in my arms, my mom, Maggie, and Allie are sitting on the old floral couch in what used to be the storage area, but has since been converted into a decent-looking living room. Allie is playing peacefully, but they stand up immediately when we walk in. Layla's still frozen in my arms. I should feel an ache from holding her like this for so long, but I don't. My chest hurts—it physically fucking hurts—when I realize that this was what I'd been training for all year. Fuck the FDNY. This was the only rescue that ever mattered.

My mom's sharp eyes dart over Layla while Maggie raises a hand to her mouth and draws Allie to her side.

"Holy shit," she murmurs. "What happened to her?"

I ignore her and look to my mom, who's looking Layla over with perfect understanding.

"Gabriel's room," she says shortly, gesturing toward my old bedroom. "Take her in there."

"*Mami*, what's wrong with Layla..."

I hear the beginnings of some awkward questions from Allie, but don't wait to hear the answers, just kick the door shut. The light is off, so the room stays dim, lit only by what filters through the window between buildings outside. The room is mostly the same, changed only by a few posters Gabe stuck to the wall.

I sit down on the bed, Layla still securely in my arms. And finally, finally, I exhale.

"Shhh," I tell her, holding her against my chest as she shudders.

But she doesn't hold on. For the first time since I met her, her fingers don't curl into my shirt, don't cling to my body, like she's trying to memorize its shape. Instead, she sits in my arms, wooden and still fucking shaking. I focus on breathing. In. Out. Try to be something solid, give her a little of my strength. At least what bit of it I still feel.

"What do you need?" I ask her as I slowly rock her back and forth. That seems to work. The shaking dies, finally, though she's just as still. "Tell me, baby. Just tell me what you need. I got you."

The words seem to pull her out of whatever strange, silent place she's been trapped in. She starts in my arms, and then, in an awkward motion that makes my chest physically hurt, she slides off my lap.

"I-I need..." Her voice is hoarse, like she's out of breath. She scoots away. "I think I just need to lie down. If that's all right with you."

I hate that she even asks. I hate the way her voice sounds so small, so afraid. How tentative it is—so different from the bright-eyed, optimistic girl I know.

She doesn't meet my eyes, just stares vacantly at the sheets gripped between her hands. She's still in her clothes from earlier today—shorts and a white I Love New York t-shirt. The t-shirt was clean, but dried blood is smeared on her arms and her legs. There are even bits of it on her face, speckled over reddened skin. Where he hit her.

Reluctantly, I stand up. It goes against every instinct I have to leave her alone right now. If I hadn't done that in the first place, she wouldn't be here, bruised and broken, inside and out. She would still be herself. She'd still be Layla.

Suddenly finding it harder to breathe than ever, I back toward the door. She lies down on the bed and barely seems to notice that I'm leaving. And in a way...I'm glad. I'm not sure I can take this anymore either. Seeing her hurt. Seeing the person whose touch echoes throughout my whole fuckin' soul after she's been hit like this. I thought it was bad watching my mother go through the same thing when I was a kid. I had no fuckin' clue. There's a crazy electric current vibrating through every nerve in my body, but at the same time, it's blanketed by a horrible ache, a sadness that presses at the bleak dam of control I still have.

I need to get out of this room. I need to do...something.

"I'll be out here if you need me," I say, then slip out and close the door.

My mother, sister, and Allie are sitting on the couch again. Ma takes one look at me and shoos Maggie and Allie away; they scurry to Ma's room.

"*Ay, nene.* Come here." She pats the seat beside her.

Now I'm the one starting to shake. Lightly at first, but it's a vibration that I can't stop. Inside, I'm spinning. Something has to give. Obeying more with my body than my mind, I follow my mother's orders, collapse on the faded flowers next to her, and let her drape a small arm over my shoulders. She rubs my neck, like she did when I was a little kid, and in the end, it's that small tenderness that does me in. I crumple forward, bury my head in my hands, and fall completely and totally apart.

———

Layla

It takes me a full five minutes to realize I'm in this room alone. This familiar, yet unfamiliar white room, with its futon I've slept on so many time before, the battered old wardrobe in the corner, the small desk that's now piled with papers and textbooks instead of random drawings and bills. The walls are littered with posters of girls. I was right before; Gabe is the one with a thing for Jennifer Lopez.

For a split second, I'm taken back to a medical tent, the one my father helped set up in Brazil. It was the whole excuse for going. The medical school had invited him to come for the summer and teach a clinic. I had worked there with him for a few days, helping some of the med students dispense STD prevention kits—condoms and the like.

At the end of the third day, the clinic was suddenly flooded with bodies. Four or five people had been shot during a drive-by on the other side of the slum. It was several miles from where we were, but we were the closest medical facility, and the people needed help. Together with his students, my father removed bullets from three children and two men.

They did it all behind the curtains. I never saw more than a brief glimpse here and there of prostrated bodies. Instead, I sat on the other side with the children's families, with people who had actually seen the shooting happen. A few were crying but one of the children's mothers sat in a chair, her arms wrapped around her middle, and stared at the dirt floor of the clinic for the entire time it took my dad to take care of her son. Her face was blank, even though I'm sure that inside, she had about a million emotions pouring through her. But there was nothing.

Shock. That's what this is. It's shock.

My stomach roils. I tell myself it isn't that bad. No one was killed. I'm not seriously hurt. A little bruised, probably, and my ankle, though sore, will probably heal within a few weeks. The blood on me is Giancarlo's, not mine. It was just a messed-up day. I'm going to be fine.

But I don't feel fine. I feel like I've just been dragged through a war zone. No one has ever touched me like that before in my life, and in two days, I let the same man do it twice. My skin feels like it's shut off in response to everything that's happened. Even sitting in the cab, Nico's arms locked around me while I shook, I felt nothing. Not even his touch could bring me back to normal.

A cry, low and broken, like a dying animal, careens through the door. I sit up, pulled toward it as it happens again. Slowly, I push myself up and limp to the door. I open it and hop across the hall, where I find Nico crumpled into himself on the couch, his broad shoulders shaking violently while he groans into his mother's shoulder.

Carmen sees me and waves me over. Like a magnet, I limp across the room and fall onto the couch next to Nico. I slide my hands across his quivering back. My fingers seem to work outside of my still-numbed body, but Nico's big frame falls into me, and we topple into the couch cushions while I absorb the waves of emotion pouring from him.

"Oh, God," he whimpers into my shoulder before launching into an unintelligible mess of Spanish and English, muttered into my clothes. "It's my fault," he keens. "Oh, God, it's...shit...I—baby—if..."

"Shhh."

I stroke his back, do everything I can just to hold him, like he did for me in his car and in the bedroom. He inhales deeply like he's trying to take all of me in. His hands tug at the bottom of my shirt like it's a security blanket, and he rocks slowly back and forth. His control is spent. This beautiful man, who carries the world on those broad shoulders for so many people, who runs to the rescue of his mother, his sisters, his brother, and now me. I broke him.

"I can't," he groans. "I can't...I can't..."

"You can't what?" I ask. I'm starting to get scared now. My voice chokes. "N-Nico, you can't what? What is it?"

With what looks like a massive amount effort, he manages to sit up. And it's then, when we are finally face-to-face, that I see what this moment has cost. His eyes are red and puffy, glossed over while the skin around them is dark with fatigue. There are frown lines crossing his brow, and his face looks haggard with the exception of the thick wet lines crisscrossing his cheeks, running down his nose.

Nico is crying. Not tiny, small tears. Great, heaving sobs that ripple through his entire body. His face is tracked with tears, a few hanging off the razor-edge of his jaw. He swallows, and the muscles in his throat quiver.

"It was my fault," he whispers, but makes no move to wipe his tears away. "If I...if I had told you about my plans. You wanted to be together. But I always said no...and now...God, Layla. Look at you!"

Unable to finish the sentence, he falls forward, his big shoulders shaking us both violently.

"I'm sorry," he keens. "I'm so fuckin' sorry."

"What?" I ask suddenly, like I'm waking up out of a nasty, terrible dream. "You're sorry? Oh, Nico..."

Because it's then, as his voice cracks over the last "sorry," that the numbness that's trapped me since I first saw him bust into that bedroom shatters. We grasp at each other, hands tearing at the edges of shirts and jeans, hair and skin. It's not violent— never violent—just a desire to be close. A desire that comes from the deep because I can't be okay when he's not. His pain is my pain. And apparently, mine is his.

"It's not your fault," I murmur into his neck.

I inhale his scent—his earthy, un-nameable scent of soap, sweat, and man. A scent I'll crave for the rest of my life. And then, somehow, I manage to sit him up. I frame his face with my palms, then press my forehead to his in that small, sweet gesture he always used to bring us closer together. He did it when his emotion are too much for him. When words aren't quite enough.

"It's not your fault," I whisper, shaking again myself. Fine, then. We'll shake together.

Nico blinks, his eyes still wet with tears. I can barely see them because of the moisture clouding my own sight. But his love is unmistakable. And I wonder, for what definitely won't be the last time, how I ever could have mistaken something so ugly for the way this man is looking at me right now.

"You came for me." I trace his cheek in awe. "You came."

Nico closes his eyes for a moment, as if the memory is too much to bear. Then he nuzzles his nose with mine and presses a gentle kiss on my mouth. I shudder at the feeling, eager and scared at the same time. But his lips, his warm, soft lips, are home to me. I hate that I ever looked elsewhere.

"I love you," he tells me. "I would *always* come for you."

He kisses me again. And again. His lips track his love all over my face—cheeks, jaw, nose, eyes. He kisses my tears away, even though I doubt they'll stop completely anytime soon. He drops kisses until both of us are out of breath, until finally my hands slide around his neck and I start meeting them with my own.

But then Nico pulls away.

"Don't," I mewl, trying to tug him back. "Don't stop. Please."

He makes me forget. A few more kisses, and maybe I can leave this horrible day behind. A few more, and maybe this entire year will eventually melt away. He's here. I'm here. No one is going anywhere. Finally, *finally* things can maybe go back to the way they were always supposed to be...

But Nico, holding me still by the shoulders, presses me gently back so he can look me in the eye.

"Baby," he says softly. "You've got his blood all over you. And so do I."

I look down. Oh, God, he's right. I'm covered with the rusty red stains on my shirt, shorts. It's smeared over my arms, and probably on my face. I shudder. I'm a mess. I've *been* a mess. And by following what's become my modus operandi, I was fully prepared to pretend it didn't exist.

Nico, on the other hand, has a hand that's got two split knuckles and looks like it might even need stitches.

I don't even need Quinn's voice to tell me that. This time I can see it for myself.

"Shower?" Nico asks hopefully.

I gulp. I'm no longer shaking, and neither is he, but both of us feel...fragile. Like if we stop touching, we might actually break.

The numbness returns a little. Maybe I still need it. I'm just too breakable without it.

"Shower," I agree with more strength than I'm feeling. I stand up. "I'll be right back."

———

Nico

Fifteen minutes later, my mom and Maggie have reemerged from Ma's room and are sitting with me on the couch while Allie watches *Sesame Street*. Layla, having showered before me, emerges from Gabe's room looking bashful. She's wrapped in my brother's t-shirt and a pair of his sweatpants. The look of another man's clothes causes jealousy to rip through me again, even if my heart has calmed down some. Still, she looks better than before. Not so small, not so scared. But still uncertain. And still beat-up.

There's a ring of fingertip bruises flowering all around her neck—from the way he choked her last night. The blood is gone, but a few scratches remain on her face, along with a big red welt under her right eye.

She tugs on her wet hair nervously and looks between me and my mom. I stand up immediately and move to her.

"Hey," I say as I take her hand, enjoying the feel of her fingers entwined with mine. "Feeling better?"

She nods. "Um, yeah. I am. Thanks."

Behind me, Maggie clicks her tongue, then shoves her way between us. "Excuse me," she says irritably as she bustles down to the bathroom. Layla and I both watch, confused, as she disappears, then quickly returns carrying a small jar of something.

"Come here," she says, but doesn't wait for Layla to respond before she takes her arm and pulls her, limping, to sit on the couch between her and Ma.

"Mmmm, he got you good, huh?" Maggie says as she looks Layla over. She gestures to Ma. "*Mira, Mami.*"

Keeping perfectly still, Layla watches me, her eyes wide while my mother and sister look closely at the bruises on her neck and face. I shrug. I have no idea what my sister is doing, but I know Maggie. She's a little hard, but she doesn't give anyone the time of day unless she cares.

Without waiting, Maggie unscrews the lid and uses some kind of sponge to swipe a bunch of skin-colored cream out of the jar and starts dabbing it on Layla's surprised face.

"Jim—" She stops, glancing at Allie, but my niece is zoned out on the television. Then, back to Layla: "Her dad nailed me there a couple times. I had a black eye once that lasted a week, and this stuff covered it up perfect for work."

"Oh my God," Layla says. "I'm so...sorry."

"Keep still." Maggie holds Layla's chin as she works. "And don't be sorry. I finally got rid of his abusive ass last year. It's hard to know better, sometimes, when you grow up with it."

Layla glances at me again, but doesn't say anything so she can keep her face still. But her eyes, so big and expressive, ask the question just the same—*is it true?* I give a quick nod, and immediately, her eyes gloss over. She blinks quickly and turns her gaze away. I'm glad. We don't need more waterworks. I feel like a sponge, drained.

"But Allie—that's my daughter —she had seen him do it," Maggie continues. "And I just thought, I can't let my daughter see me like that, you know? She deserves better."

"*Nena, te faltó un lugar,*" my mother puts in, pointing at a spot on Layla's neck that Maggie missed.

"I was getting there," she responds irritably, setting off a cascade of bickering between them.

Layla bites back a smile, and I cover my own. In a way, watching my mother and sister argue is comfortably normal. It makes the shit that just went down seem...a little farther away. But only a little.

"It's a little too dark for your skin," Maggie says as she applies the thick cream to Layla's neck. "But at least you'll be able to take the train without people looking at you funny."

Ma nods in agreement and hums. I swallow back another wave of anger as I remember her applying the same kind of cream to her face not so long ago. Sitting at the mirror she kept in her bedroom and drawing it over her cuts and bruises with a finger like she was a fancy lady preparing for a ball. Except in my mother's case, the ball was the rich lady's apartment, and she was just putting on makeup so the people whose toilets she cleaned wouldn't think she was unstable and fire her.

"Hey," I say, interrupting the love fest. "You gonna be okay here for a few?"

Layla looks up, her big blue eyes full of fear and concern. "You're leaving?"

My fist clenches at my side, but when she looks at the small movement, I have to force myself to make it relax. "I won't be long. I just need to take care of a few things. Ma?"

My mother looks up, her face full of understanding. "Go," she orders me, in English so Layla will know. But as I turn around, she beckons me back. "*Papito.*"

I turn around. "Yeah?"

My mother presses her lips together. She knows, better than anyone, what's going through my mind.

"Be careful," she says, this time in Spanish, more so Layla won't understand than anything else.

I nod. "Okay."

CHAPTER THIRTY-THREE

Nico

I JOG TEN BLOCKS, UP AND DOWN RIVERSIDE DRIVE, ABOUT THREE TIMES BEFORE I FEEL LIKE I'm calm enough to return to the building on 144th. It looks different now, even though I've been coming here for years, since Flaco first moved in. I glare at the brick exterior—tall and dark, just like him. Just like that motherfucker who put his hands on my girl.

Every time I think I'm okay, that I can go there and figure out how the fuck to deal with Evita without tearing him in two, visions of his hand meeting her face appear again, followed by my sister's fingers covering her bruises. And I have to sprint another three blocks to get my brain to calm down.

Your fault. Your fault.

The words chant with every footstep. I don't care what she says. This whole fuckin' mess *is* my fault. I always knew I'd be bad for Layla, but I never thought it would be my absence that would make way for the poison. I never thought I'd ruin her life if I was gone. Well, here we are. I'm not going to make that mistake again, but first I have to set things right. Time to suck the poison out.

By the time I finally stop in front of Flaco's building, my shirt is sticking to me with sweat. I pull the bill of my hat around to cover my face, check for people who might notice me off the street, then call up to Flaco.

"You here?" he answers on the first ring.

"Yeah," I say. "Let me in."

The buzzer on the door sounds immediately, and with another suspicious glance around, I bound inside and up the stairs. I don't need people placing me here in case of...well, I don't know what. I'm honestly not sure what I'm going to do when I get up there.

Flaco's standing in the doorway of Tango Fuckface's apartment, looking around with the same suspicion.

"Did anyone see you?" he asks as I enter.

"No." I shake my head and turn the bill of my hat backward. I'm going to need to see straight for this.

We're acting like criminals, even though nothing's happened yet. But we both know why. We both know there's a chance that when I walk back into that room, I'm going to lose my shit, and this time Layla won't be there to call me back. Flaco and I have been friends for a long time. He knows what I'm capable of.

"Does he have a roommate?" I ask as we walk down the hall.

Flaco shakes his head. "Ain't nobody here but the *cara de culo*."

I nod in approval. "The cops. Are they on their way?"

Flaco shakes his head. "Not yet. I thought you might wanna see this first."

We enter the room, where Giancarlo is still slumped on the floor by the far window, his hands now tied behind him. I take in the remnants of the scene—the drops of blood that smatter the tousled sheets and the dirty gray carpet, the knocked-over lamp by the bed, a few books and other belongings of Layla's that were tossed around. When I turn back to Giancarlo, he's watching me with one eye open; the other one, the one I hit, is swelled shut.

I turn to Flaco. "You tied him to a radiator? That's a little much, don't you think?"

Flaco shrugs, then gives me a horsey grin. "It's not on. It could be, but it's not. I think that shows pretty good restraint, don't you?"

I just snort.

"That's not what I wanted to show you, though. C'mere."

Flaco leads me to the closet, where a bunch of Layla's clothes hang. That's one more thing I need to do: get her stuff together, because she's sure as shit not coming back here. My shoulders tense as Flaco pushes the clothes to the side. I get a noseful of her flowery scent, mixed with the stale odor of dried blood and sweat already filling the room. It's a heady combination—not very good for my state of mind.

With his foot, Flaco toes open an unzipped duffel bag on the floor, just enough so I can see what's inside. At the bottom, wrapped in plastic, lies at least a key of cocaine, ready to be cut and distributed.

"Jesus," I murmur, squatting down to examine it. I glance at my friend. "*Coño*, you didn't touch that, did you?"

Flaco scoffs. "What do I look like, *papi*, a fuckin' moron? I wasn't about to leave fingerprints."

I stand back up and turn toward Giancarlo, who's still watching us.

"I knew you were into something," I growl. "I fuckin' *knew* it. I ought to beat your ass all over again for dragging Layla into it."

"Nah, Nico, don't," Flaco chimes in behind me. "He wouldn't live through it. Yo, man, I ain't seen you get like that since we were kids."

I rub my face, trying to push away the memories from my past that keep bubbling up. Right after I got back from Tryon, the detention center upstate, I was angry. I wasn't a bully—exactly—but I didn't shy away from using my fists. My hands clench. My knuckles are sore and will be bruised as fuckin' hell tomorrow. But right now, I wouldn't mind giving fuckface another taste of his own medicine.

"Nico. You don't want to..."

Flaco nods at the bag behind me. I know what he's thinking. It would be easy to leave with it, sell it ourselves. That much blow would pay both our rents for a year in just about any neighborhood in the city. But aside from the fact that it would be risky as fuck—whoever Giancarlo got that shit from is going to want the money it makes, and if the FDNY found out about it, I'd be fuckin' toast—there's something better I can do with it.

I turn to Flaco. "Call the cops. This motherfucker's gonna get what's coming to him."

Flaco raises a skinny brow. "You sure?"

I press my lips together and nod. I hate cops. Like every brown kid in New York City, I grew up fearing the words "Stop and Frisk," especially after I got back from juvie during the mid-nineties. There's a decent enough chance that just by being here, Flaco and I will both find ourselves with our noses pressed to the carpet, our wrists cuffed together.

But I'm willing to take that chance to get this asshole off the streets. To keep my girl safe. To help her sleep at night.

Flaco nods and pulls out his phone. "You got it," he says and walks out of the room as he dials.

I pace for a minute in front of Giancarlo. He watches closely, but says nothing. He's waiting to see what I'll do.

Finally, I stop and crouch down in front of him. "You hear that, *culo*?" I ask him, my voice weirdly even. "The cops are coming for your ass. And I'm gonna tell them everything."

Giancarlo rolls his head to the side with a lot more disdain than any guy tied to a heater has any right to be.

"And what will you say?" he retorts, more sharply than he looks capable of. "Who is the one with half a face right now? Whose blood is on your clothes? On *her* clothes?" He sneers. "Why do you think I cut myself instead of her, eh?"

My face twists as I glance at the nasty cut on his wrist. It's not bleeding anymore, but it needs stitches. It's fucked up. I don't even want to think about why he would do that—threaten to slit his own wrist, bleed all over someone else. This guy is sick, really sick. But that doesn't mean I give a shit about him.

Giancarlo spits, and it lands dangerously close to my shoe. Murder rises through me all over again.

"You tried to rape her," I snarl through my teeth. "We saw it. We *all* saw it. That's five people—me, Layla, Flaco, Gabe, Jamie, and Shama—*all* saying the same thing: that you're nothing but a fucking woman-beating rapist who belongs behind bars."

"She wanted it," Giancarlo replies and gives a nasty smile, baring teeth slightly stained from the bloody lip I gave him earlier.

I recoil. I can't help it. "Fuck that."

"She likes it rough," he continues, sticking his chin out, like he's daring me to punch him again. "Why do you think she kept coming back to me? I gave her everything you cannot."

I lean in. "You need to stop talking now."

"And *you* left her, no?" he continues. He clicks his tongue. "She thinks I didn't know. I knew. I saw the messages. I saw that you would call. Well, you think she will be the same? I made her *mine*, and you know it. No matter how many times you try, I will always be there in the back of her head. Every time she shows you her body, you will know that I touched it too. Her legs, her lips, her tight little pussy—"

I break off his words with an open-palmed smack across his cheek that sends his face flying to one side, his glasses to the floor.

"Oh *shit!*" crows Flaco as he strides back into the room. "*Puñeta*, you just got bitch-slapped, for real!"

I shake out my hand as I cross the room. "This motherfucker doesn't deserve a real punch. And he really doesn't know when to shut the *fuck* up."

When I turn back around, my red handprint glares on Giancarlo's pale white cheek. It makes me smirk. I like it more than I should. The darkness inside me grows, threatening to take over again. It would be so easy just to let him have it. Cut off that tape and make it a real fight, even though I know he wouldn't stand a chance.

His tongue slips out, and he licks his lips, like he's imagining some kind of dessert.

"You know it's true," he calls to me. "Every touch. Every taste. I did things to her. She will *never* forget me, no matter what. And when you try to fuck her too, you won't forget it either."

"I said you need to shut the *fuck* up!"

It takes me a second and a half to swing across the room, lift this motherfucker up as far as his bound wrists will let me, and shove him against the back of the radiator so we're nose to nose. I'm shaking, I'm so mad, like a steam kettle about to blow. He laughs. He's ten seconds from getting me to lose my shit completely and clearly enjoying it.

But in the end, it doesn't work. He doesn't realize that even with the rage the images cause, his words still remind me of the one person who puts it all out. Her face calls me back from the darkness inside me. She's the light to my dark—just like I am for her.

"Nah," I say, releasing his collar. He falls back into the chair with a thump and scowls. "You ain't worth it." I turn to Flaco. "You called?"

Flaco nods. "Yeah, *mano*. Cops are on their way." He turns to Giancarlo with a face full of glee. "You goin' to jail, *puto*. What do you think they're gonna do with your Paco Rabanne-wearing ass, huh? What goes around comes around; that's all I gotta say."

Giancarlo turns about five shades of white. He looks at me, suddenly full of desperation. "What do you want?" he asks. "Money. I have money. How much do you want?"

His eyes, so dark and deep-set, have lost all cockiness, now just scared and knowing at the same time. He looks over my clothes—the scuffed Converse, the jeans that are worn and faded at the knees, the wrinkled t-shirt I grabbed off Gabe's floor. Even though it's stained with his own blood, Giancarlo's own shirt is ironed and buttoned, like a lawyer or a banker, not a twenty-something college student.

I roll my eyes. "I don't want your money, you pathetic piece of shit. Nothing's worth not seeing you locked up."

Giancarlo mutters a long string of something under his breath to himself.

"What's that?" I ask.

He looks up, defiant, haughty even as his end is coming. "It's Spanish," he says. "A language people like *you* don't understand."

I lean down so my face is by his ear. Shit, Flaco really wasn't kidding about the Paco Rabanne. Whatever cheap cologne this dude wears, he's fuckin' doused in it.

"*Maldita sea la madre que te parió*," I growl. It's a nice, nasty curse, one I probably wouldn't be able to translate completely, but which roughly damns the bitch who gave birth to him. Then I back up so he can see my face. "How's that for fuckin' Spanish, *cabrón*?"

Behind me, Flaco bursts into laughter and long strings of profanity in both Spanish and English, most of which makes fun of the miserable asshole on the floor. A loud knock at the apartment door interrupts his teasing.

I blink at Giancarlo. "Guess who?"

Flaco answers the door and ushers a pair of police officers into the bedroom. They take a look at the mess—the ripped sheets, the bloodstains, the guy tied to the radiator, and open bag of coke in the closet—and sigh. One pulls out his walkie-talkie and requests backup while the other turns to us.

"Well, fellas," he says. "Who wants to go first?"

———

THE WHOLE THING takes more than two hours. They immediately put cuffs on Giancarlo, but only after they determine that the cut on his wrist is superficial. But between them and the two other officers that arrive later, they take our statements, separately, then together before they switched to cross-examine the details. Flaco went to his apartment to be interviewed the last time, which is where he still is.

No doubt Giancarlo has some very different things to say about what happened, so I come clean about my part. I tell them about every punch I threw and why we kept him tied up. I tell them everything and hope for the best.

"Her name is Barros, you said?" asks the cop, the one named Barrett. "How do I spell that?"

"B-a-r-r-o-s," I tell him. "She's at my apartment. I'll bring her to the station, if that's okay."

The officer frowns. "I can just come to you."

I shrug. "Either way. She needed to clean herself up. She was pretty upset." I'm playing it nonchalant, but having a cop at the apartment is the last thing I want, especially with my mom there.

Officer Barrett shrugs. "No, that's okay. If you can bring her, there's no reason for us to come."

He checks that he has the names of Jamie and Shama so he can request their information from Layla tomorrow, then stands up. A few other cops exit the bedroom, carrying the duffel bag in a plastic evidence bag along with a few other things I didn't see before. A gun. A stash of pills. Another three officers confiscate several more bags from a closet. Jesus. The thought of how much time Layla was spending here makes it hard to breathe all over again. She had no fuckin' clue.

"Thank you," says Officer Barrett. "I think we're done, finally. You're good to go."

As I stand up, two more cops escort Giancarlo out of the bedroom, his hands still cuffed behind his back. I give him a little wave as they pass. He doesn't fight them, clearly out of energy after being tied up for half the day and interrogated for the rest. But before he leaves, he struggles against his escort, managing to turn around to deliver one last line in Spanish that turns my blood cold.

"*Tu madre*," he says. "*Yo sé*."

Your mother. I know.

CHAPTER THIRTY-FOUR

Layla

I WATCH A LITTLE MOURNFULLY WHEN NICO DISAPPEARS DOWN THE DARK, NARROW HALL. I don't want him to go, but I can also see the pain on his face while his sister applies her makeup to my bruises. I should tell her it's unnecessary, but what do I know?

"Where-where did my friends go?" I ask, finally aware that Jamie and Shama aren't here.

"Friends," Maggie repeats under her breath with a knowing look at her mother. Carmen purses her lips and raises her eyebrows, but says nothing. "They went home."

The fact stings. But I remember the looks on their faces as they glanced around Giancarlo's apartment—their shock that I was spending so much time in a neighborhood that didn't have perfectly pruned trees or buildings that weren't power-washed.

"It's hard for him," Maggie says as she continues applying her makeup in big, broad strokes. I'm going to look a little like a mannequin when she's done, painted a completely different color, but I don't dare stop her. "He's seen this kind of thing a lot. Too much."

She glances at Carmen, who is watching us from her seat on the chair. I wish my Spanish were better. Carmen is so quiet, so I want to know what she's saying when she does speak up.

Guilt sweeps through me all over again. I don't know everything his family's been through, but I know enough. I know that Carmen has had her share of nasty men around in her life

"When we were kids," Maggie says, "well, when *we* were all kids, not Nico, there was this time, right after he came back from juvie, when Gabe's dad was living with us."

Carmen breaks in suddenly with a quick stream of Spanish, but Maggie just frowns and waves it away.

"*Mami*, hush," she chides her. "She should know. No one is going to think less of you, okay? Just look at her."

Carmen mutters something else, but in the end, she nods her head and flips her hands at us, as if to say "Go with God." Maggie rolls her eyes.

"Anyway," she says. "It was Gabe's father. He's wasn't a good person. For a long time, he didn't treat my mom so good."

I stay quiet while she moves down my neck with the sponge.

"When Nico got out of juvie, David was living with us, and he used to, um, well, he was hard on our mother."

From her chair, Carmen snorts, then emits another long string of Spanish.

I look curiously at Maggie. "What did she say? I couldn't catch most of that."

Again, Maggie rolls her eyes. Their relationship is the kind you'd imagine a close mother and daughter to have. Bickering, but also fond. My mother and I have never had that. She cares, sure. But we don't joke. We don't tease. We don't really know each other.

"She says if I'm going to spill our family secrets, I might as well do it right. *De verdad, Mami?*"

Carmen pushes her full lips out in agreement and gives her daughter a sardonic look. Maggie just laughs.

Carmen turns to me. "He hit me," she says in stunted English. "Gabriel father. Here and here and here." She points to different spots on her face: her eyebrow, her cheek, her chin. "My kids, they see. And my daughter, she...the same." She opens her mouth, like she's going to say something else, but instead sits back in her chair and folds her hands in her lap.

Maggie watches her mother, but her attitude has vanished. She's clearly used to the matter-of-fact way Carmen has when she speaks, but the candor takes me off guard.

"It was Nico who stopped it," Maggie says as she continues applying makeup. "Every time."

I frown. "What do you mean?"

"When he was in juvie, he started boxing. Did you know that?"

I shake my head. I know he likes to box for exercise, but he never said how he started. Nico never liked talking about his past, and it's not like we had the chance much this year to get into it. I only know a little about why he ended up in detention to begin with.

Maggie pauses, probably wondering whether to continue. But she keeps talking. "Well, after he got back, he saw David beating on *Mami*, so he gave him a taste of his own medicine."

At that, Carmen breaks in with another long string of Spanish, then nods at me. "Tell her," she says impatiently.

Maggie sighs. "She wants you to know that he also told Ma he would take away me and Selena and Gabe if she ever saw David again. We were still minors, you know? And Nico was eighteen, Alba—that's K.C.'s mother, you remember?—she transferred guardianship to him."

I swallow. This is news. I always knew that Nico took responsibility for his siblings' welfare, but I didn't know he had legally been their guardian since he was eighteen. I'm twenty, and I can't imagine having that kind of responsibility. And I definitely can't imagine threatening my own mother with it.

"That sounds incredibly hard," I say. "For everyone."

"It was," Maggie says. "'Specially since five years later, he did the same with me. Told Jimmy if he didn't get his ass into rehab, he wasn't going to be able to see me or Allie anymore. And that if I let him back before then, he would call social services and sue for custody." She emits a heavy sigh. "At first, I was mad. But now I'm glad he did that. It gave me some space, you know? To do what was right for me and my daughter."

It makes sense now, as Nico's words from March filter back to me, asking me all over again to leave Giancarlo. He made me angry. So angry. At that point, he was just one more person who was leaving me, one more person turning their backs, one more person who also thought they knew better. It never occurred to me that he already knew what it was like to watch someone you care about be hurt. And that because of that knowledge, he already knew what was going to happen to me.

"Do you...do you still see Jimmy?" I wonder.

Maggie nods. "Yes. But mostly for Allie. I gave him one more chance last year, but it didn't work out. We aren't good together because I make him too mad, and he drives me crazy." She grins at Carmen. "I have a temper. Just like *Mami*."

Carmen snorts again, but I don't miss the warmth in her eyes as she looks at her daughter. Still, there is sadness there too.

"We learn," she puts in. "From family. Your father, he do this too?" She taps her cheek.

I almost want to smile in spite of the question. She really does know a lot more English than her kids give her credit for. A year ago, I would have said no. I would have said my father wasn't the slightest bit abusive and laughed at the idea.

But it would have been an uncomfortable laugh. High-pitched and over-exuberant, it would have been a laugh that covered up the truths of how he treated my mother and me. The insults. The condescension. The control. I don't know if that makes him abusive. I don't know what it means. But I do know that he caused us both a lot of pain, and that my mother always took it.

"He didn't hit us," is all I say in the end.

Carmen appears to weigh the words for a moment or two, but eventually she nods with understanding and sits back.

Maggie finishes applying the makeup, then sits back to survey her work. "I think that will be okay." She screws the lid on the jar and hands it to me. "That's the brand you want. I got it at Duane Reade. It's the only one that will cover everything up."

I stare at the letters scribbled across the lid, imprinting them into my mind, then hand it back to her. "Thank you. I guess...I guess I should go home now."

Maggie looks at me like I'm nuts. "Are you crazy? Do you have any idea what my brother will do if he comes back and you're gone?"

"What-what would he do?"

She clicks her tongue. "I don't know. You're the only person he's ever loved. That's why you're not going anywhere."

She glances at Allie, who's conked out on the floor, then turns the channel to some kind of show in Spanish—a telenovela, like the ones my grandmother in Brazil likes to watch. The women all wear flashy colors and too much makeup. And the men are all tall, dark-haired, and impossibly handsome. But none as handsome as Nico.

I settle back into the couch. *You're the only person he's ever loved.* Even if I don't deserve it, God, I hope it's true.

———

THE DOOR OPENS AGAIN several hours later, and heavy footsteps tread down the hall. I'm half-asleep on the couch, and Allie is playing on the floor while Carmen is in the kitchen, making something to eat. Maggie stayed with me all afternoon, as if she and Carmen both understand how bad it would be for me to be alone. Our conversations have been minimal, content as we've all been to let Allie or the television fill the space. We've all just sat together. It's been...peaceful.

Nico appears in the doorway, looking both tired and beautiful. There are shadows under his eyes, and his shirt and jeans are wrinkled. He finds me and gives me a weary smile.

"Hey, beautiful," he says softly. Then he frowns. "What's wrong with your face? You look...yellow. Like you're sick or something."

"*Coño*, it's my makeup, okay? Don't be a dick!"

Maggie throws a pillow at him, which Nico deflects onto the floor with a chuckle. It causes Allie to glance up from her dolls and grin. Nico winks at her, then turns back to me.

"How you doin', baby?" he asks.

I shrug. It's only five o'clock, but I feel like I could sleep for a week.

We just watch each other while Allie sings a song to her toys. Maggie glances back and forth between us, frowning.

"*Papi*," she snaps. "Stop lurking in the doorway. You gonna take care of your woman, or what?"

Nico blinks. "What?"

Maggie nods at me. "Layla. I know that look. She needs you right now. She's your woman, isn't she?"

Nico gulps while he crosses and uncrosses his arms. His hesitation stabs, hurts more than I thought it would. After talking to Maggie and Carmen, I knew this was a possibility. That whatever he did, wherever he went, something about it might finally cross the line. That after this is all over, he might want nothing to do with me.

"No," he says, loud and clear.

I try to ignore the way my chest feels like it's going to cave in. It hurts. Oh, God, it hurts so much worse than Giancarlo's hands or my ankle.

But Nico doesn't look away. His gaze remains steady, bound to mine. "She's her own woman. I'm just lucky enough to love her."

Then he crosses the room and collapses next to me on the couch. Pulls me into his arms and cradles me to his broad, warm chest.

"I got you, baby," he says, repeating those sweet, simple words that flood my body, my heart, my soul with warmth. With homecoming. "I got you."

Slowly, my arms find their way around his waist. Slowly, I'm holding him too.

"I got you, too," I murmur into his chest. The lines of his compass tattoo, black and broad, show through the thin white cotton. I kiss him there, and a low rumble, so low only I can hear it, stirs in his chest.

"I know, baby," he says. "I know."

We sit like that for several minutes, until Carmen emerges from the kitchen holding a spatula.

"*Ya la comida está*," she tells us.

As we all gather around the small table to eat the chicken and rice that Carmen has made, Nico sighs as he looks over the food. It's a good look. This room used to be where the TV was, and the other room was storage area for his and his siblings' things. But since Carmen moved here, this apartment, which always felt more like a bachelor pad, turned into a home.

"*Mami*," he says sadly as he dishes up some food. "*Tienes que mudarte para tras a* Hell's Kitchen."

I glance between him and his mother, not understanding what he said. But Carmen freezes as she dishes up Allie's food.

"What? Why does she have to move back?" Maggie's voice is sharp.

Carmen sighs wearily and finishes putting rice on Allie's plate. "*Por qué?*"

Nico rubs his face and pulls off his baseball cap so he can run a hand through his hair. Carmen snags the hat and tosses it onto an extra chair behind her.

"He knows. Layla's—the guy—he knows about Ma. Flaco and I found a whole bunch of coke stashed in his closet, so we called the cops. But when they were taking him out..." Nico sighs and takes his mother's hand. "He said he knew, Ma. I think he's gonna tell them about you."

The desire to eat vanishes as my stomach drops to the floor. This is my fault. Yet another way I'm causing this family damage.

"Oh my God," I say. "Oh my God, oh my God."

Carmen is strangely still.

"I'm so, *so* sorry, Carmen. I told him because I—" I cut myself off, suddenly remembering the catalyst of everything that's happened. The passage. The book. "Where did you put my stuff?" I ask Nico as I stand up.

His brows screw up in confusion. "By the door. Why?"

"Hold on," I say. "I have to show you something."

I hop down the hall and root around the trash bags until I locate the textbook I had been reading when I came across the paragraph on Cuban immigration. Quickly, I flip to the page, carry it back to the table, and set it down in front of Carmen.

Nico scoots his chair over to look on with his mother. "What is this?"

"Look at the second paragraph," I tell them.

Carmen scans the page, but it's clear she can't read English much better than she can speak it. She looks to Nico, whose dark eyes are flying over the text, his lips moving silently with it.

"*Mira, mira,*" he says, pointing at the paragraph. "'Any close relative of a Cuban national can visit the country.' Ma, do you understand this?" He looks at me, suddenly alert. "Does this mean what I think it means?"

I swallow and nod. "I think so. I think it means you can go to Cuba to get her birth certificate. I was on my way here to tell you that when Giancarlo, he—"

My voice fades away, and Nico, with obvious understanding, reaches around the table and takes my hand.

"This is why he got angry?" he asks. "Because you were trying to help my family?"

Wordlessly, I nod. "He found me here, about to press the button. This was before—before I called you."

Nico says nothing for what feels like several minutes. He blinks, his long, black lashes sweeping across his cheeks in slow-motion.

"He would have done it anyway," Maggie says, more to Nico than to me. She obviously understands his tendency to bear the blame for more than he has to. "Whether it was this or something else."

"I know," I say, more to Nico than to her. "I know."

He blinks again, his eyes deep with emotions I can't quite read. Then he leans over and pulls my hand to his lips. "Thank you," he says quietly. He kisses my knuckles again. "Thank you."

I don't respond, just squeeze his hand.

He turns back to the book, flipping the pages back and forth, though he doesn't let me go. "There's nothing else in here about how this works. Baby, do you know anything more?"

I shake my head. "No, I'm sorry. But—I could find out. I could ask my professor or someone who would know. I only saw this myself, and I tried to come and tell you as soon as I could."

"Nah, baby, that's okay. We'll find an attorney." Nico looks up suddenly. "Why didn't we know about this?"

The entire family looks guiltily at each other around the table.

I shrug. "I don't remember this being in the papers. It wouldn't have been front-page news."

Nico's shoulders relax. He turns to his mother, who is still staring at the book, frozen. "*Te comprendes*?" he asks her softly.

Slowly, Carmen nods. She doesn't shake or cry—something tells me that Carmen Soltero rarely does either of those things. But her stillness has the whole table frozen right with her, even little Allie.

"Well, then," Nico says, looking back to me with shining eyes. "Looks like I need to get a passport, huh?"

CHAPTER THIRTY-FIVE

Nico

It's dark that night when I take Layla back to her apartment. After finishing dinner with my family, I brought her to the police station and literally held her hand the entire time while she told the cops what happened, then waited for another hour while she went into a room with a few of them and did it again. It was...hard. Harder than I expected to sit there and stay silent. She cried at least twice, and I practically ground my teeth into dust listening to her recount, again and again, the way Giancarlo cut his wrist and tackled her on the bed.

She wiped off that god-awful yellow makeup that Maggie painted on her face and let the officers photograph her bruises. I don't know what's worse—the yellowy brown, caked-on crap or the blues and purples that make her face and neck look like a fuckin' Jackson Pollock painting. But in the end, I think I'd take the latter. I want Layla, real Layla, however she looks.

I waited in the front of the station while she signed her statement. If I didn't know I loved her before, I do now. I wouldn't have sat in front of a suspicious row of cops for anyone else.

So, it's close to eleven by the time she unlocks her door, me right behind her with the three garbage bags full of stuff I got out of Giancarlo's place. I'm guessing she hasn't been home in a while. she wasn't exactly moved in at his place, since her things were just sort of stacked in dickhead's room, but there was a lot there. For whatever reason, she felt safer there than she did here. That's how far this dude had his claws into her.

It just makes me feel that much more guilty.

When we walk in, Jamie and Shama are gone, out for the night to let off some steam after giving their own statements earlier tonight too. Quinn sits in the common area, surrounded by a pile of books. She pulls at a couple of the doll-like curls hanging around her face while she reads. Her hair reminds me of the stuff they had on my sisters' dolls when we were kids.

She turn around when the door shuts, and her expression turns ugly. "Oh. It's *you*."

In front of me, Layla stiffens, but keeps hobbling in.

I frown. "How you doin', Quinn? How was the rest of *your* day?"

I'm not exactly sad when she shrinks a little at my sharp tone. This bitch is supposed to be Layla's friend, and she skipped all of it. I might feel guilty about everything that's happened, but this chick has no fuckin' excuse. She thinks she has the right to give *me* attitude? Yeah. Fuck that.

Quinn swallows when she catches my glare, then gets a better look at Layla when she limps into the kitchen for some water. "Jesus. Are you—are you okay?"

Layla turns around, and the fluorescent kitchen light reveals the real extent of her injuries. Quinn cringes. My grip on the bags is so tight I might pop a blood vessel.

"I'm fine," Layla replies.

"You don't look fine." Quinn walks into the kitchen to examine Layla more closely. "You look like you just came back from a war zone. Have you seen a doctor? Called your parents?"

"I said I'm *fine*," Layla repeats testily. She finishes her water and sets the glass in the sink with maybe a little more force than she needs. "No thanks to you."

Quinn's mouth falls open with disbelief. "Babe, you aren't seriously mad because I didn't join the cavalry to save you, are you? It doesn't sound like they needed my help."

"I'm not mad," Layla replies coldly. "And don't call me babe."

They stare at each other, and it's like the air between them is hard enough to smash. I've never seen Layla talk to her best friend like this before. Well, supposed best friend. I've heard enough about their banter to know that Layla and Quinn usually give each other as good as they get. Quinn's goading her a little, probably trying to reestablish the pecking order. I heard enough last spring to know the score. Quinn usually talks to Layla like a big sister. Condescending, but caring.

But older siblings don't leave their little sisters in the lurch when they need help. I should know.

Layla's not having it either. Without responding to Quinn, she limps back to me, takes my hand, and pulls me into her room, where she shuts the door. I drop the garbage bags on the floor, and while I sit down on her bed, Layla immediately starts pulling things out of them and putting them away, despite her limp, moving in that fast, forceful manner I recognize clearly. They're the same jerky motions my sisters use when they're pissed off about something but trying to hold back. Human equivalents of a kettle put on to boil.

Slam, two pairs of boots hit the floor of the closet. Smack, smack, belt buckles flying into the door of the closet. A bag of makeup hits the desk hard enough to send stray papers flying.

"Hey, NYU?" I ask as I pull my hat off and set it on the desk. Her shoulders tense. "You, um, you sure you don't want to rest or something? That stuff can wait."

My girl is about to drop. Her movements are sure, but her body droops. She pauses for a second at her closet. The only thing I want to do is curl up with her on this tiny-ass mattress of hers and fall asleep. I'll hold her until she starts to forget. Forever, if I have to.

But forever is going to have to wait.

"What the fuck?"

Quinn marches into the room without knocking with a determined look on her porcelain face. I sit up straight. Fuck, no. This bitch is not about to start something with Layla. Not now.

Layla turns around wearily from the closet. "Quinn, what is it?"

"You just gave me the silent treatment, that's what!"

"Quinn," I warn from the bed.

"Hush, FedEx!" she snaps at me before turning back to Layla.

Her hands find her hips, making her look a little like Peter Pan. A curly-haired, imperious, crazy bitchy Peter Pan. I sort of want to toss her out the window. Be all like, you can fly, bitch.

"You're unbelievable," she snaps. "You waltz back in here looking like Night of the Living Dead, with Special Delivery on your heels, and you expect me not to say anything? Give me the cold shoulder and expect me to take it?"

I bite the inside of my cheek to keep from saying anything. This chick has always looked at me like that, unable to see past the day job. She's the kind of person who likes to box people in. Layla was fine as long as she was willing to play her part: best friend, whatever. But she didn't stay in her box, and Quinn isn't taking it well.

"My ex-boyfriend just sprained my ankle," Layla points out as she limps toward Quinn. "I hardly think that allows me to waltz in anywhere. I'm just tired. I was going to put my stuff away and go to sleep, if that's all right with you."

Quinn rolls her eyes. "This is my room too," she continues. "And you need a reality check. I don't think I've been out of line by asking you not to screw my life up with yours. Speaking of which, what's *he* doing here?"

Quinn nods at me like I'm a fucking lamp or a coat rack. For real, this girl has always bugged me. She has that way about her, that thing rich people do when they treat everyone else like inanimate objects. Like they don't fucking matter.

"Don't talk about him like that," Layla says as she steps toward me. "He just saved my life."

Without thinking, I take her hand and squeeze it so she knows I'm here if she needs me. I'll save her ten times daily. And tossing this chick out would be no hardship.

"Look," Layla tries again. "I'm sorry. I've just...this day has been really hard, okay? I need some space."

"Because it's about you, right?" Quinn's tone turns nastier with every word. "I forgot. It's always about you. So fucking selfish."

Layla wilts into herself, wrapping her arms around her waist. It's a posture that, if you know her at all, is a dead giveaway for when she's feeling like shit. Unsure. Saddened. Worried. I glance between them, seeing clearly for the first time just what my girl has been going through all year. A family that basically checked out of her life, friends who chink away at her self-esteem, and a boyfriend who took advantage of that vulnerability.

You should have been here. The thought rages through my head.

Maybe I should, maybe I shouldn't have. But I'm here now.

"Quinn," I say as I finally stand up. I keep Layla's hand firmly in mine. "Step off. She's had a day. *We've* had a day, all right?"

"Oh, *she* doesn't need this?" Quinn whirls around to me, her Peter Pan face twisted into a wicked witch. "Are you *kidding* me? You've been gone all year, Romeo. You have no clue what kind of ridiculous fucking drama she's put the rest of us through."

"I think I do." I grit out, fighting like hell to keep my patience. "I think I know because *I'm* the one she called. And do you know why she'd call me instead of her supposed best friend? Because she knows *I'm* the one who will actually show up instead of judging her half to death."

"Right," Quinn says. "Showing up to jump into her bed. Half this shit is *your* fucking fault, FedEx! She was fine before you came around, and now you're here, just like you always were, to fuck her and leave her!"

"You know what?"

Layla's small voice behind me somehow breaks through the conversation. She hops in front of me, and instinctively, I wrap an arm around her waist from behind. I don't want to admit it, but some of Quinn's nasty words hit a little too close. Some of this is my fault. And I'll carry that guilt for the rest of my life.

"Stop talking about me like I'm not here," Layla says to both of us. She presses gently on my chest, forcing my arm to unwind and let her free. "You've done enough fighting for me today."

I open my mouth to tell her that I'd fight for her any day, all day. That I'll fight for her for the rest of my life if she'll let me. But her face is defiant, and for some reason, it sparks a little pride. She needs this, to stand up for herself, to say what she has to say.

So I step back, hands up. "Whatever you need, baby."

Layla turns to Quinn. "*You* don't need to worry about me anymore either," she says in a voice that's a lot softer than I think she wants it to be. If it were any other day, she'd be shouting. But right now my girl is tired. Broken. She needs a rest.

That Peter Pan fantasy starts to sound better and better.

"What?" Quinn balks. "Of course I do. We all do, clearly. You need to get your shit together and—"

"*No*," Layla puts in again, her voice quivering. "I mean *you* don't have to worry about me. You made that pretty fucking clear when Jamie and Shama walked into that room without you." She shakes her head and pulls on the end of her ponytail. "I don't blame you for what Giancarlo did or the choices I made with him. I really don't. But, Quinn, you could have helped instead of pushing me away. You could have called my parents. Even just listened sometimes instead of telling me everything that I was doing wrong. In the last nine months, I have never felt more alone in my entire life, and a lot of that has to do with the way my best friend treated me."

Quinn stills. I smirk a little. She was spunky enough in the beginning, with her little threats to me. What'd she say? That she'd feed my balls to the pigeons if I ever hurt her girl? I thought at first that she was that friend, the one who was protective, who wouldn't let her roommates come to any harm. But where the fuck was she when Layla was hanging around a guy like El Tango Shithead? Where was she when her friend was in danger? I've watched and heard enough to know that Quinn's the other type of girl—the catty kind my sisters cycle through from time to time. Layla's better off without her.

Layla continues: "I learned today who my real friends are. Who will really be there for me when things get legitimately tough. Not tough the way we think of it, with tests and final papers and oh, my dad forgot to call me. But really, really fucking hard.

Quinn, I'm sorry, but I just don't have room in my life for people who can't hack it. And I guess...that includes you."

Her hand reaches for me. It's a slight movement, maybe six inches from her hip, but I see it. She needed space before, but now she's ready to take it back. And I thread my fingers through hers and squeeze.

I got you, baby. If there's one thing I want her to know in all of this, it's that. I got her back. Always.

Quinn's mouth falls open, reminding me again of a creepy doll. The old kind with the eyelids that open and close and the porcelain skin that cracks over time. She looks between us, at our joined hands, then shuts her mouth, her eyes glazed and angry.

"You don't want to be friends?" she asks finally. I don't miss the way her voice quavers. "Fucking *fine*. I'm better off without your dead weight anyway." She looks between us. "I'll take the couch tonight. You two losers fucking deserve each other."

She spins out of the room and slams the door behind her, leaving Layla to fairly collapse into me.

"Oh, God," she whimpers into my chest. "That was hard."

I wrap my arms around her slim form, pulling her as close as I can. "It was the right thing to do. She's a bitch."

"She's my best friend."

"Not anymore." I tip Layla's head up. "Best friends don't say that kind of shit to each other. She should have had your back. She didn't. Case closed."

I kiss her, gently, if only because now I finally can again. She's still, unmoving without a sound. Even with her red-rimmed eyes and banged-up face, she's still the most beautiful woman I've ever seen.

Layla sniffs. "You should probably go, huh? It's getting late."

I pause. "Do you want me to go?"

She doesn't have to answer. Her blue eyes, so uncertain, so conflicted, spell it out. I brush some loose hairs out of her face so I can see it clearly, then tip her chin so she has to look at me.

"I'm not going anywhere," I tell her solemnly. "I belong with you." I nod at her bed. "Even if we do have to sleep in this tiny-ass bed of yours."

She giggles. It's small and sweet, and I wouldn't have heard it if I hadn't been standing inches from her face. But it was there, and the sound of it lights something inside me I haven't felt in a really long time, and something the day's events had doused like gallons of water on a campfire. But there it flickers in her smile: hope.

"Can we—can we turn out the light?" she asks quietly.

"Sure, why?"

"Because," she says. "I'm tired of you looking at me like that."

"Like what?"

"Like I'm about to break."

CHAPTER THIRTY-SIX

Layla

We listen to the sounds of Quinn bustling around the apartment, gathering her stuff before slamming the front door behind her when she leaves. I know her. She'll be back later, after she goes to the gym, maybe studies at the library. She'll have a bunch of backhanded apologies, and she'll expect me to forgive her, just like always.

Except this time, I don't think that's going to happen. I'm not sure what the immediate future looks like right now—I honestly don't have the strength to think about it —but I doubt it's going to include Quinn.

After the door shuts, Nico flips off the light, casting the room in sudden darkness lit only by the street lamps shining through the window blinds.

I'm not sure what I'm doing. What I'm asking him to do. Two days ago I was staying with another man. Someone who was supposed to love me, who had convinced me that he was the only person in the world I could trust, right before taking that trust and shattering it—and me—completely.

I'm still not sure what to do with that. What to do with my mangled body. I knew, of course, that these things happen. That women get caught up in all sorts of unhealthy relationships. That studies and facts and things like that say that it's the people closest to you who often do the most damage. But it's something totally different when it actually happens to you.

The one thing I do know is that I want Nico here if he's willing. From the second he burst into that room, at the front of the small cavalry of people still willing to help, it was like the earth shifted a little on its axis. Like it had been misaligned somehow and was put right. My body reached for him before my mind and my heart. It reaches for him now, despite all its pain.

Slowly, ignoring the way the muscles in my neck and arms ache with fatigue, I remove my jeans and crawl into bed in my shirt and underwear. A statue cast in silvery-blue light, Nico watches. I curl against the wall, hugging a pillow to my chest while I look up at him.

His face is blank, though the muscles of his neck are still corded in frustration. He was holding back with Quinn. This man has the urge to save others written into his DNA. How anyone could look at him and not see that is beyond me.

I close my eyes. How lucky am I that he is what he is? That he came when he did? The numbness of the afternoon is finally wearing off, and what replaces it are the cold chills of what might have happened if he hadn't arrived when he did. The only cure I can think of is his warmth—his strong, solid warmth that will banish this feeling.

"Please," I say, glad the darkness hides the way my chin trembles. I extend a hand. "Come here, will you?"

Nico swallows, blinks like he's pulled out of some kind of trance, even though he's been staring at me the entire time. "Um...I don't have pajamas or anything."

The coldness spreads. "Nico?"

He crouches down so we're eye to eye. "Yeah, baby?"

I bite my lip. He already said he was staying, but now I'm wondering if he was just being nice. "I just need you here, okay? Please?"

Nico blinks, then shakes his head. "Fuck. Yeah. No, of course, baby."

I watch as he strips off his clothes hurriedly. He does so without pretense. It's not a strip tease; he's just taking off his pants and t-shirt so they don't get wrinkled. But even in my wretched state, I can still appreciate the raw beauty of him. The rigid blocks of muscle that have somehow become even more chiseled since last year. The elegant lines of skin and sinew. The way his tattoos, over his right shoulder and the compass over his heart, ripple with his movements.

He folds his clothes and puts them on my desk chair, then faces me, in just his underwear. He looks down at himself then back at me. "Shit...should I put my shirt back on?"

I should probably say yes. I'm in my shirt too, and I'm not exactly sure what would happen if I had all of *that* pressed against me that way. But the chill persists, shaking me through. Having his warm body pressed against mine sounds like the best thing in the world. All afternoon, we haven't stopped touching. But it was always small, almost platonic. Handholding. This won't really be that different.

So I pull back the covers and make room for him to slide into bed with me. He crawls over so his back is against the wall, then pulls me against him, my back to his front, my body fitting to his like the petals of a flower. I hum. We've been lost, floundering around apart, finding only after the damage has been done that it's together that we're found. Right here, with him. This is where I belong.

His chest rumbles with contentment as his arms coil around me.

"You okay?" he asks.

I'm not. Obviously I'm not, and I probably won't be for a long time.

"I'm okay," I whisper into the darkness. Because what else should I say?

I squirm around suddenly, twisting until I'm facing him instead of the open, empty void of the room. Him. That's all I want. Him.

His hands thread through my hair, pulling slightly when they find a tangle or two. Sometimes it hurts a little, but he always smooths it out, runs his fingers back over my scalp to allay any lingering pain. Almost automatically, his lips find my forehead, pressing that same tenderness into my skin. It's a small movement, but it takes my breath away.

I didn't realize until today how badly I needed to feel a touch, physical or mental, that didn't hurt. But more than that, I didn't realize how badly I needed that touch to be his.

My lips find his shoulder before I can stop them. Nico stiffens slightly. I press them to his neck.

"Layla." His deep voice thrums in the dark. "Sweetie, what are you doing?"

I inhale, my nose buried in the hollow just over his clavicle. The hands in my hair tense, but I can feel the stirrings of something else stiffening lower down. I'm not sure what I feel about that.

"You make me feel good," is all I say to him.

Nico pushes up on one elbow, cradles his head in his hand so he can look over me. He gazes through me, with eyes as black and deep as the night sky outside. He's searching for something. What, I don't know.

"I do?" he asks me.

Wordlessly, I nod. Please, I want to say. Please kiss me. But the words don't come.

Slowly, he leans down and places his lips right under my jaw, to that sensitive spot that used to make me squirm. My breath catches as he flickers his tongue just there. My heart speeds up a little, but in a way that's good, not bad. This isn't fear. It's desire. It's heat. The opposite of a chill.

Then he closes his teeth around my earlobe and bites sharply, and I freeze.

He stops immediately. "What's wrong?"

I close my eyes for a second. "That...please don't...Nico, I just...I."

I can't even get the words out. I'm not sure what they should even be. But his teeth —that tiny hint of pain—struck something deep within me, and something that I thought would be an escape from the horrors of this day suddenly bring it all rushing back, and then some.

"I can't," I squeak. "Please...I..."

The look on Nico's face breaks my heart in two. "Did he..."

His brow furrows without waiting for my answer, and he closes his eyes as if in pain too. He rolls his lips together—his beautiful, soft lips—and exhales forcefully through his nostrils while he rubs his head. He's processing something. I wanted to forget him, but Giancarlo is in this room right now. I hate him for it. I hate him for all of it.

Nico opens his eyes, suddenly full of direction.

"Tell me what he did," he prompts.

I pause. "I—Nico, you don't want to hear about that, do you?"

He puffs out his cheeks and blows out another breath slowly. "No, not really. But I think I should."

I grimace. "Why?"

"Because," he says softly. "Why do you think I flew across the country the second you called? Your pain is mine, baby. So let me bear it with you."

I blink for a moment as his words seep in. The idea that I'm not alone in this. That maybe I really can talk about it with him.

"He—he liked it rough," I whisper finally, terrified of the reaction I might get here. Nico hasn't exactly hidden his disdain for me being with someone else, even before that someone turned out to be an abusive asshole. "Sometimes that was okay. I...I didn't want things sweet with him. I never did. Being with him was always like a punishment, you know? Did you ever feel like you needed something to hurt for it to feel good?"

I close my eyes, working hard to keep my control. I'm terrified of what he might think of me for this. That he might say what a voice in my head also says sometimes. That whatever harshness Giancarlo dealt out, maybe there was a part of me that was asking for it. That felt like I deserved it.

Nico chews on his lips again, clearly processing my words with varying amounts of anger and sadness. But in the end, he retains that direct, open expression.

"Okay," he says. "So tell me what he didn't do, baby. Tell me that."

"He didn't..." I pause. Tears are threatening now. "He didn't kiss me."

Nico arches a black brow in surprise. "Seriously? He never kissed you at all?"

I blush. I doubt he can see it—not with my technicolor face and the dark lighting. But I can feel the heat rising up my neck. "No, he kissed me. I just meant...he never kissed me like you."

Nico blinks. "Yeah?"

The blush deepens. It's hard not to look away. "Yeah."

Carefully, with movements scattered with micro pauses to check and check again that I'm actually all right, Nico shifts so that he's lying between my legs. It's not a lecherous move—just one that allows him to balance with his forearms on either side of my head so his hands can cup together at the crown of my head. We stare at each other. His black eyes glimmer with the glow of the city that sneaks into the room.

Slowly, slowly, he leans down. And finally presses his lips to mine.

"Like that?" he asks, his breath warm and heavy.

I nod. "Like that."

So he does it again. And again. Slowly, slowly, my mouth opens to his. His tongue slips out to taste me again, to flicker with curiosity and want. I twist mine with it, finding again that delicate dance that always made me feel like I was floating two feet off the ground. Nico sucks lightly on my bottom lip, savors the top, licks and nibbles until a low moan emerges from my chest. My hands have somehow found their way into the hair at the back of his neck, and with a sudden yank, I pull him deeper, forcing his body to collapse over me. And this time, the hardness now pressing between my legs is unmistakable.

"Shit," Nico breathes in between the deep, long kisses that I'm driving now as much as him. "Fuck, Layla."

But when he thrusts his hips, something deep inside me stills again. My chest squeezes, and I freeze again. Nico pulls back, searching my face again, even though his lips are wet with our kisses.

I shut my eyes. Fuck. What am I doing? I want this, even though I shouldn't. I need this, but I can't do anything about it. I'm so fucked up. Quinn is right. Maybe the best thing for Nico is to just leave me alone. My needs shouldn't matter when they just screw everything up.

"Look at me, baby."

So I do. Because even in this tortured state, I also know the truth: that I'd do just about anything right now because he wanted me to.

"Did he make you come?" he asks.

At first I'm not sure he actually asks me that out loud. But then he draws a finger over my cheek, plays with my lower lip for a moment, and asks it again. His lips are soft as he drifts kisses down my body, over my t-shirt, between my breasts, down to where the hem rises just above my underwear.

I stare as his mouth hovers over the elastic band. "N-no?"

It's a question more than a statement. But it's also true. The few times I did orgasm with Giancarlo, I had to do it myself. And more often than not, he would get too impatient waiting for me to find the focus to do it. I've been faking it. For months and months, I've been faking it.

Nico props his chin on my stomach and gazes up at me with eyes full of love, free of judgment. "No?"

"N-no. I just...I just couldn't. Not really. Not with him."

Nico lays his cheek on my stomach, closes his eyes and smiles an impossibly sweet smile. Like my disclosure solves all of his concerns. Like he's thinking of the countless times he's brought me to the peak of pleasure, with just a few touches, a few choice phrases, a few breathless kisses.

Men.

Then he presses one kiss, then another over my stomach. "Is this okay?"

Quickly, all deprecating thoughts vanish as his mouth toys with the elastic band of my underwear. When they pull away, I look down to find Nico fingering the sides.

He looks at me, unsure. "Is this...is this okay? You can say no. I won't be mad, baby, I swear."

I believe him. I believe that in this moment, all he wants is to give me some pleasure. And even though I should say no, I can't for the life of me think of a reason why.

In response, I lift my hips and watch as he removes my underwear. He kneels over me. With the moonlight shining in, bouncing blue gray off the windows of New York, he looks like an ancient warrior, standing over me. Protecting me.

He leans down and kisses me again, keeping it kind, but doesn't bother to mask his hunger. My hands rub up his arms, over the dips and curves of his finely honed muscles, grazing the ridges of his abdomen. Christ, he really is beautiful.

"Did I make you come?" he asks before he steals another kiss or two.

"You used to all the time."

There's that smile—the impish, cocky smile I remember. The one he reserves just for me. I let him tug off my shirt, and he kisses down my neck, humming slightly into the soft skin between my breasts. My hands clasp his head, holding him there.

"Do it," I whisper. "Please."

With a rumbling groan, Nico kisses down my body all over again, worshipping my nipples, my stomach, my hips, all in ways I never felt with...him. A name that even this quickly, starts to grow distant. I look my worst, but Nico looks at me as if I'm at my best. As if he can't see anything else but me.

He feathers his mouth over my inner thighs, and I shiver at the touch, moaning slightly as my legs spread. Spread for him.

"Please." I'm so close to begging. I will if he wants. "Please. Kiss me there."

But I don't have to beg. Nico's mouth finds my most intimate spots with the ardor of a starving man. Like he lives to do this, to feel me twitch and moan under his exquisite lips, feel my body shiver with each stroke of his tongue. As he sucks lightly on my clit, he hums again, creating a delicious vibration. My body, desperate for release, seizes almost immediately. My body isn't frozen at all anymore. The heat of desire is almost too much to take, and yet, with him it feels like it could last forever.

"Oh, God!" I cry out, holding his head firmly in place. He doesn't stop, even as the first orgasm fades. Instead, he chases it, urging another one right on its heels. "Nico!" I shout as the next one hits. "Oh my fucking *God!*"

He makes me come again and again, with his lips, then with his tongue, and finally with his hand, reached over my hip while he holds me securely against his body, absorbing the tension I didn't know I had to release. It's only after the fifth and final orgasm that he finally allows me to return to earth, still holding me close while his breath plays at my ear.

"I love you," he murmurs, almost in a daze himself. His fingers strum across my stomach lazily. "I belong to you."

The words catch in my throat, and unbidden, tears prick at my eyes. How often did I dream of him saying just that, of me being able to say it back to him as easily? I open my mouth to say it. I feel it, after all. I love this man more than anything. All I've wanted, since the day we met, was him.

But the words don't come. And suddenly I am all too aware of his erection pressing at my back. Of that fact that I have taken and taken and taken from this man all day and given him nothing in return.

"I..." I trail off, feeling unsure. Awkward. "Hold on."

I move clumsily, turning in his arms and reaching down to his underwear.

"Whoa!" he hollers as my hand takes hold of his solid length. "Baby—*shit*—what-what are you doing?"

I keep him in my grip, holding tight. I don't move, but that's only because I'm shaking again. Once again...frozen.

"I just thought," I whisper, even though I can't look at him. "I just wanted to make you feel good. Like you did for me. Because I...I love you too."

The words linger between us. Nico stares at me, holding my gaze to his. Then slowly, he reaches between us, and unwraps my fingers from his cock. My heart sinks.

"Not now," he says softly, refusing to let me look away. "One day. But you're not ready."

Still he holds my gaze, like he's demanding me to see the truth in his eyes. Maybe we moved too fast. Maybe he's regretting his actions too. But the longer I look, the more I thaw. The more his warmth surrounds me, infiltrates me. Body. Soul. Mind. Everything.

Nico takes my hands and presses them to his mouth, kisses to my knuckles.

"One day," he murmurs again. "I promise."

"That's patient of you," I say, though relief floods through me at his words.

"No, baby," he says as he gathers me into his chest. "That's love."

CHAPTER THIRTY-SEVEN

Layla

MY FACE HURTS. MY ANKLE HURTS. EVERYTHING HURTS. BUT EVEN WITH THAT AND THE fact that I have an avalanche of stuff to deal with today, the world still feels a little lighter.

And a little colder too. It takes me a second to realize that the arms that were wrapped around me all night are gone, and that I'm alone in my bed, covers draped over my bare shoulder.

Quinn's not in the room. In the wake of our fight, she really did take the couch. I feel bad. We may not be friends anymore, but that doesn't mean she shouldn't be able to sleep in her own bed.

Nico walks in, fully dressed in his t-shirt and jeans, his hat on backwards, cell phone to his ear. My cell phone, I quickly realize.

"Sure," he says. "Thanks, Cheryl. Yeah, I'll make sure she prints out the ticket." He catches me looking and winks. "Okay, you too. Take care." He sets my phone on the desk before pulling up a chair in front of me so he can take my hand. "Morning, beautiful," he says softly as his thumb plays over my knuckles. "You slept like the dead, you know that?"

I blanch. "Is that a good thing or a bad thing?"

Nico shrugs and gives me a sly half-smile. "You snore too. It's okay. I'll make sure to bring earplugs next time I see you."

"I do not snore!" I search for a pillow to whack him, but by the time I swing it around, he dodges it easily, chuckling.

"It's okay," he says. "It's just a little snore. A baby snore, like a kitten."

I tug my sheet over my head. "Kill me."

Nico just chuckles and waits patiently until I pull the sheet back down. He lounges back in the chair, content, it seems, to just sit with me.

"Was that...was that my mom?" I ask a few moments later.

His gaze flickers around the room uneasily. "Um, yeah."

Without explaining anything else, he stands up. I hold the sheet awkwardly to my chest and watch as he walks to the dresser by the closet. One of my suitcases is on the floor, open and half packed with clothes, I realize. Nico opens one of my drawers and starts transferring stuff into it.

"What-what are you doing?" I ask, completely confused.

"I talked to Shama," he says as he folds a t-shirt. He's clearly not used to folding small pieces of fabric. He has to try three times before he can get it into a square, which he puts on top of the others he's already done.

"You talked to Shama..." I repeat.

Nico looks up from dubiously examining a tank top. "Yeah. She emailed your professors and got extensions on your final papers through the summer. You already finished your language finals, so the rest are just essays. You just have to email them to confirm."

He folds the tank top in half, but it keeps falling apart every time he tries. Snorting with disgust, he balls it up and shoves it into the bag with a lot more force than a piece of cotton deserves.

I sit up and push my hair out of my face. "I don't understand. Why are you packing my stuff up?"

Nico stops. He takes off his hat and passes it in between his hands a few times. The sounds of my roommates making breakfast filter under the door. He looks around the room guiltily, shifting on the balls of his feet like a caged animal.

"You, um, you wanna go for a walk or something?" he asks abruptly. "How's your ankle?"

I swallow. This is out of nowhere, and I probably look even more like a punching bag than yesterday. If he wants me out of the apartment to talk, this can't be good. But already the place feels suffocating. I need to get outside.

"Um, it's kind of sore," I say. "I can probably just take some ibuprofen, I guess."

I swing my legs out of the bed, and Nico's eyes follow them down to the floor. His eyes dilate slightly before he blinks and looks away.

"I need to stop at Duane Reade for some of that makeup your sister showed me anyway," I tell him.

And just like that, the look is gone. Nico blinks, and his gaze hardens as he looks back at my neck and face, takes in the real extent of my bruises. I hate that look. It makes me want to throw a paper bag over my head and be done with it.

"Just, um, give me a second to get dressed," I say, looking pointedly at the door. "I need to take a shower, okay?"

He pauses, clearly unwilling to leave me alone, even for a second. But I sit there, waiting, until finally he nods.

"Okay," he says as he moves toward the door. "Take your time."

———

Nico

For the next thirty minutes, I wait on the couch, chatting with Shama and Jamie while they eat their breakfasts and staring moodily out of the windows that look out toward Union Square. Quinn is nowhere to be seen, although according to Shama, she slept on the couch before leaving early to keep studying for her finals at the library for the rest of the day. Good. Layla doesn't need any more stress today, especially since I'm pretty sure she's not going to want to hear what I have to say.

But while she slept through most of the morning—seriously, if I hadn't known before how hurt she really was, inside and out, the fourteen hours of sleep my girl just took would have told me—her friends and I were busy. Now that they've really clued in to just how messed up Layla really is right now, they jumped right in, helping me get things squared away.

Because there are only two things on my mind at the moment.

One: I love her. I love her more than anything. More than myself. More than my job. More than the need I have on a fuckin' cellular level to touch her, smell her, taste her. Those are things that suit me, but this love goes beyond that. It's not about me, it's about *her*.

And so the second realization beats loud and clearly, painfully through my skull: She needs to go home.

I barely slept last night, staring at the ceiling, looking around the posters on her walls while I recounted the past two days. The terrified phone call from the street. The plane ride where I thought I was going to chew off my own arm with anxiety. Arriving at her dorm to find her missing. Busting into that apartment to find her being attacked.

His blood. My fists. Her bruises.

But it would always come back to the present, lying there with her in my arms, snoring peacefully. Occasionally she would cry out a little, or murmur something unintelligible under her breath. My baby is fuckin' adorable when she sleeps. I never knew. I hate that I never knew. That I let a whole year pass between us without learning all these small things about her. That I'll have to put at least another three months more between us before I can start learning them again.

But my baby is broken. I was happy to give her a little pleasure last night—let her know that someone could touch her again without cruelty. I would worship her body all day every day if she'd let me, especially if it would convince her of that. But the look in her eyes that flashed every so often—pure, unadulterated fear—felt like a lightning bolt through my chest. It's the last thing I *ever* want her to feel around me. Her wounds go so much deeper than a few bruises on her face. My baby needs time, real time to heal.

And she can't do that here.

I went over it, over and over again in my mind, trying to figure out a way we could make it work. But I can't for the life of me figure out how I'll be able to pay for an apartment for the two of us and give her the attention she needs while I'm at the academy for the next four months. Me, I can deal with living in whatever shithole place I can afford on a cadet's salary, but Layla deserves better than some basement room in Queens or my brother's couch. She needs a place where she doesn't have to worry about things like paying the electricity bills or dealing with seedy landlords, where she's not going to be left for eighteen hours a day while I'm learning how to become one of New York's Bravest. She needs a place where people can take care of that shit for her. Where she won't be alone.

Still, it wasn't until I called her mom that I was absolutely sure that sending her to California was the right thing to do. Cheryl has been hurting too this last year. I don't even have to know her to hear that in her voice when I told her what had happened to her daughter. To hear the guilt that echoed there as she realized that her negligence was a primary cause of all this chaos. If Layla is really going to heal from all of this stuff, she needs to make peace with her family and the changes they've gone through.

So yeah. She can't do that here.

Layla emerges from the bathroom, dressed and looking much more alert, even though the hot water gave her a rosy complexion that darkens the purple and yellow colors around her neck and face. She's more bundled up in jeans and a sweatshirt than a sunny spring day in May really needs.

I stand up and go to her. We really are like magnets, and it's more intense now than it ever was. Which is why today is going to be that much harder.

"You ready?" I ask as I kiss her forehead.

She nods, then waves at her roommates. "Let's go."

———

I ESCORT her to the drugstore on the corner, walking slightly ahead of her with her hand clenched in mine, like I'm her bodyguard. This city has a tendency to chew people up and spit them out. I've seen it again and again. I never wanted that for her. She came to New York to follow her dreams, even if she's still figuring them out. But in the end, it still got the best of her.

"Hey," she asks as I tug her around a subway grate. "What happened with your mom? What's going on with that?"

I pull her close and kiss the side of her head. This is my girl—even when she's down, she's still thinking of others.

"Gabe is helping her move to Alba's guest room for a while," I say. "That's K.C's mom."

Layla nods. "I remember. The one who threw the party, right?"

I smile at the memory. Up until the end, that party, dancing with my girl, was one of the best nights of my life. "Yeah. She's going to stay there until one of us can go to Havana and track down her birth certificate."

I sigh. I'm starting the academy next week and going to be living on a cadet's salary for the next four months. I don't know when I'm going to have time or the money to go to Cuba, but I need to figure it out. See exactly what I need to do to get permission. I honestly don't trust any of my siblings to take care of it the right way, but one of us needs to go. Soon.

Still, we wouldn't even know about it if it hadn't been for Layla. I squeeze her hand and kiss her cheek again. She smiles.

We're quiet as we walk through the drugstore. I watch solemnly as she uses a sample of that cakey shit my sister gave her to cover up the marks on her skin. It still looks like she's wearing pancake batter, but at least this time the color is closer to her actual skin tone. About halfway through, she catches my gaze in the tiny mirror attached to the wall and smiles again, but neither of us says anything while she finishes and buys a jar of the stuff at the counter.

We're quiet as we walk around the craft market set up in the middle of the square, meandering around the stalls, my arms sometimes around her waist, sometimes slung around her shoulders, sometimes just holding her hand. But always touching. Never apart. I haven't told her the plans yet, but I think maybe she knows.

In spite of her limp, which is already getting better, we make our way across town, all the way through the East Village and Alphabet City, and eventually I steer her south toward East River Park, where we walk on the wide concrete path that winds around the river's edge.

"It looks nice over there," Layla says, pointing to some of the brownstone buildings you can just make out across the river in Brooklyn.

I nod. "That's Williamsburg. It is a nice area. Getting expensive, though."

Layla chuckles. "Everywhere here is expensive."

I shrug. She has a point.

"Sometimes I think it would be nice not to live in Manhattan," she says, still looking across the water. "This island is so crowded. I don't know…I haven't really been to other parts of the city…but it seems like maybe getting away from all these tall buildings, all these people shoved together might be…a little more peaceful."

Her words only make my resolve that much firmer. And that much more painful.

"Your flight's at six thirty," I say abruptly. I might as well get it out there.

Layla turns. "What flight?"

I chew on my lip. "The one I asked your mom to book for you this morning." I take her other hand so she can't turn away. "You need…fuck, Layla. You need to go home for a while, sweetie."

Her gaze flickers around the park for a moment. It might just be the wind blowing off the river, but she looks like she's about to cry.

"What home?" she asks finally. "My parents are split, Nico. My 'home' is an empty house in Pasadena where I've spent maybe five nights my entire life." A tear tracks down her cheek, and she swipes it away angrily, smudging some of the makeup onto her hand. "No, that's wrong. My home is with *you*. It's always been with you. That's why this whole year I've been so—"

Her voice cracks, and she looks out to the river while another few tears fall. I'm not going to lie. I'm struggling to keep it together too. The last thing I want to do is say goodbye to her again. But she needs this. She knows she needs this.

She also needs to know that we're for real. That no matter how far away she goes, for how long, I'll be waiting for her when she gets back. Or maybe it's me that needs to say it. To hear us both acknowledge that fact.

"Hey."

I let go of one of her hands and tip her face to look at me. Her eyes are bluer than the water, bluer than the sky above us. They shine, glossy with tears, but she looks at me straight. Already she has more strength than she did yesterday. The thought spurs me on.

"You've been so what?" I ask as I stroke her cheek.

She takes a deep breath and leans into my hand for a moment before answering.

"Lost."

It's a whisper, so low the word almost flies away on the wind. But it still rocks my soul to its core.

"Ah, baby." I cup her other cheek and press my forehead to hers. My heart is shaking. This is harder than I ever thought it would be. "I've been lost without you too."

"I feel like I'm being punished," she says, her voice choking a little. "Like I'm such a mess, I have to be banished. Is this about last night, that I couldn't...? I'm sorry—so sorry. I'll be better. I'll do whatever you need, I swear, I—"

"Shhhhh." I cut her off gently, kiss the tears off her cheeks. "It's not about that. Last night was perfect."

Her willingness to compromise herself breaks my heart. She doesn't understand what she's offering. I'm humbled by it, honored by her desire to make me happy. But my girl needs to figure out her own worth again without pleasing other people at her own expense. She needs to know that she doesn't have to sacrifice her comfort, her limits, with someone who really loves her. That I would love her more for being true to herself anyway.

I fold her against my chest, wrapping my arms around her as we turn to look out at the river together. There's a water taxi carrying a bunch of tourists on a tour of the boroughs, and if I look up the river, buildings in Brooklyn and Queens block the river's edge on the other side. Even farther up the river is Randall's Island, where I'll be spending the majority of my time until October. It's blocked by Roosevelt Island, but I know it's there. The Academy, the place I've dreamed of since I was a kid.

I just wish it didn't feel like a choice between my dreams and her. Because it took everything I had not to tell Cheryl to book me a ticket too. Beg her to let me stay in that big house. Let me trim their hedges, clean their gutters, whatever it would take to earn my keep.

But I know in the end, my presence won't help Layla. And I need to do this not just for myself, but for her too. I have to believe that a few more months might spell the difference between a life together that will last forever and a life bandaged together that could fall apart. We both deserve to be the best people we can for each other. I want to be worthy of this woman, inside and out.

Layla sniffs every now and then as she cries silently toward the river. I don't say anything. Sometimes you just have to let it out. I'll be her shelter while she does.

———

Layla

We walk around the East Village for a little while longer, but soon my ankle can't really take much more, and Nico tells me gently that we need to go back to the apartment. It's already almost two, and there's a lot to do if I'm going to be on a six-thirty flight to Los Angeles.

Shama and Jamie have been hard at work while we were gone. My things are already in boxes, and they're just about finished packing my clothes too.

"Hey," I say. "I can take over from here."

We spend a few more hours packing and cleaning my side of the bedroom. Nico and my roommates have already done so much. I don't want them to take on more than they have to. Shama has already said she's going to keep my stuff with hers in a storage facility, and Jamie is footing the bill to have one of the boxes of things accumulated through the year sent back to my grandparents.

Soon, too soon, it's time to say goodbye.

"I'll pay you back," I say as I hug each of them. "I'll send a check as soon as I'm home."

"Shut up," Jamie says. "My parents send me too much money anyway. I'm a spoiled brat, if you hadn't noticed."

Behind me, Nico snorts as he lugs the two suitcases I'm checking on the plane out of my room. I have to laugh. I'm pretty sure we all qualify as spoiled brats to a lot of people.

"Thank you," I say as I give my roommates both another round of hugs. "You guys saved my life. Really."

We hold tight, the three of us, before Shama and Jamie finally let go.

"Get out of here," Shama says. "We'll take care of putting the rest of your stuff in storage, okay? Just come back better."

"Okay," I say. "I promise."

Nico lugs one of my bags over his shoulder and picks up the other while I grab my messenger bag and my coat. We turn toward the front door, which opens on its own. Quinn steps into the room, and stills when she's confronted by the four of us.

"Oh," she says surprised. "You're leaving?"

I nod. Beside me, Nico tenses visibly.

"I'm going home," I tell her. "I'll, um, finish my work there."

Quinn looks over the bags and glances toward the stack of boxes in our bedroom. She nods. "That...makes sense." She looks up. "Will you be back in the fall?"

At that, I look to Nico. Uncertainty flashes over his features, but I can tell he's trying to put on a strong face for me.

"You bet," I say.

And for the first time since he showed up yesterday, a smile appears. A real smile, the kind that lights up the entire room. The kind that grabbed me from the start.

I turn back to Quinn. "I have to catch my flight. Um...have a good summer."

Quinn looks at me uneasily. "You too." She sniffs, but all of the vitriol from yesterday is gone. "Take care of yourself."

There are no hugs between us. I'm pretty sure that when I get back, Quinn will not be one of the people waiting for me. But when I close the door behind me, I do feel a peace between us at last. An acceptance that maybe wasn't even there in the first place.

———

Nico rides with me to the airport, doing his best to make small talk the entire way there. He gives me a laundry list of places to visit while I'm in LA—restaurants to try, which beaches I'll like best. I don't really hear most of what he says. I'm too busy taking all of him in: the way he talks with his hands, the way a dimple shows up on one side of his face when he laughs, the way his dark eyes flicker expressively, fringed with those lashes that frame such brightness. No matter what he's feeling—happy, sad, angry, confused—those eyes always sparkle, like two black diamonds.

Finally we arrive at the airport, and he accompanies me while I check my bags and find my way toward the security line for the gates.

"Fuckin' 9/11," he swears, glaring at the security that prohibits him from going any farther. "I miss the days when I could come with you. Watch your plane take off, like in the movies."

I lean my head on his shoulder. "I wish you could fly there with me."

He sighs and kisses the top of my head again. "Me too, baby. Me too." Then he turns to face me. "So. Here we are again."

It's hard to know what he means. At the airport? Saying goodbye? Sometimes it feels like that's all we ever do. But this time I hope, I pray, will be the last time.

He reaches down to take both of my hands and lays them palms down on his chest. Right over his heart. Right over the compass tattoo that I can see through his t-shirt if I look hard enough. The one missing its north symbol.

"You listen to me," he tells me. He presses his hands over mine, like he's trying to stamp my handprints over his heart. "I'm not going anywhere. You got that, baby? I'm going to be right fuckin' here, right in this spot when you get back. I don't care how long it takes. Three months. Two years. But in the end you better come back, all right? Because I'll be waiting."

Wordlessly, I nod. The tears are coming again—fuck, I am *so* tired of crying. But I can't seem to help it. I'm not spiraling like I was before, but I'm definitely shattered. It's going to take longer than a day or two to put my life—put myself—back together. Nico was right all along.

I tip my head up, waiting for a kiss. And dark eyes, so deep I want to dive into them, take me in for a second. Then his hands weave into my hair, and he sets his lips to mine.

It's a kiss full of promises.

Saudade. The word echoes through my soul, a legacy of my family, the undying desire for something that hasn't even happened yet. Nothing captures better what I feel for this man.

"This feels like the end of something," I whisper against his lips. I feel like a shadow of myself, a whisper of a person. Like the wind might blow me away.

"It *is* the end," Nico agrees as he pushes some hair out of my eyes. He presses a kiss to my forehead, and lingers there for a moment. "But when you come back, it'll also be a beginning." He takes my hands and lifts them solemnly to his lips, kissing one, then the other. "We aren't lost anymore, baby, because we found each other."

I close my eyes taking in his words. And then, because there's nothing else to do, I turn and start walking toward security.

"Layla!"

I pause. I'm barely keeping it together. But slowly, because I have to, I turn around.

That's when Nico captures my mouth with one last kiss. But this kiss isn't full of sadness, full of goodbyes. It's full-bodied, a kiss that holds desire, hunger, all the promise of love and tomorrow and what the world might hold for us. It's a kiss that sweeps all the doubts out of my mind, that will emanate through me for days to come.

My bag drops to the floor, and I welcome him as he holds my body to his, hovering my toes off the floor while he tells me again and again, with his lips, his tongue, the rumbling vibrations in the back of his throat, all the things that words can't ever seem to say. That he loves me. That he's mine. And that as long as we really know that, we won't ever be lost again.

"I love you," he says, with a voice that's lost its breath. "Now go."

I nod, not even trying to wipe away my tears. "I love you too. Thank you. For-for everything."

"Don't thank me," he says. When I look up, there's a tear sliding down his cheek too. He laughs and pushes it away. "Just come back to me, okay?"

"You sure you'll still want me to?" I joke, but it's laced with uncertainty.

But he smiles again, that bright, thousand-watt smile that would light up the black of night.

"Always," he says.

Hours later, when I'm stepping off a plane on the other side of the country, the word still echoes through my heart.

Always.

EPILOGUE

AUGUST 2004

Nico

I check my watch for what's probably the fifteenth time in the last hour. But fuckin' *finally* it shows me the time I want to see.

I pop up from my fiftieth burpee and jog around the other cadets to where Lieutenant Meyers stands, staring at us with his hands on his hips.

"It's three, Lieutenant," I tell him, showing my watch. "I gotta go."

Meyers, the barrel-shaped man who's been in charge of my group of cadets for the past three months, pushes his aviators up his nose. He reminds me a lot of Frank, the gruff older guy who trained me when I got out of juvie. He knew how to help me in the right direction, but also never put up with my shit. When he died a few years back, it hit hard.

Meyers frowns at me. "What are you leaving for? You gotta pick someone up at the fuckin' airport?"

I exhale through my nose. We've been through this about five times, twice today. I should have known he was going to give me shit in front of the other cadets.

"Not someone, Lieutenant," I tell him. "My girl."

Immediately, a chorus of "ooohs" and whistles and catcalls rises from the ground, where all the cadets are finishing their pushups.

"Fuckin' girl," Meyers mutters to himself, but it's all for show. I cleared this with him on day one. Every day, I show up usually a solid thirty minutes before our training begins, and I usually stay late too. I'm the best cadet in the class, and he knows it. But I was always leaving early today, even if it meant getting tossed out of the entire program.

"Hey, Lieutenant, I'm feelin' pretty hard up too!" Reilly, one of the guys I get along with pretty well, shouts out. "Can I go see my girl too? She's waiting for me at a bar in Long Island City."

"Mine too!" shouts Carson, one of the younger guys who looks like he could still be in high school.

"Mine too!" Shouts echo through the group until suddenly there are forty-five guys shouting about the different bars in the city where their nonexistent girlfriends are waiting for them.

"Twenty more!" shouts Meyers, and with a hush, everyone quiets down and starts grunting with their efforts. "An hour early tomorrow, Soltero," he says to me, nodding his consent. "Now get the fuck outta here."

———

I MILL AROUND the baggage claim, shuffling awkwardly with my hands shoved into my pockets while I scan the crowds for Layla. Occasionally a few people glance at me curiously. It's something I'm going to have to get used to: being looked at with admiration instead of suspicion. People see this uniform—the blue cargo pants and blue shirt with FDNY printed on the front—and they start asking questions. They like firefighters, especially in New York. Little kids look at me, want to be just like me. Their mothers encourage them to talk to me instead of guiding them away. It's a good feeling. For the first time in my life, I feel accepted in the city of my birth. Like I'm wanted. Like I really belong.

I check my watch again. I know she's here. I got a text from her about fifteen minutes ago saying her plane had landed. I'd already been pacing around JFK for about an hour at that point, but she doesn't need to know that. She doesn't need to know that I'm basically a puppy jumping in its cage, I'm so excited to see my girl.

We talked every day this summer, usually multiple times. It was hard sometimes to connect. Five days a week, I'm at Randall's Island from morning to night, getting back to the apartment in time to collapse on the pull-out until the next morning. On the weekends, I spend most of my time studying for the tests the next week and working the door at AJ's and the Roxy. One day, I won't have to check IDs anymore for extra cash. But cadets and rookies make shit money, and I still have bills to pay.

Layla's been busy too. In between seeing a therapist and trying to reconnect with her mom, she's also taken a couple more language classes at the local community college and worked a summer job at the YWCA. She watches the kids while their moms, women who are coming out of worse relationships than hers, talk to the lawyers and social workers to help them get out of their situations. I thought at first that it would be too hard for her to be around that kind of environment, that it might trigger some of her own traumas. But I think it's actually been cathartic. Helping others in similar situations seems to be its own kind of therapy.

But still, no matter what, we've always made time to talk. Sometimes it's early in the morning, 2:00 a.m. her time when I call her as the sun rises here. Or maybe it's close to midnight in New York, when she gets home from her classes. On the weekends, we talk for hours, eager to get lost in each other's voices. And if we're lucky enough to catch each other when we're both alone, things get a little dirty. I never thought I'd be good at phone sex, but apparently I have a knack for it. Layla's always saying how much she likes my voice, and if I toss in a little Spanish here and there, my girl pretty much goes nuts.

Every conversation ends the same. "I love you," I tell her. "Always." "Always," she repeats. "I love you back."

But I'm tired of "I love you back." I'm tired of jerking off with a phone pressed to my ear, of wishing I could jump through the receiver and *show* her all those things I've been growling into her ear.

It's been more than three months since she got on that plane. And I'm here, standing in the same place, just like I promised, ready as fuck to say all those things, dirty and sweet, to her face.

A new group of people spills down the escalators, I search their faces, looking for those blue eyes I still see every time I close mine. Will she look different? The same? She sent me a couple of pictures of her on the beach, but I still see her bruises in the back of my mind.

Then she appears at the top of the escalator. She's glowing with the effects of a summer spent in the California sun. Her skin is darker than I've ever seen, but the top of her normally black hair is bleached a little bit lighter. Her hair is down, waving around her shoulders and face, and the tiny shorts she's wearing show off long legs. She turns to the side to pull something out of her bag, and I get a peek of her ass in profile.

Shit, her ass. I was a gentleman the last time I saw her, but that body part alone has starred in weekly dreams I have. The really fuckin' dirty kind. The kind that either make me reach for the phone and pray she's alone or else force me into an ice-cold shower where I have to imagine K.C.'s *abuela* to calm myself down. And even then...yeah. Let's just say another part of me is *very* ready to get reacquainted with my girl again.

Finally, she catches sight of me, and her face bursts into the biggest, brightest smile I have ever fuckin' seen.

"Hi!" she shouts over the crowd, causing several people in front of her to turn around with cranky expressions.

Fuckin' New Yorkers. Sometimes people here forget to smile. Well, fuck 'em. I've got a grin on my face a mile wide, and I don't give a shit.

When she's finally able to get off the escalator, she starts jogging awkwardly through the crowd, her bag and purse banging on her sides. By this time, I'm hopping like a fuckin' rabbit on the other side of the barrier, ready to catch her the second she passes security. My girl is practically a linebacker as she elbows through people waiting for their bags. But I can see on her face the same thing that's probably written all over mine.

But just before she reaches me, doubt shakes through me like a thunderclap. Is she okay? Will she want what I want? Will she be the Layla I used to know? Will I be okay if she's not? Suddenly the fact that Layla and I have never really had *time*, plain and simple, to know each other and be sure of one another, looms ahead. My heart is thumping in my chest, and as the rest of the questions filter away, a final few remain:

Will she still love me for exactly what I am? And will I love her too?

She comes to a stop, and for a second, the entire airport disappears. I guess there's only one way to find out. I open my mouth.

"Welcome home, baby."

Thank you for reading Lost Ones!

Layla and Nico's story finishes in True North. Keep reading for the first two chapters or go here to download the whole book:
http://bit.ly/TrueNorthNovel

A NOTE FROM THE AUTHOR

Thank you for taking the time to read Lost Ones. A great deal of research and work went into this book, but I feel that I should call attention to a few potential inaccuracies. The first, and most glaring, is the expedited order of Nico's application with the FDNY. The FDNY *was* actually hiring in 2002 in the wake of the horrific events of 9/11, but I moved that up a year to fit the events of the story. I also expedited and shifted around the order of the application process slightly to fit the characters' other plot progressions. Similarly, I might also point out that physical conditioning like in the final scene might be more likely for new cadets rather than someone about to graduate. What can I say? I just wanted a hot pushup scene.

On a more serious note, this was easily the hardest thing I have ever written. Harder than my academic writing. Harder than my first, second, third, fourth, or fifth book. It was so difficult because, more than anything I have ever written, *Lost Ones* was a catharsis of events I've kept long buried.

When I was a sophomore in college, I ended up in a physically abusive relationship. It's funny—I think that's the first time I've ever written that down. It's strange to see it there, in print form. It's so permanent. It will never go away.

But such are the lasting effects of abuse, of all types. My story is not unique. We are living in an incredible moment where, for the first time, millions of women are coming out of the shadows to tell their stories of mistreatment. People misunderstand, perhaps seeing many of these stories as a pursuit of vengeance. I think they are about catharsis, the process of purging demons that stay inside you long after your original persecutor may be gone. Of finally having a moment to say your truth out loud and have people listen. Validate. Believe.

So this book purged some of my own demons, yes. But I also wanted to write a story about people who come from histories of abuse in multiple forms, and to understand the social foundations for a person's willingness to tolerate mistreatment. It was to understand that such foundations exist for all of us in a society, not simply people who belong to one class, one class, one identity or another. But most of all, my purpose was to write the ultimate truth: that love, in its purest form, is the cure to that terrible logic. Like so many of us, my characters frequently cannot believe that someone else would love them the way they love each other. But in the end, of course, their willingness to believe in that love, to believe that the other is worth it, that *they are worth it*, is what really defines their mutual salvation.

If you or anyone you know is suffering from the effects of an abusive relationship, please consider contacting one of the many resources out there that can help people cope, escape, and recover from abuse. You are loved. They are loved. And you are all worth it.

xo,

Nic

TRUE NORTH

BOOK THREE OF THE BAD IDEA SERIES

I

THE BITTER AND THE SWEET

CHAPTER ONE

AUGUST 2004

Nico

LONGING. DESIRE. EXCITEMENT. ABSOLUTE FUCKIN' JOY.

Finally, fuckin' *finally*, Layla Barros is in my arms again, right in the middle of John F. Kennedy airport, having launched herself at me with the force of an NFL football player.

"Hey!" I shout as I swing her around and around.

Layla's legs come around my waist with a strength I didn't know she had, forcing me to drop my hands and get two handfuls of my favorite body part in order to hold her up. Jesus fuckin' Christ. I'm already hard and she's the only thing hiding that fact from the dozens of other people milling around the baggage claim.

But before I can say anything—a smart-ass comment that's about to roll off my tongue—she's kissing me. And it's not a tentative kiss either. Gone is the fear she had when she left over three months ago. This isn't a gentle kiss. It's hungry, forceful, full-throated. Her thin arms are vises around my neck. My girl is fuckin' devouring me, and I'm consuming her right back. Three months—no, scratch that, over a fuckin' *year* of pent-up longing is released in this kiss. I'll kiss her forever if that's what she wants. God knows I'll never get tired of it.

Around us, there's even a smattering of applause—our joy is infectious. And that's the thing about New Yorkers—they might be grouchy as fuck sometimes, but when it comes down to it, they're also real. And when they see joy that's honest, authentic, as deep as what Layla and I feel for each other, no one in my city would be anything but happy for us.

Fuck me, we really can't stop kissing each other. We need to find a room, an empty closet, fuck, even a bathroom somewhere. But I know I can wait. Right now, in this moment, I might be happier than I've ever been in my life, and if the look on Layla's face is any indication, she feels the same way.

"All right," I tell her as I take her hand. "Where's your bag? We need to get out of here. I need to get you home."

Layla lays her head on my shoulder. Even just that simple touch sends tremors of happiness through my chest.

"What do you mean?" she asks with another bright smile. "I am home. I'm with you."

Her tongue dips around mine again as her legs. I groan as I squeeze her ass, which I've been dreaming about all summer. I've While I waited for her to heal after the year from fuckin' hell she had last year. While we talked on the phone so long I thought I was going to burn my ear off. While we breathed, hot and heavy, late at night, listening to each other lose control from three thousand miles away. Just the memories of that make me feel like I'm about to lose control now. I need to get my girl alone, like *yesterday*.

"Layla?"

Her lips break from mine, and I growl. I actually growl, like I'm a dog, and someone is trying to take away my bone. Or, you know, boner. Same difference right about now.

"Who the fuck is that?" I ask, seeking her mouth all over again.

But she's done for now. Layla sighs, rolls her big blue eyes, and drops her feet to the ground. She tries to step away, but I'm not having it. So she tugs on a handful of her dark hair, which, if I'm not mistaken, looks even shinier than it was before. Her pale skin is just a little sun kissed. Damn. Three months of enjoying the California sun has done my baby *good*.

"Surprise," she says weakly. "Nico, this is my mother, Cheryl."

Her...mother?

My hands fly off Layla's ass like I'm touching a hot plate. Shit. *Shit*. This wasn't the impression I was looking to make when I met her parents for the first time. I already know I'm not really the type of guy they probably want to see her with. Older, tatted up, and with a record to boot. I'm a long shot from the kind of guy they want in family pictures. Her father's a doctor, for fuck's sake, and I've seen her grandparents' mansion in Pasadena. Not exactly the one-bedroom apartment I grew up in, shared between me, my mom, and three other kids.

But Layla doesn't see any of that. She doesn't care about where I come from; she never did. And she's the only one whose opinion I give a shit about anyway.

So I straighten up and turn to her mother, glad that my skin color hides my flush.

"Hi, Mrs. Barros, how you doin'? It's nice to finally meet you."

"Cheryl, please."

I tip the brim of my Yankees hat. I feel like an idiot when I do it. Who the fuck am I, an old timey cowboy? John fuckin' Wayne? Should I just go all out and say "Howdy, ma'am?" Have a little hoedown in the middle of JFK arrivals?

Layla giggles, like she can sense what I'm thinking. And she probably can, too. She knows me better than anybody. I roll my eyes, but I have to grin. Whatever. It's polite, right?

But then my smile falls when I catch the look on Cheryl's face. A dark-blonde brow arches over one of her bright blue eyes—the same eyes she shares with her daughter. She's imperious. And currently very suspicious.

You wouldn't know that Cheryl and Layla are related unless they told you. I've never met her dad, but Layla probably has the coloring of her Brazilian father: dark-brown, almost black hair, deep-set eyes that get circles when she's tired, full pink lips that I would like to go back to sucking on, thank you very fuckin' much. But Cheryl Barros definitely gave her daughter those eyes the color of a bluebird sky, sharp as a kitchen knife. And right now, I've got two pairs of them zeroed in on me.

Bam. Gutted. Just like that.

"You must be Nico," she says evenly.

She says it like she knows me. And to be fair, she probably does. Cheryl and I have only spoken once, but it was one of the most intense conversations I've ever had. Imagine calling your girl's mom for the first time, and you tell her that her daughter is basically in pieces—not because you did anything, but because you found her that way. After I moved to LA for a year and her dad left her and Cheryl for Brazil, Layla spiraled all last year. In her vulnerability, she was taken advantage of by the worst possible person. Giancarlo—*fuck*, I don't even like thinking that piece of shit's name, let alone saying it—was a monster if I ever met one, the kind of dude who cuts a woman down to make himself feel stronger. The kind of guy who takes his anger out on her face in the end.

A pang of guilt shoots through me. I'll never forgive myself for what happened, knowing that if I had just stayed in New York, Layla wouldn't have gotten wrapped up with that abusive motherfucker. It's a memory I'll never shake: Layla crushed under a much larger man, with blood all over both of them while he used her beautiful face like a punching bag. If I hadn't gotten there when I did…

I shudder, same way I do whenever the memory reappears. No. I'm not going to go there. Returning to that day is the quickest way to bring me to The Dark Place, as I've come to know it. The place where harder Nico lives, a Nico who knows himself for the asshole he can really be, the Nico I've been working really fuckin' hard to keep buried for the last several years.

Layla gives a hopeful smile. Her face shines with that light that only my girl has. It lightens me too.

Not today, asshole, I tell myself. Maybe not ever again.

Cheryl holds out her hand, palm down, like she's expecting me to kiss it or something. Should I? I start to lean down, but end up standing up straight. Going from John Wayne to Prince Charming is a little much, don't you think? Instead, I shake it a little, accepting her light squeeze before she pulls away, looking like she wants hands sanitizer.

Okay, yeah. My hands aren't exactly clean. Thirty minutes ago, I was doing pushups on concrete with a hundred other FDNY cadets, and there are still smudges of dirt on my palms. Well, sorry, lady. I wasn't planning on touching anyone else but your daughter, and I'm pretty sure *she* doesn't mind if I came straight for her instead of washing up first.

"Mom's here to help me find an apartment," Layla says as she takes my hand. See? I knew she wouldn't care about the dirt.

I turn to her. "You're not living at the dorms this year?"

For whatever reason, Layla and I haven't spoken much about her living situation. We talked every day this summer, when we could get the spare moments to do it. But we've both been crazy busy. I'm at the academy five days a week, usually from sunup to sundown, and then I've been doing security again at AJ's, the nightclub where I used to work. The extra cash helps supplement the shitty probationary salary I get as a new recruit with the FDNY. Layla took a couple more language classes to keep up her Spanish and Portuguese requirements for her degree, and I know she's been working a lot at a local women's services center too. So when we did talk, it wasn't about monotonous shit like apartment hunting or bills. It was usually what we did that day for a few brief moments before we both fell asleep. Just enough time to reassure her that I was still here, waiting for the day she was coming back.

I didn't really think about what would happen when she did.

Layla shakes her head. "Jamie and Quinn are still rooming together, so Shama and I decided to find a place off campus..."

She drifts off, but I know where she's going. Up until the end of last year, Quinn was Layla's best friend, her roommate through the first three years of college. But their friendship was tested when Layla's life fell apart, and Quinn couldn't handle it. Bitch. Layla's better off without her.

"Okay," I say. "So we need to find you an apartment. You know, you could just stay with me—"

I can't quite cut myself off in time before I realize what I'm saying. While I'd like nothing more than to wake up and fall asleep with Layla right next to me every day— I probably like that idea *too* much, if we're being honest—all I have to offer is a pullout couch in the living room of a crowded apartment uptown. My old place is currently occupied by me, my brother Gabe, my sister Maggie, and her daughter. I'm on the couch until the academy's done and I can even start to think about finding a new place of my own. What kind of offer is that?

I frown to myself. It's just another reminder of how little I actually have to offer someone like Layla. She says she doesn't care, but I do wonder every now and then if she really knows what that means.

"Do you have a car?" Cheryl interrupts my brooding before Layla can respond. "Or do we need a taxi? We have an appointment with a realtor at six, and we need to drop Layla's bags at the hotel."

Her toe taps on the linoleum floor so loudly I can hear it over the crowd.

"Ah, no," I admit, feeling suddenly weird about it even though most people in New York don't have cars. "We'll have to get a cab."

"All right." Cheryl looks me up and down. She's dressed casually in short white pants and a striped shirt, but the woman has a presence that would intimidate my sergeant. I don't know why Layla ever described her mother as meek. This lady is anything but. "I suppose we can drop you in the city on your way home."

"Mom," Layla starts, but I cut in anyway.

"That's all right, Mrs. Barros," I say. "I'm happy to help out. You'll need a local anyway to make sure you don't get scammed by the brokers."

I wink, even though I don't really know what the fuck I'm talking about. I've only had one apartment here in New York, and it was a rent-controlled lease passed to me from K.C.'s cousin. I don't know the first thing about hunting for an apartment in the city, even though I'm about to learn myself. But right now, there isn't a thing that could stop me from being by Layla's side. Definitely not a little white lie.

Cheryl opens her mouth, surprised, then closes it again. If I'm not mistaken, there's a little quirk of lips before she looks away.

"Well, let's go," she says and turns abruptly toward baggage claim.

I pick up Layla's carry-on and heave it over my shoulder, then sling my other arm around her waist so I can sneak another kiss. She stops walking and returns it, with a lot more tongue than I was initially planning, but hey, I'm not going to argue. Fuck me, she tastes good. Like vanilla and some kind of fruit and maybe some kind of soda she was drinking on the plane. But mostly she just tastes like Layla. She tastes like home.

"Damn," I whisper when we break again. We have *got* to find a room.

"Yeah," Layla whispers, keeping her nose to mine.

It's still there: that magnetic pull that always made us feel like we couldn't get close enough. Fuck the fact that we're in the middle of an airport. Fuck the fact that her mother is ten feet away, watching me carefully. I'd take Layla right here if she said the word. I'd take her for the rest of my life.

"Come on," Layla says, finally stepping away and tugging me forward. "She's right. We do need to get going."

I just nod and follow her through the crowd. But I don't let go of her hand. Not now. Not ever.

CHAPTER TWO

Layla

N<small>ICO WAITS IN THE HOTEL LOBBY WHILE</small> M<small>OM AND</small> I <small>CHECK INTO OUR ROOM AND CHANGE.</small> He looked like it was physically painful to stay behind, and I get it. Those brief kisses in the airport were *not* enough. Not even close. I'd been waiting for that moment all summer, and the complete and utter rightness of being in his arms again was enough to banish the shadows I've been fighting for the last year. It was enough to make me feel unafraid for the first time in so, so long.

At least for a moment.

I run a brush through my hair, checking my face still for bruises. It's a habit, considering it took nearly a month for all of the damage Giancarlo inflicted to disappear. Three months ago, Nico yanked my ex-boyfriend off me, but only after I'd been kidnapped and viciously assaulted. It took me weeks to walk without a limp from my sprained ankle. I had stitches in my eyebrow for two, and a thin white line still runs through my brow line. Mom wanted to have a surgeon clean it up, but I told her no. I'm not sure I ever want to forget what happened completely. I want to keep it as a reminder. Of what, I'm not sure. But I'll figure it out at some point.

I blink in the mirror, and for a second, I see his face. Not Nico's. Giancarlo's. Long, lean, with deep shadows under his dark eyes and a mop of thick black hair. The Wayfarer glasses that were cracked by Nico's fists before I was carried out of that room. The complete and utter hatred seething through his pain.

It's a face that still haunts me, that wakes me up at night. I grip the edge of the counter, wondering again why I chose to return to the city where my attacker still roams free. His trial isn't for a few more weeks, and though I won't have to stand as a witness, I know that my statement will be read aloud. Nico thinks they'll ask for a plea bargain, but he's hoping for maximum penalty. I just want it to be over. I just want to move on. But if he's acquitted, I'm not sure I can.

"Layla? Are you ready?"

Mom pokes her head into the bathroom and checks me over. It's a look I've been getting since she helped me off the plane, when it finally registered what kind of hell her daughter had been dealing with all year. She had gotten medical privileges to meet me at the gate, like I was an unaccompanied minor. They wheeled me off the plane in a wheelchair, even though I could actually walk, and when she saw me that first time, I genuinely thought my mother was going to pass out.

She's calm now, but flashes of fear and shock still cross her face every so often. She hasn't said anything because I was so adamant, but I think she's as nervous about me coming back here as I am. There were hints all summer, mild suggestions that I might want to stay in Pasadena, maybe even transfer to UCLA to finish my degree. It's why she insisted on coming with me to find an apartment this time. It's why, I suspect, she won't leave until she knows for sure when I'm returning to Pasadena.

But I had to come back. I don't want to be the kind of person who runs away when things are scary or hard. And, like my therapist says, facing your demons is as important as understanding them. New York feels like a city full of demons to me right now, but it didn't always. For a short period of time, it felt like home, more than the house I grew up in. Maybe it can feel that way again.

Plus, there's him. Nico. If the events of last year forced me to confront the reasons why I would allow myself to be abused in the first place, they also forced me to realize the other truth in my life: that Nico is where I belong. It was his deep voice that spurred me on this summer, whispering sweet statements of faith and sex and longing and love. He believes in me when I'm not sure I can. He assures me, again and again, that I'm stronger than I feel.

If you had asked me two years ago if I believed in soul mates, I would have said no. But here is a person toward whom, from the start, every cell in my body seemed drawn. I just don't make sense without him. And I don't want to, either.

The thought reins in my fears. He's here. I'm here. Together, we can move forward.

"Yep," I call out. "I'm ready."

————

NICO'S SITTING in a chair in the lobby when we arrive, chatting up a little kid who spotted the big FDNY letters displayed across his broad chest. I used to think he looked hot in his FedEx uniform, but that thing had *nothing* on the FDNY gear. The plain navy t-shirt hugs his biceps in a way that should be illegal, and it was really hard not to stare at his ass pretty much the entire time he was leading us to the taxi line at JFK.

The thing is, he's completely unaware of the effect he has on people. He takes off his hat and sets in on the kid's head, making him giggle, and Nico laughs right along with him. His smile lights up the room, but he's oblivious to at least five women, including the kid's mother, and likely a few men who are outright ogling him. I don't even blame them. The man is impossibly gorgeous.

"See you, buddy," he says, clapping a hand on the kid's head as Mom and I approach. He stands up, all smiles for me while he fixes his hat. "So, where are we headed?"

My mother looks him up and down. She isn't a talker—while my dad was full of lectures and opinions, Mom always sat next to him, watching. Her eyes are the quickest things about her. Her expression is veiled, but I can see hints of appreciation there. Great. My mom thinks Nico is hot too.

"The office is in…" She pulls a printed email out of her Coach bag. "Murray Hill." She looks up. "Where is that?"

Nico takes the paper and glances at the address. "Oh, that's only about ten blocks from here, Mrs. Barros. We could walk, unless…" He sneaks a look at her shoes, pristine white pumps that aren't exactly made for the grimy August humidity. New York in the summer is gross. "Come on," he says with a grin. "I'll get us another cab."

———

Nico

It's a little awkward walking around with Layla and her mom from apartment to apartment for the next two hours, but after the first, Cheryl seems to figure out that I'm here for good. I'll give her credit. She's not treating me like a piece of furniture or a derelict the way most women like her—rich and white, I mean—would usually treat someone who looks like me, to the point where I kind of feel bad for assuming she would. But she's also a little wary. I catch her giving me the eye up and down a few times, sometimes resting her gaze on the tattoos that snake around my right arm. I can't really help the way I look. I can't help my dark skin, the tattoos, or the fact that to women like her, I look dangerous.

But Cheryl and I share something more important than appearances: Layla. And again, I remind myself, her opinion is the only one that matters.

"Oh, Mom!" Layla murmurs as we walk into the final apartment of the night.

The places that we've looked at have varied. One was a crazy nice place in Murray Hill, complete with a doorman, which Cheryl clearly liked, but the price was way too high. Honestly, my jaw dropped when I heard it, and I've lived in this city my whole life. If this is what I'm up against when I look for a place in a few months, I'll be sleeping on a pullout for the rest of my life.

The others have all had different problems. One was above a nightclub, which Cheryl and I both vetoed before we even went upstairs. No fuckin' way am I having Layla live above a bunch of drunk assholes who would just as soon follow her as flirt with her, and Cheryl seemed to agree completely, even though Layla liked the neighborhood. Another was in a decent building, but was about the size of a drainpipe. My shoulders literally touched both sides of the hallway.

This one isn't perfect either, but it's easily the best we've seen. Down where Chinatown, the Lower East Side, and Little Italy all meet, it's in a newly renovated walk-up that looks over Delancey Park, which, as far as I can tell, isn't one of those parks you'd spend a lot of time in, but also doesn't seem to be a magnet for junkies either.

The apartment itself is on the top floor of the six-story building. The top two floors are the only ones that are available yet, and the owners are eager to get them rented to subsidize the construction going on below. Cheryl sniffs her nose at the term "construction," and Layla rolls her eyes and nudges her. I'm more interested in looking around the actual apartment.

It's nice. A lot nicer than any place I've ever lived, although that's not saying much. Two big bedrooms look over the rooftops of Chinatown. A kitchenette next to a pretty big living room, with new fixtures in the kitchen and the bathroom.

Layla wanders into one of the bedrooms, and I follow to find her at the window, looking over the rooftops of Chinatown. Maybe ten blocks away, I think I see the top of her old dorm, the one where she was living when I first met her. A final few rays of sun are setting through the buildings, lighting up her face. The room has great light. I could sketch Layla in here for hours. Laid across a big white bed. Preferably naked, and giving me that look she does when she's about to go down—

"How much?" Cheryl's voice echoes as she and the realtor follow us into the room.

I turn toward the windows to hide the, ah, *evidence* of my imagination. Shit, I really need to get my girl alone before I embarrass myself completely.

"They're asking nineteen hundred a month," says the realtor, a kid who looks like he should be in a punk band, not showing apartments. Everyone needs to make a living, right? "But I think we could negotiate down to eighteen, maybe even seventeen-fifty. They really need to rent the available units."

I raise an eyebrow, and so does Cheryl. We've seen enough today to know that's a damn good price for an apartment like this.

"Dude," I say. "Why didn't you just bring us here first?"

The realtor shrugs. "Honestly, I didn't know it would be available until about thirty minutes ago. They literally just posted it. You're the first ones to see it."

Cheryl examines the space appreciatively, checking things like the tile in the kitchen and the molding around the doors. The rooms are big, with ceilings that are about three feet taller than the average apartment in New York. Layla's not going to find better than this, not anywhere. I'm not going to lie. I'm a little jealous.

Cheryl turns to her daughter. "What about a roommate?"

"Shama's coming tomorrow."

Layla turns to me and smiles. Even if I sort of wish I was the one who got to stay with her, I'm glad she's still rooming with Shama, one of the few people who really stood by her last year. Out of all her friends, Shama's the one I like best.

"She didn't want to help find the place?" I wonder.

Layla shrugs. "She said it was fine if it was just my name on the lease. I'll send her some pictures before we sign anything. But…" She trails off, looking around the bedroom appreciatively. "I don't think we'll find anything better than this, do you?"

"Do you?" Cheryl's voice repeats, and she looks straight at me.

It's a direct look, one without any judgment. She just wants my opinion. She trusts me. It's scary, but it also feels kind of good.

I clear my throat. "I agree. This place is a steal for an apartment without rent control."

Cheryl nods. "Still, the building isn't secure. What do you know about the neighborhood?"

Again, she's asking *me* this question, not her daughter or the realtor. I straighten up a little and look her in the eye.

"Mom," Layla says. "I used to live maybe ten blocks from here. Remember my dorm sophomore year? That was in Chinatown too. I was fine."

Cheryl says nothing, just waits for my answer.

"I'm not going to lie," I say. "You walk about five or ten blocks east of here, you might end up in a place you wouldn't want to be at night alone. But honestly, that's everywhere in this city. And Layla's smart. This is a well-lit street, and Delancey Park is safe. She'll be all right."

I want to add that I'll keep her safe, but I feel like that might be overkill. Still, Cheryl seems to get the message.

"Okay," she says, turning back to her daughter. "This is where you want to be?"

Layla gazes at me, her blue eyes full of promise. *Shit*, I really need to get her alone.

"Let's get things started. We can sign the lease tomorrow, if you want," Cheryl tells the realtor, who immediately flips open his cell phone and starts tapping away. "Is there anywhere around here to eat that won't make us sick?"

Laya snorts. "Mom, this is New York, not New Delhi. There are a ton of good Chinese and Italian places within walking distance." She turns to me. "You're coming, right?"

I grin. "Wild horses couldn't stop me, baby."

———

WE MAKE IT THROUGH DINNER, an overpriced meal of pasta and salad at one of those places in Little Italy where the tourists like to go. Cheryl chose it because it seemed "authentic" to her, and I didn't have the heart to tell her that most of the servers are probably Latino, not Italian. She seemed to enjoy the fact that they were all dressed like penguins and served our dinners on white linen tablecloths.

Afterward, Cheryl decides that she wants to go have a nightcap somewhere with her daughter, and gives me a knowing look that says "get lost" in the nicest possible way. With some regret and a lot of guilty thanks after Cheryl pays the tab in full, I have to say goodbye. It's almost eleven o'clock, and I have to be at the academy early in the morning, which means an even earlier wake up to get the train on time.

"Thanks again for dinner, Cheryl," I say as I stand up from the table. I drop a quick kiss on Layla's cheek. "I'll call you tomorrow, sweetie."

It's late, but Mulberry Street is still crowded, full of tourists out and about during the last few weeks of summer. Green, white, and red lights are strung between the fire escapes, casting a romantic glow down the alleys, while occasionally you can hear a cheesy violin or accordion filter out from one of the restaurants. It's dumb, but as I walk by couples finishing up their meals on the sidewalk tables, I'm irritated I had to leave. This is just the kind of place I wouldn't mind walking around with Layla. Where I could kiss her on the corner under these lights, like I did on our first date. Sweep her into a dark alley and let her know how much I missed her.

I'm still fighting the disappointment when my name echoes off the old brick buildings.

"Nico!"

I turn to find Layla barreling through the crowded sidewalk toward me.

"Hey," I say. "Everything okay?"

"Yeah," she says, breathing hard. Her face is flushed. "You just forgot something."

I frown, patting my back pocket for my wallet. "What's that?"

Layla grins. "This."

Then she kisses me. It shouldn't surprise, the way she's willing to do that in the middle of a crowded street, where everyone can see her. Layla has never been shy about showing how she feels. It's one of my favorite things about her.

So of course, I kiss her right back, wrapping my hands around her waist and lifting her into my chest. I tease her mouth open to taste her, taste the remnants of coffee and tiramisu still lingering on her tongue. Fuck *me*, she's so sweet. Somehow, I have a feeling that waiting for her mom to fly back to Pasadena is going to be harder than waiting an entire summer. Things go from zero to sixty in about two fuckin' seconds with this girl. They always did.

"Fuck," I breathe as she breaks away. I steal another kiss, then another until she giggles, and I set her down. "I missed you so goddamn much, you know that?"

Her eyes flutter shut. "I missed you too."

She leans her head on my shoulder and hugs me tight. There's still desire there. I can feel it in the way she presses her entire body into mine, including the part that's missed her in an entirely different way this summer. Then she sighs, full and long. I know the feeling. I don't ever want to let her go.

"She leaves the day after tomorrow," Layla whispers in my ear. She leans back to look at me. "Do you have to work tomorrow night?"

"No." The answer is knee-jerk. And also wrong. "Wait. Yes. Coño, I have a shift at AJ's tomorrow night." I rub my nose to hers. "I'm sorry, baby. I thought we'd, you know, have tonight..."

"It's okay." She kisses me again, this time more softly, sweetly, sucking lightly on my bottom lip before releasing it. "Maybe I'll have to come pay you a visit at work." She bites her lip. "I mean, if you don't mind. Crap, I didn't mean to assume—"

I cover her mouth with one more kiss, shuttering her doubt. I want more, but I'll take whatever I can get. After all, now we have all the time in the world.

"Baby, you don't *ever* have to ask to hang out with me," I tell her.

I'm rewarded with another sweet smile.

"Okay," she says. "Then I'll see you tomorrow night."

CHAPTER THREE

Layla

"Isn't that what they say?" I asked. "That we all fall in love with our parents?"

Through smudged glasses and under a hat that never seems to stay on straight, Dr. Parker, my therapist, watched me kindly.

"Well, it's a very Freudian way to think about relationships," she replied. "Or have you been reading too much Sophocles in your classes?"

I shrugged. Oedipus Rex was required reading for most college students at some point. I wasn't sure a parable about marrying your mother and killing your father applied here, but I knew the origins of Freud's theory.

"I don't think it's as simple as that," continued Dr. Parker. "Do you think you were trying to replace your father with Giancarlo, Layla?"

It got right to the heart of the issue. The idea was grotesque. Who tries to replace a family member with a lover? Ew. But when she said Giancarlo's name, it hurt. I saw his stern look, the one that was half-terrifying, half-erotic. Sometimes, when he would pin me down to the bed, controlling every part of me so I couldn't move, I was shocked by how much I liked it. By how strangely…familiar it felt to be controlled that way.

Until the last time, when he did it to hurt.

Or maybe it hurt the whole time. I never could tell.

"No," I said too quickly. Suddenly it was hard to speak. My chest felt like it was bound in cement. I couldn't breathe.

"Close your eyes. Inhale deeply. Focus on where you are now. The room. My voice. The here and now, Layla. The here and now."

It wa a routine Dr. Parker came up with about two weeks after I started seeing her, when she diagnosed me not just as a trauma victim, but also with mild post-traumatic stress disorder. It was common, she said, for women coming out of abusive relationships to experience some measure of PTSD. Flashbacks. Shortness of breath. Dizziness. Those, she said, were my symptoms. We were working on learning my triggers.

"Say it out loud," she urged gently.

"The here and now," I whispered. I didn't shut my eyes. Instead, I opened them wider, trying to let the light of the room banish the darkness that threatened.

"He's gone, Layla," hummed Dr. Parker. "He can't hurt you anymore."

"But he's not gone." Those are the words I could finally muster when my breath started to return. "He's not."

———

"LAYLA?"

My name interrupts the memory, and I blink at my reflection in the mirror. The dark circles that have been stamped under my eyes since last fall are still there, but they are slowly starting to fade a bit more.

I run the water in the pristine new sink and splash a bit on my face. It's been a long day. After signing the lease this morning, Mom and I went to get my stuff out of storage, and then spent the rest of the day getting the other furniture I'll need. Shama and I can figure out the main room when she gets here, so we just bought a bed and a desk, along with the necessary sheets and basics that I'll need, along with a few things for the kitchen. I'm actually really thankful she came—my mom knows a hell of a lot more about setting up a new house than I do.

But now it's done. The living room is still completely empty, but I am the proud owner of an entire taxi cab full of linens and kitchenware from Bed, Bath, and Beyond, plus a brand-new double mattress set and a plain oak desk and chair.

"It's late. I'm going back to the hotel to pack," Mom says as I exit the bathroom. "Are you sure you wouldn't rather just stay at the suite with me? You'll have the rest of the year to sleep here."

I shake my head. "You have to leave at four a.m. to catch your flight home. I'm good."

Mom looks at her tasteful white-gold watch and tucks a nonexistent flyaway back into place. "Hmmm. Yes. I suppose."

Then she looks up, and her blue eyes, the same bright shade as mine, float over me, in that same way they always do. Checking to make sure everything is there. Nothing's broken. Nothing's out of place.

"Maybe I should stay until your roommate gets here." Mom taps a nail on the wall. "Maybe this is too soon. I don't like you being alone."

I sigh. I'm so tired of being looked at this way. It's been three months of this, of her and my grandparents treating me with kid gloves, walking around me on eggshells. It's almost like they thought I beat myself up last spring, like if they left me alone, they'd come back to find me bruised and bloodied all over again. Ever since Dr. Parker mentioned the letters PTSD, everyone has treated me like a basket case. Everyone except Nico, who doesn't know.

Things like that don't happen in her family. In Pasadena, abuse is done nice and neat, behind closed, carved-wood doors and the pretty white stucco walls. It's done with cutting words, neglect, and bank accounts, not knives and fists. But abuse is abuse. And I think my mother took her fair share for years.

"I'll be fine, Mom."

I cross the room and give her a hug. Her thin form is stiff in my arms. We've never been a touchy-feely family. But eventually her hands clasp my waist, and she squeezes tightly before letting go.

"What about your prescription? Do you have enough?"

I cringe. There's an orange bottle of pills sitting in a drawer of my new desk—a low dose of Valium that I'm supposed to take in the event of a trigger. I don't like them. They push away the shadows, but they veil the rest of the world too. Somehow, I don't think I'm going to find my way back to my old self when I'm on a bunch of mood stabilizers.

"There's plenty," I assure her. "I'll be *fine*."

"That boy…"

At that, I look up. Mom hasn't said much about Nico since we've been here. She watched us, carefully, when he accompanied us from apartment to apartment the night before. She listened and laughed at his jokes, but always focused sharply whenever he brushed my arm, held my waist, snuck a few kisses. I think she was relieved that he had to spend the day at the academy today before going straight to his weekend job.

"The way he looks at you…Layla, he's very in love with you."

I frown. She says it like it's a bad thing.

"Well…I'm in love with him." I don't know why it makes me so nervous to say it out loud. It's the truth.

She cocks her head and worries her lower lip. "Yes. I see that too."

I know what she's thinking. That the connection between Nico and me is too much, too soon after everything I went through. That if I was smart, I would take more time away from him or any relationship. That I wouldn't jump into anything too quickly.

Too bad that's not an option. Not with him. Not now, not ever.

"Mom, you don't have to worry about Nico." I clasp my arms around my waist. "He'll take care of me."

I wish that were true. On some level, I believe it. But another part of me, the scared, anxious part, can't contain its echo: *he sent you away.*

But that was after he saved you, I tell myself. Before he flew across the country to rescue you. He sent you back to your parents so you could be together again, the right way. So you could pull yourself back together.

Still…I'm not the same person I was when we met, or even when he put me back on that plane last May. He loved me then. Will he love me now?

I shake the question away. "I'll be fine."

Mom purses her lips, like she doesn't quite believe me.

"Mom?"

She blinks, like she thinks I've changed my mind. I haven't, but I do have one question that's been bothering me for a long time. It's taken me all summer long to ask the question my therapist and I bandied back and forth again and again. How did I learn to be loved this way?

"Did Dad…did he ever hurt you?" I ask.

Mom pauses and takes a long time to examine the grooves of one of the door-frames. When she looks up, her blue eyes, the ones that are so like mine, are serious and wide.

"Not like you're asking," she says. "But in small ways, yes."

I don't need to ask what she means by that. I know my father. I know what kind of a demanding, overbearing, unforgiving bear he can be.

"You never really forget," she says quietly. "And you shouldn't. Because if you forget, then it might happen again."

I narrow my eyes. I don't like what she's insinuating. The only person in my life who could "do it again" is the same man who saved me. That's not fair to him at all.

"Okay." Mom looks me over one more time and nods. "I'll call you when I land."

"Fly safe."

With one last lingering look, she leaves, and I'm alone in my new apartment, with no one here to pull me out of my daydreams. Memories. Nightmares.

I didn't want to tell her how scared I really am to be here again. How the corners of the city, painted gray with time and people, felt all day today like they were hiding the face that's been tormenting me all summer. He could be anywhere.

I wander back into my bedroom and sit down on the mattress. I pull out my phone, thumbing the keypad. Nico and I talked every day this summer. Mostly at night, when he was off from the academy. He didn't know why I had a tendency to call him at twelve at night or even later. How I'd wake up in the middle of the night shaking, and the only thing that could calm me down was the deep burr of Nico's baritone, even lower when he'd been sleeping. But it would hum me back to a calm place while he sleepily told me about his day, told me to be good. Told me he loved me.

He never cared that I would wake him up in the middle of the night. Never asked why. He was only ever happy to hear my voice and fall back asleep on the phone with me. He doesn't know yet that his voice is the only thing that really keeps those nightmares away.

Almost as if on cue, the screen lights up with his name. I smile. At least this time, I don't have to call him.

"Hey," I answer. "I was just thinking about you."

"Good things?"

I grin into the new mirror propped against the wall. "Of course."

"Naughty things?"

My face practically splits, but I can't quite answer. Nico laughs, like he knows my face is bright red. I don't know why. It's not like we haven't had *much* dirtier conversations this summer.

"I just wanted to make sure you were coming up to the club tonight," he says. "I need to see you."

I can't stop smiling. My cheeks are starting to hurt.

"Is your mom there?"

"No," I answer. "She went back to the hotel to pack."

"So…she's not staying at your place tonight?"

I glance around the empty room. "No…"

"So, does that mean I can?"

I freeze. For a split-second, there's a war within me, one I quickly quash. How could there even be doubt about that? This is what we've been waiting for since spring.

"Of course," I say quickly. Maybe too quickly.

"And, baby?"

"Yeah?"

"I'm not saying you have to or anything…but if you *did* want to come up to AJ's tonight, I wouldn't mind seeing you in something short. And tight."

I bite my lip. Again with that weird freeze. I don't know what's wrong with me. I used to love it when Nico talked about me like this. I can easily imagine the look on his face when I walk up in one of the tiny dresses I used to wear at nightclubs. The way his full mouth will drop as his gaze sears over every curve I have. It's a look of pure, unadulterated desire. Like there is no one in the world he sees but me.

"I'll, um…I'll see what I can do."

There's a chuckle. "Okay. See you later, beautiful."

The phone hangs up before I can reply—before Nico can hear the doubt in my voice. I push away that cold feeling and focus on the night ahead as I unzip my suitcase and start pulling out clothes to change into. But one thing is bugging me. Outside, it's dark. The shadows are long beyond the telephone poles. And beyond the safety of this room, people lurk. A person, maybe, lurks.

I pick up my phone and dial the first safe person who comes to mind. Vinny, my old friend from freshman year, picks up the phone.

"Whaddya know?" he crows. "Barros is back from the dead! What the fuck is *up*, yo!"

I snort. We didn't really hang out much last year because we were in totally different dorms, but Vinny, a business student who was always determined to sound as bro-y as possible, seems like he's the same as ever.

"I'm back," I say. "Just finished moving into my new place over in Chinatown."

"No shit," Vinny says. "I'm at Lafayette again, if you can believe that. But I got one of the senior singles. Dude, it's *sweet*. I'm going to get so much ass this year."

I grin. Vinny talks like a douchebag, but he's totally harmless. I can't really see him using his single room as anything other than a gaming area. "Awesome, Vin. Let me know how it goes."

Lafayette was our dorm sophomore year, where I used to live with Jamie, Shama, and Quinn, my former best friend. The thought makes me ache a little. We had fun in that dorm. It was a good year.

"So I heard about what happened last year…" Vinny drifts off, waiting for an opening.

With one finger, I press a circle into my comforter. "Oh, yeah."

"Jamie mentioned it when I saw her at the student union yesterday."

My shoulders drop with relief. Jamie wouldn't tell much, and she wouldn't make me sound atrocious.

"Damn, Lay. I wish I was around. I coulda beat that dude's face in a long time before then. You guys always looked out for me."

I smirk. Chasing away the silly girls Vinny likes wasn't exactly a hardship. Those girls had voices like Disney characters and were ridiculous.

But what hurts more is the fact that I'm calling Vinny right now instead of Quinn or Jamie. Even though Jamie came with Shama and Nico to help me last May, she's barely said a word to me all summer. It was like she saw what was really happening to me and just couldn't handle it. Quinn and I totally parted ways when I left last spring. After the way she treated me, there's no love lost there. Best friends don't stand aside when their friend is in trouble. They don't scold and hate on them when they need to be held the most. I'm better off without her, as Nico frequently tells me.

But, I realize, it's going to be a little lonely without a posse. Starting over might be harder than I thought.

"So hey," I say, "I'm supposed to be meeting Nico—"

"Nico? FedEx guy? You back with him?"

I sigh. I'm going to be hearing that a lot, and I know Nico doesn't like it.

"Well, he's a firefighter now," I correct Vinny, enjoying the little thrill I feel when I say that out loud. I'm so proud of Nico for what he's doing. Not to mention he looks insanely hot in his uniform. "He graduates from the academy in a few more weeks. But yeah, we're back together. He's, um…he still works the door at AJ's on the weekends. Any chance you want to go up there tonight? I could be your wingman…"

"Are you kidding? I've been trying to get into AJ's for months! They *never* let dudes in!"

"Well, good," I say with a grin as I pull one of my shortest dresses out of my suitcase with renewed enthusiasm. "Then it's a date. Here, I'll give you my address."

CHAPTER FOUR

Nico

"Sorry, ladies. You'll have to go elsewhere tonight."

The three girls in front of me stick out their lips, looking even more like the children they are. I doubt they're even eighteen, let alone twenty-one. How their parents let them out of the house looking like two-bit prostitutes almost makes me feel sorry for them, but not sorry enough to let them into the club.

The taller one, who's wearing the tightest jeans I have ever seen and earrings so big they would give my sister Selena a run for her money, cocks her head and extends a finger to run up and down my shoulder. I glare at it. It's hot tonight. We're in the thick of late summer in New York, and the city smells like sweat, hot garbage, and alcohol.

"Come on, handsome," says Earrings. "I bet we could make it worth your while."

She leans in so I can smell the gallon of perfume she's wearing. I cough.

"We come as a package deal, you know," she purrs. "And my friend's parent' have an empty penthouse on Fifth."

Ah, so that's what's going on. Rich Mommy and Daddy are probably at the Hamptons for the weekend, just like all the other rich people in the city, leaving their very underage daughters to play house for the weekend. I stare at the hand on my shoulder until she removes it, looking slightly scared.

"Look…*Wanda*." I flip her shitty ID back at her. "We don't let kids in here. And word to the wise, asking strange men to your apartment is gonna get you into trouble. Go home before I call the cops, and they call your parents for you."

The girl's lip trembles, and her friends, both of them wearing so much makeup they look like sad, underage clowns, stare at the concrete. For a split-second, I almost let them in, thinking that maybe it's better if I keep them here. Then at least I could keep an eye on them. Make sure they don't go home with anyone they shouldn't.

Shit. I'm not these girls' dad. The last thing I want to be doing is babysitting, especially when my girl is going to be here any second. Then I have an idea.

"Tell you what, lemme see your IDs again, sweetheart," I say. "Maybe I was wrong."

I almost feel bad about the hopeful looks on their faces when I collect the plastic cards. Even if the pictures hadn't been grainy as fuck, their flimsy weights would have told me they were fakes. Wanda, Josephina, and Marilyn. Jesus, these are the worst fake names I've ever seen. They probably spent good money on these too. Poor kids.

I pretend to examine them closely while I fish a pair of scissors out of my pocket. And then, before they can stop me, I slice them in half, then hand them back the broken pieces.

"Hey!" "Wanda" cries out, holding the broken pieces while her friends look on in horror. "What the hell!"

"You'll thank me in about five years," I say. "Now go home, before I really do call the cops."

With a few more cries of protest, the girls finally leave, with nothing more to do. I know that most likely, they'll just buy new IDs. Maybe this week, maybe next month. But at least tonight they won't be going anywhere that sixteen-year-olds have no business going. I swear to God, the day I check my last ID will be the last time I ever set foot in a nightclub again. Ten years of my life I've spent working in these shitholes.

And now. Maybe a year. Maybe less. Once I'm off a probate's salary and making a regular income from the fire department, I won't have to do this shit. Any. More.

I settle back on my stool and run a hand through my hair. It's too long, the tight curls getting a little bushy on top, which means more shit I have to comb through it to get it to behave in this humidity. Normally I keep it short, but the memory of Layla's hum when I mentioned it to her last month stuck with me. I close my eyes, remember the way her fingers wove through it at the airport. My girl is a hair-puller. I'd like to make her pull on it *really* hard. Soon.

"That was kind of harsh."

I look up at the familiar sweet voice that brings an instant smile to my face, and immediately, every thought I have about protecting innocent girls' decency flies out the fuckin' window, because right here is an innocent girl I want nothing more than to corrupt.

I can't remember the last time I've seen her like this, all dressed up for a night out. Twelve months? Eighteen? Maybe more?

She's in a slinky black dress that's short enough to be underwear and leaves absolutely *none* of her curves to the imagination. Her hair curls over her shoulders, and she's got a pair of high-heeled shoes that make her legs look indecently good. Is it just me, or did her waist get even smaller this summer? If that dress clings the same way from the back, I'm not going to be able to focus for shit the rest of the night. Which, let's be honest, I wouldn't mind at all.

You asked for it, asshole.

"Hey, baby," I greet her as she leans in for a kiss. Fuck, she smells good. Like coconut and flowers. Familiar and exotic at the same time.

Her lips open to mine a little more than I was intending, but just when things are getting good, she breaks the kiss. I keep an arm around her waist, keeping her trapped between my legs. It's all I can do not to press my nose into her cleavage, street traffic be damned. What can I say? My girl is smokin'.

"I guess you're glad to see me, huh?" she whispers.

My hand hovers low on her back, just below where's really decent. "I'm always glad to see you, baby."

I tip my head up for another kiss, but she smiles coyly, and to my disappointment, steps away. She gestures behind her, and it's only then I realize she hasn't come alone.

"You remember my friend Vinny, right?"

For a second, I'm all glares at the well-dressed schmuck behind her. He looks just like all the Wall Street jokers, in a pair of perfectly distressed jeans and a button-up shirt, with his hair mussed with too much gel. But then I recognize him. He's a little more filled out now, but this is the kid who used to live in her dorm in Chinatown. The gawky, awkward kid who used to look out for her and her friends.

He extends a hand, looking uncertain. I shake it and smile. He immediately relaxes.

"How you doin', man? I'm Nico."

"I remember," says Vinny. "Nice to see you again, bro."

I nod. "You too. Thanks for keeping my girl company tonight."

Vinny nods. "Hey, this was my lucky night. I can never get in here."

I quirk an eyebrow. "You twenty-one?"

Vinny nods and hands me his ID. "Yeah. As of last week, anyway."

I check his New Jersey ID, which looks pretty damn legit, not that it would matter. He's Layla's friend, which is good enough for me.

I hand it back and nod. "Happy birthday, man. Go on in. Nah, you're good. Cover's on me, so have fun."

Gleefully, Vinny practically runs into the club. Layla gives me a grateful smile, then turns to follow. She pauses for a second at the doorway. It's brief, but I don't miss the way she bites her lip and examines the handle like it's about to bite her. Just when she's about to step inside, I reach out and snag her hand, making her jump.

"Hey," I say. "You okay, beautiful?"

She holds a hand to her chest, and it drifts up to the delicate skin around her neck —the skin that was a mosaic of bruises last May. I tug her back for another kiss, one that's deeper than before, since we don't have an audience other than the random passersby. She sinks into it, and slowly, that tension that was written all over her melts away. Good.

"Mmmm," she hums once I'm certain that her body is totally relaxed again. "That was nice."

I nod and close my eyes for a moment, enjoying the feel of her smile against mine. "Tell the bartender who you are, okay? He knows you're coming. I'll be inside as soon as I can."

She giggles as I bite her lip lightly, then absorbs me in another soul-searing kiss.

"Okay," she says, finally stepping away. "Don't make me wait too long."

With a grin, I watch her walk into the club. And Jesus *fuckin'* Christ, that dress is even more dangerous from the back than I thought. I groan and rub a hand over my face, then check to make sure there's no one watching before I adjust myself. Twice. It's going to be a long night.

———

ABOUT AN HOUR LATER, I head inside for my thirty-minute break, in search of one thing: Layla. AJ's has a great band tonight—a local trip hop group that basically sounds like sex on a stage. They're in the middle of a synth set while the singer croons against the beat. The combination of the sultry keys and the bass line basically has the whole crowd writhing together like snakes, lost to the rhythm. It's hot. It's sticky. It's foreplay.

Like a magnet, I'm drawn to her. Layla stands on the edge of the crowd, a drink in one hand with her other arm wrapped around her middle as she sways a little from side to side. She's stunning, of course, but that's a posture I know well—one that says she's feeling a little uncertain. Immediately, I feel terrible I didn't just take the night off. It's her first night in New York by herself. I should be there for all of it.

I approach from behind and she jumps about three feet when I slide my hands around her waist.

"Ohmygod!" she shouts, then softens when she turns around and finds me there.

"You okay?" I ask her, chuckling when she smacks me on the shoulder.

She sighs. At first I think I see a tremble of her lips, but it disappears by the time I pull her close. The taste of whiskey and Diet Coke is strong on her breath—I'm guessing she's had at least two.

"You all right there, baby?" I ask again.

Layla smirks, her hazy expression sharpening when it lands on my mouth. "I am now."

Then she kisses me, and this one is different from any kiss we've had since she got back. It's a far cry from the downright Amish kisses when her mother was around, but it's not exactly the joy or love that I'm feeling right now. This is a kiss that's only about one thing: lust.

"Jesus," I breathe when we finally come up for air. "That was—"

But I can't continue before my girl fuckin' swallows me whole all over again. Jesus, she's voracious, and the effect is immediate. Suddenly my hands are every-where, and the only thing I can think about is the fact that it has been a *very* long summer—no, fuck that, a very long year—and I need this body. I need to be *inside* this body. Right fuckin' *now*.

"Nico," she breathes as she presses every single one of her curves against me, especially one part that is aching to be let out.

"Ah." I literally lose my voice as she grinds into me again. *Coño*, I didn't know it was possible to want someone this bad. But I do. I always do with her.

"Where can we go?" she asks, somehow without removing her lips from mine. "I...I don't want to be here anymore. I need you now."

My throat constricts with need as my fingers dig into her hips. It's been a long time since we were like this, and I'm hit with flashes of when we first met. Layla has always had a voracious streak. I wouldn't call her an exhibitionist—it's not like we ever did it in front of people. But there were times, like in Central Park or in the back of a cab, where my girl just could not wait to get her hands on me.

"Seriously? You don't want to wait until—"

"*Nico*." Her hands drop to my ass and squeeze. Hard.

That's usually my move, but the fuck if it doesn't have an immediate effect on me too. I groan into her neck. "Ahhh. Okay. Yeah. Follow me."

I turn and guide her through the mass of gyrating bodies., including her friend, who's rubbing up on some blonde girl. This isn't where I'd do this if it were totally up to me. It's not that I don't want to fuck Layla. Fuck me, I've wanted to do the dirtiest things imaginable to this girl since I met her, things I'd never even say out loud because I'm pretty sure she'd slap me, things that make a fuck in a nightclub seem downright demure. But for our second first time, I'd have wanted it to be nicer. Special.

But apparently, that's not what my girl wants. And if she wants me to give it to her right here, then that's what she's going to get. I tow her down the employees' hallway in the back, checking for my manager before I knock on the door of the employees' bathroom. It's nothing much. A bunch of stored paper towels, some cleaning supplies, and a toilet and sink that haven't been used by two hundred people. But it's not exactly the most romantic spot in the world.

I lock the door, suddenly filled with uncertainty. *You asshole. She deserves better than this.*

I turn around. "Sweetie, you sure you want to—"

Again, my words are cut off by her kiss as she rams me against the door.

"Stop talking," she mumbles. "Just fuck me."

Her raw, brutal words undo the last bit of restraint I've got. In about a half a second, I've flipped us around so she's shoved against the bathroom wall while I devour that sweet, filthy mouth. Another half second and my pants are unzipped. My cock falls out, throbbing against her thigh. She moans while I hurry on a condom. Almost as quickly, I toss her legs around my waist, yank her strip of underwear to the side, and thrust inside her with all the fury that's been mounting since I left her for California over a year ago.

And she feels. So. Fucking. Good.

Tight. Wet. This body was fucking made for me to do this. Made to be taken in every possible way. Made for me to slip inside, made to undo me completely. Her body squeezes, and as she moans loudly into my mouth, I just about come right there. With two handfuls of the sweetest ass on the fuckin' planet, I'm the happiest man alive as I pound home again and again.

Any time. Any place. That's how it's always been with us. Once again, I'm taken back to memories of everywhere we gave into this need all over the city. Central Park. A restaurant downtown. The far corner of a subway station. Another in Chinatown. It doesn't matter that I've lived here my entire life. This city will always be marked by Layla and me—marked by us and the connection that can't be denied.

"Baby," I moan against her neck. Her legs are in a vise-grip around my waist—I'm not going to be able to hold it much longer. "Baby, are you close?"

"I…" She drifts off as her head bumps into the wall with one particularly hard thrust. The sound brings me even fucking closer. *Fuck.*

"Just do it," she whispers, her voice low and guttural. "I want to feel you come."

Fuck. That's all I need.

"Jesus *Christ*!" I shout, slamming my fist into the wall behind her head while my other arm holds her up.

She arches against me, her entire body quivering. We come together, our bodies clenching tight, and, at least for me, the world goes black. Gone is the thump of bass vibrating through the walls, the dingy walls of the bathroom, the stale scent of alcohol and cleaner. All I can hear, see, smell, touch, *feel* is her. Layla. Only Layla.

I shake out the rest of my orgasm, and she shakes too. Her feet fall back to the floor while we both collapse against the wall together to catch our breaths. But it's not until the world comes back into focus that I realize she's still shaking long after I'm done—but not from ecstasy. From tears.

"Oh, *shit*."

I yank up my pants, not even bothering to zip everything up, and gather her into me. She curls into my chest and sobs. What the *fuck* is going on?

"Shhhh," I croon as I stroke her hair. "What's going on? Talk to me, baby. This wasn't the right place, was it? Shit, I'm so fuckin' sorry. The bathroom of a bar—what the fuck was I thinking, right?"

"N-no," she stutters as she stands up fully. She wipes the makeup bleeding under her eyes, but remnants of tears make her blue eyes glow. She's so beautiful, even when she's sad. "I'm sorry. I–I don't know what's wrong with me."

I run a finger over her cheek, then through her hair before I pull her back to my shoulder. She sighs as she lays her head there, and we just stand for a minute as her emotions settle. I don't press her with the questions swirling around in my head. Something about this was totally wrong. At some point, I'm going to need her to tell me. But not now. Right now, I just want her to feel better.

"I think I should probably go home," Layla says after another minute or two. She stands back up and gives me a sad smile, but doesn't maintain her gaze.

I toy with her fingers. I don't want her to go. Or actually, I do, but I can't leave work just yet. I have at least three more hours of tossing drunk assholes out on the street before I can climb into bed with her and hold her until she's herself again.

Damn.

"Okay, sure. Give me a minute and we'll get you a cab."

She nods and waits patiently while I put myself back together. She doesn't have much to do. That dress of hers is short enough that one tug puts it back into place. I give her forehead another quick kiss before we go back through the club.

"What about your friend?" I ask her as we step outside.

Paul, the other bouncer, gives me a nod as he gets off the stool. I gesture that I need a minute as I lead Layla to the curb.

"Vinny will be fine," she says. "He was cozied up with some girl. I'll send him a text that I went home."

I hail a cab, then turn to my girl and cup her face, urging her to look at me. Her blue eyes, usually so bright and full of attitude, right now are clouded with uncertainty.

"I love you, you know that, *mami*?" I've said it to her a million times all summer, but it occurs to me I haven't said it once since she got off that plane. Fuck, I really am an asshole.

She cracks a smile, and her small frame relaxes a little. Okay, we're on the right track.

"I love you too," she whispers. "So much."

I kiss her again, this time gently, even though I can already feel that yearning for her that never stops. Put it away, asshole. That is *not* what she needs right now. I don't know what exactly that is, but it's not a boner pressed against her leg in the middle of the street.

"Can I come over after my shift is up?" I ask. "Not for that, I promise. I just… goddammit, baby. I just want to fall asleep with you in my arms again. Would that be all right?"

Again, that sweet smile appears, and it just about lights up the street at damn near close to midnight.

"Sure," she says. "Just call when you're on your way. Don't worry about waking me up."

I give her another more innocent kiss before she gets in the cab. I have questions, so many questions. But for now, I'm content just to be with my girl. I'll take Layla any way I can get her. That will never change.

CHAPTER FIVE

Layla

IT'S NOT UNTIL PAST FOUR THIRTY THAT MY CELL PHONE BUZZES ON THE WINDOWSILL.

Nico: Still up? I'm downstairs.

Oh, I'm awake. I've been lying in this room for hours, staring up at the ceiling and listening to the hum of the city outside my window. Every sound makes me jump. Every creak of the fire escape. Every blare of a horn. Every drunken shout on a street corner. This is a decent neighborhood, but it's true what they say. New York really never sleeps.

I buzz Nico in and unlock the door before I pad back to bed, turning on my side toward the window. Beyond the fire escape, the city twinkles against a sky that never quite grows completely dark at night. At the edges, the glow of the sun is already starting to make itself apparent. I've been watching it for hours, staring at the lights, burrowed under my covers, and trying to make sense of what happened at the club.

I still don't have any good explanation. Just one that I don't want to say.

Trigger.

I listen to the door open and close, then the sound of Nico locking up before he enters the room. He pauses for a minute at the door and smiles when I turn to look at him.

"Hey," he says. "Sorry to wake you up."

I sit up. "I wasn't asleep."

"No?" He enters the room and sits on the bed to remove his shoes. "So, you gonna tell me what that was about back there?"

"What do you mean?" Wow, he's not wasting any time, is he?

Nico cocks his head. "NYU, come on. You can't hide things from me. Layla, you totally froze. One second we were going at it like rabbits; the next, it was like I was doing a dead girl." He leans over and slips a finger under my chin. "I'm not into necrophilia, baby. I like you alive"—kiss—"and kicking"—kiss.

His lips feel good. Soft. Full. Pliant. But my lips, damn them, don't move.

Nico sits back. "Okay, really. What is going on?"

I scoot farther into my pillows and lie down. "I—"

Nico kicks off his other shoe, then scoots up the bed so he's lying on the other pillow, facing me. A hand drapes over my waist, and gently, he turns me toward him. His eyes are wide and kind, full of concern.

No.

The word echoes through me, and I hate myself for it. I don't want to feel this way. And a big part of me doesn't. A big part of me just wants to lose myself in him again, like I wanted to do in the club. For a little while, it worked. The combination of whiskey, music, and Nico made me forget for a minute what a damaged person I am. Let him touch me the way only he can, the way that makes me forget my name, where I am, everything but the nameless notion of what we are together. I was close, so close, until his hand hit the wall next to my head. Just like someone else used to do.

My shadow threatens. My muscles tense. That ability to let go isn't back yet. I stare at the wall behind him. I don't want to see the disappointment I know is all over Nico's beautiful face.

A finger tips my chin up again.

"Hey. It's all right, *mami.* I got you."

My lower lip trembles before I can stop it. Nico's face clouds.

"Hey," he says again, pulling me to him just as the tears start all over again. "What is it? Talk to me, Layla."

"Fuck," I whisper. *"Fuck."*

He chuckles. "That's usually my line."

I shake my head, rubbing my nose into his chest. He smells so good—like detergent and sweat and soap and man. Nico. I want nothing more than to get lost in him —get lost in this perfect, strong body that's never done anything but protect me.

But I can't.

"I don't want to be this girl. I wanted tonight to be perfect. You've been so patient, and I'm just…"

My voice warbles irritatingly as I trail off, but Nico just chuckles.

I frown. "What's so funny?"

"You."

He strokes the side of my face, and his grin is contagious. I smile back, despite the fact that I have no idea what he's laughing about.

"What about me?" I demand.

"The fact that you think I'd be disappointed by literally anything about you." He touches his forehead to mine. "I lived almost twenty-seven years loving you, and I didn't even know you. I spent another year and a half dreaming about you, day and night. Layla, I'll take whatever you have to give and still be the happiest fuckin' bastard on the planet. You want to fuck in the nightclub, I'm down, obviously. But if you decide you want to wait until marriage or some shit like that, I'll do that too. I'd do anything for you, baby. Don't you know that by now?"

I can't help it. I grin. His words are balm to my aching heart, my aching soul that's still not quite healed. He pulls me close, and so I do what comes naturally and kiss him. His mouth stills—he's surprised, since he was just moving in for a hug. But quickly, he adapts, and before long, we're right back against the brick wall, the back of the cab, the stairwell of my apartment. It's several more seconds—minutes?—before we break again, both of us heaving.

Nico gulps and smiles bashfully. "I mean, it's going to be a *little* harder if you keep kissing me like that."

I giggle, and he sighs contentedly.

"God, I love that sound. You mind if I make myself a little more comfortable, sweetie?"

I shake my head, then watch openly as he gets up and strips off the black pants and t-shirt he wears when he's checking IDs. It's been a long time since I've seen him like this, casual and at ease in his own body, uncaring that he's on display in front of me. He grins when he catches me ogling, but I don't care. He's mine to look at. Right?

And he's beautiful. His skin is smooth and golden, and practically glows in the moonlight, which casts shadows on his chest and stomach, playing over the ridged lines of hard-wrought muscle. His lips are full and open, and his eyes glitter, two black diamonds as they settle on me.

"Come here," I beckon, and he immediately obeys, sliding under the covers and tucking me comfortably into his warm body.

I don't have on anything but a thin camisole and my underwear. His warmth surrounds me, skin to skin. We lapse into silence, remembering the feel of each other again. This is good. This is right. My first night in this apartment, my first night back in the city, and he's here. With me.

We lie there a moment, letting the sounds of our breathing fill the empty space of the apartment, until Nico puts a few inches between us so we are looking at each other across the pillow.

"Tell me what happened," he says. "If you can."

I worry my lower lip between my teeth, thinking hard until Nico reaches a hand and plucks my lip free.

"And maybe don't do that," he suggests sweetly. He arches a sly brow. "It makes it hard to focus."

I open my mouth, then close it and exhale through my nose. "Okay. Um...I..."

How do I say this without giving it all away? Without making myself sound like a complete lunatic? A deranged girl? Nico doesn't need another burden to carry in his life on top of all the people he already supports. He doesn't need to know that the bathroom was just the start of it. That I rocked back and forth in the back seat of the cab, repeating "here and now" all the way back to my apartment while the Sudanese driver gave me strange looks. That I stared at the tiny pill in my palm for close to thirty minutes before I put it back in the bottle, choosing to feel crazy over feeling numb.

"I don't...I don't want to think about...him."

It takes him a second, but when he figures it out, Nico's eyes widen. "*Him*? I made you think about that motherfucker? How?"

"When you...on the wall...with your hand."

His brow crinkles. I don't blame him for not remembering—he was in the middle of an orgasm at that moment. I doubt he can remember his own name when he's coming like that, much less what he's doing with his hands.

"Is this...do you think about him a lot?"

Yes. "No, not really." I am such a liar.

Nico seems to think so too. "Baby, come on."

I sigh. "I'm still working through it, okay? I was doing really well this summer, actually. I thought I was ready to come back here. But last week, the police called to let us know that his trial date was scheduled, but that he was still out on bail…"

I trail off as a chill settles over me. Nico rubs my shoulder. His touch is a welcome warmth.

"He's still here," I whisper. "He didn't go back to Argentina. Nico, he's still here."

Nico's expression turns black, and a muscle in his jaw starts ticking. "When's his court date?"

I swallow. "In a few weeks. September seventeenth."

"That's a Friday," he says. "What time?"

"The police said one thirty."

My voice grows small. Nico looks like he wants to punch something. It takes me back to that day again, when he lost himself completely with Giancarlo. I don't want to tell him that some of my dreams involve him and the rage I witnessed that day. That sometimes, very, very rarely, I dream that he might turn it on me.

I shiver and resist the urge to rock myself.

"Baby, I know you don't want to hear this, but you gotta go."

My head jerks. "What? No!"

"Baby—"

"*Nico.* I don't want to see him!"

The words are more vehement than I intend, spitting out like bullets. Suddenly my voice is choked, and I can't breathe. *The here and now. The here and now.* I chant the words over and over again to myself. But it doesn't work. Everything feels tighter. My breath draws shallow, and everything starts to spin. I gasp for breath, but none of it seems like enough.

"Layla."

It's Nico's arms folding around me that open up my lungs again. It's his lips on my neck, the soft vibration of his voice on my skin. He hushes me, holds me until I calm. Until I'm ready to push away the memories of Giancarlo's looming face and terrible touch instead of this man, a man who truly loves me.

The here and now.

"Okay," I say. "I'm okay now. Um…sorry."

"You don't have to be sorry about anything," Nico murmurs. "But, Layla…"

I sigh. "What?"

"I have demons too," he says. "Which is why I know they'll stay with you until you face them. You don't want that shit chasing you forever. Don't let those memories hold you hostage."

I blink into his chest. There are times from his life that Nico hates to discuss. The years when Gabe's father lived with them and used to beat their mother, and probably the kids too. The two years he spent at a detention facility in upstate New York, which is all but a mystery to me, mostly because Nico absolutely will not go there. Plus, I've seen the tiny, terrible apartment where he grew up. Poverty is its own kind of trauma, and his lasted a lot longer than the six or so months I was with Giancarlo.

"You won't be alone," he says. "I'll be with you."

I look up. "You will?"

He snorts lightly and gives me a surprised half smile. "Of *course* I will, baby. What kind of man do you think I am?"

I blink. "I…I guess I don't really know, do I?"

We stare at each other as the reality of the words sinks in. For as much time as we've spent this summer flirting and talking, we haven't really *been* together in well over a year, and even then, it was tenuous, with his departure to LA hanging over us the whole time.

"Yours," he says softly. "I'm *your* man, Layla. No matter what, I'm here for you. You can believe that."

Just as quickly, the shadows fade away. His warmth envelops me.

"I'm yours too," I whisper back.

Nico smiles, almost a little sadly. Slowly, he takes one hand to his lips, then the other.

"Not yet," he whispers. "But I have faith."

He's honest, but without judgment. There's no doubt in his words, just the knowledge that things *will* be all right if we just give it time. It's a knowledge I didn't know I needed until now. A knowledge that scoots me across the pillow and back into his arms.

I kiss him again, and just as quickly as before, what starts sweet almost immediately turns into something more potent. Nico gasps into my mouth and tries to pull away, but I don't let him. I want more. I want to be *us* again, whatever that means. His hands drift down my back, and he groans lightly as he finds my ass and squeezes that favorite body part of his, pressing me into the hard length that's suddenly tenting the front of his shorts.

"Okay!" he shouts suddenly, rolling away and forcing some space between us.

I scowl. "What are you doing?"

"You're not ready, baby. I…gah. That's not why I came here tonight." Nico folds inward, like he's protecting himself. Almost like he's in pain.

The blanket has fallen down, and I can see the obvious bulge in his shorts. It turns me on, but just when I go to move his hand away, I stop, stricken again with fear. And immediately, shame.

Why do I have to be like this? My body wants nothing but him. All day. Every day. But some other part of me is screaming to put on the brakes. It's ruining everything.

"Let's just go to sleep," Nico's saying, but I can barely hear him over the fighting thoughts in my head.

"I…"

I can't stop staring at the bulge in the front of his shorts. Almost unconsciously, like he's not even aware of it, Nico's hand drifts down to adjust himself, then rests there.

I look up. "I can't."

"What do you mean, you can't? Just turn over."

"What if…I don't want to?"

Nico sighs. "Layla…"

"I could watch you," I blurt out and immediately flush. Holy shit. I am some kind of pervert. I could *watch* him?

A black brow rises playfully. "What?"

I gulp, and the flush gets worse as my gaze drifts back down to the, ah, package he's now casually stroking. On purpose. Yep, I'm still going to ask.

"If…if you'd let me," I say, mesmerized by his gentle strokes. "I wouldn't mind watching you…do that."

Nico follows my gaze to his cock, and, as if he just now registers what he's been doing, his eyes brighten considerably. With a bit more purpose now, his hand cups the bulge, straining against the thin black fabric. It's perfect—not too big, not too small. Slightly curved. I remember exactly how it feels when it presses into that one, perfect spot inside me. How it completely undid me only a few hours before.

Well, almost.

Nico licks his full lips. Then, without a word, he tugs down the waistband, revealing himself completely. When I meet his eyes again, they sparkle with knowing, and he leans in for a kiss.

"This okay?" he asks as his hand starts to move. "Can I kiss you again?"

I nod. "You can always kiss me."

So he does, moving slowly, softly, until our tongues are wrapped up in that delicate dance together that sets both our bodies alight. It's a light that can't be banished, even when the darkness threatens.

"What about you?" he murmurs a bit later. "This ain't just the Nico show, baby. I have another hand I can use here."

I glance down to where he works. There's an ache between my legs now, one I wouldn't mind taking care of either. But there's something about watching...I'm not quite ready to give it up.

"I...I think I can do it."

"Then can I watch too?" That sly brow is back up.

I bite my lip and nod. His eyes dilate as I slide my fingers down and under the band of my underwear. He's as transfixed by the movements as I am by the way his hand works his solid length. His breathing grows harsher as I find my sweet spot, that small bundle of nerves that makes me come undone. It's a good interim, a touch I know, a feeling I know. We've listened to each other do this countless times over the summer, but this is the first time either of us has watched.

The idea turns me on even more.

"Oh, *God*," I groan as my fingers pick up their pace.

Nico grunts, and his hand also moves faster. "Can you see this?" he asks, his deep voice somehow even deeper. "Do you see what you do to me? This isn't me, Layla. This is you. All you."

I can't answer. I'm too busy, too mesmerized by the tension in his body. Nico's not a big man, but he has the presence of one. This close, seeing the way each well-defined muscle ripples with every flick of his wrist. The way his bricked abdominals squeeze with the effort to keep his cool. The way the compass tattoo over his heart seems to tick ferociously every time his breath picks up a notch.

"Layla," he croaks, and his other hand snakes around my head and pulls me into him for another fierce kiss.

I return it with as much vigor, finally lost in this moment, lost in him as my fingers work to join him.

"Layla!" Nico cries as his body seizes up suddenly. Every muscle is cast suddenly in high relief, caught in the shadows of the night and the city.

The knowledge of his undoing spurs my own. I shout my release as suddenly as his, but he swallows my cries with yet another kiss as we come together, side by side as the world falls apart, but we come closer to being one.

"Fuck," he breathes slowly as he comes down. "You wanted to watch..." He chuckles. "I love you so goddamn much, you know that? You're bananas, but I love you like crazy."

I can't do anything but giggle, but his wide, lazy smile tells me he sees everything I'm feeling on my face.

Nico looks down sheepishly to the mess in his hand. "Got a towel? I don't want to mess up your sheets."

"Bathroom," I tell him.

I enjoy the view while he walks away in nothing but his birthday suit, admiring the prize-winning ass that literally stopped me on the street once. I wait patiently while he cleans up and returns to bed. For the first time all night, I feel a sense of peace, which is only heightened the second he slips back into the bed next to me.

"I love you," he says again as he gathers me close.

I smile behind closed eyes. "I love you too. Good night." Then I turn over and scoot to the other pillow.

"What are you doing?"

I turn back. "Giving you space."

He looks at me like I'm crazy. "Baby, why the fuck would you think I need space? When the fuck did I *ever* want space from you?"

I open my mouth to answer, but just as soon, realize the answer. Never, of course. That was Giancarlo who always insisted on a full three feet between us at night. Who pushed me to the edge of the bed so he could splay his long limbs while he slept.

As if he sees the answer on my face, Nico tugs me back toward him immediately. His arm slips under my neck, and the other one drapes over my stomach, pulling my back firmly into his chest. The man is a furnace, and I crave his warmth.

"I just want to fall asleep with you in my arms again," he murmurs into my ear, his low voice vibrating over the sensitive skin as he repeats his earlier request. "Is that okay?"

I sigh and nod. I want to tell him that this would be okay every night for the rest of my life. That when I'm with him, I have this feeling like nothing out there could hurt me. Instead I let him gather me close, hold me the way we've both wanted for so, so long until his breaths grow deep and regular.

But as the room grows cold again, and the darkness outside fades, that sliver of fear still lingering at the edges of my heart remains. I shut my eyes and focus on the sound of Nico's breath. The fear will be back tomorrow, and probably the next day too. But for now, I'm safe. For now, I'm where I belong.

CHAPTER SIX

Layla

"Happy birthday, baby."

There's a bright light shining in my face, visible even through closed eyelids. When I open them, I see the source: a flash glinting off bright gold. The whole bedroom seems cast in light. Bouncing off the east-facing windows on the other side of me, the early morning sun casts everything with a warm glow.

It's the first solid night of sleep I've had in months. The first night where I didn't wake up in the middle seized with terror. The first where I didn't have to spend an hour or more chanting myself back to sleep for another few pitiful hours.

I turn back to the trinket next to me and the eager man holding it. "It's not my birthday. That was way back in June."

"I know," Nico says, holding out the jewelry. "But I wanted to give this to you in person."

Gingerly, I take it from him, and it's only when my vision comes fully into focus that I realize what it is.

A gold watch. More specifically, it's *my* gold watch. The watch my dad gave me for Christmas last year, which I had to pawn when Giancarlo sent me, unwittingly, to pay off a drug-related debt of his in the South Bronx. Nico helped me sell it in order to avoid much, *much* worse happening if we didn't. I turn it over and find the engraved inscription: *a minha filha*. "To my daughter" in Portuguese, my father's native language. It's a little bittersweet to see, since he refused to teach me Portuguese while I was growing up, insisting that I needed to be as Americanized as possible to succeed. It was one of the reasons why his absence last year hurt so badly. Not only did he shield me from a half of myself I had always wanted to know, but then he abandoned both my mother and me to run back to it just the same.

———

"*WHAT DID he say when you told him what happened?*" *Dr. Parker's face was kind and patient. Everything my father is not.*

I stared at my hands, braced in my lap. "*I didn't tell him.*"

There was a long pause. Then: "*Would you like to tell me why not?*"

I sighed. No, I wouldn't. But I knew I should. Dr. Parker didn't ask questions she didn't think I needed to figure out. And unfortunately, the hard ones usually ended up helping the most.

"*I…I don't really want to hear what he would have to say,*" *I whispered.*

She said nothing, just waited for me to gather my thoughts. I wove and unwove my fingers, suddenly remembering the old nursery rhyme I used to play with my dad. The one he would do to get me to go to church. Here is the church. Here is the steeple. Open the door, and look, all the people.

It was a rhyme that always made me laugh, until he launched into his lecture on piety. That I needed to be one of the people inside, or else I'd burn with everyone else. My father, so concerned with my mortal soul, seemed to have given up on his own in the end.

"*He will tell me I earned it,*" *I said.* "*That I brought it on myself.*"

One word about last year would deliver endless lectures over the crackling line from Brazil. It would be questions about what I did to provoke it, just like the police asked me. What did I wear, what did I drink, when did I skip church, who was I hanging out with? But most of all, the conversation would spell out his disappointment. That his *daughter would never let this happen to her. That we get what we earn.*

The worst part is, I asked myself those questions too, all the time. No matter how many times Dr. Parker told me it wasn't my fault what Giancarlo did, I still wondered what I should have done to stop it.

It was the same reason I never said that I had lost the watch he had given me. The last thing he had given me, one that, after months of silence, explicitly recognized me as his daughter. His blood.

———

I SHAKE MY HEAD, then clasp the watch around my wrist. Nico blinks, trying to gauge my response.

"How…" I shake my head, overwhelmed. "When did you do this?"

A dimple appears with a shy smile. "About a day after I put you on the plane."

"But this must have cost you…Nico, it's too much."

The watch was taken in exchange for a debt of a thousand dollars. I sincerely doubt the pawnbroker would have taken anything less than that plus interest.

"I…I don't know." He rubs the back of his neck, like he's nervous. "I needed to do something, you know? To make things right again. This was a start."

The memories from last spring darken the morning light before either of us can stop them—I see them playing clearly across Nico's face, and feel them just as clearly on mine. The dingy apartment. The stained floors. The slam of bodies on wood and plaster. Blood dripping down my face.

My chest squeezes again. My breath recedes.

No. Not this morning.

So I do the only thing I can think of that will banish the shadows and protect this light. I tackle Nico.

"Thank you," I say as I cover his face with kisses. "Thank you *so* much. This is crazy. *You're* crazy."

He laughs, the bright sound bouncing around the high ceilings, and I nuzzle into his neck, eager for the light he exudes to permeate through me.

"It's done, all right? I had some cash from selling my truck. It's fine."

"I'll repay you, I promise. Every cent."

He shakes his head. "No way. It's a birthday gift."

"It's too much. I have to do something to show you how grateful I am."

That sly smile reappears. "I'm sure I can think of some ways."

I set my chin on his chest, enjoying the solid feel of him. "So what's your plan today? Saturdays are laundry day, right?"

Nico lies back on the pillow and nods. "Laundry. Cleaning. Pay my bills. Shit like that since I'm usually ready to drop by the time I get home during the week. You want to meet up later for dinner?"

Reluctantly, I shake my head. "I can't. Shama should be here by tonight, and I promised her we'd hang out. Chicks before dicks, you know."

Nico pouts. "I'd ask if I could come over later, but I doubt it would be the best impression to jump off with, having your boyfriend stay over on day one, huh?"

Sadly, I nod. Shama's my friend, and we've shared an apartment before. But things are different now. She's seen me spiral away with a man, and I doubt she'd be comfortable with me jumping straight into something intense all over again, even if it is with Nico. But the thing is, I don't want him to leave. I want to sleep like this every night, wound up around each other, and I want to wake up in the morning to his bright smile. Still, that's a little too much to say to him on literally our first day back together. It's a little much for anyone.

Nico appears to have the same reluctance as he stretches out his limbs across the bed. It's not a huge mattress—just a double bed—but it's certainly better than the saggy pullout he's been sleeping on since May or the twin mattresses the college gave us in the dorms.

"*Coooooñoooo*," he yawns, almost looking like a cat. "I'm already gonna miss this bed tonight. Shit. I need to start looking for an apartment too. I can't deal with my siblings anymore." He rubs his face. "Maggie is driving me crazy. It's the oatmeal, man. She decided last month that oatmeal is the best thing for Allie to be eating in the morning because, I don't know, it's high in iron or some shit like that. But Allie's five, so she hates it, right? And every damn morning I have to listen to the two of them squawk like chickadees about fuckin' cereal. With no damn door to shut."

I chuckle. "The apartment's feeling small, huh?"

Nico groans. "You have no idea. I got spoiled over the years with my own place. My own room."

"It doesn't seem quite fair that you get stuck with the couch," I remark. "You're the one who pays for it, right?"

Nico sighs. "Gabe's been putting in some, actually, and so has Maggie. We basically split it three ways now. I can't afford to pay for everyone anymore. Wanna know something, baby? The FDNY doesn't pay shit the first year and a half."

"Well, then there's no way you're paying for dinner every time we go out," I reply as I stroke a hand over his smooth skin.

"Nah, it's fine. I got it—"

"No." I say it gently, but firmly. "That's not what I need from you anyway."

Nico opens his mouth, then closes it. "I just want to get off the couch. Oatmeal. Too much Marc Anthony. Listening to Gabe beat it every night before he falls asleep."

"Wait, *what*?" I turn bright red. "You listen to him *what*?"

Nico grins. "I swear to God. I love my little brother, but that's all he does: study and jerk off in *my* bedroom. Do you know he talks to himself when he's doing it? He's like a cheerleader. I can hear him muttering, 'get it, *papi*, get it.'"

I'm laughing hard now. "You don't know he's doing that to get off. Maybe he's revving himself up for a test or something."

Nico gives me a look like I'm crazy. "You think I don't know when my baby brother is jacking it? Trust, I wish I didn't know what that particular groan sounds like. But we grew up sleeping next to each other, NYU. That shit is ingrained."

He contorts his features into a fake-orgasm face, and I dissolve into giggles all over again. Nico grins, clearly pleased by the response.

"You're one to talk," I tell him once I've recovered. "You look pretty tortured when you do that too."

In response, one side of his face quirks with an impish half smile. "What's the saying? 'Hurts so good'?"

He rolls over and cages me against the pillow with his arms. The sunlight makes his tan skin look awash in gold; the twisting lines of his tattoos shimmer.

"You can hurt me like that anytime you want, *mami*," he rumbles, low and suggestive before pressing his lips to mine.

We sink into the kiss together, and it's not long before I feel another part of him ready and willing between my thighs. Half of me is dying to surrender to it, open my legs and take him inside where he fits so perfectly, feels good in a way that really does border on torture. But at the same time, the word "hurt" causes me to stiffen, and Nico senses it.

"Ah," he mutters as he pushes off me. "Another time, then."

I grimace and bite my upper lip. "I'm sorry. You shouldn't have to deal with this."

"Hush. You're fine, baby." He kisses me one more time, then rolls back to his side of the bed. "Besides, I'm a patient man. Most of the time, anyway." He sits up, then pauses, looking over his shoulder. "It's not me, is it? I don't gross you out all of a sudden, do I?"

"*No*," I insist, sitting up myself and tugging his arm until he faces me again.

His handsome features are drawn with sudden doubt and vulnerability that makes my stomach drop. This is exactly what I was afraid of.

"Nico, I swear. It's hard to explain. I want you like crazy, you know? I just…it's like when we get started, something just…"

I trail off, unable to finish the sentence as sudden tears rise. I feel defective. Like I broke something last spring, and now I'm starting to wonder if it will ever be fixed. I thought for sure that when I came back, when he touched me, it would. And truthfully, I *do* feel better when we are together—better than I've felt in so long. But there's a wall I can't quite climb yet. And I don't know how to start.

"Hey." Nico strokes my shoulder, and then his fingers float around to clasp my chin. His lips touch mine, and tenderly, he opens up another long, lingering kiss that seems to last for hours. "However I can get you, remember? That ain't ever gonna change, Layla."

His words, his patience soothes. I bury my nose into his chest, the divot between his strong pectoral muscles. The tattooed compass under my cheek thumps with his heartbeat, and I close my eyes while his hands play up and down my back. He wants to do more, I know. But for now, he seems content to just be together. Finally, we have the time to do that. It will take some time to trust. To get used to the fact that maybe, just maybe, I'm not going to lose him all over again.

I'm just about to say as much when the angry cry of the buzzer cuts through the apartment. I look up, confused, while Nico glares in the direction of the door.

"Who the fuck is that?" he growls, clearly as annoyed as I am to have the moment ruined.

I swallow and get out of bed, pulling on a pair of shorts before going out to the entry to answer.

"Who is it?"

"Layla?"

I frown and press the button again. "Yes?"

"Dude! It's Shama! Let me up!"

"Oh my God! Of course!"

I buzz her in, then scurry back to the bedroom to get dressed. Nico is already pulling on his clothes from last night, staring at his wrinkled shirt and pants with disgust. They are covered with dust left over from setting up the furniture yesterday.

"Jesus," he mutters, brushing off the black material. "I look like I spent the night in a sawmill." He looks up. "Is it too soon to ask if I can keep a change of clothes here, baby?"

The shy hope on his face makes me want to tackle him back to the bed all over, but instead, I just step up on my tiptoes and give him a quick kiss. "Of course. I'll free up a drawer for you."

He grunts, kisses me again, then goes back to fixing his clothes while I pull on a sundress. Nico looks me over with appreciation and shakes his head ruefully.

"All right," he says. "I'm gonna go, let you guys have your time. Are you free for dinner at Alba's tomorrow night? I know everyone wants to welcome you back."

Again, the thought warms. A year ago, I would have found spending the evening with Nico's family terrifying. To them, I was *la blanquita*, the rich white girl slumming it with their brother, to whom they were *very* loyal. And with good reason, since Nico has basically carried all of them on his broad shoulders his entire life.

But in the spring, something changed when Nico carried me into their apartment and put me into the care of his sister and mother, both of whom had their own stories of abuse. What Nico's family lacks in money, they more than make up for with love and community. They had taken care of me when no one else would. Shared their stories. Given me a safe space. In their own ways, his mother, brother, and sister rescued me last spring just as much as he did.

I grin. "Absolutely."

Nico grins right back. "Perfect. You wanna come to Mass too? You'd probably make my mother the happiest person on the planet. If you can deal with her and Alba planning our wedding, that is."

Immediately, a flush blooms over my face. Wedding? That sounds like a great way to send most twenty-eight-year-olds running for the hills. But to my surprise, Nico's dark-brown eyes don't waver as he waits for my answer.

I nod. "Of course. Just let me know what time to show up."

His wide smile makes the warmth in my chest bloom throughout the rest of my body. A knock sounds at the front door, and with a kiss to Nico's cheek, I skirt through the empty living room to answer with Nico at my heels. I open it to let Shama in.

"Hey!" she cries out, practically tackling me with a hug the second I open the door.

We twist around and around while Nico pulls in her two suitcases. When she finally lets go, Shama looks at Nico curiously. "I was wondering if you two had reconnected yet. Not wasting any time, huh, FedEx?"

Nico returns from her room looking less than pleased by the nickname, giving Shama a tight smile before he kisses her on the cheek.

"How you doin', Shama?" he says, his voice low and rumbling. "You have a good summer?"

Shama nods, her dark eyes twinkling. "I did, yeah! I had an internship at this advertising company in Philadelphia, and after that, I went to Florence with my folks for a few weeks. Oh my *God*, Italian men are crazy hot. Actually, a lot of them look kinda like you, FedEx."

Shama looks Nico up and down, assessing him openly. For a second, I see what she must see: a disheveled, obviously muscled man dressed completely in black, with his arm tattoo snaking over his elbow from one sleeve. That, combined with the black stubble dusting his absurdly strong jaw and eyes that are so dark they're almost black, makes him look anything but harmless.

Nico rolls his eyes. "I think that's my cue." He lands a brief kiss on my cheek. "See you tomorrow, beautiful."

When the door closes behind him, I turn to Shama. I already know this afternoon is going to be spent recounting the last strange twenty-four hours, and I'm not quite ready to have my mental state of mind pulled apart.

"Well," I say with a shrug. "I guess I should show you around."

"That's right," Shama says as she follows me inside. "And then…it's time to dish!"

CHAPTER SEVEN

Nico

WHEN THE THICK GREEN DOOR CLOSES BEHIND ME, I IMMEDIATELY WANT TO POUND MY WAY back inside. Is that fucked up? I feel like a Neanderthal, for real. She's been back for three days, and it's a little scary how much I just want to stay with her. She's doing her best to make a new home for herself. I don't care how pathetic it makes me: I just want to be a part of it. I don't want to leave.

But it's not only that. The fear on her face last night just about killed me. It's not that she doesn't want to be close—we spent the entire night wrapped around each other like vines. But anytime things got to that point where a little bit of fury, a little bit of crazy entered into our touch, she'd pull away.

Maybe other guys would be running for the hills, but that's not an option here. Layla is my heart, my soul. My other half. I know it, and I'm pretty sure she knows it too. So really, it's taking everything I have not to go back in there and face whatever crap is going on in her head together.

I want to spend the rest of the weekend making her remember what we are together. I want to lie there straight through the next two days until I have to be back at the academy. Call off from AJ's tonight just to hold her and touch her until I can chase that terror away whenever things get just a little too much.

She's scared. To an outsider, it might be nothing. We're just getting used to each other again, right? It's only been a few days. So, it shouldn't feel as terrible as it does that she froze the way she did, refused me the way she did.

But I know her. We've been laughing, joking, flirting all damn summer. It's been three months of foreplay, and last night, I was about ready to explode. I thought she was too. There is nothing—*nothing*—more I wanted to do last night than give it to my girl. I mean really give it to her, not just with my body, but with my whole fucking heart and soul. Here we are, finally with our chance to be together, and there's this hulking ghost between us, taunting with his shadows.

I shake my head. She's not hiding anything, is she? No, we're past that. After everything we've been through together, I know Layla just wants to move forward.

And so every thought I have keeps spiraling back to one:

Fuck that guy.

Seriously. *Fuck* that guy. Fuck that Lurch-looking, drug-dealing, nineteen-fifties-glasses-wearing Don't-Cry-For-Me-Argentina mother*fucker* who beat up Layla last spring and turned her into a scared mouse. It's his ghost she sees. On the street. In the club. In our fuckin' bed. Yeah, that's right. *Our* bed. Because the fuck if anyone else but me is gonna end up there ever again.

I clench my fists, resisting the urge to shove one through the new plaster in the hallway. Because the thought of that guy interfering with what used to be magic every damn time makes me feel like committing murder. I take a deep breath and start jogging down the stairs. I'll run out this frustration for as long as I have to. And then, tomorrow, the next day, however long it takes, Layla and I will face it. Together.

———

TWO HOURS LATER, I'm walking out of my boxing gym in Hell's Kitchen. It used to belong to Frank, a gristly old dude who took me in when I got out of juvie. I started fighting in detention, but it wasn't until Frank took me under his wing, gave me a job and a room to sleep in so I could stop being a burden to my mother and start helping her, and started training me to boot, that I really grew up. He died a few years ago, and I miss him like crazy. He was the closest thing to a father I ever had.

After he died, Nate, one of the fighters Frank used to train, bought the place. I was his sparring partner when he got a title match and won back in the day. You could say he's grateful. I have free access to the gym for as long as Nate owns it.

I'm out just in time to meet my mom and sister for lunch, but the workout has done nothing for my mood. After beating the shit out of a heavy bag for two hours, my fists are still balled up at my sides. Every few minutes I'm taken back to that terrible day last May, when I tore into that shitty apartment uptown and let loose the rage I've managed to beat into submission at the gym since I was eighteen. It's still simmering now, and every time I see Layla's face, I want to break out some vigilante justice on this city. Track down that asshole and do the job the police are taking their sweet fuckin' time with.

Whoa. I can practically hear K.C. sitting on my shoulder, saying *slow down, papi.* I shake my head and pull out my phone. I could use some sense talked into me right now. If anyone can calm me down, it's K.C.

"*Acho*, what the fuck? It's before noon, asshole. You know what time I got in last night? It was light outside, that's what time. *This morning,* that's what time."

Shit. Of course. I knew K.C. was spinning last night, like he does just about every Friday and Saturday. He wouldn't have gotten home until close to four or maybe even five. And if he brought home company like he usually does…

Right on cue, there's a very female voice purring in the background.

"Nah, honey, it's all good. I'll be right back. Go back to sleep. Or, you know, *don't.*" Then, to me: "Hold on, man." The sounds of movement filter through the speaker as he switches rooms. "All right, *cabrón.* What the fuck is up that got you pullin' me out of my beauty sleep?"

I sigh. "I'm sorry, man. We can talk later. I'm about to get some lunch with Gabe and *las gatitas* anyway."

"Well, fuck that. I'm up now, so you better tell me why you're walkin' around Hell's Kitchen instead of holin' up with your girl this weekend. Everything okay with NYU?"

I swallow. That's the thing about best friends. They always know.

"She's…" I sigh, staring down the busy street.

K.C. just keeps talking. "I'm surprised you're even walkin' around right now. If I went as long as you without gettin' that cookie, *mano*, I'da gone full Cookie *Monster*, y'know? I'da torn that up—"

"That's enough," I bite through his words. I open my mouth to tell my friend what happened last night, but then pause. I'm not sure I want to share Layla's secrets when I'm not actually sure she has any. Right now, this is just a gut feeling. So I tell him the other truth instead: "Her roommate just arrived. They needed some space, so I went to the gym."

"Is she hot? The roommate?"

I roll my eyes. And just like that, he's distracted from the fact that I am definitely not where I should be right now. "Don't you have a girl in the other room?"

K.C. clicks his tongue suggestively a few times. "Eh. She can wait. Answer the question."

"It's just her friend Shama," I say. "Indian girl from New Jersey. I don't think you ever met her, did you?"

"Don't think so…she sounds worth meeting, though. Hot girls always run together, am I right? Maybe I need to come with you to pay NYU a visit. Make sure the apartment is safe and all."

I chuckle. "We'll see, man. I don't need you getting me in trouble with Layla's friends." Something else occurs to me. "Hey, you gonna be at your mom's tomorrow?"

I can hear K.C.'s brain churning on the other side of the phone. "Yeah, I was planning on it. You gonna bring NYU?" He doesn't ask about Shama, but that's no surprise. K.C. doesn't like to mix his, ah, personal exploits with his family.

Leaving Layla here was the worst mistake of my life. The consequences almost cost Layla her life, and she's still paying for it psychologically in some ways. I just want her back. I want *us* back. I don't have much to give a girl like her, someone who comes from money, but I do have family and friends in spades, and all of them are ready to welcome her with open arms.

For the first time this morning, I feel like I have a plan to help.

"Yeah," I say. "She's coming. I'll mention something to Alba too for Sunday. Let's make it a thing, all right? Welcome her back the right way."

I come to a stop in front of my family's old apartment building on Forty-Ninth Street, the one where my mother lived up until last year. The one where K.C. and I grew up together. The vigilante thoughts disappear as I look at the crumbling bricks that now have a demolition notice in front of them. Looks like Mr. Pineo finally sold out to a developer. It's a shithole, but for a long time, this place, the people in it, they were home. Until I met Layla. I may not be able to give her much, but I can at least give her that. Family. Home.

"All right, man," I say. "Go back to your, ah, morning. I'll see you tomorrow."

I keep walking until I get to the pizza joint where I'm meeting my siblings for lunch. Ma is taking my niece, Allie, for the afternoon, giving us some time to get together without her knowing. According to Gabe, there is some stuff to go over.

"Hey," I say as I slide into the booth my sisters and brother have staked at the end of the restaurant. "I'm starving. Did you order a pie, or do I need to get a couple slices?"

"I'm on a diet," Selena says, twirling her curly hair, which she's letting grow natural now. "I'm doing a cleanse. I can't eat anything but fruit for a week."

"So basically, you're planning to gain ten more pounds at the end, right?" Maggie retorts.

"Maggie, be nice," I say. "Sel's an adult. She can eat fruit all day if she wants to. It's just more pizza for us."

"I'm only telling the truth," Maggie says. "It happens every time she does one of those crazy diets. Lose five, gain ten. Maybe if you just ate normal, you'd lose your spare tire instead of adding to it."

"*Gata*, don't be sayin' shit like that," I cut in just as Selena starts spouting a round of expletives.

Gabe just rolls his eyes at them and purses his lips like he's whistling. His expression is bright through his smudged glasses. For a second, I smirk. My little brother has turned out to be such a damn brain—he finally had to get some specs this year. I won't tease him though. He's killing it in school, and I couldn't be prouder.

"We ordered a pie," he says, finally answering my question. "And in the meantime, maybe we can stop talking about Selena's dumb diet. This came in the mail yesterday."

Gabe drops a thin white envelope in the center of the table, and his hand shakes a little. I glance suspiciously at him, but then I see the words "U.S. Department of Treasury" printed in the return address.

"*Coño*," Selena mutters to herself while Maggie looks at me expectantly.

"Well, open it," she says. "We've been waiting since yesterday, and it's addressed to you, big brother."

A little over two months ago, the four of us were crowded with Ma in the office of Ileana Perkins, the immigration worker helping with Ma's case. Up until last spring, none of us thought there was any hope for our mom, who was born in Cuba, but immigrated illegally to Puerto Rico as a toddler. Her father drowned during the voyage, taking her documentation with him (or so she thinks). After being taken in by K.C.'s grandparents and flying with them into the country, she spent the rest of her life dodging authorities, mistakenly operating under the assumption that as a Cuban citizen without a birth certificate, she was not ever going to qualify for amnesty.

Shows what we knew. It nearly cost her life to tell us, but as Layla learned in one of her Latin American history classes last year, there were ways for us to return to Cuba to get our mother's birth certificate. Maybe it was even possible to get relief without it, but Ma was always too scared to try. And as a Cuban citizen who has been in the U.S. for a *lot* longer than two years, she would automatically qualify for permanent residency.

That said, the textbook chapter that Layla read us was a little misleading. Cuba doesn't require documentation to enter, but the U.S. government sure as fuck does, and weirdly, it's the U.S. Treasury that processes the licenses to go. That's right. It all comes back to the money. According to Ileana, money is the real reason family visitations to Cuba were cut off at the knees this past June.

"They decided that U.S. visitors were spending too much," she told us when we met her in June, literally a few weeks after a new law was passed making it even harder to go unless you had an immediate family member still living there. "Freakin' Bush and his cronies. They just want all the money to stack in their coffers, don't they, the vultures?" she spat as she helped us fill out the application for a general license for me to travel to Santiago.

I didn't know what to say. Ileana is nice, but she's definitely a type: about as liberal as you get, ready to denounce any politician she sees, and certainly no fan of the president. I'm fine with that, even though I don't really know anything about politics. Her taste for vengeance is going to help my mother get her freedom.

The pizza arrives, stacked on an elevated plate. But we don't touch it, staring at the letter in the middle of the table. I pray to God it contains what we need. I'd like to wipe that scared look off my mother's face too.

"Well, what does it say?" Maggie asks as I tear open the letter.

I scan the short paragraphs, and my shoulders drop.

"What does it say?" Gabe asks.

"Fuck," I say as I drop the letter into the middle of the table. "We're fucked."

Maggie snatches up the letter and reads it out loud:

Dear Nicolas Soltero,

This is in response to your application dated May 24, 2004, requesting authorization to engage in travel-related transactions involving Cuba for the purpose of a family visit.

The Cuban Assets Control Regulation 31 C.F.R. Part 515 (The Regulations) prohibits all persons subject to U.S. jurisdiction from dealing in property in Cuba unless the Cuban National has an interest, including all Cuba travel-related transactions for the purpose of visiting a member of a person's immediate family who is a national of Cuba.

We have reviewed your application and determined that the issuance of a specific license is inconsistent with current U.S. policy because there is no record of the family member you have listed as a Cuban national. Accordingly, your request is hereby denied.

We note that, consistent with §515.561 (a), it would be inappropriate for you to make an application with the Office of Foreign Assets Control for a specific license to visit a member of your immediate family without documentation of the relation.

Sincerely,

Ethan Farrow
Sanctions Coordinator (New York)
Office of Foreign Assets Control

"What?" Selena glances around at us. "What does that mean?"

Gabe reads the letter, mouthing the words softly to himself. "Inappropriate?" he scoffs. "Who the hell are they, your homeroom teacher? Are they gonna send you to the principal's office?"

I snort. "No. They're gonna stop me from going to school in the first place." I drop my head into my hands and groan. "Fuck. *Fuck*. What are we gonna do?"

But when I look up, my sisters and brother have no answers. The pizza sits on the table, growing cold while they look to me for the next steps.

I got nothing. No ideas. *Nada*.

It's a feeling I'm really getting sick of.

CHAPTER EIGHT

Layla

"WHAT ABOUT THIS ONE?"

I turn around to look at the futon Shama's pointing at and shrug. "It's all right." I sit down and immediately scowl. "Okay, I wouldn't want to have a movie marathon on it, though. You try that."

Shama flops down on the mattress with me and shakes her head. "Don't people sell discounted furniture that's actually comfortable?"

"Maybe we should try that craigslist site instead."

"Yeah, but I don't want to get ax-murdered."

I giggle, but she has a point. We get up and start looking around the other selection of couches. We have a small allowance, supplemented by Shama's parents and my mom, that's supposed to help us furnish our living room. But I can't help but notice that my friend hasn't been that interested in picking out couches. Or unpacking her bags. Or really looking for anything.

"So...I saw Quinn and Jamie last week. We went to lunch."

I pretend to be interested in a really ugly pink sofa. "Oh, yeah?"

"Yeah. Jamie says hi."

I narrow my eyes. It doesn't escape me that Quinn didn't say anything at all. Jamie, on the other hand, has disappeared from my life, like a distant relative you keep forgetting to call back.

"For what it's worth, I do think Quinn feels bad about everything," Shama remarks as we both flop down onto a very brown couch. "This one is comfortable."

"This one looks like a cow pie," I reply, making Shama laugh. "And that's great that she feels bad. But I still think it's better if we're not friends. I miss J. I miss our group, actually. But the more I think about it, the more I realize that maybe it wasn't good for me to be around Quinn."

Last spring wasn't just about extracting myself from one toxic relationship—it was about getting out of all of them. With her constant belittling and negativity, Quinn definitely qualified as toxic. I need people in my life who can be supportive and constructive. People who don't have to cut down others to feel good about themselves.

"I just hate that it puts you in a weird position," I say. "Jamie sort of peaced out over the summer and ended up taking Quinn's side. I think when she really saw how bad things were, it freaked her out."

Shama nods. "Well, it was pretty crazy to walk in on you like that. But it's not like it was your fault. I think Jamie at least knows that." She sighs. "I remember when I was going through everything with Jason…"

"I'm sorry I wasn't there for you more," I say. I squeeze her wrist, and Shama gives me a sad smile.

"Yeah, well. You had your own stuff going on."

"Quinn and Jamie were there?"

She shrugs. "Jamie was. Mostly. Quinn, you know how she is. She had a lot to say about it. Mostly criticizing why I let him come back so many times."

I nod. "Yeah, I do know how she gets like that."

"Yeah. Well. One day they are going to have hard shit to deal with too. They think they're above it, but they're not. You and I are just early bloomers."

We collapse together, giggling, even though the casual mention of her heartbreak cuts me through again. I really wasn't there for her the way I should have been. I've been a pretty awful friend.

"What about Romeo?" Shama asks. "He's been around a lot? You guys pretty much back to normal?"

I shift uncomfortably, and Shama raises a black brow.

"Dish," she says. "What's going on?"

"Nothing," I say lamely. "I just got back. Everything is fine."

"You're such a terrible liar, Lay. What is it?"

I give a heavy sigh. "It's not him. It's me. I'm…I'm still so messed up, Shams."

"What do you mean?"

I pull absently at my hair. "It's weird. We started hooking up. And it's like it always was, you know? That crazy chemistry."

Shama smiles dreamily. "Yeah, you guys always had that going for you. Damn, if I could get a guy to look at me the way he looks at you, I don't think I'd ever be walking."

I giggle. "That's how I usually feel. I met up with him last night at AJ's, and dude, we couldn't stop. I practically chased him into an employees' bathroom."

"Sounds good so far," Shama says.

I nod. "It was. In the beginning." That familiar chill hits. "But then…we almost got to the end, and he lost it, slammed his hand into the wall. And it…it freaked me out a little, that's all."

"Just the one time?"

I sigh. "I…no. The rest of the night, it was like, we'd get to a certain point, and he'd start to get, you know, really, um, passionate."

"Like, toss you against a wall and screw your brains out?"

Sometimes I really think my friend is psychic. I sigh. "Well, yeah."

"Good. You gotta put those muscles to good use, right?"

I smile to myself. "He's good at…letting go."

Shama leers. "Oh, I know. I shared an apartment with you before, remember? Lafayette had reeeeeally thin walls, my friend."

I blush. "Are you serious?"

She nudges me in the shoulder. "Please. You never cared. We had headphones."

I'm surprised by how un-embarrassed I actually am. But that really was how Nico and I were with each other. Anytime. Anyplace.

"So, what's the problem?"

"I freeze." I stare at my hands, now clasped in my lap. "One second he's making me lose my mind, like he always does. And the next, I'm a scared rabbit, in full-on flight mode. I just want to stop."

"And *does* he?" Shama's tone sharpens significantly.

"Oh, of course. It's not like this has happened a ton, Shams. I just got here a few days ago. But it's…I wasn't expecting it to be like this. And I don't know what to do."

Shama sighs, then slings a thin arm around my shoulder and pulls me close. I lay my head on her shoulder and sigh.

"I hate it," I admit. "I thought we would be good. All summer, it was hot phone sex and sweet conversations. He loves me so much, Shams, and I just want to make him happy. He doesn't deserve this, having a freaking basket case for a girlfriend."

Shama rubs my back for a minute, letting me get past my thoughts. "Layla, you went through hell last year. And then you had to go to Pasadena for three months, which is basically the seventh circle, right?"

I snort. Pasadena, boring and suburban, isn't my cup of tea, but it wasn't that bad. I filled my time with therapy, volunteering at the YWCA, and taking Spanish and Portuguese classes. It could have been a lot worse.

"You just need time, dude. And if he loves you like you say, he'll give you that."

I nod. "He will. He's the best. I just want to make sure he gets what he needs too."

"Correct me if I'm wrong, Lay, but I'm pretty sure Special Delivery just needs you. He never really seemed to care how."

I cringe. "Let's *not* keep that terrible name going, shall we? Quinn made that up, and he really, really hates it. Not to mention she's not his favorite person either."

Shama chuckles. "Fair enough." Then she sighs. "I have to tell you something, Lay."

I twist my body to look at her. I had a feeling something was coming. Time to be a good friend back. "What's up?"

"I feel really freaking bad about this. But…okay. I applied to do this study abroad thing through Oxford last spring."

"What? Shams, that's so cool! What a great thing to do!"

"Yeah, I thought so." She brightens a little, considering it. "My dad went there, you know. When he left India, he originally went through Oxford to do his degree, and then he came to the U.S. to do his Ph.D. stuff."

I listen curiously. I've met Shama's parents a few times, but they are pretty private people. I know they emigrated from India before Shama and her older brother were born and then settled in New Jersey after her dad finished his graduate work at MIT. He works for some kind of engineering firm in New Jersey, and her mom stays home.

"Anyway," she continues. "I never heard back, so I didn't think I was accepted. But last week, I got a call. A spot opened up in the program, and…" She trailed off, looking at me with her big eyes. "Look, I don't want to leave you in the lurch. I know you need a roommate, so I'll pay the rent for as long as you need. But, Lay…I just really need to do this. I feel like I need to get out of the city. Away from Jersey, New York. All of it. See what else is out there."

I'm quiet for a second, processing the news. Shama watches me nervously.

"Are you mad?" she finally asks. "I know it wasn't supposed to be this way. Are we done? Am I written out?"

"Shama…" I shake my head and turn to her with a smile. It's hard. I had expected to get through this year with my friend, and I can already feel the loneliness threatening again. But I manage it, because I know this is what she wants, and when I think about it, I'm actually really happy for her.

"Shams, of course I'm not mad," I tell her. "This is so great for you. You must be psyched."

Relief floods her face. For the first time, I can really see her fatigue. Last year wasn't an easy year for her either, what with her boyfriend cheating on her. Shama dealt with her heartbreak much more quietly than I did, and managed to help me with mine too. She spent most of her summer working, not really dealing with the stuff that happened. She deserves, more than anyone, the change of pace she so obviously craves.

I give her a giant hug, ignoring the fear at the idea of being alone in that apartment. "I'm super freaking happy for you."

She grins, a bright smile that lights up the room. "Thanks, dude. I'm actually crazy excited. I have to leave on Monday to get there in time for classes to start. But, you know, holy shit! I'm moving to England!"

We hug again. But another question pops into my head. "Why are you looking for a couch with me if you aren't going to stay?"

Shama snorts. "I like shopping. Plus, I couldn't let you do it by yourself."

We sit there for a moment, a lull falling between us. We're both thinking the same thing. I'll be in an apartment alone, at least for the time it takes to find a new roommate. Alone, and with a tendency toward breakdowns.

But Shama sees me as alone in this city without her. I realize it's not quite true.

"Hold on," I say as I pull out my phone. "I have an idea." A few rings later, and Nico's deep voice echoes down the line. "Hey. Do you think Alba would be okay with another at dinner tomorrow? I was thinking maybe Shama could come too."

There's a pause. And for a minute, I think he's going to say no.

But after another beat, his deep voice rumbles, speaking to a place deep inside me, like a match that's lit to start a fire.

"Sure, baby," he says. "Anything you want."

I grin. "That's not necessary. Just tell us what to bring."

CHAPTER NINE

Nico

AT SIX O'CLOCK THE NEXT DAY, I FIND MYSELF ESCORTING NOT ONE, BUT TWO GIRLS UP TO Alba's apartment. Ever since she moved into the classy west-side high-rise courtesy of the dough K.C. started raking in a few years back, K.C.'s mom loves to host just about anything. Parties, dinners, backgammon nights, whatever. It's from her that K.C. gets his party skills. He's just as social as she is.

She also knows exactly what Layla did to help my family, and once she heard that Ma wanted to get everyone together to welcome her back, she insisted on hosting there instead of at our railroad apartment uptown.

"So, your friend," Shama says as we enter the lobby. "He, um, does all right, huh?"

The doorman gives me a quick nod. He sees me enough that I don't get any suspicious looks. Shama looks around, her eyes growing big. I smirk. After she saw my place up by City College, I bet this is the last place she expected me or mine to be.

Layla elbows Shama in the side, and she immediately grimaces. "Sorry. I sound like a total bitch, don't I?"

I shrug, staring at the elevator buttons. "Hey, no worries."

When we get to Alba's floor, the sounds of my family laughing filters all the way down the hall. When we enter the apartment, Layla and Shama take in the decent-sized living room, the picture windows, and the simple furniture. It's a nice apartment, but it's nothing crazy. Alba has a knack for making it feel homey.

Layla looks around curiously. "It looks different when there isn't a giant party in here."

I nod. "Alba always moves all the furniture into the back room when she does her holiday stuff."

As soon as everyone sees us, they're up from the table to greet Layla. I watch happily as my sisters, my brother, and even my mom all take turns giving her bear hugs and kisses to the cheek. Layla's blue eyes shine and her cheeks flush as she returns every one of them. Having met her mom, I get how different this is from what she grew up with. Cheryl is nice, but stiff, and even with her daughter she keeps her distance. Mine, on the other hand, has absolutely no concept of space.

"Dang," Shama murmurs beside me. "Your family really loves her, huh?"

I grin. I didn't realize how much this meant to me until right now. "Yeah. They really do."

"What's up, *mano*? Who's your friend?"

K.C. pops up after he's done giving Layla kisses like everyone else does, even though they've only met a few times. It's just what you do. She's already being dragging into the living room to play dolls with Allie and chat with my sisters. I open my mouth to introduce Shama, but she takes care of that for me.

"His *friend* is right here. And her name is Shama."

K.C. darts a suspicious look at me, but I just shove my hands in my pockets and pretend the pigeon on the balcony is the most interesting thing I've ever seen. I purse my lips, sucking back a laugh, but behind K.C., Gabe doesn't bother hiding his.

"She told you!" he crows, through several bouts of laughter. "Damn." He extends a hand to Shama around K.C.'s glowering form. "How you doin', Shama?"

"Hey, good to see you." Shama accepts Gabe's awkward kiss to her cheek. His hand lingers a little too long on her waist. When Shama's eyes bug at me a little bit, I choke on another laugh, though she continues to look suspicious.

"*I'm* KC." My friend recovers his shock and gives his trademark smile. It's funny, with his thin frame and ghost-like skin, K.C. isn't what you would call a stereotypically handsome man, but somehow he makes up for it with swagger.

When Shama takes his hand with a snort, he kisses her cheek, dodging a little with her first. "You'll want to remember that name, pretty."

"Man, shut up." I elbow him in the ribs. "She's not here to get picked up."

"I can handle myself, thanks," Shama says. "If you'll excuse me…I'm sorry, what's your name again? Kaylen?"

Gabe breaks into another round of hyena-like laughter, and I can't help but join him as K.C. steps back, glowering. Shama skips neatly around him to join the girls on the couches.

"Don't feel too bad, man," I say as I rub K.C.'s shoulder. "It's broad daylight. We know the real K.C. magic happens at night."

"Damn right," he mutters. "Whatever. I'm ready to eat. We've been waiting for you for*ever*."

———

Layla

Dinner is good. And when I say good, I mean amazing. Alba, K.C.'s mom, really likes to pull out all the stops, and she and Carmen filled the table with about ten different kinds of Puerto Rican food, including a mashed plantain dish called *mofongo*, which I discover is Nico's favorite after he eats close to half of it. Carmen's wink and nod tells me she'll pass on the recipe at some point. I don't know, though. I'm not much of a cook, and I'd be kind of upset it he didn't devour my version the same way he does his mom's.

But the best part of the evening, other than being surrounded by this family that, for all of their difficult history, is incredibly close, is seeing Nico in his element, including with his best friend.

For most of the time I've known Nico, K.C. has lived in LA, pursuing his growing career in music. I knew he had done well for himself. Just the fact that he can afford this place for his mother, not to mention the beautiful brownstone he has in Hoboken, tells me that. He's not a billionaire or anything, but his job pays well, and considering the way he shares his fortune with the people around him, I like K.C. already. Generosity is something he and Nico have in common. Honestly, it's something both of their families share, through and through.

It's so different from my family, people who have everything but who, for most of my life, maintained their wealth with iron fists.

After dinner, which is loud, boisterous, and consists mostly of Allie doing imitations of Elmo, K.C. flirting with Shama while his mother smacks his wrist, and Selena and Maggie bickering, everyone helps clean up, and then the boys collapse on the couch to watch the last of the Yankees game while the girls sit back at the table to enjoy coffee and gossip. Alba and Carmen speak in rapid Spanish that I can't understand very well, but Selena and Maggie have stopped translating, piping up every now and then in English or Spanglish here and there.

"Hey, you okay?"

I look up from washing dishes in the kitchen. At some point, I drifted away from the table when Selena and Maggie started debating whether or not Selena could *really* be confused for a young J.Lo. Maggie's position on the matter was firmly in the negative, and it was not being received very well.

Shama hands me a plate. I glance behind her to where Alba and Carmen are chattering as they stow the leftovers, then back to Shama. I turn back to the sink and shrug.

"I'm fine," I tell her. "This is great."

I should feel happier than I do. I'm in Alba's beautiful apartment with its view of Midtown. I'm surrounded by people who care about me, people who took me in last spring when I needed it the most. Nico's family and I still don't know each other very well, but we all have a connection. I'm a part of that now, both because of what they did for me, and what I did for them too.

But I don't miss their concerned glances every so often. I don't miss the way Maggie, Nico's sister, floated her gaze over my neck and cheeks, where, three months ago, she applied makeup thick enough to hide the nasty bruises. I don't miss Gabe's featherlight touch on my shoulders, or the way Selena scooted away from me at the table now and then, reacting to my every movement like I was about to break.

But then again...aren't I? Sometimes I still feel it. It's why I'm in here instead of the living room with the rest of the younger people. Through the kitchen door, we can hear them all playing some kind of game.

"You should go back in there," I tell Shama. "I'm almost done."

She shakes her head in faux horror. "It...was getting a little awkward. K.C. and Gabe kept taking each other's seats next to me. K.C. wouldn't stop calling me pretty, and Gabe kept trying to slide his arm around my shoulders while he yawned, *Grease*-style. Then they brought out Twister, so I was done."

Another round of laughter and a few unintelligible Spanish phrases bounce through the room. I smirk. "Awww, who's the prettiest girl at the party, Shams?"

I'm rewarded with a giant eye roll. "Shut up. Gabe is about fourteen, and K.C., well..." She looks behind her to see if Alba's within earshot. She and Carmen have gone out to the living room. Shama turns back to me. "Let's just say that I've been there, done that, you know?"

I set a casserole pan in the dish rack and start on a handful of forks. "Gabe's only a year younger than us, Shams. And come on, K.C. is nothing like Jason."

"They're both DJs. It's a solid start."

"That's like comparing a Big Mac and a steak. K.C. gets to travel the world to do what he does. He bought his mom this apartment, and his place in Hoboken is super nice too. Jason plays shitty college bars."

Shama pulls a hand through her long black hair and gives me a grim smile. "Can you really tell me he's not the womanizing type? I feel like I have to walk out of a room backward if I don't want him to wolf-whistle me."

I open my mouth to argue on K.C.'s behalf, even though I don't really know him that well. He's a person I know more from Nico—the surrogate brother he grew up with, one who features heavily in his stories. The guy I know has given Nico places to stay, helped him find jobs when he needed them, basically just given him the best support he's had in his life. For that reason alone, I like him.

But then I'm taken back to the first night Nico and I were together. Nico was housesitting and took me to K.C.'s apartment. During a tour of the place, we ended up in the master bedroom, with its cheesy, all-white decor except for a giant splattered painting of a man biting a woman's nipple. It was the opposite of subtle. For a room that screamed sex like that, there wasn't a drop of intimacy in it. As badly as I wanted to be intimate with Nico at the time, I had absolutely no desire to do it in that room or anywhere near the white canopy bed. I wasn't about to become another notch on that particular bedpost.

"Fair enough," I say, even though the memory of what happened later that night does cause a tingle between my thighs. Nico's hungry lips. His hands, urgent and slightly rough. His slap on my thigh, the flip of my body. From the living room, I hear Nico's deep voice joking with his brother and his friend. The tingle heightens.

I scrub a little harder than necessary at a couple of knives. Other than our moment in the club, it really has been a long time, and even longer since I had the kind of sex that used to make me ache for someone like this. The thought makes me swallow, hard, just before another cloud of dread settles over me.

Will I ever be able to get there again?

"Anyway, I have to get going," Shama says.

I look up. "What? Why? I'm pretty sure Alba still has flan or something like that."

Shama gives me a tight smile. "I, um, said I'd meet up with some people."

I frown at first at her oblique references. Then it hits me. "You're meeting up with Quinn and Jamie."

Shama sighs. "Well..."

I turn back to the dishes. "It's fine. Tell Jamie I said hi."

"Lay..."

I stop washing. "It's okay, really. Have fun. I'll see you later. Or, depending on how good your night is, tomorrow." I plaster on the widest grin I can manage until finally, Shama starts laughing.

"You're a terrible liar," she says. "And you look like a zombie when you smile like that. But I love you anyway. Have fun tonight. And give your man some. He's starting to look like he's going to shrivel up from blue balls."

I nod, but turn back to the sink, ignoring the clench in my stomach at her words. She doesn't need to know just how much it hurts that I can't give someone I love what he wants. What he probably needs.

———

Nico

"She seems sad," Maggie remarks after Shama says her goodbyes.

K.C. tries to escort her to the elevators, but I have to laugh when Shama practically shoves him back into the apartment. I haven't seen my boy work that hard for a girl's attention in a very long time.

"Who, Shama?" I ask. "Why?"

"No, you fool. Your girl. The one playing Cinderella in the kitchen."

I follow her gaze to where Layla's doggedly scrubbing a pan. She's cleaned almost the entire damn kitchen. Since she started, Ma and Alba have disappeared into the bedroom to look at some hand-me-downs, and we just switched the Yankees game back on after Allie cleaned the floor with her uncles and aunties at Twister. Seriously, who knew a five-year-old could be that flexible?

I twist my lips guiltily. "I think she just wanted a second alone, Mags. We can be a little much, don't you think?"

I nod to where Gabe and K.C. are busy punching each other in the shoulders, like they're actual brothers instead of surrogate ones. Selena is lying facedown on the floor while Allie braids her hair. No one has even started putting away the mess of games that are out.

Maggie doesn't say anything. She knows what I mean.

"She's not quite herself yet," I admit quietly, folding my hands together.

"I can see that," Maggie replies. "She was really different at Thanksgiving last year. Sad then too, but in a different way."

K.C. and Gabe shout something at the screen, but I'm not even watching anymore. It was right here in this room, filled at the time with family and friends celebrating the holiday, that Layla let me teach her salsa in front of all of those people. Then she cried in my arms on the balcony. Then let me hold her for hours. Back then she was mourning the loss of her family, but not the loss of her innocence. She wasn't completely broken. Not yet.

I have to close my eyes while anger punches its way up and then recedes. I hate that she's like this—one minute sunshine, the next a rain cloud. I hate that there's nothing I can do to help. I want to make her happy, connect with the one person on this planet I'm supposed to be with. She needs time, more time to heal, but it's so fucking hard when she has to hold me at arm's length to do it, and all I want to do is come close.

"You know what helped me the most?"

I look at my sister, whose face has been marred like Layla's, also by a man who was supposed to love her. Maggie was pretty once. When she was younger, she was one of those girls who would laugh louder than everyone else. Her moods were always a little crazy, but when she smiled, so would everyone else. Now she's as stoic and hardened as ever. It's a look I understand. Everyone from my neighborhood looks like that sometimes. It's a look of self-defense, one that knows better than to be vulnerable, because that's how you get hurt.

But it's also a look I never, ever wanted to see on Layla. At some point, the numbness she has is going to turn into that hardness. And it's going to kill me.

"What's that?" I ask.

"Do you remember showing me how to throw a punch after...what happened with Jimmy?"

I squint. I remember showing Jimmy what *I* could do with my fists, but not much more than that. I was too angry to think about what I was doing. "Sort of. I took you to Frank's."

Maggie nods. "Yeah. You showed me how to use my legs and make a fist that wouldn't break my thumb when I hit someone. We did it for maybe an hour? I don't know."

"Yeah, yeah. I remember that now."

"Well, it helped," Maggie continues. "The next time I saw Jimmy, I clocked him in his stupid face. He never saw it coming. And I think *that*'s why he never did it again neither. Not just because he knew you would fuck him up. But because he knew maybe I could too."

I almost choke on my water, imagining Maggie, who's maybe five foot three with heels, coming at her ex, a guy at least as tall as me, with a balled-up fist. "*Mana,* you never told me that."

She shrugs. "Broke his nose too. We got into some fights after that, but Jimmy always knew he would get as good as he gave. He never hit me again."

I look at her for a long time, but she keeps her gaze on Allie. My siblings are a lot stronger than they seem. It's easy to look at Maggie and see someone who kept going back to a man who mistreated her, just like our mom did. It's easy to think that she was weak, even though she was also doing it to keep a family for her daughter. In the end, she got them both out when they came to live with me for good. That alone took more strength than I give her credit for.

I forget sometimes that I'm not the only one who grew up fast in our house. That they don't need me to take care of them the way they used to.

"My two cents: give her something to hit," Maggie says. "See the way she's scrubbing that pan in there? She's not just sad, Nico. She's angry. And right now, she has nowhere to put it."

We both watch Layla in the kitchen, the way her small shoulders tense as she goes to fucking town on the pan. Maggie's right. Layla"s wielding the sponge like a weapon, and her rose-petal mouth is twisted together, her forehead bunched.

It's a look I know well. Really, really well. Anger and me, we got a long history together. And for once, that history makes me happy. Because as I watch my girl take out her frustrations on the dirty dishes, I finally feel like I might have a way to help her.

CHAPTER TEN

Nico

"Where are we going?" Layla wonders when I steer her across Tenth Avenue instead of back toward the train.

It's dark outside now, and a few blocks away, the bars around the heart of Hell's Kitchen echo through the streets, even though it's a Sunday. I sling an arm around Layla's shoulder, trying to ignore the way she tenses slightly before melting into my side. I bury my nose in her hair and inhale her flowery scent. I don't know what goes into her shampoo, but it's addictive.

"I want to try something with you, baby," I say. "Do you trust me?"

Her blue eyes dart up at me suspiciously, but she nods. "Yes. I do."

I guide her toward the unlit end of the street, then up Eleventh, past some new nightclubs that have taken the place of the old, empty warehouses that used to be here when I was a kid. But the next corner is the same as it used to be. Still darkened, without the benefit of a streetlight. An old concrete building with crumbling sides. It's the first place I ever lived without my family, other than juvie. The first place anyone ever gave me a chance to be something more.

"Come on," I say as I push on the scratched glass door. "I want to show you something."

I hold her hand tightly as we walk into the gym. Even though Frank died a few years back, Nate's kept it pretty much the same. Still three rings, one after another. Still a row of heavy bags hanging from creaky chains on the back wall. Still a bunch of training equipment on the right side, bathrooms to the back. And beyond that, the storage room where I used to sleep. I wonder if it still has the cot, ready for some other poor kid to get his chance.

"What the fuck. Nico motherfuckin' Soltero. How did we get so blessed to see you twice in one weekend?"

I turn around as Nate jogs over from the front ring. At this time of night, barely anyone is here. Only the hardcore boxers, the ones who aren't pro yet, but want to get there. Nate still competes, but it looks like he's on his own tonight. Even his trainer is gone.

"Hey, man," I say after we slap hands. "This is my girl, Layla."

"Oh! NYU, huh? I've heard a lot about you." Nate extends a quick, sweaty handshake, and Layla, still a little shy, accepts and murmurs a quiet greeting back.

"Can we get on the back ring for a bit?" I ask. "I want to show Layla some stuff."

Nate nods. "All yours, man."

He flickers a kind smile over Layla. I do my best to ignore the way it skims over her curves, which are fully on display in a pair of leggings and her t-shirt. I know I can't help the way men look at her. And Nate's good people. I've known him for almost ten years, back when Frank was training me and let me be Nate's sparring partner. I might as well ask him to poke out his eyes than not notice my girl. But it doesn't mean I like it.

I lead Layla to the back of the gym, past the last few fighters still here. We take off our shoes, and then I hold up a rope to let her in. She steps onto the padded blue surface. I jog to the storage room and return with some equipment: a spare set of wraps, gloves, and some punch mitts. I approach Layla and turn her to face me.

"Hold your fingers out, sweetie."

I turn her palm up so I can weave the long strips of fabric around her knuckles, through her slim fingers, around her wrist, and back up. The repetitive movements are kind of hypnotic. When it's done on one side, I switch to the other. She watches silently as I do the same to my own hands, then put the gloves on. She still hasn't asked me what we're doing here, a fact that kind of kills me. The Layla I know would be questioning every damn thing. Not in a critical way. She was curious. Naive, maybe. But never afraid to ask.

"These are a little big," I say quietly as I pull the Velcro tight around her wrists. "They'll work for today, but we should get you some in your size."

When I'm done, I look her over. With the massive boxing gloves hanging off her thin arms and her eyes all big and wary, she looks like a cartoon bunny. A scared, beautiful cartoon bunny.

So what does that make me? The big bad wolf?

"All right," I say as I grab the mitts and slide them over my hands. "First up, let's fix your stance. You want to be on the balls of your feet, and hold your body at an angle, with one foot just ahead of the other. Good, good."

I adjust her a little bit, then mimic the stance back. I bounce back and forth between my feet, and she automatically starts to do the same.

"Okay, so, rule number one is: protect your face. Frank—that was my old trainer— used to tape my left hand to my neck so I wouldn't let it down. That's how important it is. Here's where you want to put your hands."

I hold the mitts up around my face, and Layla mimics me awkwardly, clenching her lower lip with her teeth as she practices. She's so damn adorable, I almost bat the gloves out of the way so I can kiss her, but hold off. There will be time for that, and maybe more if this works the way I hope.

"All right, baby. Let's start with a jab. Turn your wrist like this. Then, real fast, just tap the mitt with your knuckles, and pull them back to your original position. Try it."

I hold up the mitts, ready to take her punch. Looking uncertain, Layla looks at the pieces of foam. Then, she offers a weak punch with her right glove. It's…pathetic.

"NYU, come on now. I know you can give better than that."

Layla's not a boxer, but she's no slouch after playing soccer for as long as she did. I've had her legs wrapped around me enough times to know exactly what kind of muscle she's got going on down there. It's firm, but just soft enough so that when you get a really good handful...

I shake my head. Stop it, you asshole. This is not the time to be thinking about that.

She frowns. "I don't like it when you call me that, you know."

"What? NYU?"

She nods. "It makes me sound like a spoiled princess."

I cock my head. "Well, then, maybe you should stop acting like you're afraid to break a nail."

She scowls harder. "I don't want to hurt you."

I stifle a laugh and drop the mitts. "Baby, you're not going to hurt me. You wouldn't be able to do it even if I didn't have these things on, I promise."

She still looks doubtful. I sigh, then take a chance. Maybe another strategy will work.

"Yo, Nate!" I call out. "You got a second, man?"

From one of the heavy bags, Nate lopes over to the ring. "What's up?"

"You mind showing my girl a quick combo? I want her to see what it looks like when it's done right."

Nate shrugs, then steps into the ring. He's covered with sweat, and I try not to notice the way Layla's eyes bug out a little while he starts throwing punches at the mitts. We run through a few basic combinations, ones we've been doing to warm up with each other for years. He's a lot better than me now, of course, but until I left for LA, we'd still get in the ring here and there.

Layla watches, transfixed, and she mimics the movements slightly with her gloves. It's adorable, even though I don't love the way her eyes catch on Nate's muscles. It's distracting enough that at one point, he pushes past the mitt and lands a soft cross on my chin, waking me from my daze.

"You're getting soft, Soltero." He chuckles with a wink at Layla. "You getting love handles too?"

Without another thought, I tear off my shirt and toss it in the corner. Nate's cut, sure, but I'm not exactly a doughboy over here. That's what a summer at the academy, heaving fuckin' tractor tires and running incessant laps around Randall's Island, will do for you.

"My turn," I say, tugging off the mitts and hurling them at him.

Nate laughs while he puts them on. He knows exactly how to push my buttons. I turn to Layla for her gloves, and enjoy the way her tongue slips out of the side of her mouth a little while she watches me put them on. That's right, baby. Now who's got drool-worthy abs, huh? I remind myself to keep my sit-up regimen going no matter what. If it'll make her look at me like that, I'll do planks until I'm eighty.

"No wraps?" Nate asks when I turn around. "You're looking to break a knuckle."

"Fuck you," I shoot back. "Okay, baby, this is what you want to do. Ignore this joker's shitty form. That's why he got knocked out in his last fight."

"Oh, you just *had* to go there, didn't you?" Nate shakes his head. "All right, pretty boy. This ain't the heavy bag like yesterday. Let's see if you remember how to do this for real, huh?"

I whip through a bunch of punches and combination moves, much more complex than the ones Nate was doing. He blocks them like the pro he is, but I can see his muscles straining with the effort to keep up.

It feels good. I'm out of practice, having done barely anything in the gym since starting the academy. My muscles strain, even though they've been working hard in other ways all summer. After just a few minutes, I'm drenched in sweat and breathing hard.

"Last three, two, *one*," Nate calls before I smack the mitts one last time with a loud pop that tosses Nate back a few steps.

I step away, breathing hard and wiping sweat off my forehead.

"Fuckin' waste," Nate says, shaking his head as he pulls the mitts off and tosses them into the corner. "Why you never went pro, I'll never know." He mops his head with the towel he brought in, then steps out of the ring. "Don't let him push you around, beautiful. Just clock him in the kidney, and you'll bring him to his knees."

And before I can toss him another for calling my girl beautiful, Nate skips back to the other side of the gym to continue his regimen, laughing all the way. I turn back to Layla, unsure of what I'm going to find as I take off my gloves. I just wanted to show her the moves, show her she could do it, but I ended up showing off a little instead. I just wanted her to stop looking at me like she's scared.

Well, mission fuckin' accomplished. Except now the way that Layla's staring at me with her mouth open, a wrapped hand at her heart, does absolutely nothing to stop a whole bunch of energy straight to my dick.

"Holy shit," she breathes. "Nico, that was…incredible. I didn't know you could move like that."

I bite back a grin as I towel off my face. "It was just a little warm-up."

She shakes her head, her blue eyes dark and heavy as they drift over my body. "I, um…I don't think I could ever do that."

I finish mopping off my chest and arms, then toss the towel on the mat and grab the mitts. "Sure you can. I just wanted you to see that you can give it whatever you got, baby. I can take it, okay? Let it go."

It takes her a bit, but soon she starts hitting the mitts with a satisfying pop every time. I guide her through some of the other basic punches—cross, hook, uppercut—until she can do them on command. Layla's a natural athlete. She picks up the moves quickly, and it's not until Nate comes back and slaps the mat that I realize just how long we've been going at it.

"Hey," he says before leaving. "I'm done for the night. Lock up when you're finished, all right? You still have your key?"

"Yeah. Thanks, man." I turn back to Layla, who's breathing hard.

Her t-shirt clings a little to her stomach, more than a simple white t-shirt should. She's red in the cheeks, and tiny tendrils of hair stick to her forehead and neck. She looks crazy fuckin' beautiful. And also tired.

"You want to go?" I ask.

She inhales heavily, but shakes her head. "No-no. I'm…can we keep going a little while longer?"

I'm tired. She's tired. We've been at this for over two hours, and my stomach has been growling at me for half that time, having already burned through the three servings of *mofongo* I had at Alba's. But the look on Layla's face—a look of pure determination—is worth every rumble.

I nod and hold up the mitts. "Let's go, baby."

———

Layla

It must be close to midnight when I finally can't throw another punch. I don't know why I wanted to keep going like I did. It was seriously addictive. Every time my fist hit the weird foam blocker, it was like I was punching through the haze of doubt, anxiety, worry, fear that always seems to hug me close. The heaviness of the last year starts to break down. Pop! There went last week. Pop! The week before.

"Oh, God," I groan as I flop backward onto the mat.

Nico collapses next to me. Allowing me to remain still, he gently removes my gloves, then the hand wraps. My knuckles are going to be black and blue in the morning. I couldn't care less. I haven't felt this exhausted, this sated, in, well, years.

No, since the last time Nico and I slept together. It was after Thanksgiving, when he'd made me feel more adored than I'd ever been in my life, and then taken me back to my apartment and demonstrated every bit of that devotion all over my body. I try and fail to ignore the lines of sweat dripping down Nico's naked torso. His muscles ripple as he sits up to toss the wraps and gloves into the corner, and when he twists back to me, he pauses.

"What?" he asks. "What are you looking at?"

I sit up, and then, on a naughty impulse, I do something I've been wanting to do for the last fifteen minutes. I lick him. On the shoulder. Around the dip of his triceps and up to where I nip at the curve of his deltoid.

"What the…" He looks at his shoulder, then back at me, his dark eyes dancing. "You nasty, NYU." This time, there's not a hint of resentment in the name. It's a tease, a taunt. Playful.

So I do it again, this time on his neck, then tracing my tongue around the other side of his jaw. The taste is salty, and his skin is warm. It's divine.

"Layla." His voice is low as I suck a little on that right-angled corner of his jaw.

"You taste good," I whisper against his cheek. "I want to…" I look down his body, the way it glistens from our workout, and I linger on the two, muscled ridges that disappear under the waistband of his pants

I bite my lip and look back up. Tiny lines have erupted over his forehead. He looks like he's almost in pain.

"I want to taste you," I say as I reach out and slide my hand across the zipper of his jeans. "Here."

His body lurches slightly as I unzip his pants and reach under his boxers to take him firmly in my hand. My breath hitches right along with his. He's so hard. So ready for me. And I've barely even touched him.

"Are you—" He gulps. "Are you serious?"

"Nico?"

"Yeah?"

"Take off your damn pants so I can give you a blow job you'll never forget, okay?"

If he'd been eating anything, he'd have choked on it right then. But then another wide grin spreads on his handsome face.

"Fair's fair," he says with a smirk. "Take yours off too, baby. Spread those beautiful legs for me."

I balk, even though I'm already shimmying out of my leggings. "You want to...do that...right here?"

Nico tips his head back and laughs, a booming, joyful sound that ricochets off the high metal pipes hanging from the ceiling.

"Baby," he says in between wheezes. "You just offered to suck my cock in the middle of the gym. What does it matter if I'm eating your pussy at the same time? *Now* you wanna be coy?"

My mouth drops. He's been so gentle, so cautious with me. All summer. When he got back. And now he's talking like a dirty magazine and I...love it. Should I love it? What does that say about me?

"Hey. *Mami*." His deep, curt voice pulls me out of my spiral. He raises one black brow. "I didn't say no, did I?"

I open my mouth, then close it. Then I grin. "No. You didn't."

One side of Nico's full mouth pulls wide in that sly half smile I love. "Then lie back down, baby. And spread your legs. Don't make me ask again."

Slowly, I do as I'm told. I lie down on my side, curled inward with my knees together. Nico reclines on his side and kisses my ankles, up my legs, tracing his soft lips over my thighs until he reaches my underwear.

"We're not going to need these," he says as he tugs them off and tosses them across the ring.

He presses a hand between my thighs, nudging them apart again. His tongue slips out and licks the sensitive skin on either side, his tongue flickering between that slight gap. I shudder.

"I said"—Nico wrenches my legs apart—"spread 'em."

And before I can answer, he dives between my thighs, his warm, urgent mouth immediately finding my clit. With closed eyes, I lounge on the floor, opening more as I grind into his mouth—oh, that magical mouth. He hums a little while he licks, sucks, even bites lightly, both of his hands palming the backs of my legs and kneading every often.

My eyes fly open as his teeth lightly close over my clit, and I'm confronted with his own *very* strong desire. Thick. Perfect. Pointing right at me.

I lick my lips. Would he be shocked if I did it? Maybe that's what I want. I don't want to be cautious. I want to taste him, all of him. I want to do it while he's tasting me.

So I don't say anything, just take him in my mouth, relax my jaw so he can slide in nearly all the way.

"*JESUS!*" Nico shouts.

And *oh*, he tastes so good—a salty essence mixed with his own unnamable flavor. I close my eyes, relishing in the feel, the utter control we have over each other's pleasure at exactly the same time. As his mouth works intensively at that most sensitive of places, and I savor every dimension of his, I forget that I'm in the middle of a freaking boxing ring, laid out on a mat, where anyone could see us if they just walked in the door. I forget about all of my worries, frustrations, anger. All of it fades away as we feast on each other's bodies and lose ourselves to the animalism of the moment.

"Mmmm," Nico groans, then slams a hand to the mat. But this time, I don't freeze. In my mouth, he grows just a bit bigger, and the knowledge makes me shake. Oh, *fuck*. He's going to come. He's going to come in my mouth, and I'm going to take it, and I'm going to come in his, and together we're going to—

Suddenly, every thought, the thrill of what we are doing is too much, and without warning, my entire body seizes up as my orgasm hits. It crashes through me, tossing me around, tightening every muscle I have. Nico grabs my thighs roughly, keeping them apart so he can finish me off, not letting up for a second as wave after wave of tension ripples through my limbs. I moan around his cock, my body quaking as his hips thrust forward lightly as he comes as well. We grasp, claw at each other, eager to get closer, yet somehow unable to take it all completely. I savor every bit until I'm completely sure he's finished. And then, just as my legs fall limp, forcing him to roll out from between my thighs, I release him too, and flop onto my back, completely out of breath.

"Holy. Shit." Nico's deep voice is raw, like he's been shouting. His chest rises and falls visibly. "Holy *shit*."

I loll to the side, curling against the mat. "Good?"

"Fuckin'…" He sorts through a few strings of unintelligible Spanish, then blows out a long breath. "No words, baby. No fuckin' words for what you do to me."

"Mmmm, good." I close my eyes. "Do you think…" The adrenaline starts to fall, and immediately, I miss it, along with the strange high that accompanied my earlier exhaustion. "Do you think we could do this again?"

When my eyes open, Nico's twisted around so we're lying face-to-face. His dark eyes sparkle, and his mouth is spread in a peaceful grin. I grin back.

"The boxing or the sixty-nine?" he asks cheekily, and his dimple on one side comes out to play. He strokes my face, and even through his joke, there is tenderness in his expression.

I blush, and immediately he laughs. It's infectious, simmering through me. I shove him playfully in the shoulder, which only makes him laugh louder.

"Why not both?" I tease.

Before he answers, Nico scoots in closer for a kiss. His tongue gently seeks entry, looking to mingle in a delicate dance that still carries the lust of the moment, but is mostly made of something deeper: contentment.

"Any time you want, sweetie," he says as he breaks away. "It's a date."

CHAPTER ELEVEN

Layla

NICO DROPS ME AT THE TRAIN STATION WITH A KISS AND A PROMISE OF MORE BOXING LATER in the week. I'm disappointed—I had hoped we might continue things at my apartment. But aside from the fact that he has to be up early to get to Randall's Island on time for the academy, we both know we can't push it. I'm just not ready for what we both want to do.

Still, I feel lighter than I have in months. I never knew how much I wanted to hit something, maybe even some*one* like that, until the pop of glove on mitt cracked through the air. Nico has said before that learning to box saved him. It was the one good thing that came out of his time in a detention facility, and it kept him from going down some really bad paths. I feel like I get it now, just a little. If he'd been carrying this kind of pent-up anger and frustration for most of his childhood, an outlet like that must have changed his entire life.

But it's not just that. Wrapped up in each other like that on the mat, a sticky, sweaty, pheromone-soaked mess of desire, only made me want more. We were animals, diving into one another, wanting only to be closer, get closer. That wall, the familiar block on my senses didn't rise when things got too heated. A veil has lifted, and even though I'm not totally at the point where I feel open and free again, I feel like I can imagine it.

Dr. Parker would call that progress, I think.

Once I'm home, I sit at my desk, fingering the bottle of pills, which I've been taking at night, if only to calm my anxiety enough to sleep. Shama's still out with our —her?—friends. The apartment is empty, with the streetlights outside casting shadows through the fire escape outside of my window. For the first time in months, my heart beats at a regular pace at the thought of being alone. Maybe I can sleep by myself tonight.

And at that, my heart thumps loudly. My hands grow cold. A shiver passes through my body.

Okay, maybe not.

My phone buzzes in my pocket. I pull it out.

Nico: I forgot to say *te amo*, baby.

I smile at the text. When he's not smiling, he looks like he could mess up your face if you looked at him wrong, but underneath it all, Nico is really just a big softie.

Me: I love you too. Thanks for a great night. ALL of it.

The phone buzzes again almost immediately.

Nico: Anytime. Can't wait for more.

I stare at the words for a few minutes, ignoring the way my heart continues to beat a little too fast, and instead focusing on the warmth that grows through my belly when I think of him. I close my eyes and imagine the feel of his hands on my skin, his mouth between my legs, his skin pressed to mine. One of my hands creeps down and slides under the waistband of my pants, toying a little bit with the sensitive spot his tongue worried into a frenzy earlier.

A few moments later, I get up to take a shower, and finish what I've started. While the hot water runs over my body that aches for just one person, I'll think of Nico the entire time.

It doesn't take long to find my release, though my body wants more, wants the other part of me who is sleeping on a couch uptown. But when I come back, I slide into bed and fall asleep quickly and peacefully. I leave my pills where they are.

I TAP MY WATCH. The hands don't move. I'm sure Nico's late, but the watch has been stuck at ten o'clock for what seems like forever. It's lonely on this street corner, this part of the city so desolate it doesn't even have street signs. Over the tops of grimy brick buildings, I can see the glow of Manhattan, a halo over the jagged lines of skyscrapers and high-rises, the dips where the apartment buildings only reach five or six stories. Even from this far away, the city hums. But I'm here, waiting in one of the pockets that never make it into movies or the news.

"Come on, Nico," I mutter to myself. A shiver passes through my body. I hug myself, but stop when bruises appear on both shoulders. "Dammit. I'm out of makeup."

Heavy footsteps echo down the empty street. I look up, eager when I see the outline of a dark male form striding toward me.

"You're late!" I call out, though I'm already running toward him. My anchor. My everything.

"I would have been here earlier if you hadn't called the cops."

The voice, low and heavily accented, stops me in my tracks. The man's deep voice curves around me like a snail's shell. You can practically hear his lips curl as he speaks. He steps under a streetlight, revealing a long body dressed entirely in black, a mop of thick black curls that have been tamed with wax, and a thin, brooding face with eyes like obsidian, framed with Wayfarer glasses.

Giancarlo.

"Mi joya," he whispers, extending a hand while he pronounces that name he loves to use for me. Joya. Jewel. "I have been waiting for you."

I take a step back, then another. "Where's Nico?"

"Nico? Who? He left you. He went back to California. But it's you and me, joya. It always was, no? No one else matters."

I scramble back another few steps. Giancarlo looms in the dark, like he just grew another few inches. Only a few steps bring him close.

"Say it," he demands as he grabs for my hand. "Say you're mine."

I shake my head. "No."

His face, always long and gaunt, grows longer, gaunter. He stretches taller, nearly as tall as one of the buildings, until he blocks out all the lights—the stars, the moon, the lights of New York. The world is black, except his pale, hollow face.

I take a step back into an unknown street, yet another darkness in this city.

"No," I whisper, even as I turn to run.

"Say it!" Giancarlo shouts.

From an impossible distance away, he grabs me by the neck and yanks me into his chest, his long arms seeming to wrap multiple times around my body. He grows, one, two more feet, picking me up off the ground,

"Stop it!" I flail. "I don't love you! I never did!"

A hand claps over my face to shut me up. I can't breathe, struggling to move until I manage to stick my nose through a crack in the giant's hands.

"Let her go!"

I look up, barely able to see. But I do catch a glimpse of white: the stitching on a Yankees hat glows as a man charges through an alley. Nico.

"All right, cabrón, I tried to warn you," he says before spilling into Spanish I seem to know, but can't totally understand.

Giancarlo jerks at the sound. Nico pulls his fist back, ready to throw the punches, the blows he's been practicing all of his adult life. I brace myself.

But Giancarlo grows again, seemingly unaffected as Nico rains down fury onto his legs, his calves, now his ankles, a tiny David to this giant Goliath.

"Nico!" I scream again and again, voice muted by the slippery, cigarette-stained palm.

Giancarlo picks up one long, black-soled shoe and takes aim at the Yankees hat. Then he brings it down.

"NO!"

———

I WAKE UP, my heart pounding wildly. My sheets are half-soaked with sweat, twisted around me like I just traveled through a tornado.

"Lay?"

Shama's voice calls from the other side of my door. I glance at it, but remain curled into a ball while I rock.

"You okay?" she asks.

"I...I'm fine," I manage to call back, cursing myself as my voice quivers. "I was tossing around in my sleep, that's all."

There's a pause. "Um, okay. Do you need anything?"

I shake my head, even though she can't see me. "N-no. I'm good. Go back to sleep, Shams."

There's another pause before finally I hear her shuffle back to her room and shut the door. I grab my pillow, flipping it over so it's no longer damp with sweat.

On my nightstand, my phone sits innocuously. I could call him, let his deep, soothing voice lull me back to sleep, a lullaby for my soul. He'll never know the way he does that, the way his whole presence brings me peace the way no one else can.

But it's three in the morning. He needs his sleep, and so do I. And he doesn't need to know that I'm going a little crazy. I don't need to be yet another burden on his life.

So instead, I reach for the pills on the other side of the nightstand. I clap one to my mouth and swallow tightly without any water. I'm going to spend the next twenty-four hours feeling like a zombie, but that's better than feeling like a crazy person.

"The here and now," I whisper to myself as I burrow back under my sheets, waiting for the numbing effect of the drug to work its way into my system. "The here and now."

But the mantra doesn't work. Because right here, in this small, cold, white room, I am scared. Right now, I am alone.

CHAPTER TWELVE

Nico

"Time's up."

I set my pencil down onto the table next to this week's exam. It's Friday, and I'm ready to get the fuck out of here for the weekend. All week I've been cooped up on "The Rock," as a lot of people call the academy, trapped half the day in this cinder block of a room with fifty other dudes who smell like feet and Old Spice, and spending the other half of the day puzzling my way in and out of smoke-filled buildings. Don't get me wrong: I love it. I love everything I'm doing, but it's fuckin' intense. I'm looking forward to getting to work in a real station. With real hours. And real people.

I flex my fingers and shake out the cramp in my hand. I swear to God, if I never take another test in my life, it will be too soon. I've got one more month until I'm assigned a station—one more month before we take our final exams and graduate. I can't fuckin' wait.

The sergeant collects our exams, raising his brow a little at me as he passes back the last ones.

"Nice job, Soltero," he mutters, then keeps moving.

I flip over the packet and see the perfect score I got on the last test. I might hate doing them, but having Layla in my ear all summer, coaching me on study methods, has helped me more than she knows. I might even graduate top of my class if I'm lucky. Who would have thought?

I thought, you goon. I can see Layla looking at me, her bright eyes smiling with pride while she chases away my doubts. She hates it when I think badly about myself, and while I used to brush it away as naivety, the truth is, I'm starting to believe her faith in me. I'm starting to expect myself to succeed rather than fail. It's a weird feeling. But a really good one.

"You doing anything fun this weekend, Soltero?"

I turn to Mike, one of the probies in my class, as we're filing out of the classroom. He's a nice enough kid from Staten Island who just barely managed to squeak into this class. He looks at my test score and breathes a "damn" under his breath. I roll up the paper and shove it into my backpack.

"Probably hang with my girl tonight," I say, feeling a little excitement in my stomach even as I say it. God, I love calling her that again out loud, not just in my head. My girl. "Then I gotta work tomorrow, family stuff on Sunday. Do some studying. Nothing too crazy. You?"

Mike nods his head. "Nah. I'll probably sit at home and watch *Fear Factor* or something. By this time at the end of the week, I usually just want to sleep all weekend. Who's your girl?"

I can't even hide the smile this time. "Layla. She's a student at NYU." I pull out my phone and flip it open to the picture. She doesn't know I even have the stupidly blurry snapshot from my phone that I took from across the room when she was laughing.

Mike nods approvingly. "Aww, that's nice, man. She's cute. You're a lucky man."

I nod. "Sure as fuck am."

"So, what kind of stuff you doing with your family?"

"The usual. Church. Family dinner. That sort of thing." I don't mention the fact that on Sunday we have a meeting with our social worker to talk about my mother's status and our travel license to Cuba.

We file out of the building, most of us making our way toward the bus stop.

"You need a ride?" Mike asks as he sees me turning that way. "What direction are you going?"

I chew on my lip. I should go home and change out of my uniform, but I remember Layla's face when I picked her up at the airport in my regulation gear. I wouldn't mind seeing her look at me like that again.

"If it's not too out of your way, you could drop me in Williamsburg," I say.

———

"So seems like you're doing good on the tests," Mike says once we're on our way.

I look out the window at the mostly boring buildings of Queens. "Um, yeah. I'm doing all right, I guess."

"Top recruit in your class means something," Mike says as he turns on to the freeway. "Friend of my brother's was top recruit. I heard he made lieutenant in less than a year."

I roll my eyes. It's not out of the realm of possibility, but you hear stories like that all the time. Would I like to make lieutenant? Sure. But honestly, I'll just be happy to graduate and be a legit firefighter, same as I've wanted since I was just a little kid. That alone is enough for me.

"You have a degree?"

I frown. "Nah. I started community college way back, but it wasn't for me." I don't want to get into the real reasons I didn't stay in school. Truthfully, my head wasn't in it, but I needed to work. I needed to support my family when my mom couldn't.

"Too bad," Mike said. "The guys like you. They listen to you. I heard the sergeants are always looking for people to groom, you know? You could probably be a battalion chief at some point. But you need a degree."

I blink in surprise. "What? Why?"

Mike nods. "Yeah, some bullshit requirement about leadership. Ain't that some garbage? Like, what the fuck is a bunch of college courses gonna do to teach you about being a firefighter? What is writing a bunch of crappy papers going to teach you about leading other guys? Nothin', that's what."

He switches gears, talking about the last Yankees game, but I only give a couple of nods and yeahs here and there. My mind is still lingering on that bombshell. I started this job because I wanted to do something real with my life, not just push boxes around all day. Even though I didn't have any major goals of jumping up the ranks immediately, it feels fuckin' shitty to realize that even from the start, I'm doomed to stay at the bottom.

———

MIKE DROPS me off at a J stop in Williamsburg with a shout that we should get a beer next Friday. I give him a maybe. Mike's a nice guy, but I'll be real. By Friday, after five days of not seeing Layla, I'm not really interested in anything else but tackling her.

Too bad she's not freakin' here.

"Hey," Shama says as she lets me into the apartment. "She's on her way back from the gym, I think."

"Oh yeah? She been working out?" She hasn't said anything about that to me, not since our little session at Frank's last weekend.

Shama nods with a funny look on her face. "Every day. She hasn't told you?"

I frown. "No. But I'm glad she is again. She seemed to have a good time on Sunday when we did some boxing."

"Yeah, I saw her knuckles. They were bruised all week."

Immediately, a pang of guilt shoots through me at the thought of Layla bruised again. And I did that.

"She seemed happy," Shama continues as she moves a bunch of books around a cardboard box. She gives me a look that tells me my instinct to keep on my uniform was a good one. I give her a knowing look back, and she snorts.

"Don't get too excited, Special Delivery," she says, using the nickname that Quinn, their old roommate, started when I first met Layla and was working at FedEx.

Immediately, my shoulders tense. I fuckin' *hate* that name. It's a name that reminds me that to some people, I'm always going to be some rat from the street. A blue-collar schmuck not worth their time.

"Ah," Shama says as she catches my face. "Sorry. Force of habit, but I didn't mean anything by it."

I relax, a bit surprised. "Maybe don't call me that anymore. I haven't worked at FedEx in more than a year, you know?"

"Well, maybe don't look so damn pleased with yourself that you look good in your uniform. That's what uniforms do. They would make Shrek look hot."

I chuckle, and Shama goes into the kitchen, where she grabs a beer from the fridge and tosses it to me. I sit down on the couch, the only furniture still in the mostly empty living room. They bought it last weekend, but other than that, there's not much else in here yet.

"I forget you guys are twenty-one now," I say as I crack open the can. "No more fake IDs, huh?"

Shama snorts. "Now who's stuck in the past?" she asks as she goes back to the boxes.

"How'd the week go, with your classes starting and everything?"

Shama shrugs. "Mine don't start until next week."

I frown. And then it registers that Shama's putting stuff in the boxes, not taking shit out. Through her bedroom door, everything is packed up tight. "Didn't you just move in here?"

"Ah, not really. I got a late acceptance to a study abroad program in London. I'm leaving next week."

For a second, I'm not sure if I heard that right. "You're *what*?"

Shama sets the tape down on the box and comes to sit next to me on the couch. "She didn't tell you?"

I shake my head. "Layla didn't tell me anything about that."

Shama shrugs. "I just found out last week. I'm guessing she didn't want you to worry about her."

I'm about to say there's nothing to worry about, except, of course, there is. It's not that Layla's not old enough to be living on her own—obviously that's fine. But I know my girl well enough to know that she doesn't actually want to be alone. That she's felt alone most of her life. I honestly think she liked living in the dorms, sharing a tiny apartment with three other girls, because it made that feeling go away.

But last year she lost most of those friends, and now Shama's taking off too? Shit. Now I know why she was so sad last weekend. One more thing this week she didn't tell me during our brief conversations at night. I try not to let it bug me, but it does.

"So, hey," Shama says. "I think maybe you should know something."

I look up. Shit, what else?

Shama glances nervously toward the front door, but obviously no one is there. She gets up and scurries into Layla's room, then comes out carrying a small orange prescription container. She tosses it to me with a light rattle, then comes to sit on the couch next to me.

"What's this?" I examine the bottle, reading the label. "Diazepam? This says Layla's name on it."

"Valium," Shama clarifies. "It's for her panic attacks."

I look up. "Panic attacks? What the hell?"

Shama sighs. "I knew she hadn't told you. But I'm leaving on Monday, and someone here needs to know. She was diagnosed this summer with PTSD after everything that happened with Giancarlo."

I stare at the bottle, unsure of what I'm hearing. "Did she tell you this?"

Shama shakes her head. "I called her mom after I heard one of the attacks. Cheryl told me a lot more than Layla probably would want."

"PTSD? Isn't that what like, combat soldiers get?" I've heard of war vets having PTSD, but not normal people.

"I looked it up, but honestly, I don't know that much about it," Shama says. "But I think anyone who's endured significant trauma can experience it. And I would consider what happened with...*him* to be a trauma, don't you think?"

In a second, I'm back in that room. I'm looking at that guy, who sliced his wrist just to fuck with Layla's mind, dripping blood all over her while he slams his fist into her face again and again. Forcing himself between her legs.

I rub my hand violently across my face. "I mean, sure. Yeah. The guy abducted her, abused her, pummeled her, and tried to rape her." I close my eyes, shoving away the image before that wave of rage overtakes me again. Fuck. Instead I focus on where I am. This conversation. Right now. "Why are you telling me this?"

Shama takes another long drink of her beer. "I'm telling you because I'm worried about her. You know Lay. She won't say anything because she won't want to burden you. She loves you like crazy—I hope you know that."

I nod. "I know. And, just so you know, the feeling is mutual. She—she's *everything* to me, Shama. I love her so fuckin' much."

She nods . "I know you do. She's lucky to have you."

For some reason, her endorsement feels really, really good. I don't know why it means so much to me that this rich, twenty-one-year-old chick from New Jersey gives me her approval, but it does.

"Thanks," is all I say. "So…these attacks. What do they look like?"

Shama presses her lips together. "She's pretty good at keeping them secret. But honestly, I think that's why she doesn't go out much. I think she's afraid of being psycho around people. The city freaks her out." She passes her beer from hand to hand a few times. "I'm kind of worried about what she'll do without someone here with her. That's the real reason I'm telling you."

I weigh the words. Suddenly, a lot of Layla's behavior becomes clearer. Her skittish looks. Sudden withdrawals. The way she freezes up, shies from my touch. I don't say anything to Shama about our challenges in the bedroom, but I bet she knows. Girls tell each other everything.

"I hear them," Shama says sadly. "Sometimes she'll wake up at night, and I'll hear her shouting about it. A few times I've gotten home when she's in the shower, and she sounds like a wild animal."

My chest constricts. Fuck. What has Layla been dealing with? And why the fuck hasn't she told me?

"She's supposed to have weekly sessions with a therapist, but she hasn't gone since she got to New York," Shama says as she stands up. She puts her empty can into the trash in the kitchen. "If you can help her see someone again, I think it would be good."

Dumbfounded, I stay on the couch, processing. Shama stops on her way back to her room, standing behind the couch.

"Hey, Nico?"

I look up. "Huh?"

Her expression is sympathetic. "I know it's a lot. But for what it's worth, she doesn't have those episodes when you're around. I think you make her feel safe."

She holds out her hand for the pills, then leaves me to brood while she returns the bottle to Layla's room and goes back to packing boxes. I just sit on the couch, lost in thought. Because as glad as I am that I'm something good in Layla's life, there's the other reality to contend with: I can't always be with her. At some point, she needs to feel safe on her own.

The front door opens with a bang, and my girl herself strides in, red-faced and bright-eyed when she spots me on the couch. She drops her bags on the floor, and before I can even get up, she's flying at me, covering my face with enough kisses to make me laugh and forget about the bomb her roommate just dropped.

"Ah! I missed you this week," she exclaims as she nuzzles her nose to mine.

I open my lips and pull her close for another hungry kiss. She has no fuckin' clue.

All day long, I have to think about things like escape routes and oxygen levels. But then I come back to my apartment, hungry for her voice more than I want my Dominican takeout. I fall asleep thinking about her, and I wake up dreaming about her face.

It's only been five days since we saw each other last, but it feels like five weeks. Which is why suddenly we're zero to sixty in about ten seconds flat, I'm hard as a rock, and Layla's got her hands up my shirt while we're devouring each other.

"Dudes, get a room," Shama says loudly as she pulls a loud piece of tape across her box.

Layla breaks away with a flush. I can't do anything but grin.

"You really shouldn't wear that uniform unless we're alone," she murmurs, pulling down my shirt.

My grin just about splits my face. Oh, I'm *definitely* going to wear the uniform again. I may not ever take it off.

Layla bites her lip, then turns. "Sorry, Shams. We'll be good."

"Nah, don't worry about it," Shama says as she closes the last box. "But I'm sorry I can't give you the house tonight. I have to finish packing before the movers come in the morning."

"It's okay." Layla turns back to me and delivers another kiss that's sweeter, but could easily turn feral if she just gave it a few more seconds. "I'm glad to see you," she says, blue eyes glowing. "Pizza and a movie? Or do you want to go out?"

I shake my head. I'm dead tired. Vegging out on the couch with a pie and my girl sounds like a winning lottery ticket. Shit, *she's* my winning lottery ticket.

I turn my baseball hat backward so I can kiss her again, more thoroughly. God, I really can't stop. "You order the pizza. I'll pick through your DVDs and see if I can find something that won't cost me my man card."

Layla giggles, but seriously. She and her friends have *way* too many chick flicks in their movie collection.

Within an hour, we're on the couch like we've been there all night, lounging lengthwise over the cushions, Layla's back spoons against my front with my arm draped over her middle as we fit together, two pieces of a puzzle. Every now and then, she turns over, nuzzles into my chest, and sighs. Every so often, I get a whiff of her scent—coconut. Midway through the movie, Layla's asleep on my chest, and I'm almost out myself, but I keep waking myself up because I don't want to miss it. Not the movie—I've seen *Top Gun* about a million times. Her.

Sometimes I can't believe that we're finally here again. That finally we have something like normal together. Layla sighs and burrows into me a little more. I drop a kiss on her forehead, and she murmurs something sweet and unintelligible against my shirt. My heart hurts, but in a good way. Like it can't totally understand this level of happiness.

Still, even as I watch Tom Cruise whizzing his jet all over the Indian Ocean, I can't help if any minute, Layla's going to wake up with that look of terror in her eyes. I wonder if she took one of those pills today or not. And mostly I wonder what else she's not telling me.

CHAPTER THIRTEEN

Layla

AT SOME POINT, NICO MOVES US BOTH TO MY BED FOR THE REST OF THE NIGHT, AND WE spend the majority of Saturday morning there too, including a solid forty-five minutes he spent mostly under my sheets while I shouted at the ceiling. He wanted to do more. I wanted to do more. But every time he crept over me and I felt *him* there, right between the slipperiest parts of me, I would freeze. I wanted it. *So. Bad.* But the rest of my body would stiffen and close up. And Nico would move to the side, turn me in his arms, and hold me until the feeling passed.

I hate it. I hate it so much. I just want to be normal again.

We sleep in and study together for another several hours while Nico reads his assignments for the weekend, I start my first assignments for a class I'm taking on Brazilian political history, and the movers come for Shama's stuff. The normal comes back, little by little. So in the middle of the afternoon, when I return from taking a shower to find Nico sitting at my desk, passing the prescription bottle of Valium back and forth between his big hands, the realization of the farce slams into my gut like a freight train.

"Where did you get that?" I ask as I enter, shaking out my hair.

Nico looks up. He's dressed again in his uniform, which is now creased, but still makes him look indecently handsome. "I was looking for a pen and found them in your desk. But actually, Shama showed them to me last night." He sets the bottle on the table like it might explode and looks at the instructions that come with them. "Those have some serious side effects, baby."

I sit down on the bed, pulling my robe tight over my body. "I only take them at night. When I—when I can't get back to sleep." I shake my head. "I don't like them. They make me feel woozy."

He frowns. "Why can't you sleep?"

I sigh and wrap my arms around my waist. Nico watches the motion, and his frown deepens.

"I just...I worry."

That's all I can say. How can I tell him about the psychotic dreams I have when I don't take them? Dreams about giant Giancarlo stepping on a tiny Nico. Dreams about long, skeletal hands encircling my neck and never letting go. Dreams about losing my breath. Losing my life.

Nico drums his fingers on the desk top for a moment and sets down the instructions. "They used to drug us with this kind of shit at Tryon, you know. Way worse than this, actually. But this is bad enough."

I cringe. He barely ever talks about the two years he spent at the detention facility, mostly because I know it hurts. They aren't memories he likes to relive, but here he is, bringing them up for me.

When Nico looks up, his big eyes have softened. "I hated it too."

I sit down across from him on the bed. "Why did they give it to you?"

"They overmedicated us. A lot of kids had real problems. Kids who came from homes where they'd had seriously bad shit happen to them all their lives, way, *way* worse than mine ever was. Their minds couldn't deal with it, and they really didn't have many ways to learn how." He fingers the bottle again, then pushes it away before looking back up at me. "But this doesn't fix things, baby."

"You make me sound like a crazy person," I whisper, staring at the floor.

I don't blame him. Sometimes I do feel crazy. Everywhere I look, that same shadow follows me. At school. In my sleep. When I close my eyes. And sometimes when they're open too. Only two things seem to make him go away: these pills and Nico. And Nico can't be around me all the time.

A finger tips up my chin, and I find Nico looking at me with sympathy. Understanding.

"No, baby," he says. "I've just been there. And what that fucker did to you last spring, I don't want it to poison you for the rest of your life. Take these pills if you need 'em, but they won't make it go away. You gotta find a way to deal with what's going on inside you, not numb it."

I take a deep breath, suddenly unable to prevent a tear from sliding down my cheek. Silently, I get off the bed and crawl into his lap, where he pulls me close and strokes my back, humming softly. He really is the best therapy I could ever ask for.

"I'm sorry," I whisper. "God, I'm so fucked up, aren't I? You can't even have sex with your own girlfriend because she's too freaked out."

"Stop. I'm not here for that. I'm here for you. All of you. However you come."

He looks down and catches a glimpse of my cleavage, then exhales like he's in pain. His full lips purse, and I kiss them, because I can. Reflexively, my hips roll into the length suddenly pressing between them.

"Mm," Nico groans. "You don't make it easy on a guy, though, NYU. And fuck. I gotta go. I'm supposed to be at AJ's by eight, and I still have to go back uptown to get my fuckin' monkey suit."

"You need to just bring a bunch of clothes here, not just a change," I say as I get up and go look for some clothes of my own. "That way when you come on Fridays, you can just stay until you absolutely have to go on Saturdays."

I stop, realizing what I'm saying here, and flush. "I mean...if you want to. No pressure."

Immediately, I want to smack myself in the head. Stupid, stupid! You only just got back together all of five minutes ago. You've had sex one terrible time in a nightclub, and now you're offering him closet space?

But before I can turn around, Nico encircles me from behind, his strong arms wrapped around my waist.

"You really want me here all weekend?" he asks, his low voice rumbling against my neck. One hand slips under the fabric of my robe, playing over my bare stomach.

The effect is immediate. I sigh, melting into his touch as the rest of me wakes up fully. "I do."

There's another low rumble of contentment. "Good. I want to be here too. Probably too much."

He trails a few delicious kisses up and down my neck, running his teeth over my earlobe and catching it between them for a split-second.

I press back into him and moan. "Do you…do you have to go right away?"

Slowly, my head is tipped back, and with an open, warm mouth, Nico delivers a kiss that erases all doubts. Our tongues twist together delicately, a dance we never forget. I press back more against his tented pants—he's ready now. He wants this as badly as I do.

"Are you? Are you sure?" he murmurs.

Am I sure? I'm sure I want to feel good. I want to feel normal, and this—*this* insane, magnetic connection we've always had—is our normal.

I nod and then suck on his full lower lip. Nico groans. The hands at my waist slowly undo my robe so that it hangs open over my still-damp, naked body.

Nico sucks in a breath as he looks down my front. He cups my breasts with both hands, brushing his thumbs over my aching nipples.

"Can I make you come, baby?" he asks as he sucks on my earlobe again.

I hum. "Mmmmmm."

In the mirror hung over my closet door, we both watch, transfixed, as he slides a hand down my front and places two fingers over my clit.

"Look at you," he says as he runs his teeth up and down my neck. "So fucking beautiful. You drive me crazy, baby, you know that?"

I can feel his rigid length pressed against the cleft of my ass. In the back of my mind, I see us clearly: me pressed against this mirror, bent over so he can thrust his cock into my depths. I want it so badly…and at the same time, I'm content to fall against him and let him continue the insistent caresses he's started. His fingers continue their work while his other hand drifts from my breasts, over my stomach, and around my back. It palms my ass and squeezes lightly, playing with the curves of Nico's favorite body part.

"So fucking luscious," he growls as he squeezes again. He slides his tongue over my neck. I can't stop watching.

"Wrap your arms around my head," he says as he continues to knead my backside. I obey, and the motion causes my robe to spread further, leaving nothing he's doing to the imagination.

The fingers in front press a little harder and move a little faster. The ones behind slip further south, between my legs, nudging them apart. I suck in a breath as a finger enters my dark, slick entrance. One at first, then two.

"Do you need to come, baby?" Nico asks, his low voice vibrating lightly over my skin.

I lean back into him as both hands work my body from the front and back, the fingers inside me thrust lightly in time with the ones at my clit.

"Fuck!" I hiss as he slips a third inside. He curves them slightly, pressing them against the sensitive bundle of nerves there, the ones on the other side of my clit. That same spot inside my body is getting this delicious treatment from both sides.

"Come on, baby," Nico says. "Let it go. I got you."

His teeth close down on my ear, and the slight tinge of pain is my undoing.

"Oh, *fuck!*" I cry out as the orgasm shoots through me. The fingers inside thrust harder, deeper, causing pleasure to ricochet through my limbs with a force that makes me shake.

"I got you," Nico murmurs again and again through his teeth. "Take it, baby. I got you."

And he does. I shake in his arms for what seems like minutes until slowly, slowly, I fall from the high where only he can take me. I collapse backward against his strong form, feeling a different kind of wooziness—one where my body feels alive and contented all at once.

"What about you?" I murmur, still slouched into his shoulder. He's still long and hard, pressed against my backside. I nuzzle backward, noting with a little satisfaction the shudder that passes over his face at the motion.

"Later," he replies with a sharkish grin at me through the mirror. "I'll bring clothes tomorrow. That reminds me: what are you doing tomorrow? What do you think about going to Mass?"

I turn around and grin. "Are you going to save me with Jesus?" I ask, poking him in the stomach. I don't bother to close my robe, enjoying the way his gaze plays over me.

Nico tips his head back and laughs. "What the fuck kind of hypocrite would I be to do that?" But then he sobers. "No, I'm going to save you with family. Mine's a little crazy, but they love you. Come with us."

I don't have to think twice. I used to hate going to church as a kid, and even now, I only ever go out of guilt or maybe nostalgia. But the idea of going to Mass with Nico's family, a roomful of people who love, pester, annoy, and care for each other, seems really nice.

"I'll be there," I say just before he delivers another kiss. "Just tell me where and when."

CHAPTER FOURTEEN

Layla

WHEN TURNS OUT TO BE FIVE THIRTY IN THE AFTERNOON, AND THE WHERE TURNS OUT TO BE a familiar church on Forty-Ninth Street. I find myself standing, looking up at the red brick exterior, my palms sweating while the priest stands at the door, greeting all of the parishioners in Spanish.

"Hey, baby."

I turn around to find Nico approaching with Gabe and Carmen trailing behind. He gives me a lingering kiss on the cheek, and it's only then that I take in his blue button-down shirt and black pants. His dense, curly hair has been tamed a bit, and the blue of his shirt makes his skin glow. He looks way too delicious for church.

"Hi," I greet him with a tame kiss, then accept kisses on the cheek from both Carmen and Gabe. "Where are Maggie and Selena?"

"The *gatitas* went to the zoo for the day," Gabe says. "Allie was driving everyone crazy this morning, so no church. Thank God—er, I mean, thank goodness."

"Why do you call your sisters little cats?" I ask.

Next to us, Carmen rolls her eyes and shakes her head.

Nico gives me a lopsided smile. "*Gata* is a common phrase for girls. We called them that when they were little because Selena and Maggie used to fight like cats. Now Allie sometimes acts like one too."

"Ah," I say with understanding.

Their apartment is a packed place at the moment—one small bedroom for Gabe, one for Maggie and her daughter, while Nico sleeps on the couch. I wouldn't be surprised if a five-year-old was acting out here and there.

"I'm glad you're here," Nico says as he takes my hand. "You look way too beautiful for church, but I'll just have to deal with that."

I look down at my clothing, a green sweater dress that fits the slight nip marking the beginning of fall. It makes my eyes pop and sets off the olive tones in my pale skin.

"Thanks," I murmur. "But you're one to talk. You'd corrupt a priest any day."

Nico gives me a lopsided smile that brings out the dimple in his left cheek. But just before I can tell him to stop doing that lest I combust completely, Carmen calls for us to greet the priest and file inside.

"What did you do this morning?" I ask as I follow them into one of the pews near the front.

Nico shrugs. "Gabe and I had to patch a hole. A mouse got in last weekend and chewed up half the food in the kitchen. And then we had an appointment with the social worker."

He says the last sentence in a hushed voice and glances around while we sit, and I know he would prefer not to talk about that particular meeting right here. Places like this would actually be a perfect place for an immigrations officer to eavesdrop.

"Did it…did it go well?" I ask, careful not to give anything away.

Nico looks around again sharply, but his eyes soften when they land on me. "It is what it is. The last license was rejected, you know. But Ileana says we can apply for an informational one, since Gabe's in school. Maybe he can apply to travel as a student on a research project. We'll see."

I understand by his clipped tone that there isn't anymore he wants to say about it, so I drop it. But I can't help but feel like there has to be something more that I could do.

I look around the church, and before I can stop it, memories of the last time I was here come floating back just as the altar boys walk down the aisle carrying the incense. Last Christmas, for another Spanish-language Mass with…

Suddenly, that familiar freeze is back, along with a deep fear that hits me in the belly.

"I see him here sometimes," Gabe says on my other side in a low voice, clearly checking to make sure his brother doesn't hear him.

I jerk my head around. "What?"

Nico immediately turns from a conversation with his mom. "What's going on?"

Gabe looks uneasy. "I, um, was just telling NYU that I've seen her, ah…you know. Evita. Here sometimes." He shrugs. "Maybe once or twice."

Nico's eyes practically bug out of his head. "And you didn't think to fuc—you didn't think to tell me?"

Gabe frowns. "So you could get yourself into trouble while you're in the academy? Yeah, no. I thought that would be a bad idea."

Nico practically growls, earning a light slap on his shoulder from his mother, urging him to calm down before the Mass begins.

"See, that's what I'm talking about," Gabe whispers harshly. "Your temper gets you in trouble. He has a court date, doesn't he?" He looks at me for confirmation.

I nod. "Next week," I murmur. Is it really that close?

Gabe looks back at his brother. "Nobody needs you playing superhero anymore, *mano*. That's how you got yourself into trouble in the first place."

I wince, and I don't have to look next to me to know that Nico's hurt. Gabe's talking about the stint at Tryon after Nico helped rob a bodega to feed his brother and sisters. It's correct, yes. But it's also incredibly unfair.

But the church quiets before I can say it, so instead, I edge closer to Nico.

"Hey," I say.

I nudge him in the shoulder. His muscles barely move, but I can still see the shape of them, evident in the way they test the confines of his dress shirt. He looks at me sadly, but doesn't say anything.

"You're *my* hero," I whisper. "And I'll never be more grateful than I was when you busted through that door and saved me."

Nico stares at me for a moment with an expression that's a cross between pained and relieved. Then briskly, he stamps a hard, close-mouthed kiss on my lips, completely ignoring Carmen's smack on his shoulder as he does it.

"I love you," he whispers fiercely, and squeezes my hand so hard I wonder if he'll ever let it go.

The priest begins the service, and we both straighten up. But I know that neither of us are really listening to what he's saying. Even if I could understand the entire Mass in Spanish, like Nico can, I would be just as busy scanning the crowd. Watching for the face I pray I'll never see again.

─────

By the end of the Mass, I couldn't have told you a single thing the priest said. Seriously, you try focusing on Holy Scripture when you've got a hundred and eighty pounds of muscled man next to you who smells like heaven and licks his lips every time he looks at you. Church is doing *nothing* to temper all the illicit thoughts going through my head as I file down the aisle with a prime view of Nico's ass in those pants.

"*Gracias, Padre. Próxima semana.*"

The sound of the voice stops me in the middle of the center aisle. Gabe and Carmen have already left the church, but Nico, still holding my hand, looks up when I jerk to a violent stop.

"What's…"

He doesn't even finish his sentence when he sees my face. I'm still staring ahead at the tall, pale man, chatting comfortably with the priest. Giancarlo adjusts his glasses and runs a big hand through his full head of wavy black hair. And then, like he knows he's being watched, straightens and turns his head. His eyes land on me, and his mouth drops slightly.

"Layla?" he asks.

The priest steps out of the church to speak to other parishioners who are leaving. Giancarlo blocks the exit, whether on purpose or not.

"You ruined me," he says, just loud enough that I can hear him across the three or so pews.

Nico takes a step forward, shielding me with his body. Still frozen, I'm happy to let him.

"Move on, man," he says. "Let's not do this here."

"This is my last week here," Giancarlo continues, staring a hole through me over Nico's big shoulder. "My lawyers, they say I will go to jail or to Argentina." He gulps, and for a second, I can see genuine fear in the eyes I never remember as anything but stern and threatening. "All because of *you*."

He holds me captive with his glare for what seems like several minutes. Move, Layla. Don't give him the satisfaction of watching you crumble.

By some miracle, I manage to turn to Nico. "Let's go," I murmur, tugging on his hand. "Please."

After pausing for a second like he's genuinely trying to decide whether committing murder—in the middle of a church no less—is really a mortal sin, Nico finally nods. With eyes as dark as night, Nico leads me down the aisle, making big movements that force Giancarlo down one of the pews. Nico's doing his best not to lose it. Every muscle in his neck looks like it's about to snap, and his teeth grind together as we walk.

But just as we reach the door, my other hand is snatched, and when I look up, Giancarlo is glaring at me with eyes like death.

"Say something!" he hisses. "You cannot just walk away. *You* did this to me. God will not forgive you for it!"

"W-what are you talking about?" I finally sputter. "You did this to yourself. N-no one made you do the things you did to me."

"Let her go," Nico orders as the vein in his temple throbs visibly.

"You'll never get away from me," Giancarlo replies in a low, gruesome voice. "You haven't yet, have you?"

I see his face again, but in the back of my mind. All the times it flashed before me at school. On the street. Around every dark corner.

Was it ever him for real? I honestly don't know. It doesn't really matter.

Before I can ask, Giancarlo pulls on my hand, like he wants to yank me out of the church. My heart is beating out of my chest, but before I can even think about fighting, Nico drops his arm down and breaks Giancarlo's grip like he's snapping a pencil in half.

"Just try it," Nico growls, so low that only the three of us can hear him. "You do, and ain't no church gonna protect you, motherfucker. You think God's above vengeance? I guaran-fuckin-tee he'd be on *my* side of this fight."

"Don't," I murmur as I start to shake. "D-don't. Nico, just leave it."

"Layla." Nico's gaze flashes down at me, and I grip his shoulder, desperate for the warmth I need to calm my thrashing heart. When we both look up, Giancarlo is gone, having fled the church without a sound. A muscle in the side of Nico's neck still ticks. He looks like a feral cat dying to set out on the chase. But I squeeze his hand again, willing him to calm down even though my heart is beating wildly.

Then he looks back down at me. "How many times have you seen him?"

I take a step back, ignoring the people leaving the church who are watching us with interest.

"I—none."

"Goddammit, Layla," Nico hisses, earning a shocked look from one of the parishioners, an old lady who mutters "*Vergüenza!*" under her breath before automatically crossing herself. Nico grabs my arm and tows me toward one of the small apses, where an array of candles burns. "How many times?"

I bite my lip. "I...I don't think it was him. He was surprised to see me too."

Nico frowns, staring at the open door again, like he thinks Giancarlo might reappear. "Then what the fuck did he mean, you haven't gotten away from him yet?"

I shudder. "I...honestly, I don't know. Maybe he just knows that he's inside my head. I was never sure it was him. Honestly, I've just been imagining him."

"What do you mean, *imagining* him?" Nico's voice cuts, still sharp.

"I-I see him sometimes," I admit. "And then I shake my head, and he's not there.

The doctor—my therapist in Pasadena—told me they were flashbacks. That they're c-common for victims of trauma."

I hang my head, grateful that no one else appears to be hearing this conversation.

Nico exhales, long and heavy. "But maybe he really was there?"

I shrug, and even the possibility causes a pit of dread to spread throughout my stomach. "I…I don't know. Could be."

Nico shoves his hands up and down his face. "We gotta tell the police."

I frown. "Tell them what? That we ran into him at a church he attended long before I ever did? That I think I've seen him around, but we've never made contact, and that I'm not really sure which of those times were hallucinations or which were real, if any of them were? What do you think they're going to do?"

Nico groans through his fingers. "Fuck!"

"You really shouldn't say that in a church," I whisper.

"*Fuck*," he says again, more vehemently, though he still glances back toward the altar guiltily. Like the crucifix hanging on the wall can hear him. "Come on. We're getting out of here."

Outside, he looks around for Gabe and Carmen, shouting across the street in a rapid Spanish that I can barely translate, roughly meaning we're going somewhere else. Gabe, knowing better than to question his brother when he looks like this, just nods and starts shepherding Carmen back to Alba's apartment. Nico grabs my hand and tows me toward the Hudson.

His head is on a swivel as he practically jogs me through Hell's Kitchen. He's keeping an eye out for Giancarlo, I know, but that tall, slouching form is nowhere to be seen. It's not until we're a block from Frank's gym that I realize his intention. Nico pushes through the door, startling a group of people working out together on the open floor in the front.

Nate appears from the office at the top of the stairs.

"You got a free ring?" Nico asks.

Nate checks his watch. "In about an hour, yeah. Can you wait?"

Nico growls, but nods his head. "It's fine. We'll do some bag work first."

I'm towed toward the lockers at the far side of the gym, where Nico stops and unlocks one. Out of it he pulls some workout clothes for me, and a bag of his own stuff.

"How—what is this stuff doing here? Hey, I was looking for this sports bra!"

"Shama gave it to me before she left," Nico says, his voice still abrupt and curt. "I thought you should have some stuff to keep here for when we came back." He jerks his head toward the changing rooms in the back. "Get dressed and meet me by the heavy bags."

"But, wait, shouldn't we talk about what just happened? You're obviously mad, and I'm kind of freaked out." Now that I'm finding my voice again, I can't stop talking. "We need to figure out what to do—"

"Layla." His deep baritone stops my babbling.

I blink. "What?"

"We'll take care of all of that. Right now, I *really* need to do this, okay? This is what I do when I'm about to lose it."

I open my mouth to say something, but my words escape me. "Okay."

CHAPTER FIFTEEN

Nico

AFTER WE CHANGE, WE TAKE SOME TIME TO WARM UP, AND THEN SPEND ABOUT A HALF hour on the heavy bag practicing combinations until we're both breathing heavily. Layla clearly likes throwing punches, but I barely notice, going harder than I've gone in months. With every punch I throw, it's that motherfucker's face I see. It's his glasses I'm breaking. It's his teeth I'm knocking out.

Fuck. *Fuck*. Why didn't she tell me? From what he said, it sounds like this guy has either been stalking her since she got here, or else she's literally *seeing* the asshole everywhere she goes. No wonder she's been acting like a scared rabbit. She's terrified, and for good reason.

Eventually, the gym clears out after the evening classes are over. Nate comes over to tap me on the shoulder. It's past eight, and he's about ready to lock up early.

I look up. Layla is sitting on the bench, taking a drink of water.

"It's all yours," Nate says, jerking his head at the empty gym. "Lock up, okay?"

"Thanks, man." I nod and watch until the door swings shut behind him. Then I turn to Layla.

"Come on, baby," I say. "In the ring. And take off your shoes."

I toss my sneakers and gloves toward the lockers and hop into the ring. Confused, Layla follows, and then we're standing, facing each other.

"You can take off your hand wraps," I tell her. I'm not wearing any, and my knuckles are going to fuckin' throb tomorrow. But I don't really care. The pain actually feels kind of good.

Layla does as I say and drapes the reams of black fabric over one of the ropes. Then she faces me. "What are we doing?"

"I wish I could be with you all the time," I say quietly. "It's crazy, but I do. I just want to protect you from fuckin' everything."

Her blue eyes are wide, scared. The expression guts me every time. I walk around this city feeling like I have a hole in my stomach. I just want that look to disappear. I want her to look at the world, at *me* with confidence again. With openness, love, excitement, optimism. Just like she used to.

"I know," she whispers, clenching her hands together. She looks down.

I sigh. "But I can't, baby. It's not...that's not reality. So...I want to show you how to protect yourself."

"Isn't that what we started doing this last month?"

I smirk. She's learning to throw a decent punch, but she's still only a hundred and twenty pounds soaking wet. Things like height and weight matter in boxing. But there are other things she could learn to do better.

"If a guy like *Giancarlo*"—fuck, that name really does put a bad taste in my mouth —"forced you down again, do you think you'd be able to fight him off?"

Layla bites her lip and shuts her eyes. I'm taking her somewhere she doesn't want to go. But I have to. *She* has to.

I shut mine and say a quick prayer, asking God, whoever that is, to forgive me for what I'm about to do.

Then, I attack.

"What the—WHAT ARE YOU DOING?" she screams.

It doesn't take much. A quick twist of her wrist and a knock on her knee to push her to the ground, pinning her under my weight. I'm sprawled on top of her, and to my surprise, she barely fights, lost more in the confusion.

"Nico," she cries as her voice wavers. Tears start to fall down her face, and it just about breaks me. "Nico, please. W-what are you doing to me?"

"Listen to what I tell you to do." I'm going for soothing even as my heart breaks.

I don't want to do this. I don't want to hurt her ever again. But she needs it. Just a little more pain to fight through.

"You have strong legs," I tell her. "Maybe even stronger than mine. Push up on your heels, and twist your body as hard as you can. Throw me off, baby. You can do it."

She opens her mouth like she's going to argue, but then she tries, lifting her pelvis into me, and then twisting around. I move a little—it's actually hard to stay on top of her like this when she does that—but I don't fall completely off.

"Keep going," I tell her as I brace her wrists. "Come on. I'm not a good guy right now, NYU. I'm a fuckin' asshole. I'm taking advantage of you. Get me the fuck off!"

"I can't," she whimpers.

Beneath me, her body deflates. It wrecks me, inside and out. My girl, my *strong*, beautiful, incredible fucking *woman*, withers like a blade of grass without water.

But she can do this. I know she can. She has to.

"As hard as you can," I growl into her ear.

"Stop," she mewls. "Please stop."

"Make me."

And then I release one hand and draw it down her face, closing it around her neck. I take a deep breath and close my eyes, repeating a prayer again. God, forgive me. Lord, give her strength.

And then I squeeze.

"NO!"

Layla howls like a wolf, her body suddenly coming to life. She pushes with her hips, once, twice, gaining momentum for a third, final push, combined with a twist that's more awkward than anything else. But, as if she just stuck her finger in a light socket, a shock of power courses through her body. She throws me off, forcing me a solid two feet away, giving her enough space to roll over, wheezing while she clutches her neck. I lie on my back, rubbing my sore ribs where she kicked me on the way out. I couldn't have stopped her if I'd tried. But I'm so fuckin' glad of that fact.

I turn to her, unsure of what I'm going to see. Layla's scrambling up, her hand still at her neck. She glares, her eyes lit up like blue fire.

"*What* the fuck was that?" she spits. "What were you *doing*?"

"Teaching you to protect yourself." I clamber up, a silly, stupid grin on my face despite the fact that my head is fuckin' throbbing. Knuckles *and* headache in the morning. I couldn't care less.

"Fuck!" Layla shouts, kicking at the ground. "Why-why are you fucking *smiling*, you asshole?!"

"Because you did it!" I crow. "You fuckin' did it, woman! And if you can do that to me, a trained fuckin' fighter, you can protect yourself against anyone, baby. Don't you see that?"

But when I look at her, ready to see victory all over her face, she's crying. Her beautiful face is marred with tears, her blue eyes shining and red-rimmed, her rose-petal mouth screwed up in misery. Fuck me. This isn't what I wanted. To break her even more.

Immediately, I scramble to her side and pull her into my arms. Fuck the sweat. Fuck all of that. I just want her to stop crying. I can't fuckin' take it when she hurts like this.

"Shhhh. I'm sorry. I'm so fuckin' sorry, baby. I shouldn't have pushed you like that. What was it? The pressure at your neck? The holding you down? Fuck me, I'm so goddamn sorry."

"*No!*" she shouts into my neck, even as her hands cling at my arms, tight enough that her fingernails dig into the skin. Several more sobs wrack through her small body into mine. "Don't be sorry. It's-it's not that," she stutters as her tears slow to a trickle. She looks up and wipes them away angrily. "It's not that. It was…it was fine."

I lean back. "It was?"

She nods. "I'm glad you did it. I sort of hate you right now, but I'm glad I could do it too."

I push a lock of hair out of her face. "Then what is it?"

She sniffs, and when she looks up, the pain blotting her gorgeous blues, as deep as the ocean itself, sends another ripple of hurt through my body.

"I liked it," she admits, even as her lower lip trembles. "It hurt. Your hands around my throat. Holding me down. I hated it. And I fucking liked it too." She shivers. "Love shouldn't hurt, right?" Her voice shakes when she looks up. "That's what I learned from all that mess. *That* wasn't love, and it took me months to figure that out. So why…why do I like it?"

I exhale, not out of frustration, but because finally, *finally* we're getting somewhere. I see it clearly now. She wants what she wants, just like we all do. But she hates herself for it.

"I know why I ended up with someone like that," she whispers. "It's because a part of me…a part of me liked it." She looks up, her blue eyes wide and pained. "Why is that? He kept hurting me, but I kept going back. Just like I did with you."

Her words are straight and true and pierce me like arrows. Because she's right—I did hurt her. Several times, just like she did to me. And like addicts, we both kept coming back to each other, looking for more of that same, bittersweet rush.

"Some of us just learn it like that," I murmur.

I realize that this is one of the few things Layla and I have in common. We might come from totally different worlds, she and I, but we both learned in our own ways that it was normal for people to hurt us.

But maybe that knowledge is also what might set us free.

"You know what I think?" I ask. I stroke the side of her arm, and she closes her eyes. But this time I don't scratch. "I think maybe it's okay to hurt sometimes."

Her eyes open, confused. "What?"

"People like us, well, a lot of people, really...maybe we need a little bitter to make sense of the sweet."

I turn my finger over and press my nail lightly into her skin, just enough for it to bite. The sharp twinge causes the same reaction in her—a shiver of pleasure, and then a pained look on her face. She shudders, but the goose bumps that rise all over her tell me it's not an unpleasant feeling. Her breath hitches, and so does mine.

"You feel this," I say as I draw my hand up her chest.

I place it, palm down, over her heart and thrill in the solid beat of it. She's affected by what I'm doing—that much is clear. Almost immediately, she places her hand in the same spot on my chest, directly over the compass I've had tattooed there since I was nineteen. The same age she was when I met her.

"I'm *never* going to break that again," I tell her. "That's a promise."

"But, you don't know if—"

"*Never,*" I cut in.

I don't even blink, urging her to see the truth in my eyes. She searches my face for several moments.

"We can do it in ways that are good for each other. *I* can do that for you, baby. You just gotta tell me: what do you need?"

She swallows, then glances down at the other hand resting on her thigh. Slowly, she covers it with her hand, then clenches her fingers, forcing me to grab her thigh, hard enough that it might actually bruise. And then she kisses me. Hard.

"Ah!" she cries out as I nip her lower lip. But she doesn't pull away. This time she bites back.

"Again," she hisses after she sucks voraciously on my mouth.

And just like that, I'm hard as a fucking rock. It's been over a year of waiting for this, waiting for the moment where we really, truly connect again. I didn't plan for it like this. I didn't plan for the fuckin' bathroom of a shitty nightclub either, or the mat of a boxing gym. But if this is where Layla gets herself back, where we learn to be us again, I'll take it. However it comes.

"Okay," I say. "But only if you give it back."

I give her the rough, almost painful kisses she seeks, knead her legs, her thighs, her ass hard enough to hurt just a little while I grind myself into her. My cock finds her ready, just a few strips of fabric between us. There's nothing more I'd like than to bend her over and take her right now. I'd find her wet and willing, I know it.

But there will be other times like that, when we can go fast and furious. Right now, I need to make sure. I need to make sure it's right.

"What else?" I say as I take another harsh handful of her ass with a light slap. She moans lightly into my mouth. "What else do you want?"

"I want…oh! I want…*more*."

Her hands thread into my hair and yank. That hint of pain shoots down my neck, but it only turns me on more. Her mouth crashes into mine, and we're a sudden tangle of tongues and limbs. It's like a light turned on—my gamble paid off. I opened up a door, and Layla's sprinting through it. Right into me.

"Take—take these off," she says through a few more torrid, biting kisses. She paws at my shorts, and in about two seconds, I've kicked them to the floor along with my boxers. When I look back at her, she's done the same thing with her pants and is in the middle of taking off her top and sports bra. I watch, fuckin' mesmerized, as her breasts bob free. She cups them lightly.

"You said once you were a biter," she says with a sly smile. "Did you forget how?"

On my hands and knees, I cross the mat until I'm positioned over her, with Layla's back to the floor, a lot like we were only a second ago when she threw me off. The knowledge that she can even do that at all makes me want her even more. I bury my face in her breasts, licking, sucking, and even biting. She moans and arches her back.

"Does that seem like I forgot?" I growl before taking one nipple between my teeth and pulling a little.

"More," she beckons, a hand sliding around my head and urging me to one side. "Now."

I take her nipple deeply into my mouth and earn another low, long moan as I suck hard enough for it to pinch. I roll her nipple between my teeth, then bite a little, then a little more, until Layla starts to shake.

"Nico," she whispers, breathy as her legs open under me.

I'm pressed between her strong thighs, hard as one of the steel pipes crisscrossing the ceiling, and her slick heat moistens as I grind into her core. The tip of my cock slips in, and we both jerk as I switch to her other breast and continue that torture she desires. The torture she needs.

"Condom?" she whimpers even as her hips tilt, taking me a little further.

The hands in my hair pull harder, and with her breast still in my mouth, it's all I can do not to shove all the way in and drive her down to the mat. But I swear to God, I really *am* a fuckin' superhero, because I manage to pull out, my cock just hovering at her aching entrance. A different kind of torture. A different kind of sweet.

"Do we…" I pause, weighing the question. "Do we need it?"

Sometimes real closeness hurts a little too. But it's a pain that I crave also, just like she needs it from me. The knowledge that even if they don't, someone could hurt you. Layla's the only girl I've ever been with bare, and I know I'm the same for her. And it's been almost six months since…*him*. More than that for me. We've both been tested, and we talked about birth control before she came back to New York. There's nothing stopping us if this is what we want to do. Which, I realize, I do. I want it more than maybe anything I've ever wanted in my life. Just to be close to her. To know there's literally nothing between us, physically or mentally. To know that we belong to each other so much that our bodies actually become one.

The thought sends a convulsive shiver through me from head to toe.

In response, Layla arches up to kiss me, and her hands reach around to grab my ass and guide me fully inside. She's tight—*so* damn tight—enough that it takes a moment for her to get used to me. I'm not huge or anything, but big enough to stretch her small body. As I push inside her completely, she flops back onto the mat, breathing hard as I take her breast into my mouth again and bite down.

"Nico!" she cries out. It's not a whimper, but a shout. And it echoes, again and again off the cinderblock walls and concrete floors of the gym as I drive into her.

Her voice, its strength, lets loose some animal in me that's been dying to be free. With Layla, I am never anything but my purest self. I have no name. I'm barely a man, but whatever I am was made for her, her essence, her body. Made to devour, pillage, ravage, feast on this body that has only ever fit mine perfectly.

Her muscles tense and her legs squeeze around my waist. The movement squeezes the rest of me too, and it only makes me pound into her that much harder.

"Fuck!" she cries out, hands grasping at the mat while she urges me onward.

"Is it...is this okay?" I can barely get the words out, I'm so fucking overwhelmed with want. Fear. Lust. Passion.

"Nico."

I swear to God, if she didn't say it, I wouldn't even be able to remember my own name. But her eyes flash as she swallows.

"Harder."

It's the only encouragement I need. In a half second, I have her flipped over onto her hands and knees, two handfuls of her ass in my grip as I yank her hips toward me and impale myself into her waiting warmth.

"Yessssss!" I hiss as I pound into her.

"Yessssss!" she cries, her hips pressing back, hit for heavy hit.

"Again!" she shouts.

So I do. Rhythmically, my hand finds the solid flesh of her with a satisfying crack once, twice, a third and final time that causes both of us to fall apart completely. Layla's body starts to convulse as my hands take two harsh handfuls of flesh so I can ram into her for the last time before I fall over her. We come together, and the walls of the gym seem to disappear. I can't see two feet ahead of me. I can't hear a damn thing. All I can do is feel, and what I feel is her. Layla.

CHAPTER SIXTEEN

Layla

"WELL, I GUESS THAT'S IT."

Shama sets her rolling bag by the door, then turns to me with a lopsided smile.

"Here," she says, holding out her key. "For your new roommate, whoever that will be."

I turn the brass piece over and back. I don't have a new roommate yet. Actually, I haven't even started looking, even though I really should. Shama promised to pay rent for at least a month or two until I find someone decent, but I haven't even put an ad on the off-campus housing site or craigslist. Something is stopping me from inviting a stranger into my house. I've been too burned by strangers in this city. I want my home to feel safe.

I shove the key in my pocket and give Shama a hug. Her flight to London is in three hours. There's a cab waiting to take her to the airport, off to embark on her newest adventure. Tears spring to my eyes as Shama returns my tight embrace.

"I'm sorry I can't be there today with you," she says. "I want to see the look on that bastard's face when he gets his."

I step back, swiping away the tears. The truth is, I'm not just upset about her leaving. The DA informed us that Giancarlo's trial was finally moving forward this week after months of delays. So far, he has refused to take a plea, and today the jury will announce the verdict. And on the recommendations of Nico, my therapist in Pasadena, and the counselor I started seeing at the student center, I decided to attend after all. Because like Nico said, I needed to face him on my terms.

Therapy. Self-defense. It's only been a week since our explosive reunion at Frank's, but already I feel like I'm on a better path forward. My fears haven't totally faded. Not even close. But I'm feeling stronger. Like maybe one day I can chase them away.

"It's okay," I say. "It was moved to five, so Nico will be there. And I think Gabe and Maggie are planning to come too."

"You're not alone here, dude," Shama says, like she knows what's going through my head. "You have Special Delivery. You've got his family too. It's not just you."

I shake my head. "He hates being called that, you know."

"I know. It makes me want to do it more now. But seriously, he is kind of special, you know? It fits."

I smile. It's true. Nico *is* special. He's been special since he delivered himself into my life. Inwardly, I can see Nico shaking his head even as his dark eyes dance. Mumbling, *Baby, you are corny as fuck,* even as he leans in for a kiss. The thought just makes me smile more.

"Wear something blue," Shama says. "To make your eyes pop. Then stare that dickhead down as they cart his ass back to jail, say good fucking riddance, and move on with your life."

I nod. She makes it sound so easy. "I'll do my best."

———

AT FIVE O'CLOCK, the court is running late, and so is everyone else. There are several cases being tried today, and the small gallery is mostly full. Giancarlo is being held in the back, waiting for the bailiff to call his name, and I'm alone in the third row of the gallery, my arms wrapped around my waist, feeling much colder than I should in an overheated room full of people.

"It's in your favor," the DA said earlier in the week when she called with an update. "You never know what a jury is going to do, but I doubt this one will be lenient."

They chose to go for the drug crimes instead of domestic violence, since it was easier to prove, and on top of that, the fact that Giancarlo's wounds from Nico had been much worse than the ones I had incurred from Giancarlo made it difficult to prosecute him on that account. He hadn't shown any desire to file charges against Nico, considering the number of witnesses there. But the drugs in the closet were another story adding up to charges of possession, intent to distribute, and trafficking.

The second hand on my watch ticks while I wait—the watch I can't ever look at without remembering how it was taken from me. I squeeze my eyes shut and wait some more. As the courtroom murmurs rise, the colder and colder I feel. I start to rock slightly.

"The here and now," I whisper to myself, keeping my eyes closed. I'm not sure how much more of this I can take, and it hasn't even started. "The here and now."

"Hey, baby."

I open my eyes to find Nico filing into the bench seats, with Maggie and Gabe right behind him. Warmth blooms inside me. Thank God.

Nico wraps an arm around me and pulls me in for a kiss. "You okay? You look a little freaked out over here."

I snuggle into his arms, which I swear have gotten even bigger over the last few months. He's come straight from the academy, still in the uniform, which under normal circumstances, would excite me. He smells slightly of smoke, sweat, and men's deodorant. It's the best smell in the world.

"How was the day?" I ask after I wave hello to Gabe and Maggie.

"Fine, just fine. Two more weeks, and we're done." He sighs and leans back against the bench. "I can't wait. Oh, by the way, they're getting things together for the graduation. You, um, you don't want to come, do you?"

I turn so I can look at him in the face.

"Of *course* I'm coming to your freaking graduation, you goon," I tell him. "I wouldn't miss it."

Nico breaks into a wide smile that injects another shot of warmth into my chilled heart. He practically glows as he kisses me again. It's a chaste kiss—after all, we're in the middle of a courtroom—but it's full of promise of something more later. This is what love is supposed to feel like, I remind myself. Where you feel joy for your partner and only want them to succeed. Where their victories feel like your own. I hope I never forget that again.

But as Nico settles back into his seat again and pulls me close, a bit of tension vibrates through his broad shoulders. It takes me a few minutes to figure out what it is.

"Is this…is this where you were sentenced?" I wonder, looking around the room.

Nico glances at me, clearly surprised.

"No," he says, but the flash in his eyes and his quiet, resigned tone tell me I was right on the money. "It was at the family court in Brooklyn. They handle most of the juvenile offenses there."

"Was it a lot like this, though?" I ask as I look around.

It's a lot like the courtrooms you see on TV: a few rows of pew-like bench seating, a barricaded area for the lawyers and the judge, and a few other designated spots for the jury.

There's a long pause.

"Yeah," he says finally. "It did."

We sit there together silently, collectively lost in thought while Maggie and Gabe are chatting about who's going to babysit Allie next week while Maggie goes to a job interview. I assume Nico's still remembering that day when his life changed forever, the day he officially became the criminal so many think he is.

Except he's not, I think as I toy with the FDNY stitching on his rolled-up, navy-blue sleeve. And honestly, he never really was. I wonder sometimes if the perception of Nico as a criminal is more in his own head than anyone else's. The residue of a single mistake. He's been the savior of so many in his life—his family, his mother. Me. And in just over two weeks, he'll be a bona fide public servant, one of the good guys. The fact has made a visible difference too. He walks different now. Straighter. Taller.

Nico twists some of my hair around one finger, playing with it the same way I'm playing with his sleeve. I don't know if it's just because we're getting used to each other, but I like to think that maybe it's our new normal. I like the constant touching. It provides comfort in a world where I so frequently feel alone. His presence makes me feel like I can overcome almost anything. Maybe both of us will be able to say goodbye to something dark in our pasts today.

"Layla?"

We swivel to the left, to where a woman in a bland gray suit beckons. I recognize her voice. Dana Delaney, the district attorney who's been prosecuting the case. She gestures for us to follow her out of the courtroom just as the bailiff calls for everyone to stand, and another defendant enters the room. Maggie and Gabe follow us out, but give us an extra few feet of space.

Outside, we're eclipsed by the echoing stone corridors of city hall. The DA ushers Nico and me to a quiet corner and gives me a regretful look.

"He took a plea," she says frankly, flipping a pen between her fingers. "It's done."

Everything in me wilts. I hadn't realized until now how much I'd been counting on this. A moment to face him, my attacker, and put the demons to rest while the jury gave him what was coming to him. He was going to be served justice. He just had to be. I had been building myself up for this all week. And for what? To be told in the end that he was going to walk away?

"What's the deal?" Nico's strong, deep voice, breaks through my internal cacophony. He pulls on the bill of his hat, and it doesn't escape me the way the DA's gaze flickers appreciatively over his broad, trim body.

"It was last minute," she says. "But the Argentinians came through for him. It's complicated, involving a four-part exchange that basically gets the U.S. government a nasty member of a Mexican drug cartel in exchange for some intelligence and Giancarlo. I can't really go into details, but what you need to know is that his trial is going to Argentinian courts, and he's being escorted to the next flight out of New York." She shrugs. "I'm sure I don't have to tell you that his father had a bit to do with it. I'm sorry."

I wilt even further. It doesn't take a genius to realize that this means salvation for Giancarlo. He's the son of one of the wealthiest families in Buenos Aires, and his father has his fingers in plenty of politicians' pockets there. He'll get a slap on the wrist, if he's even tried to begin with. So much for justice.

I sag into Nico's side, and he mutters a few expletives under his breath.

"Hey." The attorney pulls my attention back. "He won't be allowed back in the country. As far as the USA is concerned, he's a *persona non grata*. The marshals are escorting him to holding now, and from there he'll be put on a flight out of here. That's something."

Nico's hand squeezes my shoulder.

I nod. "Yeah. It is."

A heavy door down the hall opens, and as if on cue, Giancarlo comes out, rubbing his wrists that must have been cuffed moments ago. He's flanked on either side by two agents—likely the marshals the DA was just talking about.

"I'm fine. I'm *fine*," Giancarlo spits as one of the marshals tries to escort him via the elbow. He shakes the man off as they approach the exit.

I'm frozen as I watch him, and next to me, Nico stiffens. As if he knows I'm there, Giancarlo straightens and turns his head.

"You!" he shouts from across the hall.

Nico moves in front of me, but for some reason I push him back. Giancarlo points a finger at me, and like he's suddenly acquired some kind of superhuman strength, breaks free of his captors and comes charging toward me at a run.

"You have *ruined* me!" he shouts. "You stupid whore! Do you know what will happen to me in Buenos Aires? Do you know what my father will do?"

He lunges forward, and beside me Nico tenses like a spring, his fists balled, one foot shifting automatically as Giancarlo approaches. The marshals sprint to catch up.

But before Nico can pounce, my right arm shoots out like a snake and strikes him in the belly. Giancarlo isn't hard like Nico—he's long and lean, but was always a little soft. The last thing he expects is for my fist to catch him in the belly, and the effect causes him to keel over immediately, like he's had the wind knocked out of him.

"Bitch!" he wheezes even as he drops to the floor, clutching his stomach. "You will pay for that!"

"No," I state clearly, staring down at him. "You don't get to hurt me anymore."

With a black look, Giancarlo scrambles to his feet, but before he can lunge again, the marshals grab him by both arms and haul him away, this time in handcuffs.

"You ruined me!" Giancarlo shouts again and again, his voice a chorus down the arched stone hall.

I open my mouth to reply, but think better of it, only now letting Nico wrap a strong forearm around me, almost like he's holding me back more than protecting me. We watch the marshals hustle Giancarlo down to the other end of the hall, out the double doors. New York, with its incessant noise and constant movement, swallows him up.

———

As if he knows that I need some kind of outlet, Nico takes me up to Frank's, where we spend the next hour grappling, fighting the demons that seem to follow us wherever we go. Despite the "knock-out" I managed to deliver in city hall, I feel even more defeated.

Giancarlo's gone. I'll never see him again.

But strangely, I still feel some compassion for him, regardless of what he did. I did care about him once. Giancarlo isn't totally evil. Some terrible darkness swallowed him up, but from time to time I saw glimpses of vulnerability. It was around that vulnerability that we connected. It was what made me stay with him for as long as I did. Now I find myself wondering what made him the way he is. Where his darkness came from to begin with.

It's well past eight by the time Nico and I flop back on the mat after over two hours of sparring together. He's taught me several other moves I could use in the event of another attack, although I think it's more to soothe his own worries than mine. He's been quiet all evening, letting me process the events at the courthouse, but also maybe processing his own thoughts. There was no vicious lovemaking on the mat this time around. It was all business; we barely spoke, going at it until we were both literally falling down from exhaustion.

"You want to get something to eat, sweetie?" Nico asks as we exit the gym.

I nod, taking his hand. I'm hungry, and we can pick up something quick. But I have something else in mind first.

I tow us down Ninth Avenue until I find the exact thing I'm looking for.

"A tattoo parlor?" Nico looks at me, confused. "Seriously?" He fingers my hand, then drops it so he can cup my cheek. "Tattoos...they don't go away, baby."

I lean into his touch. The warmth that has nothing to do with his body temperature seeps through me, balm to my wounds, thaw to my frozen insides. Nico heals me, just like he always does. Just like he always will.

"I need to do something more," I say. "Something that makes this day more than just about the day my ex tried to kill me. Again."

Nico's mouth is a straight line. "He wouldn't have touched you. *I* would have killed him first." Then he looks down. "I don't know if today is the best day to be making snap decisions, NYU. Especially with something permanent."

I shake my head. I'm saying this wrong.

"It's not like that. It's more like..." I tip my head to the side, trying to come up with the right words. I tug down Nico's shirt collar so I can see the edge of the big compass tattoo over his heart. "Why did you get this?"

He's told me this story, but he reiterates it anyway. "It was to remember," he says. "Not to lose track of who I was. My direction."

"Do you remember my bruises? The cuts on my face?"

His face darkens. "How could I forget?"

I chew on my lip. "This city, other people. My dad. Giancarlo. Other people marked me. Today, I want to mark myself. I want the next intense thing I feel to be because *I* wanted it, not because someone else did it to me. Does that make sense?"

Nico watches me for a moment, his black eyes burning under the streetlight. "You want control," he says softly, in a voice that's almost dangerous.

Slowly, I nod.

Nico examines me for a few more moments, like he's trying to figure out some other puzzle about me. Finally he nods back and pulls the brim of his Yankees hat down low.

He glances at the shop, then takes my hand. "If you're going to do this, we're doing it right," he says. "Come on. I know a much better place."

CHAPTER SEVENTEEN

Nico

Fifteen minutes later, we're standing in front of the tattoo shop on Second Avenue where my friend Milo has worked since we finished high school. Milo did my ink back then too, when he was an apprentice still learning his trade. Most of the art on my shoulder and half sleeve was me providing a canvas for him to practice on. I'd sketch, he'd trace, and I'd zone out on his table, half-enjoying the pinch of his needle. I figured I was already a fuckup, so I might as well get some badass art to look like it. My mom freaked when she first saw the swirling lines that Milo put all over my shoulder and arm. She said it made me look like a thug.

"Isn't that what I am?" I asked her at the time.

"*No,*" she replied, in both Spanish and English so I'd know she really meant it. Even if it's the same word in both languages, my mother has a way of making them sound different. Again and again and again.

Turns out, of course, that she was right. But I didn't really believe it until I met the girl standing next to me, a person in the same exact place I was when I stood outside these doors, back for Milo to put the compass on my chest. I had just gotten my first legit job, the one with FedEx. I wanted something that was *mine.*

I don't regret any of my tattoos, and I'll probably get more one day. They're a map of who I am, who I thought I was, what I wanted. Reminders of a life I wanted to put behind me, and another I wanted to have. If Layla wants that grounding, I'll help her get it. And I won't have her do it alone.

The bell above the door to the shop jingles when we enter. A white girl with blue hair, dime-sized gauges in her ears, and skinny arms full of multicolored tattoos, some of which I recognize as Milo's designs, is paging through a book at the glass counter.

She gives us both a bored look. "Can I help you?"

"Is Milo free?" I ask. Layla drifts away to check out the tattoo designs on the walls

"WHO THE FUCK IS THAT?" A loud voice calls from behind the red curtains that protect the rest of the shop from prying eyes.

I roll my eyes at the gauges girl. "Looks like he found us."

She shrugs and turns back to her magazine. Layla comes to my side as Milo charges through the curtain in the doorway.

Average height, wearing a white t-shirt, jeans, and a red backward Giants hat, Milo looks pretty much like your average Irish kid, with the exception of one thing: everything but his face is completely covered in tattoos, including his fingers and neck.

"What the fuck. Nico fuckin' Soltero—how you been, man?"

I slap my friend's palm and let him pull me in for a quick embrace before he steps back to look me over.

"I heard about you and the FDNY," he says, noticing my uniform. "That's the shit, Nico. Congratulations."

"Thanks, man." I shrug, like it's no big deal, but I don't know if I'll ever get tired of hearing people say this. Talk to me with that kind of admiration. Beside me, Layla grins. Yeah, I'll never get tired of that either.

"And who's this?" Milo sticks a hand out to Layla, who shyly takes it. "How're you doin'?"

"Milo, this is my girl, Layla. Layla, this is Milo. He's the talented bastard who did all of my work."

Layla brightens at the mention of my tattoos, and I stifle a grin. She never says anything, but I can tell she likes them by the way her eyes light up whenever I take off my shirt, or the way she traces the black lines with her fingers.

"Nice to meet you," she says. "I, um, I'm an admirer."

Milo leers. "Yeah, I bet you are, sweetie. But you know I just put down the ink. Your man here is the one with the real talent. You ever seen him sketch?"

Layla immediately blushes. She's thinking of some of my sketches of her; I'd bet money on it. She then turns beet red when I lay a kiss on her cheek.

Milo winks at her, then turns to me. "So what are we doing? Are you looking to add to your sleeve? I have this crazy new pattern I've been wanting to try out. If you want something new."

I shake my head. "Maybe after I graduate. Today we're paying customers. Actually, Layla's the one who wants something."

I look down at her, asking wordlessly if she still wants to do this. Her full lips quirk into a half smile before she turns to Milo, who's looking her over more appreciatively. I just focus on her.

"All right," he says. "Come on back. I'm pretty much done for the night, so I think we can figure something out."

We follow him behind the curtain to his booth in the back of the shop. It contains a padded table that's curtained off for privacy and the various equipment Milo needs to do his thing. He gestures for Layla to take a seat on the table, and she hops up while I lean back against it next to her, my hand on her thigh.

"So," Milo says as he leans against the counter across from us. "What are we doing today, pretty? Something on the wall?"

"Easy," I warn him, but my friend just rolls his eyes.

"You gotta keep this guy on his toes," he tells Layla. "Now that I know he's going to get all big bad wolf on me, I'm going to have to flirt with you all day. You down with that, honey?"

I growl. I can't help it. Layla just laughs and drapes her arm around my neck.

"I'm okay with it," she says before she kisses my temple. "I kind of like the big bad wolf sometimes. But he knows deep down that he's the only one that matters anyway."

I know he's joking—they're both joking—but her words still calm me, and I relax into her touch. I can save my growls for later, when we're alone.

"I…want a script," Layla says. "I was looking at some of the ones on the wall, but actually…" She shifts uncomfortably, and I turn to find her blue eyes wide and uncertain. "I was hoping you'd write it for me."

I frown and turn completely so I'm facing her. "You want my shitty chicken scratch on your body?"

Layla strokes my cheek lightly. She opens her mouth, then glances at Milo, like she's not sure she wants him in the room. Then she swallows and speaks in a low voice.

"I want *you* on my body. You're already there. Knowing you has changed me. You make me stronger. Your *love* and belief in me makes me stronger. I…"

She blinks, and for a split-second, a slight shimmer glosses her eyes. She's trying not to cry in front of Milo, and damn if it doesn't make me choke up too.

Layla looks straight at me. "I don't *ever* want to forget it."

For several seconds, I can't speak. It feels like my heart is lodged in my throat while every emotion I have buried inside is rushing to my head.

"I love you," Layla whispers. "*So* much."

"Fuck," I finally breathe, sliding my hands around her waist and pulling her flush to me. "You have no idea, *mami*. No fuckin' idea how much I love you."

We stand like that for a few moments until Milo clears his throat behind us. I swallow and turn around.

"I guess I'm writing something down," I tell him.

Milo chuckles and shakes his head. He's looking at me the way we used to look at our other friends who paired off with girls. Like they were jokers, the poor schmucks, totally pussy-whipped. And maybe I am. But I couldn't be happier about it.

Milo gets me a piece of paper and a Sharpie. "Don't worry about size," he says. "I can blow it up before I make the trace. Just make sure it's written the way she wants it." He glances at Layla. "Don't forget, pretty. This ain't comin' off."

Layla smiles shyly. "I know."

Milo leaves to get the materials to do the trace for the tattoo, and I turn to Layla with the paper and pen. "What am I writing, baby?"

Layla bites her lip, then leans over the paper with me. "Three words. The first word is spelled s-a-u-d-a-d-e."

It's not until I've written out the letters that I realize what I've spelled. I look up. "Saudade?"

Layla nods shyly. "And then write, *para ti.*"

I finish scratching out the words on the paper, then stare at the uneven black letters as I register what she's telling me. A little over a year ago, right before everything went to hell, Layla and I sat together on a beach in California and confessed what was in our hearts. At the time, it felt like there was nothing to lose. We were apart, with no real future ahead of us. It was a moment, just a recognition of what we were. How we really felt.

―――――

"Brazilians have a word for that, you know," she said as she played with my fingers. "Saudade. It's...it's hard to explain because there isn't a translation. But the way I had it explained to me, it's like when you yearn for something or someone. Like your heart speaks to their heart, and when they're gone, it's that emptiness that remains. It's a longing, maybe for something that never even happened."

In Portuguese, they say it: "eu tenho saudade." And to that, I whispered in Spanish: "para tí." For you.

―――――

I blink, pulling myself back to the present.

"But you have me now," I wonder aloud. "How can you miss something you have? Because you do have me, Layla. I ain't going nowhere."

Layla shrugs, her cheeks flushed. "I'll always miss you a little," she says. "The bitter and the sweet, right?"

I watch her for a moment as I begin to understand. She's right. No matter how much I love Layla, no matter how close she lets me come, a part of me will always want to be closer, will always want more of her. It's the feeling I have when our bodies are joined, when I'm buried so deep in her I think she might split in two. We devour each other, again and again, and still my heart, my soul, my entire fucking being shouts for more.

Saudade. A longing that never leaves. The bitter *and* the sweet. Just like us.

"Okay," I say. Then I hand her the pen. "Then you have to write it too. How do you say 'for you' in Portuguese?"

Layla's soft pink lips quirk into a half smile. "Are you...?"

"If you're doing this, I am too," I tell her. "It's something we *both* have, right? Write it down."

With another shy smile, Layla writes out the phrase *"saudade de voce"* in her neat, slanted cursive. Her handwriting is delicate and curling, unlike mine. I run a finger over it, and when Milo comes back in, I hand him the paper.

"We're doing two," I tell him as he examines the paper. "That one's hers. The other's mine."

Milo nods, not even bothering to challenge me. He knows me too well. "Where are they going?"

"Right here," Layla pipes up. She points to her ribs, the side of her torso, just under her arm.

Milo bares his teeth. "You sure about that, pretty? That spot is really, really painful. I wouldn't recommend it for your first time."

Layla presses her lips together and nods vehemently. "I want to *feel* it," she says fiercely as she looks at me.

I nod, then turn to my friend. "Me too," I tell him. "Let's do it."

―――――

Thirty minutes later, after Milo enlarged and then sketched our messy writing onto the transfer paper, my words are stamped on Layla's side. She lies on the table in only her bra, side up, while Milo scoots on his stool next to her as he snaps on a pair of thick latex gloves.

"Are you sure you want to do this?" I ask again.

Layla props up on her elbows, which pushes her breasts together, putting some *very* inappropriate thoughts in my head. It's been a long time since that night at Frank's. I'm not exactly crazy about the fact that my buddy is seeing her like this, and unfortunately, the wild look in her big blue eyes is only making the effect that much worse. I shift awkwardly on my chair, trying to adjust myself without giving it away.

"Do you think it will look stupid?" she asks.

"No!" I protest. "As it happens, I think you'd look fuckin' hot with a little body art," I answer before I can stop myself. Well, it's the truth. "I just don't want you to hurt."

"Well, that's just the reality, man," Milo puts in. "You know that better than anyone. But I don't think you've had anything as bad as the ribs, to be honest."

He turns on the needle. The buzz fills the small space, enclosed by the red curtains.

Layla looks back at Milo. "I said I *want* to feel it," she says clearly over the buzz, to both him and me. "I'm not going to hide from pain anymore. Do it."

Milo looks at me. I nod, even though my stomach clenches. Here we go.

Layla flinches the second the needle meets her skin, and I flinch with her as I watch. Her sweet face screws up as Milo starts drawing over her delicate skin and moves across bone. It's a feeling I know well. The slight pinch when the needle first sinks into your skin, followed by a slight burning as the area around it reacts. It's a shock at first, but slowly, your body acclimates until it moves over a nerve or a particularly sensitive spot. But until then, the pain doesn't fade. It just regulates, steady like the hum of the needle.

"It hurts," Layla whispers, even though just moments before she was demanding the pain.

She extends a hand, clearly struggling to keep still as the needle digs into her ribs.

But for a second, I'm not sure if she's actually talking about Milo's needle. Her eyes are wide, and her lip trembles. Yeah, baby, I know, I want to say. This life we chose together was never going to be easy. And I'll never stop feeling guilty about that.

But then her gaze drops to my mouth, and there's a very different thought practically shimmering across her face. Take it away, those baby blues seem to say. Or maybe…balance it out.

I take her hand between mine and press my lips to her knuckles.

"Ow," she whimpers as the needle passes over her ribs again.

I wince myself. They say it's closest to the bone that hurts the most. I wouldn't know—mine are all over muscle.

"Hey," Milo puts in when Layla jerks again. "I'm going to screw it up if you keep doing that." He looks to me. "Can you help her stay still?"

I look back at Layla. She wants this, I know. So when Milo's needle starts buzzing again, I do the only thing I can think of to distract her, to take the pain away. I kiss her.

Almost immediately, she sighs, and her fingers relax their iron grips. Deep down, this is Layla's sweet spot, just like it is mine. For better or for worse, neither of us ever learned to take the good without the bad, the pleasure without a bit of pain. Love always had to hurt a little.

She moans as our tongues twist together. Suddenly I don't care that my buddy is two feet from us with his face six inches from Layla's breasts, close enough that he can smell her flowery scent or know the curves of her body. I don't care that we're sitting in a "room" divided only by flimsy fabric, surrounded by an entire shop of people who can hear everything we do. I can feel the vibration with her, feel the sting of the needle along with the sweetness of her kiss. And the combination is like a powder keg that's just been lit.

"All right," Milo says several minutes later. "I'm done."

Layla blinks at me as I pull away. "What? Already?"

She sits up, her long, dark hair falling like a waterfall over her shoulder. Her wet, pink mouth falls open, and just like that, I'm zero to sixty. Jesus, she's so fuckin' beautiful. And it's a *really* good thing I'm sitting down.

Milo smirks. "Maybe you should make out with all my clients when they get something painful," he says. "She went stone-still after you started with that."

"I don't think so," I say with a grin. "Layla's the only one I'm kissing anymore."

"Lucky you," he replies.

Layla blushes while Milo applies a bit of Vaseline and then a light bandage over her new tattoo, and then scrambles back into her t-shirt. She hops off the table, and I whip off my shirt and take her spot almost as quickly.

"All right," I tell Milo as he reaches for the other transfer. "My turn."

I sit still, watching Layla's eyes light up as her handwriting is printed onto my ribs, the opposite side as hers, so that when we stand together our words will face each other. Milo hums as he presses the paper down, and then removes it a few seconds later.

"All good?" he asks.

I check myself in the mirror on the opposite wall. "All good."

The machine starts again as I lie on my side.

"Come here, beautiful," I say, pulling Layla down for another kiss just as Milo's needle starts to pinch. "I'm going to need you to help me bear this pain too."

CHAPTER EIGHTEEN

Layla

It's late by the time we get back to my apartment. After grabbing some food by the tattoo shop, we meander in a quiet daze, hand in hand down Second until it morphs from the hipster crowd of the East Village past Houston, where the street sign turns to Chrystie, and the tattoo parlors turn to laundromats and kitchen supplies. As we approach Delancey, we pass an open basement door that seems to be housing some kind of banquet. Shouts in an Eastern European language tumble into the night.

New York gets a reputation for loneliness, for being one of the most cutthroat cities in the world. People come here, and they get chewed up and spit out; I know that better than anyone. Places like this force you to find your tribe, because if you don't, you might not last. You'll become cold, bitter, jaded. Maybe you don't even survive. Nico wraps a big arm around me and I smile up at him, grateful that he's adopted me into his tribe. If he hadn't…I might not have survived.

We cross Delancey and eventually come to a stop in front of my building.

"You want to go up?" Nico asks. "Or do you want to keep walking?"

I hesitate, staring through the thick glass door toward the vacant stairwell. Most of the apartments are still empty, since the landlord's only just finished remodeling them. They'll be rented soon, but for now, the building is big and silent.

"Baby?"

"I don't want you to leave." The words fall out of my mouth, quick and heavy.

When I look at him, Nico's brows are lifted in surprise. "Well, I kind of assumed I'd be staying the night, if that's cool with you. I have to get up early to get things done tomorrow, but I don't mind."

I blink, shaking my head. "No, I mean I don't want you to leave at all." I rub my face. This day has been exhausting, and I'm screwing this up. "Nico, I—"

Nico gently pulls my hand from my face. "Baby, it's okay. Let's just go upstairs.

We'll watch a movie or something and crash on the couch." He rubs my shoulder and cocks his head. "You look like you're about to fall over."

I shake my head again, causing my hair to toss around my face. There's still one more thing I want to do. Say. A thought that's been swirling around my mind since Nico kissed me in the shop. If I'm being honest, it's probably been there since I stepped off the plane. But for some reason I can't quite get it out.

So instead of trying to speak, I pull out the key that's been in my back pocket since Shama handed it to me this morning. Wordlessly, I hold it out. The brass gleams under the streetlight.

Slowly Nico takes it. "What's this?" he asks, although cautious understanding is already spreading over his face as he examines the small piece of metal.

"It's Shama's key. Well…maybe your key. If you want it."

Nico looks back up, but I can't quite read the expression on his face. For a few moments, we just blink at each other like a pair of owls, and I'm struck again, like always, by just how handsome he really is. His beat-up Yankees cap is turned backward, allowing the lights above us to cast shadows under his chiseled jawbones, dusted slightly with black stubble. When he blinks, his eyelashes, a thick fringe, sweep across his cheeks. But it's always his eyes that really transfix. Almond-shaped and so dark brown they almost look black, they are fathomless.

I was lost in them from the start.

"Just to be clear," he says slowly. "When you say mine…do you mean the key? Or…the apartment?"

I tug on the ends of my hair. "It's…" Just say it, you chicken. "Look, I don't want another roommate. I want…I want you. You're living on a couch right now. You should come live on my bed. Um, *our* bed. If you want it to be ours, I mean. Shit."

Nico's eyes widen as I trail off.

"You just…Nico, when I come home at night, I want to come home to you." Finally, I force myself to look back at him, terrified of what I might find. "Is that—is that crazy?"

He's still, a statue on this empty street corner. Beside us, cars are racing up and down Delancey, but we might as well be in a vacuum, the way the noise is rushing out of my head. Nico's full mouth is open. Still, he doesn't move.

"It's too soon," I murmur, more to myself than to him.

My heart drops in my chest, and I steady against the wave of disappointment that's coming with the realization. I hadn't known just how badly I wanted this until I actually said it out loud. Oh my God, what if I lose him because of this? What if he turns and runs from the crazy girl who's given him nothing but grief and drama, and who now wants him to play house with her?

"God. I'm so sorry. Nico, I'm not trying to pressure you at all, I swear. I know it's only been maybe a month since I got back, and we've been taking it kind of slow, and oh my God, I'm screwing this up, aren't I—"

I'm cut off with a kiss as Nico yanks me close and covers my babbling mouth with his. It's the same kiss from the tattoo shop, the one that burned deeper than any needle. The one that spurred me through the pain that's still burning slightly on my side.

"Stop," he says, breathless, his broad chest heaving, though he refuses to let me move away. "Just stop. Honest to God, baby. I thought you'd never fuckin' ask."

On this lonely corner, a golden halo of warmth surrounds us.

"Yeah?" I whisper, suddenly unsure. Did he really say what I think he said?

"What's the word?" Nico asks after he kisses me again. "Home?" He tightens the arm around my waist, careful to avoid the tattoo, and lifts me so that only my toes graze the ground. "That's what we are together, Layla. Home." He kisses me again. "Now come on. Let's christen *our* new place. Together."

———

A FEW MINUTES LATER, we're practically tearing down my door. Nico uses his new key to open it, and as soon as it's shut, he's dropped his bag to the floor and pulled me in for another kiss, the kind of kiss that might get us arrested if we ever did it in public. His hands are everywhere—up and down my arms, cupping my breasts, squeezing my ass, and without a thought, mine are flung around his shoulders, pulling him tight against me.

We just want to be close. As close as we can possibly get. For the first time, there are no ghosts threatening us from far away. It's just him. It's just me. Just…us.

Keeping his lips fused to mine, Nico guides us toward the bedroom, shedding clothing as we shuffle. His shirt. My shoes. His belt. My jacket. By the time we cross the threshold, there's a trail of clothing from the front door through the living room, up to my bed, and we're standing before each other in nothing but our underwear. Nico in those black boxer briefs that fit him like a second skin; me in plain black underwear and a bra, our matching white bandages skimming our sides.

Nico cups my face and kisses me again. In the blueish light that streams through my window—no, *our* window—his smooth skin glistens, and his black eyes shine with love.

I run my hands over his body, taking my time, just enjoying the feel of it when my fingers graze the frayed edge of athletic tape over a piece of gauze on his chest. I break away and look down.

"What is that?"

Nico looks down to where I'm staring at a small white bandage at the top of the hand-sized compass over his heart. He looks back at me.

"I, um, had Milo do one other thing while you were up front paying. You…you want to see it?"

I nod. Nico swallows heavily, then slowly peels the bandage off. He turns to toss the bandaging into the trash bin under my desk, but when he turns back, I can see the black script clearly: *layla*.

My name. Nothing more. In small, almost unintelligible letters, right where the missing North symbol should have been on his compass. But it's there, for anyone to see.

"Why?" The word slips out, even as tears start to cloud my vision.

"Because that's what you are," he says softly, pressing my hand firmly over the small, reddened words. It can't feel good—it's a fresh wound, just barely scabbed over. But he holds my hand firmly, and his gaze doesn't waver as he speaks. "Layla, I knew it before I came back to New York. A part of me even knew it before I met you."

I shake my head, unable to speak. This is…*he* is so utterly overwhelming.

"Do you remember your trip to New York with your dad? When you were, I don't know, maybe in junior high?"

It was a long time ago. I was thirteen, almost fourteen. My dad took me to New

York for a birthday present when he had to attend a conference. I spent most of the time in his hotel doing homework, but we went out at night to restaurants and shows. Even a Broadway musical.

"You went to see *Phantom of the Opera*, right?" Nico asks softly.

I frown. "How did you know that?"

"Because I was there, baby. I was on my way to the subway with K.C. and Flaco. Flaco told me right then that I had gotten the job at FedEx. My first real job that wasn't hustling at some nightclub or helping my mom clean houses." He cocks his head and traces his thumb across my cheekbones. "We were going to celebrate, and the first stop was the tattoo shop, where Milo gave me my compass. I bumped into this girl. She was kind of awkward, and she had a mouthful of braces. But her eyes were like the bluest sky I'd ever seen. And even though she didn't say a word, I knew she saw right through me."

The memory rushes back with the force of a tidal wave. The trio of boys, maybe nineteen or twenty, laughing and joking loudly in the street with a mix of Spanish and English. "Ruffians," my father had called them, mostly referring to their backward hats and low-slung jeans. One bumped into me, then grabbed my arm to steady my fall. He was thinner back then, without quite the same level of swagger, but still strong and solid. His deep-black eyes and bright white smile cut through me, and I was stuck there on the sidewalk, staring at him until my father pulled me into the theater.

I blink, suddenly unable to stop the tears that have been threatening since Nico started talking. How could I have forgotten that moment? Something had always called me back to New York since those first visits...but I had never been able to say exactly what it was. What if it was him? What if it was Nico from the start?

"Every good thing that's ever happened to me has had you in it," Nico says as he brushes hair from my face. His thumbs wipe away the tears that spill, one by one. "I knew that one day I would find my true north. I just never imagined that would be a woman. The she would be this beautiful, inside and out. I never imagined she would be you."

"Nico," I whisper as he pulls me close again. His skin is so warm. He practically glows.

"It's you, Layla," he whispers back before he fits his mouth over mine. "It's always been you."

My mouth opens naturally to his as he literally sweeps me off my feet and lays me down in the bed. Our tongues tangle, lips grapple, but his touch is soft, floating over my skin like a feather. His kisses drift down my body as he removes my bra and underwear, and I watch, lovesick, when he stands up to remove his boxers. I forget sometimes what a work of art he really is. The way years of training have sculpted his body into perfectly cut lines, marred slightly with a few scars here and there, accented by the tattoos on his chest and arm. And now, of course, the words on his side and my name over his heart.

"Come here," he rumbles as he peppers my neck and chest with kisses. He sucks one nipple, then another into his mouth with vigor and just a little bite, but I don't shy. I don't need to. There is no one here but us.

"Fuck, you're ready," he groans as his hard, eager cock brushes against my entrance. "Always so goddamn ready for me."

I hiss lightly as his hand tickles over my bandage. He pulls away, looking down with concern. In response, I push him to his back, rolling over so I'm straddling him.

When he looks up at me, his eyes are big and open. "I don't want to be rough tonight," he says softly as his hands grasp my thighs.

His thumbs come together over that most sensitive spot at the juncture of my legs, and he presses lightly, eliciting a moan from deep in my chest. I rock into his touch, my eyes closed.

"Layla." His deep voice beckons. "Please tell me it doesn't have to be rough."

My chest tightens to the point where it almost hurts, but it's not a pain I hate. It's a pain I love. This is what it feels like to love someone so much you want to burst. The heart can only take so much, but what I feel for this man overflows any vessel.

I know that this time I won't need him to grab my skin so hard it bruises or bite my neck, shoulder, breasts like a beast. I won't need to claw at him or wrestle with him across the floor. We won't need to be rough, because we already did it to ourselves. Today. Yesterday. Most of our lives. I float a finger over his chest, hovering down over the bandage still on his side, the one that matches mine. These are wounds we've given ourselves on purpose. Wounds that, like all the others, will make us stronger. Together.

"It doesn't have to be rough," I say as I lower, slowly, surely, taking him inside.

His other hand finds mine, entwining our fingers as he sucks in a breath. The words on my side—his words—burn slightly, but I don't feel them. As I start to move, all I feel is him.

Nico tips his head back and shudders as I sink lower, taking him further inside me. I rock back and forth, luxuriating in the friction between us, even as his thumbs continue to circle my clit in time with the movement. We watch each other as I move, letting the sounds of our bodies joining, our hitched breaths, skin meeting skin, fill the room. Black eyes meet blue. Dark hands meet light.

I wonder now why I've been so scared to do this, to open myself to him this way. But at the same time, it's totally clear. Here, naked with him, body and soul, I am my most vulnerable. No one can hurt me like he can; maybe no one has. But I also know without a shadow of a doubt that he'll protect me with everything he has. He shelters my heart. He's more than just a lover. He's a partner. And there's nothing for me to fear in that.

"Come," I murmur as the knowledge flows through me, a river of pleasure channeling straight to where we join. It's fast. It's furious. And it's approaching faster than I anticipated. "I want you to come with me."

"Already?" Nico wonders, though I'm already starting to shake.

"Y-yes," I manage as I tip my head back, rocking my hips downward to take him even deeper. Oh *God*, he feels good.

Suddenly, Nico sits up like it's nothing, the rows of hard abdominal muscles flexing until his chest meets mine.

"Ah!" I flinch as his arms encircle my waist, landing on the fresh tattoo.

He tries to pull away, but I keep his hands where they are,

"No." I clasp his face between my hands. "I like it."

And I do. I start to move again, rotating my hips slightly to take him deeper with every movement. Nico groans, pressing his face into my breasts as his hands drop to my hips to guide my movements.

"Layla," he murmurs as I start to move faster. He tips his head up again, seeking my mouth like a drowning man.

"Nico," I whisper in between long, torrid kisses.

Balanced on one hand while the other maintains its iron grip around my waist, he meets each movement, pounding into me from below while I take him deeper, from above. He penetrates me. My heart. My body. All of me, in ways no one else ever will.

"Layla," he chokes out. "Fuck, baby. I'm...oh, God, I'm *here!*"

His teeth find my shoulder, and he bites down as he starts to shake. The slight sting is my undoing, and together we come apart in our own beautiful corona that banishes the cold glare of the city. It's the knowledge of that warmth that keeps me going, and builds my strength.

If I am his true north, then he is mine. Together, we'll never lose our way again.

II

VALIÓ LA PENA

CHAPTER NINETEEN

Layla

ALL WEEK. ALL FREAKING WEEK I'VE BEEN WAITING FOR THIS. IT'S BEEN FIVE DAYS SINCE we saw each other at the airport, when I came home from a very long month in Pasadena for Christmas. It was…nice. Safe. Boring. Sure, it was perfectly pleasant to take a break once my semester was over and spend some quality time at my grandparents' pool. My mom and I have continued to grow closer, and Dr. Parker agreed that I didn't need another prescription for Valium. Apparently Nico is all I need to sleep well at night, even though no one in California is currently aware that he's been acting as that cure for close to three months now.

But even after that month, it's still been another five days since Nico had to take an extra forty-eight hour shift at the firehouse in order to get this weekend off. Five days since our first fumbled coupling at 7 a.m. after he picked me up from my red-eye flight. Five days since he left me in bed that morning, desperate for more of him, but drowsy in the knowledge that there would be more, so much more, for as long as I wanted it. Five days of tapping my pencil irritably on my desk and squeezing my legs together in anticipation. Five days of texting and talking here and there before another bell went off and he had to dash out to be a hero.

In other words, it's been five days of pure torture.

Somehow, since October, this neighborhood, this tiny slice of New York that's not quite Chinatown and not quite Little Italy, became more than just an apartment. Nico moved in the weekend after Giancarlo's trial, and it was the perfect way to close that chapter of my life and start a new one based on *us*. We've celebrated multiple milestones there already: his twenty-eighth birthday with all of his friends and family crammed into the little two bedroom. Just before that, his graduation from the fire academy, which was much, much bigger.

It was a sight I'll never, ever forget. Nico stood on the bleachers with the other two hundred or so cadets in his graduating class. They were all kitted out in their dress blues—formal, navy-blue suits with the military-style hats that should have looked stiff, but instead just made me want to do very dirty things to my man. Nico stood taller, much taller than his not-quite-six feet. I sat with Carmen in the front row, and she held my hand on one side and Gabe's on the other while Maggie and Selena whistled loudly with Allie straddled across their laps. And after the presiding officers called everyone's names and shook their hands, Nico ran down the stairs and swept me up in a giant kiss before the rest of his family crowded around him with hugs, kisses. This man vibrated happiness and pride—more, I think, than he'd ever felt in his life. And therefore, so did I.

But that was months ago, and since then, he's lived the life of a rookie FDNY firefighter. He's stationed in Queens, which means long commutes from our place in lower Manhattan. He works forty-eight and seventy-two hour shifts for low pay, which he'll continue to supplement with shifts at AJ's until next year, when his probationary period is up, and he'll start making a real salary. It means that sometimes we barely see each other, particularly if his off days fall on an exam week for me. I'm one semester away from finishing school, and I spent the majority of November and December taking the GRE and applying for graduate school. In three months or so, I'll find out whether or not I'll be going to the school of social work at Columbia, Fordham, or NYU, or if I'll be waiting tables for a year while I try again.

Social work. Not law school. Because the other relief of living with someone who supports me and cultivates this feeling of safety is that I felt confident enough to pursue a future that isn't the one planned for me. My father, who still has barely spoken to me for most of the past year, has no idea about the change of plans, and my mother hasn't asked. But watching Nico's family's frustrations over Carmen's status inspired me more, especially when I compare it to my father's relatively easy naturalization. The more I see them struggle, the more I understand just how much of my family's fortune is just that: fortunate. Not just a product of hard work, but one of luck. I want to give back, but that's going to take work. And time. And probably a lot of debt.

So our lives aren't exactly easy. They're busy and our budget is tight, especially when we consider just how we are going to afford this apartment after I'm finished with school and my mom won't be paying my half anymore. But those are concerns for a few months from now, and these days, we both get to come home to each other. That's what counts.

I practically skip out of the 6 station on Spring Street, knowing he's at the apartment waiting for me. Normally I slow down, enjoying the eclectic window displays. On this block alone, there's a bodega, a rice pudding shop, an antique furniture store, and a kimono designer whose royal textiles loom over the sidewalk like emperors. But today, I'm practically running.

My phone buzzes in my pocket, and I pull it out as I dodge around a couple perusing a restaurant menu. They give me a dirty look. I ignore them.

"Hey, baby. You almost here? I forgot my key."

The anticipation in his deep voice vibrates against my cheek. It's that same feeling that spiraled between us, between coasts, for the last month. It thrums between us like a guitar string that's just been plucked, pulling me closer and closer to him. To Nico.

"T-two blocks," I stutter just as I turn down Elizabeth. God, I can barely speak.

I turn onto Delancey, the massive boulevard that cuts across Lower Manhattan, pouring across the Williamsburg Bridge into Brooklyn. I can see the corner of the six-story walk-up with the Chinese laundromat on the bottom, facing the still-green trees of Delancey Park. But I can't see Nico yet.

"Hurry," he says, his voice suddenly breathy and a little hoarse. "I'm…cold."

He's not cold. It's unseasonably warm for late January, and the man is a furnace. Whenever he's not out on a call, he spends most of his time in the firehouse gym. His metabolism could power all of lower Manhattan.

"I'm here," I tell him as I reach the corner. "I see you."

Across the street, he turns around. He's still in FDNY-issued navy pants and a t-shirt that pulls across the taut lines of his chest under his thick black jacket. He could change at the firehouse, but he rarely does because he knows how much I love seeing him in uniform. His favorite Yankees cap, curled tightly over his brow, casts a shadow over his eyes.

When he spots me, though, that hat doesn't hide his smile as he claps his phone shut and shoves it in his pocket. It's a bright, shining beacon; its light emanates, calling me to him. Calling me home.

"Baby! What the fuck are you waiting for?" he shouts, laughing. "Get your ass over here!"

He looks up and down Delancey. The big street, for once, is somewhat empty, the next round of cars at least four blocks away. Unable to stifle my grin, I jog across the six lanes, right into his arms just as another rush of cars arrives.

"You," he says as he pulls me close, "have been on the West Coast too fuckin' long, NYU. Waiting for streetlights. Pssh."

I can't help but grin. No one in New York waits for lights to turn to cross an empty street. But I don't even care that he's teasing. That's how happy I am to see him.

We stare at each other, until our mutual smiles start to fall, eyes drift to mouths, and the street corner, despite being mostly empty, starts to feel crowded. Too crowded.

Nico exhales heavily through his nose, chewing on his lip as he stares at mine. Every cell in my body vibrates for him.

"Um—come on," I manage. "Let's go inside."

He blinks, like some kind of spell was broken, then follows me to the door of our building. Behind me, he hovers, his broad hands at my waist while I pull out my keys.

"Stop that," I murmur as he nuzzles into my neck. "I can't get the keys into the lock when you're doing that."

"Mmmm." His deep voice rumbles against my neck. "I can't help it—you smell crazy good, and *fuuuuck*, I've been thinking about this all week." His tongue slips out, causing us both to shudder. "Baby, open the fuckin' door. I'm not waiting more than a minute, and then I swear to God, I'm taking you right here."

I smirk, even though the sudden hard length pressed into my back makes my hands fumble all over again. If anything, the last three months have made this yearning worse, rather than better. He's ready for me too. It's been a month of heavy breathing, daydreaming, and phone sex. And then another week of classes and training, with only a city between us. He wants me? I'm about ready to combust.

"Nico!" I squeal when his fingers travel under the waistband of my jeans.

His fingertips brush the elastic of my underwear, dipping a little further to tease at the dampness already building there before he pulls them out. Then, before I know it, I'm spun around and pressed to the glass door, and Nico's mouth is on mine. Warm, open-mouthed, and demanding, his kiss encompasses me completely, renders me starving in about a quarter of a second. My hands knock his bill up his forehead and grab his thick black hair. We're eating each other alive, right in front of my building, while more than one person passes us with hushed whispers and even a wolf whistle.

"Oooh, look at them."

I couldn't tell you who said it. Nico reaches around, pulls me into him and grinds into my waist while he messes with my keys. I can't even think. His taste consumes me.

Then with a click, the lock opens, and we topple inside. Jesus. I don't even care that the door is transparent. He could take me right here on the stairs if he wanted to, in front of all the neighbors that have slowly filled up our building, and I wouldn't argue one bit.

"Up," I mumbled in between kisses. "Up. Stairs."

"Fuck the stairs," Nico growls, and in a single, fluid motion, he squats down and hoists me over his shoulder like a sack of potatoes.

"Aah!" I whoop in surprise, but he's too busy stomping up the stairs like a caveman to answer.

From my vantage point, I have the privilege of watching his extremely round ass as it moves. Back and forth, back and forth. I reach down with one hand and squeeze, which only causes him to yelp and jog faster.

One of my neighbors' doors opens as we pass the fourth floor.

"Hi, Mrs. Dukakis!" I call through a bout of laughter as Nico continues his stampede.

"Are you all right, dear?" she asks as she follows our stumbling forms.

"She's fine, Mrs. Dukakis!" Nico shouts as he starts on the fifth flight. He's not even breaking a sweat. Apparently being a firefighter has given him some serious stamina.

"Is the door locked?" he asks as we climb the last set, his voice only slightly winded from his little run with an extra hundred and twenty pounds slung over his shoulder.

"Of course it's locked."

With another exuberant growl, Nico winds his way around the final post and charges to our door, which he practically kicks in after he unlocks it.

"What's so funny?" he asks after he hauls me inside and dumps me on the couch.

I can't stop giggling—I've been laughing all the way up. I yank him down to me, and his hat topples to the floor along with my purse, allowing me to sink my fingers into his flattened curls. Everything is forgotten. I'm not even sure we closed the front door.

"It's nothing," I say between kisses. "Just that I've literally wanted you to do that since the first time I met you." His tongue is slick and urgent, and I open to it completely. "I remember thinking that your shoulders would be really good at carrying a girl some place."

Nico pushes himself up to examine my face. When he realizes I'm serious, he rewards me with a grin, this one is even broader than before. It lights up my room, even in the dark. My body hums in response.

"Baby," he said as he leans back down, "you only had to ask."

CHAPTER TWENTY

Layla

"Should we order some takeout?"

I open my eyes lazily. After conking out for about two hours after our little "reunion," Nico and I are only barely starting to wake up. And if the grumbling under my ear is any indication, so is his stomach.

Mine responds with a loud growl. I prop up onto my elbow and look at Nico, who's peeking at me through one open, squinted eye. I grin.

"Want me to get Chinese?" he asks. "I'll even get dressed and go pick up those dumplings you like instead of calling the place that delivers."

I pinch his side. "You don't want me to cook for you? I thought maybe you would have missed my skills in the kitchen."

He flops back onto the pillow. "Hmm. Did I miss chicken strips cooked in straight vinegar? Lemme think about that...I mean, it did almost blind me when I got home that night."

He twists his full mouth around, like he's really weighing the option, which makes me want to sock him and kiss him at the same time. Okay, so I'm not the greatest cook. I elbow him in the gut, causing him to keel over laughing. He grabs me and starts tickling my side, which he discovered about six weeks ago is incredibly sensitive.

"Okay, okay!" I shout as I thrash around. "I give, I give! Uncle! *Tío*! You win! I'm a terrible cook, and you didn't need to miss any of it!"

When Nico releases me, he's straddling my waist, naked in all his glory and laughing like a maniac. I sigh. I could probably go another round...but I need sustenance first.

"I missed *you*," he says leaning down for a kiss. "Like fuckin' crazy. But it's a good thing I can make chicken and rice, is all I'm saying."

I roll my eyes, but we're both still chuckling as we clamber off the bed and get dressed. The bedroom is ours now—my desk was moved into the other room, across from the other desk and easel that turned into a sort of studio for Nico. He usually has a few days off a week when he's not at the firehouse, and when he's not sleeping or taking care of stuff for his family, sometimes he'll escape to the other room and draw for a while. Most of the time those drawings end up looking a lot like me, but I don't like to pry. When he's ready to show them to me, he will. Which usually it ends up with us on the floor, since I can't help myself after I see them.

"Sesame chicken?" Nico calls from the kitchen, where he's dialing our favorite Chinese place on the next block.

"Egg drop soup for me. It's freezing outside. I still need to warm up."

I pull my hair into a messy bun, then walk into the living room just as Nico's flipping on the Knicks game, kicking his heels on the coffee table in a pair of joggers and a t-shirt that's threadbare enough I can see his tattoos right through the thin white cotton. He looks comfortable, and totally at home. It makes me want to pounce on him all over again.

The open space has changed a lot since he moved in. As soon as we had a little extra cash, we went to a consignment shop and bought a small dining set, a TV to replace Shama's, and a coffee table to go in front of the couch. The walls have a weird mix of both of our belongings—a few art posters I had from my dorm, the tribal masks Nico had hanging in his old room uptown, and a few small pictures of St. Mary and St. Christopher that Carmen gave us and Nico surprised me by hanging right away.

"It's good mojo," he said with a casual shrug.

I didn't argue. It seems to have been working.

The cupboards aren't empty anymore either. Nico, I discovered, is an incredibly clean eater and a reasonably competent chef. Remnants of his boxing training. He'll splurge once a week or so to eat out, but when he cooks, it's usually something simple: chicken and salad, or fish and a vegetable, but always tasty. Considering that I'm not much of a cook at all, I'm usually happy to do the dishes on the nights when he's home, and grab something cheap out on the nights he's not.

"You're going to ruin your liver if you keep eating that crap," Nico says as I flop down onto the couch with an open bag of Doritos and a book. But he grabs a handful of chips for himself and plucks the book from my hand, flipping through it for a second before handing it back. "Borges, huh? Sounds like some nice light reading. I liked the Neruda you read last semester better."

When he wasn't at the firehouse, Nico basically took half my classes with me last semester, browsing through almost all of my books as I finished the first term of my senior year of college. He bent over my shoulder while I wrote my essay on Caribbean trade patterns and another on Cuban immigration history (he was *very* interested in that one). He quizzed me before I took the GRE exam in December and read and reread the admissions essays I sent out for graduate school.

"What did Ileana say last week?" I ask as I snuggle into Nico's side. I inhale his scent, which is warm and a little smoky. He must have been called to a live fire today.

Nico's hand drifts over my shoulder, and he starts playing with my hair. He likes it curly because he can twist it around his fingers. I think he finds it soothing.

"We're still waiting on Gabe's application," he says. "It's been almost three months. We should hear back any day."

He rubs his face. After resubmitting the application for a travel license to go to Cuba, this time on an informational license, he and his family have been waiting on pins and needles for the Treasury to get back to them. It's a long shot, Ileana said back in October. Since they weren't journalists or government employees, it was unlikely an informational visit would be granted. But they still had to try. And keep trying. Otherwise, Carmen would be at the mercy of an immigration judge who may or may not believe her claim to Cuban nationality. And if they didn't, Ileana said, it wasn't a given she would be allowed to stay. That entirely depended on the judge.

"I don't know," he says sadly. "I'm starting to think I should just try to sneak in. I've heard of people doing that. They fly through Venezuela or some place like that and change their money there so they don't break U.S. law by spending money in Cuba."

I frown. "Couldn't you get in trouble for doing that?"

Nico shrugs. "I don't know. But I doubt it would be worse than my mother being deported."

We sit there quietly for a bit, letting the basketball game fill the awkward silence. He's tense, and I hate that there's no way for me to solve this problem for him. I've been doing my best to pay attention to the things I've learned in school about Cuban immigration, but it always comes down to one thing: to guarantee residency, Carmen needs documentation of her birthplace, or else she has to risk court. But getting those documents is another matter entirely, and I'm not sure I like the idea of Nico risking everything he's worked for to do that.

"So, I forgot to ask you earlier since we were, ah, busy," Nico says as I flip through my mail I still haven't gone through from the last month. His fingers draw absent circles around my shoulder. "What did your mom say when you told her we were living together?"

I gulp. This has been a sore spot for a while. Nico has been patient, knowing that I wanted to tell her face-to-face after we spent some time together again. As far as my conservative mother knows, I have a roommate, but it's another NYU student. She likes Nico, but she wouldn't be so keen on him if she knew we were living together without being married. I don't want to think about what my father would do if he found out. We may barely speak these days, but I'm pretty sure the idea of his daughter living in sin would have him on a plane within twenty-four hours.

"Layla."

I sit up and turn to him. The guarded look on his face tells me he already knows what I'm going to say.

"I'm sorry," I squeak out. "I just…I couldn't. Not yet."

His face falls. And it just about kills me.

"Layla. Two months I've had to pretend I'm not here when she calls. Had to listen to you tell her about another roommate. It's fucked up, baby."

I hang my head. "I know." I sigh. "But, come on, you know how it goes. Your mom is Catholic too."

It's a stupid excuse, and the look on Nico's face tells me he thinks so too. "Yeah, she is. And she knows exactly where I'm living. She lights a candle, prays for our forgiveness, and then she's done with it."

"Yeah, but your mom doesn't pay your rent and your tuition."

"Maybe your mom shouldn't either, then."

We stare at each other, wrapped in a standoff. I feel terrible. I know hiding this is the wrong thing to do, and I hate it.

"Is that what you want?" I ask quietly. "I'll do it. But it will make things really hard. I'll have to drop out, probably. Apply for loans until summer or maybe fall semester and graduate then. I'll have to delay graduate school for another year if I do that."

Nico blinks, and the hardness in his face softens. "Would your dad really cut off your tuition if he knew?"

I shrug. "He's threatened it for a lot less."

"And you think your mom would tell him?"

I bite my lip. "Nico, it's just that my mom thinks I'm only barely able to stand up again by myself. She sees my last relationship as one that I need a lot of space from. If she knew that I had jumped right into living with you"—I pause when I see another round of hurt fly across his face—"not that *I* think that, but you know how she would get, well…she might…Nico, it probably would be the reason she'd finally call my dad."

Nico opens his mouth like he wants to say something else, but then his eyes drop, and he closes it.

"Fine," he says as he gets up. "I'm going to go get dinner. You have a bunch of other mail on the table, by the way."

"Please don't leave mad," I say, grabbing for his hand as he sidles around me.

He stops, and again, the hardness in his face melts a little as he looks at me. He leans down and gives me a kiss on the forehead.

"How the fuck can I be mad at a face like that?" he murmurs. Then, with a quick squeeze of my hand, he swipes his jacket off the floor and leaves.

My stomach is still in knots when I get off the couch to retrieve the rest of my mail. I hate that I made him look like that. There's nothing in the world I want to do more than shout to everyone I meet that I hit the freaking jackpot in New York City with Nico Soltero.

But my parents are a different story. On top of being conservative, Catholic, and, in my dad's case, ridiculously strict, they're also bitter after going through their own painful separation this last year. My mom likes Nico okay since she knows his role in extracting me from Giancarlo last spring, but she's definitely not too keen on seeing me jump back into anything serious. Since moving back to Brazil, my dad went from being overbearing to virtually absent in my life. I can only imagine him roaring back in with a vengeance if he found out I was living in sin with a firefighter seven years my senior.

The thought makes me tingle. And probably in a way my parents would *definitely* not like.

I flip through the mail I missed last month, sorting out spam from bills until coming to a large, stiff envelope. But it's not the weight of it that stops me. It's the familiar handwriting on the front.

The apartment door opens, and Nico comes back in carrying a plastic bag containing my soup and his beef broccoli. He sets it on the kitchenette counter and starts grabbing plates, only stopping when he realizes I haven't moved from the table.

"Hey," he says. "Everything all right over there?"

"I'm…I'm not sure." I shuffle into the kitchenette and hand him the letter. Nico squints, stumbling a little as he reads aloud my father's terse, slanted script.

Layla,

It has been too long since I have seen my daughter. Your cousin Luciano graduates from medical school at the end of summer term, and there will be a celebration before Carnaval. You should be here too, to be a part of your family. Everything has been arranged. It is the right thing to do.

I look forward to seeing you soon.

Your pai

Nico hands back the letter, and for a moment, I run my finger over the word *"pai,"* the Brazilian term for "dad." My father has never used it with me. We visited his family once when I was in high school, and after hearing my cousins call their fathers the same thing, I tried it with him and was shot down immediately. "Father," he always insisted, but when that eventually failed, he accepted "Dad." After he proclaimed most of my life that I am American, not Brazilian, it seems that now he's finally ready to open up that side of his life to me. Maybe he really did need to leave in order to do it.

"When is *Carnaval*?" Nico asks as he opens up his box of beef broccoli and starts eating directly from the container. "And what did he mean by 'everything has been arranged'?"

"He means this, I think." I pull out an airplane ticket, the old-fashioned kind that are still printed on card stock, hand it to Nico.

He flips it over and back again, examining it. "This is three weeks from now."

I nod.

Nico's mouth quirks a little. "You leave the day before Valentine's Day."

I glance down, suddenly guilty. I shouldn't go. It's Nico's and my second anniversary of sorts. Our first one since coming back together. I'm not going to miss that.

"Layla." Nico's deep voice calls me back. "You should go. Brazil? Of *course* you should go. This is great, baby. You should be happy."

Happy. It's a funny word. But as I look at the sturdy, mint-green paper of the ticket, all I feel is dread. Trepidation. There's an inquisition waiting for me in another hemisphere, and he has a barrel chest and responds to "Dad." He'll look at all of the progress I've made over the last six or seven months and rip it to shreds. To my dad, I'm never quite enough.

We bring our food to the dining table and sit down, and before we've eaten anything, I know what I want to do.

"You should come with me," I blurt out.

Nico frowns through a big bite of broccoli. "What, to Brazil?"

I brighten, full of vision. "It's the perfect idea. He can't say no to someone who just flew four thousand miles to meet him. Even my dad would have to admit that's a pretty great thing to do."

"And what am I supposed to do when I get there?"

I grin. Yes. I like this idea. I *more* than like this idea. Suddenly, facing my father again without Nico next to me sounds impossible. "You're supposed to tell him how much you love me. And then we'll tell him that we're living together, and there isn't a damn thing he can do about it."

His black brow arches high. "You must really think I'm whipped, don't you?"

My mouth drops. "Oh, I..." Shit. I hadn't thought about that. I didn't mean to imply that he was at my beck and call or anything like that. Anything but.

Nico chuckles. "I'm just playin', baby. But honestly, even if I get the money together for a ticket, I don't know if I can swing the time off. Rookies don't really get their pick of the schedule, and I have no vacation time. *Nada.*"

"What if I paid?"

With a mouthful of rice, Nico gawks. "Hmm?"

I nod, even more convinced. "I have enough in my savings. I could swing it, and you could pay me back later if you really want to. Everything else would be taken care of, like he said. We'll probably stay at his apartment, or maybe my aunt's if there isn't room. We'll eat with them, so there won't be a bunch of extra expenses. No car, we'll be right by the beach. We'll go to my cousin's thing, and then come back. Or, you know, you could do stuff on your own if you wanted a break—"

"Layla." Nico pushes his food to the side, stands up, then lifts me bodily onto the table so that he's standing between my legs, my hands on his shoulders. "Do you really think I'd go with you to Brazil and then ditch you?"

I push my fingers through his thick black hair, so densely curled I almost can't do it.

"Please don't make me go alone," I whisper. "I want him to meet you. I want him to know the real man in my life these days. The one I can't live without."

Nico gazes up at me, his dark eyes wide and uncertain. Then he presses his forehead to mine and sighs.

"Fuck," he mutters. "It's those damn Bambi eyes. I can't say no."

I blink when he pulls away. "Does that mean you'll come?"

He sighs, even though his mouth quirks on both sides. "It means I'll try." Then his eyes drift down to my lips, which I just happen to lick at that moment.

There's that hunger again—not for food, but for something else. Something in both of us that we can't ever seem to sate completely.

Nico traces his nose across my chest and places a kiss on my sternum. "If I go." Another kiss on the shoulder. "You'll tell him?" One more on my neck. "And your mom too?"

He looks up with gleaming, hopeful eyes, and I clasp his face gently.

"We can tell him together," I say.

Nico's face is blank while he chews on his lower lip. He looks scared. It's not a look I recognize.

"Would you believe I'm not usually the guy girls want to take home to meet daddy?" he jokes as he presses his nose to mine. "Seriously, NYU. What's he going to think?"

"He'll think you're the kind of man who takes care of his girl," I say. "And if he doesn't, he can stay in his hemisphere when we go back to New York together. Because he might have everything to say about my life...but I belong here. With *you.*"

"And what would he think if he knew I was doing this to his daughter, huh?" A big hand snakes underneath my pajama shorts and takes a thick handful of flesh that makes me hiss.

"I don't know," I purr as I tip my face up to his waiting lips. "What would Carmen think if she knew the things I do to you?"

A low chuckle emerges from the back of Nico's throat, but he maintains the kiss for a few more seconds.

"Why do you think my mother goes to Mass three, four times a week, NYU?" he asks just before slipping his tongue around mine in that dance I know so well. "She's praying for my poor, corrupted soul. And now, yours too." He kisses me again. "Welcome to the family, baby."

CHAPTER TWENTY-ONE

Nico

The next day, my brother, two sisters, Layla, and I are all crowded into one tiny office at Family Immigration Services, which is housed in the third floor of a walk-up in Spanish Harlem. Ileana, the caseworker assigned to our mom, is holding the newest letter from the Treasury Department, tapping insistently on her beaten-up desk with a pencil. She looks pretty much the way you'd expect a social worker to look: a granola-eating white lady wearing a wrinkled blouse and a sweater that looks like she borrowed it from her grandfather, with mousey brown hair and a mouth that moves too fast.

Layla sits next to her desk, watching with keen interest as Ileana flips through all of the paperwork we've submitted trying to get this damn permit. I can't help but chuckle a little bit when I think of the fact that this is going to be Layla in a few more years. My girl has absolutely no idea how gorgeous she is. Inside this ugly, tiny room, she shines like a diamond.

Layla catches me watching her and gives me a shy smile. I wink, give her body a look up-and-down, and she immediately blushes.

"*Coño*," Maggie puts in, shoving me hard in the shoulder. "Stop undressing her with your eyes. You're embarrassing yourself." She turns to Selena, who's trying hard not to laugh. "He acts like no one is here. I feel dirty."

"*Gata*, I didn't say anything. You always gotta read so much into things, don't you?" I retort, though I don't drop my gaze. I'm enjoying the way Layla's biting her lip and squeezing her thighs together.

"Ahem." Ileana calls our attention as she sets down the paper.

And as much as I'd like to keep flirting, I turn to the desk along with the rest of my siblings, all dirty thoughts flying out of my head. This is too important.

"It's bad, isn't it?" asks Gabe. He rubs his chin, which is showing signs of a goatee. I smirk. My little brother is actually starting to get some facial hair.

"It's not great," Ileana says frankly.

She leans back in her chair and surveys all of us, looking everyone in the eye. It's one of the things I like about this chick—she might look like a mouse, but she's a firebrand, and she's never treated anyone in my family with anything less than respect.

"Look," she continues. "We had a window last spring, because the new adjustments were passed in June. But they didn't process the family license before then, and since June, the administration has pushed through much stronger restrictions. Basically, they're grandstanding, you know? Creating conflict where there is none to get people all riled up. You know, so we'll conveniently forget about the human rights violations they're committing all over the Middle East."

Maggie and I raised our brows at each other as if to say "here we go again" while Gabe shakes his head. We've all heard Ileana go off about the current president more than once, usually about the current war. I don't know. It's not really pertinent to our situation.

"So, what's left?" Layla asks as she picks up the different letters of rejection. "What else can we do to help Carmen? She has every right to be here by U.S. law. It's ridiculous that losing a piece of paper when she was two will force her to live in the shadows for the rest of her life, especially when she has every legal right to be here!"

The passion in her voice ignites a warmth in my chest. It's fucked up, but I love watching Layla get riled up like this about my mom, my family, her blue eyes full of fire. I have to stop myself from kissing her right there. I meant what I said last night: she is part of the family now. Moments like this show it more than anything else.

But Ileana sighs, and blows all of those good feelings out of the room.

"I'm sorry," she says. "I'll keep researching, but we're running out of options. The best way would be to find someone who actually has living family in Cuba to do this for you. Otherwise, it might be time to start putting together a case for relief. You mom doesn't know any Cubans in New York?"

Beside me, Layla brightens at the idea, but Maggie shakes her head.

"*Mami* came here with a Puerto Rican family. She's been sheltered by Puerto Ricans her whole life. All her friends are Puerto Rican, other than David..."

She trails off, looking at me and Gabe uneasily. David, Gabe's father, is Dominican, but I haven't seen or spoken to the guy since I beat his ass and kicked him out of our apartment for beating on Ma and the rest of us one too many times. That was over ten years ago now, but it's the family's worst kept secret that sometimes our mom would still find her way up to the Bronx to see him in a moment of weakness. Maybe she still does. None of us really know or want to know.

"What about Luis? Isn't he Cuban?" Gabe pipes up, giving Maggie a dark look at the mention of David. I know he speaks to his dad sometimes, but he doesn't mention it to me, knowing there is no lack of bad blood between me and that violent asshole.

I sigh. Everyone in my family has a big damn mouth, but we still keep too many secrets.

Maggie and Selena both look like they want to beat Gabe's ass at the mention of their father, Luis, who hasn't been seen since Selena was about three. He's Cuban, it's true, but the dude dropped off the face of the earth.

Yeah, you could say our family has some daddy issues. One more thing Layla has in common with us, as it happens. She doesn't exactly get along with her father either. The dad she wants me to meet. I press my face into my palms. I have no idea how I would be able to do that without punching the guy who broke his daughter's heart last year.

"One of the girls in my Spanish class has some family in Havana," Layla pipes up. "I don't really know her, but she seems nice. I bet she would be willing to go to Cuba over spring break or something if we could get her the permit."

"Has she gone in the last three years?" Ileana asks.

"Yeah, she went last summer to visit her grandparents."

"Then she's out. The new laws only permit visits once every three years anyway." Ileana looks at the rest of us. "And let's be clear. Your mother says she was born in Santiago, not Havana like you originally thought, and they aren't exactly close. You can't substitute one for the other. What about the rest of you? Do you know *any*one with family in Cuba?"

I shake my head, and beside me, Maggie rolls her eyes at Selena. I could see it all too easily—someone taking our money, a free trip to Cuba, and disappearing on us. Scammers in New York are a dime a dozen; no one in this room other than the two white girls think that's even an option.

"Then it's either keep trying with a family application for one you," Ileana says in a resigned, stern voice, "or we need to turn your case over to a lawyer and get you ready for court. You never know, they might allow one of you a permit. Or else, and I'm not officially suggesting this, you understand, you could also fly there from another country. There's no guarantees you won't get caught, and spending any U.S. currency there is illegal, but you can get there from somewhere like Venezuela. Maybe Toronto or Montreal."

"I'll do it."

Gabe glances around the room, his voice grim and determined while he toys with the bottom of his blue t-shirt. The glasses he started wearing this year are slightly crooked over a fierce expression.

I frown. "*Mano*, you don't have to do that. We'll keep applying. Ma's all right staying at Alba's. They're practically having a slumber party over there, you know?"

"Ma and Alba are driving each other up the wall," Maggie puts in. "I was there yesterday, and I thought they were going to toss each other over the balcony. I don't care how much you love your best friend. After a while, you need some space."

"There was a rumor of some immigrations people sniffing around the church last week too," Selena mentions.

I jerk my head at her. "*What*?"

Selena shrugs. "We heard about it from the priest, who said some of the other parishioners were talking about it outside. I don't know if anyone was taken, but…"

I exhale forcibly. "Sel, you can't be taking Ma to a church where there are fuckin' immigrations officers hanging out!"

"I'm sorry, but have you met our mother? *You* try getting Carmen Soltero to attend any other church but St. Andrew's."

"Fuckin' *fine*," I spit. "But anyway, we can't just get all crazy because of some rumors. I hope you didn't tell Ma about those."

Selena shrinks a little. "She was there, Nico. What the fuck did you want me to do? Cover her ears, like we do to Allie?"

"Not unless you want a slipper," Maggie murmurs, setting off another round of snickering between her and Sel. I fall forward onto my knees, burying my head in my hands and relaxing only slightly when Layla starts to massage my neck.

"What about Brazil? Can you fly to Cuba from there?"

Layla's sweet voice cuts through the bickering, and everyone quiets as they turn to her. She casts me a nervous glance.

"No," I say automatically.

"That's an idea," Ileana murmurs. "You're going to Brazil?"

"Who's going to Brazil?" Maggie asks sharply.

"I am," Layla says. "And maybe Nico too, if he can get the time off. To visit my dad. I don't know if they have travel restrictions to Cuba, but if they don't, maybe we could work a trip in. I, um, could probably cover the cost..."

She drifts off, no longer meeting everyone's gazes. I know it's because Layla doesn't like to talk about money in front of my family. She thinks it makes her sound like a rich girl, like the *blanquita* people sometimes call her when they first meet her. She hasn't figured out that keeping silent about that sort of thing is a rich girl thing to do. Nothing says you have money like pretending it doesn't exist.

"No," I say again, but it's like no one in the office hears me.

"Nico, I could probably go," Layla says. "I have dual citizenship because of my father, so I could travel with a Brazilian passport—"

"*No.*" I stand up in a rush. "I'm not sending you to fucking Cuba by yourself, Layla. End of fucking story."

I grab her hand and pull her up with me. This office that smells like stale coffee and french fries suddenly feels like a strait jacket. I want to get out of here before this conversation ends the way I think it will.

I glare at Ileana, who's still looking at Layla thoughtfully. "Resubmit the applications under all of our names," I bark at her. "One for each. You need anything else?"

Ileana frowns. I'm acting like a caveman, but I can't help it. I've had enough of this office. I've had enough of doors being shut in my family's faces our entire fuckin' lives. I've had enough of being told no. So now I'm the one who's going to say it.

"I'll get that paperwork going again," she says carefully.

"I'm sorry about him," Maggie's saying. "He's just worried."

For some reason the apologies make me even angrier."Come on," I say as I tow Layla behind me. "Let's get the fuck out of here."

CHAPTER TWENTY-TWO

Nico

Layla's quiet as we walk through Astoria, marching down the icy sidewalk toward the subway. I'm being an asshole, I know. And Layla, reading my mood, keeps trying to give me space. But every time she steps away, my hand only tightens its grip, as if by reflex.

I take an automatic sharp right off the main street.

"I forgot my charger at the firehouse yesterday," I say shortly before Layla can ask where we're going. "I'll just run in and get it."

Layla frowns. My next shift starts tomorrow afternoon—I could just borrow hers, like I did last night.

I'm helpless. It's a feeling I know too well, one I was slowly starting to think might finally be fading out of my life. But all I learned from that meeting was that there's not a damn thing I can do to help my mother, and it's killing me.

The firehouse, on the other hand, hasn't quite lost its gleam. Three months after I graduated from the academy and was assigned a station in Queens, I still get a little thrill every time I arrive. The door to helping my mom get residency still might be glued shut, but this one finally opened. My job. My girl. If I can just focus on the good stuff, maybe I'll be able to pick that last lock.

"I'm sorry for being such a dick back there," I say as we stop.

Layla looks up at the three-story brick building, her eyes bright in the cold winter sunshine. It's her first time here. With the business of the semester and then her leaving for Christmas, she never got the chance to come up and see it, but I know she's been curious.

"I think you owe Ileana the apology," she says. "You weren't very nice to her."

I sigh. "Yeah. I know. I wouldn't blame her if she told us to fuck off."

"She's not going to do that. But you should make it right too." Layla looks up at the firehouse. "This is so cool. Can you show me around?"

The look on her face—the pure, unadulterated pride—lifts me out of my shitty mood in about ten seconds.

I grin back. "You fuckin' bet."

Still holding her hand, we cross the street, and I push open the heavy door.

"It's one of the oldest firehouses in the city," I tell her proudly as I walk her around the bottom floor. "They used it on a set of some movie, but I forget which one."

Layla's all eyes as I give her the grand tour through the downstairs, showing her the lockers where we keep our stuff, the dispatch room. I lead her into the big garage, where we keep the trucks. She walks around curiously, examining the interactive map on one side of the room, the rows of helmets and jackets hanging on the walls, the boots with pants bunched around them, ready to be pulled on as soon as an alarm goes off. She drags her fingers over the red paint of one of the trucks in awe. It reminds me a little of my first day on the job. I'd been in the trucks at the academy plenty of times before, but on that day, I was starstruck. I stared at the ladder I was assigned to for a solid ten minutes before I could do anything else.

Layla takes a look at the ladder eagerly. "This is *so* cool, Nico. So if the bell rang, everyone would come racing down here?"

I shove my hands in my coat pockets and nod. "And they'd probably thank us to get the fuck out of the way too."

I glance around the garage nervously. I'm a rookie, so I'm still getting used to the way things work, although the job is beginning to commit itself to muscle memory. Still, I'm pretty sure I'd catch some serious fuckin' heat if the chief caught me in here with my girlfriend when they get a call.

"Come on, sweetie," I say, nodding toward the door. "There's more."

I take her up the stairs to where most of the guys are crowded in the kitchen. Mike, who's about the same size as the industrial-sized refrigerator behind him, is stirring a big pot of sauce while pasta boils on another burner. Four other guys are leaning over the counter with Cokes, probably wishing they were beers. They're laughing, teasing Mike about his bad habit of putting too many onions in his sauce. On the other side of the kitchen, a few other guys are watching a basketball game in the lounge area. It's a typical scene. I never knew how much of this job was just waiting around for something to happen.

"Rooooook," Joe, a younger guy from Staten Island who's on his fourth year, calls from his spot at the counter, starting off a round of the same calls all around the room.

Layla grins until the chorus ends. They all sound like dogs barking at the damn moon. I'm rolling my eyes, but I'm not going to lie. I kind of like it.

"You just can't stay away, can you, rook?" Mike says as he ambles over. "What the fuck? Are you obsessed with us, or something? Are you like that chick Herrera's dating, the one that shows up at the firehouse at all times of the night and day?"

A bunch of other guys chuckle while Damien Herrera, the guy in question, rolls his eyes from the couch. He's the butt of a lot of jokes like that, but the dude really does bring it on himself. His woman is a legit psycho.

"And who is this beautiful thing?" Mike asks as he looks over Layla frankly. "And what the hell is the rookie doing with a girl as fine as you, sweetheart? He should know better than to bring you around here with all of these hooligans."

"Hey, hey, take it easy," I warn him. "This is my girl, Layla."

"We got a live wire, I see. How you doin', sweetheart?"

Mike waggles his eyebrows as he kisses Layla's hand. He's a teddy bear of a dude, and he's just giving me shit, but that doesn't make me like another guy hitting on my girl. I shake my head. I'm not jealous by nature, but I think a part of me might always feel that way a little bit with her.

"Yeah, you can stop that now," I retort, unable to help myself completely as I tug Layla out of Mike's reach. I don't care that technically he's my superior, the ranking lieutenant in the house tonight. I just want him to stop fucking touching my woman.

Fuck. Maybe coming here was a bad idea. I was all excited to show the place off to Layla, but now it's just making me tenser.

"Is there more?" Layla asks, having been pulled tightly into my side.

She looks up at me, and the teasing and laughter surrounding us dies. Suddenly, the only thing I want to do is go home, lose myself in her gorgeous body for an hour or two, and reset my mind.

I soften. "Yeah, there's more. I'll show you the upstairs, grab my charger, and then we'll go."

We bid our farewells to the guys as I take her up the third flight of stairs to the sleeping quarters and the small weight room where I work out between calls. About half of the small single beds have sheets on them, dressed for the people who are currently on live shifts overnight. The rest are just plain vinyl mattresses, waiting for the next shift to come.

Layla turns and leans against one of the beds without anything. "It kind of reminds me of a fraternity house," she remarks.

I nod, although I've never been in one. "Do they sleep twenty to a room like this?" I joke. "We're like sardines in here."

But Layla nods. "Sometimes. It depends on the frat and school, obviously. The ones at NYU are basically just on a floor of one of the dorms, but a few have pretty big common dormitory rooms. At least you don't have bunk beds." She looks around. "Which one is yours?"

I raise a brow. "You tryin' to get me into bed, NYU?"

Right on cue, Layla blushes, sending a familiar flutter through my stomach. I could make her do that all damn day.

"You're terrible," she says. "I was just curious."

I walk up to her so we're standing close enough to be nose to nose. "It's right…"

I bend and trace my nose down her neck, just under her collar. Just a taste, I tell myself. In her tight black jeans and clingy sweater, she's looking particularly fuckable at the moment, but I'm not going to do that here. I shouldn't. Not with all the guys downstairs. Not when Layla can't always control her voice when I'm in her. No, I won't. Even if the look in her eyes tells me that she really, really wants to.

"Here," I say, as I tap the bedpost just behind her and stand up.

The pupils of Layla's eyes have dilated slightly. "Do you ever think about…you know? Getting busy when you're in here without me?"

Honest? Pretty much never. Late at night, when we're all mostly asleep in here, it's a chorus of snores, grunts, all of the sounds men make when they're asleep. Pretty much the unsexiest thing on the planet.

But right now, with the room empty, the door closed, and the afternoon sunlight making Layla's hair glow like that… We shouldn't do anything. I know that. But I'm also not so sure I can wait until we're home. And by the way she's chewing on her lower lip right now, I don't think she can either.

"What's the chance anyone is going to come up here right now?" she asks, her voice low and throaty as she links two fingers through my belt loops and pulls me closer.

"Unlikely," I say. "No one comes in here except at night."

My mouth hovers over hers, not quite taking what I want. I'm teasing myself here, but I couldn't care less. Sometimes half the fun is anticipation.

Layla glances at the door, which is still cracked closed, then looks at me and licks her lip. And when I say licks it, I mean runs her tongue slowly around her plump, pink mouth until it shines, ready to be kissed.

Jesus Christ.

"Keep lookout," she says, and before I can ask what she means, she's sliding down to her knees, unzipping my jeans, and freeing the pipe I've had going down there since I watched her walk up the stairs in front of me.

"Layla, you don't have to—oh, *shit*, that feels fuckin' good."

Her mouth slides over me, with her small hand gripping around my base where her lips don't quite reach. My head falls back as I lose myself in the sensation of her sweet mouth, and it takes me a few seconds to remember that we're not in the privacy of our bedroom and I need to be watching the door.

"Fuck," I hiss as she takes me even deeper. Her mouth is fucking magic. "I—Jesus, Layla. Baby, I—" I'm practically incoherent, but something's missing. I want more. I *need* more.

Suddenly, I'm acting completely on instinct. I pull her off me and yank her up my body. Layla's mouth, warm and wet, hangs open as her heated gaze drags over me. The uncurbed desire in her bright eyes just gets me that much harder.

"Nico—" she starts to say, but I cover her mouth with mine as I walk her backward a few steps, rip open her jeans, and shove them down her legs before she topples backward onto the empty mattress I usually claim for myself.

"I don't want to come in your mouth," I say as I sweep her legs across me so she's facing me on her side.

Her pants, still twisted around her ankles, keep her thighs together, but that just makes her that much tighter when my cock finds her slick passage. She's basically bound sideways as I hold her down, her sweet, full body open for me to do what I want.

I close my eyes in half-pain, half-pleasure as I slide into her warmth. *Fuck.* It really never stops. It doesn't matter how many times we do this—her tightness, her depth, the way she squeezes around me as I fill her completely—it feels better every time.

"Why?" she whispers, barely able to get the words out as I start to move. She shudders, and I get even harder knowing I have the same effect on her.

I lean down to kiss her again, needing to taste her in that moment more than I need anything else—food, water, air. I need Layla more. I pull out, teasing her slightly with just the tip. Her breathing grows shallow as I look down, entranced by that scant few inches where our bodies are joined.

"Because," I say as I shove back in with one hard thrust. "I want to come in you."

It's hard to make jokes when we're like this, but Layla still manages one, breathy and light. "But you would have."

She shudders when I deliver another punishing thrust. I give her the wickedest smile I can, thrilling in the way her entire body responds, then deliver a quick slap across her ass. Her nipples perk, even through her sweater, her back arches, her muscles tense, and she tilts her hips slightly to take me even deeper.

"Yeah," I tell her in between more unforgiving thrusts. "But this way, I get to feel you come too."

My hand reaches between her thighs to find that warm, soft spot that I know will push her over the edge. I circle my thumb over it, working in tandem with my hips. I'm close—if we were at home, I'd stop, change positions, bring her to the edge and take her back down three, four, five times before letting us both explode together. But here we could get caught at any time.

My brothers could walk in at any second, find me eight inches deep in the sweetest pussy in New York. And you know what? I'd have no fuckin' regrets.

But for her sake, I wrap it up fast. Press a little harder until her body starts to shake and she loses a bit of its control, unable to keep as quiet as before.

"You know it's better like this, don't you, baby?" I ask, bending down and keeping my voice low so only she can hear me. The sounds of the guys' voices filter from downstairs, and it only turns me on more. "When you get to feel my cock in your tight, wet pussy? When I get to feel you squeeze and shudder around my dick?"

"Ummmmm," Layla groans into my neck, her teeth biting into my skin. She's robbed of speech at this point, that slight pain brings me even closer.

"*Fuck*," I swear as I pound into her. "This body was made for me, you know that? I fuckin' *dream* about this body, Layla. I don't care who sees me, baby. All they would see is the way I *own* this gorgeous. Fucking. Body. *Whenever. Wherever.*"

"Nico!" she gasps, now clawing hard. Her nails are going to leave marks, and I couldn't be happier about it.

I take her clit between my fingers, and watch as she falls apart completely. Her entire body seizes, a lithe line of muscle quivering around my hips, squeezing me like a fuckin' vise.

"Nico," she whimpers as she holds on for her life, taking pound after punishing pound. "Please."

"Fuuuuuuuuccccck," I growl as I follow her into oblivion.

Layla opens her mouth to cry, and I stifle both our moans with one last demanding kiss that matches the final few thrusts of my cock. *This* is what I needed for the last hour. This banishes the last of my hopelessness, because when I do this for Layla, when I do this for both of us, I feel like I could rock the whole fucking world with what we are together.

If only it would last.

I work out the rest of my orgasm and hers until slowly, slowly, the room comes back into focus. Her body softens into mine, and I lean my head on her shoulder as I catch my breath. The sounds of the city call from the other side of the window, and the guys' voices filter up the stairs. My mind puts itself back together. I can lose myself in Layla for sure, but when we're done, the world is always waiting.

Slowly, I pull out, then point Layla into the bathroom to clean herself up when she asks. We haven't used protection in months; things get a little messy. When she's done, she comes right back to where I'm leaning against the window at the far end of the dormitory and lets me fold her into my chest. My hands float down and rest on her ass—that sweet curve that's always seemed like it was molded for my palms.

"Yo." I squeeze lightly. "You're filling out a little more here, huh?"

"*What*?" Layla arches back to stare at me open-mouthed. "I'm *what*?"

I look her up and down, not even bothering to mask my open leering, and squeeze her ass again. "I know this ass like I know my own name, Layla. We've been eating well, huh?"

"Oh. My. *God*! You just told me I'm getting fat!"

Layla smacks me on the shoulder, and I can't help but start laughing, which only makes her smack me harder.

"I didn't say anything like that!" I shout, turning her around and binding her arms down in front of me. "And besides, I like it. More of you to love, right?"

"Ewwwww!" she cries, and now I'm practically wheezing because I'm laughing so hard. I'm being a dick, teasing her about a few extra pounds. I grew up with girls—I know better than to say a damn thing about their bodies at all, much less something that's not exactly complimentary.

"We'll see what you have to say when I start pointing out how you're losing your six-pack," she retorts, reaching down to pinch at the nonexistent layers of fat around my belly. "You're going to be thirty in two years, old man. Time waits for no one."

I just deliver another grin, the kind that always makes her stumble a little, and pull up my shirt. "These ain't goin' nowhere, baby. As long as you look at me like that, I'll be doing my sit-ups every night before bed. That's a promise."

Layla's mouth drops a little as she looks over my abs, and then she bites her lip all over again. *Fuck.* The problem with teasing my girl is that her response usually gets me even more hot and bothered. And since we already tested our luck in here once, I'm not about to tempt fate by bending her over the mattress again, as much as I want to.

"I'm sorry," I say as I nuzzle close for a kiss. She's tight-lipped at first, but then she gives in, sucking gently on my lower lip. "I'm just teasing. You look perfect, sweetie. You always do."

And yet. She does look a little different. What do they call it? Puppy love pounds, or something corny like that? I noticed it last night too. It's a good thing—she never did gain back all the weight she lost when she got sick, and she seemed to lose some last year too. Not much of a surprise, considering what kind of stress she was under.

I search for the words to tell her what I mean. Because really, she's even more beautiful than she ever was. Luscious. A little fuller. The word ripe keeps tripping off my tongue, but I'm pretty sure if I used any kind of word that could also be applied to produce, I'd earn myself another punch, and Layla's starting to punch hard these days after training at Frank's with me once a week or so.

So instead I fold her against me again, her back to my front while I rest my chin on her shoulder and enjoy the way her breasts—which, yeah, I think are a little bigger now too—push up under my forearms.

"You know I think you're beautiful," I murmur before inhaling deeply. Layla's sweet scent surrounds me, and immediately, I feel at peace. "You'll always be beautiful to me. No matter what."

Layla sighs and relaxes in my arms as we look out the window, over the rooftops of Queens toward the taller buildings of Manhattan.

"Let me do this for you," she murmurs.

I sigh. She's not talking about sex anymore, I had a feeling she was going to bring it up eventually. Layla and I have been living together long enough now that we're starting to know some of each other's patterns. I know when something triggers her back to Giancarlo, and a little clowning around with some well-placed kisses can usually nip a full-on panic-attack in the bud.

She, on the other hand, has an uncanny habit of knowing exactly when I feel like the world is trying to bury me, and that my instinct is to fight back. Hard. Sometimes I lash out, and that's usually when I have to walk away from people before I hurt them.

But Layla never lets me walk alone. And sometimes she can steer me back to the bedroom to distract me from my worst thoughts. Two handfuls of my favorite body part usually solve that problem, and Layla is usually all too happy to let me lose myself in her until my mind is clear enough to think straight and listen to whatever she wanted to say to begin with. Like right now.

"It would be a simple trip," she says as she leans into my neck. "Get there, go to the records office, go home. That's it. Ileana can walk me through it."

And then, of course, that's usually when she lays down her predictably clear logic. I press a light kiss into her hair as my breathing returns to normal. But when it does, and the pounding of my heart lessens, that heaviness is still there. I'd risk a lot for my mom. I'll put myself, my record, all of it on the line for her. But there's no way I'm risking Layla.

"No," I say quietly, hugging her a little tighter. "I love you for wanting to, baby, but the answer is no. We'll find another way."

CHAPTER TWENTY-THREE

Layla

THERE'S SOMETHING THAT HAPPENS WHEN YOU STEP OFF THE PLANE IN A FOREIGN country. It doesn't even matter if it's the same climate—something in the air shifts. A smell. A weight. Something changes, and you know you're in a completely different place.

As we walk down the steps of the small plane and follow the line of passengers across the runway toward the Vitória terminal, Nico's head is on a swivel. This is the first time he's ever been out of the country, which I didn't realize until we had gotten on the second leg of our flight in Miami.

It took a lot of trades, overtime, and basically giving up every holiday for the rest of the year, but Nico managed to get a week off to come with me to visit my dad. He basically worked nonstop for the past three weeks while I did extra credit in my classes so I'd be able to leave too. It's not an easy trip to be making for either of us, but I'm definitely glad we're here.

"It smells…" Nico wrinkles his nose adorably, looking around for something, then back at me, confused. "Sweet. What is that?"

I grin. "Chocolate. There's a factory a few miles from here. *Garoto* is like the Brazilian version of Willy Wonka."

Nico grins. "Oompa Loompa? Brazilian style?" He leers at me. "I would doom-pity-do you right now, baby. Jesus *fuck* it's good not to be on an airplane anymore." Even with his backpack, he jogs a second next to me. For someone as active as Nico, sitting for fifteen hours straight was tantamount to torture.

"Oh my God, you're corny." I nudge him in the shoulder. "Only you could make a song by tiny orange men sound dirty."

Nico leans in to nip my ear. "I could make a *lot* of things dirty with you, baby. 'Specially after having to sit next to you for that long without so much as a kiss. Who knew joining the mile-high club would be so damn hard?"

Nico drapes his arm around me, tipping his head up to the sun so its light can shine under the brim of his Yankees cap. In New York, it's freezing, with snow on the ground and another round predicted while we're gone. Here, Brazil is in the middle of summer, and it's hot here on the coast.

I'm laughing and blushing at the same time as we head into the airport terminal. That is, until I see the person standing with his arms crossed on the other side of the small barrier.

Tall, stolid, with thick black hair threaded with only a few strands of silver. Wearing an impeccably ironed blue button-down shirt and neat slacks in spite of the heat. He's the kind of man who looks about six inches taller than he is only because of his stern presence. Who's had frown lines since his twenties because of how little he smiles. Whose fingers tap impatiently even when he's not waiting for someone.

My father.

Nico's arm falls from my shoulder, and I take his hand as we follow the crowd through the glass doors and into the terminal. He squeezes, but whether it's to comfort me or himself isn't clear. Nico, my strong, unflappable New Yorker, has a sweaty palm.

"Dad," I say as we approach the barrier between people waiting for passengers and the tiny baggage claim area. "Hi."

My father leans over the barrier and gives me kisses on each cheek, Brazilian style, barely even grazing my skin. It's like he's greeting a stranger for the first time. There's no hug, no smile. He's not a particularly affectionate man, but I had at least hoped for some thawing of his normally stern personality, considering we haven't seen each other in over a year and a half. But it looks like any chance of that happening vanished when he caught sight of the tattooed, backward-cap-wearing bad boy walking beside me.

"*Alô, Senhor Barros,*" Nico pronounces, working extra hard on the Brazilian pronunciation of the name that I taught him on the way over. "*Tudo bem?*"

"Who is this?" Dad asks me abruptly, reverting back to his terse English, more heavily accented now than I remember.

I frown. "Dad. I told you weeks ago that Nico was coming. This is Nico Soltero, my boyfriend." I know I shouldn't like the way that sounds so much, but I do. I really do.

Nico's face has suddenly turned blank. Shit, I know that expression. It's the same one he wears when he sees cops on the street or when security guards follow him around a store. It's the face he wears when he feels trapped. Stereotyped. Pigeonholed.

"Nico," I say, reaching for his hand to tug him over next to me. "Babe, this is my father, Sergio Barros."

"*Doctor* Barros," Dad corrects me, though his gray eyes don't stray from their stern perusal of Nico.

I'm basically witnessing one of those nature videos when two male lions are facing off. My dad puffs out his chest, but keeps his arms firmly crossed while he stares, unblinking. His sooty eyes, with their dark circles that I get, which almost make him look like he's been rubbing his eyes with ashes, are unwavering. Nico, to his credit, also refuses to look away, and if it weren't for the way his hand squeezes mine almost hard enough to hurt, I wouldn't even know he was bothered. The thick silence between them actually stunts some of the other chatter around us as people look up from greeting each other to watch the standoff.

Slowly, Nico extends a hand again. Dad looks at it as if Nico's offering him a dead fish. Then, slowly, he takes it, and they commence a white-knuckled handshake that seems to last about an hour. When they finally let go, both of them flex their fingers, relieving the pressure.

"Soltero," Dad says. "And what kind of name is that?"

"Dad!"

The last thing I need is my dad fishing around for Nico's pedigree. I'm already mortified by his frosty reception, although I don't know why I expected this to be better. There was a reason I never had a real boyfriend through high school. Still, Nico's going to be on the next plane out of here if things don't perk up.

"My mother's from Cuba, sir," Nico answers gamely. "My dad was Puerto Rican and Italian."

"Was?" Dad asks. "What do you mean, 'was'?"

A muscle in Nico's jaw ticks, but otherwise he maintains his plain, open expression. "I guess is. I don't really know, sir. Honestly, I've only met him a few times, and not since I was a kid."

An awkward silence falls. Nico really, *really* doesn't like to focus on the fact that his dad was one of the first who dropped his mother and her kids like a hot potato as soon as he got the chance. I will him to know the truth—that I couldn't care less. None of that changes who he's become. In fact, it might have contributed to it.

"Well," Dad says finally, dragging his harsh gaze back to me. "Where are your bags?"

I look down at my small carry-on and the beat-up duffle Nico has over his shoulder. "This is it. We're only here for a week, so we didn't want to check anything."

Dad frowns as he starts walking toward the end of the barrier, where the gate opens. "That's it? Did you forget the banquet?"

Nico and I follow him, shuffling by other passengers in the crowded airport.

I frown. "Of course I didn't forget it, Dad. Don't worry, we brought some dress clothes. We'll just need an iron, that's all."

Dad darts a narrow-eyed look at Nico's duffel bag. "What kind of man packs his tuxedo in a sack?"

"Tuxedo?" Nico asks. He glances at me. "I was supposed to bring a tux?" He holds up the garment bag that was slung over his other shoulder. "I brought a suit. I hope that's okay. I guess I could rent something…"

"The banquet is black tie," Dad responds, not even bothering to look up as he checks his watch. "Layla, I tell you these things so you will listen. Does that expensive school teach you anything? How to read a basic email?"

Nico just glances at me, alarmed, but I shake my head, willing him to trust that I'll figure it all out. My father said absolutely no such thing. And even if he did, it doesn't really matter. I doubt that Nico will be the only one to show up in a suit instead of a tux.

We walk around to the other side of the barrier, and I set down my bag, ready, finally to embrace my father the way everyone else in the terminal seems to be doing. But even though it's been more than a year and a half since I last saw him, Dad just keeps walking toward the exit, his step as brisk as ever. It's only when he notices we've fallen behind that he stops and turns around.

"Layla," Dad barks, loud enough to startle a few clusters of passengers. "Are you coming?"

Without waiting for an answer, he walks out of the airport. I take a deep breath. A hand slides around my waist, and Nico pulls me protectively into his side.

"Your dad could host a comedy show," he mutters. "He's like a real bundle of laughs."

I chuckle, but lay my head on Nico's broad shoulder and inhale. "I'm so sorry. We've been here two minutes, and he's already being an asshole."

"He just loves you. I'd probably freak out if my daughter walked up with a guy who looks like me too."

"Stop. If our daughter ended up with someone like you, I'd be over the moon."

Nico freezes, and it takes me a second to realize what I just said.

"Shit," I say. "Don't freak out. I didn't mean anything by it."

But instead, I'm rewarded with a sweet smile that sets my insides alight.

"Relax. You're good. I got you," Nico murmurs into my ear.

His scent and the warmth of his breath on my neck immediately cause my shoulders to fall back to their normal position. I sink into him slightly and recharge for a moment before standing up straight and turning my face toward his.

"Thanks," I whisper, giving him a quick kiss. "I got you too."

"Anytime, baby." Nico smiles into my lips. "Now let's catch up with your dad before he drop-kicks my ass onto the next flight home."

WE DRIVE through Vitória in silence while my dad listens to the news, which, in its rapid Portuguese, is mostly incomprehensible. Nico and I just gaze out our windows, taking in the sights. The airport sits on the north side of Vitória, and we'll have to drive all the way through the island in the center of the C-shaped bay to get to Vila Velha, the twin city on the other side of the bay. Nico and I sit together in the back of my dad's Mercedes, since his front seat is full of paperwork he couldn't be bothered to move. I don't mind. I actually preferred to be close to Nico, even after spending a whole day straight on three different planes together.

There isn't much to see for the first part of the drive. The green foliage that surrounds the narrow highway hides a lot of the houses lurking beyond. Nico smiles when we pass the Garoto factory and starts humming the Oompa Loompa song until Dad clears his throat loudly enough to make him stop.

Eventually the highway curves into the city, and we start zooming through the hills of crumbling housing that encircle the low-lying island on which Vitória is built, where the beaches and high-rise buildings are. Occasionally Nico points to things and asks me what they are, but honestly, I don't know much more about the city than him, having only been here once in my life. I know that my dad's sister, whose son is the one graduating this week, lives in Vitória proper, in an apartment looking over a beach called Praia da Camburi. My dad lives on the other side of the massive arched bridge that crosses the bay into Vila Velha. I know from pictures that his apartment is also beachfront, on the sixteenth floor of a building in the shopping district of Praia da Costa.

"How do I say that?" Nico points to a road sign for Vila Velha, as we start crossing the bridge. "Vee-la Vel-ha?"

I shake my head. "The 'h' is pronounced kind of like a 'y' when it's paired with a vowel like that. That's why when you see it after the n, it's pronounced like ñ in Spanish. *Claro, Senhor* Soltero?"

Nico gives me an almost wicked look in response to my sudden Portuguese, one that has me wishing very badly we'd just gotten a hotel for at least one night instead of spending the whole week in my dad's apartment. There is absolutely no way we'll be allowed to share a bed. When Nico catches my hand, scratching his finger on the inside of my palm. It sends a shiver down my back.

"You're so damn smart," he whispers as he squeezes my hand, then turns and keeps looking out the window at the city fading away behind us and the other one approaching as we descend the tall arch. He nods at the hills that are piled with ramshackle housing that resembles multicolored cinder blocks stacked on top of one another. "Projects, right?" he asks with a half smile. "What did you call them?"

My lips quirk in response as I remember one of our early conversations together on the subway, passing some of the public housing projects on the way up to Nico's apartment at the time. It was during the first weekend we spent together, just after our first date. The first time Nico began showing me sides of New York, of himself, that I'd never been exposed to.

"Those neighborhoods are called *favelas*. But 'projects is just a word,' you know," I repeat his own words from one of our first dates.

That earns me a full-on grin, and Nico lifts my hand to kiss my knuckles.

"No doubt," he murmurs.

We both lapse into silence as we continue the ride—me lost in my thoughts as I watch my dad through the rearview mirror, and Nico murmuring to himself from time to time. It's only after I listen for a bit that I realize he's reading signs to himself, followed by the translations in Spanish.

"*Praia. La playa*," he says before he catches me watching him. "Beach, right?"

I nod. "Yep, you got it."

He looks back out the window, taking in the even mix of palm trees and tall buildings that make up one of Brazil's smaller cities. "Spanish and Portuguese aren't really so different, once you figure out the little things."

"They are *completely* different." My father's voice cuts in from the front, and he narrows his eyes at Nico through the rearview mirror. "If they were the same, they would be one language, not two."

"Actually, they are pretty close structurally, Dad," I say. "I've been taking both for my program, remember? It doesn't really feel like I'm learning two completely different languages. They share almost all of the same roots and cognates."

"Still," Dad says. He continues to stare bullets at Nico, who shifts uncomfortably in his seat. "Different enough."

CHAPTER TWENTY-FOUR

Nico

Dr. Barros pulls the car into the underground parking garage of a giant high-rise that's basically beachfront. It's right across the 4-lane thoroughfare that runs alongside one of the major beaches in Vila Velha right on the main Praia da Costa, according to all of the street signs. The two cities, like Layla told me earlier, separated by only a small bay, are basically one big one. Each side is probably about the size of one of the boroughs in New York.

Praia da Costa is on the other side of a giant—and I mean *giant*—arched bridge that towers over the bay and drops down into Vila Velha, next to a big white building that looks like some kind of church, perched on one of the egg-shaped hills that seem to rise everywhere up and down the coast.

"We should walk up there tomorrow," Layla says as she points to it. "It's this old convent. Nico, it's *so* pretty."

I nod. I wouldn't mind jogging up that hill right about now. I just spent way too many hours crammed into three square feet on three different airplanes. My body needs movement. But first things first: I gotta get this guy to stop looking at me like he wants to toss me off that bridge we just drove over.

I've known him for less than an hour, but I don't like Dr. Barros. I don't like the way he's barely said hello to his daughter even though he hasn't seen her for eighteen months. I don't like the fact that he keeps correcting and chiding her like she's seven years old. I don't like the fact that he keeps glaring at the tattoos on my arm like I have 666 printed on my bicep.

And I *really* don't like the sad way Layla keeps looking at him—like a beautiful, blue-eyed puppy begging to be pet. Yeah, it's taken me all of twenty fuckin' minutes to understand how a girl like Layla got wrapped up with that asshole last fall, and it has everything to do with *this* asshole in front of me.

You could say I'm having a hard time giving the guy a fair chance.

"So, you must be really proud of Layla, Dr. Barros," I venture as we take our bags up the elevator from the garage.

Dr. Barros turns around with an arched brow. "Proud? Of what?"

Beside me, Layla wilts, and I have to smother the growl in my chest. Is it fucked up that I want to punch that smug look off his face? What the fuck does he mean, "proud of what?" Layla's a fucking incredible person, and you'd think the guy who fucking raised her would understand that. Dick.

"Well, to start, she's killing it in school," I say, receiving a grateful smile from Layla. "You know every school of social work in the state is going to be throwing money at her for next year."

"Social work?"

The elevator doors ring open, but no one leaves. Dr. Barros steps in between them so they won't close, then turns to face his daughter.

"What is he talking about?" he asks.

Beside me, Layla shrinks into my shoulder. Fuck. I didn't want to get her into trouble with her dad—I was just trying to focus on the good stuff. I thought she would have told him about her applications by now. A quick glance at her, and she shakes her head imperceptibly—no, her dad did not know anything about her plans to switch to social work. And clearly, he's not happy about it.

"Answer the question, Layla."

She sighs. "Do you think we could talk about this somewhere else besides the elevator, Dad?"

Dr. Barros worries his jaw back and forth a bit before exhaling heavily through his nose.

"Bring in your things," he says in a much lower voice. "Take a rest. And then we will *talk* about whatever this… 'social work'…is."

He walks out without another word, and Layla gulps.

"Sorry," I whisper.

She gives me a weak smile and shrugs. "It's my fault. We don't talk enough, and I was too chicken to tell him before. *I'm* sorry he's being so rude."

"Please," I say. "Like I ain't seen scarier dudes than your dad a hundred times before."

I'm not about to tell her that even though I don't like her dad, and I'm positive I could take him in a fight, I actually find the guy pretty fuckin' intimidating. Sergio Barros isn't a slouch. He's obviously intelligent, ambitious, and successful. You don't have to see his nice car or his fancy degrees to know he's the kind of dude who doesn't settle for less. And I already know he extends those expectations to his daughter. More than that, though, his opinions matter to her.

Yeah. That makes me nervous.

But instead of stressing out my girl, I shrug back and stamp a quick kiss on her cheek when he's not looking. Layla giggles, and I relax a little. In the end, it doesn't really matter if any of the Barros family likes me at all. Layla is the one whose opinion counts.

We walk into one of the nicest apartments I've ever seen, and that's saying something. I may have grown up in a crappy little place, but I've seen some sweet digs in New York. This place is nicer than some of the posh spots my mom used to clean on the Upper East Side. Nicer than K.C.'s townhouse in Hoboken or Alba's view on the West Side. This place is huge. Apparently a plastic surgeon's salary buys you an entire floor of beachfront property in Brazil. It has me wondering why I wanted to be a fire-fighter.

The living room alone is bigger than Layla's and my entire apartment, covered with dark wood floors that aren't even a little scuffed. The room has not one, but two sitting areas that include a bunch of spotless white furniture, including some arranged around a fireplace. Why would you ever need a fireplace in Brazil?

The walls are decorated with tasteful and expensive-looking modern art. Not really my preference, to be honest, but it definitely looks nice. No chintzy religious pictures or movie posters for this guy. But I also can't help but notice the lack of pictures. No photos of his daughter or family. No mementos of his travel or knick-knacks that show anything about his personality.

I don't know…Dr. Barros might be the kind of guy who likes interior design, but I'm betting he had this place decorated for him. This is the kind of place that screams high maintenance and makes me miss our secondhand couch and beat-up dining table. I'm here for less than five minutes, and I already want to get back to me and Layla. Our small piece of New York. *Home.*

"Dad. Wow. This place is amazing."

Layla's even taken aback as she stares around the giant living room, with its picture windows that look out over the promenade and hills rising to the southeast. Is it weird I'm glad she's impressed? That she's not really used to this kind of luxury?

"Remove your shoes. Then come."

Dr. Barros waves us down a long hallway off the other side of the living room, but as Layla and I awkwardly take off our sneakers, I can't help but notice that her dad keeps his on. I follow them down the hall, holding my beat-up Converse like a bum while Dr. Barros gives us a lightning-quick tour of a bathroom, his bedroom, another bathroom, his housekeeper's quarters (holy *shit*, this guy has a live-in housekeeper?), and the three more rooms at the end of the hall.

"You will stay here," he says to Layla, pointing through an open door to a simple bedroom with a double bed and a dresser. "Guest room." He gestures at me, but doesn't make eye contact. "I didn't know you were coming, but I will have the maid make up this room."

Dr. Barros jerks his head toward another room, which looks like some kind of rec room, with a TV and a couch. No bed.

"*My* bedroom is here. In the middle." He gives me a knowing look. "I am a light sleeper."

It takes everything I have not to look away, but I'm not going to be ashamed. I want to tell him that if I grew up sneaking out on creaky New York fire escapes, he's not going to hear shit if I want to sneak into Layla's room. I want to tell his smug face that I already know his daughter Biblically in every sense of the word, that we share a bed every single night. But I'm pretty sure I wouldn't be allowed to know her that way ever again if I spilled that secret for her. Not right now.

"Couch sounds great, Mr. Barros."

I give him the biggest grin I can manage—the one that Layla calls my lady killer when she thinks I'm not listening to her talk to Shama. It's the one that shows my dimples, and I enjoy the way that Layla blushes when she sees it. I also enjoy the way Dr. Barros scowls when he notices his daughter's reaction.

He frowns, the lines on his forehead deepening. "*Doctor.* It's Dr. Barros."

I grin even wider and nod. Yeah, asshole, I know. Some people just need to be fucked with.

Dr. Barros turns to Layla, clearly about to launch into a new tirade, probably about the little bomb I dropped in the elevator. But just as his mouth opens to reveal two silver fillings, the pager on his belt goes off.

Dr. Barros mutters to himself in Portuguese, something that I'd guess isn't too polite by the look on Layla's face. He looks up, twisting his mouth around into another deep scowl. I swear to God, it's like a frown is this dude's default expression. I wonder if he goes out of his way to make himself look like an asshole.

"I have to return to the hospital," he says. "I will be back, maybe for dinner. Benedita is doing the shopping, I think, but she will have the cooking done by eight." He looks up. "Layla, there is a key for you in your room. I already told the guards downstairs your name. Can you give your...*his* name to them if he leaves?"

Dr. Barros tips his head at me, like I'm not even there, and I'm practically grinding my teeth to keep from shouting, "Nico, you arrogant fuck! My *fuckin'* name is Nico!"

Layla sighs and nods. "Yeah. I think my Portuguese is good enough to do that."

Dr. Barros clears his throat while he glares between us. "And no...you do not go into her room. This is a *decent* house. You are not alone. *Entende?*" He lapses into Portuguese, like he almost can't help himself. Like the very thought of his daughter being defiled by the likes of me makes him lose his mind.

And you know what's fucked up? I like it. It makes me a dick, but I *like* that the one thing that really disturbs this cocky asshole's perfect cool is his awareness that his only daughter is probably getting it good on the regular from a tattooed, working-class *me*.

We glare at each other, and I stand as tall as I can. I can't help it. I arch one eyebrow, and Dr. Barros sucks in a breath. He knows *exactly* what I'm thinking.

"Dad."

Layla's voice breaks the standoff. We both turn to her, and suddenly, it's very clear my girl is ready to drop. And of course she is. We've been traveling for way too long, starting with a red-eye out of New York. Her eyes are bloodshot, and her skin is pale. As badly as I might want to fuck with her dad by fooling around with Layla while he's gone, there's obviously no way she's going to do anything but sleep in his absence.

Dr. Barros seems to know it too. For the first time, a little softness crosses his face as he looks—really looks—at his daughter for the first time since she arrived. His eyes travel over her weary body, taking in her rumpled t-shirt, the way her hair is piled atop her head, the dark circles, a lot like his, that have gotten worse for lack of sleep. He reaches out a hand and gently strokes her cheek. And as if she can't help it, Layla closes her eyes and leans into his palm.

Fuck. It physically hurts to see how badly she wants her dad's love. And honestly, who doesn't? I remember when I was a kid, when I tracked down my dad at the grocery store in the Bronx where he worked. I was dying for his attention, and when he barely looked at me, it just about killed me. I can't imagine how painful it is to have someone turn their back on you when they spent the first eighteen years of your life actually being present.

And yeah. It makes me hate the dude that much more.

"Go rest, *linda*," he tells her, and then, with another nasty look at me, he leaves.

When the elevator doors close behind him, Layla practically melts into the doorway. The high of landing in Brazil and seeing her dad is gone now, and what's left is exhaustion.

"Shit, sweetie," I say as I pull her against me. "Come on. Let's get you into bed."

She lets me tow her into her room, despite the fact that her dad just told me explicitly *not* to enter. But despite the fact that her body feels as good in my arms as it ever does, I just help her lie down on the bed and sit next to her, stroking her hair back from her face as she looks drowsily up at me, her blue eyes the only light in the darkened room.

"Sorry my dad was such a jerk," she murmurs, one hand clasped lazily around my wrist.

I smile down at her. "Don't worry about it. I'm sorry I blew your news, baby."

She sighs and shakes her head. "It's fine. He needed to know anyway. I keep too many secrets from him."

Like me, I want to say. Like the fact that I'm not just your boyfriend, not just some dude you go on dates with. Like the fact that I'm the love of your life, right? That we live together? That we're starting to make a real life together?

Aren't we?

It's kind of crazy how much I liked what she said at the airport. The idea of having a daughter of my own one day scares the shit out of me, but the idea of Layla pregnant, our kid growing inside her…yeah. I probably like that too much. And it didn't escape me how quickly she walked it back.

So I try not to overthink why Layla hasn't told her parents about the real extent of our relationship yet. I try not to wonder if maybe, just maybe, she hasn't really told them because she's ashamed of me. Because maybe she doesn't really think we'll be together forever.

The thoughts press like a knife that's always poised right over my heart, holding me hostage, and these doubts are the blade. Nothing's cut through. But the possibility is always there.

Just ask her, cabrón. K.C. is sitting on my shoulder again, telling me not to be such a pussy. Flaco and Gabe are right behind him, shaking their heads and muttering to each other that I need to get my head out of my ass. *After all that you've been through, what the fuck are you waiting for?*

Ask her what? I want to say back. How she feels? If she really loves me? She tells me that every day, multiple times a day. Should I cut off my own balls too, just to make it clear that I have no fuckin' ability to restrain myself when it comes to this girl?

I open my mouth to let it out, because why the fuck not? I'm here. And if I want her to be honest, maybe I need to start doing that too.

Layla sighs as her eyelids flutter shut. I close my mouth and stroke her hair back again. She leans into my hand, just like she did with her dad, but now her expression is peaceful, without any trace of pain. She knows I love her. She doesn't worry about that anymore.

So, once she's asleep, I decide to do what I normally do when shit gets a little too much to handle. Something I feel like I'm going to have to do a lot while we're here.

I work out.

CHAPTER TWENTY-FIVE

Nico

Layla sleeps through most of the afternoon and into the night. My girl was *tired*, and any idea I had about sneaking across the hall into her room late at night was put straight to rest by those circles under her eyes. So in the morning, when I get up and run awkwardly into Dr. Barros in the kitchen, where his housekeeper is serving him, I'm a little irritated by the suspicious looks I'm getting. Fuck that. I'm behaving like an altar boy.

Benedita, the housekeeper, gives me a hooded look, like she knows me, even if she doesn't really. She looks over my faded shirt, my sweat-stained hat, my running shoes that haven't been white for a really long time. It's like she knows we're cut from the same cloth; that my mother cleans up rich people's shit for a living too. Like she knows I'm not really supposed to be here.

"*Cafe*?" Dr. Barros asks, gesturing at the shiny silver set on his bright white tablecloth, at the rolls, cut papaya, some kind of creamy white cheese kept in a jar, and a square loaf of something that looks like jelly. He shakes out his newspaper, but doesn't look at me. He's being polite and rude at the same time, in a way only rich people seem to know how to do.

"*Obrigado*, but I'm good. Just going to go for a run."

"Another run?"

He looks me up and down, like he's appraising my body. He's a doctor, so I can't help but wonder what he's looking for.

The coffee smells good, but I need to exercise before this day starts. First up is Mass with Layla's entire family, followed by some giant barbecue at her aunt's house, with cousins, If the Barros clan is anything like Layla's dad, I'm going to need at least ten miles just to relax.

I ran up and down the promenade last night before coming back to the house. But I'd forgotten to have Layla call down to the doorman for me, and he made me sit on the front steps until Dr. Barros showed up sometime past eight. I followed his shiny black Benz into the garage. He wasn't too happy that I was loitering outside "like a common street urchin," as he put it. Well, he didn't give me much of a choice, did he? And who the fuck talks like that except Disney villains?

I grab my ankle to stretch out my quad, lingering in the doorway. "Yeah, I tend to be pretty disciplined about it. If I don't do something most days, I get a little cranky. What do you guys say? Everyone is supposed to get an hour a day?"

I don't mention that if I don't exercise, my version of "cranky" isn't the nicest thing in the world. Running. Boxing. Lifting. These are things I realized a *long* time ago that I needed to keep the darkness in my life from swallowing me up.

"Some people need to be very...physical," is all Dr. Barros says.

I choose not to respond, even though it's clear what he's trying to say: that I'm the kind of person who uses my body because I don't have a mind.

"We leave for the church at nine thirty, is that right?" I ask him.

"Nine," he says, and with another loud shake of his paper, turns back to his coffee. "We will not wait, either."

"Don't worry, Mr. Barros. I'm never late."

And before he can correct his title, I jog out.

I make my way up and down the promenade in front of the beach, the same run I did yesterday, but the relatively short distance isn't enough for what I need. To start, there are too many people. Even at this time of the morning, it's packed with other joggers, roller-bladers, cyclists, and people just walking around the busy neighborhood. But really, it's the equivalent of running around the Upper East Side, and considering I'm going to get enough of *that* side of Brazil over the next few days, I wouldn't mind taking a break when I can.

The cities here are really different than New York, or even LA. The rich people are packed down on the beaches in thin strips of high-rise buildings that block out the hills behind them, covered with poorer neighborhoods. But you can't get away from the poor here. In New York, you actually have to get out of the wealthy neighborhoods to see the city's poverty, or even just peel back a layer or two to realize it's right there with you, like my family's apartment. But despite their proximity, the poor go out of their way to stay nice and hidden.

Here, poverty looms all around, staring down at you from the hills that surround the low-lying beaches. People like Layla's dad might live in high-rise buildings, but they can't block out the *favelas*.

So as soon as I finish jogging down the promenade and back up, I turn off the main drag and start exploring the interior of Vila Velha.

I jog up side streets, vaguely noticing the way the buildings slowly morph from the glossy apartments into smaller, plainer structures that house businesses and shops, and eventually to places that basically look like stacked, multicolored cinder blocks, terraced up the hills that stick up from the land like fingertips. They look familiar, like the pictures of the slum in San Juan where K.C.'s family (and my mom) originally lived. Eventually there are fewer cars on the street and more bikes, sometimes a flimsy motorcycle or two. I actually pass a donkey around one corner. It's still busy up here. People are passing back and forth between their houses; others look to be on their way to work. But although I get a few curious looks, most of them are friendly, nodding their "*alôs*" or "*bom dias*" as I pass.

It takes a while before I realize why I feel more comfortable up here than down on the beach. This isn't a good part of town. Most of the people I pass wear clothes that are dirty and stained, several of the compartments have dirty floors and graffiti on the outside, and more than one kid glances at me from windows with hardened eyes. The farther I go, the fewer kids have shoes.

But unlike down on the beach, the people in this part of town don't give me a second glance. The reason is clear: I look a hell of a lot more like them than I do any of the rich, light-skinned *brasileiros* jogging up and down the promenade. Most of the people in this neighborhood are mixed like me, with skin colors that range from light brown to black. It's a neighborhood that's about as diverse as my own back home. A neighborhood where I don't look or feel out of place, even though I've never been here before.

Layla told me about this. That Brazil, maybe even more than the U.S., has its own racialized caste system. Up in the north, it's more common to see black people, especially in states like Bahia, which, according to Layla, has a stronger African community, though it's definitely not reflected in their politicians or leadership. Just like back home, most of the people in power here call themselves white, even if by American standards, they aren't. Still, Layla and her family look like they just walked off the boat from Portugal or Italy, and so do most of the people living down there by the beach.

One thing's for sure, though: soccer really is a national sport here. Whether it's on the beach or on top of this hill, I've counted at last six different soccer games this morning, all played with balls in worse condition the farther up the hill I go. The last one looks like it's missing most of its air and got into a dogfight a while back, but the kids seem to be having a good time with it.

Yet another ball comes flying at me as I round a corner close to the top of the hill. I just manage to stop it with my foot before it goes rolling down the street behind me, and I look up to find four little kids, all barefoot, watching me, their hands on their hips.

"*Chute!*"

The littlest one of the four jumps up and down on the rough pavement, waving his hands at me. Skinny, with a few teeth missing and a mop of light-brown hair that sticks out in a few different directions, he looks like he can't be much older than five, though his large brown eyes look much older.

I kick the ball back, and he passes it to his friends, but he's obviously lost interest in their game. He shuffles down the street to me, not seeming to care much about the fact that his little feet are kicking loose rocks on the dirt road or that he's just ditched his friends to come talk to a strange man.

He spits a quick stream of Portuguese at me, but I have no idea what the fuck he's saying. Sometimes when Layla's dad speaks, I can recognize a few of the words, but this kid speaks something much less formal. Something that belongs to the streets.

"What's that, little man?" I ask in English, and then, thinking better of it, in Spanish. Something tells me these kids aren't exactly in school all day long learning the English alphabet.

His eyes pop open. "*Americano?*"

Ah. That I understood.

"Yeah, man," I say as I sit down next to him on one of the blocks of concrete that's been set up around their little makeshift field. "*De Nueva York.*"

His eyes get even bigger at the words. Everyone knows where New York is, even clear on the other side of the planet. John Lennon wasn't wrong when he called it the center of the universe.

I hold up my fist for him to bump, and he stares at it for a second, before mimicking the action. When he knocks his knuckles against mine, I spread my fingers and imitate the sound of a bomb blowing up. The kid's face lights up with a grin.

"So, what's your name, *papi*?" I ask him, venturing into Spanish. "*Tu nombre*?" When the word doesn't seem familiar to him, I tap my chest. "Nico." Then I point to him. "*Tú*?"

"Ahhhh." The kid nods in clear understanding. He slams his palms down on his chest with more force than I would think a little squirt like him would be capable of. "Bruno."

I grin. "That's a big name for a little man, Bruno. You better grow up to be strong, you got that?"

Bruno just nods, even though he has no idea what I said. Instead, he's absorbed with my arm, which is bare in the tank top I'm wearing.

"*Isso*." Bruno floats a little finger over the swirls of my tattoo. He rattles off another long round of Portuguese, and when it's clear I don't understand what he means, he just says, "*Tatuagem*? Ouch?"

It's not really that hard to communicate in different languages if you can keep everything to one-word sentences.

I nod. "Yeah, man, they hurt. But they were worth it. They remind me who I am. To be strong. *Fuerte. For-te*?" I'm guessing at the potential translation again, and the second version seems to work. I flex my arm for good measure, and Bruno's eye pop open again.

"*Forte*," Bruno repeats with a nod, though he pronounces it like "foh-chee" instead of the way I did: "for-tay."

"*Forte*," I echo him, and we fall silent as he examines the tattoo some more.

"Bruno!"

A woman's voice calls from across the field, and Bruno's head spins around.

I might have grown up in a building with doors that locked, but I know what it's like to have my mother call for me like that, with fear threaded through her voice, looking out the window to where her kid is running around a neighborhood full of junkies and gang members. Ma had about as much choice as this kid's mother does. There was no way you could keep four kids confined to five hundred square feet, as much as she would have liked to. She had to work, and she had no way to watch out for us other than to teach the difference between right and wrong and hope we'd stay out of trouble. It's funny. I didn't think about it much then, just stayed away from needles we'd sometimes find on the sidewalks, or walk down the middle of the street whenever we saw dealers or junkies crowding the sidewalks. But now that I'm older, the idea of raising my own kid in a place like that scares the shit out of me. Just one more reason my mother is a fuck lot stronger than I ever imagined.

Bruno stands up and waves to his mom, and I wave at her too, trying to be friendly, let her know I'm not a bad guy. Let her know that right now, at least, she doesn't have to worry. Her expression softens, but she doesn't stop watching. Then Bruno turns back to me with another long round of Portuguese that I can't understand.

"*Eu vai*," he says simply, which is close enough to the Spanish for "go" that I get it.

He points his little thumb toward his mother, who is watching us impatiently with her hands on her hips. The action causes his t-shirt sleeve to fall down his arm, revealing just how skinny he really is.

"Ah, here. Hold on, man."

I stand up and fish a few *reais* out of my shorts pockets. It's all I brought with me —maybe the equivalent of ten U.S. dollars, in case I got lost somewhere and needed a cab or a bus back to Praia da Costa.

But it's obviously a lot more than this kid has seen in a while, or ever, if his wide-eyed gaze is to be trusted. He turns, obviously to gloat to his friends, but I pull him back toward me.

"Hey," I say.

Bruno blinks up at me.

"That's for your mom," I tell him. "*Para tu mamá, entiendes?*"

It's close enough to Portuguese that he gets what I'm saying and nods immediately.

"Go, give it to her now," I tell him, nodding again toward the woman who is looking at us curiously. "*Ahora.*"

Bruno nods again, but before he leaves, he opens his little mouth. "Thank you," he says in clear English. "*Tchau*, Nico!"

He scurries over to his mother, who takes the awkward collection of coins and small bills before looking to me with surprise. Her features aren't any less hardened, and are maybe a little bit ashamed, but she nods before she puts the money in her pocket. It's another combination of expressions I also know very well. The same look my mom had every time we stopped at the food bank, or when Alba or one of her friends would slip a few extra dollars into her pocket. Gratitude. Surprise. Relief. Shame.

Before he follows his mom back into their house, though, Bruno looks at me one last time. He sticks his little chest out, and gazes at me with emotions that are so different from his mother's. Pride. Curiosity. Intelligence. Determination. Features that this neighborhood will probably do its best to erase, but if he's lucky, won't be snuffed out completely.

I wave at him, and he disappears, but his expression stays with me. He's so damn tiny, but such a strong reminder that people are so much more than where they come from. That no one is born being nothing.

It's easy to forget sometimes. But, I realize, maybe more important to remember than anything else.

I stand there for a few more minutes, looking out over the two cities spread out below. I examine the arched bridges that connect the two sides of the bay, the green hills in the distance that are mirrored by the ones closer to the city, the ones covered by houses just like these, kids just like these. It's just one city, but it seems so vast from up here. A king's view from the poorest seat. And this country is filled with them.

For the first time in my life, the world seems much, much bigger than New York. But I'm also seeing how many of the differences I've always taken for granted maybe don't matter that much at all.

CHAPTER TWENTY-SIX

Layla

NICO WAS QUIET THROUGH MOST OF THE MASS. HE ARRIVED FROM HIS RUN ABOUT THIRTY minutes before we were supposed to leave, much to my dad's obvious irritation, and with a quick kiss on my cheek (also to Dad's irritation, which I think Nico intended), jumped in the shower and changed into a nice pair of gray pants and a white button-down before stealing some bread and guava jelly at the table. I should be annoyed that he's going out of his way to bug my dad, but weirdly, I'm not. No one gives my father shit.

He sat next to me in the car, looking up at the hills as we drove out of Vila Velha to Guarapari, a suburb where my aunt keeps a vacation house by the beach. He was lost in thought as we filed into the small chapel where my family goes to church, and he only gave distant smiles when we wave hello to my aunt, uncle, and their kids: David, their oldest son, Luciano, the new graduate, and Carolina, their daughter, who is only a few years older than me. David, an engineer, is even older than Nico and has a kid of his own and another on the way. Nico remained quiet through the rest of the proceedings, watching the priest lead the small congregation through service that was just about exactly the same, speaking only when prompted by the familiar rhythm of the rites and liturgies, except saying the words in Spanish instead of the unfamiliar Portuguese.

We linger a little after the ceremony, telling everyone we want to explore the small chapel, even though really we just want a minute to ourselves before facing the inevitable barrage of curious faces at my aunt's.

"Ma would like this," Nico finally remarks as we look over one of the stained-glass windows, a portrait of St. Christopher. "Do you think they have postcards or anything? I want to send her one."

It's hard not to kiss him for wanting to send his mom a memento. But this is a tiny church, and doesn't have the same array of pamphlets and cards you find at the bigger cathedrals.

"Ah, well," Nico says with a shrug when I say so. "I can take a picture and light a candle for her instead."

My heels echo on the stone floors as we walk toward a small apse where there is an array of prayer candles. Another thing that doesn't change, no matter where you are in the world.

Nico lights a few of the candles and murmurs a prayer under his breath, then crosses himself. If I'm counting right, it looks like he lit four in all: one for each family member back home. He kisses his fingers before dropping a few *reais* in the donation box.

"Are you feeling okay?" he asks me as we continue to walk around the church. "You didn't seem to eat much at breakfast this morning when I got back."

I shrug. The truth is, I haven't really been feeling that great since we landed. I'm guessing I picked up something on one of the planes on the way down. Those things are disease incubators.

"I'm all right," I say as we continue to walk down the aisle on the other side. "I just wasn't that hungry. You've been pretty quiet, though."

Nico shrugs. "I like this place." He looks around, taking in the tall stone walls and the rows of pews.

"Yeah?" I look around, enjoying the simplicity of the space. "I was worried you were bored since you couldn't understand much."

Sun shines in the arched windows on one side, casting blocked rays of light onto Nico and a few other places. He smiles, and the room is suddenly even brighter.

"I understood enough," he says as he swings our hands slightly between us. "I've sat through enough of those to know what's happening. The Eucharist is the Eucharist no matter where you go, *verdad?*"

I smile at his casual use of Spanish. It's another word that's only different from its Portuguese cousin by a single letter. "*Verdade.* So it is."

I gaze around the chapel. It's stark and relatively bare, so unlike my father's ornate apartment or the bigger cathedrals you might find in Rio or São Paulo. But I know from my last visit to my grandparents' house that my dad's family hasn't always been rich. My grandparents still live in the same house on a farm in Colatina, a small town about two hours north of Vitória. *Vovô* made his fortune growing tobacco and coffee, enough to send his children to a private Catholic school that allowed both of them to qualify for Brazil's notoriously difficult public universities. Now most of the farm has been sold, and the old house, the *fazenda*, and a few acres of land around it, are all that's left. It's a long way from the glossy surfaces and rich textures of my father's home. Much, much closer to this church.

"When I saw this place the other time I came, I dreamed I'd get married here," I remark absently as I draw my free hand over the polished wood of the pews.

It's only after it's out there that I realize the gravity of that kind of statement to Nico. Super smooth, Layla. Ugh, he's going to think I'm dropping hints or something crazy like that. I ignore the fact that I *do* imagine getting married to him sometimes. It's a daydream that's *way* too easy to fall into.

I open my mouth to apologize, but instead find Nico looking at me softly.

"Did you?" he remarks. He lifts my hand to his lips in a motion that's strangely chivalric, even for him, but fits the ancient setting of the church. His black eyes twinkle, but not just from the sunlight. "It's not a bad dream. I kind of like it, you know." He looks around at the simple beauty. "It fits you, this place."

We watch each other for a minute, tension and some other kind of strange magic building between us. Nico opens his full mouth, like he wants to say something else. My chest constricts—why, I'm not sure. But neither of us looks away; neither of us even blinks. It's the same feeling I get when I want to kiss him, but even now, it's something more. Something that goes so much deeper than what my body does with him. From the start, everything with Nico has been on a cellular level. Past the body. When he looks at me like this, he penetrates my soul.

"Layla—" he begins, but is cut off when the heavy doors to the church open, and my father strides in with his customary frown as his footsteps echo off the high ceilings.

I look to Nico and mouth "sorry." He shrugs and gives me a lopsided smile, as if to say, "What can you do?" Dad immediately zeroes in on our joined hands as he approaches.

"Layla," he barks, giving Nico a dirty look. "*É uma igreja. Respeito!*"

I'm annoyed by that enough that I barely even care that he spoke to me in Portuguese for one of the first times in my life. "Dad. We're just holding hands."

As if in response, Nico's fingers tighten their grip instead of pulling away. I know it's partly just to get under my dad's skin, but I'm feeling kind of territorial myself. I don't like the way my dad acts around the love of my life. Especially when he's interrupting moments that are important.

Dad glowers, and Nico mutters "*Oye, tranquiló, viejo*" under his breath. I give him a wide-eyed look, and he winks at me so I have to stifle a smile.

"What was that?" Dad demands.

I gulp. I doubt my dad would appreciate being told to calm down. Or being called "old man."

Nico just blinks innocently. Well, as innocent as he ever really looks. Then, deliberately, he holds up my hand and drops it. "I just said we need to go, Dr. Barros," he says. "It's also disrespectful to be late, right?"

With a huff, Dad spins around and leaves, but when Nico follows, I tug him back. He turns around, a shit-eating grin on his handsome face that makes me start laughing.

"Dude," I chide, though I'm still giggling. "You have got to cut it out. You sound like a troublemaker caught at the principal's office."

Nico snorts. "I'll cut it out when he stops talking to us like we're high school students. Until then, he's lucky I haven't started calling him Principal Skinner. Now, come on. I wasn't kidding about not wanting to be late. I might like busting your dad's balls a little since he's never going to like me that much anyway. But I don't want to piss off the rest of your family."

———

FOR ALL HIS BRAVADO, though, Nico grows quiet again as we drive with my dad to my aunt and uncle's house, a big place in a gated community down by the beach. It's a really quiet neighborhood. Most of the people here only use their houses as vacation homes, places where they come on the weekends after working in the city during the week. But Fabiana—known to me and the more extended branches of my dad's family as Bibi—and her husband, my uncle Manuel, moved here semi-permanently after their kids left for university, although Manuel still uses their apartment in Vitória a few days a week when he's working.

The two-story house is big and airy, with the downstairs walls all opening through four different French doors onto a large yard bearing a cashew tree, a small pool, and patio where we'll eat lunch. When we arrive, all of the doors are open to reveal the Spanish-tiled ground floor, and Bibi's selection of comfortable, lounge-ready furniture. The barbecue on the side of the house has been started up while their cook and a maid hurry dishes to and from the kitchen to the patio table.

"Damn," Nico mutters as he takes in the spread already laid out. "That looks…amazing."

It really does. Bibi's gone all out, using our presence as an excuse to make real *churrasco* this afternoon for her family and a bunch of her neighbors. There is a big shank of meat rotating over a rotisserie, and the man at the grill is flipping sausages and smaller pieces of meats and fish. On the table I spot the classics of Brazilian barbecue: *feijoada* (black beans stewed with pieces of sausages and pork), *farofa* (a ground yucca dish made with beans, pork rinds, and egg), fried plantains, a massive fruit salad, and pitchers of mango and cashew juice. My aunt, uncle, and cousins are mingling with neighbors, and I recognize a few other faces from church.

"*Linda!*" Bibi's high-pitched cry sounds from the other side of the patio, and my father's magnanimous older sister practically sprints across the yard to greet us, closely followed by Manuel, her husband. "I saw you in the church, but we had to come back here so quickly. Come, let me look at my baby!"

Her exuberance makes me smile despite the fact that I've only met my aunt twice. Trips to and from Brazil are expensive, and considering that she and Manuel had three kids, they only managed to visit us in Seattle once when I was little. The other time, of course, was only a few years ago, when Dad, Mom, and I visited for *Carnaval*.

The memory hurts. It was a whirlwind trip, but I wonder now if it was the start of Dad's change of heart about his country. He hadn't been back for so many years. Maybe it was that visit that catalyzed his decision to leave.

Bibi hugs me tightly and kisses both my cheeks before passing me off to my uncle, a sober, smaller man whose personality seems to be the opposite of his vivacious wife. I wonder how she and my dad can possibly be related. They seem to be polar opposites.

"*Tudo bem,*" Manuel greets me kindly as he kisses my cheeks.

"*Tudo boa,*" I answer automatically. "Good to see you again, *Tio.*"

Bibi pats her carefully coiffed black hair, which looks like it's slightly tinted red in the sun, and winks while Manuel nods at Nico, then ambles away to say hello to other men closer to his age.

"Now, *who* is this?" Bibi asks, looking Nico up and down. She grins, her red lips tugging slyly and her black eyes sparkling. "Do all the men in New York look like this? Carolina, you might want to visit your cousin in New York. *Gua-*po!"

Nico leans in to accept her kisses on his cheek. "*Brigada, senhora,*" he murmurs, and grins when my aunt pretty much trills like a bird in response.

"*Oi,* my *goodness,* that voice! He sounds just like…who is that singer? That one with the low voice? Did you hear that voice, Lina?"

"*Sim, Mãe,*" replies a crabby voice in Portuguese. "I heard it. And it does not sound like Barry White at all. Stop embarrassing yourself."

Nico and I both turn toward my cousin Carolina, who is the closest to me in age at twenty-four. Tall, willowy, and blonde (a hair color that is definitely not natural, given all of our family's dark hair), she stands with the slouch that only certain girls affected with wealth and beauty can pull off.

"*Oi, tudo bem.*" She greets me with another round of kisses on the cheeks while I murmur "*tudo boa*" in return. She follows the same process with Nico. "Don't pay her attention. She just likes to make trouble."

"Stop," Bibi chides her daughter. "He's so handsome! And polite! Sergio, *você não está feliz que sua filha tenha um homem tão forte e guapo*?"

My father, who is walking around our little party, just strikes up a cigarette and grunts before he walks away to join a few other men sitting around a table by the pool. I watch for a moment, slightly astounded by the sight. My dad never smoked when I was growing up. He obviously knew how terrible it is for you, not to mention how bad it looks for a doctor to be a smoker in the first place. But here, it's different. Almost everyone smokes. There doesn't seem to be the same kind of stigma, even for health professionals.

Nico chuckles at Bibi's remarks, and I just shake my head. We both know my dad is not particularly happy that his daughter has "such a strong and handsome man," as Bibi said. But I'm glad to know the rest of my family doesn't necessarily feel the same way.

"Come on," I say to Nico, taking his hand in mine to guide him through the rest of the party. "We need to say hi to everyone else. And then we're going to eat."

———

FORTY-FIVE MINUTES LATER, we've been thoroughly welcomed into the fold. Even Dad seems to have forgotten that Nico is with us, since he's happily entrenched in conversation with my uncle and a bunch of other men from the neighborhood.

I sit at the end of the long table, watching as Nico lets my cousins and some of the other younger men usher him into a game of horseshoes at the other end of the lawn. Bibi takes a seat next to me, carrying a pitcher of water.

"It's too hot to eat so much without a drink," she says. "You want wine? I can get wine."

"No, no, Bibi, I'm fine. Thank you though."

A burst of laughter erupts from the horseshoe players, where Nico turns triumphant after making his first score. He blows me a kiss before starting another turn, and I finger my straw, enjoying the warm feeling his bright smile puts in my belly.

"I like him," Bibi says.

I turn to her and smile. "I know. You made that pretty clear earlier, Bibi. I think he still has lipstick on his face."

She smiles as she lights a cigarette, but shakes her head. "That was…well, yes, he is very handsome. But mostly I just like to, how do you say, tease your father. But I watch. And now, I like *him*. He is kind, yes?"

I swallow and nod. "Yes. Very kind."

Her eyes soften, the slight wrinkles around them become a little less pronounced. With all of her glamor, it's hard to remember sometimes that my aunt is actually in her sixties. She looks and acts like a woman much younger.

"And he is smart?"

Again, I nod. Strangely, I'm a little teary. I hadn't realized how badly I wanted people besides me to recognize all of Nico's amazing qualities.

"And he is good to you, yes?"

I use my index finger to swipe away the tears threatening to fall. "Very. He's the best, Bibi."

She nods, satisfied as she takes another puff. "Good. Then I like him the best too."

I sigh. "I just wish Dad felt the same way. He doesn't like him at all. He treats him like he's dangerous, or like he's going to corrupt me."

In response, Bibi produces a very unladylike snort. "My little brother is a fool some days, Layla. He only act this way because he was the same, you know."

I raise a skeptical brow. "I don't remember Dad having any tattoos, Bibi."

She waves away the thought with her cigarette, causing ash to fly into the air along with the snaking lines of smoke. "He didn't need them. He was bad enough. Out all the night, chasing the girls. Sergio, he was *so* handsome, *so* charming when he was younger. All the girls, they love him. And then, he go to America, and…things, they change. But not so much. That was when he meet your mother."

I don't reply, sensing a story coming. Bibi takes a long drag of her cigarette as she watches my dad. Of all the men standing around the table, he has the most presence. Late fifties, yes, but with a full head of hair, olive skin, and dark eyes. He makes a joke, and the other five or six men around him burst into laughter. He might be my dad, but his charisma is obvious, even to me.

"Sergio is hungry," Bibi says. "He was *always* hungry. You know, we grow up okay, but not with so much money, not like this. He made our father very angry when he did not want to run the farm. But then he go to university, and after that, to America, to Stanford. And he becomes a big doctor, and he meet your mother…he thought he has everything. But still, it was never home. There, he was foreign, you know? And I think that after a long time, it make him bitter. This man…" She waves her cigarette toward my father, who has resumed his normal scowl. "He is not my brother. My brother is still coming back sometimes."

We watch them for a bit more while I pick at my food, and Bibi puffs away.

"So, maybe he sees himself in your Nico," she remarks. "Maybe he worry that in time, you will be with a man who will be bitter too."

I frown, staring down at my juice while I swirl the straw around meditatively. Is that it? Is that why Dad hates Nico?

From across the yard, Nico catches my eye. He winks, and that familiar warm feeling spreads again.

"Yeah, but Nico doesn't have to go anywhere to find home, Bibi," I tell her. "Neither of us will. Because his home is me. And mine is him."

Bibi is quiet for a moment while she finishes her cigarette, then lights another. She watches Nico with me, and her red mouth quirks when he laughs with her sons as one of them makes another score. He turns to me for another grin. Unaware of my aunt watching him, Nico mouths, "I love you" before he turns back to his game.

"Yes," my aunt says with an approving nod. "I see it."

———

"Oh, God."

One slice of steak, two sausages, and countless scoops of *feijoada, farofa,* and fruit salad later, I am stuffed. Sated.

And losing just about all of it in my aunt's bathroom on the second story.

"This is what happens when you eat too much, Barros," I mutter to myself as the nausea dies. I stand up, flush the toilet, then go to the sink to wash my hands, rinse my mouth, and splash water on my flushed face. It was the weirdest thing—fifteen minutes ago I felt fine. Way too full, but fine. And then suddenly I had to make a beeline up the stairs to the bathroom so that no one would hear me puke up all the delicious food that had been so painstakingly prepared for me.

And now that it's gone…I'm fine again.

"It's your American stomach," I tell my reflection, dabbing a damp cloth over my cheeks.

"Is it?"

I flinch, then turn to find Carolina standing in the doorway. She strides in, her long, lithe form about as droll as her features. She reaches around me to a drawer in the sink, pulls a zipper makeup bag from the back, and removes a plastic-covered pouch that looks like a tampon.

"Here," she says as she flips the package at me.

I frown. "Oh, I'm not—it's not that time of the month for me, yet."

"It's a, how do you say? Pregnant test? Not tampon."

I stare at the flimsy package for a moment, digesting her words. "What?"

Carolina pulls it back. "We have them from when David and Erica were trying to have a baby last year. But you…*oh.* You mean you and your man, you don't…"

"No, um, we do," I admit, somewhat bashfully. My cheeks redden all over again, but for different reasons.

"Good," Carolina says. "Because if I had that at home…I know we are supposed to be good Catholics and stay virgins forever, but come on. It's a new generation." She shrugs. "What do they expect?"

I shrug too, unsure of what to say. I don't really know enough about the sexual politics of Brazil to know what I should say and what to keep to myself.

"How long since your last, you know?" Carolina checks her reflection and messes with a few strands of hair.

"My…" I start counting the days back since my last period, and slowly it dawns on me that I'm late. And not just a few days. It's been…close to two months.

I freeze.

Carolina clicks her tongue and holds out the test expectantly. "Yes. See? Take the test. Better safe than sorry, no?"

With a shaky hand, I take the test and examine it.

"You pee on it," Carolina says. "Then we wait. Don't worry, I will wait with you."

She leans back expectantly on the counter. Through my suddenly addled brain, I remember that it's one of the differences I noticed last time in Brazil—the way women, especially my cousins, have no shame about their bodies in front of each other. Bathrooms. Changing rooms. Locker rooms. Women here don't have secrets.

"Ah…okay," I say as I move awkwardly back to the toilet and proceed to pee on the stick, as directed, while Carolina watches matter-of-factly. When I'm done, she gestures to a few paper napkins she's laid on the counter.

"Put it there," she says. "We will wait."

CHAPTER TWENTY-SEVEN

Layla

"YOU ARE OKAY?"

Carolina pauses as she strides back into the bathroom. I'm sitting on the toilet, my hands braced on my knees while I try to breathe properly. This explains so much. The slight weight gain. The tiny changes in my body. The fatigue. The sudden nausea.

Carolina looks alarmed. "Should I go get *Tio*?"

"No. *No*. Do *not* get my dad. I'm fine. I'm just…" I swallow, barely able to believe it myself. I stare at the test where it's perched on the edge of the bathtub. The two pink lines cross over each other in a terrible parody of chastity. "I am pregnant. You were right."

Carolina looks at me sympathetically, then sits down on the edge of the tub, careful not to disturb the test. She pats me on the knee.

"Don't worry," she says. "I won't say anything. At least you are lucky. In America, you don't have to keep, no?"

I frown. That is literally the last thing on my mind at the moment.

"Um, no," I say. "We don't *have* to keep." But obviously what I'm thinking is all over my face. "Not keeping" is not an option. Not for me. Not in this world. Not in any.

"Ahhh," Carolina says and gives me a sweet smile. "Well, I will not say anything to *Tio* either. We don't want him to kill your man before you can marry him, no?"

Oh, God. Marry? Is that the only other option?

"It's okay," Carolina soothes, but I can barely hear her voice as the thoughts continue to rush through my head all at once.

Nico barely makes enough to live on by himself, and what little extra he has goes to taking care of his mother and siblings. Raising a baby in New York City can't be anything but crazy expensive, and I'm supposed to be going to graduate school next year. He's going to freak. *I'm* going to freak. Holy shit, what are we going to do? What is *Nico* going to do when he finds out he's going to be a father?

Numbly, I follow Carolina out of the bathroom after shoving the test, wrapped in its plastic, into my purse. Carolina babbles something more about bad contraception methods and how long I have until people realize I was pregnant before we got married instead of after. If we get married at all. Do I even want to get married? Would Nico?

My head is spinning, and suddenly, I can't take it anymore. Halfway down the stairs, I stop her, tugging on her arm so she'll face me.

"Hey," I say. "Carolina? No more, okay? This…this is just our secret for now. *Secreto*," I add in Portuguese, just for good measure, even though my cousin speaks decent enough English.

Her brown eyes, which haven't shown much more than droll curiosity since she walked upstairs, perk a little sympathetically.

"*Sim*," she says with a nod that sends her blonde tresses waving. "Of course."

We enter the patio to find everyone mostly where we left them—the boys still goofing around the yard as they finish another game, the older men having moved inside a bit to check the latest soccer scores, the women chatting around the tables by the pool with their cigarettes and coffee.

I slip around the back of the house before anyone catches me. I need a minute to myself.

There's no one back here, only a small concrete walkway that leads to the circuit breaker and a generator, along with vines that cover the hillside leading almost directly up from the house. I step over the vines, breathing deeply from air that isn't laced with cigarette smoke or chlorine, and when I reach the concrete, I lean against the wall and bury my face in my hands.

Immediately, several faces start flashing through my head. They're all disappointed. My mom. My friends. Nico. My dad. All of them frowning with concern. Disdain. Dread.

I can hear their voices too.

This isn't you, Layla.

I thought you were better than this.

What kind of girl are you?

But the thing is, I don't feel the dread I should. I'm scared, of course. Terrified. I have no idea what's going to happen—if I can afford this, do it on my own if I have to. I don't even know if I'll be a decent parent at all.

Still…I can't regret anything I'd ever make with him. Nico is my heart. My air. My breath. Even if he can't deal with this—and I know deep down that it will probably terrify him too, more so than it scares me—he'd never abandon us.

Right?

He did leave you for LA.

It's a small voice, adding to the others, but somehow it echoes even louder.

He did leave you once.

My hands clench the thin fabric of my sundress, and I keep my eyes squeezed shut as I will the doubts away. It's not fair to me. It's not fair to him.

But instead, they grow louder.

"There you are!"

I open my eyes to find Nico bounding through the vines, a broad smile on his face.

His slacks are wrinkled from too much play, and his shirt, with its sleeves rolled up to his elbows, has a couple of grass stains on it. But he looks perfect. Happy.

"Holy *shit*!" he crows. "I just took your cousin to *town*, baby. Straight up owned his ass in horseshoes, my first time out!" He pulls a wad of crumpled Brazilian currency out of his pocket and shows off his spoils. "Fifty-five *reais*, yo! Steak dinner on me!"

I can't help it. I giggle, looking down at the bills and back up at him. "You know that's about fifteen dollars, right?"

Nico's face falls slightly, but he gives me a horsey grin anyway before he tackles me with another hug and a bunch of kisses around the neck. Whether it's the thrill of competition or just having fun, he's definitely riled up. Within a few seconds, so am I.

"Beers on the beach, then," he says as his tongue flickers against my neck. "Damn, you smell good. Are you wearing something new?"

"I think it's the flowers back here. Bibi loves jasmine."

"No, it's you." He continues to trail his nose down my neck. "Do you know how long it's been?" he asks in between kisses that grow longer every time. I open to them, taking him deeper. Each one works to banish my doubts.

"Um, about three days?" I wonder as I wrap my arms around his neck, amazed, as I always am, at just how easily he's able to distract me from my worries.

"Baby, are you losing your memory?" Nico leans back and frames my face with his hands. "I had to do three straight shifts back to back to get this time off, remember?"

I grin. Oh, I remember. Three straight shifts meant nine days of barely seeing him. It meant me hoofing it up to the station twice just to sneak kisses in the bunkroom. Both times we'd been interrupted by a call, and then we were on a plane to Brazil. It has actually been a *very* long time, at least by our standards.

I pop on my toes so I can kiss him, long and hard, enjoying the faint tastes of beer and barbecue that mingle with his unique flavor.

"Mr. Soltero," I say. "Who do you think you're talking to? It's been exactly twelve days." Kiss. "Four hours." Kiss. "Twenty-four minutes." Kiss. "And thirteen seconds since you were last inside me."

Nico raises an eyebrow. "Where's your stopwatch?"

I giggle. "Okay, maybe I made up the last three. But it has been over twelve days."

His teeth graze my jawline before he fixes his mouth on the skin just under my ear and sucks, hard, until it pops from his mouth. "Exactly," he murmurs as he traces his tongue around to the other side. "Too. Fuckin'. Long."

He takes my hand and places it on the tented front of his pants. He's hard and long, and I take hold of him and squeeze, enjoying the way he moans in my mouth as I do it.

"Tell me you need it," he says, his voice lowering half an octave as I squeeze again. "Shit."

"Need what?" I squeeze again. This time he groans slightly.

"You need what?" he repeats. "Don't play with me here, baby. Just fuckin' say it, Layla. I need to hear you say it."

I *should* say what I came out here to mull over. I should tell him the news I only just found out a few minutes ago myself. But like always, I'm not thinking clearly when he's pressed between my legs, when his full mouth is working that strange voodoo on my lips, my jaw, my earlobe, my neck.

"Your cock," I mutter as he drops kisses down my chest, testing the collar of my dress to find the sensitive hollow between my breasts. "Fuck, Nico, I need your cock."

I don't know if it's pregnancy hormones or what, but I'm all over the map. One minute I'm about ready to cry out of anxiety and fear, and the next, I can only think of tearing off this man's pants. It doesn't matter that my family is literally on the other side of the house. It doesn't matter that I can still hear their voices clearly filtering through the late afternoon breeze. I need him. Inside me. Freaking yesterday.

"Your wish is my command, baby," Nico growls before capturing my lips in yet another soul-searing kiss as his hands drop down to take two harsh handfuls of his favorite part of my body.

"Nico." I try to push him away, but it's hard, too hard. Especially when I'm also half-clawing at his shirt, grabbing him by the collar and yanking him closer. He just groans and kisses me like a starving man, practically eating me alive right there in the yard.

"What in the *hell* is going on here?"

Nico and I fly apart to either side of the patio, but neither of us can hide our flushed faces, swollen lips, the way Nico's shirt is half-untucked and unbuttoned a bit too low, or the way my dress strap is falling off my shoulder.

My father glares at us, then marches through the vines, kicking them away viciously. "*What* were you doing to her?"

Nico, to his credit, stands his ground. He doesn't run or skulk away like a naughty teenager. He holds his chest out firm and crosses his arms over it, like he's ready for anything my dad has to say.

"Dad, calm down," I try weakly. "Nothing was going to happen." Other than the fact that something definitely already has, of course.

"*Nothing* was going to happen?" Dad growls. "His hands are all over you, and *nothing* was going to happen?"

"He's my boyfriend!" I cut back without thinking. "What do you think we do? Hold hands and stare at each other all day?"

Nico snorts, but immediately shuts up when my father practically castrates him with a hard, black glare. Still, Nico says nothing—just continues to meet that stare head-on.

"What are you doing with him?" Dad asks me. "This is not my daughter. *My* daughter does not sneak away with boys at a family party. This is not what our family does!"

I can't help an eye roll. "Seriously? Go check the pantry, Dad. Pretty sure Luciano and his girlfriend are having a *really* good time in there."

"Well, *my* daughter does not!" Dad roars. "Especially not with this...this..."

"This what?" Nico's voice is low, but I can hear it shaking. "This what, Dr. Barros?"

My heart rises in my throat. It didn't take long, but it's been clear this confrontation was going to happen all along. I had just hoped to push it until the end.

Dad looks Nico up and down, dragging his gaze over his faded pants, his rumpled shirt, the tattoos peeking out from under his sleeves.

"Keep your hands off my daughter."

Nico steps forward, his chest puffing out slightly. "With all due respect, sir...no."

Dad stomps his foot hard enough that I swear the ground shakes a little. "This is *my* family's house. My family's property. And if you cannot respect me, if you cannot respect *them*, you can leave. I will pay for your ticket back to New York myself."

"And if I don't?"

Dad opens his mouth again, his face twisted deeply with his anger. And then his pager pierces the air. A few seconds later, he starts, as if he has just realized what's happening. Slowly, gradually, the flush falls from his face, and he pulls his pager off his belt to check the number. With a long exhale and a death glare at Nico, he whips his cell phone off his belt and flips it open to dial the number that's appeared.

"*Alô*," he says when a voice answers almost immediately.

Nico and I stand silently while Dad speaks in rapid Portuguese to the other person, too fast for me to follow. There's too much specialized language for me to understand. I'm guessing it's medical jargon. They continue a brief exchange, which clearly doesn't please my father, because by the time he hangs up the phone, his face is back to being bright red.

"What's going on?" I ask, suddenly aware that he's pulling his car keys out of his pocket. "We're not going, are we? We just got here a few hours ago."

I look back at Nico, who shrugs. Fifteen minutes ago, he had the biggest smile on his face that I've seen in weeks. He's actually having a good time, and the last thing I want him to do is have to jump into a car with a man who looks like he would rather just take him to the airport and damn the cost of a ticket back to the States.

Dad wrinkles his nose and blows out another long exhale. "I have to go," he says curtly. "To São Paulo for a surgery. I will be back tomorrow." He frowns at us. "You will stay here in Guarapari with Bibi and Manuel and your cousins until the party. I will be back for that."

Nico raises his brows slightly at me, and immediately I know he's thinking the same thing. With my dad gone, we'd have the apartment to ourselves, with only the housemaid. We'd have space to do…a lot of things.

To tell him, an internal voice says. Okay, sure, that's totally what I was thinking about, looking at the way Nico's broad shoulders and chest muscles ripple through his button-down shirt. Absolutely.

I turn back to my dad. "That's okay. We can just stay in Vila Velha with Benedita. You can ask her to chaperone if you really need that."

"*You will stay in Guarapari*," Dad practically spits out. "Clearly someone needs to keep an eye on you, and Benedita is not up to the challenge. Manuel will take me to the airport, and he will pick up your bags on his way back."

"Dad, come on," I try again. "Please don't make a big deal about this."

He glares at me. "You cannot possibly think I would allow my unmarried daughter to stay alone at my apartment…with *him*. Don't be a fool, Layla!" He pushes a hand through his thick salt-and-peppered hair. "Although, maybe it's too late for that."

I wilt, crossing an arm over my stomach reflexively. If this is what he has to say about a kiss in the garden, a child out of wedlock will probably get me disowned. Although, honestly, I'm starting not to care what he thinks of me anymore.

"Dr. Barros."

Nico's deep voice cuts across the yard, turning my dad's deadly glare on him. My cousins, clearly used to my father's temper, quiet at the sound of the conflict.

"I think that's enough, sir," Nico says in a tone that is calmer, lower than my dad's, but somehow just as threatening. He takes my hand, and squeezes. "We got it."

"Stay *here*," Dad spits, and then turns on his heel and leaves.

CHAPTER TWENTY-EIGHT

Nico

As upset as Layla is when her dad leaves for São Paulo, I'm not a bit sorry he's gone for a few days, even if the whole point of coming here was to see him in the first place. I can't pussyfoot around it anymore. The dude's a straight-up asshole.

I don't care that he dealt with some bullshit when he was younger. Looking around what his family has here, what he had back in the States, I can promise I dealt with a lot more. And I don't fuckin' treat people the way he treats his daughter. Period.

So yeah, it probably wasn't the best thing in the world for him to see me getting handsy with Layla. And yeah, he might have seen a lot more if he had interrupted about a minute and a half later. I'd probably be facedown in the pool right now, or on my way back to the airport.

But I also kind of don't give a shit. It's fucked up, but I kind of wanted the guy to know she doesn't belong to him anymore. Shit, she doesn't belong to me either, but she's mine just the same. And if I want to mess around behind some palm trees, I know she will too. So he can fuck off about it.

Now that he's gone for a bit, Layla and I are both able to relax a little, even if it is with a bunch of other cousins around. Most of the neighbors clear out before dinner, which ends up being the leftover spread that we just pick at while we spend the rest of the evening lounging around the open-air living room, watching soccer with her cousins. It reminds me a lot of my family, the way they tease, laugh, and shout at each other over the table. The older ones have started families of their own, so there are a few little kids around. Luciano and David, Bibi's sons, have pretty much accepted me —a hell of a lot more than their uncle has, anyway. Bibi keeps finding excuses to kiss my cheek. If it weren't for Dr. Barros and his shitty attitude, I'd probably like this side of Layla's family. A lot.

Layla starts to relax too after her dad leaves. She lounges with Carolina and

Marcella, Luciano's girlfriend, joking around in stunted Portuguese that, from what I can tell, is better than she thinks. I can only catch maybe fifteen percent of what's said, but I'm proud of my girl. Layla laughs as she takes in her aunt's stories, giggles when one of her cousins makes a crazy joke. Her happiness shines. She's practically glowing.

So I'm not even mad when Bibi sticks me on a stiff trundle in Luciano's room and Layla on the floor in another with Carolina and Marcella. This house is packed for the rest of the weekend, with three or four people shoved into the four bedrooms while everyone prepares for the banquet coming up. Even though I'm dying to finish what we started behind the house, I actually don't want to go around disrespecting Bibi and Manuel for the same reason I kind of want to get it on in Dr. Barros's apartment just to piss him off. It's just about how they treat Layla and me—with basic goddamn respect. It's also obvious that every second Layla spends getting to know her family erases some of the sad-puppy look that comes when her dad snaps at her. So, yeah. I'll take all the blue balls in the world if it keeps making my girl shine.

As luck would have it, the next day Bibi and her kids are pretty much consumed with prepping for Luciano's graduation party. Apparently this kind of thing is a really big deal here. They have to leave all day, and although they invite us to come tag along to their clothes fittings and last-minute shopping, it's clear they would probably get it done faster without us. Manuel stays behind, but is too absorbed with watching soccer to do more than wave when Layla and I tell him we're going to the nearby beach for the day. Dr. Barros seems to be the only one who gives a damn about us having a chaperone.

Which is how I end up walking on a mostly deserted stretch of fuckin' paradise, hand in hand with my girl. Since, like she told me, most of the people in this neighborhood work in the city during the week, everywhere on the beach that the mostly empty neighborhood borders is pretty much deserted. Just dunes and cliffs of yellow-white sand, bright blue water rippling through lagoons, and gullies that lead out to a wider beach and the ocean beyond. And nobody here but me and my girl. Me and Layla.

"You okay, baby?" I ask her after we choose a spot to hang out for a while at the base of one of the dunes, next to a lagoon so clear I can see all the way to the bottom.

I don't know why. But I haven't been able to shake the feeling like something is up with her. She's been happy, but also looks…I don't know. Preoccupied.

Layla pauses. "I'm fine. Why?"

I pull a corner of one of the big beach towels tight and give her a look. "Layla. I know you better than anyone else. I know when that beautiful brain is moving like crazy, and you've been thinking up a storm all morning. So, *que pa'o, mami?*"

Layla's rose-petal mouth quirks a little at the Spanish. She likes it when I call her *mami*, of all things. It's not like the other women I've known, the ones who think it's exotic or some shit like that. Layla's been around my family and me enough to know it's the most common word in the world. Some men use it for every girl they know: their mom, their sisters, their friends, their lovers. Layla's been in New York long enough that *some* random dude has probably called her *mami* on the street. But hopefully she knows that from me, it means she's family. At least, that's what I hope I'm seeing when her eyes sparkle like that.

"I just…" She sits down on the towel and leans back, draping one arm over her stomach. "Do you think it's weird that I like it better when he's not around?"

I sit down on the towel next to her, and then, by habit, move through a set of sit-ups while we talk. I went on another long run this morning before everyone got up, but my belly is gonna turn to mush with all of this rich food if I'm not careful.

"Who?" I ask as I touch an elbow to my knee. "Your dad? No, I don't. I'm not gonna lie, sweetie. I think he's a dick, especially to you. But I don't have to like him because I'm not his daughter."

Layla's eyes brighten as she watches me push through a bunch of Russian twists. "What? Oh. Yeah."

I stop moving and grin up at her. "Should I stop doing this while we're talking, blue eyes?"

She blushes and looks away toward the ocean. "No. I can handle it."

She doesn't *look* like she can handle it if her flushed skin is any indication. Even just being here a few days is giving her a glow, even more than before. But I like the effect too much to stop, so I start doing some boat raises instead.

"What's a chan-cle-ra?" Layla asks a few minutes later.

I do three more reps, then stop. "What's a what?"

"A… whatever your sister says when Allie's being naughty. Sometimes you tell her she better be careful or your mom might come after her with it too."

I sit all the way up and scrunch up my face for a moment, then burst out laughing as I finally figure out what the hell she's talking about. "Oh! You mean a *chancleta*?"

"Yeah," Layla says, nudging me on the shoulder. "What's that?"

I grin. "It's a house slipper. Like your shoes." I gesture toward her flip-flops. "It's sort of a joke, something Puerto Ricans say, right? You do something bad, your mom's gonna smack you with her *chancleta, la chancla*. You talk in church, you're gonna get slapped. You say something rude, she'll fling it across the room at your head. And it always hits, no matter what."

"So it's just a joke?"

I turn my head from side to side, considering. "No. I mean, it's mostly a joke. We make it a joke. But we all got smacked with that or plenty of other things when we misbehaved. I'm sure Maggie does it with Allie. She always gets spooked if you bring it up, you know?"

Layla nods. "I get that. My dad…he used to do that with the kitchen spoons. The wooden ones. He did it until I was about ten or so."

For a second, it feels like the glory of the day dims a little. I don't know what Sergio did. I don't know what Layla did. If you asked me yesterday if I thought people spanking their kids was okay, I would have said sure, even thought getting smacked by a foam sandal is a lot different than a wooden kitchen implement. I would have said there are going to be times where your four-year-old probably isn't going to listen to reason.

But I also get what it feels like to have the shit kicked out of you when you're a kid. I get what it feels like to be scared of the people who are supposed to take care of you. There's a thin line between discipline and abuse for some—and people like Layla and me don't always know completely where it is. That confusion starts young.

Layla shrugs and wraps her arms around her knees, hugging them close. "It is what it is."

I'm quiet for a second. "It's shitty, is what it is." I shake my head. "A lot of Latino men are like that. We grow up in a culture that tells us, like, being a man means being to be stronger than other people. To dominate, especially the women in our lives. Macho bullshit."

"I *never* want to hit my child," Layla murmurs fiercely as she stares out at the water. "With anything." When she turns to me, there's a look of desperation on her sweet face, one I'm not sure I totally understand.

But I do know one thing: I'm there with her. I'm there with her all the fuckin' way.

"Never," I tell her, reaching into her lap to take one of her hands. She looks at our hands linked. "We'll never do that. I promise."

Layla lays her head on my shoulder and sighs. Her shoulders relax, and she hums a little.

"My counselor," she starts to say, pausing a little, like she's trying not to stumble over the words. "She says...she says we learn how to love and be loved by our parents."

I nod. "It makes sense." It's something we've talked about before. The fact that neither of us ever really learned how to be loved the right way. The way it made it so hard for us to believe that we even deserved to be loved. That it always had to be painful. Hard.

"Really, who's easy to love at all?" Layla wonders, so softly I think maybe she didn't mean for me to hear it.

But I do.

"You are."

I can't help the shake in my voice. I hate that she questions this about herself. She knows her dad is the reason why she's gone through what she has. Why she lets so many people walk over her, treat her like she's nothing. The fucked-up thing is that I think Dr. Barros actually does believe in his daughter. He knows she's smart, knows she can do great things with her life. But her failure to meet his expectations drowns out anything good he sees. And it makes Layla see herself as less than she is.

"You are," I say again. But my head drops. Because I know I can't blame all of this on Dr. Barros. "I know I left you too," I say as I stare at the bright blue patterns in the towel. "And, Layla, fuck...you have no idea, baby. If I hadn't...I think about..."

A tear drops down my cheek before I can help it. Not too many things make me break, but the memory of Layla, battered and broken last spring is one of them. I'll die before I let that happen again. I squeeze her hand tight enough that her fingertips turn a little white.

"Stop," she says quietly, squeezing right back. She's crying now a little too, but her voice is steadier than mine. "It's done. That's all done. It wasn't your fault, and then you brought me back, Nico. You saved me, over and over again."

"Ah, shit," I mutter as I let go of her hand to swipe away another few tears. Fuck. She really does turn me to mush.

But there's one more thing I need to say. Something I need her to know more than I need water to drink, air to breathe. I slide a hand around her neck and pull her close so our foreheads touch and our breathing mingles on the sea breeze.

"You listen to me, baby," I say, willing her to feel every word down to her bones.

Layla inhales through her teeth and closes her eyes while I speak.

"No one is easier to love than you. You're right, baby. Some people are easier to love than others. But *no one* is easier to love than you."

Sometime, maybe a few minutes, maybe an hour later, I wake up as the sun is falling below the cliffs behind us and the houses perched on top of them. I stare up at the palm trees that hang over us, their wide leaves casting shadows across the sand, and a breeze floats through the hot air.

I'm not tired. No sirens are going off. No blare of traffic outside my window. No crazy people trying to get out of my way.

The only time I've ever really spent outside the city was in upstate New York, when I was confined to the youth jail. The country there was so silent it was deafening, and for years I avoided that kind of quiet like the plague.

But here…with the heat and the sun. The lapping of water a few yards away. Here with my girl, the love of my life…this is fucking paradise. And I never thought I'd live to see it.

I turn to tell her just that, but my girl is nowhere to be found. I push up, looking up and down the beach to see where she might have gone, but it's not until I'm on my feet that I finally spot her.

Layla floats in a sea of aqua, her sun-kissed body cradled in the calm waters of the lagoon. The late afternoon sun blinks off the water, clear down to the sandy bottom, and she lies on her back, eyes closed, arms akimbo while she drifts.

The sight of her takes my breath away. I mean, literally, I can't breathe, and all the air in my chest exits at once. But it's not just her physical beauty that does it, even though she is and always will be a work of art to me. It's the look on her face as she floats. The circles under her eyes have disappeared, and her full mouth quirks to the sides with a small, secret smile that's only for her.

Here, together, in this perfect space, just her and me…my girl is finally happy. She's finally at peace. It's a look I thought I'd never see again.

Her eyes blink open, and they are bluer than the water that surrounds her. She smiles, then twists onto her belly and dives below, touching the bottom like a porpoise before she surfaces again. I watch, my voice caught in my throat as she emerges again, then swims closer until she can stand up fully. The water rises only to under her breasts, and I watch, transfixed, as droplets of water roll over her shoulders and down her chest, hanging for a second off her curves before slipping the rest of the way to the water. She's an angel dipped in gold, a woman from dreams I never knew I had…until I met her.

And she's smiling. At me. Like a man under a spell, I get up and wade out to meet her.

How the fuck did I *ever* get so lucky?

"Hey," she says, waving her hands through the water. "I just went for a swim. When did you finally wake up?"

"Marry me."

The words tumble out of my mouth before I can even register the thought. Like they've been waiting in the wings, ready to charge forward the second my vocal chords could release them. And now that they're out, it's like I've been waiting since before I knew her to say them.

Layla stills, her hands floating palms-down in the water. "Wha-what?"

"I…"

I swallow. Holy fucking shit. Did I really just say that? Everything blurs.

"I…shit. That was not at all how I was going to ask you that."

"You were going to ask me?"

"No. Yes. I...I don't know..."

I look up, and her blue eyes are glossy and worried. They shimmer like the water.

"Layla," I say softly, taking her hand under the water. I thread our fingers together, then pull them up so I can kiss her fingers. "Hey."

She finally looks at me, and though her eyes are still uncertain, there's love there too. She looks at me the way I never knew anyone could. The way I know I look at her.

"Marry me," I whisper again. And this time, it doesn't catch me by surprise. This time I fucking mean it.

CHAPTER TWENTY-NINE

Nico

<small>HER WIDE BLUE EYES ARE AS BIG AS THE OCEAN.</small>

I swallow, suddenly terrified. "It's not how I planned to ask, you know."

I keep going, babbling the way Layla usually does when she's nervous. I'm glad that out here in the water, she can't feel my palms, the way I'm sure they're sweating right now. I take her other hand now for good measure. Otherwise, I'm honestly scared I might fall over.

"I was going to...maybe in a few years or something like that. Save up for a ring, do it right, you know?" I glance around, the water swishing with the movement. *Coño*, what the fuck am I looking for? A fuckin' fish to come save me? "Shit, I can't even kneel here, can I? Fuck...but, baby, I..."

I drift off when I look back at her. Her eyes are still shining, but the surprise and shock from before is gone. Instead, she looks the same way I feel whenever I look at her—really look at her. Like she can't breathe. Like her happiness threatens to swallow her whole. Her slender hand is over her chest, and the one still in mine is clutching it so hard her knuckles are white.

"You...you okay, baby?" I ask, stepping closer.

"Say it again," she whispers. "All of it."

There's a warmth in my chest whenever I look at Layla. Before I met her, the world felt cold most of the time. Now it expands, so much I feel like I could burst.

"Layla," I whisper, taking one last step closer so I can pick up her other hand. We're almost nose to nose now, but I don't want her to turn away. "I never...you are... how do I say it? I'm not smart like you, baby. I don't have the words. But when I look at you..." I swallow. "I see the world differently because of you, Layla. And I swear to God, if you give me a chance to make you happy, I'll never stop try—"

My awkward words are swallowed by her kiss. Her lips are soft, just a little salty from the ocean, but they open quickly, welcoming me home. And that's really what this is. I want to marry Layla, because she's already my home. That's what we are and always have been for each other.

"Yes," she whispers against my mouth. It's so soft, and at first I'm not actually sure that I heard her.

"What?"

I can feel her mouth spread against mine, a wide smile that makes that warmth in my chest expand even more. "Yes," she pronounces, and then she laughs.

It's not a giggle, even though I fucking love that sound too. But this one is even better. It's a full-bodied laugh that bounces off the rocks and waves. It's full of life, and calls back to the girl I first met over two years ago. Someone who wasn't afraid to open herself up to a stranger. Someone who showed me what it meant to love.

"Yes?" I ask her, suddenly picking her up by her waist. I swing her around in the water, making her laugh even harder. "Yes? *Yes?!*"

I ask again and again, because I really can't believe that someone like Layla Barros wants to marry someone like me. Or maybe I can. Because really, that's what Layla has been teaching me all along. That maybe I'm not such a bad idea after all. That together, we're the best idea in the whole fuckin' world.

"Yes," she repeats every time. We settle into the water, submerging our bodies as she wraps her legs around my waist. Her arms rest around my neck, and our noses touch. "A million times, yes, Nico Soltero. I'll marry you."

I close my eyes, so caught up in the moment, in the gravity of what the fuck we are about to do, that I can't speak. Marry. Wife. Husband. It's what we were always meant to be. But *holy shit.* Still.

"Nico?"

When I open my eyes, I still can't speak. The low, golden light of the sunset casts around her like a halo, lighting up even the darkest corners of her tortured heart. *Our* tortured hearts. I have never wanted my sketchbook so badly, but even so, I know I'll never forget the way she looks right now.

Her black hair lies glossy and wet over her shoulders, and her fair skin, flushed from a day outside, gleams as the light skims its wet surface. The thin blue material of her bikini hugs her body as the light shimmers over her curves, and I know it's not the warm breeze floating around us that has her nipples—which somehow seem fuller, a little riper than normal—pressing through the fabric. Her blue eyes fucking glow. The electricity crackles between us. The lines between lust and love are really, really thin. Right now, I genuinely can't tell the difference.

"Jesus," I finally exhale. "Holy shit. I just…sometimes I can't believe you're really mine, Layla."

Her legs drop, and I tug her forward so she's standing between my knees. I run my hands up her bare, smooth legs until my fingertips meet the fabric of her bikini. My heart feels like it's about to explode, along with something else that just got hard as a rock. Thirteen days now it's been. *Fuck.*

I bury my face in her neck and inhale her scent. It's not strong—something a little flowery—a soap she likes, blended with something a little sweet that's only hers, something evident with the salt water glistening on her skin. It's a smell that makes me feel warm and home and turned on all at once.

"Um, Nico?"

Her hands rest lightly on my shoulders. I pull back. "Yeah?"

"Can you…do you think…"

"What is it, sweetie?"

She peers down at me with a fuckin' adorably determined look on her face. Then she sucks on her lower lip, causing it to puff slightly when she releases it from between her teeth. She watches me watching her. I know she's nervous. I know I should say something. But she's so goddamn beautiful, I can't think straight, much less say anything coherent. And she's all fuckin' mine.

"Can you just kiss me again, please?" she finally asks. "And this time...don't stop."

I blink in surprise. Of course. Don't fuck this up again, you pussy. Especially since there are no asshole fathers lurking around the next corner. This tiny lagoon is deserted. It's just me and her.

Layla shivers as my hands wrap around her tiny waist, but I doubt it's because she's cold. The water out here is like bath water, and even with the sun starting to sink, it's probably close to ninety degrees outside.

She tips her head back, waiting for me to do what she asked. So I do. I start gentle; trying to keep from eating her alive like I did behind the house. I want to savor her, worship her, treat her like the queen she is to me. She needs it slow, teasing. She needs me to tease her mouth open like this, lead a sweet slow dance with our tongues as we unravel bit by bit. At her speed, not mine.

Remind her that she's worth it.

Her fingers thread into my hair, and the slight pull sends a current of need through me. *Fuck.* God, this girl makes me manic. One second I'm trying to pull away, let her cry on my shoulder again if she needs to. The next I'm a fuckin' animal.

Slowly, because I don't want to scare her, I unhook the front straps of her bikini and let them fall down her back, then pull down the front so her breasts bob free in the water, allowing me to suck one nipple, then the other into my mouth.

Part of me wants to rip the whole thing off her, but I'm pretty sure she wouldn't be too happy if she had to walk back in nothing but that scrap of fabric she calls a cover-up. Gentle, I keep telling myself, even though all I want to do is lift her up and take her against the rocks a few feet away. I want to spread her legs and drive into her, make sure she knows deep down within that she's mine, leave my mark, my seed, my essence or whatever the fuck you want to call it. I understand now what makes men want to do things like hide their girls' pills and creepy shit like that. It's primal, the need to leave something of yourself inside your woman. Make the two of you truly one.

Layla moans as I drift back to her other breast, biting a little at the end before I release it from my mouth with a slight pop. But I keep my eyes shut, because I know if I actually look at her, I'll lose the tiny bit of control I have left. Her legs are locked around my waist again. I'm hard and pressed against the core of her, and she's already rubbing up and down the whole fuckin' length of me. She wants this as bad as I do.

My fingers play over the slightly raised edges of the tattoo along her ribs, the one that matches mine. *Saudade*, they both say. A yearning for something you never knew. Something we both wanted before we ever even met.

I feel the curve of her waist. The swell of her hips. Her ass, oh *God*, that ass that I dreamed about for months when we were apart. That I'll probably dream about for the rest of my life.

"Oh!" she cries, breathy and light as I grab just a little bit harder. Her hips roll into me, and I groan into her mouth.

"You like that?" I ask before I land a kiss on her neck, then draw my tongue to lick the tiny drops of salt water away.

She shivers again, so I do it again. And again. When I graze my teeth like this, she usually moans a little. She likes it when I bite too, when I pulled just enough on her nipples to make it hurt. A tug, a nip, the casual use of my teeth on her earlobe, and then with a well-placed growl, my girl starts panting for me to fuck her. And god*damn*, do I ever.

But not right now. This is about love, not lust. I saw the look on her face after her dad caught us yesterday. She was scared. Terrified. Right now she needs it soft and slow, and that's okay. I don't care how I get to be with her as long as I just get to be with her.

"Nico."

Layla's voice, sharp and cutting, stills my mouth on her shoulder. I pull back. *Shit.* I was trying for gentle. Maybe I need to stop with the teeth completely. Like a feather, you asshole. You need to be like a fuckin' feather.

"*Nico,*" Layla says again. She grabs my jaw and forces me to look straight at her.

I blink. "Fuck, I'm sorry. What is it, baby? I'm being too rough, aren't I? Tell me what you need, okay? I'll do whatever you want…"

Layla frowns. "Stop treating me like a china doll."

"What?"

Quickly, while I stare in disbelief, she reaches down the front of my shorts and grabs hold of my cock. There's no question in her firm grip, no nerves in the way her thumb circles lightly over the tip. A shudder, the best kind, ripples through every muscle I have.

"I think you know," she says, and her eyes, a darker blue than I've ever seen them, dare me to look away. "Stop it."

———

Layla

His cock twitches in my hand. I squeeze a little harder, and his whole body shakes. I'm not going to lie; the power is a little thrilling. He wants this just as badly as I do.

"Nico," I say as evenly as I can. "Just fuck me already. Or did you forget how in the last two weeks?"

A change filters over his body. His muscles tighten. His shoulders straighten. His black brow rises slyly, and his half smile matches it while his hand slides around my waist, and I'm wrapped around him like a cobra while his cock stiffens even more in my hand.

"I would *never* forget how to do that, NYU," he growls before he takes my mouth again.

His kiss consumes me, even more than it did moments before. But where that was a kiss of gratitude, of wonder, this is one of pent-up lust and frustration, the kind that both of us have been feeling for days. The last remnants of his self-control disintegrate, and suddenly Nico's hands are everywhere: my arms, my waist, sliding down to take two solid handfuls of my ass again and squeeze. *Hard.*

"*Fuck,*" he groans as he kneads my skin. His cock, iron between us, bulges through his pants. "Are you—are you sure…"

"Sure about what?" I mutter as his teeth graze my neck. "That I want to fuck my future husband? Out here? Where anyone could see us?" I lean back to look him in the eye. "You bet I am, *papi.*"

With nothing more than a sly smile that lights up his face—whether because of my casual use of Spanish or because he can see just how badly I want him—Nico slams his mouth onto mine. His arms wrap around my waist and shoulders as his tongue and lips invade, while his cock, stiff and ready, teases between my legs.

"Say it again," he murmurs as he takes one breathless kiss, then another, all the while reaching down, around my legs, to tug my bikini bottoms to the side.

As he suckles my lower lip, his hips rock forward, and the tip of his cock, eager to bury itself in my depths, makes us both shudder.

"I…need…you," I whisper as he pushes forward, teasing me ever so slightly, even while his hands maintain their death grip around my thighs.

Nico closes his eyes, taking a deep breath before he latches his mouth to my neck, my ear, my jaw.

"Not," he croaks, his voice a current. "Not like I need you."

He consumes me like a starving man, his lips, his teeth, his hands, anywhere and everywhere, all over my body while my hips rock automatically, seeking the angle to take him deeply, that angle he never quite permits.

"Nico!" I cry as his teeth find my breast again and bite, harder than before. In that way that only he understands, Nico walks the line between pleasure and pain.

"Touch yourself," Nico rumbles into my neck as his cock continues to tease. "I want to watch you come."

"I…can't," I whimper into his neck. The tension ebbs and flows, a current that will take down a waterfall, just slightly out of reach. I want to fall, I do. But I need him to do it.

"Yes, you can, baby," Nico says.

He shelters me with his body, dipping down to lick my collarbone or worry a nipple between his teeth while he urges my hand down between us. But his lips always find mine again, and his tongue twists and turns, driving the tension that my hand begins to match until that edge approaches far faster than I ever thought possible.

"I feel it," he says as my fingers move a little faster, press a little harder. "You're shaking, baby. You're so fucking close. Can you feel it too?"

"Mmmmm," I groan into his lips, sucking on the lower one like it's a piece of candy. "I want to feel *you.*"

"Yeah?" he murmurs before taking another kiss, this one much, *much* deeper than before.

"Yeah." And before he can respond, I take hold of his long length and guide him back to that slick, dark space where he fits best.

"*Shhhhiiiittt.*" Nico's breath is hoarse, guttural as he slides inside, so deep, so… home. Then he starts to move.

"Tell me again," he says, lifting one of my legs to wrap around his waist while his other hand slides between our grinding bodies, finding that spot I need for release.

I arch backward into the water, thrusting my breast toward his waiting mouth. But his name is the only word I can say. "Nico."

"Tell me," he insists. His eyes squeeze shut as he moves; this is all instinct for him. For both of us.

But he needs to hear it. He needs to hear that thing I could never say to anyone else. Because it was only ever the truth with him.

"I need you," I whisper, threading my hands into his hair and pulling him close. He fills me, body and soul, so deep, so strong. With him, I am stronger. He is the reason I can be what I never was before.

My body starts to shake. I'm close, so close. "I need you," I whisper again. "Nico... I....oh, God...I do, I *need* you!"

"Fuck!" he shouts. His hips move a little faster, a little more erratically. He drives deeper, harder than he had intended. But I take it, every delicious, punishing blow. The hand at my hip slides up my body and behind my head. He thrusts even deeper, and as I lift my head to meet his hungry kisses, Nico winds my hair around his fist. And then he pulls.

"Nico!" I shout, as my legs squeeze his waist impossibly tight. My body seizes, up toward the sky, a world as limitless as us. With his kiss, this pull, the ultimate pleasure blended with just the tiniest prick of pain, Nico makes me fly right along with him.

"Layla!"

His groans echoes around the sandstone cliffs as he loses himself completely. The hand in my hair keeps the knot in its unrelenting grip as he buries his face into my neck and shouts out the rest of his release.

Slowly, surely, we come back to earth. Back to these waters that drift around us, as peaceful as before. Back to these palm trees, that whisper a little with the wind. Nico's broad, strong body keeps me afloat, lifeless except for the slight twitches of his muscles as they slowly release their tension.

"Fuck," he breathes. "God, I love you."

The words sing through me, though I'm almost too dazed to hear them.

"I'm sorry," he mumbles.

My eyes close. "Huh? Why?"

He leans back so he's looking at me. "I...I kind of lost myself there."

The concern on his face is so sweet. And it only strengthens my resolve that one day I'll convince him I'm strong again. Enough for him. Enough for our baby.

"Yeah, but if we lose ourselves, at least we do it together," I say.

My hand drifts up and down the length of his back. Nico sighs in contentment and pulls me back down to lie on his shoulder. Then he presses one last sweet, soft kiss to the top of my head. "Well, thank God for that."

———

Nico

We swim for a bit longer, but as the sun starts to fall a little lower, Layla throws on her cover-up and suggests we walk through the town to get back to her aunt's house, where everyone will be arriving for dinner.

I just want her. I'm thinking I'm going to have to figure out a way to sneak her to a hotel tonight, even if it's just for a few hours. Fucking her—if that's what you can even call it—in the lagoon didn't do anything to quench the thirst I've been feeling for days. If anything, it just made it worse. We're engaged. She's going to be my wife. And fucking *hell* if I don't want to celebrate that.

But instead, we walk back through the rural part of Guarapari, hand in hand or with our arms around each other's waists as we wander in and out of shops. In one, Layla ducks into a dressing room with a handful of sundresses, leaving me to linger uncomfortably around the register, waiting for her.

"You are American?" the salesgirl asks me, taking in the tattoos on my arm and sticking out the top of my tank top. It's something I've noticed here—there aren't as many people with body art. It's the first time I've been in a place where I look the same as so many other people, but even so, I stick out. No one else has an arm full of tattoos.

But that's not what I'm thinking about when a glint of gold catches my eye.

"Yeah," I answer her as I lean over the glass counter. "Yo, how much is that one? *Combien?*"

I point to a gold ring that's wedged with a bunch of others in a velvet display. I glance over my shoulder, but Layla's still busy behind the curtain. When I turn around, the salesgirl has already pulled it out and set it on a small plate.

The ring is small, but obviously nice. Its metal has been spun so finely that it almost looks like lace. There are no stones in it, no diamonds or rubies or anything like that. I couldn't afford them anyway. I won't be able to get Layla a real engagement ring for a long time, and even then it won't be anything impressive. But maybe while she waits, she could wear something like this. Something beautiful and pure, just like her.

"Is it real?" I ask the girl. I look up sharply. "Like her finger's not going to turn green or anything, will it?"

The salesgirl's face screws up in confusion. "Ahhh…"

"*Verde,*" I repeat in Spanish. Shit, how do they say that in Portuguese? I have no fuckin' clue. I try my luck again in Spanish, slowly. "*Debido al metal, entiende?*"

Luckily, it seems to be close enough to Portuguese that she understands—it dawns across her face, as she vigorously shakes her head. "Ah! No, no. No green, gold. We buy from Ouro Preto, you know?"

I shrug. I have no idea what she's talking about. Instead, I examine the ring more, even scratching a little with my thumbnail to see if anything comes off. But she seems to be telling the truth.

"All gold," the salesgirl repeats. "All gold."

I look up. "How much?"

That one, she knows. After looking down a list of prices next to the register, she scratches out a number on a piece of paper and turns it around. I do the mental calculation in my head of converting *reais* to dollars. It's not cheap, but it's a song compared to what something like this would fetch in New York.

Without thinking about it too much, I pull out my wallet and thumb through the cash I have left. "Ummmm," I say. I take out about half of it. We leave in a few more days. I'll just have to be frugal. "Here. And you can put the rest on this?"

I hand her my credit card, the one with a tiny limit that I only have for emergencies. I glance over my shoulder, checking to see if Layla's coming out yet. "Can you hurry, please? *Por favor?*"

The salesgirl nods with a wink and continues processing the payment. She puts the ring in a little cardboard box, and I shove it in my pocket and sign the receipt like a crazy man. And it's just as well, since as soon as I'm done, Layla walks out with two dresses over her arm.

"You can't look," she says as she shields them from me. "They're a surprise."

Surprise? She has no idea.

I do my best to look casual and totally normal as she pays for the dresses. But all I'm thinking is that now that I finally have a ring to give her, how am I going to ask her to wear it?

CHAPTER THIRTY

Layla

"*O que você acha?*"

The hairdresser spins me around so I can see myself fully in the mirror.

It's a small salon, almost completely full of all of the women in my extended family—Bibi, Carolina, her sons and their significant others. Even my grandparents came from Colatina for the big party tonight. She's having her ancient gray strands set into curls around her head. It's more pomp and circumstance than I've seen for anything other than a wedding, but apparently this is totally normal in Brazil, at least in a certain set. The night before, when Carolina mentioned taking the day to get ready for the banquet, and I'd mentioned Nico's and my plans to go to the beach again before the graduation Mass and ceremony the next day, my cousin had looked at me like I should be committed, and then promptly dragged me downstairs while shouting for her mother.

Which is how I found myself in the salon for almost the entire afternoon following Luciano's graduation ceremony. After attending yet another Mass and then watching my cousin receive his degree along with the other twenty or so members of his class also graduating at the end of the summer term, I'd been swept into a car with Carolina and everyone else to be primped for the banquet tonight. Though I'd tried to be demure the day before, not wanting to be a burden or lose more precious time with Nico, Bibi took one look at me, windswept, sand-covered, with my hair a curly wind-blown mess from the salt water and hours spent at the beach, and informed me that she wasn't taking no for an answer. And as much as I like Bibi, I don't think she was doing it to be nice. This was one of those events, apparently, where her family would be *seen*.

But now I'm glad I went. It was only after watching all of the women in my extended family get waxed, buffed, and primped like it was no strange thing to have all of this done for a relatively small event, that I realized just how out of place I would be if I *didn't* do it. Compared to them, I'd end up looking like a cavewoman. I don't want to admit that a small part of me doesn't want to disappoint my dad either. Or, at least, I don't need another reason beyond the one growing in my belly.

His daughter. Pregnant. Out of wedlock. It sounds bad enough as it is, but when you add to the equation that my father is so Catholic he refuses to divorce his estranged wife who lives in a total other country…well, it's basically going to be like splitting an atom inside my father's head.

Of course, I need to tell Nico first. Sitting in the chair while a woman from Recife paints my toenails, I twitch my ring finger, imagining a ring, any ring, on it. Nico isn't rich—neither of us are—and I hope he doesn't think he has to get me anything expensive, or anything at all. All I want is him, as I've told him time and time again. He gives me so much more than any of this. Just like he'll give our baby.

My hand drifts over my still-flat belly from time to time, and occasionally Carolina looks knowingly from the other side of the room, where she's having her roots touched up. She's wondering if I've told him, I'm sure. Wondering if I've told anyone. But for now, this secret is mine. Just me and whatever it is. A little bean, a little creature, a little something made of love and nothing else. Whatever happens in the next few days before we go back to New York, I'll never forget that.

I look at my reflection. My hair has been blown into soft, silky waves, which the hairdresser has braided into a fishtail look over one shoulder, leaving a few escaped tendrils to frame my face. It's a style that looks a lot less complicated than it is, considering the number of pins and amount of hairspray she used. But the overall effect is ethereal and romantic, and fits the floaty white gown with the gold threaded embroidery over the bodice and down the skirt that's hanging in the salon's dressing room. Bibi brought it back after yesterday's shopping expedition with equally adamant insistence that I wear it instead of the four-year-old dress I still had from my senior prom. I fought it at first. After all, I used to love the light-blue dress with the sparkly fabric and color made my eyes pop. But it was the kind of dress that a high school student would buy, made of cheap polyester materials in a trendy design, more like dress-up than real life.

Bibi's dress is for a woman, not a girl. And when I tried it on, saw the way the embroidered chiffon floated over my curves, accentuating without looking tacky, and the way the combination of white and gold actually made my eyes look even bluer than normal, I knew one thing: Nico needed to see me in this dress.

"*Eu gosto,*" I tell the hairdresser, giving her the thumbs-up. "I love it."

She nods, then points to the smaller station in the far corner of the salon where one of my cousins is having her makeup done and says something in Portuguese. It's a little faster than I'm used to, but the meaning is clear: I'm next.

———

THE BANQUET TAKES place at a rented hall close to Luciano's university, in a circular building with open-air walls through which we can see into a park that surrounds it. In the center of the room, a DJ is spinning all the greatest hits from the last few decades, while most of the graduates and their families are still mingling, getting drinks from the open bar on one side or enjoying hors d'oeuvres from the buffet at the other. Even though the class had all of twenty-five people in it, it seems like the entire law school and their families showed up to celebrate. It's true what they say. Brazilians like to party.

I stand a bit awkwardly with my cousins around one of the tables that are laid around the dance floor in the center of the room. It's empty, but Carolina has assured me it will fill soon, once everyone is drunk enough. The boys are nowhere to be seen. We're a little early, having come straight from the salon.

"You almost look like a bride," Carolina says, looking me over again critically. "Your eyes...gah! Do you wear contacts?"

I shake my head.

Carolina exhales again. "I'm *so* jealous. I wanted to get contact to make my eyes blue like yours, but *Mamãe*, she says no, not while I live with her. For now, anyway."

I look down at my dress, then back up. I look good—I know that—but I haven't been this dressed up in ages, maybe not ever. I look like money in this expensive dress and the diamond earrings my aunt lent me. But that's not what I care about anymore. If I ever did.

"You don't think it's too much?" I wonder, suddenly worried she can see past the light chiffon to the truth. Nico and I haven't told anyone about our new engagement. So far it's just been our sweet secret. I'll have to tell my dad before I leave, but right now, it's been nice to just have it between us.

Carolina shakes her head. "No, no, it's perfect. I was just teasing, you know?"

I exhale. "Okay. Do you know when the boys will be showing up?"

Carolina shrugs. "They were coming from Guarapari, so it's hard to say. Maybe they find some traffic, I don't know."

"Wow."

His deep voice, the only one speaking English, curves through the air and wraps me in its warm embrace. I turn around and I'm immediately blown away. I forget sometimes how well Nico cleans up. And...wow is right. For him, not me.

Unlike most of the other men in the room, who are dressed, as my father stated, in standard black-tie regalia—black tuxedos with white shirts—Nico's in his all black suit, with a matching shirt, tie, and vest. I've seen this suit before. It's his only one, the all-black ensemble he wore at Thanksgiving, which was also his uniform when he worked at a swanky club in LA. But I haven't seen it since he moved back.

He should be a shadow, but instead the monochromatic outfit just makes his skin glow. His thick black hair has been tamed a bit, swept off to the side slightly, and the sole bit of color in his outfit is a red pocket square. He looks elegant. Maybe a little dangerous. And he's all mine.

His gaze burns over me as he takes in my dress, my hair, the jewelry, even the dainty gold cross gifted from Bibi.

"Damn," he murmurs under his breath, pulling slightly at his collar. When his eyes finally meet mine again, they gleam. "Wow. You look insane, baby. For real, you look *amazing*."

I blush under the heat of his gaze. He doesn't hold back, just continues to stare in awe—an emotion he rarely hides when he feels it, but which I haven't seen this naked before.

"Thanks," I whisper. "You—you look—I mean...gah."

Behind me, Carolina laughs. "I think she mean you look nice too," she clarifies before walking away.

Nico takes my left hand and strokes my knuckles, lingering over the bare ring finger. "Sorry I'm late."

I shake my head a little. "Please. There's nothing to be sorry for."

"We had to wait for your dad to get back from the airport. And then, well...let's just say he wasn't too happy when he remembered I didn't have a tux." Nico's mouth twists sardonically as he remembers. "He cares a lot about what other people think, huh?"

The clouded expression makes my fists clench. I hate that look, that lingering insecurity that comes out every now and then. I hate anything or anyone who makes Nico feel like anything less than the amazing person he is.

"He cares too much," I tell him. "It's his Achilles' heel. *I* think you look incredible. Isn't that what matters?"

Nico brightens, a shy smile replacing the frown. "You bet your ass it is, sweetie. So riddle me this: do you care too? Or would you be willing to dance with me on an empty floor?"

I glance at the dance floor, which is indeed mostly empty with the exception of a few younger attendees and an older couple swaying off to the side.

I turn back. "I am *always* willing to dance with you, Mr. Soltero."

———

AN HOUR LATER, the dance floor has filled up along with us, and we're both a little sweaty and worn out after dancing to song after song that could probably be pulled from cheesy pop albums of the eighties and nineties.

"I gotta say," Nico calls before he spins around on his heel. "I wasn't expecting to get down to Shania Twain on my first trip to Brazil. It's like they didn't get out of the nineties pop hell, huh? K.C. would be freaking out down here."

I giggle. "I think it's just this DJ. You don't 'feel like a woman'?"

Nico grins. "Nah. But I liked watching you scream it with everyone else. You're so cute when you sing, baby. Off key, but really damn cute."

I shove him in the shoulder, which he just takes as an excuse to pull me closer. As if on cue, the Spice Girls stop singing, and for the first time, the DJ puts on a slower song. Mariah Carey's "Honey" isn't anything that's going to kill the mood, but the tempo, a little slinkier than the manic pop songs, gives Nico an excuse to pull me closer, swaying me back and forth to the lazy rhythm.

"What is it with you tonight?" he murmurs as he starts to roll his hips in a way that obviously comes from the years of practicing salsa in his mom's kitchen growing up. "You look...you look different. Something's different." He spins me out, then pulls me back in. He looks across the room to make sure my dad is still engrossed in a conversation with a few other men, then sneaks a quick kiss. "You're fucking glowing, baby."

Now is the time. I should tell him now, right? But before I can, Nico stops dancing and reaches into his jacket pocket, though his other hand remains firmly on my back, keeping me close.

"I, uh, picked something up the other day," he says as he withdraws his hand. "I saw it and thought of you. I was going to wait until we were back home, but..." He looks over me again, taking in the apparent beauty he hasn't stopped talking about for the last hour solid. "I don't know. Something…I feel inspired. I want you to have it now."

He opens his hand, and what I see makes my heart stop.

It's a ring. A simple gold ring that gleams against the fine lines in his palm. It's delicately engraved, like the gold has been spun together to weave an imperfect, yet perfect design all the way around the thin band.

I look up. "Nico…"

Nico chews on his upper lip for a second, then gives me a shy smile. "I know it's not a diamond, Layla. One day I'll get you one, I promise. If that's what you want, baby, I'll do whatever I need to do to buy you the biggest diamond in Manhattan, I swear to God. Layla, I just want to make you happy. That's it—"

I lay my hand over the ring, a gesture that stops his babbling.

"I don't want a diamond," I tell him, keeping our eye contact solid so he knows I mean it. Then I look down. "I want this. It's so perfect, Nico. It's simple and beautiful. It's so us."

"I want you to have it," he says. "I didn't do it the right way the other day. I didn't get to tell you how beautiful you are to me, inside and out. How brave. How much I love the way you open your heart to the world, again and again. How much you want to make it better. How you inspire *me* to be better, every damn day."

His words make me giggle, the awkward kind that only happens when you feel so much your chest might split open. I reach up to swipe away a few errant tears that spring unbidden—not from sadness, but from joy.

"Layla," Nico says, tugging me just a little closer. "Will you marry me?"

I bite my lip, then hold out my left hand. "Of course I'll marry you, Nico Soltero. Tonight. Tomorrow. I'm yours, body and soul. Don't you know that by now?"

He slides the ring on my finger, and it fits, just like I knew it would. Nico knows me sometimes better than I know myself—why would my ring size be any different?

"What are you thinking?" he asks tentatively.

I look back up at him to find, even now, a little insecurity playing across his chiseled features. "I think I'm the luckiest freaking woman on the planet right now," I say honestly.

Nico grins, that signature smile that lights up every room he's in. That lights me up. "I think we need to celebrate. I'm going to get some champagne from the bar."

He turns to leave, but I tug his sleeve back. "Just…just water for me, okay? I don't want to drink."

His face screws up with immediate concern. "Baby, you're not going to go crazy if you have a glass of champagne with me. Come on, it's our engagement. We should toast, don't you think?"

I shake my head. He thinks I'm stopping him because I'm afraid of taking a step backward, to that dark, crazy time when I was spiraling without him. That I'm so scared of going there that I won't even have a cocktail. But that's not it.

"Layla," Nico says, taking a step closer. "What is it?"

He waits patiently, the expression on his face kind and open. And I know in that moment, that nothing I could tell him would ever push him away. Nico loves me, loves *us*, unabashedly, with all that he is. There's nothing to fear.

So I open my mouth to tell him the truth, the news that's going to change both of our lives. The news that has me petrified and overjoyed all at once. That I'm dying to share and at the same time, terrified to say out loud.

"I'm—"

"*What* is that on your finger?"

Before I can say a word, my father comes charging through the crowd, his voice booming over the music. He storms between Nico and me and grabs my hand, the one with the gleaming new piece of delicate gold jewelry, practically ripping it off my arm Behind him, Nico's face turns black. He *really* doesn't like my dad, and clearly he's not cool with the way he's touching me at the moment.

My father, however, doesn't care. He shakes my finger, and the two veins over his temples look like they are about to burst.

"Layla," he demands. "*What*. Is the meaning. Of this?"

CHAPTER THIRTY-ONE

Nico

I FREEZE. WE BOTH FREEZE. BUT I DON'T MISS THE WAY LAYLA TAKES A STEP TOWARD ME, like she's looking for shelter. I hate that her own father makes her feel that way, but I get it. Goddamn, do I get it.

"*What*?" Dr. Barros shakes Layla's hand, then drops it like it's burning.

He takes a long drink of something that looks like whiskey, then sets his empty glass on a nearby table before standing up, swaying a bit. Great. He's mad *and* shitfaced.

"What is the meaning of this?" He lets out a long string of Portuguese, and from the way some people's eye bug out, I'm guessing it's pretty foul.

"W-we're getting married," Layla says.

She holds out her hand with the simple ring that barely stands out in this room full of rich, flashy ladies with even flashier jewelry. But the gold on her finger still gleams in the light.

"Nico asked me. And I said yes, of course," she tells Dr. Barros, sticking her chin out a little in this fuckin' adorable away that would make me want to kiss the living shit out of her if I wasn't so worried about her dad right now.

Because I know that look. I've worn it a few too many times myself. It's the look you get when you're about to explode.

"Married," Dr. Barros repeats, and I can practically see the steam coming off his head. "To—*this*?" He gestures at me like I'm a piece of fuckin' furniture. Like I'm a thing, not a person. "No. I forbid it."

"Well, that's too damn bad," I pipe up. I can't help it. I'm so tired of this guy treating me like I'm less than him, treating Layla like she's a fucking puppet. He has no fuckin' right. "Last I checked, Layla and I are both adults. And I'm pretty sure you haven't given a shit about her for the last year and a half anyway."

Layla shakes her head at me, clearly telling me to shut the fuck up. "Dad. Please. Let's just talk about this somewhere quiet…"

"He's a criminal," Dr. Barros states a little too loudly, and the word causes another few onlookers to murmur a little.

Slowly, people around us are taking in what's happening. The dance floor is growing still, even with Montell Jordan blasting on the speakers.

It takes everything I have not to stare at the floor when the English speakers in the crowd look at me with renewed, slightly fearful interest. No. I'm not guilty of anything but falling in love. That's not who I am anymore. It's not who I've been for a long time now. Maybe I never was.

"What are you talking about? Of course he's not," Layla snaps as she comes to stand in front of me. It makes me proud. My baby is valiant, guarding me from her dad. In her white and gold, she's an angel, but the good kind, like Gabriel—the kind that don't fuck around, you know?

"You think I don't look him up? You think I don't find that he was in jail?" Dr. Barros demands wildly, his English uncharacteristically sloppy, the work of a few too many scotches. "Layla, he is nothing. He comes from nothing. He is becoming nothing. He is not good enough for you!"

"He's a hero!" Layla hisses defiantly, reaching behind to take my hand. "He's a firefighter in the best city in the world. He saves *lives*, every day, and he definitely saved mine. What do you do besides give women bigger tits?"

A laugh bursts out of my chest before I can stop myself. I should be angry—fuck, I *am* angry. But the look on Dr. Barros's face when his daughter says the word "tits" in front of a whole bunch of fancy rich Brazilians is fuckin' priceless.

"That's enough!" he shouts. His face reddens even more as he looks around. Yeah, the dude has definitely been pitching back the sauce. "We are leaving. Now."

"No," Layla replies.

"*Sim.*"

"No!"

"Layla, we are *going!*"

Dr. Barros grabs for Layla's wrist and jerks her forward, twisting her arm painfully and forcing her to kneel slightly next to him. Any trace of humor disappears completely, and just as fast, blood roars in my ears when Layla tries to fight it, her face contorted in pain as she does.

Oh. Hell. Fuckin'. No.

It takes me less than a second to dart in between Layla and her dad, grab his wrist, and twist it enough that he has to let hers go. I thrust him away from her, allowing Layla to step backward behind me, suddenly released. Out of the corner of my eye, I notice her rubbing her wrist where he had grabbed it. Now I'm the one barely holding onto my temper.

"Get out of my way," Dr. Barros orders. "This doesn't concern you. This is a *family* matter."

"Well, then it does concern me, Dr. Barros," I say. "Since Layla *is* my family, sir. And I'm hers."

He turns to me with a face full of rage, and surprises me when he walks close enough to make us almost nose to nose.

"*You* will never be her family," he informs me through capped, white teeth. "*Never*. Not you. *Never* someone like you."

I grind my teeth. I don't like this guy at all, but I never wanted him to hate me. This isn't someone Layla may ever be able to walk away from. You just can't ask someone to do that with their own dad. I don't want Layla to hate me either for messing up their relationship more. Because when I look at her, see her blue eyes full of curiosity, fear, but always, always trust in me. In us. I don't doubt it anymore. In fact, the insinuation that we're *not* inextricably bound together makes me pretty fuckin' angry.

"Is that right, *Doctor* Barros? Well, where the fuck were you last year, or the year before that, sir?" I take a step forward, forcing him one step back. "Because I'm the one who's been there. I'm the one that carried your daughter out of some asshole's apartment after he had beaten her black and blue. *I'm* the one who talked her into going home even though I wanted her with me. Your daughter is my heart and soul, sir. I would do anything for her. Lay down my life for her in a heartbeat. So there ain't *no fuckin' way* that anyone gets to talk shit about her, about *us* like that. Not while I'm alive." I pull myself up as tall as my five feet, almost eleven inches will let me. "I don't care if you're her father. I don't care if you're the Pope. You mess with Layla, you mess with me."

Dr. Barros blinks, his dark, shadowed eyes burning into me and everyone else. Into his daughter. But my words fly right by him. Maybe he's too angry to really hear them in the first place.

"Layla," he tries again, straining, it's clear, to keep his voice down. "We go. Now."

"No, Dad."

Dr. Barros gulps, hard enough that it makes his bow tie twitch. "Layla," he tries again.

"She doesn't want to go with you," I tell him.

And then I make my biggest mistake, one that in all my years of training with fighters, of living in bad neighborhoods, of growing up in a city where you *always* look over your shoulder, I should have learned by now. I turn my back.

"Come on, baby," I say, taking Layla's hand and pulling her close. I press a kiss to her forehead, willing her to know that whatever happens tonight, I'm still here for her. I'm always here for her. "Let's get out of here."

Maybe it's the kiss, innocent as it was. Or maybe it's the way that his daughter is looking at me, with big blue eyes full of love, the kind that drives me every day to be something better than I am. Whatever it is, Dr. Barros sees something that sets him off. And he attacks with a roar.

"NOOOOO!"

In a split-second, I'm wrenched away from Layla, and I've got a pair of slim, well-groomed hands flying at me. One cuffs me on the jaw, a sucker punch I'd be able to dodge on literally any other day, any other moment.

"Sergio!" screams Layla's aunt.

"Dad!" Layla shouts.

But I don't know where they're coming from, because I'm too busy fighting off the best of Brazilian society right now. Frank, my old trainer and mentor, used to say that half a good fighter is skill, and the other half is adrenaline. And that if you pit one against the other, adrenaline wins every time.

Dr. Barros might be older and weaker than me, but he's got fury on his side.

Still, I've got a little of that too. A well of it, really, that will probably never totally go away. And when I think of the way he looks at his daughter like she's nothing, that anger bubbles up in no time, and I'm ready to swing back.

"Dad!" Layla shouts as Dr. Barros scrambles at me again, his fists flying toward my face.

The guy is no fighter. His hands are soft, the slim fingers of a surgeon, not a soldier. I duck easily, parry him away as the crowd naturally spreads into a circle around the dance floor. He comes at me again, and this time, I parry away his fist, deliver an easy cross to his cheekbone, and as he falls back, grab hold of his wrist and twist him neatly into a half-nelson under my much bigger shoulder. I'm an inch or two shorter than the guy, but that means nothing in a situation like this.

"How does it feel?" I growl at him, close enough to his ear that only he can hear me. "How does it feel to be yanked around like you're nothing, huh? You like it? Because I sure as fuck know your daughter doesn't."

People are shouting in Portuguese all around us—calling for help, for someone to grab me, grab the thug American beating up the eminent surgeon, no doubt. I figure I have about two more minutes of this until I'm going to have to sprint for the door.

"Let...me...go!" Dr. Barros shouts, jerking his chest two and fro, his face turning red like a tomato.

"You gonna calm down, *cúlo*?" I ask, unable to keep the profanity from slipping out. Somehow swearing in Spanish is worse here than at home, but I can't help it. I don't want to use his title. I don't feel anything resembling respect for the guy anymore.

Dr. Barros stiffens, which tells me he knows exactly what it means. "*This* is what you call respect?" he shouts, his face screwed up as he continues to thrash around. "*This* is how you wanted to ingratiate yourself to me?"

"You're not leaving me much of a choice," I reply evenly as I struggle to maintain my hold. I'm stronger, but my anger is fading. His, however, is going strong. But not strong enough. "If you calm down, I'll let you go."

My arms are straining, but I'm immovable. He's going to hurt himself if he doesn't stop. But then again, I'm not sure I care.

"You will *never* be with my daughter!" he howls. "I will die before allowing some filthy, *moleque* to pervert my family! You will *never* deserve her! You will *never* end up with her—over my dead body!"

"But it's already done."

The crowd and Dr. Barros hush at the sound of Layla's voice.

"What does that mean?" he hisses, still struggling against my hold.

Layla steps forward, suddenly having found her voice. She glances around nervously, then zeroes in on her dad. "I'm pregnant."

The words ricochet around the room like one of those pinballs at an arcade. I should know, because they basically hit me in the head. The DJ turned off the music long ago, probably hoping the absence would shut down the fight. And within a few seconds, the only sound is a light murmur as the people around us digest what Layla's just said.

And when I do...I can't feel a thing. Dr. Barros and I both freeze, and a half second later, he flops to the floor with a thump while my hands fall limp to my sides. Dr. Barros lies on the tile for a few more seconds before he sits up, rubbing his head, as if he's not sure he heard what he just heard. But I just stare, unable to move. Did I hear what I thought I just heard?

"I'm pregnant," Layla repeats softly, this time only to me.

She steps closer, her eyes bright and wide. The people around us strain to hear, but these words are for me.

"I only found out a few days ago, at the barbecue…I was planning to tell you when we got back to New York." She swallows, looking guilty. "I'm sorry, I just…needed some time to digest it myself."

At the sound of her voice—her sweet, kind, unsure voice, I jerk. "You're…pregnant?"

Layla nods. "I am."

I take a step back—not because I want to, but because I'm having a problem standing up straight. Pregnant. Holy shit. A baby. *My* baby. Holy shit.

Dr. Barros stumbles off the floor, pushing people away so he can make his exit as quickly as possible. Before I can say anything, Layla reaches out to me, her eyes eager and scared all at once.

"Nico?" she whispers. "Say something."

But when I open my mouth, nothing comes out. Not a sound. Not a breath. I look at her, and then I look at the people still watching us openly. And then I turn around and walk out of the building.

CHAPTER THIRTY-TWO

Layla

I WATCH AS MY FATHER STUMBLES ONE WAY, BLOODY-MOUTHED AND HUNCHED OVER IN THE direction of the parking lot, and Nico strides in the other, toward the beach that's only a block or two away. Whatever I was expecting when I dropped this news—from either of them—this wasn't it. These are the men in my life who are supposed to love me more than anyone. This isn't how I wanted to tell either of them, by dropping the word "pregnant" like a bomb in the middle of this glitzy party. I'm lucky that only a few people around us probably really understood what was going on. But even those few are enough to bring shame on my family.

I stand in one place, swiveling between the two directions aimlessly until Bibi approaches and puts her hand on my shoulder.

"Go to him," she says.

She looks at me kindly, and her brown-eyed gaze, so like my father's, but invested with humor and kindness I've never seen from him, drops to my stomach, over which my hand lies. There's nothing there to cup yet. It's a flat expanse that's more of a dream still than a reality.

I don't know whom she's referring to. But I know whom I need to follow. So I turn toward the beach and make my exit.

The pavilion that's housing the party sits in the middle of a grassy park, criss-crossed with the looming, sharp-ended shadows of palm trees, while the bougainvillea climbing the walls sneaks up the sides, black against the glare of the moonlight. The grass eventually opens onto the promenade in front of this beach, like all the others. When I step into the light, I can see the outline of Nico's broad shoulders across the four-lane street as he strides, head down, toward the ocean. He pauses for a second on a rise in the sand, stares out at the waves, and then falls, ungracefully, to sit and shoves his head in his hands.

Even from here, little more than a shadow, he's so beautiful. Streetlights glint off the sheen of his hair, and the broadness of his shoulders still captivates me from afar. They sag, though, clearly feeling once more the weight of the world.

I never meant to add to his burdens.

I make my way across the street, ignoring the whistles out of the cars that pass, and remove my high-heeled shoes before crossing the beach to where he sits. Once I'm there, I sink into the sand quietly.

He hasn't looked up at me yet, but he knows I'm there. He always knows I'm there—he probably knew I was watching him from across the street.

For a while, we sit in relative silence, listening to the low roar of the cars behind us filling the air along with the sound of the waves beating the surf.

I wonder where my father has gone. If he went back to his apartment, just over the big bridge in the distance, to continue drinking himself silly while he ruminates on his daughter's shame. He was already drunk at the party. I doubt he would have made such a scene otherwise. And then I had to add to it by admitting to being pregnant out of wedlock in a roomful of staunch Brazilian Catholics. To my father, to his family, it doesn't get much worse than that. It's not like it doesn't happen; it happens all the time. But the appropriate way to deal with it would be to get married quietly, before anyone could notice completely, or else get rid of it, equally as quiet.

What must my father be thinking now? He left the United States to escape social castigation. And here I am, bringing it to his feet. All my life I've tried to make him proud. He'll never look at me the same way again. He'll never forgive me.

It occurs to me, right then, that I legitimately may never speak to him again. This isn't the kind of thing he would ever be able to forget.

Nico shifts where he sits, bringing me out of my dark thoughts. He lifts his head to look out toward the ocean, and I see waves of worry flowing from his beautiful, strong face. He rubs his hand over his eyes, down his rounded nose, over his full lips and up his chiseled jaw. Then he sighs, long and low.

What my dad thinks no longer matters. What's most important to me is right here, I realize, with some measure of peace. What matters is the man next to me, the man who owns my heart. What matters is us. Our future. Together.

If we still have one.

"What am I going to do?" Nico wonders softly, so low his voice almost has the same timbre as the waves on the shore.

My heart drops, heavy at his words. I say nothing at first, just wait patiently until Nico leans his head on my shoulder. It's warm, solid, though I can feel him shaking.

"Are you...so you're upset then?" I ask, unable to stop my voice from quaking slightly. I toy with my ring, twisting it around my finger. Maybe he'll want it back.

The idea crushes me. My chest feels like it's caving in. I know I'm too young. I know it's too soon for us. I know to everyone else, we're just a couple of poor, crazy kids who have no business jumping into a marriage, much less starting a family.

But even with that, a part of me had hoped that Nico would be happy about this news that we had created something out of the bond between us. I've only carried this knowledge with me for a few days, but already it's a part of me. Already, I would do anything for it.

"Upset?" he repeats. "No, baby. I'm not upset."

I turn to look at him, take in his beautiful profile—the jaw that could cut glass, sprinkled with the slightest stubble. The nose that's rounded at the end, just a little too long, but which fits his face. The dark eyes, lined with thick lashes, that look at everything with so much soul.

"So…what are you?" I wonder.

Nico just stares out at the ocean for what seems like an interminable amount of time. Then, finally, he turns to me with eyes so wide they could swallow me whole.

"Layla," he whispers as a lone tear tracks down his cheek. "I'm so fuckin' happy I feel like my chest is about to split open. But, baby, I can hardly speak, I'm so scared."

His calm is eerie. I want him to do something. Laugh. Run. Cry. Shout. Anything but this strange stillness that seems to have taken over.

"I just…fuck. I don't know how to be a dad," Nico says, his voice shaking slightly. "I never had one. The closest thing I saw was David, Gabe's dad, who…"

He closes his eyes, as if in pain as he trails off, pressing his forehead into his arms. He doesn't want to voice those memories out loud. I know the feeling.

"I know," I say. "Your mom told me. After Giancarlo."

He's alluded to it as well. David was abusive. He would take things out on his kid, the mother of his son, and her other children. It was Nico who chased him out for good. But with violence. That I know. It was always with violence.

It's a side of him I've only had glimpses of, but never seen until tonight. But I'm not scared. I could never be scared of him.

Nico turns his head on his forearms and gazes at me, eyes slightly glossed over. Fear shines through their black depths. "What if…what if I end up like that?"

Oh.

"Nico," I begin. "You would never—"

"Hush," he cuts me off, taking my hand in his.

In the bright moonlight, gleaming off the waves, the contrasts between us seem to be that much starker. Nico plays with his fingers, his darker skin weaving with my lighter. The glow of the moon blinks off the gold embroidery of my gown, the watch on my wrist, and probably from the diamond earrings hanging from my ears. His suit, which is slightly threadbare at the hems from years of use, swallows the light instead.

His eyes, dark though they are, still shine brighter than any diamond.

"I'm not a nice man," Nico states plainly. "Why would I be a nice father?"

"Nico—" I try again.

"No," he says. "Look."

He flexes his right hand. There's a bruise already spreading across his knuckles and a cut on the middle one. And on top of that, the evidence of other tiny nicks, calluses, and other marks of heavy labor are evident. It's the hand of a warrior, in more ways than one.

"Do you see that?" he asks quietly. "Baby, that's the hand of someone who is violent, just like your dad says. I just hit my future father-in-law in the face, Layla. In front of a whole crowd of people. What if—what if I did that to our kid?" His eyes finally meet mine, and his lower lip trembles. "I don't think I could live with myself if I ever did that. But what if that's all I know? What if, I don't know…what if I'm like your dad? Or Gabe's dad? What if I get mad at it or something and I just…snap?"

He clenches his fist suddenly, then drops it to the sand. His eyes squeeze shut, as if he's in pain, and my heart squeezes right along with them. I hate that he sees himself like this. Doubts himself so much. And I hate that my family made him do it again.

"Can I ask you something?" I venture.

He looks up. "What's that, sweetie?"

I tip my head. "Have you ever hurt someone for any other reason than protecting someone else?"

Nico rubs his neck and sighs. "When I was in high school, right after I got out of juvie…there was this kid, Jaden. He was…well, let's just say he was partly responsible for me being in the joint in the first place. What they locked me up for—he was the one who did it."

I nod, somewhat familiar with the story. We had only known each other a short time when he revealed his past—the fact that he had been sent to a detention facility for almost two years for a violent crime that would always blemish his public record. It isn't fair really, holding someone hostage for the rest of their life for something they did when they were only fifteen. And while he certainly had a dark side, Nico wasn't even the one who had actually beaten the bodega owner with a crowbar while he and two other kids had robbed it. He was just the one holding the weapon when the police arrived on the scene.

"Anyway, Jaden was always a bully, and he was even worse when I got out. I remember seeing him steal this kid's hat in school, this kid who couldn't do anything, couldn't stop him. Later that day, Flaco, K.C., and I saw him walking down the street. And I don't know…I just flipped."

Nico looks up, his brow furrowed with the memory. He folds his hands into casual fists, and the movement causes the muscles in his forearms to ripple.

"What kind of man does that?" he wonders. "I beat the shit out of a kid for stealing some guy's hat. I lost it, Layla, plain and simple. And two months later, I did the same thing to David, Gabe's dad. Told him to stay away from my family, or I'd kill him." He turns to me with a steely glare. "And I meant it, too."

I take a second to digest the story. But one thing is clear.

"So the answer is no. It doesn't sound like you've ever been violent just to be violent. You just…Nico, you protect. That's what you do."

"Baby, the way I felt back then…it's nothing to what I feel for you. For…her. Him. Whoever that is inside you." He swallows, and the movement makes a muscle in his jaw flutter. "I would do *anything* to keep the two of you safe. It scares me. That day with Giancarlo…Layla, I would have killed him if you hadn't called me back, I know I would have. What if my anger goes the wrong way? What if…what if I hurt our kid?"

Relief and sorrow flood through me. Because if that's all this is, just a fear that he won't be a good father because he never had one himself, then I have nothing to worry about at all. If anyone in the world could be a good parent, it's Nico. I have no doubt about that. I just wish he could see it too.

"Don't you know?" I ask him as I gently stroke his cheek.

His eyes close with my touch. "Know what, sweetie?"

"You said…" I pause, trying as hard to swallow the warbling in my voice as to put the right words together. "You said that no one was easier to love than me? Well, no one loves like you. Nico, it's what you do. It's who you are. You are the most giving, thoughtful, loyal, big-hearted person I have ever met. No one could have rescued me, rescued your family, the way you did, and I'm talking about in here"—I tap my chest lightly—"and out there. Nico, there is no doubt in my mind you would be an incredible father to our baby. You might be scared, but honestly? I'm not."

He's quiet for a minute or two as my words sink in. Slowly, his breathing grows more regular, and his chest doesn't rise and fall quite as intensely. He turns his head.

"We're going to have a baby?" he asks again, like he's not sure this is really happening. But this time, his voice is full of awe. Wonder. Joy.

I nod, and bite my lip, unable to stop smiling.

"And you still want to marry me?"

I fling my arms around his neck, and we topple backward into the sand. Nico barks a laugh as his arms come around me.

"A million times over," I whisper as I burrow into his neck. "I'd marry you every single day if I could. And I can't *wait* to start our family. Together."

We lie there for a moment, oblivious to the fact that we're getting sand all over our nice clothes, in our hair, and everywhere else. Above us, the stars are slightly blocked out by the lights of the city, just like they are in New York. But farther out, over the dark ocean, they twinkle clearly, harbingers of some brighter, unknown future.

"A baby," Nico murmurs, over and over to himself. He pulls me into his chest. "You and me. That's all we really need, huh?"

I tip my head for a kiss, and he delivers, his mouth warm and inviting, his tongue gentle and sweet.

"It's all we need," I agree. "But we have so much more."

His chest rumbles with agreement as he kisses me again. "I love you. So fuckin' much."

I smile against his lips. "*Te amo tambien.* I'm going to have to learn Spanish better now. I want our baby to be fluent. Like you."

My poor Spanish earns me another ear-splitting grin and an even deeper kiss. When he's done, Nico sits us back up and brushes sand out of my hair and off my dress.

"Portuguese too," he says with a lopsided smile. "Come on. We better go face the music with your family. And then…I think it's time to go home."

CHAPTER THIRTY-THREE

Layla

It's close to midnight when we creep back into my dad's apartment. He and Nico had brought all of our things from Bibi's house before coming to the party. All we have to do is pack up, and we can leave in the morning.

"There's got to be some way to get on an earlier flight," Nico says as the elevator doors open onto the living room. "If your dad doesn't want us here, do you think your aunt would let us sleep at her apartment? Or maybe there's a hotel near the airport or something."

Our tickets aren't scheduled for another day, but he's right. It's time to go home.

But I don't reply, caught instead by the sight of my father sitting in one of his lounge chairs in the living room, a crystal glass half full of brown liquid—probably more whiskey—in his hands.

He looks up at our entrance, and his eyes are bloodshot, with a big bruise blooming across his left cheek where Nico punched him. He glances between us, landing where our hands are joined. He opens his mouth, then sighs and takes another large gulp of his drink.

"We just came to get our things," Nico says stiffly, keeping me close to his side. "We'll stay at a hotel. It's fine."

But it's not fine. Nico wants to protect me, but this is my father. He's in pain, and I hate the fact that I caused it, even if his anger hurts me too.

"Dad?" I whisper. I release Nico's hand and walk toward my father, then squat down next to his chair so we are eye level. "Daddy?"

When he looks at me, his eyes are full of hurt and sorrow. "*Meu docinha*," he murmurs, with a gaze that's softer than anything I've seen from him in years. "*Linda.*"

I don't respond, just hold still as he reaches out slowly to brush a few stray hairs out of my face. His hand lingers on my cheek, a tender touch I haven't gotten from my father for longer than I can remember. A tear trickles down my face, followed by another as one falls down his as well.

My father. Crying.

"You're not mine anymore, are you?" he asks sadly. "Not my daughter anymore."

More tears fall, but I don't deny his words. Because it's true. Although I'm his daughter, through and through, I don't belong to him anymore. Not since he left my mother and effectively left me too. Really, not since I left him and moved to New York.

"What happened?" he asks hoarsely.

I brush a few more tears away. "What do you mean?"

"He said he found you in an apartment…beaten, he said." Dad sits up and swipes the damp tracks off his cheeks. "What happened to you?"

"Dad…" I twist some of the fabric in my dress. This isn't a story I can tell easily, even to a therapist.

"Tell me." It's not a request.

Nico takes a step forward, and my dad looks up wearily.

"I deserve to know," he says, his voice creaking slightly, "what happened to my daughter. At least give me that."

I open my mouth to tell him he doesn't deserve anything. That he left Mom and me last year to fend for ourselves. That he called maybe three times for an entire year, and basically abdicated any rights he had as a father. That it's because of that hurt, that neglect, that I chased people and places all last year to ignore the pain and loneliness I was feeling inside.

But instead I move to the couch that faces the chair. Nico automatically comes to sit next to me, wrapping a protective arm around me that clearly announces his role as my protector all over again. Dad glares at the hand clasping my shoulder, but says nothing.

"It was last year. Just after you went back to Brazil," I begin. "I met a man—"

I'm interrupted almost immediately by Nico muttering, "Please. Ain't no *man* that I saw."

I elbow him in the side, and he casts me a lopsided smile before tugging me closer.

"Sorry," he says. "It's the truth, though."

I roll my eyes and turn back to my dad, who tips back more of his drink.

"Was he American?" Dad asks.

I shake my head. "No. He was from Buenos Aires. He was studying business at CUNY and lived close to where Nico used to, up by Harlem. He…"

I drift off. I don't want to go through the details anymore. I've spent most of the last year combing through them, recovering from the trauma of that short relationship. What it did to my body. My heart. My mind. It's only been in the last few months that I've really started to feel like myself.

But my father needs to know. He needs to know because he's partly responsible.

"He was a lot like you, actually," I say.

Dad's head whips up and he winces, like it gives him a headache. His eye is already turning black. "What do you mean, he was like me?"

I gulp, and Nico squeezes my shoulder encouragingly.

"Proud. South American. He came from a strict, wealthy family, and he was very, uh, bossy. Hard to please. He was…familiar to me. I didn't understand that at the time, but I do now."

I look directly at my father, forcing myself not to look away as he studies me and ingests my description. But it's true. Giancarlo was, in many ways, a placeholder for the other authoritarian in my life. The order and control he exerted over me, the manipulations, echoed the normality of my father's control, and so, in a fucked-up way, made me feel loved. In my confused heart, one that was already in pieces after Nico had left, after my father had left, that attention made sense. And for a while, it felt better than nothing.

Until it felt so much worse.

"And so what happened?" my father inquires. "How did you end up…" He trails off, unable to complete the sentence before he has to take another drink.

I exhale heavily. "He was…not good to me," I say quietly.

Beside me, Nico tenses.

"What do you mean, 'not good'? Layla, be more specific."

"I mean like that!" I blurt out. "He would yell at me, just like you do. Demean me. Talk down to me, all the time. He'd make me second-guess myself and all the important relationships in my life. I never felt so alone until I was with him, and at the end, when I fought him about it, he took it out on me physically!"

My voice is shaking at this point, as if I never knew how much I really did blame my father for all of this. Would I have been attracted to someone like Giancarlo if I hadn't learned this kind of thing at home? I'll never know. But maybe not. Maybe…

"He hit me here." I point to my cheek, while tears start to roll down it all over again. "And here." To my eyebrow. "And cut himself too, and bled all over me. And tried to force himself on me. He would have succeeded too if N-Nico hadn't shown up when he did."

By the time I finish, my voice is almost a whisper, and the tears are flowing freely. Nico's arm drops to my waist so he can hug me as close as possible. He presses a long, lingering kiss to my forehead, like he's trying to absorb the memories and take them away.

He doesn't have to say those three words he does when I'm scared, but I feel them anyway. *I got you.* And he does, he always does.

Dad, however, has no idea. He flashes an angry look at Nico. "And where were *you* this whole time?" he demands. "You say you love my daughter. You want to protect her. Why did you only come at the end?"

"You are *not* trying to blame this on him, Dad," I put in.

Nico inhales, but keeps his arm tightly wrapped around me. "I was in Los Angeles, trying to make an honest living. A future instead of being a nobody," he says, recalling Dad's harsh words from earlier. There's no more pretense in his voice. No more "Dr. Barros" or "sir." Things are real now, and he has nothing to lose.

"Nico saved me," I say. "Dad. Dad!"

Finally, my father turns back to me, and it's then he sees the truth in my eyes.

"I'd be dead without him," I say. "You owe him my life. *I* owe him my life."

Dad tips back the rest of his liquor, then sets the glass on the side table with an audible clink. I can't imagine what he's feeling, discovering all of this about his daughter on top of the fact that she's marrying a tatted-up bad boy from Hell's Kitchen and carrying his child.

"You know he's a criminal too?" he asks. "First day you were here, I did a background check. I knew you were no good. He beat a store clerk within an inch of his life, just like he did to me. Do you know this, Layla? Does that make him a hero too?"

Nico wilts slightly beside me—the motion is so small, that I can barely sense it. But I can. I know him too well. I slide my hand to Nico's knee and squeeze. *I love you,* I try to convey.

"Dad, I know about Nico's record. And for what it's worth, he didn't do the crime he was convicted for. Either way, it's in the past. He was just a teenager. Should we hold all of the indiscretions of your youth against you?"

"That's not the point," Dad spits. "He's not good enough for you, *linda.* You deserve the best, not a boy who, good as he might be, only wants you for your money." He glares at Nico. "How do we know he's not still wrapped up in some kind of criminal organization? You are so naive, Layla. I know how these things work. You do not."

"What the fuck…" Nico says, but before he can reply, I sit forward so I can look my father in the eye.

"You are intoxicated, which is the only reason I'm not walking out the door right now," I say clearly. "But if you want me in your life, you need to stop. Stop making up stories. Stop trash-talking the very best person in my life, a person to whom you actually owe a great debt. Just *stop.*"

Dad swallows, looking between us, taking in our connection. We are unbreakable. Internally, I beg him to know it.

"I'll cut off your tuition," he says, though his voice is already weakening. "I'll cancel my check for this semester. I won't pay for your school next year, or any year after. You want to go to this silly school so you can take care of poor people like this? I won't do it. Not if you are with him."

"Then I won't go to school next year," I say. "I'll work and pay for it myself."

"*We'll* pay for it ourselves," Nico adds beside me. He sits up a little straighter. "Layla's going to finish school, with or without you, Sergio."

At the sound of his Christian name echoing through the room, Dad winces again. But he doesn't argue with it.

"I'm not leaving New York, Dad," I say. "I'm not leaving Nico. We're a family, he and I. That's what we are now. Maybe what we've always been." I stand up, and Nico follows suit."You can be a part of it or not," I tell my father. "I hope you will. But if you're going to be in it, you can't boss me around anymore. And you need to treat my fiancé, your grandchild's father, with respect. Otherwise…that's it. We'll live our lives, and you can live yours."

I exhale the breath I didn't know I'd been holding at the end of all of it. It's the hardest thing I've ever done, putting my foot down with my father. All my life I've been his little girl. Someone he coddled early, but disciplined more and more, trying to make into something he could never be: someone he was satisfied with. But all it taught me was that I was never enough. It made me scared. It kept me from understanding what love was.

Until I met Nico.

Like a magnet, Nico moves close, wrapping both of his strong arms around my waist as he pulls me against his front. It's a move that's typically affectionate for him, but given the context, in front of my father, marks me as his as much as I've named him mine. In this room, we are a unit, more so than I have ever been with my parents.

Nico flattens his palms over my middle, over the child that's still barely more than an idea yet. But it's there, nonetheless. And now it's all that matters.

My father sighs. He's a man beaten, withered. And for the first time in my life, he looks old. He gazes at us for a long time, tapping his lips like he's wishing for a cigarette or something to take off the edge. Then he sighs, long and low, and says something that genuinely shocks me.

"Thank you," he says formally. He stands up, and to my surprise, extends a hand to Nico. "For my daughter's life."

Nico stares for a minute, then unwraps his right hand from my waist and accepts the handshake.

"Right," he murmurs. "You're, ah, welcome."

"I'll never be happy about this marriage, you know," Dad says. "She's too good for you."

I cringe, but Nico just tucks both arms back around me.

"She is," he agrees. "But that never stopped me from loving her. It's happening whether you like it or not, Sergio. We're a family now, like she says. That's all there is to it."

Dad's weary eyes drop to my stomach. They float over me, over Nico, as if for the first time registering us together. Whole.

"Yes," he says. "*Deos me ajude*...I know."

And with a squeeze of my shoulder, he turns and trudges down the hall, a man defeated, but I hope, a man who is also learning to accept what he can't change.

Nico and I watch until Dad disappears into the darkness. My chest feels hollow, but I'm also strangely calm. I may never fully have peace with my father. You can't undo twenty-some years of anger, control, and abandonment in a few minutes. But the catharsis feels good. Right. And maybe we can both move forward.

"Let's get some sleep, baby," says Nico, rubbing my shoulder sympathetically. But before I can ask whether or not he thinks we should keep sleeping separately or risk my dad's continued wrath by sleeping in the same room, his phone rings.

It rings. At one o'clock in the morning. And the number is from New York. Where they're only an hour behind. Everyone we know understands we're in Brazil right now, where cell phone roaming charges are ridiculously high.

"What the fuck..." Nico murmurs as he flips it open. "Maggie. What's going on?"

I watch as he collapses back onto the couch and thrusts a hand through his hair. His sister's voice is as loud and insistent as ever; though I can't understand her, I hear her urgency. Her fear.

"Fuck," Nico keeps whispering as she talks. "Okay, calm down. Mags, I said *calm the fuck down*. Listen, I'll be back as soon as I can, okay? First flight out tomorrow. *Gata*, don't worry. It's gonna be fine."

She says a few more things, and I fall next to Nico. He clutches my hand while he listens.

"Tomorrow," Nico reassures her. "Okay. Yeah, call Ileana. I don't care if it's late. Blow her shit up until she answers. We'll figure this out. Okay, bye."

"What's going on?" I ask as soon as he closes his phone.

When he turns to me, most of the color in his beautiful tan face is gone. The fierce light, the sparkle in his eyes is gone, replaced by utter hopelessness.

"They got her," he whispers. "My mom. Immigration arrested her tonight. She's... they got her."

And that's all my strong man can say as his greatest fear comes true: Carmen, his mother, who was brought illegally to Puerto Rico and then to the United States when she was just a small girl, has finally been discovered after more than thirty years of living in the shadows of New York.

Without thinking and while my father watches, utterly confused, I pull my phone out of my clutch and start dialing automatically. Nico's face is blank. There's not much I can do, but one plan of action lies before me. My father is probably passed out by now, and unlikely to help at any rate. But there's one other person who understands what Nico has done for me. Maybe, just maybe she'll help.

"Mom?" I ask when I hear her familiar voice. "It's Layla. I'm still in Brazil. But, Mom…I need your help. Nico needs our help."

CHAPTER THIRTY-FOUR

Nico

"I don't want you to go. It should be me."

"Shhhh. We've been over this." Layla looks up from checking her passports and tickets and strokes my face. "This is the quickest option if you don't want to be tied up in court for months or even years."

I have to hand it to my girl. While I sat there in a daze, getting sand all over her dad's fancy white couch, she was on the phone with her mom for at least two hours, giving her the details on the situation and figuring out a solution. It was clear at first that Cheryl didn't want to help. She wanted to wait until the morning and talk to Ileana. But in the end, I wonder if Layla didn't call her mother first just to get her dad to spring into action. Because as soon as the dude realized Layla was on the phone with his wife, he shot out of his bedroom, not giving a shit that it was almost three in the morning at that point. He snatched the phone from Layla and took over the situation immediately, and we just sat back while the two of them argued about who was going to help us the most.

Which is how we found ourselves here at the airport the next morning, me holding one ticket back to the States, and Layla clutching another for Santiago.

I hate this. I fuckin' hate this, and so does Sergio. But, as Ileana confirmed when we talked to her this morning, it was probably the easiest way. Layla has dual citizenship, so she doesn't need a special permit to fly to Cuba from Brazil. So the plan is for her to do just that: fly to Santiago, get a copy of my mother's birth certificate, then go to Montreal and on to New York. Sergio helpfully upgraded her flights to first class all the way and shoved a credit card into her hand, along with a massive pile of Cuban pesos that he got from the bank on the way here.

"Fifty if they hassle you," he reminds her as her flight to Rio echoes over the airport loudspeaker. I smirk. For all his polish, Sergio Barros is clearly a man familiar with the art of bribery. "One hundred to speak to a supervisor. Say it with authority. You're *my* daughter, Layla. Don't forget this."

Layla blinks up at him. "I won't, Dad. I promise."

"You don't have to do this," I tell her again. "I'll do it. I'll sneak in through Venezuela or somewhere like that. Some place where they won't stop Americans."

Layla places her hand on my arm. "Stop. I'll be fine. I'm not violating any laws here, and I'll meet you in New York in a few days, okay? I promise."

I sigh. This is so damn wrong. Here I am, sending my brand-new fiancée and my unborn baby on a plane to a country where U.S. citizens aren't supposed to go. And to top it all off, Layla doesn't even really speak the language. They're going to take one look at her big blue eyes and trusting face and eat her alive. *Fuck.*

It goes against everything I know to be right. And yet…it's the only thing to do.

"*Nico*," she says again, pulling me out of my misery. "Take care of your mother. I'll be there in a few days."

The loudspeaker calls the number and the boarding information of her flight one last time. Layla presses a final kiss to my lips, and I pull her closer, taking a little more. I'd rather walk through fire than put her in danger. But this is how it has to be.

"Three days," I murmur against her lips. "If you're not back in three days, I'm coming after you myself." My hand drifts up her side to where, underneath her thin t-shirt, the words "*saudade para tí* " are etched over her ribs—just like the Portuguese equivalent is on mine. Fuck. I miss her already, and she's not even gone.

She bites my lower lip softly. "Promise. I love you."

"You have no idea."

And then, because I can't not do it, I pick her clear up off the floor and kiss her again, the kind of kiss that I shouldn't do in front of her father or any polite company. Fear. Love. Lust. Worry. I kiss her until we're both breathless, ignoring the whistles flying around the terminal, the glares from her dad, the fact that the flight attendants are making the last boarding call right now.

And when I finally put her down, those big blue eyes see straight through me. They always have. She clasps my face and presses one last kiss on my lips.

"I know," she murmurs. "I know."

And with a touch of her forehead to mine, she turns and leaves.

"Baby!" I call out when she's halfway out the door, about to follow the last of the passengers toward the small plane waiting on the runway.

She turns and looks at me.

"Be good!" I call out.

As the words register, Layla grins—that bright smile that shot an arrow through me the first time we met. And for the first time all day, I think that maybe things might really turn out all right. Because who could resist a smile like that?

And then it's just her dad and me, standing side by side as Layla's plane taxis around the runway and eventually takes off with the woman we both love. When it finally disappears, Sergio turns to me, his face sagging with guilt. I get it. Layla isn't someone who is ever easy to say goodbye to. And as much of an asshole as he is, I also know that deep down, Sergio loves his daughter.

"Your flight," he says. "It leaves…"

"In an hour," I tell him.

His relief is obvious. He's glad he won't have to share his apartment with me for another night, and he won't have to keep me company much longer either. Well, I feel about the same. The guy is a dick. He's a sorry dick right about now. He realizes, on some level, that he pretty much lost his daughter, and to the kind of guy he never wanted her to be with in the first place. Well, fuckin' tough. I'm done being made to feel like I'm not good enough for her.

I wasn't able to fly with Layla to Rio. The quickest way back to New York that I could still afford was routed through São Paulo—though how going an hour and a half in the wrong fuckin' direction is quicker, I'll never know. But it is what it is.

Sergio turns, and to my surprise, holds out his hand. I pause for a second, then take it. He squeezes it tight, more tightly than I would have thought someone with such slim hands could. Skilled hands. A surgeon's hands.

"Thank you," he says again. "For what you did for her."

I don't say anything, just nod. I wonder if he remembers thanking me for the same thing the night before, or if he was too drunk. But I don't say anything, because what else is there to say? He still has a nasty purple bruise on his face from where I hit him, and my right knuckles have a nice scab building from where they split on his cheekbone. And the thing is, I'm still not sorry.

"Will we see you at the wedding?" I ask.

He blinks, like he's forgotten all about that. Then he closes his eyes, almost as if he's in pain, and rubs his forehead. Whiskey makes for a hell of a hangover.

"Yes," he says in the end. "Of course. Yes, I will be there."

"Good," I say. I couldn't care less if he came, but I know Layla will. It's important to have your dad there when you get married. I get that.

He nods, then turns to go.

"Take care, Dr. Barros," I call after him, sending a quick wave. I figure I can give him that. He's not Dr. Barros in my head anymore, but I can pay him the small respect he asked for in the beginning. It's the least I can do for taking away his daughter.

He pauses, frowns a little, then surprises me.

"Sergio," he replies. "My name is Sergio."

And then he's gone.

———

FROM THERE, I take three of the longest fuckin' flights of my life. The hour and a half to São Paulo feels like four, and the eight and a half to Miami feel like twenty. By the time I stumble off the last three-hour flight into the arrivals gate at JFK, I've been traveling for close to twenty-four hours. Twenty-four hours, and I have no fuckin' clue what happened to Layla after she left. There isn't much in the way of cell phone service in Cuba, and what little they have sure as shit doesn't service American cell phones.

For now, there's nothing on my voicemail. Not a hey, I'm good. Don't fuckin' worry. Nothing.

I dial Maggie's number as soon as I'm off the plane, but it goes straight to voicemail. Next up is Gabe, who picks up right away.

"*Coño!*" he shouts so loud I have to hold the phone away from my ear. "There you fuckin' are. We've been waiting for hours for you to land."

I yank my duffel and garment bag over my shoulder as I truck out to the curbside, looking for the shuttles into town. It's more expensive, but there's no way I'm taking the train back into the city. I need to be able to communicate with everyone and get up to speed.

"My flight was delayed in Miami," I tell him. "But I'm here now. What's good?"

Gabe gives me the low-down on Ma's situation. "She's being held in a detainment facility upstate," he says. "In Albany."

"Albany? Are you fuckin' kidding me? With all the illegals in New York, immigration doesn't have a holding center in the city?"

I hand a porter the fare and let him take my bags, then board a bus headed for Manhattan.

Gabe's laughing in my ear. "Real estate, *mano*," he says. "That's what Ileana said. Too expensive."

I'm glad he's laughing because I'm fuckin' not. Not while my mother is locked in a fuckin' detainment center hours away, ironically close to the other facility where I wasted two years of my life. I shiver. I remember what it was like to be carted away in some shitty van. I'd never left the city before. And suddenly I was in the middle of nowhere, staring at vacant lots of snow, tiny towns full of trailers and bare-branched trees. It was the perfect place to send criminals. A place where they could abandon you. Forget you.

I imagine my mother, who hasn't left New York since she first arrived in the mid sixties, when she was maybe ten, at most. She's a woman who barely speaks English, who's lived her life behind the thick curtain of the Puerto Rican community in New York for fear of exactly what is happening to her right now. I imagine what she must be feeling, and *fuck*, it makes me want to hit something. Because for the first time, I can't get to her. I can't protect her.

I never should have gone to Brazil.

"It's going to be okay," Gabe's saying, breaking me out of my thoughts. "Ileana's up there now. She says the deportation officer set a bond, and—"

"A bond?" I ask. "They can do that? I thought if you were caught, that was it."

"*Claro*, they can," Gabe replies. "And they do. Her hearing is set three weeks from now downtown. She has to appear before a judge, I guess, just like any other charge."

"So they had to cart her all the way up to Albany just to assign her a court date back in New York? That makes no fuckin' sense." I shake my head.

Gabe chuckles again. "That's the government, right? That's why they shipped you upstate too instead of Spofford, am I right?"

I snort. A few more people get onto the bus, and eventually the porter swings on and shuts the door behind him, calling out the stops in Manhattan coming up.

"So where are you?" I ask as the van starts moving. "Give me the address, and I'll meet you there. We can go get Ma together."

Gabe just laughs, and in the background, I swear I can hear the sound of my sisters cackling.

"I don't think that's going to happen, bro," he says plainly. "We're on a bus to Albany. Me, Maggie, Selena, and even Allie."

"What?!" I practically explode out of my seat.

"Shhh. You're going to wake up Allie, man. She's asleep. It's just a little road trip," Gabe says, way the fuck more playfully than he should, considering. "Go home. Get some sleep. We'll be back tonight, and Ma will be with us. Don't worry, *mano*. We got this."

———

IT'S ALMOST dark by the time I finally get back to the apartment on Chrystie Street. My mind is still working a million miles a minute, but all of the thoughts are sloshing together, lost in a haze of jet lag and worry. Gabe and my sisters will stay the night in Albany. There's no way they'll be able to get up there soon enough to get Ma out tonight. Which means I'm stuck here like a buster, playing the waiting game for everyone else to fix shit.

Not a role I'm used to.

I trudge up the five flights of stairs and unlock the door, breathing in the familiar scents as I do. They're stale, since the apartment has been shut up for a week, but still there: leftover coffee, a little bit of Lysol, linens and towels, and the vanilla-scented candles Layla likes. It's barely been a week, but I'm glad to be back. I don't know why it surprises me still that this place feels so much like home. But not now, I realize. Not without her in it.

"There you are."

"*Jesusfuckin'Christ!*" I practically jump out of my skin at the sound of a low, female voice coming from the couch on the far side of the living room.

The voice laughs lightly as I turn around, and then Cheryl Barros stands up and smooths out the front of her pants.

"What the…"

I stare, dumbfounded, until she's standing in front of me: Layla's mother.

"You look tired," she says. "It's a terrible flight, isn't it? I always hated going there, just for that reason alone. Did you go to the farm too?"

Wordlessly, I shake my head. What the fuck is happening?

Cheryl shrugs. "You didn't miss much. It's awful. Two hours of winding roads up a river, and the place is absolutely swarming with mosquitos. Layla liked it when we visited, of course, but I could never sleep well in a house without screens on the windows."

My mouth works, but still, no words come out. I don't even know what she's doing here. How she got in here. But…*of course.*

This apartment is in Cheryl's name. It's her lease. Of course she has a key. Of course she can get in. Of fucking course.

"I came to help," she says. "But also because my husband had some very interesting things to tell me after the two of you caught your flights." She walks around the couch, takes a seat at the dining table, drums her fingernails on the lacquered wood, and looks expectantly at me.

"I think," she says, "you'd better come sit down. And tell me exactly where my daughter and grandchild are at the moment. And how it is you came to have a key to her apartment in the first place."

CHAPTER THIRTY-FIVE

Layla

THE CITY HALL BUILDING IS OLD, WHITE, AND THE STUCCO GLEAMS UNDER THE BRIGHT Caribbean sun. Unlike many of the buildings I passed while riding in the back of the 1950s taxi here, it's relatively well maintained, with its Spanish-style architecture that lords over the palm tree-laden square. It's not the picture that we're often painted of Cuba in the U.S.—a dilapidated country full of old cars and inadequate systems. There is certainly some of that; I've seen more vintage cars here than I ever thought existed in the world. But this building stands tall and bright. There's nothing dilapidated about it. If anything, it's pretty intimidating.

Not for the first time, I shake my head, wishing Nico were here. It feels wrong, somehow, that I'm seeing the country where his mother was born before him. Of course, I'm barely seeing it, I'm so tired. It took me three flights to get here. Vitória to Rio to Santo Domingo to, finally, Santiago at about 10 a.m. I left my bag at the small *casa*, one of the common local accommodations that are kind of like bed and breakfasts run out of people's houses, where the Brazilian travel agent booked me. Then I went straight to the registry after receiving directions from the house owner. I've been traveling for almost twenty-four hours straight, and I'm exhausted. But my flight to Montreal is tomorrow, and then it's home. I just need this piece of paper. And the office here in Santiago, where Nico's mother was born, is open.

It takes a while to find the correct room inside the city hall, while I skirt past several men and two women in green uniforms, all with guns holstered to their waists. It's not uncommon to see a military presence in Brazil, and there were some in the airport in Santo Domingo too. But here in Cuba, the military seems stronger, or at least more ubiquitous. I was warned before coming not to take pictures of them or talk to anyone about politics. The last thing I want is to be accused of spying or insurgency.

I know I've got the right door when I walk into a room containing a single clerk at a desk in front of a back room filled with filing cabinets. Filing cabinets mean one thing: records. It reminds me of one of the NYU libraries—austere, poorly lit, and badly ventilated. A few people are slumped in the chairs scattered around the perimeter of the waiting room; others lean against the wall, while others are just sitting on the floor, looking half-asleep. I take my place at the end of the line and wait. And wait. And...wait.

When it's finally my turn, the clerk is abrupt.

"How can I help you?" she asks in Spanish that is so clipped around the consonants, I can barely understand her. But her meaning is clear enough.

"*Necesito un certificato del navidad,*" I state in my awkward Spanish. I'm not as bad as I was a year ago, but I know my pronunciation is poor. "*Para mi madre.*"

The clerk frowns. I'm guessing she gets this request a lot. I've already been informed by multiple people at the *casa* that getting records here is difficult, particularly since technically people are not allowed to take them out of the country. The process, therefore, usually requires extra money to grease the wheels. Luckily, I have a stack of that.

I take out a set of bills in the approved Cuban tourist currency, and lay them on the counter for her.

"For the fee," I say, though she hasn't mentioned anything of the sort.

The clerk examines the stack, like she's trying to evaluate what I'm doing. Everything about her expression is suspicious, and again, I'm desperately wishing that Nico were here with me. He knows how to read people so much better than me. He'd take one look at this woman, wink and make some crazy joke in Spanish that would put her at ease, and ten minutes later he'd probably have flirted ten birth certificates out of her instead of just the one I need.

The clerk reaches out slowly and taps a finger on the bills. Then she pushes it back to me and whips out a faded form before rattling something in Spanish that I'm guessing means roughly "fill this out, you idiot American."

I take the paper and pen and tuck the bills back in my bag. I'll try again in a minute. This has to work. It has to.

An hour later, I wait through the line again to hand her the paper. Again, I set the stack of bills on the counter while she goes over the paper. But this time, her response is almost immediate. She stamps a clear red mark across the top of the paper: *Negado.* Denied.

"What? No! Please, I've come all this way!" I pull out another wad of cash from my purse and slap it on the counter. What else can I do? "Please! *Por favor.* I'll pay extra, I will. *Pagaré...mucho,*" I translate poorly, lacking the vocabulary I need to make my point.

But she knows what I mean. She just doesn't want to do it. For whatever reason, the clerk shakes her head and starts waving the money away, almost like she doesn't want to look at it.

"*Por favor,*" I try again, this time more calmly. "It's not for me. It's for my fiancé's mother—*la madre de mi novio.* She needs the certificate so she can live legally in New York. She's been there since she was a girl, and now she's in custody with immigration. If I don't bring back the document tomorrow, they'll deport her. Please!"

The woman looks me over, her sharp eye slanted with doubt. "She is in America?" she asks in clear, obvious English.

I swallow with relief, and a little bit of irritation. She let me go through all of that terrible Spanish when she speaks perfectly good English? "Yes. Yes, she is. Please, she's been there for more than thirty years."

Again, her sharp gaze drops down over me, lingering on the watch that encircles my wrist, then travels back up to look me in the eye. "Then maybe it's time for her to come home."

My entire being droops as I turn from the desk. I failed. I have six people waiting for me to return to New York with the document that will keep their family intact, and I have no idea what to do next. This was the end of the line, and there are no other choices, other than Carmen begging clemency from the court system. The money I have didn't work. What the hell am I going to do?

"Layla."

I look up, and to my surprise, find my father standing in the doorway of the office. His face is covered with a sheen of sweat, like he ran all the way here from Brazil, but otherwise, he is dressed the same as always, in a button-up shirt and slacks. Relief slides over his face when I turn around.

"Dad?" I wonder. "What-what are you doing here?"

He shrugs. "I took the next plane after you. Your mother wouldn't have it any other way, and she was correct. You left. The boy left. And I…" Before I can say anything, he goes on. "I wondered what in the hell I was doing, allowing my daughter to travel to a strange country like this by herself. Not when I could come and help her."

I stare at him for a moment, and then, by instinct, fall against his chest to give him a hug. He's still at first, then wraps his arms around me and strokes my hair, the same way he did when I was a child. I have to focus on breathing not to cry into his shirt. The people in the office are all watching us curiously, and I don't think crying in the middle of the vital records office is going to help anything.

I'm so angry at him. I was ready to leave Brazil and never come back. I was ready to leave my father, cut him out of my life since all he wanted to do was control it.

And yet…now that he's here, I've never been happier to see him in my life.

"Please," I say, handing him the paper. "Help."

He examines the denied application, then faces the clerk, who is watching him curiously out of the corner of her eye. I sometimes forget that for an older man, my dad is still quite handsome. That women notice him.

I roll my eyes. It cannot possibly be as easy as that.

And then I watch as he strides up to the counter like he owns it, cutting in front of the three other people waiting, and starts speaking in Spanish—a language I didn't even know he spoke!

No. They're not going to let him get away with this. I can't hear what he's saying, but I watch the clerk as she listens, watch the people behind him standing with their arms crossed, watch my father smile and laugh and gesture at me and the paper like he's sitting across from the woman at an adorable bistro table instead of a dank government office.

At one point, the woman laughs. My father reaches out a long finger and strokes her chin. The woman blushes, and I'm sickened slightly by the sight of my father being more affectionate with a stranger than he's ever been with me or my mother in my life. A smile brightens his stern face, and for a moment, he looks pleasant. Kind. Handsome.

I can't hear what they're saying, but the woman twists and turns from side to side, playing with her curly hair like a schoolgirl flirting with her crush. She keeps shaking her head, saying no, but her smile and body language clearly say otherwise. With his other hand dropped below the counter, my father beckons to me with a flick of his fingers. It takes a second for me to understand what he wants, but as soon as it registers, I glance around, then take some of the cash out of my purse and set it in his hand.

He flips it onto the counter between him and the woman. She examines it for a moment, and my father whispers something else. I catch the word *linda* float on the air, and watch as the woman grins again and then slides the money under the counter. Then my father stands expectantly while she turns and disappears into a back room. He turns to me and winks. I'm still too shocked to reply.

A few minutes later, the woman returns holding a flimsy envelope. She clutches the birth certificate against her chest for a moment, and a flash of fear crosses her face.

"You can't take it out of the coun—" she starts, but stops talking when my dad lays another stack of bills from his pocket on the counter.

He leans back across the counter, and slowly traces a finger up her forearm. Even from my place on the opposite wall, I can see her shiver with desire.

"*Creo que está perdido, no?*" he asks with a sly smile.

The clerk bites her lip, then after looking around to see that no one else is watching, pulls the money across the counter and below with the rest. "*Sí,*" she says. "I think it *was* lost."

Dad plucks the birth certificate out of her hand and gives it to me. I promptly tuck it into a folder in my purse, treating it like the gold it is: Carmen's salvation.

"*Gracias, linda,*" Dad says to the clerk, who proceeds to blush all over the place. But to me, he resumes his stern mask. "Let's go."

———

AN HOUR LATER, I find myself sitting in a wicker chair in a square a few blocks away from the *casa* where now both my dad and I will be staying the night before the flight we are apparently both taking to Montreal in the morning. He's taking no chances, or so he said, of making sure his daughter gets home safe. I sort of wonder if it's because he wants to speak his mind one last time to Nico, but for whatever reason, he's insisted on coming with me, seeing my apartment, inspecting the life I'm now living. I'm not sure what I think about it, but I accept. For the first time in a few years, my dad is actually showing some interest in my life again. Now it will have to be more on my terms, but I'm willing to try if he is.

Music floats down the street, the casual cadence of Cuban salsa, with drums. There is music everywhere in this city. Every time we turned a corner to get here, I would hear it, swimming through doorways and out of open widows. It's not quite the same type you would hear in the Bronx, but the rhythms are similar and remind me of the parties at Alba's apartment. I wish I were there now.

The waitress drops a glass of rum for my dad and a coffee for me on the table before she winks at him. I roll my eyes. The attention he gets from women here really is ridiculous.

We sit for a minute, and I watch as my dad pulls out a pack of cigarettes and lights one.

"I can't believe you smoke now," I say, watching the habit that's been so strange to me since arriving in Brazil.

He looks up, curious. "You are? Everyone smokes in Brazil. Here too."

"Yeah, but you're a doctor. You know exactly what that's doing to your body."

He takes another drag, then examines the cigarette carefully, like he's never really considered what it does to him.

"I do," he admits. "But...do you know, I do not think I care so much. Everyone is going to die in the end."

We lapse into silence again as we drink and my dad smokes, and I do my best to ignore his newfound nihilism.

"We could have been like this," he says in a low voice, gesturing around the square.

There's another cluster of military personnel in one corner, loitering in their green uniforms and berets, and a group of students in the other. It's not a bad scene. People are laughing, cars are driving by. But it is strangely...quiet...for such a public place. Not silent. But you'd expect it to be a little louder.

"Who?" I ask. "The U.S., you mean?"

He darts a warning look at me that clearly says I need to be quiet.

"No," he says quickly. "Brazil."

I blink, unsure of what he means. In my classes, we learned about some of the destabilizing events of the sixties and seventies in South America, including the military coup in Brazil that was sponsored by the United States. But it's a history that was always a little unclear. The coup ended the rise of socialism in Brazil, I thought. But then it became a military state for the next twenty.

"When I was starting university," my father continues as he sips on his rum, "that was when Jango was overthrown."

I nod, somewhat familiar with the events from my classes. João Goulart, also known as Jango, was the president during the early sixties, one whose proposal to nationalize a variety of social services earned him the ire of right-wing nationalists and the military.

"My professor last year thought that was a reflexive maneuver," I said. "He thought it was more because the U.S. saw it as another situation like, well...here."

I was hesitant to say Cuba out loud. Talking politics was frowned upon.

Dad shrugged. "It was. I remember being very angry about it at the time, actually. My father, he supported it. But, like so many young people, I was very interested in what was happening here in Cuba and in Colombia. I liked the idea of people receiving free healthcare. Better social services." He looks at me pointedly. "When I first became a doctor, I wanted to help, you know. I wanted to do more than clean up scar tissue or help women, ah, enhance themselves."

I smirk. I can practically hear Nico on my shoulder, urging me to say "tits" again in front of my dad.

"So you wish that the coup hadn't happened?" I wondered. "Do you wish that Jango had stayed in power?"

Dad looks around, like he's evaluating the state of the country. I've read plenty about Cuba, what information is available to Americans. My professor, clearly a leftist thinker, was always careful to temper the critiques of Fidel Castro with other facts: like that Cuba has some of the best public health records and highest literacy rates in the world. Its economic conditions, he argued, were due to the embargoes by the U.S., not because of the way that Castro and the communists actually ran the country. I didn't know. It was hard to say one way or another. A country where people had to watch what they said for fear of being accused of being a government usurper also seems oppressive.

Dad just shrugs again and finishes his rum. "Fifty years is a long time for one man to be in power," is all he says, and I know he's referring to Fidel. Then he turns to me. "I was angry, yes. But then we watched what happened in Argentina. In Chile. We watched as people disappeared, again and again. And I looked at my government, at the men who guarded every building with their guns, and the people who were scared to talk out loud...just like here. And I decided I would leave before maybe they wouldn't let me."

It turned out to be unnecessary. Because, as I knew, Brazil held elections again in 1985, two years after I was born. But by that point, my father was well into establishing a practice in Seattle. He had married my mother, gotten his citizenship, started a life in America. A life that gave us all so much, but isolated him even more despite the freedoms he sought.

It was a strange paradox. And one that explains his tight-fisted grip on our lives. He sought stability. He sought reassurance. He sought the knowledge that his family would never have to struggle the way he did.

"Why did you come here?" I ask finally. "Besides to keep me safe, I mean. You didn't have to help with the records. You don't like Nico at all. And you don't even know his mother."

Dad's dark eyes soften. "You speak as if keeping you safe isn't the most important thing. I am your father, Layla. That is all that matters to me."

I don't say anything. My other questions still stand.

Dad clears his throat. "I know what it's like to grow up in a country toyed with like a figure in a game," he says. "I don't know this Carmen, but why should she have to come to a country she's never known? A country her father left for the same reason I did—because in the end, it was being enchained by a country that claims to be the land of the free?" He shrugs and takes a long pull of his cigarette. "Free for itself, maybe. But at the expense of everyone else."

I frown. "Do you really think it's as simple as that?"

He shakes his head. Of course it's not. But as he stubs out his cigarette and stands up, resignation falls over his stern face. It's strange. This is the most honest conversation I've ever had with my father. It's the first time he's admitted that maybe his decisions in the past were less than perfect. That things didn't always turn out the way he planned.

"I don't know this woman, this Carmen," he repeats. "But everyone deserves to be free."

CHAPTER THIRTY-SIX

Nico

YOU KNOW THAT SAYING, "LIKE SITTING DUCKS?" IT'S A DUMB SAYING. I'VE BARELY EVER seen ducks sitting. They're usually paddling or waddling around Central Park. Sometimes they quack at you because you had the balls to interfere with their fishing or whatever. Maybe they fly south for the winter, or just across the pond. But they don't really sit, and if they do, it's in some bushes or someplace like that where people won't be able to get them. They don't just sit there, waiting around like idiots for the firing squad.

But right now, that's what I feel like, sitting with my family in a row that feels strangely like a church pew, while we wait for my mother's case to be called into the small courtroom. The room is packed, full of other people also waiting for their fates to be sealed by the few judges who sit on the city's immigration court.

It's two o'clock. Layla's flight was supposed to arrive early this morning from Montreal, but I haven't heard from her in more than four days. Her phone must be dead. The calls have been going straight to voicemail since we left.

I rub my chest, the spot where her name is tattooed over my compass. I miss her like crazy, but it's really the not knowing what's about to happen that's the worst part of all. Is she okay? Is my mom going to be okay? The only thing I had to do the last few days was work, pulling a forty-eight-hour shift at the firehouse. I have twelve hours off, but then I'm right back on at midnight for another three days. I should be tired—well, I *am*—but I wouldn't have been able to sleep anyway.

"Somebody tell me again how the fuck this happened?" I whisper to Gabe.

That earns me a sharp look from Ma, who's sitting quietly with the lawyer that Cheryl hired to represent her. I have to hand it to Cheryl. For someone who's basically just been a housewife for the last twenty years, she knows how to come in and put shit together. And damn, it really is a whole different story when you have money for someone to go to bat for you. Christina, the lawyer, got the court date moved up several weeks to today.

She rolled her eyes a little at the plan to get the birth certificate, which made me want to punch through a wall all over again. Ma was probably eligible for relief, she said. The bigger issue would be that she had worked under the table for so many years and hadn't paid taxes. Still, documentation wouldn't do anything but help, and if my mother can prove she's a Cuban citizen, she's covered under the Cuban Adjustment Act to apply for permanent residency.

But, of course, that means my girl needs to get here fast. Because if this hearing starts and we don't have documentation…that means more court dates. More lawyers we can't afford. More possibilities that in the end, my mother might still be forced to leave.

Fuck. I can't think about that right now.

"Relax," Gabe says. "Christina said even if they start deportation proceedings, it takes months, maybe even years. And unlike Ileana, she actually thinks she has a good shot at getting relief because she's been here for so long."

"No," I say. "I mean, how did we end up here? I want to know how *exactly* immigration ended up tagging Ma."

It's a story I've asked for over and over, and no one seems to be able to give me a good answer. Maggie was at home with Allie. Selena was at work. Gabe was in class. We know that at some point after attending a Wednesday Mass by herself, which she doesn't normally do, Ma was cornered and arrested in the space of five minutes on her walk back to Alba's apartment. And from there, a message was left on Gabe's cell phone before she was taken to Albany.

When she came back with Gabe and my sisters, she didn't want to talk about it. Shut herself up in her room at Alba's for over an hour before she would come out.

She's ashamed. After being careful for so many years, she's ashamed that she was caught. That she's putting us all through this. But most of all, more than I've ever seen her, my mother's scared.

I glance down the row, to where she's sitting in her Sunday best, flanked on one side by Maggie and by the lawyer on the other. On the other side of the lawyer sits Cheryl, blonde and stiff while she looks over the room. She looks taller than everyone else, but it's only because she sits up straight, whereas most of the people in here are slumped. Fear does things to your posture, I guess.

Cheryl and I still haven't quite figured each other out. Layla's mom is a lot like her—soft spoken and a good listener, and the kind of person who looks you right in the eye. She wasn't surprised, for instance, when I told her about the engagement or about the fact that Layla is pregnant, since Dr. Barros called her that night. She was, however, pretty damn surprised to find out that I had been Layla's new roommate for almost four months.

"If it wasn't a problem, why do you think she hasn't told me?" she kept asking as she walked around the apartment that, slowly, Layla and I made our own.

I hopped up on the counter after getting myself a big glass of water and watched her pace, trying to see what she sees. It wasn't the empty place she left Layla with in August. We'd hung pictures. Bought a few more pieces of old furniture. We had mail on the counter and food in the cupboards. Coats hanging from hooks I installed after Christmas, and a bunch of framed photos of the two of us placed on bookshelves and a few windowsills. We made it a home. Our home.

Cheryl picked up one of the pictures—one of me and Layla at another of Alba's parties, just before Christmas. Layla loves my family's parties. In the weeks before, I taught her some more salsa moves so we could rip it up a little. I didn't even care that my sisters teased me like crazy because I fell in love with a girl who likes Marc Anthony now as much as they do. I just really, really liked the way Layla sways her hips.

I looked around the apartment, suddenly aching for my girl. It wasn't right, being there without her.

"So my twenty-one-year-old daughter is suddenly pregnant and engaged. And now Bibi tells me she's in Cuba," *Cheryl said.* "Alone."

She looked up, and her blue eyes pierced, just like her daughter's. It was unnerving, if you want to know the truth.

I hung my head. Hating myself for letting her go to Cuba without me. Hating that I didn't know where she was. If she was safe. Convinced I really was the worst person in the world.

"Which is why," *Cheryl continued,* "I told Sergio to do the right thing and follow her."

I practically fell off the counter when she said that. I smacked my hand on my forehead, causing my baseball cap to fall into the sink. "What? Is he there now? Can we call them?"

Cheryl sighed. "I've been trying. But the last time I tried to call him, he was already gone. He should be in Santiago by now."

I slid off the counter. "Jesus. I mean, geez." *It's not like Cheryl hadn't heard me swear or anything, but I figured I shouldn't test my luck.*

She tapped her fingernails on the table and slid her lower lip around her teeth. It was another habit she gave her daughter, and it was unnerving as fuck to watch another woman do it.

"Yes. Well. Apparently he does love his daughter after all." *Cheryl turned that deceptively deep stare of hers on me again.* "And now I think you had better tell me exactly what my daughter is marrying into that requires her to fly on your behalf to a country where Americans are not supposed to go."

I told her everything and then some. After all, she was right. Layla and I were family, even if we weren't married yet. There was a piece of me growing inside her, so no matter what, her family and mine were linked forever now.

To her credit, Cheryl didn't say anything while I told her my mother's story, much more than Layla gave up when they spoke. She just took a calm seat at our scratched dining table and listened, occasionally cocking her head a little when I came to an exciting part.

And at the end, she asked only a few questions. Who was Ileana? Where exactly were we getting our information from? And when exactly was the court date? Once she had that information, she picked up her phone and proceeded to hire our family a real lawyer. The other stuff —the baby, the engagement, the fact that I'd been living with her daughter in sin—would have to wait for later.

———

FINALLY, I can't take the waiting any more. Gabe watches curiously when I get up and start pacing around the room. I can't sit still. I feel like a trapped animal.

"Nico!" Maggie hisses at me. "You look like a psycho. Stop!"

"I can't help it." I really can't. I don't know if I've ever been this worried in my life.

Christina looks over with an understanding smile. "You know, we probably have about an hour or more."

At the end of the row, Cheryl catches my eye, and a slim, blonde brow rises. Cheryl seems to read me well for someone who barely knows me. Too well. Maybe it's in the genes.

"Go take a walk," she tells me, in words that barely float down the row to where I'm about ready to combust. She holds up her cell phone. "Stay in the building. I'll call."

I hesitate, glancing at Ma. With her hands clasped in her lap, avoiding Cheryl's gaze, all of our gazes, she watches me with tired eyes. She's scared too, a lot more than me, and suddenly I feel bad for going as crazy as I am. But I also see plainly that I'm not helping shit treading holes through the cheap carpet. A walk would be good —for me and for her.

"Okay," I say. "I'll be back in fifteen minutes."

"Take thirty," says Christina.

"Take an hour," mutters Maggie, causing Gabe and Selena to laugh. Even Cheryl quirks a smile.

I decide instead to jog up and down one of the big concrete stairwells on either end of the building. I zigzag up, then back down, doing it again until I land on the second floor and start walking, not really knowing where I'm going.

I need her here. Layla always knows how to cool me down, how to find my center. But what if something happened to her? What if she's lost somewhere in Cuba, with no money, no phone, no way to get back? What if she's hurt? What if someone hurt her?

The nervous energy doubles and triples over again. Fuck. Maybe walking wasn't the way to go.

I stop in front of an office, but it takes me a second before I can actually read the words written on the glass door: "Marriage Licenses."

I stare at them for a long, long time. I don't know how long it takes to get a marriage license in New York. Maybe they'll make us wait months. Years. Maybe they'll want her to have enough time to think it over, decide it's a terrible mistake to marry a bad idea like me.

Except I'm not. For once, it's not Layla's voice saying that—it's mine. It's the one thing I've come to understand since I met her. To Layla, I'm somebody, and the longer I've known her the more I've realized that I'm somebody to other people too. She did that. She does that every day. And now I'm actually starting to believe it.

I push open the door.

There are four other couples in the waiting room for the judge, three of them dressed in their little white dresses and rented tuxedos. They look gooey and in love. It just makes me miss my girl even more.

"Can I help you?"

I turn to the desk, where a clerk is looking at me impatiently over a pair of aviator glasses straight out of the seventies. I approach the desk nervously.

"I, um. I'd like to apply for a marriage license."

The clerk looks around. "Who you gonna marry, honey? Yourself?"

I swallow. I don't know what the fuck I'm doing here, but now that the words are out of my mouth, I know what I want.

"No," I say. "I have a fiancée, thanks. I just wanted to get the forms, so we could, you know, do this?" I chew on my lower lip for a second. "*Can* we do this today?"

The clerk tips her head and gives me a smile, the kind you'd give a little kid pretending to be a policeman. "You have to wait twenty-four hours after you're granted a license," she tells me. "Your fiancée. Is she here, honey?"

I shake my head, pulling on my hat. "No. But she will be. Could we…could we just get it started?"

The clerk gives me a look like she feels sorry for me, then reaches out and taps my hand. "Sorry, hon. The law says both parties must be present to apply for a license. No exceptions. When she gets here, come back. In the meantime, take the application and fill it out so everything is ready to go." She looks me up and down, takes in my uniform, the jacket with the FDNY patch, the letters embroidered on my hat. "Tell her to hurry too, honey. Because if she doesn't want to marry you, I just might take her place."

I gotta give it to her, the lady can make me grin. I tip my hat, and take the application to a table to fill out, while the giggly couples get called back, one at a time. I smile at them as they go, thinking to myself that maybe, just maybe, that might be me in twenty-four hours. If Layla wants a big wedding, wants to spend every penny we have on dresses and cakes and flowers and food, we'll do it. Because I don't want to wait. I want Layla Barros to be my wife as soon as fuckin' possible.

If she can just get here.

As I finish the last line of information that I can, my phone buzzes in my pocket.

Cheryl: It's time.

"Thanks," I tell the clerk as I take off at a jog. "I'll be back." And she smiles, like she knows I will.

———

I ENTER the formal courtroom just as my mother is sitting down at the table in front of the judge on the other side of the barrier. The lawyer sits next to her, while a government attorney sits on her other side. The lawyer already explained to us how today would go. The judge would confirm the claims of the state and confirm that they were there in response to the charges. Ma would have to sit in a witness stand, like it's a trial, and from there she would be questioned by both attorneys. The judge would then decide whether there needs to be another hearing, or if the case could be dismissed.

I slide into another pew (I can't think of them as anything else) next to Gabe, then turn around to greet the other members of my family who have arrived: Alba, K.C., Flaco, and a few other extended aunties and uncles who showed up to support my mother. This isn't anything compared to everyone in New York City who considers Carmen Soltero family. If this were the final hearing, I know that half of Hell's Kitchen would be here to speak on her behalf. She doesn't just have a village—she's got a city of millions. The knowledge gives me faith that everything is going to be all right.

In a bored voice, the judge announces herself to the court, then, just as Christina said, confirms the case and then has Ma swear in. The representative from ICE stands and drones a quick statement about Carmen Soltero entering the country illegally and requesting deportment proceedings to begin. With every word, my mom shrinks into her seat. And at the end, she's practically a child again, that little girl who first came off a plane in the sixties, following a family who had adopted her because she didn't have any of her own.

"Counselor?" The judge turns to Christina, who stands.

Christina proceeds to inform the judge that under the terms of the Cuban Adjustment Act, my mother has every right to be in the United States. "As a national of Cuba and having resided in the United States for a duration longer than two years, she is legally entitled to permanent residency status under the terms of the Cuban Adjustment Act," she states.

The judge takes a deep breath, and with a raised brow, turns to Ma. "Ms. Soltero, would you like to say anything?"

Shakily, Ma nods. Next to me, Maggie starts chanting the Hail Mary under her breath, and down the row, I catch Alba crossing herself. Ma's English still isn't great, but we've all been practicing with her for months now—even Layla.

"I come to New York when I am ten," she states in a clear, shaky voice. "With a family from San Juan de Puerto Rico." She turns and smiles at Alba, who waves. "That is Alba Ortiz, my sister from this family. Her parents are not alive anymore, but she come with me in the plane."

The judge looks between them. "But you were born in Cuba?"

Ma nods. "Yes. I was born in Santiago de Cuba. My mother, she died when I was a baby. When I was two, almost three, my father had saved enough for us to take a boat. This was after Fidel came into power."

The whole room is silent as she tells this story, to the point where every shake of her voice vibrates through the air.

"I don't remember the boat except for the last part. I remember the ocean. The waves, they were very big. The boat, it went up and down, side and side." She mimics the motions with her hands. "It make me sick. My father, he put me under the boat, in a tiny room. Then he go away. Maybe to help. I don't know. But I lose him in that storm. And when we come to Puerto Rico, I was alone."

She blinks several times, and I can tell she's trying not to cry. I've maybe seen my mother cry twice in my life. Once when I was sent away. Once when I came back. But now the judge is asking my mother to remember things she keeps buried. Stories she never wants to tell.

"Alba's family...I don't know how I come to them. I remember I was scared. And a woman bringing me to their house in San Juan." She clears her throat. "They took me in. Make me part of their family. And when they come to New York, I come with them."

"Without identification," the judge murmurs more to herself than anyone else. "And I don't suppose you had a birth certificate on you at two or three years old." She looks up. "How do you actually know you're from Cuba to begin with? You were so young. A lot of people come by boat to Puerto Rico. You could be Dominican or from somewhere else."

"My father told the men of the boat," Ma says. "They tell *Señor* Ortiz. He tell me."

She shrugs, but my eyes are on the judge. I wonder how anyone could hear this story and deny her is beyond me. But thousands of people have similar stories. How many people come here looking for a better life, trying to escape countries ripped up by wars and poverty, so much of it caused by this country and others like it? I've known plenty. New York is full of them.

"I come to New York without a family," Ma says, her voice a little stronger now. "And so I make my own. There they are. All my children. My granddaughter."

She turns around and points to us: me, Maggie, Selena, Gabe. Even Allie on Maggie's lap. Maggie grips my hand hard enough that I'm going to bruise, and Selena is practically plastered to Gabe.

"Please," Ma says. "Don't break up my family. In Cuba, I have nothing. Everything I have is here."

The judge looks over all of us, her eyes plainly sympathetic.

"I'm sorry," she says. "But, Ms. Soltero, unless you can provide documentation of the fact that you are a Cuban national, I cannot grant relief based on this evidence. Therefore, we will schedule another hearing to give you enough time to procure documentation—a birth certificate, for instance."

"But she has one!"

The judge looks up, both curious and annoyed. A murmur rises in the court, everyone wondering who would have the balls to interrupt a federal judge. But I know who it is. The second I hear her voice, a wave of relief washes over me. She's all right. She's here.

I twist around, and there's Layla, striding down the aisle with Sergio following behind her as she whips a yellowed piece of paper out of her backpack. She stretches across the barrier to hand the paper to the lawyer. With a brief clasp of my mother's wrist, Layla backs away until I can grab her hand and pull her onto the bench next to me.

"Hey," she greets me with a short, thorough kiss. The circles under her blue eyes are darker than normal. She's tired, and not just because of traveling for three days straight, I realize with guilt. Traveling for three days straight can't be good for the baby.

I pull her tight, nosing her and placing a hand on her stomach. "Hey, *mami*. You okay?"

Blue eyes shining, she nods. "I got it," she whispers fiercely as I wrap an arm around her shoulders, eager to feel her body, know she's safe. Know she's real.

"Shall we continue?" asks the judge in an irritated voice.

Christina looks up from the document. "Your Honor, permission to approach the bench?"

The judge nods, and Christina and the government attorney walk up to the judge. We strain to hear them, but none of their conversation is clear from our perspective. All that's left to do is wait.

After a few minutes, both lawyers return to their tables, while the judge continues examining the birth certificate.

"All right," says the judge. "In light of the evidence at hand, I believe we have a different outcome. I hereby cancel removal proceedings for Carmen Soltero and order the immediate processing of her application for permanent residency under the Cuban Adjustment Act."

With a bang of a gavel, she closes the session, and the bailiff stands up to call the next case. In the meantime, my mother gathers her birth certificate and returns to the gallery, where she's immediately embraced by all of her children. Layla lets me go long enough to sweep my mother up in a bear hug. She's crying. We're all crying. Every single one of us a big teary mess as we shuttle out of the room so we stop interrupting the court.

Once all ten of us are in the hall, my mother locates Layla and pulls her close. Layla's crying too, her big blue eyes glossy with relief and happiness. My girl is part of this family too. She knows it. Everyone knows it.

"Thank you," my mother says, again and again as she strokes her hair softly, the same way she used to do to all of her kids when we were small. "My other daughter, you know that? I am so, so happy you come into my boy's life."

"Me too," Layla whispers as she returns the embrace. "Me too."

When at last she's released, I pull her close and kiss her the way I wanted the second I knew she was there.

"I'm glad I came into your life too," Layla says as I practically squeeze the life out of her.

I nuzzle her, touching our noses and close my eyes. My heart might truly explode. I never knew this kind of happiness, this kind of peace, was possible, and it's all because of this girl.

"Me too, baby," I whisper, squeezing my eyes shut as the tears keep coming. "Me too."

CHAPTER THIRTY-SEVEN

Layla

If there is one thing Nico's family knows how to do quickly, it's throw a party. Literally as soon as we're outside city hall, Alba, Flaco, K.C., Carmen, and *all* of the Soltero kids practically explode right there on the sidewalk, cheering and jumping on each other like it's the Fourth of July.

"You fuckin' did it!" Nico cries as he lifts me into the air, then pulls me back down to kiss me again, longer this time.

I'm immediately grabbed and hugged and kissed by everyone, their joyful tears rubbing on my cheeks as they pass me around.

"It wasn't me," I'm finally able to get out with K.C.'s arm slung around my shoulder. He grew up with Nico. To him, Carmen is like a second mother.

"What's that, NYU?" he asks me, rubbing my head like a kid.

"Easy," Nico warns playfully, but he still pulls me back to that familiar place under his arm. I can feel his concern in the clutch of his hands. He's still checking to make sure I'm here for real. My man was scared while I was gone.

I turn to where my parents are standing awkwardly together on the sidewalk. They're both smiling a little, bemused by the Solteros' open displays of affections, but basically statues compared to the boisterous display of joy going on. They take in the movement of this family, and my mother in particular studies Nico's mother and sisters. Why, I'm not so sure.

"It was my dad," I say, and when I say it, Dad meets my gaze.

His dark eyes are as tired as mine, and he looks much different from his usual polished self. His clothes, after wearing them for two days straight, are as rumpled as my pants and jacket—his usual white button-down creased into oblivion, his gray slacks wrinkled terribly. He clutches his thin blazer around his body, a poor ward against the mid-February wind.

"What do you mean?" Nico asks, his brow furrowed in confusion. He pulls his hat backward so he can see me clearly, and for a moment, I'm taken aback by the beauty of his face, even in its confusion. The curl of his lashes, the almond-shaped eyes. The carved cheekbones and full lips. It's not a face I'll ever tire of.

I clear my throat. Okay, pregnancy is seriously doing things to my libido. I've barely slept in two days, we've just accomplished a major victory in his mother's life, and all I can think about is getting this man into bed. Where are my priorities?

"Well, I tried," I say. "But the clerk really didn't want to give me the birth certificate. She said no, rejected the money I brought. I was freaking out, and then…my dad showed up."

I look at Dad, who actually looks somewhat bashful. It's a weird look for him. His olive skin is slightly flushed, and for the first time, he can't totally make eye contact with me. It's…sweet.

"She didn't like me," I tell Nico. "But she liked my dad."

Everyone else listens to the story as I relay the rest as best I can, considering I didn't completely understand the entire exchange. But in the end, the meaning is clear, and everyone, even my mom, is gazing at my dad with gratitude.

"You did good, Serge," Mom murmurs, earning a soft look from my dad. Huh.

Nico steps forward, and his family quiets a little, despite the hum of the city moving around us. Nico extends his hand—the same hand that gave my dad the bruise over his cheek.

"Thank you," he says solemnly. "I mean it. Me, my family. We're in your debt, Sergio."

They shake hands for what seems like an eternity, and it really does seem like something passes between them. Something big.

Carmen pushes her way through her kids to stand in front of my father.

"*Dios le bendiga*," she says. God bless you. "Dr. Barros. Thank you."

Dad blinks, a sheen clear over his deep-set eyes. He shakes his head—something about the blessing got to him, but I'm not sure what it is. She beckons him down, and to my surprise, he obeys, allowing her to kiss him on both cheeks on a busy street in the middle of New York.

"'*Brigado*," he murmurs, seemingly unaware that he's lapsed into Portuguese instead of Spanish.

"Time to celebrate!" calls out Alba. "My house, now! Food, everything. It will be perfect. K.C., you go pick up some pizzas, okay?"

K.C. shrugs, like he's not a semi-famous DJ at this point, just a kid who takes orders from his mother. "Sure, Ma. Whatever you say."

"Come on. Sergio and Cheryl, you too!" Alba calls. And before my parents can answer, she gets into a cab with K.C., followed soon after by the rest of us.

———

"So, *habla español*, huh?" Nico asks my dad as they both sprinkle their slices with extra hot chili flakes.

Mom watches as Nico folds his massive slice in half lengthwise so he can hold it without it flopping over, then gingerly does the same with what's probably the first piece of pizza she's had in ten years.

Dad quirks a sardonic smile and gives a brief nod. "Some, yes. I learned in Argentina when I was a boy. Not so bad for a *culo*, eh?"

Nico raises a brow, though he has to suppress a smile. "Good to know. Now if the baby's first language is Spanish, you'll be able to speak to it."

Dad looks less than pleased by the idea, but he says nothing. Mom just takes another tiny bite of her pizza and pretends not to have heard anything.

Nico looks at me. "What do you think, baby? Should we try to speak Spanish at home?"

I shrug. "I mean, sure. I bet just having Carmen as its grandma guarantees the baby will be fluent, don't you think?"

"Baby?" Carmen's voice cuts through the clamor around Alba's big table. "*Quién va tener un bebé, papito?*"

Nico pauses mid-bite, his face slightly reddened. I immediately flush everywhere. *Oh.* Of course. In the craze of everything, no one knows our big news.

He swallows heavily, then sets his slice down on his paper plate. "Ah, well, *Mami*…"

He reaches out an errant hand, and immediately I take it in my lap and squeeze.

"We found out in Brazil that…well, Layla's pregnant. And while we were there, well, I asked her to marry me, and"—he grins—"she said yes."

"What?" Selena cries out.

"That's amazing!" Maggie shouts, just as Gabe reaches around me to slap Nico's shoulder.

Immediately, almost everyone in Nico's family is on their feet, and we are too, accepting another round of kisses and congratulations and hugs like crazy from everyone in the room. Allie immediately jumps up and demands to be the flower girl, while Alba starts talking about dates with Carmen. I grin at Nico over K.C.'s shoulder. His eyes shine with happiness.

"Was it a shotgun proposal, Dr. Barros?" K.C. jokes.

Everyone turns to my dad, who still hasn't gotten up. My mom sits next to him, blank-faced, though clearly she already knew. There is no surprise on her face. My heart falls. *No, Dad, I will him. I know what's coming.*

"No, asshole," Nico shoots back at K.C. "I asked her before I knew, if you really have to know." He turns to me and presses a sweet kiss on my lips. "So we're getting married. Soon, I hope."

There's a loud clearing of a throat. I shut my eyes. *Shit.*

"No, you're not."

Just like that, all of the joy in the room vanishes as everyone turns once again to my father. Dad pushes a hand through his hair, then crosses his arms over his chest. His pizza sits on his plate, growing cold. I doubt it's going to get eaten now.

"I am sorry," he says slowly, looking at me, not everyone else. "I didn't want to do this now. Not with the celebration and everything. But you're too young, Layla. He is…even with the baby, he is…this boy is not a good fit for you. He will not be able to give you the same life you have. The life you know. You are too…different."

He gestures toward Nico, like there is something there that I should see in him that's self-evident. Whether it's the tattoo on his arm or the darker color of his skin, the fact that he has a delinquent record or that he grew up in relative poverty…it's all just surface. None of it matters.

His arm still around my shoulders, Nico shrinks. His eyelashes sweep across his cheeks as he looks down.

No. Absolutely not. I am *not* having that.

I turn to my dad, ready to tell him to get the hell out, but Nico's family beats me to it.

"Are you *kidding* me?"

"Who the fuck do you think you are, man?"

"*Coño*, who the fuck *is* this dude, huh?"

Nico's family and friends all speak at once, practically jumping over themselves to shout at my dad. Maggie looks like she's about ten seconds from taking off her earrings, and even Carmen looks like she wants to take a swing at my dad for insulting her son.

But it's the last voice that surprises me the most.

"Sergio, that's absolutely ridiculous."

My mother's voice drops through the cacophony and cuts them all off at the knees. In utter shock, Dad turns to his wife—if you can even call her that, since they've lived apart for close to two years now. But if I'm not mistaken, looking at her pains him a little. I wonder if, despite everything they said, the church wasn't the only reason they didn't want to divorce.

"You don't know, Serge," Mom says, speaking directly to him in a voice that is stronger than I've ever heard her use with my dad. "We owe that boy Layla's life."

Sergio glares at Nico, but his anger fades when he turns back to Mom. "So he says. But we don't know *really* that—"

"*I* do," she corrects him. "Layla stepped off that plane utterly broken, Sergio. Her face. Her soul. She had a cut from here to here." With a delicate hand, Mom gestures across her eyebrow and up her forehead. I actually still have a delicate scar there, but the surgeon Mom took me to see did good work last spring. You can barely tell anything is there.

Nico buries his nose in my hair, but I can feel him vibrating next to me.

"A man did that to our little girl, Serge," Mom continues, like there isn't an audience of nine staring at her. "And would have done worse, I'm *sure* of it, if this boy hadn't stepped in! And she would be an absolutely shell of herself if he hadn't been there for her every day since." Her voice is shaking now, and then she turns to Nico. "I never thanked you properly," she tells him. "But I'm doing it now."

"Cheryl, let's talk about this another time."

"We'll talk about it *now*," Mom bites out. "Before you insult Layla's new family even more."

Dad bites his lip, but has the courtesy to look contrite.

"What I know is this," Mom says. "This boy is the kind of *man* who would step in and do what needed to be done…when we were too wrapped up in ourselves to see what was going on." She pauses and darts a glance at Nico again. "We are very lucky, I think, to have someone like this, like *all* of the Soltero family, love our daughter. I don't think we could ask for more."

I swallow a sob, and behind her, I see both of Nico's sisters swiping at their eyes. It means a lot to this family to have the oldest of the kids, their caretaker—the one other people always seemed to see the worst in, but in whom they see and have the best—validated like this. Nico clenches my hand like he'll never let it go. He's watching my mom now too, and to my surprise, his eyes are also glossed over. This means more to him than he'd ever want to admit.

Mom clears her throat. "And if you don't think so, well, I'll just have to make sure they don't *need* your approval to live. You're not the only one who can pay tuition, Sergio."

I turn to Nico, willing him to look at me, to see the belief in us that I have in my eyes. There is *nothing* I know better than the fact that we are supposed to be together. I would go to hell and back for this man. I would give up everything I know to follow him anywhere. He just needs to see it.

"Where's the license?" I ask quietly.

His black brows quirk, and the side of his mouth twitches. Damn. I *really* want to kiss him—actually, I want to do a lot more than that. Freaking pregnancy hormones! Focus, Layla!

Nico pulls out the piece of paper we got at the clerk's office today, when everyone thought we were going to the restroom after leaving the courthouse. We weren't.

———

*"*LET'S DO IT NOW,*" he whispered in between kisses as his black eyes shined with happiness. "I don't want to wait. Today's a day for new beginnings, baby. I want ours to start right now."*

I grinned and pressed my nose to his. "Show me the way."

———

THE MEMORY still fresh in my mind, I unfold the paper and hand it to my dad.

"Tomorrow," I say, then turn to everyone else, speaking loudly, though my voice shakes. "We're getting married tomorrow. We decided to elope, and we're getting married at city hall in exactly twenty-two hours and forty minutes. Dad, I really want you there. I understand if you can't. It's a lot to take. But this baby deserves to have its family intact when it comes into the world. So now…it's your choice. Support us. Don't support us. But this is my family too now. And if you can't treat them with the respect they deserve, then maybe you shouldn't be here at all."

Dad looks at me for a long time, then glances between the two of us. Eventually the energy in the room subsides, but no one moves from the table. Finally, Dad stands with a screech of the chair leg on the floor and comes to stand in front of me.

"Come," he says, draping an around over my shoulder and pulling me close.

Nico releases my hand, and I stand up to lean into my father's embrace. His familiar scent—Hugo Boss cologne, scotch, and a hint of cigarette smoke—overwhelms me. My eyes well up. When I look up, my father's eyes are closed.

"This is what you want?" he asks. "This life? It won't be what you grew up with, Layla. Not like the one I made for you."

I shake my head. Like that matters. Like any of that ever mattered at all. "I don't need you to make a life for me, Dad. I want to make it for myself."

He gazes down at me for a long time with a look I barely remember: one of pride.

"With him?" he asks.

"He's the best man I've ever met," I whisper fiercely. I don't have to say the rest of what I mean. It lingers anyway: *even better than you.*

Dad winces, but holds me that much tighter. "I guess…" He sighs. "Tomorrow, then. But you're not getting married at city hall, *linda*. Do it right. We'll find a church, okay?"

"*Sí, sí!*" Carmen cuts in on top of my dad. I hear, rather than see her smack Nico on the shoulder. "You were not getting married in a church?" she demands in Spanish. "I raised you better than that!"

I'm released, and when I turn around, Nico is grinning while he fights off his mother's light smacks on his shoulder. He gives me a lopsided smile, as if to say, "What did you expect?" When we had planned to run off and get married, we hadn't counted on having our two very religious parents fighting our every step.

"Well, we do already have the license," he says to me.

I shrug. I don't really care where we get married—just that we do.

Nico turns to his mother and my dad, who have unwittingly bonded over the one thing the both of them care about most: being good Catholics.

"You find us a church by tomorrow," he tells them, "and we'll show up. Otherwise, it's city hall. Because I'm not waiting more than a few days, and neither is she."

CHAPTER THIRTY-EIGHT

Nico

I should be nervous, but I'm not. Cold feet, that's what they call it, right? Well, as I let my mom fix a new red tie around my neck, my feet are anything but cold. They're perfectly warm and ready to take off at a run the four blocks to the church where I went almost every Sunday for Mass my entire life.

I don't know how she did it, but somehow Cheryl managed to convince the priest to officiate a wedding before the six o'clock Mass, the day after Layla and I applied for a marriage license. Turns out that if Layla's dad has a way with clerks, her mom has a way with priests. And I can't tell you how fuckin' awkward it was hearing about Cheryl charming the pants off Father Boylan. Layla said the man actually blushed.

Layla and Cheryl stayed at our apartment the last few nights while her dad got a hotel close by, and I went back to work another seventy-two-hour shift that ended this morning. So I haven't seen Layla in three days, and when I do see her again, I'm going to marry her.

Cold feet? Try blazing hot.

"Ma, it's *fine*," I tell her, batting her hands away.

I straighten the knot in front of the mirror, then spread everything down. It's the same suit I've been wearing for years, but I splurged for a new white shirt, and was surprised when Sergio presented me with a gift from him and Cheryl this afternoon—the red tie.

"*Ay, bendito,*" Ma murmurs behind me as I check over everything. "You look so handsome, *papi.*"

I turn around to face her, and I soften when she reaches up to smooth back my hair.

"*Un hombre,*" she says as her hand drifts over my chest.

I smile. It's the same thing she said to me when I got dressed for my first real job. I was eighteen and trying to knot a tie for the first time in my life. The new job as a part-time doorman was a step up then, at a time when I wondered if I'd ever be able to get a real job. But slowly, I came to realize that my past didn't have to define me. That it doesn't have to define any of us.

I look over my mother's shoulder to where my sister plays dominoes with Allie. My niece is about to start school next year, a scholarship spot at a private school on the Upper East Side. Maggie catches me watching them and winks. They're both dressed up, Allie in her little red dress so she can be our impromptu flower girl, and Maggie in a flowery green thing that makes her look really pretty. I don't normally think of my sister that way, but she is. She's strong and solid, just like our mom, and usually doesn't have time to bother with things like getting her hair done or wearing the kinds of clothes that get her a lot of attention. But today, she really does look beautiful.

Gabe strides out of the back room, fixing his glasses and his tie, followed by Selena, who's just as gussied up as the rest of us. We're all in more than our Sunday best. But then again, this isn't any normal Sunday.

"I look like a penguin," Gabe says as he comes to stand next to me and look in the mirror. He's wearing the same as me: a black suit, white shirt, but his tie is black.

"No, you don't," I tell him. "You look like a waiter."

"*Pare,*" Ma orders us. "All of my children look beautiful today." She surveys us, real joy beaming out of her face. "Every single one." She turns to the kitchen, where Alba and K.C. are having a drink, and beckons Alba to take our picture.

"Ma!" Selena protests. "I hate having my picture taken!"

"Sel, hush," I tell her, already moving toward the picture window that looks over New York. "Come on. I'm getting married. Pictures are a requirement."

With only a little bit of groaning, we assemble together, the four of us standing on either side of our mom. Ma comes to just above my shoulder, taller than I remember her being before. The flowers she put in her hair today tickle my nose; the smell of gardenias filters all around us. But then I realize that for the first time, my mother is standing up straight. She's not cowered down, trying to hide from the world. Instead, she stands with her head held up, her chest out, looking straight at the camera with an unabashed grin on her face. The realization makes me stand tall too—it makes all of us do it. I toss an arm around Gabe on the other side and pull my sisters close. We're all grinning already, and it's not because Alba's telling us to. Our smiles are real. Even Allie, clutched by her grandmother, can't stop giggling.

This feeling won't last. Life is like that—bad things happen. People get sick. They lose their jobs. Shit happens that make things hard, but they also make the sweet moments like this that much better. My family has dealt with the bitter for a long time. I close my eyes for a second. For just a moment, we finally get to enjoy a little bit of the sweet.

———

WE WALK the four blocks to the church, where the priest is setting up for Mass. It's the same church where I was baptized and was confirmed. The same place where my mom found solace for so many years, and the same place where we thought our family was going to be split apart.

Cheryl scurries around lighting candles in the sconces, but most of the dim light in the church actually comes from the rows of prayer candles in the apses, where people light candles for their loved ones. Their well wishes float through the air and all around us. We have thirty minutes to do this, but that's about twenty-five minutes more than I need. I just need to say the words. Tell her I love her. Say: "I do."

There are only a few people here to see us off. My family, Alba, K.C., and Flaco. Cheryl, Sergio, and Vinny, Layla's friend from school, and Shama, who actually flew back from England to be her maid of honor. All the aunties and uncles will be meeting us at Alba's for a party after, but for this, we just wanted it to stay small. Just the people who know us. Who know our story.

"You good, man?" Gabe claps me on the shoulder as I take my place in front of the altar, next to the priest. On his other side stands Shama, holding a small bouquet of tulips—Layla's favorite flower. She gives me a smile, though I notice her glancing every so often to the piano at the side of the chapel, where K.C. is tapping out a soft melody.

I smile to myself. "Yeah," I say. "I'm more than good. Let's do this."

Everyone feels the love at weddings. But not like me. Not like when my girl steps out of the atrium, flanked on either side by her parents. Sergio looks the picture of a patrician, older father, distinguished in what looks like a brand-new suit, and maybe a little sad as he walks his daughter down the aisle. Cheryl is dressed in blue, the same shade as her and Layla's eyes, and her dark-blonde hair shines like a halo. She finds me and nods, and I return the gesture.

But neither of them can hold a candle to my girl. She wears a lace dress that comes down past her knees and hugs her hips. With its delicate sleeves and modest skirt, it's not a dress that puts everything on display, and yet, it frames her curves perfectly. Her hair is down and pulled back from her face, curling around her shoulders in a way that makes me want to pull on it and stroke it all at once. She carries a bouquet of pink tulips that match the color of her lips, and even from the far side of the atrium, her blue eyes find mine and fucking sing.

The wedding is small and perfect. The priest gives a brief speech about the sanctity of marriage, reading out names off the card provided to him an hour before. Layla and I repeat after every vow he states, unblinking as we clutch each other's hands, moving our lips around the sacred words that we both mean with everything we are.

There's no doubt. No fear. Just love. Just the knowledge that everything we've been through in the last two years—no, in all of our lives—has been leading us here, to this moment, and to the future ahead of us.

"Do you take this woman?" the priest asks, but by that point, I can barely see him. All I see is her.

"I do," I whisper. "Always."

Layla's face shines.

The priest smiles, and asks for the rings—the simple gold ring I bought just last week, and another gold band that was gifted from Cheryl and Sergio this morning. Another peace offering of sorts.

We slide the rings onto each other's hands, both of us fighting tears the whole time. A cheer rises as he says those final words I've been waiting for: "You may kiss the bride."

So I do. And I swear to God, before all that is holy, I'll never, ever stop.

———

Two HOURS LATER, we're back at Alba's house. Just like at her holiday parties, all of the furniture has been cleared out, making space in the living room for all of the aunties and uncles, cousins and friends who've shown up last minute to dance and laugh and eat and wish us well. Everyone is full of *pasteles* and chicken, beer and wine, and whatever else we could rustle up around town. Cheryl bought out half the flower markets in New York. Alba's apartment looks like a florist exploded in here. K.C. set up his turntables in the corner and has been spinning a mix of Latin music that includes both samba, bossa nova, merengue, and salsa—a perfect mix of the two of us.

Even Sergio and Cheryl are having a good time. I've caught Cheryl's laugh a few times when she lets her estranged husband spin her around the floor. Layla watches them closely. I get the feeling she's never seen them let loose like this together. But I get it. The look on their faces tells me they're remembering things that happened long before she was born. They're remembering what it was like to fall in love.

Layla and I sway in the middle of the crowded dance floor, mostly too caught up in each other to follow the beats. My jacket's been long tossed aside, and she lies with her cheek on my shoulder, burrowed into me after we finally finished accepting all of the blessings from everyone here.

Suddenly, she stops moving and pulls away. She looks down, her mouth dropped in shock.

"What?" I ask. "What is it?" Shit. *Shit.* Something's wrong, I know it. We just couldn't have one fucking day to ourselves, could we?

But then Layla bites her lip, and her eyes open with a look of wonder.

"I felt it," she whispers, pulling my hand to her still-flat belly.

I know it's too early to feel kicks. Maggie didn't feel anything with Allie until she looked like she had a mini basketball sticking out of her. But Layla clearly feels something, and who am I to tell her it's anything other than indigestion?

"Like a butterfly," she tells me, keeping my hand pressed under hers. "Can you feel it?"

I shake my head and grin. "No. But I will." I can't wait.

The clear, recognizable notes of a bass line and piano sound through Alba's speakers, and like that the party really starts up. Just try to tell a room full of Puerto Ricans not to sing at the top of their lungs when this dude comes on. I dare you.

Layla tips her head, listening. "Is this Marc Anthony?"

I chuckle. "You've been hanging around Maggie too much. I'm impressed."

She taps her foot, unable to keep her hips from twisting and turning with the beat that's already started. I stare. It doesn't matter how many times I see her do that; the way Layla moves her body is fuckin' mesmerizing.

"You like it," she says. "Don't even pretend."

I laugh. "Now you *really* sound like Maggie."

But she's right. My hips are already moving, feet shuffling back and forth in the familiar rhythm. I can't help it. Salsa is infectious, and it's in my blood. And now that there is a part of me inside Layla, it's in hers too.

I grin and take both of her hands. "Come on, then," I tell her. "Let's show them some new moves."

I start twisting her around in the combinations we've practiced over the last few months, even trying a few new ones that I didn't know I had in me. Layla's laughter filters around the crowd, her happiness beaming through her entire body, just like I know it is through mine. All around us, our family and friends watch with smiles and laughter that joins ours. I know it won't always be like this. I know our life will still be hard sometimes. That we'll fight. Make mistakes. Struggle for money, jobs, places to live, maybe even more when there's a baby.

But no matter what's coming, we'll always have this. We'll always have us. And that knowledge will keep me going for the rest of my life.

"Hey," Layla says as I pull her back in. I kiss her, because I can't not, and she returns it and smiles. But it's a normal smile, because I'm always kissing her.

"What's that?" I reply when I let her go again.

"What does *'valió la pena'* mean anyway?" she asks, quoting the song lyrics.

I cock my head. "It means, 'it was worth it.'"

A slow, knowing smile spreads across Layla's face. "That sounds about right," she says. "It was *definitely* worth it."

She stumbles a little as I take her around a particularly difficult turn. She falls into my arms, and when she looks up, she's breathless.

"It's okay," I assure her as I pull her upright. "I won't let you fall. I got you, baby."

"I know," she says as she pulls me close. "I got you, too."

Layla grins, that smile that lights me up, that sets me on the right path every time. The smile that guides me home. My true north.

EPILOGUE

Nico

"WHAT DO YOU THINK, *PAPI*? RED OR PINK?"

Mattie shakes his head, making his black curls flop over his forehead.

"*Violeta*," he pronounces. "Mommy likes the purple best."

My son's Spanish is probably better than mine, courtesy of the fancy-ass preschool he's attending. Thank you, Grandma, although if my mother-in-law ever hears me use that word, Layla says I'll get a drink in my face. Of course, that only makes me want to say it more.

I look back at the rows of flowers, searching for the dusky shade of eggplant he means. It's the color I usually buy my wife, the one I've been bringing her since we first met. I would see it at sidewalk stands just like this one, and the purple, the same color as the flags hung from the downtown buildings owned by her school, would remind me of that sweet, beautiful girl I met in the middle of my delivery route. The one I should have stayed away from. The one I could never forget. The nickname is a joke now, since she graduated almost four years ago, but Layla will always be my NYU.

I turn back to Mattie, who's giving the flower selection the same critical eye. Mateo Christopher Barros Soltero, otherwise known as Mattie (because that name is way too grown up for a person who still can't tie his own shoes), is picky. Too picky for someone who barely comes past my knee.

"*Papi*, they don't have purple," I say, holding out the two bunches again. "Come on, man. We need to meet up with *Abuela* so I have time to pick up Mommy. We got an appointment, and we can't be late."

Mattie scowls at the flowers and shakes his head again. "*No.*"

I sigh. That was a Spanish *no* right there, the kind he learned from Ma and Maggie and Allie and Selena—all of the women in my family who manage to shove "what the fuck are you thinking?" and "are you fuckin' kidding?" and "try again, you idiot" into two tiny letters. This kid has two very strong personality traits: he's stubborn like his aunties, and he fuckin' adores his mother, maybe even more than me. Only the best for her, and he doesn't settle. Even at three.

I put the flowers back. "Okay, okay, fine. You choose. But for real, Mattie, you got two minutes."

Mattie strides up the sidewalk and back to reexamine the selection, his chest sticking out. He's short for his age, but a little soldier, no matter if his shoelaces are always untied or he always has a little bit of chocolate smudged on his cheek.

When he comes back, he's carrying a spray of bright blue flowers that pretty much match his eyes, the ones he inherited from his mother. Everything else on the outside is all me, from the thick black hair to the shoulders that promise to be a little too wide for his frame one day. But his eyes? His heart? That's all Layla.

"These," he says. "Because they match her school now." He frowns. "Wait, is it still her school since she finished yesterday? The funny hat means she was done, right?"

I smile. It's stuff like this that amazes me about this kid. Three years old, and he remembers that the school colors for Columbia are blue and white. I doubt I could have remembered my own name at that age.

"Close enough, man. It's still her school." I take the flowers and hold them up to the vendor. "Yo, man. How much are these?"

"For the hydrangeas? Ten dollars."

I fish a crumpled bill from my wallet and hand it to the guy before turning to Mattie. "All right, kid. Let's go. We got a train to catch."

———

WE SPEND the forty-five-minute subway and then PATH ride across the Hudson into Hoboken chatting about pretty much whatever goes through Mattie's head. Super-heroes and why does that guy have a funny ear and how his friend Henry has a superhero cape and he'd like one too and, and, and...

"Daddy?"

"*Que pa'o, papi?*"

I look down at my little man. That's really what Mattie is. Living in the city makes kids grow up faster than they should. I would know. And as much as Layla and I try to keep his innocence intact as best we can, the truth is, you see shit in this city, whether you grow up on Park Avenue or in the projects. I wish Mattie didn't know what it sounds like to have his mom catcalled or see someone with so little they have to sleep on the street. But that's New York. Highs and lows. Skyscrapers and tent cities. You can't tell a three-year-old to keep his eyes closed; just teach him how to understand it all as best you can.

But I'll give him this: you can't tell a three-year-old to be quiet either. And when Mattie sees someone doing wrong, *especially* if it's to his mom, he calls that shit out. I almost fainted when he yelled "GIVE THAT LADY BACK HER WALLET!" across a subway car two months ago, but you know what? The asshole did, and then he was tossed out of the car on the next stop. And then the entire, jam-packed subway car started clapping. For my kid.

Yeah, you could call me a proud dad.

Mattie looks up at me, twisting his lips around in thought. "Why don't you call Mommy Columbia instead of NYU, since that's her school now?"

I mimic his expression. We both do that when we're thinking—make weird shapes with our mouths. Layla laughs at it all the time, which, to be honest, only makes me do it more. I love that sound.

At first I'm not sure how to answer. I mean, I can't really tell Mattie that I call his mom NYU because it makes her turn the color of a ripe peach, the exact color of her skin after I smack her on the ass. I can't tell him that it reminds us both of when we first met, when I'd shove her up against the brick wall of her dorm and kiss her until she'd run out of breath. Or that just a name will sometimes make her do the same thing to me, even after four years of marriage.

"It bugs her," is all I tell him. "And she likes it."

Mattie frowns. He's a very literal little dude, and usually if something doesn't make sense, he'll push me until it does.

Luckily, he doesn't press it this time. A group of panhandlers starts singing at the other end of the train, their rendition of "A Hard Day's Night" a distraction from slightly naughty nicknames and even naughtier memories. The singers are pretty good. You can't be busking for money in this city and not have some talent.

When they're done, Mattie turns to me, and I already know he's going to ask for change. He's so much like his mother—he can't stand to see people hurting, people in need, without doing something to help. Unfortunately, there are a lot of people in New York who need help. My wallet doesn't have enough singles.

"Here," I say, pressing another few bills into his chubby hand.

He grins, and when one of the singers comes around with his hat, Mattie gleefully drops the dollars in it.

"Good song!" he tells the guy, and the man grins, showing a big gold tooth in the back of his mouth along with a few others that look like they need some dental work. Mattie, to his credit, just keeps smiling. It's just another way he's more like his mom than me—he sees the best in people, no matter what.

About twenty minutes later, we get off in Hoboken. At one point, I hoist Mattie up with one arm to help him avoid the rush. Some people are just dicks, through and through—they won't even slow down for a little kid.

"I'm *fine*, Dad," he says, kicking his little legs to be put down when we emerge from the station.

"I know, I know," I tell him as I set him on the sidewalk. "I just gotta look out, you know?"

He brushes out his sweatshirt, then goes about taking off his backpack and digging out his baseball hat—a little black Yankees cap, just like mine. He claps it on, looks back up at me, and grins.

"Now we're twins," he says. "See?"

I nod. I can't help but smile back when my kid looks at me that way. "Yeah, *papi*, we're twins. Come on, everybody's waiting."

We walk the few blocks to K.C.'s townhouse near the river. The girls are all almost ready for the party—there's a bunch of big blue balloons tied to the iron rail of the brownstone. When we enter the apartment upstairs, I'm hit in the face by a giant cluster of blue, white, and gold streamers and a shit ton of tinsel hanging from the doorframe.

"Ah!" I cry, spitting them out while Mattie runs into the decor.

"Be careful!" snaps Maggie as she walks out of the kitchen carrying an armful of blue and white plates.

I toss the streamers over my shoulder and stride in. My sad blue flowers look ridiculous compared to the fuckin' flower shop my sisters—and I'm guessing Cheryl, because some of these bouquets look expensive—have set up in here.

"Maggie, what the fuck—I mean, freak?" I hastily correct myself when Mattie beelines back across the room. Shit. I mean, shoot. It's a habit I still haven't been able to break since having a kid. It doesn't help that everyone in my family swears like sailors, and the guys at the firehouse are twice as bad.

"That was a curse, Daddy," he calls out with his tiny palm turned over. "A dollar for the swear jar at home. I'll put it in my pocket for later."

Maggie snorts. "Please. *Papito*, you gotta bill him more than a dollar if you want your daddy to quit using the f-word. I've been trying to get him to clean his mouth out since Allie was born."

"Please. Like you got any right to call me out. You need to take some Palmolive to your own mouth, *gata*, that's what's up." I roll my eyes, then fish out my last dollar and hand it to Mattie. "Don't tell Mommy," I tell him, and clap him on the head while he runs off to find his cousin.

"Ma's here?" I ask. "Where is she? Or Selena and Alba?"

Maggie tosses her head back toward the kitchen. "Alba and Selena are in there making the rest of the *pasteles*, and Ma went with Scott to the store to get some more fruit for the punch." She clicks her tongue. "I'm glad. They are freaking nauseating."

I snort. After Ma got her green card, the first thing she did was start taking English classes. And wouldn't you know it, she fell for her teacher, Scott. Scott is a nice dude, a retired community college instructor who teaches free ESL classes for immigrants at the library. Apparently Ma was his star student, and since then, they've been pretty much inseparable. Ma moved into his apartment in Queens last summer, and two weeks ago, the dude actually asked my permission for her hand in marriage.

"Head of household," he said, like that was supposed to make a difference.

But the thing is, it does. It matters that for once, my mother found a man who cares enough about her to care what her family thinks of him. It matters that he treats her like gold, like a whole person, not someone to clean his shit and do whatever he says. And it matters, *really* fuckin' matters, that she's happier than I've ever seen her in my life.

So of course I said yes and bought the guy a couple of beers. Now we're just waiting for the announcement.

"Seriously, though," I say as I take the plates from Maggie and bring them over to the table. She takes my flowers and examines them critically. "You don't think this is a bit much? It looks like a *quinceañera* in here. It's just her master's degree. Layla doesn't like this kind of craziness."

"Boy, please. You are not the only person in this family proud of my sister. First person in our family to go to graduate school. And now she's going to do good with it? Your fucking sad little flowers don't cut it. Everyone wanted to do this for her, and she deserves it, so let us throw her a real party."

I look around, waiting for Mattie to charge back in, but he doesn't. Of course not. I'm the only one who ever gets caught cussing.

I can't argue with my sister's words, though—that she considers my wife a sister or that her accomplishments are something to be fuckin' proud of. I can't lie. I was practically busting at the seams when I watched my girl accept her diploma yesterday. I was maybe even prouder than when she graduated from NYU, because this degree was hers in a way that first one wasn't. After Layla was accepted to Columbia, she worked her ass off and won four different scholarships to pay for school and living expenses so she could get her master's in social work instead of going to law school like her dad wanted.

Sergio never stopped bugging her about it. In fact, once he knew his daughter was pregnant, would you believe the asshole actually took a sabbatical and moved to New York for the birth? Three fuckin' months I had to put up with that dickhead poking his controlling face around my apartment, checking on my kid, giving me dirty looks every time I had to pull a two or three-day shift, criticizing every damn thing I did, from the way I put on a diaper to the way I warmed up milk. If it wasn't for how pissed he got every time I called him *Mister* Barros instead of Doctor, I don't know how I would have survived.

But I can't say I wasn't ever grateful, either. Like that time Mattie got croup, Sergio was the only one who knew how to loosen that shit in his throat to keep him from choking to death. Scared the fuck out of me, let me tell you. Or when Mattie got hand, foot, and mouth disease from his first daycare, Sergio was the one to calm us down over and assure us that Mattie wasn't dying of measles.

So, yeah. Maybe the guy's not all bad.

In another year, though, Sergio Barros won't be the only doctor in the family. Gabe has two more years at NYU medical school, and then he'll officially be Dr. Soltero, ready to start an internship in family medicine. And even though I know we'll be throwing a *hell* of a party when he does graduate, Maggie's right. Layla is the first to get some fancy initials after her name. After Soltero. It is something to celebrate.

"Hey." Maggie snaps me out of my thoughts with her fingers two inches in front of my face.

"Yo!" I cry out, batting her hand away. "Why do you *always* have to do that?"

Maggie smirks. "Because you *always* ignore me when I'm talking."

I frown. "What is it?"

"I said, don't you have an appointment you need to get to?"

I blink, then check my watch. Shit, yeah. If I'm going to have time with the graduate herself at home, I have to jam.

I grab the keys to K.C.'s Yukon off the table and start for the door. Mattie won't miss me—he's probably knee-deep in Allie's Barbie collection by now, poor kid.

"K.C. know you're taking his car?" Maggie asks as she heads back to the kitchen.

I jingle the keys. "It's all part of the plan. See you at seven."

"Don't be late!" Maggie shouts, but I'm already halfway out the door.

———

Layla

I glance at the wall clock, but it still says the same time. Still five after two. Still twenty minutes past the time my freaking husband was supposed to be here to pick me up.

I stand up from the couch and smooth out my skirt. After our appointment, Nico and I are meeting with my parents, who both came to town for my graduation last night, for a small celebration. I should probably go change my shirt, a thin cotton tank top that's more comfortable than dressy, but Nico's unreasonable enjoyment at irritating my dad seems to have rubbed off on me. He'll take one look at my outfit, a

simple red skirt and cotton tank top, and give me a lecture for lacking appropri-
ateness.

Well, whatever. Going for drinks at the Plaza isn't really my idea of celebrating,
especially these days, but it's fine. It's their comfort zone. Really, though, a master's
degree isn't *that* big of a deal. Not compared to the fact that Gabe is going to be a
freaking doctor in a few more years. It's a two-year degree that I finished with the
help of a lot of people. If anyone should be celebrated, it's them.

I glance around our small living room, checking for things out of place. This is the
first time in a long time I've actually had some time to myself without the threat of
papers to write or housework to catch up on. Since we moved here, I've been in
school, balancing the hectic life of having a husband whose job takes him away for
days at a time, living with a toddler who would just as soon knock things over as look
at them, and trying to get through the intense two-year program that would allow me
to do the kind of work I've dreamed of since that day I watched Carmen find her
freedom.

My job starts next week, but first things first. As soon as my final paper was
submitted, Mom, Carmen, and I went through every piece of junk that Nico and I had
accumulated over the past few years and tossed it, getting ready for the changes up
ahead. And today I spent the morning cleaning my house.

It's weird to call it that—*my* house. I mean, I'm still not quite twenty-six. Most
people my age spend their extra money on drinks or vacations. No one is spending
them on a new furnace or toddler clothes.

But honestly, I couldn't be happier. We're so lucky. Our little townhouse is nothing
massive, maybe a quarter of the size of the house where I grew up outside of Seattle.
But it's a lot bigger than most apartments in New York, with three full bedrooms, an
actual living room, even a washer and dryer. Is it weird that a washer and dryer
excites me now? There is a *lot* more laundry to do with two boys in my house.

I wouldn't have thought I'd like living this far from Manhattan, but things change
when you have a kid. We kept the apartment in Chinatown until Mateo was about a
year old, but you get tired of walking up and down five flights of stairs *really* quickly
when you're carrying a baby, a stroller, and all the other crap that somehow magically
materializes when you have a kid.

Mateo brought other changes too. When he was born, something clicked in both of
my parents. They might have finally gotten their act together and finalized their own
divorce, but they also realized that this life I had been building in New York wasn't
going anywhere. So instead of alienating my new family and distancing themselves
from what I had embraced, they gifted Nico and me with a down payment on this
place in Riverdale, just in time for our first anniversary. Nico was speechless. Really,
he literally couldn't speak for almost an hour.

I wander out the back door, to the tiny patio that makes up our "backyard," if you
could even call it that. Having a yard at all in New York City is a luxury. This space
was my birthday present last year from Nico and Gabe. Together they landscaped the
two hundred square feet of nothing into a mini-paradise, laying down a brick patio,
exchanging the chain-link fence for a taller wood one, and building a fire pit in the
middle. They planted a few trees that now block out most of the surrounding buildings, and a bunch of different flowers that make it smell sweet in the spring. It's my
happy place.

I sit down on one of the lounge chairs and look up through the foliage, past strings of lights to the blue sky that's dappled with clouds. Even from here, you can hear the chatter of the city, although it's quieter in this part of the Bronx. We're not far from the Metro line we both take into Manhattan almost daily, and the sounds of kids playing at the park a half a black away filter through the fence. But the noises blend together with the wind coming off the Hudson and laughing through the trees. It's peaceful, not frenetic. Just what I need.

I close my eyes and listen, turning my face to the sun.

Please, I find myself praying to a God that, over the years, I've come to believe in more and more. *Please protect it. Please don't take it away.*

I listen, but there's no answer. There never is, but I know He's there. He must be.

"I thought you might be out here."

Nico's deep voice seeps into me, and even though I'm annoyed he's late, I'm immediately calmer. That's just what his presence does. It's why, though he'll never know, I'm that much more anxious when he goes to work. Nico's job isn't the safest in the world. As interesting as his stories about climbing into burning buildings or broken sewers are, there's a part of me that doesn't want to hear them. Is it terrible that I kind of wish my husband were the type of firefighter who rescued cats in trees?

But I'd never stop him from talking about his job, one of the loves of his life, because I love every damn bit of himself that Nico Soltero has ever been willing to share with me. Even the scary parts.

I turn and smile. "It's so nice, and the weather is beautiful. We have to enjoy it while we can, right?"

Nico leans against the doorframe, making no move to come get me, though I kind of wish he would. He looks as freaking delectable as ever in his uniform—the navy pants that hug his slim hips and round backside *just* right, the short-sleeved button-down shirt that really doesn't leave enough room for his biceps, the curved-bill Yankees hat that he'll never, ever toss out. He smiles and crosses his arms, making the tattoo sleeve that now extends down his forearm ripple. He let Milo try out a few more patterns, blending several dates into the curving lines. The day he was released from Tryon. The day he graduated high school. Our first date. The day he was accepted into the FDNY academy. The day his mother was granted permanent residency. Two days later, when we got married. Mateo's birthday.

There are others too, etched so small in black you can only see them when you're close enough to kiss them, as I often do. His arm has become a map of his life, and I'm honored to be a part of it.

By the time my gaze drifts back up to meet his, Nico's no longer smiling. Suddenly the air, despite the balmy spring weather, crackles.

Even more than six years after we first met, it's still like that between us. There's an energy, something between us that connects on a cellular level. Something in Nico's body, in his blood, his veins, calls directly to mine. Sure, sometimes it gets swallowed up by everyday life. It's hard to want to jump each other's bones when a baby is crying and you've got a term paper due in two days, or when you've been working for seventy-two hours straight and the water heater's broken. But even so, there are still times when he will just look at me—across the dinner table, over a mountain of laundry, when I walk in the front door—and I swear, it's like the wind was knocked out of me. Every single, solitary part of me reorients toward him. And for just a moment, it feels like there's nothing else.

"You're late," I whisper, although I'm done caring about that. It's occurring to me, just as I'm sure it's occurring to him, that we have the house to ourselves, which almost *never* happens.

Nico smiles again, this time slow and deliberate, gradually baring his bright white teeth in that sly way that hints of something much more wicked. "No, I'm not. I borrowed K.C.'s car. No train today, so we have plenty of time."

His deep-brown eyes, almost black, slide over my body, tracing over the shirt that clings to my breasts and waist and the skirt that stops mid-thigh. It's not a particularly revealing outfit. Comfortable and light, appropriate for the warm May weather. As if on command, though, goose bumps rise all over my skin, down my bare legs. Nico's eyes gleam, and finally, he pushes off the doorway and joins me on the lounge.

"How you doin', Mrs. Soltero?" he asks as he squats down for a kiss. "You're looking pretty fine over here in the sunshine."

"You are so corny. Nice rhyme."

He doesn't answer, just reveals one of his dimples before he slips a big hand around the nape of my neck and plants a long, slow kiss on my lips. His tongue teases them open, and I oblige, eager to taste him thoroughly. We don't often get moments like these when we can take our time.

"Mmm." His voice rumbles low in his throat as he pushes me back into the chair. His other hand drifts down my shoulder to palm one breast. "What the…" He breaks away and looks down. "Baby, you're not wearing a bra."

I raise a brow and bite my lip. "I was home alone. Didn't really see the point."

"Yeah, but…" He licks his lower lip. "Baby, look at you. What if you had to answer the door like that?"

I follow his gaze. Okay, to look at me, you'd probably think I was freezing. But to be fair, that's *his* fault, not mine.

I look back up and grin. "Afraid I'm going to attract the attention of another deliveryman?"

That only elicits a growl and a kiss that's much more possessive than the first. Both hands find my breasts now, knead and caress while mine slide up his neck and into his thick black hair, knocking the baseball cap to the ground. Nico drops his lips down my neck, and then, as he breaks away, plays with the straps of my shirt, pulling one strap over my shoulder, then the other until the entire neckline is below my breasts.

Keeping the straps wound around his fingers, he teases my nipples with the tightened fabric. Up and down over the sensitive nubs until my breath grows shallow, keeping his eyes on mine the entire time. When I moan a little, he drops the straps, and his thumbs feather down over the soft skin of my breasts, then over my nipples, making them rise even more. My back arches into his touch. Then he pinches, and any and all thinking ceases entirely.

"You got jokes, huh?" Nico asks as he tugs lightly on the ends of my aching breasts. They're more sensitive than ever, and I know that feeling is only going to get worse in the months to come. If it's anything like it was with Mattie, I'll be tempted to run to the firehouse in the middle of the night just so Nico can take care of it.

He pulls again, this time harder. My eyes close against that intoxicating combination of pain and pleasure as he pulls again, forcing me to follow the movement and sit completely up until my lips meet his full, eager mouth. He kisses me deeply, pairing a bit of sweetness with the pain he inflicts.

Then, just as suddenly, his hands and mouth pull away, and I'm released back against the chair cushion with a light thump.

My eyes fly open. "Are you kidding?"

Nico sits up, black eyes dancing. "What?"

I shake my head. "There is no way you're going to get me all turned on like that and stop midway. That's just cruel for a woman in my condition."

That wicked smile returns, just like I knew it would.

"And what condition would that be?"

I tip my head. "Pregnant, as you well know. And everyone knows you're supposed to do what your wife tells you. You're not supposed to stress her out, so you have to give her what she wants, whether it's weird foods at three a.m. or sex with her hot firefighter husband."

Nico tips his head back and laughs, and then, before I can say anything else, he slips one big arm under my back and another under my knees, and sweeps me off the lounge against his very broad shoulders. There won't be any carrying me over his shoulder for the next several months, but that won't stop him from picking me up in other ways. He'll do it when I weigh an extra thirty pounds, too, as he proved the last time around. I was honestly scared he was going to break his back, carrying me up six flights of stairs, but the man is stubborn as a mule. Considering our son, it appears to be a family trait.

"We could just stay out here, you know," I suggest as I bury my nose into his neck, inhaling his salty-sweet scent. Soap. Sweat. Smoke. The combination is intoxicating.

"We could," he agrees, though he's already moving toward the house. "But the last time we tried that, Mrs. Mariano gave me dirty looks for a week." He kicks the door shut behind him and gives me a long kiss, full of tongue and promise. "Face it, NYU. You're too damn loud."

I smack him on the shoulder, but I don't argue as he continues carrying me up the stairs and into our bedroom, maintaining our kiss the entire time. The man is seriously talented with that tongue of his. I should have known better than to let him use it when we were outside, where the neighbors could hear.

He lays me on the bed, but when he tries to stand up, I snake a hand around his neck, keeping his face close for a moment more.

"Please," I whisper. "You know. You know how I need it right now."

Nico stands up, clearly checking me over. It's not often I make this request, and when I do, it's usually because I'm scared of something. Sometimes he doesn't know what. The demons that used to visit me from time to time rarely stop by these days, but our life has replaced them with some others. I have more to lose now, just like him.

I stare as he removes his shirt, reveals every delectable muscle, every beautiful line of his chest and stomach, one button at a time. The funny thing is, I don't even think he notices the way I'm drooling over him. He's too busy thinking about what I'm asking, making sure I'm really okay.

"I don't—I don't want to hurt you. Either of you," he says, though I can see by the way his hands are clenching at his sides that he wants to do exactly what I'm asking. Today, we're both scared. We're both searching for a bit of control, in the best way we know.

"If it's going to happen again, it's going to happen again," I say, struggling to keep my voice from warbling. It's one thing to think it to myself, but it's another completely to say it out loud. "But you remember what the doctor said. Sex has nothing to do with it. Neither do any of the other things we normally do. The best thing we can do is just be ourselves. Together."

Nico swallows, causing a muscle in the side of his jaw to tick. His hands flex again. He's dying to do it. Flip me over. Ram inside. Release his frustrations onto my body the same way I'm dying to let him.

But still, he pauses.

He thinks too much. At least, that's what I always tell him. Even though we've been together for as long as we have, Nico still doesn't always believe I completely understand what I'm asking for. Or maybe he still can't believe I like it as much as he does. Nico understands that deep inside, there is always going to be a part of me that burns a little, an anger that needs to be let out, a need to hurt, just a little. He gets it because he feels it too. But that doesn't stop him from feeling bad about it.

Even though he spends most of his down time at the firehouse working out, he still has to take off for Frank's a few times a week just to rid himself of the tension that builds up. Sometimes it's just too much for my man to bear, and hitting something, whether it's one of the heavy bags or Nate's mitts, is one of the only ways to get rid of it.

This is the other. I wish he didn't feel guilty about it, but the reality is, we both get what we need when he takes control, gets a little aggressive. I need to feel just a little pinch of pain. And sometimes he needs to give it.

I get up on my knees and shuffle to the edge of the bed, where I slip off my shirt and skirt so that I'm kneeling in front of him, almost naked. He watches me unbuckle his pants and pull them down so that, after he removes his shoes, he can shimmy out of them the rest of the way. I toy with the elastic of his boxer briefs, but only tug them a little lower than his hip bones. There is something so crazy sexy about the combination of muscle, bone, and tendon that converges right above that band. I lean in and lick the spot, then sit back up to kiss him properly.

"Please," I whisper against his lips. "I'm not going to break. We're not going to break."

Then I clap his hand to my ass, which is *still* his favorite part of my body. Seriously, I could probably get this man to do anything I wanted if I kept his hand right here. It's not a privilege I take advantage of a lot, but it's nice to know it's there.

Nico moans into my mouth, and his hand automatically kneads the full flesh.

"Fuck," he breathes before sucking on my lip again with a slight bite. His other hand grabs the other cheek, and he massages them together, pulling me up against his hard length. "Jesus. *Christ.*"

I reach behind and cover his hands with mine. Then I clamp down, grabbing with him, and make him do it hard. Hard enough to leave a bruise.

"Ah!" he bites out.

Suddenly, I'm flipped over so I'm on my knees, my face pressed into the bedding while my hands are held together behind my back. My underwear is dragged down my legs, and before I know it, he's pressed against my entrance, sliding in slowly at first, and then thrusting deeply into that warm, slick place where he still fits so perfectly.

There's no wait. No gentle touch or kisses to get me ready. He doesn't take the time to lick or play with his hand—but he doesn't need to, not today. His little game on the patio had me ready and willing well before he picked me up, and he knows it too.

And he knows I'm looking for something else anyway.

The crack of his hand meeting my flesh echoes through the air, and I shudder, in the best possible way.

"Again," I call, low because my voice is muffled in the sheets. But he hears me.

His hand smacks my ass again and again, alternating between a light, brushing swat, and a full-on smack as he pounds harder, filling me completely with every push, every grunt. I press my elbows down, pushing back against each blow, groaning into the sheets every time his palm lands on my skin. I'll be bright red by the time he's done, and I'm absolutely loving it.

With the last, particularly rough slap, I scream into the sheets, and Nico pauses.

"Layla," he barks. "Up. Now."

I push up awkwardly, and he helps me the rest of the way so that I'm resting against his chest, both of us on our knees together while he remains buried inside. He twists us toward the shelves mounted over the bed, the ones that are doubly reinforced for moments like these, and sets my hands on the edge of the lowest one so that I'm bent at a slight angle, It's one of our favorite positions, one that allows me to take him deeply, yet gives him full access to the front of my body.

He lifts one knee and sets his foot down on the bed, almost in a parody of a proposal, except he's buried seven inches deep and giving me one of the hardest fucks of my life instead of an engagement ring.

"Is that how you want it, baby?" he asks as his hand slams down again. "You want it hard like this?"

"Ummmmmmm, yesssssss!" I shout, holding onto the shelf for dear life. When he takes me this way, I can barely think, much less speak in full sentences.

Nico's hands float up my sides, resting briefly over my ribs, where my half of our matching tattoos stretches over my skin: in his handwriting, *saudade para tí*. His fingers trace the lines as he continues to thrust, harder and harder, while his fingers curl and his nails scrape my skin just a bit as he drops that hand down between my legs.

The effect is instantaneous. He pinches my clit, and it's that tricky combination of pleasure and pain, the one that Nico always manages to find *exactly* right, that sets me off.

I begin to shake. He pulls the hand away.

"Nico!" I cry out hoarsely as my muscles tense. "Oh...*fuck*! Baby, I'm so close, *sooooooo* close."

He slams in again, and again, but his words are no longer intelligible. I can feel him expand within me, growing bigger, longer, harder. It only brings me even closer to that critical edge, the place where I can't hold myself back any more.

"Hold on, baby," he grunts. Thrust. Smack. He winds a hand into my hair and yanks me back up against him. The hand at my clit works a little harder, then pinches a bit and pulls.

"Now, Layla," Nico croaks. "Come with me, baby. *Now!*"

His teeth find my neck, and he bites. Hard.

"FUCK!" I shout as my orgasm launches through me.

My entire body shakes, seizing up against his strong, solid warmth, kept from toppling over by the arm around my hips and the other hand clasping my hair. I don't know how he doesn't come apart too, but it's Nico's strength that keeps us from falling over together. He's shattered too. I can tell by the way every part of him wound around me is flexed, muscle, vein, and tendon all in high relief. His teeth still clamp down hard enough that I swear he's going to draw blood, and he emits a long, almost pained groan against my skin as his release floods me.

Our life together has never been easy. We've had our battles to fight to be together, both coming from inside and outside of ourselves. Money. Family. This city and all the memories it holds.

We both have our outlets, our ways of coping, so that when we come together, we can give each other the best we have to offer. Most days they work, but sometimes they aren't enough.

But this. This connection. This outlet. This heat. This love. This is *always* enough.

———

The End...for now.
(Click here for the Extended Epilogue)

NEED MORE NICO AND LAYLA? You can catch sneak peeks of these two in my upcoming forbidden romance, The Other Man. www.nicolefrenchromance.com/theotherman

Need more Nico? You can read about his early life in the Bad Idea prequel novella, Broken Arrow, free only to newsletter subscribers: https://BookHip.com/BBXWVX

AFTER PARTY

A BAD IDEA STORY

CHAPTER ONE

Shama

THE WALLS ARE SHAKING.

No, not those kinds, you dirty bird. I mean the *actual* walls of my hotel room are shaking. The windows rattle in their frames, the big platform bed shuffles on the carpet, and the big brass mirror over the vanity claps against the plaster.

"Don't drop, don't drop, you fucker," I mutter without opening my eyes. How many earthquakes have I experienced in five years of living in L.A.? Ten? Twelve? Twenty?

I don't even know. This thing is barely a tremor, hardly audible over the noise bubbling up from Santa Monica Boulevard. The only reason I can feel the damn thing is because I'm flat on my back. And, no, not in that way either. Jeez, you guys really are perverts.

Three. Two. One. The shaking stops. The mirror is crooked but has the good sense not to fall. No seven years of bad luck. I exhale. I need coffee. But to do that, I need to get up.

Seven years I've lived in L.A. Five since I took the job with National Records as a video production assistant. I did the job, and I did it well. Worked steadily up the ladder until I was eventually producing music videos on my own.

And now, two days since I left my apartment and officially began my ten-years-coming vacation here at the Santa Monica Marriott, not four blocks from my old studio.

You think you know how hard the music business is? No one tells you about behind the scenes. No one tells you about the boys' clubs. The way they treat women like playthings. No one tells you just how hard you have to fight to make *any* of them listen to you. They hear a name like Shama Sandhu and assume I'm there to provide the "catering," not to be the damn boss.

But now I'm finished. No more producing. No more music industry. No more of these assholes who, starting with my old DJ boyfriend, can't seem to keep their dicks in their pants for more than five minutes.

You want to know something crazy? I originally wanted to be a video journalist. I started at NYU thinking I'd travel the world making docu-shorts and video essays for publications like *The New Yorker* or *The Atlantic*. Instead, it's been seven years of telling people how best to "back that ass up."

But I'm done. I paid off my bills. I saved my money. And now I have enough to take a full year off with my camera and return to the dream. I just have to tie up loose ends.

My cell phone blares its sickly sweet tinkle on the nightstand. The bed frame squeals as I grab the phone.

"What up, bitch?"

"Hey, girl. Just wanted to make sure you're still alive before your trip. Are you ready to go?"

I smiled. My best friend, Layla Soltero, is seriously one of the sweetest people on the planet. Maybe too sweet. We lived together for three years in college, and she's been a rock ever since. Unlike most, she's never put off by my, ah, "harsher" moments. She's one of the few people who love me for exactly who I am.

"Dude. I am more than ready. We just had an earthquake. I think this city is literally trying to throw me out."

"An earthquake? Oh my God, Shams, are you okay?!"

A clamor sounds on the other side of the phone, like dishes jumbling on a table, followed by the squirrely voices of two small children. I smile.

"*Mami,* is Auntie Shama okay?"

I grin, shoving my hair back from my face. Mateo, Layla and Nico's son, is the cutest damn kid in the world. Their three-year-old daughter, Camila, better known as Coco, is a close second.

"Tell Mattie I'm fine," I say as I haul myself out of bed.

"He wants to know when you're coming for a visit."

I study myself in the mirror, drawing a finger over the dark circles under my eyes. "Lay, I was just out there at Christmas."

"That was six months ago. You're really not going to come back before your year-long travel extravaganza? What if you die over there, Shams? What if you get eaten by a crocodile?"

I smile into the mirror. "She perished by way of crocodile" isn't a bad thing to have in your obituary.

"This is the beauty of video chats, my friend," I say. "God bless smartphones. And the fact that there are no crocodiles in New Delhi. At least, I don't think."

There's a long sigh. I don't tease her more, because I know it's partly jealousy that's motivating these comments. Well, I'm jealous of her too. Layla might not get to travel, but she's got the rest of her life buttoned up. Two adorable kids. A job she loves as a social worker. And a sexy-as-sin, fire-fighting husband. Yeah, I don't feel so sorry for Little Miss Domestic.

"So, what's your plan before you leave?"

"I give the keys to the landlord at eleven, and then I get to check into the hotel. Two days as a tourist in L.A. I never thought I'd see the day, but I don't want to leave the City of Angels on bad terms, you know?"

"Stupid city. I'm glad you're leaving. They don't deserve you."

I have to grin. Layla has a personal vendetta against L.A. after Nico moved here for a year when they first met, and then when I moved here too.

"Eh, it's not that bad. I'll miss Huckleberry for one. Oh my *God*, those lemon croissants…I should go there today for breakfast." I smack my lips, imagining the butter-soaked pastry that only me and about two other women in this stupid city are willing to enjoy. Only the people behind the cameras in L.A. ever eat. Whatever. More for me.

"Yum. Have one for me."

"And me!" Mateo's voice chirps behind her, and soon after that, Coco's lisped drawl follows. Damn. I will miss seeing those kids for a whole year.

"One year, babe. And then it's back to New York. Or London. Or wherever else I happen to land."

She tuts at the idea, but inside, I'm thrilling. I love the idea of not knowing the future for the first time in my life.

"Maybe I should come visit you…" Layla daydreams just as another call rings through.

I frown at the number. Why is the head of A&R at National calling? The guy has spoken to me maybe once in seven years.

"Hold on, Lay. I'll call you back, okay?" She agrees, and I switch answer the new call. "Hello?"

"Shama, this is Gary Clayburn. How are you?"

I sit down on the edge of the mattress. "Ah, fine, thanks."

"I hear we're losing you to…a private project. Is that right?"

My frown intensifies as I look in the mirror. Damn, I really should have cut my hair before leaving. Maybe a trip to the salon is in order…

"Yes," I say as I hold my hair up, trying out a mock bob. Yeah, no. I need my long hair. "I'm leaving on Monday, actually. Right now I'm taking a little downtime before my flight to Delhi." I meander over to the closet and shrug on the maxi dress I'm planning to wear for the next two days when I'm not on the beach.

"Good, good, so we haven't lost you yet. Any chance you're available this weekend for an emergency? We lost the producer on the DJ Cairo video. Apparently Cairo didn't like the final mix and refuses to appear in the video until it's fixed."

"He's back in the *studio*?"

"He's an EP, and his agent got him final cut."

The irritation in his voice is palpable. I don't blame him. Final cut makes for tyrants. I've heard of DJ Cairo, of course—everyone has. He's one of the most talented music producers in the business, the next Dr. Luke. He was the most recent get for National, and they bought his entire album, which, rumor has it, he recorded in his own apartment over several years. They say it's a damn masterpiece. I haven't heard this single, but I do know he's stepping out as a performer for the first time, and National is putting everything they have behind it.

So sure, maybe the guy has first-time jitters, but that's no reason to hijack an entire production and cost the studio thousands of dollars a day just to redo some auto tuning.

"We need someone to step in, Shama. Take the reins. Make sure everything gets done. We need you."

Now my frown is an all-out scowl. I quit this job precisely because I was done babysitting all the narcissists in the industry. The last thing I want to do on my mini-vacation is to chase some prima donna beat boy into performing like a trained monkey. No. I want the beach. I want sunshine. I want margaritas.

Then Gary offers exactly five times what I've ever gotten paid for one of these projects. It's more than I usually make in six months. More than I made in my first two years as an assistant producer. It's enough to fund my entire year-long project on top of the money I've saved.

I cough profusely.

"Everything okay, there?"

"Sorry," I said. "I just didn't quite hear what you said."

So he says it again. And this time, I'm sure.

"Wow." The word pops out before I can stop it.

"So you'll do it?"

"Um, well. I only have three days before I leave L.A. How involved is the project?" I'm not staying past Sunday. Absolutely not.

"Not too bad. They've already started filming," Gary replies. "The director has a pretty clear vision for the video too. Beach party. They're doing it mostly on location in Redondo Beach. You know Jeff de Soto?"

I nod, though he can't see me. "Oh, sure. Jeff and I have worked together a few times." I glance at my maxi. So much for vacation. "All right. I'll do it."

"First things first," Gary says. "We need to get Cairo out of the studio and back on set."

CHAPTER TWO

K.C.

"It's still not right."

I flip off the track and sit back in my chair, tapping my lips for a second while the studio stops shaking. The motion makes the big watch on my wrist slide forward, a gift from my agent after she signed me to National. Funny thing…we were so excited at the time. I could never have guessed how the transition from producer to performer would have turned out.

"I think it sounds dope," says Joaquin, my personal assistant. "The bass is poppin'."

I just roll my eyes at the soundboard. I like Joaquin. I do. One of my cousins from New York, he's been my body man since he graduated high school. He's loyal, trustworthy, and doesn't snort his paycheck like half the people in this industry. And more than that, he always has *yes*-es when I need to hear them. But right now I don't need a yes-man. I need someone who's going to tell me what the fuck is wrong with this track.

Problem is, when you're the producer on top of the talent, everyone expects *you* to have that answer. Today, though, the magic is not happening.

"Here." I pull off the two fat chains around my neck, the diamond-encrusted pinkie ring, and the watch I bought with the royalties from the first Billboard hit I ever produced. I hand the whole kit over my shoulder. "'Quin, this shit is weighing me down. Take it back to the hotel and have them put it in the safe, all right?"

Joaquin whips out a velvet cloth to take the jewelry. He knows I don't like my ice getting his fingerprints on it. And this happens often enough that he's usually ready for it when I've had it with the hardware. The funny thing is, I don't even like it that much. When I'm by myself, I keep it simple. T-shirt. Jeans. That's about it.

But when you don't come from much, you feel like you need to insulate yourself once you have something. Like somehow a little gleam makes it real.

I remember that feeling when I started making some money. First came a record with my first job at The Hit Factory. Then someone picked up my mixes. They started hiring me at bars. Clubs. Festivals. More records. More gigs. They just kept coming and coming.

But the numbers didn't seem real until I saw what they could buy. Nothing —*nothing*—will ever compare to the feeling of handing my mother the title to her very own two-bedroom condo on the west side of Manhattan, four blocks from the falling-down building in Hell's Kitchen where I grew up. From there, she could look over New York like the queen she was, not the servant she'd always been forced to be.

I turn to Barry, the sound tech. "What do you think?"

"Needs more bass," he says, directly contradicting Joaquin. "You knew I was going to say that. It needs bounce."

I turn back to the console like it's going to give me all the answers. I did know that. Barry's in-house here at National—a good guy who's worked on some other projects with me. Old school, though, and very L.A. He wants to make my shit sound like Dr. Dre. I'm not having that. I'm from New York City, not Compton. *Boricua*, not Crenshaw.

"Joaquin. Phone. Call Nico." I hold out my hand behind me, and like magic, my phone appears, the number to my best friend already ringing.

"Yo, *mano*. Where the fuck you been? I tried to call you, what, five times last week?"

I grin as the voice of Nico Soltero, my best friend, echoes through the room. Joaquin grins too. Everyone loves Nico.

Me most of all, though. Because out of everyone in my life, my boy is the only one who keeps it real. He tells me when I'm being a jackass. He tells me when I'm getting too big for my head. And he tells me when I'm getting shit right too.

"Where else, man?" I reply. "I'm in the studio."

"Don't you have that video shoot? I thought today was the day you become a real rap star!"

I grimace at my reflection in the window. "Yeah, the video's on hold."

Behind me, Joaquin snorts. Okay, fine. So I ran off set to fix the damn track. What the fuck is the point of doing a video if the track's not right?

"Layla good?" I ask, deflecting. "Family good?"

I can practically hear my man's grin over the phone when I mention his wife. Cha-*ching*, if there was ever a man whipped by his woman. But I don't blame him. She's fine as hell, and really fuckin' good for him to boot. We should all be so lucky as those two.

"Yeah, man, she's good. Got a promotion at work last week. She's director of the whole damn office now. You believe that?"

I nod. "Yeah, yeah. I can believe that. How about you? How does it feel to be a fuckin' FDNY lieutenant now, *mano*?"

There's another deep chuckle before he launches into some updates. He probably thinks I'm humoring him with these questions. But really, who's doing better things for the world, huh? A firefighter and a social worker with two beautiful kids? Or an asshole making records about shaking ass and popping tags?

"Yo, man. I need you to listen to this track," I say. "You got a minute?"

"Ah...sure, I guess. But you know I don't know anything about music, bro."

"Just tell me if you like it," I say. I don't have time for this song and dance. Nico isn't a musical talent, but he knows good shit. If anyone else has an ear for the vibe I want, it's him.

"I'm trying to make it sound like home," I clarify.

Before he can ask any more questions, I flip on the song, hold the phone up to a speaker, and let it play for a solid minute before turning it off.

"Okay, what do you think?"

There's a long pause. Shit.

"I mean, it's nice...I'm sure it would play well with the younger crowd these days...they seem to like that auto-tuned business that got so popular."

I groan into my palm. I knew sampling this girl was the wrong way to go. National demanded fuckin' "synergy" on this project, and they gave me straight-up shit.

"It's weak," I translate. "And Katie Derek sounds weak on it."

"Well...yeah. *Claro*, man. I'mma be real, I'd probably change the station. The beat is tight, but you need a better voice with it, you know? If you're gonna use that rhythm, you need a hook to match. Maybe...shit, Kayce, I'm not a producer."

I groan again. "Nico, cut the shit. I asked for your help, so just tell me what you're thinking of."

"*Coño*, calm the fuck down all right. God, you're such a sensitive fuckin' artist, you know that?"

I snort. "Shut the fuck up."

"*You* shut up. You want my opinion or not?"

I sigh. I do want his opinion. Honest to God, Nico and I are probably...what's the word...codependent. "Hit me."

There's a long pause while he thinks. "All right...I hear the lyrics...and I hear that beat you got going. It's a rumba, right?"

"Right."

"It reminds me of those Sunday mornings, you remember? Remember our moms, they used to hang laundry out the fire escape while they listened to that Ghetto Brothers album?"

My eyes pop open. "Oh *shit*. I forgot about that album. The one with those licks like Dusty Springfield? Like it's echoing in a glass goblet? *Viva Puerto Rico Libre*..."

"Ah...I guess? But yeah, that song. That's the one I mean."

I can already hear it. Sultry harmonies, a lazy hum liquid as the ocean. In a flash, I'm back on the fire escape in Hell's Kitchen, watching the sway of my mother's skirt in the summer heat while she sings along and pins my shirts to the clothes line. In those moments, she was back in Santiago, sitting under the palm trees, watching the ocean as blue as the sky.

"Tell Layla I said what's up," I say in a hurry. "I gotta go." I hang up—Nico knows there's no more time for goodbyes, not when I've got *the sound* locked in my head. I swing around to Barry. "Yo, we need a guitarist."

Barry nods—he's been listening to my end of the conversation. "You want me to call Danny, the cat who worked on Drake's last album?"

"How about Elian Ramirez? I think he's in town. He could do it." I'm rocking now to an unheard melody. Ba-da-da-dahhhh. I can hear it clearly, swimming over the beat I wrote, but with a different voice. I shake my head. "We need a new singer too."

But Barry's got no suggestions. Shit.

"Who, Barry, who?" I demand. "Goddammit, who's available right the fuck now?

Deeper voice, kind of husky, but Latin? *Coño*, who am I thinking of? I need to get this shit down before it flies."

Barry taps a finger on his lips while Joaquin's expression ping-pongs between us. "I don't know, man. National ain't gonna like it if you ax Katie Derek…"

I wave him away. "They're gonna like it fine when I give them a platinum record. She doesn't work with this, and you know it."

"Ariana can do it the way you're saying—"

"Nah, she's touring in Australia with Katie Derek right now," I say. "Who else?"

I'm snapping my fingers like a guy who needs his fix.

Barry opens his mouth and rattles off a few more names, but none of them work. Fuck, *fuck*. I'm sitting here rapping my brains, trying to think of someone, *anyone* who can sing this fucking hook for me.

And then, before I can name anyone else, the studio door opens, and *the voice* enters.

"All right, where's the bastard who delayed an entire video production to adjust a few fucking beats? Where's the spoiled brat who thinks the entire fucking industry revolves around him? Which one of you assholes is DJ Cairo?'"

I swear to God, I don't even remember what she said after my stage name comes out of her mouth. She practically sang it, like she was making fun of a singer, but it was melodic, and the deep, husky tone shot through my bones.

Without even turning around, I raise my hand. "That would be me, sweetheart."

"Damn," Barry murmurs behind me. He bats me on the shoulder. Then he does it again.

Finally, I swing in, wondering what he's on about and ready to get this intruder into the sound booth so we can finish this shit. Then I look up, and I can't think at all.

CHAPTER THREE

Shama

He's just...staring at me.

I won't lie. I stare too for a second. But I did it the nice appropriate way through the tiny window on the studio door. Because it was a shock—a *shock*, I tell you—to walk in here and see world famous, yet oddly reclusive producer DJ Cairo sitting there with no jewelry, no flashy clothes, no posse, brow furrowed while he listened to a track over and over again. Lost in the zone. Totally floating away on his music.

Look. It's not like I've never seen a hot musician before. Shit, I've been brushing these assholes aside like flies since I started in this business. Get it done, get it done. The number one rule of being a producer.

But this...somehow this is different.

I stride over and snap my fingers in front of his face. "Hey! Rapper boy, you there?"

He blinks and bats my hand away. "*Coño*! No need to get into my face, damn!

"*You're* DJ Cairo?" I let the name slides of my tongue with disdain so thick it's practically molasses.

He's not at all what I would expect a Puerto Rican rapper to look like. Where's the hat? The chains? The baggy jeans? This guy is pale enough that he probably passes as white most of the time in spite of the deep-set eyes and close-cut hair that's even blacker than mine, and the full mouth set in a never-ending smirk. And with nothing on but a simple white t-shirt, completely *normal* jeans, and a pair of Adidas sneakers, he looks like any guy off the street.

I must have seen his picture before somewhere. A newspaper. Maybe a press release. Of course I have. That must be why he looks familiar.

At that, he blinks, then gives me a lazy smile and raises his hand. "*Claro*, that's me. But I'm going to need you to say that one more time, sweetheart. This time, into the mic, *por favor*." He points toward the studio, and another guy, whom I'm guessing is the technician, is already standing, ready to escort me inside.

I push his hands away. "Get off me! I'm not a back-up singer, you asshole."

"Then who are you?" Cairo grabs a red Yankees hat off the soundboard and claps it on backward. He absently toys with a small chain around his neck, pulling out a medallion of what looks like a Catholic saint while he scowls up at me. Ah, there's the rapper I was expecting.

I cross my arms. "I'm Shama Sandhu, your new producer. The studio ruined my first vacation in seven years to get you back on set. Do you have any idea how much time you're costing them by tinkering with the auto tune?"

The scowl deepens, which could be hot if I wasn't so fired up.

"No use making excuses," I say. "You might be a hitmaking veteran, but you're a virgin performer. In this economy, you're lucky the studio gave you any kind of video budget for your first single, and if you squander it making the crew wait, you won't get another."

"Oh, really?" he sneers. "According to who?"

"According to *me* and my seven years wrangling idiots like you. Do you want to do this or not?"

He taps his lip again. It's distracting. And then that smile reappears, and for a second, I have to balance myself against the wall.

"Fine," he says. "You want me on set?"

I nod sharply.

A wide, slow smile spreads across Cairo's face. "Fine, sweetheart. I just need your voice."

CHAPTER FOUR

K.C.

THE SECOND SHE SAID MY NAME, LIKE A WOMAN WHO'S PISSED AND TURNED THE FUCK ON all at once, the syllables dripping off her tongue like honey, I knew *that* was the exact thing this track needed. Sultry and stubborn, right where it belongs, like a call and response to the lilt of my rhymes.

> Porque eres mi gatita *(DJ Cairo)*
> Porque eres mi mamita *(DJ Cairo)*

When I first asked, she stared at me like I was crazy. And for a moment, I thought I knew her. I must have seen her around, maybe in the studio, or at an industry party somewhere. I can't pace it, but something about her feels right.

But I ignore it, because there's a part of me that turns on like a button at the weirdest fuckin' things. A tone. A new pitch. And then I can hear it. Not just that one sound, but I can hear how it fits in a whole fuckin' symphony in my mind.

It takes us less than two hours to finish. For real, I don't know if I've ever laid a track that quickly. It's not just because Shama's a damn natural, purring into the mic like she wants to make out with it later. No, it's that with her, everything just *works*. She might scowl at me every time I ask for another take, but damn if her husky, somewhat imperious vocals doesn't add exactly what this track need.

Pop star out, cranky producer in. Add the extra riffs from the guitarist Barry wrangled, and we're on our way back to the video set by noon. And apparently, not a moment too soon.

"Finally!" shouts Blake, the director, as Shama practically drags me across the beach toward the section of the Santa Monica pier the studio blockaded for the shoot.

"I know, I know," Shama says, accepting a hug from the director. He kisses her on the cheek, and I have to fight not to be jealous. I just spent the last two hours with no one but her, Barry, Joaquin, and the guitarist. Now, standing here on a beach full of extras and crew members, I'm feeling a little invaded. I want our privacy back.

And why would that be, mano? Nico's laughing on my shoulder. That motherfucker. He knows what's up. Whatever, I'm a professional. And this pain-in-the-ass chick is my boss. At least for the next two days.

I accept a slap on the hand from Blake.

"We done?" he asks. "You got the new track?"

I nod. "Joaquin?"

My body man holds out his phone with headphones for Blake to listen. "Here you go. It's so hot, man. You're gonna love it."

Blake just rolls his eyes, but puts in the earbuds and starts bobbing his head almost immediately. "Yeah. Yeah, that is much better." His eye pop open right when the hook thumps through the tiny speakers. "Who's the girl?"

"That would be me." Shama looks bored, but I can tell she's kind of proud. She knows the goods as well as I do. "Porque" is going to be the song of the summer. It's gonna be her voice bumping through every open window between L.A. and New York.

Blake gives the headphones back to Joaquin. "Ah...you know we don't have a model for this. Shit, I know it's good, but she's all over this track, and I can't do a whole new shot list. And we didn't hire anyone to lip-sync..."

"Nah, Shama's gonna be in it," I say, only just realizing I mean it. "Just add her to my shots during the hook. That's all you gotta do."

At that, Shama swings around, her soft-looking lips open. "Um, *excuse me*?"

Behind me, Joaquin chuckles, but already, Blake is sizing her up. I want to tell him not to bother. Shama's just as gorgeous as any of the girls we got out here. Tall and slim, with an ass that doesn't quit. Yeah, I was looking on the way out to the car. And on the walk down the beach. No shame in that. The fabric of her dress clings, and wasn't nobody doing any harm, all right?

But it's not just the body. Shama is fuckin' gorgeous in a way that's a hell of a lot more real than most of the bimbos crowding the sand around us. Her hair is blacker than mine, if that's even possible, and her skin is deep brown and glows like she's been out in the sun a little too long recently. But it's her eyes, which sparkle like black diamonds and are glaring right at me that will really make the video come alive. The push and pull that was in every utterance of my name—that's going to fuckin' *jump* out of the screen. I know it.

"Yeah." Blake nods appraisingly, and I can tell he sees what I see. "Shama, you got it, baby. We need you."

Another thick scowl. "Blake, I am here as a producer, not a performer. You need me here to keep this on track not to get off course!" She tugs at her hair, which is falling over her shoulders in thick waves. For a second, I imagine what it would look like spread across a white sheet. While I cage her under my body, undulating in time to the rhythm.

Whoa, there, you horny motherfucker. One look at this girl, and suddenly you're a Backstreet Boy? What the fuck is going on?

"Come on, Sparks," I say, cuffing her lightly on the shoulder.

"Sparks?" She whirls to me, and Blake covers a smile. "Who the hell is Sparks?" she demands.

But the fire I see only makes me like the nickname more. Not caring whether or not anyone is watching, I reach out and tug the end of her hair.

"You are," I say, enjoying the feel of the silky strands between my fingers and the fire that rises in her eyes. "All we need are these lips"—I drag a finger over the bottom one—"saying my name"—I smile, and I swear to God, I think she shudders —"into that camera. You think you can do that for me, sweetheart?"

For a second, it's like the hustle and bustle of the beach fade away. It's just her and me standing there, my finger poised over her mouth while I'm wondering what the inside looks like. Her tongue sneaks out to one side.

She stares at me for a long second, and just then, I wonder if she can see through more than just my bravado. Shama's eyes are dangerous. They pierce right through you.

Yeah. Sparks, for real.

"But I'm not a video girl!" Shama suddenly bursts out. "Look at me. Do I look like these girls?"

She gestures wildly toward the models and extras milling around the set, all of them in the smallest of small bikinis, asses oiled, done up to the nines. They're hot, yeah. A few of them I've probably hooked up with at some point. But so is Shama, with her jet black hair and skin that looks dipped in gold. And she's got one thing none of those girls have: spark.

"Shama," I say. "You want me to get this video done today, right?"

She opens her mouth, then presses it shut again and nods succinctly.

I shrug and hold my hands out. "Well, you better get to makeup, sweetheart. Because we ain't got time to run new auditions, right?" I tap the watch on my wrist. "Chop, chop."

Shama opens her mouth like she wants to argue all over again. But instead, she turns toward the tent set up for wardrobe.

"Fine!" she shouts as she stumbles over the sand. "But I am *not* parading around in my underwear. I have to work between takes, you know. And one more thing: under no circumstances will I *twerk*."

CHAPTER FIVE

Shama

Two seconds into this shoot, and I'm already regretting it. It's chaos on the beach, we've got about two hours to get a party together that will last for five hours, and I have a director, crew, and about two hundred extras to wrangle. Instead I'm sitting around playing dress up with the makeup and wardrobe people.

At least I get to choose my own damn clothes instead of wearing the dental floss the models and extras considered bikinis. If, by some chance, my parents stumble upon this video, I'd rather not horrify them more than I have to by my association with someone like DJ Cairo.

And so, the DJ himself and I end up sitting in makeup at the same time, me getting rubbed all over with gold shimmery body makeup before I put on the magenta cover-up, him getting smeared with and oil and water substance that makes him look like he just walked out of the ocean.

"She's a class act," he keeps muttering to himself, winking at me when he catches me looking at him.

It would be easier to do this if he wasn't so damn good-looking. Most musicians aren't, really. People love them because of their talent, their glamor, but when you're up close, nine out of ten of them look like regular people.

Not Cairo. I see now why the studio courted him so hard. The second the guy takes off his shirt, it's clear he either has a *really* good metabolism or a hell of a trainer. Abs for days. Coated in a light sheen of oil, just enough that he looks like he's been diving into the ocean recently. It's all very…lickable.

Curiously, he cringes when they settle a few of the thick gold ropes around his neck and give him a pair of diamond-encrusted aviators sent over from Gucci. This is basic stuff. A music video is just a marketing tool, and you have to speak to your audience. People are looking for the next Daddy Yankee, even if the guy looks more like Enrique Iglesias.

"Come on, Cairo," I jeer from my chair, where another hairstylist is putting the finishing touches of beachy waves into my hair. "Can't you handle a little bling?"

I hold up my own wrists, which are loaded with gold bangles to match the diamond-laced hoops the costume designer assigned me.

Can you imagine if you brought him home, Shams? Layla's voice giggles in the back of my mind. I chuckle with her. I can imagine perfectly the expressions on my stolid Indian parents' faces if their daughter brought home a Puerto Rican rapper.

"Carlos," Cairo says quietly as he stares at his newly ringed fingers. He looks up, and his eyes pierce, even though the sunglasses. "That's my name. Not Cairo. I used to be DJ Carlos when I first started mixing. But I did this tour opening for Abel Rodriguez in Europe when I was maybe twenty, twenty-one. The German announcer couldn't read my name or something and pronounced it Cairo." He shrugs. "My manager thought it was hot, so we kept it. It's dumb, but I can't lose it now."

I can't deny its appeal. DJ Cairo is a much better stage name than DJ Carlos, which just sounds like some kid messing around on turntables in his dad's basement. But his voice lacks the bravado it had ten seconds ago, and when he looks up, his eyes are pleading. I've been involved in this industry for years, but still I forget how lonely it can be. When everyone thinks they know some version of you, eventually no one knows you at all.

Time to put on the nice producer hat. Sometimes talent needs their ass kicked. But sometimes they need a little coaxing to get the job done.

"Hey," I say, sliding off my chair and padding across the tatami mats to where he stands. "Are you okay there, slugger?"

All right, so empathy isn't really my best face.

Carlos tips the aviators down and examines me over the rims with a sardonic expression. The sun hits the silver edge and gleams. "Why, you gonna cheer me up, pretty?"

The cocky musician is back.

I scowl. "I just need to make sure you can perform. I'm not your fluffer, asshole. I'm the producer."

"No, *I'm* the producer," he corrects me.

"Not on this video, you're not."

This time he takes off his glasses completely, and I'm struck once more by how penetrating his gaze is. "Do you always talk to talent this way?" he asks.

I snort. "Did you just refer to yourself as the *talent*?"

His gaze doesn't waver, but before he can answer, Blake pops up between us.

"Okay," he says. "We're about ready to film the first sequence. The original plan was to juxtapose three separate parties, back and forth between them, so the audience can see how Cairo rolls. The pre-party, the beach party, and the one at night. Make sense, Shama?"

"I like it," I said. "What comes first?"

"First we need to do the pre-party. The set-up. Just a few friends hanging out at the beach. Cairo starts rapping. It's chill, everyone is drinking, laughing, having a good time, and as the beat heats up, so does the party. We've already done a lot of the basic shots of the beach crap—hot bodies, volleyball, you know. But we need you two. This is where you meet."

Carlos grins at me, his teeth bright white. "You should give me a dirty look like you did in the studio."

I glare at him.

"Yeahhhh," he says. "Just like that."

Blake smirks.

I just shake my head. "Okay, so after that, then what?"

"Then we'll do some work with the group as the sun starts to go down," Blake says. "That's got to move the fastest so we can get the light. I'll be working with Cairo while the other cameras are on the crowd."

"Show me," I say, beckoning for the shot list. It's pretty simple. There are five cameras rolling at the same time to get as much as possible to edit later. I've seen Blake's videos before. His work tends to be on the spontaneous side.

"The end is at night. After everyone goes home." He looked to Carlos. "Originally we were going to shoot you by yourself, but since you added Shama's voice to the hook, I'm thinking it should be with her too."

Carlos nods. "Yeah, I like that. Sort of what happens when the lights go out?" Again, he shoots me his cheeky grin. "The after party, right?"

The way his voice slides over the words leaves no doubt what kind of party he's envisioning.

I scowl even more.

"Just like that," Carlos says again.

I hand the shot list back to Blake. "Everything else ready?"

He nods.

"Good," I say. "Because thanks to this guy, we don't have any time to lose." I yank on Cairo's arm, ignoring the way his slick, oiled skin feels warm and *very* hard under my hand. "Come on, you. Let's get this over with."

CHAPTER SIX

Shama

TWO DAYS LATER, I'M TIRED, HOT, AND REALLY CRANKY. UNFORTUNATELY, BLAKE IS AS much of a perfectionist with his videos as Carlos is with his songs. Shot after shot after shot after shot, which meant that when I wasn't actually being filmed myself, I was working double duty to make sure the extras wouldn't wander off, help the crew prepare for the next shots, while we were all racing the sunset.

So now I'm sick of the beach, sick of this song, sick of baby sundresses, sick of being covered with gold body paint, and *really* sick of watching silicon-lipped models gyrate all over Carlos. It's not because I've spent approximately eight-five hours with the man staring into my eyes like I'm the only person he sees. It's not because we had to pretend to almost-kiss for at least an hour or because I can still remember what his cologne smells like. It has *nothing* to do with the fact that I fell asleep last night with my vibrator in hand because I cannot get the asshole out of my head.

And he knows it. He has to fucking know it. Every time he catches me scowling at one of the girls, he smiles. Every time he sees me staring at his finely-formed ass or those should-be-illegal arms of his, he smirks.

It's getting harder and harder to keep others on task when I'm losing my focus. That's what's making me cranky.

But finally, it's Saturday night. It's the last scene of the video, the one where it's just me and Carlos, alone on the beach at night. The "after party."

"You two can rest on the blanket for a while if you want," Blake says, gesturing toward the giant setup at the top of a dune. "Just don't move, okay? We don't have time to start from scratch."

Carlos and I sink down onto the rug. The designer basically created any woman's dream date, with a giant kilim rug dotted with cushions, candles, scattered fruit, and tiki torches all around us. It's basically a sex pad in the middle of the beach, and if we weren't surrounded by a crew, it would probably be doing the trick.

We sit for a long time while the lighting crew works to get things right. No one knows how much waiting happens on a video set.

Carlos lays back on the rug, and eventually, his eyes closed. Not for the first time, I notice how thick his eyelashes are, resting against his pale skin. In the moonlight, he looks almost ghostly, like a pirate.

His eyes open, and he offers a lazy smile. "You checkin' me out over there, pretty?"

I snort. "Just making sure you don't pass out."

"Whatever. You've been staring a hole at me for two days, *mami*. How long has it been? One year? Two?"

My jaw drops. "Um, excuse *me*, Mr. Sexual Harassment. That is none of your business."

He shrugs, lying back again and closing his eyes. "You gonna tell Blake on me? Report me for a couple of jokes when you've been throwing shit at me for days?"

Finally, I lie down too. I'd rather look at the stars than his smug face. "I just want to finish this crap tonight so I can start my vacation properly."

"Vacation? What vacation? Don't you live here?"

I shake my head. "Technically, not anymore. I was taking a few days on the beach, staying at a hotel when Gary called. I'm leaving tomorrow."

"Leaving for where?"

I toy with the hem of my skirt. "Delhi. I'm taking a year off to do some documentary work."

I wait for that familiar "how nice" or something equally trite. It's the response I always get when I tell people my plans. They look at me like I'm a child who wants to play make-believe, not a grown woman with her own dreams. I might as well say I'm leaving L.A. to find a frog to kiss.

"Passion project?"

I turn. There isn't a drop of placation on Carlos's face. In fact, he's watching me intently.

I nod. "Yeah. Yeah, it is. I'm just really tired of producing."

"Well, it's not your work, is it? It's managing someone else's."

I perk up more, surprised that he gets it. "That's right."

He sits up and balances his arms over his knees. I sit back up too.

"It was like that with this album. I worked on it in secret for...shit...two years? Maybe more?" He draws a line in the sand with his finger, tracing a box and then a circle inside it. A turntable. "For ten years, I made music for other people. Wrote their beats. Mixed their shit. Charted artist after artist."

"Hey, you did win a couple of Grammys."

That sly smile makes another appearance. It's tinged with an adorable shyness, though, instead of the cockiness that comes out around others. "I was a producer, like you. I wasn't onstage or nothin'. Those wins never really felt like mine."

I shrugged. "It's still an impressive achievement, especially considering how many voters don't like hip hop."

"Impressive, maybe." Carlos shrugs, his big shoulders rippling under the moon. "But a real artist has their own voice. They need to speak their truth."

His words echo my truth, the truth that was driving this whole crazy trip I was about to begin. "So what's the documentary about?" Carlos asks.

"I...I don't know yet." I stare at the weave of the kilim rug, wondering who made it. If it's authentic, lifted from a souk in Marrakech, or if it's a knock-off from Bangla-desh. Both places sound worth exploring with my camera. "I'll have to see what I find."

The other truth is, I want to create my own art, but I don't know if I'm really an artist. I won't know if I have a real voice, a real truth, until I try to speak at all.

The idea is terrifying.

Carlos sighs and looks up at the stars. "I'll never get tired of this."

I look up too, welcoming the change of subject. "The stars? I guess there are a few out tonight. Better than most nights."

He nods. "You can't see them in New York at all, ever. It's the only thing I like better about the West Coast."

I nod. After spending four years at NYU, I remember yearning for my parents' house in New Jersey. The glow of Manhattan obscures everything but its own corona.

"So where'd you grow up, Sparks?"

"Montclair," I say. "Not far from the city, but close enough."

He whistles. "Montclair is nice."

I nod. "Yeah, it is. I was lucky." I consider my parents, who still live in the same split-level house where I grew up. Still have the same La-Z-Boy furniture that smells faintly of cardamom and coriander. Every day, my mother cooks and cleans, tending to her empty nest while my dad goes to work. In another few years, maybe he'll retire.

"What about you?" I ask. "You're from the Bronx, right?"

He shakes his head. "Nah, the Kitchen. Forty-ninth Street."

"Really? That's funny." I smile. "I actually have a friend who grew up on that street too. Well, he's my best friend's husband. You don't know a Nico Soltero, do you?"

For a second, Carlos gives me a funny look, and again, I'm struck with that faint sense of déjà vu.

"Ah, I've heard the name," he says. "It's a big city, though."

"He and Layla are the best," I continue. "They live in Riverdale now with their kids. Tiny happy little family."

"You sound a little jealous." Carlos lies back on the rug.

I sigh and lie back again too. Above me, Cassiopeia spreads her arms wide like she wants to give me a hug. It really is a magical night. Usually you can't see more than the brightest of stars here.

"Maybe I am a little," I admit. "I don't know. I'm not in a hurry to get married or anything, but I think it would be pretty amazing to have the kind of partnership they have. It's hard to explain if you don't know them, but from both sides, it was love at first sight. They had their hard times, but I have never met a couple more devoted to each other."

My parents suddenly spring to mind with their quiet dedication. Not all love is passionate—they are a good example, an arranged marriage that evolved into a beau-tiful partnership over the years. That's not something I could ever do, but I respect them for it.

"It would be pretty amazing," Carlos agrees. "Ambition has its own price. It's tough being alone."

I turn. "Are you really alone? It seems like there are always people with you. Or who want to be."

Carlos just shrugs. "You can be with all sorts of people and still feel alone."

I ponder that for a moment, considering who has been around him. Video girls. Techs. That kid Joaquin who seems to exist just to pump him up. I definitely spotted a few people trying to slip him tapes or cards. To DJ Cairo, the hitmaker.

I wonder if anyone knows his real name.

"Yeah," I say. "I can see that."

For a few more minutes, we gaze up at the stars, and it's like the crew bustling around us doesn't exist. All I can feel is Carlos's warm shoulder against mine, sense the gentle shift of skin on skin as our breath causes our bodies to move.

For a moment, I don't want to leave L.A. at all. Not if I could stay on the beach with him.

Whoa. Where in the hell did that come from?

"All right, guys, ready?"

We stand up to find Blake poised with a couple of camera guys. The hair and makeup team come in to fluff my hair and straighten my dress (blue this time).

Carlos gives me another shy smile. "Ready to finish this thing, Sparks?"

Unaccountably shy myself, I nod.

"All right, guys, this is the seduction scene. Third verse, Cairo," Blake calls out.

"I'm sorry I ruined your vacation," Carlos says, reaching for my hand. He pulls me close while the lilting beat we've all come to know so well starts. "I...I didn't mean it to be like this. But I didn't know I needed you until you walked into the room."

I open my mouth to respond, but find I don't know what to say. I'm caught in the depth of his dark eyes, drawn to him like a moth to a flame. But I need to leave L.A. I can't stay here just to get burned.

"I—"

"Let's go!" Blake shouts from behind a camera.

And I watch as Carlos launches into another lip-sync, moving his lips while sound emits from speakers next to the camera. It reminds me that this is fake. None of these moments are designed for anything but performance. And this world is something that after tonight, I'll be leaving behind forever.

Still, Carlos's deep eyes never leave mine. And as I watch his mouth move silently in time with the music, I find myself wondering how I'm going to feel knowing he might never look at me like this again either.

CHAPTER SEVEN

K.C.

"Room 714."

That was what she whispered after Blake called, "That's a wrap." Right before she pressed a piece of plastic into my palm.

"For what?" I asked just before she disappeared.

She turned and grinned, looking almost devious under the remnants of the moonlight. "For the after party, of course." And before I could reply, she slipped into the wardrobe tent to change out of the slinky blue dress, leaving me to wonder just what this party might be like.

Shocked the fuck out of me, lemme tell you. Two days ago, this woman hated me. For two days I've been staring at her whenever I wasn't looking at the camera. Wondering why I dreamed about her nagging voice at night, threaded with the husky sound of my name coming through her lips.

But now I know.

Because she's not a strange woman. She's a someone.

Layla. Nico. Pretty little family in Riverdale.

It wasn't until she mentioned their names that I realized why Shama seemed so familiar. It's because we've met before, at my mother's freaking apartment, no less. Thanksgiving. Almost ten years ago.

She didn't remember me either, but back then, I was still just a skinny, pale-faced asshole with a goofy grin and some corny-ass game. It's amazing what a trainer and a few extra years will do. I also had no (major) name for myself yet, and she and Layla had just finished school. Money was coming, but fame was a long ways off.

And Shama...damn...yeah, she looked different back then too. Her hair was shorter, her cheeks were a little rounder, smooth with the naivety only someone just out of their teens has. But she was beautiful. I remember that. And she still had that attitude.

I palm the card back and forth in my palm before sliding it into the back pocket of my jeans. She wants one night before she leaves. A game with a famous musician. Take advantage of this cat-and-mouse game we've been playing for two days before she takes off.

I'm undecided on the ride back to my own hotel on Wilshire. Undecided while I shower off the residue of the video and change into a pair of black pants and a black t-shirt, keeping just the chain my mother gave me.

I stay undecided while I tell Joaquin that he's done for the next two days. As I sneak back downstairs to grab a taxi. When I stop at a supermarket for a bouquet of cheap pink roses, champagne, and some strawberries, like I do for a lot of the girls I meet at events.

And yeah, I'm *still* undecided when I find myself standing on the seventh floor of the Marriott, turning the card key over and over in my palm while I stare at the numbers next to the door.

714.

Then, before I make my decision, the door opens.

Shama stands there, looking ten times more gorgeous than she did on the beach. Gone is the makeup, the jewelry, the glitzy fuckin' dresses. She's in nothing but a t-shirt and these little shorts that ride up her smooth brown thighs. Her hair is tossed over her shoulder, wavy and slightly wet after a shower. A drop of real water, not makeup, still glistens on her cheek. After two straight days of work, she looks tired. But also relaxed. Back on vacation.

I blink. I know what this is. I might have the feeling like once we cross the line we've literally be dancing around for days, the earth is going to shatter, but the reality is, Shama has a flight tomorrow morning. She's leaving L.A., maybe for good.

And I'm leaving too. After this video is done, the tour starts. The promotional blitz. I've got real money to make, a project to finish, and it's not going to help if I'm pining after some girl I can't have.

But there's no doubt in my mind anymore.

We have one night.

And the fuck if I'm not going to make the most of it.

Suddenly the roses, the champagne, the strawberries—all of it seems cheap. Every bit of game I have seems ridiculous.

I consider the painting that hangs in my apartment in New York—the picture of a woman's nipple that I thought was a sex magnet when I was twenty-three. Nico still teases me about that thing. Apparently when he brought Layla to the apartment one weekend, she took one look at that thing and ran in the opposite direction.

Smart girl.

I wonder if that's when he knew she was worth the trouble of settling down. A woman who knows her worth is a woman worth having.

Who said that?

Papito, please. Ah. Ma. Yeah, I should have known.

I press the Santa Cecilia medallion to my lips. I haven't taken it off since my first communion. A gift from my mother, who knew I had my own gifts to share with the world. The patron saint of music to guide me through this crazy life. Maybe she knew I was going to have it before I did.

A woman who knows her worth, papi, *is a woman worth having.*

"Ahem."

Shama's husky voice pulls me out of my daze. A woman who knows every inch of her worth, from the top of her shiny black head to the tips of her perfectly painted toes. Shama knows she's worth the fuckin' world. I knew it the second I heard her voice. *That*'s what I needed on the record. That worth.

"H-hi," she says. But then she straightens. That confidence—it's so much more than swagger—is back. "Are you coming in?"

But I don't answer. I just stare for a few seconds longer, taking in this beauty in front of me.

And then I kiss her.

CHAPTER EIGHT

Shama

HIS KISS BEGINS SUDDENLY, AND AT FIRST, I'M FROZEN, STUNNED BY THE GRASP OF HIS hands and the feel of his body fully pressed against mine. Tall. Hard. Extremely solid.

It's not like I didn't know what I was doing, inviting him up here.

What was the harm in giving in to a fantasy for once in my life? Especially when I was leaving the very next morning?

But then he walks me into the room. The door slams shut behind him, the bottle and flowers he carries fall to the carpet, and my body springs to life.

"Oof!"

"Fuck," he hisses as my hands slide into his thick, cropped hair.

My mouth opens to his, accepting his tongue, his full lips, his bites, and licks. He tasted like caramel and just a hint of the Hennessy that was floating around the set tonight. Only one word runs through my mind, fast and hurried like an electrical current.

Carlos.

"Get this off," I mutter, yanking his shirt over his shoulders, revealing the finely toned chest and delicious set of abs that have been taunting me for days. Only this time I can actually touch them.

"Play fair," he says and he steals another kiss. His hands reach down to take ample handfuls of my ass, and he groans against my mouth as he squeezes. "Goddamn, I've been wanting to do that for fuckin' days, Shama. You know that? *Days.*"

"Is that right?"

I smile against his mouth, before nipping his lower lip. He captures my mouth with his eyes, and I sink into it. Because holy *hell*, the man can kiss. His tongue is hypnotic, twisting me into a trance so within seconds, I barely know where I am.

"You drive me crazy, you know that?" he growls as his hands travel up and down my sides, squeezing here and there, mapping the terrain of my body as he peels my clothes off. Soon I'm standing in front of him in nothing but my underwear and bra. He takes a step back.

"You look like you're examining a piece of art of something," I remark.

His eyes travel back up to meet mine, and that wicked grin makes another appearance as he reaches down lazily and unbuckles his pants. "I am."

I try and fail to ignore the way my heart gives an extra thump when he says it. But before I can say anything else, he backs me up against the wall, reaching down to lift me against it. He fuses our mouths together and grinds between my legs. I mean...wow. That's not just a belt buckle down there, if you know what I mean.

"What?" I ask as he pulls my panties to the side. "Am I not good enough for the bedroom?"

He stills. Shit. If I had a dollar for every time I killed a guy's mojo after opening my big mouth, I'd...well, I wouldn't have had to work quite as long as I did.

But Carlos doesn't move away. Instead, he smiles again. It's not the same smile as before. There's no swagger there, no game. This is charming, almost shy. It brings out a dimple in his left cheek I didn't see before in the bar, and his full lips purse together while his dark eyes twinkle, like he's trying to figure out exactly what to say.

"You're too good for the bedroom, if that makes any sense," he says, then drops my feet to the floor, takes my hand, and leads me past the bed and out to the balcony.

We're on a corner, looking out to the beach. Maybe people could see us if they really wanted, but there are no lights here other than the moon slicing through a few clouds in the summer sky. Carlos pulls me close and kisses me again, kisses me until I'm dizzy and can't breathe right. Whoa. Those lips. Fucking hell, that shouldn't be legal.

"Sit," he says, gesturing at the big lounge chair. "I'll be right back."

He disappears into the bedroom, and I wait, wondering what he's rustling up in my little hotel room. I'm just starting to wonder if I should go in there after him when the doors reopen, and Carlos emerges carrying my comforter and at least three of the massive pillows from the bed. I get up to help him, but he sets the pillows by my feet and proceeds to spread the comforter onto the balcony floor.

"You know they don't clean these things regularly after use, right?" I ask him.

"They do at this chain," he says with a smirk. "Ma was a maid for a long time, and she worked for this hotel in New York. I used to help her for extra money when I was younger."

The idea of him cleaning rooms is...charming. And disarming. Though I knew that Carlos, like a lot of artists, didn't come from much, it's hard to imagine when he pretty much drips wealth.

"They are not going to be happy about cleaning that," I say.

Carlos stands and shimmies out of his black pants, revealing arousal that hasn't faded under a pair of plaid boxers. "Send me the bill, pretty," he said. "Just get down here with me."

Slowly, I slide down next to him and allow him to gather me into his arms.

"You make me...you make me..." he says again and again, in between kisses that smear across my shoulder, neck, between my breasts.

I clasp his head to my breasts, urging him on. "I make you what?"

His mouth finds mine again. "You make me want to be better. Live better," he says in between an avalanche of kisses. "I want to be good enough for a woman like you."

Oh, hell. This is going to be one hell of a night if he keeps saying things like that.

You have to leave, Shama. You're on a plane in the morning.

"You *are* good enough," I manage to get out as I slide my hands over his strong, defined arms, then reach down for the waistband of his boxers. "You're perfect."

He groans as my hand wraps around him, then presses me backward so he cages me against the ground. The roar of the ocean sounds below us, and the stars twinkle over him, but all I can sense is him.

"Please," he gasps as I guide him between my legs. "Please. Fuck, Shama. I need you so bad. I—fuck!" he exclaims as he finds the entry he desires. He fills me in one deep thrust. "Tell me," he orders. "Tell me again. Tell me you need it too."

He's long, but not too long. Big, but not too big. I arch against his movements, my legs wrapping around his waist of their own accord.

"I...need...it." The rhythm he's setting makes it hard to speak at all, but I manage it for him. I'd manage just about anything. If he would just ask.

He sits up, takes hold of my thighs and spreads them wide so he can watch himself pound into me. "Fuck, that's hot."

My eyes shut tightly as I take every rough pound, every harsh lunge he has to give. This isn't what you'd call making love—it's not sweet and soft; it's not gentle and slow. But it doesn't feel easy either, the way a fling should. It's intense and furious, like the waves pounding on the sand. Like we both know there isn't a moment to lose.

When I look up at him again, his eyes pop open, two hazel stars as a supernova flashes through us both.

His thumb slips between us, brushes lightly over my clit. And in that moment, that's all I need.

We fall apart together in cries of desperation that neither of us expects. But above, the stars just twinkle on, like they knew this would happen the whole time.

CHAPTER NINE

K.C.

I DIDN'T SLEEP. NOT AFTER SHE CLIMBED ON TOP OF ME ABOUT FIVE MINUTES AFTER WE finished together the first time. Not after I spent an extra ten minutes tasting her *every-where* until she shouted my name for the whole city to hear. Not after she conked out on my chest right there on the balcony, then woke up and surprised me with the best fuckin' BJ of my life. And definitely not after we fell into this crazy daze, a new song still ringing in my ears. Music. Our music. This melody in my head that seems to be her.

Santa Monica twinkles below us, the ocean a black, dark space beyond the promenade. For the first time since I was a kid, I'm sleeping on the floor, wrapping up this incredible, irreplaceable woman and staring at the ocean she's about to cross. Wishing to God I was going with her.

Absently, I pull the Santa Cecilia medallion to my lips and kiss it for good luck.

I've worked too hard for this day to leave it all for some girl. And even if it was a good idea, I'm still contractually bound. To a tour. Promotions. Appearances.

Too much to leave without paying a massive price.

But…

"When's your flight?" I ask. The sun is starting to peek over the horizon.

Shama stirs on my chest. I watch the elegant lines of her shoulders ripple a little as she stretches to check her watch.

"In about five hours," she replies. We have some time."

Time.

"You really want to go all the way over there?" I'm a dick for asking, but I can't help it. "Seems…hot."

Hot. In India. Way to fuckin' go, Captain Obvious.

Shama just chuckles. "Yes. It will be hot in some places."

"What are you going to film? In Delhi, I mean?"

She sighs. "I honestly don't know. I need to see what I see first. See what speaks to me. I'll stay with some family first while I get my bearings. And then I'll go where inspiration leads, I guess."

"What if..." I toy with her hair, combing out some of the tangles I put there. *No, you can't say it.* I shouldn't. She's doing her own thing, and I'm doing mine. I don't have time for more than one night. I'm about to spend the next year on the fuckin' road.

Most people ain't her, mano. There's Nico again, telling me what's what. And you know, he's right.

I open my mouth to tell her that I knew her before. But instead, something else comes out:

"Come with me instead." I blink, shocked by the words, but also by how much I mean them. Quickly, I recover. "You could do your documentary everywhere we go. Do it on the tour or something. But we'll be on the move. Shama, you'd get to see the world, just like you want. And you can film anything, everything. *Te prometo.* I promise."

My words become babble, a ridiculous string of nothings in Spanish and English. Anything to get her to reconsider her plans and come with me instead. I'm crazy. This is crazy. I barely know this girl, and she barely knows me. But nothing has ever felt more right than holding her like this. Sometimes you don't know you're searching for something until you've found it. And I can't be the only one feeling what I'm feeling. I can't be the only one who sees beyond just tonight.

Shama sits up, unabashed as the blanket falls from her shoulders. But I'm too entranced by her face to be distracted by her curves or the beautiful shadows of her body. I could go another round or four with her. But everything I need right now is on her face.

And it's going to break my head.

She cups my cheek and runs her thumb over my lips.

"Carlos," she whispers, and her eyes glimmer, almost like she's about to cry. "Carlos, I know. I so, so want to..."

I swallow. "But the answer is no."

Slowly, she nods, and I watch as a tear slides down her cheek. Sadly, she shakes her head. "I've been waiting years to do this," she says, her voice cracking over the words. "*Years.* I can't...I can't just back out now, you know? This is the first time I've ever done something just...for me."

I get it. Fucking hell, do I get it. How many people did I leave behind in New York every time I flew out to L.A. for months, even years to get my career going? How many hearts have I broken, never willing to settle down because if I did, I would have ended up just another bodega owner or janitor in New York, working two or three jobs to get by.

You only get so many chances in this life to be yourself. I'm not about to take hers.

"Don't cry, Sparks," I whisper though the words only bring out more tears. "Not for me, pretty. I don't deserve your tears."

She hiccups back a choked sob and gives me a grim smile. "You deserve anyone's tears, Carlos," she says. "Least of all mine. I hope you know that."

I press a kiss to her lips, and pull her close so she's lying on top of me. "I believe it now, Sparks. I think you could get me to do just about anything. That's what you've been doing all weekend too."

She laughs, then lets me pull her down for another kiss that turns into something more than just a peck. I keep doing it, let her slide down, feel how much I want her again. She guides me inside her, wincing slightly as she lowers herself onto me, then tips her head up with pleasure.

"Don't hurt yourself," I whisper, though I'm already starting to thrust from underneath her.

Another tear falls. She doesn't fight them, because we both know this is goodbye.

"Shut up and take it, Carlos," she mutters, laughing and crying all at once.

I slip a hand around her neck and pull her down for another kiss. If these are our last moments, I'm going to make them good. "Whatever you say, Sparks. Whatever you need."

EPILOGUE

ONE YEAR LATER

Shama

THE CAB PULLS UP TO THE TOWNHOUSE IN RIVERDALE, A SHABBY, YET SPACIOUS HOME IN the Bronx that houses two of my best friends.

I'm tired. Not just from the multi-day flight that somehow got me back to New York from the tiny town in Bali where I finally finished my documentary on South Asian indigenous music. I'm fall-down exhausted from the entire year I just spent documenting tiny indigenous communities all over South Asia, getting their native music forms on camera for the docu-series commissioned by none other than HBO halfway through the year.

Thank you, Gary, I suppose. I never wanted to produce that last music video in LA, but it changed my life. In multiple ways. One call from the A&R executive kicked off the career I never knew I wanted—as a music documentary filmmaker.

The other way, of course, was Carlos.

It's not like I never heard from him again. I had a cell phone, after all, and when I returned to a city here and there to send my films back to New York, I'd always be cheered by the sudden flurry of texts and emails. Carlos would give me the news along with pictorial reminders of just what I was missing out on. Carlos onstage, usually shirtless, while he gave the crowd what they wanted. Carlos standing next to his record, first certified gold, then platinum. Carlos at the Grammys, accepting his first-ever award as a performer, not just a producer. "Porque" won Song of the Year. And I won't lie. I cried a little when I watched him thank me on a scratchy broadcast I managed to track down in Hanoi.

"I'll hold onto this until we meet again, Sparks," he said, holding up the shiny gold statue and blowing a kiss to the camera just before the music played him off.

But the texts and emails, just like everything else, eventually petered off. I spent a month riding a bike around Indonesia while "DJ Cairo" was back in the studio. Naturally, we were both relegated to a memory, a lark at the beginning of a vacation, at the end of both of our previous lives. One magical night that might have ruined me forever, but which I wouldn't give up for anything.

I knock on the door and wait eagerly as tiny feet pitter-patter to the door. It swings open, and almost immediately, I'm bowled over by Mateo, my godson.

"Auntie Shama!" he cries as he wraps his thin arms around my waist.

"Hey, you!" I love this kid so damn much. Even though he's almost eight, he's never too big for hugs.

"Shamashamashamashamashama!" Mateo's sister, Coco, squeals behind him, and like a flea, the doll-like four-year-old plasters herself to my legs. "Did you get me a present?"

"Coco!" the deep voice of Nico bounds through the hallway as he comes to collect his kids. He scoops the little girl up and sets her on his hip. "*Mija*, you got better manners than that."

"What's up Special Delivery?" I say as I accept Nico's kiss to my cheek.

Nico scowls at the old nickname, a remnant of his days at Fedex. "Trouble," he says as he stands back to let me into the house. "Always giving me shit, girl."

"Where is she? Where's my best friend?" calls another familiar voice.

I look up to see Layla running down the stairs, and a few seconds later, I'm tackled by *my* best friend.

"Ahh!" she cries as she rocks me back and forth. "Look at you. You look amazing!"

"Thanks, dude," I say, squeezing her back just as hard. "I also look like I haven't slept in two days—which I haven't. I need to crash for about a decade, but I wasn't going to miss your birthday. Speaking of."

I pull out a little box from my purse and hand it to her. Layla opens it and lifts the delicate gold bracelet.

"Oh my god, Shams," she murmurs. "This is too much."

"It's not. I got it from this amazing artist in Bangalore," I said. "Hold out your wrist. I'll help you put it on."

She does while Nico shepherds the kids out the back door to the deck, where a bunch of other party attendees are mingling. As Layla admires her gift, I spot some familiar faces, mostly people from college and some of Nico's family. Another man stands with his back to the door. His shoulders look familiar in that Giants jersey.

I shake my head and turn back to Layla. It's been way too long since that night in Santa Monica. One whole year of nothing but me. Every pair of shoulders looks like Carlos.

I need a drink. And a date.

"I see you checking out K.C.," Layla says slyly.

"Who?"

"Nico's best friend." She nods toward the deck. "He's back in town."

"No, I wasn't checking anyone out. Just…remembering."

Layla frowns. "Remembering what?"

"Oh, you know. That guy just kind of looks like Carlos. That DJ whose video I did before I left."

I peer at him again. He still hasn't turned around, but I can't shake the image now.

Layla looks back and forth between me and the guests. "Carlos…you mean Cairo?" Her eyes widen. "Oh, my God, Shama. You mean you didn't…you didn't know that—"

I frown. What is she talking about? I told her all about my little tryst with Carlos. None of this should be a mystery. "Know what?"

Her mouth opens and closes a few times before she stands up straight and grabs my hand. "You know what? Let's just join the party."

But I'm stuck on the guy, and suddenly, I don't want to go out there. I don't want to meet some new guy who reminds me of the one I haven't been able to get out of my head. I'm too tired for a poor substitute. Especially when it's for someone I can never have.

"I'm just going to get a glass of water," I try, but my friend isn't having it.

"Don't be rude. It's my birthday. You have to do what I say."

She leads me to the tiny backyard, and then, to my horror, reaches out and taps the Giants fan on the shoulder.

"Shams," she says with a sneaky smile, "you remember K.C., don't you?"

But I can't answer. My throat is caught in my chest.

DJ Cairo.

Carlos.

A complete and total stranger, but also someone I know...very well.

"K.—K.C.? *You're* K.C.?"

His dark eyes are diamonds, sparkling under the lights. The dimple in his left cheek appears. The one I still see almost every time I close my eyes.

Carlos smiles, warm and bright but without surprise. He knew I'd be here tonight.

"Kevin Carlos," he says softly. "Or at least, that's the name my mother gave me."

I turned to Layla. "Why didn't you tell me?" I hiss.

She shrugs. "I thought you knew."

"Almost everyone important to me calls me K.C." Carlos says.

"*Almost* everyone," I whisper.

He takes a step closer. "That's right. All except one."

I blink. An awkward Thanksgiving is coming back to me. Nico's little brother and player-looking best friend spend the entire evening hitting on me before I escaped to my parents' house. We were just in college. It was eons ago. We were both younger. So much...different.

And yet, still the same.

"Shama."

Our friends fall back into the party, but all I can see is him.

"Where...where did you go?" I ask. "I stopped hearing from you. After the Grammys, you stopped—you forgot about me."

"My tour ended." He takes yet another step closer, his broad shoulders lumbering. "I went back into the studio. I had all these rhymes. Beats in my head. Sounds like the ocean." One more step. "Like us."

He holds out a flash drive, and I know without asking what it contains. Songs, rhythms. New music this incredibly talented man has concocted.

I don't want to tell him that he's been in my ears for the last year. That after I left L.A., I downloaded his album once it was released, plus every artist he ever produced. I listened to our song, "Porque," on repeat every night for a month. No music I recorded could erase the rhythms we made together.

His hand touches mine, and by instinct, our fingers entwine. In the periphery, I can see people watching us curiously, but Carlos's gaze doesn't waver.

"Sparks?" he asks.

My bottom lip quivers. "What?"

One step, and he's only a few inches from my face. His hand cups my chin, and his thumb gently brushes over my cheek.

"I could *never* forget you, sweetheart," he whispers. "I came back to New York to wait. Because I knew when you got back from whatever you needed to do, *I* needed to be here. For you. I spent a year apart from you, Sparks. I'm not doing it again."

I look around, though my vision can't focus.

"But...but what if you have to go away again? What if *I* have to go again? I left the industry for a reason, Carlos."

"Shama, who are you kidding? Even when you left the business, you were still in love with music. Your whole series is about it."

I blink, now genuinely shocked. "How did you know that? It doesn't air for another three months."

That smirk returns, the one that makes me want to punch him and kiss him at the same time. But mostly, I realize, the latter.

"I haven't missed *anything* you've been doing, Shama," Carlos says. "A few phone calls from my agent made sure I was always in the know. It's beautiful work, Sparks. It really is." He slips a hand around my waist. "I'm so fuckin' proud of you."

It's not until he says it that I realize how much I needed to hear it. That I needed to have *someone* validate this long path I've been on to find myself.

"So what do you say, Sparks?" Carlos whispers. "You ready to continue this journey together or what? I'll be recording for another three months or so...and then I'm going to need someone to film my next tour."

I open my mouth to argue, but find I can't. He's right. Music calls to me. Films calls to me. *He* calls to me. And all the questions I ever had about him melt away as I realize that his arms are where I'm supposed to be. That maybe it's not about whether or not we grow apart, but whether we can grow together.

I press a kiss to his lips, and his hands cup my chin while his mouth teases mine. A few whistles sound in the background, but he doesn't release me until he's good and ready.

"So what do you say, Sparks?" he asks again, this time when we are both out of breath.

"What else, you idiot?" I'm grinning so hard that tears are about to fall. "I say yes."

The End

Thank you so much for reading the Bad Idea Series!
Get more updates from Nicole French here: www.nicolefrenchromance.com

Need more Nico and Layla? You can catch sneak peeks of these two in my upcoming forbidden romance, The Other Man. www.nicolefrenchromance.com/theotherman

Need more Nico? You can read about his early life in the Bad Idea prequel novella, Broken Arrow, free only to newsletter subscribers: https://BookHip.com/BBXWVX